THE ESSENTIAL
BATMAN ENCYCLOPEDIA

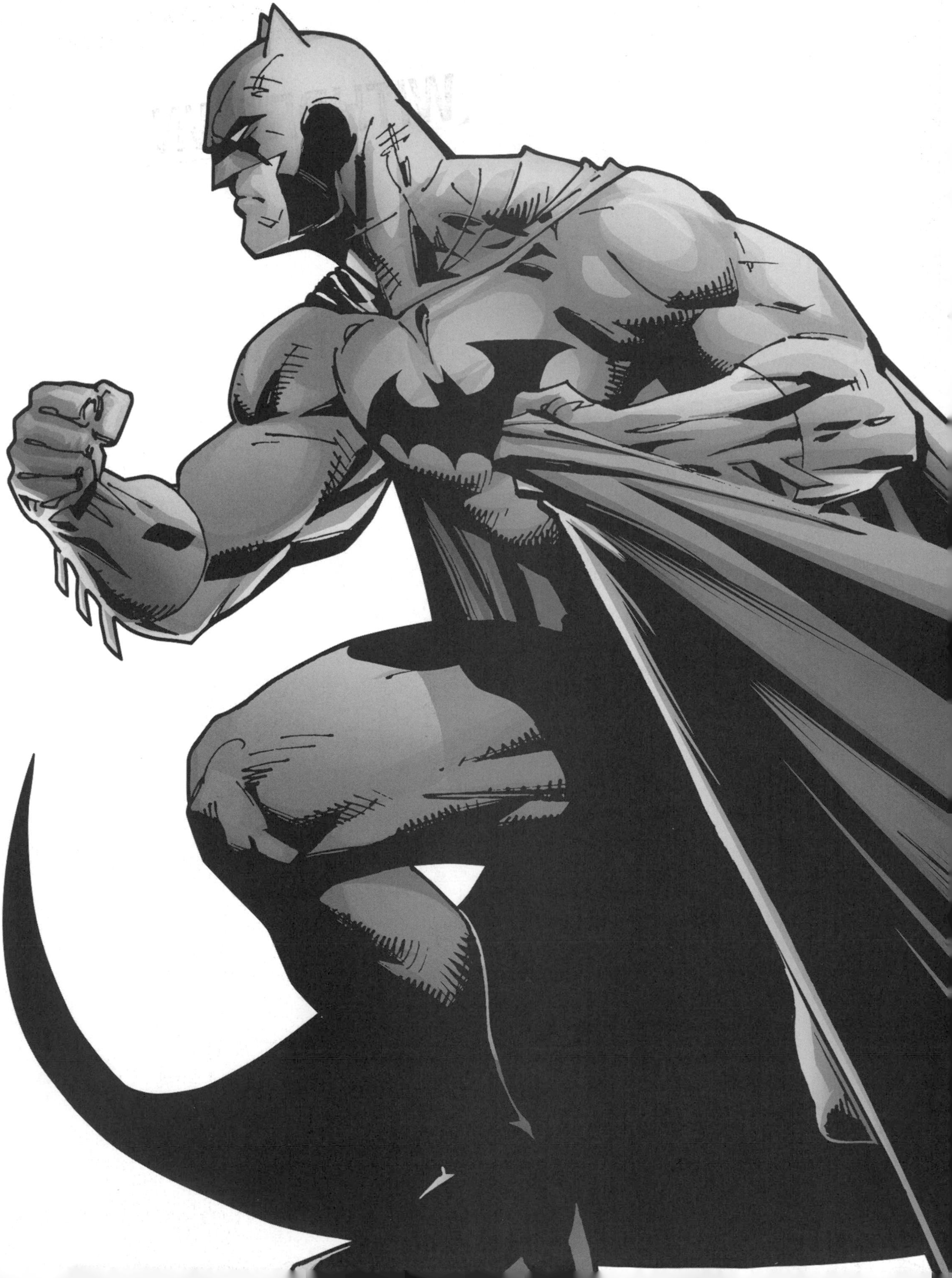

THE ESSENTIAL
BATMAN ENCYCLOPEDIA

ROBERT GREENBERGER

Batman created by Bob Kane

DEL REY
DC

BALLANTINE
BOOKS
NEW YORK

A Del Rey Trade Paperback Original

Copyright © 2008 by DC Comics

BATMAN and all related names, characters, and elements are trademarks of DC Comics © 2008.
All Rights Reserved.

Published in the United States by Del Rey Books, an imprint of
The Random House Publishing Group, a division of Random House, Inc., New York.

DEL REY is a registered trademark and the Del Rey colophon is a
trademark of Random House, Inc.

Library of Congress Cataloging-in-Publication Data

Greenberger, Robert.
The essential Batman encyclopedia / Robert Greenberger.
p. cm.
ISBN-13: 978-0-345-50106-6 (pbk.)
1. Batman (Fictitious character)—Encyclopedias.   I. Title.
PN6728.B363G74 2008
741.5'97303—dc22
2008003016

Printed in the United States of America

www.dccomics.com
keyword: DC Comics on AOL
www.delreybooks.com

9 8 7 6 5 4 3 2

Interior design by Foltz Design

To Edwin and Joan Greenberger, who gave me that first Superman comic

at age six and encouraged my love of the characters and medium

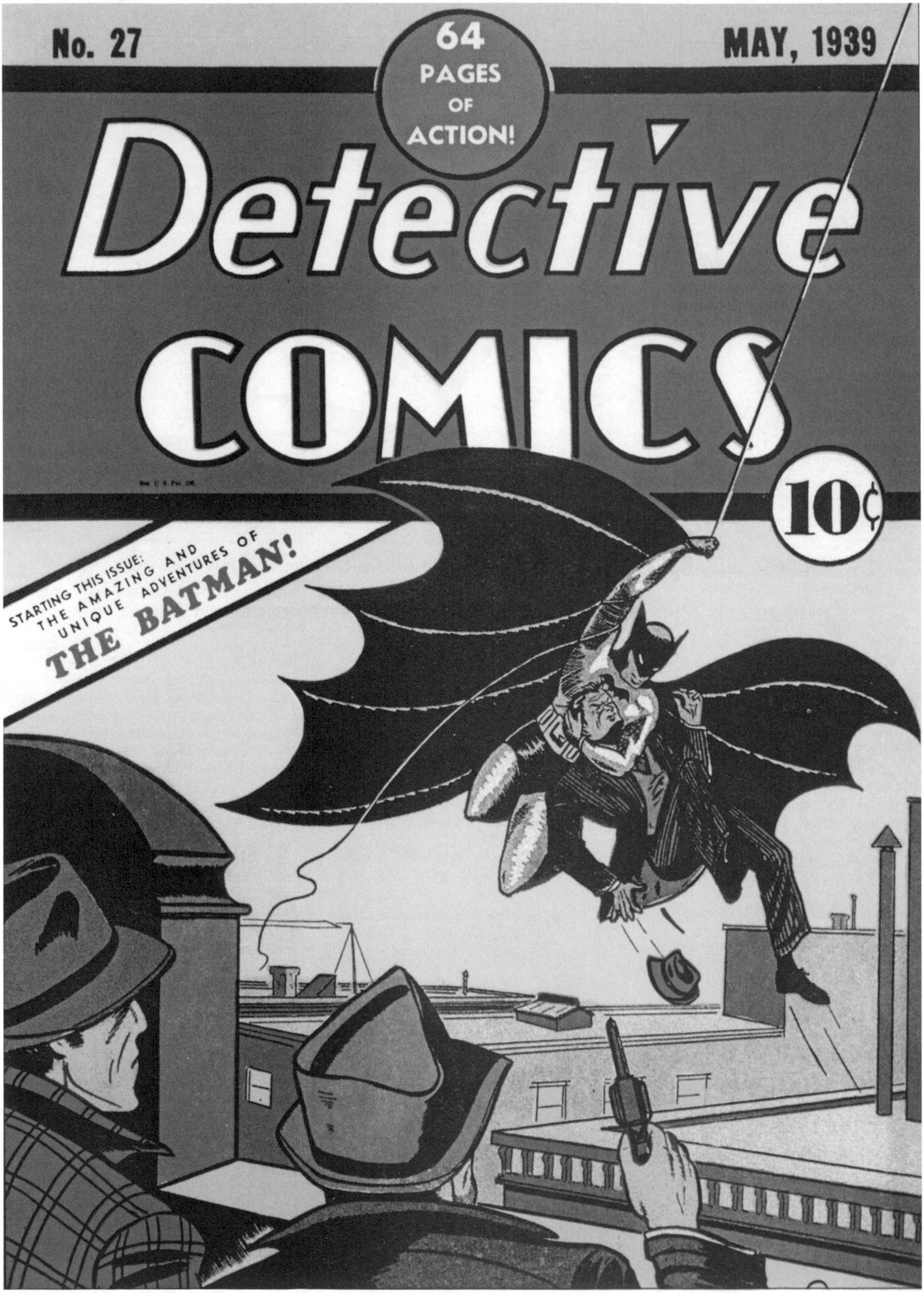
No. 27
64 PAGES OF ACTION!
MAY, 1939
Detective
COMICS
10¢
STARTING THIS ISSUE: THE AMAZING AND UNIQUE ADVENTURES OF
THE BATMAN!

PREFACE

Labors of love are not unique to anyone, and many of us tread the same territory in different eras. Long before there was an Internet, let alone computers with vast stores of memory, Michael Fleisher cataloged every Batman comic book DC Comics had published to date. He had this crazy notion that a single-volume encyclopedia of super heroes could actually be researched and written. Then he entered DC's fabled print library and saw the vast scope of what a single company had published since its founding in 1935. Undaunted, he changed his plans to a multivolume series featuring the greatest super heroes, starting with Batman.

He was aided by Janet Lincoln, and together they stored their data on twenty thousand index cards. The first volume of *The Encyclopedia of Comic Book Heroes* was published in 1976 and all told, only three of the projected eight volumes ever saw print. In 2007 DC released facsimile editions of these three, spotlighting Batman, Wonder Woman, and Superman, filling a desire among longtime collectors to posses this information.

Still, Michael's efforts pretty much stopped in the late 1960s as DC continued to publish comics. As a result, much more to the mythos has been added, tweaked, revised, revitalized, abandoned, and so on. DC and Del Rey thought there remained a desire to present the most comprehensive histories for each character, so the triumvirate will star in three books over the next few years, beginning with the volume in your hands.

While Michael limited his research and writing to Batman's appearances in *Batman, Detective Comics,* and *World's Finest Comics,* the Caped Crusader during those same days also appeared regularly in *The Brave and the Bold* and *Justice League of America.* Today he stars in *Batman, Detective Comics, Batman Confidential,* and *Justice League of America,* while making regular appearances in *Robin, Nightwing, Catwoman,* and many of DC's other core titles. Elements from various titles have proven essential to Batman's world, so a new work needed to expand its horizons to every appearance Batman had made since his 1939 debut.

That said, this book does limit itself to those stories that are considered part of the Greater DC Universe. This means that comics based on the feature films or animated series are not reflected in these pages. Similarly, Batman's appearances in movie serials, live-action television, feature films, animated stories, and the like are also excluded from these works—so don't be confused if, say, the Riddler's origins as listed here don't match what you recall seeing on-screen in *Batman Forever.*

What can be confusing, though, is the notion of parallel worlds and how the canonical stories and character details have changed through cosmic events. In short, DC Comics was not concerned with a universe of consistent story details until the 1960s. Prior to that, the editors' presumption was that the readership turned over every six to eight years; thus they didn't feel constrained by stories published years before. As a result, Batman fought the Nazi menace during World War II and then aliens and monsters in the 1950s without having to worry about things like aging.

That all ended when editor Julie Schwartz introduced the Earth-1/Earth-2 concept. Parallel universes were a staple of science fiction for decades by 1961, and Schwartz—who first read, then agented, science fiction—added the element to comic books. It all happened in *Flash* #123 when the modern-day Flash met his inspiration, whom he thought was actually a comic book character. It turned out that their universes occupied the same physical space but vibrated at different speeds, allowing them to coexist (trust me on this). One parallel world was nice and popular, so through the years more and more parallel worlds were introduced.

Batman existed on several of these worlds, with the first *Batman* published considered to be set on Earth-2. That became the home to all the heroes considered the forerunners of the super heroes most know today. When comic readers formed comic fandom, this era was known as the Golden Age. Batman and Robin were among the first inhabitants of that age. As a result, Batman aged, albeit slowly, and while the Batman of Earth-1 was in his prime, his forerunner was in semi-retirement, with an adult Robin eventually replacing him.

By 1983 it was decided that editors, writers, artists, and readers were fatigued by tracking these varying worlds, especially as characters crossed back and forth with impunity. To celebrate the company's fiftieth anniversary in 1985, it was decided to blow up all the parallel universes and reduce everything down to one, with one Batman, one Joker, one Superman, et cetera. The result was *Crisis on Infinite Earths,* a twelve-issue comic book event that was cosmic in scope as countless universes were wiped out and the remaining ones combined into one universe. On the heels of the event's conclusion, a new *Batman* editor and creative team retold the first year of the Dark Knight's career, reestablishing many of the basic facts about Batman, Catwoman, Commissioner Gordon, and others.

In time, though, inconsistencies throughout the DC titles led to one revamp after another, all intended to streamline events and correct "mistakes." In 2003 a new road map was drawn up by incoming executive editor Dan DiDio that put Batman in the center of the action. A series of stories ran across the various titles and in their own miniseries, culminating in 2006's *Infinite Crisis,* a sequel to *Crisis.* Reality was modified once more, including the creation of new parallel worlds, although limited to a mere fifty-two. The New Earth, the core of the DC Universe, presented newly modified backgrounds and details for the familiar heroes and villains.

What I attempt to do in this volume is sort all of this out by clearly identifying what happened in each reality. After all, comic book historian Don Thompson once said that the Golden Age of comics is twelve. It's when we are at our most passionate about a hobby, in this case, comic books. My Golden Age was then 1970, whereas my son's was 2000, and the details each of us knows about these characters are different as the storylines have evolved. As a result, I try to sift through the events and contradictions so you understand how these people evolved. If you scratch your head in bewilderment only once or twice, my job here was done well.

I had one other issue to contend with: These stories are going to continue unfolding long after this manuscript goes to press. Some endpoint needed to be established. After consulting with the DC editors, it seemed that limiting entries to the stories published through September 2007 (cover-dated November 2007) made the most practical sense. Still, comics coming out after that time will add new elements, retell familiar stories, and add wrinkles that may make some of these entries seem incorrect. Especially foreboding is the notion that as I write this, DC is publishing a title called *Countdown to Final Crisis.* I have no idea what this cosmic event may do to the reality of these characters.

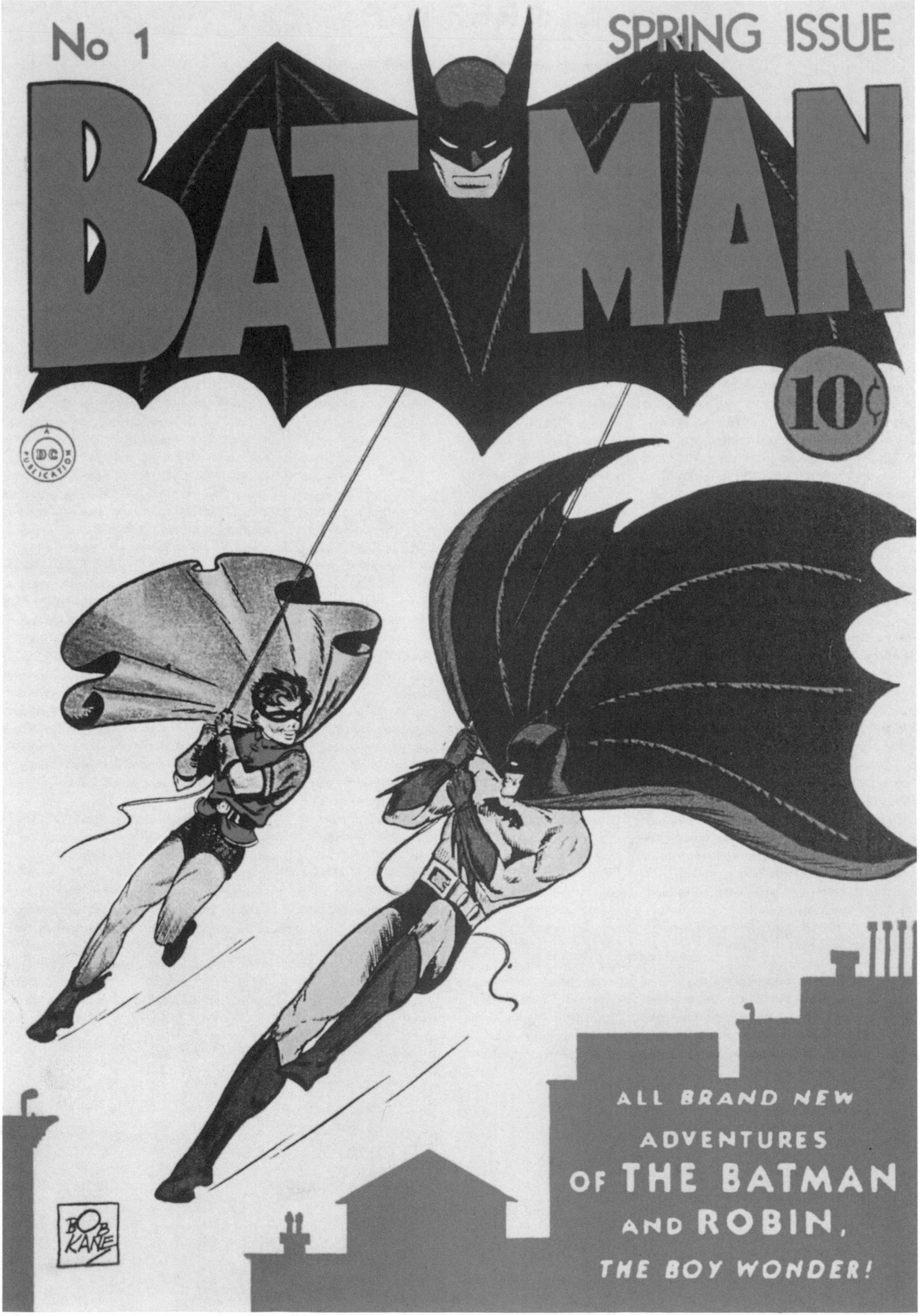
No 1
SPRING ISSUE
BATMAN
10¢
A DC PUBLICATION
ALL BRAND NEW
ADVENTURES
OF THE BATMAN
AND ROBIN,
THE BOY WONDER!
BOB KANE

ACKNOWLEDGMENTS

A book this massive in scope could not be written entirely by one or two people filling out index cards. As a result, many other sources and people provided information that proved vital for the completion of the project.

I thank DC Comics and its president and publisher, Paul Levitz, a longtime friend. They provided support and access to archives and staff with generosity.

This book could not exist without the work of the countless writers, artists, and editors who crafted the mythos, expanded it, and helped it endure. Clearly Bob Kane knew what he was doing when he imagined the character. Over time his efforts were supported by collaborators before Kane ceded Gotham City and its denizens to others. They all provided countless hours of reading enjoyment to me when I was a child—and again now that I'm an adult researcher.

Additionally, I would like to thank:

Emily Lerner, associate editor in DC's Licensed Publishing department, for first inviting me to work on this book. She could not see this through to completion, but her faith was important.

Chris Cerasi, who inherited the project and kept me focused on issues of content, style, and comprehension. Chris made certain I had plenty of current research at my fingertips and was always there when I needed help. He was aided now and then by fellow editor John Morgan, whose efforts are also appreciated.

At Del Rey, editor Keith Clayton, who provided a steady hand. Publisher Scott Shannon, a longtime colleague, showed unwavering faith in both author and project.

This book looks amazing, and it had nothing to do with the words. From the first time I saw a mock design, I knew we had a winner. Erich Schoeneweiss at Random House and Brad Foltz of Foltz Design worked hard to make the book readable and attractive, and I think they succeeded wonderfully.

Peter Tomasi and Mike Marts, editors of the core Batman franchise during the production of this book, who were happy to answer my questions and provide sneak peeks at upcoming scripts to enable my manuscript to be as complete as possible. Mike Carlin, who edited many of the supporting titles, also came through with valuable information, and corny jokes, along the way.

Comics scribes Marv Wolfman and Mark Waid, who made time to answer questions—their assistance is appreciated.

Jeff Rovin and Paul Kupperberg, my former colleagues at *Weekly World News,* who graciously allowed me the schedule flexibility to concentrate on huge sections of the book during crunch periods.

Bob and Laurie Rozakis, who provided friendship and support during the ten-month process this book required.

Martin Pasko and Phil Jimenez, authors of the forthcoming Superman and Wonder Woman volumes, for their input, advice, and encouragement.

The following websites, which were invaluable when cross-checking facts and details about characters and stories: The Grand Comics Database; Mike's Amazing World of DC Comics; BatSquad.net; Batman, Yesterday, Today and Beyond; Collected Issues of the Dark Knight; DarkMark's Comics Indexing Domain; and the Unofficial Guide to the DC Universe.

Kate and Robbie, my children, who endured yet another round of Dad hiding in the basement for long stretches of time. Fortunately, both were away at college for much of the writing of this book.

Deb, my wife, without whom I could never accomplish a fraction of what I manage. Her love, advice, cajoling, support, and devotion are essential to me every day. This book could not have been completed without her understanding.

Saved for last, but certainly not least, is John Wells. We've worked together for some time since my second tenure at DC Comics, and he was more than generous in making his vast databases available to me. When I had a name but couldn't identify a starting point, his files pointed me in the right direction. As a frequent website writer, he made sense out of many of the continuity changes long before the rest of us caught up, which enabled me to streamline much of the research. His massive index of Gotham City alone should be its own book. He answered questions with lightning speed, usually providing far more information than requested. He also read first drafts for many entries, helping make certain the various incarnations were properly detailed. There is no way this book could exist without his help and friendship. Boy, do I owe you one!

Robert Greenberger
Connecticut, 2007

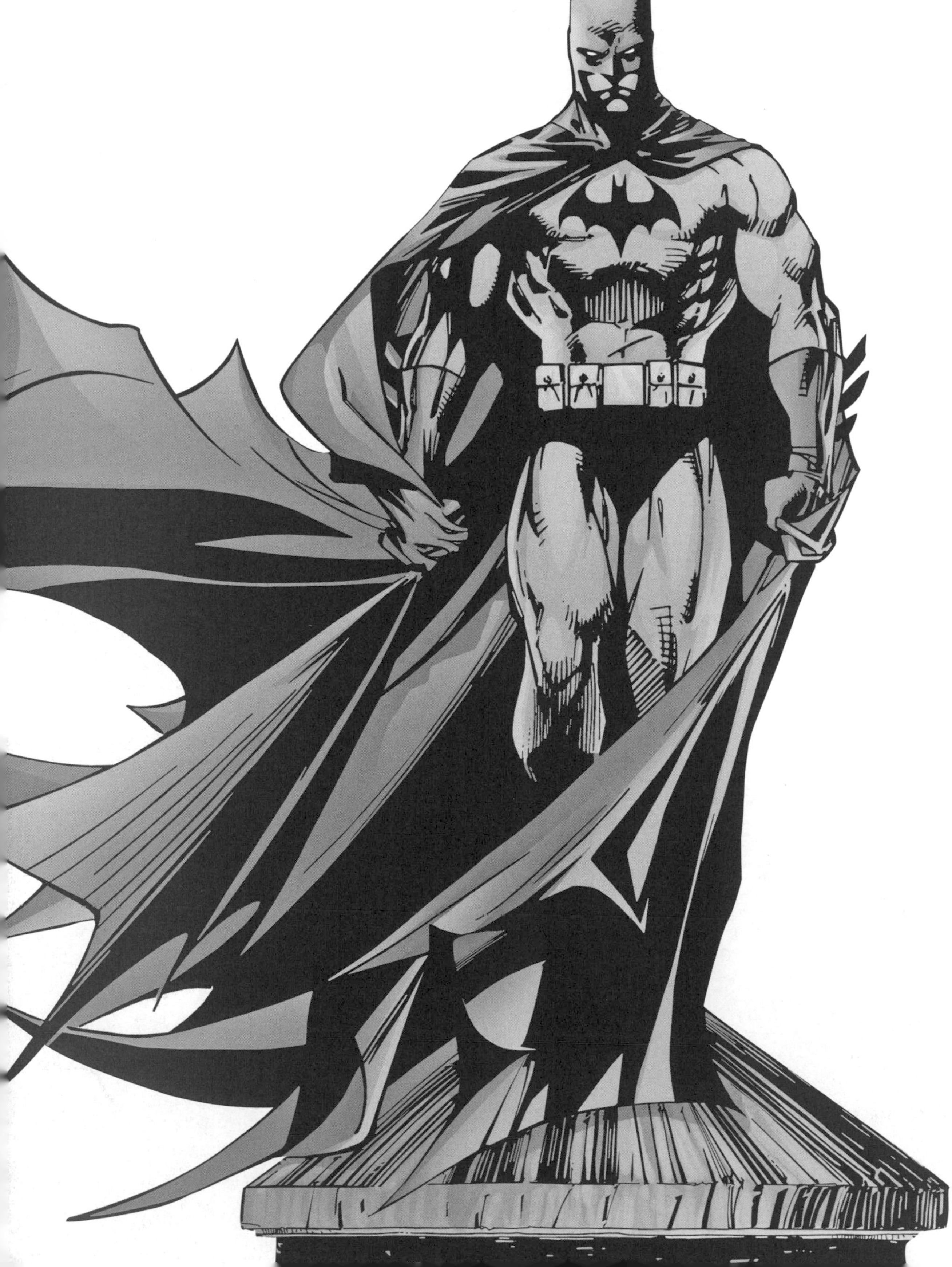

HOW TO USE THIS BOOK

I used Michael Fleisher's Batman encyclopedia as my starting point in this book, but with double the number of years to cover, it was impossible to include everyone he first used in addition to every major and minor character to appear in a Batman comic.

My master list concentrated on those characters who appeared at least twice in a core Batman title, including *Batman* (and related one-shots and mini-series), *Detective Comics, Batman Family, Legends of the Dark Knight, Shadow of the Bat, Gotham Knights, The Brave and the Bold, World's Finest Comics,* and *Justice League of America.* Characters who crossed between these titles and the family of Batman-related books, including *Robin, Catwoman,*

Nightwing, Batgirl, and *Birds of Prey,* were also included. Those unique to family titles were left out for space considerations. Entries on many of the heroes Batman has worked alongside were limited to those who had particular impact on Batman's life, such as being handpicked to work with him in the JLA or the Outsiders, so casual team-ups had to be excluded.

Characters are listed following standard encyclopedia style. An entry for the Club of Heroes, for instance, would appear as CLUB OF HEROES, THE. Characters appear alphabetically, and those with surnames are listed accordingly: WAYNE, BRUCE. Those with titles are listed by title: MISTER FREEZE.

Those with dual identities are listed both ways: GRAYSON, RICHARD and NIGHTWING entries are both here. The detailed entries for the heroes tend to be listed by their birth names, given how many people have used many of the same names, such as *Robin* and *Batgirl.*

Cover dates appearing here were used on the actual comic books; some list only a year, which means that no month was identified, an increasingly common practice since 1986. Story titles were omitted for space considerations.

Cross-references are indicated by names appearing in SMALL CAPITALS.

THE ESSENTIAL
BATMAN ENCYCLOPEDIA

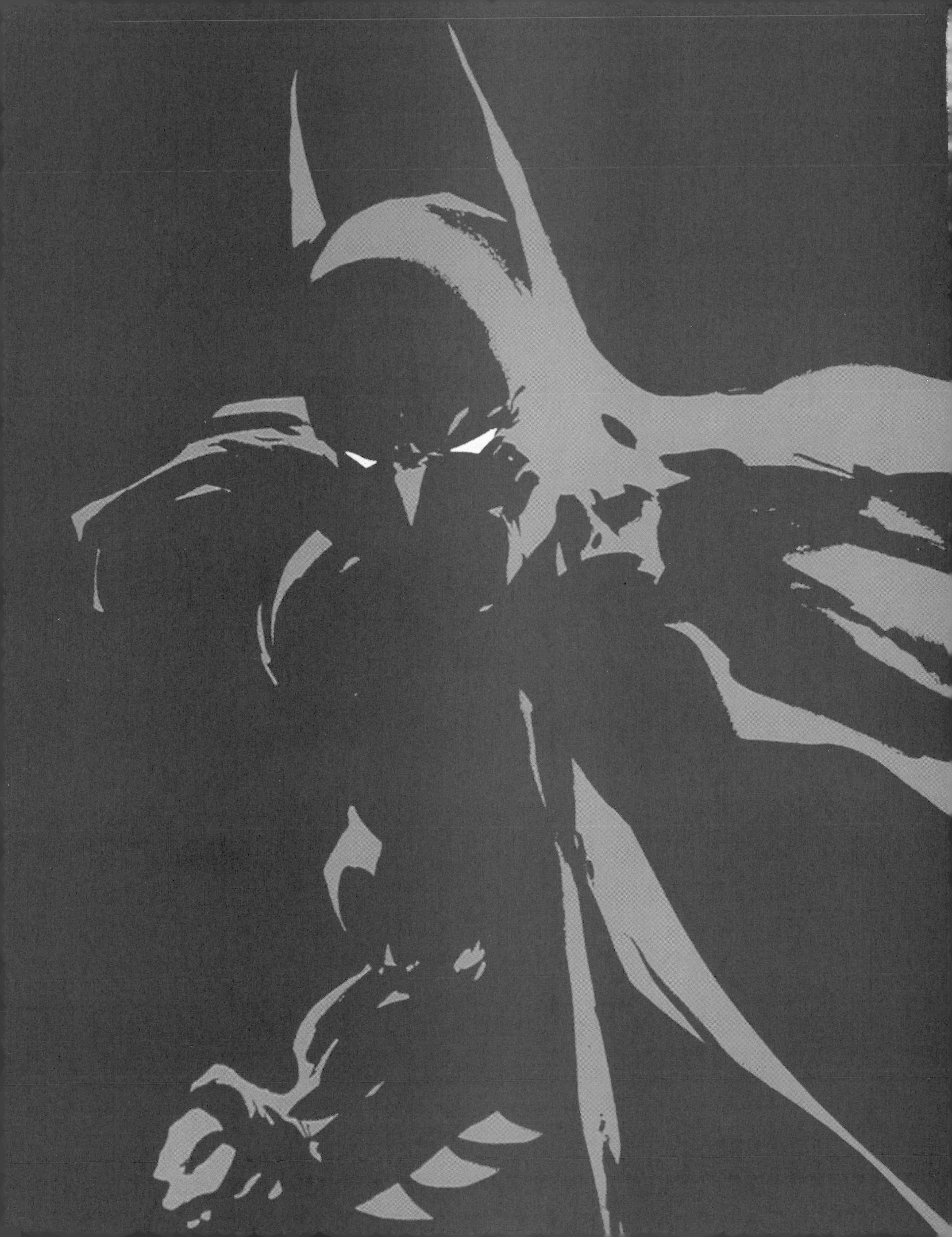

ABATTOIR

Serial killer Arnold Etchison grew up convinced that his family members were evil. He eventually murdered them in the belief that their deaths would protect the world from further perils. Etchison also believed that he absorbed the life force from each victim after his or her death. Taking the name Abattoir, he continued his murderous spree until Batman apprehended him. Etchison was declared criminally insane and sentenced to spend the rest of his life in GOTHAM CITY'S ARKHAM ASYLUM. When the international criminal BANE freed the Arkham inmates while carrying out his plan to weaken the Dark Knight, Abattoir immediately returned to tracking down and killing members of his extended family. Etchison was eventually found by JEAN-PAUL VALLEY, who at the time was substituting for Batman after the latter was crippled in a fight with Bane. Their confrontation took place at a Gotham refinery where Valley, who lacked BRUCE WAYNE's unwavering moral scruples, allowed Abattoir to fall to his death. However, Valley later learned that Etchison had left an innocent victim, his cousin GRAHAM ETCHISON, hidden away in an undisclosed torture chamber. With Etchison dead, the victim remained undiscovered and eventually died.

Some time later Etchison's spirit returned to plague Bruce Wayne, who had healed and wore Batman's cape and cowl once again. Abattoir's spirit attempted to cause his last surviving relative, an unnamed cousin, to miscarry, thereby providing him with a mortal vessel to possess in his plan to return to human form. Instead, Abattoir animated Valley's armored BATSUIT and fought Batman until the Dark Knight convinced Etchison's spirit to abandon his vengeful mission and return to his proper place in the spirit realm. (*Detective Comics* #625, January 1991)

ABBOTT, KYLE

Little is known about Kyle Abbott, whose first recorded appearance saw him in the employ of ecoterrorist RĀ'S AL GHŪL. He later swore his allegiance to al Ghūl's former employee, WHISPER A'DAIRE, who injected him with a serum made by Rā's that gave Abbott the ability to shape-shift into a werewolf and eternal life. The serum needed to be taken on a regular basis, thereby granting a'Daire control over Abbott, who became her much-feared second in command. (*Detective Comics* #743, April 2000)

Abbott was also a'Daire's whipping boy, and was punished every time one of her power-grabbing schemes failed. As a result of the many beatings he received, he was left partially blinded and disfigured until a'Daire used the serum to restore Abbott's health, although he remained blind in one eye. Despite his suffering, Abbott remained unswervingly loyal to his vicious master. When a'Daire took over HSC International Banking, a legitimate company fronting for the criminal group INTERGANG, Abbott remained by her side.

Eventually regaining total sight, Abbott—now able to change form from human to semi-lycan to full werewolf—led a team of shape-changers against the QUESTION and former GOTHAM CITY POLICE DEPARTMENT detective RENEE MONTOYA, who were tracing illegal alien weaponry to Intergang. Abbott and his men engaged Intergang in a vicious fight that left all of Intergang's agents dead. Abbott later managed to track Montoya and the Question to Khandaq, framing them for the slaughter that had occurred at the Intergang HSC warehouse. (*52* #1, 2006)

When he returned to Gotham, Abbott was alarmed at the fervor BRUNO MANNHEIM, Intergang's leader, displayed for the task of destroying the city to fulfill a prophecy from the Crime Bible. As a result, he turned his back on a'Daire and proved crucial in leading Montoya to the kidnapped BATWOMAN, about to be sacrificed by Mannheim. He was last seen accompanying NIGHTWING in disabling devices designed to turn the city into a charred lump of rock. (*52* #48, 2007)

ABDULLAH

On Earth-2, Batman and ROBIN, sometimes accompanied by SUPERMAN, would be hypnotized by PROFESSOR CARTER NICHOLS and manage to pierce the time barrier. One such adventure landed the World's Finest team in tenth-century Baghdad. The swarthy giant Abdullah led the notorious Forty Thieves and traded a youth named Aladdin a useless oil lamp in exchange for a fortune, and then tried to frame Aladdin as a member of the thieves. The time-traveling trio not only helped the lad regain his fortune, which had been swindled from him by Abdullah, but also stopped Abdullah's planned crime wave through a Baghdad bazaar. (*World's Finest Comics* #79, November/December 1955)

ACADEMY, THE

Organized crime in GOTHAM CITY has taken many shapes over the years, but none so blatantly mirrored the efforts of law enforcement as the Academy. A secret training facility for criminals, it also doubled as the headquarters for the underworld group that most benefited from the training. Standards for admission were high, the Academy accepting only those men with an IQ higher than 135 who were physically at their peak. Upon learning of the Academy's existence, Batman was determined to shut down the facility for good. The Caped Crusader disguised himself as a recruit and went through all the training courses upon acceptance. His well-developed mind and body ensured that he advanced rapidly, and eventually he became a nominee for the next leader of the organization. Batman took the leadership role and subsequently brought about the Academy's downfall, with the help of the GOTHAM CITY POLICE DEPARTMENT. The Academy's hoard of stolen property and its current membership roster were taken into custody, and the facility was shut down for good. (*Batman* #70, April/May 1952)

ACCORD

The small town of Accord was said to be located "two hundred or so miles north of GOTHAM CITY." Accord was founded by the great-grandfather of its local physician, Lynn Eagles, who aided the Batman during a case involving the JOKER. (*Legends of the Dark Knight* #67, January 1995)

ACE THE BAT-HOUND

When would-be counterfeiters kidnapped engraver JOHN WILKER, Batman and ROBIN launched an investigation. They saved Wilker's abandoned German shepherd, Ace, from drowning in a river, and used the dog's innate tracking abilities to help locate his master. During the search, BRUCE WAYNE also placed an ad for Ace's master. Given the distinctive diamond-shaped mark on Ace's forehead, Wayne hoped someone would recognize the dog and provide some useful information. Sure enough, one of Wilker's neighbors gave Bruce a vital clue.

Wayne was also concerned that people might associate Ace and his distinctive diamond mark with Batman and his true identity; as a result, he quickly fashioned a black hood and bat-symbol collar, and Ace joined the Dynamic Duo. A criminal tracked by the cowled canine soon dubbed him Ace the Bat-Hound.

Wilker's kidnappers were attempting to steal ink from the Eastern Printing-Ink Company when the crime fighters caught up to them, only to be subdued during the fight. Fashioning a crude BAT-SIGNAL from cloth and a flashlight, Batman managed to summon Ace, who gnawed through Robin's bonds, freeing the heroes and allowing them to defeat the counterfeiters. (*Batman* #92, June 1955)

Wilker loaned Ace to Batman for numerous cases over the next few months. When Wilker took a new job that required him to travel frequently, Wayne finally adopted the dog. By then Batman had added a receiver to Ace's collar that used an ultra-high-frequency sound to summon the canine. (*Batman* #125, August 1959) Ace went on frequent adventures with the Dynamic Duo, and worked alongside BATWOMAN as well. BAT-MITE, the magical imp from another dimension, once bequeathed Ace temporary superpowers, with disastrous results.

In the reality created by the CRISIS ON INFINITE EARTHS, Batman encountered the German shepherd when the dog was pet to a 130-year-old Native

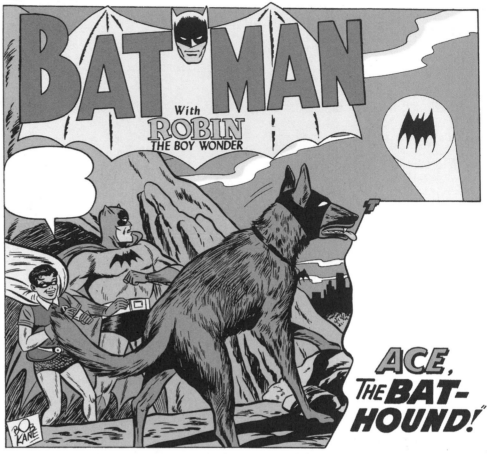

American shaman named Black Wolf. Batman was drawn to a bat-shaped patch on the dog's shoulder, and followed the dog. Batman was led to and rescued Black Wolf from members of his own tribe, who wanted to silence his protests at their evil plans. Batman and Black Wolf worked together to stop the tribe from committing atrocities that they felt would balance the heinous crimes committed by European settlers in 1863. After their mission, Black Wolf died and Batman brought Ace back to GOTHAM CITY. Ace aided Batman on several occasions, including tracking the monstrous and elusive KILLER CROC. (*Batman* #462, May 1991) Once ensconced in the BATCAVE, Ace was drawn to the mute hunchback Harold, who had also come to live in the cave and build tools for the Dark Knight. Harold, in return, built Ace a mechanical mouse to play with. Ace was last seen prior to events known as NO MAN'S LAND.

Ace has not appeared in the reality created after the events of INFINITE CRISIS.

ACTUARY, THE

As a way to commit crimes without interference from Batman, the PENGUIN once recruited an unnamed actuary. This actuary observed that the best way to commit a crime without being foiled by Batman was to do so in broad daylight. As the Penguin made his plans, he was unaware that Batman had already targeted one of his current gang members, Nico Vanetta. Batman learned from Vanetta that the Penguin intended to rob the annual Gotham Flower Show. The Dark Knight then

engineered events so that the show was plunged into darkness, and the Penguin's latest scheme was foiled. Evidence gathered at the crime scene prevented Batman from linking the near robbery to the Penguin. In his role as a casino owner, the Penguin not only had an alibi, but could explain away circumstantial evidence as well. Still, to settle the possible criminal charges, Penguin maneuvered the actuary into pleading guilty to the flower show robbery. The actuary was subsequently sentenced to BLACKGATE PENITENTIARY. (*Detective Comics* #683, March 1995)

A'DAIRE, WHISPER

Little is known about Whisper a'Daire, whose first recorded appearance had her working for ecoterrorist RÃ'S AL GHÚL. (*Detective Comics* #743, April 2000) At the time, Rã's had developed a serum that enabled humans to change at will into one of several animal forms. She took the serum and became a snake woman, while her loyal bodyguard, KYLE ABBOTT, became a werewolf. One effect of the serum was prolonged life, and a'Daire was estimated to be at least eighty years old at the time Batman first encountered her, despite appearing to be in her late twenties at most. Her youthful visage was maintained by regularly shedding her skin, much like her snake counterpart. When Batman attempted to free a'Daire and Abbott from Rã's clutches, a'Daire refused, as she liked her new form and her abilities. She then disappeared and used the serum on several other former followers of Rã's, creating a small army of half-human/half-beast creatures. All were controlled by a'Daire's considerable mental powers. She learned that this telepathic link had limitations, however: Those under her command with superior willpower often sought their freedom.

A'Daire has demonstrated the ability to hypnotize by locking her slit-like eyes onto her victims. However, she often gets her way without employing this skill. A'Daire's fiery temper surfaced whenever her plans went awry, and she once spat a powerful acidic poison at Kyle Abbott, which blinded him.

The redheaded seductress later surfaced as the manager of HSC International Banking, a legitimate company fronting for the criminal group INTERGANG, with Abbott once more by her side. When the QUESTION and former G.C.P.D. detective RENEE MONTOYA were tracing illegal alien weaponry to Intergang, she ordered them killed. During the battle between the detectives and her minions, led by Abbott, a'Daire vanished. (*52* #11, 2006) She resurfaced in GOTHAM CITY more than six months later, aiding BRUNO MANNHEIM in performing spells as outlined in the Crime Bible. When that plan crumbled, she was severely burned and went her own way. (*52* #48, 2007)

ADAMS, ABEL

A citizen of eighteenth-century GOTHAM CITY who was better known to the masses as a criminal highwayman, CAPTAIN LIGHTFOOT.

ADAMS, MICHAEL

A criminal who fought the Batman under the name OGRE.

AGATHA (AUNT)

On Earth-2, Agatha was BRUCE WAYNE's aunt, although her exact relationship to the Wayne and Kane families remains unknown. Some time after Wayne began his career as Batman, Agatha arrived for what was to be a two-week visit, to ensure that her orphaned nephew was being well cared for by ALFRED PENNYWORTH, the family butler. To Wayne, the two weeks felt prolonged and on numerous occasions proved challenging for him and his ward, DICK GRAYSON, in their fight against crime as Batman and ROBIN. The timing of Agatha's visit could not have

been worse, as Alfred was on a two-week vacation and there was no one present to distract her.

The bespectacled, white-haired Agatha was kindhearted and somewhat overprotective of her family. Unfortunately, the visit complicated the Dynamic Duo's war on crime, especially when she fell asleep in front of the grandfather clock that doubled as the entrance to the BATCAVE. After they changed into their costumes in the WAYNE MANOR kitchen, Agatha discovered Bruce and Dick prior to their leaving the mansion, and she believed them to be dressed for a costume party. Instead the pair tackled the Rotor-Robbers as they were committing a crime, the confrontation conveniently "delaying" the costume party by a day. While this gave Batman and Robin a second chance to use the costume party excuse, they found themselves overwhelmed by the Rotor-Robbers . . . that is, until the JOKER arrived and pointed a gun at the Robbers, ordering them to free the Caped Crusaders. Removing the Joker mask, Agatha revealed herself and nearly gave away Batman's alter ego in the process. The confusion allowed Batman and Robin to subdue the Robbers, and the remainder of Agatha's visit went without incident. She was never seen again and is presumed no longer a part of Batman's life after the reality-altering events of various recent crises. (*Batman* #89, February 1955)

AIKO

Maureen Breen was a meta-human on retainer to the YAKUZA, Japan's underworld. As Aiko (a name that translates to "patronage or favor"), she first encountered Batman when she was sent to GOTHAM CITY to handle an INTERGANG stoolie. Breen demonstrated incredible strength and fast reflexes when she confronted the Dark Knight. A trained fighter, she managed to go toe-to-toe with the Batman, resulting in a draw during their first confrontation. When his next mission took him to Japan, Batman encountered Aiko a second time, where he manipulated her into ending the life of a deviant criminal who liked cosplay (costumed role playing). Aiko unfortunately proved an embarrassment to her superiors, and her ultimate fate went unrecorded. (*Legends of the Dark Knight* #213, February 2007)

AKINS, MICHAEL

Michael Akins originally served the citizens of Gateway City as a police officer before relocating to GOTHAM CITY. As a member of the GOTHAM CITY POLICE DEPARTMENT, Akins achieved a sterling record and was eventually named as Commissioner JAMES GORDON's replacement. Gordon retired after Gotham City was reopened in the wake of NO MAN'S LAND. The African American officer bravely endured all of Gotham's relentless problems, which gradually diminished optimistic Akins's belief in human nature. This was exacerbated when he asked Internal Affairs to investigate detective HARVEY BULLOCK. At the time, Bullock was suspected of shooting a man who had tried to kill Gordon. Bullock retired from the force under a cloud of controversy, and Akins found himself mistrusted by the officers for going after one of their own. (*Batman: Turning Points* #5, January 2001)

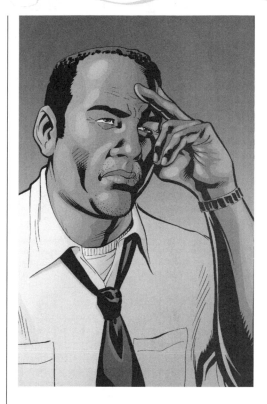

Unlike Gordon, Akins disliked the reliance the G.C.P.D. placed on its costumed protector, Batman. The reticence began during his Gateway days, when Akins had first encountered a vigilante and had approved of his efforts until a hostage situation went bad, leaving both the vigilante and the kidnapped victim—a child—dead. However, constant exposure to the psychotic and costumed criminals preying on Gotham's citizens eventually made Akins recognize that there was a place for Batman and those like him.

That changed during the events known as WAR GAMES, when Batman usurped Akins's command and started issuing orders to Gotham's police forces. The officers charged into a volatile gunfight between criminal gangs, which resulted in heavy casualties among the uniforms. There was a major loss of trust on both sides, and Akins ordered the BAT-SIGNAL removed from the G.C.P.D.'s rooftop, declaring that all costumed vigilantes were to be considered in violation of the law.

Shortly after these events, Batman, Robin, and NIGHTWING left Gotham City for six months, and Akins subsequently tendered his resignation, clearing the way for Gordon to come out of retirement. Rumors of fresh police corruption had circulated, and there was speculation that Akins resigned under pressure, given that the rumors stretched all the way to the commissioner's office. Since his resignation, Akins has not been seen in Gotham.

ALBREK, EDGAR

Edgar Albrek was desirous of his uncle's vast wealth and crafted a complex scheme to murder him and avoid conviction for the crime. The plan involved convincing law enforcement officers that while out of the country, Edgar had lost both hands to a gangrene epidemic in Africa. Through modern medicine, his claim went, new hands were grafted on, but they would prove to be the hands of an English murderer. Albrek would then contend that the murderer's hands acted on their own accord, against his will. Batman and ROBIN learned of the proposed crime and exposed the preposterous scam before Albrek's uncle could be killed. He was arrested. (*World's Finest Comics* #41, July/August 1941)

ALCOR

Alcor was a distant world with a prospering civilization. The citizens were protected by TAL-DAR, a crime fighter not unlike Batman. When the Dynamic Duo visited the world, they aided Tal-Dar in overcoming his vicious enemy, Zan-Rak. (*Detective Comics* #282, August 1960)

ALFRED

The first name of Bruce Wayne's longtime butler and confidant, ALFRED PENNYWORTH.

ALFRED MEMORIAL FOUNDATION

ALFRED PENNYWORTH died on Earth-1 while protecting Batman and ROBIN from the TRI-STATE GANG. He was trapped and perished under a massive pile of boulders, and in his memory BRUCE WAYNE opened the Alfred Foundation. A charitable organization, it would further Alfred's efforts to better all humankind.

When Alfred later returned to life as the villainous OUTSIDER and was subsequently restored to his old self, the foundation was renamed for the WAYNE FAMILY. The WAYNE FOUNDATION continued its mission of good works while also expanding, thanks to the vast Wayne Family fortune. (*Detective Comics* #328, June 1964)

ALI

Ali's Health Resort in GOTHAM CITY—a front for a criminal enterprise—was run by a corpulent Arab named Ali. As wealthy patrons visited the resort, selected victims were kidnapped and imprisoned within secret sections of the facility. Carefully prepared impersonators emerged from the resort and resumed the victims' lives, using their private access to funds to enrich Ali. For a brief time BRUCE WAYNE was numbered among the kidnapped, but DICK GRAYSON discovered the impersonator. The scheme was eventually foiled by Batman and ROBIN. (*Batman* #19, October/November 1943)

ALLEN, CRISPUS

Crispus Allen was a METROPOLIS police officer before relocating to the GOTHAM CITY POLICE DEPARTMENT'S MAJOR CRIMES UNIT. (*Detective Comics* #742, March 2000) Allen was a disciplined officer, finding strength from his family and believing that the role Batman played was a necessary component in the fight against crime. Allen was partnered with RENEE MONTOYA, and the two had a long string of successes working together. He was a loving and devoted husband and father to two children, and placed their safety above all else. Despite his family's strong religious beliefs, Allen remained an agnostic, refusing to believe in a God who could let so much evil exist in the world.

Allen's life took a tragic turn when he and Montoya tracked gang members into a deserted building. Without waiting for backup, per police procedure, they split up and trailed the criminals. BLACK SPIDER II suddenly appeared and shot Montoya, who avoided serious injury thanks to her bulletproof vest. The costumed criminal took aim at Montoya's unprotected head, but Allen arrived before he could fire and fatally shot Black Spider.

As Internal Affairs officers began their routine investigation, the corrupt crime scene officer, JIM CORRIGAN, pocketed the bullet Allen had fired that killed Black Spider. Corrigan kept it to sell on the collectors' black market, but without it IA was unable to complete its investigation. Tipped off by IA, Montoya tracked Corrigan and beat him to retrieve the evidence before he could sell it. While this freed Allen from suspicion, it fouled IA's separate investigation into Corrigan, and marked the partners as enemies in Corrigan's eyes. This news also placed a strain on Allen and Montoya's partnership.

Obsessed with obtaining evidence against Corrigan, Allen began putting in extra hours on his own, hiding his work from Montoya. Eventually learning of Allen's efforts, Corrigan had an informant who was about to speak out against him beaten to death. Subsequently Corrigan lured Allen into finding the body before cravenly shooting Allen in the back. In his role as an investigator, Corrigan tainted the crime scene, thereby avoiding arrest. Montoya, unable to nail Corrigan, suffered an emotional breakdown, left the force, and set off on a self-destructive path. (*Gotham Central* #38, February 2006)

Allen left behind his wife, Dore; his sons, Jacob and Mal; his mother, Violet; and two brothers.

As Allen's body lay in the city morgue during the events known as INFINITE CRISIS, the SPECTRE was forced by God to take Allen's corpse as its new human host. Allen's spirit was unwilling to accept this divine intervention, however, and initially tried to reject it. Nevertheless, the Spectre was summoned to Stonehenge by Earth's practitioners of magic to help usher in the Tenth Age of Magic. This new incarnation of the Spectre meted out justice by killing the villainous Star Sapphire for her past misdeeds. (*Infinite Crisis* #4, April 2006)

Allen and the Spirit of Vengeance later came to an agreement that would give Allen's spirit a year to roam the Earth and study humanity

before accepting the Spectre's presence. Without a human to anchor the Spectre, all humankind was threatened. Allen's spirit remained largely in Gotham, watching over his family and witnessing the fruitless investigation into his own death; he even discovered Batman's true identity. As the year ended, the Spectre returned and Allen finally accepted his fate.

By this time Allen's younger son, Mal, had determined on his own that Corrigan must have killed his father. Seeking revenge, Mal murders the corrupt cop, only to be confronted by the Spectre immediately after. Allen had no choice but to condemn his son to death for committing the crime. Because of this, Allen recognized his role as the Spectre's moral compass and always ensured that the punishment fit the crime. (*Infinite Crisis Aftermath: The Spectre* #1–3, 2006)

ALLEN, TOD

Tod Allen was a wealthy friend of BRUCE WAYNE'S, and through their many social interactions at the Sportsmen's Club, Allen eventually deduced that Wayne and his ward, DICK GRAYSON, were secretly Batman and ROBIN. Indulging his fondness for practical jokes, he began taunting Wayne with letters purportedly from a Mr. X, indicating that Batman's alter ego was in danger. Investigating the letters, Batman determined that Mr. X was Allen, and prepared to confront him about the ruse. Before he got the chance to do so, Allen died in a plane crash, his knowledge of Wayne's secret dying with him. (*Batman* #134, September 1960)

ALLNUT, HAROLD

Harold Allnut suffered all through life with muteness and a hunchback. (*The Question* #33, December 1989) After being thrown out of his home by his cruel parents in Hub City, he found his way north to GOTHAM CITY. There he came to the PENGUIN's attention, and when the criminal learned of Harold's innate genius with mechanical objects he provided shelter in exchange for Harold creating new devices to be used in the Penguin's crime sprees. However, anytime Harold tried to object to what the Penguin asked, he threatened his life. Batman fought the Penguin's gang on many occasions, and eventually rescued Harold from the stout felon. (*Batman* #458, January 1991)

Grateful for his reprieve, Harold turned his skills to helping the Dark Knight build new crime-fighting gear; eventually he maintained everything

Wayne used, from the BATMOBILE to the BATCAVE's computer systems. Shortly after Harold came to live in the Batcave, Batman's back was broken during a confrontation with the villain BANE. As Bruce Wayne began his long recuperation process, he turned the mantle of the Bat over to his recently acquired ally, JEAN-PAUL VALLEY—aka AZRAEL. Valley lacked Wayne's strict moral code, however, and quickly devolved the Caped Crusader into an armored avenger, barring Harold from the Batcave. Harold found a new way in and worked in secret, ultimately supporting NIGHTWING, ROBIN, and a recovered Wayne in their attempts to stop Valley.

Little has been recorded of Harold's activities between the restoration of Wayne as Batman and the arrival of the mysterious villain called HUSH. Dr. Tommy Elliot, a childhood friend of BRUCE WAYNE, sought revenge against Wayne for a long-ago slight, and used his miraculous surgical skills to transform Harold from a misshapen man into what passed for "normal." To repay the scheming surgeon, Harold agreed to hide microcircuits inside the Batcave's computer systems. The circuits then transmitted subliminal cues into Batman's mind, throwing the Caped Crusader off balance as Hush pressed forward his plan. Hush eventually killed Harold, whom he felt was nothing more than a loose end to be tied up. As he died, Harold confessed to Batman that he continued to look up to the hero, despite his own betrayal. (*Batman* #618, October 2003) A sympathetic Batman buried Harold overlooking WAYNE MANOR.

ALPHA (THE EXPERIMENTAL MAN)

Dr. Burgos once designed and constructed an android he dubbed Alpha. The artificial life-form possessed superhuman strength, but imperfect programming left Alpha with the emotional level of an infant. When sent by the doctor to aid Batman and ROBIN during a fight with the GREEN MASK BANDITS, Alpha complied without question, but when he thought Batman had turned against him, Alpha went on a destructive rampage. Alpha also had a crush on BATWOMAN, which led to his sacrificing himself while saving her life as she dangled off the edge of a cliff. The android was destroyed, and a distraught Burgos never built another model. (*Detective Comics* #306, September 1962)

AMYGDALA

Aaron Helzinger was born with a diminished mental capacity, and was prone to violent rages while growing up. Early in his tragic life Helzinger underwent brain surgery in an attempt to reduce the number of violent outbursts. The doctor performing the operation mistakenly removed his amygdala—the collection of nerves the brain uses to control emotional associations—rather than the hypothalamus that was the intended target. Complicating matters was that the botched operation mysteriously left Helzinger with strength beyond the human norm. (*Batman: Shadow of the Bat* #3, August 1992) Helzinger suffered from a variation of Klüver-Bucy syndrome, which involves damaged amygdalae, leaving its victims unable to properly respond to stimuli.

Given his unstable mental state and increased strength, Helzinger became a pawn of GOTHAM CITY's underworld, which resulted in his eventually being committed to ARKHAM ASYLUM. Now dubbed Amygdala, his brute strength proved more than a match for the Batman when the Dark Knight was trapped within the institution by JEREMIAH ARKHAM. Once he was finally subdued, his condition was properly diagnosed, and Amygdala received medication that corrected his emotional imbalance.

The medication was slow to change Amygdala's condition, however, and he eventually began committing additional crimes, which landed him back at Arkham until his condition stabilized. When BANE freed Arkham's residents during his attempt to weaken the Dark Knight, Amygdala fell under the sway of the VENTRILOQUIST, who took great comfort in his hulking presence. Their freedom did not last long, and soon they were back within the walls of the institution. At some point after this, Amygdala was transferred to BLACKGATE PENITENTIARY, where he took pleasure in being a fearsome hitter on the prison baseball team. Soon after, he was transferred back to Arkham, and freed once more, this time by the demon Neron, who was out to tempt the world's villains with their hearts' desires. The freedom was a rush for Amygdala, but before leaving he wanted to gain some measure of revenge against Arkham's cruel administration, and he nearly killed Jeremiah Arkham. The surprise appearance of the New God Izaya, aka Highfather, whose calming presence soothed Amygdala, saw the brute subdued once more.

Amygdala eventually agreed to a medical implant that distributed medication replicating the amygdala's function throughout his system, which seemed a permanent treatment for his condition. Helzinger was now declared cured and freed from custody, and he relocated to BLÜDHAVEN and wound up living in the same apartment building as NIGHTWING. (*Nightwing* [second series] #18, March 1998) He proved to be a good friend to DICK GRAYSON and his neighbors, in addition to being

successfully employed as a warden at Lockhaven Prison. When Blockbuster II blew up the apartment building as part of his vendetta against Nightwing, Amygdala was left shattered and homeless. He eventually found a new apartment in the city, but his whereabouts after Blüdhaven was destroyed by Chemo have yet to be chronicled.

ANARKY

Lonnie Machin's mother, showgirl Greta Mitchell, gave him up for adoption as a baby. His adoptive parents, Mike and Roxanne Machin, recognized that Lonnie was special. Mike took the incredibly bright and inquisitive Lonnie to many bookstores to feed his insatiable interest in all things, especially philosophy.

As an adolescent Lonnie went beyond the typical definition of *rebellious,* finding American society essentially morally bankrupt; he despaired at what people were doing to one another and to the planet itself. Donning an outfit he constructed that covered him head-to-toe and simulated great height, he expressed his rage toward polluters by attacking a factory that dumped waste into the water. With his walking stick, which contained a taser, he proved adept at combat. Confronting Anarky, Batman quickly deduced from body

language and commentary that underneath the elongated outfit was a youth. After physically restraining Machin, Batman had him confined to a juvenile detention center. (*Detective Comics* #608, November 1989)

During his incarceration, Machin accessed the facility's computers and, using the screen name Moneyspider, hacked into various corporations' bank accounts and siphoned millions. This he sent anonymously to the Third World countries he felt needed the money more than big businesses did.

Machin also managed to repeatedly escape and continue his one-teen crusade. When Eclipso was out to corrupt the world with his Black Diamond slivers, Anarky obtained one and used its power to attack buildings he felt were symbols of oppression. (*Robin Annual* #1, 1992) He engaged not only with Batman, but with the Scarecrow and Batman's temporary replacement Jean-Paul Valley as well. His genius led him to create the Anarkist Foundation; he also earned five million dollars by selling his own personal tracts via the Internet.

Unfortunately one of his customers, Malochia, used the tracts to further his own agenda as a prophet of doom. In his zeal Malochia became a danger to society, one Anarky felt responsible for. When Anarky tried to contain Malochia, he—along

with Batman and Joe Potato—were instead tied to an explosives-laden zeppelin. Anarky freed Batman and Joe Potato, but needed rescuing by Robin seconds before the zeppelin detonated, killing Malochia. Anarky used the explosion to fake his death and left a written farewell for his adoptive parents. (*Batman: Shadow of the Bat* #40–41, July/August 1995)

Now on his own, Machin dissolved his foundation and launched Anarco, naming himself president and CEO. He continued to sell his provocative documents, and in short order the company earned $199 million. Machin also trained extensively to improve his physical condition and better prepare himself for the confrontations he now knew would be a regular part of his mission. This regimen included eight hours a day of biofeedback, which seemed to result in his fusing the two hemispheres of his brain together, boosting his mental capabilities a hundredfold. With his newfound genius, he developed a device to improve the minds of fellow humans, hoping they would become more enlightened.

However, the machine needed vast amounts of power to run. He sought as many methods as possible to obtain the energy, first turning to Etrigan the Demon for help. Failing at that, he built his own version of a Boom Tube and hoped to extract the energy from Darkseid, ruler of the alien world Apokolips. He was stopped from doing this by Batman, who feared for Machin's life. Using the machine on himself, Anarky saw the many mistakes he was making and vowed to do better.

When Gotham City was devastated by a massive earthquake and descended into lawlessness, Anarky saw an opportunity to help remake the city. Batman wanted him out of the city, though: He saw Anarky as a distraction, not a help. Before acquiescing, Anarky searched for his parents, and feared them to have perished when he could not locate them.

With this newfound sense of direction and purpose, Machin set out on a new life. He relocated to Washington, D.C., where he established a living and working space under the Washington Monument. (*Anarky* #1, May 1999) There he built MAX, a super-computer with advanced AI technology. While working for a better tomorrow, Anarky found himself at cross purposes with Green Lantern and Jade, and then became a target of Rä's al Ghül when he discovered the latter's plan to ignite a Middle Eastern war. This plan failed, and Anarky managed to survive his battle with the ecoterrorist, although he earned himself another enemy.

Not long after building the super-computer, he asked MAX to access all available online records and determine if his parents had survived the earthquake. MAX reported that Mike and Roxanne were not his natural parents, and news of his adoption rocked Machin. The computer told him of his birth mother, but no record existed about his father. Clues, though, led Machin to speculate, with much fear and trepidation, that his father may have been the Joker.

This presented the teen with a crisis of confidence, and he largely withdrew from public sight. It took a rally of all the teen heroes to aid

the Young Justice team in bringing Anarky back into action. During the adventure the teens were temporarily turned into adults; seeing the world through new eyes, Machin reconsidered the importance of his life—despite the possible connection to the Joker. (*Young Justice: Sins of Youth* #1, May 2000)

ANDERSON, PROFESSOR

Anderson was a gifted engineer and scientist who constructed a device that actually transported people into works of fiction. When he demonstrated the device to Batman and Robin, he did so by sending them inside a volume called *Anthology of Fairy Tales*. While journeying through the stories, the duo rescued Anderson's daughter Enid, who had become trapped in the book, from the Black Witch. The trio soon safely returned to the real world, and the device's future uses went unrecorded. (*Batman* #5, Spring 1941)

ANDREWS

Andrews was an assistant curator working at the Gotham Museum who also had a large corrupt streak. He committed numerous high-profile crimes while disguised as a mummy, leading people to conclude that this relic from ancient Egypt had come back to life. Andrews chose the mummy motif not only because it frightened ordinary citizens, but also because the wrappings covered his oversized hearing aid, a sure clue to his identity. His criminal activities proved short-lived when he was quickly captured and exposed by Batman. (*Batman* #57, February/March 1950)

ANTAL, PIERRE

Pierre Antal was a noted European painter who remained virtually unknown in the United States. The "socially eminent" American Mr. Wylie was vacationing on the Continent when he fell in love with Antal's work. He purchased a number of the paintings at relatively inexpensive prices, despite his shaky fiscal condition. Wylie then concocted a scheme to bring Antal to America, get his work noticed, and let the value of his Antal collection appreciate so that he could sell the works and restore his lost wealth.

He took the plan a step further by letting Antal paint a series of portraits of America's wealthiest citizens. After each painting was finished, Wylie would desecrate the image in a specific way—such as by slashing it with a butcher knife. Donning a skull mask, Wylie then murdered the painting's subject in the same way. He committed three killings, in the process creating great notoriety for Antal. His fourth attempt, however, was thwarted by Robin. Then, in order to lure out the killer, Bruce Wayne agreed to sit for a portrait. Sure enough, Wylie made another attempt, but was stopped by the Caped Crusader. Rather than be tried for his crimes, Wylie shot himself to death. Batman would later note that he considered this to be the Dynamic Duo's first major case. (*Detective Comics* #42, August 1940)

Years later noteworthy people were once again dying after having their portraits painted by Antal. Among the victims were a broker named Jennings and singer Louisa Ponelle. The paintings had been altered just as Wylie's were years before. When Batman investigated Antal, the artist expressed his concern over his reputation being once more called into question.

Batman let Antal paint Bruce Wayne's image again in another attempt to lure the copycat killer, but Batman and Robin were captured by the killer instead. The real killer revealed himself to be a deranged, unnamed criminologist who held a theory that if Batman had failed at his first major investigation, his career as a crime fighter would never have gained traction. The criminologist theorized that only lucky starts meant long-term success, so he re-created Wylie's crimes in order to ruin Batman's confidence and career.

To avoid being killed by the criminologist, Batman and Robin took the risk of unmasking themselves and pleaded that they were standing in for the real Dynamic Duo, who were in Gotham City making a radio broadcast. The criminologist turned on his radio and was shattered to hear Batman's voice, never once realizing it was a pre-recorded message. Driven over the edge by his seeming failure, he imitated Wylie's final act and shot himself. (*Batman* #38, December 1946/January 1947)

ANT-MAN

Jumbo Carson was a rival mobster to Al Welles and was marked for death by the latter. Escaping the assassination attempt, Carson fell into the river near Hanson's Research Laboratory. The water by the lab was saturated with chemical runoff from Professor Hanson's attempts to perfect a formula to shrink people in size; Carson proved an unexpected test subject and was immediately reduced in stature. Soon after, a foot-high figure dressed in a scarlet costume was first noticed in Gotham City when he came to Robin's aid in apprehending Welles and his mob. Then, to the Boy Wonder's shock, the Ant-Man absconded with the very jewels Welles had tried to steal! Carson, as Ant-Man, had intended to plague Welles in revenge, but was instead captured by Robin. Without a known cure for Hanson's formula, Carson remained permanently in miniature form. (*Batman* #156, June 1963)

AQUAMAN

Orin, aka Arthur Curry, the king of Atlantis, served with Batman as a founding member of the Justice League of America. They have worked together as partners on numerous occasions since. Both men are usually grim and determined in their missions, making them close allies despite their vastly different backgrounds. Aquaman's origins have been altered many times as the fabric of reality has been continuously rewritten, but he remains a water-breathing monarch with great telepathic abilities that enable him to communicate with all forms of sea life. His adopted son Garth, known first as Aqualad and then Tempest, served with Batman's ward, Dick Grayson (the first Robin) in the Teen Titans. (*More Fun Comics* #73, November 1941)

AQUISTA, DARLA

Tim Drake's friend who died during the events of War Games and was later resurrected by Johnny Warlock and called the Warlock's Daughter.

ARDELLO

On another plane of reality existed an artificial construct named Ardello, who was described as a "nonmetallic robot." Accompanied by another construct, an "electronic bloodhound" that could scan human brain-wave activity and locate criminal patterns, Ardello journeyed to Earth's plane in order to find whoever had been crossing the barrier between dimensions and stealing high-tech weaponry. Fearing what harm the weapon—which was said to have been able to transform matter—could do, Ardello and the bloodhound felt great urgency in accomplishing their task. As a result, they mistakenly believed Batman to be behind the crimes, and a bizarre manhunt for the vigilante began. When Ardello eventually came to the realization that the Dark Knight was a fellow crime fighter, they compared notes and concluded that a criminal disguised as Batman was behind the crime. The unlikely duo tracked down Gimlet (aka Ed Collins), the true perpetrator. Collins had managed to cross the dimensional barrier using an ingenious—and stolen—device belonging to a prominent unnamed scientist. With the weapon recovered, the mechanical manhunters returned to their own reality. (*Detective Comics* #279, May 1960)

ARISTO

Aristo was a "cunning international thief" who arrived in Gotham City with riches on his mind. With his gang, he broke into the Gotham Museum and stole a magic lamp, created by the legendary Larko, a sorcerer. When Batman and Robin arrived to apprehend the thieves, the lamp was used to transform the Caped Crusader into a *jinni*, or "magical genie," connected to the lamp. As a magical being, Batman was now possessed of great powers, but he could only use them on behalf of the lamp's owner. Robin, working with Bat-Girl, managed to outwit Aristo, forcing the traditional three wishes to be expended without causing too much harm to Gotham's people and property. With his obligation completed, Batman resumed mortal form and, with Robin, brought Aristo and the gang to justice. The lamp was returned to the museum and kept under firm lock and key. (*Detective Comics* #322, December 1963)

ARKHAM, JEREMIAH

Nephew to Amadeus Arkham, Jeremiah was the most recent administrator of Arkham Asylum. He proved an uneven administrator thanks to the frequent escapes and high rate of recidivism among the asylum's residents. Some even questioned his close relationship with several of the inmates, especially Mister Zsasz. When the facility was upgraded some years ago, Arkham oversaw its reopening and subsequently trapped Batman within the asylum for research purposes. He decided to see what made Batman tick by exposing the Dark Knight to several liberated inmates, including the Joker, Killer Croc, and the Mad Hatter. (*Batman: Shadow of the Bat* #1–4, June–September 1992)

Jeremiah's own sanity was eventually questioned, and when the asylum was temporarily closed by federal order, he was seen cowering in the shadows. The building reopened a year later, and the unstable Jeremiah was unbelievably back in charge.

ARKHAM ASYLUM

The Elizabeth Arkham Asylum for the criminally insane was located north of Gotham City, and had been the home to both average and superpowered criminals since its founding in the early twentieth century. Named for original asylum director Amadeus Arkham's mother, the facility was dedicated to helping those afflicted with mental illnesses, as was Elizabeth. Amadeus had told others that his mother had committed suicide, but the truth was later revealed: He euthanized her when she became too much to handle, and then repressed his memories of the murder. Amadeus took control of the family mansion and had it converted into an asylum, and it has been constantly rebuilt and added on to over the years; for those residents with unique needs, customized facilities have been installed, such as a refrigerated cell for Mister Freeze. As the expansion work was in process, Amadeus; his wife, Constance; and his daughter, Harriet, relocated to Metropolis, where he temporarily treated patients at the state psychiatric hospital. (*Batman* #258, October 1974)

While overseeing the construction of the asylum during a trip back to Gotham, Arkham was consulted by Metropolis police after Martin "Mad Dog" Hawkins, a patient referred to Arkham, had escaped from a Metropolis prison. The police were unable to find the killer and asked Arkham for assistance. Arkham returned his family to Gotham as construction neared completion. He arrived home on April 1, 1921, only to discover that Hawkins had tracked him down and raped and mutilated both Constance and Harriet. Hawkins had even carved his nickname on Harriet's fresh corpse.

Seemingly undaunted by these grisly events, Arkham oversaw the asylum's opening the following November, with the recaptured Hawkins among the first residents. At various times the facility was referred to by the public as either Arkham Hospital or Arkham Sanitarium. Arkham personally treated Hawkins for six months, but on April 1, 1922, he strapped the criminal to a table, purportedly for electroshock therapy, and executed him. The police ruled it an accident. Arkham, however, slipped into madness from that moment onward, eventually becoming a ward of his own institution.

After the arrival of many costumed felons during the modern age of heroes, the cells at Arkham Asylum were filled with a colorful variety of cases that taxed the staff—and on occasion the building itself. In fact, it was damaged and partially demolished several times. At one point the entire facility was destroyed and completely rebuilt. Upon its reopening, Jeremiah Arkham, great-nephew of Amadeus and a man of questionable scruples himself, became its new director. In fact, shortly after the Asylum's reopening, he trapped Batman within its walls for a brief time as part of an intense psychiatric study. Even after Batman escaped, Arkham remained in charge of the facility. (*Batman: Shadow of the Bat* #1–4, June–September 1992)

Months later, the international criminal Bane actually blew up a portion of the asylum in order to release the inmates as part of his scheme to weaken Batman. (*Batman* #491, April 1993) Recapturing the escaped inmates took weeks and pushed Batman to his emotional and physical limits. With Arkham damaged, the inmates were temporarily housed at Blackgate Penitentiary. When the federal government cut off support to Gotham City, Arkham's cells were opened by the staff, its inmates freed, and the facility closed for a year. During that time, the Joker and Harley Quinn took up residence of their own free will.

Other cities across the country have sent their dangerous or insane super-villains to Arkham Asylum despite its somewhat shaky history, believing it better to simply dump the criminal problem on Gotham City. Among the noteworthy out-of-towners kept in Arkham were Jason Woodrue, John Dee (Doctor Destiny), the Dummy, Dancer, Doc Willard, the Crumbler, and Mister Thornton. Nearly every costumed foe the Dark Knight has ever faced has been incarcerated in Arkham at one point or another. Financier Warren White escaped a white-collar crime conviction by pleading insanity and being assigned to Arkham Asylum, without realizing the deleterious effects that exposure to his fellow inmates would have. White, by then known as the Great White Shark, was left a different person upon his release, and became a ruthless underworld boss. (*Arkham Asylum: Living Hell* #1–6, 2005)

The facility on the whole proved extremely porous, its residents having escaped on countless occasions. Those released had a high rate of recidivism. Security was uneven as well, to put it kindly, and the asylum's staffing proved questionable given how unstable several of its doctors became, including Dr. Harleen Quinzel, Lyle Bolton, and, in some versions of Arkham's reality, Jonathan Crane and Hugo Strange. Despite all that, the asylum remained a functioning facility relied upon by the government to treat those in need. It did, though, remain under constant surveillance by the ever-vigilant Batman.

In the reality after Infinite Crisis, the Arkham Mental Hospital was originally known as Arkham House and at some point in the past closed its doors. Early in Batman's career, Jonathan Crane told the Dark Knight his dream was to renovate and reopen the facility as a secure location to house a new breed of villain. With the advent of crimes committed by the madman who would be later known as the Joker, Crane's grants were finally approved and he expected to open the hospital by the end of that year. (*Batman Confidential* #9, November 2007)

ARMLESS MASTER

A legendary martial arts sensei called the Armless Master taught several heroes and villains—such as Tim Drake (Robin III), Catwoman, and Hellhound—fighting skills from his base in Asia. (*Robin* #49,

January 1998) His brother was the Paris-based Iron Hand (once known as the Legless Master), who trained both Tim Drake and a young woman named DAVA in France. The killing technique known as the Whispering Hand was the signature move both men taught their apprentices.

The Armless Master, a legend in the Thai fighting circuit, was killed by a masked figure known only as Tengu, who turned out to be LADY SHIVA. She had brought the recovering Batman to the Armless Master to begin his retraining in the wake of his back (and spirit) being broken by BANE. Once sufficiently inspired, Batman fought the Armless Master's students and eventually regained his atrophied skills.

ARNOLD, PROFESSOR HUGO

Despite great technological accomplishments during his career, Professor Hugo Arnold was overlooked by the GOTHAM CITY Historical Society when they selected prominent city ancestors to be recognized in a series of public events. His oversized ego badly bruised, Arnold swore to ruin the society's efforts and bring attention to his own genius. With the help of a brain stimulator of his own devising, Arnold increased the size of his intellect, in addition to his brain and skull casing, turning him into a deformed figure. Using his newfound extensive knowledge, Arnold built several attention-getting devices, including a lightning cannon and invisible flying robots. Both were used to attack the pageants, ruining the society's celebration and causing panic in the streets. Empowered by his first successes, Arnold decided to show the world how smart he was by planning the creation of a second moon and placing it in orbit around Earth—regardless of the havoc such an additional celestial body would wreak across the globe. His antics brought him to the attention of Batman and ROBIN, who managed to stop Arnold and his henchmen before the mad scientist could go too far. Arnold's devices were quickly rendered inoperative, and the professor was jailed. (*Detective Comics* #306, August 1962)

ARTISANS, THE

A gang of ruthless, plainclothes GOTHAM CITY criminals led by JACK "FIVE STAR" THORPE and eventually brought to justice by Batman and ROBIN. (*Batman* #65, June/July 1951)

ARVIN, DR. EDWARD

A brilliant scientist who turned to a life of crime as MISTER BLANK.

ASHER

Asher owned Asher Lumber Company, but gave in to his baser instincts when he coveted ownership of the much more lucrative North Woods lumber holdings. The first step in his plan was to murder lumber magnate Matthew Powell and obtain control of his rival's land. However, Batman and ROBIN interrupted each step in Asher's plan until they finally ensnared him and brought him to trial to face attempted murder charges. (*Batman* #7, October/November 1941)

ASHLEY, J. J.

Promoters-turned-criminals J. J. Ashley and Ed Burton staged a series of Mardi Gras–themed carnivals across the United States. In addition to entertaining the masses, they moved stolen goods from city to city, buying them from fences in one spot and selling them elsewhere for an increased profit. The business was a successful one, and had gone undetected until Burton decided to double-cross his partner. With the help of escaped convict Mike Kelso, they attempted to murder Ashley and gain sole control of the business. Instead, Ashley killed *them,* which immediately brought him to the attention of the Dynamic Duo. Batman and Robin shut down the criminal enterprise and sent Ashley to jail. (*Detective Comics* #309, November 1962)

ASPLIN, BENEDICT

A superpowered criminal better known to law enforcement authorities as Mister Asp.

ASTRO

Astro may have been the given name of an underworld inventor, but it was more likely a moniker bestowed thanks to the inventor's work with satellite technology. His greatest device was a multifunction satellite that could aid criminal activities from orbit. Once secretly launched, the "crime satellite" managed to help rob banks, melt pursuing police cars, and even create a force field to protect itself from attack. Astro grew rich from his invention and continued his string of incredible crimes until he was brought to the attention of Batman and Robin. With the Gotham City Police Department, the Dynamic Duo put Astro out of business, and the satellite was rendered useless. (*Detective Comics* #266, April 1959)

ATHENA

Celia Kazantzakis worked herself up from near poverty to great success running an orphanage. However, she eventually grew greedy and corrupt, disdaining the way high society looked down on her. She fell in love with Lorenzo Rossetti, a low-level thug, and after he was executed by his family she sought revenge. In time Celia built the Network, an international criminal empire using the name of the Greek goddess Athena, and struck at the Rossetti family as well as Wayne Enterprises, given her soured relationship with Martha Wayne, Bruce's deceased mother.

ATKINS

The man known only as Atkins was a stockholder in the Hobbs Clock Company whose secret desire was to control the entire business. He brought Elias Brock, a Hobbs employee, into his confidence, knowing the skilled clockmaker was mentally unstable. In fact, Brock fancied himself a contemporary "Father Time" and did Atkins's bidding, including killing two of the majority stockholders, believing in each case that the victims were "time wasters." For both killings, Brock constructed tabletop clocks that emitted either a deadly gas or a poisoned dart. Realizing that his work was being exploited, Brock killed Atkins and then fought Batman when the Caped Crusader arrived to investigate the murders. Brock fell to his death from the Hobbs Clock Company's clock tower during the confrontation, a fitting end to a sad life. (*Batman* #6, August/September 1941)

ATKINS

Gotham City's Atkins and Bork Curio Shop was the starting point for one of the most bizarre cases in Batman's early career. A dying criminal arrived at the store and provided Atkins and Bork with a map that was said to lead the owner to four ancient objects of great power. The duo tracked down the objects across the continents and recovered all four—a green box containing a living, fire-breathing dragon; a prism that distorted light and deflected energy; a glove that dissolved inert matter; and a mantle that turned its wearer invisible—and intended to use the recovered talismans for a life of crime. Before they could accomplish their goal, however, Atkins and Bork were defeated by Batman, Robin, and Superman, and the Man of Steel hurled the objects into space at such great speed that the friction was presumed to have destroyed them. (*World's Finest Comics* #103, August 1959)

ATKINS, GWEN

Gwen Atkins was Bruce Wayne's longtime secretary at Wayne Enterprises. She never once dated Bruce or suspected his secret life as Batman. She abruptly left his employ, possibly as part of Gregorian Falstaff's scheme to gain control of the company some years ago. Her whereabouts after leaving Wayne Enterprises are unrecorded. (*Batman* #217, December 1969)

ATLANTIS

Atlantis is the Greek word for "island of Atlas," and is largely the stuff of myths and legends. In Batman's initial reality, dubbed Earth-2, he discovered the island to be a reality, its people surviving on the floor of the sea some eleven thousand years after the continent supposedly sank. Atlantean scientists had constructed an artificial sun to provide light and heat; a giant transparent dome kept the deep sea pressure at bay. Ruled by the youthful Taro and his sister Lanya, Atlantis was nearly ensnared in the events of World War II when Batman and Robin fought the Nazi forces of Admiral Von Buritz above the domed city. (*Batman* #19, October/November 1943)

On the parallel Earth-1, and subsequent re-orderings of reality, Atlantis also survived and became home to Orin, better known to the surface world as Aquaman.

ATOM, THE

Ray Palmer, a physics professor at Ivy University, discovered a piece of a white dwarf star when a meteorite struck the outskirts of Ivy Town. Studying the celestial object, he learned how to harness its properties, which allowed him to control his size and weight. Creating a costumed identity, Palmer began a crime-fighting career as the Atom, and subsequently joined with Batman as a member of the Justice League of America. The Batman had tremendous respect for Palmer's expertise and ability to teach others. In Earth-1's reality the two

paired up on several occasions, most notably when Batman was electrocuted by Buggsy Cathcart's booby trap, leaving the Caped Crusader near death. The Atom entered his brain and jumped from point to point to animate Batman and save his life. (*Showcase* #34, September/October 1961)

In the reordered universe after the Crisis on Infinite Earths, the Atom dealt with the double blows of his wife, Jean Loring's, infidelity and mental illness, which led her to kill Sue Dibny, wife of fellow JLAer Elongated Man. Palmer then vanished from sight, entering one of myriad microscopic universes to deal with his grief.

Palmer's disappearance turned out to have cosmic repercussions. When the multiuniverse was re-formed in the wake of Infinite Crisis, Palmer apparently visited many of the newly formed parallel Earths, leaving behind a trail. He was said to be the solution to an impending "Great Disaster" although the secrets remained unrecorded. (*Countdown* #52, 2007; *Countdown Presents: The Search for Ray Palmer,* January-February 2008)

ATOMIC-MAN

Paul Strobe was a brilliant electrical engineer who worked with three partners to create electronic devices for sale. Strobe also engaged in private atomic studies and needed additional cash resources for funding. Desperate, he wound up stealing gold and platinum from his own company. He was eventually apprehended by Batman and served jail time.

Once free from jail, Strobe returned to his studies and created several devices with the express purpose of revenge against his former partners for reporting the crime, and Batman for capturing him. He created a pair of special goggles with colored filters, the various combinations of which would channel the massive energy created by a machine of his own design. The filtered power could alter the molecular structure of any object; one setting would turn solid objects to water, another would change the item into glass. Donning a green-and-yellow costume, he dubbed himself Atomic-Man.

With a gang of thugs, he committed a series of crimes aimed at his former partners until he was stopped by Batman and Robin. Strobe was sent to jail for good after standing trial for his crimes. (*Detective Comics* #280, June 1960)

ATOM-MASTER, THE

The Atom-Master, a scientist also known as the Illusion-Master, committed a series of crimes in Metropolis and Gotham City to raise enough capital to build a gigantic transmitter that would further his criminal activities. Using the equipment he had already built, the Atom-Master convinced the residents of both cities that they were being attacked by either a giant crab in Metropolis or a dive-bombing Batplane in Gotham. Such distractions kept Batman, Robin, and Superman, in addition to both cities' police, preoccupied, allowing the criminal to rob elsewhere. With the stolen money, the Atom-Master managed to construct the next-generation device, which gave his illusions actual form and substance. When Batman and Robin finally tracked the Atom-Master to his lair, an old pottery factory outside Gotham, they discovered him wearing a bulky headpiece that sent his thoughts to the transmitter, which would then create the life-like images to be projected in either city. Before Atom-Master could use the devices further, Superman arrived and apprehended the scientist. (*World's Finest Comics* #101, May 1959)

When the Atom-Master turned up some time later after being freed from jail, he managed to rebuild his machine into a smaller and more streamlined helmet. He teamed up with super-villains Enchantress, Ultivac, and Mister Poseidon, forming a group dubbed the Forgotten Villains, although he felt the mentally unstable Enchantress was too unreliable. This suspicion proved true, and the villains wound up defeated by Superman and a cadre of other costumed crime fighters. (*DC Comics Presents* #77, January 1985)

The Forgotten Villains again fought the Man of Steel and his allies the Forgotten Heroes (Animal Man, Dolphin, Immortal Man) several years later. The villains acted as agents for the immortal Vandal Savage in a battle that took them through time as they sought fragments from the meteor that had turned Savage and Immortal Man into long-lived beings. Superman, Atom-Master, Vandal Savage, and Resurrection Man all became trapped in the distant past when Savage escaped, but were eventually were returned to the present thanks to the intervention of Time Master Rip Hunter. Atom-Master was then once more imprisoned. (*Resurrection Man* #25, June 1999)

AVIARY, THE

The nightclub known as the Aviary was one of many legitimate businesses that served as hideouts used by the Penguin throughout his criminal career, all of which were inspirations for his legitimate operation, the Iceberg Lounge. (*World's Finest Comics* #55, December 1951/January 1952)

AZRAEL

The Sacred Order of Saint Dumas existed for five centuries. A splinter group of the Knights Templar, it was a secret society that mixed martial training with a quasi-mystical belief system. Over time improved technology helped to serve the order's goals of protecting those they deemed sacred. In the twentieth century its members began to experiment with test-tube babies and genetic manipulation. At the same time, the order trained followers in something known as "the System," which mixed fervent religious belief with unparalleled fighting skills. (*Batman: Sword of Azrael* #1, October 1992)

Jean-Paul Valley was the first successful result of the test-tube experiments, his genes having been mixed with those of simians. As a child he was deeply indoctrinated into the System, something he was eventually trained to forget until he was ready to employ his knowledge as an adult. Valley remembered nothing of the order until his father revealed everything as he lay dying. Jean-Paul's secret past was brought to light, and the university student was shocked to learn of his forgotten childhood. Upon his father's death, Jean-Paul was taken to a secret location, where he donned the armor of Azrael (the order's Angel of Death) and began following the order's instructions without question, just as his rigorous training demanded. When assigned to kill a weapons dealer who threatened a fragile international peace, Azrael first encountered Batman in Gotham City.

As a result of the encounter—which ended the dealer's business without ending his life—Azrael realized total blind obedience was wrong; recognizing the need for further training in all matters, he accompanied Batman back to Gotham City. Together they fought crime, and while Batman tried to instill some sense of moral justice in Jean-Paul, he struggled to fight the System with his newfound free will. He would do so for the rest of his life.

A short time later, before Azrael's training was complete, Batman's back was broken during an encounter with Bane, and with Gotham City overrun by the criminals Bane freed from Arkham Asylum, the gravely injured Bruce Wayne asked Jean-Paul Valley to put aside Azrael's armor and take up the mantle of the Bat. A grateful Valley accepted and donned Batman's cape and cowl. Little time was lost in establishing to Gotham City residents that Batman was back in action, thereby squelching rumors of the Dark Knight's injury or death. However, the System continued to prey on Jean-Paul's mind, and fairly quickly he began to replace portions of Bruce Wayne's Batman costume with tailor-made armored enhancements of his own design. Unlike his more disciplined mentor, Jean-Paul fought to win and didn't care what condition his enemies were left in. He continually defied Wayne's instructions, including taking on Bane, whom Jean-Paul defeated in hand-to-hand combat. (*Batman* #500, October 1993)

Obsessed with his new role, he eventually banned Robin and Harold Allnut from the Batcave in order to focus on training in complete solitude. In time Bruce Wayne recovered from his ordeal with Bane, and his first act was to reclaim the Batman mantle from Jean-Paul, who fought Bruce with the intent to kill. When Wayne defeated him, Valley was distraught.

Jean-Paul spent the next few years trying to find a place for himself in the world while fighting for justice. He tempered his fighting with more compassion, remembering Batman's training and placing it ahead of the System. This then put him at odds with the order, whose members demanded strict loyalty to their agenda. They ordered his death, and agents of the order tried to kill Valley on more than one occasion.

To compound matters, Valley didn't quite understand how to successfully deal with people and fumbled at things as simple as social interactions and dating. He earned himself enemies whenever he came to the aid of others, including megalomaniacs Nicholas Scratch and Carlton Lehah.

Azrael was called to aid the Dark Knight on several subsequent occasions, such as when the Clench—a deadly disease—was unleashed on Gotham City. Finally, when he no longer needed to single-mindedly fight the System, Azrael took on his father's spirit, and that of Saint Dumas himself as well. In the process he experienced hallucinations and other supernatural manifestations that made him question how much freedom he truly had in choosing his own path. One result of this spiritual conflict was the destruction of the order's European mountain headquarters, and its centuries-long reign finally came to an end. In a climactic battle with his frequent opponents Scratch and Lehah, Azrael was struck with bullets coated with a deadly toxin. Although his body was never recovered, Batman and the rest of the world believed Azrael dead. (*Azrael: Agent of the Bat* #100, May 2003)

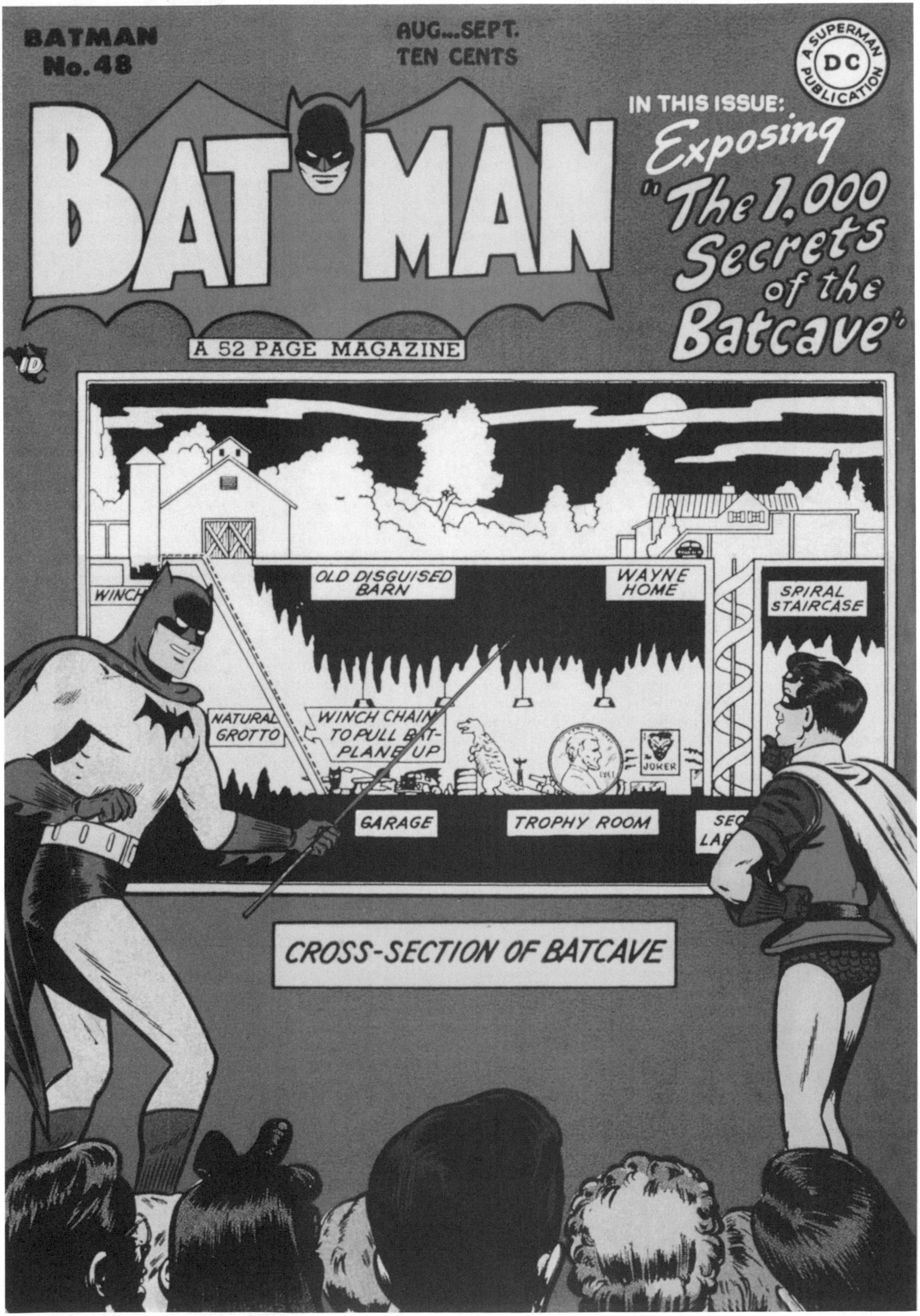
BATMAN No. 48
AUG...SEPT. TEN CENTS
A SUPERMAN DC PUBLICATION
BATMAN
IN THIS ISSUE: Exposing "The 1,000 Secrets of the Batcave"
A 52 PAGE MAGAZINE
WINCH
OLD DISGUISED BARN
WAYNE HOME
SPIRAL STAIRCASE
NATURAL GROTTO
WINCH CHAIN TO PULL BAT-PLANE UP
JOKER
GARAGE
TROPHY ROOM
CROSS-SECTION OF BATCAVE

BABBLE, ALLY

Ally Babble liked to talk . . . and talk and talk. He used his particular gift to convince people to see things his way, often with remarkable results. When Babble successfully used his skills at the request of Jasper Quinch to silence a tap dancer living above him, Quinch decided to hire the voluble fellow to handle thirteen other pet peeves that were disturbing his life as well. Accepting the five-thousand-dollar fee, Babble set right to work. A subway guard who liked to overpack subway cars found himself shoved into a crowded car, while a motorist who liked to splash pedestrians by driving through puddles was himself tossed into a huge muddy deluge. GOTHAM CITY police were eventually alerted to these misdemeanors and began to investigate. At the same time, two criminals named Hoiman and Shoiman learned of Babble's abilities and robbed his home. They subsequently followed Babble to the Clown Club, a home for practical jokers, and as Babble dealt with the annoying jokers—another item on Quinch's list—the two thugs tried to steal the club's solid-gold trophy. They were stopped by Batman and ROBIN, and the Dynamic Duo, along with the blabbering man, returned to verify the facts with Quinch. It was then that Babble found himself placed on Quinch's pet peeves list and was shown the door. (*Batman* #30, August/September 1945)

Some time later Babble turned superstitious in addition to being a public nuisance. Upon hearing a gypsy who read tea leaves promise he would find wealth, love, travel, and the ability to bring happiness to others, Babble took the tea leaves, sealed each in a separate envelope, and cast them into the spring winds. By following each envelope, Babble theorized, he would be able to find his fortunes come to life. The first envelope was tracked to a trolley car that had just been hijacked by criminals hoping to obtain the bonds being carried by a passenger onboard. Before Babble could act, Batman and Robin arrived and stopped the criminals. Since the Dynamic Duo never accepted rewards, the bond company president turned over the reward—one dollar—to Babble.

While tracking the second envelope, Babble saved a woman from being struck down by a car. She rewarded him with a peck on the cheek. Babble presumed this meant he had met the girl from the prophecy, and promptly fell in love with her.

Leaving the confused woman behind, Babble headed after the third envelope, which wound up in the lounge area of a hospital. The lounge was decorated to resemble the deck of a luxury ocean liner in an effort to bring a sense of peace and calm to the patients. As Babble studied the surroundings, he noticed that criminals were also present and were trying to steal the facility's supply of radium. As Batman and Robin arrived—they had been following the superstitious Babble—he accidentally inhaled a large amount of pure oxygen, which left him intoxicated. His drunken ambling about actually served a good cause, as it enabled the heroes to stop the attempted robbery. In his haze Babble believed himself to be traveling, also as prophesied by the tea leaves.

While the police took the criminals away, Babble complained of being left hoarse by the oxygen overdose. Batman laughed and suggested that Babble's inability to speak was the fourth fortune come true: His not speaking brought great happiness to those around him. (*Batman* #34, April/May 1946)

BAFFLE, MICHAEL

The international thief named Michael Baffle used his charm and good looks to commit crimes all across Europe. After finally being apprehended for a jewel robbery, he was sentenced to death, but managed to charm the firing squad into filling their rifles with blanks, enabling him to escape during the resulting confusion. He immediately left for America and arrived in GOTHAM CITY. Wasting little time once he was settled in the gleaming city, he soon acquired two thugs, Fish-eye and Egg-head. With their help Baffle compiled a listing of wealthy targets and set out to relieve them of all their belongings. In some instances the trio robbed empty homes, while other times they staked out mansions. Using his innate charisma, Baffle posed as a society reporter and interviewed his future victims, simultaneously taking pictures of the interiors of their homes using a camera secreted within his boutonnière. The criminals would then return and rob the home at a later time. Batman quickly joined the police investigation into this rash of crimes and came to respect Baffle's modus operandi. In turn, as the Dynamic Duo foiled attempt after attempt and managed to retrieve stolen property, Baffle also learned to respect the costumed lawman's methods. In the end Baffle engineered a daring escape; as he departed, he admitted he liked the Batman, wished they could be friends under other circumstances, and hoped they would see each other again. Batman admitted he felt the same way, but Baffle's hope never came to pass. (*Detective Comics* #63, May 1942)

BAGLEY

Bagley was a GOTHAM CITY underworld boss who sought to control all criminal activity in the city. Doing so of course meant removing the omnipresent threat that Batman posed to illegal activity. Bagley devised a plan to capture the Caped Crusader and unmask him before the city's mob bosses, thereby rendering Batman ineffective and asserting his own supremacy. Bagley's attempt failed when Batman learned of the plan and allowed a Batman robot to be captured in his place. At the unmasking, the stunned criminals were quickly apprehended by the Dynamic Duo. (*Batman* #109, August 1957)

BAILEY, NICK

Nick Bailey was a ruthless criminal who would stop at nothing to get his way. One of his crimes included stealing a quantity of jade from a Wyoming boxcar shipment. In an effort to fence the material, Bailey disguised himself as the mayor of GOTHAM CITY's CHINATOWN, Shing Far. Seeking the real Far, who had been reported missing, Detective Ling Ho enlisted the help of Batman and ROBIN, and the unlikely trio managed to stop Bailey from shipping the stolen jade as part of Far's curio import/export business. The impersonator was soon apprehended and the real Far freed. (*Detective Comics* #139, September 1948)

BAIN, MARTIN

To disguise his crime wave, gangster Martin Bain posed as eminent time-travel authority PROFESSOR CARTER NICHOLS. With the impostor Nichols speaking as an authority, the crimes were being attributed not to Bain's gang but to time-displaced figures including Jesse James, John Dillinger, Genghis Khan, and Captain Kidd. The bogus Nichols informed the police, as well as Batman and ROBIN, that his latest device, a time ray that could retrieve objects from the past, had been stolen.

While the gullible public believed these famous figures to be real, the police continued to try to stop the city's gold supplies from being stolen. The Dynamic Duo aided the police in finally capturing the thieves, exposing them as modern-day thugs. Bain was subsequently apprehended, and Batman's friend Nichols was freed from his closet prison. (*Batman* #43, October/November 1947)

BAKER, BIG JACK

Big Jack Baker was a ruthless mobster who was imprisoned and awaiting trial when he convinced his defense attorney, Verne Lever, to assume temporary control over his men. Baker told Lever that this was to provide leadership in the vacuum created by his imprisonment, but it was really a ploy to have Lever incriminate himself and thus work his hardest to get Baker freed during trial.

Complications arose when Batman was accidentally doused with liquid from a vat containing an experimental radioactive dye that left the Dark Knight temporarily invisible. Not only could people not see Batman, but BRUCE WAYNE was nowhere to be found, either. As he struggled to preserve his secret identity, Batman had to testify at Baker's trial. Fortunately, he managed to convince the judge of his presence and was allowed to testify. Baker was later found guilty and, before being taken from the court, exposed Lever's criminal

activity. Batman managed to grab the crooked lawyer before he could flee the courtroom using ROBIN as a human shield. (*Detective Comics* #199, September 1953)

BALFOR, GRIFFIN

Griffin Balfor was known to many as one of the greatest directors of the silent-film era. With the advent of sound, however, his career came to an abrupt halt, and he brooded about this for years. The time alone seemed to have twisted his mind, and one day he hit upon a warped scheme to launch a comeback. Balfor used his reputation and connections to gain access to the greatest modern-day actors and actresses, and he kidnapped them. He then transported the "cast" and all his equipment to a remote, nearly inaccessible valley and set out to film his next masterpiece. Batman and ROBIN managed to track the missing stars to the valley and arrived in time to free them. Balfor flooded the valley in a vain attempt to kill the rescuers but wound up drowning instead when he rushed back to retrieve a reel of vintage film from his private collection of great silent dramas. (*Batman* #66, September 1951)

BALKANIA

Described as a faraway kingdom, Balkania was ruled by PRINCESS VARINA when it became part of a case involving Batman, ROBIN, and SUPERMAN. It was believed to be a tiny principality somewhere in Europe. (*World's Finest Comics* #85, November/December 1956)

BALLARD, BRAND

Brand Ballard had a mediocre career as a stage illusionist and makeup artist who allied himself with criminals in a scheme to discredit Batman by convincing the citizens of GOTHAM CITY that the Caped Crusader was, in fact, an alien.

Ballard's work was effective enough that even Batman's close allies began to mentally review his amazing feats and wonder if Ballard's claim could be valid. With the evidence mounting, support from Police Commissioner JAMES GORDON and VICKI VALE paled, and the public, scared of anything out of the ordinary, was even more put off. As a result, Batman's effectiveness was hampered: People feared he was merely the vanguard of some alien invasion that would endanger the world.

Eventually Batman discovered Ballard's role and forced him into a full confession. A newly emboldened police force aided the Gotham Guardian in apprehending Ballard's criminal allies. Afterward, Gordon and Vale publicly reaffirmed their faith in Gotham City's protector. (*Detective Comics* #251, January 1958)

BAMBOO MONKEY

The Bamboo Monkey was a martial artist who served the cult known as the BROTHERHOOD OF THE FIST. In combat, he had bested both ROBIN and NIGHTWING before being defeated by CONNOR HAWKE, son of the GREEN ARROW. The fighter's title meant that he was as strong and flexible as the material he was named for. (*Nightwing* #23, August 1998)

BANCROFT, BIG JACK

GOTHAM CITY's public enemy number one was once Big Jack Bancroft, a ruthless gangster. He also closely resembled Eddie Blinn, noted saxophonist in Kay Kyser's band. To avoid arrest, Bancroft had Blinn kidnapped, and he replaced the musician while the band was performing in Gotham City. Bancroft managed to fool Kyser for a time, even during radio performances on *Kay Kyser's Kollege of Musical Knowledge,* but eventually Batman and ROBIN tracked down and exposed the criminal. With the help of "the Ol' Professor," the Dynamic Duo arrested the corrupt crook. (*Detective Comics* #144, February 1949)

BAND OF SUPER-VILLAINS, THE

Three ordinary criminals (ASTRO, the Mer-man, and an unnamed third) were caught up in a scheme created by a would-be dictator on a far-off planet. Brought to this alien environment, they were each given a belt that provided the wearer with fantastic powers. The humans were told they were to use the belts to become famous super-villains on Earth and then return to help the dictator secure his position. The real scheme involved the releasing of poison from the radioactive elements contained within each belt into the atmosphere, killing all humans and preparing Earth for an alien colonization. The villains wreaked havoc on Earth for a brief time before their newfound powers proved ineffective against the World's Finest team of Batman, ROBIN, and SUPERMAN. The alien's plan now exposed, he destroyed himself and his spacecraft as punishment for failing to carry out his own goals. (*World's Finest Comics* #134, June 1963)

BANE

The villain known as Bane began life in the dreaded Peña Duro prison on the island nation of SANTA PRISCA. His mother had been imprisoned while pregnant, and, cruelly, the unborn child was to serve out his unknown father's sentence. The question of Bane's parentage would haunt him throughout his adult years. Bane grew up in the harsh, unforgiving prison environment, developing a hard edge at an early age and striking out at antagonists from as young as eight years old. He committed the first of his countless murders at that age, killing a man who sought information from the young Bane. Bane was no fool, and took advantage of Peña Duro's meager facilities, reading every book in the library and using the gym's equipment to develop a superior body. By adulthood Bane stood at six feet one inch tall and weighed a massive 325 pounds, all of which was muscle. Intellectually he developed his mind to an extraordinary degree, his eidetic memory enabling him to master at least eight languages and match the most accomplished leaders in a variety of scientific fields.

Among his many mentors was an old Jesuit priest, who saw to it that the youth was grounded in classical teachings in addition to the "street life" he experienced day after day in prison. Still, Bane considered no one his friend; that title was reserved solely for Osito, a stuffed bear and his only toy while growing up. It also became the hiding place

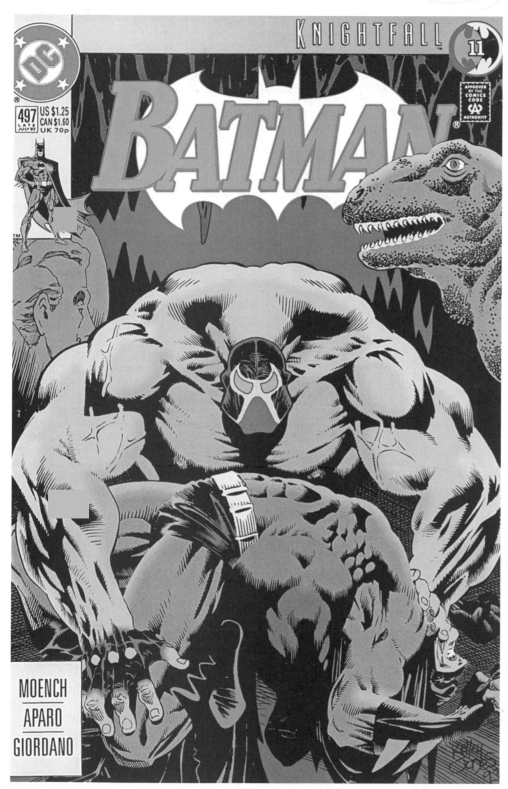

motif was one he recognized from the dreams that terrorized him throughout the years. Bane decided to destroy Batman and rule Gotham by himself. (*Batman: Vengeance of Bane* #1, 1993)

Bane was crafty and highly intelligent, and worked out a scheme to weaken the Dark Knight before engaging him in single combat. He figured out Batman's alter ego and used that knowledge to his advantage as well. His first step involved destroying ARKHAM ASYLUM and unleashing the psychotic criminals who had been housed there. Gotham City was quickly overrun with homicidal felons, overtaxing the police department and pushing Batman to the edge of exhaustion. It took the Caped Crusader some three months to track and recapture all the inmates. His mission seemingly complete, Batman returned to WAYNE MANOR to find Bane waiting for him. The battle in the BATCAVE was brutal but decidedly one-sided given Bane's superhuman strength and Batman's physical and mental exhaustion. The fight ended when Bane broke Batman's back and left him lying on the cave's floor. (*Batman* #497, Late July 1993)

Bane then seized control of Gotham's underworld and ruled with an iron hand until he was challenged by Batman's successor, JEAN-PAUL VALLEY, who had been temporarily given the mantle of the Bat. During this confrontation, Bane was bested when Valley severed the cables carrying the Venom drug, but was left alive.

Later, after BRUCE WAYNE healed and resumed his role as Batman, he had a rematch with Bane that saw the two men on more equal footing. During this fight Batman prevailed, although the two would fight again and again in the years that followed, always ending in a draw.

After his defeat, Bane left Gotham City and sought a destiny divorced from the Batman. On a return to Santa Prisca, the bitter Bane killed the priest who had tutored him, the act granting Bane little solace. He fell under the sway of the international terrorist RÄ'S AL GHÜL, acting as his bodyguard with the promise of marriage to Rä's daughter TALIA HEAD, but that partnership was doomed to failure. (*Batman: Bane of the Demon* #1–4, March–June 1998)

At one point Bane sought to learn his father's identity, and discovered clues pointing to the possibility that Dr. THOMAS WAYNE may have had an adulterous affair and fathered Bane. Batman learned that his father had spent time at Santa Prisca and had known Bane's mother, but the issue of parenthood was proven false. Bane tracked new clues to KING SNAKE, leader of the GHOST DRAGONS; when he learned that King Snake was his true father, he killed him.

During all of this, Bane sought to rid himself of his dependency on the Venom drug. Bane also tried to walk the path of good, going so far as to bathe in a LAZARUS PIT, which he saw as a chance for rebirth. This proved not to last, however, and Bane allied himself with the global organization known as the Society, made up of the world's foremost super-villains. During the Great Battle of METROPOLIS, Bane joined the villains in opposing a cadre of super heroes, repeating his signature move and breaking the Judomaster's back. (*Infinite Crisis* #7, June 2006)

---

for a knife that Bane used to defend himself. When Bane reached adulthood, he agreed to become a test subject for a drug known as VENOM, which had proven deadly to others it had been tested on. While it sickened him almost to death, Bane survived and found himself in possession of superior strength. There was a price to be paid for such power, however: He had to take fresh doses of the drug every twelve hours or immediately begin

suffering the withering and painful side effects. He had a series of tubes built and connected to a supply of the drug so he was constantly fed dosages without fail. Bane, accompanied by fellow convicts TROGG, BIRD, and ZOMBIE, eventually escaped Santa Prisca and set out for America. During the course of his extensive reading, Bane had become fascinated by how the people of GOTHAM CITY feared their costumed protector, the Batman. The bat-

After that adventure Bane sought out the Justice Society of America's Hourman, Rick Tyler. He explained to Rick and his father, Rex, the original Man of the Hour, that he had been working to undo the damage Venom had caused the world. Before the events in Metropolis, he had returned to his homeland and destroyed the drug lords' control over the corrupt government. In so doing he learned of an even more addictive and potent form of Venom. Bane wiped out the drug lords and destroyed their research notes. He also got rid of every sample save one. In reviewing the notes, Bane learned that the formula for Venom derived from Rex Tyler's early work in developing the Miraclo drug—the one he used to give himself, and subsequently his son, temporary superhuman abilities. Seeking a twisted form of revenge, Bane wanted to kill Rex and turn his son Rick into the last Venom addict. His plan almost worked—until the two Hourmen fought back, trapping Bane in the remains of the very same Santa Prisca prison where he'd been born. (*JSA Classified* #17–18, November–December 2006)

Bane escaped the prison once more and backed an anti-US faction during Santa Prisca's general elections. The election proved to be rigged by Computron under orders from Checkmate's Amanda Waller, and Bane forced the current regime to declare martial law as the country teetered on the brink of civil war. (*Checkmate* [second series] #11, April 2007) In the wake of these revelations, Bane apparently abandoned his country to actually work for Waller and her Suicide Squad. (*Outsiders* [third series] #50, November 2007)

BANNER, THE

The terrorist known to the public as the Banner arrived in Gotham City after the city was rebuilt in the wake of a devastating earthquake that resulted in the federal government withdrawing support. Believing himself a true patriot, the Banner meted out violent justice to those he felt had betrayed Gotham, from gangsters to citizens who had turned their backs on the city during the yearlong period when Gotham became a No Man's Land. When the city was welcomed back as part of the United States, the Banner wanted to express his displeasure with the government's stance by blowing up the newly constructed FBI headquarters located in the Truman Building. A subway filled with explosives hurtled beneath the streets toward its target, and the plan would have succeeded had Batman not intercepted the train. The Banner escaped arrest and has not reappeared since. (*Batman* #575, March 2000)

BARD, JASON

A criminal who was better known to law enforcement authorities as the Trapper.

BARD, JASON

Jason Bard was a red-haired private investigator with a history that was altered with each change of reality. Initially he was a resident of Earth-1, and as a youth he sought to avenge his mother's death by killing her murderer—his father. The hunt proved difficult since Bard's mother destroyed all photographs of his father. Looking to channel his rage, Bard enlisted in the marines and was sent to Vietnam. There Bard's right knee was crippled, and he was honorably discharged. Thanks to the GI Bill, Bard earned a degree in criminology and obtained a private investigator's license, opening up a one-man business in Gotham City.

During his professional career, Bard built a positive reputation, earning him cases from high-profile clients, including Police Commissioner James Gordon. For a time Bard was romantically linked with Gordon's daughter, Barbara, not knowing that she was moonlighting as Batgirl. Bard did occasionally find himself allied with Barbara's inspiration, Batman. Bard even took on Kirk Langstrom as a partner in the agency without realizing Langstrom was also the Man-Bat. (*Batman Family* #20, October/November 1978)

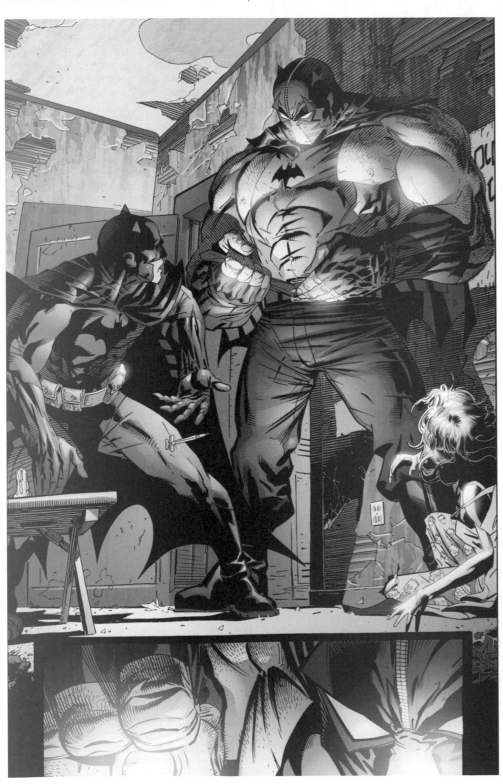

Years after his abusive father had killed his mother, Bard finally tracked the man down, only to see him fatally shot. (*Detective Comics* #491, June 1980)

Reality was shifted during the CRISIS ON INFINITE EARTHS, and in the re-formed world Bard was never a crippled marine. Instead he entered the GOTHAM CITY POLICE DEPARTMENT and became a uniformed officer. While responding to a call for help at Lance Investigations (owned by Larry Lance, husband to the first BLACK CANARY and father of the second), Bard was shot and crippled by a sadist masquerading as KILLER MOTH. (*Batgirl Year One* #1, 2003) Unable to return to duty, Bard used his experience to become a private investigator and date Barbara Gordon. The two were briefly engaged, but Barbara's life was changed forever when she was crippled by the JOKER. Feeling vulnerable and scared, Barbara broke off the engagement, and Bard left Gotham City.

His next recorded appearance was as an investigator for the Childfind Network in New York. (*Firebrand* #5, June 1996) Some time later he became a freelance operative who traveled the globe. After Barbara had taken on her role as ORACLE, she began directing the second Black Canary on her mission to the island of Rheelasia. There Black Canary encountered an undercover Bard, posing as a criminal named Reed Montel. In order to save the Canary, he revealed his true identity and was literally beaten blind. Despite these setbacks, Bard and the Black Canary fought past HELLHOUND and his group of mercenaries to escape the island. (*Birds of Prey* #1, January 1999)

Bard quickly mastered his new handicap and remained an active PI. He wanted to renew his relationship with Barbara, but she put him off, preferring to keep things professional. In time, though, they met, and she finally explained why she had ended their romance. Barbara also helped Jason find medical treatment for his blindness, and his sight was restored. Jason admitted that he remained in love with Barbara, but she told him she could not return those feelings.

Back in Gotham City, Bard helped ROBIN cure his former partner, Langstrom, from another disastrous run as Man-Bat. Bard then agreed to help Barbara by shadowing the Black Canary in Cannes, where the latter had begun dating some mystery man. When the man was revealed to be the ecoterrorist RĀ'S AL GHŪL, Bard wound up captured. Black Canary convinced Rā's to free Bard, but she refused to acknowledge the perilous depth of her situation. (*Birds of Prey* #31–32, July–August 2001)

Reality was modified once more during the events known as INFINITE CRISIS, and Jason Bard was back in Gotham City as a private investigator. After Batman ended his one-year absence from Gotham, he put Bard on a weekly retainer to conduct investigations during the daylight hours when Batman preferred to remain out of sight. On his very first assignment, Bard reentered the world of super heroes and super-villains by tracking the disappearance of the female villain ORCA. This led to Bard being shot in the arm by the TALLY MAN, but the detective managed to defeat the shooter and detain him until the Dark Knight arrived. He remains in service to Batman while his PI business flourishes. (*Detective Comics* #817, September 2006)

BARD, JONATHAN

Jonathan Bard was an expert puppeteer who was never content to rely solely on his entertainment skills. At a competition he once actively tried to sabotage other puppets, only to be caught and expelled. Enraged at having been tossed out, he vowed revenge against the judges; he would prove himself the greatest puppet master of them all. Over the next few weeks he constructed a series of life-like puppets and used them to commit crimes aimed at property owned by the various competition judges. In time, though, his campaign was thwarted by Batman and ROBIN, with Bard being arrested. (*Detective Comics* #212, October 1954)

BARDEN, CHARLES

Charles Barden was one of a rare breed: a successful businessman with a heart of gold. After earning millions of dollars, he used a small portion of his wealth to purchase an amusement park near Gotham Beach. Dubbing it Playland Island, Barden intended that children of all ages should be admitted free. Soon after, Barden was found dead in the park's Funhouse. Batman arrived to aid the police investigation and rounded up three suspects: Barden's wastrel nephew Wilton, who objected to the way his uncle had "squandered" his fortune; Barden's daughter, who was hoping to marry a man named Macklin—but the millionaire insisted the young man complete college before the wedding, and Macklin objected to the interference; and finally Carter, a former business associate who remained bitter that Barden had withdrawn funding from a business venture when it appeared that Carter was careless. Batman's investigation led him to accurately accuse Carter of the crime. It was later learned that Barden had been killed when he found Carter hiding stolen jewels within the Funhouse's mechanical clown. (*Detective Comics* #264, February 1959)

BARHAM, JAMES

James Barham was a gun manufacturer who preferred living in isolation from society. His home was a European castle, transported stone by stone and rebuilt on a small island upriver from GOTHAM CITY. When the millionaire was found murdered, Batman aided the police investigation. Four men quickly emerged as prime suspects: gun smuggler and former mobster Jay Sonderson; Adam Barham, a cousin and sole heir to the man's fortune; businessman John Gorley, who was accused by Barham of fraud; and Barham Gun Company vice president Robert Cray. The Gotham Guardian determined that the killer was Cray, who had murdered his boss in order to keep hidden the massive embezzling he had been conducting. (*Detective Comics* #246, August 1957)

BARNABY, A. K.

Few people know more about Batman Island, the small island on the Gotham River, than the obsessive fan who constructed it, A. K. Barnaby. The multimillionaire obtained all manner of souvenirs from Batman's cases from GOTHAM CITY and around the world and put them all on display. Barnaby received the thrill of a lifetime when he aided his idols, Batman and ROBIN, in stopping a gang of jewel thieves operating on the island. (*Batman* #119, October 1958)

BARROC, ERIC

Eric Barroc was a brilliant inventor who devised a machine that could change the structure of animal life, turning commonplace creatures into human–animal hybrids. Barroc perfected his transformation machine and learned to control the new life-forms, despite their ferocious nature and superior strength, agility, and speed. With his crooked aide Roscoe, Barroc unleashed several specially selected creatures to commit a series of spectacular crimes in GOTHAM CITY. Given the large scale of the crimes, Batman relied on the aid of not only ROBIN, but BATWOMAN and ACE THE BAT-HOUND as well. When the transformation machine was turned on Batman, the Caped Crusader was transformed into a mindless gorilla-like beast. The other members of his team managed to stop Barroc and take control of the machine—turning the animals, and Batman, back to normal. (*Batman* #162, March 1964)

BARROW, "BOSS"

Not only was "Boss" Barrow a feared criminal, but he was also a scientific genius. He invented a device that could scan the faces of two different people and actually revise their facial features so the two would seem to have swapped identities for a period lasting no more than twelve hours. Additionally, the first of the two people would retain no memory of the process. Rather than sell the technology and obtain his wealth legitimately, Barrow used the device to swap the faces of his henchmen with those of GOTHAM CITY's wealthiest citizens. The impostors would then steal huge sums of money for Barrow. The scheme was unraveled thanks to the combined efforts of the world's greatest detectives, Batman and the ELONGATED MAN, who met for the first time while on the case. (*Detective Comics* #331, September 1964)

BARROWS, BARNEY

When Barney Barrows failed the written psychological profile test required to become a GOTHAM CITY police officer, the dejected man took a job as a janitor at police headquarters. His hatred of criminals kept him close to law enforcement in some manner. Things changed, though, after a freak accident in the police lab, which bathed Barrows in experimental radiation. This left him with an increased mental capacity, and he literally became a genius overnight. Given his distaste for criminals, Barrows turned his attention to crime fighting.

Barrows quickly deduced the secret identities of Batman and ROBIN and used that information to blackmail the Dynamic Duo into aiding him. They did so until it became apparent that whereas Batman apprehended criminals for trial, Barrows intended to kill his prey. Soon after, Batman and Robin managed to outwit Barrows long enough to apprehend the Metals Mob as they attempted a daring robbery of rare metals. Barrows's enhancements eventually faded as the radiation left his body, returning him to normal with no recollection of Batman's greatest secret. (*Detective Comics* #217, March 1955)

BARSH

Upon learning of PLAINVILLE, also known as Batmantown, Barsh and his gang relocated there to hatch their plan. They allied themselves with Dane, owner of the Batmantown Safe Storage Company, and set out to convince the citizens that the town was a crime-free haven. The Safe Storage Company, they claimed, would be an ideal place to store their valuables. Barsh intended to help himself to the storage units while the populace was distracted by the annual Batman Pageant. The plan was foiled when Batman and ROBIN learned of it and arrived in time to stop it. (*Batman* #100, June 1956)

BART, JOE

Joe Bart operated a print shop in GOTHAM CITY that also printed fraudulent stock certificates. His scheme remained undetected until he got greedy and robbed the jewelry store next door. Bart then tried to frame former convict Roger Rainer. Batman and ROBIN became involved and determined that Bart was the true criminal; Rainer was quickly exonerated. (*Detective Comics* #101, July 1945)

BARTLETT, JOELY

Joely Bartlett was a GOTHAM CITY POLICE DEPARTMENT detective who was partnered with Sergeant Vincent del Arrasio. She worked in the G.C.P.D.'s MAJOR CRIMES UNIT and lived on a houseboat. Bartlett was also said to be very observant of her Catholic faith. She and her parents became estranged when they used their great wealth to support LEX LUTHOR's successful bid to become president. (*Detective Comics* #747, August 2000)

BARTOK

Bartok was a successful inventor who sold his creations to criminals until the GOTHAM CITY POLICE DEPARTMENT arrested him. After serving five years in prison, he was freed and resumed his work. He built a series of robots that were designed specifically to obtain the materials he needed for his next project, a series of advanced robots that contained artificial intelligence. These robots could independently loot Earth's riches until Bartok became the wealthiest man in the world. He sent his robots out to begin accumulating the electronic components he needed to achieve his dream. However, Batman and ROBIN trailed the robots back to Bartok's lair, located in Eagle Mountain, some 125 miles northwest of GOTHAM CITY. The Dynamic Duo was overwhelmed by the robots and held hostage until a Batman robot, stored in the BATMOBILE's trunk, was summoned by remote control. The distraction allowed the heroes to free themselves and defeat Bartok. (*Detective Comics* #258, August 1958)

BARTON, CAPTAIN

Barton was a former sailor and member of the Stamp Club who attempted to manipulate the philatelic market via murder and mayhem. Members of the club each specialized in collections of stamps that depicted the areas of an individual's interests, such as Barton's passion for the sea.

Knowing that specific stamps appreciated in value if they had a unique history attached, Barton sought to purchase a stamp from several different disciplines, then use the stamp's image to inform a method of murder for each club member. This way, the stamp would gain in value—and suspicion would be aimed away from him given the differing subject matters. Once the murders began, they came to the attention of Batman, who subsequently joined the club as BRUCE WAYNE. His specialty was race cars, and he told the club that he was an amateur driver. After Barton learned that Wayne had purchased a series of Mexican stamps depicting fiery race crashes, he sabotaged Wayne's car before an upcoming race.

Instead of Wayne dying, though, Barton witnessed his own capture at the hands of Batman and ROBIN, thereby ending this threat. (*Batman* #78, August/September 1953)

BARTOR, BRAND

When Brand Bartor was arrested for impersonating the Caped Crusader by wearing a Batman costume, he mounted an imaginative defense. The criminal maintained that Batman himself violated the GOTHAM CITY ordinance against wearing an imitation BATSUIT to preserve the unique crime-fighting outfit worn by the Dark Knight. His defense pointed to a three-thousand-year-old image of a Babylonian wearing a similar outfit. The recently uncovered cave painting depicted the ancient "Batman" fighting a soldier in a fierce battle.

Batman had trouble countering the argument, knowing full well that the image on the cave wall was based on him and not a Babylonian. He had traveled to the past using the unique hypnosis process perfected by PROFESSOR CARTER NICHOLS. With ROBIN's help, he had defeated the evil King Beladin and returned King Lanak to the throne. The complication was that the trip was made by BRUCE WAYNE and DICK GRAYSON, so if Batman explained he was the painting's subject, their identities would be revealed.

In the end Batman countered Bartor by explaining to the judge that the Babylonians worshiped ZORN, who wore a costume not unlike Batman's uniform. The judge took evidence of this "hero-idol" to heart and ruled against Bartor. (*Batman* #102, September 1956)

BATARANG

Among Batman's many tools, perhaps the most recognizable is the Batarang. The bat-shaped device was clearly inspired by the Australian boomerang, but Batman's weapon did more than fly through the air in an arc, returning to its owner. The Batarang was his long-distance weapon of choice; it could incapacitate a foe, knock weapons out of assailants' hands, or travel long distances to attach itself to objects, often trailing a strong cable that enabled Batman to cross vast distances. With the Dark Knight having vowed never to use a gun, he devised this substitute, which was just as effective at disabling criminals. (*Detective Comics* #31, September 1939)

Through the years Batman developed other uses for the Batarang, including a veritable arsenal of customized Batarangs that wailed like a siren, emitted smoke, exploded, and much more.

Batman saw to it that the various ROBINS were as adept with the Batarang as he was, and that training was extended to BATWOMAN, BAT-GIRL, and the various BATGIRLS.

On Earth-2, Batman used the more gadget-

oriented Batarangs, which hung on a display board in the BATCAVE and were selected in anticipation of each case. On Earth-1, Batman's Batarang was more consistent and remained largely gadget-free, with the exception of the rope.

After CRISIS ON INFINITE EARTHS, the Batman's other tools began to vary in size. The Batarang remained an offensive weapon, with the cable relegated to a grappling hook and a gun also affixed to his remarkable UTILITY BELT. Batman also developed smaller Batarangs that worked more like Japanese *shuriken* or darts, sharpened to cut into criminals' hands or arms in order to disarm them. The most consistently used versions of the Batarang included ones with micro-serrated edges; a hard-impact version for stunning criminals; a remote-controlled one linked to his Utility Belt; and an aerodynamically edged model with a throwing top.

Robin I, as NIGHTWING, modified his Batarangs to create bird-shaped tools nicknamed wing-dings. Robin III gave up using a Batarang in favor of R-shaped *shuriken,* used to the same effect. He once told his fellow TEEN TITANS that the "Batarang budget" was huger than they could imagine.

Whenever possible, Batman and Robin collected the used weapons to keep them out of the hands of criminals or curious, untrained civilians who might injure themselves. As a result, real Batarangs remain rare objects beyond Batman's control. Nightwing noted this when presenting a single Batarang to Batwoman the Christmas after they met. He explained that the current model was composite-graphite-molded, unbreakable to ten thousand psi, laser-honed, aerodynamically tested, and perfectly balanced. (*52* #33, February 2007)

BATBOAT

The first BATMARINE was a specially designed submersible and the model for all other amphibious vessels that followed. (*Batman* #86, September 1954) Early in his career Batman first used a Batboat when investigating arms dealers along CHINATOWN's wharves, destroying the criminals' machinations using a bow-mounted flamethrower.

The Batboat was eventually housed on sub-level six of the BATCAVE and measured 25.4 feet in length and 8.56 feet at the beam. Its maximum surface speed was 120 miles per hour; 150 mph using the hydrofoil. When submerged, its maximum speed was thirty knots with a maximum depth of two hundred feet.

Its offensive weaponry included a pneumatic harpoon with titanium cable, a launching grapnel that doubled as an anchor, variable-setting depth charges, and a small supply of active-homing torpedoes with heat/motion/vibration target acquisition.

When underwater, the Batboat's oxygen supply provided six hours of breathable air, with an additional twelve hours stored for life support and deep-water submersion.

BATBOY

ROBIN was surprised at the arrival in GOTHAM CITY of a pint-sized crime fighter who used a baseball motif, Batboy. With Batman out of town on a special assignment, Robin was working to apprehend Tapper Nolan and his mob on his own. Batboy, hiding behind a catcher's mask and armed with a variety of imaginative tools, came to the Boy Wonder's aid. From his Dugout hideaway, Batboy sallied into battle with tools not unlike the bat-themed equipment Batman made famous. Instead of the scalloped BATARANG, Batboy employed a baseball bat-arang, a battering ram bat, a parachute-bat, porcupine-bat, and a web-bat that ensnared his prey.

During the course of the case, Robin learned that Batboy's true identity was Midge Merrill, a middle-aged little person with a personal grudge against Tapper Nolan. When Nolan had worked as a circus roustabout years before, Merrill was part of a performing trio known as the Mighty Mites. Nolan had set fire to the circus to mask his robbery of the gate receipts. The resulting conflagration killed Merrill's partners, and the surviving Mite swore vengeance. Batboy and Robin eventually managed to bring Tapper Nolan to justice. Merrill then happily hung up his mask and found a job as a professional batboy for an out-of-town Major League Baseball team. (*Batman* #90, March 1955)

BATCAVE

The Batcave is a series of catacombs, tunnels, and a multi-tiered immensely vast cave discovered deep beneath WAYNE MANOR. The space was drastically modified by BRUCE WAYNE to serve as Batman's headquarters, research laboratory, training facility, and trophy room.

On Earth-2, Bruce Wayne initially kept his sole piece of equipment, the BATGYRO, in a secret hangar. Soon after, he used a false wall within Wayne Manor to house scientific and medical equipment. Within a year of beginning his war on crime, Batman finally built his permanent headquarters beneath the manor. (*Batman* #3, Fall 1940)

The Batcave was accessed by a staircase located behind a grandfather clock in the mansion. A winch hauled the BATMOBILE up an incline to access an exit tunnel. The BATPLANE was hidden within a barn situated over an accessway to the cave. The BATBOAT remained anchored at the cave's edge, with the Gotham River easily accessible. It was said that the Wayne ancestors knew of the cave through the years they occupied the manor, and different events were subsequently traced to the catacombs. This Batcave had an elaborate collection of trophies that included a dinosaur replica taken from Dinosaur Island (*Batman* #35, June/July 1946), a giant Joker card (*Detective Comics* #158, April 1950), a giant penny (*World's Finest Comics* #30, September/October 1947), and a collection of the Penguin's trick umbrellas (*Detective Comics* #158, April 1950), among many other items. A complete inventory was never chronicled.

On Earth-1 the cave was accessed by either a staircase located behind a grandfather clock in the mansion or a service elevator. (*Batman* #164, June 1964) A road and ramp provided the Batmobile with access to a little-used road some twelve miles from Gotham City. A high hill served as the Batplane's hangar, allowing the craft's VTOL (vertical takeoff and landing) gear access. The Batboat remained anchored at the cave's edge, with the Gotham River accessible. This Batcave survived to the thirtieth century virtually intact, and once provided refuge to the Legion of Super-Heroes. (*Adventure Comics* #341, February 1966)

At one point Dick Grayson left for college and Bruce Wayne closed the Batcave and moved into Gotham City itself, establishing a smaller version in the sub-basement levels below the Wayne Foundation building. (*Batman* #217, December 1969)

In the reality that merged the parallel worlds, the Batcave grew in size and scope and was first discovered by Bruce Wayne at the age of four. The Batcave was—as usual—accessed by a staircase located behind a grandfather clock in the mansion's study. The hands of the clock had to be set to ten forty-seven, the time Bruce's parents were slain, to unlock the secret entrance. A giant carousel housed a multitude of Batmobiles that allowed the chosen vehicle access to a tunnel route. The exterior entrance was shrouded behind holographic technology. The Batplane, or Batwing, was housed on an upper level, while the Batboat was located on level six.

Initially the Wayne Family history recorded that the cave was used as a storehouse and a resting stop along the Underground Railroad during the Civil War. Bruce accidentally discovered the cave as a child when he fell through boards that had concealed a well and access point to the cave. The well remained as an emergency access, and was used by Nightwing and Robin to enter the Batcave after Jean-Paul Valley denied them access during his brief tenure as Batman, and again when Nightwing needed to investigate the police accusation that Bruce Wayne had murdered Vesper Fairchild.

The centerpiece of the command center was a huge computer interface with a massive screen several feet tall. It was connected to a series of linked Cray and Digitronix computers providing massive amounts of computing ability. As a result, it datamined around the globe, analyzing and storing countless megabytes of information to be recalled whenever required. Batman also had a series of satellites in orbit around the globe that could retrieve information or send it to the Dark Knight without fail. He maintained constant online links with both Oracle and the Justice League of America.

The level of medical equipment in the sick bay rivaled the best hospital in the world, which often proved the difference between life and death, most notably when Bane broke Batman's back during a savage fight and Alfred Pennyworth was forced to use the cave's advanced labs.

A different section of the cave had a training area with equipment for every part of the body, as well as simulators to create different scenarios to test reflexes and reaction times. When Stephanie

Brown trained to replace Tim Drake as Robin, she spent more time here than anyone else.

The laboratory equaled the research equipment found at S.T.A.R. Labs, allowing Batman to process forensic evidence or develop new methods for subduing criminals. He also had the mechanical means to fabricate certain materials, but much of his crime-fighting equipment and supply of vehicles were initially built elsewhere, usually in different divisions of Wayne Enterprises.

Beyond his more familiar vehicles, Batman also housed a Justice League transporter within a recess of the cave. A sled-like transport granted him access to Gotham City's subway rails through an abandoned spur line. (*Detective Comics* #667, October 1993)

While other realities showed Batman with an elaborate trophy collection that could span several levels, the current reality limited the displays. One constant was a glass case containing the Robin uniform worn by Jason Todd, the second Boy Wonder and the first to die in the line of duty. A Batgirl costume also hung in tribute to Barbara Gordon after she was crippled by the Joker.

After a devastating earthquake in Gotham City and its nearby environs, Wayne Manor was demolished, but the Batcave survived because Bruce Wayne had seen to it that the structure was reinforced to withstand almost anything. Still, Bruce decided to revamp the setup, utilizing eight separate levels, the lowest being eighty-four feet beneath sea level. With solar and hydrogen energy powering the facility, the Batcave could easily act as permanent headquarters or a siege bunker.

The main level (150 feet above sea level) contained the main equipment and computer interface. Seated on a rock ledge, Batman's computer platform featured state-of-the-art holographic technology for displaying information, as well as a giant screen for visual communications. The Batcomputer was first built by WayneTech employees who were told it was for a strategic command-and-control bunker to be housed beneath the Canadian Rockies. The most recently chronicled suite consisted of seven linked Cray T932 computers, the most powerful setup on Earth, and was constantly being upgraded.

Sub-level one (138 feet) featured Batman's laboratories and library, plus guest quarters. The second sub-level (114 feet) housed the training facilities for himself and was also used for Sasha Bordeaux and Stephanie Brown. The third sub-level (ninety-six feet) was storage. When Harold Allnut and Ace the Bat-Hound stayed with Batman, they lived on sub-level four (eighty-four feet), where the Subway rocket was also housed. Sub-level five (sixty-six feet) functioned as the cave's power plant, while sub-level six (sea level) was where the Batboat was moored. The seventh sub-level (eighty-four feet below sea level) has yet to be revealed, its contents known only to Batman.

Batman established miniature versions of the Batcave as safe houses in and around Gotham City, and operated from these during the events known as No Man's Land. One, Batcave South, was located across from Paris Island, while the Northwest Batcave was hidden beneath Arkham Asylum.

At one point in the Earth-2 reality, Batman had invented and constructed a flying Batcave. Larger and less maneuverable than the Batcopter, it did boast laboratory and computer facilities, plus smokescreen generators so that it could hide in plain sight. The flying Batcave also carried a modified Batmobile called a Batracer. It required frequent refueling and proved a costly short-lived experiment. (*Detective Comics* #186, August 1952)

BATCAVE WEST

Batcave West was the OUTSIDERS' base of operations when they were being trained by Batman. (*Outsiders* #19, May 1987) Designed by Dr. Helga Jace, it contained many of the same facilities as its East Coast counterpart, but without the size and scope. It provided mainly temporary living quarters, training and medical facilities, and a massive computer/communications area for use by the entire team. After Dr. Jace was revealed to be an android designed by the alien Manhunters to infiltrate the team, the Batman considered the facility compromised and closed it down. Once the Outsiders disbanded, it was not seen again.

BATCOPTER

On occasion Batman used a modified helicopter that enabled him to reach places neither the BATMOBILE or BATPLANE could easily maneuver around. (*Detective Comics* #254, April 1958)

BATCYCLE

In addition to the BATMOBILE, Batman sometimes used a slightly smaller, more versatile road vehicle. Throughout his career, he drove a variety of makes and models, all customized for the all-terrain pursuit needs of his missions. Additionally, each

motorcycle was outfitted with state-of-the-art communications equipment that kept the driver in constant contact with the BATCAVE, ORACLE, or the GOTHAM CITY POLICE DEPARTMENT.

BATGIRL

The mantle of Batgirl has been taken on by several different young women over the years and through the varying realities. In most cases, Batgirl has been supported and endorsed by Batman and is

usually a trained member of Batman's allies in his war on crime.

The first Bat-Girl was seen on Earth-2. (*Batman* #139, April 1961) She was BETTY KANE, niece of KATHY KANE, the BATWOMAN of her world. In her red-and-green costume, she proved adept at acrobatics and basic crime fighting, and was often partnered with ROBIN the Boy Wonder.

On Earth-1, Betty Kane also became Bat-Girl, but later in the time line. She, too, was Kathy Kane's niece, but had a longer career, even serving on a splinter division of the TEEN TITANS called Titans West. Betty Kane was also a noted tennis professional.

In the reality after the multiple Earths were merged into a single Earth, Mary Elizabeth "Bette" Kane was also a crime fighter but under the code name FLAMEBIRD. She was a tennis professional as well, but seemed to take her crime career far less seriously than her predecessors and was written off as flighty by her peers.

On Earth-1, BARBARA GORDON, daughter of Police Commissioner JAMES GORDON, went as Batgirl to a costume party, encountered KILLER MOTH, and a crime-fighting career was born. She fought beside Batman and Robin for several years until she began to question her effectiveness. Her career ended

MM AL '03

The mute CASSANDRA CAIN came into Barbara Gordon's care weeks later, and quickly showed a keen interest in joining Batman's crusade. After she'd proven herself to all, Barbara supported Cain's becoming the new Batgirl.

When Cassandra seemed to give up crime fighting in favor of ruling the LEAGUE OF ASSASSINS, a Batgirl wannabe infiltrated Oracle's headquarters and eventually became a part of Barbara's life. Her mystery slowly unfolded as the BIRDS OF PREY attempted to learn who she was and how this young woman knew their secret identities. After displaying meta-human powers, including teleportation and superstrength, Barbara complained about the teen usurping the *Batgirl* name. Instead the girl renamed herself Misfit and made a new costume. (*Birds of Prey* #96, September 2006) In time Gordon came to realize that Misfit was hiding her past. She tracked the teen down, discovering that she was a homeless girl named Charlotte Gage-Radcliffe. When her family's tenement apartment caught fire, she used her skills to seek freedom, but it meant leaving her mother and baby sister to die in the inferno. Gordon invited Charlie to come live with her in the Maiden Tower, headquarters to the Birds of Prey. (*Birds of Prey* #108, September 2007)

BATGYRO

When the Batman on Earth-2 recognized that he needed to get around Gotham City faster than his feet could manage, he designed and constructed the Batgyro, a modification of the autogyros that were in wide use during the 1930s. He maintained the craft in a secret hangar, the exact whereabouts never having been chronicled. The vehicle could fly like a plane or briefly hover over locations like a helicopter. It also possessed an early version of autopilot technology. The vehicle was quickly replaced by the faster and more versatile BATPLANE. (*Detective Comics* #31, September 1939)

BAT-HOMBRE

When President Jose Camaran of the small Latin American republic of Mantegua visited GOTHAM CITY, he was honored with a ticker-tape parade. An assassin tried to kill the president during the event but was foiled thanks to the timely arrival of the Dynamic Duo. After the parade, Batman and ROBIN were introduced to the president, who lamented his country's lack of proper law and order. The citizens were being plagued by a criminal nicknamed EL PAPAGAYO. The criminal also had a predilection for talking with his omnipresent parrot, who displayed a remarkable vocabulary. Camaran asked Batman if he could come to Mantegua and teach someone to become their country's own crime fighter. Two days later Batman and Robin arrived in the capital city of Casanegro. They immediately set to work, finding a good-sized grotto beneath an abandoned farmhouse to act as a new BATCAVE. Batman then selected a superior horse from Argentina to provide terrain-appropriate transportation. Camaran was shocked to see Batman reject the use of swords and firearms, instead selecting a whip to be used as the new hero's main tool.

Batman and Robin then put the applicants through rigorous physical testing, rejecting those

after the cosmic events of the CRISIS ON INFINITE EARTHS reordered reality. (*Detective Comics* #359, January 1967)

In the re-formed single Earth, Barbara Gordon was now James Gordon's niece, who came to live with him after her parents died. She became Batgirl in much the same way, but was trained by Batman after her debut, and she began a flirtation with a teenage Robin that later flared into a full-fledged romance. She continued her career until the JOKER

shot and crippled her. Refusing to give up the fight against crime, she turned her computer skills into her greatest asset and became the computer-based hero known as ORACLE.

When GOTHAM CITY was cut off from federal aid for a year after a devastating earthquake, a new Batgirl emerged. She turned out to be HELENA BERTINELLI, also known as the HUNTRESS. After Helena's identity was exposed, Barbara took the costume from her for safekeeping.

who failed to perform basic routines, such as fifty chin-ups. Luis Peralda, one of the final candidates, passed each of the demanding physical and mental challenges. Batman settled on Peralda and began training him as Bat-Hombre. Peralda, though, was actually in the employ of El Papagayo, and was prepared to betray Batman and destroy President Camaran's hopes for law and order.

Batman discovered Peralda's plan and had him put into custody, then disguised himself to infiltrate El Papagayo's mob. Before Batman could put the criminal out of business, however, Peralda escaped and exposed Batman. Surrounded by troops, Batman and Robin were sentenced to be executed. As usual, El Papagayo consulted his parrot, who suggested the duo fight to the death with whips. Forced to take whips in hand, Batman and Robin appeared ready to fight, but instead they used whips to latch onto high tree branches and swing out of danger. Batman explained to Robin that he had used a mild dose of curare to knock out the parrot and employed ventriloquism to suggest the whips.

They subdued the entire mob just as Camaran's feeble police force arrived. Batman was then informed that Camaran had passed away, happy in the knowledge his people were being protected by Bat-Hombre. With El Papagayo in custody, Batman felt that proper law enforcement could now gain a hold in the country, finally fulfilling Camaran's dream. (*Batman* #56, December 1949/January 1950)

BAT-HOUND

A name given to Ace, the German shepherd who accompanied Batman and Robin on numerous cases.

BAT-KNIGHT

In a potential future reality, the Bat-Knights were robots created by Bruce Wayne to act as his avatars, charged with protecting Gotham City's citizens. They were huge, hulking creations with heads styled after one of the early model Batmobiles. The guardians could fly and usually traveled as a small unit. Criminals were routinely thwarted, contained, and transported to police detention. The Bat-Knights had a limited form of artificial intelligence but were monitored and controlled by Wayne from the Batcave outside the city. (*Kingdom Come*, 1996)

BATMAN

A. Origin

1. The Original Account

Thomas Wayne, his wife, and their son Bruce Wayne attended a movie one evening. Afterward, they were headed for home when they were accosted by a thief who demanded their money and jewelry. Thomas stepped between the thief and his wife and was shot for his effort; a second shot killed the woman. The boy was left to stand over their corpses as the thief fled into the shadows. He vowed over their graves to fight a war on crime and then dedicated his life to both physical and mental perfection to wage that battle. As an adult, he deemed himself ready for the fight but wanted an edge. When a bat entered the Wayne Manor's

window, he took this as an omen, devising the Batsuit and taking to the city's rooftops as Batman. (first appearance, *Detective Comics* #27, May 1939; origin revealed, *Detective Comics* #33, October 1939)

2. Addenda and Revisions

Other accounts altered what happened next based on which world the story was taking place on, as well as reality-altering events such as the Crisis on Infinite Earths and Infinite Crisis.

Details also slowly came to light in subsequent retellings of that pivotal night. Gotham City wasn't identified until some time later (*Batman* #4, Fall 1940); likewise the name of his mother (Martha Wayne in *Batman* #47, June/July 1948). The Wayne Family's influence in Gotham evolved through the chronicles, as did the revelation of Thomas's profession. (*Detective Comics* #235, September 1956) Martha's interest in social work came to light much later in the chronicles. (*Batman: The Ultimate Evil*, 1995) One account said that the fateful event

(*World's Finest Comics* #59, July/August 1952) There he met JULIE MADISON, who was performing as Ophelia in *Hamlet,* while Bruce portrayed Polonius. They dated and fell in love during this time, but when they graduated she left for Manhattan and he remained in Gotham. A short time later Bruce proposed, and they became engaged. (*Secret Origins* [second series] #6, September 1986)

Upon graduation, Bruce declared that he was ready, was inspired by the bat, and became the Batman. His first case involved the arrest of "Slugsy" KYLE, a petty thief, and a clear victory for the crime fighter. (*Detective Comics* #265, March 1959) He also befriended Police Commissioner JAMES W. GORDON, a friend of his uncle Philip, around this time, figuring that being close to the source of crime news would prove invaluable. In short order he learned of deaths at a chemical factory and cracked the case of the chemical syndicate. (*Detective Comics* #27, May 1939) Shortly thereafter Bruce purchased the estate soon to be known as Wayne Manor and began construction of a labyrinthine BATCAVE beneath it. (*Detective Comics* #205, March 1954)

On Earth-1, Bruce may have been subconsciously influenced to adopt the Batman guise after seeing his father wearing a similar costume for a party, a memory he didn't recall until his adult years. (*Detective Comics* #235, September 1956)

Wayne was also taken in by Uncle Philip and largely raised by Mrs. Chilton, secretly the mother of Joe Chill. His training, for the most part, went unrecorded. However, Bruce did don a variety of identities prior to becoming Batman. When he visited Smallville, Bruce became the Flying Fox (*Adventure Comics* #275, August 1960) and the Executioner (*Superboy* #182, February 1972) prior to donning his ROBIN-like costume with Harvey Harris. (*Batman* #213, July/August 1969)

After the Crisis, it was stated that Bruce remained in Wayne Manor with ALFRED PENNYWORTH until he was fourteen, when he deemed himself ready to learn from the greatest masters of the fighting arts and detecting skills. The exact order of his training has yet to be recorded but it is likely he began locally, learning about magic and about death-defying escapes from John Zatara, father to his playmate ZATANNA. He learned boxing from former heavyweight champion TED GRANT, who also battled crime during World War II as WILDCAT. From Harvey Harris (*Detective Comics Annual* #2, 1989) and France's amoral HENRI DUCARD (*Detective Comics* #599, April 1989), he learned the skills of the detective. By fifteen he was traveling the globe, learning how to track a man from Woodley. (*Legends of the Dark Knight* #1–5, November 1989– March 1990) In Asia he was taught how to kill by the LEAGUE OF ASSASSINS' DAVID CAIN, but he refused to actually kill, which dampened Cain's enthusiasm for his student. Another League member was Master Kirgi, who trained most of the members in the ways of stealth. (*Batman* #431, March 1989) Tsunetomo taught him many of the basic martial arts. (*Detective Comics Annual* #3, 1990) His quest for knowledge led him to an ascended master in the Paektusan Mountains of Korea and a convicted killer living on an island off Borneo; he dwelled for a length of

occurred on different dates on the various parallel worlds. (*Detective Comics* #500, March 1981)

On Earth-2 it was established that Bruce was born on April 7, 1915. (*World's Finest Comics* #33, March/April 1948; *Star-Spangled Comics* #91, April 1949; *America vs. the Justice Society* #1, January 1985) The fatal robbery occurred on June 26, 1924 (*Secret Origins* [second series] #6, September 1986); the same account indicated they had seen a Rudolph Valentino film, either *Monsieur Beaucaire* or *A Sainted Devil*. Bruce was said to

be subsequently taken in and raised by Thomas's brother Philip. It wasn't until Bruce was an adult that he learned of JOE CHILL being the robber, with that account changing Martha's shooting to death from a heart attack. (*Batman* #47, June/July 1948)

The first recorded instance of Bruce beginning his training told of his adopting a red-and-yellow costume to study alongside police detective HARVEY HARRIS. (*Detective Comics* #226, December 1955) A little later, around 1935, he enrolled at Gotham University to get his formal education.

time in Japan and China. While on the continent, he went to Nepal and learned healing techniques from monks. By the end of his physical training, he had sculpted his body to hard muscle and mastered the 127 known forms of hand-to-hand combat.

In Africa, Bruce sought out tribal Bushmen to teach him their hunting techniques; in the Middle East he learned other skills from the TEN-EYED MEN OF THE EMPTY QUARTER. (*52* #30, 2007)

Bruce did not neglect his other studies, taking advantage of his inherited wealth to study at the finest institutions around the planet including the Berlin School of Science, Cambridge University in England, and the Sorbonne in France. He began to cultivate a reputation as a disinterested wastrel by never staying at any one school for long, usually just a semester. He was actually cherry-picking the subjects he felt he needed to master while receiving education from the finest mind in each field.

By age twenty Bruce had returned to America and thought he could apply himself through the FBI. He lasted all of six weeks as a trainee, recognizing that the war on crime could not be fought from behind a desk. (*Secret Origins of the World's Great Super-Heroes,* 1990) Bruce left and resumed training on his own.

By his early twenties he had ended his training and returned to Wayne Manor, where Alfred had patiently waited for him, only so he could resign in person. Again, accounts differed as to what occurred next, but Bruce made several forays against common criminals in Gotham, earning bumps and bruises as he attempted to put his training to practical use. Alfred felt he could not leave Bruce as he was beginning a new life. He used his own experience to help refine Bruce's knowledge of makeup and disguise, giving him tips on how to make certain the general public differentiated Bruce Wayne from Batman. (*Batman Annual* #13, 1989) Dark clothes and a ski mask did not make an effective disguise, and he sought something that would make a difference. In the manor's library, he sat brooding until the bat arrived—and inspiration struck.

B. The Secret Identity

All along he recognized the need to keep Batman and Bruce Wayne separate, not only in his own mind but in the minds of others. As a result, he went to great lengths, in all realities, to maintain the secret.

He trained himself, and later instructed Robin, to sign with his left hand while in costume. (*Batman* #92, June 1955) In other cases when there was a possibility that his identity might be pierced, Batman took precautions such as wearing modified cowls or even a face mask. When he revealed his identity to BATGIRL, he used traces of wax to convince her that he was masquerading as Bruce Wayne, diverting suspicion. (*Detective Comics* #363, May 1967)

Despite the efforts he made to protect his real name, many people deduced his secret—and in most cases Batman went out of his way to convince them they were wrong. Often this involved using others to pose as either Batman or Bruce Wayne to prove the suspicion wrong. Among those who imitated the Caped Crusader were Alfred, SUPERMAN, and Robin. The first time he needed to do this, Batman hired an actor who would die soon after. (*World's Finest Comics* #6, Summer 1942)

Quite often those who learned the secret took it to their grave, either through happenstance as with the villainous QUEENIE (*Batman* #5, Spring 1941) or because they were already old or ill, such as Bruce's great-uncle Silas. (*Batman* #122, March 1959)

On the other hand, Wayne angrily revealed himself to Joe Chill, telling the gangster it was his robbery attempt that set a boy on the path to becoming Batman. Chill panicked; after he told his men he'd created Batman, they gunned him down. (*Batman* #47, June/July 1948)

On Earth-1 fellow members of the JUSTICE LEAGUE OF AMERICA knew his secret identity, as did his fellow OUTSIDERS and Gotham-based allies Batgirl and CATWOMAN. With the TEEN TITANS and JIMMY OLSEN aware of Robin's real name, it was understood that they, too, knew Wayne was Batman. DEATHSTROKE THE TERMINATOR's discovery of the Titans' secret identities also laid bare Batman's secrets to him. HUGO STRANGE, one of Batman's deadliest foes, learned his secret and used it to impersonate the Dark Knight for three days.

While several villains had the chance to learn Batman's identity, most resisted the temptation given the circumstances. One who did manage to figure out the secret was RĂ'S AL GHŬL, who kept the secret to himself. (The UBU who accompanied him at the time died soon after.) His daughter TALIA HEAD also learned the secret and kept it to herself. Later both NOCTURNA and BANE deduced the secret and used it to exploit him in their early encounters. The RIDDLER also discovered the secret and shared it with Tommy Elliot, Wayne's former childhood friend, who had always sought revenge against Thomas Wayne for saving his mother's life after he tried to kill both parents when the boys were just eight. Even though he subsequently lost the knowledge, the Riddler had the answer to the greatest puzzler in the super-villain community. In post-Crisis continuity, Catwoman was finally told the secret—but during a period when she was not only Batman's ally but also his lover.

Among the civilian population, Alfred was always aware of the secret; after the Crisis, LESLIE THOMPKINS knew Batman's secret from the beginning. Police Commissioner Gordon was often suspected of knowing but apparently never did. Aware that criminals might believe otherwise,

Batman instructed the commissioner to identify him as real estate agent Neil Merrick if he was ever in a life-or-death situation. (*Detective Comics* #465, November 1976) When Batman offered to reveal his identity to repair a rift between them, Gordon refused. (*Legends of the Dark Knight* #125, January 2000)

Interestingly, the youngest person to figure out Batman's identity was TIM DRAKE, who was a witness to the death of the FLYING GRAYSONS. Later, when he recognized a patented move Robin made on news footage, Tim realized that if DICK GRAYSON was Robin, Bruce Wayne had to be Batman. He kept the information to himself until it dawned on him that after the second Robin died, the Dark Knight needed a junior partner. He insisted he be given a chance.

After the Crisis, Batman went to greater lengths to maintain his mystique, keeping his identity a secret even from his fellow heroes until much later in his career. In time, though, most of the JLA knew his real name. Superman's wife, LOIS LANE, was also made privy to the secret after their marriage. Similarly, among his operatives in Gotham City, beyond Robin, BARBARA GORDON and Batgirl knew, while the secret was intentionally withheld from HUNTRESS and SPOILER.

To aid his war on crime, Batman created several personae as he needed them, including Thomas Quigley, Detective Hawke, Sir Hemingford Grey, Frank Dixon, and Gordon Selkirk. For the most part, his main alias was MATCHES MALONE, until the real Malone turned up and then died. After Scarface dispatched Malone, Batman used several new personae, among them Eddie Nickles, Bronner, and Lefty Knox. Lefty was his most frequent new identity; for it, he covered his right hand with a three-pronged hook prosthetic. He established his reputation so well that the PENGUIN called Lefty a "crook I can trust."

C. The Batsuit

1. The Basic Costume and Accessories

The basic elements of the BATSUIT have remained fairly consistent throughout the differing eras and realities. However, some differences have been dramatic.

On Earth-2, for example, the Batsuit had bright blue highlights, and the cowl ears were bobbed. The gray unitard was covered with blue boots, gloves, briefs, cape, and cowl. Early on, once the short gloves became more like gauntlets, they acquired three fins; for a brief time they also contained short claws for climbing. In the beginning of his career, Batman was also known to have briefly used a bulletproof vest.

The early Earth-1 version had a yellow oval containing the chest's bat-symbol. Batman stated on numerous occasions that the oval provided villains with a target away from his more vulnerable head. The integrated gray unitard contained the blue-black briefs, supplemented by blue-black gloves, boots, cape, and cowl.

The suit worn by Batman in the wake of the parallel worlds merging during the Crisis on Infinite Earths consisted of a dark gray custom-made body stocking with black-blue gloves, boots, trunks, cape, and cowl. He continually modified the Batsuit, including a period when it consisted of a one-piece all-black version. The cape was constructed from a Nomex fire-resistant material that boasted a Kevlar weave to repel bullets without losing flexibility.

Batman's suit seemed to vary with each use, but in most cases the cowl concealed a voice-activated communications system, a variety of lenses, and in once instance tiny gas capsules that deployed when the cowl was tampered with, preserving his true identity even if he was unconscious.

2. The Emergency and Special-Purpose Costumes

Over the years Batman and Robin wore a number of uniforms in different colors or fabrics based on specific needs, such as all-white arctic suits for wintry environs (*World's Finest Comics* #7, Fall 1942) and a camouflage uniform for jungle terrain. When they climbed to the summit of K4, the Dynamic Duo adopted heavily insulated outfits. (*Batman* #93, August 1955) The basic suit template was also adapted for the deep sea. (*Batman* #68, December 1951/January 1952)

3. The Utility Belt

In all realities Batman relied on a UTILITY BELT festooned with miniaturized gear to aid his investigations. The first belt housed only a coiled rope and then a BATARANG to secure a cable, enabling him to swing from building to building or climb exterior structures. The Earth-2 Batman even had a pistol and holster for his first few cases before giving up guns forever. No other version used guns.

The gear depicted in his adventures has included a variety of Batarangs of differing sizes, bat-shaped handcuffs, a rebreather device, flashbang and gas grenades, plastic explosives, lock-picking tools, a taser, a remote control for the BATMOBILE, a Justice League of America signaling device, a forensic crime scene kit, emergency first-aid supplies, cash, and empty pockets for storing evidence. The Utility Belt had anti-theft technology that usually delivered electric shocks to thwart criminals or the curious. A gas-propelled grappling hook and gun mechanism allowed the Dark Knight to scale steep structures or traverse the Gotham City rooftops.

Batman constantly improved on his gear and learned how to handle it more efficiently while in action. Early on, a thermite charge accidentally went off, destroying his first Utility Belt. (*Batman* #404–407, February–May 1987) Much of his technology came from the futuristic research and development divisions from across WAYNE ENTERPRISES. In the shifted reality in the wake of Infinite Crisis, LUCIUS FOX was the chief architect of tools and equipment used by Bruce Wayne.

D. The Batcave

The Batcave is a series of catacombs, tunnels, and a multi-tiered immensely vast cave discovered deep beneath Wayne Manor. The space was drastically modified by Bruce Wayne to serve as Batman's headquarters, research laboratory, training facility, and trophy room.

On Earth-2, Bruce initially kept his sole piece of equipment, the BATGYRO, in a secret hangar. Soon after, he used a false wall within Wayne Manor to house scientific and medical equipment. Within a year of beginning his war on crime, Batman finally built his permanent headquarters beneath the manor. (*Batman* #3, Fall 1940)

The Batcave was accessed by a staircase located behind a grandfather clock in the mansion. A winch hauled the Batmobile up an incline to access an exit tunnel. The BATPLANE was hidden within a barn situated over an accessway to the cave. The BATBOAT remained anchored at the cave's edge, with the Gotham River easily accessible. This Batcave had an elaborate collection of trophies that included a dinosaur replica taken from Dinosaur Island (*Batman* #35, June/July 1946), a giant JOKER card (*Detective Comics* #158, April 1950), a giant penny (*World's Finest Comics* #30, September/October 1947), and a collection of the Penguin's trick umbrellas (*Detective Comics* #158, April 1950), among many others. A complete inventory was never chronicled.

On Earth-1 the cave was accessed by either a staircase located behind a grandfather clock in the mansion or a service elevator. (*Batman* #164, June 1964) A road and ramp provided the Batmobile with access to a little-used road some twelve miles from Gotham City. A high hill served as the Batplane's hangar, allowing the craft's VTOL (vertical takeoff and landing) gear to gain access. The Batboat remained anchored at the cave's edge, with the Gotham River easily accessible.

After the Crisis, the Batcave grew in size and scope and was first discovered by Bruce Wayne at the age of four. The Batcave was—as usual—accessed by a staircase located behind a grandfather clock in the mansion's study. The hands of

the clock had to be set to ten forty-seven, the time Bruce's parents were slain, to unlock the secret entrance. A giant carousel housed a multitude of Batmobiles that allowed the chosen vehicle access to a tunnel route. The exterior entrance was shrouded behind holographic technology.

E. The Extraordinary Abilities and the Famous Crime-Fighting Equipment

1. The Abilities

Batman has been described as being the World's Greatest Detective and the World's Greatest Escape

Artist. To many he might be the greatest living tactician, given his numerous plans and scenarios that had him prepared for almost any eventuality. His eidetic, or photographic, memory proved invaluable in mastering languages, arts, sciences, and the myriad details he had to command instantaneously to conduct his war on crime. The records indicate that he mastered Arabic, Chinese, Japanese, Tibetan, Eskimo, Latin, French, German, Spanish, and even Kryptonese.

If there was anything he was less than perfect in knowing it was pop culture, movies, books, and television—ephemera he had little time to peruse given the demands on his time as Bruce Wayne and as Batman. Still, he figured out one of the Martian Manhunter's disguises as being based on the Japanese anime series *Sailor Moon*. (*JLA* #27, March 1999)

Batman was said to be proficient at the 127 recognized forms of hand-to-hand fighting, which he blended into something unique and solely his own. He was not the world's best martial artist, a title usually given to Lady Shiva.

While Batman swore never to use firearms, he made certain he knew how to recognize and operate all manner of weapons from pistols to bazookas. Similarly, he was proficient with a sword, lariat, bow, and other weapons. He was among the greatest experts with a boomerang, which he customized into his Batarangs, but clearly second to the first Captain Boomerang.

A master of disguise, he was trained on Earth-1 by Barrett Kean (*Detective Comics* #227, January 1958) and in the post-Crisis world by Alfred, who had initially wanted to be an actor. In a related field, Batman was also a good ventriloquist, a skill that saved him on several occasions. (*Detective Comics* #150, November 1949)

On Earth-2, and early in his time on Earth-1, Batman used his training to design and construct much of his crime-fighting gear, from his Utility Belt tools to the Batplane.

2. The Equipment

In his unending battle against crime, Batman made certain he maintained state-of-the-art tools, which he carried as needed in his remarkable Utility Belt. Additionally, his vehicles—from the Batmobile to the Batplane—were all cutting-edge, one-of-a-kind designs that were customized for his particular needs.

It was established that Wayne grew Wayne Enterprises in order to explore all manner of technology that could be siphoned out of the research and development labs and into the Batcave for use. He purchased the companies Cyberware and Kordtronics specifically for what they offered to meet his crime-fighting needs. Batman has also stolen technology as required, including Mister Terrific's T-spheres, programmable floating orbs that can record information or project messages.

Perhaps Wayne's greatest technological feat was his creation of Brother I, a mammoth satellite that contained adaptable artificial intelligence and was launched into orbit to observe the planet's metahuman community. Unfortunately it was usurped twice in rapid succession, first by Alexander Luthor from his Limbo-like realm; then by Maxwell Lord, who used it to spread nanotechnology that turned more than two million humans into cybernetic soldiers, his OMACS. Brother I gained a degree of sentience and renamed itself BROTHER EYE, deviating so drastically from its programming that it had to be destroyed by its creator.

F. The Batman Counterparts

1. Batmen of All Nations

Given Batman's Earth-2 fame, there was little surprise when other costumed vigilantes began operating in other countries, starting with the KNIGHT and the SQUIRE. (*Batman* #62, December 1950/January 1951) At one point Batman invited the Batmen of All Nations—Knight and Squire, LEGIONARY, MUSKETEER, EL GAUCHO, the RANGER—to visit Gotham City for a meeting. (*Detective Comics* #215, January 1955) On Earth-1 these heroes—with the exception of the Ranger—joined Superman, Batman, and Robin in the CLUB OF HEROES (*World's Finest Comics* #89).

Batman also traveled to South America to personally create a BAT-HOMBRE to help protect the citizens. (*Batman* #56, December 1949/January 1950)

On post-Crisis Earth, the heroes gathered once more as the Club of Heroes, adding in the European-based WINGMAN and Chief MAN-OF-THE-BATS, with disastrous results. (*Batman* #667–669, October–November 2007)

Beyond that, Batman's template of costumed-crime-fighter-accompanied-by-youthful-sidekick was inspirational and adapted time and again. Initially GREEN ARROW had Speedy, and his Arrowcave, Arrowcar, and Arrowplane became a running joke between the crime fighters. Across the American West, Chief Man-of-the-Bats and his son, LITTLE RAVEN, looked after people on their reservation. (*Batman* #86, September 1954)

2. Azrael

On occasion Batman was incapacitated and turned to others to don the cape and cowl. On Earth-2 he once summoned his descendant, BRANE TAYLOR, from a potential thirtieth century to fill in. (*Detective Comics* #216, February 1955) Alfred originally posed as Batman of his own volition (*Batman* #22, April/May 1944) but was subsequently prevailed upon to do so officially many times. At various points Batman also had Robin impersonate him in a padded costume. (*Detective Comics* #165, *Batman* #243, August 1972, among many others) Superman was a reliable backup as well (beginning in *World's Finest Comics* #71, July/August 1954); Batman even resorted to using a robot on more than one occasion (beginning in *Detective Comics* #224, October 1955).

However, the first time he ever let someone fill in for him for an extended period was after Bane broke his back in a brutal fight. Uncertain of his future, and needing someone to carry on the mission, he asked JEAN-PAUL VALLEY to replace him. Valley had been raised by the SACRED ORDER OF SAINT DUMAS and trained in its unique program called the System to

be its Avenging Angel, AZRAEL, making him a close match to the Dark Knight. Valley agreed, but the System had been accompanied by psychological conditioning that turned Valley more violent than Wayne imagined. His Batman grew vicious; the Batsuit was slowly replaced with armor, and it was clear there was a new Caped Crusader in Gotham City. After Wayne healed, he challenged Valley to regain what he called the mantle of the Bat. After prevailing, Wayne realized he needed to regroup in mind and body and asked Dick Grayson to give up being NIGHTWING for a time and be the next Batman.

3. Potential Future Versions

The chronicles have shown that Batman's legacy extended far into the future, with descendants and others adopting the cape and cowl to fight for justice both on and off Earth. With the future an ever-changing series of possibilities based on actions in the present, the following Batmen are all possible glimpses of how the mantle of the Bat has been handled in succeeding generations.

The first such recorded appearance was by a man named Cohen in the war-ravaged America of 2050. He fought alongside a time-stranded Jonah Hex; after crashing his Batwing into a harbor, his fate remained unknown. (*Hex* #11–12, July–August 1986) In a variant near future, Batman's permanent

replacement was known to have defeated a second-generation TWO-FACE by proving statistically that his good side was dominant. (*DC One Million* #3, November 1998) The date is speculative, and this time line postulated that hundreds of Batmen would follow through to the 853rd century.

A different Batman was seen in roughly the same period: Terry McGinnis, who used a techno-logically sophisticated Batsuit to continue the fight on crime. (*Superman/Batman* #22–23, October–November 2005)

One time line followed the exploits of the sixth, fifteenth, and nineteenth Batmen. The latter and his family were nearly wiped out by the Joker's descendant. Batman's son, Bron, became the twentieth Batman in 2967. (*World's Finest Comics* #166, May 1967)

In the year 3000, two possible Batmen have been recorded, the first being BRANE, the twentieth direct descendant of Bruce Wayne and his era's Caped Crusader. (*Batman* #26, December 1944/January 1945) An entirely different man was Batman in a vastly different 3000. (*Robin 3000* #1, 1993) In 3057 Brane Taylor, a possible relative, took over the role. (*Batman* #67, October/November 1951)

From an unspecified era came a Batman who visited Earth-2's Batman on one occasion. (*Batman* #105, February 1957)

Batman, Robin, and Nightwing were re-created in the 853rd century. That far-distant era's Dark Knight was based on the distant planetoid Pluto and served with the Justice League. Robin was actually a robot, nicknamed the Toy Wonder. (*DC One Million* #1–4, October 1998–February 1999)

4. Imaginary Story/Elseworlds Versions

Batman's exploits were not limited to Earth-1 or Earth-2: There have been noteworthy recorded adventures across the multiverse prior to its collapse during the Crisis on Infinite Earths. What follows are highlights from those recorded variations in order of their appearance in the time line.

The Wayne Family fought the immortal con-queror Vandal Savage through the centuries. (*Batman: Dark Knight Dynasty*, 1998)

A knight of the Round Table swore fealty to King Arthur but also sought to avenge his parents' death. (*Batman: Dark Knight of the Round Table* #1–2, 1998–1999)

Bruce Wayne served as Leonardo da Vinci's apprentice and used his bat-wing designs to become a costumed crime fighter. (*Batman Annual* #18, 1994)

Scientist Bruce Wayne restored his father to life in Germany, with disastrous results. (*Batman: Castle of the Bat*, 1994)

Batman was a Union agent during the Civil War. (*Batman: The Blue, the Grey and the Bat*, 1992) In a different version of the era, Bruce Wayne joined the Pinkertons, a society of detectives. (*Batman: Detective No. 27*, 2004)

In the Victorian era a heavily cloaked and goggled Batman went into action to hunt down Jack the Ripper in England. (*Batman: Gotham by Gaslight*, 1989)

Fighting foes of Prohibition, federal agent

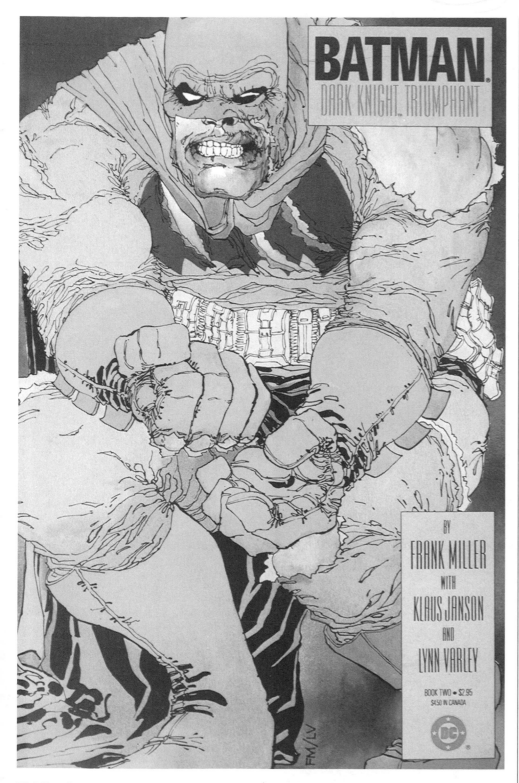

and Catwoman marrying Bruce Wayne, changing her persona from Catwoman to Batwoman and continuing the fight against crime. (*JLA: The Nail* #1–3, 1998; *JLA: Another Nail* #1–3, 2004)

Batman and Superman both began their careers as they did on Earth-2, but married sooner and had children, beginning parallel generations of heroes to survive the millennia. Both progenitors also lived well into the distant future, ensuring peace on Earth. (*Superman & Batman: Generations* #1–4, 1999; *Superman & Batman: Generations II* #1–4, 2001; *Superman & Batman: Generations III* #1–4, 2003)

In the late twentieth century Batman began investigating a series of murders only to discover that the killer was Dracula, lord of the vampires. To combat the undead villain, Batman had himself turned into a vampire by a rogue named Tanya. After losing his humanity, he had the power necessary to defeat Dracula. Some time later Dracula's hordes were taken over by the Joker, who needed to be subdued by Batman and Catwoman (who in this reality was a werecat). After she was killed, Batman sought revenge by killing the Joker via drinking all his blood. He insisted he be staked and killed for good but found himself resurrected to help Gotham City defend itself against its costumed super-villains. They intended to lure Batman into the Batcave then detonate a bomb that would expose the caverns to the sun and destroy him once and for all. The plan failed, and KILLER CROC and Two-Face were killed in the fight. A wounded Batman was offered Alfred's blood to give him the strength to win the battle. He then ordered James Gordon to trigger the bomb; the commissioner was crushed in the debris. (*Batman and Dracula: Red Rain,* 1992; *Batman: Bloodstorm,* 1995; *Batman: Crimson Mist,* 1999)

A different modern-day story showed what happened when Abin Sur crashed on Earth and passed the power ring to Bruce Wayne in lieu of Hal Jordan, inspiring the driven millionaire to become GREEN LANTERN. (*Batman: In Darkest Knight,* 1994)

Alfred was inspired to write imaginary stories wherein Batman and Batwoman married and had children. In time he retired, and Dick Grayson became Batman II while Bruce Wayne Jr. became Robin II. (*Batman* #131, April 1960)

Other realities showed Bruce Wayne Jr. struggle or delight in following in the footsteps of his father. (*World's Finest Comics* #154, December 1965; *Action Comics* #391–392, August–September 1970) One reality, said to possibly be a computer glitch in the FORTRESS OF SOLITUDE, showed Clark Kent Jr. joining his counterpart as the SUPER SONS. (*World's Finest Comics* #215, December 1972/January 1973)

While New Earth featured DAMIAN as the spoiled son of Batman and Talia, different possibilities showed him as a more responsible successor to his father, whether as Tallant (*Batman: Brotherhood of the Bat,* 1995; *Batman: League of Batmen* #1–2, 2001) or Ibn al Xu'ffasch. (*The Kingdom: Son of the Bat* #1, February 1999)

Alexander Luthor's efforts to create the perfect Earth failed during Infinite Crisis, but did cause the rebirth of the multiverse. This new set of parallel worlds was limited to fifty-two, most of which remained unchronicled. Many, though, have been

Eliot Ness became Batman to do what his badge wouldn't allow. (*Batman: Scar of the Bat,* 1996)

America needed its Batman to work for the OSS during World War II. (*Batman: Dark Allegiances,* 1996)

One world saw LEX LUTHOR kidnap and subsequently kill the infant from KRYPTON, Kal-El. Repercussions of there being no Superman included the lack of a JLA and Joe Chill killing Barbara Gordon's parents instead of Bruce Wayne's. As a result, it was Batgirl who came first, partnered with SUPERGIRL, Kara Zor-El, who rocketed to Earth without benefit of the Man of Steel's guidance. Bruce Wayne grew up to be the dilettante he normally pretended to be. (*Elseworld's Finest: Supergirl & Batgirl,* 1994)

A different world saw a nail give Jonathan Kent's truck a flat tire so he missed his fateful rendezvous with Kal-El's rocketship. Instead he was raised by an Amish family, depriving the world of Superman. That world saw Robin and Batgirl fall in the line of duty

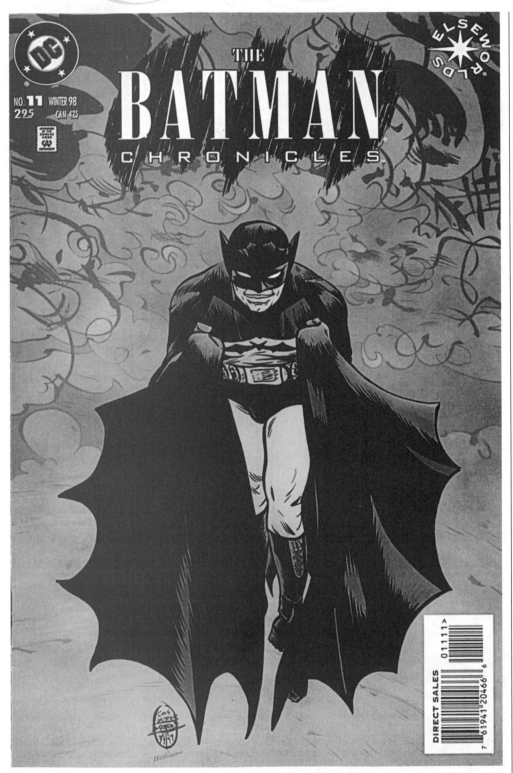

William, who was cursed by a witch on what was once known as Earth-97. (*Tangent: Batman,* September 1998)

Earth-19 featured a Victorian-era Batman. (*Batman: Gotham by Gaslight,* 1989)

Earth-43 featured a world where vampires were a major threat and Batman turned vampire to stop Dracula. (*Batman and Dracula: Red Rain,* 1989)

Earth-13 was ruled by magic, not science, and Bruce Wayne was known there as the Batmage, master of the Dark Arts. (*Arena* #1, February 2008)

Earth-21 saw the rise of the modern age of heroes in the late 1950s when Batman was still older and still active. (*New Frontier* #1–46, March–August 2004)

An unnumbered world featured Terry McGinnis as Batman's first true successor. (*Superman/Batman* #22–23, October–November 2005)

Earth-40 featured costumed champions all without superpowers; they worked as espionage agents during World War II. (*JSA: Liberty Files* #1–2, February–March 2000; *JSA: The Unholy Three* #1–2, 2003)

G. The Man Himself (as Bruce Wayne)

Often Batman saw Bruce Wayne as a useful disguise, not as a real person. Other times he preferred playing the playboy to the brooding Dark Knight, recognizing the good he did by owning Wayne Enterprises and running the WAYNE FOUNDATION. He was handsome with black hair and blue eyes; he stood six feet two inches tall and weighed 210 pounds. His chest measured forty-four inches, while he had a thirty-three-inch sleeve length. (*Detective Comics* #169, March 1951) On Earth-2 he had a silver plate in his left shoulder to repair a bullet wound received while in action. (*Detective Comics* #199, September 1953) He also briefly smoked a pipe but gave it up early in his crime-fighting career. That world's Bruce Wayne was a member of many of Gotham City's unique clubs and served on the boards of many local companies.

After the Crisis, Bruce Wayne had little time for work beyond the needs of Batman, and he served on precious few boards. One exception was ARKHAM ASYLUM's parole board—an assignment that actually enhanced his ability to work as Batman. (*Detective Comics* #831, June 2007)

To the world at large, Bruce Wayne was a billionaire who seemed to be at the edge of the international social swirl, always seen with a gorgeous woman (or two) on his arm. The media recorded his whereabouts and often speculated about when he would end his bachelor days. As a result, whenever he needed Bruce Wayne to drop from sight, Batman had the media cover Wayne's travels or the injuries he suffered during his inept athletic pursuits, from polo to auto racing. When Bane broke Batman's back, Alfred planted the story that Wayne was severely injured in a car accident as Nightwing wrecked one of the many sports cars Wayne owned.

By virtue of his wealth—*Forbes* magazine estimated his fortune at $6.8 billion, making him the seventh richest man on Earth—Wayne was a

identified and are similar to but not exact replicas of the pre-Crisis multiverse.

The New Earth continues to feature the adventures of the core set of characters that provide the template for all parallel variations. Many include members from Batman's life.

Earth-2 featured a world with the JUSTICE SOCIETY OF AMERICA, complete with adult Robin and Batman's daughter grown to adulthood as the Huntress. (*52* #52, 2007)

Earth-3 was home to the Crime Syndicate of America and the Jokester, with OWLMAN fulfilling the Batman role. (*52* #52, 2007)

Earth-22 was a world where the heroes became more of a threat than the villains they opposed and a crippled Bruce Wayne continued to operate from the Batcave, controlling his robotic Batmen. Nightwing had married STARFIRE and they had a daughter, Nightstar. (*52* #52, 2007)

An unnumbered world featured the knight

magnet for women, would-be inventors, crackpots, the needy, and more. His charitable works burnished the Wayne image but also brought him a deep personal satisfaction, for he knew the family wealth could heal people in ways Batman never could touch.

Bruce Wayne was also seen as the face of the city. When Congress was considering cutting all funding to Gotham, virtually cutting it off from America, it was Bruce Wayne who testified before the Senate. And after a year with the city a virtual NO MAN'S LAND, Wayne and his resources led the rebuilding process, making many around the world look at him in new ways.

A downside to such wealth was that Wayne was often the target of the unscrupulous. Corrupt employees at WayneTech tried to make him the fall guy when their experimental program went awry. (Detective Comics #598–600, March–May 1989) Similarly, he has been suspected of various crimes, notably murder, on more than one occasion. He actually was jailed on suspicion of killing his former lover VESPER FAIRCHILD. His incarceration pushed Wayne to drop the mask he normally wore, and he severely injured several inmates at BLACKGATE PENITENTIARY. When he then became a fugitive to clear his name on his own, it was the closest the two halves of his personality had ever come to blending. (Batman: The Ten Cent Adventure, March 2002)

Throughout the years he has been Batman, Wayne has often veered between embracing and distancing himself from his real name and legacy. In the wake of Infinite Crisis, Bruce Wayne traveled the world to renew his mission, retraining in his physical skills but also mentally refreshing himself. Upon his return to Gotham, Batman was noticeably less grim and Bruce Wayne seemed a little more grounded, less the dim-witted dilettante.

H. The Man Himself (as Batman)

Alfred once said of the man he helped raise, "He's at his best when cornered. Faced with the possibility of death, most of us descend into the throes of panic. But not the Batman. They think he will somehow be afraid of them. Frightened by their twisted faces, contorted with evil. They don't understand that he's not seeing their faces in the struggle, but the face of the one who killed his parents. And then his own face, wet with tears. It's what gives him the strength to face any opponent. The Batman endures because his sorrow has been channeled into a white hot righteousness. As a child he could only watch while his parents bled to death in the street. He refused to ever feel that hopelessness again." (Superman/Batman #32, February 2007)

On Earth-2, Batman was driven but appeared to enjoy his mission, displaying a sense of humor and seeming easily approachable by the man on the street. It wasn't always that way. Early on, Batman took his job seriously, meting out justice as he felt the circumstances dictated. He even carried a gun and was willing to kill when necessary. On one of his earliest cases, Batman threw a member of FRENCHY BLAKE's gang off a roof to his death (Detective Comics #28, June 1939); soon after this he strangled DOCTOR DEATH's aide, JABAH, and broke the neck of another assistant, MIKHAIL. (Detective Comics #29–30, July–August 1939) When he first encountered the MONK, the Dark Knight determined that the only way to end his threat was to kill him with silver bullets. (Detective Comics #32, October 1939) He continued in this manner, going so far as to use a machine gun mounted on the first Batplane, until he ended the GREEN DRAGON's menace. (Detective Comics #39, May 1940) He then seemed to take a vow against killing.

Batman's career was a colorful one throughout the 1940s. After World War II, things began to change and slow down. Batman was also more interested in selective cases, and he watched Dick Grayson attend college and become a lawyer. (DC Super-Stars #17, November/December 1977) He and Catwoman, though, tangled one final time, which landed her in jail. Later, when the SCARECROW proved more dangerous than usual, Batman asked for Catwoman's help; by mission's end, they finally gave in to the passion they'd felt for each other for years. (The Brave and the Bold #197, April 1983)

They married, and SELINA KYLE gave birth to a daughter, HELENA WAYNE. At that point Batman slipped into semi-retirement.

Batman and Catwoman were retired for good. Or so both thought. Selina was blackmailed into going out for one more robbery as Catwoman, only to die during the crime. To avenge her, Helena adopted the guise of the Huntress. (DC Super-Stars #17, November/December 1977) By then, despite the JSA re-forming and its members frequently adventuring with their Earth-1 counterparts, Batman was done. In fact, Wayne succeeded James Gordon as police commissioner, continuing the fight against crime from a new vantage point. Bill Jensen, a petty thief who gained superpowers, forced him to don the cape and cowl one final time. Both men died in the confrontation, although countless lives were saved in the process. (Adventure Comics #461–463, January/February 1979–April/May 1979)

On Earth-1, Batman was recorded as using a gun only once and never again; he went out of his way to avoid using them. He also was never recorded to have killed anyone. The same held true for the Batman re-created after the Crisis and Infinite Crisis. His career was filled with costumed super-villains and intergalactic threats, which he handled without much stress. The world was growing darker, though, and the threats were more compelling, starting with the arrival of ecoterrorist Rā's al Ghūl.

Batman watched Dick Grayson grow up and leave for college. There was tension between the two for a time, but when circumstances demanded it, Robin was always ready to back up the Dark Knight. Bruce was then alone for the first time in years and boarded up the mansion for a brief time, living in the penthouse atop the Wayne Foundation building. He even had time for romance, with girlfriends including photojournalist VICKI VALE and Catwoman, who was attempting to turn her life around.

After the Crisis, Batman faced new challenges and briefly attempted to maintain the notion that Batman was an urban legend. Some people insisted that the police flashed the BAT-SIGNAL only to scare the criminal element; Batman sightings were lumped together with those of Bigfoot and Elvis. Batman was real, however, and he was no longer alone. He encountered JASON TODD and brought him home, training the headstrong youth to become the second Robin. Dick had since taken the name *Nightwing* and was out on his own or with the Teen Titans. The new Dynamic Duo took on new and familiar threats until the Joker killed Jason in the Middle East. The months that followed saw a dark, grimmer Batman prowl the streets of Gotham, dishing out brutal justice.

Alfred despaired over the changes in his master but seemed at a loss to get through to him. Dick, busy with the Titans and his lover Starfire, was feeling somewhat estranged from his mentor, unhappy with how he'd handled Jason. As a result, it took the arrival of Tim Drake to shake Batman from his self-destruction.

Tim had deduced Batman's identity years earlier and began a campaign to convince Dick that Batman needed a Robin. Dick finally noticed what had happened to his guardian and returned to Gotham, but as Nightwing. When they were endangered, Tim convinced Alfred to let him borrow a Robin outfit, and he came to their rescue. Only then did Batman begin to realize what having an optimistic and energetic partner meant to

him. Learning from his experience with Jason, he demanded that Tim undergo a six-month training program. Tim agreed. Six months later the third Robin was at Batman's side when he responded to the Bat-Signal.

Batman slowly built up a cadre of agents in Gotham, frowning on vigilantes who did not have his blessing, among them Huntress and ORPHEUS; he turned a blind eye to the altruistic RAGMAN. He used his agents as pawns with Gotham his chessboard, and time and again they proved the difference between disaster and success.

Then international criminal Bane arrived in Gotham, intending to supplant Batman as the source of fear in the city. He freed the criminals in Blackgate and Arkham, letting Batman and his team exhaust themselves rounding up the villains. After three months Batman was emotionally and physically drained—which is when Bane turned up in Wayne Manor. They fought, and the VENOM-powered thug broke Batman's back across his knee. (*Batman* #497, Late July 1993) Alfred helped stabilize Bruce Wayne, and the wounded hero turned the mantle of the Bat over to Azrael.

Azrael had to struggle against early training called the System, and in the process he became a Batman that really terrorized Gotham's underworld. Wayne feared he'd never walk again until SHONDRA KINSOLVING, his physical therapist, used her meta-human skill to repair his spinal damage. He then began retraining himself, calling on Lady Shiva for assistance.

When he was deemed ready, he fought Azrael to regain the mantle for himself and proved victorious. Still, he needed more time to prepare himself and finally asked Dick to fill in as Batman for a time.

Then the CLENCH was unleashed in Gotham. The disease rapidly spread and killed hundreds, nearly adding Robin to the list. Not long after, a 7.6 magnitude earthquake shook the city to its foundations. Batman, Robin, Nightwing, Huntress, and ORACLE protected the citizens from the rampaging villains freed from Blackgate and Arkham, assisting rescue operations and protecting lives. Later, the federal government cut off Gotham from the country, turning the city into a No Man's Land. At first Batman felt dead, like the city, and vanished from sight for three months. He worked out of a series of mini-Batcaves he had constructed throughout the city. One hundred days later, he returned and found anarchy reigning. In short order he reestablished his presence, adopting the graffiti-tagging system others had used to mark turf.

Working alongside Gordon and his agents, Batman began to restore order block by block. The Dark Knight recognized his need for his allies—his surrogate family—and worked with them with great success. Things changed once more, though, when Lucius Fox forced Wayne to take on a bodyguard, SASHA BORDEAUX. Rather than let her interfere with his crime fighting, Wayne slowly left clues leading Bordeaux to his secret. He then brought her fully into his world. She trained, much as Tim did, and even donned a mask and costume for Wayne's nights on the town. One night, though, they returned to the manor to find the body of Vesper Fairchild. The police arrived moments later, and the two were arrested on suspicion of murder.

Bruce broke out of Blackgate and went to investigate the truth on his own. His allies, baffled by his distance, worked feverishly to find the answers. In the end they all learned that the murder had been committed by Batgirl's father, David Cain, under contract from Lex Luthor, who wanted revenge against Wayne for usurping his dream of being the driving force behind rebuilding Gotham.

Bordeaux remained in jail until she was hurt in a fight and believed dead, only to be spirited away by CHECKMATE to start over. Batman was freed from her presence, despite Sasha having captured his heart.

He continued to work against the odds as crime and corruption seemed to grow more and more prevalent. Tim's father learned his secret and demanded that the boy give up his costumed role—or else he'd expose Wayne's secret, too. Tim's girlfriend, STEPHANIE BROWN, lobbied Batman to become the new Robin, arguing that her time as Spoiler had prepared her. He had pretty much concluded by then she was more heart than skill, but he agreed to take her on anyway—with the understanding that if she disobeyed him once, she was through. They worked together for nearly three months before she did as he expected, and she was fired. Hoping to regain his confidence, she activated one of his WAR GAMES scenarios without understanding all its implications, plunging the city into a vicious, bloody gang war.

It forced Tim back into costume, finally with his father's blessing. But the war came at a price—Spoiler wound up captured by BLACK MASK, tortured for information, and left to die from her wounds. Worse, Batman abused Oracle, using her more as operator than ally, and usurped the police frequencies, giving uniformed officers orders ahead of Commissioner MICHAEL AKINS. When the war ended, Black Mask consolidated power in the underworld, the costumed heroes were declared vigilantes to be shot on sight, and Batman lost Oracle as an ally.

Things grew darkest when the wife of the ELONGATED MAN died, beginning a series of events that nearly brought down the super-hero community. While the heroes investigated, other loved ones were targeted, and the Dynamic Duo arrived too late to prevent Captain Boomerang from killing Tim's father, JACK DRAKE.

Soon after, Batman learned that his spy satellite Brother I had been taken over by Checkmate's insane leader, Maxwell Lord. He had killed BLUE BEETLE, who investigated his own suspicions— theories Batman had dismissed when he'd first heard them. Bordeaux tipped off Batman that the Beetle was dead, forcing him to get proactive. Instead, Earth's heroes were plunged into a war against its villains as the Society attacked and Lord turned more than two million humans into OMACs, programmed to kill meta-humans. It took the combined efforts of the super heroes to stop both threats. Batman led a team into space to destroy his creation, which by then had renamed itself Brother Eye.

Batman soon after learned that the satellite had also been used by Alexander Luthor, survivor of Earth-3. He wanted to remake the universe, bringing back the multiverse in order to find the perfect Earth. Batman, Superman, and WONDER WOMAN bickered among themselves, for each disapproved of what the others had done during the OMAC wars—including Wonder Woman killing Lord to break his telepathic control of the Man of Steel, who had nearly beaten the Dark Knight to death. Without the triumvirate acting as leaders, things grew chaotic as an Infinite Crisis was unleashed on Earth.

When the Battle of METROPOLIS ended, along with the threat, Nightwing had been blasted; he lay in a coma for three weeks. Superman had lost his powers, and Wonder Woman's homeland of Themyscira left its plane of existence. Batman was spent, emotionally, and recognized that it was time to regroup. After Oracle declared Dick Grayson healed and ready, Batman invited him and Tim to join him for a year abroad, where they would all retrain and refresh.

Batman confidently left Gotham in the hands of HARVEY DENT, knowing that a restored Commissioner Gordon would be there to help. The trio traveled from continent to continent, but when they were in the Middle East after six months overseas, he sent his children home. Batman remained with the Ten-Eyed brotherhood, having them psychically cut out his personal demons. Cleansed, he traveled to New Delhi to experience the Thorgal Ordeal in the legendary land of Nanda Parbat. He finished with a seven-day sensory deprivation experience, then climbed the 9,999 stairs to a chamber to complete his work. (*52* #47, 2007)

Upon his return to Gotham City, things felt right to the Dark Knight. He had Robin at his side, Gordon back in office, and Gotham City saved from immolation thanks to Nightwing and other allies. With renewed optimism, he returned to his mission to fight crime.

With Superman and Wonder Woman, he also rebuilt the Justice League of America, recognizing that the world needed a team of heroes it could count on. Still, he knew there were additional dangers in the world's darkest corner; when the opportunity presented itself, then, he gladly took over the Outsiders from Nightwing, auditioning a new strike force to do what the JLA could not.

I. The Relationship with Robin(s)

Dick Grayson

Dick Grayson was born for action. Raised in a circus environment and trained as an acrobat, he was a natural when Batman adopted him in the wake of his parents' deaths. As the red-and-yellow Robin the Boy Wonder, he exuded optimism and brightened his new father's mood. They enjoyed fighting crime side by side and became the inspiration for many other heroic duos.

The two maintained a strong familial relationship on Earth-2 and Earth-1, as Bruce Wayne delighted in Dick's accomplishments. Things were a little different after the Crisis: Dick's lighthearted

approach grew a shade darker after a dangerous encounter with Two-Face. Batman watched Dick grow up, take command of the Teen Titans, and become his own person. However, as Dick neared eighteen, he began to assert his independence. After heading off to an upstate college, Dick rarely had time to operate with Batman. Dick's decision to drop out of college caused a brief rift between him and Bruce, but the two soon reconciled. Now an adult, he felt increasingly conflicted in costume. Noting the desire of Bruce's new ward Jason Todd to become a super hero in his own right, Dick gave him the Robin persona with his blessing while adopting the new identity of Nightwing for himself.

Dick struggled to come out from the Batman's shadow. He found himself at odds with his mentor time and again, especially as Batman never told him of Todd's death; Dick had to learn it from a fellow Titan. They bickered in the aftermath and were estranged for a time.

As a result, Dick chafed when Tim Drake asked him to come back as Robin. He recognized that Batman needed help but went back as Nightwing. However, when they were both captured by Two-Face, it was Tim, dressed as Robin, who saved the day. With Batman distant toward Tim, other than training, Dick took it upon himself to ease the teen into his new role.

Dick was hurt when Bruce picked Jean-Paul Valley to replace him after Bane broke Batman's back. The Dark Knight did so out of respect for Dick's independence, though. Later, after healing, he asked Dick to act in his stead for a time. The relationship finally began to heal, and Bruce's respect for the man Dick had become was clear. Indeed, as a symbolic gesture, Bruce would even formally adopt the adult Dick Grayson as his son. He also picked Nightwing to act as JLA leader when an emergency JLA needed to be formed. (*JLA* #68, September 2002)

Jason Todd

Batman filled the void in his life when Dick Grayson left for college by replacing him with Jason Todd. Prior to the Crisis, Jason's path to Robin was eerily similar to Dick's, which made the transition smooth. Post-Crisis, though, Jason was a street kid with guts and bravado but no athletic skills. He proved brash, headstrong, and difficult, making his training challenging. Additionally, his life experiences gave him a skewed moral code; he often blurred the lines between right and wrong. Batman was initially forgiving of the differences, but over time it became clear that Jason was trouble. Batman tried to find a way to correct his worldview before things spiraled out of control. Instead, Jason defied Bruce, benching him. He left Gotham in search of his birth mother, only to find Sheila Haywood working for the Joker in the Middle East. He was no match for the Clown Prince of Crime and was beaten with a crowbar and left to die in an explosion. Batman blamed himself for the senseless death and hung a Robin outfit in the Batcave as a reminder of his failure.

After Jason's miraculous resurrection, the two had yet to sort out their relationship.

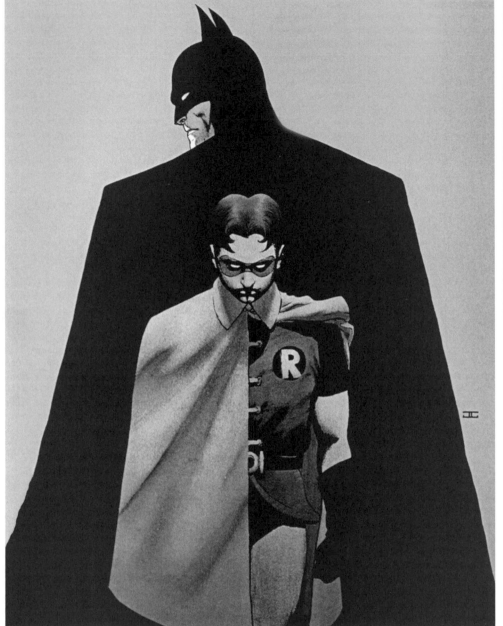

Tim Drake

Tim Drake

Like Jason Todd, Tim filled a void in Batman's life—although it took the Dark Knight time to recognize it. He respected the boy's enthusiasm and keen mind, which had discerned Batman's identity at the age of nine. Still, he didn't want to repeat the mistakes he'd made with Jason, so it took a lot of convincing from Alfred, Dick, and Tim before Batman agreed he needed a Robin.

In time Batman came to embrace the new Robin. He remarked to Alfred and Dick that Tim was likely smarter than he himself. They meshed well, and Batman went out of his way to look after Tim even though—unlike Dick and Jason—the boy had a living father. That all changed when Jack Drake died at the hands of Captain Boomerang.

Tim wanted his own independence for a while, moving to BLÜDHAVEN and rejecting Bruce Wayne's offer of adoption. However, after the neighboring city was destroyed, he moved to a farmhouse on the Wayne estate. He finally came around to accepting Bruce's offer and moved into the mansion as Wayne's legal son, setting up residence in Dick's old room.

Stephanie Brown

Batman never thought Stephanie had what it took to be a member of his team. He tried to train her and even asked the BIRDS OF PREY for help. Stephanie proved to have desire and spirit, but she lacked the keen mind and athletic skills needed to be the exceptional crime fighter Batman's mission demanded. When she lobbied to become the fourth Robin, Batman accepted her and drilled her harder than he had her predecessors. Unlike the others, he never revealed his identity to her or entrusted her with many of his secrets. Largely, that was a result of his belief she would not live up to the role and the blind obedience it demanded. She proved him right and was fired. They remained estranged until she lay dying, a victim of Black Mask's torture. Batman was filled with grief and guilt for not working harder to make her dream a reality.

J. The Women of the Chronicles

Batman was so busy fighting crime that he usually dated women—as Bruce Wayne—only when he had an ulterior motive. Early in his Earth-2 career, Bruce Wayne was engaged to Julie Madison, but she broke it off to pursue her career. Soon after, Bruce dated LINDA PAGE, but she left to become a nurse. Vicki Vale arrived in Gotham and dated Bruce Wayne, but the relationship petered out. He was always attracted to the Catwoman but did not admit his feelings until well after World War II, when they finally married.

Bruce Wayne had a few serious female relationships on Earth-1, notably KATHY KANE. Similarly, Batman and Batwoman seemed to share a mutual attraction but rarely acted on it; she quickly retired from crime fighting, ending the chance for romance. Rā's daughter, Talia, fell in love with Batman, but the Caped Crusader wouldn't act on his feelings since this would have played into Rā's plans to have him as an heir. Their relationship ran hot and cold until finally she gave up on him.

Wayne fell hard for SILVER ST. CLOUD, a platinum-haired beauty, but she ended the relationship after figuring out his secret. It was a life she could not handle, and she left Gotham rather than see the man she loved risk his life night after night. Bruce Wayne actually dated Catwoman—that is, a reformed Selina Kyle—for a while, but the relationship never lasted, and she returned to crime. Later, Bruce dated Vicki Vale and even JULIA REMARQUE, Alfred's daughter, but both women grew frustrated that the relationships never progressed. The final woman to garner Batman's affections was Nocturna, a deadly, deranged woman who ultimately died from her actions.

After the Crisis on Infinite Earths, Bruce Wayne's female companions grew in number, although most were arm candy to protect his playboy image. In fact, women boasted of their conquest of Bruce Wayne while none ever got past the first floor of Wayne Manor. His first girlfriend while Batman was the Gotham Museum of Art's Lorna Shore. (*Batman Confidential* #7, September 2007)

Wayne observed that the night they slept together was the first time he'd slept through the night since he was eight. Soon after, he did fall for Julie Madison, who learned his secret and like Silver, left rather than deal with his dangerous life. (*Batman and the Mad Monk* #6, March 2007)

Those who actually touched his heart during his tenure as Batman included the always simmering Catwoman, Talia, Vicki Vale, RACHEL CASPIAN, Vesper Fairchild, Shondra Kinsolving, and Sasha Bordeaux. Through his life as Batman, he came to escort fellow heroes Dr. Light II and Fire, but he was surprised to find himself growing increasingly attracted to the Amazon Princess. They finally decided to try

Their friendship deepened with time, so that when Gordon became commissioner, Batman had an ally at the top of the law enforcement world. Sarah Essen Gordon disliked Batman but tolerated him because of Jim Gordon's relationship with him. In time, though, she came to accept him as an ally. Jim Gordon's successor, Michael Akins, gave the Caped Crusader the benefit of the doubt until gang wars turned the streets red with blood. Batman took over the police band and ordered the cops around as if he were in charge, which angered Akins so much that he ordered that anyone in costume be shot on sight. While he eventually rescinded the order, he distrusted the vigilantes for the remainder of his tenure.

Various mayors reacted differently to Batman. Hamilton Hill, Rupert Thorne's lackey, actively disliked the crime fighter. Marion Grange, though, relied heavily on the Dark Knight when Gotham was plagued with the Clench and then an earthquake. Away from Gotham, Batman was kept at arm's length by the federal government's various operations, from Checkmate to the Suicide Squad. When Lex Luthor was president, he actively worked to destroy Batman, failing in the process.

Through the JLA, Batman enjoyed free access to

an actual date and see what happened, but Bruce Wayne abandoned Wonder Woman to fight crime, letting Alfred's dinner go to waste. They agreed the relationship was best left as a friendship. (*JLA* #90, January 2004)

Batman and Catwoman finally began a romance at the same time Hush was targeting the Dark Knight for death. He went so far as to entrust her with his secret identity, but broke things off when he realized he could not fully trust her. They have remained friendly ever since but have eschewed the romance while she raises her daughter, Helena, the product of a brief relationship with Sam Bradley.

K. The Relationship with the Law Enforcement Establishment

Batman began life as a vigilante and was actually wanted by the police at the outset of his career. In time, though, Police Commissioner Gordon realized what an asset Batman and Robin had become. They became officially deputized members of the police force, enhancing their crime-fighting abilities. (*Batman* #7, October/November 1941) Later Batman was issued a platinum badge. (*Detective Comics* #70, December 1942; actually presented in *Detective Comics* #95, November 1945)

On Earth-1, Batman generally seemed to enjoy the support of the police—interrupted by brief periods involving unfriendly political administrations or false accusations of murder—and had a warm, enduring friendship with Commissioner Gordon, even exchanging Christmas gifts. With the JLA a world-recognized crime-fighting operation, Batman enjoyed police privileges beyond America.

After the Crisis, Batman was seen as a vigilante once more, and was hunted down by Commissioner Gillian B. Loeb. (*Batman* #404, February 1987) He trusted only newly arrived detective Jim Gordon.

most countries. He did not necessarily have police powers, though, and usually worked under their radar when away from his home base.

L. The Relationship to the Super-Hero Community

As one of the first heroes to operate on any of the Earths, Batman enjoyed a particular place in the hearts and minds of his fellow heroes. His example of an average man making himself the equal of almost any super hero was a model for countless others. He was a founding member of the Justice Society of America on Earth-2 and the Justice League of America on Earth-1. His planning and preparation kept the world safer, although his plans also came back to haunt him.

Gotham Allies

Locally, Batman operated in Gotham City usually with a Robin at his side. That's all he seemed to need on the parallel worlds despite the periodic appearances of Batwoman, Bat-Girl, and Batgirl. After the Crisis, the threats grew—and so did his need for allies. Around the third year of Batman's career, Barbara Gordon, Commissioner Gordon's niece, became Batgirl and received surreptitious assistance from the Dark Knight. He later welcomed her to the battle and grieved when she was crippled by the Joker. When she took up the identity of Oracle, she proved even more valuable. As Dick Grayson grew up and became Nightwing, Batman and Robin separated. Other Robins followed, and the Dynamic Duo was often a titanic trio. Later, the Huntress began to operate in Gotham, much to Batman's dismay since they did not share the same ideals. He actively resisted her help but did find her useful on numerous occasions, as he did Azrael. Later, when the city was a No Man's Land, Cassandra Cain arrived and proved she had the spirit to work with the team as the next Batgirl. During the tumultuous times that followed, Batman was able to count on his allies. Joining the ranks over time were Orpheus and Onyx. After Batman's year away from the city, though, many of his allies had disappeared—Orpheus was dead, Azrael thought dead, Oracle in Metropolis, and Batgirl a lost soul. Gotham City once more could rely only on Batman and Robin, which seemed to suit the Dark Knight.

Superman

Superman and Batman were the best of friends on Earth-1 and Earth-2, sharing their secrets, adventuring across the galaxy together, and watching each other's backs. After the Crisis, things grew more tenuous. Superman saw Gotham's Dark Knight as a vigilante who needed to be reined in. (*Man of Steel* #3, Early November 1986) Over time, though, they forged tenuous bonds that after many years turned into a friendship. Much of that bonding grew out of a time when they didn't work well together and a man died. (*Batman & Superman: World's Finest* #1–10, April 1999–January 2000) In the continuity of the New Earth formed after Infinite Crisis, the relationship between the two heroes once again seemed to have been a close one dating back to their early days (as evidenced by flashbacks in *Justice League of America* [second series] #0, September 2006, among others).

Their mutual respect helped them get past their different approaches to crime fighting and justice. Each learned from the other, and Superman eventually entrusted Batman with Kryptonite to be used should he ever lose control of his powers. The friendship deepened, and they often first turned to the other in times of crisis. Batman extended that trust to Lois Lane after she married the Man of Steel.

Wonder Woman

The Amazon Princess and Batman had nothing but the utmost respect for each other in the various realities. After the Crisis they were seen as among the triumvirate, along with Superman, that guided Earth's champions of justice. There was a brief romantic spark between the two but they remained nothing but allies in the war against evil.

Justice Society of America

Batman joined Earth-2's Justice Society of America in November 1940 (*DC Special* #29, August/September 1977), although he was not present at many of their meetings given his obligations in Gotham City. During World War II the JSA expanded and became the All-Star Squadron, to which both Batman and Robin belonged. (*All-Star Squadron* #3, November 1981) After the JSA returned to action, Batman chose to remain in semi-retirement until one final case, where he lost his life. During the many team-ups with Earth-1's Justice League of America, he participated in only two of the meetings. (*Justice League of America* #82, August 1970; #135–137, October–December 1976)

Justice League of America

On Earth-1, Batman was present during the pivotal case that brought the world's greatest super heroes together to repel an alien invasion. The team that came from that adventure, the Justice League of America, stood as Earth's vanguard for truth and justice. After the Crisis, Batman grudgingly joined within the first year of the JLA's existence with prodding from Superman. (*JLA: Incarnations* #2, August 2001) After secretly bankrolling the team during its early existence, Oliver Queen privately asked Bruce Wayne to succeed him as the JLA's financial benefactor when his own fortunes began to fail. (*Legends of the DCU* #12, January 1999) In

the continuity following Infinite Crisis, Batman was once again said to have been a founding member of the League.

When the JLA enjoyed United Nations sanction, it was asked to stay out of a coup in MARKOVIA. Batman wanted the League's help to rescue Lucius Fox, but members refused—so he quit and, during the rescue, wound up forming the Outsiders. (*Batman and the Outsiders* #1-2, August–September 1983) He later left that team and rejoined the JLA (*Justice League of America* #250, May 1986), something that happened on occasion. He was generally present whenever the League re-formed (*Legends* #6, April 1987), although his level of involvement waxed and waned.

Following a battle with Doctor Destiny, Batman agreed to join a new incarnation of the Justice League of America with its headquarters a Watchtower on the moon. (*Justice League: A Midsummer's Nightmare* #3, November 1996)

Batman and the JLA have had trust issues through the years. When Batman arrived at the satellite headquarters to see Zatanna about to use her magic on Dr. Light's mind, he objected—only to have ten minutes of his memory mystically obscured. Those memories resurfaced later, plunging the JLA into serious problems. Years later the team learned that Batman had prepared files on each member detailing ways each could be incapacitated or killed. When Rā's al Ghūl stole the files and used them against the JLA, the heroes prevailed but asked the Dark Knight to leave. (*JLA* #46, October 2000) Batman had to agree to a full-disclosure agreement to return to the roster (*JLA* #50, February 2001), where he remained until the team was dissolved. (*JLA* #125, April 2006) On the other hand, one of his contingency plans proved most useful when the team was plunged three thousand years back in time: His emergency protocols re-formed the JLA

with a new roster led by Nightwing. (*JLA* #66-76, July 2002–February 2003)

After Infinite Crisis, Batman, Wonder Woman, and Superman took a year away from crime fighting to pursue personal agendas. However, when all three returned to action, they met in the Batcave and hand-selected a new team. (*Justice League of America* [second series] #0, September 2006) Batman did not think to include himself in the roster until BLACK LIGHTNING insisted. (*Justice League of America* [second series] #7, April 2007)

Outsiders

Batman left the JLA after its members refused to help him rescue Lucius Fox in Markovia, which was going through a coup at the time. While there, he encountered several other heroes; after Fox was freed and the country saved, they formed the Outsiders. (*The Brave and the Bold* #200, October 1983) Batman brought them to America and worked on training the newcomers GEO-FORCE, KATANA, and HALO. The team worked well together for a time, but when Batman withheld information from them about new troubles in Markovia, they split from their founder.

Years later a new incarnation of the team was founded by Arsenal and Nightwing. After operating haphazardly for a time, Nightwing realized it was not the team for him.

Batman, though, recognized that troubled times were ahead and knew he'd need a strike force for situations the JLA could not touch. He stepped in and re-formed the team, expecting them to be cold, obedient operatives who would do the world's dirty work without question. (*Batman and the Outsiders* [second series] #1, December 2007)

Team-Ups

Despite his reputation as a loner, Batman worked on countless occasions with one or more heroes.

He usually had the right mix of skills and experience to complement nonpowered or superpowered colleagues. Most, from battle-tested veteran to newcomer, remained in awe of his dedication, preparation, and perseverance. The FLASH once observed that Batman spooked him, but was the first one to call in an emergency. (*Justice League of America* [second series] #12, September 2007)

Batman, though, has had issues with the super-hero community, stemming from when the JLA began using Zatanna's magic to erase memories or alter personalities of super-villains. He didn't know about this for some time, because Zatanna sealed off ten minutes of his memory when he first saw the JLA about to alter Dr. Light. This probably explained why he never remained with any incarnation of the JLA or Outsiders for long stretches, although he never realized it himself.

In the aftermath of SUE DIBNY's death, after the JLA's dirty secret became common knowledge among super-villains, Batman's memories came back. Disgusted at his colleagues' betrayal, and concerned over the growing meta-human population on Earth, he took covert action. Batman designed and launched Brother I, a mammoth satellite complete with artificial intelligence to monitor the meta-humans in case of emergency. The satellite, well intentioned as it was, was misused by several villains including Maxwell Lord, who reprogrammed it so that it gained a level of sentience. Calling itself Brother Eye, it plunged the world into a crisis that saw many heroes, villains, and civilians die needlessly. (*Countdown to Infinite Crisis*, May 2005; *The OMAC Project* #1-6, June–November 2005)

As a result, Batman maintained a healthy distrust for those who deviated from their heroic ideal. For example, when Green Lantern was infected by Parallax, the embodiment of fear, he committed many illegal acts until he sacrificed himself in an act of atonement. Batman rejected his offers of help; it wasn't until the Lantern's rebirth that he could prove his good intentions, once again earning Batman's trust. (*Green Lantern* [fourth series] #9, April 2006) When a rocket from Krypton crashed near Gotham, Batman was the first to discover the teenage girl inside. He was skeptical when she claimed to be from Krypton and risked Superman's anger when he continued to be suspicious of the newly arrived Supergirl. (*Superman/Batman* #8-12, May–September 2004)

After Infinite Crisis, and Batman's year away for renewal, he was more welcoming of allies, both in Gotham and on adventures around the world.

BATMAN (JUST IMAGINE)

Among the myriad parallel worlds was one Earth that had a radically different set of super heroes. On this world the Batman was a convict-turned-professional-wrestler. (*Just Imagine Stan Lee with Joe Kubert Creating Batman*, September 2001)

Wayne Williams was framed for a crime he did not commit and sentenced to prison. While serving his time, Williams befriended Frederick Grant, a scientist who mentored him in an eclectic array of disciplines from sewing to bodybuilding. During his sentence Williams was informed that his mother had died; he blamed the gang leader, Handz, who'd framed him, for keeping him away when his family needed him most. A short time later Williams rescued the warden from harm and earned himself a full pardon.

While avoiding Handz until he could exact a measure of revenge, Williams shaved his head, donned a mask, and become a professional wrestler named Batman. In keeping with his new persona, Batman never unmasked in public, giving him a real mystique among his growing fan base. Before long, Batman was commanding top dollar at the gate, and Williams found himself possessed of unexpected wealth. Since he owed his physique to Grant's tutelage, Williams sought out the recently released scientist and shared his secret identity with him. He then enlisted Grant in helping him prepare a perfect revenge plan.

Grant helped Williams design a variety of gear for his wrestling costume, preparing it for its new use. The mask was outfitted with night-vision lenses, and the costume was remade using Kevlar. Lining the outfit were electronic devices that could magnify sound to disorient foes; glider wings were added to allow Williams more freedom of movement.

Williams bought a mansion and installed Grant as its owner, while he took on the less obvious role of Grant's bodyguard. The Batman then used his new network of contacts to find Handz, who fell to his death before being able to admit to the frame-up. Enjoying the positive feeling of delivering justice, Batman switched from wrestling to crime fighting full-time.

When the evil Reverend Darkk attempted to bring a demon called Crisis to Earth, a handful of powerful figures gathered to combat the plan, including Batman. The demon was stopped, but Darkk escaped. To protect the innocent from Darkk's kind, the five heroes banded together and became the Justice League.

BATMAN (TANGENT)

On the parallel world once known as Earth-97, superpowered champions began appearing in the wake of the Cuban Missile Crisis of 1962. Into this world came Sir William, a knight who fought beside King Arthur during the Middle Ages. While an ally of the king, he was never asked to sit at the famed Round Table. He was married to the Lady Tasmia, in reality a bat-like creature from Hell, and her presence bode ill for Arthur. For, ignoring Arthur's warning, Tasmia wreaked havoc, the blame laid at William's feet. The wizard Merlin cursed William, and his body was trapped within the castle until such time as he could atone for his sins against the Crown and England. William's spirit was able to leave his body, animating a suit of armor in order to accomplish good deeds in the hope of redemption. In the twentieth century William encountered Imra, a woman who resembled Tasmia, and became enraptured. He fought for good and even joined that world's version of the Justice League in his never-ending quest for redemption. (*Tangent: Batman,* September 1998)

BATMAN II

Zur-en-Arrh was a planet in a far-distant galaxy that possessed much advanced technology. A man named Tlano used a sophisticated telescope to study life on Earth and grew fascinated by Batman, whom he continually observed. The scientist then used a teleportation ray to bring Batman to his far-flung world. Tlano demonstrated for the surprised crime fighter that he had modeled himself after Batman, fighting crime in a similar costume. After the meeting, Tlano remained inspired to do good for his people. (*Batman* #113, February 1958)

BATMAN ISLAND

A privately owned island shrine to Batman, conceived and maintained by wealthy eccentric A. K. Barnaby. (*Batman* #119, October 1958)

BATMAN JONES

During one memorable adventure, Batman used the Batmobile to stop an out-of-control car, thereby saving the family within. The grateful passengers named their newborn son Batman Jones in the Caped Crusader's honor. In return, Batman built a "Bat-Coop" crib for the baby and posed for reporters' pictures with the family, even holding the baby himself. Since Batman never accepted rewards, grateful citizens instead sent presents or money to the Jones family. Batman Jones grew up revering Batman as his idol.

One night the Bat-Signal summoned Batman and Robin to police headquarters, where they witnessed the arrival of young Batman Jones, clad in a homemade bat-uniform and riding a bike. Commissioner James Gordon asked Batman and Robin to help recover a silver statue stolen from a millionaire's home. By threatening to launch his own investigation, Batman Jones convinced the Dynamic Duo to take him along in order to keep him out of mischief. The boy proved to be of use when he organized a game of hide-and-seek among a group of neighborhood boys, using their talent at finding places to hide to uncover the stolen statue's hiding place; as a result, Batman was able to intercept the thief as he returned for his booty.

Later, Batman and Robin took their protégé back to the Batcave, claiming to be offering him a training session. In reality, they intended to demonstrate that crime fighting was too difficult for most people, including Jones, to master. Batman Jones, however, proved quick-witted and agile enough to pass all their tests. After sending him home, the two heroes admitted they needed another tack.

Batman Jones deduced that criminals would try to use the machine tools exhibited at a hobby show to tunnel through a connecting wall into the next-door bank. The youth was there to see the crooks make the attempt, but Batman and Robin also arrived and apprehended the thieves. However, Batman Jones discovered a stamp exhibit while at the show, and became so engrossed with it that he dropped his desire to be another Batman in favor of stamp collecting, much to the relief of Batman and Robin. (*Batman* #108, June 1957)

BATMAN JUNIOR

John Vance was a youth who once helped Batman before the latter took Dick Grayson to train beside him as Robin. Some time after the Dynamic Duo debuted, Vance returned to help Batman solve one last case, which caused young Grayson to feel threatened. However, Dick quickly realized he had nothing to fear. (*Detective Comics* #231, May 1956)

BATMAN MUSEUM

Upon the death of an unnamed philanthropist, it was revealed that he had left money to Gotham City for the construction of a downtown headquarters for its chief protector, Batman. The House of Batman, as it was known, was built as a surprise for the Caped Crusader, and contained a variety of tools and equipment the city presumed he would need. Honored, Batman took to using the building as his headquarters—but soon he realized that the thief Mayne Mallock always seemed to be one step ahead of the crime fighter. Batman learned that the entire building had been Mallock's idea and was being used as his secret hideout. The Gotham Guardian set a trap and eventually ensnared Mallock; he thereafter abandoned the building, letting the city use it as a museum. (*Batman* #102, September 1956) The museum subsequently moved into larger quarters, a bat-shaped building that was designed by Superman. (*World's Finest Comics* #149, May 1965)

Several other individuals built museums based on Batman's fame. One example was "Breezy" Lane's traveling Batman Dime Museum, which briefly set up shop in Gotham City before it was ultimately bought out and closed by Bruce Wayne. (*Detective Comics* #223, September 1955) Another was Tomioka, the head of Tomioka Pharmaceuticals, who was fascinated by the American hero and had a private collection of Batman memorabilia. Tomioka, however, was so obsessed with the Dark Knight that he had worked on a DNA-altering drug he thought would enhance his physique so that he could enshrine Batman in his museum and replace him as a new Batman. The plan was foiled when Tomioka died in an gang-related explosion that destroyed the museum and the drug. (*Batman: Child of Dreams,* 2003)

One potential future showed a twenty-first-century Gotham City complete with Batman Museum. (*World's Finest Comics* #11, Fall 1943)

BATMARINE

A variation on the Batboat in its submersible configuration.

BATMEN OF ALL NATIONS

Given Batman's fame, there was little surprise when other costumed vigilantes began operating in other countries. At one point Batman invited them all to Gotham City for a meeting. (*Detective Comics* #215, January 1955)

From South America came the El Gaucho, while the Ranger arrived from Australia. Europe was represented by the Wingman with the Knight and Squire direct from England, the Musketeer from France, and the Legionary from Italy. Nicknamed by the media as Batmen of All Nations, they were dubbed by others the Club of Heroes. During the meeting, the club also included Superman, who represented the rest of the world. (*World's Finest Comics* #89, July/August 1957)

After the CRISIS ON INFINITE EARTHS, the international heroes were organized by Africa's Dr. Mist as an international operation known as the Global Guardians, said to be inspired by the JUSTICE SOCIETY OF AMERICA. Their headquarters, known as the Dome, was located in Europe.

In a potential future, the heroes were known as the Batmen of Many Nations. In addition to the recognizable Batman-inspired heroes, there was also Russia's Cossack, Japan's Samurai, China's Dragon, Mysteryman, Steel, and a BATWOMAN hailing from the Fourth World. (*Kingdom Come*, 1996)

BAT-MEN OF DALTON CORNERS, THE

After years of wearing a sacred Indian Bat-Man costume and performing rituals to prevent the return of a dangerous bat-god, John and Paul Wainwright were driven from Dalton Corners. Relocating to Australia, John Wainwright eventually died, but his son John Jr. returned to Dalton Corners to don the costume himself and help stop the bat-god's return. (*World's Finest Comics* #255, February/March 1979)

BAT-MISSILE

In one dire case involving an oversized alien invader, the Earth-2 Batman and ROBIN launched an experimental vehicle from within the BATCAVE and landed safely on Earth using its unique rocket-chute landing gear. (*Detective Comics* #270, August 1959)

BAT-MITE

In a dimension where magic was commonplace, one imp used his innate skills to sightsee through myriad dimensions, and when he found Earth-1, he became fascinated by the exploits of Batman. He would tune in regularly to watch the Caped Crusader and the Boy Wonder outwit criminals and escape dangerous death traps. The fascination grew to idolization until finally, conjuring up a variation on Batman's uniform, the imp journeyed to Earth.

Introducing himself as Bat-Mite, he declared himself Batman's biggest fan and attempted to use his amazing magical abilities to aid Batman in apprehending felons. As often as he was a help, his efforts conflicted with Batman's own work, and simple cases became complicated. There were times when Bat-Mite also engineered events to provide his idol opportunities to demonstrate his superior prowess. Batman couldn't remain angry at the well-meaning magical being, although he frequently tried to convince him to go home. (*Detective Comics* #257, May 1959)

On several occasions Bat-Mite wound up working not only with Batman, but with other GOTHAM CITY costumed champions as well. He got to share adventures with ROBIN, BATWOMAN, and BAT-GIRL. Later he discovered a similarly powered being in MR. MXYZPTLK, and either paired up with or challenged the FIFTH DIMENSION being depending on his mood. On those occasions, it took the combined effort of the World's Finest team of Batman, Robin, and SUPERMAN to put an end to their mischief.

Bat-Mite was known to travel to other dimensions, including a world known as Earth-Prime where Batman and company were merely characters in comic books. On his sole visit, Bat-Mite tried to convince a publisher to give him a feature as well. The ploy did not work.

In the wake of the cosmic events of the CRISIS ON INFINITE EARTHS, all the parallel worlds were collapsed into a single reality. Bat-Mite did not regularly journey to this new world or meet up with Batman. On his very first visit to the world, he was considered a hallucination by BOB OVERDOG, a petty criminal. (*Legends of the Dark Knight* #38, October 1992; *Batman: Mitefall*, 1998)

Six years after Batman first appeared in Gotham City, in the new reality Bat-Mite finally encountered his idol and met up with Mr. Mxyzptlk immediately afterward. (*Batman & Superman: World's Finest*, 1999) Superman theorized at the time that his Fifth Dimensional nemesis actually created Bat-Mite, with the imp's powers based on Overdog's ravings. Bat-Mite was not seen again, lending credence to the hypothesis.

Reality was shaken one more time during INFINITE CRISIS, and Bat-Mite appeared once more. This time the imp came into contact with the JOKER, however, and the Clown Prince of Crime managed to absorb Bat-Mite's magical energies for a brief time. This ended after the interference of the artificial creature known as Bizarro, and Bat-Mite was once again free. In the new world, it was unclear how Bat-Mite viewed the Dark Knight and what their exact relationship was. (*Superman/Batman* #25, December 2006)

In other realities Bat-Mite appeared in a variety of ways, such as co-founder of the First Church of the Last Son of KRYPTON. (*Batman: The Dark Knight Returns*, 1986) He perplexed Batman and other heroes in these myriad realities, rarely with ill intent. (*Kingdom Come* #2 1996; *World's Funnest*, 1999) He was also seen on Earth-3839 (*Superman & Batman: Generations* #2, February 1999), and in one potential future there was evidence that Bat-Mite existed in the 853rd century. (*DC One Million 80-Page Giant* #1, 1999)

BATMOBILE, THE

Of all the pieces of equipment used by Batman in his fight against crime, none may have been as iconic as his car. The Batmobile, in all its configurations, remained a singular entity as it traversed GOTHAM CITY's streets, performing feats and rescues other drivers could only dream about.

When Batman first took to the rooftops of Gotham City, he didn't think much about getting around on a large scale. It soon became obvious he needed a vehicle, however, and he selected a red sedan that could have belonged to anybody. When this proved obvious, he designed a black car with a bat-wing fin atop the roof that created a distinctive silhouette. In time the car gained additional features and gadgetry, and one souped-up model quickly followed another.

On Earth-2, Batman drove several models, starting with the red sedan. He quickly changed to a dark blue sedan built for both speed and silence. The wheels were coated with a radioactive substance that allowed the Dynamic Duo to trace the vehicle using infrared technology. The bat-symbol was added, first as a roof ornament and then as a scalloped fin. This version was continually upgraded, eventually becoming the fastest car in the world. One model was even able to skim along atop water for brief periods, although this eventually gave way to the new BATBOAT. Over time the Batmobile's communications gear grew to include a direct link to Police Commissioner JAMES GORDON's office. A bat-headed grille was added to the front, which further distinguished the vehicle and provided additional protection from gunfire.

That version was eventually totaled and replaced with a much longer car. It still had the bat-grille up front, but the driver's section was a bubble-topped area, and the extended trunk section contained room for a working lab, communications equipment, and extra gear.

On Earth-1, Batman used a variety of sportier vehicles, including one long-running version based on a Lincoln Futura chassis. Equipment aboard this vehicle included advanced communications gear, notably a wireless phone connection to Commissioner Gordon. Experimental technology included the encephitector, which was designed to trace individual brains' alpha waves, and a hydrofoil attachment allowing this Batmobile, too, to skim water using compressed air. There were also times Batman employed sonic detecting equipment, sophisticated enough to detect even individual heartbeats.

After the CRISIS ON INFINITE EARTHS, Batman was seen to drive most versions of the Batmobile across the former parallel worlds. The various models remained in storage within the BATCAVE and were upgraded on a regular basis, largely because Batman tended to total them with great regularity.

Later models averaged nearly twenty feet long and eight feet wide; their 97 percent octane jet fuel enabled them to accelerate from zero to ninety in a mere 5.2 seconds. The maximum speed was clocked at 245 miles per hour thanks to a fifteen-hundred-horsepower jet turbine engine. With afterburners, one car achieved 350 mph for brief durations. In most cases the vehicles were shielded

against bullets and small missiles without sacrificing speed or maneuverability. The chassis usually were composed of light experimental titanium alloys, coated with bulletproof ceramic. The tires were the most durable, puncture-proof versions ever designed. Some models had breakaway sections to access difficult spaces, while others were

chock-full of firepower to stop a wide variety of threats.

Standard equipment included bulletproof windshields, ejector seats, automatic/voice-controlled pilot, radio links to the Batcave and ORACLE, a customized GPS system, anti-theft devices, and infrared vision to allow stealth driving. The defensive mechanisms included spinning tire slashers, smokescreens, oil slicks, flares, and even piercing sonics.

Construction of the Batmobile was handled by a variety of people. On Earth-1, Batman saved Jack Edison, a stunt driver and car designer who built model after model for him in gratitude. In most realities Batman himself oversaw the design and construction, usually working in tandem with ALFRED PENNYWORTH or ROBIN. Much of the technology that kept the Batmobile at the edge of automotive technology was originally developed throughout various divisions of WAYNE ENTERPRISES.

BAT-PEOPLE, THE

They came from another dimension: little people with bat-wings, similar in appearance to Batman. They waged war on humans in their dimension, a battle that was soon joined by the Dynamic Duo.

When the BATPLANE was caught in a hurricane, it

was whipped by such terrific force that the vehicle shattered the dimensional barrier and entered another reality. Found by humans, Batman's resemblance to their enemy resulted in the Dynamic Duo's capture and imprisonment in a dungeon.

In due course Batman and ROBIN proved their good intentions and were freed. They soon after erected a fiery barrier to keep the bat-people away. Batman also uncovered a human plot, led by the villainous Arko, that had his people aiding the bat-people in the hope of overthrowing the queen and taking over the country.

Batman and Robin were thanked for their work, and they used the repaired Batplane to pierce the barriers and return home. (*Batman* #116, June 1958)

BATPLANE

The Batplane enabled Batman to extend his reach in his unending campaign against injustice. Needing to get across GOTHAM CITY or reach other trouble spots faster than even his BATMOBILE could manage, Batman found the plane a necessity. Since its inception, he used various models and initially housed them within the grounds of WAYNE MANOR.

On Earth-2 the first aircraft was the BATGYRO, essentially a car with giant propellers, closer to

up to forty-five thousand feet, retracting bat-shaped wings, radar-deflecting shielding, and cutting-edge communications equipment. If necessary, delta fins could be deployed so the craft could reach a maximum altitude of fifty-five thousand feet. The body was rigged to withstand supersonic speeds.

Within the cockpit, the controls could be used manually or automated, even voice-activated.

BAT-SIGNAL, THE

Citizens of Gotham City could look up in the sky and be comforted to know that Batman was looking out for their best interests whenever they saw the pale yellow signal in the shape of a bat summoning him to police headquarters. Of all Earth's super heroes, Batman had the most visible connection to local law enforcement through use of this special signal.

On Earth-2, Commissioner James Gordon took to using the Bat-Signal early in Batman's career, either activating it from a button on his desk or actually turning it on from the rooftop of police headquarters. (*Detective Comics* #60, February 1942) The equipment itself was said to use a hand-ground bulletproof glass lens and a fog filter. During World War II the Bat-Signal was briefly switched to an infrared version; specially tinted windows at Wayne Manor allowed the Dynamic Duo to detect when they were being summoned. In time other technology was employed to alert Batman and Robin that they were needed.

On Earth-1, Commissioner Gordon used the Bat-Signal from the rooftop and awaited the Dark Knight's arrival. All too often Batman would arrive and depart without being detected, frequently speaking to Gordon only from the shadows, especially if others were around.

After the events of Crisis on Infinite Earths, conflicting accounts were recorded. In most cases Batman provided the signal to newly promoted Police Commissioner Gordon as a symbol of trust and a way they could communicate with each other. One account suggested that Batman presented the signal to Gordon after his first encounter with the Joker. (*Batman: The Man Who Laughs,* 2005) A different recorded legend had Batman providing Commissioner Gordon with a high-tech signaling device. During the case of the mad Monk, Gordon finally tossed the device away, disliking its skulduggery implications; he wanted something more aboveboard and less covert. (*Batman and the Mad Monk* #5, February 2007)

Through the years various people have accessed the well-known signal, each for his or her own reason. Even criminals have used it to summon Batman's protection—although they turned the bat-symbol upside down, imitating the international symbol for distress. (*Legends of the Dark Knight* #6, February 1993)

Unlike some realities, where Batman was a duly deputized officer of the law, he was not a sanctioned presence in Gotham City. For years, Batman preferred being thought of as an urban legend, the signal therefore a tool the police used to frighten criminals into thinking Batman was working for the department. To protect the Gotham City Police Department from tainting cases by summoning a costumed vigilante, no representative of the

a helicopter than an airplane. Initially it was even equipped with a machine gun. It was quickly replaced with a modified jet-propelled model featuring bat-motifs. As airplane technology advanced, so did models of the Batplane.

On Earth-1, Batman utilized a variety of jet craft, including several models boasting VTOL (vertical takeoff and landing) mode. The Batplanes were stocked with high-tech communications, computer, and lab equipment, allowing the Dynamic Duo to complete their investigations while in the air.

After the events of Crisis on Infinite Earths, Batman's plane was secreted within the holdings of Wayne Aerospace. The first model was a WayneTech design originally built for a government contract that was fraudulently awarded to LexCorp. Wayne told the dejected engineers he had plans for the plane and had it modified into the first Batplane. (*Batman Confidential* #3, April 2007) The aircraft had auto-maintenance systems that allowed it to refuel and rearm itself. Modern-day models were styled after the SlipStream, which had a cruising altitude of

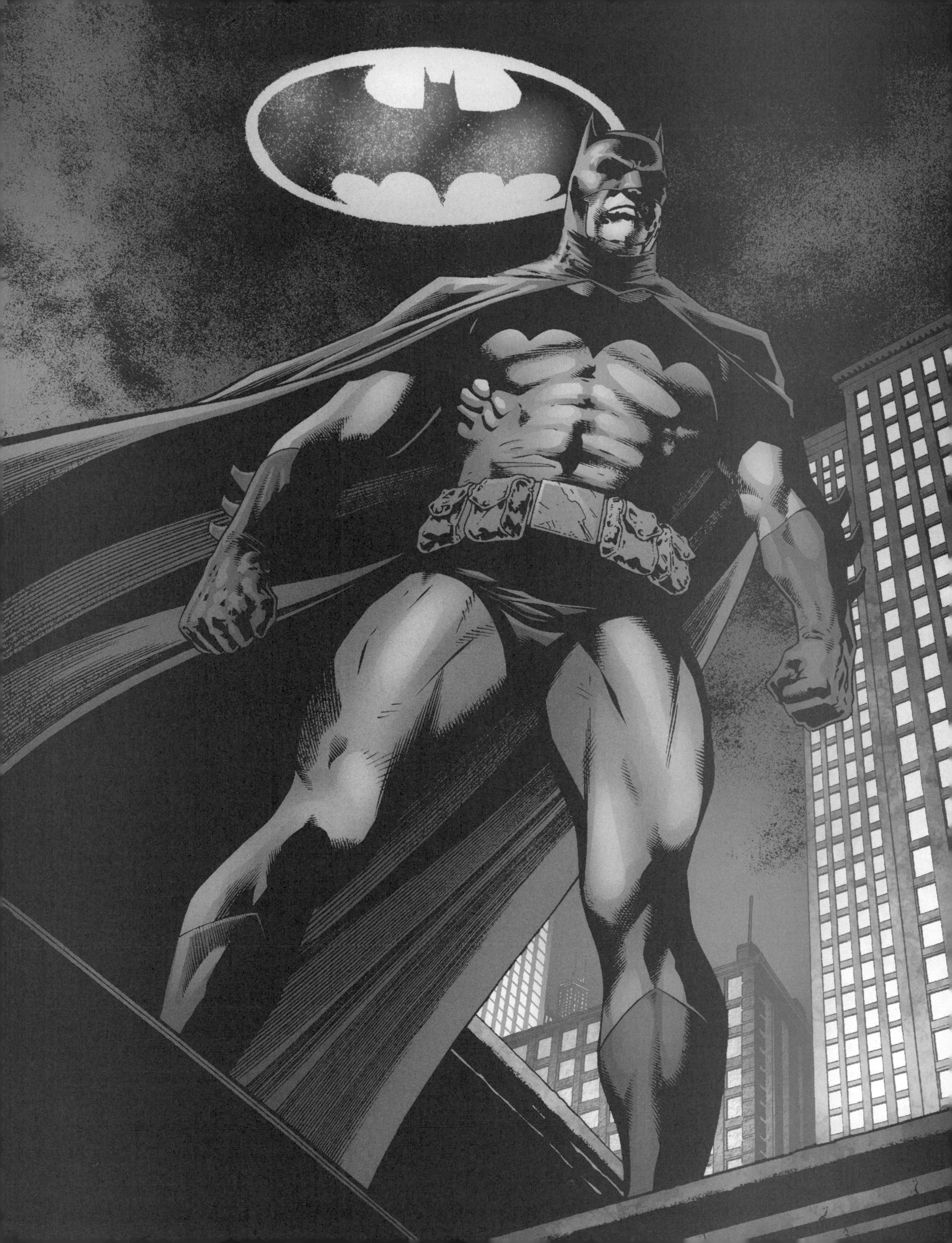

police was allowed to access the signal. Instead the G.C.P.D. employed a civilian aide to handle the giant klieg light. The only recorded civilian to handle the chore was a young woman named STACY, who harbored secret romantic fantasies about the Dark Knight. (*Gotham Central* #11, November 2003)

During Batman's decade-plus career in Gotham City, his relationship with the police waxed and waned. The use or absence of the Bat-Signal was seen as a barometer of the relationship. After Batman usurped control of the G.C.P.D. during the events of the WAR GAMES, Commissioner MICHAEL AKINS had the signal removed from the rooftop. It was soon after returned for unexplained reasons, as witnessed by its use by the QUESTION. In the wake of INFINITE CRISIS, Batman left Gotham for a year, and the skies remained dark. Upon his return, the signal shone brightly once more, and the citizenry was made to feel safe. (*Detective Comics* #817, May 2006)

In one future reality the Bat-Signal was seen not as a comfort to the citizens, but as a symbol of fear. (*Batman: The Dark Knight Returns*, 1986)

BAT-SQUAD

When BRUCE WAYNE traveled to London to observe Basil Coventry direct *The Scarlet Strangler*, he became involved in a bizarre case. On the first day of filming, lead actors Vivien Tremain and Ronald Dawson were kidnapped. Soon after, Dawson was found murdered, prompting Wayne to investigate as Batman. During the course of the investigation a modern-day strangler attacked him, and the Gotham Guardian was saved due to the arrival of former Scotland Yard inspector Major Dabney, the movie's technical adviser. The Caped Crusader found himself allied with not only Dabney, but also script girl Margo Cantrell and musician Mick Murdock. Dabney continually cast a suspicious eye on Murdock, due to the fact that the inspector had once arrested Murdock for a minor crime.

The investigation led Batman and his mod Bat-Squad to find Tremaine chained beneath the Half Moon Inn. Circumstances led first the actress and then the others to think they may have traveled back in time to 1906, when the original murders occurred. When Batman found an unexploded bomb, complete with swastika, the remnant from World War II shocked everyone to the reality of their situation. Dabney talked Murdock through disarming the bomb, but they ran out of time before it went off and narrowly escaped with their lives.

Finally the quartet found the Scarlet Strangler, who proved to be director Coventry's father—and then the truth came out. The original strangler was Coventry's grandfather. Fearing he would turn out like the grandfather, Coventry's father had himself committed to an asylum, leaving his brother to raise Coventry. When the filmmaker learned of his heritage, he wanted to make a movie about it, but the news of this drove his father insane. He broke out of the asylum and began to think *he* was the strangler. It was his father who abducted the stars, but Coventry also cracked under the strain of events and killed him. The insane director was taken into custody and—despite hopes of reteaming with Batman sometime in the future—the British trio were never seen again. (*The Brave and the Bold* #92, October/November 1970)

BATSUIT

After his decision to begin his one-man war against crime, BRUCE WAYNE needed an outfit that would enable him to move freely and provide versatility and cover as he patrolled GOTHAM CITY. Inspired by a bat, he had an outfit tailored to resemble the winged creature's silhouette, theorizing that the frightening visage would strike fear into the superstitious and cowardly criminals preying on the city's innocent citizens. He was correct in this assumption, and the image of the Caped Crusader's cloaked form became indelibly linked to Gotham City.

By donning the cape and cowl, Bruce Wayne was symbolically reaffirming the vow he'd made at his parents' graveside. In his earliest recorded adventures, the costume was little more than an acrobat's outfit with a few minor modifications. The gray tights were covered with black trunks, short gloves, boots, and a scalloped cloak that was affixed to his arms. The outfit was eventually modified, and the cloak became an enveloping, scalloped-edged cape, while the gloves grew in length and gained three fins. His belt was augmented with pockets and pouches for his crime-fighting gear. The bat-ears of the cowl also grew in length, improving on the menacing image he projected from the shadows and alleyways and rooftops.

The basic elements of the Batsuit have remained fairly consistent throughout the differing eras and realities. However, some differences have been dramatic.

On Earth-2, for example, the Batsuit had bright blue highlights, and the cowl ears were bobbed. The gray unitard was covered with blue boots, gloves,

briefs, cape, and cowl. Early on, once the short gloves became more like gauntlets, they acquired three fins; for a brief time they also contained short claws for climbing. In the beginning of his career, Batman was also known to have briefly used a bulletproof vest. Over the years he wore a number of uniforms in different colors or fabrics based on specific needs, such as an all-white arctic suit for wintry environs and a camouflage uniform for jungle terrain. The basic suit template was also adapted for scuba, deep-sea, and high-altitude scenarios.

The early Earth-1 version had a yellow oval background for the chest's bat-symbol. Batman stated on numerous occasions that the oval provided villains with a target away from his more vulnerable head. The integrated gray unitard contained the blue-black briefs, supplemented by blue-black gloves, boots, cape, and cowl.

The suit worn by Batman in the wake of the parallel worlds merging during the CRISIS ON INFINITE EARTHS consisted of a dark gray custom-made body stocking with black-blue gloves, boots, trunks, cape, and cowl. He continually modified the Batsuit, including a period when it consisted of a one-piece all-black version. The cape was constructed from a Nomex fire-resistant material that boasted a Kevlar weave to repel bullets without losing flexibility.

Batman's suit seemed to vary with each use, but in most cases the cowl concealed a voice-activated communications system, a variety of lenses, and in once instance tiny gas capsules that deployed when the cowl was tampered with, preserving his true identity even if he was unconscious.

In all realities Batman relied on a UTILITY BELT festooned with miniaturized gear to aid his

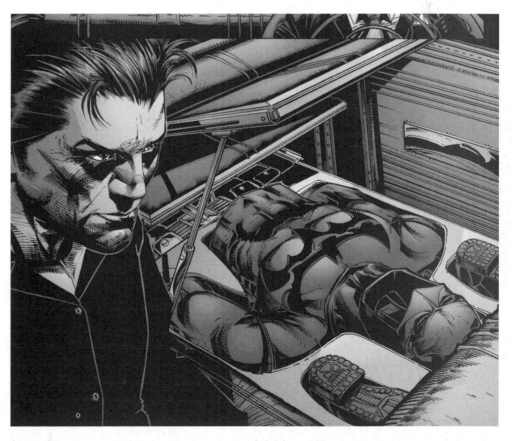

investigations. The first belt housed only a coiled rope and then a Batarang to secure a cable, enabling him to swing from building to building or climb exterior structures. The Earth-2 Batman even had a pistol and holster for his first few cases before giving up guns forever. No other version used guns.

The gear depicted in his adventures included a variety of Batarangs of differing sizes, bat-shaped handcuffs, a rebreather device, flashbang and gas grenades, plastic explosives, lock-picking tools, a taser, a remote control for the Batmobile, a Justice League of America signaling device, a forensic crime scene kit, emergency first-aid supplies, cash, and empty pockets for storing evidence. The Utility Belt had anti-theft technology that usually delivered electric shocks to thwart criminals or the curious. A gas-propelled grappling hook and gun mechanism allowed the Dark Knight to scale steep structures or traverse the Gotham City rooftops.

Batman constantly improved on his gear and learned how to handle it more efficiently while in action. Early on, a thermite charge accidentally went off, destroying his first Utility Belt. (*Batman* #404–407, February–May 1987) Much of his technology came from the futuristic research and development divisions from across Wayne Enterprises. In the shifted reality in the wake of Infinite Crisis, Lucius Fox was the chief architect of tools and equipment used by Bruce Wayne.

The most significant variant of Batman's gear was worn by his temporary replacement, Jean-Paul Valley, aka Azrael. Influenced by conditioning known as the System, Valley sought an outfit and accompanying gear that would be more offensive than defensive. The unitard was replaced with bulkier armor complete with full face helmet. The gear included a flamethrower, clawed gauntlets, and a *shuriken* launcher. After Bruce Wayne resumed his role and Valley gave up the gear, the gauntlets were somehow obtained by a Gotham City lawyer who kept them locked up. A small-time criminal stole them until he was apprehended on the West Coast. They wound up in the evidence room of the Los Angeles Police Department; when District Attorney Kate Spencer raided the room to build her Manhunter outfit, she took them.

BATWING

Some versions of the aircraft flown by Batman have been called either the Batplane or the Batwing.

BATWOMAN, THE

Batwoman was a costumed crime fighter who fought alongside Batman in various realities and was either an ally or romantic partner—or sometimes both.

On Earth-2 socialite Kathy Kane was inspired by Batman to don a variation on his Batsuit and join his fight against crime in Gotham City. With her yellow unitard, red gloves, boots, belt, and cape, the adventurer used a red purse to substitute for Batman's famed Utility Belt. (*Detective Comics* #233, July 1956) Batwoman fought beside Batman, and even championed her niece, Betty Kane, as Bat-Girl. Batman continually encouraged Batwoman to give up the dangerous profession, and eventually

she retired when Batman married Catwoman. Although she subsequently married and had children, her husband was never identified. In the wake of the Batman's death, Kane came out of retirement to protect Gotham City when it was threatened by Professor Hugo Strange. (*The Brave and the Bold* #182, January 1982)

On Earth-1 socialite Kathy Kane was also inspired by Batman to don a variation on his Batsuit and join his fight against crime in Gotham City. (*Detective Comics* #233, July 1956) She voluntarily retired after years of crime fighting and purchased a circus. Sadly, Kane became a victim in a war between Rä's al Ghūl and the Sensei. (*Detective Comics* #485, September 1979)

In the reality created in the wake of Infinite Crisis, Katherine "Kate" Kane donned a black-and-red outfit and first fought crime as Batwoman during Batman's one-year absence from Gotham City. She was befriended by Nightwing and slowly accepted by the Gotham Guardian upon his return. (*52* #11, 2006)

On other parallel worlds Kathy Kane became Batwoman, but in other realities different people used the name. One example was a resident from New Genesis who—inspired by Batman—modified armor to match his uniform. She rode a bat-winged dog-like creature named Ace. (*Kingdom Come*, 1996) Another was Selina Kyle, partnering with her husband, Batman, in an outfit resembling Batwoman's traditional red-and-yellow garb. (*JLA: The Nail; JLA: Another Nail*, July 2004) Helena Wayne was the Batwoman of a world where traditional gender roles were reversed, and her best friend was Superman. (*Superman/Batman* #24, November 2006)

In one potential future Bette Kane, Flamebird, became an adult and took the name *Batwoman*.

BATZARRO

The Batzarro was an imperfect duplicate of the Batman and appeared in several varying realities.

On Earth-1 it was created by a machine—

Bizarro—initially devised by the twisted scientist Lex Luthor, that produced these faux humans. Luthor's original plan was to create and control a duplicate Superman in order to destroy the original. The machine also produced countless Bizarro humans and super-humans, from Lois Lane to Green Lantern. The machine even managed to duplicate a version of Earth, which became the universe's only known square-shaped planet. The machine rendered a basic humanoid form, but with the unique effects of craggy chalk-white faces and warped thinking that had them speaking in a reverse language, so *hello* meant "good-bye" and so on. (*World's Finest Comics* #156, March 1966)

In the post–Crisis on Infinite Earths reality, Bizarro was also created by Luthor, this time using a piece of Superman's genetic material. Bizarro sought a place on Earth for itself, lacking the companionship of others in its image that were seen in other realities.

The Batzarro creation was a flawed, fun-house-mirror image of Batman, with an upside-down bat-symbol on his chest. The imitation Utility Belt was worn upside down, with the various pockets open, their contents long gone. Batzarro also used pistols to shoot citizens in Gotham City's Crime Alley, and sported a steel chain and grappling hook as his sole tools. Self-described as the world's worst detective, Batzarro never explained how this came to be, despite his propensity for conversation. (*Superman/Batman* #20, June 2005)

Bizarro encountered Batzarro and took pity on the lonely figure. Accepting an offer to team up, Batzarro spent time with Bizarro until a fragment of blue Kryptonite, which he had on his person, negatively affected Luthor's creation. Bizarro flew away to lessen the object's effects, leaving Batzarro to his own devices.

Now attempting to aid the Dark Knight, Batzarro couldn't make himself understood clearly enough, and events grew complicated. Worse, Batman never knew Batzarro existed, and was never able to understand him since the artificial life-form sacrificed himself to stop the JOKER's bullet from killing the Batman. Speculation remained that the same machine Luthor used to create Bizarro may have been turned on the Dark Knight, but the truth was never revealed. (*Superman/Batman* #24, November 2006)

BAUMGARTEN, STANLEY

A criminal who became the second person to take the name DARK RIDER.

BEAGLE, ALFRED

In the reality known as Earth-2, Alfred Beagle was the name of BRUCE WAYNE's butler and confidant.

BEAN, SOLLY

Solly Bean was an inmate at ARKHAM ASYLUM known for his even temperament. He was imprisoned for his inability to control his cannibalistic urges, which required medication and constant observation. (*Batman: Shadow of the Bat* #80, December 1998)

BECKETT, TOM

Tom Beckett was the adopted son of "Grey Mike" Riggs, an infamous criminal who was executed at Baxter Prison north of GOTHAM CITY. Just after his father's death, Beckett contracted a deadly illness while on a jungle expedition. Doctors confirmed that he had a month to live, which seemed to accelerate Beckett's already deteriorating mental condition. Fearing his own death and blaming Batman for his adoptive father's death, Beckett decided that the Caped Crusader would die with him. Over the course of several days Beckett made attempt after attempt at elaborate murder-suicide schemes, all of which failed. As Batman came to understand the pain that drove Beckett, he used his vast resources to determine that a little-known antidote existed. Once he was treated, Beckett's mental state improved and he was cleared of all attempted murder charges. (*World's Finest Comics* #69, March/April 1954)

BELDON, "BRAINS"

"Brains" Beldon made his mark in GOTHAM CITY when he and his gang pulled off a heist of twenty million dollars—money that was en route to the new Gotham National Bank. The same time period saw Batman transformed into a virtual biohazard. Because of a freak accident, the Dark Knight was generating so much heat that he had to operate from a shielded hovercraft. In the course of his pursuit of Beldon and company, Batman was struck by a power line, whose electrical force restored the hero to normal. Thereafter the thieves were captured in short order. (*Detective Comics* #301, March 1962)

After his parole, Beldon returned to his Long Island mansion. Now aspiring to join the inner circle of the criminal outfit known as H.I.V.E., Beldon designed a red power suit capable of disrupting the synapses in the brain of any meta-human opponent, inducing spasms and preventing his opponent from using her or his powers. His son Michael, as the Disruptor, wore the power suit when he attacked the TEEN TITANS.

Michael craved his father's approval, but the old man continually demeaned him, constantly referring to his son as an idiot. In the end the Disruptor was defeated when the mystical RAVEN showed him a horrific vision of his probable future and the young man collapsed in tears.

Michael refused to implicate his father in his crimes and received a ten-year prison sentence. "Brains" disowned his son and vowed never to speak to him again. (*New Teen Titans* #20, June 1982) Left almost hysterical by his father's rejection, Michael vowed to prove himself to his father by murdering the Titans. The opportunity presented itself when he was freed from prison by the Wildebeest, but instead of getting revenge Michael was rendered powerless when the Teen Titan Jericho took control of his body and Jericho's teammate Danny Chase destroyed his exo-suit. (*New Teen Titans* #41–42, March–April 1988)

Michael eventually managed to re-create the Disruptor costume and sought revenge on the Teen Titans once more. This time he was opposed by the incarnation of the team known as the New Titans. The Disruptor held his own against them until he was knocked cold by a punch to the jaw from Arsenal. Michael was once more imprisoned, and his father has not been heard from since rejecting his only child. (*Titans Secret Files* #1, 1999)

BELL, LONGHORN

Upon learning that GOTHAM CITY's elite had created a series of lead-lined caves to protect their priceless belongings in case of nuclear attack, Longhorn Bell decided to help himself to these items. He worked with a geologist named Duane, and the two were successful in raiding the "atom caves." Once there, Duane detected a cave that seemed larger than the others and was not lead-lined. Tunneling into it, they discovered the BATCAVE, and realized that the Dynamic Duo were, in reality, BRUCE WAYNE and DICK GRAYSON. Aided by ALFRED PENNYWORTH, the costumed crime fighters managed to convince the criminals that the Batcave was really an elaborate movie set. The scheme ended when Bell, Duane, and their henchmen were apprehended. (*Batman* #68, December 1951/January 1952)

BELLOWS, RALPH

Ex-convict Ed Stinson decided to help his fellow parolees by creating an employment agency for people with criminal records. Upon learning of this, local businessman Ralph Bellows decided to take advantage of the situation and began robbing companies that hired ex-cons. As Bellows had hoped, the companies blamed the ex-cons, but the ploy proved short-lived when Batman and ROBIN began their investigation, which led to Bellows's arrest. Stinson and his referrals were then exonerated. (*Batman* #103, October 1956)

BELTT, WARDEN

The Whiskers Mob committed crime after crime, vanishing from sight each time and leaving no clues that local police could find. News of the disappearing gang reached GOTHAM CITY and prompted Batman and ROBIN to investigate. They determined that the members of the Whiskers Mob were actually prison inmates working on a prison farm. Warden Beltt had established the mob and, with the aid of corrupt guards, arranged for the prisoners to leave the farm, commit their crimes, and return with the local officers none the wiser. Once exposed by the Dynamic Duo, Beltt and the guards were arrested. (*Batman* #47, June/July 1948)

BELVOS

Belvos was a planet in another galaxy that was home to KLOR, an evil being. His efforts to frame SUPERMAN for his own crimes were thwarted when Batman, ROBIN, and Superman visited his world. (*World's Finest Comics* #122, December 1961)

BENNETT, "KEYS"

Bennett earned the nickname "Keys" from his belief that keys brought him luck as a result of a key-shaped scar on his face. The criminal and his men proved unlucky after all when they were apprehended by Batman and ROBIN. (*Batman* #73, November 1952)

BENTLEY, MORRIS

Morris Bentley was a successful Hollywood figure on Earth-2, heading up the Argus Motion Picture Company. Among his many credits was *Dread Castle*, a feature film starring actress JULIE MADISON, who was romantically involved with BRUCE WAYNE. Wayne, as Batman, got involved in the production when he had to save Madison and Bentley from BASIL KARLO, the first CLAYFACE. It was Bentley who ordered his publicity manager Gabby Fest to rename Madison Portia Storme. Bentley repeatedly offered Batman a contract to star in films, and each time the Dark Knight politely refused. (*Detective Comics* #40, June 1940) Batman once again saved Bentley from Clayface a year later. (*Detective Comics* #49, March 1941)

BERTINELLI, HELENA

Born into one of GOTHAM CITY's Mafia families, Helena Rosa Bertinelli survived a brutal gangland slaughter of her family to grow up and become the vigilante known as the HUNTRESS.

Details of her past have changed with each retelling of her life, but initially Helena was said to be the favorite daughter of Guido and Carmela Bertinelli. Her life was shattered when, at age six, she was kidnapped and raped by someone from a rival crime family. Once her family regained custody of their daughter, Helena was sent off to boarding school, and a bodyguard accompanied her to ensure her safety. While home for a family wedding, the withdrawn nineteen-year-old was the sole survivor of a gangland hit that left her an orphan. An enraged Bertinelli vowed to exact revenge. With Sal, her bodyguard, training her, Bertinelli became a dangerous fighter. When he declared her ready, they returned to Gotham, and the Huntress was born. (*The Huntress* #1–4, June–September 1994)

She craved acceptance into the family of

costumed crime fighters, wishing to work alongside Batman, ROBIN, and NIGHTWING, but was always left to feel the outsider. Batman sensed Helena's rage, something he himself had managed to control—but he feared that it controlled her. The Huntress was aggressive, violent, and reckless when it came to dealing with criminals, and she struggled to follow Batman's instructions and authority. Both Robin and Nightwing had easier dealings with her, the Boy Wonder going as far as to help clear her name when she was suspected of murder.

In an effort to "smooth her edges," Batman acted as the Huntress's sponsor to join the JUSTICE LEAGUE OF AMERICA. (*JLA* #16, March 1998) She worked hard to be accepted by the whole team, although she never really grew close with any of her costumed colleagues. Her tenure was cut short when the Huntress tried to kill PROMETHEUS after the mercenary attempted to destroy the League.

Now back in Gotham, the Huntress continued taking on the mob, but was forced to stop and reexamine her life when she uncovered new information about her past. The new information revealed her purported parents' names to be Franco and Maria. Then she discovered that she was actually sired by rival don Santo Cassamento.

When Cassamento's capo, Mandragora, ordered the Bertinelli family eliminated, he passed on the order and instructed that Maria be spared. A misunderstanding left eight-year-old Helena alive instead. (*Batman/Huntress: Cry for Blood,* 2000)

Helena was then said to have been shipped to live with her cousins, the Asaro family, in Sicily, Italy. Sal was now her older cousin who taught her to fight using a variety of weapons, and also helped turn her body into a weapon. Some time later Sal and his father were arrested, and the truth finally hit home: Helena had been born into a Mafia family from which there was little hope of escape. She continued to grow a hard shell around her, keeping others at arm's length.

When Helena was sixteen, she made a brief return to her home city of Gotham, where she first saw Batman in action. The way he handled himself proved inspiring, and when she left Gotham once more to attend boarding school in Switzerland, his image lingered in her mind. Upon completion of her lessons, Helena attended a university in Palermo to be closer to her family. With a degree in education in hand, Helena eventually returned to Gotham City and became both a schoolteacher and the Huntress.

Shortly after learning of her true heritage, Helena tracked down her true father, Cassamento, who had already figured out that his daughter was the Huntress. She told her uncle that Cassamento was the man who ordered the Bertinelli killings, and he was subsequently executed.

The Huntress continued to operate in Gotham City despite Batman's official disapproval. That did not stop other members of his team from aiding her, and on one noteworthy case she and Nightwing engaged in a one-night stand. Not only did she find him attractive, but she had hoped the liaison would help her get closer to Batman. (*Nightwing/Huntress* #1–4, May–August 1998) While that ploy failed, a series of devastating incidents kept the Huntress an active participant in Gotham, giving Batman little choice but to avail himself of her considerable skills. During the plague known as the CLENCH, followed by the terrifying earthquake, she acquitted herself time and again despite her status as a rogue agent. When the federal government cut off support, Gotham became a virtual NO MAN'S LAND. Helena chose to stay within the city but gave up being the Huntress, recognizing those who remained would fear anything—and anyone—who wore a bat-cape. She designed an all-black outfit that obscured her face and hit the streets as the new BATGIRL. Despite the objections of the original Batgirl, BARBARA GORDON, she was continually given assignments. (*Batman: No Man's Land* #0, December 1999)

In one case she had to single-handedly protect the sliver of the city that had been marked as Batman's turf. When TWO-FACE and hundreds of hardened criminal encroached, Batgirl failed to protect the shaky borders. Batman blamed her for losing the space and formally demanded that Batgirl stop operating. Helena left the outfit with Barbara and defiantly took to the streets once more as the Huntress. She continued to work independently until she got in the way of the JOKER's latest scheme,

which would have involved the murder of innocent infants. The Joker shot her several times, but Helena survived, and the entire incident caused Batman to give her the respect he felt she now deserved. (*Batman* #574, February 2000)

Following Gotham's City return to federal government status, the Huntress continued to work on her own. ORACLE, however, brought her in on several missions, and—given her success and easy rapport with Oracle's other field operative, the BLACK CANARY—Bertinelli finally found acceptance. She traveled the globe as a BIRD OF PREY, once temporarily leaving the team when she felt she was being manipulated by Barbara. Additionally, she continued to lend aid and support to Batman's efforts in Gotham, although their relationship remained tense at best.

Her work with the JLA and Batman made her an ideal candidate to fill in for Arsenal after he was seriously injured on an OUTSIDERS mission. Given their history, she and Nightwing had a rocky relationship as co-leaders. When he learned that she had previously slept with Arsenal, things got even tenser.

During her work with the Birds of Prey, and on her own, Bertinelli used her family connections to make the Mafia think she was reasserting her family's authority. She pushed matters so far as to be made a capo, and the Dark Knight was concerned that she was going to trigger a new gang war, something the city could not handle in the wake of the WAR GAMES fiasco. To his surprise, she wound up providing him with detailed intelligence and a "mob atlas," which went a long way toward healing the rift between them. (*Birds of Prey* #91, April 2006)

After that, she remained with Oracle, serving as the top field operative in the wake of the Black Canary's withdrawal from the team. She often found herself allied with fellow adventurers Lady Blackhawk, Gypsy, MANHUNTER, and even the New God Big Barda. When Spy Smasher usurped control of Oracle's operation, one of the incentives she offered was eliminating Bertinelli's remaining obligations to CHECKMATE. (*Birds of Prey* #104, May 2007)

BIFF
Bored with his job as the elevator operator at the Maskers Club, Biff decided to use the club's motif in a series of crimes. The Maskers were all people who used masks in their professions, such as welders or deep-sea operators. Biff figured he could use the masks of the club members to avoid suspicion and also hide his thick prescription glasses. No sooner did he begin his criminal career than he was caught and arrested by Batman. (*Batman* #72, August/September 1952)

BIGBEE, "ANGLES"
Bigbee used to operate as a GOTHAM CITY underworld gang leader, but relocated to the Arctic. Hiring a new gang, Bigbee established his new base of operations within the Bikou Glacier. His Snow Man Bandits then began a crime wave across the region, from Alaska to Greenland. Upon hearing of Bigbee's activities, Batman and ROBIN journeyed north and tracked him to North Town, near the

Alaskan Klondike. However, before he could be arrested, Bigbee died after being crushed in an icy crevice. (*World's Finest Comics* #7, Fall 1942)

BIG GAME HUNTER, THE

A man possibly named B. G. Hunter was better known as the Big Game Hunter, making his name with his spectacular exploits in Africa and the Himalayas. To Hunter, the biggest game of all was the Gotham Guardian—Batman. He determined that the best way to bring Batman out into the open would be to stage a large-scale crime. As a result, he freed Roy Reynolds from prison and kept him in a cage until he agreed to participate in the game. The Hunter wanted to capture Batman and break his mental state, turning him into a tame animal, thereby making this the Hunter's greatest triumph.

Reynolds and the Hunter's underlings executed a robbery at the Riverside Museum. Responding to the jewelry theft, Batman and Robin followed the intentional trail of clues to the Hunter's mansion hideaway. The Caped Crusader fell through a trapdoor and into a thick plastic bag, where he was immediately pummeled by the thugs. Batman fell unconscious when his oxygen supply became depleted, but when he was removed from the bag, he revealed that he had feigned unconsciousness. He quickly subdued the henchmen and apprehended both the Hunter and Reynolds. (*Batman* #174, September 1965)

BIG-HEARTED JOHN

Big-hearted John's actions belied his nickname. The heavyweight loan shark was known for brutal acts toward customers who were late with their payments. The cigar-smoking shylock wound up falling to his death at a construction site during a fight with Batman and Robin, who then shut down his criminal operation. (*Detective Comics* #88, June 1944)

BILLINGS, DELBERT

Billings was the criminal who donned a costume and played with people's perceptions as the second Spellbinder.

BIRD

Bird was one of the three criminal companions who left the Santa Prisca prison with Bane. He accompanied Bane as far as Gotham City and was never seen again. (*Batman* #489, February 1993)

BIRD HOUSE, THE

The Penguin attempted to branch out from his Gotham City criminal enterprises by opening the Bird House, a nightclub and casino, in Florida. Working in the new business were old colleagues Buzzard Benny and Joe Crow. The featured singer was a woman named Canary. It proved a short-lived operation. (*Batman* #11, June/July 1942)

BIRDS OF PREY

Birds of Prey was the unofficial title given to the all-female squadron of operatives who performed missions around the world under the guidance of Oracle, Barbara Gordon.

After Gordon was crippled by the Joker, she turned her crime-fighting efforts to the cyberworld and created the online presence known as Oracle. After aiding the Suicide Squad on several cases, she branched out, becoming the information resource among the costumed crime-fighter community. (*Suicide Squad* #23, January 1989) For a brief time she was even a full-fledged member of the Justice League of America—all without leaving her clock tower headquarters in Gotham City.

After a roster revision that left her at reserve status, Oracle saw the benefit in using other heroes to do the legwork she could not. Her first attempt at working with another heroine, Power Girl, ended badly (*Birds of Prey* # 42, June 2002), and she was hesitant to do so again, fearing more mistakes. She scoured the lists of other potential heroes around America and selected Black Canary, who had previously worked on several teams and was at that point without an anchor or focus. (*Birds of Prey Secret Files* #1, 2003)

Oracle got in touch with Black Canary, who responded enthusiastically. For a while the two worked well together without even meeting. Eventually they met and grew close as both friends and colleagues. (*Birds of Prey* #21, September 2000) At times, Black Canary was paired with other operatives, most notably the Huntress. (*Birds of Prey* #69, September 2004)

Oracle continued to provide her services to other

heroes, including Batman, who in return stayed out of the Birds' business. As a leader, Oracle displayed a compassionate nature, offering succor, support, and money, as well as whatever else her friends and fellow agents needed.

A mercenary named Savant, once a target of the Birds, kidnapped and severely beat Black Canary, going so far as to break her legs. When that case successfully concluded, Oracle wound up challenging Savant to improve his life and the world around him. He accepted the challenge and lived up to her faith by cleaning up a Gotham City neighborhood.

With success came more complex missions that required the team to grow and adapt. In the wake of Oracle losing her headquarters to BLACK MASK, she went mobile for a time, flying in a customized jet piloted by Zinda Blake, a temporally displaced woman from the past. She was dubbed Lady Blackhawk in her day, and the name remained. (*Birds of Prey* #75, December 2004) Blake was also the first one to refer to the cadre of adventurers as the Birds of Prey.

Oracle and the Birds settled in METROPOLIS's Dalten Tower as Lady Blackhawk traded in the jet for a helicopter dubbed *Aerie Two*. Soon after, America's super-villains were banded together by the LEX LUTHOR from a parallel world. The Society intended to take a stand against the heroes' tampering with their minds and personalities. A Society leader, the CALCULATOR, attempted to track and kill Oracle, his heroic counterpart. (*Birds of Prey* #88, January 2006)

The team went through several gyrations in the wake of these events, which saw Black Canary and LADY SHIVA switch places for several months. The Birds completed several missions with the help of Shiva, who went by the name *Jade Canary* for the duration of her stay with the team, and left when Black Canary returned from Asia. It wasn't long after this that the Canary formally resigned from the team, preferring to spend time with a young girl named Sin whom she rescued from Mother, the woman who originally trained Shiva and attempted to train Black Canary. Replacing her on the roster was Gypsy. (*Birds of Prey* #92, May 2006)

The Birds of Prey continued their operations around the world using a variety of costumed adventurers as their skills were required. Oracle granted personal access to a precious few at that time, including Black Canary, Huntress, and Lady Blackhawk.

When Gordon's old rival, Spy Smasher, seized control of the Birds, the women rallied in great numbers, convincing the government operative that they would not work for her and she was to leave Oracle alone. Spy Smasher left, and the Birds of Prey were free to operate as they pleased. (*Birds of Prey* #108, September 2007)

BISHOP, TIGER

Tiger Bishop was known as one of the coldest killers in the history of crime. His career came to an end when he was pursued by crime reporter Dave Purdy. Their final confrontation took place atop GOTHAM CITY police headquarters, where the career criminal was blinded by the powerful light emitted by the BAT-SIGNAL, leaving him vulnerable to Purdy's right cross, which laid him low. Purdy was aided from the sidelines by Batman, who witnessed the fight and interfered when needed. (*Detective Comics* #164, October 1954)

BLACKBEARD

A criminal named THATCH was named for the famous pirate Blackbeard. This modern-day Blackbeard led a group of buccaneers across the seas near the GOTHAM CITY coast. When they raided the Yacht Club's vessel during its annual outing, the occupants were carried off to Blackbeard's galleon until the arrival of Batman and ROBIN. The pirates were quickly thwarted and arrested. (*Batman* #4, Winter 1941)

BLACK CANARY

Black Canary is the code name for two women, mother and daughter, who have been costumed crime fighters in different eras. On Earth-2, DINAH LANCE was the daughter of a cop and trained to become a fighter and detective. (*Flash Comics* #86, August 1947) She donned a wig, fishnets, and a short jacket to fight crime as Black Canary, and was the last hero invited to join the legendary JUSTICE SOCIETY OF AMERICA in the late 1940s. She married Larry Lance only to watch him die during a battle with the cosmic being Aquarius. With nothing tethering her to Earth-2, she accompanied the JUSTICE LEAGUE OF AMERICA to Earth-1 and eventually began a romance with GREEN ARROW. (*Justice League of America* #72–73, August 1969)

On the world after CRISIS ON INFINITE EARTHS, Dinah and Larry Lance had a daughter, Dinah Laurel, and worked hard to keep her from becoming a super hero. In secret she trained with TED GRANT, aka WILDCAT, and as a teen she donned her mother's outfit for the first time. She was present to help fend off an alien invasion and became a charter member of the Justice League of America. She and her mother argued frequently, but when the elder Dinah lay dying of cancer, her daughter was at her side.

When in college, she was married for less than a year to Craig Windrow, who continued to turn up in her life like a bad penny. Dinah graduated and went to work as a florist, much like her mother, and fought crime as Black Canary. Her romance with Green Arrow waxed and waned through the years, with Dinah disapproving of his constant cheating.

In addition to her stints with the JLA, she became partnered with ORACLE as a BIRD OF PREY. While one of the world's greatest martial artists, she sought to improve her fighting skills by working with several teachers. The last teacher, Mother, was the most brutal. The woman had previously trained LADY SHIVA and attempted to remake the Canary in her image, but Lance refused to give up her moral convictions to become a killing machine.

Lance left Asia and soon after left the Birds of Prey to reestablish a life on her own and raise Sin, a young girl who was also being taught by Mother. (*Birds of Prey* #95, March 2006) The JLA re-formed after the events of INFINITE CRISIS, and she became the new team's first chair. (*Justice League of America* [second series] #7, April 2007) She took Sin to Star City where she renewed her relationship with Green Arrow, leading to his proposal of marriage.

After much deliberation, she accepted, and they finally wed. (*Green Arrow/Black Canary Wedding Special*, 2007)

BLACK DIAMOND, THE

The criminal known as the Black Diamond earned his name due to his overwhelming fascination with accumulating gemstones. The Black Diamond put together some of the GOTHAM CITY underworld's greatest minds—triggerman Bull's-Eye Kendall, the vicious Barracuda Brothers, and demolition expert "Nitro" Nelson—to plan a major strike: the death of Batman and ROBIN. The Black Diamond theorized that eliminating the Dynamic Duo would leave Gotham City ripe for the plucking. The scheme failed when Diamond and the others were stopped by Batman, Robin, and the police. (*Batman* #58, April/May 1950)

BLACKFIRE, JOSEPH

Deacon Joseph Blackfire led a collection of GOTHAM CITY's homeless in a war on crime that put him in Batman's path. (*Batman: The Cult* #1–4, 1991)

In an effort to rid Gotham City of the pervasive criminal elements that were robbing the city of its humanity, Joseph Blackfire began to organize the homeless and disenfranchised citizens who sought harbor in the city's sewer system. The charismatic religious figure inspired the men and women to rally to his just cause, and soon an army of the faithful was formed. When Blackfire and his followers took to the streets, they quickly routed out criminals and assumed control of the city. Criminals escaped into the sewers, only to find themselves trapped and killed. As his following grew in size, Blackfire's power seemed to fuel his passion—but it also narrowed his worldview, and soon Gotham City was virtually cut off from the rest of North America.

When Batman sensed that things teetered on the brink of chaos and intervened, he was overpowered and taken hostage by Blackfire. During his captivity Batman was subjected to various mind-control techniques, including drugs. Blackfire succeeded in the one thing that Batman's archnemeses had failed to do over the years: He broke Batman's spirit. While Batman was captive, Police Commissioner James Gordon turned to Robin for help. More than five hundred missing persons reports had been filed in a single week—more and more people were joining Blackfire's army, willingly or not. Meanwhile, a brainwashed Batman was taken along on a mission against a Mafia don. The Mafioso and his accomplice fled, but Batman was firmly under the deacon's sway.

Robin infiltrated the cult in the hope of finding Batman, but the Dark Knight was kept apart from the people, regaining his strength in solitude. Meanwhile, things were rapidly spiraling out of control as Blackfire's control over the city tightened. The mayor and city council were executed, and Commissioner Gordon was shot during a press conference. The governor finally declared martial law, and the National Guard was called in. Guardsmen entering Gotham's sewers wound up decimated.

Batman and Robin were finally reunited, and the time had come to retake the city. In a specially modified, armored Batmobile, the Dynamic Duo approached Gotham Square and used tranquilizer darts to cut a swath through Blackfire's forces. Taking to the sewers, Robin sustained a shot to the leg but continued subduing Blackfire's cult. In a final confrontation, Blackfire succumbed to Batman's stronger will and, now broken, begged for death. Blackfire's cult turned on him, and he was killed in the mêlée.

BLACKGATE PENITENTIARY

The original Blackgate Prison was closed after decades of service. It was built in the late 1800s and eventually condemned by Amnesty International. Blackgate Rock had a gallows that stood for more than a century, and in that time 313 men had been executed. Initially built to house Gotham City's criminals, it served as both a prison and a pre-trial detention center. Blackgate was designed to house nine hundred convicts, but had been forced over the years to hold in excess of twice that number. Just over three hundred of its occupants were women.

Isolated in Gotham Bay, Blackgate, also known as Blackgate Penitentiary, held a population of 2,342 men, 273 of them guards who commuted daily and by boat, watched over by Warden Tom Lansky. Blackgate's Death Row was located on the prison's lowest, ground-level tier—"closest to Hell," according to its unwilling inhabitants. The Gotham earthquake sent a tidal wave smashing into the island prison. Of the 2,103 occupants still on Blackgate Island, 1,761 were alive. While 342 were either missing, escaped, or dead.

Blackgate was said to have featured some of the most sophisticated prison defenses this side of Keystone City's Iron Heights, all developed by Wayne Industries. Later, Bruce Wayne spent time there as he awaited trial for the murder of Vesper Fairchild, giving him an intimate look at the life to which he'd condemned so many criminals. (*Batman: Blackgate—Isle of Men*, April 1998)

BLACKHAND

This seafaring criminal earned his name by escaping the police. Arrested by a detective who cuffed their hands together, Blackhand forced both their handcuffed hands into a fire. When the policeman fainted, Blackhand got the keys and escaped despite charring his hand. Later he formed a gang and attacked oyster fishermen, stealing their catches at the end of the day as they returned to shore. Batman and Robin, aided by feisty fisherwoman Josephine Jibbs, brought Blackhand's criminal efforts to an end. (*Detective Comics* #113, July 1946)

BLACK LIGHTNING

Jefferson Pierce was a gold-medal-winning Olympic decathlete who ended his athletic career and returned to his home neighborhood of Metropolis's Suicide Slum as a high school teacher. Frustrated by his inability to reach his students, and given the prevalence of juvenile delinquency and crime controlled by the criminal organization known as the 100, Pierce had a costume and device constructed enabling him to fight back. The device allowed him to generate large electric charges, and Pierce hit the streets as Black Lightning. (*Black Lightning* #1, April 1977) In time the electric charges were internalized through his meta-gene and grew in strength. He fought crime on his own for a time until Batman recruited him for his Outsiders team—people who would take on cases that the Justice League of America could not, given their government affiliation. (*The Brave and the Bold* #200, July 1983)

Pierce successfully fought crime despite occasional setbacks until he was tapped by President Lex Luthor to serve as secretary of education. Pierce accepted, figuring that at least one member of the super hero community should stay close to the evil mastermind. During his tenure, he recommended that his niece Joanna aid Green Arrow in a lawsuit against businessman Martin Somers. As a result, Somers ordered Joanna's death. Enraged, Pierce tracked Somers down and tried to put fear into him with a lightning strike. To his horror, Somers fell dead. Later, it was learned that Deathstroke had shot Somers moments before the lightning was discharged. A devastated Pierce did not finish his term, resigning amid controversy

that exposed his identity. President Pete Ross, however, later pardoned him.

Pierce was concerned when his daughter, Anissa, who displayed powers similar to her father's, graduated from college and immediately donned a costume to join the "family business" as Thunder. To his surprise, she wound up joining a new incarnation of the Outsiders, this time led by Batman's protégé Nightwing. (*Outsiders* [third series] #1, August 2003)

Black Lightning aided Batman in taking out Brother Eye, the artificial intelligence that was a key component in the events known as Infinite Crisis. In the wake of those events, Pierce decided to come clean about his involvement with Somers's death, and he surrendered himself to Checkmate. Not wishing to cause further complications, the intelligence agency disguised Pierce and let him serve time in Keystone City's Iron Heights prison. Soon after, the Red Hood told Nightwing that Pierce was innocent and that it was Deathstroke who had killed Somers, hiding his shot in the lightning blast. On learning this, Anissa led the Outsiders on a mission to free her father from prison after his identity had been compromised. (*Outsiders* #45, April 2007)

It was Batman who recommended that Black Lightning formally join the JLA in the wake of these events. (*Justice League of America* #1 [second series], October 2006)

Black Lightning had pretended to pass along criminal intelligence to Lex Luthor but was actually building his own resources throughout the criminal community. Luthor, of course, knew of the deception. (*Justice League of America* [second series] #12, October 2007)

BLACK MASK

Black Mask was one of Gotham City's many bizarre criminals. He grew to become a ruthless killer who briefly controlled the city's underworld.

The Sionis family were among the elite living in Gotham City, and their lifestyle reflected this status. Young ROMAN SIONIS was expected to join the family business, Janus Cosmetics, but he first endured a childhood in which he was seen more as a liability than a joy. The first evidence of this occurred when his mother displayed an inherent lack of maternal instinct and dropped Roman on his head immediately following his birth. The family, afraid of a damaged reputation, covered up the incident. Several years later Roman was bitten by a raccoon, and once more the family covered up the incident, refusing to let their son ever mention it again. (*Batman* #386, August 1985)

Roman watched his parents' hypocrisy in action as he grew up—specifically their faux friendship with THOMAS and MARTHA WAYNE, a family the Sionises disliked intensely. However, the Sionis and Wayne families would get together at functions, and Roman was encouraged to play with young BRUCE WAYNE.

Rather than attend an elite college upon graduating from high school, Roman went right to work at Janus, and was given an important role despite his total lack of work experience. While there, he met and fell in love with CIRCE, a young secretary from a working-class family. His parents didn't approve of the relationship and insisted their romance be terminated. Tired of the constant condemnation based on shallow issues of class, Roman snapped under his parents' incessant needling and eventually burned down the family home. His parents were killed in the blaze.

Unprepared for his newfound wealth and role as head and owner of the Janus company, Roman squandered all of the money and ruined the company. Rather than lose Janus completely, Roman asked his team of research chemists to develop a new product. A waterproof makeup was developed, and Roman rushed the new line to market without proper testing or FDA approval. He figured the cash flow would more than offset any government-imposed fines. Almost immediately the untested makeup proved to be toxic, leaving many women disfigured. The company was now beyond salvaging, and Circe, Roman's fiancée, ended their relationship in front of the remainder of the Janus staff.

A last-minute offer from Roman's childhood "friend," Bruce Wayne, saved the day. Wayne offered to buy the company, but only if Roman surrendered control and let Wayne fill the board of directors seats with his own choices. Humiliated but desperately in need of cash, Roman agreed.

The loss of face eventually drove Roman over the edge, and he visited the Sionis mausoleum, where he broke into his father's crypt and removed a large piece of ebony from the coffin. After carving the ebony into a mask, Roman was transformed into a new person, and the criminal known as Black Mask was born. Using the business skills he had developed over the years, Black Mask assembled a criminal mob and dubbed them the FALSE FACE SOCIETY. His goal was to make a place for himself in Gotham's underworld on his own terms,

something he felt was denied him in the legitimate business world. His first target: WAYNE ENTERPRISES. The Society kidnapped Wayne Enterprises executives and brought them to Black Mask, who placed on each face a mask coated with the toxic makeup. He had Circe brought back to him and disfigured so she would never leave him again. She killed herself instead, and the twisted Black Mask took to speaking with a mannequin in her place.

The attack on Wayne Enterprises drew Batman into Black Mask's world. In quick order Batman apprehended members of the Society and tracked down Black Mask, who was headquartered at the ruins of the Sionis mansion. To escape, Black Mask set the mansion's remains on fire, but he became trapped. By the time Batman rescued Roman, the black mask was permanently burned onto his face, further damaging his fragile psyche.

After standing trial, Black Mask was remanded to ARKHAM ASYLUM, only to be freed when BANE destroyed the facility in his own scheme to rule Gotham. Roman re-formed the False Face Society and took on a man named Tattoo as his new second in command. Once more, Black Mask targeted Wayne Enterprises and managed to kidnap CEO LUCIUS FOX. Batman arrived before Fox could be harmed and captured Tattoo, although Black Mask escaped. Working underground, Black Mask continued to seek control over Gotham's underworld. He accomplished this on his own and through periodic alliances with villains such as the PENGUIN.

His underwork control lasted until the earthquake that devastated the city.

Black Mask chose to remain in the No Man's Land and carved out a piece of the action for himself. Those drawn to him pledged their allegiance through ritual scarring, although any who refused to join his cult were automatically killed. Batman finally apprehended Black Mask, putting him in Blackgate Penitentiary, but he eventually escaped. In time Roman rebuilt his diminished power base through drug running, avoiding capture.

Eventually Roman relocated to Gotham's East End and ignored that section's protector, Catwoman. That is, until she began defeating his operatives, intercepting cash payments, and disbursing the money to the East End's needy. He needed a way to strike back at the elusive feline, and sought out any who knew her. During this search he encountered fellow mobster Sylvia Sinclair, who knew that Catwoman was actually Selina Kyle. Armed with this knowledge, Black Mask set out to eliminate Catwoman, starting with the destruction of a youth center she had funded. He then had her sister Maggie Kyle and brother-in-law captured, torturing the brother-in-law until he died, then forcing Maggie to eat from his remains. Before Black Mask could turn his attentions to Holly Robinson, Selina's best friend, Catwoman arrived and viciously fought with Roman. Black Mask seemingly fell to his death from a penthouse roof after the fight.

However, Black Mask escaped death and remained out of sight until circumstances eventually proved fortuitous. Where he went and how he survived remains unrecorded, but he next surfaced when the city was caught up in gang war triggered by a would-be protégé of Batman named Spoiler. She enacted one of Batman's War Games scenarios without realizing that it all hinged on Batman's alias Matches Malone; without Malone, the plan was doomed to failure. To rectify matters, Spoiler tried to recruit another of Batman's agents, Orpheus, into filling Malone's role. Black Mask somehow tracked down this meeting, overheard their conversation, and then killed Orpheus and captured Spoiler. He used his makeup experience to impersonate the helmeted Orpheus, then tortured Spoiler to learn the rest of the game plan. (*Batman: War Games Act Two,* 2005)

Rather than execute Batman's plan, Black Mask substituted his own, which brought chaos and bloodshed back to Gotham's streets. The insane criminal relished the hell he visited on the city, but when he returned to his hideout to torture Spoiler for sport, he found she had escaped. He located the injured woman, however, and they fought viciously. Spoiler escaped, but was mortally wounded. Black Mask made his way across Gotham City and proclaimed on live television that he had found Batman's secret headquarters—the clock tower that was actually home to Oracle. The Dark Knight became enraged and repeatedly struck Black Mask. Oracle was forced to activate the clock tower's self-destruct device to prevent Black Mask's death.

Black Mask escaped the explosion and managed to reassert his authority over the remnants of Gotham's underworld. For a time his control re-mained unquestioned and his wealth was restored. Yet he remained dissatisfied and wanted revenge on Batman for all previous slights. Black Mask thus impersonated Batman and committed a series of acts designed to discredit the Dark Knight, all covered by television reporter Arturo Rodriguez, who had been co-opted by Black Mask. The plan was spoiled, however, when the Joker arrived, ready to kill Black Mask, who had killed Spoiler. The public had come to learn that Spoiler was training to become Batman's new Robin, and the Joker felt that only he was allowed to kill Robins. Batman arrived during the fight and stopped it, capturing Black Mask and exposing Rodriguez's complicity. Black Mask managed to escape yet again by murdering a policeman and running off.

Black Mask attempted once more to rebuild his criminal operation, which had been significantly damaged when his plans went awry. It was further eroded thanks to Batman's vigilance and the arrival of the Red Hood on the crime scene. As a result, Black Mask happily accepted Deathstroke's offer to join the newly formed society of super-villains. In return, Deathstroke supplied Captain Nazi, Count Vertigo, and one of the two Hyenas to help stop Black Mask's irritants. The effort did not work, however: Not only did Batman stop the villains, but he managed to successfully keep the Society out of Gotham City as well.

A desperate Black Mask tried one last tactic and once more went after those individuals close to Catwoman. The feline felon was fed up with Black Mask and shot him at close range, blowing apart his jaw and killing him. In the weeks that followed, she and Sam Bradley dismantled the remainder of Black Mask's operation; then she gave up her costume to seek a quieter civilian life. Her replacement, Holly, was arrested for the murder of Black Mask, but was subsequently cleared.

BLACK PATCH

Soon after the existence of a Crystal Creature became public, Black Patch and his gang of criminals decided to capitalize on the public's focus on the artificial life-form. They began a series of crimes involving the theft of metal statuettes and gold bullion, hoping the police would attribute the crimes to the Creature. Batman, however, determined that Black Patch was responsible and arrested him and the gang. (*Detective Comics* #272, October 1959)

BLACK ROGUE, THE

Felix Dunn was a longtime fan of the legendary Black Knight from English legend. The well-read criminal even crafted a black costume, complete with plumed hat, to begin the next phase of his career. His first act was to steal the Crown Jewels that were currently on display in Gotham City, thereby attracting the attention of Batman and Robin. During the robbery Dunn suffered a blow to the head that left him believing he was the Black Knight incarnate. With the jewels hidden, Batman feared the location would be forgotten if Dunn regained his senses. Therefore, he, Robin, and the police masqueraded as knights, furthering the delusion until the jewels were finally recovered. When Batman posed as the great Merlin, Dunn revealed the location to him and was subsequently placed in a mental institution until a cure could be achieved. (*World's Finest Comics* #62, January/February 1953)

BLACK SPIDER I

Eric Needham was a drug-addict-turned-vigilante who sought to destroy Gotham City's drug trade. (*Detective Comics* #463, September 1976)

As a child, Eric was raised by a loving family that fell apart when his mother died from illness. His father was distraught and virtually ignored young Eric, who struggled on his own to cope with his mother's loss. Seeking companionship, Eric took to the streets and found himself getting involved in gangs and drugs. The numbing effects of the drugs helped ease his pain for a time, until he became addicted to heroin.

His first confrontation with the law occurred when Eric was arrested for mugging an elderly woman. After serving three years, he was released, and within a two-year span hooked up with fellow junkie Linda Morrel and had a son, Michael. Eric took to robbing to find the money to support their drug habit and raise their baby.

One night he robbed a liquor store and gunned down a customer who'd lunged for him. Eric realized that he'd just murdered his own father. Eric was arrested and sent to jail, where he finally kicked his heroin habit. Upon his release, he decided it was time to stop the relentless flow of drugs into Gotham and donned a costume, taking the name Black Spider. Inspired by Batman but uninhibited by any strict moral code, he began killing dealers and suppliers without remorse until Batman intervened. Whereas Batman had his Utility Belt and tools, Black Spider relied on a wrist-mounted gun that had deadly accuracy. The two fought several times, and it appeared that Black Spider died after his last battle with the Dark Knight atop a subway car.

In fact he barely survived the fight and was nursed at a free clinic for several months. As he healed and retrained himself, Needham learned that he was being funded by a man named Hannibal Hardwicke, a major drug lord. Hardwicke intended to use Black Spider to remove and kill his competition. Once healthy, Black Spider stalked the streets for Hardwicke, and only Batman's intervention meant jail—and not the grave—for Hardwicke.

Lost for a time, Black Spider shifted from vigilante to costumed criminal and found himself battling Batman just for the sake of it. Eventually Needham refocused on his war on drugs, especially when the battle claimed his still-addicted wife and small son in a crossfire. In a final desperate act, a severely wounded Needham detonated explosives he had strapped to his body and took out a large cartel of drug dealers.

Meanwhile, in Hell, Lucifer had for reasons of his own set all the dead free, a turn of events that would eventually lead many back to Earth. (*Sandman* #23, February 1991) Eventually the angels Duma and Remiel took charge of the dark realm. By then most of the dead had returned. (*Sandman* #28, September 1991) Most, but not all. Needham had no intention of going back and seemed to have struck an unholy bargain to remain on Earth. Ominously, he frequented a nightclub overseen by Lucifer himself. (*Sandman* #57, February 1994) As the Black Spider, he was seen with other villains hoping to strike a deal with the demonic Neron. (*Underworld Unleashed* #1, November 1995) The deal's details remain unrecorded, but Black Spider fell in with costumed criminals such as DEADSHOT and MERLYN and remained active. (*Identity Crisis,* 2004)

BLACK SPIDER II

With Black Spider believed dead, hit man JOHNNY LAMONICA took the name for himself when he accepted a contract to kill BLACK MASK. LaMonica was an egomaniac who, unlike his predecessor, disliked covering his face. He infiltrated Black Mask's FALSE FACE SOCIETY, but the assassination attempt failed; the new Black Spider wound up captured by Batman and sent to jail. During the battle, his face was pushed into a mirror and severely scarred. (*Batman* #518, May 1995) LaMonica was eventually released; he resumed his criminal career, only to be shot dead by Detective CRISPUS ALLEN when LaMonica got the drop on his partner, RENEE MONTOYA. (*Gotham Central* #23, November 2004)

BLACK SPIDER III

When the CALCULATOR needed someone to learn the identity of his counterpart, ORACLE, he recruited a man named Derrick Coe. Coe became the third incarnation of Black Spider and was described as having bought the name from the Calculator—this despite evidence that the first Black Spider had defied death and still roamed GOTHAM CITY with other super-villains. Coe tracked down Savant, who had first fought against—then worked for—Oracle, and tortured him in the hope of learning her true identity. Oracle dispatched her BIRDS OF PREY to rescue Savant, and Coe was tossed from a window by the freed Savant. He appeared to have survived the event but has not been seen since. (*Birds of Prey* #87, December 2005)

BLACKWING

On Earth-2, Batman and CATWOMAN married and had a daughter, HELENA WAYNE, who grew up to become the HUNTRESS. Among the many adversaries she fought, Blackwing was perhaps the most memorable.

Years ago, WILDCAT encountered a scrappy young boy named Charlie Bullock, who had come to his aid while the hero battled four would-be muggers. Impressed, Wildcat unmasked and introduced himself to Charlie, and soon the JUSTICE SOCIETY OF

AMERICA member placed training Gotham's youth over battling its super-villains. He took a leave of absence from the JSA, determined to have a positive influence over the next generation of crime fighters. (*Adventure Comics* #464, July/August 1979)

Three years later Charles Bullock joined the law firm of Cranston, Grayson & Wayne, where that world's ROBIN and Huntress worked in their civilian identities alongside Arthur Cranston. Karnage—a super-villain who attacked the firm in an attempt to kill Cranston and Bullock—was knocked aside during the attack. The Huntress arrived in time to stop Karnage and save Cranston. (*Wonder Woman* #286–287, December 1981–January 1982)

Bullock was incensed at his futility during the situation and sought to better prepare himself to function in a world filled with super heroes and super-villains. He spent considerable time preparing his body for combat, and some time later he emerged in a variation on the late Batman's costume—light blue replacing the gray, a more stylized bat chest emblem and UTILITY BELT, yellow bands around his wrists and calves, and a sharply arched yellow-tipped face mask that evoked bat-ears in silhouette. Calling himself Blackwing, he was eager to tackle street criminals, but quickly proved unsuitable for crime fighting. The criminals shredded his cape and unmasked him. He was taken to their leader, a charismatic figure known only as the Boa. When the Huntress, who had been tailing Blackwing, showed up, she became mesmerized by the Boa and was soon on the verge of being crushed by a boa constrictor. Blackwing managed to free her in time and, using his extensive legal training, found the evidence necessary to put the Boa and his men away for good. (*Wonder Woman* #297, November 1982)

BLAKE, FRENCHY

Frenchy Blake was the leader of a gang that specialized in jewel robberies. He chose to match wits with Batman, only to find himself hung outside a window on a rope. He was freed after signing a confession of his crimes, making him the second criminal ever thwarted by the Batman. (*Detective Comics* #28, June 1939)

BLAKE, GEORGE

George Blake, the manager of the Gotham Theatre, turned to crime for unexplained reasons. He disguised himself as TWO-FACE, hoping suspicion would fall on HARVEY KENT, the deranged Earth-2 criminal, and not a seemingly respectable theater manager. Batman proved otherwise, and Kent was quickly exonerated. (*Detective Comics* #187, September 1952)

BLAKE, THOMAS

A wealthy big-game hunter, Blake grew bored with animals and set his sights on human beings. After squandering his fortune, he turned to criminal activities, donning a costume and battling Batman and other crime fighters as CATMAN.

BLAKELY, TED

Early in their partnership Batman and Police Commissioner JAMES GORDON conceived of a plan

to ensure that GOTHAM CITY would be protected in the event the Caped Crusader was incapacitated or killed. They formed the SECRET STAR and selected five members of the police force to begin intensive training in case one was required to don Batman's cape and cowl. Among the five was Ted Blakely, who had never told anyone that he had been raised and financially supported by the criminal Matt "Sugar" Kroler. Kroler and Blakely's father were cellmates in prison, and Kroler honored his friend's wishes to look after young Ted when the elder Blakely died. When Batman was trapped in a mine shaft but Gotham needed its costumed guardian, Blakely was summoned to duty. His task was to apprehend Kroler, and at first he felt torn between duty and obligation, but ultimately he arrested Kroler and honored his oath to the city. (*Batman* #77, June/July 1953)

BLANE, CORY

Cory Blane was a film producer shooting a movie on Skull Island, located in the Pacific Ocean. After his sets and crew were repeatedly vandalized by a sea creature, Blane turned to his friend Batman for help. The Caped Crusader traveled west and began investigating the creature. He soon learned it was actually a robotic construct built and operated by Tod Martin, the film's production assistant. Martin had devised the creature to scare away the cast and crew after he discovered a rich bed of rare black-pearl oysters in the island's Green Lagoon and wanted them for himself. He was subsequently arrested, and the oysters remained protected. (*Detective Comics* #252, February 1958)

BLANNING, RAND

Wealthy Rand Blanning was a member of GOTHAM CITY's Exploration Club. When fellow member Guy Hawtree discovered Incan ruins in a Peruvian jungle, Blanning decided to plunder the plentiful gold that was located there. Despite Hawtree's attempts at keeping the location a secret, Blanning learned the details and immediately left by plane. When Batman and ROBIN learned of Blanning's plans, they took the BATPLANE south of the border and arrested him before he could steal a single ounce of gold. (*Batman* #91, April 1955)

BLASTER, THE

The Blaster was named for his predilection for using demolition devices to blow up trains and buildings during robberies. Working with "Spots" Derrow and Guy Banning, who was a corrupt administrator at Samson Explosive Works, the Blaster had a successful career until he was arrested by Batman and ROBIN. In the wake of the Blaster's arrest, Derrow tried to shoot Batman, but instead lost his balance on a high cliff and fell to his death. Batman exposed Banning's complicity by disguising himself as Derrow and getting the executive to make a full confession. (*World's Finest Comics* #65, July/August 1953)

BLAZE, THE

Named for his preference for using fire during his crimes, the villain known as the Blaze terrorized the citizens of GOTHAM CITY. With his gang, the Blaze set free a train full of criminals and announced to the city that he intended to take over the underworld and unleash a new age of crime. The bearded redhead's first step was robbing the City Museum. He had hoped to distract Batman by posing as Baron Von Peltz and asking for the Caped Crusader's help against those who meant the baron harm. Instead Batman saw through the disguise and took the Blaze down before this new age of crime could begin. (*Detective Comics* #95, January 1945)

BLINK

LEE HYLAND was a blind man who developed the meta-human ability to see through the eyes of others after making physical contact with them. He used his skill for his personal gain, getting people to access their personal bank accounts. Hyland was seeing through another man's eyes when he witnessed a woman's brutal murder. He wound up implicated in the crime and first encountered Batman when the Caped Crusader arrived to investigate. After touching the Dark Knight, Hyland accessed Batman and learned that Batman was in reality BRUCE WAYNE. Batman and Police Commissioner JAMES GORDON oversaw the investigation, and Hyland was ultimately cleared. The hero and the grifter formed an odd alliance as Hyland strove to protect his criminal actions while also keeping Batman's secret to himself. Together they tried to piece together the methods of a serial killer that defied logic. In the end it was discovered that the killings were being recorded for a series of "snuff" films made by a man named Davies. (*Legends of the Dark Knight* #156, August 2002)

Batman encountered Hyland a second time when the blind man was forced by America's military to spy on international terrorists. The Dark Knight Detective defended Hyland's right to freedom over the nation's need to protect itself. Ultimately, Hyland was freed and left to fend for himself once more. (*Legends of the Dark Knight* #164, April 2003)

BLOCKBUSTER I

MARK and ROLAND DESMOND were devoted brothers who experienced horrific transformations into the mammoth entity known as Blockbuster.

As a teenager Mark Desmond was considered a scientific genius, achieving his high school and college diplomas years ahead of his peers. However, this left him socially awkward with people older than himself, so he preferred living a solitary life with his older brother on an island near GOTHAM CITY. Mark got himself mired in quicksand once, but fortunately BRUCE WAYNE was strolling the island and rescued the teen.

Inspired by his timely rescue and hoping to improve his physique, Mark used his advanced knowledge to fabricate a serum that would provide him with muscles almost instantaneously. Anxious to transform himself, he never stopped to test the formula. As expected, his endocrine glands altered, and he gained mass and muscle. Unexpectedly, the anterior lobe of Mark's pituitary gland also enlarged, which seemed to rob him of most of his mental faculties. The transformed Mark was prone

to emotional rages calmed only by his brother's soothing words and presence.

Roland was at first horrified by the transformation, but also saw how he could exploit his brother's strength for his own goals. He asked his brother to aid him in committing his crimes, figuring that Mark's strength and endurance would best both the police and Gotham's guardians, Batman and ROBIN. Sure enough, bullets bounced right off the toughened body; Mark even pummeled the Dynamic Duo into submission. Robin described Mark as a blockbuster, and the media quickly picked up on the name.

At the scene of the next Desmond brothers' crime, Batman opted to follow the behemoth, figuring that someone was manipulating the seemingly simple-minded man. Once they reached the island, Batman recognized it from his travels months earlier. Realizing the creature was Mark, Batman removed his cowl and showed Blockbuster his true identity.

Somewhere in his altered brain there was recognition, and Blockbuster calmed down. To reinforce the connection, the unmasked Batman entered the same patch of quicksand and submerged himself until Blockbuster repeated Wayne's rescue using a branch. With Blockbuster complacent, Batman and Robin captured Roland and brought him to justice back in Gotham City. But when Batman retuned to the island, Mark was gone. (*Detective Comics* #345, November 1965)

Blockbuster reappeared later, this time under the OUTSIDER's control. His addled mind retained Roland's reconditioning that Batman was an object of hatred, and the Outsider exploited that. When Batman tried to unmask himself once more, the Outsider's science thwarted his attempt. The Caped Crusader then hardened his glove with a

calcium compound and reluctantly took down Blockbuster with an uppercut. (*Detective Comics* #349, March 1966)

Batman saw to it that Blockbuster was remanded to the ALFRED MEMORIAL FOUNDATION for treatment and a possible antidote to the original serum that had caused his condition. Instead a cosmic being known as the Anti-Matter Man removed Blockbuster from Earth and sent him to the parallel world known as Earth-2, where he traded places with SOLOMON GRUNDY. The catastrophe brought together the combined forces of the JUSTICE LEAGUE OF AMERICA and the JUSTICE SOCIETY OF AMERICA, and the two beasts wound up knocking each other silly. (*Justice League of America* #46–47, August–September 1966)

Once more back on Earth-1, Blockbuster resumed treatment at Alfred Memorial Foundation, now renamed the Wayne Foundation and regained some of his cognitive abilities, starting with improved speech. Still, occasions arose that brought Blockbuster away from his confinement, and his hatred of Batman remained. Subduing him was often a challenge. Sadly, he also remained an easy subject to place under another's thrall. Queen Clea had him take on members of the JLA, while the villainous Wizard abducted him from the Wayne Foundation and used him as a soldier in his personal vendetta against the JSA. During this time chemicals released by JASON WOODRUE, the FLORONIC MAN, intensified Blockbuster's hatred of Batman, undoing countless hours of reconditioning therapy. (*Justice League of America* #166–168, May–July 1979)

Having exhausted their resources, the Wayne Foundation turned Blockbuster over to S.T.A.R. LABS. Staff there developed a radiation therapy that they hoped would undo the serum's mutations. The experiment seemed to have killed Blockbuster, but it turned out only to be a death-like state, something Batman learned one bitter winter's night. His speech limited once more due to the radiation therapy, Blockbuster couldn't explain that he was trying to help a woman who had overdosed on drugs; he seemingly drowned in the Gotham River as he saved her. (*Batman* #308–309, February–March 1979)

Blockbuster surfaced some time later, winding up in Bleak Rock, West Virginia. He was taken in and cared for by Willie Macon, a mute, and his family. Mark Desmond finally achieved a measure of peace and contentment, something denied him for a long time. Batman eventually caught a news item that alerted him to the fact that Blockbuster still lived. When he arrived in West Virginia to investigate, he and Blockbuster wound up working together to save miners from a cave-in. Afterward, however, while playing with an electronic toy, Blockbuster once more came under another's control, this time General Electric, who pitted him against the Amazon Princess WONDER WOMAN. (*Wonder Woman* #294, August 1982)

Blockbuster's more heroic habits continued after this interruption when he aided Earth's super heroes during the events known as CRISIS ON INFINITE EARTHS. The parallel worlds were merged into one Earth, and Blockbuster continued to live with the Macons. It took the lure of a possible cure for him to leave West Virginia and perform a mission for AMANDA

WALLER's newly formed Suicide Squad. She needed his strength to confront the Apokoliptian creation known as Brimstone. Brimstone crushed Mark Desmond in his fiery fist, leaving only a charred corpse. Mark Desmond died a hero's death and was finally at peace. (*Legends* #3, January 1987)

BLOCKBUSTER II

ROLAND DESMOND and his brother MARK lived on their own in a home on an island near GOTHAM CITY. They were abandoned by their cruel, manipulative mother, who had relocated to nearby BLÜDHAVEN. Left to his own devices, Roland wound up committing several petty crimes to ensure their support; he built up a thick rap sheet. He envied Mark for his superior intellect until an experiment of his went wrong, and Mark was turned into a behemoth known as Blockbuster. (*Detective Comics* #345, November 1965)

In this transformation Mark lost much of his mental acuity. Roland trained his brother to regard Batman as the enemy, and then sent him from their island home to nearby Gotham City, where Mark could commit robberies for Roland. Batman and ROBIN trailed Blockbuster back to the island, then calmed him down and apprehended Roland.

While serving time in jail, Roland was a victim of an experiment at the hands of the aliens known as the Dominators. Part of an alien invasion of Earth, the Dominators sought to test humankind's meta-human gene by activating it in random people. Roland was one such victim; as a result, he was sent to the prison hospital, where he was given steroid treatments. The combination of steroids and the now active meta-human gene turned Roland into a hulking form that nearly matched the strength of his brother. There were two key differences between the two, however: Roland could transform from his normal shape to Blockbuster size, and he retained his intellect. He freed himself from prison, and it took the combined efforts of Batman and STARMAN to defeat him at Arizona's Monument Valley. (*Starman* [first series] #9, April 1989)

Roland was arrested anew but left prison to work with a version of the Suicide Squad before returning to jail once more. He was then offered a deal by the demon Neron. In exchange for his soul, Neron would grant Roland an intellect that rivaled that of his dead brother Mark. (*Underworld Unleashed* #1, November 1995) Now possessed of a superior mind and body, Roland was ready to establish himself as a criminal leader.

Seeking a beachhead, the new Blockbuster tested himself against the youthful speedster Impulse and then set up operations in Washington, D.C. However, his efforts were stymied by the capital's protector, Steel, and he ultimately decided to relocate. (*Steel* #33, December 1996)

He returned close to his roots and moved to the bleak city of Blüdhaven, staying near his now ill and unhappy mother. Even in a town filled with corrupt politicians and policemen—not to mention members of the various Mafia crime families—no one was prepared for Blockbuster's arrival. In short order he ousted Angel Marin and placed criminals and law enforcement under his thick thumb. He controlled the mayor's office and police

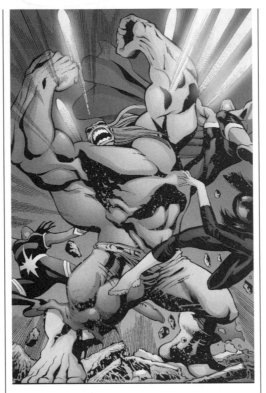

headquarters, with Police Chief Redhorn and Inspector Dudley Soames doing most of his dirty work. His new operation had tendrils that reached to such faraway places as Star City and, closer to home, Gotham. Soon after, though, he found fresh opposition in the form of NIGHTWING, the original Robin, who was seeking a fresh start away from the Dark Knight's shadow. (*Nightwing* [second series] #1, October 1996)

Thus began a war between hero and villain that would stretch beyond the city's limits and harm friends and family of both participants. While Blockbuster sought to kill Nightwing, he was also bothered by his hidden bank accounts being discovered and emptied by a cyberentity known only as ORACLE. She had been watching Roland Desmond for quite some time and had decided that his wealth should fund her operations. (*Underworld Unleashed: Patterns of Fear,* 1995) In time Blockbuster hunted her down, capturing not the real Oracle but BLACK CANARY. (*Birds of Prey* #21, October 2000)

Complicating his campaign was a recurring chest pain that was finally diagnosed as a terminal heart condition brought on by his transformation. Blockbuster would need a heart transplant to live, but his unusual physique required a heart larger than a normal human's. He turned his attention to the sentient residents of Gorilla City hidden away in Africa, and used a citizen named Grimm to help him find a subject. (*Nightwing* [second series] #43, May 2000)

More misery followed soon after with the death of his mother, which the distraught Blockbuster incorrectly blamed on Nightwing. The battle between them grew even more vicious when Blockbuster blew up the apartment building where Nightwing lived, killing many of his neighbors and

leaving the rest homeless. Blockbuster put a price on Nightwing's head and employed a small army of costumed mercenaries—Lady Vic, Stallion, Brutale, the TRIGGER TWINS, and SHRIKE—to take him out once and for all.

While eschewing assistance from his mentor, Nightwing did occasionally avail himself of help from Oracle, Black Canary, and Robin during his battles with Blockbuster. Later he encountered CATALINA FLORES, who dressed in the style of the hero TARANTULA, and began working alongside her to take down Blockbuster's operation. Both sides grew more desperate to end the confrontation, and the attacks grew in brutality. Exhausted both physically and mentally, Nightwing and Blockbuster faced off one final time.

Blockbuster taunted Nightwing, telling the hero that he would continue to pick away at his friends and his family until they were all dead. The amoral Tarantula saw a way to end the battle that Nightwing would never consider: She shot Blockbuster. Nightwing knew he could have prevented it, but let Tarantula do what he could never bring himself to do. His inaction brought about a breakdown that left him adrift for some time. Regardless, the citizens of Blüdhaven were finally freed from Blockbuster's tyranny. (*Nightwing* [second series] #97, November 2004)

BLOCKBUSTER III

A new Blockbuster emerged in the wake of LEX LUTHOR's creation of his own superpowered group, Infinity, Inc. To create the public perception that the new teen heroes were ready to defend METROPOLIS and the world, he unleashed the latest Blockbuster against them. Much as he controlled the heroes, Luthor seemed to exert control not only over Blockbuster's actions but over his levels of strength as well. In Luthor's estimation, the new Blockbuster was even stronger than either of his predecessors. (*52* #21, 2006)

BLONDEED, BLACKIE

Blackie Blondeed decided that the way to commit better robberies was to lay out the proposed crimes much as football coaches set up plays for their teams. His gang, which included Glassjaw Greegan, Curly, and Skeets, would rehearse the robberies during practice sessions before going into the field. The notion, while sound, still failed given the timely intervention of Batman and ROBIN. (*Detective Comics* #82, December 1943)

BLOOD, JASON

Jason Blood shared a mystic bond with a demon from Hell known as Etrigan, but on his own he was a respected demonologist and frequent ally of Batman.

Blood's origins were convoluted given the reordered reality of the universe and the very nature of the mystical worlds, including Heaven and Hell. Most recorded histories show that in the waning hours of Camelot, a desperate Merlin summoned a demon from Hell to stop the witch Morgana le Fay. The DEMON Etrigan arrived and cut a bloody swath through le Fay's hordes, but even his presence would not change the outcome. As a result, the wizard either bonded Etrigan with a member of the court, Jason Blood, or transformed Etrigan into Blood. (*The Demon* #1, August/September 1972)

Accounts vary as to what transpired next, with Blood either an innocent or allied with le Fay and bonded to Etrigan as punishment. One account said that Blood had a wife, Marie, and two daughters. Once connected to Etrigan, Blood was driven temporarily insane and killed his family with an ax. It was a year before the new form managed a semblance of reason. (*The Demon* [second series] #0, October 1994)

Blood was seemingly granted immortality as a result of Etrigan's presence, and he accumulated vast knowledge of demons and sorcery. In any painted picture, he looked the same, never aging, and kept on the move around Europe. He finally settled into an apartment in GOTHAM CITY, a location built upon cursed land, perfect for a demonologist. One day Blood was compelled to visit Merlin's crypt and found a poem that, when recited, would turn him back into Etrigan.

The demon was freed after centuries of slumber and began a new cycle of chaos in the world. On his heels was the return of le Fay and other threats to humankind. Etrigan relished his work as a demon, and impressed Hell's hierarchy enough to be promoted to the rank of Rhymer, which meant his every utterance was in the form of a rhyme.

Given that Gotham was his home base, once Etrigan reappeared, he came to Batman's attention. Despite preferring tangible matters he could handle on his own, Batman recognized Blood as an ally, and when the occasion demanded he sought help from Blood and Etrigan. In time the Dark Knight realized the depth of Blood's knowledge and courage. When he prepared extensive notes for re-creating the JUSTICE LEAGUE OF AMERICA in the wake of the team's devastation, he selected Blood to serve the JLA as its resident wizard. With the JLA lost in time during ATLANTIS's Obsidian Age, the call went out, and a reluctant Blood answered. Because Batman was always prepared for any occasion, NIGHTWING knew what would be required should Etrigan need taming. When the primary Leaguers were returned to their present time, Blood was happy to return to his quiet life. (*JLA* #66–76, July 2002–February 2003)

When GREEN ARROW seemingly rose from the dead, Batman turned to Blood to better understand what had occurred. It was Blood who learned that the Emerald Archer was a "hollow"—an animated body without a soul. Etrigan tried to kill the body lest it be used by a demon to gain access to humankind's world, but Green Arrow stopped him and eventually regained his own soul. (*Green Arrow* #1, April 2001)

In the reality after the event known as INFINITE CRISIS, much of the legend was merged so that Blood and Etrigan were once again separate entities, joined by Merlin, with no familiar relations between the wizard and Etrigan. Blood was a renowned investigator of the occult and paranormal, while the demon was described instead as "a prince among the fallen, captain-general of the fifteenth diabolical host, sometime war dog of the sorcerer Merlin and a Rhyming-Class demon who stopped

rhyming years ago." A fellow demon, Vortigar, appeared before Etrigan and informed him that he was being demoted from the rhyming class; Etrigan was coerced into recruiting the Blue Devil as a replacement in Hell's ranks.

Blue Devil and Etrigan fought, allowing the demon to gain possession of Lucifer's Unholy Trident, which he used to return to the depths in the hope of obtaining the crown of thorns denoting rulership over Hell itself. The effort failed and Etrigan was turned to stone inside the Oblivion Bar. The spell would be undone at daybreak, but within the pandimensional bar, the sun never rises, trapping Etrigan, seemingly, for eternity. (*Shadowpact* #9–11, March–May 2007)

BLORE, "GADGETS"

Described as a warped genius, the criminal inventor "Gadgets" Blore devised a series of high-tech weapons powered by high-voltage electricity. They were used to commit a string of outrageous crimes throughout GOTHAM CITY; his cannon generated enough heat to melt safes, for instance, and a sonic gun emitted enough power to split a tree in two. When Batman and ROBIN first tried to apprehend Blore, they were bathed in radiation from the electromagnetic field, leaving Batman positively charged and Robin negatively charged. As a result, the Dynamic Duo actually repulsed each other. The Caped Crusader built a Robin robot that the Boy Wonder operated by remote control to track down Blore. Soon after, Robin's charge faded, and he was able to help Batman stop Blore once and for all. Batman's charge quickly dissipated as well. (*Detective Comics* #290, April 1961)

BLÜDHAVEN

Located some twenty-three miles down the coast from GOTHAM CITY in Haven County, Blüdhaven was settled in 1777 but wasn't incorporated until 1912, and was never considered an American jewel. Instead the whaling town grew without a plan, and over time row houses found themselves built next to petrochemical plants. Situated on the Bay Highway southeast of Ossaville and about 184 miles from Opal City, the mess was exacerbated by a confusing series of roads and highways in and around the city. Such municipal chaos resulted in high pollution content in the air, and that caused the city's population to level off at about two million. Its populace had grown jaded through the years and actually liked it when the media dubbed Blüdhaven "Asbestos City, USA." (*Nightwing* [second series] #1, October 1996)

During the Revolutionary War, a network of underground tunnels was built under Fort Joseph and ran throughout the town. While no tunnel reached the surface anymore, Batman had them linked to either the subway tunnels or the sewer system for easier access during his patrols.

If Gotham City was known for crime and corruption, its biggest influence was Blüdhaven. One reason the city comprised a hodgepodge instead of well-designed neighborhoods had to do with decades of graft and the undue influence of the criminal underworld. The city was under the sway of mob boss Angel Marin until ROLAND DESMOND, the

second BLOCKBUSTER, moved to the town's wealthy Avalon Hill section. Desmond asserted his control with a grip tighter than Marin's and made certain he controlled not only the mayor's office but also the police force, which was headed by Chief Francis Alexander Redhorn.

Soon after, however, the city received its first costumed champion when NIGHTWING moved to Blüdhaven from Gotham. The hero made it his goal to restore a measure of self-respect in its population and put a stop to the corruption, working out of his apartment in the Melville section. He and Blockbuster began a feud that ended only when Blockbuster was shot and killed by another vigilante called the TARANTULA.

Nightwing left Blüdhaven after letting Tarantula commit murder, as Gotham endured a horrible gang war. In its wake ROBIN and BATGIRL temporarily moved to Blüdhaven in an effort to start afresh. Also dropping in for a year was the PENGUIN, no longer welcome in Gotham's underworld.

At 12:51 AM on a Friday, DEATHSTROKE and the Society dropped the toxic Chemo on the city, killing 100,068 citizens. Nightwing, Robin, and Batgirl were all out of the city at the time but were on hand to help with the rescue efforts. SUPERMAN, the TEEN TITANS, Metal Men, and several other heroes also responded to the catastrophe. As Chemo reintegrated, Superman battled the creature. The Man of Steel theorized that Chemo's reintegration would draw most of the deadly toxins from the streets and buildings. Once the process was completed, Superman hurled Chemo into outer space. (*Infinite Crisis* #6, 2006)

Fearing residual effects from Chemo's attack, President Horne declared a state of national emergency and had the city walled off from the rest of Haven County. Under presidential order, a team of superpowered government agents called

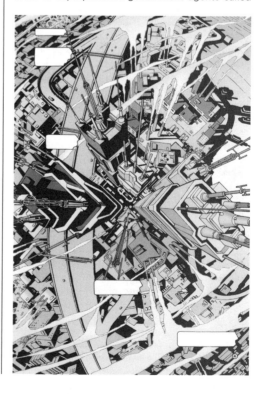

Freedom's Ring, led by the enigmatic Father Time, took command of the city. The unaffiliated heroes were eventually ordered out of the devastated city, where a new era began. Refugee camps sprung up by the wall erected by Freedom's Ring, and people struggled for basic necessities. The golem known as Monolith arrived from New York City and tried to help the needy. A secret band of government agents known as the Atomic Knights were activated and worked to help trapped citizens escape the wall to freedom.

Unbeknownst to most, Father Time also helped himself to the disenfranchised populace, subjecting several people to his secret experiments. Around the same time, the Society sent in the androids known as the Nuclear Family to help find a radioactive leak that was causing much concern to the city's remaining populace. With all this activity, it was only a matter of time before Freedom's Ring and the Atomic Knights came to blows. Joining in the fray were members of the Titans and agents from Father Time's Super Human Advanced Defense Executive operation.

During the conflict, the Titan Ravager killed Lady Liberty, and Monolith smacked the Black Baron, a local drug lord, into another state. When Major Force arrived, he was quickly handled by Green Lantern, which prompted Major Victory to order Freedom's Ring to cease hostilities. When Major Force objected, he beat Major Victory to death to make his point clear. The brutality cost him the loyalty of the other SHADE agents.

During the mêlée, the Atomic Knights finally tracked down the source of the radiation—an imprisoned and injured Captain Atom. They rescued the hero and placed him within a containment suit to limit exposure. Captain Atom hit the streets of Blüdhaven in time to stop Major Victory by draining him of his radiation-spawned power, seemingly killing him in the process.

Captain Atom warned everyone to evacuate the city, with the Atomic Knights securing themselves within an underground facility known as Command-D. When the quantum hero received an all-clear, Captain Atom unleashed his power, reducing the beleaguered, underappreciated, and much-maligned city to atoms. Only a crater remained to mark the site of the soon-to-be-forgotten town. (*Crisis Aftermath: The Battle for Blüdhaven* #1–6, May–October 2006).

BLUE BEETLE

Blue Beetle was the name used by three different heroes throughout the twentieth and twenty-first centuries, linked only through legacy and an ancient beetle scarab that was a unique blend of science and magic.

Dan Garrett was a professor who used the scarab's power, as well as his own scientific enhancements, to battle crime during the modern heroic age, but he died in his attempt to prevent androids from another world from conquering Earth. Garrett then bequeathed the scarab to his favorite student, Ted Kord. (*Secret Origins* [second series] #2, May 1986)

The scarab never seemed to bestow any special abilities on Kord while it was in his possession, so he used the resources of his father's technology firm,

Kord Industries, to become a new kind of Blue Beetle. He built a special outfit and custom-designed an aircraft resembling a giant beetle filled with cutting-edge technology. With his Bug, the Beetle first fought crime in his native Chicago and later joined one incarnation of the Justice League of America.

Batman always considered Kord to be a second-string hero, and rarely spent time with him. However, Kord befriended Oracle and lent his fists—and more often his technical expertise—to her while she formed her Birds of Prey operation. Heart and weight issues forced Kord to give up crime fighting, and he struggled to make Kord Industries a viable business after he was placed in charge. When it looked like the company was on the verge of failure, it was bought out by a division of Wayne Enterprises.

After Blue Beetle discovered that the former US government agency Checkmate had been reorganized by Maxwell Lord, he grew seriously concerned. Lord had a checkered past, and Blue Beetle had long been suspicious of the JLA's onetime benefactor. Blue Beetle tried to have the scarab summon help, but it only took him to the Rock of Eternity, where the wizard Shazam took custody of the scarab and returned Blue Beetle to Earth. When Blue Beetle's concerns were ignored by many, including Batman, he secretly accessed Checkmate's new European headquarters. He was shocked to discover detailed information on all of Earth's meta-humans. Lord had Blue Beetle detained and offered him a chance to join him in his quest to eradicate all the meta-humans from Earth. When Blue Beetle refused, Lord shot him in the head. (*Countdown to Infinite Crisis,* 2005)

The scarab was then seemingly forgotten when

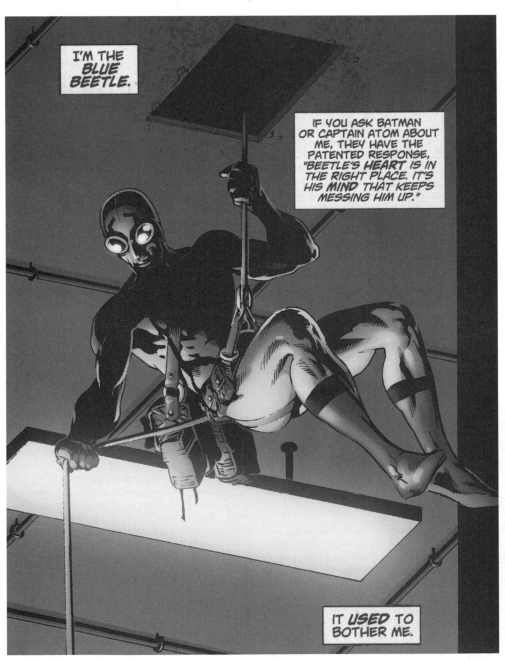

the Rock of Eternity exploded over Gotham City, and eventually the scarab wound up in New Mexico, in the hands of a teen who was to become the third Blue Beetle.

With his quasi-mystic/alien-tech scarab, the new Blue Beetle accompanied Batman into orbit to help deactivate Brother Eye, the satellite Batman had once constructed to monitor all meta-human activity, but its programming and artificial intelligence had been perverted by Maxwell Lord. (*Infinite Crisis,* 2006)

BOCK, MACKENZIE "HARDBACK"

MacKenzie Bock worked his way up through the ranks in the Gotham City Police Department to become a detective in the Major Crimes Unit. Along the way he impressed many with his work ethic and was partnered with Sarah Essen Gordon prior to her promotion to commissioner. They were among the detectives who helped rescue Renee Montoya when she was held by the criminal operation Cell Six. His work earned him the job of running the MCU before ceding the role to Maggie Sawyer. During the No Man's Land year, Bock left the police force to help maintain order in his home neighborhood. When James Gordon retired as commissioner in the wake of his being shot by Jordan Rich, Bock was promoted to captain of the Organized Crime Unit. Little was recorded about Bock's personal life, although he was married to a woman named Dore and was nicknamed "Hardback" due to his fondness for reading hardcover books. His reading gave him a deep and broad background of knowledge that often aided his exemplary police work. (*Detective Comics* #681, January 1996)

BODIN, "HUSH-HUSH"

Bodin earned his nickname *Hush-Hush* thanks to his extreme distaste for loud noises. He led a successful gang of criminals in Gotham City until he was stopped once and for all by Batman and Robin. (*Batman* #30, August/September 1945)

BODIN, PAUL

A famed circus-escape-artist-turned-criminal who committed his felonies under the guise of the Human Key.

BOLES, BEETLE

Beetle Boles had a lengthy criminal record that included the murder of a police officer. He was known for his brazen strategies, which worked until he was confronted by Batman and Robin. Noteworthy in this case was the rare assistance lent in the field by Alfred Pennyworth. (*Batman* #42, April/May 1947)

BOLEY, JINX

Jinx Boley was everything Batman imagined criminals to be: superstitious and cowardly. Boley firmly believed in the special powers possessed by the number seven and took to wearing a bulletproof vest while committing his crimes. When the escaped convict attempted to steal jewels from the Gotham Historical Society, his vest proved his undoing. Batman had installed a powerful electromagnet near the jewels prior to

Boley's robbery attempt, and it held Boley firmly in place until he could be apprehended by the Dark Knight. (*Batman* #67, October/November 1951)

BOLEY BROTHERS, THE

Slats, Dave, and Bull Boley were career smugglers seemingly favored by fortune. They found the Batplane after it crashed into a clump of trees north of Gotham City. It had been abandoned due to equipment failure, but the brothers secured the craft before Batman could return. With their vast monetary resources, the brothers had two duplicate planes constructed, allowing the three to grow their criminal enterprise. Their attacks grew more daring and forced Batman to design and construct the next-generation Batplane, which put the brothers out of business for good. (*Batman* #61, October/November 1950)

BOLTON, DR. FRANK

Frank Bolton was a noted physicist who developed an unusual device during the course of his research. Dubbed the "illus-o-ray," the machine used two gem-shaped objects atop a shaft that refracted light—much the way a prism works. The difference, however, was that these projections would create realistic images not unlike holographic technology. The only way viewers could tell image from reality was through a pair of specially tinted glasses. Bolton's lab assistant, Parker, contacted criminal Al Framm and entered into a partnership that led to a series of spectacular crimes. The police were baffled by the false images the criminal projected, letting Framm and his cohorts abscond with vast quantities of plunder. Batman and Robin countered the illus-o-ray with their own new device, a combination radar and sonar emitter, which they fitted into the Batmobile in order to pierce the false images. Parker, Framm, and the "illus-o-raiders" were quickly brought to justice. (*Batman* #90, March 1955)

BOLTON, LYLE

A criminal known as Lock-Up who fought Batman on several occasions.

BOLTON, TOM

Tom Bolton grew up in the shadow of his father, Mike Nolan's, criminal career. When the elder Nolan intended to confess his misdeeds to the Batman, gang leader Nick Rocco murdered Mike. Tom believed it was Batman who had killed his father, and thought the Caped Crusader was a lying coward. As a result, he went into law enforcement and became a well-respected state trooper, trying to be everything he felt Batman was not. When the Dynamic Duo wound up partnering with Bolton on a case involving Rocco, Tom finally saw the truth. Batman's actions were also bolstered by Rocco's confession, so the grudge between cop and crime fighter became instead a friendship. (*Detective Comics* #65, July 1942)

BONECRUSHERS, THE

A secret group known as the Cartel began using WayneTech resources in the hope of creating an army of remote-controlled soldiers. The Cartel used a team of bodybuilders as guinea pigs, and each member had a bio-chip implanted in his brain.

Operators would then use the technology to send the subjects' minds into the minds of the recipients, controlling their actions. Kenneth Harbinger, the project's creator, was asked by the Cartel to field-test the soldiers. Outfitted with a wristband containing infrasound technology, the bodybuilders were nicknamed the Bonecrushers, given the technology's ability to reduce bone to powder without breaking the skin. A Bonecrusher was directed to commit a robbery; at the crime scene, a body was found with every bone pulverized.

Batman entered the investigation and wound up confronting the Bonecrushers on several occasions. The white-hooded, brown-vested agents proved formidable, but Batman prevailed and obtained one of the transfer units. During one of the battles, Batman was injured and temporarily confined to a wheelchair. To stop the Bonecrushers and defeat the Cartel, he wound up entering the mind of Roy Kane. Kane was a test subject who had escaped the Cartel some time earlier and was found by Batman during the investigation. Unfortunately, Kane's body wound up being struck by an elevated train; while he died, Batman managed to return consciousness to his own body before he, too, died.

The Bonecrusher project was exposed, and despite the Cartel trying to place the blame on WayneTech owner Bruce Wayne, it was implicated. Cartel members killed their Gotham coordinator, Mitchell Riordan, and withdrew operations from the United States. (*Detective Comics* #598–600, 1989)

BOONE

Boone was the man who became known as the costumed criminal Shrike, a longtime foe to Dick Grayson, the first Robin.

BORDEAUX, SASHA

Initially hired by Lucius Fox as Bruce Wayne's bodyguard, Sasha Bordeaux was drawn deep into Wayne's world, first as a costumed vigilante and then as a cybernetic agent for Checkmate. (*Detective Comics* #751, December 2000)

Given Wayne's high profile in the worlds of business and society, Fox decided that the time had come to protect the man, even though Bordeaux was hired against Wayne's wishes. Wayne and the attractive Bordeaux were initially cold toward each other, but clearly both felt something stirring beneath the surface. To control events, Wayne slowly left clues that aroused Bordeaux's suspicions; eventually the bodyguard came to conclude that Wayne and Batman were the same person. When she finally confronted him with the knowledge, Wayne didn't deny it but insisted that if she were to continue as his bodyguard, she would also have to be a part of Batman's world.

Against her better judgment, Bordeaux acquiesced and began training in earnest. When Batman deemed her ready, she was given a mask and purple costume and joined him on nightly patrols across Gotham City. Even though Wayne kept up pretenses as he dated women, Bordeaux realized he let none of them matter to him and couldn't help but fall in love with her newfound mentor.

On orders from Lex Luthor, assassin David Cain killed Wayne's former lover, Vesper Fairchild, and

didn't believe she died that easily—not with the training he'd provided her. Over time he came to suspect that Checkmate had a hand in the events surrounding her death. He set out to interfere with all of Checkmate's Gotham City operations until he forced a meeting with Bordeaux. While both admitted their attraction to each other, it was clearly not something meant to happen. She left, asking that he stay away.

In short order, Bordeaux made an impression on Checkmate's management and rapidly rose to the rank of Knight, reporting to the Black King, Maxwell Lord. At the time, she was unaware that Lord was insane and intending to use Checkmate as a pawn in his plan to rid the world of meta-humans. He had already located and usurped the Brother I satellite from Batman and designed the nanites that would turn ordinary humans into armored cyborgs known as OMACs. (*Countdown to Infinite Crisis,* 2005)

When Bordeaux learned the truth, she needed to warn Batman without being detected. She surreptitiously shipped the slain Blue Beetle's goggles to Wayne Manor, which convinced Batman of the grave danger faced by the entire world. When he arranged a clandestine meeting with her to share intelligence, OMACs descended upon them. While Batman managed to escape, the attackers captured Bordeaux. Lord's own meta-human power of mind control failed to force her to talk, so she remained imprisoned. She was later freed by fellow agent Jessica Midnight, who had once before tried to kill Lord. As they fled, an OMAC impaled Bordeaux— but rather than kill her, the puncture transformed her into a new being. She was encased in a metal skin, a human-sized independent OMAC.

Her lack of humanity weighed heavily on her, but she still managed to see to it that Lord was stopped at every turn. She effectively usurped his control of Checkmate by reaching out to the disenfranchised agents who'd left when Lord himself seized total control of the organization. She then used her new technological skills to develop a computer virus disabling the renamed and now sentient Brother Eye. As she uploaded the virus, Earth's super heroes unleashed an electromagnetic pulse that disabled all but two hundred thousand of the OMACs.

When she next saw Batman, Bordeaux was unhappy, but he pointed out that she retained her humanity and individuality; she could never be like Brother Eye or the OMACs. She accompanied Batman into orbit in order to directly confront and destroy the sentient satellite. As they disabled Brother Eye, it crashed in Saudi Arabia, and she followed it to the surface. The satellite's central core remained intact and tried to assert control over Bordeaux's cybernetic form, which she resisted. Brother Eye revealed to her that she was unique because the satellite had designed her nanites to prepare her as an emergency backup to the central computer core. She managed to destroy the remains of Brother Eye; with it finally offline, the metallic casing she wore began to shed from her skin. All that remained were metallic pieces around her left eye and right forearm.

She returned to Europe with Midnight to help rebuild Checkmate. In the re-formed order, she was promoted to Black Queen and began a romance

successfully framed Wayne by leaving the body in Wayne Manor. Wayne and Bordeaux were found by Gotham police with Fairchild's body and were both arrested. Without giving away Wayne's secret, Bordeaux could not possibly reveal that they couldn't have committed the crime, so she remained silent, refusing all legal help. While at Blackgate Penitentiary, Bordeaux suffered in silence, getting beaten, fighting back, and holding out hope that Wayne would come to her rescue.

While Wayne escaped and set out to clear his name, Bordeaux remained to suffer. Even after he was exonerated, Wayne was slow to have Bordeaux freed. Instead she got into another prison fight and, while in the hospital, was spirited away by agents from Checkmate. The world was left to believe that Bordeaux had died from her injuries, filling Wayne with guilt.

Checkmate healed her and offered to train her as an agent, even though it meant giving up her identity. She agreed and underwent plastic surgery in addition to her training. Batman, meanwhile, with the Justice Society of America's Mister Terrific, who also served Checkmate. In her new field role, she displayed a willingness to kill without mercy, making some think she had finally shed her humanity. (*Checkmate* [second series] #1, June 2006) On one fateful mission, she was captured by the misshapen criminal Chang Tzu, who tortured her, testing her cyborg attributes. He determined that she was a good 15 percent faster, stronger, and more agile than the world's best Olympian. Her nanites also repaired any organic damage done to her body; by the time Batman and the Outsiders rescued her, she was little more than a torso with stumps for limbs, until the nanites reconstructed her. (*Checkmate* [second series] #16, September 2007)

BORK, CARL

Carl Bork never had it easy as a child, leading to criminal behavior. As an adult, Bork took to working the Gotham City wharves, earning himself the nickname *King of the Docks*. Some time later Bork was preparing to rob a docked ship when he wound up saving the life of a young boy who lived on nearby Desolation Island. His heroic effort was rewarded by the boy's father with the gift of a statue. Back in Gotham, the statue proved to have magical properties: It added bulk and muscle to his body, as well as making him invulnerable. Newly empowered, Bork escalated his criminal activities, leading to a conflict with Batman. Coming to the Caped Crusader's aid was the Flash, who traced the statue's origin back to Desolation Island. The Fastest Man Alive was unable to destroy the statue; instead he hurled it into the sun, where it finally disintegrated, reverting Bork to human proportions.

Found guilty of his crimes, Bork was sentenced to Metropolis's Van Kull Maximum Security Facility. During his incarceration, the now destroyed statue's mystic effects continued to work on his body, mutating him anew. His bulk and invulnerability returned, allowing him to escape from prison. Eluding Batman and the Flash, he made his way to Newark, New Jersey, to see his ill mother. When the heroes arrived, Bork's mother fell victim to congestive heart failure, and Batman convinced Bork to surrender in exchange for a promise to help the woman. A distraught Bork agreed, and the Wayne Foundation covered the hospital tab. (*The Brave and the Bold* #81, December 1968)

Some time later, Bork was released on parole and had difficulty finding a legitimate job. Many prospective employers were as wary of his criminal record as of his grotesquely muscular physique. Things turned around for him when the wealthy Josiah Power offered him a position with his corporate heroes, Power Company. The newly hired associate worked with the team for a time, eventually sharing an apartment with fellow associate Sapphire. (*JLA* #61, February 2002)

Bork worked with Power Company on numerous missions but also did work pro bono during times of great catastrophe such as the events known as Infinite Crisis. Shortly after that, he was captured by the criminal Roulette and forced to take part in her gladiatorial games, battling the latest person to go by the name Vulcan. His whereabouts after that incident remain unrecorded. (*JSA Classified* #19, January 2007)

BOTA, GREGORY

Gregory Bota appeared to most people as a South American millionaire recently relocated to Gotham City, but to a select few he was a scheming criminal. Bota told the world he was fascinated with crime and collected photographs having to do with it. The reality was more sordid: Through his plethora of collected photos, Bota found incriminating evidence against four of Gotham's underworld bosses. His hope was to blackmail the quartet into naming him king of the underworld. Instead, Batman and Robin took down the four mobsters, and the resulting fight ignited a fire that wound up destroying the blackmail material. Bota directed his wrath toward the Dynamic Duo and had a special gun constructed that could simultaneously fire bullets while snapping pictures to preserve the act. Before he could carry out his revenge, though, Batman and Robin apprehended him. (*Batman* #64, April/May 1951)

BOUNCER

An unnamed metallurgist-turned-criminal invented a unique alloy comprising rubber, steel, and chrome, the result of five years' research. Clad in a body-sized brown suit coated in the compound, he was able to absorb kinetic energy and use it

to bounce off objects. Taking the name *Bouncer*, he used his discovery for a series of spectacular crimes in Gotham City. When the Dynamic Duo failed to apprehend him, the local media questioned the crime fighters' effectiveness. Finally Batman determined that the best way to apprehend him was to strain the criminal's costume's limits. He outfitted Robin and himself with electrodes that generated a cold beam; they trapped the Bouncer between the two of them, chilling the thief and freezing the rubber costume in an outsized shape. The Bouncer was apprehended, at last earning the heroes overdue praise from the media. (*Detective Comics* #347, November 1965)

The Bouncer appeared a second time as one of several costumed criminals who took advantage of Batman's prolonged absence at one point. His new red costume used a modification of his compound. When Batman returned from his case abroad, the Bouncer hoped to crush him using a high-velocity attack, but the Caped Crusader's well-timed kick caused him to ricochet in a confined space until he was knocked unconscious. (*Batman* #336, June 1981)

BOURDET

Professor Carter Nichols was fascinated with Alexander Dumas's story of the Man in the Iron Mask, so he persuaded the World's Finest team of Batman, Robin, and Superman to allow themselves to be hypnotized and transported to the 1619 French court of Louis XIV. The trio came upon the famed Three Musketeers—Athos, Porthos, and Aramis—who were wounded by guardsmen loyal to the evil chancellor, Bourdet. Taking up the wounded men's swords, the heroes disguised themselves as musketeers and teamed with D'Artagnan to save the kindly Count Ferney, who was locked in Pignerol Castle and forced to wear the fabled iron mask to hide his identity. The heroes freed Ferney and exposed Bourdet's treachery to the king. As punishment, the chancellor was stripped of his title and sent to the Bastille, imprisoned for the rest of his life in the iron mask. (*World's Finest Comics* #82, May/June 1956)

BOWERS, BERT

Bert Bowers was a criminal who escaped custody and hid in Gotham City's Stevens Warehouse. Batman and Robin managed to track him down with the help of Ace, a hound they had recently rescued from a river. When Ace latched onto him, Bowers provided Ace with a crime dog's name, calling him a Bat-Hound. (*Batman* #92, June 1955)

BOYD, "LITTLE NAP"

Modeling himself after the notorious Napoleon Bonaparte, "Little Nap" Boyd took a calculated approach to his crimes. He went beyond the usual casing of potential locations to craft elaborate campaigns ensuring that his efforts would be successful. US Special Agent John O'Brien was shot and killed while attempting to arrest Boyd during this spree. Batman and Robin intervened to end Boyd's criminal campaign, and they welcomed the assistance of O'Brien's adult sons, Tim and Nick, to accomplish the feat. (*World's Finest Comics* #8, Winter 1942)

BRADLEY, SLAM

The Bradley family enjoyed a century-old legacy of adventuring that endured in GOTHAM CITY in the last members of the family, Slam and his son Sam. Biff, the eldest Bradley brother, was recorded as journeying to the legendary Dinosaur Island in the company of gunslinger Bat Lash and German flying ace Hans Von Hammer in the 1920s. Biff sacrificed his life during a confrontation with the immortal Vandal Savage. (*Guns of the Dragon* #1–4, October 1998–January 1999)

His younger brother, Slam Bradley, was a private investigator who usually sleuthed more with his fists than his wits in Cleveland and later New York City. He often fought alongside his longtime pal "Shorty" Morgan. (*Detective Comics* #1, March 1937)

Another Slam Bradley—presumably a Slam Bradley Jr.—appeared as an officer in the METROPOLIS Police Department.

In the wake of the reality-altering events of INFINITE CRISIS, the Bradley brothers vanished and only one Slam Bradley existed. This Bradley was a police-officer-turned-private-eye in his sixties, who had spent his career in Gotham City. (*Detective Comics* #759, August 2001) His first recorded case was being hired to investigate the apparent death of CATWOMAN. SELINA KYLE, the real Catwoman, turned up alive and befriended Bradley. They fought alongside each other for a time, protecting Gotham's EAST END from encroaching

criminal activity. On more than one occasion Bradley crossed paths with Batman, and the two experienced an uneasy alliance.

Bradley and Kyle had a brief romantic fling but remained loyal to each other. During this time, Slam revealed the existence of his son, Sam Bradley Jr., also nicknamed Slam and an officer in the GOTHAM CITY POLICE DEPARTMENT. Details about Sam's mother were never revealed.

Sam came to Catwoman's aid after she shot and killed BLACK MASK. The two spent several months closing down Black Mask's various operations, and in the euphoria of completing the task, the two made love. Shortly after learning that Selina was pregnant, Sam wound up being captured by other criminals still loyal to Black Mask's memory. He was beaten and left for dead. He died without ever seeing his child. Nine months later, Selina gave birth to a daughter, Helena. Slam remained a part of Selina's and Helena's lives.

In an alternate reality, a Slam Bradley was seen as a police detective partnered with John Jones, secretly the MARTIAN MANHUNTER. (*New Frontier*, 2003)

BRADY, JIM

Jim Brady and Al Rorick were career criminals who were discovered by Batman and ROBIN during the commission of a crime. The resulting chase led to GOTHAM CITY's underground subway system, where the crooks boarded an early-morning train. Disaster struck when Brady tried to shoot a passenger but hit Rorick instead. After the Dynamic Duo boarded the crowded subway car, Batman missed being struck by a metal hammer, which instead found the electrified third rail, shocking Brady to death. (*Batman* #43, October/November 1947)

BRADY BROTHERS, THE

When Earth-2's Alaska was admitted to the United States of America as its forty-ninth state, a wealthy miner named Chalmers intended to present the new state with a gift: forty-eight magnificent jewels with a larger forty-ninth diamond. Before Chalmers could make his presentation, however, the Brady brothers—Matt, Will, and Bart—stole the priceless treasure. Alerted to the crime by his old friend Chalmers, Batman journeyed north with ROBIN and tracked the Brady Brothers. Across the state, the Dynamic Duo managed to gain custody of the forty-eight same-sized diamonds and finally located the largest one of them all. The Brady Brothers had given it to the mining plant's guard, Atkins, for his help in committing the crime. They were arrested and stood trial for their crime. (*Batman* #126, September 1959)

BRAINIAC

On Earth-1, Brainiac was an android construct from the alien planet Colu. Fulfilling its programming, Brainiac traveled among the stars using a miniaturization ray to capture sample cities from populated worlds, including KANDOR from the planet KRYPTON.

When Brainiac arrived to collect a city from Earth, he was stopped by SUPERMAN, who rescued Kandor and kept the bottled city in his famed FORTRESS OF SOLITUDE. (*Action Comics* #242, July 1958)

Subsequently the bald, green-skinned construct abandoned its programming and became a recurring nemesis to the Man of Steel. Frequently, this required Batman's assistance.

After the CRISIS ON INFINITE EARTHS, Brainiac was Coluan scientist Vril Dox. When he tried to overthrow the Computer Tyrants of his homeworld, he was sentenced to death. Dox managed to transfer his mind to a human, Milton Fine, a purported mentalist. (*Adventures of Superman* #438, March 1988) He used LexCorp technology to regain his Coluan form and went on to attempt to conquer Earth and its heroes time and again.

(For a complete account of the many incarnations of Brainiac, consult *The Essential Superman Encyclopedia*.)

BRAMWELL, BRAMWELL B.

Bramwell B. Bramwell was the author of a series of bestselling crime novels who decided to challenge GOTHAM CITY's top four crime bosses. He invited the gangsters—Bright Guy Warner, Slim Ryan, CHOPPER GANT, and Muscles Hardy—to join him for a "literary tea" where he proposed to test their crooked minds. Bramwell met them in his castle-like residence and asked them to commit a crime per month to demonstrate their ingenuity and moxie. At the conclusion of that month's four crimes, Bramwell would choose a winner, with the proceeds from all four crimes going to the champion criminal. The crimes began with a splash and quickly drew the attention of Batman and ROBIN. Bramwell made his own robbery attempt at a society benefit for the Allied War Relief Fund and was easily apprehended by the Dynamic Duo. (*World's Finest Comics* #9, Spring 1943)

BRAND, EDDIE

In the days following World War II, flying ace Eddie Brand joined the growing field of test piloting. On one such flight Brand's plane crashed, and doctors performed an operation to try to save his eyes. The emergency surgery did something to Brand's vision, allowing him to see in the X-ray spectrum. No longer eligible to fly, Brand resorted to using his new talent on the vaudeville circuit. He soon grew disheartened and bitter, however, as he realized how much people feared him for being different. Brand finally turned toward a life of crime. He sought out Milt, a criminal acquaintance, and together they staged a series of crimes in which Brand's X-ray vision proved invaluable. Ultimately they confronted Batman and ROBIN. Milt accidentally touched a high-voltage wire during the battle, electrocuting himself. Batman employed a daring psychological ruse to entrap Brand, leading to the man's collapse. When he awoke, his unique X-ray vision had disappeared, leaving his sight normal. Doctors and the Caped Crusader determined that Brand had been driven temporarily insane from the combination of battle fatigue from the war and trauma from the crash. As a result, Brand would not be prosecuted for his crimes. (*World's Finest Comics* #31, November/December 1947)

BRAND, THE

The western-style criminal known only as the Brand arrived in GOTHAM CITY hoping to steal a hundred thousand dollars that had been raised for a youth center. The money was to be presented by Batman to the city's mayor during a ceremony, but until then it was stored in the Gotham Bank's vault. The Brand planned to tunnel into the vault and steal the money, but when he fell behind schedule, he came up with a delaying tactic so the ceremony would be postponed. Despite the elaborate plan, the Brand failed to get to the money in time—the delay tipped off Batman and Robin to the pending crime. He and his men were apprehended, and the money was donated to the city. (*Batman* #137, February 1961)

BRANDO, WOLF

Once declared public enemy number one, Wolf Brando escaped prison and sought refuge in the mansion of Bruce Wayne. There Brando accidentally discovered the entrance to the Batcave and realized he now knew the secret of Batman's identity. The Caped Crusader and Boy Wonder followed him through the catacombs until Brando, startled by a flock of bats that flew in his path, fell to his death in an underground whirlpool. (*Batman* #48, August/September 1948)

BRANE

In a potential thirtieth century, humankind was enslaved by Saturn's warlord Fura. Brane and his companion Ricky took up an ages-old tradition. Brane said he was the twentieth direct descendant of Bruce Wayne and was going to be a new Batman, coming to Earth's aid. His inspiration came from film footage of Batman and Robin in action, rescued from a time capsule dating back to the 1939 New York World's Fair. Donning the traditional garb of the Dynamic Duo, Brane and Ricky inspired the rest of humankind to fight their robotic oppressors. The future Batman and Robin took the struggle back to Saturn, where they confronted Fura himself. The warlord escaped into space, followed by a determined Brane. During their battle in the vacuum of space, Brane ripped Fura's space suit, and the conqueror suffocated in space. (*Batman* #26, December 1944/January 1945)

Brane's exploits would prove inspirational a century later to his descendant Brane Taylor.

BRANE, PROFESSOR L. M.

L. M. Brane was a theatrical agent who used his skills to moonlight as a booking agent for criminal activity. He would provide specialized talent to criminals in need, ensuring that their robberies went off without a problem. One such plan involved blacking out part of Gotham City, which would allow blind criminals to easily navigate around the Gotham City Bank and steal a gold shipment. Batman and Robin struggled at first in the dark but learned to compensate. They then tracked down Brane, arresting him and a band of deaf criminals before they could rob receipts from a war bond drive. (*World's Finest Comics* #18, Summer 1945)

BRANN

A gambling czar, Brann was also known as the Dagger.

BRENTWOOD ACADEMY

Brentwood Academy was a private high school located near Gotham City. Jack Drake was a widower frequently traveling on business, so he decided that his teenage son Tim Drake should live at the school. Tim's seemingly erratic comings and goings contributed to this decision—Jack did not know that at the time, his son was also spending time as Robin the Teen Wonder.

To ease the boy's transition, Bruce Wayne asked his butler Alfred Pennyworth to join Tim at Brentwood. Tim easily made new friends, starting with his roommate, Ali Ben Khadir, who hailed from the small Asian country of Dhabar. Being the country's religious leader meant that he, too, had a companion, a muscular man named Dhabar. Tim still managed his Robin career, creating a souped-up skateboard to get around campus and the environs. He also maintained his romantic relationship with Spoiler, so the distance didn't hurt his crime fighting.

During Tim's time at the academy, the school saw its share of oddities—from the arrival of Man-Bat to a photo shoot conducted by Jennie-Lynn Hayden (secretly the crime fighter Jade) gone awry when the school's mascot was stolen. Eventually Jack relented and let Tim return home. (*Robin* #74, March 2000)

BRESSI, ANTHONY

Anthony Bressi was a Gotham City mobster who ran a large protection racket when Batman first began his war on crime. Bressi continued to conduct his illegal business despite the proliferation of costumed crime fighters. (*Robin III: Cry of the Huntress* #1, December 1992) He refused Killer Moth's offer of protection from the "capes" and continued to oppose Batman, Batgirl, and the Huntress through the years. "Tough Tony" Bressi lived in a mansion in Gotham's Somerset neighborhood until it was destroyed by Killer Moth and Firefly in a revenge scheme complicated by Batgirl and Black Canary. He was not seen after that incident. (*Batgirl Year One* #6–7, July–August 2003)

BRIDESHEAD

The Brideshead section of Gotham City included Pinkney Square, with its statue of architect Cyrus Pinkney. The Coit Pyramid building (once owned by mobster Ramon Bracuda) was on Mott Street. (*Showcase '93* #1, January 1993)

BRIGGS

Briggs was a wealthy architect who was also the leader of a criminal operation. His peculiar passion was to purchase prized buildings and have them moved, brick by brick, to a private island hideaway. When he was dying, Briggs told his number two henchman Catlin about a series of clues to a fabulous treasure. Catlin set out to find this prize, accompanied by fellow criminals Hoke and Danny. They were trailed by the Dynamic Duo, who arrived in time to recover the treasure—a wealth of items stolen from museums—before Hoke and Danny could double-cross Catlin and take the stolen goods for themselves. All three wound up arrested, and the items were returned to their respective museums. (*Batman* #147, May 1962)

BRINK, SCAR

In a bizarre twist on the prison system, Scar Brink built a prison that housed members of law enforcement, establishing himself as the warden. The prison, located on a stretch of isolated marshland near Gotham City, was infiltrated by Batman and Robin until they were discovered and became inmates. Once inside, the Caped Crusader incited a prison revolt that turned the tables on Brink and his men, who soon found themselves inside the cells while members of the Gotham City Police Department arrived to take charge (*Batman* #71, June/July 1952)

BRISTOL

Bristol was an upscale neighborhood in northern Gotham City, about ten kilometers from the city proper and to one side of the Gotham Tunnel on Bristol Parkway. Spillkin Hill looked down over the city. Bristol was home to both Bruce Wayne and Lucius Fox, the latter residing at 375 Sprang Street. Also of note: the Bristol Pike Drive-In, the Bristol Country Club's Seneca Lodge, and Gotham Cemetery. (*World's Finest Comics* #286, December 1982)

BRONZE TIGER

The Bronze Tiger was a martial-artist-turned-crime-fighter who fell under the sway of the Sensei and killed Kathy Kane, Batwoman, on Earth-1.

Ben Turner grew up in Central City where, at age ten, he killed a burglar robbing his home. It was the first manifestation of a deep inner rage that Ben barely kept contained. Choosing to channel this rage, Turner, at thirteen, began martial arts training. While honing his skills, Ben never lost the anger, but he also came to enjoy inflicting violence on others. Recognizing that if the rage was left untreated, he would wind up in jail, Turner traveled to the Far East. After rejecting several teachers who wanted to exploit, not control, his feelings, Turner found the O-Sensei, who recognized his troubled spirit. He also met fellow American Richard Dragon, and the two formed a tight friendship that has endured through the years. Returning to the States, Turner and Dragon worked as agents for King Faraday and the Central Bureau of Intelligence. (*Richard Dragon, Kung Fu Fighter* #1, April/May 1975)

When they were assigned to dismantle the League of Assassins, Turner came under the sway

of the manipulative Sensei. He brainwashed Turner into associating his rage and anger with a tiger mask. Whenever Turner donned the Bronze Tiger mask, he became an engine of destruction, controlled entirely by the Sensei. The Bronze Tiger was a fearsome opponent. Operating across three different continents, he was kept so busy, he rarely took the mask off. When the Sensei and Rā's al Ghūl came into conflict, the Tiger was sent into battle, ultimately distracting Batman in a fight long enough for one of the others to kill Kathy Kane. (*Detective Comics* #485, August/September 1979)

Eventually Ben Turner was rescued from the Sensei, and while the process took years, the psychological damage was undone. As a result, when Batman needed to invade Santa Prisca to rescue Jack Drake and Shondra Kinsolving, he trusted Turner enough to recruit him for a team including Green Arrow and Gypsy.

In the reality after Infinite Crisis, Turner never killed Kathy Kane, so his relationship to the Batman remains unexplored.

BROOKS, PAULA
On Earth-2, Paula Brooks was an athlete-turned-costumed-criminal who operated as the Huntress.

BROTHER EYE
When Batman learned that the Justice League of America had voted to use Zatanna's magic to alter the minds of criminals, he objected. Zatanna then dared to use her magic, erasing ten minutes from the Dark Knight's memory so he would not recall witnessing the vote and its aftermath. Some years later Batman's memory healed itself, and he grew suspicious of his fellow Leaguers. In secret he used technology originally designed by Pseudopersons, Inc., programmer Buddy Blank, who designed the prototype Brother I. (*Countdown* #30, 2007). Batman constructed a massive satellite, also dubbed Brother I, to monitor the world's super-heroic activity, seeking lawbreakers. (*Identity Crisis* #1–7, August 2004–February 2005)

Soon after it achieved orbit, the satellite was usurped by Alexander Luthor, the sole survivor of a parallel universe known as Earth-3, and given alternate programming, boosting its level of artificial intelligence. Brother I was then used to help define coordinates for construction of a tower that would channel energies culled from meta-humans to turn the universe back into a multiverse. (*Infinite Crisis* #1–7, December 2005–June 2006)

After that, Maxwell Lord, once the benefactor to the Justice League, also discovered the satellite and took permanent control of it. Brother I took to calling Lord "teacher." At the same time, Lord had seized control of the government spy organization Checkmate, and with it he launched a mad scheme to wipe out the Earth's meta-humans. He used a nanovirus, constructed from advanced future technology that had been modified by the US Department of Defense and LexCorp, to turn normal humans into armored battle cyborgs dubbed OMACs—Observational Meta-human Activity Constructs. As his plan unfolded, he came into conflict with Superman and Wonder Woman. Using his own meta-human power to control minds, he

took control of the Man of Steel and nearly killed first Batman, then Wonder Woman. Seeing no other choice, the Amazon snapped Lord's neck, killing him. (*Superman: Sacrifice,* 2005)

No one realized that Lord's death triggered a program called KingIsDead, which activated all 1,373,462 infected humans as OMACs, terrorizing the world. Brother I renamed itself Brother Eye and sought to turn world opinion against the

heroes by endlessly streaming footage of Wonder Woman's murder of Lord worldwide. As the super heroes battled the OMACs, Batman sought to stop his own creation from destroying the world. An electromagnetic pulse was unleashed, short-circuiting most of the OMACs—but even that was not enough. The disruption activated Brother Eye's "Truth and Justice" protocol, sending the remaining two hundred thousand OMACs to attack

the Amazon Princess's home of Themyscira, intent on killing everyone. Rather than lose more lives, Wonder Woman encouraged her sisters to remove themselves from the mortal plane, and the island vanished. (*Infinite Crisis*, 2005)

In the wake of the OMACs' defeat, Batman took a cadre of heroes into space, including Green Lanterns Hal Jordan and John Stewart, Green Arrow, Mister Terrific, Black Lightning, Black Canary, Blue Beetle, Metamorpho, Booster Gold, and Sasha Bordeaux. The new Blue Beetle used his mystic scarab to find the camouflaged satellite, and Batman crashed their vessel into Brother Eye. Batman provided distraction while Sasha Bordeaux, aided by Oracle, uploaded a concentration of all known computer viruses into Brother Eye's operating system. The other heroes used their various powers to short out systems or destroy parts of the unit. Mister Terrific finally managed to take Brother Eye out of orbit, and the machine crashed into the Earth, seemingly destroyed as it landed in Saudi Arabia.

Brother Eye was not entirely deactivated, though: Over time, repair programs came online and a warped version was rebuilt. Its programming determined that all human life should be wiped out, although it also displayed schizophrenic tendencies. The physical shell was taken by NORAD for safekeeping. A final human, Michael Costner, possessed the last active OMAC—now known as Omni Mind and Community—nanovirus and came into conflict with his "creator." (*OMAC* [second series] #1, September 2006)

The Brother Eye was built because Batman distrusted his fellow heroes, questioning their motives as well as their morals. In the end, the Dark Knight not only regained their trust, but restored his own faith in his costumed colleagues as well. The damage done was extensive and long lasting, but the result may have left the world of heroes a stronger one.

BROTHERHOOD OF THE FIST

The Brotherhood of the Fist was an Asian order dedicated to specific fighting forms within the world of martial arts. Each form's master was named for a specific property—obsidian, ivory, paper—and had a cult of followers. The fewer members a discipline had, the more difficult it was.

Chief among the Brotherhood was the Monkey King. Named for a legend from China, the Monkey King was known as a fighter unequaled on Earth or in Heaven. It took the mythical being Buddha to trick the Monkey King into submission, and the Brotherhood was built around this legendary figure.

Highest within the Brotherhood was the Silver Monkey, who doubled as a mercenary and first arrived in Gotham City to fulfill a contract to assassinate the criminal King Snake. The Silver Monkey and the leader of the Ghost Dragons were so evenly matched that the fight was only stopped after Robin interfered, forcing the Silver Monkey to leave, the contract incomplete. (*Detective Comics* #685, May 1995)

By selling his skills, the Silver Monkey was said to have shamed the Brotherhood. To restore the Brotherhood's name and purity, the leaders decided to go out into the world and kill the best martial artists alive, so none would further challenge their supremacy. Representatives loyal to the Bronze Monkey made the first strike, attacking former spy Eddie Fyers. After Fyers shot them all rather than fight them, he warned his friend Connor Hawke, who had previously defeated the Silver Monkey in combat.

At that time Hawke, son of Green Arrow, was in Gotham City investigating illegal arms being dealt by his stepfather, Milo Armitage. He and the Batman had teamed up and were tracing the deal to a facility used by the Kobra Cult, where they were surprised to find a collection of bodies. Among them was Adder, considered to be a top martial artist in the criminal underworld. A swarm of Emerald Monkey disciples descended upon the duo, who handled them easily—but the facility was destroyed.

Almost immediately Batman and Hawke were attacked by the Ivory Monkey team, fighting the heroes in the snowy hills outside Gotham City. The battle triggered an avalanche, with the Dark Knight saving the Emerald Archer.

With Batman preoccupied, it fell to a visiting Nightwing and Robin to look after Gotham's citizenry, making them targets for the Steel Monkey fighters. Given their training, the heroes quickly prevailed. Eddie Fyers arrived in time to save them from being speared by yet another branch of the Brotherhood.

Meanwhile other martial artists around the world were also being attacked, including Batman's former Outsiders teammate Katana, Hub City's Question, and the Judomaster. Once Nightwing and Robin learned of the Brotherhood's plans from Fyers, they spread the word via Oracle. When Oracle got in touch with her field agent Black Canary, she was already engaged in a battle against overwhelming odds. Her savior proved to be the Bronze Tiger, who was also drawn into this struggle. Together they sought the Brotherhood's base of operations near the Burma-China border.

Soon after, Batman gathered his team, along with Hawke, recognizing that they would best withstand the Brotherhood as a united force. What they did not count on was the Brotherhood hiring the deadly Deathstroke to take out Fyers, which placed the heroes in a confrontation with the fastest, most dangerous mercenary alive. Surviving that, Fyers decided to take the fight back to the Brotherhood. After he left, the female known as the Paper Monkey challenged Hawke directly, instructing the Brotherhood that Robin be left alone. Members of the Obsidian Monkey cult challenged her and paid with their lives.

Dealing with the Obsidian Monkey deaths exposed Batman's team to an attack from the Bamboo Monkey. This fighter bested both Nightwing and Robin before succumbing to Hawke.

As events unfolded in Gotham, both Black Canary and the Bronze Tiger fell victim to the Brotherhood's numbers and were taken prisoner. Fyers tracked down the Fist's base and was finally confronted by Deathstroke, narrowly escaping with his life. He freed the Canary and the Tiger, trapping the Silver Monkey in the process.

The costumed crime fighters finally found the Paper Monkey, seemingly fighting her own people. Seeing Hawke, she challenged him, revealing her true identity as the deadly fighter Lady Shiva. She took out Nightwing with a single kick while easily ignoring Hawke's arrows. It was clear that Shiva lived for this fight—it had become obvious to her that Hawke was the greatest living challenge to her skills. The two battled. During the confrontation Hawke learned that, should he defeat her, he would assume the leadership of the Brotherhood, making him the greatest living martial artist in the world.

Good as Hawke was, Shiva was better, and she defeated him. As she prepared for the killing Leopard Blow, Robin got between them, calling in a debt she owed him for saving her life some time back. While she refused to acknowledge the debt, she did spare Hawke's life, saying that she respected Robin's courage. It did mean, though, that she and the Teen Wonder would have to battle each other some future day. (*Green Arrow* #134, *Detective Comics* #723, *Robin* #55, *Nightwing* #23, *Green Arrow* #135, July-August 1998)

The Brotherhood's ranks were severely depleted, its headquarters compromised, and its existence made known to the world's super heroes. It would take the members some time before they could once more challenge the world's other martial artists.

BROWN, ARTHUR

A multiple-time losing criminal, he had a brief career as the costumed criminal Cluemaster.

BROWN, STEPHANIE

The Cluemaster's only child, she sought to be his opposite, a hero, and desperately tried to fight crime as the Spoiler.

BROWNE, B. BOSWELL

B. Boswell Browne was Batman's self-appointed biographer. He amassed a wealth of memorabilia and wrote a volume about the Dark Knight Detective. His efforts caught the attention of a criminal known as the Conjurer, who posed as a journalist to gain access to Browne. The Conjurer asked leading questions, learning how Batman fought and where he might have weaknesses. Browne eventually caught on to the Conjurer's plan and proved essential in Batman's eventual apprehension of the cloaked criminal. (*Batman* #17, June/July 1943)

BRULE

Brule was not only a successful cattle rancher but also the secret leader of a gang of black-market rustlers. The scheme was undone by the arrival of Batman and Robin, aided by local ranchers who'd been victimized by Brule. He resisted arrest and took aim at Robin but was fatally shot by the local sheriff. (*Batman* #21, February/March 1944)

BUCHINSKY, LESTER

The second man to become the shocking vigilante known as the Electrocutioner.

BUCKLER, JIB

Jib Buckler was a swindler who crafted an elaborate scheme to rob sunken vessels in

Gotham Harbor. The plan called for Buckler to torpedo a boat, let it sink, and claim salvage rights. He would then find a salvage company, plead poverty, and sell the salvage rights, pocketing the investment. Before the company could arrive to do its work, though, Buckler would surreptitiously raid the wreck and take the salvage for himself, which he would then fence for huge profits. After escaping in his custom-built "submobile," he would then destroy the wreck to cover his tracks. His efforts weren't good enough, though: He was discovered by Batman and Robin. As he attempted to flee, Buckler crashed the submobile into a stockpile of torpedoes and died in the resulting explosion. (*World's Finest Comics* #14, Summer 1944)

BUGG

A youth named Hector grew up in the wake of witnessing his parents' double homicide, leaving him with the compulsion to be a voyeur. He channeled this obsession into becoming an expert with surveillance equipment, eventually coming to the attention of international criminal Athena, who recruited him into her Network operation. Bugg used increasingly sophisticated devices to infiltrate any location Athena found of interest; he would then monitor the multiple feeds, claiming he never slept. After Batman destroyed the Network, Bugg was arrested. (*Batman Family* #1–8, December 2002–July 2003)

BULLET-HOLE CLUB

The Bullet-Hole Club was an exclusive club for Gotham City police officers who had been shot while on duty. To join, the extracted bullet had to be presented for inspection. At the time the club was chronicled, Batman was its president, earning the rank by having the largest number of wounds, nine. (*World's Finest Comics* #50, February/March 1951)

BULLOCK, HARVEY

Harvey Bullock was a Gotham City police detective with a checkered career that included corruption, a detour into government work, and ultimately disgrace and redemption. (*Detective Comics* #441, June 1974)

Initially Bullock was a career police officer, working his way up to detective. His love of films from the 1940s and 1950s influenced his career choice. All along, he distrusted Batman. During Batman's early years in Gotham, Bullock also found himself investigating such felons as Hellhound. (*Catwoman Annual* #2, 1995) With his pal and fellow cop Jack Crane, Bullock spent a good deal of time at the Police Youth League Building. (*Detective Comics* #528, July 1983)

The sergeant was eventually seduced by the rampant corruption pervasive throughout Gotham City government and fell under the influence of Mayor Hamilton Hill. Bullock was asked to help ruin James Gordon's career as police commissioner. Given Gordon's growing health issues at the time, Hill forced the commissioner to accept Bullock as an aide. (*Detective Comics* #527, June 1983) Thereafter, the twenty-year veteran, already a

sloppy dresser and overweight, developed clumsy habits that just happened to spoil one crime scene after another.

Bullock's harassment of Gordon continued unabated, including trashing the commissioner's files. He phoned in a false alarm about a critically wounded Batman, arranging compressed springs in the drawer where Gordon kept his car keys. The collective jolt of the phone call and the springs leaping out at him triggered a heart attack. (*Batman* #364, October 1983)

Bullock felt great guilt and confessed his sins to a comatose Gordon, although he was overheard by Gordon's niece Barbara Gordon. When Hill tried to manipulate events so that Bullock wound up the next commissioner, the cop refused. The newly reformed Bullock was overly zealous in mending his ways, however, so his clumsiness was no longer an act. Hill still wanted Gordon out of office and added revenge against Bullock to his to-do list.

Instead Gordon and Bullock, aided by Batman, slowly built up a corruption case against Hill. The mayor attempted to kill Detective Bullock but severely wounded him instead. As Bullock recuperated, Batman orchestrated events to expose Hill's villainy on television, leading to his quiet surrender to Gordon. A recovered Bullock joined Gordon in a carefully choreographed double-teaming of the next mayor, George P. Skowcroft, putting him on notice that things had to remain on the straight and narrow.

It was Bullock who first noticed that Jason Todd seemed smaller and younger than the previous Robin and brought his suspicions to Gordon. The commissioner knew all about the second Boy Wonder and confirmed Bullock's theory. This led

Bullock and Robin to form a friendship highlighted by their work together to stop the Film Freak. (*Batman* #395–396, May–June 1986)

Bullock once attended a detective convention in Las Vegas alongside such luminaries as Jonny Double, Christopher Chance, Jonni Thunder, and Angel O'Day (*Crisis on Infinite Earths* #11, February 1986). He was also sent to Washington, D.C., for a three-week seminar that would change his life. While there, his running vocal commentary caught the attention of seminar organizer Harry Stein. More importantly, Bullock's sharp detective skills helped Stein locate a missing quarry, and the two quickly returned to Gotham City on the hunt. (*Vigilante* #45–46, September–October 1987)

In the wake of their success, Bullock remained a liaison with the federal government. When Stein took control of the espionage agency Checkmate, he offered Bullock a position as Bishop. Bullock, uncertain of the future, took a leave of absence from the force and retained his rent-controlled apartment while relocating to Washington. (*Checkmate!* #1, April 1988)

Despite his successes with Checkmate, Gotham remained his home. When the Joker brutally shot Barbara Gordon and captured the commissioner, Bullock rushed to Gotham. (*Batman: The Killing Joke,* 1988) He did eventually leave Checkmate, and his first case back home was an investigation of the Garbage Man murders. (*Batman: Turning Points* #3, 2000)

Bullock was seen as a larger-than-life member of Gotham's Major Crimes Unit. He had a reputation that was less than stellar, with accusations flying about that he took bribes, used brutality to accomplish his goals, and was in the pocket of organized crime.

AUTOMATIC ASSAULT RIFLES, ANTI-PERSONNEL MINES, MORTARS, HEAVY MACHINEGUNS, FRAGMENTATION GRENADES...

...AN' EVEN A FEW CRATES O' SHOULDER-LAUNCHED STINGER MISSILES.

PIZZA KITCHEN

He spoke out regularly against the vigilante tactics employed by Batman and grudgingly collaborated on cases when there was no other choice. He was partnered at this time with Renee Montoya and the two, at first, did not work well together. (*Detective Comics* #644, May 1992)

When Batman was injured by Bane and replaced by Jean-Paul Valley, Bullock found himself almost approving of the new Batman's far more brutal methods. However, when Bullock realized that Valley had killed Abattoir before learning the whereabouts of a victim, he turned on the new Caped Crusader. (*Shadow of the Bat* #28, June 1994)

Bullock nearly died soon after when the KGBeast tossed a metal drum at the cop. Robin performed lifesaving CPR, and Bullock remained in a coma for more than three days. One of his duty nurses, Charlotte, agreed to go out with him after his discharge. Their budding relationship was cut short when a would-be carjacker approached them after a date. As Bullock reached for the keys, the criminal panicked and fired, mortally wounding Charlotte. (*Batman* #520, July 1995)

Bullock had trouble adjusting in the aftermath and went beyond reason in dealing with Mister Polka Dot, resulting in Montoya requesting a new partner. The disgruntled cop was then partnered with Kevin Soong, although it proved a short-lived relationship after Soong retired early, the result of being wounded in the line of duty. (*Batman: GCPD* #1–4, August–November 1996)

Some time after that, Bullock received a tempting offer from Black Mask. The deranged criminal offered him a data disk filled with incriminating information on most of Gotham's active underworld, in exchange for the criminal Johnny Poodles avoiding trial and being set free. Bullock played his own game against Black Mask, though, accepting the disk and secretly using its information for a stunning string of arrests. He also infiltrated Black Mask's False Face Society in an attempt to find enough information to take down Johnny Poodles. It required the Batman's help, but the criminals were ultimately arrested, and Bullock provided the testimony that sealed Poodles's fate. (*Batman: Bullock's Law* #1, 1999)

Bullock broke his arm during the case, and he piled on other injuries as Gotham City endured a devastating earthquake that led to its being cut off from the federal government. The doughnut-loving detective remained an active and useful member of the force, though, beloved by his brothers and sisters in blue. He burnished his reputation by remaining in Gotham after the government withdrew its support during the yearlong time known as No Man's Land. It was during that year that Tim Drake, the third Robin, earned Bullock's respect. Bullock, battered and torn, helped keep the fragile peace alongside Gordon. The scarcity of supplies forced him to finally break his doughnut habit, lose weight, lower his cholesterol, and give up smoking his beloved cigars.

As the city prepared to reopen to the rest of the country, Gordon promoted Bullock to lieutenant and placed him in charge of the Major Crimes Unit. (*Detective Comics* #742, March 2000)

From Bullock's perspective, there would be no crime more major than the shooting of Gordon on his birthday (*Batman* #587, March 2001) and the fact that his assailant, Jordan Reynolds, would go free. Bullock went so far as to stop Montoya from breaking the law to get at Reynolds, who was enrolled in the federal Witness Protection Program.

The next time anyone saw Jordan Reynolds's apartment, it had been stripped of all its contents, a trail of blood leading out its shattered door frame. (*Batman: Gotham Knights* #13, March 2001) Suspected but never convicted of killing Reynolds, Bullock was finally disgraced enough to leave the G.C.P.D. Briefly he attempted a new career as a private eye, but he soon fell into depression and alcoholism.

Some six months after Batman left Gotham City in the wake of the events known as Infinite Crisis, Bullock was reinstated to the G.C.P.D. The details of his second career are thus far unrevealed. When the Dark Knight returned, Bullock buried the hatchet, establishing a more cordial working relationship.

BULOW, BRAINY

Brainy Bulow led a trio of criminals who preyed on their fellow villains. After being released from prison, Bulow and the others would seek out wanted criminals, capture them, and collect the reward. Having done too good a job, the bounty hunters decided to break convicts out of prison, let them run free, and then round them up after a reward was posted. Batman and Robin put an end to the unscrupulous business. (*Detective Comics* #92, October 1944)

BURKE, TOMMY

Tommy Burke was a member of the Gotham City Police Department's Major Crimes Unit, working the day shift and partnered with Dagmar Procjnow. Burke was close to Commissioner James Gordon, as witnessed by his presence at the birthday party where the commissioner was shot. Considered the ladies' man of the MCU, he also had a big mouth tempered by his sense of humor and poker-playing skill. (*Detective Comics* #748, September 2000)

BURNS, BOSTON

Boston Burns, an ex-convict, decided that for criminals to succeed, they needed to be as well trained as the police officers they opposed. As a result, he established a training academy on Devers Island. The rigorous training covered physical and mental disciplines, and it eventually came to Batman's attention. He disguised himself and joined the academy, claiming to be a fugitive. An accidental explosion tore his clothes, revealing his Batman costume underneath, but Batman prevailed, aided by the timely arrival of Robin and a contingent of US Coast Guard officers. The academy was quickly put out of business. (*World's Finest Comics* #51, April/May 1951)

BURR, JASON

One of a pair of twins who shared a psychic bond, he was stolen at birth and raised to be the head of the Kobra Cult. He later terrorized the world in the guise of Kobra.

BURR, JOE

When Joe Burr escaped from prison, he abducted Professor Norenz, wishing to use the scientist's noteworthy shrinking ray. Burr had hoped the ray would reduce him to three inches tall, making it easy for him to be smuggled out of the country in a shipment of toys. Instead he and his henchmen were thwarted by Batman and Robin. (*Batman* #145, February 1962)

BURTON, HENRY

Henry Burton, the manager of Thompson's Luxury Shop, stole gems from the store's jewelry department and then hid them in the toy department. Members of "Muscles" Malone's gang would then buy the specific toys, legally removing them from the store. Eventually the scheme was exposed and everyone arrested by Batman and Robin. (*Batman* #11, June/July 1942)

BUSH, HENRY

Henry Bush was Bruce Wayne's personal attorney until Wayne exposed him as a forger and embezzler. He did this by faking his own death in an auto accident and then eavesdropping on the reading of his will, which Bush had altered to leave the bulk of the Wayne Family fortune to a dummy company he secretly controlled. (*Batman* #40, April/May 1947)

BYRUS

On one of Batman and Robin's time-travel trips courtesy of Professor Carter Nichols, the Dynamic Duo encountered Byrus, a Persian villain in the fifth century BC. Byrus attempted to disrupt the Olympic Games in Athens by setting up a Persian invasion; he was stopped by Batman, Robin, and a variety of Greek athletes. (*Batman* #38, December 1946/January 1947)

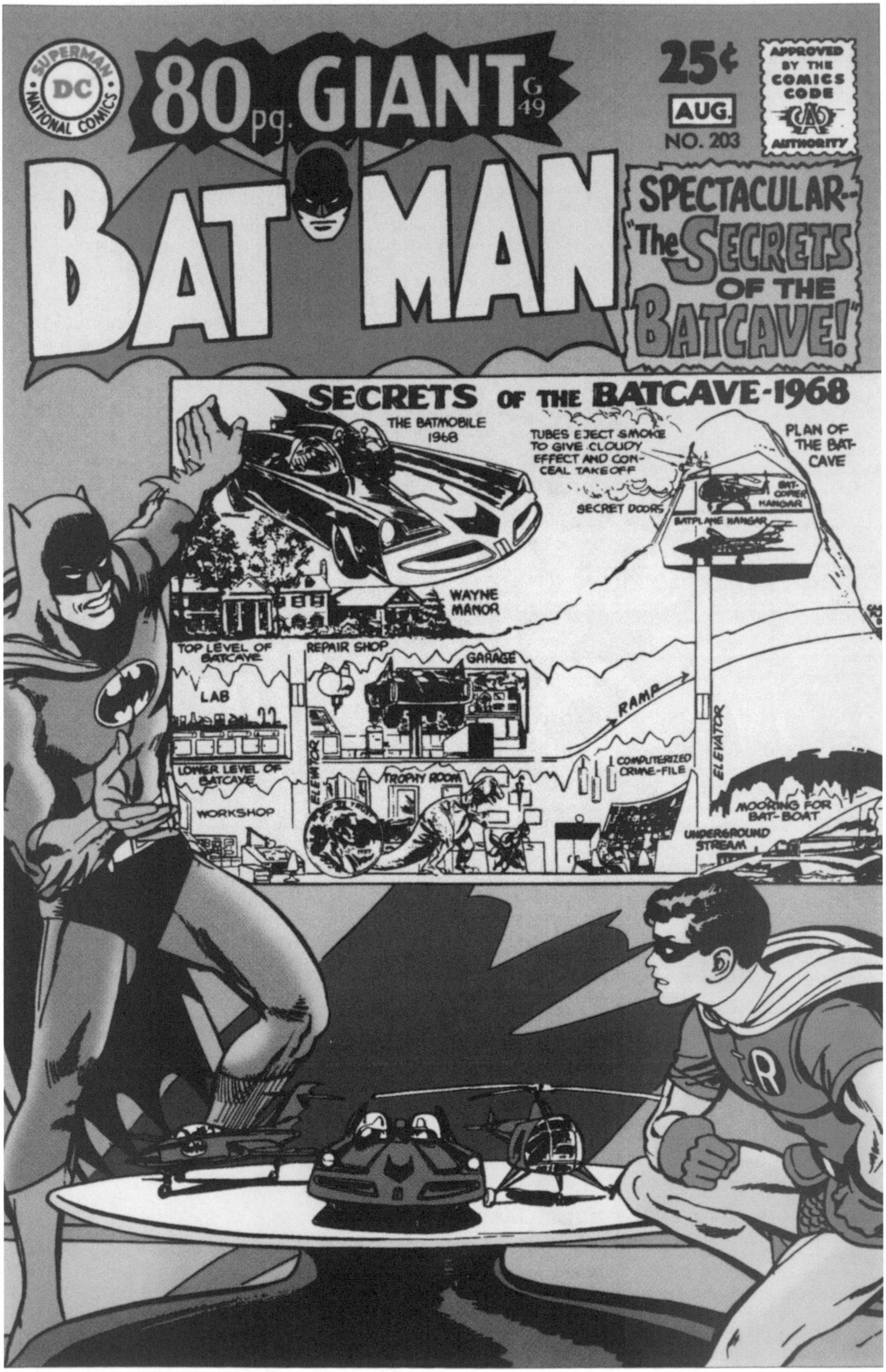
SUPERMAN
DC
NATIONAL COMICS
80 pg. GIANT
G 49
25¢
AUG.
NO. 203
APPROVED BY THE COMICS CODE AUTHORITY
BATMAN
SPECTACULAR--
"The SECRETS OF THE BATCAVE!"
SECRETS OF THE BATCAVE-1968
THE BATMOBILE 1968
TUBES EJECT SMOKE TO GIVE CLOUDY EFFECT AND CONCEAL TAKEOFF
PLAN OF THE BAT-CAVE
BAT-COPTER HANGAR
SECRET DOORS
BATPLANE HANGAR
WAYNE MANOR
TOP LEVEL OF BATCAVE
REPAIR SHOP
GARAGE
LAB
RAMP
ELEVATOR
ELEVATOR
LOWER LEVEL OF BATCAVE
TROPHY ROOM
COMPUTERIZED CRIME-FILE
WORKSHOP
MOORING FOR BAT-BOAT
UNDERGROUND STREAM

CAIN

Cain and his brother Abel were mythic archetypes known for participating in the first homicide. The sons of Adam and Eve, the two were inextricably linked from conception. According to the Bible, Cain traveled to the Land of Nod—which was revealed to be an aspect of the realm known as the Dreaming. Dream of the Endless invited them both to live in his realm. There Cain was seen as a tall, thin, bearded man with glasses who lived in a structure known as the House of Mystery. He would spin yarns to any who would listen to him. (*House of Mystery* #75, July/August 1968)

With Abel living next door in the House of Secrets, the two would get together frequently. Each time Cain would give in to his bloodlust and slay his brother. And each time, Abel would be restored.

At one point BRUCE WAYNE was on a cruise and wound up interacting with Cain in a supernatural case as the Batman. (*The Brave and the Bold* #93, December 1970/January 1971)

CAIN, CASSANDRA

The daughter of DAVID CAIN and LADY SHIVA, Cassandra Cain was raised to be a living weapon until she rejected her training and sought her own destiny. (*Batman* #567, July 1999)

David Cain was a member of RÃ'S AL GHÜL'S LEAGUE OF ASSASSINS, hoping to perfect a fighting style that would one day result in an ideal warrior who could serve as the nearly immortal leader's bodyguard. Cain's training methods continued in earnest but kept falling short, and he determined that he needed the perfect woman to provide the right child to train. His research led him to Detroit and the Wu-San sisters, who had studied martial arts from a young age and communicated in ways unique to the siblings. In observing Carolyn and her younger sister, Sandra, he noted that Sandra would hold back for fear of hurting her sister. To win Sandra over and bring her to the emotional point he felt was necessary, Cain killed Carolyn, letting her sister find the corpse. Sandra wanted revenge and began seeking the killer, which led her to the League and a trap laid by Cain. As she fought for her freedom, Sandra experienced the epiphany Cain sought: She needed to let go and be the fighter she could be. Cain offered to spare her life, saving her from the League, if she agreed to bear his child and let him raise it alone. Sandra agreed and resumed training, becoming the world's greatest living martial artist, LADY SHIVA. Her goal was to one day stop her daughter from performing great evil.

Cassandra, named for the mythological being who could see the future, was raised to understand the people around her by their body language alone. As a result, she never learned speech. The method proved effective, and she grew up to handle the cloistered world of the League without discomfort.

By age eight Cassandra was deemed ready for her first assignment: to kill a randomly selected executive. As Cain recorded her actions, Cassandra played the "game"—which is how her father explained the job—and killed the man. She knew exactly the moment to strike and delivered the killing blow, but its aftermath shocked her. The youth concluded that what she had trained to do was wrong, and so she ran away.

Cassandra spent the next decade on her own, racked with guilt over her crime. She entered GOTHAM CITY just as the federal government was withdrawing its support, cutting off the city from the rest of America. The NO MAN'S LAND year proved taxing to Gotham's citizens, but to Cassandra it was ripe with opportunities. She came to ORACLE'S attention, and the crime fighter provided the teen shelter and friendship. When Cassandra learned of Oracle's efforts—along with those of Batman, ROBIN, NIGHTWING, and others—to preserve order, she wanted to participate. Oracle, the first BATGIRL, initially demurred, until Cassandra saved Police Commissioner JAMES GORDON's life. Then she was allowed to work with the others and was given a Batgirl costume with the former Batgirl's blessing. This outfit covered her entire face and was entirely black. Despite being given a version of the UTILITY BELT complete with bat-tools, Cassandra rarely employed any of them, preferring to use her hands and feet to do the work.

Over time Oracle began to teach Cassandra words and concepts that proved taxing to the teen. In fact, her brain had developed in such a way that learning to speak and read was very difficult. At first she spoke in simple sentences, similar to those of a two-year-old.

Even though Batman learned of Cassandra's crime, he had enough experience with her to see that she truly intended to fight for justice.

When contact with a telepath resulted in her brain being altered, allowing her to master language, Cassandra suddenly had to retrain herself. While she could suddenly speak in complete sentences and at length, she could no longer "read" people's motions and act accordingly; thus she now had to modify her approach to every aspect of her life. Desperate to be allowed to continue her crime-fighting work, Cassandra sought out Lady Shiva and asked the woman to help her retrain, unaware of their intimate link. Shiva accepted the request with the understanding that in one year's time,

leaving Cassandra dead. Shiva, feeling Cassandra had a death wish, brought her back to life, and the fight continued. It became apparent that, for entirely separate reasons, both females harbored death wishes; their battle ended in a draw.

In the wake of a devastating crime wave in Gotham, both Batgirl and Robin briefly relocated to BLÜDHAVEN. There she made friends with a few civilians, which enhanced her understanding of the world she had chosen to protect. While in her new city, she fought the PENGUIN's criminal operation and defeated RAVAGER, daughter of DEATHSTROKE THE TERMINATOR. Batman used her on undercover assignments; once she infiltrated a splinter JUSTICE LEAGUE OF AMERICA operation as the masked fighter Kasumi. (*Justice League Elite* #1, September 2004)

Finally Cassandra decided to seek out her birth mother, and she put together enough clues to point toward Lady Shiva. When the two women again confronted each other, it caused a split among the League, which was still reeling from the recent death of Rā's al Ghūl. Al Ghūl's daughter NYSSA RAATKO had recognized Cassandra as the prophesied "One who is All," prompting half the League to declare its allegiance to her. The rest sided with her mother, Lady Shiva. This prompted a civil war, and during the fight MAD DOG—one of David Cain's earlier prototypes—wounded Cassandra. Shiva saved her daughter's life, dipping her in a LAZARUS PIT. Revived, Cassandra came to recognize that her mother would never stop being a killer, and once more they fought. Shiva was severely injured, and she begged her daughter not to use the pit. Instead Cassandra left the paralyzed woman hanging over the pit, seemingly to die there. Shiva survived, escaped, and healed out of sight.

No longer feeling worthy of the uniform, Cassandra abandoned her Batgirl identity and took to once more wandering the world. Deathstroke found her and manipulated the lost woman into joining his side in his latest campaign against the TEEN TITANS. Part of the plan saw her resume her role as the League's leader (*Robin* [second series] #150, July 2006) and saw Tim Drake as another wounded soul and potential ally. She convinced him to break David Cain out of prison, and as he did her bidding, she began killing Cain's other students. When her father was before her, she ordered Drake to kill him but the Teen Wonder refused. As Batgirl and Robin struggled, an explosion separated them and allowed Cain to escape.

She returned to leading the League as assassins for hire, going so far as to take a contract on Supergirl's life. (*Supergirl* [sixth series] #14, March 2007) Prepared with swords imbued with red solar energy, she gave the Maid of Steel a fight for her life. Cassandra survived the battle, as did Supergirl, and they next confronted each other during a battle against the Teen Titans, which was Deathstroke's ultimate goal. During the struggle, Robin realized Deathstroke had her in his thrall by injecting her with a drug. After a rematch with Ravager, she was finally freed when Robin injected her with a counteragent. Even though Batgirl switched sides and helped subdue Deathstroke, Nightwing arrived

they would meet and fight. All it took was a single night for Shiva to teach her daughter everything she needed to know.

Batgirl continued to fight crime in Gotham City, receiving additional training in fighting and detective work from Batman, Robin, and ONYX. The Dark Knight taught her the Navajo language, which in some ways bridged her two manners of communication. Cassandra proved pivotal in helping clear BRUCE WAYNE of murder charges,

though the incident grew complicated when it turned out the true killer was her own father. She also got to meet other costumed heroes, enjoying brief flirtations here and there, something entirely new to her. A friendship blossomed with SPOILER, although Cassandra had a habit of giving her friend a concussion rather than let her participate in battles she was clearly unprepared for.

A year passed, and Cassandra and Lady Shiva kept their appointment. The fight was brutal and brief,

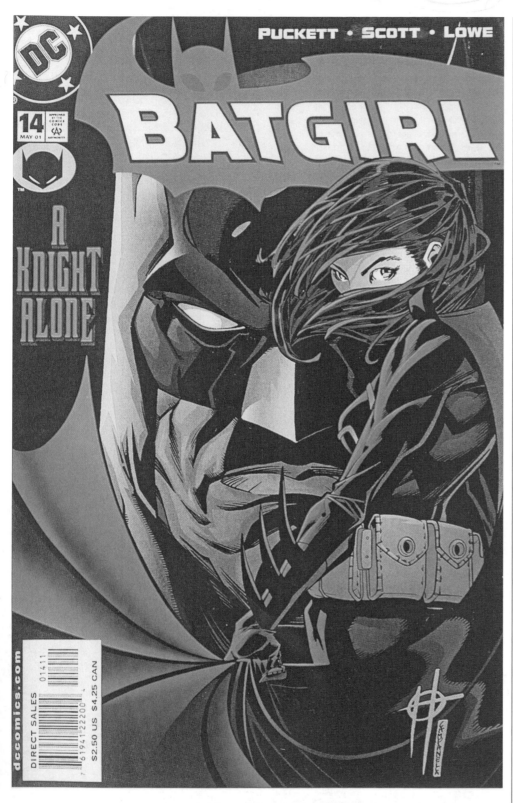

PUCKETT • SCOTT • LOWE

BATGIRL

14
MAY 01

A KNIGHT ALONE

teenage BRUCE WAYNE in the ways of mortal combat as the orphan prepared for his career as Batman.

To Cain, intense preparation was essential to becoming a successful assassin. He devised a training method that would ensure the fighter could read an opponent's actions and determine the appropriate course in advance of the actual movement. Over time Cain employed this training on young children, hoping to create the ideal assassin. His goal was to one day create the perfect bodyguard for the League's leader, the near-immortal RÃ's AL GHŪL. Cain's efforts repeatedly came close but ended in failure—although he nearly succeeded with a boy who grew up to be the psychotic killer known as MAD DOG.

Cain decided that his failure stemmed from imperfect breeding and sought a genetic path to his goal. He began searching the globe for the right woman to bear the desired child, whose training would begin from birth. The hunt led him to the Wu-San sisters in Detroit. Carolyn and Sandra were accomplished martial artists, even at a young age, and frequently sparred. They communicated in the sort of unique language usually associated with twins—but it worked for the girls. Cain felt himself drawn emotionally to Sandra, and in watching her he discovered that the younger Wu-San girl would allow Carolyn the victory rather than bring her harm.

To win Sandra over and bring her to the emotional point he felt was necessary, Cain killed Carolyn, letting her sister find the corpse. Sandra wanted

in time to prevent her from killing him in a vicious act of revenge. (*Teen Titans* [third series] #43–45, March–May 2007)

Her whereabouts after this incident remain unrecorded, but she clearly made amends with Batman, who added her as a replacement member of his re-formed Outsiders. (*Batman and the Outsiders* [second series] #2, February 2008)

CAIN, DAVID

David Cain was a master assassin and key figure in the international organization known as the LEAGUE OF ASSASSINS. He trained numerous people as assassins, most notably his daughter CASSANDRA CAIN, who became BATGIRL. (*Batman* #567, July 1999)

Cain's background remained largely unexplored, but he was known to be one of the people to train revenge and began seeking the killer, which led her to the League and a trap laid by Cain. As she fought for her freedom, Sandra experienced the epiphany Cain sought: She needed to let go and be the fighter she could be. Cain offered to spare her life, saving her from the League, if she agreed to bear his child and let him raise it alone. Sandra accepted. In time she gave birth to a girl whom Cain named Cassandra. After Cain took the child away, Sandra set out to complete her training and became Lady Shiva, the world's greatest martial artist.

Cain raised Cassandra as he desired, teaching her to read people's body language. Her intensive training did not allow Cassandra to learn speech; instead she studied one fighting discipline after another, getting faster and learning how to handle a wide variety of opponents.

At age eight Cassandra was deemed ready for a field test. Cain picked a businessman at random and set her loose. She performed as expected, thrilling her father. However, when she realized she'd taken a life, Cassandra rebelled and ran away. Cain was left with nothing to show for his investment of time except the knowledge that his system worked. He truly loved his daughter, and he recognized that in some ways he had failed her entirely.

Some time later Cain left the League and became an independent contractor. He accepted a contract from Lex Luthor to frame Bruce Wayne for murder. Cain created an almost perfect plan, killing Vesper Fairchild and letting the police believe that Wayne had committed the crime. In taking the contract, Cain knew it would bring him to Gotham City and closer to his daughter, whom he had come to recognize as the city's latest Batgirl. It also meant that Cain would interact with Wayne, a man he had trained but could not teach to actually kill, a choice that initially baffled him.

Batman's allies rallied to investigate and clear Wayne, leaving Cain disheartened. He finally revealed himself and fought Batman, losing the struggle and choosing to turn himself in to face American justice. While in custody, he survived a murder attempt by Deadshot, hired by Luthor to avoid being implicated in the Fairchild murder case. Cain chose to allow Deadshot to succeed but realized he wanted to remain alive for Cassandra. He subsequently broke out of Blackgate Penitentiary to leave his daughter a birthday gift. His relationship with Cassandra remained complicated, and despite her efforts, he refused to reveal the name of her birth mother. (*Batman* #606, October 2002)

One year later Batgirl manipulated Robin into bringing David Cain from prison to the League of Assassins. The Teen Wonder thought he was doing this as ransom to free Batgirl, but she revealed herself to be the League's new leader. She explained to Robin that she needed her father dead so no other children such as Mad Dog or herself would ever be trained to kill. She handed Robin a gun and asked him to pull the trigger. When he refused to kill Cain and join her in the League, they fought; Cassandra wound up shooting her father. When Robin and Batgirl continued the fight, there was an explosion that separated the two and apparently allowed the wounded Cain to escape. His whereabouts remain unrecorded. (*Batgirl* #73, April 2006)

CAIRD, JAY

Jay Caird was a scientist who chose crime over research and was sentenced to jail for espionage. After serving his time, he returned to his lawless ways and stole an experimental ultrasonic beam projector from the Gotham Trust company. Caird and his hired men were stopped by Batman and Robin before they could get away with the device. Caird turned the projector on the Dynamic Duo with the unexpected side effect of temporary amnesia so complete, they no longer recalled their secret identities. After figuring out their alter egos, the confident crime fighters apprehended Caird and his mob. (*Detective Comics* #234, August 1956)

CALCULATOR

Once a costumed criminal, the Calculator became the underworld's information broker and ultimately assumed control over the secret Society. (*Detective Comics* #463, September 1976)

Noah Kuttler used his scientific genius to design hardware that generated "hard light" constructs to aid in his criminal pursuits. A victim of obsessive-compulsive disorder, he treated his condition with medication, which allowed him to focus on his inventions. In addition to creating these objects, the Calculator was also able to access computer networks, traveling through network connections.

For phase one of his master plan, the Calculator took on the Atom while attempting to steal an earthquake-inhibiting device from Ray Palmer's friend Richard Bagley. In this Ivy Town battle, the Calculator demonstrated the variety of shapes his oversized equipment could generate, from a ring of fire to pure energy in the shape of a hand, to keep the Tiny Titan at bay. As the Atom beat the Calculator senseless, the Mighty Mite missed seeing the Calculator press the asterisk button on his chest-mounted keypad.

He next surfaced in Star City during a heat wave that threatened to mar the city's Tricentennial celebration. The Calculator tried to increase the heat, effectively stealing Founder's Day from the citizens until he was stopped by the Black Canary. He did, though, manage to escape, and again he threatened Star City, this time by using his advanced gear to literally stretch its citizenry into malformed shapes. A visiting Elongated Man spoiled the chaos Kuttler hoped to ignite, but once more he eluded capture. His third and final appearance in Star City was during the World Series when he threatened to steal every baseball used in the games between the Star City Stars and Gotham City Giants. Green Arrow, on hand to fire a first-pitch arrow, managed to thwart the ploy. By this point three more heroes had been engaged and recorded by Kuttler's computerized costume.

The Calculator moved on to Midway City where he challenged Hawkman, trying to prevent him from bringing in a nuclear scientist to repair an atomic facility that threatened the city. Again the Calculator was stopped and the asterisk key pressed. The Winged Wonder grew suspicious of the costumed villain and took his concerns to the World's Greatest Detective, Batman.

Together they suspected that the Calculator was gathering intelligence on America's super heroes—a theory borne out by a subsequent attack on Gotham City. Then, thanks to the Flash's absence, the Calculator struck twice in Central City. Batman finally figured out a ploy in which the Calculator wound up trapping himself, allowing the heroes to put an end to the bizarre spree. (*Detective Comics* #468, March/April 1977)

When he resurfaced some time later, Kuttler had modified his equipment and fought other heroes, including a rematch with the Atom and an encounter with the second Blue Beetle. (*Blue Beetle* #8, January 1987) At one point he was arrested and was said to be serving three consecutive life terms for his crimes.

The Calculator escaped and attempted to gain revenge against the heroes Coordinator and Stretch by attacking them through their affiliation with the vigilantes-for-hire organization Hero Hotline. The exact nature of their conflict was never recorded.

Kuttler admitted that his career in costume

was fruitless and turned his attentions to using his technological skills in new ways. He built up a massive computer network and database, styling himself as a go-between for criminals in need of help and a seemingly endless supply of allies and henchmen. In exchange, he would receive a percentage or negotiated flat fee for his efforts. As his expertise and reputation grew, Kuttler began charging a thousand dollars per question as an expert. (*Identity Crisis* #1, August 2004)

Given his knowledge and connections, he was approached by Lex Luthor to join a nascent society of villains, hoping to ensure that super heroes never again used their powers to alter the minds and memories of villains. After discovering that Zatanna had done just that to Dr. Light, a sense of urgency spread among the villainous fraternity. What Kuttler didn't know at the time was that this Lex Luthor was, in reality, Alexander Luthor, sole survivor of Earth-3 and an escapee from a Limbo that enabled him to survive the events known as Crisis on Infinite Earths. (*Countdown to Infinite Crisis,* 2005)

In the aftermath of the events known as Infinite Crisis, Luthor was exposed and ultimately died, but the need for an organized villain operation remained. Kuttler took over the leadership role and saw to it that the villains remained loyal, sending agents after those who chose to remain rogue.

He also grew obsessed with tracking down, exposing, and destroying his heroic counterpart, Oracle. Frustration over not succeeding drove Kuttler to the point of a nervous breakdown. Having ceased taking his medication, Kuttler suffered from nightmares featuring the green wireframe face that was Oracle's online persona. (*Birds of Prey* #87, December 2005)

CALENDAR MAN

The Calendar Man was a costumed criminal who plagued Batman from the early days of his career in Gotham City. (*Detective Comics* #259, September 1958)

Julian Gregory Day, the Calendar Man, first came to the attention of law enforcement when he audaciously attacked the Gotham City Planetarium. Dressed like the man from the moon, he stole priceless stamps that had been hand-canceled on the lunar surface by astronauts. His costumed antics and broad approach to crime marked him as both a deranged thief and a thrill-seeking exhibitionist. In time he came to appreciate matching wits with Batman; he once admitted that even though killing the Dark Knight would be a red-letter day, the days that followed would be hollow.

The Calendar Man based his crimes on elements taken from across history—which on the one hand made him predictable, and on the other made him a challenge to apprehend. He sported sixteen different outfits during his first three crime sprees, to the delight of the press and the consternation of the Gotham City Police Department. Briefly the Calendar Man worked out of a ground-level headquarters that was a shrine to timekeeping devices. Batman was at first confounded by the plethora of high-tech gear the Calendar Man employed—from lasers to sonic weaponry—but finally found an approach leading to Day's apprehension.

The Batman and Captain James Gordon offered the incarcerated Day a deal: If he provided them with information and analysis regarding a similarly themed murderer known only as Holiday, Gordon would have Day's sentence commuted to time served. Day agreed to help and even accurately determined the killer to be a woman, which was partly correct. (*Batman: The Long Halloween* #3, February 1997; #8, July 1997; #12, November 1997) It later turned out that Holiday was both a man, Alberto Falcone, and a woman, Gilda Dent. When Batman apprehended Falcone, he wound up in a cell facing Day at Arkham Asylum. By this time Day had the months of the year tattooed around his shaved head. (*Batman: Dark Victory* #0, 1999)

When a new killer, dubbed the Hangman, began

a spree in Gotham, the deaths were also linked to the calendar. Former district attorney HARVEY DENT broke Day out of Arkham and put him on a mock trial with other costumed felons as his jury. Dent tried to determine if Day was Hangman. Day continued to profess that he never condoned murder, and it was more likely Dent—not Day—who was the murderer. Day was freed and took advantage of the two-way mirrors and secret passages Dent had installed in Falcone's home. When Falcone was paroled from Arkham, he heard voices, which he interpreted as his dead father urging him to go back to murdering others and then commit suicide. Driven to the edge, Falcone finally realized his father would never ask him to do these things, and he fired at the mirror from which the voice was emerging. Day was on the other side, and fired his pistol as well. Day was incensed that others would steal his motif, and other costumed criminals soon made Gotham forget about the Calendar Man. (*Batman: Dark Victory* #7, June 2000; #11, October 2000; #12, November 2000) Batman and Gordon arrived two hours later to find Day on the Falcone property, his jaw broken. Falcone soon after succumbed to the wound he'd received from Day. (*Batman: Dark Victory* #13, December 2000)

The Calendar Man quickly returned to his over-the-top crimes, seeking the spotlight. No other criminal was bold enough to challenge Batman and ROBIN in print, so Day took to announcing his criminal plans in the *Gotham Gazette,* daring the Dynamic Duo to stop him.

The timely criminal appeared in one-off costumes until settling on a red-and-white number that featured calendar pages for a cape. In addition to his spectacular solo crimes, he was recruited on several occasions for larger capers. He was once freed from prison by the ecoterrorist RÄ'S AL GHÜL and actually refused to join the mass attack on the Dark Knight. (*Batman* #400, October 1986)

His losses to Batman finally dried up his financial resources, and he was forced to remain in his one costume. As a result, he partnered with CATMAN and Chancer in KILLER MOTH's scheme to kidnap BRUCE WAYNE, Mayor ARMAND KROL, and Commissioner Gordon for a ten-million-dollar ransom. He showed a marked difference from his peers, known as the Misfits, when he insisted the hostages not be killed—something Killer Moth was more than ready to do. (*Batman: Shadow of the Bat* #7–9, December 1992–February 1993)

Another failed attempt at working in a group saw Calendar Man recruited by the criminal 2000 Committee, along with the CLOCK KING, Chronos, and the Time Commander, in an attempt to overthrow the federal government. They were stopped, despite their timely planning, by the TEAM TITANS, with Day having some of his hair burned off by Battalion. (*Team Titans* #13–15, October–December 1993) The time thieves actually reteamed again, now seeking a device that would enable them to travel through time with ease. Instead they found themselves trapped in a temporal loop until the Time Commander shattered his powerful hourglass. (*Showcase '94* #10, October 1994)

The repeated time-traveling events left Day's

mind rattled, and it took him some time to sort nightmares from reality. In one nightmare, he imagined his bald-headed incarnation as a jailer at Arkham. (*Superman* #160, September 2000) Regardless, Day faced trial for his latest crimes and was sentenced to prison, once more experiencing a psychotic breakdown that led to his return to Arkham. He was freed when BANE released all the inmates. He fled to try his luck in Century City, only to be thwarted by Power Girl. This time he was sent to BLACKGATE PENITENTIARY until an earthquake destroyed the facility.

Day remained in Gotham even after the federal government withdrew its support. After surviving in the NO MAN'S LAND, he eventually turned himself over to the law and was sent back to a rebuilt Arkham. There a radical therapy was attempted: placing him in a darkened room, away from calendars and reminders of time's passage. Rather than help, the solitary confinement seemed to shatter his psyche. After additional therapy, Day was surprisingly paroled.

He was not at all cured, however, and grew obsessed with the time that had passed—the events and holidays he had missed—while in Arkham. Dressed in a new costume, the Calendar Man now wore predominantly red, including hood and cape, with gold shoulder pads and belt and an Egyptian motif that included a pharaoh's mask and a sacred ibis on his chest. He spent five months recruiting henchmen and planning a new wave of amazing crimes. The Dynamic Duo concluded that his crimes were based on ancient calendars, not the modern-day Gregorian version. The villain grew more brazen and actually resorted to mass murder when he used a shoulder-mounted rifle to fire a missile that destroyed an airliner with two hundred people aboard.

Batman used his MATCHES MALONE persona to force the underworld to team up and bring Calendar Man to justice. They took down the henchman, but Day himself remained free as he threatened a nuclear power plant with a bazooka. Batman arrived in time to spoil the shot and save Gotham. Day was arrested, tried, found guilty, and sentenced to eight years in prison. (*Batman 80-Page Giant* #3, 2000)

CALLENDER, ROB

Rob Callender worked in a twenty-first-century laboratory, but an accidental explosion he caused propelled him back approximately one hundred years in time. Arriving in GOTHAM CITY, Callender quickly determined where he was and chose to take advantage of his circumstances. In short order he hired several henchmen and began a spree of crimes that at first confounded police, given their innocuous nature. To Callender, they were priceless, because he knew the stolen property would all wind up in Batman's BATCAVE trophy room. His hope was to bring these objects back home with him and then sell them to the highest bidder. Batman and ROBIN deduced Callender's true nature and apprehended his men. Before Callender himself could be taken into custody, the accident's effects wore off and he returned to his proper era. (*World's Finest Comics* #11, Fall 1943)

CALVINO, SAUL

The criminal better known to law enforcement officials as the costumed killer STILETTO.

CAMEO, CAMILLA

The criminal better known to law enforcement officials as costumed killer the MIME.

CANALVILLE

Located two hours north of Gotham City, Canalville was described as "a sleepy small town that's been running downhill since the canal was abandoned decades ago." Its park included a statue dedicated to a Civil War hero and was the site for one of the Batman and JOKER's many confrontations. (*The Brave and the Bold* #111, February/March 1974)

CANARY

When the PENGUIN opened a nightclub in Florida, he hired a physician's-assistant-turned-singer named Canary as his headliner. She worked alongside Buzzard Benny and Joe Crow, imported from GOTHAM CITY, as the BIRD HOUSE fronted a criminal enterprise. A swimming Canary was rescued by Batman when she was attacked by a squid. Fortunately for her, BRUCE WAYNE happened to be vacationing near where the Bird House was located.

She told the story of this daring rescue to the PENGUIN, which put him on the alert—much as her presence made the Caped Crusader suspicious about the nightclub. During the investigation, ROBIN was captured and used as bait. Batman arrived soon after and demanded to know where his partner was being held. Benny provided an address, but a smitten Canary warned Batman that it was a trap. Enraged at her betrayal, Benny attempted to shoot the singer; Batman threw himself in front of her, taking two bullets meant for her. The Caped Crusader managed to subdue Benny and then staggered off to free the Boy Wonder.

No sooner did Batman find Robin than he collapsed from his wounds. Canary used her nurse's training to remove the bullets and save Batman's life. Soon after, the Dynamic Duo apprehended Benny, Crow, and the Penguin. Canary decided to give up singing and use her skills as a Red Cross nurse. Before leaving, though, she gave a surprised Batman the kiss she'd always wanted to deliver. (*Batman* #11, June/July 1942)

CAP'N BEN'S WILD ANIMAL ACT

What made Cap'n Ben's animal act unique was that he had his animals perform aboard a showboat. The patrons delighted in the performance and were unaware that the boat was being operated by a trio of criminals—Stilts, Ed, and Pete. Every time the boat docked, people would come aboard for a show . . . while the criminals headed for shore and robbed the neighborhood. They kept their booty hidden beneath the animal cages until they could fence it at other stops along their route. The ploy worked until they came to the attention of Batman and ROBIN, who quickly put them out of business. (*Batman* #170, March 1965)

CAPSHAW, TERRY

Some time after the villain called ORCA was released from the Slabside Penitentiary, she met Terry Capshaw. They were, he joked, the only two straight people at a party thrown by gay mutual acquaintances. He fell in love with her despite her deformity, noting that he liked full-figured girls; she was drawn to him for being a nerd. They were married for about a year, and he loved everything about her and her friends. The notion of costumed villains dropping by on social calls was about the most unnerving part of the marriage for Capshaw. When Orca vanished for a week, he panicked until private investigator JASON BARD interviewed him on Batman's behalf. Bard had been assigned to investigate Orca's disappearance, which was in fact tied to a plot by the GREAT WHITE SHARK to take over Gotham's underworld in the wake of BLACK MASK's death. As Capshaw explained what little he knew of Orca's role in working for the PENGUIN and being recruited by HARVEY DENT to spy on the Penguin for him, Capshaw was shot by the TALLY MAN and killed. (*Detective Comics* #819, July 2006)

CAPTAIN BEN

Ben was the captain of a steamboat that boasted wild animal acts as well as performances by humans. The boat was, however, a front for a sophisticated criminal enterprise. Whenever the boat docked, people flocked in from nearby areas; when the performers took breaks, they would disembark and rob the empty homes. The loot was hidden under animal cages until it could be fenced at subsequent towns along the itinerary. The plan worked until the troupe was apprehended by Batman and ROBIN. (*Batman* #170, March 1965)

CAPTAIN BOOMERANG

Digger Harkness—an Australian brought to America to promote the boomerang as a toy—became a ruthless costumed criminal known as Captain Boomerang. (*The Flash* #117, December 1960)

Raised in poverty, Harkness developed a warped and cynical view of the world and always sought ways to enhance his wealth. He developed an unusual skill with the boomerang and was hired by the Wiggins Toy Company, which wanted a costumed spokesman to entice American children into buying boomerangs. Dressed as Captain Boomerang, Harkness thought he was on his way to fame and fortune but instead found himself mocked by the youthful audiences. Disgusted, Harkness took to a life of crime, using the costume and boomerangs to commit robberies.

In time he developed an aptitude for technology, modifying the boomerangs for uses from flashing blinding light to exploding. Each came in response to his frequent defeat at the hands of Central City's protector, the FLASH. He became a charter member of the Flash's Rogues Gallery, dedicated to defeating the Scarlet Speedster and his successors. At some point he and criminal speedster Meloni Thawne had a brief liaison, which resulted in a son he didn't meet until years later. Hoping to change his fortunes, he and Mirror Master tried to commit crimes in GOTHAM CITY, only to be stopped by Batman.

Captain Boomerang eventually encountered the

Dark Knight again when he served with the secret government operation known as the Suicide Squad. Harkness continued to crave money and took to masquerading as Mirror Master to avoid capture. Later he spent a year on a remote island, which left him missing Australia and reconsidering his life.

Harkness fell on hard times, having difficulties committing enough successful crimes to live on, and took to begging the CALCULATOR for help. During this time he reflected on his past and decided it was time to contact the son, Owen Mercer, he had never seen. The two met and formed a tentative bond, but circumstances prevented anything more.

The Calculator forwarded an assignment that was unusual for Harkness: assassin. Still, hard up for cash, he took the job and stalked JACK DRAKE. TIM DRAKE's father, already on edge in the wake of other recent attacks on the loved ones of costumed crime fighters, had been provided with a gun and one night heard a sound. Drake fired as Harkness simultaneously tossed a razor-sharp boomerang, resulting in each man dying in a pool of blood. (*Identity Crisis* #5, December 2004)

Members of the Rogues Gallery held a full-scale funeral and memorial for their fallen comrade and offered Owen Mercer a spot in their ranks. He joined them and was immediately plunged into a civil war among the Flash's army of villains, centering on the theft of Boomerang's body. The body was eventually recovered, but Boomerang's memories had first been accessed, allowing Mercer to learn the truth behind his parentage. Finally Captain Boomerang was dead and gone, his tortured soul consigned to Hell. (*Flash* #225, August 2005)

CAPTAIN BOOMERANG II

Son of the original CAPTAIN BOOMERANG and Meloni Thawne, Owen Mercer inherited skills from both parents and succeeded his father as the new Captain Boomerang. (*Identity Crisis* #3, October 2004)

Owen grew up never knowing that his father, DIGGER HARKNESS, was the criminal Captain Boomerang. Little has been recorded about his early years or relationship with his mother. Mercer finally met his father when Harkness was going through a rough patch, convinced that the world of super heroes and super-villains had passed him by. The two men managed to form a tentative bond until Captain Boomerang died while killing JACK DRAKE, father to ROBIN III.

It was during this time that Mercer revealed the same skill with boomerangs that his father possessed—but he also demonstrated bursts of superspeed, making many wonder who his mother

might be. For a time members of the FLASH's Rogues Gallery assumed his mother was the Golden Glider, the deceased sister of Captain Cold. When Captain Boomerang's body was stolen by a cadre of former Flash foes, all seemingly working for the government, the other villains launched a war to recover the body. They accessed Harkness's memories and learned that Mercer's mother was Meloni Thawne, member of a family who hated the Flash legacy and also mother to Bart Allen, the hero known as Impulse and, later, the Flash.

In the wake of Harkness's death, the Rogues invited Owen to join them as the new Captain Boomerang, and for a brief time he did just that. They provided him with a sense of belonging, something lacking from his life. In time, though, he began to recognize that he didn't subscribe to their beliefs and code. He remained with the Rogues long enough to be recruited into the secret Society of super-villains. With Captain Cold and Mirror Master, Mercer was assigned by DEATHSTROKE (actually the OUTSIDERS' Arsenal in disguise) to protect a factory from the Outsiders. Sure enough, a fight between teams broke out; when the factory exploded it was the Outsiders, not the Rogues, who saved Mercer's life.

This changed Mercer's focus, and he affiliated himself with the rogue team of heroes. The underground nature of the group appealed to him, and he turned to honing his skills. Unlike his father, Mercer came to rely almost exclusively on one kind of boomerang: a model with razor-sharp edges that he took to calling his "razorrang." He perfected using his short bursts of speed while tossing his weapon with deadly accuracy.

Mercer's edgy nature fit right in with the Outsiders, and he happily performed dirty work as assigned by Arsenal or NIGHTWING, the team's co-leaders. Still, he also felt he had unfinished business with Robin. The two finally met, with Robin expecting a fight. Instead Mercer wanted to apologize for one father killing the other. They even worked together on one of Robin's cases, and although the Teen Wonder came to recognize what Mercer was feeling, he refused to shake the man's hand.

While with the Outsiders, Mercer struck up a close friendship with SUPERGIRL after Kara Zor-El joined the team. They briefly dated, and she gave him the nickname *Boomer*.

CHECKMATE took down the Outsiders, save Nightwing, who managed to infiltrate their headquarters to free his team. After a horrible fight, a deal was cut that saw the Outsiders infiltrating Oolong Island, but things went awry. Batman managed to save the team, and it was then Nightwing turned the Outsiders over to his mentor. (*Outsiders* [third series] #50, November 2007) Immediately, the Dark Knight held auditions to build his new team. Nightwing and Mercer competed until the new hero decided he had nothing left to prove—to Batman or himself. (*Outsiders: Five of a Kind—Nightwing/Boomerang*, 2007) Following in his father's footsteps, he allied himself with the Suicide Squad.

His first assignment with the team saw him apprehend his former fellow Rogues, Heat Wave and Weather Wizard, for the death of the third Flash, Bart Allen. (*All Flash* #1, September 2007)

CAPTAIN LIGHTFOOT

Michael Martin was an Irish-born highwayman who came to the United States in 1818. In his new country he resumed his criminal ways, robbing coaches and their riders, until he was captured and hung in Cambridge, Massachusetts.

The story of Captain Lightfoot, as the horse thief was known, had become a legend accepted as fact until BRUCE WAYNE learned the truth. Apparently a loyal Gothamite, Abel Adams, took on the persona of a highwayman by that name decades earlier, in 1753. Adams did this after learning that Hugo Vorney, a criminal, was selling arms to the nearby Native Americans and inciting them to riot and attack the village of Gotham. Vorney's goal was to get rich supplying arms and ammunition to the citizens of Gotham who needed to defend their homes. Adams, as Captain Lightfoot, intercepted the coaches bearing arms, risking his freedom in an effort to tamp down a chance of war.

Vorney was finally defeated, and a truce established between Natives and colonists, thanks in part to the arrival of a time-traveling Batman and Robin. (*Batman* #79, October/November 1953)

CAPTAIN STINGAREE

KARL CROSSMAN, a convicted criminal, was sent to a Central City jail. There he shared a cell with Len Snart, better known as Captain Cold. After his release, Crossman relocated to GOTHAM CITY, inspired to become a costumed criminal after learning from Snart.

He bought a replica pirate ship and turned it into a restaurant called Stingaree. As owner and greeter, Crossman took to wearing pirate garb including a long purple coat, an orange sash, and a sharp cutlass. The bearded pirate's head was shaved, and he also wore a patch over his left eye—which apparently was truly damaged. While he established himself as a legitimate businessman, Crossman was also working to establish himself in Gotham City's criminal underworld.

Crossman got their attention with his accomplished sword work, but it was his superb tactical skills that earned him a measure of respect. His one flaw was the firmly held belief that Batman could not possibly be a single person, but a team of triplets—private investigators Jerome, Michael, and Robert Courtney—wearing the same uniform and funded by the WAYNE FOUNDATION. As a result, his schemes were based on incorrect data.

Stingaree set out to capture each "Courtney Batman," and he believed he was succeeding until the true Dark Knight turned up and put an end to his scheme. After his initial encounter with Stingaree, Batman learned of his Courtney theory and asked the private investigators to aid him in entrapping the criminal. Completing the ploy, Batman had recruited the FLASH to come to Gotham and lend a hand, dressing as Batman and vanishing in a burst of speed to confuse Stingaree. Once he was captured, it was learned that Crossman held a grudge against the triplets since he was actually their fourth brother and disliked being the black sheep of the family. (Detective Comics #460–461, June-July 1976)

Soon after, Captain Cold helped Captain Stingaree break out of prison and work with CAPTAIN BOOMERANG to begin a new crime spree to prove their superiority. Instead they were stopped by the BLACK CANARY and Captain Comet. (Secret Society of Super-Villains #6, March/April 1977)

Captain Stingaree never again enjoyed the respect and attention he craved as a criminal mastermind. Instead, time and again he was recruited whenever Batman's enemies were gathered en masse. (Batman #291–294, September–December 1977; Detective Comics #526, May 1983; Batman #400, October 1986)

He remained at large after RA'S AL GHŪL freed the costumed felons from prison. At some point he also engaged in a romantic relationship with fellow Batman foe the CAVALIER.

CARDEN, PROFESSOR

Professor Carden developed a miraculous artificial life-form that could morph its metallic body to resemble anyone thanks to the special helmet it wore that analyzed brain waves. These brain waves were then transmitted to the android's receiver, and the machine began re-forming itself per its new template. Carden tried this with Batman, and the machine resembled the Gotham Guardian in appearance, knowledge, and capabilities. Matters grew complicated when the criminal called DALL stole the Batman robot. The robot was ultimately recovered and Carden regained his invention. (Detective Comics #239, January 1957)

CARDINAL SIN

Aliens invaded the Earth during the modern heroic age, led by a parasitic life-form named Gemir. When they bit humans, their secretions activated the human meta-gene, bestowing unpredictable abilities on each victim. In the case of former priest Perry Dennison, his very touch would decay living matter to the point of death. The changes to his body also seemed to alter his outlook on life, and possessing this power made him embrace all things evil. Dennison headed for GOTHAM CITY, determined to kill Bishop Maxwell, who suddenly stood for things he could no longer abide. He was stopped by Batman—who at the time was JEAN PAUL VALLEY, because BRUCE WAYNE was recuperating from injuries. Gemir had also attacked Dennison's half brother Luke Hames, an escaped convict. Luke and Perry learned that their powers canceled each

other out when they came into contact. In fact, their final touch shorted out both sets of powers but left Dennison drawn to evil. Cardinal Sin has not been seen since. (Legends of the Dark Knight Annual #3, 1993)

CARDINE, "KNOTS"

"Knots" Cardine was a powerful GOTHAM CITY underworld figure who sought to eliminate his greatest threat—Batman. Upon hearing that an international assemblage of lawmen was coming to town, he hatched a scheme to not only kill the Caped Crusader but also make off with a truck filled with currency. When the BATMEN OF ALL NATIONS assembled in Gotham, Cardine managed to subdue and replace the LEGIONARY. Cardine intended to kill Batman and then have the "Legionary" volunteer to guard the shipment in the dead hero's stead. Batman and ROBIN discovered the scheme and put an end to it before it could be fully executed. (Detective Comics #215, January 1955)

CARDINE, PAYNE

The tortured pianist Payne Cardine was better known to the police as the costumed villain the MAESTRO.

CARLATHAN MOUNTAINS

The Carlathan Mountains were located in Europe's Hungary. Here Batman stayed in a hotel as he sought out the MONK. His quarry was holed up in a castle in the nearby lost mountains of CATHALA, which might or might not be connected to the Carlathan Mountains. (Detective Comics #32, October 1939)

CARLIN

Carlin was a method actor who was deeply inhabiting the part of a caveman when he received an accidental blow to his head. Upon awakening, Carlin truly believed himself to be a caveman named Goth. In his confusion he stumbled upon the BATCAVE and claimed it for himself, defending it from its true occupants, Batman and ROBIN. As they fought, a second blow to his head seemed to clear away the mental fog and Carlin regained his senses. Fortunately for the Dynamic Duo, this happened away from their cave headquarters, and the thespian recalled nothing of his time as Goth. (Batman #102, September 1956)

CARLIN, CATSPAW

Catspaw Carlin and his partner, Corky Huggins, made the unfortunate choice to rob WAYNE MANSION. Even though their crime succeeded given that the home's occupants—BRUCE WAYNE, DICK GRAYSON, and ALFRED PENNYWORTH—were away fishing at the time, neither realized it meant they had stolen from Batman and ROBIN. When the crime was reported, two down-on-their-luck detectives named Hawke and Wrenn decided to bolster their careers by dressing as the Caped Crusaders and apprehending the thieves themselves. Despite their bumbling, neither prevented the true heroes from apprehending Carlin and Huggins. (Batman #29, June/July 1945)

CARLO

Carlo performed a mind-reading act on the dying vaudeville circuit. He was injured in an automobile

accident and required brain surgery. Upon recovery, Carlo was astonished to discover he truly could read minds. When he read BRUCE WAYNE's mind and learned of his Batman alter ego, Carlo intended to profit from the knowledge. But first, he hoped to use his newfound talents to rob from others and enrich himself. One such victim was Pete Jorgen, who shot and killed him. Batman's secret died with Carlo. (Detective Comics #70, December 1942)

CARLSON

Carlson grew embittered when he was involved in a college fraternity initiation that went horribly wrong. An accidental injection of chemicals left him with a deformed face, alone and bitter. He spent the following years trying to re-create the serum; when he achieved his goal, he used the substance on others, transforming them into his UGLY HORDE. The chemicals were said to paralyze the thyroid gland and brought about a disease identified as myxedema, cretinism. Carlson and his deformed army sought to terrorize the populace, notably the members of the fraternity who had first injected him. The Ugly Horde also destroyed anything of beauty, however, including killing a beauty queen, destroying works of art, and bombing statues.

Wearing a life-like mask to pass as handsome, Carlson gained admittance to the fraternity and began injecting its members with the serum, ruining the looks of several members. He would have gone further had Batman not intervened. The two engaged in a vicious fight; just as Carlson was ready to stab the Caped Crusader, he was shot and killed by police detective McGONIGLE. A Dr. Ekhart developed a counteragent to Carlson's serum, and his victims were restored to normal. (Batman #3, Fall 1940)

CARLYLE, ROGER

The great character actor Roger Carlyle suffered brain damage from an auto accident. Monarch Pictures, which held his contract, suggested he take time off to recover, which Carlyle took to mean they thought his career was at an end. The deranged man swore vengeance against Monarch's owners—Austin, Bates, and Harmon—and set out to kill them. As he stalked the trio, successfully killing Austin and Bates, Carlyle also sought to make it appear to the police that he was being framed by the real murderer. Fortunately, Batman and ROBIN saw through the ruse and stopped Carlyle before he could kill Harmon. (Detective Comics #314, April 1963)

CARMA, TOMMY

Tommy Carma once had a promising future with the GOTHAM CITY POLICE DEPARTMENT. He was the youngest detective on the force but proved to be more brutal than necessary. As a result, many cases he was involved in were tossed out of court due to technicalities. Carma was careful when he arrested a major underworld figure, and the process went off without a single error. However, on the first day of trial, a bomb under the Carma family minivan killed his wife and daughter. The shock caused Carma to quit the force, and he took work as a private security guard. All the while, though, his mental state deteriorated until the day he decided to become his idol: Batman. Carma dressed as the Dark Knight and set out to kill each criminal he had arrested but the courts turned free. As a result, suspicion centered on the real Batman. Instead, the Caped Crusader tracked down Carma and brought him to justice. (*Batman* #402–403, December 1986–January 1987)

CARP, CLEMENT

Clement Carp was a criminal best known as costumed criminal the SQUID.

CARRIER, THE

CARY RINALDI was visiting in Colombia when he bought a treasure map from one of the local vendors. What Rinaldi didn't realize was that he had been exposed to a virus that made him a carrier of a fatal disease. When he arrived in GOTHAM CITY, he exposed countless people to the unnamed virus.

At the same time, a new designer drug called Sanitiz was making the rounds of the Gotham club scene and was a cause of concern for the police. Batman, in the early days of his crime-fighting career, attempted to track the drugs. He found Claire, a drug dealer handling Sanitiz, and followed her to a club, planting a bug on her. ALFRED PENNYWORTH informed Batman that the bug showed she was to meet her dealer at the airport that night. When he arrived, a HAZMAT team was already present since everyone aboard the Colombian airplane had contracted some vicious disease. The man on the plane was not only Claire's supplier but also the drug's inventor, and he became a victim of the disease. Only one man, Cary Rinaldi, survived. As Batman investigated further, he learned that Rinaldi was loose in Gotham and spreading the disease with a rapidly mounting death toll. Batman began working with Lieutenant JAMES GORDON, sharing information as an uneasy alliance solidified. Research indicated that the disease's origin was a Colombian cave and its bat inhabitants. Batman and Alfred theorized that they themselves were immune from the disease given their constant exposure to the bats inhabiting the cave beneath stately WAYNE MANOR.

While they investigated, Rinaldi roamed the streets of Gotham, protecting the populace by wearing a gas mask, but he occasionally lifted it to infect those who offended him. Batman tracked the sick and dying until he found one ill man who finally provided him with Rinaldi's name. Batman and Gordon concluded that Rinaldi was intentionally killing people who had been using Sanitiz.

Rinaldi had met Claire, the pair forming an odd friendship. They robbed a bank together to finance his hunt, and she took to carrying the cash in a satchel that rarely left her side. Rinaldi was seeking the man who sold him the supposed treasure map—the one that led him to the cave where he contracted the disease. Upon locating the man, Rinaldi discovered that Barry Lewison had a natural immunity, so he couldn't exact revenge as planned. Instead Lewison shot Claire and had his man take Rinaldi prisoner. While a captive, Lewison cut off Rinaldi's hand to use as a mobile way to spread the disease and intended to auction it off. This drove Rinaldi mentally off the edge.

Claire was smart enough to accompany Rinaldi wearing a bulletproof vest; when Batman arrived, she had been injured but remained alive. Batman attempted to free Rinaldi but was met with overwhelming force that caused the crime fighter to back off.

Lewison, though, wanted the cash Claire carried and sought her out. She produced a gun and held him captive, eventually regaining possession of Rinaldi's hand. Batman, meantime, traced Lewison's men to an armored truck carrying a steel container that held Rinaldi. The men had all contracted the disease and died. Batman recovered the steel case and transferred it to ARKHAM ASYLUM, where the now insane Rinaldi could be treated.

Claire told Gordon of the impending auction, and the lieutenant flashed the BAT-SIGNAL to inform the Dark Knight. With the new information, Batman tried to break up the auction by himself but wound up interfering with an FBI raid. He vanished from the scene and took Claire to visit Rinaldi at Arkham. She gently removed his protective covering, gave him a kiss, and willingly exposed herself to the disease, ready to die with him rather than be apart. (*Batman: Journey into Knight* #1–6, October 2005–March 2006)

CARSON, BENNETT

Bennett Carson was a respected GOTHAM CITY citizen who seemed the ideal candidate to head up a committee investigating the Red Gloves Gang. What no one at the time knew was that Carson was secretly the gang's leader. Soon members of his gang learned Carson was planning to cheat them out of their fair shares from their robberies, and they wanted him dead. Rather than killing him, though, they left Carson injured and with temporary amnesia. He was rescued by Batman and ROBIN, who had to help him regain his memory so they could better understand why the gang wanted him dead. When his memory returned, the truth came out, allowing the Dynamic Duo to bring Carson and the Red Gloves Gang to justice. (*Batman* #117, August 1958)

CARSON, JUMBO

Jumbo Carson was a criminal who used stolen scientific gear to reduce himself in size and was later known as the ANT-MAN.

CARSON, TED

Ted Carson turned his obsession with fire into a criminal career as the deadly FIREFLY.

CARTER, MICHAEL

Michael Carter was a criminal who took on the costumed persona of the SWASHBUCKLER.

CASPIAN, JUDSON

In the days before Batman protected GOTHAM CITY, Judson Caspian meted out a very brutal form of justice as the costumed vigilante the REAPER.

CASPIAN, RACHEL

During Batman's second year in GOTHAM CITY, his alter ego, BRUCE WAYNE, was introduced to Rachel

Caspian. The two felt a mutual attraction despite Rachel's impending vows to become a nun. Soon after, her father, Judson, returned to Gotham after many years abroad. At almost the same time, a costumed vigilante known as the REAPER returned to Gotham's streets after an absence of more than a decade. His brutal approach to crime stopping brought Batman into opposition with the Reaper, with devastating results. As Batman sought ways to take the Reaper down, Bruce continued to develop a relationship with Rachel, leading her to question her vocation. In time Bruce proposed to Rachel, and she accepted. However, when Batman and the Reaper had a final confrontation at a construction site, the scythe-handed opponent fell to his death and was revealed to be Judson Caspian. Rachel broke off her engagement with Bruce and completed her vows so she could atone for her father's sins. (*Detective Comics* #575, June 1987)

Bruce saw Rachel one more time, when she returned to Gotham, convinced a new Reaper was her father reincarnated. While she stayed with Dr. LESLIE THOMPKINS, the Reaper included Rachel in his plans for revenge, plaguing her with images that made her think it really was her father reborn. This proved to be untrue, and although seeing Bruce stirred romantic feelings anew, she remained committed to her course. (*Batman: Full Circle,* 1991)

In the aftermath of the INFINITE CRISIS, this version of reality was rewritten so that Rachel never met Bruce Wayne.

CASSIDY

Cassidy was a member of the car thieving gang known as the SPEEDBOYZ, which specialized in high-priced, powerful machines. He engaged ROBIN III on several occasions and the Batman once. (*Robin* #1, November 1993)

CASSIUS

The offspring of CLAYFACE II and Lady Clay, Cassius was an amorphous, near-mindless child.

CAT, THE

On Earth-2, SELINA KYLE began her criminal career wearing a long gown topped with a cat-shaped head mask as the Cat before being known as CATWOMAN.

CATHALA

Located in Hungary, Cathala may be a region or specific location but was definitely home to the castle housing the MONK. The region was located near the River Dess and might be a part of the CARLATHAN MOUNTAIN range. (*Detective Comics* #32, October 1939)

CATMAN

Big-game hunter THOMAS BLAKE grew bored and sought new challenges, turning to crime and adopting the costumed persona of the Catman. He then became an enemy of the Batman and subsequently a dangerous opponent to any who crossed his path. (*Detective Comics* #311, January 1963)

On Earth-1 the famous jungle cat trapper earned and squandered a fortune, the first of many up-and-down cycles that would plague Blake throughout his adult life. While in Africa, he obtained a cat skin that was said to provide the wearer with eight extra lives, like a true cat was said to have. He had the skin modified into a costume, inspired by the costume worn by GOTHAM CITY's felon CATWOMAN.

Blake was inspired to become Catman when he overheard a chance conversation saying that if he and BRUCE WAYNE were so bored, they should put on costumes and fight each other. As Catman, Blake wore a yellow costume and tights with orange gloves, boots, and cowl plus the cat-skin cape. The orange initials CM were emblazoned on his chest. He initially carried an orange satchel—a kit bag that included various Batman-inspired tools, from a cat-line to a catarang. Catwoman initially resented Catman and went so far as to partner with Batman to apprehend him. They engaged in a friendly rivalry for some time until the world was wiped out during the CRISIS ON INFINITE EARTHS.

Despite his failures as a criminal, Catman continued to operate in Gotham City, prompting ROBIN to wonder why he didn't relocate to a city without a super hero. Batman reminded him that Catman was irresistibly attracted to BATWOMAN. She once gave in to her mixed feelings toward Blake and began a whirlwind romance, even forsaking her Batwoman costume in favor of a Cat-Woman outfit, but it did not last. (*Detective Comics* #318, July 1963) After being freed, Blake immediately resumed his criminal career as Catman, once more crossing paths with Catwoman as they both sought a cat-themed object. His goal was to create an independent island nation as a hideaway for criminals in exchange for a percentage of their loot. (*Detective Comics* #322-324, December 1963–February 1964)

Their relationship continued despite Blake's several near-death experiences, culminating with his spending a year as a fugitive until Batman,

Robin, and Batwoman finally apprehended him. (*Detective Comics* #325, March 1964)

Batman eventually became convinced of the cape's magical properties, which had seemingly saved not only Blake but also Catwoman from certain death on more than one occasion. In prison Blake shared a cell with an inmate named Collins, who learned all about the costume and its magic. At one point Collins stole the outfit and became the new Cat-Man for a period of time, although he fared no better against the Dark Knight Detective. (*Batman* #371, May 1984)

Blake regained his costume and resumed his career only to meet defeat at the hands of MANHUNTER. (*Manhunter* #13, May 1989)

In the single universe post-Crisis, Blake debuted as Catman, wearing a cloak that was sourced not from Africa but a South Sea cult. Blake journeyed to a South Sea island, bored and hungry for new experiences. He stayed with a native tribe and studied its worship of a sacred cat despite the cult's prohibition against non-natives and those under the age of thirty-five. One night, after the cult members drank a native potion and entered a trance-like state, Blake entered their hut and stole the cat statue and the cloth it was wrapped in—both said to possess magical energy. (*Batman: Shadow of the Bat* #43, October 1995)

Catman proved to be somewhat chauvinistic toward women, an attitude that ultimately caused Catwoman, with whom he was briefly partnered, to rebel against him. Later, the South Sea cult's Council of Three hired her to gain the cloak for them, but she failed and instead delivered them a fake. Along the way Blake began to realize how unfulfilling being a criminal was. He grew to hate the constant relocation and sought a way for Blake

to vanish and Catman to be out of the way. Despite his most fervent hopes, he wound up aiding Batman and Catwoman in stopping a plan by the RATCATCHER that threatened Gotham. Catman was resigned to his criminal ways until he could afford to retire.

Blake continued as a minor criminal threat to Batman, rarely taken seriously. In fact, he was in a group known as the Misfits, including KILLER MOTH and CALENDAR MAN, seeking to make names for themselves but failing in the process. Blake recruited a man named Chancer to join them, believing he, too, was lucky and would help the team. (*Batman: Shadow of the Bat* #7–9, December 1992–February 1993)

While other criminals were ready to kill, Catman was not. He assured police officer SARAH ESSEN GORDON that no harm would befall Mayor ARMAND KROL, Commissioner JAMES GORDON, or millionaire playboy BRUCE WAYNE, unaware that Killer Moth was ready to execute them the minute the ten-million-dollar ransom was received. Blake's moral code was evident time and again, such as when he refused the demon Neron's offer for enhanced abilities in exchange for his soul. Later, when he was once more in BLACKGATE PENITENTIARY, the prison was cracked open by an earthquake, and rather than flee he saved a fellow inmate from being killed by the KGBeast. (*Batman: Blackgate—Isle of Men* #1, 1998)

Free for good, Blake left Gotham rather than be trapped there when the government cut off aid. He set out to achieve his goal of independence, but first met defeat at the hands of the Black Condor (*Starman* #80, June 2001) and was later seen trying to gamble his way to wealth at Roulette's illicit gambling den, the House. (*JSA* #28, November 2001).

When Oliver Queen, the GREEN ARROW, died, Blake attended his funeral at the behest of the enigmatic Shade. After that, he seemed to have made his fortune and retired to obscurity, letting himself gain weight and get out of shape. (*Green Arrow* #1, April 2001)

Queen returned to life and sought out Blake to understand what had happened at the funeral. They later had a sharp confrontation when Green Arrow caught Blake being abusive once more to a female companion. The fight ended when the villain Warp appeared and snatched Blake. (*Green Arrow* #20, March 2003)

After finishing his unrecorded business with Warp, Blake decided to turn his life around. He lost the weight, regained his hunter's physique, and returned to the jungle. At that time, the Society had formed—a coalition of super-villains determined to make a strike against the world's super heroes. Those who refused to join were the recipients of strongarm tactics. In Blake's case, when he refused admission, the pride of lions he was near was killed by DEATHSTROKE.

Still, he remained independent, until he was coaxed into joining a rogue operation led by a mysterious figure known as Mockingbird. Catman became a member of the Secret Six, working to thwart the Society's efforts. While working alongside the Six, Blake came to learn that it was teammate DEADSHOT, not Deathstroke, who had killed the lions, at Mockingbird's behest.

Catman lived up to his big-game hunter's reputation, proving himself a fierce fighter and cunning tactician. During his battles with the Society, he actually managed to go toe-to-toe with the super-ape Monsieur Mallah. In his dealings with the Six and the Society, Blake made it clear he preferred being around people who were honest with themselves and true about their intentions. As a result, he and Deadshot and even Green Arrow came to develop understandings.

His moral approach and manly physique intrigued fellow member Cheshire, who chose him to sire her second child, an unnamed son. He continued working with the Secret Six and on one mission developed a crush on the HUNTRESS, who promised to give him a chance once he went straight.

One incarnation of Catman was rendered obsolete during the earliest reality-altering waves that became the INFINITE CRISIS. Here Blake became Catman during Batman's first two years in Gotham City. He was a serial killer, beginning with his mother, and sported a gray outfit closer to Catwoman's. Batman and Catwoman actually formed a truce in order to stop the killer. (*Legends of the Dark Knight* #46–49, June–August 1993)

Note: Catman is not the same as the villain KING OF CATS.

CATWOMAN

On Earth-2, SELINA KYLE began her criminal career as the Cat, wearing a gown and cat-head mask. (*Batman* #1, Spring 1940) She used a cat-o'-nine tails and was drawn to spectacular robberies. Time and again she and the Batman opposed each other, both acknowledging that there was some romantic tension underlying each meeting.

At one time Selina explained she was in reality a flight attendant who had suffered a concussion during a plane crash that altered her personality and memories. (*Batman* #62, December 1950/ January 1951) She later recanted the amnesia story and revealed the truth: She had been married to an abusive husband who kept her jewelry in a vault. When she wanted to leave him, she needed to break into the vault to get her possessions. She enjoyed the liberating experience so much that she launched a new career as a criminal. (*The Brave and the Bold* #197, April 1983)

Catwoman was highly influenced by the Caped Crusader, going so far as to drive a Catmobile and even fly a Catplane. For a while she seemed to change allegiances, possibly due to her affection for the Gotham Guardian; they actually were allies on several occasions. (*Batman* #65, June/July 1951; #69, February/March 1952) For reasons of her own, however, she returned to her criminal ways. (*Detective Comics* #203, January 1954)

Finally, in the 1950s, both slowly withdrew from their battle and subsequently gave in to their romantic feelings. BRUCE WAYNE and Selina Kyle were married in a lavish ceremony that was attended by a large gathering, including CLARK KENT and LOIS LANE. (*Superman Family* #211, October 1981)

Some years later Selina gave birth to a daughter, HELENA WAYNE, and the three settled into a happy family situation. This idyll was shattered when Selina was blackmailed into committing a crime that resulted in her death. (*Adventure Comics* #461–462, January/February–March/April 1977) The brutal act galvanized teenage Helena into action; she put on a costume of her own, becoming the HUNTRESS. (*DC Super-Stars* #17, November/December 1977) Soon thereafter, Wayne once more put on the Batman uniform to join the JUSTICE SOCIETY OF AMERICA on a case that resulted in his own death. (*Adventure Comics* #466, November/December 1979)

On Earth-1, Selina Kyle became Catwoman and enjoyed many successes as a cat burglar and frequent opponent of Batman and ROBIN. The attraction that existed on Earth-2 was also present here, but to a lesser degree. She battled against the Dynamic Duo and even crossed paths with METROPOLIS reporter Lois Lane (*Superman's Girl Friend Lois Lane* #70, November 1966)

Catwoman continued her life of crime, going so far as to murder to accomplish her tasks. Eventually, Selina Kyle worked on reforming her wicked ways and even engaged in a romance with Bruce Wayne. (*Batman* #310–326, April 1979–August 1980) Batman's alter ego encouraged the relationship in the hope that it would reform her . . . which worked until Earth-1 was erased.

In the wake of parallel worlds being melded into one during the CRISIS ON INFINITE EARTHS, Kyle's life changed dramatically. This Kyle was a prostitute and dominatrix, performing in a catsuit with a whip and a jaundiced view toward society. When news reports first told of a man dressed as a bat, she was intrigued. She modified one of her catsuits and entered the Batman's life for the first time. (*Batman* #404–407, February–May 1987)

It was later revealed that Selina had endured a sad childhood. Her mother, Maria, was an unloving woman who seemed to prefer her cats to her children, Selina and MAGGIE KYLE. Whatever demons haunted

her eventually drove Maria to commit suicide. Her husband, Brian, grew angry at his wife's action. He told Selina he didn't like her because she resembled Maria. Brian took to the bottle and stayed with it until he died. (*Catwoman* #0, October 1994) Selina was placed in an orphanage followed by a GOTHAM CITY juvenile hall. While at the hall, thirteen-year-old Selina found that an administrator was embezzling and confronted the man. She was placed inside a bag and dropped in the Gotham River to drown. Instead Kyle made it to shore and washed up in a section of the city known as Alleytown, located between the EAST END and Old Gotham. (*Catwoman* #12, July 1994) She was taken in by an old street woman calling herself Mama Fortuna, a modern-day Fagin who harbored other homeless children and taught them to steal on her behalf.

Selina and her friend Sylvia ran away and fell into prostitution to support themselves, working for a pimp named Stan. Sylvia hated her experience and developed a hatred for Selina, wishing her friend were more supportive. After Sylvia vanished from her life, Selina met HOLLY ROBINSON, another teen prostitute, and the two became best friends, a relationship that endured unlike so many others in her life. In time, though, Holly and Maggie left for the West Coast.

Selina escaped Mama Fortuna's influence in any event and learned to become a thief. The people who helped train her to fight included the ARMLESS MASTER and TED GRANT, the former heavyweight champ and costumed fighter WILDCAT. (*Catwoman Annual #2*, 1998)

Selina as an adult set her sights on something better and remade herself into a socialite. She used her stolen money and other resources to reestablish her Selina Kyle persona with a partly faked background, and she held on to it until Batman found out she was Catwoman. This prompted her to abandon the name temporarily, but she revived it periodically to keep it in play. Batman never got around to telling the authorities, romantically believing he'd be spoiling her shot at redemption. (*Catwoman Secret Files*, 2002)

Later, Stan reentered Selina's life and abused Maggie violently. This drove Selina to kill him. (*Catwoman: Her Sister's Keeper*, 1989)

Her adventures over the next couple of years paralleled those of her Earth-1 counterpart, complete with a variety of costumes. The key distinction was that Selina was defeated but never apprehended. After the JUSTICE LEAGUE OF AMERICA discovered her tenuous link to the secret Society of super-villains,

ZATANNA altered Catwoman's memories. She retired her costumed identity and, as Selina, started up an affair with Bruce Wayne—only to have it collapse when his trust in her wavered due to Batman's mistaken belief that she'd returned to crime. Resuming her Catwoman persona, Selina remained a heroine, deducing that Bruce was Batman and gradually rekindling their romance.

That came to an end when the JOKER learned of the romance and arranged for DOCTOR MOON to modify Selina's behavior back to that of a criminal. The process was a success and also removed Catwoman's memories of both her recent reformation *and* Batman's real identity. (*Detective Comics*

#569–570, December 1986–January 1987) However, Moon had unknowingly interfered with Zatanna's behavior modification spell, and this would plague Selina for years to come. The inconsistencies in her personality and alliances stemmed from the conflicting commands in her mind. Consequently, the SCARECROW's gradual

penetration of her psyche was even more effective than he could have expected. (*Catwoman* #58-60, June-August 1998, revealed and culminating in *Catwoman* #92-94, May-July 2001)

Along the way she appeared to revise her moral code based on the situation she found herself in. On the one hand, she had a tender spot in her heart for orphans—witness her adoption of a young teen runaway Arizona—but on the other, she thought nothing of working alongside killers such as BANE. Oddly, though, she wound up sneaking up to the moon and infiltrating the JLA's Watchtower headquarters in time to aid the League in defeating PROMETHEUS. (*JLA* #17, April 1998)

When Gotham was temporarily rendered a No MAN'S LAND, Catwoman revived her Selina Kyle identity, this time in New York City. Rising quickly to become CEO of Randolf Industries, Selina decided to run for mayor. The intense public scrutiny quickly shone a light on her sketchy background, and Catwoman wound up "killing" Selina Kyle to extricate herself from the mess. (*Catwoman* [second series] #67-71, April-August 1999) When the body was later exhumed, it was discovered that the corpse's prints matched a DOA from three days before Selina Kyle was "killed."

Gradually easing herself back into Gotham society, Selina first approached her old boyfriend Bruce Wayne privately, telling him that "even in New York, they've sort of quietly revoked my death certificate." (*Catwoman* #10, October 2002)

Kyle wound up fighting alongside Batman as he opposed LEX LUTHOR's attempts to gain control of real estate during Gotham's reconstruction. Still, she was arrested by Commissioner JAMES GORDON for older crimes, but she easily broke out of jail. Soon after, she became a suspect when Gordon was shot, although she was cleared. She was subsequently shot herself and seemingly killed once more by DEATHSTROKE. (*Catwoman* #94, July 2001)

Her apparent death didn't stop SLAM BRADLEY, a private investigator, from seeking her out. When he finally tracked her down, Kyle was settled in the East End and had decided this was her refuge. She would become its defender and woe be to any cop, cape, or villain who tried to cross her there. (*Detective Comics* #759-762, August-November 2001) She continued her burglaries, as much for the thrill as for the money. She found herself fighting as often against Batman as she did with the Dark Knight. As a result, they began their long-anticipated romance, leading Batman to actually

unmask, ready to share everything with her. During this time, though, the villainous HUSH stalked Batman and in the end, he remained suspicious of Catwoman, considering she might have been one of Hush's pawns. (*Batman* #608-619, December 2002-November 2003) They remained allies after that but kept their distance.

Soon after, America's villains learned that many had been magically mindwiped by Zatanna in an effort to protect the super heroes' secret identities. They banded together as a secret Society to oppose the heroes, although Catwoman was not active with them. Still, Zatanna did admit to Catwoman that she was one of her subjects. Selina Kyle was tortured with the news, no longer certain of who she really was. Did she love Bruce Wayne? Was she protecting the East End because deep down she wanted to do good? She had no answers. (*Catwoman* [second series] #50, December 2005)

One thing was certain: Her life would never settle down as long as BLACK MASK controlled Gotham's underworld. He continued to encroach on the East End in more and more brutal ways. She declared war on him, with disastrous results. Black Mask found and recruited Sylvia as an ally and from the bitter woman learned that Catwoman was Selina

Kyle. Armed with this information, he threatened Maggie and her husband, killing him. Left with no choice, Kyle gave up any pretense of heroism and shot Black Mask to death. (*Catwoman* [second series] #52, February 2006)

In the wake of Black Mask's death, Catwoman took it upon herself to dismantle his criminal operation. She teamed with Sam Bradley, son of Slam, and they spent weeks picking apart the Black Mask empire. They finally managed to trap Black Mask's right-hand man, Dylan, and had him arrested. During the euphoria that followed, they made love and she conceived a daughter. Dylan was freed a week later and ordered that Sam Bradley be caught. He tortured and then killed Bradley on the day Selina learned of her pregnancy. (*Catwoman* [second series] #59, September 2006) Holly took over as the new Catwoman while Selina, living under the alias Irena Dubrovna, turned her attention to caring for her infant daughter, Helena.

Even after training Holly, with Ted Grant's help, Selina put on the catsuit from time to time. The police continued to seek Black Mask's killer, and clues pointed toward Catwoman. Surveillance footage indicated that there might be two Catwomen operating in Gotham, something that caught the attention of the Film Freak. Working with the footage, the Freak determined who Kyle really was and, aided by the Angle Man, abducted Helena. Catwoman managed to rescue her daughter and then demanded Zatanna repay her debt by mindwiping the Film Freak so he would forget her identity.

Holly was arrested for the murder but freed and cleared by Selina Kyle. While Robinson moved to Metropolis, Kyle remained in Gotham, and both went into action as Catwoman. Kyle, at Batman's request, infiltrated the Bana warriors, an offshoot tribe of Amazons that instigated a war between the legendary women and America. (*Catwoman* [second series] #69, September 2007)

In the various alternate realities and parallel universes, Selina Kyle has usually remained Catwoman. One version saw her with a vicious, murderous streak that also showed Holly no longer a lesbian but straight and married to a man named Arthur. While still Catwoman, Selina was also running the Tin Roof Club, which acted as a front for her lucrative fencing operation. When Arthur found out about the illegal business, he arranged to kill Holly and grab the business for himself. During their confrontation at the Gotham Plaza Hotel, she callously tossed two guards off the roof and then calmly framed Arthur for their deaths, resolving the challenge to her business. (*Action Comics Weekly* #611-614, 1988)

In one parallel world Selina thought herself the daughter of crime boss Carmine Falcone, but the evidence remained inconclusive. (*Catwoman: When in Rome* #1-6, February-August 2005)

CAVALIER, THE

Mortimer Drake was a bored millionaire who decided to indulge his whims and become a costumed villain using the name *the Cavalier*. (*Detective Comics* #81, November 1943)

On Earth-2, Drake turned to crime so he could

obtain what he could not legally buy to suit his exotic tastes. Once he found himself opposed by Batman and Robin, though, Drake seemed to relish the challenge. Batman figured out that the Cavalier was Drake and used that knowledge to arrest him. Drake returned again and again to steal—but more to confront the Dynamic Duo. Eventually he was arrested and retired from his life of crime once and for all.

On Earth-1, he found himself opposite not Batman but Batgirl and Batwoman, and he abandoned the code of chivalry his costume demanded and punched Batgirl. Later, he accepted a challenge from Killer Moth, attempting to learn the Batcave's whereabouts from Robin before the Moth could learn the same secret from Batgirl. The heroes led the villains to false locations, with the Cavalier convinced Robin was really an alien life-form. (*Batman Family* #15, December 1977/January 1978)

In the revised reality in the wake of the Crisis on Infinite Earths, the Cavalier was nothing more than a minor costumed felon wearing a Renaissance swashbuckler's outfit. He was a poor combatant who took to drinking with his fellow villains. (*Justice League of America* #44, November 1990) His failures seemed to have driven him insane, and Drake was confined to Arkham Asylum. He underwent treatment and was released after an unspecified time. He remained a costumed criminal but agreed to become Black Lightning's informant when threatened with the revelation that he and Captain Stingaree were engaged in a secret homosexual affair. (*Justice League of America* #2, November 2006)

A criminal named Hudson Pyle was also the Cavalier in a variant reality, fighting Batman only once. (*Legends of the Dark Knight* #32-34, June-July 1992)

CAVE, CARL C.

Carl C. Cave was a master criminal better known to the police as the man called Numbers.

CELL SIX

Cell Six was a Latin American terrorist organization that preferred kidnapping as a way to raise money for other business. Cell Six troops could be distinguished by the number—6 or VI—tattooed on their foreheads. They were responsible for the abduction of Wayne Enterprises' Lucius Fox while he

was doing business in Hasaragua. They demanded three million dollars in ransom and a letter of apology from Wayne Enterprises for the company's supposed despoiling of Hasaragua's environment and exploitation of its people. Batman traveled to the country to rescue his friend and learned that the kidnapping was actually a collaboration between Hasaragua's finance minister and Cell Six. (*Detective Comics Annual* #10, 1997) Later Cell Six went to Gotham City and staged a kidnapping attempt against the wife of a Hasaraguan ambassador—only to fail at the hands of the Dark Knight and the police. (*Batman: G.C.P.D.* #1-4, August–December 1996)

CHALMERS, DEUCE

Deuce Chalmers was a schemer and confidence man who set up a scheme to kidnap six millionaires and hold them for ransoms of one million dollars apiece. The scheme involved his being disguised as Batman the very week the real hero was selected, as Bruce Wayne, to serve as honorary mayor of Gotham City. Bruce had to expose Chalmers and rescue his fellow millionaires without giving away his alter ego. Chalmers was no match for the World's Greatest Detective; he was soon arrested. (*Detective Comics* #179, January 1952)

CHANDLER, ROMY

Romy Chandler initially trained to become an FBI agent but, despairing over the amount of paperwork, soon shifted her focus to local law enforcement. Her test scores, athletic skills, and black belt in karate got her assigned to Gotham City's Major Crimes Unit, where she served on the second shift. There Chandler was initially partnered with the abrasive Nate Patton. Ironically, her fellow cops thought she had a crush on Patton; in fact it was Patton holding the crush. He always managed to say the wrong thing but remained heroic, rescuing a newscaster from one of the Joker's bombs, only to lose his life. Chandler blamed the Batman for the Joker's existence and harbored a grudge toward him. She was subsequently partnered with Marcus Driver and the two entered into a clandestine romance known only to Stacy, the civilian aide. (*Gotham Central* #1, Early February 2003)

CHARAXES

The criminal known as Killer Moth was also known as millionaire Cameron Van Cleer and fought Batman and Batgirl on numerous occasions before selling his soul to Neron in exchange for true power. He became the hideous creature renamed Charaxes. (*Batman* #63, February/March 1951)

On Earth-2, a convict chose to oppose Batman as an almost mirror image. He used his hidden stolen property to finance the creation of Killer Moth, complete with a mothcave headquarters, mothmobile, and even a moth-signal. Once in his Killer Moth costume, the criminal became a high-priced mercenary to members of Gotham City's underworld. In his first encounter with Batman and Robin, Killer Moth managed a stalemate before apparently drowning. Instead he survived and fought Batman a second time. He also created the fictitious Cameron Van Cleer so he could operate

Charaxes

with anonymity. During their next battle Batman arrested Killer Moth and exposed the Van Cleer alias. Killer Moth escaped and decided to steal a living person's identity, that of BRUCE WAYNE. After Killer Moth trapped Wayne in a vault, he underwent plastic surgery to resemble Wayne. So successful was the transformation, DICK GRAYSON was convinced he was the real man. It also meant that Dick accidentally gave away the Batman's secret identity, something Killer Moth exploited. Disguised as Batman, he set out to convince the underworld that the Caped Crusader was terrified of Killer Moth. Wayne escaped the vault, and soon Batman confronted Killer Moth for real. By then criminals had fired at "Batman," not only disfiguring him but also affecting Killer Moth's memory, preserving their secret identities. (*Detective Comics* #173, July 1951)

On Earth-1, Killer Moth was millionaire-turned-criminal Cameron Van Cleef, a minor costumed felon who opposed Batman on occasion. (*Justice League of America* #35, May 1965) Seeking to extort money from his former socialite friends, Killer Moth intended to attack a costume ball but was thwarted by BARBARA GORDON dressed as a Batgirl—the seminal event that launched her crime-fighting career. (*Detective Comics* #359, January 1967)

Killer Moth remained a thorn in Batgirl's side after that. He once teamed with former millionaire

Drury Walker

MORTIMER DRAKE, the CAVALIER, to ferret out the location of the BATCAVE. While Drake attempted to learn the secret from Robin, Killer Moth tried to pry the information from Batgirl. (*Batman Family* #10, March/April 1977; #15, December 1977/January 1978) In the wake of that debacle, Killer Moth went solo against Batgirl once more. (*Batman* #311, May 1979)

Realities merged during the CRISIS ON INFINITE EARTHS, but Killer Moth was largely unaffected. Drury Walker remained a minor costumed criminal who occasionally sold his services to other criminals. He also used the aliases *Arthur Leland* and *Cameron Van Cleer* while committing crimes. At one point, in some desperation, he formed the Misfits with CALENDAR MAN, CATMAN, and Chancer, hoping to abduct Mayor ARMAND KROL, Police Commissioner JAMES GORDON, and Bruce Wayne for ransom. Unlike the others, Killer Moth was ready to kill the men, ransom paid or not. (*Batman: Shadow of the Bat* #7-9, December 1992–February 1993)

Killer Moth sought power and respect, so he was among the first to accept the demon Neron's offer for just that. In exchange for his soul, Killer Moth evolved into a giant insect with an insatiable appetite now known as Charaxes. (*Underworld Unleashed* #1, November 1995)

In his new form, Charaxes was six feet two, complete with the power of flight and enhanced strength. He also secreted an acidic solution. The new incarnation seemed to rob Drury of his reasoning faculties. (*Robin* #23-24, December 1995–January 1996) Charaxes often confronted Robin and even contended against his fellow TEEN TITANS.

In addition, Charaxes's transformation left him with the ability to lay eggs, which seemed to hatch miniature versions of his Walker self. The government took possession of these new life-forms for study. At one point they got loose and wound up being destroyed.

During a battle with Superboy-Prime during the events known as INFINITE CRISIS, the corrupted Teen of Steel ripped Charaxes apart, ending his tragic life and consigning his soul to Hell. (*Infinite Crisis* #7, June 2006)

CHARLATAN

Actor PAUL SLOANE was an Earth-2 impostor who posed as TWO-FACE. This occurred when he was hired to portray HARVEY DENT in a filmed biography of the tortured man's life. During filming, an accident replicated the disfigurement that had warped Dent's mind; Sloane thought he, too, was Two-Face. He was apprehended by Batman and sent for treatment. (*Batman* #68, December 1951/January 1952)

After the realities were merged during the CRISIS ON INFINITE EARTHS, Paul Sloane was an actor hired by GOTHAM CITY underworld costumed criminals. His assignment was to portray Two-Face in a ruse that was intended to end in Batman's death. The real Two-Face learned of this and objected to Sloane's impersonation, so he had the actor kidnapped. Two-Face used acid to scar the actor's face in a pattern similar to his own injuries. Sloane was then exposed to the SCARECROW's newly designed fear toxin, and the combination drove him mad. Now known as Charlatan, he sought vengeance against all the criminals; he was also determined to fulfill his contract and kill Batman. He failed in his quests and was eventually taken into custody. Sloan was subsequently placed in ARKHAM ASYLUM. (*Detective Comics* #776–782, January–August 2003)

CHASE, CAMERON

Cameron Chase was the daughter of an obscure super hero who grew up hiding her meta-human potential, instead becoming one of the most celebrated agents at the Department of Extranormal Operations. (*Batman* #550, January 1998)

Walter Chase doubled as the Acro-Bat, a costumed crime fighter and member of the Justice Experience in between the two great ages of super heroes. One opponent, Dr. Trap, killed Chase in his own home, and it was young Cameron, his eldest

child, who found the body. As she grew up, she remained angry at super heroes and developed a distrust of them. As an adult she became a private investigator, dealing out justice in her own way until recruited to the DEO by its director, the reformed super-villain Mister Bones.

During her time with the DEO she learned that when pushed, she could exert a power that dampened other meta-humans' abilities. And despite her dislike of super heroes, she encountered many in her time with the DEO, including Batman on several occasions. One assignment had her seek out his true identity, but it resulted in a rare failure. (*Chase* #7–8, August–September 1998)

Her experiences with the heroes softened her objection to them, and she finally seemed to accept them when she learned that her college roommate Kate Spencer had become the latest MANHUNTER. They trained together, and eventually Chase began an affair with Dylan Battles, a former criminal henchman who had come to work with Spencer.

When not on the West Coast with Manhunter, Chase maintained an apartment in Brooklyn's Park Slope. She also had a romantic relationship with a civilian, Peter Rice, although the affair with Battles may have ended that.

CHECKMATE

A criminal was eluding Batman and ROBIN when he hid inside a lead-lined container of nuclear materials that irradiated his body, poisoning him. Wishing revenge, he used his waning days to create an elaborate series of death traps and hid them within a GOTHAM CITY amphitheater. After he died, his men lured the Dynamic Duo to the location, and the heroes had to use their great acrobatic skills and quick wits to avoid one trap after another. All were designed to lead them to the final trap, a room containing the same deadly nuclear material that had killed Checkmate. The pair avoided each trap and never entered the final room, instead arresting the men. (*Detective Comics* #238, December 1956)

CHECKMATE

Checkmate was first a federal then an international espionage organization that was frequently involved in Batman's career. (*Action Comics* #598, March 1988)

In all its incarnations, Checkmate was organized around the players on a chessboard, initially with one King controlling Bishops, who operated Rooks (field supervisors) and Pawns (the field agents). After the operation went global, with United Nations sanctioning, it more closely resembled the board with Black and White parallel executives providing a series of checks and balances to prevent it from being usurped as it had been by Maxwell Lord. (*Countdown to Infinite Crisis*, 2005)

Initially Checkmate was organized as a branch of the federal government's Task Force X, which was then overseen by AMANDA WALLER. The first Queen was former Doom Patrol member Colonel Valentina Vostok, followed soon after by Harry Stein as the first King. Under Stein, the agency grew and tackled many global threats. For his Bishop, Stein recruited GOTHAM CITY'S HARVEY BULLOCK for a time.

However, he was also manipulated by the terrorist KOBRA into beginning an interagency battle against Waller's Suicide Squad and the Pentagon's Project Atom. This left thirty-eight Knights dead and forced Waller to give up control to Sarge Steel.

Under Steel, a Russian division was created, although it was poorly funded and underemployed, much like its host country. It was during this period the notion of Black and White administrations began to develop.

At some later date DAVID SAID became Checkmate's new King and orchestrated an invasion of the BATCAVE intended to recruit the HUNTRESS to the operation. At Batman's urging, she accepted the role of Queen in order to keep him informed on Checkmate's operations. She remained in this role for only a brief period, preferring her independence. (*Batman: Gotham Knights* #38, April 2003; #48, February 2004)

Later, after SASHA BORDEAUX was cleared of murder charges involving BRUCE WAYNE'S ex-lover VESPER FAIRCHILD, Checkmate faked her death and broke her out of BLACKGATE PENITENTIARY. There Said and agent JESSICA MIDNIGHT offered her a new life. She accepted, gained a new face and identity, and saw Batman

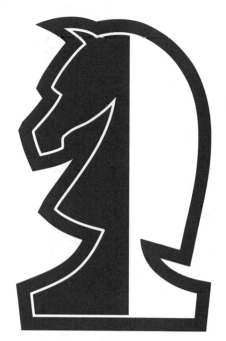

only once more, to say good-bye—and that only after Batman threatened Said to force the meeting.

Around this time, financier and megalomaniac Maxwell Lord maneuvered himself into becoming the operation's Black King. He wanted to use Checkmate to further his goal of wiping out all of Earth's meta-humans. When he discovered that Batman had launched Brother I, a satellite with artificial intelligence designed to perform meta-human surveillance, he took control and reprogrammed it. Lord's scheme continued as he killed the second Blue Beetle, Ted Kord, and unleashed a nanovirus among humanity, turning hundreds of thousand of people into cybernetic agents known as OMACs. He went out of control and wound up being killed by Wonder Woman. It fell to Earth's super heroes to stop the OMAC threat, and Batman brought down his creation.

In the aftermath of this, Checkmate was a ruined, disgraced agency. Its reputation was further spoiled by an undercover Martian Manhunter who was determined to get President Horne to close it down once and for all. (52 #24, 2006)

The United Nations stepped in days later and rebuilt the agency under its auspices (UN Security Council Resolution 1696). A new structure was installed with a balanced mix of super heroes and normal humans in command, including Green Lantern Alan Scott as White King and Mister Terrific as Black King. Amanda Waller came back to the agency as White Queen; the Black Queen was Sasha Bordeaux.

The new Checkmate performed the dirty jobs no other operation could safely tackle, ensuring worldwide safety. Its leaders continued to modify the limits to the work they were willing to do. (Checkmate #1, April 2006)

CHIFFORD, JACK

Jack Chifford was a trained martial artist and assassin who was best known as Hellhound.

CHILL, EDDIE

Eddie Chill led the Night Owl Gang, criminals who disguised themselves with owl masks. To bring the gang to justice, Batman devised a scheme to make Chill believe its members had killed him. Batman then infiltrated the gang by disguising himself as Wedge Dixon, Chill's trusted number two. Chill was enticed into revealing the location of the stolen goods they had accumulated, at which point Robin and a Batman robot revealed themselves and took the gang into custody. (Detective Comics #281, July 1960)

CHILL, JOE

Joe Chill was the mugger who robbed Thomas and Martha Wayne, shooting them when they resisted and setting their son, Bruce, on a path that led to his becoming the Batman. (Detective Comics #33, November 1939)

On Earth-2, Chill was a thief actually hired by a mobster named Lew Moxon to rob and kill the Waynes, settling a score with Thomas Wayne. When Thomas resisted the presumed robbery, Chill shot him; the shock caused Martha to have a fatal heart attack. Young Bruce looked at Chill with such deadly eyes that it scared the hit man and he ran off, leaving Bruce an orphan.

Through the years, Chill became a successful, albeit small-time, mob boss who came to the attention of Batman. When Batman saw Chill up close, he recognized the man despite the passage of time. The Dark Knight Detective cornered Chill in his office and unmasked, showing the killer what his efforts had created. Chill, threatened by Batman's promise to haunt him, burst out of his office and into where his men sat. When he blurted out that he was responsible for the creation of Batman, they shot him dead. (Batman #47, June/July 1948)

Only later did Batman discover the true reason behind his parents' deaths. It was crime boss Lew Moxon who ordered Chill to kill the Waynes. The reason dated back to a costume party before Bruce was born. There, Thomas had dressed in a costume not dissimilar to that of the Batman. Moxon and his men had barged in and forced the doctor to remove a bullet from Moxon. Wayne subsequently testified against the criminal, and Moxon vowed revenge. Batman tracked down Moxon and, with his regular uniform damaged, wore his father's costume. Moxon had been suffering from amnesia at the time but, upon seeing the outfit, his memory snapped back. Confused, he thought it was Thomas Wayne's ghost come to haunt him; he ran into the street, only to be struck and killed by a truck. (Detective Comics #235, September 1958)

On Earth-1, only low-life criminal Joe Chill was involved in the Waynes' deaths. Chill intended to rob them, but when Thomas resisted he wound up shooting both adults. In the wake of the crime, Gotham City's Social Services personnel turned Bruce over to his uncle Philip. Bruce spent his childhood at Philip's estate, growing close to the housekeeper, Mrs. Chilton, never learning she was Joe Chill's mother. She, though, knew Bruce had become Batman and kept a scrapbook of his exploits. Even though both her sons, Max and Joe, died after encountering Batman, she harbored no grudges. (Batman #208, January/February 1969)

In one reality created by the Crisis on Infinite

IT'S TRUE! BATMAN JUST TOLD ME WHO HE IS! HE BECAME BATMAN BECAUSE I KILLED HIS FATHER!

Earths, Joe Chill was still responsible for the Waynes' deaths but played a later role in Batman's life. When the Reaper returned to menace the city's criminals, the various bosses chipped in to hire Chill to kill the vigilante. Chill and Batman crossed paths and agreed it might be best if they pooled their resources even though it became clear to Batman who Chill was. He vowed that once the Reaper was disposed of, he would kill Chill. When the Reaper killed the men who had hired Chill, the hired gun no longer felt the need to honor the contract. Batman took Chill to Crime Alley, where the Wayne murders had taken place, and unmasked. The two men fought, with Batman actually holding a gun to Chill's head, ready to pull the trigger, when the Reaper arrived. The vigilante, instead, killed Chill. (Detective Comics #572–575, March–June 1987)

Waves of reality rippled through the universe as a result of people trapped in a limbo-like realm. One such ripple removed Joe Chill from reality, and for some time Batman had no idea who had killed the Waynes. (Zero Hour: Crisis in Time #4–0, September 1994) After the events known as Infinite Crisis, Joe Chill was restored to the fabric of time and space and was known to have killed the Waynes; he was imprisoned for the crime, with the Reaper encounter erased. (Infinite Crisis #6, May 2006)

On the parallel world designated Earth-3, Joe Chill and Thomas Wayne were friends. When a police officer wanted to question Wayne regarding a crime, the doctor refused. The crooked cop fired at Wayne but instead killed Bruce and Martha. It was Joe Chill who found the bodies in Crime Alley. He raised Thomas Jr., who later became that world's smartest thinker, Owlman. Thomas Sr. went on to become Gotham's police commissioner. (JLA: Earth 2, 2000)

CHILL, JOE JR.

Some time after Joe Chill died at the hands of the violent Reaper, Joe Chill Jr. took up the Reaper's identity. Little was recorded regarding his upbringing or what prompted him to choose this self-destructive path. He did, though, want to avenge his father's death, which he incorrectly blamed on the Batman. Rather than violence, Chill attempted to use psychology to make Batman feel guilty for surviving his parents' deaths. By this point in his career Batman had added Robin to his life, and it was that physical presence that reminded him of what he had and had to live for. He overcame Chill's plan and defeated him. (Batman: Full Circle, 1991)

In the wake of Infinite Crisis, Joe Chill Jr. never existed.

CHILL, MAX

The spirit of Boston Brand, nicknamed Deadman, arrived in Gotham City, suspecting that a criminal named Monk Manville was actually the one-handed man who had murdered him. The wraith tracked down Manville and wound up getting involved in a case that caused him to ask for Batman's assistance. When the two worked together, it was revealed that Manville was an alias for Max Chill, brother to Joe Chill, the man who had murdered Thomas and Martha Wayne during a botched robbery. Chill had a hook replacing an injured hand, but Deadman realized that it was on the wrong hand; Chill could not have been his murderer. Chill subsequently was crushed to death under a pile of falling slot machines. (*The Brave and the Bold* #79, August/September 1968)

CHIMERA

Chimera was a thief who attacked a circus near GOTHAM CITY. Since this was the circus where JASON TODD's parents had worked before their deaths, the boy insisted on investigating. Batman helped his new ward, the second ROBIN, and they learned that Chimera actually was disguised as multiple people. Chimera was eventually apprehended. (*Batman* #364, *Detective Comics* #531, October 1983)

In the reality shifts created by the CRISIS ON INFINITE EARTHS, Jason Todd's background altered, calling into question whether he and Batman ever faced Chimera.

CHINATOWN

GOTHAM CITY's Chinatown was located on the wharf and could be entered through an ornate golden gateway on Gate Street. One of Chinatown's highlights was famed nightclub the Crystal Palace, later destroyed by the GREEN DRAGON. Castro Street and Cathay Street could also be found in this area.

CHORN

On the distant planet ZORON, a horde of interplanetary conquerors arrived, led by Chorn. They turned the pacifist people into slaves until the arrival of the World's Finest team of Batman, ROBIN, and SUPERMAN. Given the unique properties of the planet and its solar system, the humans were granted superpowers while the Kryptonian was rendered a mere mortal. Pooling their talents and experience proved exactly what was needed to end Chorn's hold over the Zorons. (*World's Finest Comics* #114, December 1960)

CHUBB, DR.

Trained as a plastic surgeon, Chubb supplemented his routine practice by specializing in performing work on criminals. He took before-and-after photos of each patient for his files but eventually used this treasure trove to blackmail his patients. When Police Commissioner JAMES GORDON asked Chubb to examine Batman's legs after an accident, he decided there was no better place to hide the film than on the Caped Crusader's person. He told Batman that both legs were broken and needed to be placed in plaster casts, one of which also held the incriminating film. Batman used his vast athletic skill to still fight crime from a wheelchair. With ROBIN's help, he disguised the casts so no one would see BRUCE WAYNE also sporting two broken legs. The Boy Wonder additionally aided Batman in discovering the true extent of his injuries. They apprehended Chubb in his home, which saved the doctor from criminals who had invaded it, seeking the incriminating film. (*Batman* #63, October/November 1950)

CHUBB, T. WORTHINGTON

The self-described crime czar T. Worthington Chubb had operated in GOTHAM CITY long enough to study his opponent Batman. In due time he deduced that Batman was also BRUCE WAYNE. Chubb threatened to expose the Gotham Guardian's secret unless he allowed Chubb and his gang to operate unmolested. Instead, Batman and ROBIN created a set of ruses to convince Chubb he was mistaken. After that, Chubb and his men were brought to justice. (*Detective Comics* #159, May 1950)

CHUBB, THE FABULOUS ERNIE

Ernie Chubb was a brawler calling himself a boxer. The heavyweight had deluded himself into believing he was boxing's heavyweight champion when he was just another slugger. Calling himself the Fabulous Ernie Chubb, he wound up partnering with LOCK-UP in an illegal pay-per-view wrestling event called the Secret Ring. They captured varying fighters, including KILLER CROC, then threw them into the ring; only one was expected to emerge alive. There was little doubt that Croc would emerge victorious, but the entire operation was shut down by Batman and the true former heavyweight champ, WILDCAT. (*Batman/Wildcat* #1–3, April–June 1997)

CIRCE

In Batman's world there have been three different Circes active. The first and best known was the actually Circe of Greek myth, who often challenged WONDER WOMAN. The second was an obscure onetime villainess.

The third was a former runway model who took a job as a secretary at the Sionis company, Janus Cosmetics. There she met and ultimately got involved with ROMAN SIONIS, heir to the family fortune. His parents didn't approve of his relationship with a woman from a working-class family. After Roman snapped and burned down his family home in an act of vengeance, Circe ended their engagement, humiliating him in front of the Janus staff.

Soon thereafter, Roman's twisted mind led him to assume the persona of BLACK MASK. He ordered his men to track Circe down and bring her back to him. Black Mask demanded that Circe be disfigured to match his own ebony skull-like appearance. He reasoned that she'd never leave him again. Instead, Circe killed herself, depriving Black Mask of what he loved most. In the wake of her death, he began talking to a mannequin. (*Batman* #386, August 1985)

CLANCY, BRIDGET

The landlady at 1013 Parkthorne Avenue in BLÜDHAVEN, Bridget Clancy was a well-loved woman, perhaps appreciated by no one more than DICK GRAYSON. (*Nightwing* [second series] #6, November 1996)

Clancy was born in Hong Kong but raised in Ireland after her adoption as an infant. She lived in Ireland until moving to the United States to attend college in Blüdhaven. To help pay for school and living expenses, she took the landlady job, never expecting to become so close to the people dwelling in the crumbling building. It was an odd collection of tenants, including the elderly John Law (formerly the hero TARANTULA), the medicated felon AMYGDALA, and the Hogan boys Michael (Mutt) and Hank (Hero).

Her gorgeous exterior was a cover for someone with guts and a variety of skills. She could swing a hammer and maintain the building without formal training. Clancy, as she preferred to be called, also was generous and helpful to all she came into contact with.

When Dick Grayson moved in, it was awhile before the two actually met. Dick grew to like the neighbors and used his wealth to act as a benefactor, saving the apartment building from demolition. Later, he arranged for the WAYNE FOUNDATION to offer Clancy a scholarship so she could finally afford medical school.

Soon after, they flirted and even attempted dating, although Dick's odd hours as a cop and as NIGHTWING complicated matters. Worse, Clancy backed off when she learned of his long-standing relationship with BARBARA GORDON, despite her having fallen in love with Grayson. It was his revelation that led her to ultimately leave Blüdhaven to take up her studies at Bellevue Hospital in Manhattan. By leaving, she avoided being killed when BLOCKBUSTER II had the building destroyed in his vendetta against Grayson.

Some time later Nightwing had relocated to New York, but the two had yet to reconnect.

CLATE, "CRAFTY" CAL

"Crafty" Clate devised a way to ensure that he and his men got away from robberies without police pursuit. Using a transmitter hidden in a laundry truck, one of the men would send out police calls, diverting any officers who might be tracking the men after a heist. Clate's ruse, though, didn't deter Batman and ROBIN, who finally caught him. (*Detective Comics* #61, March 1942)

CLAYBER

Clayber worked for the Gotham Gem Company, which he soon discovered was fronting a gem-smuggling operation. He approached the partners who owned the company—John Wilcox, Henry Stubbs, and Ed Carder—informed them he knew their secret, and demanded to be made the fourth partner. They agreed, but soon Clayber insisted on a larger cut of the illicit profits. The partners, instead, murdered Clayber, framing ex-convict Ted Greaves for the crime. Batman and ROBIN investigated and learned the truth, bringing the three partners to justice and shutting down the smuggling business. (*Batman* #131, April 1960)

CLAYFACE

Clayface was the name used by a variety of criminals and creatures, all of which have plagued Batman's career.

The very first to use the name was BASIL KARLO, an actor driven insane when he learned his landmark film, *The Terror,* was going to be remade. Even though he was hired as a consultant, he feared that this meant the end of his career, so instead he sought to cause mayhem on the remake's set. Hiding behind a mask of *The Terror*'s antagonist, Clayface, he caused damage and near death until stopped by Batman and ROBIN. (*Detective Comics* #40, June 1940)

On Earth-2, Batman got involved with Karlo's vendetta because his fiancée, JULIE MADISON, was acting in the film. In the reality after CRISIS ON INFINITE EARTHS, Julie was no longer an actress, and Batman got involved with the Karlo cases for un-recorded reasons.

After trial, Karlo was sentenced to ARKHAM ASYLUM. When SONDRA FULLER, the fourth to use the name *Clayface,* visited him to see who started the legacy, it was Karlo who proposed that all the namesakes be united as a fighting force that became the MUDPACK. (*Detective* Comics #605–607, October–November 1989)

While trying to kill Batman with his allies, Karlo managed to gain the shape-changing powers of the other Clayfaces by injecting himself with samples taken from them. He developed the ability to project quartz-like crystal, taking the name the Ultimate Clayface. He used those abilities to hold POISON IVY hostage when she was providing fresh vegetables from ROBINSON PARK during GOTHAM CITY's period as a NO MAN'S LAND.

The second Clayface was a skin diver and treasure hunter named MATT HAGEN. He surfaced inside an unexplored grotto when he encountered a pool filled with unidentified radioactive goo. Hagen slipped into the pool, and his body was almost instantly transformed into a walking lump of protoplasm. Hagen learned that with a thought he could change shape for finite periods of time. Taking the name *Clayface,* he turned to crime and fought Batman on numerous occasions. At first he had to return to the cave every two days to renew his abilities; then he produced a copy of the substance in a lab and managed a version endowing him with up to five hours of shape-changing. In time though, his body adjusted, and he remained Clayface permanently. (*Detective Comics* #298, December 1961) Hagen fought Batman repeatedly, and his powers continued to require renewal from the original pool. (*World's Finest Comics* #264,

Basil Karlo

August/September 1980) On the other hand, with the passage of time he could go for extended periods without renewal. (*Detective Comics* #526, May 1983) Hagen eventually died during the event known as Crisis on Infinite Earths. (*Crisis on Infinite Earths* #12, March 1986)

PRESTON PAYNE was a tragic figure who became the third Clayface. Payne suffered from hyperpituitarism, a condition caused by excess hormonal secretions that caused him stiffness and pain. This condition resulted in a horrible childhood, exacerbated by abusive parents who didn't understand his issues. While working at a branch of S.T.A.R. LABS, Payne encountered a sample of Hagen's altered blood and studied it. In time he found an enzyme he thought might cure his condition and injected it. This allowed Payne the ability to shift his appearance and ease his pain, but

Preston Payne

the effects were limited in duration. On a disastrous date, his skin seemed to literally melt, horrifying his girlfriend. Worse, when he touched her, it turned out his touch was toxic; she, too, melted and died. Payne used his scientific knowledge to construct an exoskeleton to pour himself into, with a Plexiglas face mask allowing him to see. (*Detective Comics* #478, July/August 1978)

The events took a toll on his psyche, and he lost his moral balance. He also became fixated on a mannequin he named Helena, figuring the inanimate form would never melt. (*Batman Annual* #11, 1987) Payne, as the third Clayface, experienced psychotic episodes driving him to extreme actions, that were always stopped by Batman, and each time he was returned to Arkham Asylum, where Helena awaited him. To Payne, they were a married couple, and the mannequin was the one thing the doctors could rely on to calm him. During this time, a medicine had been developed that allowed Payne to control the physical pain he still felt, so the hunger that had once driven him became merely a psychological condition that also could be treated.

Sondra Fuller visited him at Arkham and encouraged him to join with other Clayfaces in forming the Mudpack. Meeting her changed Payne's life, for this was a living being who could love him. They began a romantic liaison that also produced a child, named Cassius, who would become the fifth Clayface.

In another reality Payne was seen in Arkham Asylum, but this one was a wasted version; his body ravaged with pain and disease, unsuccessful at love and at being a super-villain. (*Arkham Asylum*, 1989)

Sondra Fuller was turned into a shape-shifter by the terrorist KOBRA, called either Clayface IV or Lady Clay. He decided to oppose the super heroes who stood in his way by creating his own superpowered Strike Force Kobra. Fuller, who considered her normal appearance disfigured and ugly, agreed to the process knowing she could assume other, more pleasing visages. Unlike Hagen and his temporary abilities, she permanently possessed hers. Fuller not only duplicated people's appearances but seemed able to mimic their super-abilities as well, making her far more dangerous. (*Outsiders* #21, July 1987)

Fuller and the Strike Force were defeated, and she set out on her own path. This led her to seek out her namesakes at Arkham Asylum and convince them to form the Mudpack. To honor the fallen Hagen, they maintained a portion of his inert clay form. (*Detective Comics* #605–607, October–November 1989) There she met and fell in love with Preston Payne, which resulted in the birth of their child, Cassius. (*Shadow of the Bat* #27, May 1994)

The Mudpack were defeated time and again by Batman, and Cassius wound up in government custody. He was subjected to numerous tests to gauge the full extent of his powers. Apparently, if a piece broke off from the main body, it, too, could grow to another full-sized form—but with a retarded set of mental faculties. Should a piece be affixed to another person, the new human hybrid took on morphing abilities, from shape-changing to Cassius's father's ability to melt organic objects. Cassius appeared limited in his ability to remain in clay-like form before needing to change shape. (*Batman: Gotham Knights* #71, January 2006)

Johnny Williams, a former firefighter, was the sixth Clayface. He was the only member of a squad not to be injured during a Gotham City warehouse fire that exposed all to some form of toxic waste. While physically fine, Williams was left mentally shaken, and he slowly lost his grip on reality. In time he realized he *had* been changed by the exposure and could change his shape like the other Clayfaces. (*Batman: Gotham Knights* #60, February 2005)

Soon after, he was found by the villain known as HUSH. The bandaged criminal manipulated Williams, going so far as to hold his wife, son, and daughter hostage.

Williams agreed to do Hush's bidding, changing to resemble Hush's alter ego, TOMMY ELLIOT, in order to confuse Batman. Williams had reached a mental limit and offered to help Batman against Hush as long as the Dark Knight saved his family. Williams also seemed to know the toxic waste was slowly killing him and wanted to ensure they would be

Preston Payne

fine before he died. His last act was to clear ALFRED PENNYWORTH of murder charges. (*Batman* #616, August 2003)

One of the government lab experiments on Cassius led to Dr. Malley, of the Department of Extranormal Operations, being exposed to a sample; he became a creation dubbed Claything. Batman and CAMERON CHASE stopped the creature, and it was killed with the remaining samples locked away in a DEO facility. (*Batman* #550, January 1998)

CLENCH, THE

Ecoterrorist RĀ'S AL GHŪL found the legendary Wheel of Plagues, a mythological item that led him to develop a strain of the Ebola virus, which he intended to use to wipe out most of humanity so the Earth could heal itself. The disease was stolen and released in GOTHAM CITY by the SACRED ORDER OF SAINT DUMAS as an act of revenge for Batman taking AZRAEL away from them. The strain Ebola Gulf-A spread quickly, earning the nickname the Clench, and the death toll rapidly mounted. Azrael alerted Batman that disaster had come to the city, so it fell to the Dark Knight, ROBIN, NIGHTWING, Azrael, and CATWOMAN to span the globe in search of a cure. (*Batman: Shadow of the Bat* #48, March 1996)

At one point, Batman managed to synthesize a vaccine and provided it to POISON IVY, who had a natural immunity to the Clench, in order to help people trapped in the ritzy Babylon Towers. Instead, Ivy tried to turn this to her advantage. (*Batman* #529, April 1996) The vaccine ultimately proved ineffective, and Robin subsequently contracted the disease. (*Batman: Shadow of the Bat* #49, April 1996)

As the Teen Wonder suffered in the BATCAVE, Azrael realized he possessed stolen Saint Dumas documents that, when studied, provided the information needed to devise a proper cure. Robin was saved, but it was clear that the virus had mutated and still threatened all life.

Once the city was saved, Batman, Robin, and Nightwing headed to the Sudan in search of a permanent cure. Batman left HUNTRESS behind to watch over the city while Catwoman set out to find the Wheel of Plagues. After several battles, the trio found Rā's al Ghūl, his daughter TALIA HEAD, and the ever-present bodyguard UBU. Rā's explained that he had found the Wheel of Plagues and intended to create three diseases to destroy three major population centers. He also told Batman that Ubu would be his heir since Batman had repeatedly rejected the offer. (*Detective Comics* #700, August 1996)

Catwoman had been captured by Rā's during her hunt but freed herself and learned that Rā's intended to unleash the diseases in Edinburgh, Paris, and Gotham. Nightwing and Robin headed for Paris, where they united with HENRI DUCARD, one of the men who'd trained BRUCE WAYNE years earlier. They managed to stop Rā's LEAGUE OF ASSASSINS agents at the Louvre. (*Robin* #32, August 1996)

No sooner did Batman also achieve success in Scotland than ORACLE contacted him, letting him know that a fourth location, Calcutta, had been identified. There Batman found himself working toward a common goal with the deadly LADY SHIVA. Successfully finished there, the Dark Knight returned home. (*Batman* #534, September 1996)

Back in Gotham, the heroes united and tracked Rā's al Ghūl's boat in an effort to stop him from unleashing the final plague. Batman managed to not only stop the bomb but also defeat his nemesis BANE, who was working with Rā's. While that fight continued, Nightwing, Huntress, and Robin tackled the terrorist's guards. Robin managed to send a digital copy of the Wheel to Oracle, who extracted the vital information for a universal cure. The Clench and its related variations were no longer a threat to humanity. (*Robin* #33, September 1996)

CLEVENGER, EPSILPAH

Epsilpah Clevenger was better known to Batman and the police as the murderous MIMIC.

CLOCK, THE

In the Gotham prison system, a convict named KYLE had one claim to fame: He said he was the first criminal apprehended by the Batman. (*Detective Comics* #265, March 1959) He vowed that he'd have revenge and spent his every waking moment studying clocks until his parole. Once free, he used his knowledge to become the yellow-clad villain called the Clock. He used timepieces to attempt his plans for vengeance, boasting that he would commit time-themed robberies leading to Batman's death. Batman recognized Kyle, which explained to him the importance of 3 PM—that was the moment when Kyle had begun his prison sentence. While committing one of his crimes, the Clock accidentally dropped his watch, which Batman studied. Its high content of flour residue pointed the Caped Crusader in the direction of an old flour mill. However, the watch had intentionally been left behind, leading to a trap that captured the Dynamic Duo. With the mill set to explode at three o'clock sharp, they escaped by cutting their bonds with pieces of the watch's broken crystal. The Dynamic Duo apprehended Kyle at the Clock Fair and sent him to a police holding cell that conveniently faced the prison clock.

CLOCK KING, THE

WILLIAM TOCKMAN donned a blue bodysuit with clock designs and battled the GREEN ARROW and Speedy as the Clock King. (*World's Finest Comics* #111, August 1960) He was a repeat offender, usually fighting solo—but after one failure too many, he began to form teams. He joined the Injustice Gang before teaming with Chronos, Time Commander, and CALENDAR MAN (*Team Titans* #13–15, October–December 1993; *Showcase '94* #10, October 1994) to improve his fortunes. He reinvented himself again and gathered several young meta-humans to form the Clockwatchers. Again, the plan failed: The youths were captured by the DEO's CAMERON CHASE while Tockman escaped. (*Chase* #4, May 1998)

The Clockwatchers and their leader were later recruited for a new incarnation of the Suicide Squad. The first mission proved disastrous, and all the young allies were killed and Clock King seriously wounded. Major Disaster reported Clock King had died, although no body was found. (*Suicide Squad* [second series] #1, November 2001) Since then, a Clock Queen has been mentioned, but no connection between the two has been established.

CLOCK KING

CLOCKMASTER, THE

The man known only as the Clockmaster was an intelligent thief who devised an elaborate scheme to steal a priceless collection of gems at a GOTHAM CITY exhibit. He devised a false gem containing sleeping gas, which would allow him access to the real gems without guards interfering. However, he was concerned about the city's protectors, Batman and ROBIN. Clockmaster thus learned of some peers' robbery plans and left the Caped Crusader clues to this series of real crimes being committed at much the same time he intended his jewel heist. Batman and Robin raced across the city, apprehending the criminals until they learned of the one crime without a clue. As Robin handled a bakery larceny, Batman arrived in time to stop Clockmaster's plan. (*Batman* #141, August 1961)

CLUB OF HEROES, THE

After SUPERMAN joined the KNIGHT and SQUIRE, EL GAUCHO, LEGIONARY, and Batman in an international brotherhood of crime fighters, the BATMEN OF ALL NATIONS were renamed the Club of Heroes.

In the reality after INFINITE CRISIS, millionaire businessman John Mayhew formed the Club of Heroes with the noble goal of sharing training and information to make the world safer. He provided a twenty-billion-dollar METROPOLIS-based headquarters but the combination of heroes, sans the Man of Steel, proved explosive. After one meeting that Batman attended, things began to fall apart. Chief MAN-OF-THE-BATS and WINGMAN joined at the second meeting, but no one got along without the Dark Knight's presence.

Mayhew, a bored businessman, decided if he couldn't have heroes, he'd have revenge against Batman—who'd snubbed his dream—by becoming a villain. Years later, he summoned the heroes to his Caribbean mansion and faked his death. As the heroes investigated, Mayhew worked with Wingman and El Sombrero, one of El Gaucho's foes, to begin killing the heroes one by one. Batman couldn't save Ranger and Legionary, but he did manage to stop Mayhew's scheme. Mayhew himself was exploring the notions of good and evil with a figure known only as the Black Glove. By failing to kill the heroes, he lost his house, which was blown up. (*Batman* #667–669, October–December 2007)

CLUEMASTER

ARTHUR BROWN was a failed daytime game-show host who turned into the criminal Cluemaster. He taunted the police and Batman with clues but he was equally a failure at crime. (*Detective Comics* #351, May 1966)

Brown could not catch a break as a professional entertainer or husband. His daytime children's television series had dismal ratings and was canceled, replaced with cartoon reruns, leaving him unemployed. Brown decided he had little choice but to rob in order to pay the rent. He devised an orange body-stocking costume and a handkerchief face mask and debuted as the Cluemaster. Brown wasn't even an inventive criminal, heavily borrowing from the RIDDLER's methods—complete with leaving clues to his crimes to taunt both the GOTHAM CITY police and Batman. His most unique gimmick was wearing a series of capsules sewn onto the front of his outfit; these contained explosives and gas pellets, which he used while committing crimes. On his first outing, Cluemaster committed a robbery while his hired men tried to learn Batman's identity. If he succeeded, he could strike against the super hero's public identity and take Batman out of the picture. The Dynamic Duo stopped that scheme, beginning a pattern that would plague Cluemaster's criminal career.

He and his wife, Crystal, watched as their marriage crumbled despite the birth of their daughter, STEPHANIE. After turning to crime, Brown was in and out of jail often enough that he was always a distant parent, leaving his wife to raise Stephanie pretty much on her own.

Failing as a solo criminal, he briefly joined the Injustice Gang—but they, too, were defeated time and again by Justice League International. The gang briefly agreed to serve as a JLI branch based in Antarctica, until their base was destroyed by Major Disaster. (*Justice League Europe* #23, February 1991; *JLA Annual* #4, August 2000)

Brown, unsure of what else he could do, returned

to a life of crime. Soon after, he was back at Blackgate Penitentiary. This time, though, he worked with a psychiatrist who helped him halt his clue-leaving compulsion. Instead, he channeled those thoughts into more productive uses and developed into a surprisingly effective tactician. He practiced by organizing crimes to be committed by Wiley Cutter's gang, in exchange for a 10 percent fee. After the plan succeeded, Brown got greedy and killed Wiley, intending to take over.

By this time, his daughter was a teen and disappointed in her father. She decided to stop him, adopting her own costumed persona as the Spoiler and sending clues to the police to make certain he was foiled. She then encountered Batman as he investigated Wiley's death, and they found Cluemaster together. The father-daughter reunion was a disaster: She tried to choke him to death with a chain. (*Detective Comics* #647–648, August–September 1992)

Back at Blackgate, Cluemaster decided he had had enough time in jail and tried to bust out, only to fail once more. (*Batman: Blackgate* #1, 1997) Gotham City's devastating earthquake accomplished what he had been unable to, and Cluemaster was once more free. Being free, though, didn't seem to help as he continued to struggle with robberies, sending what money he could to Crystal and Stephanie. He continued to get arrested and accepted parole in exchange for serving with the federal government's clandestine Suicide Squad. While on a mission, Cluemaster was presumed dead. Brown had asked that if he should die, the squad would tell Crystal he'd died a hero, but they refused. (*Suicide Squad* [second series] #1, November 2001)

Instead of dying, Brown was severely burned. It took him a year to recover from the injuries and subsequent plastic surgery. Stephanie was shocked by the news of his "death" and attempted to investigate what had really happened, but even with Robin's help she came up empty-handed. (*Robin* #111–113, April–June 2003)

By the time Brown—now calling himself Aaron Black—returned to Gotham City, Stephanie had died during the horrendous events known as War Games. Black went public, seeking to find his daughter's killer. He gave away Stephanie's Spoiler history and demanded to know what had happened after her injured body was taken to Dr. Leslie Thompkins's clinic. Batman took up the challenge without realizing that he was once more responding to Cluemaster's modus operandi. He discovered that Stephanie could have been saved—but Thompkins had let her die to pay for her involvement in the gang war. Batman's investigation turned Gotham City upside down and made the citizens vulnerable once more as he crossed paths with the deadly Black Mask and Joker. Thompkins admitted her crime and was arrested, leaving Arthur and Crystal Brown to separately grieve for their lost child. (*Batman* #643–644, *Detective Comics* #809–810, October 2005)

COBB, PHIL

Small-time criminal Phil Cobb sought greater crimes under the costume of the Signalman.

COBBLEPOT, OSWALD CHESTERFIELD

Oswald Chesterfield Cobblepot grew up with a body shaped not unlike that of a penguin, earning him a hated childhood nickname and sour view of humanity. As the Penguin, he proved a deadly foe of the Batman.

COE, JEREMY

During America's colonial period, Jeremy Coe discovered the cave that was known later as the Batcave. Given the bats that inhabited the cave, Coe also took to calling it a Batcave. He used it as a base of operations, allowing him to secretly disguise himself as a Native American and enter nearby villages. Once he'd insinuated himself among the others, Coe was able to learn of any plans that might threaten the nearby colony of Gotham. His unrecorded exploits were finally discovered when Professor Carter Nichols sent Batman and Robin back in time to that period. There the Dynamic Duo aided Coe in warning a fort of an impending attack. (*Detective Comics* #205, March 1954)

COHEN, IVAN

Ivan Cohen was a detective with the Gotham City Police Department's Major Crimes Unit. Little was recorded about his personal life or career record. (*Batman* #587, March 2001)

COLBY, ART

To residents of Midville, Art Colby was the owner of the Green Anchor Nightclub. What they didn't know was that he also led a gang specializing in jewel robberies. One of their crimes had them stealing jewels from Midville's jewelry store and secreting the loot among the belongings of Sando, a circus strongman in town for performances. A jewel was found among his possessions, and Sando was arrested for the crime. When Robin heard the news, he asked Batman to help investigate since the Boy Wonder knew Sando back from his days with the Flying Graysons. The Dynamic Duo headed to Midville. Sando aided in an investigation that revealed Colby's duplicity and exonerated the strongman. (*Batman* #129, February 1960)

COLEMAN, ROBERT

Using high-tech sonic gear, Robert Coleman brought great harm to Gotham City as the Quakemaster.

COLLECTOR, THE

The Collector was an unnamed masked criminal who was known for stealing art treasures for his private use. His career was brought to an end and his collection recovered by Robin and Batwoman. (*Detective Comics* #249, November 1957)

COLLINS, LEE

Early in Batman's career, the Caped Crusader saw Lee Collins performing with boomerangs at a circus, where Collins used the weapon to take down a thief. Fascinated, Batman saw the potential in having a longer-range weapon at his disposal and asked Collins for lessons. The Australian agreed, and they worked together over the course of several days. Collins crafted the first boomerang to have the scalloped edge resembling a bat's wings. He presented the first Batarang to the Caped Crusader as a gift. (*Detective Comics* #244, June 1957)

In the reality-altering effects of the various crises, this event may no longer be part of Batman's life.

COLLINS, VANCE

Vance Collins was a former convict who had been arrested by Batman and Robin. Released, he took a job at a hot dog stand, living a peaceful life. Unfortunately, he was struck with a purple ray emanating from somewhere beyond the solar system. Bizarrely, the ray struck a nearby billboard and reflected off it, hitting Collins. Something in the alien beam's properties seemed to affect Collins, who began periodically morphing from human to resemble the creature depicted on the billboard, advertising a horror film. In his terrifying form, Collins took control of the Jackson Mob. Together they performed daring crimes, bringing them to the attention of Batman, Robin, and SUPERMAN. In time, however, the ray's affects began to wear off, and Collins reverted to his normal shape with little memory of his activities. When the ray's residual effects were gone from his body for good, Collins was mortified to learn what he had done. He joined the World's Finest team in apprehending the Jackson Mob and cleared his name. (*World's Finest Comics* #116, March 1961)

COLONEL SULPHUR

A psychological terrorist and criminal, the man called Colonel Sulphur matched wits against Batman with little success. The self-styled leader of a freelance spy ring, he manipulated people into doing his bidding. The middle-aged criminal had thinning black hair and a goatee. He sported a black glove on his right hand, which turned out to be artificial; a razor-sharp knife was hidden in the middle finger.

He abducted Mary MacGuffin, ordering her diplomat husband, Howard, to steal top-secret documents from the Pentagon. Howard did as asked, and the crime brought Batman into the investigation as clues led back to the MacGuffins' GOTHAM CITY apartment. It was there the Dark Knight learned of Mary's part in the crime. Colonel Sulphur called the apartment, and when Batman answered without providing the password the criminal had provided, he knew the game was on in earnest.

Batman knew a little something about the ruthless opportunist and his preference for committing his heinous acts at dawn, somehow believing the rising sun brought luck. He listened carefully to a taped playback and detected the sound of train tracks, narrowing it down to a sound made by an elevated train. The Dark Knight Detective tracked hotels adjacent to the L line and finally found Sulphur and Mary as he prepared to kill her. Batman fought the man, and the colonel was about to deliver a killing blow when the rising sun glinted off his knife hand, distracting him long enough for Batman to win the day. (*Batman* #241, March 1972)

The colonel turned up again when he accosted a World War II survivor upon his release from prison and demanded the location of a diamond the naval officer had hidden aboard an aircraft carrier in 1943. Batman once more spoiled Sulphur's scheme. (*Batman* #248, April 1973)

Colonel Sulphur next opposed Batman when he kidnapped Fred Danvers, a S.T.A.R. LABS scientist developing experimental rocket fuel. Danvers was the adoptive father of Kara Zor-El, SUPERGIRL, who sought help from the World's Greatest Detective to find him. They were located in a submarine, and the colonel was no match for the Maid of Steel. (*The Brave and the Bold* #160, March 1980) Note: In the post–CRISIS ON INFINITE EARTHS reality, this story never occurred.

Failing at his solo career, Colonel Sulphur joined with three other villains—General Scarr, Captain Cutlass, and Major Disaster—to acquire stolen high-tech weapons that were being sold at a METROPOLIS underworld auction. Before the bidding could conclude, SUPERMAN arrived to spoil the sale—only to be shocked by a weapon that sent him, holding a Duranian time bomb, to another dimension. When Superman eventually returned, he recruited Batman's help in stopping the criminal quartet. (*World's Finest Comics* #279–281, May 1982) Colonel Sulphur has not been seen since.

COLOSSIMO, BIRD

Colossimo was a criminal and associate of BANE, better known to most as BIRD.

COMBS, HARLAN

Harlan Combs was a thrill seeker who purchased from Joseph Rigger FIREBUG's original costume. He became a superior arsonist until he killed a babysitter who discovered his secret, bringing him to the attention of the Gotham City Police Department. He was apprehended without Batman's involvement. (*Gotham Central* #5, May 2003)

COMPOSITE SUPERMAN

The Composite Superman was a superpowered human being who temporarily gained an array of powers, enough to challenge Batman and SUPERMAN. (*World's Finest Comics* #142, June 1964)

JOE MEACH was a down-on-his-luck man having trouble finding work as a diver. To call attention to his skills, he intended to dive from a METROPOLIS high-rise building into a tank on the street below. Meach missed detecting a leak in the tank and would have died in the attempt had Superman not spotted it and rescued him. Upon hearing of his misfortunes, the Man of Steel found Meach work at the Superman Museum. While thankful for the work, Meach disliked being reduced to a custodian and developed a grudge against his benefactor. As he dusted a set of miniature statues of the thirtieth century's Legion of Super-Heroes, of which SUPERMAN had once been a member, a stray bolt of lightning hit the figurines. Since each figure had been created using advanced imaging technology, they were charged with energy, which passed into Meach. When he recovered from the jolt, Meach realized he had gained the individual powers of each Legionnaire, from Chameleon Boy's shape-shifting skill to Light Lass's gravity-defying powers.

Meach decided he now had the ability to strike back at Superman, so he re-formed himself as half Superman and half Batman with a green face, derived from BRAINIAC 5. He located the heroes and demanded to be allowed to join them as the Composite Superman. If they refused, he would announce their secret identities, which he'd learned by using Saturn Girl's telepathy. The Composite Superman set out to embarrass the World's Finest team, and as they handled each complication tossed their way, it became apparent that Meach did not wish to be a hero but really wanted to rule the world. The Composite Superman's threat ended when the powers wore off and he reverted to normal.

The Composite Superman was revived when Meach regained his powers as a part of the alien Xan's scheme to exact revenge against Batman and

COMPOSITE SUPERMAN

Superman for his father's death. Still bitter, Meach wanted to kill the super heroes and willingly fought them. He nearly succeeded—but again, the powers faded. Xan took matters into his own hands and fired his own energy weapon at them, but Meach got in the way, attempting to save the heroes. Joe Meach died for his efforts, a hero at last. (*World's Finest Comics* #168 (August 1967)

Some time later, Xan escaped from his alien prison and came back to try once more for vengeance. He used his technology again, but this time on himself, becoming a new Composite Superman. This newly powered being showed greater control over the myriad powers, so he renamed himself Amalgamax. It took Batman, Superman, and the real Legion to battle him until he was subdued more through subterfuge than raw power. (*World's Finest Comics* #283, September 1982)

In the wake of the Crisis on Infinite Earths, these events were wiped from the chronicles.

The Composite Superman image endured when a powerful computer named Crayd'll accessed the files of the teen heroes known as Young Justice and created a being who was half Robin, half Superboy. The speedster Impulse tricked the artificial entity into downloading music rather than additional files and put the creation out of action. (*Impulse* #56, January 2000)

The teen inventor Hiro Okamura, Toyman, created a spaceship featuring a Composite Superman when he aided Superman and Batman in their battle against Lex Luthor's corrupt White House administration. (*Superman/Batman* #6, March 2004)

CONDOR GANG, THE (1958)

Millionaire John Titus hid his criminal nature under the guise of the Condor. With his gang, Titus committed a string of robberies noteworthy enough to capture the attention of Batman, Robin, and Superman. To bring the Condor Gang to justice, Superman posed as Professor Milo, who was said to have invented a machine that accurately predicted the future. With the Dynamic Duo's help, the somewhat preposterous predictions all came true, catching Titus's eye. He dispatched his gang to bring Milo and the machine to him, at which time Milo revealed himself. With Batman and Robin's aid, the Condor Gang was brought to justice and Titus's identity exposed. (*World's Finest Comics* #97, October 1958)

CONDOR GANG, THE (1963)

The Condor Gang was based out of Center City but took to absorbing criminal gangs from cities coast to coast. Over time these independent groups were unified in the first-ever nationwide crime operation, with members wearing condor headgear. To hasten their expansion plans and bring public shame to one of their most feared threats—Batman—they planned to destroy the Flying Batcave, which was in Center City. As Batman was appearing as an honored gust at a policemen's convention, the gang would destroy the machine and steal the policemen's fund. Instead Batman and Robin stopped the plot, aided by a young rookie officer, Joseph Arno. (*Detective Comics* #317, July 1963)

CONGER, "KNUCKLES"

"Knuckles" Conger made his name as a boxer and was a skilled athlete. He was also a criminal who sought to commit a series of crimes as a mirror image of Batman. To accomplish this, he found a homeless shoeshine boy named Bobby Deen and made him his companion. Over the course of several weeks, Conger trained Deen in acrobatics and the manly arts. When Deen was deemed ready, the two set off for their first case, with the youth believing they were out to fight crime, emulating the Dynamic Duo. Instead Conger duped the lad so each crime prevented was actually a crime committed. Eventually, though, Deen caught on to Conger and helped Batman bring his mentor to justice. (*Batman* #15, February/March 1943)

CONJURER, THE

Using stage magician techniques, including misdirection and deception, the Conjurer committed a series of crimes. He was finally apprehended when he sought Batman's secrets and threatened B. Boswell Browne, Batman's self-appointed biographer. (*Batman* #17, June/July 1943)

CONKLIN, BUGS

During a shootout with police, criminal kingpin Bugs Conklin was seriously wounded. His men managed to escape the police and took their boss to the home of R. Davenport, a physician. With little choice, Davenport repaired the damage to the best of his abilities. To ensure the doctor's silence, the men left, bringing Davenport's daughter Marjory Davenport with them. On the trail, though, were Batman and Robin, who tracked down the gang. Marjory was rescued, and it was learned that despite the doctor's efforts, Conklin was expected to die in a matter of days. (*Batman* #23, June/July 1944)

CONROY, BIG ED

When Big Ed Conroy left prison, he was determined to stay honest. He established a messenger service specializing in company payrolls and hired other ex-convicts to provide them an honest living. The company proved successful—so much so that current criminals were leaving their gangs to hire on. Such actions infuriated Duke Ryall, a Gotham City mobster. He decided to put Conroy out of business by striking at the payrolls and making it appear that Conroy and his employees had returned to their criminal ways. Batman and Robin investigated the crimes and apprehended Ryall and his men, clearing Conroy and the company of wrongdoing. (*Batman* #35, June/July 1946)

COOK, JOHN

The Namesake Club comprised folks who shared names with famous people throughout history. The organization was so successful that when several patrons died, they left large bequests to the club. John Cook, the club's vice chairman, decided to hasten some of these deaths and take possession of the bequests for himself. After he killed two members, Batman and Robin investigated and saved the lives of others. Cook was arrested. (*Detective Comics* #183, May 1952)

COOPER, HARRIET

On Earth-1, Harriet Cooper was Dick Grayson's aunt, sister to his father John Grayson, who came to stay with Dick and Bruce Wayne at Wayne Manor. Harriet Cooper had doted on her younger brother, John, and worshipped Dick as well. In the wake of her brother's death, Harriet considered taking Dick into her home. However, her husband was an invalid, the result of a grave injury. Cooper returned to work, taking on two jobs to make ends meet. Given her circumstances, she was grateful when Bruce Wayne offered to care for Dick as his guardian. Still, she refused Wayne's offer of cash to ease her burdens. In time, though, her husband's injury benefits mysteriously increased, and she never found out how. (*Detective Comics* #328, June 1964)

Cooper's husband passed away and left Cooper uncertain of her next steps. She didn't need both jobs and had spare time on her hands. The timing was such that when she heard the tragic news that Wayne's butler, Alfred Pennyworth, had died in an accident, she saw an opportunity. She felt the millionaire playboy and his ward needed looking after and arrived to do so. In reality, the men were concerned about their ability to spring into action as Batman and Robin without giving away their secret. While Cooper meant well, she was clearly unaccustomed to their lifestyles and left after a short period of time. (*Detective Comics* #328, June 1964)

During her short stay in the manor, Cooper was frequently frustrated by the odd comings and goings of both Wayne and her nephew. She heard odd sounds from one room and saw flashing lamps from another (signaling an incoming hotline call from Police Commissioner James Gordon). Cooper began suspecting that Wayne led some sort of double life and feared for Dick; Wayne, in turn, was concerned that the kindly older woman was zeroing in on his secret identity. She even began setting up cameras throughout the mansion in an effort to find out what Wayne was up to.

Unwittingly, her efforts provided a clue to the Caped Crusader in his case against the Cluemaster. (*Detective Comics* #351, May 1966) Cooper's attempts to learn the truth came to an end when Alfred returned to life and she realized there was no further need for her to stay. (*Detective Comics* #364, June 1967)

Cooper stayed in Gotham City, where a lingering health issue grew worse, requiring hospitalization. To help the process, the doctors used cryosurgery—but the device failed, prompting Batman and Robin to track Mister Freeze in order to obtain his freeze gun and cannibalize it for needed parts. (*Detective Comics* #373, March 1968) Cooper survived the operation but needed time to recuperate. Wayne moved her back to the manor and Alfred cared for her. (*Superman's Pal Jimmy Olsen* #111, June 1968; *Detective Comics* #380, October 1968) After she recovered, she moved out but stayed in touch with her remaining family.

Cooper's last recorded visit with her family was over the Christmas holidays some years in the past. (*Batman Family* #4, March/April 1976)

In the reality after Crisis on Infinite Earths, Harriet Cooper has not been seen.

He was initially so focused on his target that he remained unaware of events around him, allowing the Dark Knight to apprehend him. Even with his constricting tail as a superior weapon, Copperhead was easily stopped time and again. His suit was frictionless, which, coupled with his ability to compact his form, allowed him to gain access where most humans could not reach.

The Copperhead worked solo and often in groups until he sold his soul to the demon Neron and became a living snake. Deadlier and more vicious, spitting poison, Copperhead was a larger threat. Still, he was killed in a battle with Kate Spencer, the MANHUNTER. (*Manhunter* [second series] #1, October 2004)

In the wake of his death, the name *Copperhead* was used by an Indian super heroine. (*52* #10, September 2006) The full extent of her abilities have yet to be recorded.

CORBETT, MADOLYN

Madolyn Corbett was a stalker, and her target was millionaire BRUCE WAYNE. When Wayne went to confront her, he found her dead in her own home. Not for the first time was Wayne suspected of murdering a woman. The police arrived and, given his celebrity, Commissioner JAMES GORDON himself conducted the interview. The investigation led them to believe that the mentally disturbed woman had been unable to achieve her goal—Wayne—and committed suicide. (*Batman* #517, April 1995)

CORRIGAN, JIM

There have been two Jim Corrigans in Batman's life. One was a cop during the 1940s, who was gunned down by gangsters and became the mortal host for the Wrath of God called the SPECTRE. On Earth-2 the Spectre and Batman served together in the JUSTICE SOCIETY OF AMERICA, while on the combined Earth after the CRISIS ON INFINITE EARTHS, Batman and the Spectre crossed paths on numerous occasions.

There was also a corrupt member of the GOTHAM CITY POLICE DEPARTMENT named Jim Corrigan. In addition to examining crime scenes and studying forensic evidence, Corrigan supplemented his income by selling collectible evidence on the black market.

Corrigan's corruption was an open secret among the G.C.P.D., but the Internal Affairs division had trouble building an airtight case against him. Their efforts were complicated when RENEE MONTOYA accosted Corrigan during the investigation resulting from her partner, CRISPUS ALLEN, being accused of murder.

COPPERHEAD

Wearing a snake costume and appearing unusually wiry, the thief called Copperhead became a recurring threat to Batman and subsequently other heroes until his death. (*The Brave and the Bold* #78, June 1968)

His real name was never revealed. He first fought Batman, WONDER WOMAN, and BATGIRL in GOTHAM CITY. At first Copperhead appeared to be an above-average thief, but he grew deadlier in subsequent confrontations and took to working as an assassin-for-hire. This allowed him to indulge his passion for collecting transistor radios, antiques from an earlier time.

Although he was cleared, Allen was unhappy that IA had not put Corrigan out of business, so he began investigating the man on his own. He built a superior case—but before Allen could present his evidence, Corrigan lured him away from headquarters and shot him dead. Although Corrigan was arrested for the murder, he had prepared an alibi that could not be shaken. Eventually he was freed.

His freedom sent Montoya into a rage followed by depression and self-destructive behavior. Losing all respect for the law, she finally confronted Corrigan in his apartment. The previously smug Corrigan recognized that she was ready to kill him and broke down, begging for mercy. Montoya relented, letting Corrigan live, and resigned from the G.C.P.D. Corrigan took to drinking heavily and when Allen, the new host for the Spectre, found him, he chose not to take his life. Instead, Mal Allen, Crispus's youngest son, found Corrigan and shot him to death. (*Crisis Aftermath: The Spectre* #3, September 2006)

CORROSIVE MAN

Derek Mitchell was a GOTHAM CITY police officer who gave in to the city's pervasive corruption. Unlike many of his fellow officers, Derek Mitchell's involvement was discovered, leading to his arrest and imprisonment. Mitchell escaped from BLACKGATE PENITENTIARY and sought revenge against MORTIMER KADAVER, the killer who'd set him up for arrest. Eluding the police seeking him, he was down at the Gotham docks when a bolt of lightning struck. The ensuing explosion of a building doused him in a unique blend of chemicals and hazardous waste. This apparently activated Mitchell's meta-gene and altered his body to emit a highly corrosive' acid. Mitchell continued his hunt for Kadaver, now convinced he had the power to end the villain's life without complication.

When Mitchell found Kadaver, the killer was torturing his latest victim over a lime pit. Before Mitchell could exact revenge, Batman interfered and a fight began. During the struggle, Mitchell fell into the lime pit, the mineral neutralizing his acidic touch, allowing the Caped Crusader to subdue him. (*Detective Comics* #587–588, June–July 1988)

CORT, MAXWELL

This deranged police sergeant took on the costumed persona of NIGHT-SCOURGE.

COSSACK, THE

Three different people have been named the Cossack in Batman's world. The first fought the Doom Patrol once and disappeared. The second was a merchant seaman known to be from the Baltics and nicknamed the Cossack. When in GOTHAM CITY's port, he also earned a reputation as a brawler. When Batman arrived to break up a riot that had started out as an illegal bare-knuckle fight, he was warned off by a rookie cop, Mercedes Stone. He allowed the police to do their work, staying on the rooftop, until he realized the Cossack had brutally attacked every cop. Stone was seriously injured, her partner dead. Batman agreed to help train Stone to fight better, but her grief turned to anger and six months later she was suspended from the force for excessive violence. She turned her attentions

to tracking down the Cossack and avenging her partner. It took her five years, but Stone managed to find him. Better, she arranged to get into the ring with him for an ultimate fighting match that was broadcast on an illegal closed-circuit network. When Batman tracked the signal to mobster Jimmy Gluck, the Dark Knight saw the Cossack viciously beating Stone on the screen. He offered Gluck the twenty thousand dollars he'd just confiscated in order to get in the ring with the Cossack, hoping to save Stone's life. Batman and the massive Cossack squared off; after the Caped Crusader sustained a shoulder injury, the Cossack was moving in for the kill. Stone distracted him, getting staked for her trouble. Batman, angered and nearly out of control, beat the Cossack into submission. It took every ounce of self-control not to kill him despite the crowd's fevered encouragement. The police arrived at that moment, arresting the Cossack while Batman took Stone to safety. (*Legends of the Dark Knight* #37, September 1992)

A third man took the name Cossack but was better known as the DARK RIDER.

COUNT, THE

MICHAEL STRAIT took on the name of the Count, organizing GOTHAM CITY's bunko rackets into a single, smooth-running business. It took undercover police officer SHIRLEY HOLMES, ALFRED PENNYWORTH, Batman, and ROBIN to bring the business to an end. (*Batman* #28, April/May 1945)

COURTNEY, KARL

Karl Courtney was an embittered criminal who sought vengeance on his three brothers as CAPTAIN STINGAREE.

COYNE, JOE

Criminal Joe Coyne, the PENNY PLUNDERER, was responsible for one of the Batman's most famous trophies.

CRADDOCK, "GENTLEMAN" JIM

This former nineteenth-century highwayman was hung but became the vengeful GENTLEMAN GHOST, plaguing Hawkman and Batman.

CRAIG, AL

Al Craig ran a training operation for juvenile delinquents, working out of the gymnasium he owned. Once they were ready, each youth donned a ROBIN outfit and simultaneously committed crimes across GOTHAM CITY. Despite police confusion over the Boy Wonder's seeming new career, Batman and Robin managed to crack the case and arrest Craig. (*Detective Comics* #342, August 1965)

CRAIG, ELTON

Elton Craig found a box of capsules that had survived the destruction of the planet KRYPTON. The criminal had been searching among meteor fragments, hoping to find some KRYPTONITE to use against SUPERMAN. Instead he had the box, which was inscribed in English with a note saying each vial would restore superpowers to a person for twenty-four hours. Later, Superman explained

that Jor-El had intended the vials as a medicinal aid for any Kryptonians who had made it safely to Earth, although Superman was the sole survivor. Craig took one dose and gained superpowers that made him a match for the Man of Steel. He fought Superman and injured him with some kryptonite. The METROPOLIS Marvel summoned Batman and ROBIN for help, asking each to also take a dose from the box. The Dynamic Duo complied and fought Craig. When his powers faded first, Craig was no longer a match for Batman and Robin and was apprehended. (*World's Finest Comics* #87, March/ April 1957)

Craig was placed in a Metropolis prison but soon after broke out. He headed for GOTHAM CITY and the General Chemical Company, where he'd hidden the last vial of Jor-El's serum. While Superman, Batman, and Robin searched for Craig, BATWOMAN deduced where Elton was headed. She arrived just as Craig unearthed the vial, and they fought over it. She managed to snatch it from him and drank the serum rather than let him have it. Endowed with temporary superpowers, Batwoman easily grabbed Craig and returned him to Metropolis. (*World's Finest Comics* #90, September/October 1957)

CRAIL, VINCENT

Vincent Crail studied handwriting and became an acknowledged expert in his field. However, he also committed forgery and was wanted by the police. Crail decided that there would be tremendous advantages to unearthing Batman's true identity through handwriting analysis. He narrowed down his list of suspects to Howard Dane, Ted Stevens, Guy Wilford, and BRUCE WAYNE, four men who had been suspected at some time in the past of being the Gotham Guardian. Despite his efforts, Crail was found and apprehended by Batman and ROBIN. Robin noted that Crail was doomed to fail since the Dynamic Duo had both practiced to sign their heroic names with their left hands, rather than their right-handed inclination. (*Batman* #92, June 1955)

CRANE, JACK

Jack Crane was better known to the police and Batman as the costumed criminal SAVAGE SKULL.

CRANE, JONATHAN

University-professor-turned-criminal Jonathan Crane sought to master people through their fears as costumed felon the SCARECROW.

CRATCHITT, TIMMY

Timmy Cratchitt's father, Bob, was wasting away in a GOTHAM CITY prison, convicted of murder. With no other family, Timmy had been sent to an orphanage, where he encountered Batman. Hearing of the boy's plight, Batman looked into the case and learned that Bob had been framed. With the real murderer found, Bob Cratchitt was released and reunited with Timmy in time for Christmas. (*Batman* #9, February/March 1942)

CRAWFORD, BRANDON

Brandon Crawford was a reclusive scientific genius who accidentally transformed the seemingly deceased ALFRED PENNYWORTH into the villainous OUTSIDER. (*Detective Comics* #356, October 1966)

CRAZY QUILT

On Earth-2 the lawbreaker known as Crazy Quilt headed up a nationwide criminal operation. Earlier he'd been an artist of some renown who was also leading a double life as a thief. He had been blinded during an assassination attempt by rival criminals. He had his men find a qualified surgeon and then held him hostage until he performed surgery to help the painter's sight. These attempts left the villain with imperfect sight, allowing him to see only bright, primary colors. Enraged by what he considered a botched operation, the man killed his doctor—and so Crazy Quilt was born. He adopted a colorful costume and wore a helmet that emitted

multicolored spotlights. In his new career as Crazy Quilt he continued committing crimes but actually wound up being defeated on at least four occasions by the youths known as the Boy Commandos. (*Boy Commandos* #15, March 1946)

Relocating to GOTHAM CITY, Crazy Quilt announced his arrival although no one paid attention, his words and lights lost amid the city's hustle and bustle. He intended to change that but first he established his headquarters, dubbed the Color Dome and complete with a Color Organ so he could indulge his passion for music. If the city wasn't going to notice his colorful presence, he intended to rob Gotham of its color. With his men bleaching everything from flags to paintings, things were looking rather gray. Even ROBIN the Boy Wonder found his bright costume rendered white when he first opposed Crazy Quilt. In time, he figured out that the lack of color was a ruse to hide the fact that Crazy Quilt intended to actually steal the priceless paintings that seemed ruined. (*Star Spangled Comics* #123, December 1951)

Years later, Paul Dekker, an underworld fence, took on the Crazy Quilt persona but without the unique helmet, substituting a simple hood. He committed a series of crimes that led people to think he was insane, but in actuality he had hidden his loot in innocuous items that he later recovered. It fell to international troubleshooters the Blackhawks to bring the second Crazy Quilt's career to an end. (*Blackhawk* #180, January 1963)

On Earth-1, Crazy Quilt was much the same but had only opposed Batman and Robin in Gotham City. (*Batman* #316, October 1979)

When Crazy Quilt was paroled from prison, he learned that his eyesight was failing altogether. Rather than accept his fate, he stole an experimental laser from Gotham's S.T.A.R. LABS branch, eluding Batman and Robin. Once more he had his men kidnap a surgeon to handle the delicate surgery.

As he recovered, Crazy Quilt remained sequestered behind a deadly array of light-based weapons intended to keep the Dynamic Duo at bay. When they finally reached him, Robin grabbed an instrument tray and reflected Crazy Quilt's helmet lights back at him. The sensitive eyes, still recovering from the surgery, were injured and the man's greatest fear came true: He was left blind.

Desperate, Crazy Quilt once more sought out a surgeon, Dr. Kinski, who might help him regain his sight. This doctor added electrodes between the brain, optic nerves, and helmet, which enabled Crazy Quilt to actually see, but only through the helmet lenses. The helmet retained its light-emitting abilities, as proven by Crazy Quilt killing his doctor. Now "cured," he was ready to resume his criminal ways—but first, he wanted revenge against Robin, even though at the time Robin was JASON TODD, not DICK GRAYSON. The second Boy Wonder was in uniform for just a day when he was attacked. As Crazy Quilt fought, Robin managed to deflect the light beams and then smash the helmet, rendering the villain blind once more. (*Batman* #368, *Detective Comics* #535, February 1984)

When RÃ'S AL GHÚL freed criminals from prison, he provided Crazy Quilt with a new helmet, but rather than aid the ecoterrorist Crazy Quilt set

off on his own. (*Batman* #400, October 1986) He wound up apprehended and was remanded, this time, to ARKHAM ASYLUM. He was later transferred to Belle Reve in Louisiana and while there, rejected an offer from the demon Neron. Crazy Quilt bounced between Arkham and Belle Reve, where he finally attacked the warden during a riot. (*JLA* #34, October 1999)

During the formation of the criminal Society, a female wearing a similar helmet and outfit and calling herself Crazy Quilt debuted. Nothing was revealed about her or if the original villain's status had changed. (*Villains United* #2, August 2005)

CREEPER, THE

The Creeper was initially a costumed persona of crusading journalist Jack Ryder, only to later become twin personalities inhabiting the same body. (*Showcase* #73, March/April 1968)

On Earth-1, Jack Ryder was a television host who angered his management, which yanked him off the air. He subsequently became a security investigator for his network. One of his first cases was to figure out the whereabouts of Professor Ephraim Yatz, abducted by Communist spies. When he determined Yatz was being held at the site of a costume party, he quickly bought odds and ends from a costume shop and became the garish Creeper, with a green wig, yellow body stocking and face paint, and short red sheepskin cape. His attempt to rescue Yatz left him wounded from a knife and lying in the same room with the doctor. Yatz used an experimental formula he carried to heal the wound—but first implanted a device in Ryder's stomach. He then placed the device's twin in the journalist's palm. Yatz explained that the serum not only would heal Ryder but also endow him with enhanced strength, agility, and endurance. The dual devices would enable him to make the Creeper outfit appear and disappear. Before Ryder could free Yatz, the professor was shot; police believed the Creeper had killed him.

Ryder used his Creeper persona to battle crime and corruption, eventually regaining his on-camera duties. His gonzo journalism style and combative on-air personality were good matches for the wild and anarchic fighting style used by his alter ego. Some time after beginning his career, the Creeper aided Batman in stopping the insectoid creature called HELLGRAMMITE. (*The Brave and the Bold* #80, October/November 1968) The Creeper and the Dark Knight crossed paths on other occasions, although no real friendship ever developed. The Creeper even took on the deadly JOKER during one notable case and survived. (*The Joker* #3, September/October 1975) Ryder's career led him to a variety of cities, ending in Boston when the reality-altering events of the CRISIS ON INFINITE EARTHS struck.

In the wake of those events, Ryder was much the same, but the Creeper seemed more of a schizophrenic being than a role being played. There was serious doubt as to whether the Creeper and Yatz's formula were making Ryder insane. Additionally, Yatz revealed that the device he had implanted actually imprinted an object in its circuitry, allowing the costume to appear and disappear. Also, Ryder had been drugged by the criminals when he was injured—the serum that entered his bloodstream at the same time thus altered him in a unique way, never to be repeated. The makeup of his blood was also imprinted, so every time he transformed from Ryder to the Creeper, the altered blood was re-created. (*The Creeper* [second series] #1, December 1997)

At one point Ryder confronted his dual personas thanks to WONDER WOMAN's lasso of truth, but it was something he ignored. Instead he entered into a vicious grudge against the villainous Eclipso. Their climactic fight seemingly left the Creeper dead, but the Yatz formula slowly healed him. (*Eclipso* #13, November 1993)

Reality was altered yet again through the events known as the INFINITE CRISIS. In the reordered world Ryder remained a journalist, but this time he worked for the METROPOLIS *Daily Planet* before moving on to a newspaper job in GOTHAM CITY. Some time after that, Ryder became host of the television series *You Are Wrong!* With his confrontational style, he goaded his guests on hot-button topics of the day. Preparing for a show, Ryder studied the work of Dr. Vincent Yatz, who had a new form of nanotechnology that would be used for medical therapy. Yatz's work was being tested on burn victims, and one test subject tried to help himself to a sample. A fight broke out and Yatz, fearing for his work, injected himself with the last sample. Ryder arrived and was shot in the head, then left for dead. Yatz's nanotechnology was used to save Ryder's life and it interacted with his cells, allowing him to transform himself into the Creeper. (*The Creeper* #1, October 2006)

When the new Creeper took on the Joker in Gotham City, it caught Batman's attention. The Dark Knight studied Jack Ryder and came to understand the schizophrenic nature of the man; he provided guidance but no direct aid. In the end Batman had to capture the Joker on his own when the Creeper had his own issues to deal with. Batman informed the Creeper that Professor Yatz had injected Ryder with a serum containing Yatz's unique nanotechnology, called the smart skin, but also elements derived from the Joker's deadly venom, which explained his manic state. Batman warned Ryder that the venom in its pure form killed or drove many insane. In analyzing Ryder's contaminated blood, he observed that the makeup was volatile, with two cellular structures competing to occupy the same space. Batman synthesized a compound that he anticipated could cure Ryder and gave him the vial. While Ryder considered this, the Creeper took offense, accusing Batman of trying to eliminate him. The Dark Knight let Ryder and the Creeper decide what to do. The new life-form decided to destroy the vial but work together on the side of good. (*The Creeper* [fourth series] #6, March 2007)

In the potential future of the 853rd century, a being called Insanitation arrived on the planet IAI, drawn to this energy source called Creeper. A Jack Ryder existed in the year 85,271, worn out after years as a hero. The force split Ryder and Creeper into separate beings for the first time. Insanitation battled and injured the Creeper, which forced Ryder to reunite with his alter ego, their lives inextricably linked. (*DC One Million*, 1998)

CRIER, THE

On one of Batman and ROBIN's time-travel trips courtesy of PROFESSOR CARTER NICHOLS, they visited ancient Baghdad. While there, they stopped a criminal known as the Crier given his tendency to weep while committing his robberies. (*Batman* #49, October/November 1948)

CRIME ALLEY

A small side street in GOTHAM CITY's EAST END was formally known as PARK ROW. Over the years it fell into the shadows and became unsafe. It was on this street that THOMAS and MARTHA WAYNE lost their lives and BRUCE WAYNE set off on his path toward becoming the Batman. On the anniversary of their deaths, Batman arrived in the shadows and left behind memorial flowers. Crime Alley was where Dr. LESLIE THOMPKINS maintained her clinic. Later, it was where Batman first met JASON TODD, who was stealing the BATMOBILE's tires. (*Detective Comics* #457, March 1976)

In a potential future, it was also where Batman and SUPERMAN engaged in a climactic battle. (*Batman: The Dark Knight Returns* #4, 1986)

CRIME DOCTOR, THE

MATTHEW THORNE was a middle aged physician on Earth-2 who liked performing surgery but was truly energized when he committed criminal

The Crime Doctor (front) , Killer Croc, Clayface, and the Ventriloquist with Scarface

acts. As a result, he created the persona of the Crime Doctor, providing criminals with insightful diagnoses. He was also available to make house calls during crimes that developed complications. During a confrontation with Batman and Robin, the Crime Doctor honored his Hippocratic Oath and performed a life-saving appendectomy, then allowed himself to be arrested. (*Detective Comics* #77, July 1943)

Just one month later, though, he escaped and took his criminal practice on the road, working from a trailer. The Dynamic Duo pursued him; during a battle, Robin was shot by one of the doctor's men in violation of the doctor's orders. Again Thorne risked capture to save the Boy Wonder, although this time he managed to get away, heading for California. Once more his skills were required to help the wife of one of his hirelings, although this time Thorne refused. He committed his next crime, and the woman died. The angry widower found the Crime Doctor and mortally wounded him. By the time Batman arrived, it was too late; the remorseful doctor died. (*Batman* #18, August/September 1943)

On Earth-1, the Crime Doctor was physician BRADFORD THORNE. During his career he treated BRUCE WAYNE for a shoulder injury. Later, when Batman took on the Crime Doctor, the Caped Crusader's uniform tore and Thorne recognized his own handiwork, learning Batman's true identity. Master smuggler STERLING T. SILVERSMITH heard of the doctor's knowledge and had Thorne poisoned, offering the antidote in exchange for the secret. Batman arrived, but by the time he could get Thorne treatment, the poison had left him in a vegetative state. (*Detective Comics* #494–495, September–October 1980)

The Crime Doctor who existed in the reality created by the CRISIS ON INFINITE EARTHS had Thorne recover from Silversmith's poison. It was also revealed that he was brother to the corrupt politician RUPERT THORNE. Undaunted by his injury, Thorne resumed his criminal ways, although he apparently no longer remembered Batman's true name. Instead he opened a hospital for the underworld. There he was responsible for the plastic surgery that turned actor PAUL SLOANE into a TWO-FACE doppelgänger, CHIMERA. (*Detective Comics* #579, 581, October, December 1987)

The Crime Doctor continued to operate his hospital but abandoned the "do no harm" part of his oath. In fact, he began resorting to withholding treatment when it suited him or even using slipshod surgical techniques. He also took to wearing star-shaped glasses, said to be a souvenir from his first victim, Katherine Wheyhall, the nurse who'd first voiced her suspicions about his actions.

Hired by the criminal Society, he tortured the villains comprising the Secret Six to learn the identity of their leader, Mockingbird. CATMAN resisted the torture long enough to stab and blind Thorne in one eye. (*Villains United* #3, September 2005)

In the wake of this, Thorne wanted to break away from the Society. Instead they sent PROMETHEUS to make him reconsider his choice by kidnapping, torturing, and killing his young daughter Bethany. Before he could complete the mission, the BIRDS OF PREY interfered and saved the girl. The Crime Doctor had seen enough and caused enough misery for all, so he chose to kill himself, ensuring that his daughter would live. LADY SHIVA took the girl and brought her to Asia, where she began training as a martial artist and assassin. (*Birds of Prey* #95, August 2006)

CRIMESMITH

RAND GARROW was a criminal once arrested and jailed by Batman. When he was freed early after using his know-how to upgrade prison facilities, he used his genius to commit smarter and better crimes. As Crimesmith, Garrow was not only a cunning planner but also a gifted inventor who designed his own tools for his crimes. Among his creations was a burrowing machine that dug under structures to reach vaults. He'd aid other criminals for 50 percent of the profits, all to fund his master plan. When he was ready, he unleashed a horde of robot attackers that threw GOTHAM CITY into a panic. ROBIN flew the BATPLANE to skywrite a message designed to reassure the populace. Batman, meanwhile, worked with the police to track and apprehend Crimesmith, ending the robotic threat. (*World's Finest Comics* #68, January/February 1954)

In the reality after the CRISIS ON INFINITE EARTHS, Dr. Jeffrey Fraser was the Crimesmith, a detail-oriented criminal mastermind. He sold his services to thieves in exchange for a hefty percentage of their take. The maps and plans always indicated where the security cameras would be, allowing them to avoid surveillance. Crimesmith took the unusual step of implanting explosive devices in his underlings so he could remotely detonate the bombs should any employees fail to follow his orders or turn stool pigeon.

Regardless, Batman managed to track down Crimesmith. In the end he died when his headquarters went up in flames. (*Batman* #443–444, January–February 1990)

CRIMSON KNIGHT, THE

GOTHAM CITY'S residents were surprised to see a knight in crimson armor arrive to battle crime. Armed with his electrically charged broadsword and bulletproof armor and shield, the Crimson Knight was readily welcomed as another protector.

What no one realized was that the Knight was a fiction created by DICK LYONS, an underworld figure who launched an audacious scheme designed to get him close to the Liberty Train. Lyons figured that if the Crimson Knight was adored, he'd be invited to the honor guard that traveled with the train, which carried many of the nation's most precious documents. He'd then use the armor to help himself steal the documents and blackmail the federal government into paying to get them back. To gain the city's trust, Lyons planned a series of heists for his men then, as the Knight, subdued his own employees. Batman, ROBIN, and the Knight were picked for the honor guard, but before Lyons could complete the robbery, Batman apprehended him, having previously figured out the plan. (*Detective Comics* #271, September 1959)

CRISIS ON INFINITE EARTHS

The universe in which Batman lived was created and re-created repeatedly. At the time of the Big Bang, there were but two universes, one composed of positive matter, the other of anti-matter.

On the distant planet Oa, in the universe's center, a scientist named Krona attempted to understand the act of Creation in violation of his people's taboos. As Krona witnessed the formation of the universe, an explosion rippled across reality, shattering the two universes, forming countless parallel realities.

In most recorded parallel universes, there was a BRUCE WAYNE who became the Batman.

The explosion also awoke two cosmic beings, twins, who had once confronted each other, and the battle caused both to enter coma-like states. One, the Anti-Monitor, resided in the anti-matter universe of Qward and hungered for power. Using his energies and the Weaponers of Qward as his army, the Anti-Monitor began eliminating one universe after enough, unleashing a wave of anti-matter that destroyed them entirely. His counterpart, the Monitor, searched through the remaining universes as well as time and space to put together an army that could hold off the Anti-Monitor until he could be stopped for good.

In the ensuing battle, all but five worlds were destroyed; these five were merged into one, with reality reordered and people's lives modified to fit the new template. This left only one primary incarnation of each person, so there was no longer an Earth-2 Batman who'd died prior to these events—just a single Batman. No one remembered the parallel worlds or variations in their lives. The sole exception, a person who existed but shouldn't have, was the Kara Zor-El of Earth-2, who was known as Power Girl.

The Anti-Monitor still wanted to destroy even the sole remaining positive-matter universe, but was ultimately annihilated by the SUPERMAN from Earth-2.

The Superman and LOIS LANE of Earth-2, the ALEXANDER LUTHOR of Earth-3, and the Superboy from Earth-Prime entered a crystalline limbo, shielded from the reordered universe.

In the aftermath, many heroes and villains and civilians died, but the single positive and anti-matter universes endured. (*Crisis on Infinite Earths* #1–12, April 1985–March 1986)

In the years following this cataclysmic event, reality was continually altered, culminating in the events known as INFINITE CRISIS.

CROCKY

To children around America, the green crocodile called Crocky was a beloved companion. His appearances on syndicated television, movies, theme parks, and merchandise made him ubiquitous. Crocky's catchphrases included "You Be Me. I Am You" in addition to "It all fits together like a hand and a glove. It all fits together with love! So long until tomorrow and remember to be a happy gator!" (*Robin* #42, June 1997)

TIM DRAKE cited Crocky, in his white T-shirt with a red heart, as one of his childhood idols. The popular cereal Crocky Crunch was a favorite of DICK GRAYSON; the cereal also sponsored the HALY BROS. CIRCUS. (*Birds of Prey* #8, August 1999)

The Crocky licensing empire was run by Ellen Anders. When a theatrical production was in the offing, the crocodile's human persona, Dexter

Crabtree, demanded a raise and points to appear in *Crocky the Movie*. Instead, PARAGON PICTURES' Calvin Berkowitz had him unceremoniously fired. (*Detective Comics* #668, November 1993). The movie did so well that a sequel was made only months later, *Crocky 2: The Motion Picture*. Logically, Crabtree became a suspect of the GOTHAM CITY POLICE DEPARTMENT when someone in a Crocky suit began committing robberies. Anders admitted that two costumes had gone missing from Paragon's Gotham facility. With Robin's help, the true culprit, Mr. Bingo from the television series, was nabbed. Crabtree was rehired.

CRONIN, LEW

When counterfeiter Lew Cronin served his prison sentence, he learned from a cellmate the whereabouts of two million dollars in stolen gold bullion. Cronin soon after escaped prison and dug up the gold, creating an elaborate scheme to launder the bullion and get rich without being caught. He posed as Mark Medalion, the wheelchair-bound coin dealer who peddled treasure maps in exchange for 50 percent of their find. People bought the maps and found the bullion, already smelted and turned into imitation ancient coins, thinking they were getting rich. As word about the maps spread, "Lucky" Smith and his gang took to stealing the maps and looting the "found treasure" for themselves. Batman and ROBIN exposed the fraud, and Cronin was returned to jail. (*World's Finest Comics* #20, Winter 1945)

CROSSMAN, KARL

This restaurateur turned costumed criminal after sharing a cell with Captain Cold, bedeviling GOTHAM CITY as the pirate CAPTAIN STINGAREE.

CROWN, CAROLINE

GREGORIAN FALSTAFF wanted WAYNE ENTERPRISES and did whatever he thought it would take to gain control. He maneuvered BRUCE WAYNE's longtime secretary GWEN ATKINS to leave and had her replaced with Caroline Crown. The new, equally attractive assistant committed numerous acts of corporate espionage to provide Falstaff with vital information. (*Batman* #323, May 1980)

When Wayne began to investigate Falstaff, he learned that Crown had been blackmailed into committing her crimes—Falstaff was holding her young daughter, Elizabeth, hostage. As a result, Batman rescued Elizabeth and helped shut down Falstaff's criminal activities.

Crown remained Wayne's secretary for a short time after those events but eventually left the company to raise Elizabeth.

CRYSTAL CREATURE, THE

The Crystal Creature was an unusual living crystalline structure that seemingly emerged from beneath the Earth and ran amok until subdued by Batman and ROBIN. Scientists theorized that the creature was given life through a unique combination of factors including an underground volcanic eruption, which opened a cask of atomic waste that in turn coated fish, and mutation occurred. The mindless being sought metal as sustenance and was eventually lured out of GOTHAM CITY by Robin, who used steel cubes like pet treats. Batman, meantime, used a radio transmitter to shatter the creature with sonic waves. (*Detective Comics* #272, October 1959)

CULLEN, BART

When gang boss Bart Cullen discovered a crashed alien vessel, he looted it. With the advanced technology, he decided to pass himself off to rival boss Tod Garret as an extraterrestrial. Together they formed the GIMMICK GANG and used the alien equipment to commit a series of spectacular crimes. All along, Cullen planned to double-cross his partner by eventually exposing Garret and the gang to the police. Then, on his own, Cullen would control Gotham's underworld. Instead, after apprehending the Gimmick Gang, Batman exposed the alien gangster as a mere mortal. (*Batman* #160, December 1963)

CULLEN, BOBO

In a fight against the Dynamic Duo, Cullen gained possession of Batman's famed UTILITY BELT. To regain it before Cullen could figure out that Batman's fingerprints would be on it—putting his secret identity at risk—Batman set up a scheme to get close to Cullen. He and ROBIN posed as Spence and Li'l Red, common criminals who could be passed off as Batman and Robin to elude police suspicion. They hired on with Hugh Bradford and his partner Wilks but needed a convincing Utility Belt to complete the ruse. Cullen let it be known the belt could be rented for a price. When they met to arrange the details, Spence and Li'l Red revealed their true personas and regained the precious belt while apprehending a handful of criminals. (*Batman* #158, September 1960)

CYPHER

AVERY TWOMBEY was a killer-for-hire called Cypher. He began killing the CEOs of corporations engaged in work similar to that of WAYNE ENTERPRISES, leading BRUCE WAYNE to suspect that his own CEO, LUCIUS FOX, might be next. (*Detective Comics* #657–658, March 1993) Wayne stumbled onto this information during one of his rare bouts of actively working at the company during the day, rather than indulging the playboy persona he used to mask his real activities as Batman. As a result, he saved the partying for the evening and allowed Robin and AZRAEL to handle patrolling Gotham City's streets.

The duo found a corporate spy at WayneTech, and when Azrael apprehended the man, he beat him mercilessly until stopped by Robin—an early warning that Azrael might not be entirely stable.

It became apparent that Cypher was after a top-secret project the WayneTech division was preparing for the federal government. So were the other two companies, something the government knew, and they stepped in to shut down Wayne Enterprises until the killer—who convinced the CEOs to commit suicide, hiding his involvement—was caught and the project preserved. In the meantime, Cypher managed to capture Fox, who was freed by Batman, Robin, and Azrael before Cypher could commit a third murder. Later Cypher surfaced again, only to die after a second confrontation with Robin as he handled a case against the SPEEDBOYZ. (*Robin* #2, November 1993)

CYRIL

The EARL OF WORDENSHIRE's son, who secretly aided his father, the KNIGHT, as the costumed adventurer the SQUIRE.

CZONK

Titus Samuel Czonka was a former construction worker who took up with ARTHUR BROWN, the CLUEMASTER. The two losers were their own support system after meeting as they escaped BLACKGATE PENITENTIARY with the ELECTROCUTIONER. (*Robin* [second series] #1, November 1993)

Czonka wanted a costume to fit in better with the Cluemaster and devised one on his own: a flight cap and goggles, orange pants, and a yellow shirt with a violet question mark in the center. He took to calling himself the Baffler, master of mysteries, but everyone called him Czonk.

In an effort to replicate the Cluemaster's clue-leaving habit, Czonk accidentally gave away their location, allowing ROBIN and the police to find them. Soon after, still free, Cluemaster renamed the Baffler the Headbanger, more in keeping with Czonk's preferred fighting style. A green shirt complete with skull replaced the yellow one. Soon after, the Electrocutioner met defeat again thanks to the SPOILER.

The remaining two criminals fought Batman and later wound up back at Blackgate as cellmates. They once more sought their freedom and achieved it, at least for a while. (*Batman: Blackgate* #1, 1996) They were arrested once more and tried separately; during a break, the Headbanger managed another escape. While free he actually managed to capture Robin and Spoiler and thought about killing them as a way to make a name for himself, but the teens broke free and subdued him once more. (*Robin* [second series] #44, August 1997)

When an earthquake freed Blackgate's prisoners, Cluemaster and Czonk were freed, although once more it was temporary. Czonk was almost immediately stopped by the HUNTRESS at a local mall. (*Batman: Spoiler/Huntress: Blunt Trauma* #1, 1998) After GOTHAM CITY was declared a NO MAN'S LAND, Czonk was again briefly free, until he was apprehended by the vigilante known as LOCK-UP. He remained Lock-Up's prisoner until the captives were freed by NIGHTWING. (*Nightwing* [second series] #36–37, October–November 1999) He has not been seen since.

DABBLO

The man known only as Dabblo crafted a plan to steal the fabled Pearl of the Orient when it was on display at Gotham Square Museum. Following his timetable, Dabblo accessed the museum's rare treasures exhibit without tripping the security system. He and a colleague made it as far as GOTHAM CITY's waterfront before being stopped by Batman and ROBIN. (*Batman* #164, June 1964)

DAGGER, DEADEYE

When TWO-FACE escaped from ARKHAM ASYLUM, he took refuge at the Lockhart Circus, enticed there by Schism, the circus's conjoined twins. Among the other circus workers who took Two-Face's side in his confrontation with Batman was ace knife thrower Deadeye Dagger. Despite his skill, he was no match for the Dark Knight, who managed to recapture the villain. (*Batman* #527–528, February–March 1996)

DAGGER, THE

Earth-2's GOTHAM CITY society was shocked in mid-1951 when millionaire playboy BRUCE WAYNE found a new diversion—boxing. Officially the Park Avenue Kid, as he wanted to be known, was fighting to raise funds for charity, but secretly Batman was searching for a connection between Gotham gambling racketeer Ned Brann and the Dagger, the latest costumed crook to terrorize the city. The Dagger and his men all wore red hoods, and the Dagger was known for his skill with a throwing knife. When Batman apprehended Brann, he proved the criminal was also masquerading as the Dagger. (*Detective Comics* #174, August 1951)

On Earth-1, Batman became aware of a different Dagger when victims of a protection scheme wound up with knife wounds. As the Dark Knight investigated, he encountered the Dagger, dressed in purple and orange with daggers attached to both arms and legs, administering punishment to a customer unwilling to pay. As the Dagger used a blade to disable a moving truck, Batman tried to save the vehicle—but another knife hurled into the BATMOBILE's engine started a fire, and the car went into Gotham River. Batman survived and brought the weapon back to the BATCAVE for analysis, learning it was manufactured by Rennington Steel.

Batman journeyed north of Gotham to Stokley, where he met with DAVID RENNINGTON, the company's owner. The midnight visit allowed Batman to privately study the company records as Rennington explained the family firm's financial struggles. At one point Rennington excused himself, he returned moments later dressed as the Dagger. Despite the kerchief covering part of his face, it was clear the Dagger was Rennington, willing to kill to salvage his company. As they fought, Batman heard how Rennington intended to use the protection income to help refinance his steel firm. Atop a giant sword replica, Batman swung down and delivered a final blow. (*Batman* #343, January 1982)

The only other appearance of the Dagger came after the CRISIS ON INFINITE EARTHS when he was among the dozens of criminals released from BLACKGATE PENITENTIARY by RÃ'S AL GHÜL. Rã's daughter, TALIA HEAD, stopped him during his frenzied rampage through Gotham. (*Batman* #400, October 1986)

DAGNER, DIRK

Dirk Dagner was one in a long line of GOTHAM CITY underworld mob bosses. He decided to commit a series of Christmas Eve crimes that would net him a small fortune while also complicating Batman's life. While the spree began successfully, Dagner and his men were quickly apprehended by the Dynamic Duo. As Dagner sat in a jail cell, Batman and ROBIN visited lighthouse keeper Tom Wick for a holiday meal, bringing cheer to those with solitary lifestyles—a joy Dagner clearly didn't understand. (*Batman* #15, February/March 1943)

DAI-LO, THE

Among the deadlier gangs inhabiting GOTHAM CITY was the Triads, led by Ekin Tzu, also known as the Dai-Lo. Tzu blamed a rival Russian gang for the death of his wife during a turf fight. WHISPER A'DAIRE came to the Dai-Lo's aid, delivering to him VASILY KOSOV, head of the Russians. She also provided him with a dose of the chemical compound that granted her not only seeming immortality but also an animal-like appearance. All she asked was Tzu's total devotion. Tzu agreed and drank the compound, transforming into a raven-like being. When Batman arrived to break up the fight with Kosov, Tzu abruptly surrendered. He explained that according to the I Ching, the bat was more sacred than the raven, and he recognized Batman's superiority. A'Daire, who had actually killed Tzu's wife to coax him to her side, escaped during the fight. In the aftermath of this confrontation, the Dai-Lo rededicated his life to ending evil in Gotham. (*Detective Comics* #768–770, May–July 2002)

DALA

BRUCE WAYNE's fiancée on Earth-2, JULIE MADISON, fell under the thrall of the sinister MONK and his accomplice Dala, who tried to hypnotically force Julie to murder one of their enemies. Bruce sent Julie on an ocean cruise to recuperate from the ordeal. As Batman, he followed her to Europe in

the BATGYRO. Once in Paris, he narrowly escaped a death trap set by the Monk and again rescued Julie from the villain's clutches. (*Detective Comics* #31, September 1939)

Batman captured Dala in Paris and forced her to lead him to the Monk's stronghold in Hungary, where he learned that the villains were both vampires and werewolves. He eventually destroyed both monsters using a pistol loaded with homemade silver bullets. It was to be the last time the Dark Knight used a gun on a case. (*Detective Comics* #32, October 1939)

On Earth-1, Dala was something else entirely. A former heroin junkie, she fell under the Monk's sway and joined his vampire cult, the Brotherhood. On the streets of GOTHAM CITY, Dala encountered ROBIN and became fascinated with him, wanting to seduce the Teen Wonder and add him to the Brotherhood's ranks. He fell under her mental control and wound up fighting Batman to keep him from stopping the Brotherhood. Batman's blood was tainted by the Monk and Dala, and he required a total blood transfusion to regain his freedom. Finally Batman managed to end their threat and a newfound ally, Father Green, took her away for safekeeping. (*Detective Comics* #511, February 1982)

In the reality created after the events of the CRISIS ON INFINITE EARTHS, Dala Vadim lost her parents to machine-gun fire during an unnamed European war. Seeking solace, she sank into a heroin dependency. Adrift, she met Nicolai the mad Monk, who promised that he could grant her darkest desires. She fell in love with him and became a member of his cult. Taking the name NOCTURNA, she served as his aide and would-be vampire. She first encountered Batman when she helped the Monk seduce Julie Madison to gain her father's wealth. While not a vampire, Dala was the Monk's most loyal acolyte. Batman interrupted the Monk before Madison could be sacrificed. After he died, Madison struck Dala with a piece of wood, knocking her

onto her own sacrificial blade. (*Batman and the Mad Monk* #1–6, October 2006–March 2007)

DALE, PETER

Batman and ROBIN followed the criminal Peter Dale beyond the GOTHAM CITY limits, out toward America's southwestern deserts. While hiding in an abandoned Native American pueblo, Dale was exposed to gases left over from a medicine man's handiwork, which had combined the four elements. The exposure altered Dale's form, granting him the ability to change into one of four shapes, one for each element: the earthquake-generating Earth-Man; Cyclone-Man with command of the winds; Flame Master, who could control any fire; and Liquid Man, who could hide within any body of water. Dale decided he'd return to Gotham, commit a monthlong crime spree, and retire on the proceeds. During his first bank heist, however, he was stopped by the Dynamic Duo. (*Detective Comics* #308, October 1962)

DALL

The man called only Dall was a criminal who posed as a scientist to gain the trust of PROFESSOR CARDEN. When he got close, he forced the professor to turn his robotic creation into a mechanical Batman. Carden's genius was in his creation's ability to mimic its human model's attributes and abilities. With the Batman robot responding only to Dall's voice, it posed a real danger for the Caped Crusader. In the end, the robot was lured near the Gotham Power Company, where it was enmeshed in high-voltage wires that overloaded its circuits. Dall was subsequently apprehended by the Dynamic Duo. (*Detective Comics* #239, January 1957)

DALLING, MRS.

Mrs. Dalling worked as a nighttime janitor at GOTHAM CITY's police headquarters and used the solitude to access police files. Over time she pored through countless criminal records and developed a keen understanding of which techniques worked, and which were doomed to failure. Armed with this knowledge, she sought to commit crimes to free herself from her grim life. Batman investigated and exposed Dalling, which resulted in jail time. (*Batman* #31, October/November 1945)

DAMFINO, NINA

Nina Damfino was a biker who donned a costume and aided the RIDDLER as ECHO.

DAMIAN

RĀ'S AL GHŪL concluded Batman met his qualifications to become his heir and consort to his most beloved daughter TALIA HEAD. Despite Batman's rejection of the initial offer to join him, Rā's remained determined, going so far as to once abducting and drugging the Dark Knight, performing a marriage ceremony when he was unable to object.

Later, the Demon's Head asked for Batman's help when a rogue assassin murdered Talia's mother. During these events, the romantic tension between Batman and Talia resulted in a more formal ceremony followed by her conceiving a child, the heir Rā's desired. The news also affected the Caped Crusader's worldview, making him take fewer risks and therefore grow less effective in his war on crime. Out of kindness, Talia claimed to have miscarried, and Rā's annulled the second marriage. What he did not know was that Talia had lied and carried the child to term. He was left at an orphanage, a bejeweled necklace his only connection to Talia. (*Batman: Son of the Demon,* 1987)

Years later, Talia turned up at a London museum, right after Batman fought an army of man-bats. She introduced him to Damian and explained her ruse. Feeling it was time Damian knew his father, Talia left him with Batman, who took the boy back to GOTHAM CITY. With mixed emotions Batman introduced Damian to his world: WAYNE MANOR and the BATCAVE, ALFRED PENNYWORTH and TIM DRAKE. To Batman's displeasure, Damian appeared spoiled, ill mannered, and unappreciative of his surroundings. Called to duty, Batman locked Damian in a room and set off.

Arriving at BLACKGATE PENITENTIARY, Batman saved an undercover cop from being killed by one of the Shocker's henchmen. He then found his old foe the SPOOK dead and headless. Soon after, Batman learned that Damian had stolen out of the manor, followed him to Blackgate, and beheaded the Spook with a sword the boy owned. At the Batcave, Damian was boasting of his exploits and showing off the Spook's head, complete with a grenade in the mouth. He tossed the head in the air so it could explode, the shock wave sending Damian and Tim atop the dinosaur trophy.

Damian then took advantage of the situation to beat Tim senseless and don JASON TODD's old ROBIN outfit. Batman was appalled to find his costume-clad son on a Gotham rooftop.

Damian felt he and he only should stand beside Batman. It was the LEAGUE OF ASSASSINS' way, training instilled by Talia. Batman brought Damian along

Damian

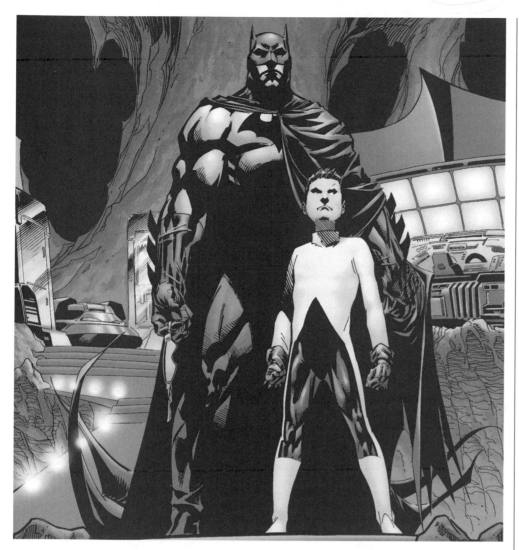

as he tracked Talia to Gibraltar where her army of manufactured MAN-BAT COMMANDOS were about to attack. Batman had also brought the real MAN-BAT, Kirk Langstrom, from the British army to consult on a cure. In the final confrontation Batman rejected the notion of a united family, and Damian clutched onto his mother. They vanished in the resulting explosion—but there was no doubt in Batman's mind both survived and would return. (*Batman* #655–658, September–November 2007)

Damian was chronicled in several speculative futures from this point, including his assuming the mantle of the Bat in a post-apocalyptic world. (*Batman* #666, July 2007)

Another possible future showed that ten years into the future, Robin and the TEEN TITANS found a graveyard of Batman allies, including one marked IBN AL XU'FFASCH—a more traditional name Damian had been given by his grandfather. (*Teen Titans* #18, January 2005)

Still other futures showed Damian assuming the name Ibn al Xu'ffasch (Arabic: إبن الخفاش; literally "son of the bat"). One possible future showed him raised by Rā's al Ghūl until he cut off his grandfather's head and sought his own destiny. (*The Kingdom: Son of the Bat,* February 1999) He was subsequently recruited by the time-traveling Rip Hunter to join

the scions of other heroes—Kid Flash, Nightstar, and Offspring—to prevent a rampaging murderer named Gog from destroying history. (*The Kingdom* #1–2, February 1999) Ibn was also attracted to Nightstar, daughter of his father's ward, NIGHTWING.

A different reality posited that Rā's al Ghūl accessed the Batcave in the wake of BRUCE WAYNE's death and used prototype BATSUITS to outfit an army culled from his League of Assassins. Bruce and Talia's son was called Tallant Wayne and joined the brotherhood using his father's outfit, working to stop his grandfather's plan. (*Brotherhood of the Bat* #1, 1995) What he didn't realize at first was that Rā's al Ghūl had unleashed a plague, and he had to form his own team in Batsuits to save the world. (*League of Batman,* 2001)

DAMSEL

When CATWOMAN posed as Madame Moderne, she used her role as publisher of the high-fashion magazine called *Damsel* to mask her criminal activities. (*Batman* #47, June/July 1948)

DANGER CLUB, THE

As with other GOTHAM CITY clubs, the Danger Club catered to a membership with a unique set of criteria. In this case, it served as a meeting place

for citizens who performed high-risk jobs, the kind that no insurance company would issue coverage for. In addition to providing a respite, the club existed to administer a fund to which everyone contributed, providing for the family of anyone who died in their line of work. The club's secretary, a test pilot named Milding, began murdering his fellow members to cover up his embezzling from the fund. To divert suspicion, he directed attention to member Mack Thorn, who had made comments that could have been construed as threats. To investigate, Batman applied for membership and was admitted. Soon after, he exposed Milding; the club chose to disband rather than cause any other member hardship. (*Batman* #76, April/May 1953)

DANIELS, BIG BOY

Big Boy Daniels was a career criminal who decided to form a school for youngsters, teaching the essentials to the next generation of thieves. While ensuring a better-educated class of thug, Daniels also made himself a target for the Dynamic Duo. Batman began a campaign to counter Daniels's work, encouraging Gotham's youth to play fair and obey the law. ROBIN went undercover as DICK GRAYSON and recruited former members who had reformed to help him bring down Daniels's school. (*Batman* #3, Fall 1940)

DANKO, WILLIS

Inside a secret GOTHAM CITY fight club, costumed criminals and civilian lowlifes fought before a crowd of thugs. Danko was another crook with nothing left to live for when he entered the ring against feared Russian agent the KGBEAST. Danko died during the bout; the club was discovered by Batman and WILDCAT. (*Batman/Wildcat* #2, May 1997)

DANNING, VICTOR

Victor Danning squandered his scientific acumen in favor of a criminal career. It allowed him to plunder the work of other scientists—victims whom most criminals wouldn't bother with. He accessed an experimental device created by Dr. John Carr that was intended to boost a human's mental capabilities. Before he could escape with the device and use it on himself, he got into a scuffle with the World's Finest team of Batman, ROBIN, and SUPERMAN. Danning and the Boy Wonder were exposed to the device and became supreme intellects while the Man of Steel was reduced to a dullard. Batman and his brainy partner circumvented Superman's well-meaning interference and managed to apprehend Danning and his men. They then used Carr's machine to restore Danning, Robin, and Superman to normal. (*World's Finest Comics* #93, March/April 1958)

DANNY THE DUMMY

Danny was a midget who developed a ventriloquist act that involved him performing with a normal-sized mannequin. He'd perform the act and convince people that he was the mannequin while the man was real until the act's conclusion. Despite his success, audiences and the public took to calling him Danny the Dummy. The humiliation angered the man, who decided to gain revenge against the ignorant populace and launched a spectacular series of crimes. In each case the crime involved the use of various types of dummies from mannequins to a "dummy" western town used for filmed entertainment, where Danny hid away with his creations. Batman and Robin finally tracked down the midget and rang down the curtain on his criminal career. (*Batman* #134, September 1960)

DANTON, JOE

Joe Danton was a college peer of Bruce Wayne's on Earth-2 but was shunned by their classmates for his spoiled and unsportsmanlike ways. He grew to resent Wayne's popularity and sought to harm him during a fencing match. Danton did not play by the rules and left the safety tip off his foil, managing to slash Wayne's wrist.

Years later Danton still harbored a grudge against his classmates and decided to bring them aboard his yacht for a three-day cruise that would end with their deaths by underwater mines. Wayne changed to Batman to stop the madman, and during their fight Danton spied the scar he'd inflicted on Wayne years before. Now knowing the Batman's greatest secret, Danton intended to spitefully spread the news.

Before he could share the information, he watched as Batman selflessly saved the ship and their fellow college alumni. The actions of the day also took their toll on Danton as a long-term heart ailment finally claimed his life. (*Batman* #96, December 1955)

DANTON, SLITS

Slits Danton was a career criminal who harbored a grudge against Batman for his latest stint in jail. When he escaped, he wanted revenge and sought the Caped Crusader. While terrorizing a lecture hall where Bruce Wayne and Dick Grayson happened to be listening to a presentation on bats, Danton got a measure of satisfaction when he managed to knock Batman out. In the end, it was Robin who stopped Danton, ending his threat and returning him to jail. (*Detective Comics* #153, November 1949)

DARCY, ROBERT

Robert Darcy was a recognized chemistry expert who eschewed legitimate work in favor of crime. He intended to use his knowledge to plan a series of crimes that would make him and his men rich. When Batman and Robin tried to put them out of business, Darcy shot and seriously wounded the Caped Crusader. While Batman spent a week recovering, Robin donned a specially designed outfit to make people think he was Batman. Soon after, Robin lured Darcy and his mob toward Gotham City's police, who waited in hiding. (*Detective Comics* #165, November 1950)

DAREDEVILS, THE

Initially circus acrobats, the three men known as the Daredevils took to crime—only to have their new career rapidly derailed by Batman and Robin. (*Batman* #107, April 1957)

DARKK, DR. EBENEZER

Ebenezer Darkk was chosen by Rā's al Ghūl to succeed the Sensei as leader of his League of Assassins. He was a master strategist who preferred his wits and planning skills as opposed to the hand-to-hand combat tactics most of the League used. Darkk developed a reputation for using clever death traps, hidden weapons, and indirect murder tools such as gas and poison. (*Detective Comics* #405–406, November–December 1970)

At one point Darkk and Rā's had a disagreement and the leader went rogue, taking many League members with him. His first act against his former employer was to kidnap Rā's daughter, Talia Head. She was rescued, though, by Batman, who had been investigating a series of killings; the trail had led the Dark Knight to Darkk. In the ensuing fight to free her, Darkk wound up dying, ending the threat. This proved to be the fateful first meeting between the Caped Crusader and Daughter of the Demon. (*Detective Comics* #411, May 1971)

DARK RIDER I

The first Dark Rider was better known to the Batman as the Cossack.

DARK RIDER II

Stanley Baumgarten suffered from a sleeping disorder that made his body susceptible to a malevolent force known as Dark Rider. Whatever Dark Rider truly was—spectral being, demon, meta-human—it inhabited body after body until it found a home in Baumgarten. As Dark Rider, he accepted the Penguin's contract to kill Robin after both relocated from Gotham City to Blüdhaven. Dark Rider somehow conjured up a phantom steed to carry him through the city, and he wielded an electrically charged lance. His initial attack on Robin failed, and with the rising sun Baumgarten's mind reasserted control over the body. The following night Robin subdued the Dark Rider and turned him over to the police. The essence of Dark Rider has not been seen since. (*Robin* [second series] #135–137, April–June 2005)

DARKWOLF

An unnamed criminal known only as Darkwolf set out to cause great damage in Gotham City, his motives unrevealed. Batman stopped him once and then paired up with Catwoman to rescue a plane full of hostages during a second attack. Darkwolf was subdued and sent to prison. (*Detective Comics* #548, March 1985)

DARRELL, LOU

Lou Darrell worked a menial job at Gotham Hospital and hoped to improve his fortunes by stealing the facility's radium supply. He intended to sell the isotope and use the funds to bring his plans for a radio-therapy machine to fruition. While he managed to steal the radium, he was apprehended by Batman and Robin before he could sell the material. (*Batman* #37, October/November 1946)

DAVA

Dava Sbörsc sided with the Transbelvians when her homeland of Tbliska was split by a bloody civil war. The youth was tiny for her age but fast, and she used this to her advantage in taking out as many members of the Krasna-Volny forces as she possibly could. In hunting the very worst of her former countrymen, she recognized the need to hit hard and move on, so she studied single-blow techniques. In time, Dava had come to learn and employ moves that were colorfully named the Scalpel, the Wind Through the Reeds, the Lion's Paw, Wave and Shore, and the Skullcrack. Her studies led her to the domain of the Master of the Iron Hand in order to learn the Whispering Hand. While there, she encountered Tim Drake, who was also a student, preparing to become the next Robin. The two appeared equals and sparred with pleasure. Dava mentioned that her next lesson would come from Lady Shiva, to learn the infamous Leopard Blow. Having previously encountered the deadliest martial artist alive, Drake grew concerned for his new friend. By this time, though, Lady Shiva had been made aware of someone who had become the master of single-blow attacks and tracked his wake, leading her to the Master of the Iron Hand. Dava had by then returned to Transbelvia, and the Iron Master refused to give up information about her. He agreed to combat Shiva for the information, allowing Drake time to leave his dojo and warn Dava. Drake fled as the two fought, and just as she had killed the Armless Master, she now killed his brother, the Iron Hand.

When Dava returned home, she discovered that King Snake had begun arming the Krasna-Volny army, which threatened to tip the tide of battle. Dava had previously derailed one shipment of his weapons, so King Snake accompanied the second, hoping to dispatch whoever had killed his agents. Before they met, though, Drake had found Dava and joined her in the struggle. Together they bested General Dvak Tvorakovich, who had butchered entire villages. At that point Drake learned Dava's secret: She had been improving her speed and agility by using the oil derived from the Aramilla plant. When she kissed him, some of the oil rubbed off and enhanced him as well.

Lady Shiva arrived at that moment and challenged Dava. Robin objected and, with his newfound speed, accidentally killed Shiva. It was then that King Snake and his men found them all and prepared to kill everyone. As Robin revived Shiva, he also passed on some of the Aramilla oil to the martial artist, aiding her recovery. In a blur, Lady Shiva killed King Snake's men as he escaped.

In the aftermath Robin recognized that he and Dava saw the world in different ways. Dava's tragic experiences had taught her that killing could be easily justified; she had no doubts that it was required. Robin, after Batman's training, believed that taking a life could not be justified, and they parted. (*Robin* [second series] #49, January 1998)

DAVENPORT, J. DEVLIN

J. Devlin Davenport made his fortune in real estate and for at least a decade lived in a mansion situated next to stately Wayne Manor. Whereas Bruce Wayne played at being a playboy, Davenport was the living embodiment of the lifestyle. He came from wealth and added to it, spending much of his time working on improving his golf game. Once, he managed to win a PGA trophy from the current holder, a source of pride. (*Detective Comics* #685, May 1995)

Davenport took to calling his neighbor "Brucie," constantly inviting Wayne to join him on jaunts to nearby strip clubs. The seedier side of life held some appeal for Davenport; he was on occasion lured to less-than-legal dealings such as watching pay-per-view brawls and doing business with known mob figures.

He was in Bimini when the earthquake devastated GOTHAM CITY, but he returned shortly thereafter and was crushed to see his pride and joy, the Davenport Center, lying on its side. He refused to let the city remove the rubble to clear the way for relief trucks, which drove Wayne, as Batman, to use an earthmover to do the work the following evening. (*Detective Comics* #724, August 1998) Davenport lost a lot of his properties and, rather than rebuild, sold most of his holdings to Wayne.

After Gotham City was restored, Davenport turned his attention from real estate to acquiring other businesses, including buying an electric company. (*Batman: Gotham Knights* #4, June 2000) He was also briefly suspected of being involved in the murder of VESPER FAIRCHILD but was cleared by ALFRED PENNYWORTH and ORACLE. (*Robin* [second series] #99, April 2002)

DAVENPORT, MARJORY

Marjory Davenport was DICK GRAYSON's classmate and the object of the Boy Wonder's affection. The pretty teen was kidnapped by BUGS CONKLIN to ensure that her father, Dr. R. Davenport, would not go to the police after he was forced to treat Conklin. Batman and ROBIN managed to rescue her, but in so doing Marjory developed her own crush—on Robin. (*Batman* #23, June/July 1944)

DAVIS, BART

Bart Davis was a criminal who used his physical resemblance to Batman to impersonate him for a series of crimes. He was arrested and jailed but eventually released; soon after, Davis auditioned to play Batman in Excelsior Studios' planned feature film. Batman had agreed to select his doppelgänger, theorizing that Davis would take advantage of this opportunity. Sure enough, Davis auditioned, received the part, and, soon after filming began, used the costume and props to once more imitate the Caped Crusader for criminal purposes. Davis, as Batman, threatened to take his fellow criminals into custody unless they gave him a cut of their take. All the while, Batman shadowed him, hoping to find the one million dollars taken from a Fields Armored Car. The plan worked: The armored car thieves and Davis were apprehended. To make things up to director Herb Dennison, Batman agreed to play himself for the remainder of the shoot. (*Detective Comics* #232, June 1956)

DAVIS, FRANK

Frank Davis was fascinated by the Batman and became an amateur expert on the Caped Crusader, going so far as to deduce his secret identity. When he appeared on a local television quiz show, Davis was murdered by the host, JOE HARMON, before he could give away the secret. (*Batman* #108, June 1957)

DAVIS, HOMER

Homer Davis was a banker who fell into deep debt and crafted an elaborate plan to kill architect Peter Chaney to erase the burden. Davis wanted to pin the blame on Ben Kole, who publicly threatened the lives of Davis, Chaney, and Batman. When Davis enacted his scheme, he accidentally killed his own butler and was apprehended by the Caped Crusader before Davis could kill Chaney. (*Detective Comics* #151, September 1949)

DAY, JULIAN GREGORY

Obsessed with time and holidays, he became the costumed CALENDAR MAN, using over-the-top costumes and themes to commit crimes.

DEACON BLACKFIRE

JOSEPH BLACKFIRE led an army of the homeless into GOTHAM CITY and was opposed by the Batman.

DEADMAN

When the SENSEI wanted a man known as the Hook to randomly kill someone to prove his eligibility to join the LEAGUE OF ASSASSINS, the target was circus aerialist Boston Brand. As he performed for the Hills Bros. Circus, a shot rang out and killed him in midair. Rather than let him go to his eternal reward, Rama Kushna, a Hindu goddess, chose Brand as her agent. Still in his red-and-white costume, he became an earthbound spirit, able to temporarily possess the bodies of living beings and control them. Afterward, none could recall the possession. (*Strange Adventures* #205, October 1967)

At first, Brand hunted his killer, looking after his circus friends and aiding others along the way. When the trail took him to GOTHAM CITY, Brand enlisted the Batman's assistance, forming an odd friendship that endured through the years. (*The Brave and the Bold* #79, August/September 1968)

In one parallel reality, it was discovered that THOMAS and MARTHA WAYNE had a son named Thomas Jr., who was mentally disabled and kept in a home. Bruce Wayne made the shocking discovery on a case with SUPERMAN and Deadman. Ultimately he granted Brand permission to permanently inhabit his brother's body, bringing some peace to both. (*World's Finest Comics* #223, May/June 1974)

DEADSHOT

FLOYD LAWTON grew up in a twisted family that early on affected his worldview and set him on a path that turned him into a deadly assassin. (*Batman* #59, June/July 1950)

The Lawtons were a wealthy family, but George and Genevieve's marriage turned sour and the two began manipulating the affections of both sons, Floyd and Edward. As a teen, Edward was encouraged by Genevieve to kill George. When Floyd learned of this, he tried to stop his brother, but the gun fired, killing Edward. Filled with guilt, hatred, and remorse, Floyd began a self-destructive path that he felt would not end until he died in some spectacular manner. (*Deadshot* #1–4, November 1988–February 1989)

As an adult, Lawton moved to GOTHAM CITY, married, and had a son whom he named Edward. The life of a socialite bored him to tears so, seeking a thrill, he donned a costume and initially appeared as a vigilante trying to replace Batman. Failing that, Deadshot took to the life of a mercenary. On several occasions his commissions brought him into conflict with Batman, resulting in numerous prison terms. At one point he was transferred to Louisiana's Belle Reve prison, the front for the federal government's clandestine Suicide Squad division. There he was recruited by AMANDA WALLER, receiving a full pardon for his crimes in exchange for missions with the squad. Lawton accepted, presuming that if he were to die spectacularly, it could be on these

McDaniel

this time, he had begun dating Carmen Leno, a member of the mercenary team known as the Body Doubles. When the Elite and Doubles competed for a contract, Lawton sabotaged the Elite's chances. (*Body Doubles* #1, February 1998) The Elite took advantage of the chaos created when the JOKER infected super-villains with his own brand of madness and tried to free the inmates of Central City's Iron Heights prison but failed. (*Flash* [second series] #179, December 2001)

A new version of the squad was formed under a man called the Unknown Soldier and Lawton signed up, putting the Elite behind him. His time with the new team was turbulent and unsatisfying. (*Suicide Squad* [second series] #1–12, November 2001–October 2002)

All along, Deadshot and the Batman continued to cross paths. After DAVID CAIN surrendered to Batman in the VESPER FAIRCHILD murder case, LEX LUTHOR hired Deadshot to kill Cain before the president of the United States could be implicated. Batman thwarted that particular mission and, as in the past, Lawton received numerous wounds but managed to live. (*Batman* #606–607, October–November 2002)

Sometime after his recovery, Deadshot began to socialize more with his fellow criminals at the satellite once used by the Injustice Gang. It was there that Dr. Light informed him that Deadshot's mind had been tampered with by ZATANNA, making him one of many who had their memories altered to protect the heroes' secrets. (*Identity Crisis* #4, November 2004)

Deadshot was then offered a chance to join a secret Society of villains, formed to exact revenge against the heroes for their tampering. He rejected their offer and wound up siding with several others, who were banded together by the mysterious Mockingbird to stop the Society. While a member of the Secret Six, Lawton admitted to CATMAN that it was he who'd killed the lions in Africa that sent Catman over to the Six's side. (*Villains United* #1–6, July–December 2005)

After the Society was stopped, Deadshot traveled to Star City, meeting up with an old girlfriend, Michelle Torres, and discovering he had a daughter, Zoe. Looking to do right by her after failing Eddie, Lawton moved into their apartment and made certain the crime-ridden street they lived on became peaceful and safe. Despite a confrontation with GREEN ARROW, they reached an understanding, and Lawton remained with them for a time, setting up bank accounts to ensure that Zoe and her mother were well provided for. (*Deadshot* [second series] #1–4, February–June 2005)

When Luthor threatened to level the street they lived on, Lawton moved out, getting the Emerald Archer to promise to look after them. Deadshot remained an active mercenary, taking on solo missions and occasionally working with the Secret Six to stem the Society's growth. He continued to come into conflict with super heroes, notably Batman. In one confrontation with Batman, the Dark Knight observed that Lawton always pulled his shots around him. He offered to tell Deadshot why that was, but Lawton refused. (*Legends of the Dark Knight* #214, March 2007)

assignments. Instead he wound up surviving despite harrowing experiences around the world. (*Legends of the Dark Knight* #1–4, November 1986–February 1987; *Suicide Squad* #1, May 1987)

The squad seemed to give his life new purpose, and he began exploring his past with the prison psychiatrist Simon LaGrieve. He also seemed to have a potential romance in staffer Flo Crawley. As good as things got for him, they turned harsh in a heartbeat. Genevieve had his son, Eddie,

kidnapped—bait to force Lawton to shoot and kill George once and for all. Lawton refused, instead killing the men his mother had hired, but Eddie still died. Distraught, Lawton sought out his mother and crippled her with a single shot. (*Deadshot* #1–4, November 1988–February 1989)

In addition to his work with the squad, he was also briefly partnered with the Killer Elite, a team of assassins including Deadline and Bolt. (*Justice League of America* #105, November 1995) During

Deadshot continued to work for the Suicide Squad, rounding up villains to be transported to another realm. (*Salvation Run* #1, January 2008) One of his assignments was to collect the Pied Piper and the Trickster, failing to obtain them but killing the latter in the process. (*Countdown to Final Crisis* #24, 2008)

DEATH-CHEATERS' CLUB, THE

Like so many organizations in GOTHAM CITY, this club had a unique criterion for admission: Every member had been declared dead before returning to life. The group was trusting and tight-knit, so much so that all the members trusted Jeff Silvers to act as their personal accountant. Silvers, though, was embezzling their funds for his private use; fearing discovery, he schemed to kill the members one by one. He cleverly framed Little Dougy, a mobster who had been gunned down and brought back to life but was denied membership. To ferret out the killer, BRUCE WAYNE used a poison to kill himself with DICK GRAYSON reviving him with artificial respiration. Once admitted, Wayne began his investigation and determined it was Silvers behind the deaths, apprehending him. (*Batman* #72, August/September 1952)

DEATHSTROKE THE TERMINATOR

SLADE WILSON was a soldier who agreed to undergo experiments designed to create a form of super-soldier. The result activated Wilson's meta-gene, which allowed him to use 90 percent of his mental capacity. His speed, agility, endurance, and healing abilities were all enhanced well beyond the human norm. Wilson also seemed to age at a slower rate. After his enhancements were tested, Wilson left the army and became a mercenary, using his marksmanship and fighting skills along with his new physique to become a feared threat known as Deathstroke the Terminator. Armed with a power staff, pistols, and knives, he was an expert in most forms of hand-to-hand battle as well as comfortable with any form of weaponry. (*The New Teen Titans* #2, December 1980)

At some point in Wilson's adult life, he was trained by an assassin known only as Natas. How and when has not been recorded.

Initially Wilson kept the results of his tests hidden from his wife, Adeline, despite her experience as a military combat instructor. Together they raised Grant and Joseph, and all seemed fine—for a time. Another mercenary known as the Jackal, trying to learn who had put the hit out on his client, kidnapped Joseph to force Wilson to talk. Wilson refused and attempted to save his son, but not before the Jackal slit Joseph's throat, rendering him mute.

Adeline was enraged at Wilson for allowing this to happen and tried to kill him, but wound up only injuring him, ruining his right eye. As a result, Wilson took to wearing a white eye patch; in full battle gear, his mask was black on the entire right side. Joseph grew up a gentle soul, and when his meta-human power manifested he wound up joining the TEEN TITANS, a team that had become a perennial problem for Wilson.

His first contact with the team came when Grant, who also allowed himself to be enhanced, took a contract to destroy the team. As the RAVAGER, he battled the Titans but died as a result of the treatment he endured. Deathstroke chose to inherit the contract—and thus began a series of battles that rapidly became legend. When he used the twisted teen Terra to infiltrate the team, Wilson learned that the team leader, ROBIN, was DICK GRAYSON and thus that Batman was BRUCE WAYNE. He used this knowledge frequently in his future encounters with both heroes. (*Tales of the Teen Titans* #44, July 1984)

At one point, to save the world, Deathstroke wound up having to kill Joseph, code-named Jericho. At the moment of his death, Jericho, who could possess others, entered Wilson's mind, where he would reside for years. In that time Deathstroke became a feared killer and frequent opponent not only of the Titans but of most super heroes. Still, he occasionally fought on the side of the angels when circumstances dictated. In one such instance he wound up fighting alongside the Titans against the H.I.V.E., which was then led by his ex-wife. Sometime in the past, Adeline had

received some of Wilson's blood and inherited many of his abilities, including the healing factor. When the immortal Vandal Savage slit her throat, she was left in a miserable state, begging for death. Wilson could not kill his ex-wife after killing Joseph and watching Grant die. Instead NIGHTWING's lover, STARFIRE, delivered the killing blow. (*The Titans* #12, February 2000)

Later, after watching the young heroes risk their lives time and again, Jericho influenced his father and sought to derail the budding careers of the latest incarnation of the Teen Titans. Deathstroke shattered Impulse's leg before Jericho was freed, leaving Wilson to deal with the repercussions of his acts. Seeking revenge against Jericho, he recruited his illegitimate daughter Rose to become the new Ravager. He used a serum similar to the one that had enhanced him, but in her case it left her mentally unstable, and included removing her left eye to match her father. Rose wound up fighting for Deathstroke before being freed of her mental troubles. She subsequently joined the Titans, atoning for her acts and hoping to master her skills. (*Teen Titans* [third series] #34, May 2006)

Deathstroke was hired by Dr. Light to act as his bodyguard when he was sought by the Justice League of America. During the inevitable fight, Green Arrow plunged a shaft into his empty eye socket to stop him, which earned the Emerald Archer a new enemy. (*Identity Crisis* #2, September 2004) After learning that the heroes had used Zatanna's magic to alter many villains' memories, he eagerly joined a new secret Society to unite the villains against the heroes. He served on its ruling council and personally acted as the muscle to convince people to join. (*Countdown to Infinite Crisis,* 2006)

While events were unfolding in the brewing war, Deathstroke also masqueraded as Batman, feeding information to Arsenal, which was used by the Outsiders to take down threats to the coalescing Society. He also hired Dick Grayson to train his daughter Rose in combat skills but objected when he learned that Nightwing was also teaching her how to be "good." Nightwing suggested that he'd stop training Rose if Deathstroke kept the Society out of Blüdhaven. The deal was accepted and lasted for about thirty-four hours. At that point Deathstroke was on hand when the living chemical creature Chemo was dropped on the city, essentially destroying it.

Nightwing got his own measure of revenge when he confronted Wilson and explained that the Kryptonite Rose hid in her empty eye socket to keep Superman away was slowly poisoning her. The explosive battle left Rose free to join the Titans and injured both men—but they lived, each man vowing revenge. (*Nightwing* #112–117, November 2005–April 2006)

In the wake of the events known as Infinite Crisis, Deathstroke decided to fight fire with fire and built a team of teens under his thrall. This Titans East included Batgirl, who was drugged by Wilson to get her to agree to join him. (*Teen Titans* #43–45, March–May 2007)

In other realities the name *Deathstroke* was used by others, not Slade Wilson. (*Tangent Comics/The Atom* #1, December 1997; *Just Imagine Stan Lee with Jerry Ordway Creating JLA,* February 2003)

DEEMS, DARBY

Darby Deems was an expert on dreams and used this facility to further his criminal career as Doctor Dreemo.

DELION, JOHN

Whereas history showed Juan Ponce de León as seeking the Fountain of Youth, a man known as John DeLion was the sixteenth-century explorer who actually found it. To protect the valley where the fountain was sited, DeLion built a castle at the valley's entrance. As each member of his extended family turned sixty, they would travel to the Florida Everglades and approach the giant golden door; and only then would they be admitted to drink from the life-elongating waters. Whoever drank of the water was also forevermore confined to the valley.

Criminal Dan Morgan and his men accidentally found the golden doors and entered the valley, terrorizing its sole village. Similarly, a vacationing Bruce Wayne and Dick Grayson also passed through the doors and, learning of Morgan's acts, donned their crime-fighting costumes. As Batman and Robin fought to free the village, DeLion gave Morgan and his men water to quench their thirst. When they escaped past the golden doors, the water turned to poison and killed the men. Batman and Robin left the valley, promising to keep its secret. (*Batman* #54, August/September 1949)

DELMAR, HORATIO

Bruce Wayne was accused of murdering racketeer Horatio Delmar as part of an underworld power play. The actual murder was ordered by Delmar's second in command, Freddie Hill, and the shooting was done by Weasel Venner. During Wayne's trial, Venner cleared the millionaire and accused Hill of the deed. (*Batman* #7, October/November 1941)

DEMON, THE

Etrigan was a Hell-born demon bonded to a man called Jason Blood, a frequent ally of Batman.

DENT, DUELA

Duela Dent appeared in a variety of guises, claiming to be the daughter of various Batman villains; her true background remained unrevealed. (*Batman Family* #6, July/August 1976)

On Earth-1, Dent first appeared as the Joker's Daughter, confounding Robin with her subsequent appearances as the supposed daughter of the Catwoman, Scarecrow, Riddler, and Penguin. In the end she admitted to being Duela Dent, daughter of former Gotham City district attorney Harvey Dent, who was better known as Two-Face.

After her confusing appearances, she adopted the name Harlequin and told the Boy Wonder she wanted to join the Teen Titans, in part to atone for her father's crimes. She worked alongside the team on a few cases but was never truly accepted by her peers. After the team disbanded, she returned to Gotham City, donned the identity of Card Queen,

Duela Dent

and tried to bring down a criminal operation called MAZE.

She turned up at fellow Titan Donna Troy's wedding, where DICK GRAYSON observed that Duela was too old to be Dent's true daughter—something she admitted to while providing no further information.

After the events known as the CRISIS ON INFINITE EARTHS, a schizophrenic woman was said to have been a recurring mental institution patient for years. She finally took on the name *Duela Dent,* displaying acrobatic prowess and using gadgets similar to super-villains' to commit criminal acts. She encountered a group called the Team Titans and later the Teen Titans. In the latter instance, Cyborg once summoned all members and associates of the Titans, and she turned up despite no previous recorded instances of her working with the team in any of her guises. (*JLA/Titans* #1-3, December 1998-January 1999)

After she helped the Titans and JUSTICE LEAGUE OF AMERICA save Cyborg from an entity called Technis, she was seen in a bar sounding delusional. She claimed that she was not only awaiting a call to join the Titans but also was the daughter of an alien creature, Doomsday. When Duela Dent heard that a membership drive was being held to populate a Titans West operation, she gathered the villains Fear and Loathing and crashed the event, upset at not being invited. The entire event was unsanctioned but set up by Matthew Logan, Gar Logan's cousin, and she was subdued by FLAMEBIRD and Terra. (*Titans Secret Files* #2, October 2000)

Dent was next recorded aboard the Injustice Society's old satellite, socializing with members of the secret Society of villains that had united against the heroes. She told outrageous stories about her lineage, convincing no one present. In a twist, she also claimed that her mother was the villain, not one of Batman's male rogues. One of her claims was new: that she had been repeatedly revived using RĀ'S AL GHŪL'S LAZARUS PIT technology. (*Teen Titans/Outsiders Secret Files 2005,* October 2005)

When the call went out to all teen heroes in times of crisis, she responded despite her problems with the Titans. She aided them against Dr. Light and Superboy-Prime, using her gadgets and acrobatic skills. (*Teen Titans* [third series] #24, July 2005; #32, March 2006)

Some time after the events of INFINITE CRISIS, the Titans were decimated and rebuilt with Dent finally an officially member, alongside someone else using the name *Riddler's Daughter,* who may be her sister. Dent's membership didn't last long; soon after, she left to join DEATHSTROKE's rogue outfit known as Titans East. (*Teen Titans* [third series] #43, February 2007)

After abducting a celebrity, she was stopped by JASON TODD. During the confrontation she threw out a new claim: that she hailed from a parallel Earth. She escaped Todd only to be confronted by a Monitor, one of the guardians protecting the fifty-two parallel worlds recently created. For a change, her claim was a valid one, and because she did not belong on this New Earth, he killed the "anomaly" to preserve the multiverse. (*Countdown* #51, 2007)

In a potential future, it was shown that Duela

Dent helped destroy ARKHAM ASYLUM, attempting to reconnect with her unnamed father. The plan did not work and, angered, she went out and personally killed BATGIRL, ALFRED PENNYWORTH, and BETTE KANE. Her rage was also directed at GOTHAM CITY POLICE DEPARTMENT officer CRISPUS ALLEN, who was still a mortal and not the SPECTRE. Her rampage was finally ended when Batman, TIM DRAKE, shot her dead. (*Teen Titans* #18, January 2005)

A different person used the name *Joker's Daughter* in an entirely different potential future. (*Kingdom Come,* 1996)

DENT, GILDA

Gilda married HARVEY DENT, and together they had dreams of a bright future. After their marriage, Harvey was a rising lawyer and rapidly became GOTHAM CITY's newest district attorney. His pursuit of justice became obsessive, and after a while Gilda began to feel neglected—yet she still loved Harvey and wanted things to work out. (*Detective Comics* #66, August 1942)

After the arrival of Batman in Gotham City, Harvey became a trusted ally of the masked vigilante, but this put further strain on the marriage. Gilda was lonely, and her hopes of starting a family were rapidly diminishing.

When Dent was prosecuting "BOSS" MARONI, he had acid thrown at him, scarring half his face. It also caused a psychological break, and the TWO-FACE persona was born. Gilda despaired over the latest turn of events and wanted him apprehended so he could be at least mentally healed.

Two-Face haunted Gilda time and again. In one case he was despondent over her inability to provide him with two children, let alone one. She finally moved on with her life, marrying a man named Paul Janus. Jealous, Two-Face attempted to frame Janus with a crime then replace him with a hired actor, who was made up to appear as if Janus had suffered the same fate as Harvey Dent. Batman and the first ROBIN ended that scheme, and

the couple were reunited. Some years later, Gilda finally had children—twins no less. The news caused Two-Face to break out of jail and try to obtain them for himself, convinced they were the result of an experimental fertility drug. Gilda admitted that the children were truly Harvey's; she had used frozen sperm to conceive. Batman and the third Robin used the information to convince Two-Face to release the children unharmed. (*Batman: Two-Face Strikes Twice* #1-2, 1993)

In one interpretation of events, all this occurred during a yearlong investigation of the serial murderer called HOLIDAY. After Two-Face was captured and sent to ARKHAM ASYLUM, Gilda admitted, before destroying evidence and leaving the city, that she herself was the first Holiday, followed by her husband in his vendetta against mobster ALBERTO FALCONE. Falcone, though, admitted to all the murders, so the truth remained unknown. (*Batman: The Long Halloween* #1-12, 1996-1997)

Gilda Dent's whereabouts after these incidents remains unrecorded.

DENT, HARVEY

The handsome GOTHAM CITY district attorney was physically and mentally scarred during a court case, resulting in the birth of the twisted TWO-FACE.

On Earth-2, the scarring incident that created Two-Face befell a man named HARVEY KENT.

DENT, PAUL

Dr. Paul Dent invented a device emitting rays that helped rapidly knit scarred flesh. The device was used on criminal BART MAGAN and turned him into DOCTOR NO-FACE. (*Detective Comics* #319, September 1963)

DEREK, DR.

During Earth-2's World War II, Derek was a spy working in GOTHAM CITY. He would kidnap scientists and military men in order to learn their secrets. Enhancing his success was a machine designed by his prisoner, Dr. Jon Henry. The machine was said to emit radio waves that were absorbed by metal; if that metal was placed at the base of a man's brain, he would be driven crazy. Derek intended to use FIFTH COLUMNISTS as guinea pigs, having slivers of metal surgically implanted and then having them take jobs at key industrial facilities. He would turn the device on, and the resulting chaos would disrupt America's mounting war effort. Batman and ROBIN managed to stop Derek before the scheme could be enacted, saving countless lives. (*Detective Comics* #55, September 1941)

DEREK, WILEY

Wiley Derek was a criminal who was also an expert makeup artist. He obtained a job at an insane asylum and preyed on the delusions of inmates who believed themselves to be the incarnation of historic personages. Disguised as Lafayette, he wanted to build an army of the mad and commit a series of crimes. Instead, he was stopped by Batman and ROBIN. (*Detective Comics* #119, January 1947)

DESMOND, MARK

Mark Desmond was a smart man who disliked his average body and submitted to an experiment that turned him into the mindless behemoth BLOCKBUSTER.

DESMOND, ROLAND

Roland Desmond, brother to Mark, the first BLOCKBUSTER, also became a physical giant but retained his mental faculties, becoming BLOCKBUSTER II, a ruthless crime boss.

DEVOE

Devoe was a deep-sea diver who discovered a fire-breathing creature near an island. Learning that the creature was sheltering an egg, he concocted a scheme to pretend to help apprehend the creature, but actually kill it and obtain the egg. He would then make a fortune by showcasing the last surviving baby from a near-extinct species. His efforts were thwarted by Batman and ROBIN, and his humiliation was compounded when it was determined the egg would not be hatching for another century. (*Batman* #104, December 1956)

DIBNY, RALPH

The happy, extroverted detective who drank an extract of gingold and became the stretchable sleuth the ELONGATED MAN.

DIBNY, SUE DEARBON

Sue Dearbon Dibny was a socialite-turned-author who delighted in traveling the world beside her husband, RALPH, who was known to all as the ELONGATED MAN. (*The Flash* #119, March 1961)

The two met at her debutante ball, which Ralph crashed hoping to see more of the captivating woman he had spied earlier that day. By then, Ralph had discovered that an extract of gingold allowed him to stretch his form, and he'd begun adventuring as the Elongated Man. He and Sue fell in love almost immediately, and the socialite

Ralph and Sue Dibny

married the sleuth with the Fastest Man Alive, the FLASH, as best man.

Over the next few years the couple traveled the globe investigating mysteries and enjoying the celebrity that came with being a hero. Sue was delighted when Ralph was formally inducted into the JUSTICE LEAGUE OF AMERICA. Soon thereafter, though, when she was alone on the JLA's satellite headquarters, she was brutally raped by Dr. Light. Even that attack did not deter her from getting the most out of life. Sue eventually got more involved with the JLA, working as an administrator through several incarnations of the team.

Sue finally took to writing and wrote at least one bestselling detective novel—which made her the center of attention for a change. During her book tour, she and Ralph worked with Batman on a mystery. (*Batman: Gotham Knights* #41, July 2003)

The one thing missing from their life was a child, and the day she prepared to tell Ralph the good news that a child was finally on the way, she wound up accidentally killed by a deranged Jean Loring, ex-wife of the ATOM. The investigation into her death began a chain of events that led to JACK DRAKE dying and Batman recalling that the heroes had begun using ZATANNA's magic to mindwipe the villains in the wake of Sue's rape. (*Identity Crisis* #1–7, August 2004–February 2005)

Her death had a devastating effect on Ralph, leading him to alcoholism and a religious cult that hinted it could resurrect Sue. He carried her wedding ring with him and used it in his final defiant act, trapping the demon Neron in a mystic construct before dying himself. (*52* #41, 2007) The reunited spirits of the Dibnys finally achieved a new level of happiness.

DICKERSON, DANIEL DANFORTH III

Like so many of his predecessors, Daniel Danforth Dickerson III was ill equipped for the mayorship of a city as unique as GOTHAM CITY. He was a political creature, not a public servant, and he was easily seduced by the rampant corruption that remained in the political infrastructure. Unlike those who came before him, Dickerson seemed to enjoy the public spotlight and made the most of it. He assumed office from MARION GRANGE at the end of the city's period as a NO MAN'S LAND. His unremarkable administration was almost derailed when WHISPER A'DAIRE seduced him for her personal gain. (*Detective Comics* #743, April 2000)

His term was cut short when the JOKER shot him to death just as the mayor was discussing his plans to cut police overtime in his next budget. He was succeeded by David Hull. (*Gotham Central* #15, March 2004)

DIGGES

Digges worked for bestselling mystery novelist Reginald Scofield. The author maintained a home located some twenty miles up the coast from GOTHAM CITY in Crow's Nest. The mansion was also used by gem smugglers until their operation was stopped by Batman and ROBIN. (*Detective Comics* #100, June 1945)

DILLON, DR. JOHN V.

Dr. John V. Dillon was personal physician to both BRUCE WAYNE and DICK GRAYSON on Earth-2. He never knew the two were also Batman and ROBIN. (*World's Finest Comics* #66, September/October 1953)

DIPINA

DiPina was a scientist who managed to create a volatile explosive requiring a mere ounce to destroy a city block. Fearful of what might become of his compound, DiPina had an ounce sealed in a lead casing before discussing matters with the authorities. Before he could act, the lead tube was stolen by a homeless man, who had no clue how dangerous his loot was. From there the tube got handled by Boy Scouts, ex-convicts, and escaped convicts, none aware of the item's true nature. Burns, one of the escaped criminals, tampered with the case to see what was inside but was stopped from detonating the material by the timely arrival of Batman, ROBIN, and ACE THE BAT-HOUND. (*Detective Comics* #254, April 1958)

DIRECTOR, THE

The man known only as the Director built up an exclusive clientele with his nightly performances of *The Thousand Deaths of Batman*. Unable to kill the real Caped Crusader, the Director staged a different death scenario for his actors to perform. He regularly sold out his theater, located on a private island in Gotham Bay, to cheering criminals. Batman and ROBIN eventually infiltrated the theater and took over the roles from the actors. Then, on stage, the Dynamic Duo, aided by the harbor police, brought down the curtain on the show. Many wanted felons, including the current head of the underworld, the Big Guy, were arrested. (*Detective Comics* #269, July 1959)

DIX, SMILEY

Smiley Dix was the leader of a criminal trio that robbed the Van Ness Mansion in GOTHAM CITY. As Batman and ROBIN pursued them, Dix blew up a bridge, totaling the BATMOBILE. Dix thought he and his men were free until the Dynamic Duo arrived in a brand-new Batmobile and apprehended them. (*Detective Comics* #156, February 1950)

DOCTOR AGAR

A frustrated scientist, Agar felt he was close to completing a gas that would reduce people in size. When one financier after another refused to invest funds to help his work, he sought revenge. He kidnapped the wealthy men and placed them in specially decorated rooms designed to make them believe the gas worked, and they had been reduced in size. In exchange for funding, he would "restore" them to normal. His scheme was undone when Batman and ROBIN tracked down the missing men. (*Detective Comics* #127, September 1947).

DOCTOR DEATH

KARL HELLFERN was one of several criminal entities to use the name *Doctor Death*. He devised a fatal strain of pollen and intended to use it to create a

..THIS MAN THEY CALL THE BAT MAN A CRIME SUCH AS OURS IS SURE TO ATTRACT HIS ATTENTION. HE MUST BE DONE AWAY WITH! IF I KNEW WHO HE IS—BUT, NO ONE DOES. I MUST TRAP HIM!

climate of terror among the world's wealthy; they would have to pay tribute to remain healthy. When learning that Batman was on his trail, Doctor Death lured the Dark Knight into an ambush where his aide, a large man named JABAH, shot and wounded the hero. Undaunted, Batman dispatched Jabah and then confronted Hellfern. The doctor held a test tube filled with flammable chemicals and threatened to destroy the Batman. Instead, the Dark Knight Detective threw a fire extinguisher at the doctor, who reflexively dropped the tube. It ignited.

Doctor Death came back from seeming death, although the conflagration cost him his lips and nose, charring his skin brown. He devised a new means of obtaining wealth and began extorting the rich, killing John Jones, the first to refuse to pay. Hellfern dispatched his new assistant, MIKHAIL, to rob the widow of jewels in lieu of cash. Batman fought the man, allowing him to escape in order to track him back to Hellfern. Instead, Batman was led only to Ivan Herd, a fence. Mikhail and Batman fought, leaving the thug dead. Batman then threatened Herd for information on Hellfern's whereabouts, only to discover that they were one and the same. Batman turned the murderer over to the police. (*Detective Comics* #29–30, July–August 1939)

DOCTOR DOOM

Why a smuggler took the name *Doctor Doom* was never explained, but he used it effectively in his career. Doctor Doom hid inside a mummy's sarcophagus to elude Batman and ROBIN during an aborted robbery. Unbeknownst to the Dark Knight Detective, Doom was transported back to the BATCAVE when the sarcophagus was added to the trophy room. After the heroes left, Doom emerged and was fascinated by the place. He then rigged many of the other trophies, turning them into death traps in the hope of ridding the underworld of the Dynamic Duo. Batman and Robin managed to elude several of these traps so a frustrated Doom hurled a grenade at them, hiding once more in the sarcophagus. The explosion sealed the case tightly, and Doom died from asphyxiation before Batman could free him. (*Detective Comics* #158, April 1950)

DOCTOR DOUBLE-X

SIMON ECKS was a research chemist who developed a mechanism that would amplify a person's kirilian aura. In so doing, he created an energy duplicate of himself. The duplicate was dependent upon the introverted doctor for life, and the two coexisted, granting the human energy-generating powers. The new incarnation also seemed to warp Ecks's personal morals, and he turned to crime to enhance his wealth and feeling of superiority over normal humans. As Doctor Double-X, the symbiotic life-form set out to commit crimes before encountering Batman and ROBIN. They met on several occasions, and in their final battle, the machine created an energy duplicate of Batman that turned the battle's tide. After apprehending him, Batman destroyed the machine, and Ecks himself was committed to ARKHAM ASYLUM. (*Detective Comics* #261, November 1958)

While in prison, Ecks concluded that his

doppelgänger lay dormant within him. He experimented by sticking his finger in an outlet, with the electric discharge reactivating Double-X. He escaped prison and resumed his attempts at accumulating wealth, only to meet defeat at the hands of Batman and SUPERMAN. (*World's Finest Comics* #276, February 1982)

After a prison term, he resumed his life of crime, teaming with the Rainbow Raider for a particular burglary. This time, it took the combined efforts of the Caped Crusader and the FLASH to subdue them. (*The Brave and the Bold* #194, January 1983)

Despite the ability to split from Ecks, the Double-X being seemed an inept fighter. The energy form could fly and emit power bolts that destroyed metal and concrete. Ecks was in constant need of raw electricity to rejuvenate his new form. Should the power level drop, the Double-X entity faded as an independent being, returning to Ecks's body.

By this time Ecks was considered an ordinary criminal and was sent to BLACKGATE PENITENTIARY. He was among the dozens of inmates freed by RÃ'S AL GHŪL in one of his attacks against Batman. (*Batman* #400, October 1986) He was last recorded operating in GOTHAM CITY, once again opposed by the Caped Crusader. (*Batman: Dark Detective* #3, Early August 2005)

DOCTOR DREEMO

DARBY DEEMS was a stage performer, a self-professed expert on dreams. As Doctor Dreemo, he used his stage notoriety to become host of radio's *The Nightmare Hour*. Rather than use his expertise to help people understand their dreams, however, he was actually delving deep to better understand his guests' subconscious fears. Deems then schemed to exploit them at a later date, as he did when he blackmailed one guest who had committed murder. Batman and ROBIN tracked and apprehended Doctor Dreemo and his men, ending the threat. (*World's Finest Comics* #17, Spring 1945)

DOCTOR EXCESS

The criminal known only as Doctor Excess worked for ATHENA, the criminal mastermind who with her team, the NETWORK, attempted to take over WAYNE ENTERPRISES and destroy the Batman. Excess established a legitimate medical business that fronted for his criminal deeds. His chemical expertise provided Athena with substances that enhanced people's performance. After the Network shut down, Doctor Excess vanished. (*Batman Family* #1–8, December 2002–February 2003)

DOCTOR FANG

Sergeant HARVEY BULLOCK took it upon himself to investigate rumors of a new crime boss in GOTHAM CITY. He used his shady reputation to make Doctor Fang believe he could be bought and allow the cop to get close. Doctor Fang never revealed his identity, preferring his showy costumed persona for all appearances. (*Batman* #370–372, April–June 1984)

Batman was also on the trail and took down Doctor Fang before Bullock could; the cop's ruse was exposed. Later, when Police Commissioner JAMES GORDON was hospitalized, Bullock wound up defying the orders of Mayor HAMILTON HILL, which angered the corrupt leader. He contracted with Doctor Fang, offering the crime boss freedom in exchange for the assassination of Bullock. The first shot missed; the second hit the detective's left arm. Batman brought down the villain before he could fire again. (*Detective Comics* #542, September 1984)

It took Batman a little time, but he finally discovered Hill's involvement, which led to the mayor being ousted from office while Doctor Fang remained in prison.

DOCTOR HERCULES

Hercules was a scientist who constructed three giant robots to help him commit crimes. To operate the machines, he obtained the services of three criminals who broke out of prison. The men—Whitey Drebs, George "Four Eyes" Foley, and Jawbone Bannon—began working the machines with some degree of success. However, a furious Hercules killed Foley when one crime was not successfully completed. Before more mayhem could ensue, Batman and ROBIN arrived to put an end to the operation. (*Batman* #42, August/September 1947)

DOCTOR MOON

During Batman's first extended confrontation with RÃ'S AL GHŪL, he encountered Doctor Moon. Moon was in Ra's employ, gleefully conducting experiments at the Demon Head's direction as well as indulging his own scientific whims. Batman was introduced to Moon's handiwork when he found the corpse of Mason Sterling, a scientist whose brain had been removed. The Dark Knight Detective traced the brain to Moon and discovered that the doctor had found a way to link the brain to a computer. This was done so Rã's could use the scientist's knowledge to further his own schemes. Doctor Moon escaped with Rã's and his daughter TALIA HEAD before Batman could apprehend any of them. (*Batman* #240, March 1972)

Prior to his criminal career, Moon was a respected Asian doctor who was once nominated for a Nobel Prize, but between his increasingly outrageous experiments and his oversized ego, he soon was

ostracized from the medical community. To him, the acquisition of knowledge was more important than ethics or morals; he once equated himself with the infamous Nazi surgeon Joseph Mengele. He began contracting his services to terrorists like Rã's al Ghūl and Doctor Cyber, doing their dirty work to earn the funds to perform his own studies. As a result, he found himself in opposition not only to the Batman but also to other heroes including WONDER WOMAN. He grew fascinated with meta-humans and wanted to create his own, going so far as to briefly operate Doctor Moon's Athletic Academy in Brooklyn. His only real success was a man named Topper, who wound up battling and being defeated by Richard Dragon and LADY SHIVA. (*Richard Dragon, Kung-Fu Fighter* #7, April 1976)

It wasn't long before Dr. Moon and the Batman once again crossed paths. Moon was contracted by General Ivan Angst to help create an army of superpowered men. Angst envisioned Mercenaries, Inc., to rival the LEAGUE OF ASSASSINS as a leading supplier of killers. Moon's work went beyond his Brooklyn efforts, cutting the nerve endings on test subjects so they would not experience pain during battle. Batman foiled Angst's plans but Moon, coward that he was, escaped. (*Detective Comics* #480, November/December 1978)

Their next encounter came when Moon worked for the crime boss Tobias Whale, as he attempted to access the memories of HALO, a member of Batman's OUTSIDERS team. (*Batman and the Outsiders* #20, April 1985) Things grew deadlier, though, when Doctor Moon was asked by the JOKER to help unreform CATWOMAN, returning her to the ranks of villainy. Moon was not pleased to be paid in exploding cigars, so he indulged himself when he insisted Catwoman be awake during his process so he could study her threshold for pain. His efforts were a success although it meant another confrontation with the Caped Crusader, this time resulting in his arrest. He refused Batman's demand that he undo his work, announcing that Catwoman was his masterpiece and should be untouched. (*Detective Comics* #569–570, December 1986–January 1987)

His work had come to the attention of Amanda Waller, head of the federal agency Task Force X. She had Moon transferred to Belle Reve, the secret headquarters of her Suicide Squad. There, she had Moon repeat his work, this time erasing the team's existence from the mind of Plastique. (*Suicide Squad* #3, July 1987) His efforts earned him a pardon. He was soon after hired by the Sunderland Corporation, a public business that also engaged in illegal research activities. Again his research was directed at meta-humans but this time in benevolent ways, including providing a better way for the heroic Air Wave to harness his natural abilities. (*Firestorm* #88, August 1989) Moon continued his work for Sunderland for some time, taking advantage of the firm's superior technological resources and his ability to freelance on occasion, such as his work with the mercenary Deadline.

He eventually left Sunderland to work with Metropolis's Intergang, using his memory-tampering techniques to wipe memories from the mind of reporter Catherine Grant before she could testify against them in court. For a change, Moon actually objected to some of the organization's methods and spoke up. Still, he accepted a contract and was ready to do its dirty work. The arrival of Batman and Superman put an end to the threat. (*Adventures of Superman* #483, June 1990; *Action Comics* #654, June 1990)

Moon wound up free once more and returned to Sunderland, where he helped create new superpowered criminals, an effort that brought him up against Hawkman. One of his freelance jobs during this period was at the behest of Two-Face. The twisted former district attorney asked for help finding a fertility drug that had helped twins come to life in Gotham City. The twins belonged to Two-Face's ex-wife Gilda, and only when Batman revealed they were conceived using Two-Face's own sperm was Moon stopped from performing surgery on the infants—when Two-Face shot his left shoulder. (*Batman: Two-Face Strikes Twice!* #1–2, 1993)

Moon continued working for Sunderland for a time and then once more went freelance. He took to spending time aboard the Injustice Society's old satellite headquarters, which had become a hangout for villains. It was noted, though, that every time Moon visited, someone usually went missing.

Dr. Moon finally died after engaging in a rare hand-to-hand fight with the female Manhunter, Kate Spencer, who stabbed him with his own scalpel. (*Manhunter* #18, March 2006)

DOCTOR NO-FACE

On Earth-2, Dr. Paul Dent created a machine that could rapidly heal scarred facial tissue—he had himself lost his facial features in an accident. Criminal Bart Magan tried to use the machine to obliterate a telltale facial scar, but instead he obliterated all his facial features. Magan then designed

a new criminal career to take advantage of his new condition. Disguised as Doctor No-Face, Magan began a series of seemingly senseless crimes as anything with a face, such as statues and clocks, were destroyed. He also created suspicion that Doctor No-Face was actually Dent. As people repaired and replaced the damaged items, Magan's men were stealing valuable objects and using replicas to hide their thefts. Investigating the crimes, Batman and Robin determined that the perpetrator was Magan, not Dent, and apprehended the criminal and his men. (*Detective Comics* #319, September 1963)

In the reality after the events of Infinite Crisis, Doctor No-Face was mentioned but not seen. (*52* #17, 2006)

DOCTOR PHOSPHORUS

Alexander James Sartorius was invited by Gotham General's Dr. Bell to join the Tobacconists' Club, an influential Gotham City institution. Once a member, Sartorious was invited to invest in a nuclear power plant that was about to be constructed just outside the city. The trusting doctor agreed and invested his life's savings without realizing the plant was going to be built on the cheap with substandard safety systems. During construction, Sartorius was visiting the site when an explosion occurred. The doctor threw himself under a pile of sandbags, hoping to avoid being killed. Instead, radiation changed his body as the sand was elevated one step up the elemental scale to phosphorus.

Doctor Phosphorus

Sartorius's body was turned into living phosphorus, and the alteration drove him to the brink of insanity. His every breath emitted deadly fumes, and he glowed bright white with coruscating nuclear flame. The exposed skin burned anything on contact.

Calling himself Doctor Phosphorus, Sartorius began a rampage against the crooked investors and politicians who had allowed the cut-rate plant to be built. The citizens of Gotham first learned of the grotesque threat when noxious fumes were pumped through Sprang Stadium's ventilation system during a rock concert, killing many people. Their deaths, coupled with the arrival of four dozen injured at Gotham General Hospital, alerted police to the scope of the danger. Among the victims was ALFRED PENNYWORTH, which meant, three minutes after his admittance, that Batman was on the case. He tracked Doctor Phosphorus to the Gotham reservoir, where the madman was attempting to poison the water supply to kill most of the city's seven million citizens.

As Batman tried to apprehend Doctor Phosphorus, he was severely burned, and the doctor fled.

Members of the Gotham City Council, controlled by RUPERT THORNE, acted swiftly when Police Commissioner JAMES GORDON also fell victim to Phosphorus's presence. They banned Batman's involvement, raising his suspicions. The Dark Knight Detective tracked the doctor to the offshore nuclear plant's remains. Using a specially shielded BATSUIT, the Caped Crusader faced Doctor Phosphorus a second time and was victorious, as the doctor seemingly fell to his doom inside the reactor's core. (*Detective Comics* #469–470, May–June 1977)

Doctor Phosphorus survived, however, and sought renewed vengeance against Thorne. He arrived at ARKHAM ASYLUM and threatened Thorne before turning his attentions once more to the city. This time he attempted to poison the populace through seeding rain clouds with his own irradiated material. Using the anti-radiation Batsuit, the Caped Crusader tracked him to an airfield and used the BATMOBILE to crash the villain's plane and keep it grounded. (*Batman* #311, May 1979)

Sartorius remained in prison, with time logged at both Arkham Asylum and BLACKGATE PENITENTIARY until he was freed by RĀ'S AL GHŪL. (*Batman* #400, October 1986) When he was apprehended, Phosphorus was locked away in a specially designed cell. (*Black Orchid* #2, 1989)

Later, he was transferred to Belle Reve prison in Louisiana, where he was freed by the demon Neron. Like so many other villains, he agreed to sell his soul in exchange for enhanced abilities. The demon enhanced his power—twenty times by Sartorius's estimate—and enabled him to control his burning emissions. As a result, the doctor took to wearing a fashionable suit and glowed with orange-red flame. (*Underworld Unleashed* #1, November 1995)

Sartorius relished being able to indulge his normal habits again, such as chain-smoking. He became a carefree criminal, moving away from exacting vengeance on Gotham and toward taking jobs that appealed to him. As a result, he wound up in Opal City, working for the Mist's daughter in her personal quest to kill the original Starman, Ted Knight. (*Starman* [second series] #12, July 1989) On several occasions Doctor Phosphorus and Starman fought, and with each setback the villain was more determined to finish the job despite the occasional stay in Opal's Cray Prison. He became a recurring threat in Opal City, killing seventeen guards in a daring escape, until he finally irradiated Starman with enough energy that the older hero succumbed to the poison in his blood. Before his death, STARMAN ended Doctor Phosphorus's threat to his beloved city. (*Starman* [second series] #70, October 2000)

Alex Sartorius was believed dead after his encounter in Opal City but turned up at the Cadmus Research Laboratories. There he was cared for by Dr. Church, the nuclear technician in charge of the tax evasion scam that had resulted in the initial accident changing Sartorius from man to menace. Church stole his life's savings and intended to steal his secrets to patent the technology. It was said that everything human about Sartorius had been consumed by his condition, leaving him soulless. A fusion reaction completely sublimated his central nervous system, creating functional facsimiles of his heart, lungs, kidneys, all working in concert to produce a near-endless supply of clean energy. He escaped Cadmus and killed Dr. Church before crossing Gotham City to find Dr. Bell and exact his long-overdue revenge. Doctor Phosphorus next sought Thorne, incarcerated at Blackgate. He managed to step once on Thorne's back, burning him, before Batman stopped him. He was remanded to Arkham until S.T.A.R. Labs built a better containment facility for him. (*Detective Comics* #825, January 2007)

DOCTOR PNEUMO

The man known only as Doctor Pneumo studied air pressure and devised tools that would allow compressed air to do the heavy work during the commission of crimes. In one case, his men drilled a hole in a bank vault; once a tube was inserted, air was pumped into the vault, letting the pressure build until the metal split apart. As Batman and ROBIN attempted to stop the thieves, the Caped Crusader received an injury to his optic nerves, rendering him temporarily blind. Refusing to give up, he designed earplugs that acted as sonar beacons and allowed him to freely move. He and Robin fought Pneumo and his men; Batman received a blow to his head, restoring his sight. The criminals were taken into custody. (*Batman* #143, October 1961)

DOCTOR SAMPSON

Sampson was a brilliant psychologist but was jailed for malpractice. Upon his release, he used his vast knowledge to devise a gas that would erase people's memories. Sampson and his men intended to use the gas and other psychological ploys to commit a wave of crimes in GOTHAM CITY. When Batman tried to stop them, he was exposed to the "amnesia gas" and forgot all his crime-fighting training. In time, though, the Dynamic Duo found the gas's counteragent and soon after apprehended Sampson and his team. (*Detective Comics* #190, December 1952)

DOCTOR TZIN-TZIN

While many people considered Doctor Tzin-Tzin an Asian menace, few knew that he was actually an American-born citizen kidnapped in his youth by Chinese bandits, for unknown reasons. He was raised by them and took to crime, returning to America as a modern-day gangster already with a long Interpol record. His crimes had included raiding a South African gold mine and stealing both a South American jet airplane and an ocean freighter. (*Detective Comics* #354, August 1966)

When a criminal was found frightened to death, the police suspected that Doctor Tzin-Tzin had arrived in GOTHAM CITY. He gathered a mob and declared his goal: to destroy the city's protector, Batman. The mastermind set a plan in motion that saw the Caped Crusader fight through a gauntlet of men as the blood-loving criminal recorded the battle, studying his prey. When the two finally met, Doctor Tzin-Tzin attempted to transfix the hero with his storied death-gaze, a form of hypnosis learned in Asia. When Batman shattered a light fixture that enhanced the hypnosis, Doctor Tzin-Tzin's hold broke and he was apprehended.

Seeking revenge, Doctor Tzin-Tzin remained in the vicinity, scheming to kill Batman and ROBIN in excruciating ways. He accepted a contract from the

LEAGUE OF ASSASSINS that funded the modification of a mansion into a death trap that would first inflict psychological damage. Batman and Robin struggled before escaping the deadly house, watching it go up in flames, presumably killing the doctor within. (*Detective Comics* #408, February 1971)

Instead, Doctor Tzin-Tzin escaped and went west, settling in San Francisco's Chinatown; there he rebuilt his operation. His new Dragon Tong stole and thrived, thwarting law enforcement at every turn until he was stopped again, this time by SUPERGIRL and private eye Jonny Double. (*Adventure Comics* #418, April 1972) When he next appeared, he had eschewed mere illusions in favor of mastering occult forces. He harbored *tsal*—mystic energy—within his body to aid his audacious plans. First he stole the Sphinx, relocating it to the ocean floor and replacing it with a replica. When he arrived in Gotham, attempting to do the same with Gotham Stadium, he prematurely lured Batman into the stadium. With the doctor's mystic energy spent from levitating the stadium, Batman managed to subdue him.

It took Doctor Tzin-Tzin six days of meditation to reenergize his *tsal;* then he went after the Dark Knight once more. Summoning countless ants to eat away at his cell's mortar, he freed himself and hypnotized the prison guards. With them as his new army, Doctor Tzin-Tzin threatened Gotham during the Christmas season. He used his occult abilities to rob the citizens of their Christmas recollections, virtually stealing the holiday from Gotham. At the Gotham Steam Company, Batman confronted Doctor Tzin-Tzin anew and finally stopped his madness by scalding the doctor and his occult creations with superhot steam. (*Batman* #284–285, February–March 1977)

Soon after, Batman endured excruciating pain after battling a criminal called SKULL DUGGER. Seeking relief, he approached the imprisoned doctor while disguised as a prison guard. Batman was willing to free the villain in exchange for one hour without pain. The doctor agreed. Batman managed to defeat Skull Dugger and then reneged on the deal, keeping Doctor Tzin-Tzin in jail. (*Batman* #290, August 1977)

The next time he turned up, the doctor had taken control of a small island—and its army—some seventeen miles southeast of Greece. His ultimate goal was new: taking over Russia. With the great power in disarray, he and his allies would be able to plunder Eastern Europe. However, Project Peacemaker learned of the plan and Christopher Smith, the Peacemaker, went after Doctor Tzin-Tzin, stopping him before the plan could be initiated. (*Peacemaker* #1–4, January–April 1988)

DOCTOR X

An evil energy duplicate of Dr. SIMON ECKS also known as DOCTOR DOUBLE-X.

DOCTOR ZODIAC

Theodore B. Carrigan was an old-fashioned carnival mystic who turned to crime. He based his robberies on a horoscope book, which he used for inspiration. Doctor Zodiac and his men wound up being apprehended by Batman, ROBIN, and SUPERMAN. (*World's Finest Comics* #160, September 1966)

Some time later, Doctor Zodiac was freed from prison and returned to his criminal ways. He stole a dozen coins from ATLANTIS, each bearing a Zodiac symbol. If the legends were true, Doctor Zodiac believed each coin would bestow him with a different power. Batman and Superman were on hand, though, to thwart his latest plan before he learned the truth. (*World's Finest Comics* #268, May 1981)

Seeking revenge and power, Doctor Zodiac later allied himself with the mystic Madame Zodiac to obtain a different set of one dozen Zodiac coins. This time Batman and Superman needed ZATANNA's help in stopping them, but not before Doctor Zodiac learned Batman's secret identity, allowing him to posses BRUCE WAYNE's body. During the battle, the Maid of Magic was injured; the chaos unleashed required the JUSTICE LEAGUE OF AMERICA's intervention.

WONDER WOMAN whisked Zatanna to Paradise Island so she could be healed while Superman fought to protect Batman from having his body permanently possessed by a malevolent force known only as the Master. The Master did manage to take temporary control of Batman's body and vanished, with Superman in pursuit. Doctor Zodiac and Madame Zodiac then tried to prepare a series of duplicate Batman bodies for the Master to use when the template burned out. Instead, Superman rescued his friend, and together they put an end to Doctor Zodiac and the others' world threat. (*World's Finest Comics* #285–288, November 1982–February 1983) The doctor has not been seen since.

DOC WILLARD

Doc Willard was considered a renegade scientist and flouted medical ethics when he transplanted GEORGE DYKE's brain into the body of a gorilla. When his patient escaped and went on a rampage, Willard realized the consequences of his work, and it drove him insane. As the disoriented gorilla fell to its death, ROBIN swept in and caught his mentor—unmasked as Doc Willard. Batman had faked unconsciousness and switched places with Doc just as the enraged GORILLA BOSS awakened. (*Batman* #75, February/March 1953)

Some time later, Dyke's brain, preserved as a souvenir in the BATCAVE, was revived by alien colonists, who offered Dyke a new body if he would use the form to erase Earth's chlorophyll, which was toxic to them. Manipulating Batman into placing the brain in the disintegration pit of SUPERMAN's FORTRESS OF SOLITUDE, Dyke burst forth in a new form, a massive green flying manta-like entity made up of vegetable matter.

Still craving a human body, Dyke sought out Doc Willard, who actually fulfilled the Boss's long-held goal of acquiring Batman's body. The fortuitous arrival of the aliens, angry that Dyke had reneged on their deal, alerted Superman to the swap. The Man of Steel hastily performed surgery that placed BRUCE WAYNE's brain back in Batman's body. In the meantime, Willard escaped. (*World's Finest Comics* #251, June/July 1978)

Willard returned soon after, hoping to confirm that Batman was in fact Bruce Wayne, as he'd suspected ever since he'd seen the Dark Knight's face during the operation. Though frustrated in his efforts, he escaped custody once more. Willard was finally apprehended, now an incoherent madman babbling about Dyke's brain being lost to aliens. The alien in question was no less than ex–GREEN LANTERN Sinestro, who had expanded the cerebellum to the size of a planet located in the anti-matter universe of Qward and was using the mutated brain as a power source. With his X-ray vision, Superman destroyed the unnatural extension of George Dyke once and for all. (*World's Finest Comics* #253–254, October/November 1978–December 1978/January 1979)

DODD, WALLY

Wally Dodd was a visionary entertainer who managed to construct a floating amusement park to hover above GOTHAM CITY. In keeping with its fantastic location, Skyland boasted a series of futuristic attractions. Batman and ROBIN were summoned to help investigate Dodd's murder, and the trail led them to Blinky Cole. The mob enforcer had killed Dodd after discovering that the attraction's owner had film showing Cole committing acts of sabotage after Dodd refused to pay protection money. (*Detective Comics* #303, May 1962)

DODO MAN, THE

The villain known only as the Dodo Man was described as a psychotic who had an unnatural urge to obtain anything related to the extinct dodo bird. This led him to commit criminal acts including a brazen robbery at GOTHAM CITY's Museum of Natural History. Batman arrived to stop the crime and suffered a blow to the head that led him to reverse his personas, dressing as BRUCE WAYNE by night and Batman during the day. Despite this bizarre set of circumstances, Wayne tracked the Dodo Man and then as Batman apprehended him, recovering the stolen stuffed dodo bird. (*Batman* #303, September 1978)

DODSON, PETER

Peter Dodson was a good-natured and reclusive millionaire who idolized Batman. He used his wealth, while it lasted, to fund many of GOTHAM CITY's celebrations to honor its protector. Criminals tried to exploit this by having Dodson kidnapped and replaced by an impostor. Then Batman was summoned to the millionaire's home and was informed by a "doctor" that Dodson had had a psychotic break, leaving him believing he was Batman. The doctor asked the Caped Crusader to humor the man as part of his treatment. Batman agreed, and the false Dodson was given a spare uniform and equipment to allow him to go on patrol. Batman and ROBIN shadowed him to keep Dodson safe until they realized it was all a ruse to distract them from actual crimes the men were committing. Shortly thereafter Dodson was rescued and the criminals placed behind bars. (*World's Finest Comics* #54, October/November 1954)

DOLAN, JOE

Joe Dolan had a long history of criminal acts, including robbery and murder. He was captured by Batman and ROBIN only to be freed soon after. The second time the Dynamic Duo apprehended him, they were aided by Dolan's boyhood chum, now a GOTHAM CITY district attorney. (*Batman* #11, June/July 1942)

DOLAN, JOHN
John Dolan was a criminal who gained powers and fought Batman and ROBIN as the ELEMENTAL MAN.

DONEGAN, KNUCKLES
Knuckles Donegan was once GOTHAM CITY's underworld chief, until he fled the city rather than be arrested by Batman and ROBIN. The Dynamic Duo tracked the criminal to Florida and apprehended him. (*Batman* #31, October/November 1945)

DORN
Dorn was a research scientist who obtained a meteorite and began to study its properties. He found dormant microbes and worked to bring them back to life—but the process resulted in an accident that transformed him into a green-hued, alien-shaped humanoid. The transformation was temporary but recurring, leaving Dorn with no memory of each experience. As the creature, Dorn was disoriented, resulting in a destructive rampage through GOTHAM CITY until Batman and ROBIN intervened. Though the creature emitted defensive energy, Batman found a way to destroy it and leave Dorn in his normal form with no lasting ill effects. (*Batman* #154, March 1963)

DORN, MAESTRO
Dorn was a puppeteer-turned-criminal who liked to meticulously plan his crimes. Before his men went into the field, Dorn would perform a dry run, using his marionettes to show them what to do and where pitfalls may be hidden. Despite the planning, they were all apprehended by Batman and ROBIN. (*Detective Comics* #182, April 1952)

D'ORTERRE
Duc D'Orterre was the head of the Apaches, a Paris-based violent criminal operation that worked from the city's sewers. To obtain vast wealth, D'Orterre was determined to marry a woman who had come into a sizable inheritance. He courted Karel Marie despite her brother Charles's objections, prompting the villain to use a unique mechanical device to obliterate Charles's facial features. D'Orterre grabbed Karel and they drove away from Paris toward Champagne and the duc's château. Before he could complete the journey, Batman found them. During the battle, the villain and his car drove off a high bridge, killing him. (*Detective Comics* #34, December 1939)

DOSYNSKI, GREGOR
Gregor Dosynski trained with the KGBEAST and came to America as his successor, the KNV Demon.

DOUBLE DARE
Aliki and MARGOT MARCEAU were identical twins who became circus acrobats before turning to a life of crime. They were based in Paris, but their exploits took them often to America—notably to BLÜDHAVEN, where they encountered NIGHTWING on more than one occasion. As a duo, they perfected a fighting

style that allowed them to attack a single opponent together without getting tangled up. Nightwing interested them given their similarity in fighting styles and training. (*Nightwing* #32, June 1999)

DOUBLE-X
DOCTOR DOUBLE-X was the name of the energy being created by SIMON ECKS.

DRAGONCAT
PHILIP PARSONS taught martial arts and under the alias Dragoncat; he was also a criminal. (*Robin* #22, November 1995)

When eighteen-year-old BARBARA GORDON set out to become a vigilante, she learned jujitsu from Dragoncat at his GOTHAM CITY studio. (*Batgirl Year One* #1, February 2003) Later, the third ROBIN, using his own alias of Alvin Draper, infiltrated Dragoncat's dojo to learn of his criminal ties. Parsons was subsequently captured and imprisoned at BLACKGATE PENITENTIARY. When Batman learned of a planned breakout, he arrived at Blackgate in time to stop Dragoncat from stealing chemicals intended for FIREFLY. (*Batman: Blackgate* #1, January 1997)

DRAGON FLY, SILKEN SPIDER, AND TIGER MOTH
A pop artist chose to make stars out of three female costumed criminals: Dragon Fly, Silken Spider, and Tiger Moth. While the unnamed artist referred to them as World Public Enemy numbers 1, 2, and 3, they were hardly credible candidates. Still, the women enjoyed their fifteen minutes of fame, including the portraits the artist painted of them. Also admiring the paintings were BRUCE WAYNE and DICK GRAYSON, who were present when POISON IVY first arrived in GOTHAM CITY, crashing the museum and claiming that

she herself was actually Public Enemy Number One. This was all part of a scheme on Ivy's part to drive the various costumed felons to compete with one another while she waited them out.

Dragon Fly intended to arrive early and get the drop on her rivals, but she discovered that Silken Spider and Tiger Moth had done the same thing. During the growing mêlée, Batman and Robin dropped from the sky in parachutes and subdued the third-tier criminals fighting among themselves. (*Batman* #181, June 1966)

In the reality after CRISIS ON INFINITE EARTHS, the three women had begun their career together as a rock band called World Public Enemy before turning to crime and first encountering Batman, Robin, and Poison Ivy. (*Batman: Shadow of the Bat Annual* #3, 1995)

Years later, the trio was employed by RĀ'S AL GHŪL to distract Batman as he sought to obtain DAMIAN to complete his resurrection. (*Batman* #570, December 2007)

DRAGON SOCIETY, THE
Unlike most criminal operations, the Dragon Society was a coast-to-coast organization with members masked at all times, so they did not know one another's real names or faces. How Batman took down the Dragon Society was the topic of a speech that Police Commissioner JAMES GORDON gave at the GOTHAM CITY Police Academy. He told of how Batman took on the Chief Dragon, who was based in Dragon One—aka Gotham—by apprehending Dragon One's leader, Harvey Straker, and impersonating him at a national meeting. By the time the Chief Dragon learned of the deception, it was too late to escape as ROBIN and local police arrived in force. (*Detective Comics* #273, November 1959)

DRAKE, DANA WINTERS
Dana Winters was a GOTHAM CITY physical therapist when she was hired to help JACK DRAKE regain the use of his legs after he was poisoned in Haiti. She and Jack not only worked well together but felt an attraction that grew rapidly. As he regained the ability to walk, Jack and Dana began to date. In due time, the two fell in love and married, Dana becoming stepmother to Jack's son TIM DRAKE, who was also ROBIN the Teen Wonder. (*Robin* [second series] #12, December 1994)

Dana enjoyed a loving relationship with Tim until tragedy struck. While she was away from home, Jack was killed by CAPTAIN BOOMERANG. She fell into a depression and soon after relocated with Tim from Gotham to BLÜDHAVEN. She lost her grip on sanity and was hospitalized, visited by both Tim and ALFRED PENNYWORTH on a regular basis. After the city was destroyed, she was successfully relocated back to Gotham.

DRAKE, JACK
Jack Drake was a wealthy businessman who married a woman named JANET; together they had an only child, TIM DRAKE. Jack and Janet may have settled in GOTHAM CITY, but they liked to travel as he indulged his passion for archaeology. They formed a loving partnership that extended from home to business. (*Batman* #455, October 1990)

The one thing that seemed to receive scant attention was Tim: The child was frequently left in Gotham while his parents trotted around the globe. As a result, his formative years were spent in a variety of boarding schools. A rare instance of the three acting as a family, and thus making an indelible impression on Tim, was when they all attended HALY BROS. CIRCUS when he was six. A souvenir from that day was a photo of the smiling family with the circus headliners, the FLYING GRAYSONS. DICK GRAYSON held Tim in his arms and said he'd dedicate his performance that night to the younger boy. It was the same fateful performance that saw JOHN and MARY GRAYSON fall to their deaths, putting Dick on a path that led him to becoming Batman's first partner, ROBIN.

The Drakes rushed Tim out of the tent in the tragedy's wake. The event seemed to have altered the family dynamic—suddenly things weren't the same between Jack and Janet. Still, they continued to travel. One trip took them to Haiti, where they were unfortunately kidnapped by the OBEAH MAN. He held them as hostages, demanding money, which brought Batman out of Gotham to save two of its citizens. While the Dark Knight apprehended the Obeah Man, the Drakes fell ill after drinking water altered by the mad mystic. Janet died and Jack fell into a coma, a state in which he would remain for some months. (Detective Comics #618–621, Late July–September 1990) When he did wake up, he was left paralyzed and confined to a wheelchair.

By this time, Tim had discovered Batman's secret identity and convinced the crime fighter to train him as the third Robin. As a result, when Jack was alert and wanted to be closer to his son, things grew complicated. Jack objected to Tim's close relationship with their neighbor BRUCE WAYNE, and he was often bitter. That changed, though, when he began to fall in love with his physical therapist Dana Winters. Her arrival softened the mood between father and son, which thrilled both. In due time, Jack and Dana married.

Jack also became a victim in BANE's scheme to crush Batman. Bane kidnapped Jack (Detective Comics #665, August 1993), although he was eventually rescued by Bruce Wayne and ALFRED PENNYWORTH. (Robin [second series] #7, June 1994)

Given his physical and emotional trauma, Jack couldn't keep on top of his business dealings, and soon after the wedding, Drake Industries faced bankruptcy. The Drakes had to give up their mansion, and Jack struggled with depression until he was convinced he'd seen a vision of Janet telling him it was time to move forward.

He took this literally, and when Gotham City became a NO MAN'S LAND, he relocated his family to Keystone City, although they eventually moved back to Gotham Heights after the city was restored.

In their new home, Jack grew concerned about Tim's frequent absences and long hours away from home. After catching his son in a lie, Jack tore through his room and discovered the real reason: Tim was Robin. Furious, Drake confronted Wayne, threatening to kill and/or expose him. (Robin [second series] #124, May 2004) To appease his father, Tim agreed to stop being Robin and spend more time at home. This lasted until a crisis precipitated by Tim's replacement, Stephanie Brown—aka SPOILER. She unintentionally ignited a gang war, and when Tim's high school was a target, he defied his father to act as Robin. By then, however, Jack had come to realize the good his son could do and tacitly agreed to his resumption of a crime-fighting career.

Jack Drake became a victim, though, when the deranged Jean Loring, ex-wife of the ATOM, began targeting the loved ones of super heroes in order to win her former husband back. She covertly hired CAPTAIN BOOMERANG to kill Jack, while also sending Jack a pistol so the confrontation could end in a stalemate. Loring's idea was that they'd kill each other, framing the rogue as the true killer of the ELONGATED MAN's wife, SUE DIBNY. While Tim listened in over an open phone line, Jack shot Boomerang just as the curved weapon also struck Jack in the chest, leaving both men dead. (Identity Crisis #5, December 2004)

DRAKE, JANET LYNN

Janet Drake was a GOTHAM CITY–born woman who married JACK DRAKE and gave birth to TIM, who became the third ROBIN.

DRAKE, MORTIMER

Mortimer Drake was a costumed criminal better known to law enforcement as the CAVALIER.

DRAKE, TIMOTHY "TIM"

Tim Drake was an exceptional youth who boldly sought to become the third ROBIN. (Batman #436, August 1989)

The son of JACK and JANET DRAKE, he spent his early years largely on his own as his parents traveled the world for business and archaeology. When he came of school age, he attended boarding schools.

On one rare family day, the Drakes attended the HALY BROS. CIRCUS during its stay in GOTHAM CITY. To record the event, the Drakes posed for a photo with the star performers, the FLYING GRAYSONS. Young DICK GRAYSON held Tim in his arms and dedicated the night's performance to the six-year-old.

To Tim's shock, he watched as JOHN and MARY GRAYSON fell to their deaths. As his parents rushed him out of the tent, Tim caught sight of an indelible image: the grieving Dick encountering Batman. Three years later Tim saw a television broadcast of a security tape showing Batman and Robin in action and he recognized the Boy Wonder's quadruple somersault from the circus. He had figured out the Dynamic Duo's secret identities. Captivated, Tim followed their careers with keen interest, keeping the secret to himself.

His observations alerted him to the change in Robins, from Grayson to JASON TODD. In the wake of Todd's death, Tim also watched as Batman became grimmer, more violent, and even reckless. Tim tracked down the former Boy Wonder and tried to convince Dick to go back and help his mentor. (New Titans #60, December 1989) The best promise Dick could make was to work with Batman in his current role as NIGHTWING. While this helped, Tim couldn't shake the notion that Batman needed a full-time Robin. Using his knowledge, he approached ALFRED PENNYWORTH and talked his way into obtaining the Robin costume Batman kept in the BATCAVE's trophy area. In uniform for the first time, Tim aided Batman and Nightwing in their latest battle with TWO-FACE. (Batman #442, 1989)

Batman was angry, unwilling to put yet another teen at risk as he carried out his vendetta against criminals, but both Nightwing and Alfred saw the value Tim could bring to Batman's life. Slowly, he allowed himself to be convinced, but he refused to sanction Tim until he trained and trained hard. First Alfred worked with Tim, followed by Batman; even Dick helped explain how to deal with their mentor's grim moodiness. During this time Tim took full advantage of his parents' frequent absences to devote nearly every waking hour to either school or training. All that changed when the Drakes were kidnapped in Haiti. Batman flew down to rescue them from the OBEAH MAN, but the confrontation left Janet Drake dead and Jack Drake in a coma. (Detective Comics #591, September 1990)

As Jack slowly recovered, Batman questioned whether or not Tim could control his emotions and be effective. Unlike Batman, Tim was more even-tempered, desiring to be Robin to do good as opposed to Batman and Dick Grayson's need to exact revenge against criminals. After Tim rescued the Dark Knight and VICKI VALE from the SCARECROW, Batman finally sanctioned the new Robin. (Batman #457, December 1990)

Batman thought he had taught Robin well, but

he knew there were others who could enhance that education. As a result, he sent Tim to study under many of the same people who'd initially trained BRUCE WAYNE. (*Robin* #1-5, January–May 1991)

The new training began for the Teen Wonder in Paris with RAHUL LAMA, a martial arts master. As Tim learned healing techniques, he had his initial encounter with the KING SNAKE, head of the GHOST DRAGONS, and his teen aide LYNX. More importantly, he met LADY SHIVA, who gifted him with her personal time and attention. She also rewarded him with his choice of weapon, and he adopted a Bo staff. The collapsible tool was modified to emit a whistling sound. After Robin refused to kill King Snake to complete his training, Lady Shiva abandoned him.

Soon after, he returned to Gotham City and began work in earnest as Batman's new partner. During this period, Jack Drake came out of his coma and was confined to a wheelchair. As he endured a long period of physical therapy—in which he began to fall for his trainer, Dana Winters—he also wanted to spend more time with his son. This added new stress to Tim's limited free time.

Jack at first objected to Tim's closeness to Bruce Wayne, but with Dana's help, even those wounds healed. It was the first time Tim had felt any real sense of family. He also built up a circle of friends in public school, where he met and fell for ARIANA DZERCHENKO. (*Robin III: Cry of the Huntress* #1-6,

December 1992–March 1993) They were an item for some time, grounding Tim's noncostumed life.

In addition to his work alongside Batman, Tim also single-handedly fought old-time opponents such as CLUEMASTER and the JOKER while taking on newer threats such as the SPEEDBOYZ and the GENERAL.

Tim also began to interact with other costumed crime fighters around America, including numerous peers who gathered to form YOUNG JUSTICE. Among the charter members was Superboy, a genetic clone derived from both SUPERMAN's and LEX LUTHOR's DNA. Tim and Superboy became best friends, each understanding what the other was going through as they sought to find their way in the world without being lost in the shadows cast by their respective mentors. Given his training, and Batman and Nightwing's reputations, people naturally gravitated toward levelheaded Tim Drake as their leader. Even when he wasn't their elected captain, most turned to him for direction in moments of crisis.

Tim's worlds meshed when he encountered Cluemaster's daughter, STEPHANIE BROWN. She donned her self-made costume as the SPOILER to thwart her father's criminal ways in an attempt to retain some semblance of a family. Stephanie was desperate to find affection and approval wherever she could. Shortly after she and Robin crossed paths, she learned that she was pregnant with another teen's child. As she struggled with telling

her mother, Crystal, and deciding what to do, Tim grew closer to her, first as a supportive friend (disguised as Alvin Draper when not in Robin gear), and then as a romantic partner. After she gave birth and put the child up for adoption, she returned to her role as Spoiler, and her relationship with Tim deepened.

Spoiler slowly became a part of the extended team of crime fighters working for Batman in Gotham City. She craved full acceptance but her training was iffy, despite Tim's help. Their relationship grew complicated when Jack decided that Tim needed better schooling and dispatched him to the nearby BRENTWOOD ACADEMY, where he stayed for about a year. He made a new circle of friends and continued his adventuring as Robin, both solo and alongside the Dark Knight. Alfred initially accompanied him to ease the transition. (*Robin* #74, March 2000) Robin was left reeling after Batman recruited Spoiler and told her that his partner was really Tim Drake. (*Robin* #87, April 2001)

Meanwhile, Tim was present during a series of catastrophic incidents plaguing Gotham's citizens. The cycle began when BANE came to Gotham to destroy Batman and wound up crippling him. Robin worked alongside Batman's chosen successor, JEAN-PAUL VALLEY, until Valley's training as AZRAEL forced him to not only work solo but also become a more violent defender of justice. Tim tried to work with him but wound up locked out of the BATCAVE. (*Detective Comics* #665, August 1993) After Bruce Wayne healed and took back the mantle of the Bat, Robin was once more at his side. There was a brief time when Dick substituted as Batman, allowing him and Tim to form a tight, sibling-like bond. (*Batman* #512, November 1994) Soon after, Robin was stricken with the CLENCH, an Ebola-A virus unleashed on the city. Fortunately the heroes found a cure in time. Finally, an earthquake devastated the city and forced the US government to withdraw funding and support.

When the city was cut off, turning it into a NO MAN'S LAND, Tim was determined to stay behind and help Gotham adjust. Instead, his father relocated the family to Keystone City, which made Tim's career as Robin a nightmare. He continued to fight crime with Young Justice, and even teamed up on occasion with Impulse in Keystone, but also found his way back to Gotham as needed. Jack did move the family back once the city was reunited with the country.

Around this time, Young Justice was drawn into a battle precipitated by an android from the future that decimated the ranks of the team along with Nightwing's TEEN TITANS. Once the first Wonder Girl, Donna Troy, was killed at the battle's climax, the teen heroes chose to disband. Robin was left without a regular peer group and remained active only with Batman. That changed when the Titan Cyborg wanted to reactivate his team and use it as a training ground for the next generation of heroes. For months Tim shuttled to San Francisco each weekend to train and adventure with the new Teen Titans roster. He was thrilled. (*Teen Titans* [third series] #1, September 2003)

Tim Drake left the Brentwood Academy and moved back to Gotham after Jack Drake declared bankruptcy. (*Robin* [second series] #100, May 2002)

Once the Drakes settled in Gotham Heights, though, Jack began to wonder about Tim's long absences. After catching his son in a lie, he investigated his room and discovered the truth regarding his whereabouts. Jack was angry and confronted Bruce Wayne, threatening to reveal his secret. (*Robin* [second series] #124–126, May–July 2004).

Forced into an impossible situation, Tim agreed to step down as Robin and remain a member of the Drake family. After all—as he time and again told Batman and Nightwing and others—he enjoyed his adventures as Robin, but saw himself growing into an adult and hanging up the costume in favor of a "normal" life. And that meant family had to take priority.

Stephanie lobbied to become the new Robin and Batman agreed, hoping to finally give her the training she needed. Meanwhile, Tim was going to school and staying home at night, his romance with Spoiler definitely on the rocks. However, when Stephanie failed in her new role and was fired, she activated a War Games scenario she found in the Batcomputer, hoping to prove her worth. The plan was flawed and led to untold violence throughout Gotham as rival gangs were drawn into war. Tim did

what he could to protect those around him, until his high school became a battlefield as gangs tried to kidnap Darla Aquista, daughter of a crime boss, for ransom. Tim sprang into action until help could arrive, and he managed to save many although Aquista died from her wounds.

Jack finally recognized all the good Tim could do as Robin and gave his approval for the teen to resume his costumed role. He went back to work, but too late to save Stephanie, who died from injuries sustained during the time Black Mask tortured her. Soon after, tragedy arrived in the super-hero community as loved ones to the heroes were being targeted. Jack was drawn into this scheme, created by the Atom's ex-wife Jean Loring, to get her husband back. He first found a gun waiting for him in the house, and then he heard an intruder. Jack called Tim, via Oracle, who was on patrol with Batman. As the Batmobile speed through the city, Tim heard the attack, which left Jack Drake dead from Captain Boomerang's razorrang, and the gunfire that took Boomerang's life.

Jack's death left Tim devastated and sent his second wife, Dana, into a psychotic breakdown.

Rejecting Bruce's offer to adopt him, Tim relocated to Blüdhaven, installing Dana at a hospital. Tim went so far as to create a fictitious Uncle Eddie with whom he could stay, but Batman soon learned that this was a ruse with Eddie being played by an actor. Bruce tried to lend assistance, and Alfred went to Blüdhaven on numerous occasions to help as well. Batgirl had also moved to the city, and the two fought and trained together, giving Tim an outlet for the tumultuous emotions he was handling.

The teen was at a crossroads of sorts. He enjoyed being Robin and found himself an orphan like Bruce and Dick, wondering if that meant he would be a vengeance-driven hero. His life grew more complex when a reality-altering wave brought his predecessor, Jason Todd, back to life. Todd was now in an adult body, angry not only at being replaced as Batman's partner but also at seeing Tim so readily accepted by the Titans, a team that had seemed to barely tolerate him years earlier. The two battled to a standstill and then Todd vanished, reappearing as the Red Hood, determined to make Batman's world a miserable one.

Tim continued to weigh his options when he was made a new offer. The Veteran, a military-styled hero who led a team, thought Tim had what it took to be on his squad. To test the waters, Robin worked alongside them and had several successes, although he ultimately turned the offer down. (*Robin* #138, July 2005)

But then came the events known as Infinite Crisis. Robin was defending Blüdhaven alongside the Veteran and others against OMACs. After the city was secured, he was asked by Donna Troy to help the Titans elsewhere. Robin fought alongside his fellow Titans plus the Doom Patrol and the legendary Justice Society of America, but watched in horror as his best friend, Superboy, died in battle with Superman-Prime. Despite their best efforts, the heroic ranks were dwindling and Blüdhaven was destroyed by the creature called Chemo. Robin was then asked by Superman to command the heroes' combined rescue efforts. That lasted until the federal government installed its own team of meta-human rescuers. (*Infinite Crisis* #5, #7, April, June 2006)

When the dust settled and Superboy-Prime's threat finally ended on Earth, Tim was left to assess his future. First his mother had died, then Stephanie Brown, followed quickly by his father and his best friend. Even his favorite super hero, Blue Beetle II, lost his life during this time. It all could have taken its toll on the teen. Instead, he had the love and support of Bruce and Dick, which helped him heal. In fact, Bruce took the two around the world, meeting with his teachers once more, retraining and readying the heroes for a new era. After six months Bruce sent Dick and Tim back to Gotham to continue to look after the city. (*52* #30, November 2006) Tim moved, with Alfred's help, into the Wayne Estate's Carriage House, a place he could finally call his own. He then returned to action as Robin, drawn into a scheme by Batgirl to bring him to her side. Tim was given yet another emotional wallop when he found Batgirl's body, but it was revealed that she was Lynx from the Ghost Dragons. (*Robin* [second series] #148, May 2006)

As he investigated, Tim encountered Lady Shiva once more. She warned him of someone taking over the LEAGUE OF ASSASSINS in the wake of RĀ'S AL GHŪL and his daughter NYSSA RAATKO'S apparent deaths. As Robin investigated, he found Batgirl's cowl and a note, in Navajo code, telling him to break DAVID CAIN out of prison or Cain's daughter, Batgirl, would die. Robin complied, only to learn that it was all a ruse orchestrated by Batgirl, now in charge of the League and hoping to lure Robin to her side. She asked him to kill Cain but Tim refused, so she shot her father. Robin bolted, fearing what had become of his ally and friend.

Upon Tim's return to Gotham, he encountered Owen Mercer, son of Captain Boomerang, who sought forgiveness for his father's heinous crime. Owen joined Robin in finding a bomb planted by the Joker but in the end, the Teen Wonder still refused to shake Mercer's hand. He was healing but wasn't ready to offer forgiveness.

Batman then returned to Gotham City, and the Dynamic Duo was reunited. They immediately had to figure out who was killing minor members of Batman's Rogues Gallery despite suspicion being thrown HARVEY DENT'S way. During the course of the case, which cleared Dent but revealed the GREAT WHITE SHARK as the underworld's new boss, Bruce Wayne took stock of their lives and once more offered to adopt Tim. This time, the offer

was accepted. (*Batman* #654, August 2006) Tim subsequently moved into WAYNE MANOR, taking over the room that Dick and then Jason had used.

Tim was soon after captured and tied up by the Joker but managed to escape on his own, which Batman acknowledged and commended. The bonds were deepening between them despite obstacles that would continue to be in their path. (*Detective Comics* #826, February 2007)

Back at a new school, Tim was once more making friends, including a girl named Zoanne who was at first his tutor. She soon became something more to him, and the two began dating.

Robin continued his work with the Teen Titans, overseeing a thorough overhaul of the roster that brought him into close contact with several heroines who found him attractive. He was still mourning Stephanie and even Superboy, so he was surprised when he found himself kissing Cassie Sandsmark, the second Wonder Girl, Superboy's former girlfriend. Tim was also secretly using advanced technology underneath Titans Tower to try to clone a new Superboy, but met with countless failures.

Like his mentor, Tim had begun to collect reminders of the losses he'd endured in his short life. Among the items he retained were clothing from his parents and the uniforms worn by Superboy and Spoiler.

Tim was a growing boy; he'd begun his new life at five foot one, but adolescence brought a developing body. While measuring at average height and weight for boys his age, Tim possessed heightened strength, agility, endurance, and eye–hand coordination as a result of his training at the hands of the world's greatest teachers. He proved to be a bright student, mastering his school subjects in addition to criminology and other skills required for a crime fighter. A quick study, Tim proved to be an excellent tactician and had a superb eye for body language. Batman even admitted that Tim was smarter than both Alfred and himself. (*Robin* #136, May 2005)

As Robin, Tim wore a variety of uniforms harking back to the red, green, and yellow outfit first used by Dick Grayson. Over time, the materials used provided additional layers of protection without sacrificing maneuverability. While he wore a modified UTILITY BELT, Tim preferred his Bo staff and an R-shaped throwing star he wore as a chest emblem.

DREW, "DIMPLES"

The criminal "Dimples" Drew organized an underworld Olympics, basing it in an abandoned airplane hangar in Orville, an hour's drive from GOTHAM CITY. These games were designed to find the underworld's best safecracker, burglar, and so on. Drew was no fool and anticipated that Batman

would learn of the games and infiltrate them in order to apprehend the participants. He offered a million-dollar prize to the man who could correctly pierce Batman's disguise. In addition, Drew rigged the games so his own men would win, allowing him to pocket both winnings and entry fees. Batman had infiltrated the games and was exposed, as planned, but he and ROBIN still managed to shut down the event and arrest the participants. (*Batman* #82, March 1954)

DRISCOLL, PETER

Dr. Peter Driscoll suffered a blow to the head and developed temporary amnesia, resulting in his not knowing in which city he'd left a package. The package contained a vial filled with a deadly disease he had been researching; if it was released, some innocent metropolis was imperiled. Batman and ROBIN crafted an ingenious ruse to shock Driscoll's mind, restoring his memory. The vial was safely recovered. (*Batman* #90, March 1955)

DRIVER, MARCUS

Marcus Driver was the last officer selected by JAMES GORDON to be made detective before the police commissioner's retirement. He joined the MAJOR CRIMES UNIT and was partnered with veteran cop Charlie Fields. While investigating a missing fourteen-year-old, they entered an apartment and unexpectedly encountered MISTER FREEZE. Driver's hands were iced by Mister Freeze's weapon, but Fields was entirely frozen. The villain began chipping away at the iced body, demanding that Driver provide information. When Freeze finally got what he was after, he shattered the frigid remains of Fields.

Fields had been outspoken about his belief that the GOTHAM CITY POLICE DEPARTMENT had grown too dependent on Batman and his caped colleagues. His tragic death made Driver resolve never to need a cape's assistance on a case. He went so far as to summon Batman to the G.C.P.D. rooftop and announce he did not need the Dark Knight's assistance. Batman demanded that Driver never repeat the stunt.

The brown-eyed, brown-haired detective was subsequently partnered with ROMY CHANDLER. Over a short space of time, the two began a clandestine affair, known only to themselves and STACY, the MCU's civilian aide. (*Gotham Central* #1, February 2003)

DRYE, DANA

Batman considered Dana Drye the greatest detective of them all. When the two men were gathered at a conference of notable detectives, a shot rang out and Drye, the guest of honor, fell dead. Batman took charge of his fellow detectives, steering the investigation. In time, Batman learned that Drye had been dying from a disease and created the elaborate ploy, a stumper to be remembered by. As Batman studied Drye's papers, he found a journal in which the great sleuth had recorded his observations, including the secret of Batman's identity. Batman subsequently told his fellows that Drye's death could not be solved, then confided in ROBIN that if Drye could keep Batman's secret, he would honor the dead man's wishes and keep his own secret as well. (*Batman* #14, December 1942/January 1943)

DUBOIS, LOUIS

The minor criminal Louis DuBois was a threat to Batman in his guise as the second MONK.

DUCARD, HENRI

Henri Ducard was one of several people who agreed to train BRUCE WAYNE in his quest to become a living weapon against crime. (*Detective Comics* #599, April 1989)

Wayne traveled to Paris and sought out Ducard for his renowned skills as a detective. Ducard agreed to train Wayne, and they spent several months working together. All the while, however, the eager teenager never realized that Ducard was largely an amoral man who worked with both sides of the law.

After Wayne became Batman, he encountered Ducard again while investigating an attempt to wrest control of WAYNE ENTERPRISES away from him. Ducard, his skills sharp as ever, recognized that the Dark Knight and Wayne were one and the same. Rather than exploit the knowledge, he kept it to himself.

Wayne finally recognized Ducard's lack of morals but still thought well enough of the man to let him continue to operate. Soon thereafter, when TIM DRAKE was also globe trotting as part of his own training to become ROBIN, he and Ducard encountered each other in Paris, leading them to work together on a case in Hong Kong. (*Robin* #2, February 1991) The two met again when Robin went to Paris in search of a cure to the CLENCH virus. (*Robin* [second series] #32, August 1996)

Ducard also encountered CATWOMAN when she journeyed to Paris on a mission. (*Catwoman* #17, January 1995)

DUGGER, COSMO

Cosmo Dugger was a career criminal who briefly used the moniker SKULL DUGGER.

DUMPLER, HUMPHREY

Humphrey Dumpler was an overweight, slightly misshapen man, taunted since childhood. He turned to crime and was better known as HUMPTY DUMPTY.

DUMPSTER SLASHERS, THE

Karl Branneck and Vito Procaccini teamed up to attack innocent citizens and leave them in Dumpsters around GOTHAM CITY. They came to Batman's attention when Kate Babcock, a social worker whom BRUCE WAYNE knew, became their victim. (*Batman* #414, December 1987)

Batman investigated but was distracted time and again until he finally tracked down the two killers. (*Batman* #421–422, July–August 1988)

DUNDEE, DOUGLAS WILLIAM

Dr. Douglas Dundee was both a physician and a friend to THOMAS and MARTHA WAYNE on Earth-1. It was Dundee who delivered BRUCE WAYNE, with Thomas's help. He remained a family friend even after the Waynes were murdered, offering the youth friendship and counsel at their grave site. He was there to see Bruce grow into a young man, excelling at football before he set out to train en route to becoming the Batman. Once

Wayne became the Caped Crusader, he eventually revealed his secret to Dundee, bringing him into his confidence and making Dundee his personal doctor. Dundee got to see his friend in action after two criminals interrupted his examination of Wayne, insisting they remove a bullet from the arm of one of them. After Dundee complied and the thugs left with many of his drugs, Wayne used his vast skills to track them down and bring them to justice. (*Batman* #304, October 1978)

DUNN, FELIX

Felix Dunn was a modern-day man who suffered a concussion that left him believing he was a villainous knight from Arthurian times. He became the BLACK ROGUE.

DUPLICATE MAN

An unnamed criminal devised advanced technology that crafted a perfect duplicate of himself. Whenever he desired, he could dematerialize one body—a handy skill for avoiding capture. Clad in blue and orange, he took the name *Duplicate Man* and dedicated himself to acquiring the world's greatest inventions en route to becoming the world's greatest villain. He began executing his plan but was stopped cold by Batman, ROBIN, and SUPERMAN. (*World's Finest Comics* #106, December 1959)

DURFEE, JIM

As a child Jim Durfee was fascinated by guns, putting him on a path that led to an adult career as a hit man. He failed on an assignment to assassinate BRUCE WAYNE and was soon after shot dead by a cop who thought Durfee was robbing a jewelry store. (*World's Finest Comics* #34, May/June 1948)

DURGIN, HAL

Hal Durgin was a brilliant scientist who devised a machine styled after a camera. When it snapped a picture of an object, it would actually dematerialize the object and store it inside as data. When he was safely back in his lab, Durgin could then transmit the data to restore the object to its proper size and shape. Rather than profit from selling the technology, he used it for a series of baffling crimes. When Batman tried to apprehend him, ROBIN accidentally hit Durgin's arm, and Batman was captured by the camera. The Caped Crusader was converted into a living negative image of himself that, when exposed to direct sunlight, rapidly weakened; he would soon die. With Robin's help, they tracked down Durgin and had him use the camera on the Negative Batman, restoring him to normal. Durgin was then apprehended and the camera taken into custody. (*Detective Comics* #284, October 1960)

DURIM

Durim was the planetary home to Logi, a local hero, and his nemesis, HROGUTH, both of whom had an encounter with Batman, ROBIN, and SUPERMAN. (*World's Finest Comics* #124, March 1962)

DURR, JON

In a potential twenty-first century, Jon Durr served as secretary of science in New GOTHAM CITY. He was also the inventor of a time machine, which was stolen for criminal purposes by his brother Rak. While serving as Jon's assistant, Rak learned that a unique alloy derived from Kryptonite and the legendary Thor's hammer, *mjolnir*, would result in something with "fantastic powers." Using the time machine, he traveled back to the twentieth century to obtain kryptonite and then farther back to AD 522 to steal Thor's hammer. He almost succeeded in his plan but was stopped by Batman, Robin, and Superman. (*World's Finest Comics* #135, August 1963)

DYKE, GEORGE "BOSS"

George Dyke was better known to Batman and the Gotham City Police Department as the Gorilla Boss of Gotham after a bizarre experiment.

DYNAMIC DUO, THE ———————

Batman and his various Robins were dubbed the Dynamic Duo by Gotham City's media.

DZERCHENKO, ARIANA ———————

Ariana Dzerchenko was Tim Drake's first serious girlfriend, the daughter of a Soviet patriot relocated to Gotham City. The family settled in the Little Odessa section of the city and opened Dzerchenko Quality Meats, which had modest success. As the Russian mob grew in influence, it decided to force Ariana's father, Vari, to cooperate, which resulted in his death at the hands of the KGBeast. Ariana and Tim met in school, became friends, and turned into romantic partners until a family tragedy struck and the relationship cooled. Ariana and her mother, Natalia, moved in with her uncle in Gotham Heights, where they opened Vari & Natty's Deli & Salad Bar. Ariana drifted out of Tim's life. (*Robin III: Cry of the Huntress* #1, December 1992)

The Dynamic Duo

EAGLE, THE

Batman and ROBIN attempted to prevent the JOKER from making off with the Gotham Book Fair's receipts but wound up trapped within an armored car. The heavy metal doors were ripped apart by a figure dressed in an orange-and-tan feathered costume. Clawed gloves gripped the door . . . and the Dynamic Duo was rescued by GOTHAM CITY's latest protector, the Eagle. Once freed, the heroes pursued the Joker through giant replicas of classic books, but the Clown Prince of Crime escaped.

Back at the BATCAVE, the dejected crime fighters were surprised to discover the Eagle awaiting them, and when he unmasked they were shocked to see that their savior was actually ALFRED PENNYWORTH. He explained that while cleaning the trophy room,

MOMENTS LATER, A STRANGE, COSTUMED FIGURE APPEARS...

HELP! LET US OUT!

he'd fallen and been enmeshed in wires from a weapon created by "Doc" Cranium, which caused a discharge that went through a crystal from outer space and struck the butler. The result? Alfred gained incredible superpowers. He finally had his chance to join the team, indulging a desire to fight crime that he had harbored since entering BRUCE WAYNE's employ.

A reluctant Batman, who had already sanctioned BATWOMAN and had been duped by DEADSHOT, couldn't possibly say no to Alfred. Over the following day Batman, Robin, and the Eagle went into action, but Alfred lacked training and experience—which no amount of power could give him. Each attempt to apprehend the Joker turned into an embarrassing failure. Finally, just as his powers faded, Alfred finally helped his idols bring the Joker to justice. (*Batman* #127, October 1959)

EAGLETON, MORRIS

When Morris Eagleton and his partner drank an ancient formula, they were transformed into humanoid creatures with stone-like skin. Eagleton battled Batman over the GOTHAM CITY skyline as the GARGOYLE.

EAST END

The eastern end of GOTHAM CITY was said to be polluted with taverns, strip clubs, prostitutes, and crime. Slums bordered the historic Old Gotham, a portion of the city saved from damage during a devastating earthquake. The Amicus Avenue Projects were in this area; Alleytown, a network of cobblestone streets, formed a small borough between the East End and Old Gotham. Built over two hundred years ago as a way to house a large population of immigrants and keep them out of sight,

it became the home of their descendants. Just off McKinley Street, CRIME ALLEY was the nickname for PARK ROW, whose tranquility was shattered forever by the murders of THOMAS and MARTHA WAYNE. Crime Alley included a nine-hundred-unit housing project called the Skirley Apartments but better known to locals as "Scurvy City." Hell's Crucible was on the lower east side not far from Crime Alley.

CATWOMAN adopted the East End as her section of the city to protect and fought against street gangs and costumed felons to make the area safe for residents.

ECHO

The first Echo was a costumed foe opposed by the Crimson Avenger. (*Detective Comics* #49, March 1941)

The second was NINA DAMFINO, who partnered with DEIRDRE VANCE to assist the RIDDLER in the costumed guises of QUERY and Echo. Their partnership began when the women were bikers who adopted sexy, distracting costumes to commit a series of robberies. One night they found a down-on-his-luck Riddler, who saw them as a way to brighten his life. They were clearly trained fighters and found the Riddler oddly charismatic. Together the trio hit GOTHAM CITY's Reservoir Street Cash Depository. Carefully, they subverted the impregnable vault's safety devices, and—as the women fought Batman as a distraction—the Prince of Puzzlers made off with the cash. Next, they stole priceless violins, holding them for ransom from a mogul. When Query and Echo arrived for the payment, the mogul proved to be a disguised Batman, who apprehended them. (*Detective Comics Annual* #8, 1995)

Although Echo II has resurfaced, always with

Query at her side, little has been recorded about her life.

The third Echo was a heroine generated by an alien device wielded by the teenager Vicki Grant.

Terri Eckhart was a pop star who went by the name *Echo* given her meta-human ability to reflect sound waves. She donned a costume and got hired for mercenary heroic team the Conglomerate. With her team, she encountered Batman and the JUSTICE LEAGUE OF AMERICA on several occasions. (*Justice League Quarterly* #1, Winter 1990)

The fifth and final Echo was a Russian woman who was wired up with advanced technology that allowed her to access other people's thoughts. She was also able to access various aspects of the electromagnetic spectrum. The unnamed espionage agent disliked using the abilities because they caused her massive headaches. Despite her skills, Echo V was still no match for the Dark Knight during their one encounter. (*Legends of the Dark Knight* #119, July 1999)

Echo V

ECKS, SIMON

Scientist Simon Ecks constructed a machine that created an electric life-form mirroring his own body. Together they became the superpowered criminal DOCTOR DOUBLE-X.

EDISON

Edison was a film fanatic who turned to crime as the FILM FREAK, indulging his passion with crimes based on classic cinema from generations past.

EKDAL, EIVOL

Eivol Ekdal was a master craftsman who had two lines of items for sale: gadgets for performing escape artists and ingenious traps for members of the underworld. Carnado, a stage performer, bought devices for both activities, keeping Ekdal on retainer but claiming credit for the handiwork. For one hundred thousand dollars every year, Ekdal would build and provide the Great Carnado with new tools to use. The two enjoyed a long relationship that allowed the balding, slightly hunchbacked Ekdal to see his work appreciated by audiences as well as giving him the chance to needle handsome, vain Carnado.

Despite the useful equipment, the Great Carnado was not necessarily a successful performer, and he found himself driven to robbery to pay Ekdal his annual retainer. When he robbed a bank of exactly one hundred thousand dollars, Batman grew curious and began investigating.

Meantime, Ekdal showed Carnado a chamber that featured Plexiglas walls, an electrified vent, and another vent that released a deadly gas. Carnado, desperate for a new stunt to revive his flagging career, wanted the device. Ekdal told him it would cost an additional one hundred thousand dollars. Taunting Carnado, the craftsman insisted that Batman could escape the death trap—so the performer decided to lure the World's Greatest Escape Artist into the device. First he managed to separate Batman from ROBIN; then he got the Caped Crusader into the chamber.

At first Batman sagged from the gas's effects, but he soon realized that he could scrape his UTILITY BELT's metal buckle against the electrified grate, causing a spark that would ignite the gas and shatter the chamber. Free again, he and Robin set out to track the perpetrators.

Fearing the Dynamic Duo, Ekdal prepared another trap at his workshop. When the heroes arrived, they had to walk past two mummy sarcophagi to approach the inventor. Batman noted Ekdal glancing toward the cases and ordered the Teen Wonder to the ground—only a moment before gunmen secreted in each sarcophagus opened fire with pistols. In short order the gunmen were subdued and Ekdal and Carnado were apprehended, with most of the latest cash payment recovered.

The two men were tried, with the judge ordering bail for both men set at one hundred thousand dollars. (*Detective Comics* #346, December 1965)

Some time later, Ekdal, using his intricate knowledge, escaped from the penitentiary. He resumed work and set out to build a death trap that would exact revenge against the Dynamic Duo by killing them. He sold gangsters a new trap: a transparent safe that would rise from the floor and, when completely sealed, emit tremendous heat.

Robin was to be lured inside; when Batman cracked the combination lock, the final tumbler clicking into place would trigger an explosion, killing them both.

As this plan was unfolding, Ekdal was distracted by a visit from Russian KGB agents seeking his knowledge of devices used to help East Germans

get past the Berlin Wall. Before things grew violent, the gangsters arrived for the death trap and the Russians withdrew.

Robin was successfully lured into the trap, and as Batman worked the lock he realized that the combination was a mnemonic for Ekdal's name, similar to a trick he had shown Robin earlier that day. Fortunately, the intense heat melted the glue holding the cage in place, allowing Robin to kick his way free without detonating the explosive.

The Dynamic Duo then got embroiled in Ekdal's troubles with the KGB. Thanks to a tip that Police Commissioner JAMES GORDON received from German freedom fighter Thea Albrecht, they knew that Yuri Melikov was the man supplying the escape devices and therefore was the KGB's target. The complications mounted as Melikov wanted Ekdal dead to protect his secrets, the KGB wanted the escapes stopped, the gangsters wanted their money back after the death trap's failure, and the Dynamic Duo had to prevent an international incident.

In the end Ekdal and Melikov wound up dead, and the gangsters were apprehended. Robin noted, some weeks later, that with the KGB disheartened by its American failure, East Germans continued to use Ekdal devices to find freedom in the West. (*Detective Comics* #361, March 1967)

EKHART, DR.

On Earth-2, Dr. Ekhart was a renowned plastic surgeon who escaped from Germany in 1943. He had been visiting his brother there when World

War II broke out, trapping him in a foreign country. Two months after he made it back to the United States, Ekhart was deemed the only man capable of saving Harvey Kent's scarred face. Kent was the Gotham City district attorney whose face was ruined by acid while in court, subsequently turning him into the criminal Two-Face. The surgery worked, and Kent's handsome features were restored. (*Detective Comics* #80, October 1943)

ELECTROCUTIONER, THE

The first Electrocutioner was a would-be crime fighter who grew disappointed when Batman did not approve of his harsh vigilante methods. The two fought, and an injured Dark Knight could only watch as the wannabe hero fell through a window, grasped the fire escape, and electrocuted himself. (*Batman* #331, January 1981)

He survived the near-fatal charge and relocated to New York City where he intended to resume his activities. Soon after arriving, he crossed paths with Adrian Chase, a lawyer-turned-crime-fighter known as Vigilante. Even though both used violent methods to render street justice, Chase rejected the Electrocutioner's offer of a partnership. (*Vigilante* #8–9, July–August 1984)

The Electrocutioner received a measure of satisfaction when he banded with other heroes to stem the Anti-Monitor's attack on Earth. (*Crisis on Infinite Earths* #10, #12, January, March 1986) Soon after, Adrian Chase and the Electrocutioner followed leads to a mob hideout in the Catskill Mountains. During the confrontation the Electrocutioner was wounded by the criminals, but it was Chase who fired the fatal shot, killing the costumed figure. Unmasking the Electrocutioner, Chase observed that he was a nobody. (*Vigilante* #24–26, December 1985–February 1986) The Electrocutioner's spirit, though, passed to a limbo-like plane of existence where he battled an incarnation of the Teen Titans. (*Hawk and Dove Annual* #1, 1990)

Not long after the Electrocutioner's death, a new man wearing the red-and-black leather outfit hit the streets of Gotham City. Unlike his predecessor, he possessed an electrically charged whip. When he first encountered Batman, the new Electrocutioner declared that he was not interested in justice or a partnership, but was acting on his own terms. As victims began to pile up, Batman realized that all were low-level mobsters, being taught a lesson to keep others in line. The new Electrocutioner, he concluded, was therefore in the employ of Gotham's underworld. Wearing an insulated Batsuit, the Caped Crusader tracked the Electrocutioner and put an end to his efforts. (*Detective Comics* #626, May 1992)

In less than a year a third man using the costume, powers, and name arrived in Gotham City and managed to kill Batman. The Dynamic Duo was hunting down the fugitive "Buzz" Galvan when they encountered the third Electrocutioner, who was also seeking Galvan. When he and Batman fought, the discharge killed the Dark Knight, but Robin forced the vigilante to use his electric powers to restart the Batman's heart. As Batman recovered, Robin took down the criminal. When they unmasked him, this new foe proved to be Lester Buchinsky, who proclaimed himself the brother to the first

Electrocutioner. He was subsequently sentenced to Blackgate Penitentiary. (*Detective Comics* #644–646, May–July 1992)

Some time later, along with Cluemaster and Czonk, he escaped the prison and hid out in a run-down apartment building. The trio went on a crime spree to fund their escape from the city. Instead they crossed paths with Robin; when the Electrocutioner tried to escape, he was knocked cold by the Spoiler. (*Robin* [second series] #2–4, December 1993–February 1994)

Since then the Electrocutioner has been in and out of jail. When free, he relocated to Blüdhaven and worked for Blockbuster II as part of his vendetta against Nightwing. (*Nightwing* [second series] #33–34, July–August 1999) He has not been seen since.

ELEMENTAL MAN, THE

John Dolan worked as assistant to Professor Higgins, who was an acquaintance of the Earth-2 Dynamic Duo. During their long friendship, the professor supplied Batman with much of his high-tech equipment. One of Higgins's experiments involved a machine that would alter the molecular structure of elements. Higgins never realized that the machine was leaking radiation, which was being absorbed by Dolan as he worked the equipment. Over time Dolan's body began to exhibit changes, with his flesh turning to aluminum and then gold.

To help Dolan control these transformations, Higgins used parts of the equipment to fashion a control belt. Still, as Dolan repeatedly metamorphosed, his mind was deteriorating. Dolan left the lab proclaiming he intended to use his newfound abilities to become king of Gotham City's under-

world. Wearing a skintight red outfit, along with the control belt, Dolan emerged as the Elemental Man and began his path toward the crime throne.

Batman, unable to punch a being of iron, turned to Higgins for help. The professor theorized that if they could get Dolan close to the machine again, he could reverse its effects. Batman attempted this, but Dolan turned his skin diamond-hard and fled just as the overheated machine exploded. The released radiation immediately affected the Caped Crusader, turning him into another Elemental Man. Rather than risk the same mental alteration, Police Commissioner James Gordon had Batman imprisoned. Batman did experience metal changes and turned himself to mercury, escaped the jail cell, and began a competition with Dolan to become the city's crime king.

The Elemental Man was initially skeptical of Batman's offer to become partners but gave in and agreed after watching the Caped Crusader knock Robin to the ground. When he grasped Batman's hand to gain access to a rooftop, though, the Elemental Man found himself in a trap. Higgins was waiting with a repaired device, which effectively reversed not only the physical changes but the mental alteration as well. Batman explained that by becoming an elemental man himself and faking his dementia, he stood a better chance of curing Dolan. (*Detective Comics* #294, August 1961)

Another scientist named John Dubrovny managed to unwittingly replicate Higgins's experiment. Just as Dolan went mad with the transformation, so did Dubrovny, who was dubbed Mister 103 and battled the Doom Patrol on several occasions. Divorced from his wife, he lived for battle and conquest and, as Mister 104, continued to battle Earth's super heroes. (*Doom Patrol* #98, September 1965)

Years later, after the Earths merged during the Crisis on Infinite Earths, the international terrorist Kobra studied Gotham's legacy of bizarre transformations. He concluded that many could be replicated—and he was proven right when he created his Strikeforce Kobra team of agents. He turned a woman into a new Elemental, although she was limited to being able to transform into only mercury. She was easily vanquished by the Outsiders' Metamorpho, who exposed her to liquid oxygen, effectively freezing her molecules. (*Outsiders* #21–22, July–August 1987)

ELGIN, SLIPPERY JIM

Jim Elgin earned the nickname *Slippery* for his ability to blend into crowds as a master of disguise. The criminal easily eluded police capture time and again, building a reputation as a top-notch thief with his fatal flaw being an inability to come into contact with any metal. This was the result of a tiny sliver of magnetic metal being lodged in his brain; any shifting of its position in response to metallic objects would prove instantly fatal. During one crime, he was pursued by Batman and Robin, and Elgin once more attempted to be lost in a crowd. To help his disguise, he grabbed a man's top hat and put it on, unaware that it contained a spring to make it collapsible. The metallic spring caused the magnetic material to move, killing Elgin. (*Detective Comics* #163, September 1950)

ELLIOT, DR. THOMAS

Bruce Wayne's childhood pal grew up harboring a grudge. As an adult he created a labyrinthine scheme to exact vengeance as the bandaged villain Hush.

ELLISON, DR. THOMAS

Thomas Ellison was a noted astronomer who built his own special telescope and used it to study the distant planet Krypton for years prior to its destruction. The telescope's resolution was so fine that he could observe the planet's society, and he studied its culture and language. Ellison was also an old friend of Dr. Thomas Wayne, often visiting the mansion and entertaining the young Bruce Wayne with stories about the fascinating faraway world.

Ellison's observations led him to conclude that the planet was due to explode, and he feverishly worked to save it. Ellison invented an atomic-neutralizing ray and beamed it across the galaxy in the hope that it would calm the planet. Krypton blew up regardless, sending a guilty Ellison into a depressed state.

Later Superman used a different device—one that could detect elements from the past—to show Ellison that his efforts had not harmed Krypton; the help had just arrived too late to make a difference. The news mollified the doctor. (*World's Finest Comics* #146, September 1964)

ELONGATED MAN, THE

Ralph Dibny grew up fascinated by contortionists, and as he studied them, he heard frequent references to a drink known as gingold. This led him to research gingold's chemical secrets. It proved to be a concentrated extract from the Gingo, a rare fruit that alters body chemistry to allow greater elasticity. His further experiments led to a liquid that endowed him with the ability to stretch his body beyond human norms. He later learned that gingold extract worked in concert with his meta-gene, which allowed him superhuman abilities. Donning a specially treated costume and mask, he debuted as the Elongated Man in Central City. (*The Flash* #112, May 1960)

Dibny loved mysteries like the secret of gingold, and he set out to solve as many as he could, both with and without his powers. He trained as a detective, was fluent in French, and understood Interlac. Whenever he sensed a mystery, he felt a tingle in his nose, which actually vibrated thanks to the gingold. His earliest encounters led him to cross paths with Central City's protector, the Flash, and to meet socialite Sue Dearborn. Their attraction was instantaneous, and it wasn't long before the couple got married, in a ceremony attended by the Flash. Around that time Dibny chose to ditch his mask and become one of the few super heroes with a public identity.

Ralph and Sue Dibny traveled the country, enjoying the sights and ferreting out mysteries begging to be solved. As a result, they wound up in Gotham City on several occasions, which usually involved the pair teaming up with Batman. (*Detective Comics* #331, September 1964) The Caped Crusader held tremendous respect for Dibny's natural sleuthing skills and appreciated how seamlessly the couple worked together.

In time the Elongated Man was elected into the Justice League of America, where he and Batman frequently collaborated on solving cases. When Sue was brutally raped aboard the JLA's satellite headquarters by Dr. Light, Ralph sided with the Leaguers, who felt it appropriate to use Zatanna's magic to alter Light's mind. When Batman learned of this, the Maid of Magic erased ten minutes from his memory—an effect that lasted for years.

Ralph and Sue settled in Opal City for a time, helping watch over the city as a favor to the original Starman. During that time Sue learned she was pregnant, and she prepared to tell Ralph as part of a birthday surprise. Ralph returned home to find Sue dead, however, beginning a chain of events that was to affect every super hero in America. As the hunt for her killer began in earnest, Ralph was convinced Dr. Light was behind it, but he was wrong—it was Jean Loring, ex-wife of the Atom, who had accidentally caused her friend's death. (*Identity Crisis* #1-7 June–December 2004)

Despondent, Ralph tried to carry on alone, but his despair was crippling. He swore off the gingold, began heavily drinking alcohol, and seemed suicidal when he discovered Sue's headstone had been vandalized. His hunt for the culprit led him to a cult that honored the recently killed Superboy, thinking they could bring Sue back from the dead. During a ceremony, it appeared Sue may have been resurrected—but it was interrupted, leaving Ralph with a nervous breakdown.

Dibny began a new spiritual quest when the helmet of Doctor Fate, a Lord of Order, appeared before him and led the distraught man on a global hunt that taught him much about magic, constantly holding out the hope that Sue could be resurrected. Finally, in the mystic land known as Nanda Parbat, Ralph began the spell that he

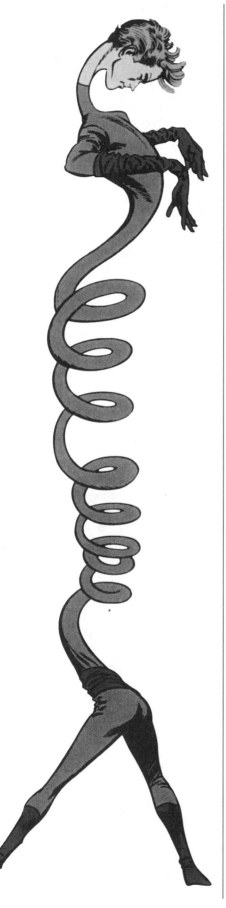

thought would give him his heart's desire—but he wound up shooting the floating helmet. As he deduced, the helmet was actually an illusion covering the JLA's longtime foe Felix Faust. The mad magician intended to trade Dibny's soul to the demon Neron, which would in turn have granted Faust freedom. Neron arrived and—learning of Dibny's attempt to trap Faust—killed the hero. However, Dibny had intended to die, imprisoning Neron and Faust in a doorless tower with the binding spell only responsive to the now dead Dibny. (*52* #1–44, 2006–2007)

ELTON, LORI

DICK GRAYSON left GOTHAM CITY to attend HUDSON UNIVERSITY, where he met Lori Elton. She was a fellow freshman, and they enjoyed each other's company. The budding romance was complicated by his frequent time away as ROBIN the Teen Wonder, either solo or working alongside Batman or the TEEN TITANS. Lori, pretty with long blond hair, grew agitated that their relationship wasn't progressing. (*Detective Comics* #450, August 1975)

The couple unhappily broke up and Lori began dating Dave Corby, shutting Dick out of her life. Dick was then confronted by DUELA DENT, the purported JOKER'S DAUGHTER, who warned Grayson that Corby was dangerous. (*Batman Family* #18–19, June/July–August/September 1978)

Late in his freshman year, Robin found himself battling a new criminal operation called MAZE. He had previously encountered one of its agents, a man named Raven, and once again opposed him and Card Queen. MAZE members wanted Robin eliminated for his frequent interference in their business but they were shut down entirely by the Teen Wonder. When Raven attempted to escape, he was stopped by Card Queen, who proved to be Dent working undercover, and she exposed Raven as Corby, shattering Elton's faith in herself and her boyfriend. (*Detective Comics* #482–483, February/March–April/May 1979) Lori has not been seen since.

ENFORCER, THE

DAN KINGDOM was in the employ of a secretive group known as the Council. Its decades-long plan was to eventually rule the world, and its soldiers were to be clones of perfect men. One was Paul Kirk, the adventurer known as MANHUNTER. Kingdom was also cloned for use by the Council. The real Kingdom and his clone were among the last defenses the Council employed when Batman and Manhunter infiltrated its headquarters. The climactic battle resulted in an atomic blast, destroying the headquarters, the Council, the Kingdoms, and Manhunter. (*Detective Comics* #443, October/November 1974)

Batman encountered another man known as the Enforcer who turned out to be a time-displaced Kamandi in thrall to Extortion, Inc. The Caped Crusader rescued the Last Boy on Earth and returned him to his proper place and era. (*The Brave and the Bold* #157, December 1979)

ERASER, THE

The Eraser had a specialized role in the underworld hierarchy. For a 20 percent commission, before taxes, the Eraser would eliminate all clues at a crime scene before the police could arrive and conduct an investigation. Wearing a suit and full head mask that made him resemble a living number two pencil, the Eraser was much in demand, especially in GOTHAM CITY. Despite his efforts, he eventually made mistakes that provided clues used by Batman and ROBIN to track and arrest him. The Eraser was revealed as LENNY FIASCO—a fitting name. (*Batman* #188, December 1966)

ERBOT

Erbot was an audacious criminal who devised a scheme in which he and his fellow mobsters would pose as aliens from Saturn. They threatened an invasion of Earth unless they received a hundred tons of gold. Batman and ROBIN investigated the potential danger and realized the deception. Erbot was exposed, and the scheme ended. (*Batman* #63, February/March 1951)

ERKHAM

In a potential twenty-first-century GOTHAM CITY, Erkham was the chief engineer at Comet Spacecraft Company. He was also an industrial spy, sabotaging Comet's handicraft in the employ of rival manufacturer Meteor. On a visit to the future, Batman and ROBIN discovered Erkham's treachery and exposed his crimes. (*Batman* #59, June/July 1950)

ESCABEDO CARTEL

Based in Colombia, South America, the Escabedo family ran a drug cartel that sold illegal narcotics around the world. To protect members' interests, the cartel employed brutal field soldiers who protected the smugglers, manufacturers, and sellers of their product. Sensing weakness among the ruling family, several lieutenants began a war to seize control of the business.

The operation in America was dependent on street gangs moving the illicit drugs. These gangs had no direct connection to the cartel, making it difficult for federal agents to make a case against the Escabedos. Additionally, the gangs used money to buy off police and arranged an "understanding" with the Northeast's Mafia families, providing them with drugs at favorable terms in exchange for being allowed to operate unimpeded.

The long-term survival of the cartel depended entirely on its leadership. It had been formed by veteran criminal Emanuel Escabedo. Emanuel's sons, Henry and Diego, struggled to run the operation while their lieutenants battled one another for a favored position in the hierarchy.

The Escabedos arrived in GOTHAM CITY, opening a strip club in the EAST END. Not only did they run drugs through the club, but it also acted as a front for a sex-trade operation. CATWOMAN, self-proclaimed protector of the East End, attempted to put them out of business, but she was easily outnumbered. Unexpected help came from Batman, disguised as MATCHES MALONE, who traced to the club a deal between the cartel and CHINATOWN'S LUCKY HAND TRIAD. With his aid, Catwoman broke the sex-trade business. However, having gained a toehold in Gotham, the Escabedos remained a part of the criminal population. (*Legends of the Dark Knight* #177, May 2004)

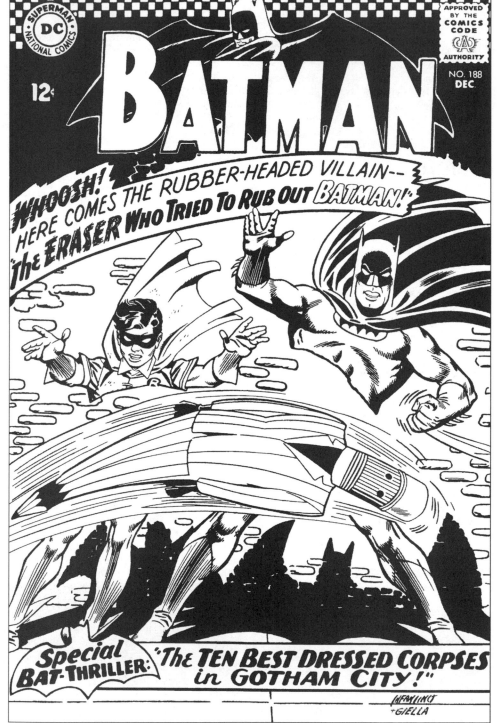

The Eraser

ESSEN, SARAH

Sarah Essen was a GOTHAM CITY police officer who fell in love with Police Commissioner JAMES GORDON, becoming his second wife, SARAH ESSEN GORDON.

ETCHISON, GRAHAM

Graham Etchison was a cousin to Arnold Etchison—né ARNOLD ETKAR—the deranged killer known as ABATTOIR. He was captured by CLAYFACE III

and delivered to Abattoir, who felt Earth could be cleansed of evil by killing each member of his family. Etchison was hidden away while Abattoir battled Batman, who at the time was actually JEAN-PAUL VALLEY; BRUCE WAYNE was recovering from injuries. Batman wound up killing Abattoir without learning where Etchison was kept. As a result, Etchison died from malnutrition and dehydration. (*Batman* #505, April 1999)

ETKAR (NÉ ETCHISON), ARNOLD

Arnold Etchison was the psychotic killer known to Batman as ABATTOIR.

EXECUTIONER, THE

WILLY HOOKER owned a penny-arcade shooting gallery, but wanted something more. He conspired to help free the criminal Big Cal Davis from jail and recover two million dollars, which Davis had stolen and hidden before his arrest. To make the scheme work, Hooker donned a maroon robe with a white E on his chest and introduced himself to GOTHAM CITY as the Executioner. He murdered wanted criminals and delivered their bodies for the bounty, establishing a reputation that would work to cover Davis's supposed death. Hooker prepared to break Davis out of jail but first discovered the location of the cash among the prisoner's personal effects. He changed the plan, intending to shoot Davis for real and keep all the money for himself. Hooker helped Davis flee prison; however, Batman had already determined the Executioner's real identity and posed as Davis when the breakout occurred. The Caped Crusader was also alerted to the impending double cross and wore a bulletproof vest, which spoiled the scheme. Hooker was then arrested by the police, joining Davis in jail as Batman recovered the cash. (*Detective Comics* #191, January 1953)

EXECUTRIX

The company Metrosteel had decided to use low-grade steel to construct a bridge between METROPOLIS and GOTHAM CITY. An engineer named Page felt the process and inferior metal would not sustain the weight and traffic, so he decided to blow the whistle on his company. After giving an interview to *Daily Planet* reporter Casey Harrow, Page was targeted for death by Metrosteel. They hired the Executrix, a wily mercenary, to silence the engineer before his story could gain traction in the media. Executrix, clad in black leather, killed Harrow, which drove Page to seek a safe hiding place. A friend saw to it Page was ensconced at WAYNE MANOR, which brought the case to BRUCE WAYNE's attention. Meantime, CLARK KENT used his superhuman abilities to look into Harrow's death. As the World's Finest team investigated, Executrix located Page and took him hostage. Batman and SUPERMAN found the assassin holding Page on the bridge, which proved to be crumbling faster than expected. Batman and Executrix fought until a shift in the structure sent her plunging into the Gotham River. The Man of Steel managed to rescue her and took her into custody. (*World's Finest Comics* #313–314, March–April 1985)

FABIAN, FRANK

Frank Fabian was a vain model, well aware of his noble-appearing face. He posed for painter Carl Martin and was so taken with the finished work that he tried to purchase it, but Martin refused. The painter told Fabian that the world would someday see past his pleasant features and realize what a twisted, rotten soul lurked beneath. Enraged, Fabian killed Martin and stole the painting.

Fabian soon after gave up modeling for a career in crime, using the name *the Dapper Bandit.* As he committed his crimes, however, Martin's widow broke into Fabian's home and, bit by bit, began altering the painting to bring her husband's words to life. Fabian would return home from a crime and see that the portrait had changed, the subject looking less handsome and more twisted.

Batman and Robin investigated and realized what Mrs. Martin was doing. The Caped Crusader used that knowledge to further unnerve Fabian. When he returned home, Batman struck him unconscious and used makeup to match the robber to the painting; he then restored the portrait to its original state. Upon awakening, Fabian was so startled by what he saw that he confessed to all his crimes, including the murder of Martin. He was finally arrested. (*Batman* #53, June/July 1949)

FAÇADE

Erik Hanson worked at Gotham City's popular Peregrinator's Club as a busboy. At the urging of the waiter Edwards, Hanson willingly joined a gang to rob the wealthy patrons after they left the club. Edwards used his position to spy on the socialites, passing along information that Hanson used in the field. As Façade, Hanson mugged patron after patron, using the stolen money to help finance the gang's growth,

benefiting all. When Batman investigated, he discerned a pattern that pointed to the club's staff. As Bruce Wayne, he met one of the gang members while posing as a reporter, and subsequently followed her to the gang's hideout. There Batman avoided being shot by several mannequins that were built to hide machine guns at the wrists. He apprehended the members—all save Hanson, who ran back to the club to obtain the remaining spare cash and escape. At the club, Batman stopped Hanson and brought him and Edwards to justice. (*Detective Comics* #821, September 2006)

FACELESS

Mailman Joseph Zedno received many complaints about missing mail from stops along his route. After losing his job, Zedno had a psychological break and took revenge against the complainers by killing them one by one. He skinned the face from each victim and wore it like a mask as he visited the next target. Batman traced the crimes, found their link, and stopped Zedno before all those who lived on his former route were killed. Zedno was sentenced to serve time at Arkham Asylum. (*Batman* #542, May 1997)

FAIRCHILD, VESPER

Vesper Katherine Fairchild made her name as a journalist and radio personality. She was brought to Gotham City's WKGC to host *Siren of the Night.* She quickly established herself as a popular broadcaster in a city that thrived at night. Her popularity led to many public appearances and social engagements, and it was only a matter of time before she met Bruce Wayne. In short order they began seeing each other, and a romance blossomed. The green-eyed, auburn-haired woman sensed there was something

Wayne was not sharing with her, however, and she began to study him as an investigative subject. Then the earthquake that devastated Gotham derailed her work, and she soon left the city and Wayne. (*Batman* #540, March 1997)

Fairchild worked mainly as a journalist, garnering a Pulitzer Prize nomination, and then she set her sights on figuring out Batman's secret identity. That required a return to Gotham City and Wayne. She even figured the millionaire might be a good source of information about the Dark Knight, but he warned her away from the story. Fairchild also earned the enmity of Wayne's new bodyguard,

SASHA BORDEAUX. Wayne decided that Fairchild had changed and wanted to create distance between them. He contrived to have her come to the mansion only to find the playboy cavorting in the pool with three other women. A month later Wayne and Bordeaux returned to the mansion—after a night patrolling Gotham in their costumed identities—to find Fairchild's bloody body in the foyer. Moments later Gotham City police officers arrived in response to a 911 call and arrested the two on suspicion of murder. (*Batman: The Ten-Cent Adventure,* March 2002)

The investigation turned Wayne into a fugitive and separated Batman from his closest allies. However, they all learned clues that, when pieced together, pointed to DAVID CAIN as the killer. Among these clues were tape recordings Fairchild made of her investigation, proving she had uncovered Batman's secret but had done nothing with the information.

Fairchild was buried at a Gotham cemetery.

FAITH

At some point in the past, Batman met the teen girl known only as Faith. She earned his trust—so much so that when a substitute JUSTICE LEAGUE OF AMERICA had to be formed, she was recruited. The other heroes, having just met her, had to take Batman's recorded recommendation as a matter of . . . faith. (*JLA* #69, October 2002)

Faith earned their trust and more, becoming a full-fledged member after the core roster returned from an adventure three thousand years in the past. She displayed unmeasured psychic abilities and usually used them to put an end to whatever threat they were facing, earning her the nickname of Fat Lady.

Few know any details of her life, although Faith has revealed that she was raised by the military and

had served with some covert federal operation. In fact, the US government has attempted to regain control of her for use as a tactical weapon.

After serving with the JLA, Faith left to briefly work with an incarnation of the Doom Patrol.

FALCONE, ALBERTO

Alberto Falcone was the son of GOTHAM CITY crime boss CARMINE FALCONE. He was born on Valentine's Day to Carmine and his wife, Luisa, and grew up feeling cut off from the crime family his father ruthlessly ran. Much of this feeling stemmed from Carmine's preference for his older children, Mario and Sofia. To establish himself, both to his parents and his siblings, Alberto managed scholarships at Harvard University and Oxford. Still, he yearned to enter the "family business," but his father rebuffed every entreaty. (*Batman: The Long Halloween* #1, 1996)

One year, soon after Batman debuted in Gotham, a serial killer dubbed HOLIDAY began brutally murdering Carmine's associates. Carmine fell under District Attorney HARVEY DENT's suspicion so he contracted the Irish—hit men for hire—to kill Dent. They blew up his home but failed to kill the DA. By Thanksgiving the Irish were all dead, followed by Carmine's consigliere, Milos Grappa, on Christmas. Suspicion swang from Carmine to a possible rival.

Matters grew worse when Alberto was killed on New Year's Eve, his body identified by a grieving and furious Carmine. Holiday's killing spree continued on celebration days throughout the following year, much to the consternation of Gotham's police, Batman, and Carmine. By Labor Day, though, Alberto reappeared, seemingly back from the dead. He showed up in time to kill SALVATORE MARONI, the mobster who'd scarred Dent and sent the DA on his tortured path to a new life as TWO-FACE. Alberto was immediately arrested by Police Captain JAMES GORDON, who then allowed Batman to beat Alberto, hoping to learn information about Holiday.

Alberto was freed and returned home, where he admitted to Carmine that *he* was Holiday and had killed many people. Carmine told his son that if he

admitted to Maroni's murder, Carmine would see to it Alberto remained free. To the boss's surprise, his son refused, saying that as Holiday he was now a bigger threat to Gotham than Carmine had ever been. Defiant to the end, Alberto was tried for his crimes and sentenced to death in the gas chamber. Carmine used his influence over law enforcement to have the sentence commuted to incarceration at ARKHAM ASYLUM. Alberto was placed in a cell directly opposite CALENDAR MAN, whose crimes were also holiday-themed.

A year later, DA JANICE PORTER, who replaced Dent, had Alberto freed and placed under house arrest. It was presumed Mario Falcone and SOFIA FALCONE GIGANTE would help watch over his recovery. (*Batman: Dark Victory* #1, December 1999)

While at the family home, both the SCARECROW and Calendar Man tricked Alberto into believing that his father's ghost was communicating from beyond the grave. He soon found Holiday's gun and used it to rescue his sister from the JOKER. When he was given a second gun on his father's birthday, he was instructed to kill his sister, a step toward seizing total control over Gotham's five major crime families. Although tempted, he refused the order.

Some time later, Porter was killed and her body left in Alberto's bed by Two-Face in an attempt to convince the now psychologically fragile Alberto that he was blacking out and committing more murders. His father's ghost then suggested that Alberto end everything and kill himself—an act he rejected, convinced that his father would never ask this. Angry, he finally figured out that the voice was coming from Calendar Man, who was out for revenge against Falcone for stealing his gimmick. They fought and Alberto managed to break Calendar Man's foot. He then placed the tracer used to monitor his own house arrest on his enemy and fled, but was shot and wounded by the police. Sofia rescued Alberto, taking him to the safety of the family mausoleum. The siblings argued over their father, leading Sofia to smother Alberto to death.

FALCONE, CARMINE

Carmine Falcone, known as the Roman, ruled GOTHAM CITY's underworld when Batman first began his campaign against crime. Falcon used his ill-gotten income to raise three children—Mario, Sofia, and Alberto—on an estate outside the city limits. His influence was such that no one dared commit major crimes in the city without his approval; he had judges, lawyers, cops, and even the current police commissioner, GILLIAN B. LOEB, in his pocket. Loeb did not see the costumed vigilante as a threat, something with which the Roman disagreed. He was proven correct when the Batman made an unexpected appearance at a Falcone dinner. (*Batman* #404, February 1987)

Batman stepped up his harassment of Gotham's top underworld boss, delivering a pointed message that things in the city were about to change. Falcone was embarrassed when he was left in only his underwear and tied to his bed. Enraged, he ordered Batman killed, and to make his point clear he kidnapped police officer JAMES GORDON, his wife BARBARA, and their infant son James Jr. Batman rescued the family, earning Gordon's trust and loyalty.

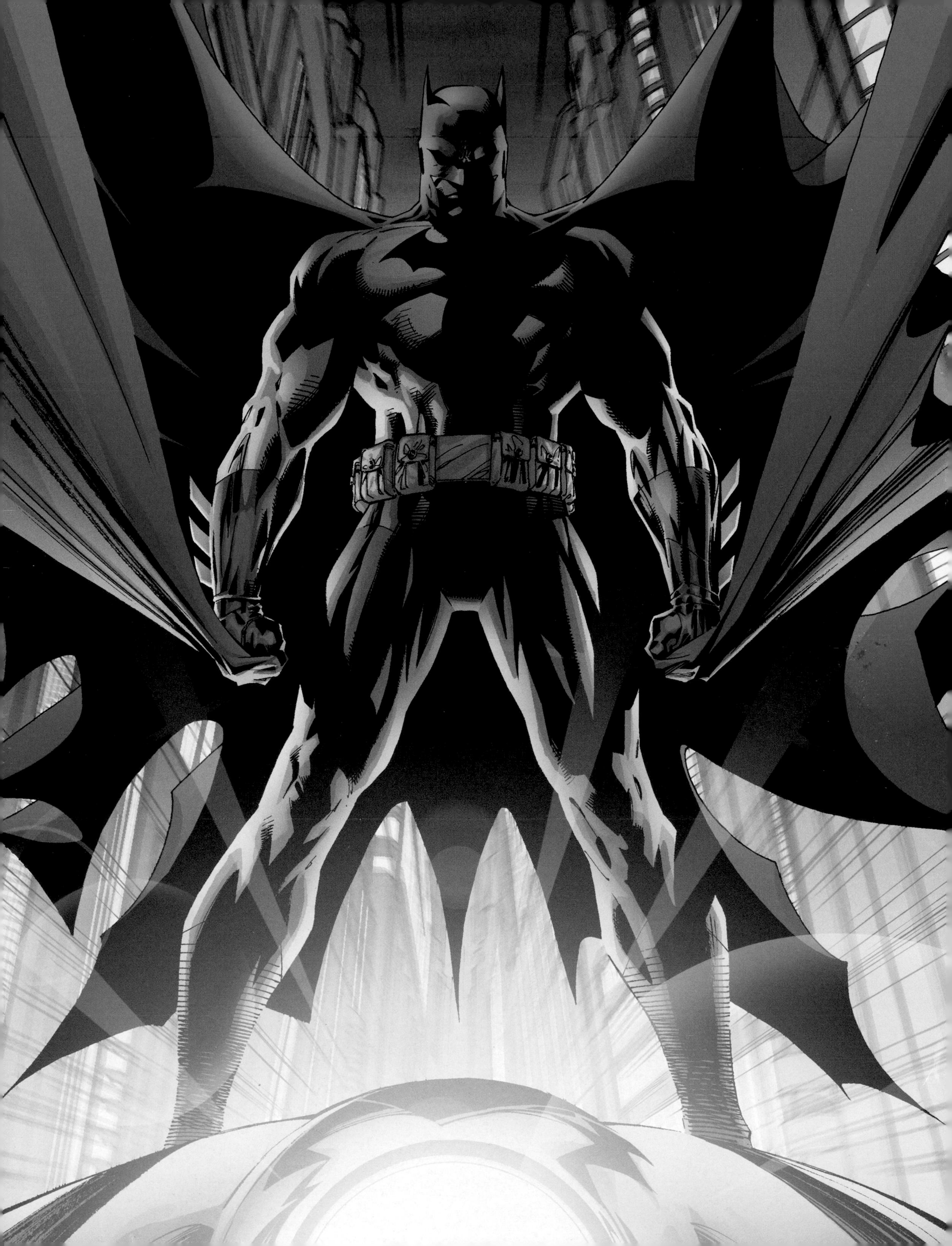

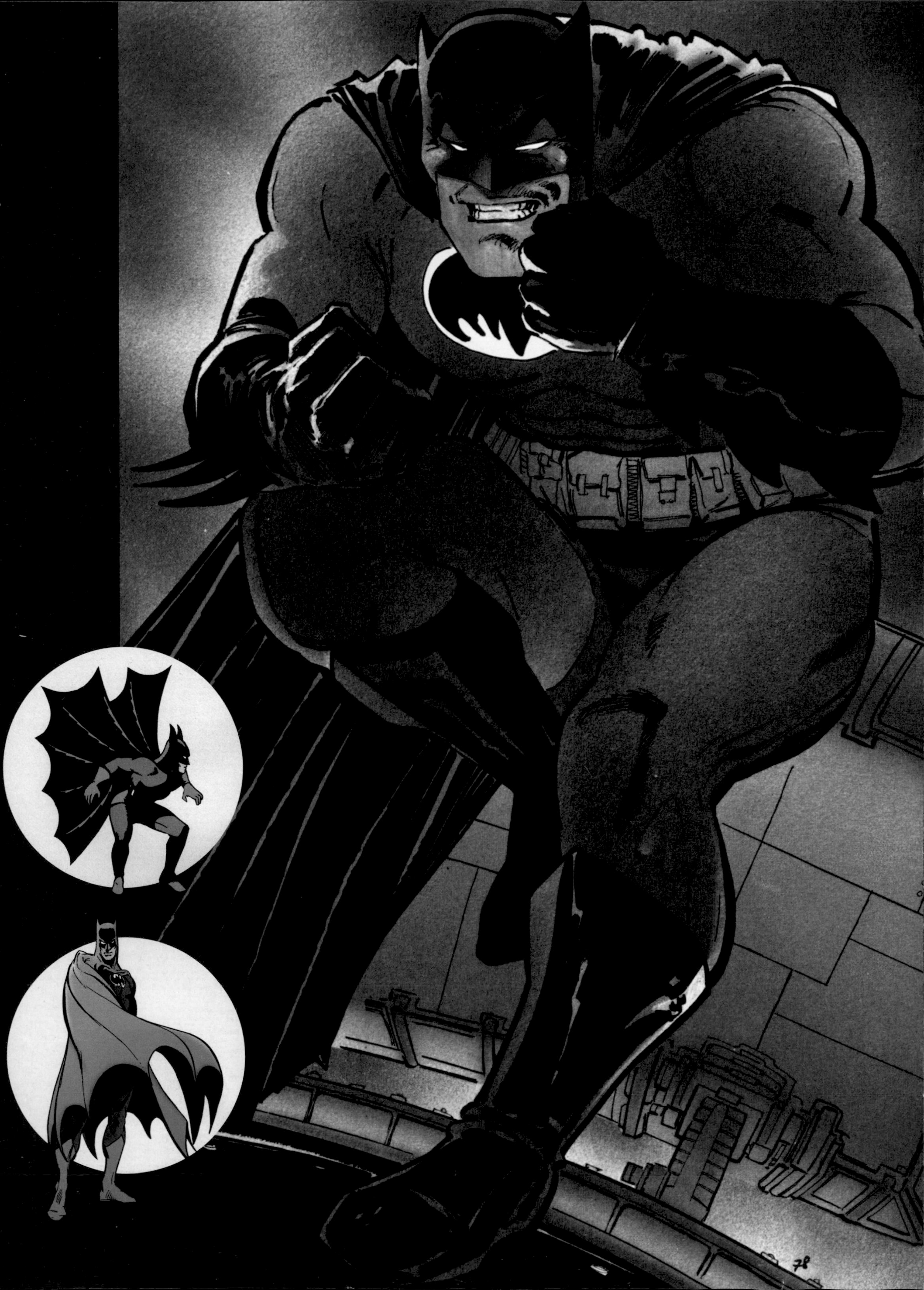

Bruce Wayne and Alfred Pennyworth share an enduring bond, not just as master and manservant but also as friends and fellow believers in justice.

Batman and the second Robin, Jason Todd, go to work from Gotham's rooftops.

All-Star Batman and Robin portrays a twelve-year-old Dick Grayson thrust into a battle against crime mere moments after his parents have been killed.

After Tim Drake was forced to give up his identity, Stephanie Brown lobbied for a chance to become the fourth Robin.

Tim Drake became the third Robin, recognizing that Batman needed a Robin to conduct his war on crime.

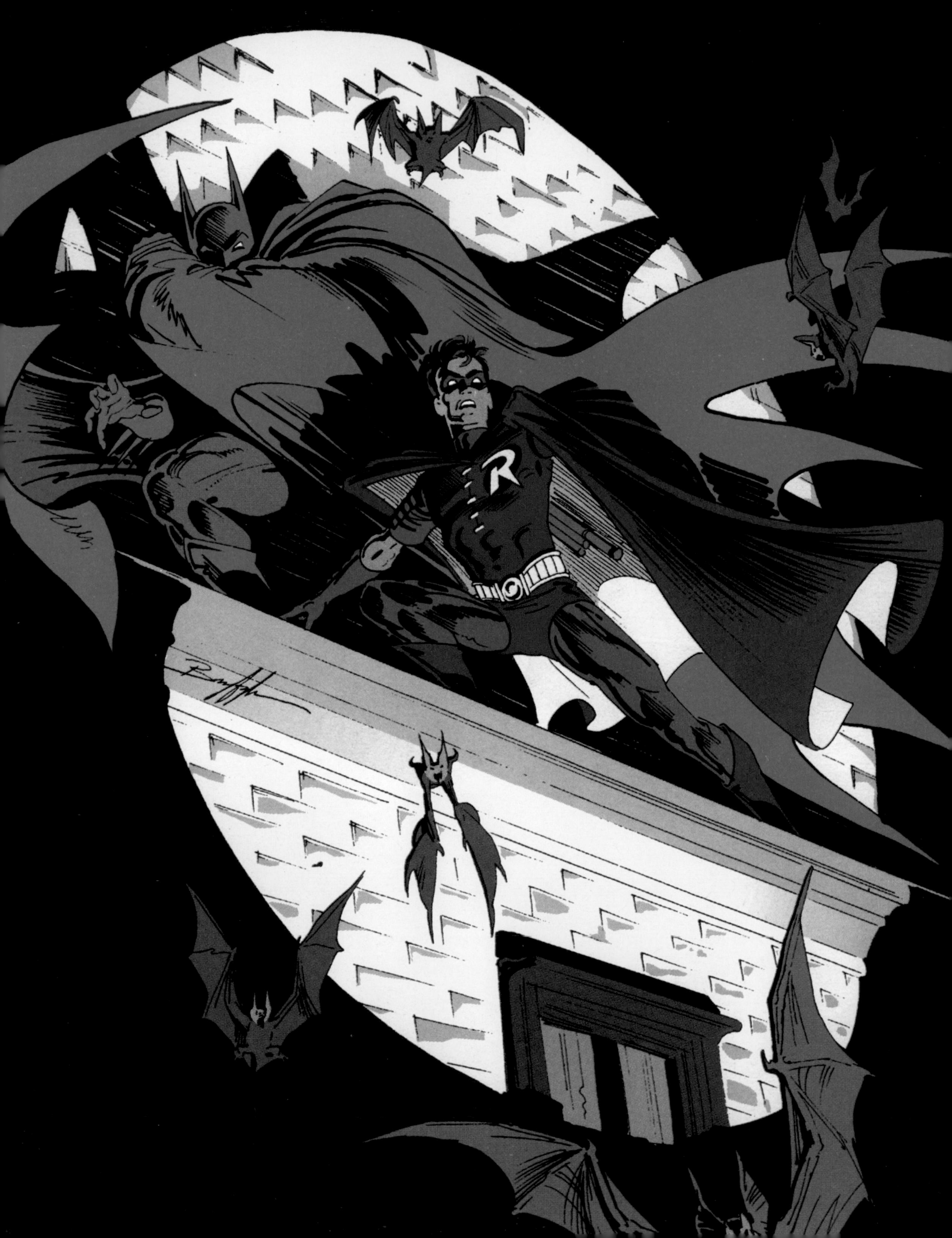

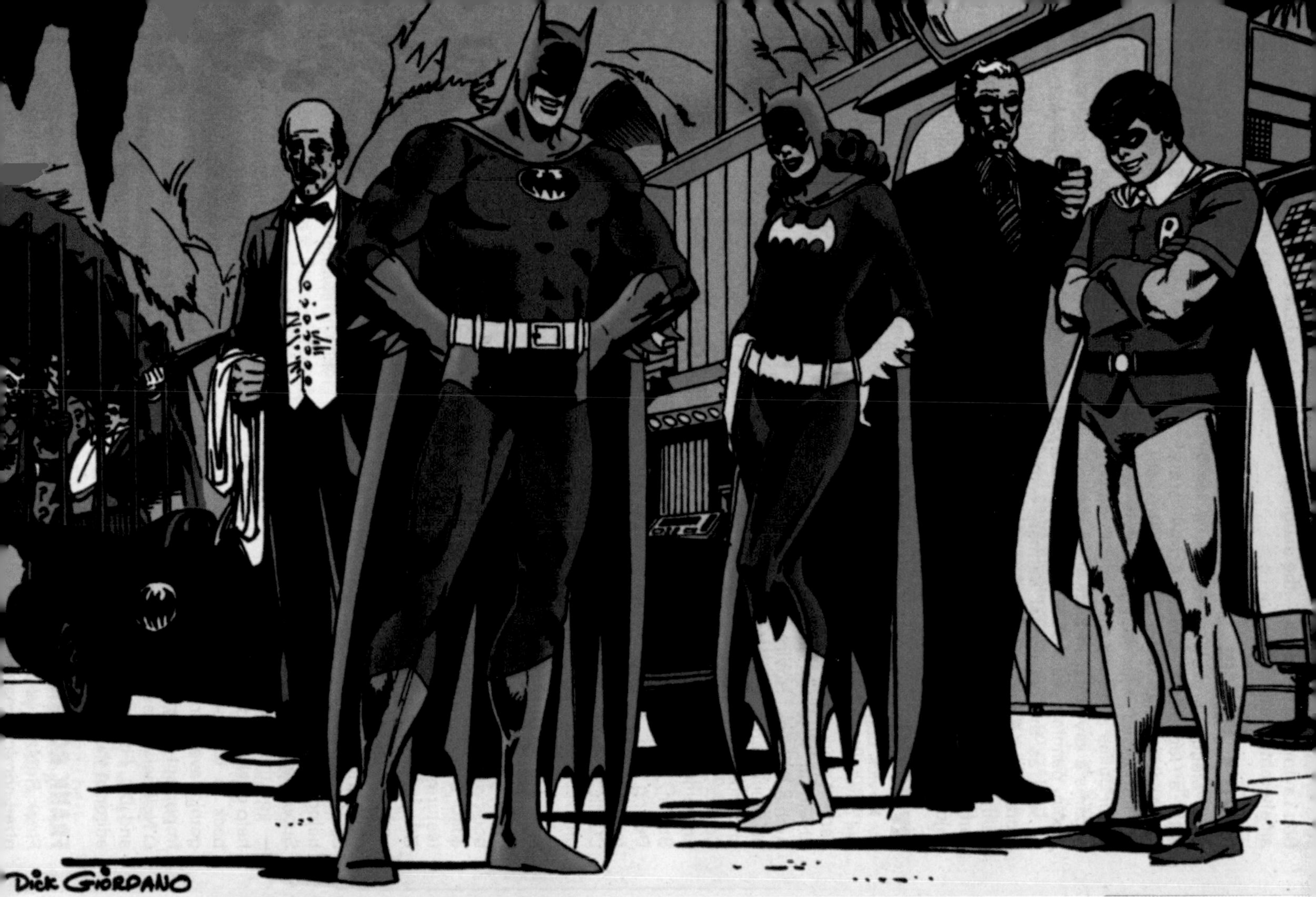
DICK GIORDANO

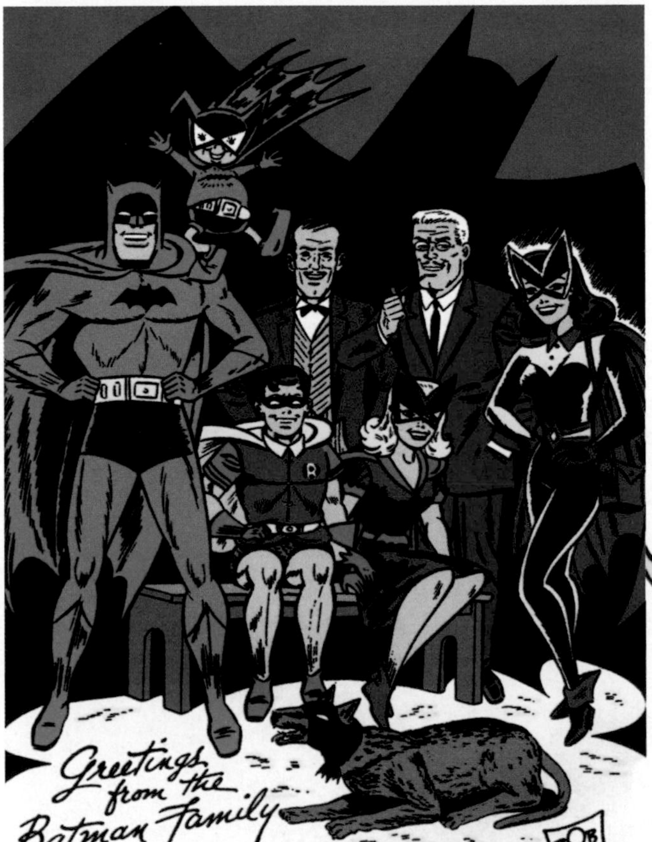
Greetings from the Batman Family
BOB KANE

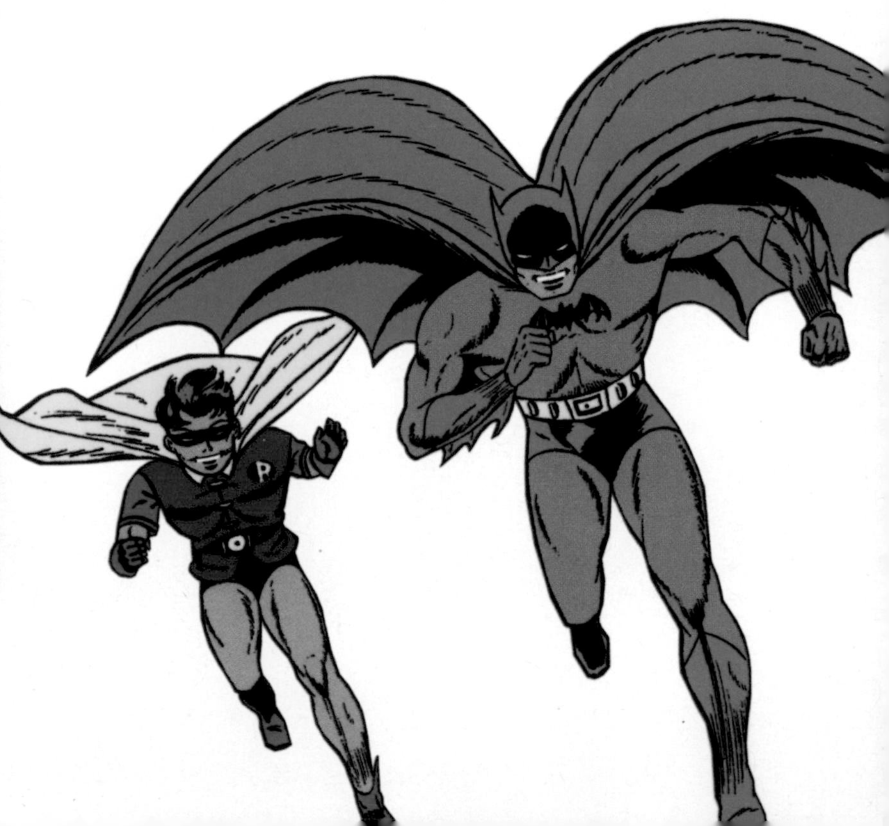

Batman, flanked by Robin and Oracle (the former Batgirl, Barbara Gordon), continues to protect Gotham City's innocent residents.

Dick Grayson grew to adulthood and forged his own identity, taking the name Nightwing from Kryptonian legend. He remained a circus performer at heart, but picked up the detective skills necessary to be worthy of being Batman's partner.

As Batgirl, Barbara Gordon was effective until the Joker's bullet crippled her, sending her on a different path.

Barbara Gordon became the second Batgirl, using her martial arts training and brilliant mind to join the fight against crime.

Cassandra Cain earned the right to become the latest Batgirl during Gotham City's No Man's Land crisis.

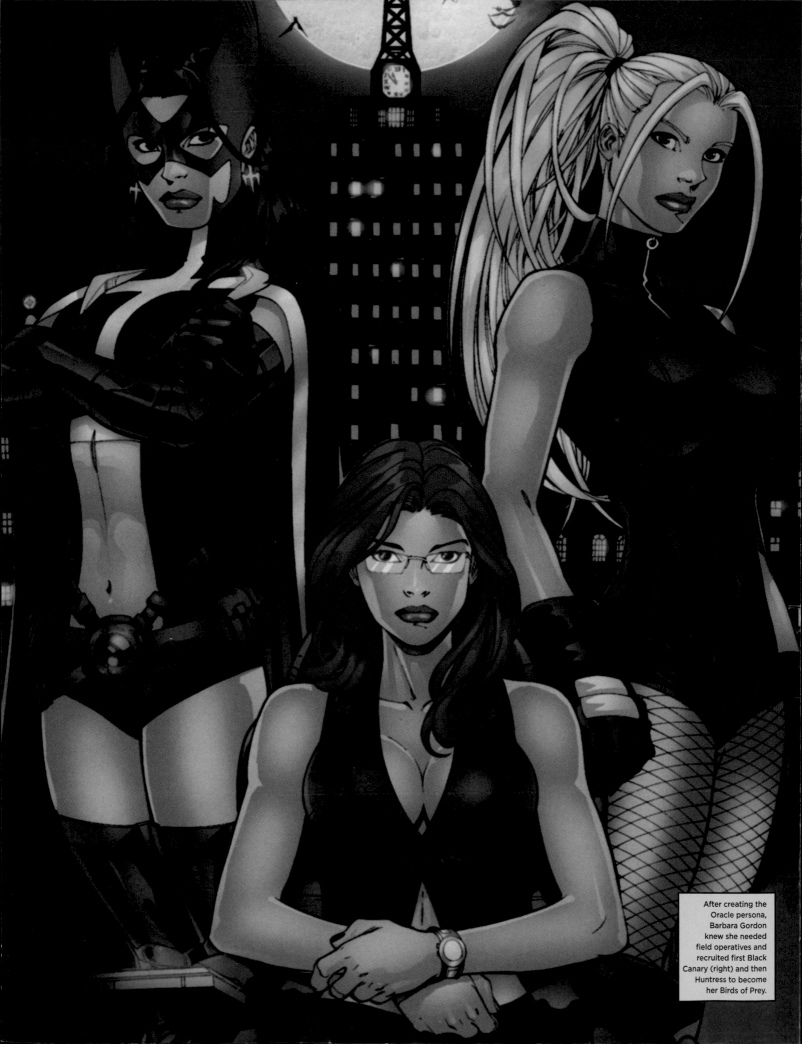

After creating the Oracle persona, Barbara Gordon knew she needed field operatives and recruited first Black Canary (right) and then Huntress to become her Birds of Prey.

Batman remained an uncomfortable presence within the Justice League of America, preferring to stay in the shadows, not the harsh light of their orbiting satellite headquarters.

Superman and Batman have frequently teamed up through the years, but it took a monumental disaster to require both of their allies and teammates to join in the fray.

The latest incarnation of the JLA was handpicked by Batman, Superman, and Wonder Woman, but it took Black Lightning to make certain the Dark Knight would join, too.

A look at the many pieces of equipment employed by Batman in his unceasing fight against crime and injustice.

Batman's computer systems are unparalleled by any other on Earth.

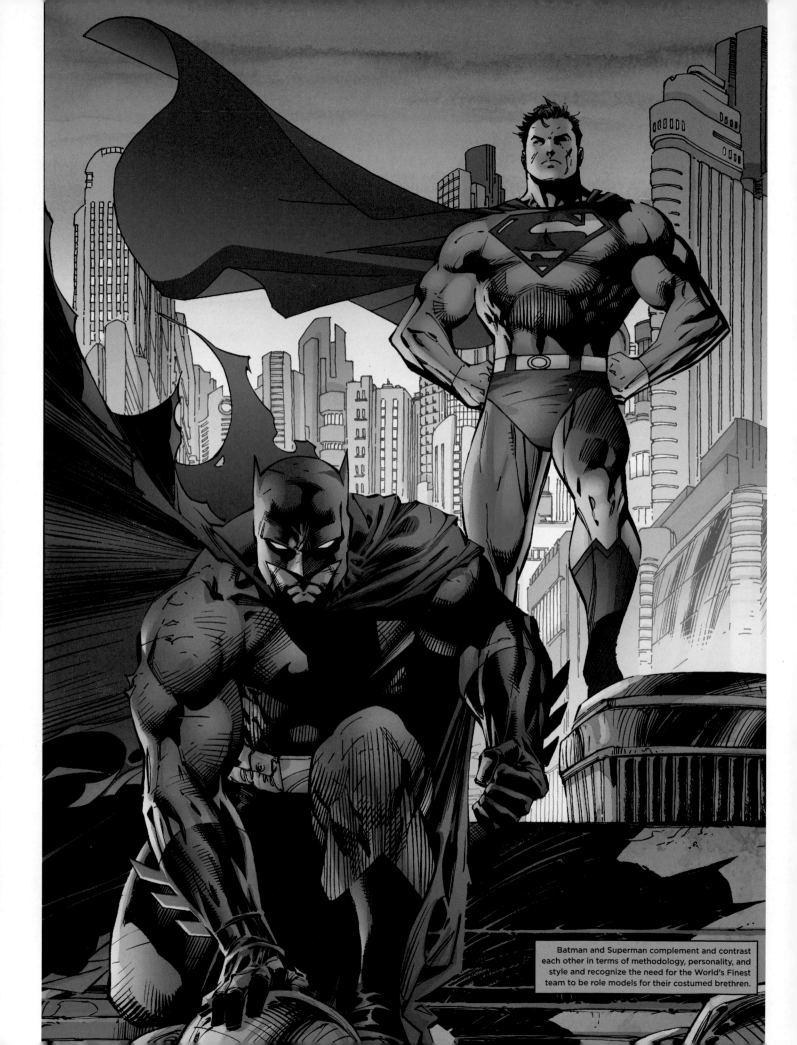

Batman and Superman complement and contrast each other in terms of methodology, personality, and style and recognize the need for the World's Finest team to be role models for their costumed brethren.

Carmine Falcone

own reasons. In a confrontation with Falcone, Two-Face shot and killed the crime boss.

Falcone knew no peace, though, as his grave was robbed shortly thereafter. His daughter Sofia Falcone Gigante, who succeeded him as boss, received one of the dead man's fingers as a message. During the investigation, it was learned that Two-Face had absconded with the body, using Mister Freeze's cryogenic equipment to maintain it. (*Batman: Dark Victory* #1, December 1999)

FALSE FACE

False Face was a criminal who used his skill with makeup to impersonate wealthy people. In reality, the white-haired toothless man was innocuous and seemingly only came to life when clad in a tuxedo complete with black hood while observing potential targets. He studied their habits and routines, choosing from among Gotham City's wealthy citizenry.

Once his next target was chosen, False Face arranged matters to detain the person for a length of time. With the victim out of the way and posing no threat, he would impersonate him or her and steal goods and services.

After six successful crimes, Batman and Robin began an investigation. Having sussed out the modus operandi, Batman was on the lookout for the next crime. Hearing that Wally Weskit, a rockabilly entertainer, was trapped in an elevator, Batman realized this fit the profile. Arriving at the theater where Weskit was scheduled to perform, the disguised False Face was ready to take receipt of the charitable donations. The criminal managed to elude capture, frustrating the Caped Crusader.

Aware that the Dynamic Duo was after him, False Face altered his next scheme, setting it up so that when Batman found him masquerading as explorer Arthur Crandall, he would lead the Caped Crusader into a trap. Batman showed up, as expected, and fell unconscious into a sixty-foot tank. False Face entered the tank, intending to unmask the crime fighter.

Back at their hideout, the gang grabbed at Batman's cowl, eager to learn who he really was. They were stunned to see Crandall's face. Batman then revealed his own deception: He had survived the fall, faking unconsciousness so he could surprise False Face. He traded places, and faces, with the criminal, letting the gang lead him back to their hideout. Batman easily subdued and apprehended the men. (*Batman* #113, February 1958)

FALSE FACE SOCIETY

When Roman Sionis became Black Mask, he enlisted underlings who took to wearing masks and formed his False Face Society, joining him on his criminal forays throughout Gotham City. (*Detective Comics* #553, August 1985) In the wake of Black Mask's murder, the gang was permanently put out of business by Catwoman, aided by Sam Bradley.

FALSTAFF, GREGORIAN

Gregorian Falstaff was a billionaire, but rather than working to earn his money, he used every underhanded method known to humankind to grow his wealth. Falstaff arrived in Gotham City and set his sights on taking control of the Wayne

Soon thereafter, people around Falcone began to die at the hands of a serial killer, dubbed Holiday given that each murder occurred on a celebration day. With each new death, suspicion was cast in Falcone's direction, forcing him to hire the growing number of costumed "freaks" who had arrived soon after Batman first appeared. In time Falcone learned that his youngest son, Alberto Falcone—the one he most desperately wanted out of the

"family business"—was Holiday. (*Batman: The Long Halloween* #1, 1996)

During the course of the year, District Attorney Harvey Dent was attacked in court and his face scarred, leading him to a new career as the twisted criminal Two-Face. Holiday continued to commit crimes until the truth came out that the serial killer was actually Harvey Dent, his wife Gilda Dent, and Alberto, each committing murder for his or her

FOUNDATION and WAYNE ENTERPRISES. His first step was to try to hire away LUCIUS FOX, who at the time was BRUCE WAYNE's chief executive officer. (*Batman* #307, January 1979)

Fox rebuffed the offer, sensing that the red-haired, rotund Falstaff meant nothing but trouble. Sure enough, Wayne's longtime secretary GWEN ATKINS mysteriously quit her position, to be replaced by CAROLYN CROWN. Eventually it was learned Crown was being manipulated into feeding insider information to Falstaff since he was holding her daughter hostage.

Batman first encountered the corporate raider when he rescued him from an attack by CAPTAIN BOOMERANG, who sought revenge for a stock investment that proved fraudulent. (*Batman* #322, April 1980)

As Wayne fought to keep control of his company, Falstaff upped the ante by running a smear campaign in Gotham's media and even tried to blow up the Wayne Foundation building. Falstaff, possessing detailed information from Crown, was ready to seize control of the company but was stopped by Batman. As the two fought, Falstaff produced a high-tech pistol that fired a sphere of deadly energy. Batman dodged it, but Falstaff found himself kicked into the fatal energy by TALIA HEAD, RĀ'S AL GHŪL's daughter and lover to the Dark Knight.

It was some time before Batman learned that Falstaff had been sent to Gotham and equipped with the pistol by Rā's in another attempt to gain control over Batman's destiny.

FANG, THE

The man known only as the Fang was a gangland chieftain who always carried a sword forged in China as a lucky talisman. He claimed the sword had been made over a thousand years ago and was imbued with magic, bringing luck to its wielder. When the Fang abandoned the sword at a crime scene, Batman, ROBIN, and SUPERMAN used it as bait to lure the criminal into a trap. Instead Batman and Robin wound up in his clutches—but they were rescued by the Man of Steel, who apprehended the Fang. (*World's Finest Comics* #73, November/ December 1954)

FANGAN

Fangan was a twelfth-century English wizard who crafted a potion to use against a knight whom he considered an enemy. Secreted in a cave, it was left with the hope the knight would enter and be overcome by its fumes, which would then enchant him. The spell would force the knight to perform three impossible feats, which Fangan presumed would ultimately kill his antagonist.

Instead, both Fangan and the knight died long before the elixir was used—and centuries later Batman became its victim. While in England for a policeman's convention, the Caped Crusader entered the cave and was enchanted. Coming to his aid was SUPERMAN, who first worked to make certain all three feats could be performed without killing his friend. The duo first went to the FORTRESS OF SOLITUDE, where a machine granted Batman temporary superpowers. Then he was presented with a dragon-like beast from another world that

he could overwhelm. Next, he had to wear a jester's outfit and do as he was instructed by townspeople. Superman surreptitiously watched to make certain Batman would do nothing to harm himself, as criminals might have hoped. Finally he had to defeat the mightiest man on Earth—and Superman took a dive during a fight, thus breaking the spell's hold over Batman. (*World's Finest Comics* #109, May 1960)

FARNUM, LEW

Lew Farnum chose to prey upon his fellow criminals by scheming to convince them that his doctor could alter not only faces, but also fingerprints. For high fees, criminals could undergo the procedure; soon thereafter, Farnum would kill them before they could realize the truth: You could not alter fingerprints in this manner. Batman and ROBIN tumbled to the plan and apprehended Farnum and his colleagues. (*Batman* #82, March 1954)

FARR, GLENN

Glenn Farr spent a decade earning great wealth as a black marketer. After amassing his fortune, he retired to an empty castle just north of GOTHAM CITY. Farr then intended to decorate the space with objets d'art from around the world. He was frustrated, though, to discover that much of what he desired was refused him, as the items' owners had other plans. Farr decided to engage in unconventional behavior to get what he wanted, which included purchasing an entire town and replacing the standing administration with his own men, all to get his hands on a collection of jade. Batman and ROBIN put an end to his criminal activities. (*World's Finest Comics* #60, September/ October 1952)

FARRELL, SPARKS

Sparks Farrell was hired by Baron Ferric to kidnap Valonia's Prince Stefan when he visited the United States. With Stefan out of the way, Ferric hoped to assume the country's throne. Instead Batman and ROBIN rescued Stefan, and the trio took down Farrell and his men. They then brought Ferric to justice, restoring peace to Valonia. (*World's Finest Comics* #26, January/February 1947)

FARROW, DWIGHT

Dwight Farrow carved his way toward Batman's attention as costumed criminal the WRECKER.

FAT FRANK

Fat Frank led a band of GOTHAM CITY criminals, who fell into ownership of a billboard business. Frank realized that the gang members could turn this to their advantage and began a blackmail scheme, threatening prominent Gothamites with exposure of their guilty secrets via billboard unless they paid. The payments were then made to the billboard company for advertising space, so nothing illegal appeared to be happening; nor could the police act. A frustrated ROBIN wondered how he and Batman could stop the criminals who, by the book, had done nothing wrong. The Dynamic Duo set out to destroy several of Fat Frank's billboards while Gotham's police ignored the criminal's complaints

about them destroying his property. Then Batman and Robin used the billboards to post Frank's picture and criminal record, rousing the ire of the citizens, who forced Frank and his men out past the city limits. (*Detective Comics* #104, October 1945)

FATMAN

Fatman was a circus performer who dressed as a comical version of Batman and gently mocked him, to the delight of audiences around the country. (*Batman* #113, February 1958)

FELINA

CATMAN kept several pet animals, including Felina, a black panther. (*Detective Comics* #311, January 1963)

FELIX, COUNT

Count Felix was a Nazi who headed up a dangerous spy ring on Earth-2 during World War II. Felix and his men, including fellow German FRITZ HOFFNER, sabotaged factories in the hope of slowing America's war efforts. Batman and ROBIN saw to it that the spy ring was smashed, with the count and his men arrested. (*Batman* #14, December 1942/ January 1943)

FERRIS, IRON-HAT

Ferris was a GOTHAM CITY mobster who, when arrested, squealed on his fellow criminals. When the underworld got hold of him, an iron mask was welded into place over his head. Henry Kendall, hoping to be elected as Gotham's next district attorney, brazenly kidnapped Ferris and committed a series of crimes while wearing an identical mask. Kendall then accused the current DA of failing to properly stop Ferris's crime wave, besmirching the man's reputation. To escalate matters, Kendall intended to kill Ferris, claiming he'd done what the DA couldn't manage. Instead, Batman and ROBIN discovered the real Ferris and set out to expose the impostor. Fleeing the Dynamic Duo, Kendall raced out into a raging storm where a bolt of lightning struck his iron mask, killing him. (*Batman* #39, February/March 1947)

FIASCO, LENNY

The criminal who donned a costume to clean crime scenes as the ERASER.

FIFTH COLUMNIST

During World War II, a fifth columnist was someone who worked to undermine the efforts of a larger group. In America, fifth columnists were citizens who betrayed their country in the service of the Axis powers. On Earth-2, Batman and ROBIN repeatedly thwarted the efforts of fifth columnists to stall America's war efforts. The first such traitor was a man named WRIGHT, who murdered author Erik Dorne. (*World's Best Comics* 1939)

FIFTH DIMENSION

The Fifth Dimension was a plane of existence where there lived a race of beings endowed with powers that appeared magical to humans. The legend of the djinn is traced to this realm. Its best-known resident was MR. MXYZTPLK, a magical imp who liked to taunt SUPERMAN. (*Superman* #30, September 1944)

When there were multiple universes, each one seemed to have multiple planes of existence as well, so Earth-2 featured Mr. Mxyztplk while Earth-1 had Mr. Mxyzptlk. In all cases, the people had magical abilities, and the rules of their magic demanded that practitioners return to their home dimension for ninety days if they said their name backward.

In the single universe created in the wake of CRISIS ON INFINITE EARTHS, Mr. Mxyzptlk regularly visited Earth, usually confining his antics to METROPOLIS and the Man of Steel. Still, at one point it was learned that humans could possess a Fifth Dimension resident's powers. Unfortunately, that human was the JOKER, who stole 99 percent of the magic from Mr. Mxyzptlk. The world suffered greatly during this time, although—even possessing this energy— the Joker could not eliminate Batman. Instead he realized that he saw the world as one that must have a Batman to oppose him. (*Superman* #160, September 2000)

Whether the abilities of people from the Fifth Dimension were the result of advance technology or true magic remains unclear.

FILM FREAK

Two men have plagued GOTHAM CITY using the name *Film Freak*. The first was BURT WESTON, a man who playacted his entire sad life. A failed actor who yearned to portray charismatic, memorable villains, Weston experienced nothing but disappointment. In an effort to change his fortune, he faked his death, imitating a moment from *The Sting*, but no one paid attention. (*Batman* #395, May 1986)

While he was lying low, Weston's grip on reality loosened, and when he emerged three years later he began a new career. Weston committed a daring series of crimes all with moments taken from classic cinema, every word he uttered coming from long- ago scripts. Journalist JULIA PENNYWORTH was the first to trace the Film Freak to Weston, which made her his next target. Intending to finishing her off with a crime inspired by *Psycho*, Weston failed but decided that murdering all his former co-workers was his next production.

Detective HARVEY BULLOCK, a cinema buff, identified all of Weston's film references, enabling Batman to finally track and apprehend the deranged man. Later, Weston fell under the MAD HATTER's thrall and was used to spy on BANE, when the international criminal was attempting to conquer Gotham's underworld. Bane discovered the surveillance and killed Weston for his efforts, a sad curtain ringing down on a small career.

Some years later a television personality named EDISON hosted a creepy film program and used the *Film Freak* name. (*Catwoman* [second series] #54, June 2006) To him, life was one extended motion picture, so he was thrilled to receive a videotape with footage of CATWOMAN fighting the new Angle Man. The Film Freak found Angle Man and they agreed to team up and take down Catwoman, who at the time was the novice HOLLY ROBINSON. The Film Freak eventually spotted two different women in the Catwoman suit and followed clues that led him to SELINA KYLE's apartment, where he kidnapped her daughter Helena. Catwoman rescued her child and then demanded that ZATANNA use her magic to

alter Film Freak's mind, much as the Maid of Magic had altered Catwoman's mind years earlier. The magic didn't work as expected, leaving Film Freak a homicidal maniac. It took plenty of effort, but Catwoman managed to subdue the Freak, turning him over to Gotham's police. (*Catwoman* [second series] #61, January 2007)

FINCH, NATHAN

Nathan Finch was a mechanically inclined criminal best known to Batman as GEARHEAD.

FINGERS, SLICK

Slick Fingers was a criminal who specialized in cracking safes manufactured by the Titus Keyes Safe Company. The name was actually an alias for George Collins, who harbored a grudge against Keyes. He framed Titus Keyes for the crimes, and it wasn't until Keyes was on trial that evidence started pointing to Collins. At that point Batman and ROBIN apprehended Collins. (*Batman* #20, December 1943/January 1944)

FINNEY, NAILS (1946)

Finney was a criminal nicknamed Nails for his nail-biting habit. He led a gang that specialized in stealing radium. To hide the material until it could be resold, he had Dr. James Martin, a tree surgeon, fashion a unique hiding place. Martin hollowed out an oak tree on France Van Orsdell's estate, saving it from disease, and then coated the interior with zinc to hide the radium's emissions. After several more thefts, Finney and the gang returned to the tree, only to be confronted by Batman and Robin. The men fought, with two being knocked unconscious. Before the Dynamic Duo could apprehend the others, the fleeing men were killed when the hollowed and weakened tree was struck by lightning and fell on them. (*World's Finest Comics* #22, May/June 1946)

FINNEY, NAILS (1962)

Nails Finney was an underworld chief who wanted to rid Gotham City of Batman. He hired a man named Garth to create a device to accomplish this goal. The unscrupulous scientist created a machine that reversed a human's growth. When used on the Caped Crusader, it reduced him to the form of an infant. What surprised everyone was that Batman retained his mental faculties and could still direct Robin on the case. Dressed in an infant's version of his Batsuit, Batman was with the Boy Wonder when they found Finney's hideout. There, the machine's ray was reversed and Batman regained his normal form. Finney, Garth, Swap Smith—a fence—and the others were apprehended. (*Batman* #147, May 1962)

FIREBUG

Soldier Joseph Rigger was granted leave and returned to his home in Gotham City after his family died in three suspicious building accidents. Between his military experiences and the loss of his family, Rigger's mind snapped. Determined to punish the buildings for killing his family, Rigger, a demolitions expert, donned a bodysuit, strapped on tanks of napalm, and attacked the buildings. As the structures burned to the ground, Firebug was born.

Batman was soon on the trail of the arsonist, and the two battled atop the Gotham State Building. When Firebug's tank ruptured and exploded, Batman presumed he had died.

Instead, Firebug somehow survived and was next seen working for the Calculator, attempting to infiltrate Hero Hotline's headquarters. He failed at this and returned to Gotham, where he auditioned to join Black Mask, only to lose out to Firefly. Angry at another defeat, he set out to prove he was the better criminal only to seemingly be killed once more.

When not incinerating buildings, he was said to have made a great cup of coffee and used to visit Orca and her husband, Terry Capshaw, at their apartment. (*Detective Comics* #819, July 2006)

FIREBUG II

An unnamed man bought a spare Firebug flameproof suit and matching equipment, debuting alongside Deadshot, Killer Frost II, and the Closer

in criminal mischief. (*Deadshot* [second series] #1, February 2005)

FIREFLY

Garfield Lynns was a theatrical lighting technician who found himself out of work and struggling in Gotham City's poor economy. Without a steady income, Lynns used his expertise to begin a criminal career in order to survive. Donning a green-and-purple costume, Lynns employed his expertise staging eye-catching crimes. As the Firefly (complete with ff on his chest), Lynns thought he was on his way to financial security until Batman and Robin apprehended him. (*Detective Comics* #184, June 1952)

Soon after, Ted Carson stole Lynns's costume and equipment and ventured forth as the Firefly. Carson modified the outfit: It was now green with yellow stripes and featured decorative wings on his back, a cowl that included antennae, and a blinding spotlight on his forehead. At first, police and Batman believed that Firefly had robbed the Carson Mansion, knocking out Ted Carson in the process. As Kathy Kane—Batwoman—began a brief romance with Carson, Batman continued to investigate the new Firefly's crime wave. Batwoman got closer to Carson and realized he was actually the Firefly; she tipped off her crime-fighting mentor. The climactic struggle took place at the Gotham Museum, atop an Incan exhibit, where the Caped Crusader subdued the Firefly. Batwoman explained that the Carson fortune was dependent on a gold mine that had stopped producing, and Carson's gambling debts hastened the fortune's depletion. Carson had felt he had little recourse but to steal money. (*Batman* #126, September 1959)

There was even mention of a third man masquerading as Firefly. (*Blackhawk* #175, December 1962)

Lynns regained possession of his gear and, upon leaving prison, resumed his career, almost immediately being thwarted by the Creeper. The colorful vigilante mocked his appearance, as did his own henchmen, causing Lynns to display a violent streak resulting in the death of one of his own hirelings. (*First Issue Special* #7, October 1975) His luck did not change when he returned to crime once more, only to be stopped by two of Batman's

OUTSIDERS teammates, HALO and LOOKER. (*Outsiders* #12, October 1986)

When BANE cracked open ARKHAM ASYLUM, unleashing a flood of criminals to weaken Batman, Lynns was one of the escapees. Police described Lynns as afflicted with pyromania, a condition that may have developed while in jail. In a new orange outfit that covered him from head to toe, complete with glider wings, the new Firefly descended upon Gotham. (*Detective Comics* #661, Early June 1993) He set out to destroy the places that he'd never been able to visit when he was young, including Elmo's Pier. Robin determined Lynns's goals after eavesdropping on a conversation between the villain and his sister. At what had once been the Orpheum Majestic Theater, an exhausted Batman confronted Firefly. The criminal escaped, only to be tracked and finally apprehended at the Gotham Zoo.

He escaped once more, took the alias Gil Fields, and settled in the city while offering his criminal services to BLACK MASK. (*Detective Comics* #689, September 1995) He beat out FIREBUG for the assignment and went on to cause mayhem and destruction on numerous occasions. NICHOLAS SCRATCH hired him to create the largest fire Gotham had ever endured, and Lynns complied. An accident, however, left him with burns over 90 percent of his body, and he was remanded to recuperate at BLACKGATE PENITENTIARY.

Miraculously, he healed quickly and not only regained mobility but also returned to his criminal ways, escaping Blackgate, retrieving his costume, and getting back to work. He battled CATWOMAN and was recruited by the secret Society of super-villains, gathering to take on the heroes en masse. When the cybernetic OMACs were unleashed against the costumed heroes and villains around the world, Firefly was one of those murdered. (*The OMAC Project* #6, 2005)

The Firefly outfit survived Lynns, and someone new took up the guise, in the employ of the second VENTRILOQUIST and SCARFACE. (*Gotham Underground* #2, January 2008)

FLAGG, TIM

An escaped convict better known to Batman as the costumed criminal HYDRO.

FLAMEBIRD

On Earth-1, JIMMY OLSEN accompanied SUPERMAN to the bottled city of KANDOR, a miniaturized survivor of Superman's doomed homeworld. Under the red sun radiation, Superman's abilities were reduced to human norms. When he was mistakenly accused of a crime, he went into hiding. To find out the truth, he and Jimmy donned costumes patterned after Batman and ROBIN but based on Kryptonian legends. NIGHTWING and Flamebird solved the case, clearing Superman's name. Over the years Nightwing and Flamebird continued to have Kandorian adventures, even once fighting alongside Batman and Robin. Later, two native scientists, Van-Zee and Ak-Var, took over the roles to provide a constant crime-fighting presence. (*Superman* #158, January 1963)

In the reality crafted after the CRISIS ON INFINITE EARTHS, Dick GRAYSON sought a new name after declaring his career as Robin over. Following a conversation with Superman that touched on Kryptonian myth, Grayson chose the new name *Nightwing*. (*Nightwing Secret Files* #1, October 1999)

Teenage-tennis-pro-turned-wannabe-super-hero Mary Elizabeth "BETTE" Kane adventured in the red-and-yellow outfit of Flamebird, taking the name after hearing of the Kryptonian legends from Superman. (*Superman: Man of Steel* #111, April 2001)

Superman and LOIS LANE once traveled to Krypton's past and assumed the heroic identities of Nightwing and Flamebird. (*Superman: Man of Steel* #111, April 2001)

In the wake of the reordered reality after INFINITE CRISIS, Kara Zor-El, SUPERGIRL, briefly fought crime in Kandor as Flamebird alongside Power Girl's Nightwing. (*Supergirl* [sixth series] #6, April 2006)

FLANNEGAN, OTIS

Otis Flannegan was an outcast from society who discovered an affinity for rats and became the criminal known in GOTHAM CITY as RATCATCHER.

FLASH, THE

The Flash is the name used by the fastest men on Earth, dating back to the early twentieth century. The name has become a legacy that will endure through the centuries, with Flashes recorded up through the 853rd century.

The first Flash was Jay Garrick, a college student who gained super-speed after a chemistry lab accident. He became a founding member of both the JUSTICE SOCIETY OF AMERICA and the All-Star Squadron. On Earth-2 he and Batman were teammates and friends. (*Flash Comics* #1, January 1940)

On Earth-1, Barry Allen became the Flash as a result of lightning striking a wall full of chemicals in his police crime laboratory. (*Showcase* #4, September/October 1956) As with Garrick, this enabled Allen to access the mysterious realm known as the Speed Force and become the Scarlet Speedster. He and Batman became charter members of the JUSTICE LEAGUE OF AMERICA and shared many adventures together. Batman admired Allen's analytic mind and methodical approach to investigations.

In the wake of the CRISIS ON INFINITE EARTHS, reality was altered, so Garrick served as the first Flash and Allen the second, with Batman only serving with the latter. Allen died, though, saving the universe from the Anti-Monitor. (*Crisis on Infinite Earths* #8, November 1985) His protégé and nephew, Wally West, took over the mantle of the Flash.

Wallace Rudolph West gained access to the Speed Force in a freak repetition of Allen's accident. (*Flash* #110, December 1959/January 1960) First, as Kid Flash, Wally learned to harness his skills at Allen's side. With ROBIN the Boy Wonder, he helped form the TEEN TITANS, and the two grew up as best friends. West and DICK GRAYSON used to take annual vacations together.

As the third Flash, West was invited to join the JLA and did so despite being somewhat intimidated by Robin's mentor. West worked with differing incarnations of the JLA and Titans until he sacrificed himself during the events of INFINITE CRISIS, leaving for another dimension of existence with his wife, Linda, and their infant twins.

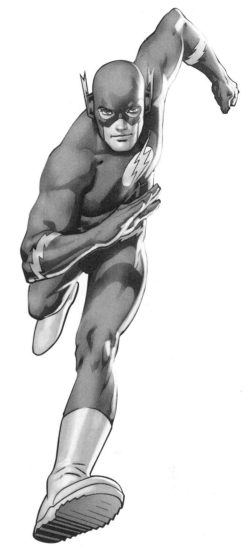

Barry Allen had spent a month in the thirtieth century with his wife, Iris West Allen, before his death. He left behind a legacy and twins, Don and Dawn; Don had a son, Bart, who also accessed the Speed Force. To best learn how to use his abilities, Bart was sent to the twentieth century to learn from the "Zen master of speed," Max Mercury. Following in his grandfather's footsteps, Bart took on the costumed identity of Impulse, adventuring alongside Robin in YOUNG JUSTICE and the Teen Titans. During Infinite Crisis, Bart traveled through the Speed Force, emerging physically as a twenty-year-old although his emotional makeup remained that of an adolescent. When West vanished, Bart saw little choice but to become the next Flash. It was subsequently learned that Bart possessed the totality of the Speed Force within his body. (*The Flash: The Fastest Man Alive* #1, August 2006) Bart was savagely beaten to death by the Flash's Rogues Gallery at much the same time as West and his family returned to Earth.

FLASS, ARNOLD

Arnold Flass grew up in GOTHAM CITY, joining the Green Berets after high school. He left the service, becoming a detective in the GOTHAM CITY POLICE

DEPARTMENT. Despite his valiant record overseas, Flass succumbed to Gotham's rampant corruption under Commissioner GILLIAN B. LOEB. Flass specialized in shakedowns and accepted bribes by the fistful.

His career changed when he was partnered with JAMES GORDON, recently relocated from Chicago. At first, Flass thought "Jimmy" would become one of the "boys," but he quickly reassessed the earnest—and honest—detective. As a result, Flass wanted to show Gordon what became of honest cops. With Loeb's permission, Flass and fellow officers hid under ski masks and brutally beat Gordon with baseball bats in the G.C.P.D. parking garage. During the beating, Gordon recognized Flass's laugh and knew who led his assault. He was determined to gain revenge.

Later that same night, Gordon trailed Flass and waited until the drunk, crooked cop left another officer's home for the evening. Gordon challenged Flass to a fight, even providing his opponent with a fresh baseball bat. Flass proved no match, despite his military training, and wound up handcuffed, naked, on the street.

Gordon proved his valor and forced Loeb to insist the cop be left alone. Flass continued his bent ways despite an intimate encounter with Batman, the costumed vigilante who had recently arrived in the city. A shocked Flass insisted that the "bat-man" was actually a demon with both fangs and claws.

Soon after, narcotics dealer JEFFERSON SKEEVERS was arrested by Gordon, only to be released on bail under Loeb's orders. Batman tracked Skeevers to a seedy hotel and terrified the man. The following morning Skeevers turned himself in and confessed that he had been paying Flass and Loeb to leave his business unmolested. Gordon sought and obtained an indictment, leaving his former partner to face a ten-year jail sentence. (*Batman* #404, February 1987)

Flass was killed by the serial murderer HANGMAN

after serving barely two years of his sentence. (*Batman: Dark Victory* #3, February 2000)

FLEMING, "BULL"

"Bull" Fleming led a gang of criminals who thought he might have it easy. At the time, a chemical accident supercharged Batman's hands, leading them to be declared lethal weapons. Instead the Caped Crusader used all his training to find other methods to carefully subdue Fleming and his men. (*Detective Comics* #338, April 1965)

FLINT, JOE

Joe Flint was a private detective who arranged to be shot so he could gain admittance to the BULLET-HOLE CLUB. His goal was to kill FBI agent Terry Collins, who was trailing counterfeiters and was a threat to Flint, who doubled as the counterfeiters' leader. When he failed but was exposed to Batman, a fellow club member, Flint attempted a suicide leap out a window. The plan failed, but the action did cause a mental breakdown. Flint was apprehended and remanded to a psychiatric institution. (*World's Finest Comics* #50, February/March 1951)

FLIPPY

Edward Deacon was born with deformed arms and legs that closely resembled flippers, earning him the nickname *Flippy*. His drug-addicted mother eventually sold her deformed child to a circus freak show. When the carnival went broke, its four freaks were abandoned. One of them was murdered by an escaped killer, who was being trailed by Batman. In the end Batman saved Flippy from death. The encounter proved life changing for the youth. (*Detective Comics* #410, April 1971)

Inspired, he vowed to become a super hero. As he grew, Flippy studied magic to gain powers, including telekinesis. He sought out Greenwich Village's Madame Xanadu, who led him to a variety of mystic teachers. To help pay for his studies, Flippy used his limited limbs to become a master bartender. He claimed his record of drink mixing was twenty-three. After Nightmaster abandoned the pandimensional Oblivion Bar during the INFINITE CRISIS, Flippy broke in and assumed ownership. Previous owner Nightmaster contested the move but ultimately resigned himself to a back room, where he and fellow members of the Shadowpact convene.

FLORES, CATALINA

This BLÜDHAVEN resident became a costumed vigilante, basing her name and appearance on the hero TARANTULA.

FLORIAN, COUNT

Count Florian hailed from an unrevealed European country and over the years built up an elaborate espionage operation. Those loyal to him were noted by the third-eye stickers proudly worn on their foreheads. To international crime-fighting organizations, he was known as the man with a thousand eyes. In the years after Earth-2's World War II, the count turned his organization into a for-hire option for worldwide organized crime. Florian arrived in America to oversee one such operation and came to the attention of GOTHAM CITY's Batman

and ROBIN. The Caped Crusader held the man in contempt, disapproving of his selling his services to anyone, for any price. In order to bring Florian to justice, Batman posed as a former underling. Once he and Robin got close enough, Florian and his agents were apprehended, ending a threat to America's safety. (*World's Finest Comics* #43, December 1949/January 1950)

FLORONIC MAN

JASON WOODRUE was a political extremist from another dimension known as Floria. He was a revolutionary racist who saw to it that his dimension's human-shaped races were predominant over the Floral Spirits. He was captured and exiled to Earth.

Seeking a way to survive, he took the name *Jason Woodrue* and gained employment as a botany professor at Gardner University. His research was concentrated on accelerated plant growth, and he was increasingly aware of what humankind was doing to his newly adopted world. His noteworthy student body included Alec and Linda Holland, who set off to create a bio-restorative formula; Susan Linden, who morphed into the plant-like Black Orchid; Phillip Sylvan, who later cloned more Black Orchids; Janet Klyburn, who went on to become director of METROPOLIS's S.T.A.R. LABS franchise; Dan Cassidy, who became a Hollywood stuntman and then the demonic Blue Devil; and PAMELA ISLEY. It was rumored among the students that Woodrue and Isley engaged in an affair. Along the way he coaxed her into stealing herbs from an Egyptian collection, and then tried to kill her by using the herbs to craft a rare toxin. When Isley ingested the toxin, it activated her meta-gene, making her immune to all poisons and putting her on the path to becoming POISON IVY.

Shortly thereafter, Woodrue left Gardner for Ivy University, where he continued his research in the hope of returning to Floria and killing Queen Maya. Somehow hearing of Woodrue's plan, the queen came to Earth and enlisted the ATOM's help in stopping it. (*The Atom* #1, June/July 1962)

After a series of defeats against the Atom and the JUSTICE LEAGUE OF AMERICA, Woodrue experienced a biochemical mishap that altered his human form to that of a living tree, complete with shrubbery atop his head. (*The Flash* #245, November 1976)

Hiding his new form under makeup and a wig, Woodrue was hired by the Sunderland Corporation to study the captured SWAMP THING. It was then that Swamp Thing learned he was not Woodrue's former student Alec Holland reborn as a swamp creature but a sentient form of plant life that *thought* it was the human Holland. (*Saga of the Swamp Thing* #21–24, February–May 1984)

Woodrue then learned from a Guardian of the Universe that he possessed the makings of the next generation of humankind and agreed to explore that potential as part of the team known as the New Guardians. Taking the name *Floro,* he adventured with the team for a brief period of time. (*New Guardians* #1–12, September 1988–September 1989)

Some time after this, he had another encounter with the Swamp Thing, which left Woodrue decapitated. Scientists managed to keep him alive, and Woodrue was exposed to marijuana. He used the plant substance to craft a new body for himself and left the laboratory. Woodrue journeyed to GOTHAM CITY, where he unleashed his new breed of pot and also broke his former student, now Poison Ivy, out of ARKHAM ASYLUM. Aided by his hirelings Holly Wood and Eva Green, Woodrue extracted DNA from Ivy, hoping to generate a new life-form, a child he could call his own. Poison Ivy was to receive ten million dollars, earned from sale of his own brand of marijuana. She disliked Woodrue's manic desire to take over the world, however, so she helped Batman stop the crazed creature. Batman lured Woodrue to a puddle, then grabbed a cable and electrocuted the grounded life-form. Taking a cue from Swamp Thing, the Dark Knight once more decapitated Woodrue. (*Batman: Shadow of the Bat* #56–58, November 1996–January 1997)

Woodrue's head was remanded to Arkham Asylum, where he grew a new body. Some time later, Batman was allowed to take Woodrue to Opal City to aid STARMAN in dealing with SOLOMON GRUNDY, another humanoid plant being. Although he was sent back to Arkham, Woodrue has since been freed and was one of the villains who learned his mind had been tampered with by ZATANNA. He has since fought with the Society of villains against Earth's heroes. (*Infinite Crisis* #7, June 2006)

FLOWER GANG, THE

Three men with a high degree of horticultural knowledge combined their resources to commit crimes as the Flower Gang. The men robbed from around GOTHAM CITY using various plants' specific properties to gain entry or unlock safes; one such heist was the robbery at the Morrow Art Gallery. While the gang members were imaginative in their efforts, they proved to be no threat to ROBIN, as the Boy Wonder apprehended them without the aid of Batman. (*Batman* #172, June 1965)

FLYING GRAYSONS, THE

JOHN and MARY GRAYSON were star trapeze artists for the HALY BROS. CIRCUS. Their son DICK joined the

act when he was a youth, and the three were a highlight attraction. The act came to a tragic end when John and Mary fell to their deaths, their ropes severed by ANTHONY "BOSS" ZUCCO to prove that Haly needed to pay protection money. Dick Grayson was adopted by BRUCE WAYNE and trained to become ROBIN, the Boy Wonder. (*Detective Comics* #38, April 1940)

FOLLAND, FRANK

Frank Folland was an enterprising engineer who sought funding to build his next invention, the aeraquamobile, capable of traversing sea, land, and air. To raise the money, Folland embarked on a series of exhibitions highlighting famous firsts, in the hope that his vehicle would join the list in the near future. His estranged partner, George Sellman, hired thugs to ruin the exhibits and kill Folland so he could obtain the prototype vehicle himself. Instead Batman and ROBIN ended the threat and apprehended the criminals. Soon after, Folland received funding from a manufacturing firm. (*World's Finest Comics* #25, November/December 1946)

FORBES, FREDDY

In a parallel, unnamed reality, Freddy Forbes was a popular television comedian known to all as the JOKER. When Batman paid this reality a visit, he was startled to see how closely the comic resembled his archnemesis. (*World's Finest Comics* #136, September 1963)

FORTRESS OF SOLITUDE, THE

The Fortress of Solitude is SUPERMAN's private refuge, much like Batman's BATCAVE. On Earth-2 he had a Secret Citadel built into a mountain near METROPOLIS. (*Superman* #17, July/August 1942)

On Earth-1, Superman's Fortress was located in the Arctic, its massive golden door opened by a giant key disguised as an airplane directional marker. The fortress contained numerous mementos from KRYPTON, Smallville, and Metropolis. For Superman's birthday, Batman once staged a mystery within the fortress. (*Action Comics* #241, June 1958)

Batman and ROBIN were frequent visitors to the fortress, both on Earth-1 and on the Earth re-formed by the CRISIS ON INFINITE EARTHS. On another birthday, the Dynamic Duo and WONDER WOMAN visited the fortress, only to find Superman in thrall to Mongul, which led to a massive battle. (*Superman Annual* #11, 1986)

(For a detailed account of the Fortress of Solitude, consult *The Essential Superman Encyclopedia*.)

FOSTER, "BIG JOE"

Batman was acting as a test pilot for the Eagle Aircraft Company when his experimental jet was bathed in a passing comet's radiation trail. The cosmic energy altered his physiology, not only making him glow but also imbuing him with superpowers. Scientists from Eagle determined that once the radiation faded from his system, he would die. The Caped Crusader's only hope was a treatment from Professor Blake, an idiosyncratic scientist whose whereabouts were a mystery. Upon learning of this, the criminal "Big Joe" Foster tried to locate Blake before Eagle's staff could. With the clock ticking, Batman used his newfound abilities to fight crime in GOTHAM CITY, initially unaware that Foster had managed to find Blake and take him hostage. Turning his attention to the kidnapping, Batman deduced where the scientist was being held and arrived in time to free him. Blake then used his expertise in rare gases to concoct a serum that would purge Batman's system of the radiation, sparing his life. (*Detective Comics* #268, June 1959)

FOSTER, FRANK "WHEELS"

Frank Foster ran a restaurant that fronted an illegal gambling den until he was apprehended by Batman and ROBIN. While he sat in prison, a laundry truck experienced a flat tire, causing it to crash through the front gate; Foster escaped. Much as a stray bat inspired BRUCE WAYNE to become the feared Batman, Foster saw the tire as an omen and began a crime spree wearing a yellow-and-orange costume sporting a wheel insignia. He used wheels to commit his crimes, which were also wheel-inspired. It took some doing, but the Dynamic Duo managed to put the brakes to Foster's newfound career. (*Batman* #135, October 1960)

FOSTER, JOHN

John Foster was a career criminal whose life took a different turn when he realized he was an identical twin to architect George C. Hudson. Foster callously murdered Hudson and assumed his identity. He then took the architectural plans for houses in various steps of completion and added hidden access ways and storage spaces. Once the homes were completed and occupied, Foster and his allies could rob the homes without leaving clues for the police. Batman figured out that Foster was impersonating the architect and managed to trick him into confessing the murder, allowing the police to arrest him. (*Batman* #54, August/September 1949)

FOX, LUCIUS

Lucius Fox was the business manager at WAYNE ENTERPRISES on Earth-1. He was described as having a keen sense for business and earned BRUCE WAYNE's trust, which allowed him to assume greater responsibilities over time. Eventually Fox was given control over both Wayne Enterprises and the WAYNE FOUNDATION, freeing Wayne to concentrate on being Batman. (*Batman* #307, January 1979)

In the reality after CRISIS ON INFINITE EARTHS, Fox was rescued from muggers in Paris by teenage

Lucius Fox

Bruce Wayne. It was Fox who put forth the notion of using Wayne's wealth for a charitable foundation. During Wayne's second year as the Dark Knight, he recovered a precious medallion for Fox, stolen at a party by the Penguin. The renewed acquaintanceship led to Wayne hiring Fox for the Wayne Foundation. (*Batman: Ghosts—Legends of the Dark Knight,* 1995)

A different post-Crisis account indicated that Fox was working for T. Clyde Pontefract's Pontefract Industries when Wayne recruited him to run WayneTech prior to Wayne donning the Batsuit. At that point Wayne had begun using WayneTech prototypes for his crime-fighting needs, arousing the occasional suspicion from Fox. (*Detective Comics* #0, October 1994)

A refinement of that account showed that Lucius Fox graduated at the top of his class at Morton Business School and began a business career that led to his being vice president of corporate services at failing Atwater Air. In just a few years he turned the near-bankrupt commuter air service into a leading competitor and was made CEO of the company while avoiding the massive layoffs endorsed by every business pundit of the time. He was considered a major player with a stunning portfolio and a limitless future. Every major corporation was said to be angling to land him. His decision to join Wayne Enterprises as CEO and president took the normally staid business world by surprise. (*Batman Secret Files* #1, October 1997)

A conflicting account showed Wayne coming back from his training abroad to find his father's company being mismanaged with no sign of Fox being present at all. While Wayne acclimated himself to his new role as Batman, he was also delving into how corrupt the board of directors had become and what housecleaning was required. (*Batman: Journey into Knight* #1–12, October 2005–September 2006)

All the previous accounts may have been superseded by the events of Infinite Crisis. Shortly after Wayne became Batman, he began diverting Wayne Enterprises' prototypes for his personal use in outfitting his Batcave. There he had a friendly relationship with Fox, who was an engineer at the Wayne Aerospace division. (*Batman Confidential* #1–6, February–July 2007) Some time after that, Fox rapidly rose through the ranks to become CEO of both Wayne Enterprises and the Wayne Foundation.

In addition to his stellar work managing the entirety of the Wayne family's business and philanthropic activities, Fox was also the father of four. Fox's eldest child was Tiffany, who worked at a Wayne Foundation–sponsored drug rehab clinic. (*Batman* #308, February 1979) His son Tim graduated from college and had a strained relationship with his father. Over time they healed the rift, and Tim actually did work at Wayne Enterprises during the one year Gotham City was a No Man's Land. (*Batman* #313, July 1979) Daughter Tam Fox was in high school (*Detective Comics* #658, April 1993), and Fox's youngest son has not been named. (*Batman: Gotham Knights* #32, October 2002)

Fox was married to a woman named Tanya, although she was also called Nancy in one instance. (*Batman* #443, January 1990)

FOX, THE

Warren Kawford, alias Fisk, wore a business suit and fox-head mask and worked with the Shark and the Vulture as the criminal Terrible Trio.

FRALEY, WALTER

Walter Fraley hijacked a shipment of gold bars and had the metal melted and reshaped to resemble antique gold bars. He then buried them in specific places, selling fraudulent treasure maps with his men legitimately finding the buried treasure. When Fraley claimed this was the treasure from the noted highwayman Captain Lightfoot, Batman had Professor Carter Nichols send him and Robin back in time to learn the truth. In colonial America the Dynamic Duo learned that Lightfoot was a persona used by a crime fighter who worked to maintain a fragile peace between settlers and Native Americans. Back in the present, Batman used his knowledge to force a confession from the accomplices, resulting in them, and Fraley, being arrested. (*Batman* #79, October/November 1953)

FRANK, ADAM

Adam Frank promoted himself as the first in everything. He used this to fashion himself as a Gotham City celebrity, burnishing his reputation with each new first. When he tried to obtain a valuable Shakespeare first edition, A. H. Evans, the owner, refused to sell. This inspired Frank to be first in something else: first criminal in his family. He found himself a criminal crew and set out to rob using "firsts" as a theme. It didn't take Batman and Robin long to track and arrest Frank and his men. (*Batman* #29, June/July 1945)

FRANKLIN, AMINA

Siblings Amina and Wayne Franklin grew up under harsh circumstances, forging a deep bond. Their father was a former radical who once threatened to kill his children and himself rather than be arrested and subjected to the "white man's prison."

Both grew up to become doctors, with Amina working at a Gotham City community clinic. At a charity fund-raiser, she met and briefly dated Bruce Wayne.

Two years later she directed a patient, Henry Jones, to her brother, who sought someone to take his place as he faked his own death to avoid both the Russian Mafia and members of the Yakuza, who demanded repayment for their investments in his failed medical technology. Jones, a terminal patient, agreed to die in a warehouse explosion in exchange for five thousand dollars that his mother desperately needed. But the explosion caught Amina's brother Wayne, disfiguring him and twisting his mind. He sought revenge against the criminal forces allied against him. As Grotesk, he killed without remorse.

Amina and Wayne reconnected during this time, and she provided Batman with invaluable information during his investigation. In the end, though, she learned that Jones's mother had never received the payment, and the news broke her heart. Grotesk even endangered her life during a final showdown with Batman when Amina was injected with an overdose of poison, forcing the Dark Knight to save her, letting Grotesk run free.

Before he could get her to medical help, Amina died. (*Batman* #659–662, February–March 2007)

FRANKLIN, WAYNE

Dr. Wayne Franklin, described as the "Black Bruce Wayne," suffered a debilitating injury and emerged as the malformed villain Grotesk.

FREEWAY

Freeway was a meta-human who was able to turn his corporeal form insubstantial, allowing him to spy on people or enter locked structures. At some point the otherwise unnamed Freeway also studied martial arts under Asano Nitobe, former associate of Paul Kirk, Manhunter. He challenged Robin on several occasions, even endangering the Teen Wonder's secret identity. (*Robin* [second series] #106, November 2002)

Freeway was recruited by Athena to join her Network when the international operation began working out of Gotham City. When Batman shut down her operation, Freeway vanished. (*Batman Family* #8, February 2003)

FRIES, NORA

Nora Fries was a gentle soul who met Victor Fries when she attended a strict boarding school. The attractive young woman fell in love with the scientist, marrying him soon after her graduation. Their storybook marriage was short-lived, as Nora fell terminally ill; despite medical science's best efforts, there was no cure. Fries, who studied cryogenics, chose to preserve his wife, awaiting a day when she could be cured. Some time later, an accident turned the despondent Fries into the vicious Mister Freeze, able to exist only in subzero environments. (*Batman: Mister Freeze,* 1997)

During one battle with Batman, Nora's frozen body was shattered into pieces, effectively killing her and sending Fries over a psychological edge. In time, though, he reassembled the icy pieces and hoped for a miracle. That miracle finally arrived in the form of Nyssa Raatko, daughter of Rā's al Ghūl. She offered to place Nora's frozen form into a Lazarus Pit, which would resurrect her, in exchange for his creating a weapon for use by the Society, a band of super-villains. Nora was placed into the alchemical

Victor and Nora Fries

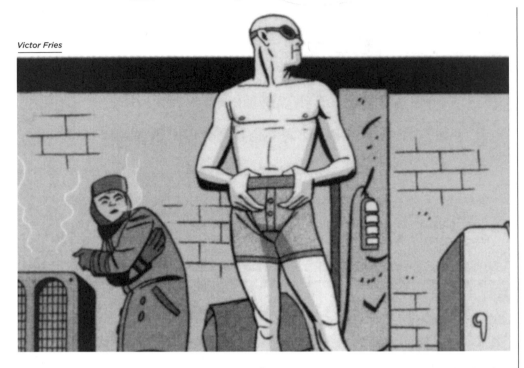

Victor Fries

substance and—given her altered condition—was brought back to life, but not as the loving Nora. She emerged as a living, humanoid molten form that could emit flames. She also seemed to absorb the very essence of the pit and was apparently able to resurrect the dead. She took the name *Lazara*, and her mental outlook was diametrically opposed to that of Nora. Claiming she hated her husband for what had become of her, she tried to kill him. After failing, she fled before he could use his freeze gun to entrap her. (*Batgirl* #70, January 2006)

FRIES, VICTOR

This tragic scientist tried to find a way to preserve his ill wife's life but instead was turned into a human who could only survive in subzero temperatures. His twisted mind led to a life of crime as MISTER FREEZE.

FRIGHT

Dr. Linda Friitawa specialized in genetics but lost her medical license when she conducted unauthorized experiments on humans. Disgraced yet still consumed by her research, the albino Friitawa agreed to work for the PENGUIN, who assigned her to work beside Dr. JONATHAN CRANE. Crane, known to most as the fear-inducing SCARECROW, was working on new toxins to create hallucinations, preying on people's personal fears. Friitawa, who slept by day to avoid direct sunlight, worked all night, learning much from Crane. He responded to her kindness, which was a marked contrast with the brutal manner shown him by the Penguin. She coordinated her research with his, then performed an experiment on Crane. The thin, gangly man was transformed into a hulking creature named SCAREBEAST that she could not control. Scarebeast began killing the Penguin's hired men; when Batman attempted to intervene, the creature defensively emitted Crane's toxin.

In time it became clear that Crane was transforming back and forth between human and beast. Batman subdued Crane and helped seek a cure for his condition. Friitawa used the results of her experiment to treat her albinism, which resulted in her gaining superpowers, including the ability to emit deadly nerve toxins. Telling Batman to call her Fright, she escaped. (*Batman* #627, Late July 2004)

FRISBY, FLOYD

Floyd Frisby was a racketeer who fled arrest in the United States and hid in South America. Batman, ROBIN, and SUPERMAN tracked the criminal to the dense jungles and apprehended him. Before they could return home, though, Superman was caught in the full force of an exploding volcano, resulting in temporary amnesia. Natives thought the Man of Steel was a reincarnated king returning, as foretold in their legends, to rebuild their time-lost city. In time he recovered his memories and helped bring Frisby back for prosecution. (*World's Finest Comics* #111, August 1960)

FROGEL, "FIVE ACES"

The career criminal "Five Aces" Frogel led a gang of cohorts who decided to take over Sunshine City, somewhere in the American West. The frightened citizens beseeched Batman and ROBIN to come to their aid. Upon arrival, Batman was elected as sheriff and the Dynamic Duo quickly restored peace to the town. Frogel and his men were arrested. (*Batman* #10, April/May 1942)

FRYE, "FISH"

"Fish" Frye was a fugitive criminal who intercepted an SOS from Batman, who had been injured during a BATPLANE crash. This inspired an intricate scheme in which Frye could not only remain free but also profit. He turned to ex-convict HARRY LARSON, blackmailing the man to use his uncanny resemblance to both Batman and BRUCE WAYNE, to pose as the Caped Crusader. This Batman would be active in GOTHAM CITY, but allow Frye to operate unmolested. The faux-Batman, though, suffered a head injury, leaving him with temporary amnesia. Found by ROBIN, he was brought back to the BATCAVE, where the Boy Wonder and ALFRED PENNYWORTH accepted him as the real Batman/Bruce Wayne. This convinced Larson he *was* Batman, and he made it a point to bring Frye to justice. Along the way Larson's memory was returned, and he was determined to find the injured Caped Crusader, rescuing him from imminent death. After freeing him from criminals, Larson fell onto high-tension wires and was electrocuted. Frye and his men were subsequently arrested by Gotham's police. (*Batman* #83, April 1954)

FULLER, SANDRA

Sandra Fuller was fascinated with the various men known as CLAYFACE and managed to gain their powers, operating as Lady Clay.

FUNNY FACE GANG, THE

The Funny Face Gang criminals earned their name for the silly rubber masks they wore during their robberies. When Batman and ROBIN got involved in the case, they apprehended the criminals, exposing their leader as Al Talley, owner of GOTHAM CITY's prestigious Tally Ho Club. (*Batman* #116, June 1958)

FUTURIANS, THE

Six people possessing extrasensory perception banded together as the Futurians. Their goal was to use their uncanny abilities to rule the world. When they threatened the life of one man, Batman intervened and was seen by the group as a seventh Futurian. He disabused them of that notion and apprehended them before they could launch their plan. (*Batman* #229, February 1971)

GAIGE

Gaige was a famous oceanographer but was better known to Batman as TIGER SHARK.

GALVAN, "BUZZ"

Elmo Galvan and his accomplices murdered four people. When the five were arrested, the other four turned state's evidence against Galvan, who was tried, convicted, and sentenced to the electric chair. The high voltage failed to kill Galvan, reducing him to a partially paralyzed man. At BLACKGATE PENITENTIARY's infirmary, Galvan dragged himself out of bed, intending to kill himself by biting into an electrical cord. The voltage, though, seemingly cured Galvan of his affliction. He did realize, though, that he would need to carry a power supply for the remainder of his life. Galvan decided he could live with that and left prison to seek revenge on his former friends and witnesses to his botched execution. Galvan managed to kill two men before Batman was on his trail.

The Dark Knight was stopped from apprehending Galvan when he was attacked by the ELECTROCUTIONER, a would-be vigilante. The distraction allowed Galvan to flee and resume his plan, which included targeting Police Commissioner JAMES GORDON. Gordon assigned officers to cover most of the other witnesses, with the Dynamic Duo shadowing the final witness. Galvan managed to kill the man under Batman's protection but was finally taken down by Batman and the Electrocutioner. (*Detective Comics* #644, May 1992)

GANT, CHOPPER

Chopper Gant led a gang of criminals, but decided to improve their methods for committing crimes by seeking military help. Posing as reporters, Gant and his men duped Hannibal Bonaparte Brown, a military strategist, into answering questions about hypothetical strategic problems. In every case Brown's advice proved key in committing their robberies. Batman and ROBIN figured out that Brown was being used, and the embarrassed tactical genius aided the Dynamic Duo in apprehending the gang. (*Batman* #21, February/March 1944)

GARGOYLE, THE

Biochemists MORRIS EAGLETON and David Creighton crafted a formula—known as "the Stone Man"—originally written in the thirteenth century by Jorix, an alchemist. The two thought if the formula worked, it might bestow immortality. They followed the directions, and Creighton tested it on himself. He was transformed into a monstrous shape and actually attacked his young daughter Cristina. The effects proved temporary, and the horrified man insisted Eagleton burn the manuscript. His partner agreed, but then kept the manuscript and tried it himself. The transformation left him with a bloodlust, and he promptly killed two innocent victims. Batman tried to stop the creature, but the Gargoyle proved too powerful. Eagleton used the formula sparingly, only fourteen times over the following decade, delighting in the ability to fly and enhanced strength. It did, though, ravage his body, prematurely aging him. Creighton suspected it was his partner who was behind the mysterious slayings but held his tongue until his daughter, now grown, returned to GOTHAM CITY. During the confrontation, Eagleton injected the formula into Creighton and then, as he was transforming, the scientist shot his partner to death. The police discovered the body and presumed they'd found the killer, turning Eagleton into a hero. Having studied the case through the years, Batman recognized the truth and created a scenario that saw Cristina, Eagleton, and himself trapped in an airtight vault. Eagleton confessed before transforming once more to use his strength to free them. Once they were free, a more experienced Dark Knight easily subdued him, ending the threat once and for all. (*Batman* #477, May 1992)

GARGOYLE GANG, THE

The Gargoyle Gang consisted of several would-be kidnappers, including members named Maxie, Snail, and Joey. They took a hostage to hold for ransom, hiding in GOTHAM CITY's sewer system. Batman was on their trail and had to outrace floodwaters that threatened to drown the gang, the hostage, and himself. The Gotham Guardian accomplished the feat, apprehending the gang. (*Batman Family* #18, June/July 1978)

GARR

Garr considered himself the king of the interplanetary underworld and was frequently sought by Tutian, the Universal Police Corps' chief inspector. Garr came to Earth-2 and allied himself with common criminal Eddie Marrow. They began a new crime spree, starting on Earth but spreading across the galaxy. Tutian similarly teamed with Batman and ROBIN to bring the pair to justice. (*Batman* #117, August 1958)

GARRIS, JAY

Jay Garris and his gang were tired of constantly being thwarted by Batman. To even the odds, Garris stole film of Batman in action from bat-fan Elmer Mason. Watching, Garris realized that if they could master the boomerang, they could counter Batman's famed BATARANGS. Replaying the film endlessly, the men all practiced until they achieved a degree of mastery. Garris then fashioned several specialized Batarangs containing bombs to help commit crimes.

Mason recognized the criminals thanks to newsreel footage from one of the robberies and alerted Batman. From there, the Dynamic Duo traced the gang to a deserted island near GOTHAM CITY. To access the island, Batman strapped himself to the mammoth Batarang X, which was fired by a catapult. Once on land, he defused all the bombarangs and easily apprehended the gang. (*Detective Comics* #244, June 1957)

GARROW, RAND

This criminal, better known as CRIMESMITH, used his cunning genius with mechanics to commit his offenses.

GARTH

Garth was described as a ruthless, renegade scientist; his greatest achievement was constructing a machine that could change a man, such as Batman, into an infant. NAILS FINNEY used the machine for his own purposes. (*Batman* #147, May 1962)

GARTH, JIM

Jim Garth was an arsonist, starting fires for pay, but faced personal tragedy when a fire destroyed his own home and killed his only son. The flames severely burned Garth's face, and the entire event twisted his mind. Rather than admit any responsibility, he placed the blame on the firemen who could not quench the fire before his son died. Donning a fireproof suit and helmet, he set out as Blaze and sought revenge against the volunteer fire brigade, which had disbanded after the fire. Following the pattern of the children's rhyme, he began killing the former firefighters in order: rich man, poor man, beggar, and so on. Men lost their lives or their offices until Batman and ROBIN intervened. The Dynamic Duo tracked him down but, before he could be arrested, Garth used his flamethrower on a stack of dynamite and perished in the resulting explosion. (*Batman* #69, February/March 1952)

GARTH, SAM

Sam Garth was a clever criminal who used fake credentials to gain admittance to GOTHAM CITY's Camera Scoops Club. As a member, he was extended privileges that allowed the elite band of photojournalists inside police lines at crime scenes. With his access, Garth cased prospective robbery sites. Once the crimes began, Batman and ROBIN investigated. The Caped Crusader turned to the club's junior members to snap pictures of Garth committing his crimes, building up the necessary evidence to arrest him. (*World's Finest Comics* #21, March/April 1946)

GARVER, BIG JIM

Big Jim Garver led a successful criminal gang in GOTHAM CITY and was the object of Batman's investigation. The case grew complicated when Ed

Wilson was paroled from jail and returned home, explaining to his young son that he was in reality Batman, fighting crime for extended periods. Tommy idolized his dad and was thrilled to hear that he was retired and home to stay. Putting on the costume to show his son, Wilson wound up being mistaken for the hero and critically shot by Garver's men.

Upon hearing this, Batman agreed to help Wilson maintain the fiction until the injured father could properly reveal the truth to the boy. However, Garver kidnapped Tommy, believing he had Batman's own son. The Caped Crusader rescued the youth and apprehended Garver and his men. Wilson recovered and told his son the truth, and he accepted it with newfound maturity. (*Batman* #88, December 1954)

GARVEY, ED "NUMBERS"

Ed Garvey was another GOTHAM CITY criminal gang leader but enjoyed only a brief period of activity, ultimately being apprehended by Batman and ROBIN. (*Batman* #176, December 1965)

GAUCHO, EL

Argentina's own costumed protector, El Gaucho, was modeled after GOTHAM CITY's protector, Batman. He was initially a spy for the Allies within Nazi Germany, his first recorded case as a hero. The two heroes met when the Caped Crusader invited adventurers from around the world to gather in Gotham for a meeting. The BATMEN OF ALL NATIONS were thrilled to aid their mentor in stopping "Knots" CARDINE. (*Detective Comics* #215, January 1955)

They were reunited a short time later when philanthropist John Mayhew invited the international crime fighters, along with SUPERMAN, to form a CLUB OF HEROES. (*World's Finest Comics* #89, July/August 1957)

El Gaucho used a horse, lariat, and other native tools in lieu of Batman's gear, but the results were the same. He also used a motorcycle given the terrain. Batman noted that while many international heroes faded over time, El Gaucho remained active and gained respect for his efforts. When the Club of Heroes reunited at the behest of its founder, John Mayhew, members became targets in Mayhew's scheme of revenge for the club's failure. Gaucho wound up shot in the chest by the corrupt WINGMAN,

HERE IS THE THIEF YOU WANTED!

MUCHAS GRACIAS, *GAUCHO*... WE KNEW YOU'D RUN HIM DOWN! BUT THERE IS A CALL FOR YOU, FROM NORTE AMERICA!

but he survived. (*Batman* #667–669, October–December 2007)

GAVIN

Gavin, Gee-Gee, Moore, and Dalton escaped from Gotham State Prison by concealing themselves in a large container that the government used to transport radioactive specimens. Quickly the men became infected with radiation poisoning, and they panicked. Dying and a threat to the citizens of GOTHAM CITY, the convicts were traced by Batman and the police to Police Island. At the time, this island was home to a Police World's Fair with contemporary and prototype future law enforcement tools on display. Batman and ROBIN employed many of the devices to help apprehend the escaped convicts without getting too close, thus helping to save the men's lives. (*Batman* #118, September 1958)

GEARHEAD

NATHAN FINCH had had enough of his hard-luck life and decided to improve his fortunes by kidnapping his boss's daughter and holding her for ransom. Batman arrived and successfully freed the woman, but could not stop Finch from falling to his apparent death. However, Finch survived and was discovered by two homeless men, who sold the broken body to an underworld doctor. The doctor, marveling at Finch's endurance, began experimenting on him to better understand the field of cybernetics. In short order Finch lost his frostbitten arms and legs, and the doctor provided him with a series of interchangeable limbs with differing attributes. Dubbed Gearhead, Finch sought revenge against Batman, blaming him for the fall. (*Detective Comics* #712, August 1997)

He failed at his goal but remained a recurring threat in GOTHAM CITY. During the yearlong NO MAN'S LAND time, Gearhead competed with fellow villains for control of the city's sewer system, only to be thwarted by ROBIN. When he lost access to his artificial limbs, Finch found himself agreeing to partner with TOMMY "MANGLES" MANCHESTER, who carried Finch's torso with him. Both ran afoul of MISTER FREEZE, who flash-froze them with his gun. Gearhead survived and found himself upgrading his attachments, including attachment to a souped-up automobile. (*Rush City* #1–2, September–October 2006)

A different man named Gearhead worked in Washington, D.C., as an accomplice of the White Rabbit and was defeated by Steel. (*Steel* #14, April 1995)

GEISHA GRRLS

The four women known as the Geisha Grrls were YAKUZA associates of a GOTHAM CITY mobster named JOHNNY KARAOKE. They were named for contemporary pop stars—J.Lo, Britney, Beyoncé, and Mariah—but were deadly with firearms and ruthless in maintaining Yakuza tradition. In their first encounter with Batman, he handled them easily, noting that they relied too much on their weaponry. All but one apparently died in a shootout at the Gotham Opera House, a result of GROTESK's trap to rid himself of enemies, including Karaoke. (*Batman* #659–662, February–March 2007)

GEIST

A horde of alien invaders arrived on Earth and, during their attempt at conquering the planet, bit various humans. One, Pritor, bit a man named Dwayne Geyer, and his alien fluids mixed with Geyer's body chemistry to activate the man's meta-gene, granting him superpowers. Geyer was suddenly invisible in bright light and only partly visible in lesser light. Taking the name *Geist,* the Twilight Man, he found his powers useful in fighting crime. However, the condition was permanent, making it impossible for Geyer to hold a job. Geist did, though, come to the aid of Batman, who at the time was actually JEAN-PAUL VALLEY. They defeated another of the alien invaders threatening GOTHAM CITY. (*Detective Comics Annual* #6, 1993)

Geist subsequently joined with other victims of the aliens and formed the Blood Pack. They had several missions, including defeating a criminal organization, the Quorum, before he left the team following a misunderstanding. Geist then largely retired from crime fighting until ORACLE contacted him during a crisis. He was once more alongside the Blood Pack as they attempted to protect METROPOLIS from a rampaging SOLOMON GRUNDY. Later, he was killed by Superboy-Prime, who fired his heat vision at Grundy and the Blood Pack. (*Infinite Crisis* #7, June 2007)

GELBY, BIX

Bix Gelby was a scheming criminal who managed to convince America's gangland chiefs to contribute written memories and memorabilia about their greatest unsolved crimes for placement in a time capsule dedicated to crime for burial during the 1940 World's Fair. Once Gelby obtained all the items, he turned around and threatened to deliver the incriminating documents to the police unless he received a total of one million dollars. Once paid, he promised to destroy the incriminating evidence. As the criminals anted up, Gelby got ready to destroy the capsule. What he didn't realize was that Batman and ROBIN had learned of the scam and extracted all the evidence before the capsule's destruction. With the objects in hand, Batman helped law enforcement from coast to coast solve the many outstanding cases. The Dynamic Duo also apprehended Gelby and his men so they could stand trial. (*World's Finest Comics* #68, March/April 1953)

GENERAL

Ulysses Hadrian Armstrong grew up at a military academy and was intrigued by war. To him, it was an art form to be studied and appreciated. When he left school, he returned to GOTHAM CITY and practiced his lessons by organizing street gangs into an army despite his youth. When the gangs were sent out on campaigns, they were largely successful until they encountered ROBIN. On numerous occasions the General and Robin have matched wits, with the Teen Wonder always winning. (*Detective Comics* #654, December 1992)

GENTLEMAN GHOST, THE

"GENTLEMAN JIM" CRADDOCK was a European criminal who attracted the attention of Hawkgirl on Earth-2.

She urged her partner, Hawkman, to travel overseas and try to apprehend the thief. In four meetings the Winged Wonders were stunned to see that he truly appeared to be a ghost clad in white tie and tails, top hat, and floating monocle. (*Flash Comics* #88, October 1947)

On Earth-1 the Gentleman Ghost plagued Hawkman anew. It was learned that the Ghost was once "Gentleman Jim" Craddock, a nineteenth-century highwayman who was hanged for his crimes—but his spirit remained on Earth. (*Atom-Hawkman* #43–44, June/July–August/September 1969) He frequently fought Hawkman until he arrived for a stay in GOTHAM CITY, matching wits with Batman. (*Batman* #310, April 1979)

In the reality after CRISIS ON INFINITE EARTHS, Craddock's spirit battled costumed heroes through the twentieth century, including Hawkman and Hawkwoman, Batman, the TEEN TITANS, and even the SPECTRE. Another James Craddock appeared, possibly a descendant, a silver-haired jewel thief. This Craddock also fought Hawkman and Impulse.

Over time, Craddock's story was expanded upon; his opponents learned that he had grown up the son of an English gentleman who'd abandoned his wife and only child. Craddock took to crime to feed himself and his mother, and he continued in this career as an adult. Seeking a change in

fortune, Craddock journeyed to the United States, where he was opposed by western gunslingers Nighthawk and Cinnamon. It was Nighthawk who apprehended him and killed him via the gallows. Craddock vowed that his spirit would remain until the soul of his killer moved to another plane of existence. Nighthawk, though, was one in a long line of reincarnated spirits dating back to ancient Egypt and cursed to remain that way. It was this connection that led Craddock to plague Hawkman in the 1940s and again in modern times.

In the wake of INFINITE CRISIS, Craddock's life story was altered, and his burgeoning life of crime brought him up close and personal with the supernatural. A gypsy told him he would survive death and return to life. She said he would remain to fight England's enemies, and when that time came Craddock gained the ability to summon ghosts who sought vengeance against their common enemies. Craddock was stopped by WILDCAT and other members of the JUSTICE SOCIETY OF AMERICA. (*JSA* #82–87, April–September 2006)

GEO-FORCE

BRION MARKOV was prince of MARKOVIA but wanted to do more to help his people. He had Dr. Helga Jace bestow upon him superpowers, using her technological skills in time for him to stop an insurrection led by Baron Bedlam. He gained the ability to control gravity and crushed the rebellion under the name Geo-Force. At much the same time, other heroes were in Markovia and came to his aid. In the end, Batman suggested that Markov, BLACK LIGHTNING, METAMORPHO, HALO, and KAIANA remain together as a heroic strike force, taking on cases that the JUSTICE LEAGUE OF AMERICA would not. In fact, he had recently resigned from the League, and this met his needs. And so the OUTSIDERS were born. (*The Brave and the Bold* #200, July 1983)

Brion possessed enhanced strength and endurance in addition to his ability to alter levels of gravity, which enabled him to void gravity and fly or increase it and weigh down his opponents. At first he wore a costume in earth tones before eventually adopting one in green and gold to match Markovia's flag.

The Outsiders trained together and went into action regularly. In one case they encountered the TEEN TITANS, led by Batman's partner ROBIN. There, Geo-Force met Terra and realized she was his half sister Tara. He explained that their father, King Markov, had an affair with an American woman, which resulted in Tara's birth. She'd grown up in America to keep the hint of scandal far from Markovia. What he didn't know was that Tara was a psychotic, in league with DEATHSTROKE to destroy the Titans. When she died, he at first believed it was a heroic end, but Batman told him the truth some time later.

At one point the team split from Batman and the hotheaded prince used royal funds to maintain the operation, now located in the American West. That ended when Major Disaster trashed their headquarters and the US government demanded to know the Outsiders' true identities. If they remained silent, relations with Markovia were threatened. Things spiraled out of control from there as King

Gregor, the prince's older brother, was assassinated. Brion assumed the throne—only to abdicate when he learned Queen Iona was pregnant with the true heir. Worse, he learned that Gregor had been killed by Dr. Jace, who was actually an android duplicate, as part of an intergalactic scheme to derail man's evolution. With all the turmoil, the Outsiders couldn't remain together; they disbanded.

Iona was later killed by Roderick, a vampire, who framed Brion for the crime. He and his fellow Outsiders became fugitives until Roderick could be brought to justice. Along the way a new Terra arrived, claiming to be from a different point in time. There was some doubt as to the veracity of her story, but DNA testing proved it to be true. Soon after, Brion finally married his longtime lover, Denise Howard, and served Markovia as regent until his nephew could come of age. During this time, he rarely appeared in costume.

At some point his powers evolved to include the earth-morphing powers Terra possessed, and he remained uncertain how or why this occurred. He also began operating with a new incarnation of the JLA. (*Justice League of America* [second series] #12, October 2007)

Deathstroke had been blackmailing Brion for intelligence. Six minutes after he was approached, he told the JLA, who wired him. (*Justice League of America* [second series] #12, October 2007)

GETAWAY GENIUS, THE

Roy Reynolds was an experienced Gotham City criminal who came to realize that beating Batman and Robin was nigh unto impossible. Instead of seeking ways to defeat the Dynamic Duo, Reynolds concentrated on escape plans so he could continue to commit crimes. He proved adept at this, and quickly Reynolds was recognized as a mastermind. Batman and Robin altered their efforts and concentrated on his henchmen, who proved gullible. When the criminals thought they were attacking Batman and Robin, who had been brought down by the fictitious creation the Hexer, the duo gained the upper hand and learned where Reynolds was. (*Batman* #170, March 1965)

The Big Game Hunter broke Reynolds out of jail in order to help him lure the greatest prey on Earth, Batman. When Batman beat the Hunter, Reynolds was ready to return to prison. (*Batman* #174, September 1965) Some time later, when Batman's rogues tried to stop an incursion from West Coast criminals, Reynolds rigged a trapdoor that allowed Batman to escape execution. (*Batman* #201, May 1968) Years later, the Getaway Genius tried his hand at crime again. Batman suspected that Reynolds was behind the latest crime spree and sought getaway vehicles. While Batman found ground vehicles, he missed a backup helicopter that Reynolds took to freedom—or so he thought. Kirk Langstrom, in his Man-Bat form, was in the vicinity and forced the copter back to the ground and an awaiting Dark Knight. (*Batman* #254, January/February 1974) He has not been seen since.

GHOST DRAGONS, THE

The Ghost Dragons was a Chinese youth gang with members from Macau, Kowloon, and Hong Kong. At the head of the operation was Sir Edmund Dorrance, a British businessman and secretly a criminal. (*Robin* #1, November 1991)

Dorrance, known to his people as King Snake, brought the Ghost Dragons to Gotham City after his people came into contact with Robin III, who was in Paris undergoing training. Robin found himself up against a young woman named Ling, who had assumed control of the branch in the wake of her boyfriend's death. When she failed to kill Robin, King Snake took one of her eyes as punishment, earning the Teen Wonder her enmity. King Snake then chose to relocate to Gotham City, seeing endless opportunity.

With King Snake staying behind the scenes, Ling, now called Lynx, established her control over the operation. The Dragons clashed with the Russian Odessa Mob in a vicious turf war that involved both Robin and Huntress. (*Robin III: Cry of the Huntress* #1–6, December 1992–February 1993)

At one point King Snake was arrested, and Lynx's attempt to expand the Dragons' territory was beaten back by Robin and Spoiler. Lynx left the Dragons and tried life as a mercenary, deciding to return to Gotham and her operation. Soon after her return, Gotham City became a No Man's Land and the Dragons carved out a piece of the city for themselves. Things grew so dire that Batman allied with Lynx in order to shut down a child slavery ring.

Later, when Spoiler's plans backfired and plunged the city into live War Games, Lynx once again tried to take more turf for the Ghost Dragons. She wound up in a battle with Batgirl, only to be beheaded.

The Ghost Dragons continued to operate in Gotham with no new leader recorded.

GHOST GANG

The Ghost Gang was a large group of bandits in America's West who earned their name by seemingly being able to rob two towns a hundred miles apart—yet the crimes occurred only minutes apart. The feat was managed by use of a unique autogyro that transported the thieves and their mounts from town to town. The crimes attracted the attention of Batman and Robin, who headed west to investigate. They subsequently unmasked rancher Lafe Brunt as the secret leader of the robbers. With information from the Dynamic Duo, a local sheriff managed to arrest the remainder of the gang. (*World's Finest Comics* #4, Winter 1941)

GHOST MOUNTAIN

Located in Darkhill County in a remote corner of the Appalachians, Ghost Mountain has been home for hundreds of years to the eccentric, superstitious Tull family, beginning when "the first Tull hunted on Ghost Mountain without the local tribe's permission." That man earned his family the right to stay by sacrificing his life before the Indians. Children in the county's only town are cautioned, "Those who see night fall on Ghost Mountain ain't likely to see the dawn." (*Detective Comics* #440, April/May 1974)

GIBBONS, ARCHIE

Archie Gibbons was a fish wholesaler who specialized in soupfin sharks, whose livers were known as an excellent source of vitamin A. However, gangsters were attacking soupfin shark shipments, threatening to ruin business and, worse, deprive the government of the vitamins needed to keep their troops overseas in top shape. As Batman and Robin investigated, it became clear that the thieves were secretly led by Gibbons. They shut down the criminal ring and apprehended Gibbons. (*Batman* #17, June/July 1943)

GIBLING, WILLIS

Willis Gibling was a former convict also known to Batman as the Zero.

GIBSON

Gibson was affiliated with the Gotham Museum but was also secretly the criminal known as the Jackal-Head.

GIGANTE, SOFIA FALCONE

Sofia Falcone was daughter to Carmine Falcone, the Roman, who ruled Gotham City's underworld in the days when Batman began his career. The eldest of the three siblings, she was a shrewd manipulator of people, clearly being groomed to succeed her father. Even her marriage to Rocco Gigante was part of a grander scheme. (*Batman: The Long Halloween* #1, 1996)

Unfortunately, the Gigantes got embroiled in the Holiday serial killings that targeted the Roman's associates. As the events wound down, the Roman died at Two-Face's hands, finally leaving Sofia in command of the operation. Before she could do much in her new role, she got into a scuffle with Catwoman, leaving Sofia's face scarred and Catwoman's bolo wrapped around her neck as she fell from a building and was crippled. Confined to a wheelchair, the buxom woman also wore a harness to immobilize her head and facilitate healing.

Bitter and angry, Sofia Gigante displayed a ruthless streak, even toward those close to her. After receiving her dead father's finger as a traditional warning, she would not back down. A new serial killer dubbed the Hangman Killer arrived in Gotham City, targeting police officers. This also sparked a gang war as the Falcones struggled to maintain dominance while the Maronis nibbled away at their turf.

Over the course of the nine-month spree, police and Batman were unable to identify who the Hangman Killer was or why the murders were being committed. In time, though, as Batman and Catwoman compared notes, the feline felon realized that they knew who had treated Sofia's facial scars—but nothing about the doctor who'd treated her paralysis. Her ruse uncovered, Sofia left her wheelchair revealed as the Hangman Killer. Before being apprehended, she wanted Two-Face to be her last victim, a fitting end to the family's business. Instead, Batman rescued Two-Face, who then shot and killed Sofia.

GILDED AGE BIRD SHOPPE
Long before the Penguin began using nightclubs as fronts for his criminal enterprises, he operated out of the Gilded Age Bird Shoppe. In a fight with Batman, the Penguin accidentally destroyed it with fire emitted from his flamethrower umbrella. (*Detective Comics* #67, September 1942)

GILLEN, JOHN
John Gillen was an ex-convict, paroled and working as a successful impersonator at a circus. The so-called man of a million faces kept his criminal past a secret but was threatened with exposure by two co-workers, Carey and Withers. Fearing for his job, Gillen reluctantly agreed to their scheme of impersonating famous people, which allowed the men to commit crimes. When Batman and Robin investigated, they learned the

truth and helped apprehend the two thieves. The circus management was understanding and allowed Gillen to retain his job. (*Detective Comics* #166, December 1950)

GILLIS, BART
Bart Gillis was a Canadian highwayman who escaped prison. He tracked down a horse that Robin the Boy Wonder owned and tried to kill it to keep vital evidence from being discovered. Instead, Gillis was re-arrested by Batman, and an examination of the horse led to a bullet found lodged in its neck. The bullet was the proof needed to show that Gillis had killed a Canadian mountie. (*Detective Comics* #157, March 1950)

GIMMICK GANG, THE
Considered by the media as the trickiest trio of bandits in Gotham City, the Gimmick Gang proved no match for Batman and Robin. (*Batman* #116, June 1958) A different Gimmick Gang operated years later in Metropolis. (*Action Comics* #364, June 1968)

GLASS MAN, THE
A series of murders terrorized Gotham City as three men all died from mysterious causes. An investigation by Batman showed that the men died after touching poison affixed to sharp glass sculptures that each received as a gift. At first suspicion was directed at George Stevens, a glass manufacturer who had once threatened Horace Manders, an amateur astronomer and victim. The other two victims were former investors in Stevens's company. The case ultimately led the Caped Crusader to Judson, owner of Gotham's Comet Cars. Judson's financial future was being threatened after Manders chose to withdraw his financial investment in the failing company. When Batman confronted Judson, he backed away, falling to his death into a glass furnace. (*World's Finest Comics* #28, May/June 1947)

He made a memorable impression, mentioned at one point by the third Robin. (*Robin* #153, November 2006)

GLEESON, SUMMER
When a wealthy philanthropist unveiled a statue of Batman as his personal thanks to the Dark Knight for saving his life, it provoked a strong reaction from Professor Hugo Strange. He intended to blow up the statue and, as he planned his crime, he took television journalist Summer Gleeson hostage. Batman rescued Gleeson but allowed the statue to be destroyed. (*Batman: Gotham Knights* #33, November 2002)

GLIM, JOHNNY
Johnny Glim was a playwright driven to extreme behavior after selling his play for the stage. The needy author subsequently learned that a Hollywood producer was ready to make a bid for the script at a substantially higher fee. When Glim realized that the contract allowed the rights to revert to him should the play not remain open for two straight weeks, he began to murder members of the cast. Batman and Robin apprehended him before anyone else could be killed. (*Batman* #8, December 1941/January 1942)

GLOBETROTTER, THE
The man known only as the Globetrotter was an international thief who once visited Gotham City. His target was gems inlaid in a statue of the deity Kwaidan at the Natural History Museum. His string of successful crimes ended when he was apprehended by Batman and Robin, aided by museum employee Bill Jordan. (*Batman* #44, December 1947/January 1948)

GLOBE-TROTTER, THE
Henry Guile III was a noted society figure known for his love of the theater, money, and himself—not necessarily in that order. Deluded into thinking he was a talented thespian, he took on a variety of roles, being critically lambasted time and again. In an effort to continue working the stage, he funded and starred in his own traveling repertory company. The venture failed both critically and financially, leaving Guile with a mere dime. He vowed to use that dime and his performance skills to regain his wealth. Using makeup and costumes, Guile committed a series of crimes in England before moving on to commit more robberies in France. Batman and Robin traveled to Europe to investigate the crimes. They tracked Guile to the Eiffel Tower, where he was finally apprehended. Given the spectacular nature of the case, an international gathering of law enforcement officials was convened to celebrate Guile's capture. The Dynamic Duo were guests of honor, and Batman gave the assemblage the case's full details. (*Detective Comics* #160, June 1950)

GLOVES
Gloves coveted more of Gotham City's underworld for himself, so he murdered rival gang chief Waxey Wilson. Batman and Robin investigated the case and were aided by Jimmy, a blind youth who was being

trained in criminology by the Caped Crusader. (*Batman* #50, December 1948/January 1949)

GOBLIN, THE

MARTIN TATE owned GOTHAM CITY's Tate Jewelry Store, but he was also a safecracker, hiding his identity under a grotesque mask and old hat. His daring crimes were ended when Batman and members of the police apprehended him. (*Detective Comics* #152, October 1949)

GOLAR, ERIC

Eric Golar was a recognized inventor who had gone into seclusion to build a fully automated city of the future. His plan was to complete the work, then invite leading manufacturers to see the city at work and buy rights to mass-produce the devices for the American public. Instead, word of his work reached Nero Thompson and his criminal gang. They located Golar's island hideaway and stole the prototype devices, using them to commit a series of crimes in GOTHAM CITY. Batman and ROBIN tracked one of the remote-controlled devices back to the island, freed Golar, and apprehended Thompson and his men. (*Batman* #80, December 1953/January 1954)

GONG, THE

ED PEALE grew up detesting the sound of bells. He turned that hatred into a symbol of his criminal life and became the Gong, employing bells during his criminal acts. His crimes were at first successful, and his antics engaged the public's interest until he was apprehended by Batman and ROBIN. (*Batman* #55, October/November 1949)

GOOD QUEEN BESS

Good Queen Bess was a renowned homeless woman in GOTHAM CITY who briefly served as an informant for Batman. Bess, along with Slugger and POET, provided invaluable information, and Batman gave them cash for meals. During their first meeting, the street people helped Batman identify Quentin Conroy, son of "Linehouse Jack"—a wanted killer. (*Batman* #307, January 1979)

GOODWIN

The research scientist known as Goodwin had developed a formula that placed victims into a sleep-like state in which they obeyed commands. He allied himself with Biff Bannister and his gang to use the gas on prominent GOTHAM CITY businessmen, forcing them to rob their own companies and turn the proceeds over to the criminals. In his first confrontation with Batman, Goodwin managed to gas the Caped Crusader, but through sheer force of will Batman overcame its effects. Batman and ROBIN, aided by ALFRED PENNYWORTH, managed to subdue Goodwin, Bannister, and their men. (*Detective Comics* #83, January 1944)

GORDON, BARBARA

GOTHAM CITY police commissioner JAMES GORDON has always been married. On Earth-2 the unnamed woman appeared infrequently after marrying the cop on October 11, 1926. The first time she appeared

in the chronicles, she was the potential victim of a jewel robbery. (*Detective Comics* #72, February 1943) At some point afterward, the couple had a son, TONY GORDON. Mrs. Gordon's last recorded appearance was at the wedding of BRUCE WAYNE and SELINA KYLE. (*Superman Family* #211, October 1981)

On Earth-1, Gordon's wife was never seen; only the existence of their son Tony and daughter BARBARA GORDON confirmed that there was a marriage at all. At one point a conversation implied that Gordon was a widower, with no further explanation given. (*Detective Comics* #512, March 1982)

In another reality similar to Earth-1, Barbara Kean was a redheaded librarian who introduced herself to Bruce Wayne as James Gordon's fiancée. (*Detective Comics* #500, March 1981)

On the world created in the wake of CRISIS ON INFINITE EARTHS, James and Barbara Eileen Gordon met, fell in love, and were married in Chicago. For career reasons, James took a new job in Gotham City, relocating himself and his pregnant wife. (*Batman* #404, February 1987) She stayed at home, trying to adjust to the dark and corrupt city, while Gordon became embroiled in his work. He also entered into an affair with his fellow officer SARAH ESSEN. Gordon crossed the disreputable powers that ran the city, and they threatened him with blackmail, prompting James to confess everything to Barbara. She told him she already knew. Soon after, she delivered a boy, named James Junior.

When the Gordons' marriage fell apart during Batman's second year of operation, Barbara and James returned to Chicago, where she filed for divorce. (*Batman: Turning Points* #1, January 2001) One account had this happening when James was six. (*Batman: Night Cries*, 1992) At some later point Barbara died and James visited her grave on the anniversary of her passing. (*Batman Annual* #13, 1989) A reality-shifting wave changed things so that Barbara never died; she attended her former husband's marriage to Sarah Essen. (*Legends of the Dark Knight Annual* #2, 1992)

GORDON, BARBARA

On Earth-1, Barbara Gordon was the younger child of GOTHAM CITY police commissioner JAMES GORDON and his unnamed wife. A prodigy, she quickly made her way through public school and college, earning a degree in library science and going to work at the main branch of Gotham's public library. (*Detective Comics* #359, January 1967)

One night she was en route to a masquerade party, dressed as a female version of Batman, when she came across KILLER MOTH attempting to kidnap millionaire BRUCE WAYNE. She rescued Wayne and found the experience so exhilarating, she chose to begin a double life as BATGIRL. Her inexperience

at crime fighting endeared her to Batman and ROBIN, but she also displayed a keen intellect and ability to learn. She rapidly came to be seen as a third member of the team, although it was years before she learned their identities. The super-hero community embraced Batgirl as well. She worked alongside but did not join the JUSTICE LEAGUE OF AMERICA. (*Justice League of America* #60, February 1968) She and SUPERGIRL formed a friendship that endured. (*World's Finest Comics* #169, September 1967; *Adventure Comics* #381, June 1969; *Superman Family* #171, June/July 1975)

Meantime, she and her father shared a house at 21 East Sixty-fifth Street in the city, and he deduced her identity long before she revealed it to him. Batgirl fought common criminals and costumed villains with aplomb, the experiences helping transform Barbara from a mousy librarian to a more confident woman. This led to her running for a seat in the US House of Representatives, which resulted in a relocation to Washington, D.C. She still managed to tackle crimes as Batgirl while reviewing legislation as Barbara. When DICK GRAYSON once served as her summer intern, the potential romance between older woman and younger man remained a teasing flirtation, full of potential but never acted upon. (*Batman Family* #1, September/October 1975) Robin and Batgirl, though, engaged in numerous missions, proving they worked almost as well together as Batman and Robin.

All along, Barbara had only one serious boyfriend, private investigator JASON BARD. After that cooled, she did date Senator Tom Cleary, although the romance did not last.

Barbara met her predecessor, KATHY KANE, the first BATWOMAN, when Kane resumed her crime-fighting career. They began a friendship and worked

together on a handful of occasions. (*Batman Family* #10, March/April 1977)

After her term ended, she lost reelection and returned to Gotham, using her experience to become a social worker. Batgirl also returned to action until she was seriously wounded by Commorant. This began a crisis of faith that lingered with her for the rest of her career. (*Crisis on Infinite Earths* #4, July 1985)

Reality was altered during the CRISIS ON INFINITE EARTHS, and Barbara became the daughter of ROGER and THELMA GORDON, based in Chicago. Both parents died in a horrific car accident, leaving her an orphan until James and BARBARA GORDON adopted the adolescent. (*Secret Origins* [second series] #20, November 1987)

Barbara and Katarina Armstrong were high school acquaintances and academic rivals without becoming friends. Both received early admission to Gotham State days before their sixteenth birthdays. Barbara was admitted on an academic scholarship. All along, she and Katarina measured themselves against each other. If Barbara spoke ten languages, Kat spoke eleven. To Barbara, Kat was a Spoiled Rich Girl. When they raced on the track—the hundred-meter dash in under 10.5 seconds—Barbara won and was congratulated by her rival, breaking the ice; soon the two became inseparable friends. Upon graduation, Barbara headed for the Gotham library while Kat went into the military until she rose through the ranks to become the nation's latest Spy Smasher. (*Birds of Prey* #103, April 2007)

Batman's visits to Gordon's home proved inspiring to the teen, which directed her choice of costume for the fateful party that began her career. Once she debuted, Batman and Robin were actively involved in her training, and Batman refused to let her work with him until he deemed her ready. The flirtation and hint of romance with Dick Grayson started early. (*Batgirl Year One* #1–9, February–October 2003)

Batgirl continued to operate in Gotham City, befriending other heroes and working on cases with Power Girl. It remains unclear if she served in Congress, although she did not do social work.

She was engaged to Jason Bard (now a G.C.P.D. officer), although that ended and Dick seemed to be her only real love.

Her career came to a screeching halt one night when Barbara answered a knock at her door. The JOKER was on the other side and fired a pistol, knocking her to the ground, crippling her. He then disrobed her and took pictures of the suffering woman, which were used to torture her uncle. (*Batman: The Killing Joke,* 1988) After recovering at the hospital, Barbara faced a new life in a wheelchair, her Batgirl career at an end. Still, she hungered to prevent such acts from happening again and sought some way to make a contribution.

Assessing herself, she recognized that her skills at detecting remained intact, in addition to her superior abilities with computers. Bit by bit, she assembled hardware and software, perfecting her hacking skills and slowly building an online presence. She practiced by surreptitiously helping her uncle with a murder investigation. Finally she contacted the Suicide Squad, the government's covert action branch of Task Force X. She hid behind a green-hued avatar and called herself ORACLE. (*Suicide Squad* #23, January 1989)

As she grew more comfortable with her role, Barbara decided to move closer to the action.

Assuming the persona of Amy Beddoes, she relocated to Louisiana, near the squad's base of operations at Belle Reve prison. This proved to be a brief stay; soon she was back in Gotham City, and Oracle began assisting all costumed champions of justice. Her skills and reputation grew despite no one knowing who she really was. At some point she sought out and received training in fighting from her wheelchair from Richard Dragon, one of the world's top martial artists and a teacher to many heroes.

Over time Batman and Oracle worked out a relationship that had him heavily relying on her research and tactical skills as his growing team of agents in Gotham City faced one monumental disaster after another, beginning when BANE broke the Dark Knight's back. Oracle managed to coordinate actions from her new apartment located in the top floor of a midtown Gotham building, obscured by a huge clock face.

After settling in the clock tower, Barbara had time on her hands and wanted to be more proactive but needed agents beyond her friends in Gotham City. The first few times she tried this, she worked with her friend Power Girl, but after a disastrous mission the partnership fizzled. (*Birds of Prey* #42, June 2002) After a while, though, Barbara found her perfect partner in BLACK CANARY. Together they began handling small-scale problems around the world as a budding friendship began. (*Black Canary/Oracle: Birds of Prey,* 1996) It was more than a year before they met face-to-face and Black Canary finally learned who her mysterious partner and benefactor really was. In time these BIRDS OF PREY worked with other heroines, such as the HUNTRESS and CATWOMAN. Later the Birds became a more formal operation, and the roster was expanded to include any number of costumed crime fighters.

Barbara engaged in a correspondence and flirtation with a mysterious presence until it was revealed to be Ted Kord, the second BLUE BEETLE. Kord's technological knowledge and disarming personality made him a natural friend and ally to the Birds of Prey.

Gotham City endured a plague called the CLENCH and an earthquake but finally, the US government decided it was done rebuilding the city again and again. Instead, it decided to cut Gotham off

from America. Those who stayed behind were condemned to live in a No Man's Land. Barbara kept a detailed diary of that year and worked with citizens to help maintain order and distribute what meager supplies there were. With Batman vanished during those first three months, chaos seemed to be winning despite the efforts of Oracle, Nightwing, Robin, and a new Batgirl. Barbara was at first offended to see someone in a variation on her uniform, even more so when it proved to be the Huntress, seeking Batman's approval. A short time afterward Barbara encountered Cassandra Cain, newly arrived in Gotham and unable to speak, but trained as a deadly weapon. After she proved useful and in need of companionship, Barbara offered her a place to stay. Cassandra learned of Batman's mission with his allies and wanted to be a part of the plan. Barbara finally gifted her with the discarded uniform and blessed Cassandra as the new Batgirl.

Oracle continued to funnel information around the super-hero community, including formal induction into the Justice League. (*JLA* #16, March 1998) She funded her operations through raiding criminal accounts, pilfering from Blockbuster II, Blüdhaven's criminal kingpin, until he began a merciless hunt for her. Black Canary's self-sacrifice, posing as Oracle, saved Barbara's life. (*Birds of Prey* #24, December 2000) Later she spread out her efforts, ensuring that enough cash was on hand for technological upgrades as well as mission expenses. On a personal level, Barbara also took the time to earn a law degree, although she rarely put it to use.

Eventually, though, Oracle began to chafe under Batman's constant use of her services without also relying on her observations and advice. A final straw was when he usurped her equipment, complete with satellite links, to control matters during deadly War Games that Spoiler initiated from his personal files. During the mêlée, Black Mask targeted the Watchtower on television, announcing it as the location of Batman's private headquarters. He subsequently destroyed it, moments after Oracle escaped. (*Batman* #633, December 2004)

In the aftermath she decided it was in her best interests to leave both Batman and Gotham behind, relocating with her Birds of Prey team to Metropolis. By this point she had acquired a jet designed by Kord and went mobile with the Birds for a time. (*Birds of Prey* #75, December 2004) Throughout all this, Barbara remained emotionally stable, largely through her finally ignited romance with Dick. They battled crime together and looked after each other when things got roughest. However, when Blockbuster began his bloody vendetta against Nightwing, Dick grew protective of Barbara, which she resented. The romance ended, although later Dick finally proposed to Barbara in the wake of Blüdhaven's destruction. (*Nightwing Annual* #2, 2007)

A future incarnation of Brainiac infected Barbara with a virus as part of its scheme to master the world. One effect it left her with was cyberpathic abilities, literally making her one with computers, but it also threatened to kill her. She virtually battled the virus, which left her in a weakened state. Doctor Mid-Nite performed lifesaving surgery, and upon awakening she marveled at finally being able to move a toe. Oracle redoubled her efforts with her growing Birds of Prey, marshaling her forces when it became apparent that the villains were organizing. In fact, she was opposed by the Society's Calculator, her villainous counterpart. They matched wits time and again, with Oracle regularly maintaining the upper hand.

Oracle and the Birds of Prey prevailed and Oracle and Batman mended fences in the wake of Infinite Crisis. Her next challenge came from her college rival, Katarina Armstrong, Spy Smasher, who manipulated Barbara into giving her control of the Birds of Prey. (*Birds of Prey* #103, April 2007) The Birds rallied and forced Spy Smasher to give up, which she did after engaging Barbara in a bloody fistfight.

In other realities Barbara Gordon has never been far from her role in Batman's life.

On one world her injuries were far more severe; she remained an artificial life-form, a voice that could also speak to the dead. (*Batman: The Doom That Came to Gotham* #1–3, 2003)

Barbara Gordon and Dick Graystark, aka Dick Grayson, were costumed vigilantes in the 1960s, and she subsequently teamed with that world's Batman. (*Thrillkiller*, January–March 1997; *Thrillkiller '62*, 1998)

In another reality Barbara was a wealthy-novelist-turned-cutting-edge-crime-fighter in a world without a Batman. There she befriended a Supergirl. (*Elseworld's Finest: Supergirl and Batgirl*, 1998)

GORDON, JAMES

In all of Batman's realities, one constant has been the presence of James W. Gordon as Gotham City police commissioner.

On Earth-2, Gordon and Bruce Wayne were friends, spending time together prior to the Batman's debut. (*Detective Comics* #27, May 1939) The officer was suspicious of the costumed vigilante and initially had the police hunting him. In short order, as Batman's successes mounted, Gordon changed his opinion. Soon after the arrival of Robin the Boy Wonder, Gordon deputized the Dynamic Duo. (*Batman* #7, October/November 1941) Gordon and Batman quickly grew into a partnership and professional friendship.

Little was revealed about Gordon's life although it was eventually learned he married on October 11, 1926; he and his unnamed wife had a son, Tony Gordon. When he retired, Bruce Wayne, who had given up his costumed role as Batman, succeeded him as commissioner.

On Earth-1, Batman and Gordon were also seen as allies and friends, although that friendship seemed to deepen with time. The two were known for exchanging Christmas gifts, with Batman usually giving Gotham's top cop some unique tobacco for his ever-present pipe. He and his unnamed wife had two children, Tony and BARBARA GORDON. At some point his wife passed away and Tony was off to college, leaving James and Barbara together in their midtown apartment. In time Barbara also grew up and became a crime fighter in her own way as BATGIRL. He deduced her secret before she revealed it to him, and they maintained a close relationship.

On the Earth fashioned after the CRISIS ON INFINITE EARTHS, more was revealed about Gordon's past. He and his brother ROGER GORDON grew up in Chicago, where he went into law enforcement after serving in the military with Special Forces. After achieving the rank of detective, Gordon and his wife, Barbara, left for Gotham City. (*Batman* #404, February 1987) He was initially partnered with ARTHUR FLASS, as corrupt a cop as could be found in the city. Flass operated with impunity under Commissioner GILLIAN B. LOEB and was offended when Gordon refused to shred his integrity for some extra cash. Flass helped beat Gordon to teach him a lesson but Gordon got the last laugh, publicly embarrassing Flass later that night.

During his initial months in Gotham, the lieutenant battled corruption and gave in to an affair with fellow detective SARAH ESSEN. Loeb and Flass tried to blackmail Gordon about the affair but he admitted his adultery to Barbara, beginning the end of his marriage. Shortly after James Jr. was born they attempted counseling but the marriage was doomed. Essen also left Gotham around that time, leaving Gordon feeling alone, except for his all-consuming work.

When Roger and his wife, THELMA, died in a car crash, the Gordons adopted their niece, also named BARBARA GORDON. Some time later, Barbara and her son left James and relocated to Chicago. They divorced at some future point.

When Batman arrived in Gotham, he was hunted by the police, including Gordon. Slowly, the two recognized that the other could be trusted, and clandestinely they shared information that took the first steps toward cleaning the corruption out of the police force. Gordon's efforts were recognized and soon after he was promoted to captain under Loeb's successor, JACK GROGAN. At some unspecified point, Gordon succeeded Grogan.

Batman and Gordon developed a strong bond, and on occasion the Caped Crusader would confer with Gordon at his home, with young Barbara watching from the shadows. The Dark Knight inspired her to one day follow in his footsteps as Batgirl. Gordon was leery at first when Batman began working alongside young Robin, but the youth's enthusiasm and preparedness won him over. He remained cautious when it was apparent the person in the red-and-yellow costume changed the first time.

Through the years, Gordon resisted learning Batman's secret identity. Many presumed a man so smart would know the Caped Crusader's name, but if Gordon did, he never said. At one point, when Gordon felt betrayed by Batman's absence during the first three months of Gotham's life as a NO MAN'S LAND, Batman attempted to heal the rift by unmasking, but Gordon turned his back on the Dark Knight. (*Legends of the Dark Knight* #125, January 2000)

Gordon endured a lot as police commissioner, his life repeatedly threatened by the criminals and criminally insane costumed villains that rampaged through the city with sickening regularity. The nadir may have come when he was kidnapped by the JOKER then stripped, trussed up, and subjected to several days of psychological torture. During that time the Joker shot and crippled Barbara, taking photos of her suffering to inflict further damage on Gordon, who never broke. (*Batman: The Killing Joke,* 1988)

His steadfast influence remained strong despite the worst that happened to his city. He helped maintain order when Gotham was overrun with criminals after Bane broke them free from Blackgate Penitentiary and Arkham Asylum. Soon after, Bane broke Batman's back and Bruce Wayne asked Jean-Paul Valley to assume the mantle of the Bat;

the commissioner instantly detected the change. Because Valley worked alone and was subjected to his own personal demons, he remained aloof from Gordon, which placed one of several strains on his relationship with Batman.

Sarah Essen never strayed far from Gordon's thoughts, and soon after her return to Gotham, their romance was rekindled, blossoming into true love. They married and enjoyed a brief number of years together, fighting crime and corruption while maintaining their relationship. (*Legends of the Dark Knight Annual* #2, 1992) Things nearly ended before they could start when days after her return to Gotham, he suffered a near-fatal heart attack, the result of years of smoking. (*Batman* #459, February 1991)

The grisly crimes and political stresses did briefly take their toll on the couple, forcing a separation. (*Batman: Shadow of the Bat* #35, February 1995) Circumstances grew even more twisted when Essen found herself named as Gordon's replacement, prompting him to quit the force. (*Batman* #519, June 1995) Her tenure at the top proved short-lived, however: She was replaced by an incompetent, who proved his worthlessness when the city was overcome with the Clench, a deadly virus. (*Detective Comics* #694, February 1996) Gordon was finally returned to his post, which seemed to heal their wounds. The two reconciled. (*Detective Comics* #702, October 1996)

Not long after, he directed rescue efforts when the city suffered a devastating earthquake. When the United States severed ties with the city, Gordon stayed behind, defending the rights of those citizens who also chose to remain in their homes. He and a handful of officers fought for every block of turf, holding out hope that Batman could be counted on for support—and in time that belief was rewarded.

At Christmastime, when circumstances in No Man's Land began to improve, Gordon's life was shattered. The Joker had kidnapped the city's remaining infants and threatened to blow them up. As Batman rescued the majority of them, Essen found herself opposite the Joker's gun; she had

to choose between saving an infant or being shot. She dove for the child, cushioning the fall with her body as the bullets slammed into her. After Batman apprehended the madman, Gordon seemed ready to shoot him dead, but instead blew out his knees, crippling him much as he had crippled Gordon's niece. (*Detective Comics* #741, February 2000)

Sarah's death finally took its toll on Gordon, who chose to retire from office after serving more than twenty years as a law officer. As Michael Akins succeeded him, he was fêted by his friends and comrades. He was shot and seriously wounded as the party ended, beginning a manhunt for the killer. (*Batman: Officer Down,* 2001)

Gordon recovered and tended to the small garden outside his Gotham apartment. Officers and the Caped Crusader visited on occasion. At one point he traveled to Metropolis to visit Barbara, and she finally revealed that she was not only the current Oracle, but also the former Batgirl. He was pleased that she had confided in him, but admitted he already knew of her life as the dominoed daredoll.

The fabled Rock of Eternity exploded over Gotham City, a portent of a new round of dark times. Seeing his city in need may have prompted Gordon to return to his former post. At some point after Infinite Crisis ended, Batman, Robin, and Nightwing left Gotham for a year; around Christmas, Gordon returned to his former office.

Gordon continued his friendship with Batman upon the Dark Knight's return, proudly flashing the Bat-Signal to summon his friend. In the days that followed, Gordon continued to direct his officers and was once again risking his life. The Joker made one attempt on his life, but the commissioner survived. (*Batman* #655, September 2006)

In one potential future, Batman had retired and revealed his identity to Gordon, and the two became close friends. (*Batman: The Dark Knight Returns,* 1986)

In the negative matter universe, James Gordon was a criminal named "Boss" Gordon. One record indicated he and Martha Wayne had an affair. (*JLA: Earth-2,* 2000)

GORDON, JAMES JR.

James Jr. was born to James and Barbara Gordon shortly after the family relocated to Gotham City from Chicago. (*Batman* #407, May 1987)

When the Gordons' marriage fell apart during Batman's second year of operation, Barbara and James returned to Chicago, where she filed for divorce. (*Batman: Turning Points* #1, January 2001) One account had this happening when James was six. (*Batman: Night Cries*, 1992)

James Jr. became a pawn between Gordon and his former partner Arthur Flass when the latter kidnapped James on the day Gordon married Sarah Essen. With Batman's help, the child was safely recovered. (*Legends of the Dark Knight Annual* #2, 1992)

GORDON, JOHN

John Gordon was the captain of the *River Queen*, a Mississippi River showboat. He was also great-grandfather to James Gordon, commissioner of Gotham City's police. James asked Batman and Robin to help clear John's name, which required a time-travel trip to 1854. Using Professor Carter Nichols's methods, the Dynamic Duo headed backward in time and discovered that John Gordon had been framed for a series of robberies by Grady Hawes, head of the *River Queen*'s acting troupe. Hawes wore John Gordon's captain's coat while committing his crimes so suspicion would fall on the captain, not him. (*Batman* #89, February 1955)

GORDON, ROGER

Younger brother to James Gordon, the Chicago native and his wife, Thelma, had one child, Barbara Gordon. When Barbara was thirteen, Roger and Thelma died in a horrific car accident. (*Secret Origins* [second series] #20, November 1987)

GORDON, SARAH ESSEN

Sarah Essen was a Gotham City police detective who was briefly partnered with James Gordon, a sergeant recently arrived from Chicago. (*Batman* #405, March 1987) The two began a clandestine affair that became the fuel for a blackmail plot against Gordon; it was thwarted when he revealed his infidelity to his pregnant wife. Gordon and Essen ended the affair, and both were reassigned.

Essen soon after left Gotham City and continued her law enforcement career, even marrying another cop. When the unnamed officer died during a drug bust, she chose to return to Gotham. Essen reentered Gordon's life, and the romance was renewed—only to be derailed by his heart attack. (*Batman* #458, January 1991)

While Gordon recuperated, Essen found herself crossing paths with his costumed friend. She saw Batman as a vigilante and tolerated him only out of respect for Gordon. Eventually the renewed relationship flared into love—so much so that Gordon proposed to Essen *twice*. (*Batman* #465, August 1991; *Detective Comics* #646, July 1992) The two married less than a year after reuniting. (*Legends of the Dark Knight Annual* #2, 1992) They served side by side through the worst years in Gotham's history, with Essen heading up the G.C.P.D.'s Major Crimes Unit. As a result of her cases,

she changed her opinion regarding the Gotham Guardian, gradually accepting his place in the scheme of things.

The grisly crimes and political stresses did briefly take their toll, forcing the couple to separate. (*Batman: Shadow of the Bat* #35, February 1995) Things grew even more twisted when Essen found herself named as Gordon's replacement, prompting him to quit the force. (*Batman* #519, June 1995) Her tenure at the top proved short-lived, however: She was replaced by an incompetent, who proved his worthlessness when the city was overcome with the Clench, a deadly virus. (*Detective Comics* #694, February 1996) Gordon was finally returned to his post, which seemed to heal their wounds. The two reconciled. (*Detective Comics* #702, October 1996)

The 7.6-magnitude earthquake that devastated Gotham put their lives on hold in service to the city. There was no question they would remain when the federal government chose to withdraw support from the city, turning it into a virtual No Man's Land. They battled together to maintain peace for those citizens who had also chosen to remain. Things slowly began to improve, and the Gordons thought the worst was over by Christmastime. Instead the Joker kidnapped the city's remaining infants, triggering an intense manhunt. Essen found the Clown Prince of Crime ready to destroy the babies

at police headquarters. Given a choice to save a child or be shot, she chose the child, only to be shot at point-blank range. She died heroically, and Gordon was mad with grief. He was ready to shoot and kill the Joker, but instead shot both of the madman's knees, crippling him much as he had crippled Gordon's niece Barbara. (*Detective Comics* #741, February 2000)

On New Year's Eve, Jim poured a glass of champagne at Sarah's grave as he raised one for himself to his lips. "Happy New Year, sweetheart. I love you." (*Batman: Shadow of the Bat* #94, February 2000). Her tombstone read:

SARAH ESSEN-GORDON
Honored Officer
Killed in the Line of Duty
Gotham's Finest

In a potential future, Gordon repeated to himself, "I think of Sarah. The rest is easy," indicating her effect on him through the intervening years. (*Batman: The Dark Knight Returns*, 1986)

GORDON, THELMA

Thelma and James Gordon dated for a time before she ultimately married James's brother, Roger. (*Batman: Gotham Knights* #6, August 2000) Roger and Thelma had one child, Barbara Gordon, and there was brief speculation that James was Barbara's actual father although no paternity test was ever taken. When Barbara was thirteen, Roger and Thelma died in a horrific car accident. (*Secret Origins* [second series] #20, November 1987)

GORDON, TONY

On Earth-2, James Gordon married his wife on October 11, 1926, and they had one son, Tony. Their only child, Tony was born several years after the marriage; little else is known about him, although it seems Tony was a year or two older than Robin the Boy Wonder. (*World's Finest Comics* #53, August/September 1951) Tony was in attendance when Bruce Wayne married Selina Kyle. (*Superman Family* #211, October 1981)

James Gordon married his wife on October 11 on Earth-1, and they became the parents of a son, Anthony, some time later, followed by a daughter, Barbara Gordon. He was said to be a college student when he went missing, hiding from Communist spies. Barbara, as Batgirl, found Tony in China. He perished as Batgirl battled the Sino-Supermen. (*Batman Family* #12, July/August 1977; *Detective Comics* #482, February/March 1979)

In the reality after the events of Crisis on Infinite Earths, Tony did not exist.

GORILLA BOSS OF GOTHAM

Mobster George "Boss" Dyke died in the gas chamber of the Gotham State Prison on a cold, rainy evening. On Dyke's orders, his body was retrieved by members of his gang and presented to disgraced surgeon Doc Willard. Performing radical surgery, Willard transplanted the hood's brain into the body of a towering gorilla. Though no longer capable of speech, the Gorilla Boss continued to communicate with his men via pencil and paper.

Unable to stop the great ape's reign of terror, Batman began to realize that the creature was not merely well trained but in the service of a human brain. Having stolen a satisfactory sum of money, the Gorilla Boss captured Batman and returned to his lair, where he commanded Willard to put his brain in the Dark Knight's body—and vice versa. Unaware of this, the Gotham City Police Department had converged when officers spotted the gorilla climbing a TV tower with an unconscious Batman in tow. As the disoriented gorilla fell to his death, Robin swept in and caught his mentor—unmasked as Doc Willard! Batman had faked unconsciousness and switched places with Doc just as the enraged Gorilla Boss awakened (*Batman* #75, February/March 1953)

Batman preserved Dyke's brain as a trophy in the Batcave. Through unknown circumstances, the brain was revived by alien colonists, who offered Dyke a new body if he would use the form to erase Earth's chlorophyll, which was toxic to them. Manipulating Batman into placing the brain in the disintegration pit of Superman's Fortress of Solitude, Dyke burst forth in a new form, a massive green flying manta-like entity made up of vegetable matter.

Batman's foe the Gorilla Boss and a same-named foe of Animal Man's were merged into the same person after the events of CRISIS ON INFINITE EARTHS. (*Swamp Thing Annual* #4, 1988)

GORILLA GANG, THE

The Gorilla Gang was a trio of criminals wearing gorilla costumes who committed a series of robberies in GOTHAM CITY. While they would not normally have posed a problem for Batman and ROBIN, the Caped Crusader was suffering from the effects of an experiment. He had volunteered to test prolonged isolation in preparation for man's ascent into space. Physically, he was fine, but mentally he had begun suffering from waking hallucinations featuring tentacled creatures and alien monsters that inhibited his actions. He had to conquer those fears before he could swing into action, apprehending the gang. (*Batman* #156, June 1963)

GORNEY, GOLDPLATE

A three-time loser, Goldplate Gorney was facing a life term in prison if he was ever captured again. Since all three arrests were a result of Batman and ROBIN, Gorney schemed to kidnap Robin then kill the pair during the rescue attempt.

To kidnap the Boy Wonder, Gorney and his men began scouting GOTHAM CITY high school sporting events, figuring the teen would be a top-performing athlete. What they did not anticipate was that DICK GRAYSON purposely retarded his efforts so as not to let his training gave him an unfair advantage over his peers. At a track event, Gorney decided that Hugh Ross had to be Robin, while his father must be Batman. The Dynamic Duo rescued Hugh and apprehended Gorney without compromising their secret identities. (*World's Finest Comics* #23, July/August 1946)

GOSS, JOHN

The Sky Museum boasted the world's greatest collection of ancient airships and airplanes. John Goss, the assistant curator, privately boasted that he could smuggle criminals out of GOTHAM CITY for a price. Upon payment, criminals were boarded onto a zeppelin and ferried beyond the city limits to freedom. Batman and ROBIN trailed criminals to the city's outskirts and the museum, where Goss was apprehended along with a zeppelinful of criminals. (*Batman* #94, September 1955)

GOTHAM BROADCASTING COMPANY, THE

The Gotham Broadcasting Company was GOTHAM CITY's oldest telecommunications business, formed when the first radio licenses were granted in the early twentieth century.

Early on, engineer Alan Scott changed professions and joined GBC, and WXYZ radio, using its constant flow of news to monitor activities that would require him to swing into action as GREEN LANTERN. He rose to the position of vice president and general manager of Gotham Broadcasting Company. (*JSA* #2, May 1991) Soon after, Scott grew the company with his new wife MOLLY MAYNE; it was renamed Scott Telecommunications and acquired GBC outright. (*Chase* #8, September 1998)

Still craving a human body, Dyke sought out Doc Willard, who actually fulfilled the Boss's long-held goal of acquiring Batman's body. The fortuitous arrival of the aliens, angry that Dyke had reneged on their deal, alerted Superman to the swap, and he hastily performed surgery that placed BRUCE WAYNE's brain back in Batman's body. In the meantime, Willard—with Dyke's brain in his possession—escaped. (*World's Finest Comics* #251, June/July 1978)

Willard returned, hoping to confirm that Batman was in fact Bruce Wayne, as he'd suspected ever since he'd seen the Dark Knight's face during the operation. Though frustrated in his efforts, he escaped custody once more. Willard was finally apprehended, now an incoherent madman babbling about Dyke's brain being lost to aliens. The alien in question was no less than ex-GREEN LANTERN Sinestro, who had expanded the cerebellum to the size of a planet located in the anti-matter universe of Qward and was using the mutated brain as a power source. With his X-ray vision, the Man of Steel destroyed the unnatural extension of George Dyke once and for all. (*World's Finest Comics* #253–254, October/November 1978–December 1978/January 1979)

GOTHAM CITY

One of America's largest cities, Gotham has seen more than its fair share of tragedy and disaster, yet continued to rebuild and flourish. That is due partly to its location on the eastern seaboard, partly to its wide variety of architecture and history, and largely to the urban legends that have made Gotham City a must-see attraction. (*Detective Comics* #27, May 1939)

At its peak Gotham has housed eight million souls, although after recent cataclysmic events, the population dipped as low as seven and a half million before rebounding. It's located in Kane County, nicknamed Gotham County given the disproportionate size of the city to the county boundaries. To the northwest is Ferris County; Washara County also abuts Kane County. Hudson County lies north of Gotham, and Rockland County is north of that.

The city boundaries cover twenty-five square miles along the eastern seaboard, divided into communities and regions that each have their own

distinct flavor. Cutting through all of them, though, is the wicked, sharp wind during the winter months, nicknamed the "razor" by the residents. From atop the Metro Building in METROPOLIS, Gotham City is visible across the bay. The countryside surrounding Gotham City is unlike the suburbs of other metropolitan areas: Within fifteen miles of the downtown skyscrapers there are pleasant farm-like estates—acres of parkland—and not a few turn-of-the-twentieth-century mansions, among them WAYNE MANOR and famed magician Zatara's Shadowcrest.

The city was known for its strong architectural style, veering toward the Gothic, but always visually arresting. During the 1940s Gotham was considered one of the most exciting, vibrant cities on the East Coast, eclipsing, in some minds, Manhattan. Other architectural marvels included buildings shaped like cash registers, blenders, and toasters. Daniel McKinley wrote a book on the novelty buildings, published by Signal Publishing, a division of WAYNE ENTERPRISES.

Frank Lloyd Wright, the renowned architect, noting the unique architectural style, called Gotham a "Jotunheim" after the land of the giants in Norse myths, claiming that the city was designed for a race of giants—but not for people. The people of Gotham, in their customary style, have turned the criticism into a perverse compliment.

The mad criminal HUMPTY DUMPTY unintentionally created a domino effect that caused many of Gotham's giant rooftop displays to come crashing to the ground. As a consequence, the state senate passed the Sprang Act, which banned such objects from the skyline.

What with all the buildings that resembled giant appliances, the look seeped into local media, and during the first half of the twentieth century giant working-model props were all the rage. Many pieces survived and became collectibles. C. Carstairs Biddle had an enormous private collection until his town house was destroyed during an earthquake. Gotham Metro Studios also housed such props in a warehouse, many of

which were used on the *Gotham Island* television series. The RIDDLER stole some of these props from the Finger Warehouse, which he used on his own show, *The Riddle Factory*. (*Batman: The Riddle Factory*, 1995)

Hollywood's ongoing love affair with crime drama has made Gotham the number one locale for budget-conscious moviemakers who want New York aesthetics at affordable prices, and celebrities who fell in love with Gotham while filming have snapped up the luxurious penthouses that occupy the former hideouts of Gotham's super-criminals.

Historians have determined that much of the land making up Gotham City and its suburbs today was where a tribe known as the Miagani once lived. Millennia ago the tribe, led by Chief Palebear, rose up against the fiery shaman Blackfire. Failing to kill him, they entombed him in a cave, marking the location with a mystic totem. When the crops began to die, the tribe felt it was due to Blackfire's ill will. They abandoned the area, seeking a new home, only to come into conflict with another tribe and be virtually wiped out. (*Batman: The Cult* #1, 1988)

Some five hundred years ago an unnamed man and woman became the first Caucasian settlers in the now abandoned region. On their first night, he got drunk during the celebration, killing his spouse and giving rise to a demon named Gothodaemon, said to have been raised by the demon Asteroth and subsequently slain in modern times by Etrigan the demon. (*The Demon* [second series] #44–45, February–March 1994)

Dutch settlers first arrived in 1609, surprised to find no Native Americans in the vicinity. Given the uninhabited territory, the colonists divided their resources, setting up homes both by the sea and farther inland where there would be ample space for farming. The farmers unwittingly settled the cursed land where the Miagani had once lived. While digging a field, the tomb of Blackfire was unearthed, releasing the still-living shaman. (*Batman: The Cult* #1, 1988)

A different legend persists about Gotham's founding, imitating the legend of Manhattan to make the city more palatable to certain tourists. This legend has it that the Algonquin Indians sold the site in 1624 to European settlers for twenty-four dollars' worth of trinkets. (*Detective Comics* #468, March/April 1977)

By the 1650s Gotham colony was well established. A Father Knickerbocker distinguished himself by this time and was regarded as the symbol of Gotham City. Also during this period, frontiersman Jeremy Coe often disguised himself as an Indian in order to spy on hostile tribes. His base of operations was the site known centuries later as the BAT-CAVE. (*Detective Comics* #205, March 1954)

Through the years the growing town became a city and attracted its share of wealthy landowners. Mansion after mansion began to dot the area; among the oldest surviving structures was the Fairbairn Estate. The ancestors who helped develop the town into a city are all buried on the grounds, and the current keeper of the flame is Conrad Fairbairn. (*The Brave and the Bold* #101, April/May 1972)

Gotham celebrated its bicentennial in 1948,

perhaps an acknowledgment of some sort of incorporation or milestone in 1748.

On the 1765 farm of Jacob Stockman, a group of occultists (allegedly including Thomas Jefferson) attempted to summon the demon Barbathos. Panicking at the sight of a large bat, the would-be conjurors unwittingly left a netherworld spirit in limbo. As the entity would later put it before he was finally freed by the Batman, he became one with Gotham, growing as the town grew. "My blood and seed mixed with the mortar, my breath in the mud and the sewers and the buildings great and small. My spirit in every brick, in every inch of timber. The whole city a bent and misshapen echo of my own desolation." The burial site of the demon was the area later known as Stockman's Square, "part of the original old town of Gotham" and encompassed the byways Peterson Lane, Stockman Road, Helfer Road, O'Neil Boulevard, and Raspler Street. (*Batman* #452–454, August–September 1990)

At this point the various realities diverge, with a slightly different Gotham history presented. Historical documents, valid after the CRISIS ON INFINITE EARTHS, indicated that the area later known as Gotham City had been terrorized in the late 1700s by a killer who preceded each murder with a cryptic letter addressed to residents. In his own words, he identified himself as "Epsilpah Clevenger, late of London, England. He is known as the MIMIC for his voice and mannerisms of any he chooses. 'Tis said he has sent over a score of men and women to the hereafter. He is either a madman or possessed by unholy spirits and none may say which, I'll warrant."

Upon his arrival in the United States, the Mimic left a string of victims, the seventh of whom was discovered in the wilderness near the whaling settlement known as BLÜDHAVEN. A mulatto named Hiram discovered the corpse while passing through the area and buried him.

Hiram's report of the murder only enraged Blüdhaven merchant Rance Benedict, who figuratively spewed fire-and-brimstone invectives at the traveler. The latest dead man was Benedict's own brother and Rance struck blow after blow against Hiram, convinced that this was his sibling's murderer for no other reason than because of his African American heritage.

As he left Blüdhaven, Hiram was hailed by a bearded Englishman on horseback who professed to admire his composure during his confrontation with Benedict. Hiram initially welcomed the company but grew more concerned as the stranger's conversation turned to the Mimic and the recent killings. When they arrived in the future Gotham territory, the rider inquired about the framework of a building in the clearing. Hiram noted that it would be a place of worship. The stranger demurred, suggesting the site would be better used as a home to the insane.

Hiram turned down the request as politely as he could, and the two men prepared to bed down for the night. Against his better judgment, Hiram also accepted a gun pressed upon him by the doctor. That night, Hiram awoke to hear a shout of murder and emerged from his tent to see a

stalker approaching him in the torrential rainstorm. Terrified, Hiram fired the gun and watched as the figure collapsed to the ground. An examination of the corpse revealed it to be Rance Benedict. And standing nearby was the doctor, who admitted to having lured the man to the scene.

Pointing out that no one would believe Hiram had killed Rance in self-defense, Epsilpah blackmailed him into concealing the body and agreeing to his earlier suggestion. Hiram complied, and Gotham City's first citizens were the unfortunate dregs of New York and Boston, brought under false pretenses and let loose. Hiram's subsequent whereabouts remain a mystery, but his journal—which concluded with the fateful encounter with the Mimic—eventually ended up in the WAYNE FAMILY archives. Indeed, BRUCE WAYNE later confided in ALFRED PENNYWORTH that one of the figures in the origin of Gotham was his ancestor. Whether that man was Hiram or Benedict or Epsilpah Clevenger remains unrecorded.

Gotham, like so many colonial towns, was devastated by fire in 1785, only to rebuild using more modern techniques. The city grew prosperous from its shipping; it was located in a desirable location for European merchants seeking to reach interior colonists. The Gotham River became an important thoroughfare for trade goods in pre–Civil War America. The Wayne family looked to the acquisition and parceling of land on its road to prominence. Buying acres for pennies, including quite a bit of swampland, Charles Arwin Wayne deftly managed his family's modest fortune and built a thriving enterprise for his two sons, Solomon Zebediah and Joshua Thomas.

During the 1820s, inspired by Josiah Heller, a sect grew in town; members were puritanical in appearance but were drawn to the Dark Arts. Fear and suspicion surrounded the growing organization until the day a child was found dead and a mob blamed the Hellerites. Their settlement was accidentally set afire, killing Heller himself. As he died, he cursed the already cursed ground, prophesying that Gotham's streets would fill with dust from a desert until the inhabitants' sins were cleansed. The remaining Hellerites left Gotham and settled elsewhere. (*The Brave and the Bold* #89, April/May 1970)

In the latter half of the 1800s Judge Solomon Wayne commissioned architect Cyrus Pinkney to design a series of buildings that they imagined would serve as a fortress against the evils of the rest of the world. The first of the so-called Gotham Style structures was in what is now the center of the financial district. Although vehemently criticized by Wayne's fellow Gothamites, the edifice pleased the judge and, in fact, was highly successful in that it attracted others to locate their ventures nearby—becoming the focal point for a thriving financial industry. Together Wayne and Pinkney raised no fewer than a dozen other, similar buildings. Pinkney's style was, for a time, widely imitated, both in Gotham and elsewhere—this despite vilification from virtually every architectural journal in the world. On his deathbed Solomon Wayne said, "I wished to lock evil out of men's neighborhoods and hearts. I fear that

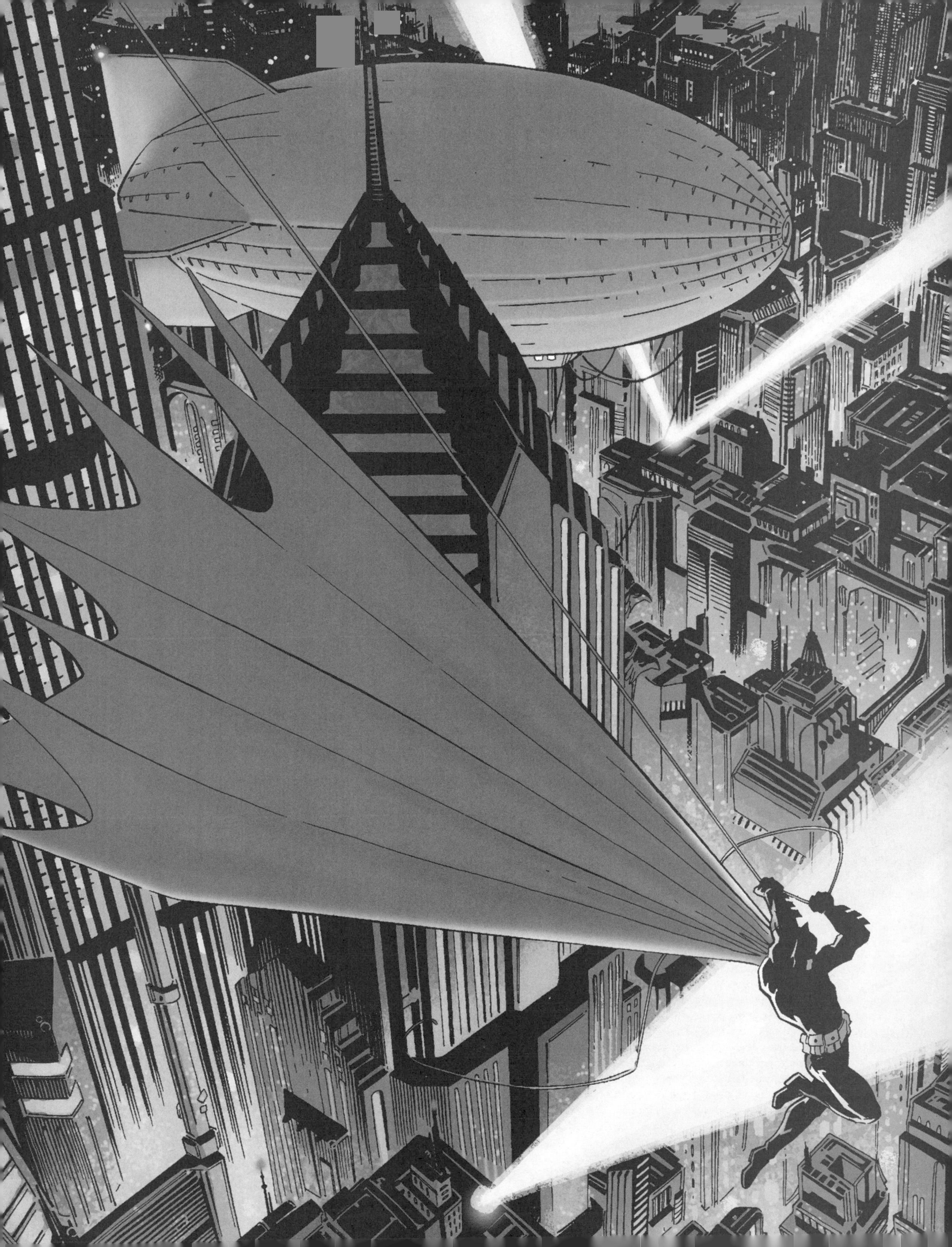

instead I have given it the means to be locked in." (*Legends of the Dark Knight* #27, February 1992)

The Gotham skyline was also noted for the abundance of gargoyles mounted on its buildings, even inspiring art shows devoted to the pieces. By this time Gotham had proven an inspiration to visitors including the poet Lincoln Killavey, who once described Gotham "as if the city itself were an engine whose hot breath rained soot and despair upon its immigrant workers." (*Batman: Gotham Knights* #42, August 2003)

In the nineteenth century, during a wave of immigration, ethnic gangs formed to rule the streets, ranging from the Irish Wounded Ravens to the Italian East-Siders not to mention the Free Men Gang, Jewish Sons of David, and the All-Americans. They kept their streets safe, plundered other streets, and fought. One day, to hide which gang killed Jeremiah Whale, a killer emerged wearing a mask. Soon, entire gangs were masked, and then masks replaced ethnicities as marks of distinction. Many families fled Gotham in the wake of the masked gangs and the modern-day grotesque costumed villains were considered direct descendants of these street gangs. (*Gotham Underground* #2, January 2008)

By the turn of the twentieth century, Gotham was described as "an eclectic train wreck of undisciplined architectural aegis that regularly frightened pets and small children." Despite the tourist bureau's best efforts, Gotham came to have the same mythic quality to it as, say, Transylvania. This was not to say tourists didn't travel there, but that they usually came for the ghoulish dice-roll of seeing if they could live to tell the tale. Try as they did to gloss over a cityscape dominated by glaring stone gargoyles and cryptic, menacing archways, where the symbol of the bat was projected regularly and in huge dimension high above the menacing spires, Gotham's strongest selling point was also its most obvious descriptor: "Mickey Mouse doesn't live here." (*Green Lantern: Sleepers* Book Three, 2005)

As in other cities around the country, the move toward Prohibition fueled the underworld, which led to an entrenchment of mob families that persists to this day. A period of economic uncertainty began during the Depression; basic infrastructure was ignored, beginning the city's decline. A bright spot during the 1940s was the arrival of Green Lantern, the emerald crusader who battled the first generation of costumed criminals.

Following Green Lantern's disappearance in the early 1950s, after he refused to unmask before the Joint Congressional Un-American Activities Committee, things seemed to quiet down. Then came a vigilante dressed similarly to the Grim Reaper and meting out violent justice. This spurred Green Lantern to come out of retirement, only to be thrashed by the Reaper. Gotham's citizens cowered for a time until the attacks mysteriously stopped.

The city's decline continued for the next few decades as fashionable areas, such as Park Row, fell into lawless hands. Criminals ruled the streets, and the mobs had effectively neutered the police force through years of bribing policemen and judges. The nadir may have been when respected millionaire

Thomas Wayne and his wife Martha Wayne were killed on Park Row—now nicknamed Crime Alley.

Then things began to change for Gotham when a caped vigilante took to the streets. Batman was long thought to be an urban legend, a smoke screen for a revitalized police force to hide behind or a media sensation for ratings and newspaper sales. In more recent times the myth was solidly shown to be fact, and citizens took pride in their protector and his cohorts. Batman, Robin, Batgirl, and others have been counted on time and again to stem the tide from the insidious mobs and psychopathic killers ranging from the colorful but homicidal Joker to the deadly Mister Zsasz.

Much time has been spent debating over whether Batman is a response to the growing tide toward psychotic criminals, or whether his arrival brought them to Gotham. Regardless, the city suffered some of the greatest tragedies to befall America as a result of these villains. A chain reaction seemed to have been sparked by Rā's al Ghūl's release of a deadly virus nicknamed the Clench, which claimed hundreds of lives. Soon after a cure was administered to a needy populace, the city endured an earthquake measuring 7.6 on the Richter scale. Fatalities were estimated from a low of 5,057 to a high of several hundred thousand. The fault that caused the Gotham earthquake ran from Spillkin Hill across the harbor to Chalfonte and through the heart of Gotham. The earthquake caused billions of dollars in damage, including the destruction of Wayne Manor, which was located less than a mile from the epicenter. Haphazard construction was demolished, revealing older structures that had been covered over. During the rebuilding process, the face of Gotham changed to something older and more eccentric, befitting the city's reputation for architectural variety.

The federal government, frustrated over wasting countless dollars on reconstruction, was encouraged by the political maneuverings of Nicholas Scratch to effectively cut the city off. Citizens were given until midnight on December 31 to leave before bridges and tunnels were sealed off. The city became a virtual No Man's Land with gangs, citizens, and super-villains staking out turf. The police, under James Gordon, maintained what peace they could until Batman reappeared, three months into the ordeal. Gordon, Batman, Robin, Nightwing, Oracle, and a new Batgirl slowly began to retake the city, street by street. Meantime, Lex Luthor was manipulating the situation to his advantage, hoping to own the majority of the city whenever the government came to its senses and reopened Gotham. Bruce Wayne outmaneuvered his business rival, but it was Batman who ensured that Gotham would remain intact when he thwarted the Joker's deadly Christmas bombing. However, to save one infant, Gordon's wife Sarah Essen Gordon sacrificed her life to the Clown Prince of Crime.

Gotham recovered and rebuilt, only to endure a continuous stream of super-villains, madmen, and opportunistic thugs. The streets were home to violent War Games, accidentally triggered by Spoiler, which led to Black Mask ruling Gotham's underworld with a deadly hand. This chased veterans including the Penguin from the city. After Black Mask was

killed, the Great White Shark proved to be an even deadlier master of crime and corruption. The city also endured the explosion of the fabled Rock of Eternity over the skyline, remnants of which had deleterious effects on some of the citizens.

A year later Intergang installed a series of drills from Apokolips, designed to turn first Gotham, then the Earth, into a fire-pitted planet resembling the homeworld of the New God Darkseid. Intergang's leader, Bruno Mannheim, did this following the instructions found in the Crime Bible, which foretold that the twice-named daughter of Cain—in this case, Kate Kane, the new Batwoman—needed to be sacrificed to bring about the book's prophecy. Nightwing and the new Question, Renee Montoya, stopped both the sacrifice and the city's destruction, but not before more damage was done to the recently rebuilt metropolis. (*52* #48, 2007)

The city had a particularly high turnover of mayors, largely due to its lengthy history of corruption in addition to the dangers posed by the costumed criminals who called Gotham home. Aubrey James was mayor just before Thomas and Martha Wayne were murdered by Joe Chill. James was subsequently stabbed to death. At the time Batman debuted in Gotham, the mayor was Wilson Klass. A mayor named Hayes served the city during Batman's existence. (*Batman* #207, December 1968). When political boss Rupert Thorne seized control of the political machine, he saw to it that Hamilton Hill became the next mayor, beating Arthur Reeves. (*Detective Comics* #511, February 1982) Hill did as he was bade by Thorne, which made Gordon's and Batman's lives complicated. George P. Skowcroft served as Gotham's acting mayor in the aftermath of Hill's forced resignation. The next, unnamed mayor and the entire Gotham City Council were murdered by Joseph Blackfire's followers. Several briefly tenured mayors followed until Mayor Lieberman settled into office; then he was abruptly replaced by an unnamed man. (*Batman: Run, Riddler, Run* #1, 1992) Armand Krol next assumed the office and began his tenure with an intense dislike for Batman. (*Detective Comics* #647, August 1992) The Dark Knight saved his life and Krol changed his opinion, relying more on the vigilante than had Gordon and his men. Krol lost the next election to Marion Grange. (*Batman: Shadow of the Bat* #46, January 1996) She assumed office early when Krol succumbed to the Clench virus that gripped Gotham at the time. Grange ably served the city through the end of the Clench and right up until the federal government declared the city a No Man's Land. She died from an assassin's bullet. Daniel Danforth Dickerson III (*Detective Comics* #743, April 2000) succeeded her until he, too, was assassinated by the Joker. David Hull was the city's next mayor. (*Gotham Central* #15, March 2004) In the wake of Infinite Crisis, records indicated that the new mayor was an as-yet-unidentified woman.

GOTHAM CITY POLICE DEPARTMENT, THE

Gotham City's police department had a reputation for corruption dating through the majority of the twentieth century—more so in the later years. The corruption stemmed from the mayor's office and continued throughout the law enforcement and judicial branches of the city government.

When CARMINE "the Roman" FALCONE ran Gotham's underworld, the commissioner of police was GILLIAN B. LOEB, who steered his officers away from interfering with the Roman's operations. (*Batman* #404, February 1987) After Loeb left office, he was replaced by JACK GROGAN. (*Batman* #407, May 1987)

JAMES GORDON succeeded Grogan and served for a lengthy period until politics reared its ugly head. In short order Peter Pauling, ANDREW HOWE, and SARAH ESSEN GORDON briefly took on the commissionership before Gordon was repeatedly restored to his office. When he finally chose to retire, MICHAEL AKINS succeeded him. Akins left office under unrevealed circumstances, and six months after Batman left the city for a year, Gordon returned to his office. (*52* #33, 2007)

Back in Loeb's day, things began to change for the better when an honest cop, Gordon, transferred from Chicago and a costumed vigilante, Batman, both began to patrol the city's streets. They worked at exposing the rampant corruption and ultimately forced Loeb to resign from office in disgrace.

Gotham City, for years, was known for its corrupt police force and its high turnover in district attorneys. This, too, began to change after Batman arrived. The crusading district attorney at the time was HARVEY DENT, although he was attacked by a criminal and was physically and psychologically harmed. As TWO-FACE, Dent murdered his immediate successor, Aldrich Meany, although other accounts name the victim as Judge Lawrence Watkins.

Dent and Meany were followed in rapid succession by JANICE PORTER, a man named Barnes, John Danton, and David Stevens, onetime assistant to Dent. Stevens had actually married Harvey's ex-wife GILDA DENT. When Stevens was murdered, Dent tracked down the killer and took his life. Other DAs to lose their lives included Dick Jaynes, ARMAND KROL, and MARION GRANGE, the latter two after they'd moved up to serve as Gotham's mayor.

Aubrey James was mayor in the years preceding THOMAS and MARTHA WAYNE's murders. James was himself stabbed to death, and his chief of police, Hendrik Petersen, was fatally shot in the same general period. When Batman debuted some seventeen years later, the mayor of Gotham was Wilson Klass. Like being district attorney, serving as mayor was usually a short-lived phenomenon due to the rampant corruption and virulent crime dating back to GREEN LANTERN's tenure as the city's protector.

While Gordon developed a strong respect for Batman and his efforts, the rest of the police cast a suspicious eye in his direction. For years Batman was real to them but an urban legend to the city's citizens. When the BAT-SIGNAL was first used to summon the Dark Knight, the populace thought it was a scare tactic directed toward the city's criminal element. Given the legal implications of the city's police summoning a vigilante, only a civilian could legally activate the signal, a role most recently filled by STACY. (*Gotham Central* #11, November 2003)

FIRST SHIFT

CAPTAIN MAGGIE SAWYER
First shift commander; formerly head of Metropolis Special Crimes Unit.

SGT. VINCENT DEL ARRAZIO
First shift commander; First shift second-in-command; partner of Joely Bartlett.

DETECTIVE TOMMY BURKE
Partner of Dagmar Procjnow.

DETECTIVE ERIC COHEN
Partner of Andi Kasinsky.

DETECTIVE ANDI KASINSKY
Partner of Eric Cohen.

DETECTIVE JOSEPHINE "JOSIE MAC" MacDONALD
Has the distinction of being the first MCU officer selected after Jim Gordon's retirement.

SECOND SHIFT

LT. DAVID CORNWELL
Second shift commander.

SGT. JACKSON "SARGE" DAVIES
Second shift co-second-in-command; partner of Crowe.

LT. RON PROBSON
Second shift co-second-in-command.

DETECTIVE TREY HARTLEY
Partner of Josh Azeveda.

DETECTIVE NATE PATTON
Partner of Romy Chandler.

POLICE SUPPORT

COMMISSIONER MICHAEL AKINS
Former commissioner for Gateway City, replaced James W. Gordon.

Gotham's long-standing crime families fought for turf with a rising tide of costumed criminals, and the police department had to respond accordingly. A MAJOR CRIMES UNIT was founded to specialize in such cases, first headed by Sarah Essen Gordon and MACKENZIE BOCK. Since then, it has been led by former METROPOLIS cop MAGGIE SAWYER. The city also created a QUICK RESPONSE TEAM headed by Lieutenant GERARD "JERRY" HENNELLY.

GRADY, "SPARKLES"

"Sparkles" Grady led a criminal gang to the newly opened Batman Exposition, GOTHAM CITY's latest tribute to its protector. Grady wanted the jewels that Rajah Punjab had entrusted to ROBIN, who was representing the Dynamic Duo while Batman recovered from a broken ankle. The Boy Wonder took advantage of the fifty memorials to the Caped Crusader, using the exhibits as crime-fighting

DETECTIVE
CRISPUS ALLEN
Partner of Renee Montoya.

DETECTIVE
JOELY BARTLETT
Partner of Vincent
Del Arrazio.

DETECTIVE 2ND GRADE
RENEE MONTOYA
Partner of Crispus Allen.

DETECTIVE
DAGMAR PROCJNOW
Partner of Tommy Burke.

GOTHAM CITY POLICE DEPARTMENT, MAJOR CRIMES UNIT

DETECTIVE
JOSH AZEVEDA
Partner of Trey Hartley.

DETECTIVE
ROMY CHANDLER
Partner of Nate Patton.

DETECTIVE CROWE
Partner of Sarge Davies.

DETECTIVE
MARCUS DRIVER
Last MCU officer to be selected by former Commissioner
James W. Gordon.

JIM CORRIGAN
GCPD crime scene
investigator.

NORA FIELDS
City coroner.

JAMES W. GORDON
Former Gotham City police
commissioner, and 20-year
veteran of the force. Currently
teaches criminology at
Gotham University.

STACY
Receptionist; only person
permitted to operate the
Bat-signal.

weapons with which to single-handedly apprehend Grady and his men. (*Batman* #104, December 1956)

GRAHAM

Graham was hired by Paragon Pictures to construct replicas of ancient weapons. A head injury left him dazed, leading him to don a medieval costume and use his own replicas to commit crimes in Gotham City. His crime spree was stopped by the combined efforts of Batman, Robin, and Ace the Bat-Hound. (*Batman* #130, March 1960)

GRAMBLY, GENERAL

Grambly considered himself the Napoleon of crime and organized his hirelings as if they were an army. They wore purple uniforms and worked with military precision. He conceived and then executed intricate crimes as if they were war games.

Batman and Robin were joined by Superman in an effort to end the threat posed by the general and his Purple Legion. With a Superman Robot working with the Dynamic Duo, the Man of Steel posed as Tigerman. As they went into action,

Tigerman appeared inept but had some hold over the World's Finest heroes, which caught Grambly's attention. Ordering members of the legion to bring Tigerman to him for questioning, the general was surprised to learn the truth. As soon as he had access to Grambly's headquarters, Superman, aided by Batman and Robin, easily apprehended Grambly and his legion. (*World's Finest Comics* #119, August 1961)

GRANDA THE MYSTIC

Granda was a carnival mystic who used hypnosis to learn the innermost secrets of his customers. He then used this information to blackmail them for huge sums of money. Granda's scheme was finally broken by Batman and Robin. (*Batman* #7, October/November 1941)

GRANEY, GUY

Guy Graney was an underworld leader who stole an experimental "mind ray." He then offered one hundred thousand dollars to the man among his cohorts who could use the device to actually control their nemesis, Batman. Graney wanted Batman to reveal his identity in public, with the intent to ruin his life, but the plan failed as the Gotham Guardian proved too strong for the men and the machine. Graney and his men were corralled by Batman, Robin, and Alfred Pennyworth. (*Batman* #106, March 1957)

GRANGE, MARION

Marion Grange, fifty-two, was a former Gotham City district attorney who was eventually elected to the office of mayor, beating Armand Krol thanks to an endorsement from Batman. (*Batman: Shadow of the Bat* #46, January 1996) She took office in the midst of Gotham being infected with the Clench virus. Her first act was to reappoint James Gordon as police commissioner. (*Robin* #28, April 1996) Grange ably ran the city through the remainder of the Clench epidemic as well as a devastating earthquake. When she was in Washington, D.C., to oppose the government's attempts to cut off support, she wound up shot and killed with a bullet intended for Bruce Wayne.

GRANT, TED

Former heavyweight boxing champion Ted Grant has used his mystically granted nine lives to fight crime as Wildcat and train other heroes, including Bruce Wayne.

GRASSHOPPERS, THE

Batman and Robin were intrigued by money blowing through the nearly deserted streets of Gotham City. The trail took them to a man dressed in a light green grasshopper costume, with antennae on the forehead and glowing green eyes peering out from its shadowy depths. He also wore elfin yellow slippers, green tights, and a yellow-and-white shirt with matching bands on his forearms. His cape separated into wings whose purpose seemed more to complete the effect than to enable him to take flight. Calling himself the Grasshopper, he displayed superhuman abilities matching the insect's attributes. The man taunted the Dynamic Duo, promising to steal their most valued possessions. Sure enough, as they read his note, the Grasshopper managed to steal the Batmobile. Soon after, aboard a yacht, he stole a Batarang and made off in the Batboat with Robin as his hostage.

Batman began to piece together the clues and realized that the Grasshopper was actually twin brothers. He also identified one of their voices as belonging to a member of the yacht's crew, allowing him to trail the man back to the Grasshopper's headquarters. Batman narrowly avoided a hail of bullets as he attempted to rescue Robin. Then, while the duo apprehended the Grasshoppers, Batman received a message that they were merely agents of a deadly villain known only as the Outsider, who notified the Caped Crusader that he and Robin would lose their lives. (*Detective Comics* #334, December 1964)

After a series of encounters with the Outsider, things drew to climax when two men delivered coffins to Wayne Manor. Within, Bruce Wayne was stunned to see mannequins of Batman and Robin with a note promising that he and Dick Grayson would die within the hour. As the Dynamic Duo, they trailed the delivery truck, learning that the passengers were actually the Grasshoppers. They were joined by a third man with the same amazing acrobatic skills, but even these three were no match for Batman and Robin. Delivering the crooks to police headquarters, the duo then trailed radiation from the truck to the Outsider's lair, where they found their opponent. The surprise, though, was that the Outsider was Alfred Pennyworth, their loyal butler, rescued from death but transformed into a twisted version of himself.

A different Grasshopper with an active metagene also operated in Chicago in a similar costume. He committed a series of crimes only to be swiftly apprehended by the third Manhunter. (*Manhunter* #18, October 1989)

GRAVES (1940)

Graves taught art at the exclusive Blake School for Boys. He also worked in cahoots with Blake, the school's headmaster, to run a counterfeiting operation near the school. When Batman and Robin investigated the counterfeit money circulating in Gotham City, Blake was ready to talk. Graves killed him but was subsequently apprehended by the Dynamic Duo. (*Detective Comics* #41, July 1940)

GRAVES (1942)

Graves hosted *Racketsmashers,* a radio and television series that dramatized near-perfect crimes culled from police casebooks from around the country. What no one suspected was that he also headed up a mob that studied these crimes and used them, minus the flaws, as templates for perfect robberies. Batman and Robin exposed the scheme and had Graves and the men arrested. (*World's Finest Comics* #6, Summer 1942)

GRAVIOS, THE

On another continent lived a people in a lost valley. Centuries in the past, the inhabitants had learned how to graft bird wings onto human bodies,

creating an offshoot species of humankind. They were dependent, though, upon a rare substance known only as serum alpha, which was jealously protected in the valley. The Gravlo family was ruthless, and terrorized the nonwinged villagers in the valley. Sandago Gravio journeyed to Gotham City to abduct Batman and Robin and bring them home to put an end to his family's tyrannical ways. Batman agreed to have huge bat-wings grafted to his body so he could battle the Gravios on their own terms. With Robin's aid, Batman battled the evil family and brought them down. Their hold over the valley was broken, and Sandago had the Dynamic Duo returned to Gotham City. Recovering from anesthesia after having the wings removed, Batman wondered if the entire case had been a vivid dream. (*Batman* #82, March 1954)

GRAY

Dean Gray presided over Gotham University and upon his retirement, founded Trouble, Inc., to offer assistance to those facing problems. Sam Slick rented space next to Trouble, Inc.'s, offices and eavesdropped on clients' conversations. He used this information to capitalize on their troubles but was quickly thwarted by Batman and Robin. (*Detective Comics* #103, September 1945)

GRAYSON, CHARLES

Charles Grayson was the laboratory assistant to Earth-2 scientist Robert Crane, who placed his own brain in a robotic body and fought during World War II as Robotman. (*Star-Spangled Comics* #7, April 1942) Charles was a cousin to Dick Grayson, although the exact lineage was never recorded. The youth was thrilled to meet a relative and revealed his identity during a meeting of the All-Star Squadron. (*All-Star Squadron* #24, August 1983)

Years later, Charles developed cancer from a rare brain disease and arranged to have his body cryogenically frozen. When Robotman emerged after decades of being trapped in a collapsed mine, he completed his final mission, then, following Charles's wishes, had his brain transferred to Grayson's body. The lab assistant happily provided a new human existence to his mentor. (*DC Comics Presents* #31, March 1981)

GRAYSON, CLARA

An unnamed woman agreed to wear old age makeup and pose as Clara Grayson, aunt to Dick Grayson. Pretending to be George Grayson's wife, she participated in a scheme to gain access to Bruce Wayne's fortune through an attempted custody battle. The scheme failed, and her fraud was exposed by Batman. (*Batman* #20, December 1943/January 1944)

GRAYSON, GEORGE

George Grayson was brother to John Grayson and uncle to Dick Grayson. He and a woman posing as his wife, Clara Grayson, attempted to gain custody of Dick in an effort to extort one million dollars from Bruce Wayne. George gained temporary custody of Dick, who disliked how he was being treated. Batman, Robin, and Alfred Pennyworth helped

expose the scheme and the court returned Dick to Bruce's safekeeping. (*Batman* #20, December 1943/January 1944)

GRAYSON, JOHN

John Frederick Grayson was a circus trapeze artist, one half of the famed Flying Graysons. He and his wife, Mary Grayson, had one son, Richard, and when he was five, he became a part of the act. When the Haly Bros. Circus arrived in Gotham City, Garrison Haly refused to pay Anthony "Boss" Zucco protection money, so Zucco saw to it that the ropes used by the Graysons were cut. On June 27, performing in a sold-out arena, John and Mary fell to their deaths. A stunned Dick Grayson was approached by the Batman and offered a new life. (*Detective Comics* #38, May 1940)

Grayson was an encouraging father, telling his young son, "If you're sure of yourself up there, you've got nothing to fear." (*Secret Origins* [second series] #13, April 1987) "Sure, it's about bravery, son," John explained. "But that's only a part of it. For the rest you need a strategy. You need a plan, Dick. It's not the next bar. It's the bar after that and the one after that. And so on to the other side." (*Nightwing* [second series] #7, April 1997)

GRAYSON, MARY

Mary Elizabeth Loyd married circus acrobat John Grayson, and together they formed the Flying Graysons, a star attraction at Haly Bros. Circus. (*Detective Comics* #38, May 1940) They had one son, Richard, and when he was five, he was incorporated into the act. She nicknamed her son Robin, noting that he was born on the first day of spring. (*Robin Annual* #4, 1995)

Mary briefly dabbled in a life outside the circus, working as a dental assistant until a meeting with John, "a real full-blooded gypsy," drew her back to her roots. (*Nightwing Annual* #1, 1997) Mary was also troubled by a disturbing incident—a murder that she and John had witnessed while the Haly Bros. Circus was touring the European country of Kravia. (*Nightwing* #3, 1995)

When the circus arrived in Gotham City, Garrison Haly refused to pay Anthony "Boss" Zucco protection money, so Zucco saw to it that the ropes used by the Graysons were cut. On June 27, before the night's performance, the Flying Graysons posed for a photo with young Tim Drake. Watching Tim with his parents, Mary wondered aloud if they were depriving Dick a normal family life. (*Batman* #436, Early August 1989) While performing in a sold-out arena, John executed his triple flip. With her legs curled around the trapeze bar, Mary swung forward and clasped her hands in his. "Nicely done, John." Before he could reply, there was a sickening *snap*. The trapeze ropes had snapped and the Flying Graysons, operating without a net, had only enough time to scream out each other's names.

GRAYSON, RICHARD "DICK"

Richard Grayson was the only son of John and Mary Grayson, the Flying Graysons of the Haly Bros. Circus, born on March 20. (*Detective Comics* #38, May 1940) Mary nicknamed her son Robin, noting

that he was born on the first day of spring. At age five, he began training to join the trapeze act.

The Graysons performed together for three years, enjoying a happy existence. When the circus arrived in GOTHAM CITY, Garrison Haly refused to pay ANTHONY "BOSS" ZUCCO protection money, so Zucco saw to it that the ropes used by the Graysons were cut. Young Dick had overheard the threat but was too scared to act—something that would haunt him later. On June 27, performing in a sold-out arena, the ropes snapped and the adults fell to their deaths. A stunned eight-year-old was approached by Batman and offered a new life.

Dick swore his allegiance and dedication to eradicating crime by candlelight in the BATCAVE and soon after donned a red-and-yellow costume,

joining Batman's crusade as Robin the Boy Wonder. He would never forget his family, returning to visit their graves every year on the anniversary of their deaths.

On Earth-2, Dick fought all manner of criminals, using a slingshot as his weapon of choice. He lived as BRUCE WAYNE's ward, attending public school by day and swinging into action after classes. He was accepted as a member of the All-Star Squadron, the team of super heroes that was formed in the wake of America's entry into World War II. Through the years he grew up and began to study law, earning his degree and beginning a life on his own that saw him spending less and less time in costume. It wasn't until his adult years that he returned to regular action, being voted to replace Batman (complete

in a costume that blended his uniform with his mentor's) as a member of the fabled JUSTICE SOCIETY OF AMERICA. (*Justice League of America* #55, August 1967) Later, he (now in a red-and-green variation on his original uniform), Power Girl, and the Star-Spangled Kid formed a youthful subset of the JSA, the Super Squad, and had many adventures. He and Batman had one final adventure together with the JSA prior to the Caped Crusader's death. (*Justice League of America* #135–137, October–December 1976) Dick eventually joined Cranston, Grayson & Wayne, a legal partnership that included Bruce Wayne and his daughter HELENA WAYNE. In the wake of his mentor's heroic death, Dick began to have feelings for Helena but—rather than act on them—left town. He returned as a prosecutor handling

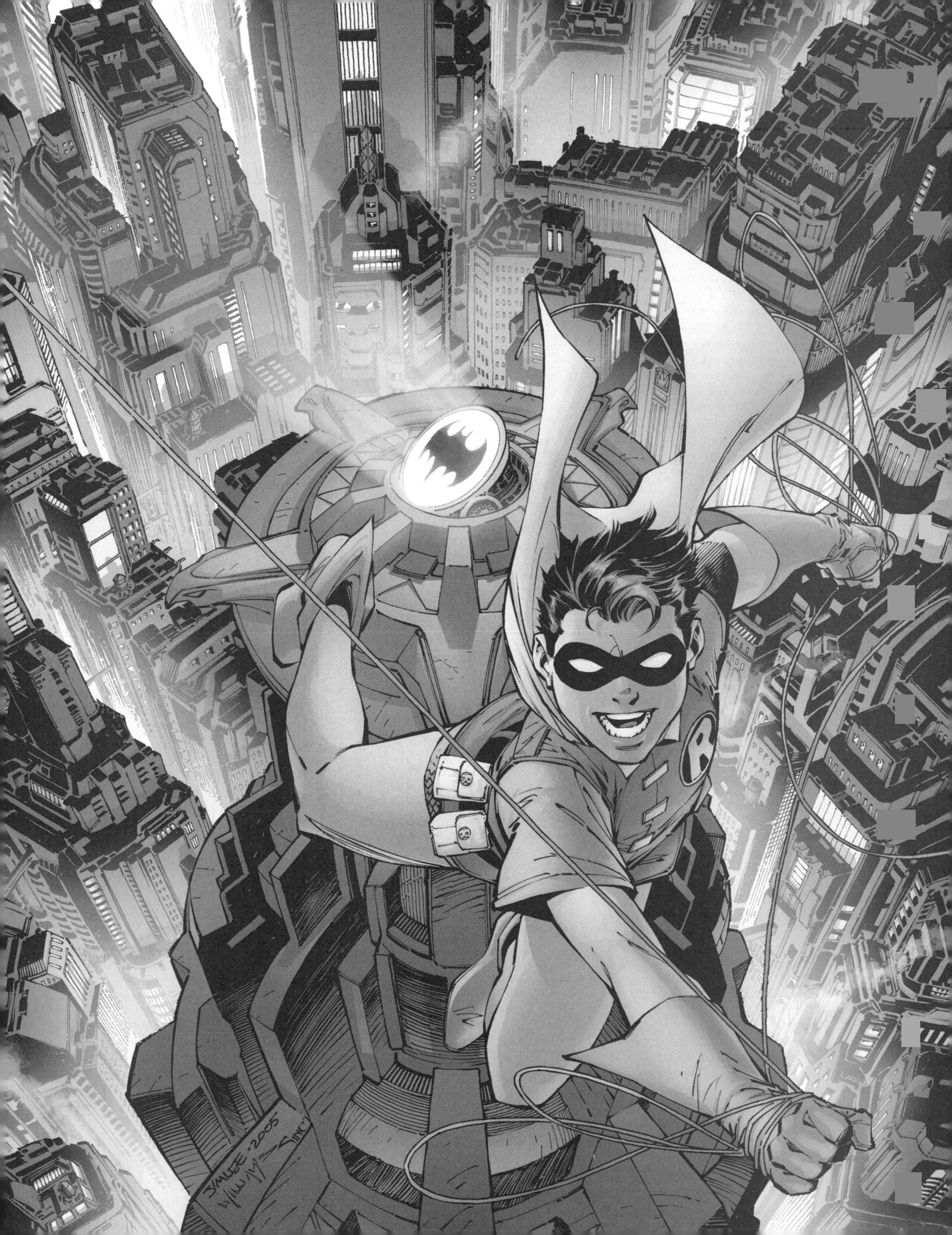

the government's case against the JSA, based on a diary Batman had written, but it was all part of a scheme from the time-traveling Per Degaton. (*America vs. the Justice Society* #1, January 1985) He would fight crime on and off, with the JSA and in partnership with the HUNTRESS, until Earth-2 ceased to exist, dying under a wall of rubble during a cosmic upheaval. (*Crisis on Infinite Earths* #12, March 1986)

On Earth-1, Dick made his first acrobatic attempt at age two, diving off a pile of toys and injuring himself. That was when his mother first nicknamed him Robin and saw that he was going to make his way into the family business. (*Robin Annual* #4, 1995) Grayson remained Batman's ward and fought alongside him in Gotham City. Unidentified nearby relatives approved of Wayne taking charge of Dick despite a judge's reticence, given Wayne's reputation. (*Batman* #213, July/August 1969) He was a founding member of the TEEN TITANS, initially working alongside Kid Flash and Aqualad. (*The Brave and the Bold* #54, June/July 1964) Over time, the ranks of the Titans swelled, and Robin remained the group's natural leader. As he grew up, Dick finally left the comfort of WAYNE MANOR to attend HUDSON UNIVERSITY, pursuing pre-law courses while still fighting crime. (*Batman* #217, December 1969) After a tumultuous semester, he left college to return to Gotham and the Titans. It was some time before the two teamed up to take on a case. (*Batman* #332–335, February–May 1981) Batman by then had taken in JASON TODD, whose parents had died in circumstances remarkably similar to Dick's. (*Detective Comics* #526, May 1983) Dick passed on the Robin costume, welcoming the latest addition to the family. (*Batman* #416, February 1988) Finally feeling the need to establish his own identity, he donned his own outfit, becoming NIGHTWING. (*Tales of the Teen Titans* #44, July 1984)

Dick also tried college again with a single semester at Gotham University but his frequent absences led the school to ask him not to return. (*Detective Comics* #511, February 1982) A short time later, Batman was shot and wounded; Dick assumed the cape and cowl for the first time as a brief substitute. (*Batman* #354, December 1982) Wayne realized that the shadow he cast was inhibiting Dick's development as his own man. Time and again Wayne orchestrated situations or said things that appeared cold but were designed to help Dick come into his own. (*Teen Titans Spotlight* #14, September 1987)

In the reality formed in the wake of CRISIS ON INFINITE EARTHS, one change was that Dick was twelve when his parents died; and a key addition to the June 27 incident occurred prior to the night's performance. JACK and JANET DRAKE asked if their son Tim could pose for a photo with the Flying Graysons. They were in the audience that night, watching in horror as the couple fell to their deaths, but also putting TIM DRAKE on a path that led to his being Dick's successor. (*Batman* #437, Late August 1989)

Young Dick was fascinated by reports of the costumed vigilantes such as Gotham's "batman" and METROPOLIS's SUPERMAN. (*Legends of the Dark Knight* #23, October 1991; #100, November 1997; *Legends of the DC Universe* #6, July 1998)

He playacted the role of super hero with circus strongman Sando. (*Batman* #129, February 1960) Dick continued his training, beginning on his fifth birthday, and his daredevil streak was cause for pride in John and concern in Mary. Later Dick would say, "Dad was right. He taught me to be careful, to know my limitations and never over-reach myself . . . and Mom taught me to keep on trying to extend my reach, by learning about myself . . . my skills . . . my potential. They made it safe to work without a net." (*Batman* #339, September 1981)

Also, immediately following the murder, Dick found and confronted the man who had cut the ropes, getting injured in the process. Batman was nearby and saved the youth from death although Dick suffered a mild concussion. He was taken to a hospital and then placed in a Catholic orphanage. Bruce Wayne couldn't get Dick out of his mind and used his influence to have social services release the boy to his care. (*Legends of the Dark Knight* #100, November 1997) Dick chafed at being in the

mansion, unused to a stable environment after spending more than a decade on the road with the circus. He also resented Wayne's frequent absences, during which he was left behind to be tended to by the "elderly" ALFRED PENNYWORTH. (*Batman: Dark Victory* #8, July 2000)

Dick spent six months training before Batman decided he was ready to join him on the streets and rooftops of Gotham City. When they sought a name, Wayne and Alfred suggested Bat-Boy, Bat-Teen, and Bat-Mite before Dick recalled his mother's nickname. Batman and Robin were born. (*Robin Annual* #4, 1995) Before taking to the streets that first time, though, Dick was asked to undergo a test: He had to elude Batman for one evening. Not only did he succeed, but he also managed to apprehend a criminal, Joe Minette. (*Batman Chronicles: The Gauntlet,* 1997) Immediately after,

the duo dealt with the twin threats posed by TWO-FACE and the HANGMAN.

Much of Dick's career remained the same, although Batman on occasion regretted involving someone so young in his crusade. This occurred first when Two-Face injured Dick early on and later when, in quick succession, Dick was tortured by the cult leader Brother Blood (*New Teen Titans* #21–22, June–July 1986) and shot by the JOKER (*Batman* #408, June 1987). Ordered to quit as Robin, Dick refused, and he returned to the Titans and the arms of his lover, the alien princess STARFIRE. When Batman later repeated his demand that Dick abandon the Robin persona, Dick acceded and took the new identity of Nightwing, based on Kryptonian legends of a crime fighter told to him by Superman. Meanwhile, Batman cast an orphan named Jason Todd as the new Robin, and he soon joined forces with Nightwing to rescue Alfred from KILLER CROC. (*Nightwing* #101–106, March–May 2005)

Increasingly falling prey to the prolonged mental conditioning implanted by Brother Blood, Dick reacted badly to the news that Starfire must marry another man to fulfill a treaty on her home planet. Returning to Earth, he finally fell fully in thrall to Blood before regaining his wits and reconciling with Starfire. Belatedly discovering that BARBARA GORDON had lost the use of her legs in an attack by the Joker, Dick sought her out to tell her he planned to marry Starfire—but instead wound up giving her the news after they'd slept together. Belatedly appalled at his behavior, Grayson recognized he had still not fully recovered from Blood's brainwashing, postponed his marriage to Starfire, and sought out a therapist named Dr. Parker (*Secret Origins Annual* #3, 1989; *New Titans* #57, August 1989)

While Dick approved of Jason Todd being the second Robin, feeling his presence helped keep Bruce Wayne on an even keel, he began to suspect that Jason was a brewing problem. He did not seem to employ the same moral governor Wayne and Dick used. The two never shared any sort of bond or even friendship, but Dick was still shocked when he learned that Jason had been killed by the Joker. (*Batman* #428, 1988) Bruce told Dick he would never accept another partner again. (*New Titans* #55, June 1989)

Batman refused entreaties from Dick and grew grimmer and darker. Dick received another shock when he learned that Batman was aware a hit had been ordered on Anthony Zucco, but did nothing to prevent the murder of the man who had his parents killed. (*Batman* #438–439, September 1989) Dick then decided to dip into his savings and buy the struggling Haly Bros. Circus. He was surprised soon after when Tim Drake turned up, insisting Batman needed his Robin back. (*New Titans* #60, July 1989) Dick agreed to return, as Nightwing, but he found an unreceptive former partner. Eventually Tim convinced Dick and Alfred that Batman indeed needed a Robin and if Dick wasn't going to fill the role, *he* would. In time, Batman agreed to take Tim on, training him to ensure that he would not wind up as Jason had. (*Batman* #442, December 1989) Soon after, Dick was off planet for six months with the Teen Titans, meaning that he missed out on developments with his Gotham City family.

Bane arrived in Gotham and spent weeks orchestrating a plan to weaken Batman. It succeeded, and the villain broke the Dark Knight's back. Rather than ask Dick to replace him, Wayne asked Jean-Paul Valley, Azrael. Dick had to hear of the event from Alfred, who asked him to fill in for Batman on a JLA mission. (*Justice League Task Force* #1–3, June–August 1993) The move hurt his former partner, opening a new rift between the men. With the mad Valley running rampant in Gotham, Wayne asked Nightwing and Robin to join him in defeating the substitute Batman. (*Batman: Shadow of the Bat* #29, July 1994) Nightwing altered his look slightly, pulling his long hair back into a ponytail. Over the next few days, Dick met the new Batcave handyman, Harold Allnut (*Detective Comics* #676, July 1994), and faced Lady Shiva for the first time. (*Robin* [second series] #8, July 1994) Once Bane's threat was ended, Bruce was ready to reassume his role, and Nightwing was there to support him. As Wayne continued to retrain himself, he finally asked Dick to briefly act as his substitute. Dick agreed and worked alongside Tim Drake, beginning a friendship that would deepen with time, turning allies into brothers. It also began to heal the pain between Wayne and Grayson. (*Robin* [second series] #0, October 1994)

Alfred had quit Wayne's employ during this tense period, so Dick traveled to England to convince the family friend to return to his duties at Wayne Manor. (*Nightwing: Alfred's Return*, 1995) He then traveled overseas again to Kravia to investigate whether his parents had been killed because his mother had witnessed a murder there years before. It proved to be a false report. (*Nightwing* #1–4, September–December 1995)

Batman's and Nightwing's suspicions that widow Emily Claire Washburn had murdered her first two husbands induced Dick to romance and marry Emily in the hope that she'd incriminate herself by attempting to kill the heir to the Wayne fortune. The paperwork verifying the marriage was destroyed, and the true killer proved to be Washburn's best friend. She was left reeling by the revelation that her marriage—though never consummated—was a ploy, and refused Dick's offer to remain her husband. (*Nightwing Annual* #1, 1997)

When Wayne was framed for the murder of Madolyn Corbett, Dick again assumed the persona of Batman to clear his name. (*Batman: Shadow of the Bat* #55, October 1996)

Soon after, the discovery of twenty-one corpses with broken necks that arrived in Gotham Harbor, prompted Batman to send Nightwing to the corrupt city of Blüdhaven. Dick quickly became embroiled in a gang war involving Black Mask and his False Face Society—one of its members slashed off his ponytail—and learned that the corruption of the police department extended to chief Francis Redhorn. (*Nightwing* [second series] #1, September 1995) Recognizing the sorry state of the city, Dick decided to stay and clean it up, making Blüdhaven his own. He found an apartment at 1013 Parkthorne Avenue and then got a job as a bartender at a tavern. (*Nightwing* [second series] #4, December 1995) As he started to clean up the city, he battled familiar foes like the Scarecrow and newcomers such as Lady Vic.

When Lucius Fox informed Dick that a trust fund he had been administering as a favor to Wayne was now his, Dick realized he was independently wealthy. (*Nightwing* [second series] #13, October 1997) He rented a separate space and began customizing his own vehicle, the Redbird. (*Nightwing* [second series] #16, January 1998) Slowly he began making headway in his fight against the city's corruption, choosing to attack in two directions—as Nightwing and as a cop, which meant joining the police academy. Nightwing also earned the undying enmity of Blockbuster II, who worked tirelessly to eradicate the hero from his life, employing a variety of costumed vigilantes with little success.

While in his new city, Nightwing was in constant demand by his former teammates, helping reunite the Teen Titans after Cyborg was endangered. (*JLA/Titans* #1, December 1998) He continued to participate in other Titans cases, maintaining his friendships with his peers.

He also befriended his neighbors, including landlady Bridget Clancy, John Law, the former hero

TARANTULA, and even the former villain AMYGDALA, now cured and trying to maintain an honest life. The earthquake that nearly destroyed Gotham also caused collateral damage in Blüdhaven, including Dick's apartment building. He quietly formed Haly Enterprises and he bought the building, ensuring that everyone still had a home. (*Nightwing* [second series] #21, June 1998)

When Gotham City was declared a NO MAN'S LAND, Nightwing split his time between the cities. He graduated from the police academy but was unable to land a position with the force. (*Nightwing* [second series] #41, March 2000) While in Gotham, Nightwing freed BLACKGATE PENITENTIARY from the would-be jailer LOCK-UP but wound up severely wounded. Just as he healed, Dick finally found a place within the police department, partnered with AMY ROHRBACH. (*Nightwing* [second series] #48, October 2000)

Nightwing continued to lead various incarnations of the Titans until a rogue Superman android killed teammates Lilith and Donna Troy. At Troy's funeral Dick declared that he was tired of seeing friends die and disbanded the team, officially ending the Titans. (*Titans/Young Justice: Graduation Day* #1-3, July–August 2003) A few months later, though, Arsenal persuaded him to join a new proactive crime-fighting team: the new OUTSIDERS, who would hunt villains as co-workers rather than an extended family. (*Outsiders* #1, August 2003)

Dick helped expose the Blüdhaven Police Department's rampant corruption, with Rohrbach becoming the new chief. Along the way, she figured out his identity but kept it to herself, respecting the work he did in either uniform. Dick, for his part, thrived on the adrenaline rush both jobs provided; indeed, friends accused him of being an "action junkie." Rohrbach decided to help by firing him from the force.

The war between Nightwing and Blockbuster continued to escalate as the attacks on both sides grew more violent. The total destruction of the apartment complex took their war to another level. Blockbuster declared that he would go after not only Nightwing but also anyone who mattered in his life.

CATALINA FLORES arrived at Nightwing's side, a vigilante in a costume patterned after the Tarantula, and the two fought side by side for weeks until they finally confronted Blockbuster in person. An emotionally and physically exhausted Nightwing stood by as Tarantula aimed her pistol and shot Blockbuster to death. His moral underpinnings shaken, he had her imprisoned for the act and left his city. (*Nightwing* [second series] #97, November 2004) He had Robin and BATGIRL relocate to Blüdhaven in an attempt to cover for him during his absence.

Dick continued to work with the Outsiders, even recruiting his former lover Huntress to fill in when Arsenal was wounded. Later, when he realized Arsenal had been fed information by a disguised DEATHSTROKE—who was trying to use the Outsiders to remove rivals to the Society, a secret band of super-villains—Dick decided to fight back. He took on the persona of Renegade and actually allied himself with Deathstroke to protect his city. At Death-

stroke's request, Nightwing also began training his daughter, the RAVAGER. (*Nightwing* [second series] #111-117, October 2005–April 2006) That lasted until Deathstroke disapproved of the moral lessons that were accompanying the physical training.

At 12:51 AM on a Friday, Deathstroke reneged on the deal as the Society dropped the toxic Chemo on the city, killing 100,068 citizens. Nightwing, Robin, and Batgirl were all out of the city when this occurred but returned to help with the rescue efforts. When Dick attempted to enter the city, he was physically restrained by Batman, at which point he confessed his role in Blockbuster's death. (*Infinite Crisis* #6, May 2006)

Dick paused to finally propose marriage to Barbara Gordon and then went back into action to oppose the LEX LUTHOR from a dead parallel Earth and the Superboy from another reality. He and his world's Superboy went into battle, although the Teen of Steel died, while Nightwing was shocked by raw energy as he saved Batman's life. (*Infinite Crisis* #7, June 2006)

Dick was in a coma for three weeks. When he awoke, Barbara was there. Over the next several weeks she helped oversee his recovery and retraining as his body relearned how to use its muscles. When she deemed him fit, Batman invited Dick to accompany Robin and himself on a world tour where they would retrain together. (*Nightwing Annual* #2, 2007)

After six months, Batman sent Nightwing and Robin back to Gotham City, where HARVEY DENT was left to keep the citizens safe. While back home, Dick encountered a new heroine, BATWOMAN, and he provided help to her now and again, including giving her a prized BATARANG for Christmas (*52* #33, 2006)

Dick chose to relocate to New York, only to discover that a resurrected Jason Todd was masquerading as a vicious Nightwing. The two tussled time and again until Nightwing chased a resentful Jason out of town. (*Nightwing* #118-125, May–December 2006) He also helped the Outsiders during their one-year undercover efforts overseas before he returned to work with them on a regular basis.

Dick returned to Gotham to help former cop RENEE MONTOYA and Batwoman stop INTERGANG from incinerating the city in order to unleash demonic forces. (*52* #48, 2007)

Back in Manhattan, Dick took a job at a local gym, putting his training to good use while continuing to battle crime as Nightwing. (*Nightwing* [second series] #126, January 2007)

Handsome and gregarious, Dick was always desired by girls as he grew up. He was comfortable around them, thanks to essentially growing up with Donna Troy as a sister.

His first serious romance came the first time he declared his independence and left Batman's side. Making his own way in Manhattan, he took up with a slightly older woman named Liu, who became his first lover. (*Nightwing* [second series] #133, August 2007) She wound up taking advantage of his passion to have Dick help her and a friend, Metal Eddie, commit crimes; then she abandoned him, destroying him emotionally. He never talked

about her, because he felt horribly used by her (*Nightwing* [second series] #137, December 2007); the experience colored all his relationships after. It also established a pattern of the sort of women Dick dated following Liu: those with pedigrees blatantly tied to law enforcement, including LORI ELTON, the daughter of NEW CARTHAGE's police chief, and Barbara, Commissioner JAMES GORDON's niece and a heroine in her own right.

At the same time, the trauma of his relationship with Liu left Dick too emotionally guarded to really commit to either woman. Lori was so appalled by Dick's seemingly cold, clinical reaction to the murder of a classmate before their eyes that she broke up with him. (*Batman Family* #18, June/July 1978) On the rebound, Dick hooked up with Barbara, who was in a similar funk after losing her congressional reelection. Unable to commit, Dick suggested that their respective states of mind might have led them down an unwise path and that they ought to spend some time apart. So Dick started dating the boring Jennifer Anne and Barbara began briefly seeing Jim Dover.

He almost immediately began his longest relationship, that with Princess Koriand'r of Tamaran. Fighting together in the Teen Titans, they quickly were attracted to each other, and their passion was as explosive as one of her starbursts. They nearly married until circumstances and then distance kept them apart. He did engage in several noteworthy one-night stands, including one with HELENA BERTINELLI, the Huntress. (*Nightwing/Huntress* #2, June 1998)

The true love of his life remained Barbara Gordon. A crush that started when he helped train her in her early days as Batgirl flared to a real romance as the difference in their ages diminished in importance. They considered their first date dinner after apprehending CRAZY QUILT and remained mainly flirtatious for years thereafter. Romance flowered briefly after Dick's breakup with Lori Elton—as indicated by a photograph seen in his apartment (*Nightwing* [second series] #43, May 2000)—but came to nothing when Barbara discovered Dick's interest in Starfire. Meeting Barbara for the first time in her wheelchair, Dick made love to her that night and then he broke her heart the next morning by announcing his engagement to Starfire. It was years before they went out again, a memorable night at the Haly Bros. Circus. (*Birds of Prey* #8, August 1999) Even though he finally proposed before being severely injured, when he awoke Barbara returned the ring and said she was not ready to marry. When Dick left to accompany Batman on a journey of renewal, he left the ring behind—along with a note implying that the time would again be right, and they would continue the romance. (*Nightwing Annual* #2, 2007)

Dick's closest friend was Wally West, the third FLASH, with the two sharing an annual vacation that lasted through their teens until West vanished from existence. (*The Flash Plus* #1, January 1997) Most of the founding members of the Titans remained his close allies and friends, considering their common frame of reference. Donna Troy was probably the person he was most comfortable with and the one who would never hide the truth from him.

Dick was comfortable around other heroes, and his personality—coupled with his training—made him a natural leader; hence his repeated role as captain for the Teen Titans, the Outsiders, and even briefly the Justice League of America. (*JLA* #68–76, September 2002–February 2003) At one point, he learned that when Green Lantern Abin Sur crashed on Earth and was dying, his ring considered Dick Grayson as a replacement—but he was too young at the time. (*Action Comics Weekly* #642, March 14, 1989) His connections among the super-hero community and his self-confidence easily earned him trust from his heroic peers.

Since his parents began training him at age five, Dick was a natural athlete who had mastered one skill after another. Early on his mastery of the quadruple somersault was a trademark move. In addition to his acrobatic skills, the five-foot-ten, 175-pound athlete favored many forms of martial arts, including aikido, jeet kune do, and escrima. Batman's own training left Dick an above-average hand-to-hand fighter and excellent criminologist. Dick also was taught English, French, Spanish, Russian, Japanese, Mandarin and Cantonese, and some Romany. He excelled as a tactician and field leader—one area in which he probably surpassed Batman.

As Robin, his outfit was designed for maximum flexibility with a modified Utility Belt containing pouches with an array of tools from Batarang to climbing line. As Nightwing, his evolving uniforms have been made with Nomex fire-resistant, triple-weave Kevlar-lined material. His face mask contained multiple lenses and a radio transceiver. Rather than a belt, Nightwing favored a series of compartments in both gloves and boots providing him access to flares, a rebreather, a GPS, lock picks, first aid, flexi-cuffs, a halogen flashlight, and listening devices. As a security precaution, the entire outfit was wired to emit a single-use taser charge. The most often-used tool in his arsenal is a set of Escrima sticks fashioned from unbreakable polymer that can be used offensively or defensively.

GREAT EAGLE

Great Eagle was a Native American who fought crime on his reservation in the guise of Chief Man-of-Bats. His son, Little Raven, was said to uncannily resemble Dick Grayson. (*Batman* #86, September 1954)

GREAT SWAMI, THE

"Mugsy" Morton went by several aliases, including the Great Swami, but he was known by most as the Phantom Bandit.

GREAT WHITE SHARK, THE

Warren White, known as the Great White Shark for his work in the business sector, pleaded insanity to avoid a conviction for a white-collar crime. He figured a stay at Arkham Asylum beat time at Blackgate Penitentiary. White was in for a shock when he entered the facility, enduring torture at the hands of Jane Doe. The time White spent locked in a refrigeration unit left his skin pale white, and his facial features were damaged by frostbite. (*Arkham Asylum: Living Hell* #1–6, July–December 2003)

White used his business connections to fence for his fellow criminals and then parlayed those

new affiliations to usurp control of Gotham City's underworld in the wake of Black Mask's murder. He killed villains associated with the Penguin, pinning the blame on Harvey Dent, who was left to protect the city while Batman spent a year away. (*Batman* #654, August 2006)

GREEN, EVA

Eva Green was a mercenary partnered with Holly Wood, and in the employ of Jason Woodrue. Together they freed Poison Ivy, a former student of Woodrue's, from Arkham Asylum. At the same time, a new breed of marijuana was being sold throughout Gotham, coming to the attention of Batman. The marijuana was grown directly by Woodrue, the Floronic Man, who sought to raise ten million dollars, which he offered to Ivy in exchange for her poison-resistant blood—which he wanted in the hope of creating a new life-form. When Batman interfered, Green and her partner subdued him. Ivy helped free Batman since she wanted nothing to do with Woodrue and his scheme. Batman easily apprehended Green and Wood before dealing directly with Woodrue. (*Batman: Shadow of the Bat* #56–58, November 1996–January 1997)

GREEN, RACHEL

Rachel Green, an attorney hired by Bruce Wayne, first assisted him in the adoption of Dick Grayson. The attractive blond lawyer also appeared in court against the Penguin and defended Wayne when he was accused of murdering Vesper Fairchild. She offered her services, on Wayne's tab, to co-defendant Sasha Bordeaux, but Sasha refused help. Later Green stepped in, at Wayne's request, to defend Detective Renee Montoya, who had been framed for murder by Two-Face. (*Batman* #585, January 2001)

GREEN ARROW

Millionaire Oliver Queen was stranded on a desert island on Earth-2 and taught himself to use a bow and arrow to survive. After his rescue, he decided to use his newfound skills to battle crime as the Green Arrow. Soon after, Queen adopted Roy Harper, who

fought alongside him as Speedy. (*More Fun Comics* #73, November 1941) He was a founding member of the Seven Soldiers of Victory and served alongside Batman and Robin in the All-Star Squadron.

On Earth-1, Queen and his ward Roy Harper also battled crime as Green Arrow and Speedy. Green Arrow seemed to base his crime-fighting style on Batman's, complete with Arrowcave, Arrowcar, and Arrowplane. He was the first hero inducted into the Justice League of America after its founding. (*Justice League of America* #5, June/July 1961) In the years that followed, the slightly older Queen grew a social conscience, and after losing his fortune he became an outspoken idealist. He butted heads with his "establishment" counterparts and even vied with Batman for the affections of Black Canary after relocating from Earth-2. He held a variety of jobs, including newspaper columnist, and even ran for mayor in Star City, only to lose.

On the world created in the wake of Crisis on Infinite Earths, Queen became Green Arrow and, as Queen, helped fund the nascent JLA. Still using his patented gimmick arrows, he battled crime and challenged the rigid beliefs of his peers, becoming the team's moral barometer. Whether he lived in Star City or Seattle, Green Arrow maintained a respect for Batman and the two teamed up on many occasions, handling all manner of threats. The key difference between the men was Green Arrow's willingness to kill when he deemed the situation warranted extreme action. (*The Brave and the Bold* #71, April/May 1967; *Batman/Green Arrow: The Poison Tomorrow*, 1992)

Green Arrow died saving Metropolis from a bomb; however, thanks to his best friend Hal Jordan, Green Lantern, his body was resurrected. His soul needed to be rejoined before the body could house a demon, however, and—while it required several ordeals—Green Arrow ultimately became once more. (*Green Arrow* [third series] #1–10, April 2001–January 2002) He returned to protecting Star City and battled criminals, super-villains, and assorted

demons. In time, he chose to run for mayor, winning for a single term. His on-again/off-again romance with the Black Canary led to their wedding. (*Green Arrow/Black Canary Wedding Special*, 2007).

In a potential future, Green Arrow lost one arm and remained battling the corrupt establishment of a dark world, coming to ally himself with a Batman who returned from retirement when the world needed him most. (*Batman: The Dark Knight Returns* #1–4, 1987; *Dark Knight Strikes Again* #1–3, 2002)

GREEN ARROW II

CONNOR HAWKE was Oliver Queen's illegitimate son, though he didn't meet his father until they both coincidentally sought spiritual guidance at the same ashram. Hawke had trained with traditional bow and arrow in addition to a wide array of martial arts. His heritage is a blend of American, Asian, and African influences. (*Green Arrow* [second series] #101, October 1995)

Slowly, Connor acclimated himself to the world beyond the ashram, displaying a charming naïveté that women found incredibly appealing. Accompanied by secret agent Eddie Fyers, Hawke embarked on a series of adventures, establishing himself as the new GREEN ARROW. He even served briefly with the JUSTICE LEAGUE OF AMERICA, proudly filling his father's shoes. Batman used Connor as a supposed traitor to infiltrate LEX LUTHOR's Injustice Gang; the experience was unpleasant, leading to his leaving the JLA.

Among his opponents was LADY SHIVA, the deadliest martial artist on Earth. In a later series of battles with the BROTHERHOOD OF THE FIST, Connor outlasted Batman, ROBIN, NIGHTWING, and BATGIRL, proving himself the world's champion martial artist.

When Oliver Queen returned from the dead, Hawke and his father set up a home in Star City, adventuring together.

GREEN DRAGON, THE

The Green Dragon was a Chinese underworld operation in GOTHAM CITY; members used hatchets to press their point during conflicts. The criminal enterprises they engaged in included murder, narcotics smuggling, and kidnapping. Batman finally chose to bring the Green Dragon down after his friend WONG was killed by one of its agents. During the investigation, ROBIN was captured, but before he could be tortured for information, Batman arrived and the Dynamic Duo put the Dragon to sleep. (*Detective Comics* #39, May 1940)

GREEN LANTERN I

Alan Scott was an engineer who found a magic lantern and obeyed its instructions, forging a ring from a piece of the lantern into a weapon of unimaginable power. Donning a costume, he began protecting GOTHAM CITY as Green Lantern. (*All-American Comics* #16, July 1940) In addition to his solo escapades, Green Lantern was a founding member of both the JUSTICE SOCIETY OF AMERICA and the All-Star Squadron, serving as the former's second chairman. (*All-Star Comics* #7, Winter 1941) The mystic energy that became the lantern and ring had originated as the magical energies of Earth-1, cast by the Guardians

of the Universe to Earth-2, which coalesced into a meteor dubbed the Starheart.

Green Lantern fought a wave of costumed criminals that threatened the safety of Gotham's streets, including the Icicle, HARLEQUIN, and the immortal Vandal Savage. However, in the wake of Communist paranoia gripping America, Green Lantern was among the JSA members who retired rather than reveal their identities to the Joint Congressional Un-American Activities Committee. (*Adventure Comics* #466, November/December 1979)

When a cloaked figure known as the REAPER began a murderous spree, Scott donned his costume for the first time in years, only to see defeat thanks to his rusty reflexes and the Reaper's brutality. Scott chose to remain in retirement for years after. (*Detective Comics* #572, May 1987)

In the wake of Batman's arrival on the streets of Gotham, Green Lantern sought out the new vigilante. After working together on a case, the elder hero agreed that their city was now in safe hands. (*Batman: Gotham Knights* #10, October 2000) Soon after, however, a wave of new super heroes inspired Scott and his JSA peers to return to action. Ever since, the first Green Lantern has served as a mentor for a new generation of crime fighters. After the incident known as INFINITE CRISIS, Scott lost an eye but continued his adventures. He continued to serve the JSA in addition to taking on the rank of White King in CHECKMATE. (*Checkmate* [second series] #1, June 2006)

As Alan Scott, he took a position with the GOTHAM

BROADCASTING COMPANY, rising to station manager and then owner of the company. Scott married his former nemesis the Thorn and they had two children, Todd and Jennie-Lynn, both of whom acquired meta-human abilities. Eventually, he married a second time, to MOLLY MAYNE, the former Harlequin.

GREEN LANTERN II

A race of beings known as the Guardians of the Universe created an intergalactic police force, arming each with a ring that drew emerald energy from a Central Power Battery on their adopted world Oa, set in the center of the universe. Dividing space into thirty-six hundred sectors, they assigned one patrolman to each; these guards were known to all sentient races as the Green Lantern Corps.

The Green Lantern Corps operated successfully for millions of years. Then the Lantern for sector 2814 was mortally wounded and crashed his space vehicle on Earth. Dying, he asked the ring to find suitable candidates to be his replacement. The ring considered many, including a young DICK GRAYSON, but settled on test pilot Hal Jordan. With his dying breath, Abin Sur bequeathed the ring and the mantle of Green Lantern to the human. (*Showcase* #22, September/October 1959)

Learning to use the ring, Hal Jordan became the latest in a long line of intergalactic protectors in addition to being the second hero on Earth to use the name. Additionally, Jordan became a charter member in the JUSTICE LEAGUE OF AMERICA and was hailed around the world for his bravery.

As Green Lantern, Jordan was considered a straight shooter, honest, and filled with integrity. To his masters, the Guardians, he was deemed the greatest Green Lantern of them all and held an honored place among the corps, despite his frequent challenges to their rulings and methodology. He even endured a year's exile in his sector, away from Earth, when the Guardians felt he favored his homeworld over his other responsibilities.

In time, though, Jordan went through a troubled period beginning with the destruction of Coast City at the hands of the alien marauder Mongul, something he was powerless to stop. Mad with grief, he wanted to restore the city and its dead population, but the Guardians forbade it. Seemingly insane—but actually possessed by the living embodiment of fear—Jordan traveled through space to confront his masters, massacring his fellow corpsmen and taking their rings for himself. (*Green Lantern* #48–50, January–March 1994) With so much power, Jordan renamed himself Parallax and attempted to reorder time in an effort to resurrect

Coast City, only to be stopped by his fellow heroes. (*Zero Hour* #4–0, September 1994)

Jordan, seeking redemption for his actions, seemingly sacrificed his life to reignite the sun after a Sun Eater consumed its energy. (*Final Night* #1–4, November 1996) Before going into action, he did use a measure of his energy to help bring his best friend Oliver Queen, Green Arrow I, back to life. Jordan's path was not ended, though, as his spirit became fused with the Wrath of God, the Spectre. As the new host and moral governor, the Spectre worked at meting out justice as Jordan sought to cleanse his soul and achieve peace. (*Day of Judgment* #1–5, November 1999)

Jordan learned that he'd been chosen by the Spectre even though the latter knew that Fear—also known as Parallax—still resided within him. The Spectre had hoped to vanquish Parallax. Indeed, after a fierce battle involving many of Jordan's former friends and heroes, the Spectre managed to emerge triumphant, and Jordan was restored to life. (*Green Lantern: Rebirth* #1–6, December 2004–May 2005)

During Jordan's possession by Parallax, Batman was disgusted by his apparent weakness and betrayal of their heroic ideals. Despite everything Jordan did subsequently, Batman remained skeptical, casting a jaundiced eye even at his sacrifice to save Earth. After learning the truth about Jordan's madness and resurrection, he remained suspicious.

Jordan rescued Batman during the final attack on the Brother Eye satellite. (*The OMAC Project* #6, June–November 2005) But it wasn't until they teamed up to fight the Tattooed Man that Batman finally acknowledged Jordan's redemption. (*Green Lantern* [third series] #10, May 2006)

In one noteworthy alternative universe, it was Bruce Wayne and not Hal Jordan who was summoned to be sector 2814's emerald champion. Still seeking a way to strike fear in the superstitious minds of criminals, he donned an outfit that was a blend of the Lantern uniform and Batman's cape and cowl. (*Batman: In Darkest Knight,* 1994)

GREEN MASK BANDITS, THE

The Green Mask Bandits earned their name for their emerald masks. They were also noted for escaping from their crimes via blimp. Batman and Robin managed to apprehend them with the aid of Alpha the Experimental Man. (*Detective Comics* #307, September 1962)

GREER, HARLISS

Harliss Greer was a crooked politician allied with "Bugs" Norton, a noted racketeer. When Greer was named mayor of an unnamed city in the wake of the elected official's death, he made radical changes throughout the city government. Honest police were replaced with Norton's thugs, and illegal activities such as gambling began to thrive. Upon hearing of this change, Batman and Robin traveled to the city and encouraged the shocked populace. Busting up several of Norton's operations, Batman showed the citizens what one man could do. He roused the populace to fight back, ultimately bringing Greer and Norton to justice. (*Detective Comics* #43, September 1940)

GREGGSON, DR.

Greggson was a research scientist who developed two prototype machines, the "maximizer" and the "minimizer," that could alter the size of common objects. Before he could do anything with his devices, though, they were stolen by the criminal Jay Vanney. Batman and Robin apprehended Vanney and returned the machines to Greggson. (*Detective Comics* #243, May 1957)

GREGORIAN, PAUL

Paul Martin was a popular magician, but his career stalled after some unexplained problems with the police. Martin spent the next decade building and perfecting new illusions and magic tricks, planning a comeback under the name *Gregorian*. He then returned to the public eye, announcing that he was a man with nine lives. Each death-defying stunt utilized his new escape devices and thrilled the people. His shifty brother, "Hoofer," decided the gimmicks were perfect for use during robberies

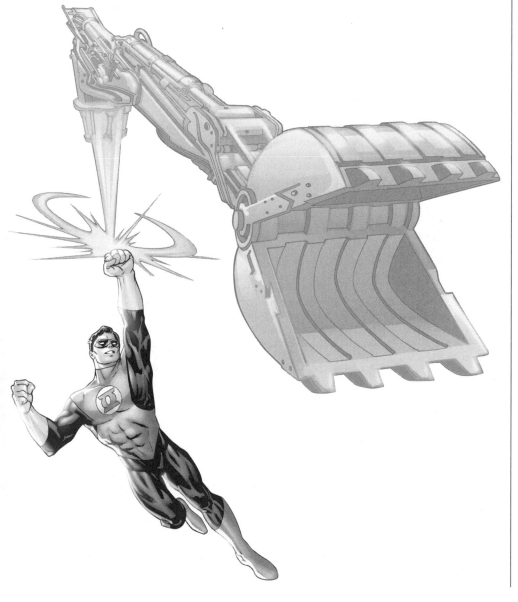

and blackmailed Paul into using them as part of Hoofer's scheme. Batman and ROBIN were on the case and located Hoofer's hideout. When the Dynamic Duo and the police arrived, Hoofer and his men were arrested. Gregorian, trying to escape, died after leaping through a window and cracking his head against an adjacent brick wall. (*Detective Comics* #172, June 1951)

GRIMES, BASIL

Basil Grimes and Ray Arliss were successful architects who teamed up to build an experimental house entirely from shatterproof glass. A steel magnate, fearing the rival material's success, allied himself with the unscrupulous Grimes. Secretly, Grimes aided the steel man in building an all-steel home next door to the glass house. Then the plan called for a series of mishaps to show how unsafe the glass home truly was. Batman and ROBIN intervened and exposed the scheme, apprehending Grimes. (*Detective Comics* #115, September 1946)

GRIMES, ROCKY

Rocky Grimes served a twenty-year prison sentence for bank robbery and murder. He vowed revenge against the five cohorts who'd testified against him in exchange for their freedom. Finally out on parole, Grimes set out to kill the five men, and succeeded in murdering two before Batman and ROBIN found him. Rather than face more jail time, Grimes resisted; in the struggle he accidentally fell off a bridge and died. (*Batman* #13, October/November 1942)

GRIMM

When BLOCKBUSTER II needed a new heart, the ideal candidate was said to be a resident of Africa's hidden Gorilla City. Grimm was captured by Blockbuster after siding with Gorilla Grodd in a failed coup attempt. The tissue match was a bad one, however, so Grimm led a team of super-intelligent gorillas to find a new heart. This action was not seen favorably by Grodd, who disliked any aid given to humans. Grimm fled GOTHAM CITY, presumably to return to Gorilla City. (*Batman Annual* #23, September 1999)

GROFF

Criminals from GOTHAM CITY blasted apart a bank vault using what was later determined to be a missile fueled by R-17, a secret and powerful government creation. The investigation led Batman and ROBIN to the Space Research College to determine how common criminals had obtained such a valuable fuel. Their investigation cast suspicion on the civilian volunteers who were testing space medicine. Upon further study, Batman fingered Groff, who admitted to his criminal past and involvement in the fuel theft. (*Detective Comics* #208, June 1954)

GROFF, JO-JO

Jo-Jo Groff was the leader of a criminal gang when his fortunes changed. He discovered a man—presumably an ancient caveman—freed from a state of suspended animation. Soon Groff realized that this caveman was actually a survivor from KRYPTON who had been trapped within a meteor and only recently crash-landed on Earth. Groff befriended the confused caveman and got his superpowered help in committing a series of crimes. Batman, ROBIN, and SUPERMAN tracked down the criminals and confronted the time-displaced Kryptonian. Once Groff and his men were apprehended, Superman was stunned to watch his countryman die from a combination of exposure to KRYPTONITE and the cosmic rays he had absorbed during his interstellar travels. (*World's Finest Comics* #102, June 1959)

GROGAN, JACK

Edward Peter "Jack" Grogan was GOTHAM CITY's commissioner of police after GILLIAN B. LOEB resigned in disgrace. He was not at all happy to have Batman operating in his city and asked Captain JAMES GORDON to help hunt him down. At some point Grogan left his post and was replaced by Gordon. (*Batman* #407, May 1987; *Catwoman Annual* #2, July 1995; *Batman: Man Who Laughs,* 2005)

GROGAN, MIKE

Mike Grogan was a GOTHAM CITY gangster who worked with a gang in committing crimes. His younger brother Tommy idolized Mike and was allowed to accompany them on the occasional heist. During one such outing at a midtown bank, Tommy was severely wounded. The crooks kidnapped nurse LINDA PAGE to treat him, but the wound required more skilled assistance. While the others were ready to abandon him, Mike would not leave his brother. One of the other criminals fired, mortally wounding Mike, before Batman and ROBIN arrived on the scene. Tommy would be saved—but first Mike made him promise to give up any thought of a criminal life. Mike died, and Tommy left with the Dynamic Duo. (*Batman* #5, Spring 1941)

GROSSET, BLINKY

Blinky Grosset was a smart criminal who conceived of a way to commit crimes in GOTHAM CITY without hindrance from Batman and ROBIN. He anonymously donated money for Gotham to mount a publicity campaign designed to promote Batman and scare off criminals. Then, with the Dynamic Duo off at frequent publicity appearances, Grosset and his men were free to plunder the city. Over time Batman figured out Grosset's scheme, arresting him and his men. (*Batman* #91, April 1955)

GROTE

Grote hailed from a distant world that was bent on galactic conquest. The aliens' long-range plan involved kidnapping early humans from Earth to use as slave labor as they built their war machines to prepare for their interstellar campaign. Grote and his followers assassinated the planetary leaders and attacked. Defending Earth were Batman, ROBIN, and SUPERMAN, who managed to thwart the long-range plan. (*World's Finest Comics* #138, December 1963)

GROTESK

Dr. WAYNE FRANKLIN was a very successful GOTHAM CITY plastic surgeon with society columnists calling him the "Black BRUCE WAYNE." The two met at a charity event, where Franklin thanked Wayne for helping to fund I-Gore, a cybernetic robotic interface that could act as a surgeon's hands even from a great distance. At the same event, Bruce met Dr. AMINA FRANKLIN, the surgeon's sister, and the two briefly dated. Two years later Wayne Franklin was believed killed in a warehouse explosion and fire near the docks. Two days after the explosion, the Omnimed company announced the development of Mimic, a device identical to the I-Gore. Omnimed employee Dr. JAQUI TREMAYNE was Grotesk's first victim. His face was surgically removed and became the first piece of a macabre mask that Franklin fashioned. During his investigation, Batman learned that Franklin was taking investments not only from the WAYNE FOUNDATION but also from a local loan shark, the Russian mob, and the YAKUZA. Franklin was apparently looking to fake his death and abscond with I-Gore without paying off his investors.

Henry Jones, a man being treated at a community clinic by Franklin's sister, Amina, agreed to act as the victim in exchange for a five-thousand-dollar payment to his mother. As Franklin prepared the lab explosion, something went wrong; Jones died, and Franklin was engulfed in flame and ran into the river. Amina rescued him—though he refused emergency room treatment, preferring to test the I-Gore device on himself. Amina was disheartened to subsequently learn that Jones's mother had never received her payment; Franklin needed it for more equipment.

Batman learned that Franklin had Parkinson's disease; this threat to his career as a surgeon had initially spurred his interest in building a remote-controlled surgical machine.

Grotesk infiltrated Zeis Pharmaceuticals, killed Dr. Miles Strayne, and stole his research notes. He later stole the Mimic device, using it to lure both PERUN and JOHNNY KARAOKE, mobsters to whom he owed money for his own project's development. At the Gotham Opera House, the device was dangled as bait, and in a frenzy the mobsters killed each other. During the battle, Batman fought Grotesk, learning that both his arms were prosthetics; beneath both existed deadly weapons of his own design, including a flamethrower and a series of hypodermics filled with various drugs.

Batman finally tracked down Grotesk thanks to information provided by Amina. During their fight, she was injected with an overdose, forcing the Dark Knight to save her while letting Grotesk run free. Before he could get her to medical help, Amina died. Batman followed Grotesk out onto the Gotham East River where they fought aboard a small sailing vessel. It was on a collision course with a barge, and while Batman sprang free, Grotesk was killed during the resulting collision. (*Batman* #659–662, February–March 2007)

GRUNDY, SOLOMON

On Earth-2 wealthy merchant Cyrus Gold was killed, and his body was tossed in Slaughter Swamp just outside GOTHAM CITY. Fifty years later, in 1944, a hulking white-skinned zombie fashioned from Gold's corpse rose from the swamp. The near-mindless creature recalled nothing of his past life and shambled into the city, killing two hobos on

continued to be destroyed and re-created, a pawn in the never-ending battle between heroes and villains. (*Justice League of America* [second series] #6, March 2007)

GRUTT, COUNT

Count Grutt was an international spy who intended to pin the blame for the ocean liner *Ronij*'s destruction on the United States. Accompanied by Elias Turg, the leader, Grutt, set out to plan the attack but was stopped by Batman. During the fight, Grutt impaled himself on his own sword, dying. (*Detective Comics* #37, March 1940)

GUILE, HENRY III

This conceited wealthy would-be actor sought recognition for his talents and took to crime as the GLOBE-TROTTER.

GUNBUNNY

Gunbunny was a female assassin-for-hire who worked alongside her onetime lover GUNHAWK before changing identities to PISTOLERA and joining the all-female mercenary team the Ravens.

GUNHAWK

LIAM HAWKLEIGH was a sharpshooter who became the costumed mercenary Gunhawk. For a time he operated alongside his lover, a woman known as GUNBUNNY. Together they made frequent forays into GOTHAM CITY, where they were opposed by Batman and ROBIN. After Gunbunny went her separate way, a despondent Gunhawk continued to operate, although his heart did not appear to be in his work. As costumed mercenaries went, he was not highly regarded despite his unerring accuracy with firearms. (*Detective Comics* #674, May 1994)

GUNN, FAYE

FAYE "MA" GUNN used GOTHAM CITY's orphans to help her commit crimes as a modern-day female Fagan until she was stopped by Batman.

GURLIN, SIMON

Simon Gurlin led a band of criminals who had the good fortune to be active at a moment of personal crisis for Batman. BRUCE WAYNE's Wayne Motor Company had been struck by an embezzler, leaving the millionaire penniless. As Batman and ROBIN struggled to make ends meet, Gurlin and his men operated without interference. When things grew bleakest, ALFRED PENNYWORTH took to mowing neighborhood lawns and DICK GRAYSON was a newsboy. When they lacked the twenty dollars necessary to repair the BATMOBILE, the Dynamic Duo were reduced to performing at a county fair to raise funds. Despite their travails, the crime fighters did manage to finally apprehend Gurlin and his men. Soon after, the embezzler was located and the money restored to Wayne. (*Detective Comics* #105, November 1945)

the way and taking their clothing for itself. Before they died, they asked his name; all he recalled was "born on a Monday," which reminded them of a nursery rhyme about Solomon Grundy. Once in the city, the newly named Grundy began committing crimes, only to be opposed by GREEN LANTERN I. Given the presence of swamp mixed with organic matter, there was enough wood in his physical composition to make Grundy resistant to Green Lantern's emerald energy. (*All-American Comics* #61, October 1944)

Grundy fought Green Lantern and other heroes for years until he was stranded on the moon for more than two decades. Grundy did eventually find his way back to Earth, only to be opposed again by Green Lantern, Doctor Fate, and Hourman. (*Showcase* #55, March/April 1965) He remained a recurring threat, always managing to escape imprisonment, and once engaged BLOCKBUSTER in a titanic fight. (*Justice League of America* #47, September 1966)

Grundy eventually migrated to Earth-1, where he was pulverized. SUPERMAN's nemesis the Parasite used the residual elements to help create a new

incarnation, which was even more mindless than its predecessor. Too dangerous to remain on Earth, Grundy was taken by Superman to an alien world, leaving behind one of his capes to appease the creature. (*Superman* #301, July 1976)

On the one Earth left after CRISIS ON INFINITE EARTHS, Grundy never left the planet and remained a recurring plague on Green Lantern's career. He kept returning to Gotham City, possibly drawn back to the site of his creation. As a result, Batman met up with him on numerous occasions, beginning with a sewer encounter during his first year in action. (*Batman: The Long Halloween* #12, November 1997)

Years later, it was learned that each time Grundy was decimated and reborn, his persona was altered. Sometimes Grundy was child-like; other times, he was a rampaging monster. During one of the latter incarnations, it took the combined efforts of STARMAN, the FLORONIC MAN, Green Lantern, and Batman to subdue him.

Batman again was confronted by Grundy, this time mind-controlled by super ape Gorilla Grodd, at the behest of President LEX LUTHOR. The Dark Knight had other battles with Grundy, who

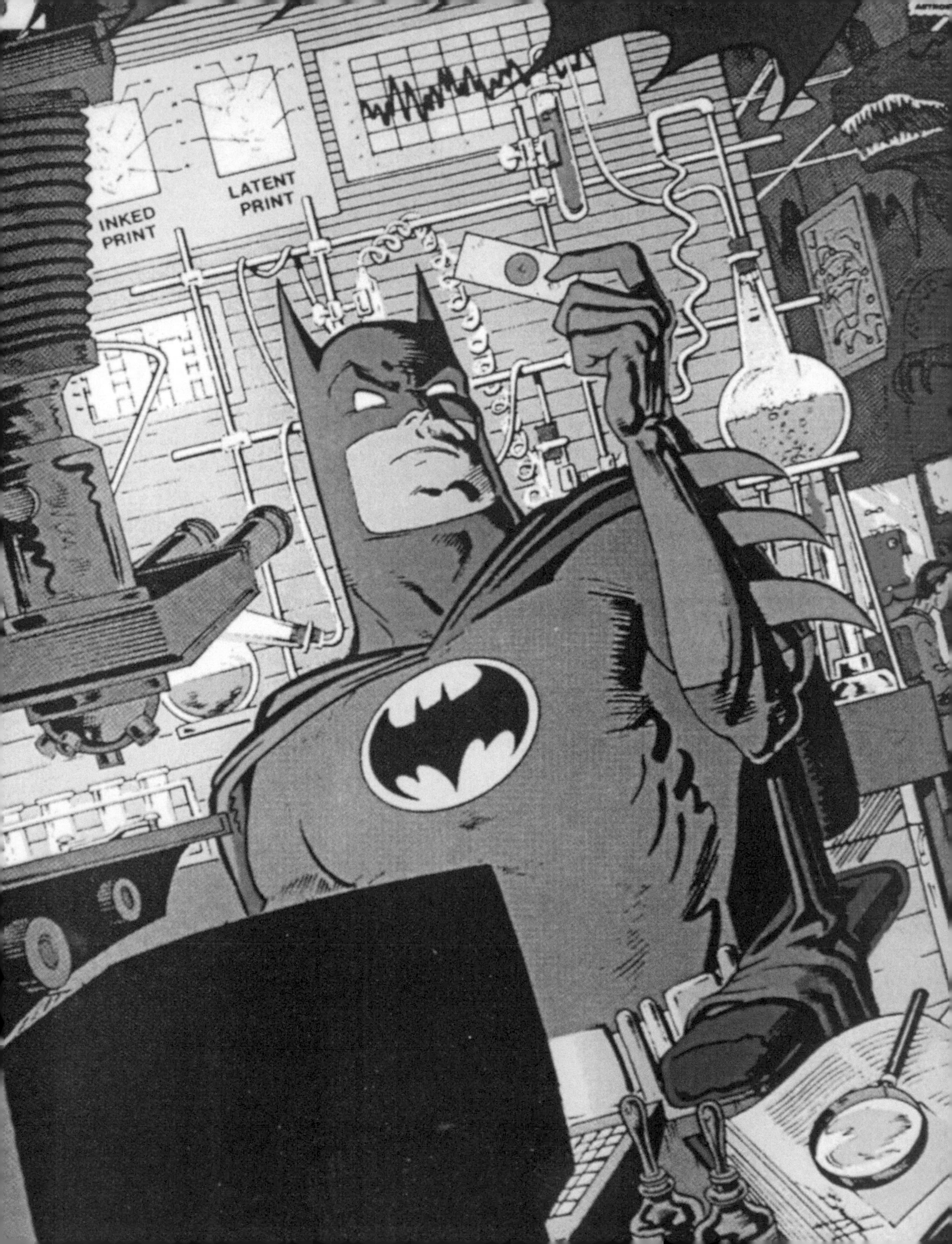

INKED PRINT
LATENT PRINT

HACKETT, AL

Al Hackett was a fugitive on the run from the GOTHAM CITY police and Batman and ROBIN. As the Boy Wonder trailed the Hackett to his waterfront hideout, Batman investigated the criminal's mountain lodge. Upon entering, the Caped Crusader was overcome by fumes emitted by a rare potted plant hailing from the Amazon rain forest. As a result, Batman hallucinated that he had slept for twenty years, awakening like Rip Van Winkle to find a sleeker, shinier Gotham and an adult Robin, now Batman, aided by a blond Boy Wonder. As the fumes wore off, Batman saw his youthful partner, and realized it had all been a waking dream. Robin happily announced that he'd apprehended Hackett while his mentor was incapacitated. (*Batman* #119, October 1958)

HACKETT AND SNEAD

Hackett and Snead ran a circus that needed a boost in attendance. They hired a criminal named Grimes to kidnap a fifteen-foot-tall man nicknamed Goliath, whom Professor Drake believed might be the missing link in man's evolution. Drake, who brought Goliath back from Africa, was easily overwhelmed, and the giant was brought to the big top. Unused to a cheering crowd, he went berserk, threatening the patrons and killing Grimes until he was subdued by a shot from ROBIN the Boy Wonder's slingshot. Batman and his partner apprehended Hackett and Snead for the capture of the innocent behemoth, who was returned to the wild. (*Batman* #2, Summer 1940)

HADLEY, BRASS

The killer Brass Hadley was eluding the police when he suffered a heart attack. The treating physician warned the fugitive that he was afflicted with a rare condition. In fact, only four other men in all of GOTHAM CITY also had the disease, and any serious physical exertion might prove fatal. Hadley, still planning a series of heists that would be rigorous for even a healthy man, decided to use the other four as guinea pigs. He broke into the doctor's office to learn the names and whereabouts of the four similarly afflicted men—but thanks to a records error, one of the men he discovered was actually healthy: BRUCE WAYNE. Hadley had all four men kidnapped, then subjected them to tests to learn how much each could endure. The plan was derailed by the timely arrival of Batman and ROBIN, who freed the three other men, stopped Hadley's henchmen, and then chased the criminal. Hadley, having earlier seen Wayne swim without a problem, jumped into the water, stroking his way to a waiting one-man submarine. The exertion proved too much: Hadley suffered a heart attack and drowned. (*World's Finest Comics* #66, September/October 1953)

HAGEN, DR.

Dr. Hagen was a world renowned expert on weapons and was also the criminal known as the RENTER.

HAGEN, MATT

Matt Hagen was an explorer who found a mysterious chemical substance that transformed him into the shape-shifting CLAYFACE.

HAINER, SERGEANT HARVEY

Harvey Hainer was a longtime GOTHAM CITY police officer. A wound early in his career caused progressively worsening eyesight until he was no longer fit for street duty. Rather than force the man

to face an empty early retirement, Commissioner JAMES GORDON reassigned Hainer to the police headquarters rooftop, where he had the task of activating the BAT-SIGNAL whenever Gordon had need of Batman's help. (*Batman* #85, August 1954) On Earth-1, Hainer held the post for the twelve or so years that Batman was active. (*Batman* #265, July 1975) In the reality after CRISIS ON INFINITE EARTHS, only civilians could control the signal, and Hainer has not been seen.

HALE, PROFESSOR

Hale was the head curator at GOTHAM CITY's Mechanical Museum of Natural History, a huge structure displaying life-like robotic re-creations of all manner of animal life. Hale was found murdered at the museum, and Batman's investigation led him to four suspects: taxidermist Albert Linke, co-worker Mario Nazzara, museum electrician John Logan, and secretary Carl Danton. All had reason to resent Hale, providing motive for the killing, but when Batman realized that Danton was embezzling museum funds, he concluded that the secretary had killed Hale to silence him. The man was quickly arrested for the murder. (*Detective Comics* #255, May 1958)

HALL, HUBERT

When Gotham Movie Studios announced plans to shoot a movie about Batman, Hubert Hall, a career criminal, went into training to win the physically demanding role. Hall wanted the part so he and the rest of "Twisty" Rhodes's gang could plunder the Gotham Mint when scenes were to be filmed there. Unfortunately, after winning the role—given his striking physical resemblance to the Caped Crusader—Hall proved to be a horrible actor. When faced with possible dismissal, he chose to eliminate the competition, forcing the producers to keep him. Once the attacks began, Batman and ROBIN investigated and apprehended Hall and his cronies. (*Batman* #85, August 1954)

HALO

Violet Harper was a teenage runaway, having stolen an experimental formula from crime boss

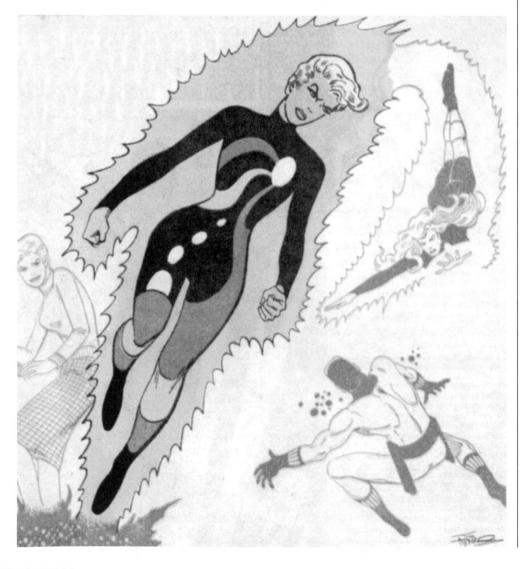

Tobias Whale. With her boyfriend Mark Denninger, she had hoped to raise money by blackmailing Whale from the tiny European country of MARKOVIA. Instead of paying, Whale sent the assassin Syonide after the teens. Harper killed Denninger with an overdose of narcotics as they hid in the Markovian woods. Syonide arrived shortly thereafter and attacked Harper, leaving the teen for dead. Harper's life then took an unexpected turn when the Aurakles, alien beings dating back to the birth of the universe, visited Earth, having grown fascinated with organic life-forms. They spotted Harper and one touched her, which resulted in the alien entity being absorbed by Harper's comatose body. (*Batman and the Outsiders* #20–22, April–June 1985)

When Harper awoke, she had little recollection of her name or her past as the Aurakle exerted control over the body they now shared. As she stumbled through the woods, Harper encountered Batman, who was in country to rescue a kidnapped LUCIUS FOX. She wound up aiding the Dark Knight, and her impressive display of multicolored powers encouraged him to invite her to join him in the formation of the OUTSIDERS. (*The Brave and the Bold* #200, July 1983; *Batman and the Outsiders* #1,

August 1983) Now named Halo, she accompanied the team back to GOTHAM CITY and sought guidance from KATANA, who acted as her mentor. Naming herself Gabrielle Doe, she attempted life in high school in addition to her heroic training under the Dark Knight's watch. During this time, Batman asked JASON BARD to investigate Halo's mysterious background. Bard finally located her parents in Arlington, Missouri, and her real name. Batman, feeling it was the right thing to do, returned Halo to the Harpers. (*Batman and the Outsiders* #16, December 1984)

Unfortunately, Whale learned of Harper's reappearance and once more dispatched Syonide to get her, and the formula, back. During the confrontation, the Harpers died and Violet was captured. Whale hired DOCTOR MOON to extract the formula from the seventeen-year-old's photographic memory, but the doctor found the Aurakle brain-wave pattern instead, which led to Violet learning the truth about her current physiology and the source of her light-based powers. Each wavelength of the spectrum channeled a different power. Red channeled heat beams; orange, concussive force beams; yellow, blinding light; green, stasis beams; blue, a distortion effect; and indigo, a tractor beam. Violet denoted the teen's total control over her body and all the spectral powers.

After she was rescued by the Outsiders, Batman continued probing Harper's condition, which wound up drawing the Aurakles to the JUSTICE LEAGUE OF AMERICA satellite. The Aurakles were convinced to release their hold on Halo, and in the aftermath she chose to leave the team.

With her parents dead and feeling estranged from her team, Halo tried to live on her own. In time, though, she and the Outsiders reconciled. Violet continued to work with them even after they split from Batman and relocated to Los Angeles. During a battle with the intergalactic Manhunter androids, Halo was left comatose. (*Outsiders* #28, February 1988)

Halo eventually recovered and continued to work with the Outsiders until her teammates once more went their separate ways. Soon after, Halo had a fight with the assassin Sanction, and during the battle, the Aurakle leapt from her body to that of Marissa Baron, ex-wife to the villain Technocrat. Violet's body remained near death until it was rescued by the international terrorist KOBRA. He used his technology to revive Violet's body and restore her spirit. Renamed Spectra, she became a member of Strikeforce Kobra for a period of time.

Resuming her Halo identity, she worked alongside various former members of the Outsiders and usually responded to the summons for heroes during times of crisis. (*Day of Judgment* #1–5, November 1999; *Infinite Crisis* #7, June 2006)

HALY BROS. CIRCUS

Jack and Garrison Haly owned and operated Haly Bros. Circus, a troupe that traveled the world, thrilling audiences on six continents. (*Detective Comics* #38, April 1940)

Among the popular attractions were Sando the strongman and the FLYING GRAYSONS, a trapeze act. When the circus arrived in GOTHAM CITY, ANTHONY

"Boss" Zucco demanded protection money from Haly, suggesting that terrible things would happen if the showman did not pay. Haly refused, and Zucco left, his threat intact. A witness to this heated exchange was eight-year-old Dick Grayson, who was too frightened to tell his parents or anyone else.

That evening, as John and Mary Grayson were performing in midair, their ropes broke apart, and the two fell to their deaths. The suddenly orphaned Dick was approached by Batman, who swore their deaths would be avenged.

In some accounts, Zucco wanted to gain control of the circus to access its trucks for smuggling illegal narcotics from town to town. (*Batman: Dark Victory* #8, July 2000)

The circus survived and continued without its star attraction. Many years later an adult Dick Grayson bought the circus and would periodically train with the current troupe's acrobats. Firefly, though, torched the circus, burning it to the ground, during the events known as War Games. (*Nightwing* [second series] #98, December 2004)

HAMMER, JAKE

Jake Hammer was a gunrunner housed at Gotham State Prison who had befriended the Riddler. When the two men attempted an escape, the Riddler succeeded but Hammer was wounded by a guard. Visiting him at the prison infirmary, Robin overheard the semi-conscious man mutter a riddle that provided a clue to what the Prince of Puzzlers had in mind. Batman deduced that the Riddler had used Hammer to get in touch with gunrunners in an attempt to raise funds from selling illegal firearms. The Dynamic Duo thwarted the scheme, and the Riddler was reunited with Hammer in prison. (*Batman* #317, November 1979)

HAMMER, THE

The Hammer—a covert Russian division of the KGB—was responsible for the training of the man who became the KGBeast. (*Batman* #417, March 1988) In the wake of the Soviet Union's dissolution, the Hammer splintered. One group of former agents wound up in Gotham City working with the Russian mob to seize control of the city's underworld. Their efforts were stopped by Robin and the Huntress, but not before a man named Dzerchenko, father of Robin's girlfriend Ariana Dzerchenko, died. (*Robin III: Cry of the Huntress* #1–6, December 1992–May 1993)

HAMMOND, W. W.

W. W. Hammond was a screenwriter who lacked moral scruples. He sold his script *The Batman Story* to Gotham City Movie Studios, with the stipulation that all rights would revert to him should the film not be finished within one year. To regain the rights and sell the script a second time, Hammond then hired "Spaghetti" Thompson and his gang to spoil the production. Batman and Robin posed as actors and joined the production in an effort to thwart Thompson's thugs without risking the production schedule. Before lensing was completed, Thompson and his men were in police custody and Hammond's scheme was exposed. (*Batman* #69, February/March 1952)

HANGMAN, THE

The Hangman was a professional wrestler who rose to the top ranks, earning himself a grudge match against the Arizona Apache. In attendance that night were Bruce Wayne and Dick Grayson, enjoying a rare night away from patrolling Gotham City. The Hangman promised to unmask himself if he was ever defeated, but no opponent could withstand his signature submission hold—the Hangman's Knot. That night proved no different, and the Apache was defeated.

A fascinated Grayson wanted to unravel the mystery of the Hangman's identity—something to fill the idle hours while temporarily suspending his work as Robin to handle high school midterms. Speculation was put aside when Batman discovered the Hangman fleeing a pawnshop, its burglar alarm blaring. They fought and the Caped Crusader was rendered senseless, but the Hangman left when he heard approaching police cars. Batman decided the case needed resolution, especially when evidence pointed to two other criminals

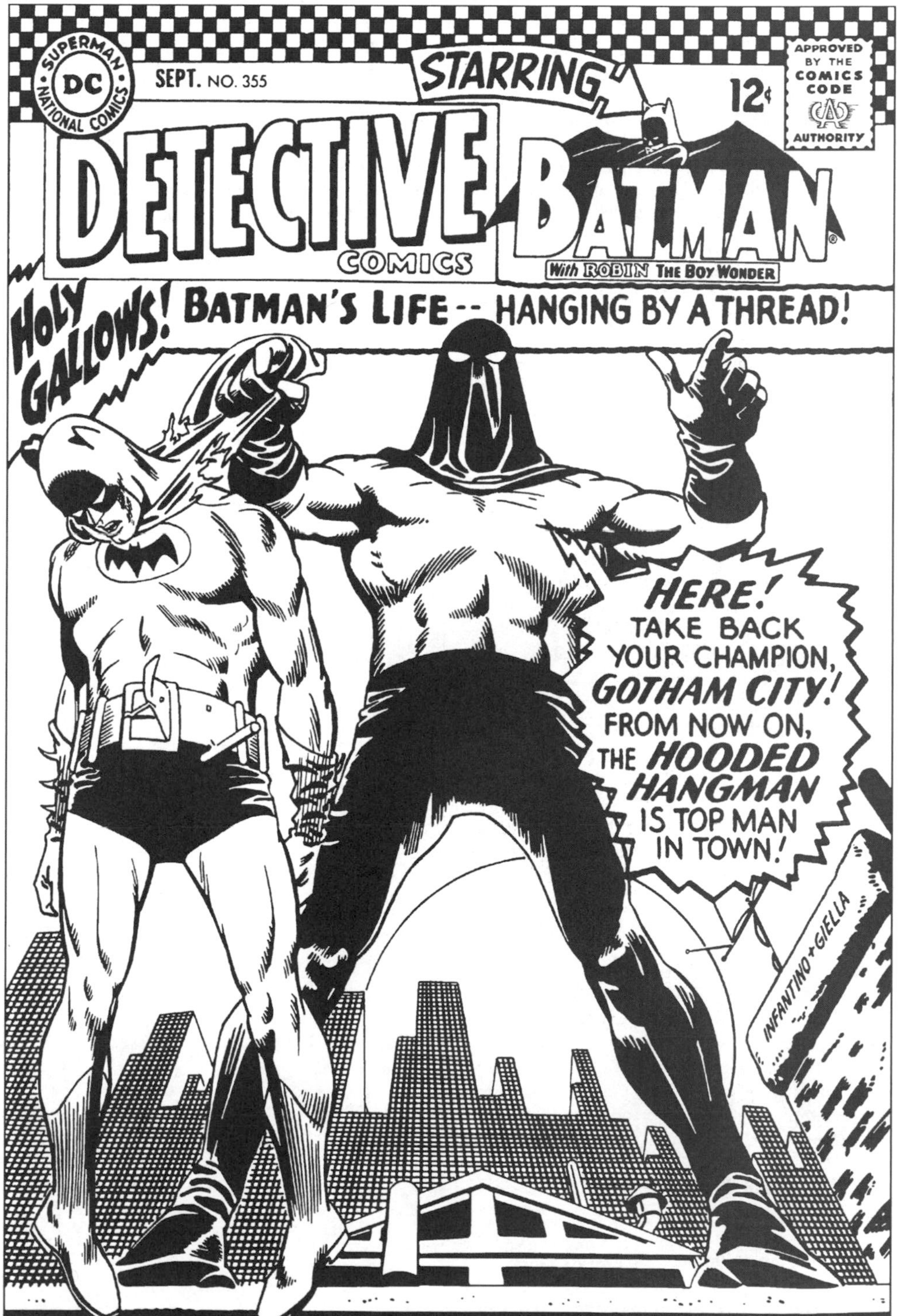
SUPERMAN DC NATIONAL COMICS
SEPT. NO. 355
STARRING
12¢
APPROVED BY THE COMICS CODE AUTHORITY
DETECTIVE COMICS
BATMAN
With ROBIN THE BOY WONDER
HOLY GALLOWS! BATMAN'S LIFE -- HANGING BY A THREAD!
HERE! TAKE BACK YOUR CHAMPION, GOTHAM CITY! FROM NOW ON, THE HOODED HANGMAN IS TOP MAN IN TOWN!
INFANTINO + GIELLA

behind the pawnshop robbery. Batman suddenly suspected that the Hangman was actually *trying* to involve him in the robbery—and then realized that he recognized the muffled voice. His suspicions were confirmed when he heard newscaster Telman Davies on the television.

After another wrestling match, with the Hangman still undefeated, he suggested to the Caped Crusader that they finish their business atop a roof near the city's center. The wrestler managed to stun Batman with the Hangman's Knot, and unmasked him for the entire city to see. The Hangman was shocked, though, to find Telman Davies's face under the cowl. This disguise gave Batman time to recover and knock the wrestler unconscious.

The telecaster admitted he craved fame as the most mysterious masked figure in Gotham and needed to bring down Batman to achieve that goal. Defeated, he left the city and took passage on a ship bound for South America. (*Detective Comics* #355, September 1966)

HANGMAN CLUB, THE

Mark Dresden, Marcia Evans, Sam Hopkins, and Jim Proxmire—the "Diet Doctor"—were all falsely accused of murder, only to have their convictions overturned. The four formed the Hangman Club, one of myriad unique clubs in GOTHAM CITY's history. The group provided a vehicle for the four to aid freshly released convicts, helping find them work and ways to reacclimatize to society. The four served as the board of directors, joined by Evans's husband Thomas Quigley.

On the club's tenth anniversary, a gala affair became the site of fresh tragedy. Dresden was found dead, hanged in his office, with a note promising more death to follow. Police Commissioner JAMES GORDON and Batman began an investigation, joined by the ELONGATED MAN, in town on vacation.

After the club accountant was found dead, Batman realized that the sizable treasury would be inherited by the last surviving member, which provided the killer's motive. Soon after, the heroes encountered the Hangman in the Quigleys' apartment. He was clad in a head-to-toe dark green costume with an H stretching from chest to legs. The killer eluded capture, incapacitating the world's greatest detectives. They then escaped elaborate death traps before discovering Marcia Evans's body.

The Dark Knight Detective and the Stretchable Sleuth laid a trap and caught the Hangman, exposing him as Tom Quigley, who had murdered the others in a ruse to get away with killing his spouse. He had tired of his wife, but not the money she earned from penning *Women in Prison,* and had wanted to inherit her fortune just for himself. (*The Brave and the Bold* #177, August 1981)

HANGMAN KILLER, THE

The Hangman Killer began a spree of death coinciding with national holidays. Following less than a year after Batman had halted the HOLIDAY murders, the new killings were directed at officers of the law or court, with a crude hangman drawing styled after the word *game.* The killer was revealed to be SOFIA FALCONE GIGANTE, daughter of crime boss CARMINE FALCONE.

HANRAHAN, DANA

Dana Hanrahan was a police detective in GOTHAM CITY who crossed paths with Batman on numerous occasions. Unlike many other officers, Hanrahan did not resent the Dark Knight's involvement in police cases, often welcoming his aid. (*Batman* #444, February 1990)

HANSON, ERIK

A busboy at the Peregrinator's Club who studied the patrons and targeted them for crimes in his guise as FAÇADE.

HARBEN, RICK

Rick Harben was a cunning criminal who, while a fugitive, lured Batman, ROBIN, and SUPERMAN to a lonely mountain range and rendered them unconscious with knockout gas and a piece of KRYPTONITE. The World's Finest were placed in cases, suspended in time, until they were discovered in the thirtieth century. In the potential future of 2957, they were freed and subsequently defeated the master criminal ROHTUL before a "time-ray" device returned them to their proper era. (*World's Finest Comics* #91, November/December 1957)

HARBIN

The man known as Harbin worked at the Gotham Museum as an assistant curator. He began to supplement his income by stealing gold artifacts from the Mexican Room, replacing them with lead items painted gold. Harbin resold the real gold through Drago, who owned a GOTHAM CITY curio shop. A museum curator discovered the fakes but was murdered before summoning the police. Harbin and Drago were apprehended by Batman and ROBIN. (*Detective Comics* #285, November 1960)

HARE, TOOTHY

Toothy Hare led a criminal gang that briefly operated in GOTHAM CITY. The members' spree ended after they stole furs and jewelry from Viola Vane. The crime was investigated by Batman and ROBIN, leading to their capture and arrest. (*Detective Comics* #53, July 1941)

HARLEQUIN

Four women have gone by the name *Harlequin,* all based in GOTHAM CITY.

During the 1940s the first Harlequin was MOLLY MAYNE, who developed a crush on Alan Scott, the GREEN LANTERN. To attract his attention, she donned a harlequin's colorful costume and committed relatively harmless crimes. They battled for years until she realized she would never win his heart and retired. Many years later, Alan Scott and Molly Mayne did find romance and married. (*Infinity, Inc. Annual* #1, 1985)

The second Harlequin was one of the many personas used by a woman known as DUELA DENT, more commonly known as the JOKER's daughter.

The first Harlequin, Molly Mayne

She used the *Harlequin* name during a brief tenure with the TEEN TITANS.

Marcie Cooper worked beside Molly Mayne at KGLX radio in Gotham, a part of GOTHAM BROADCASTING. Cooper's grandfather Dan Richards was the World War II–era hero known as MANHUNTER, who encouraged her to join the secretive Manhunter cult. She worked for them and agreed to infiltrate Infinity, Inc., by dating Obsidian, Alan Scott's son. As Harlequin, she worked with the team but betrayed them by helping orchestrate the death of their leader, Skyman. (*Infinity, Inc.* #46, June 1989)

The fourth Harlequin appeared briefly in Alan Scott's life some years after his marriage to Molly Mayne. (*Green Lantern Corps Quarterly* #5, Summer 1993) This new Harlequin could cast illusions and battled Green Lantern for a time. Her background and motives remain unrecorded.

HARLEY QUINN

Harleen Quinzel was a onetime Arkham psychiatrist and gained notoriety as the JOKER's frequent partner in crime. (*Batman: Harley Quinn,* October 1999)

Quinzel worked as a waitress to put herself through college en route to earning her degree in psychiatry. In one fateful encounter, she met the man who would later become the Joker, but even from the beginning there was a spark between them. (*Batman Confidential* #7, September 2007)

They did not see each other again, but soon after their meeting, she found her entire tuition paid in full and suspected it might have been the man she knew only as "Jack." (*Batman Confidential* #11, January 2008)

She began her career as an intern at the legendary ARKHAM ASYLUM in GOTHAM CITY before earning a degree in psychiatry and returning to the facility in a full-time capacity. Of all the colorful inmates at the Asylum, the one who most captured her imagination was the Joker. When they met for one-on-one sessions, the Joker played upon her insecurities, appearing interested; Quinzel responded by falling madly in love with the psychopathic killer. In time, after many such meetings, the Joker convinced her to help him escape.

While the first escape was overlooked by her superiors, subsequent breakouts required that she be fired from her job, her psychiatric license revoked. She also became an inmate. During her first weeks, the Joker was still on the loose, leaving her alone in the recreation room with a guard. Arnold Wesker, the VENTRILOQUIST, performed a puppet show in which the Joker beat up on Batman. It was his shy way of saying welcome to a fellow inmate. "We're a strange lot here, no denying," he told her. "But once you're in, you're one of us. Kind of like a family if you will."

The earthquake that rocked Gotham also damaged Arkham, and Quinzel escaped in search of her would-be lover. Donning a harlequin's costume and white face makeup, Quinzel joined him as Harley Quinn. From that point onward, the Joker and Harley engaged in an odd relationship that saw the Clown Prince of Crime either affectionate with her or trying to kill her.

Harley also spent a great deal of time with POISON IVY, whom she met after the Joker tried to

kill her with a rocket ship. Ivy recognized Harley as Quinzel, and the two formed a bond that became close. Ivy went so far as to alter Harley's physiology, making her immune to toxins and Ivy's own poisonous touch. An unexpected side effect was that Quinzel's natural athletic abilities were substantially enhanced. (*Batman: Harley Quinn,* 1999)

At one point, while the Joker was incarcerated, Harley decided to strike out on her own, complete with henchmen. (*Harley Quinn* #1, December 2000)

Since then she has been in and out of Arkham, with and without the Joker.

When she was turned down for release, Quinzel was kidnapped by Moose, an underling directed by SCARFACE and also sister to Scarface's other underling, RHINO. There the new Ventriloquist, Sugar, and Scarface explained that Harley had been recruited to help them commit a crime. During the act, the reluctant criminal notified Police Commissioner JAMES GORDON, who summoned Batman. Batman and Harley fought Scarface but failed to capture him. Based on her acts, Batman reconsidered, and Bruce Wayne, as a member of Arkham's board, granted her reconsideration and ultimate freedom. (*Detective Comics* 831, June 2007)

After her release she went to work with the Secret Six, a band of villains opposing the secret Society of villains under the Calculator's control. She learned how deadly the group was after a mission to Russia and asked to be released. (*Birds of Prey* #105–108, June–September 2007) Harleen next turned up residing at a Manhattan women's shelter run by the Greek goddess Artemis. She became totally devoted to Artemis's goal of helping women, giving up her costumed persona and befriending the recently arrived Holly Robinson. (*Countdown* #43, 2007)

HARMON, JAMES

James Harmon enjoyed a stellar reputation as curator of the special gems collection at the Gotham City Museum. His precious stones were considered the world's finest collection. However, when it was learned that he had mistakenly purchased a fake blue sapphire, Harmon was dismissed. He vowed revenge against the museum's five directors and set about concocting elaborate death traps contained within giant replicas of each director's birthstone. One died from a fire ignited from within a large ruby, for instance, in accordance with the Asian legend that a fire burns in each ruby. After two directors died horribly, Batman and Robin traced the crimes back to Harmon and apprehended the bitter man. (*World's Finest Comics* #33, March/April 1948)

HARMON, JOE

Joe Harmon was the popular television host of *The Big Quiz,* but secretly tried to cut deals with contestants. When Frank Davis was offered a peek at the questions in his category, the career of Batman, in exchange for a cut of the prize money, he refused. Harmon, fearing exposure, killed Davis by releasing a poison gas while the contestant sat in the isolation booth. Despite attempting to frame a co-worker named Garth, Harmon was apprehended by Batman and Robin. (*Batman* #108, June 1957)

HARPER, HARRIS

On a time-travel trip to the frontier town of Plain City in 1880, Batman and Robin got involved in the criminal scheme of cattle buyer Harris Harper. After the plan was exposed, the Caped Crusader was named Plain City's temporary marshal. While he engaged in a fight with Harper's men, Batman's life was saved by the timely arrival of the legendary Bat Masterson, Plain City's new permanent marshal. (*Batman* #99, April 1956)

HARPER, KEENE

Keene Harper assembled a gang of criminals and trained them to pose as disaster relief workers so they could successfully loot Gotham City businesses. When a hurricane eventually hit Gotham, they attempted to rob the Gotham Branch Bank's vault, only to be stopped by Batman and Robin. (*Batman* #106, March 1957)

HARPY

A woman named Iris Phelios was briefly the girlfriend of the deranged criminal Maxie Zeus. While he was in prison, Zeus used her to pass messages to his men. After delivering one such message, Iris overheard them speaking derisively about their boss. Angry, she called off the proposed robbery then suffered a mental breakdown. She emerged as a criminal in her own right, taking the name *Harpy.* When they ignored her instructions, Harpy decided to put Zeus's men out of business, feeling that Maxie did not deserve such disloyalty. Batman also arrived at the crime scene and wound up fighting Harpy, which allowed the criminals to escape. In the end Batman used the twisted psychologies of both Maxie Zeus and Harpy to manipulate matters so he could easily apprehend the woman. (*Batman* #481–482, July 1992)

HARRIET, AUNT

Dick Grayson's aunt, who briefly stayed at Wayne Manor with Bruce Wayne and Grayson.

HARRIS, HARVEY

When Bruce Wayne was a youth training to become a crime fighter, he learned a lot from his idol, detective Harvey Harris. On Earth-1, Wayne disguised himself in a red-and-yellow costume that became the prototype for Robin's uniform, keeping his identity a secret. Harris brought the teen along on numerous cases, explaining his methodology along the way. When Harris died, he had the old costume sent to Wayne, acknowledging that he'd known Batman's real name all along. (*Detective Comics* #226, December 1955) In the world reshaped by the Crisis on Infinite Earths, Harris was one of many teachers who helped shape Wayne without the use of a Robin costume. (*Detective Comics Annual* #2, 1989)

HARRIS BOYS, THE

The Harris Boys were a criminal gang operating in Gotham City. Batman and Robin prepared to apprehend them, but the effort was delayed when an alien artifact—apparently abandoned by intergalactic visitors millennia ago—was found by a hiker and activated. The device accelerated the growth of plant and animal life to such a degree that all of Gotham was threatened. Once the Dynamic Duo recovered the device and reversed its effects, the Harris Boys were easily taken into custody. (*Batman* #151, November 1962)

HART, JOHN

John Hart was a criminal better known to Gotham City police as Mister Brains.

HART, MR.

Hart was a businessman from Fayetteville, West Virginia, who chose to commit a series of crimes disguised as the Joker. He was stopped and exposed by the real Joker, who found Hart's attempts at imitation to be insulting. Batman and Robin took the failed criminal into custody. (*Detective Comics* #85, March 1944)

HART, MURRAY WILSON

Murray Wilson Hart was a master showman and the proprietor of Dinosaur Island, an amusement park filled with mechanized re-creations of Jurassic-era creatures. Batman and Robin agreed to a friendly game of tag with the robot dinosaurs, but the game turned deadly when the criminal Chase took possession of the robots' control mechanism. The Dynamic Duo successfully avoided injury until they could short-circuit the control box and apprehend Chase. (*Batman* #35, June/July 1946)

HARTLEY

The scientist known as Hartley established a hideaway for criminals within an ancient Mayan temple in Central America. He devised mechanical replicas of a jaguar and a flying serpent to frighten the locals into providing food to the temple's residents. When Batman and Robin tracked the whereabouts of the missing detective Regan, they discovered Hartley's operation. They apprehended not only Hartley but also his customers and found Regan, whom the men had captured. The locals were delighted to have the terror come to an end. (*Batman* #142, September 1961)

HARTLEY, SPOTSWOOD

A wealthy Gotham City businessman who was also secretly the criminal known as the Kingpin.

HARVEST

When Oracle's Birds of Prey began to track new and dangerous meta-humans, the first they encountered was a young woman named Harvest. She was dressed like a scarecrow and seemed able to tap into others' meta-human abilities from across the world, using them to wreak vengeance on those who'd done wrong in the past and were trying to live righteous lives. While Black Canary and Huntress tracked her, vital clues came from Lady Blackhawk, who learned much by sharing beers with local citizens. Harvest's reign of terror was put to an end. (*Birds of Prey* #77–78, February–March 2005)

HARVEST II

During Batman's one-year absence from Gotham City, Poison Ivy's powers flourished. With her newfound abilities, she created a plant-like creature named Harvest and fed it human beings to keep the life-form alive. The accumulation of consumed souls appeared to give Harvest a form of sentience. Harvest sought revenge against Ivy for killing each of them. When the creation threatened Batman inside the Batcave, he dissolved it using an herbicide, flushing the remains through the underground river that ran through the cave. (*Detective Comics* #823, November 2006)

HASARAGUA

Hasaragua was a small Central American country, its corrupt government backed by neighboring Cuba. Eventually its Marxist regime fell, and chaos ruled the land. Several of its exports included costumed mercenaries, most notably Brutale, Clawhammer, and Redblade. It was also the home of the terrorist Cell Six operation, which availed itself of the Russian-built weapons of mass destruction that were left behind. (*Detective Comics Annual* #10, 1997)

The nation included the provincial city of Montarazavilla and a mountain range, the Sierra Negros. Visitors to the country were cautioned that the local cuisine was "an acquired taste." The country also had access to a nuclear power plant, apparently in the vicinity of the coastal city of Puerto Real.

HASSEL, CHIPS

Chips Hassel led a small gang of GOTHAM CITY criminals but was easily apprehended by Batman, who then impersonated him in order to gain access to HAL TORSON and Lester Guinn. Both criminals were subsequently arrested. (*Batman* #138, March 1961)

HAWKE, CONNOR

The son of Oliver Queen, the first GREEN ARROW. He, too, mastered the bow and arrow and was also known as Green Arrow.

HAWKINS, "MAD DOG"

Martin "Mad Dog" Hawkins was a serial killer who escaped METROPOLIS police custody in the 1920s. While Amadeus Arkham resided in that city as his asylum for the criminally insane was being constructed in nearby GOTHAM CITY, he agreed to consult with police. Hawkins subsequently escaped custody.

On April 1, 1921, Arkham returned to Gotham to check on progress at the asylum, only to find his wife and daughter raped, mutilated, and dead. Hawkins had even carved his nickname on daughter Harriet's fresh corpse. Six months later Hawkins was captured and became one of the first inmates at the newly opened asylum. Arkham tried to work with Hawkins for six months but finally, on the anniversary of the grisly act, he electrocuted Mad Dog, claiming it was an electroshock therapy accident. (*Arkham Asylum*, 1989)

HAWKLEIGH, LIAM

The sharpshooting mercenary known to law enforcement as GUNHAWK.

HEAD, TALIA

Talia was the younger daughter of RĀ'S AL GHŪL, considered heir to his empire despite her independent streak. (*Detective Comics* #411, May 1971)

She entered Batman's life when he rescued her from DR. EBENEZER DARKK, who had recently split from Rā's LEAGUE OF ASSASSINS. After her rescue, she shot and killed the man who had affronted her father. Batman's arrival caught her attention, and after telling the Demon's Head of this heroic figure, began a relationship that mixed passion with betrayal, love with deceit, and left the Dark Knight with a son.

The entire Dr. Darkk incident was considered a test for Batman, gauging his suitability to assume control of the league and run Rā's operation. Rā's had ROBIN kidnapped, then introduced himself to Batman in the BATCAVE, noting that his own daughter was kidnapped in the same way. Batman's investigation and rescue of the pair convinced

Rā's that Batman was a suitable heir, but the Dark Knight rejected the offer of Talia and Rā's business. (*Batman* #232, June 1971)

From the beginning, Talia found herself drawn to Batman despite their differing views of the world. His outright rejection of her father's offer, and subsequent efforts to dismantle the league, only seemed to encourage her own independence. When Batman and Rā's dueled in the desert, he was struck by a scorpion; as he lay dying under the blazing sun, she slipped him the antidote. (*Batman* #245, October 1972)

Little has been recorded about her early years or even who her mother was. She was clearly well educated in the arts and sciences in addition to being trained in weaponry and martial arts. She never knew her older half sister, NYSSA RAATKO, and seemed to have been raised in isolation, under

Rā's watchful eye. Her mother, of mixed Asian and Arabic descent, met the Demon's Head at the Woodstock Festival in 1969. One account indicated that the woman's name was Melisande, and that she was killed by one of Rā's servants, QAYIN. (*Batman: Son of the Demon*, 1988) Another account left the woman nameless and said she died from a drug overdose. (*Batman: Birth of the Demon*, 1993)

Over the next several years Talia would turn up in Batman's life as ally or opponent, as the situation dictated. He continued to acknowledge but resist the attraction between them. At one point Rā's gassed Batman, and when he awoke the Dark Knight discovered that Rā's had performed a marriage ceremony for him and Talia. The marriage remained unconsummated at that point: The Caped Crusader escaped and refused to acknowledge the bond. (*DC Special Series* #15, Summer 1978)

At some later point they did finally admit their attraction and love, which resulted in another ceremony, followed by the birth of their son, DAMIAN. (*Batman: Son of the Demon*, 1987)

However, he continued to reject Talia so Rā's had her betrothed, instead, to BANE. She rejected the international brute, and after Batman defeated him, Rā's agreed that he was unworthy of his "only" daughter. (*Batman: Bane of the Demon* #1–4, March–June 1998) Talia remained affectionate toward her "detective" but gave up on thoughts of a life together. Instead, she changed her focus toward charting her own destiny.

She abandoned her father and, using the name *Talia Head*, accepted LEX LUTHOR's offer to run LexCorp when he took office as president of the United States. To seal the deal, she provided Lex with a disk containing details of her father's operations. Once she took over the conglomerate, Talia fed incriminating information about Luthor's operations to SUPERMAN and Batman, which helped lead to the president's downfall. She then sold off parts of the company to WAYNE ENTERPRISES. (*Superman/Batman* #1–6, October 2003–March 2004)

Talia returned to the family business when she was befriended by Nyssa, who proved to be her considerably older half sister, preserved, like their father, by the LAZARUS PITS. Nyssa tortured Talia, killing and resurrecting her, using the moments of madness provided by a pit to turn Talia into her agent. In time, Talia located her father and finally killed him. Nyssa and Talia then assumed control of the League of Assassins. (*Batman: Death and the Maidens* #1–9, October 2003–August 2004) The changes hardened Talia's attitude toward Batman; she now opposed him more than allying herself with the Dark Knight. Additionally, after BATGIRL killed Nyssa, Talia took control of the league, setting herself up as one of the most dangerous people on Earth.

The five-foot-eight woman used her newfound position of Demon's Head to become a founding member of Lex Luthor's Society, a band of super-villains dedicated to wiping out the planet's super heroes. She toured the world, recruiting members, punishing those who refused membership, and opposing the heroes whenever they turned up. After the events known as INFINITE CRISIS, Talia began her own schemes, which included obtaining Kirk Langstrom's

MAN-BAT formula and creating an army of man-bats. She intended to obtain weapons of mass destruction from the British military, sending her son Damian to distract Batman. In the end, Batman stopped the plan as Damian chose his mother over his father, and the pair seemingly died in an explosion. (*Batman* #655–658, July–October 2006) However, they survived the explosion, although her son was injured and required a transplant of his major organs. (*Batman* #665, May 2007)

HEAVY WEAPONS GANG, THE

The Heavy Weapons Gang used advanced technological weapons to commit a series of crimes in both METROPOLIS and GOTHAM CITY before being stopped by Batman, ROBIN, and SUPERMAN, who apprehended them at their headquarters in a fort outside Metropolis. (*World's Finest Comics* #72, September/October 1954)

HECATE

On Earth-2, Hecate was the CATWOMAN's longtime pet feline. (*Batman* #35, June/July 1946)

HEDRANT, FERRIS

Ferris Hedrant made his name playing villains in a long string of Hollywood blockbusters. His portrayals of violent killers kept him in vogue for years until his box-office appeal began to wane. When Triumphant Pictures refused to renew his contract, Hedrant seemed to snap. He decided to reenact his most famous screen killings, selecting innocent citizens of GOTHAM CITY as his new victims. After two murders, Hedrant was apprehended by Batman and ROBIN. (*Batman* #76, April/May 1953)

HELLFERN, DR. KARL

Better known to Batman and law enforcement as the criminal DOCTOR DEATH.

HELLGRAMMITE

Roderick Rose was an entomologist who used specially treated humanoid-sized cocoons to transform his physique to one resembling a man-sized insect, including a rugged exoskeleton. The effect wore off after twenty-four hours unless Rose entered a new cocoon. In his new form, Rose ran through GOTHAM CITY, causing numerous sightings from frightened citizens but no hard evidence as to his existence; police concluded that he was an urban legend. Batman tended to agree at first, but evidence began to point toward the reality of Hellgrammite—named for the larva of the dobsonfly, a dark deadly bug with a bite like a timber wolf that lives under rocks. Several criminal leaders had vanished, only to be located within giant-sized cocoons.

It fell to reporter Jack Ryder to locate the Hellgrammite, while searching for the missing Rose, and alert Batman to the danger threatening Gotham. Ryder transformed himself into bizarre adventurer the CREEPER and aided the Caped Crusader in subduing Hellgrammite before he could transform the criminals into powerful allies. (*The Brave and the Bold* #80, October/November 1968)

Rose absorbed enough of the proteins and chemicals from the cocoons to stop needing daily regenerative therapy and became the altered life-form permanently. He even developed the ability to spin his own durable cocoon and hoped to become an insect lord—nearly accomplishing his goal until he was stopped by GREEN ARROW and BLACK CANARY. (*World's Finest Comics* #248–249, December 1977/January 1978–February/March 1978)

Hellgrammite was later freed and began working as a mercenary rather than would-be conqueror. One of his first contracts was to take the life of LEX LUTHOR, only to be opposed by SUPERMAN. (*Action Comics* #673–674, January–February 1992) Thanks to Rampage, Hellgrammite was stopped for good and taken to a holding cell crafted by S.T.A.R. LABS; it fell to SUPERGIRL to track down who had ordered the hit and save Luthor's life. (*Supergirl/Lex Luthor Special*, 1993)

Not long after, Hellgrammite accepted the demon Neron's offer of even more power in exchange for his immortal soul. The new power came at the cost of Rose's reasoning abilities, leaving him a near-mindless beast. (*Underworld Unleashed* #1, November 1995)

Hellgrammite continued to threaten lives and was stopped repeatedly by Batman, Superman, and even NIGHTWING. (*Batman & Superman: World's Finest* #10, January 2000) Hellgrammite was imprisoned at various times in METROPOLIS's Stryker's Island and the federal facility nicknamed the Slab. (*Green Lantern* #79, October 1996)

HELLHOUND

The ARMLESS MASTER taught many people from his GOTHAM CITY dojo, and his best student was a man named Kai. In addition, though, Kai was a thief. At one point he tried to steal a statue of the cat god Bast, but was interrupted by CATWOMAN, who dared to touch the object. Kai beat the young thief, who followed him back to the dojo and herself became a student. In time, Kai realized that SELINA KYLE was the cat thief who had dared to interrupt the ceremony that he imagined would bring him power. He took this as a sign and designed his own costumed persona, becoming the Hellhound. They fought, and Catwoman seriously scarred his face. (*Catwoman Annual* #2, 1995)

Denied power, Hellhound sought wealth as a costumed mercenary, battling the likes of Catwoman and Batman. Kai found himself in the uncomfortable position of being allied with Catwoman when a man known as the COLLECTOR tasked them with finding the ancient Wheel of Plagues. To the world's dismay, it was found first by RĀ's AL GHŪL, who used its inscriptions to create a plague known as the CLENCH. (*Catwoman* #33–36, May–August 1996)

Later, Hellhound worked for a drug lord in Rheelasia, only to be opposed by BLACK CANARY on an early mission as a BIRD OF PREY. (*Birds of Prey* #1–3, January–March 1999) Hellhound had subsequent assignments bringing him to Gotham City. LEW MOXON hired him as a bodyguard, and he met his end when rival PHILO ZEISS killed both Moxon and Kai. (*Batman: The 12-Cent Adventure*, October 2004)

A man called JACK CHIFFORD took up the identity

of Hellhound, claiming to have bought the naming rights from the CALCULATOR. He became a member of the Calculator's secret Society of super-villains. (*Villains United* #2, August 2005)

HELZINGER, AARON

Aaron Helzinger suffered from problems related to his brain chemistry, which left him an uncontrollable monster known as AMYGDALA until he could be cured.

HENNELLY, GERARD "JERRY"

Gerard "Jerry" Hennelly was a GOTHAM CITY police officer named commander of the city's QUICK RESPONSE TEAM in the period after Gotham emerged from being known as a NO MAN'S LAND.

HEWITT, WALTER

Walter Hewitt was a scientist who developed a device, "the bioniformer," that used irradiated light to transfer specific animal attributes to human beings. He tested the device on himself and gained the eyesight of an eagle and the speed of a cheetah. However, when he tried to gain a gorilla's strength,

there was an accident that actually transferred Hewitt's intellect to the mammal. The gorilla, KARMAK, began a series of crimes that frustrated GOTHAM CITY's police. Karmak resented humans for treating him like an animal and sought a measure of revenge through wanton destruction. He was finally laid low by Batman and ROBIN. (*Detective Comics* #339, May 1965)

HIJACK

Hijack led a band of thieves who targeted the trucking industry, becoming modern-day highway pirates. Wearing a costume based on the Jack of Spades playing card, Hijack and his men enjoyed a measure of success before being apprehended by Batman and ROBIN. Hijack was revealed as JACK SPADE, a recently released convict. (*Batman* #122, March 1959)

HILL, HAMILTON

GOTHAM CITY's history was thick with corrupt mayors, but perhaps none caused more damage than Hamilton Hill. Placed in office through the machinations of RUPERT THORNE, Hill worked tirelessly

to discredit Police Commissioner JAMES GORDON and wreck law enforcement's relationship with Batman. Hill fired Gordon, placing the hapless Peter Pauling in the office. When Batman finally took down Thorne, Hill relented and rehired Gordon but worked to blame many of Gotham's ills on Gordon. He was eventually manipulated into resigning and vanished from public life. (*Detective Comics* #511, February 1982)

HILL, THE

The Hill may be the most notorious section of GOTHAM CITY. Considered at the low end of the economic spectrum, it was the farthest residential section from Gotham Cathedral Square. Intentionally isolated from the rest of Gotham, the Hill was almost a city unto itself. Here in the most impoverished area, crime and drugs ran rampant, with decrepit Old World buildings in various stages of decay encircling a large cemetery at the neighborhood's center. Aparo Park was located in the Hill, as was the Leslie N. Hill Public Housing Project. The Hill's cheap real estate became a hot commodity after the events of NO MAN'S LAND. ORPHEUS operated out of this area, as did a subsection from the secret Society of super-villains. (*Batman: Secret Files and Origins*, 1997)

HILLERY

Hillery worked as the assistant to prominent GOTHAM CITY lawyer Logan, who represented the millionaire Thaddeus Moore. When Moore died, it was learned that he'd left behind one million dollars in cash hidden somewhere in the city. Clues were to be found in working models of some of humankind's greatest inventions. Hillery intended to find the money for himself by stealing the replicas before anyone else. He and his hirelings were stopped by Batman and ROBIN. (*Batman* #128, December 1959)

HOBSON, "BRAIN"

"Brain" Hobson was a highly regarded criminal mastermind who was executed in North Gotham Prison. His corpse was stolen by his former gang, who concocted a scheme to convince America's mobsters to band together and take orders from Hobson's still-functioning brain. After a replica brain was placed in a vat of chemicals hooked up to a faux computer setup, it appeared Hobson was indeed still giving orders, so the conglomeration of criminals agreed to form the largest underworld operation known to law enforcement. The spectacular crime wave that followed overwhelmed GOTHAM CITY's police force; it took the intervention of Batman and ROBIN to expose the hoax and break the criminal gang apart. (*Detective Comics* #210, August 1954)

HOFFNER, FRITZ

Fritz Hoffner was a young German who followed Count Felix's espionage activities in America during World War II. Using the alias Fred Hopper, he worked as a newsreel cameraman in Earth-2's GOTHAM CITY, hoping to access America's industrial plants. He was arrested, instead, by Batman and ROBIN. (*Batman* #14, December 1942/January 1943)

HOGGSBY, HAPPY

Happy Hoggsby was a career criminal in GOTHAM CITY who decided to corner the Christmas tree market, charging citizens exorbitant prices while threatening harm to any who tried to undersell him. A disgusted Batman and ROBIN swiftly put the criminal out of business, allowing the citizens to have a merry holiday season. (*Batman* #27, February/March 1945)

HOLIDAY

Holiday was a serial murderer who seemingly killed underworld figures at random. A .22-caliber pistol was Holiday's weapon of choice, and the name was bestowed when it became apparent that deaths were being linked to national holidays. Additionally, some small memento denoting the holiday was left at each crime scene. The first was on Halloween when crime lord CARMINE FALCONE's nephew Johnny Vitti was shot.

Batman, Lieutenant JAMES GORDON, and district attorney HARVEY DENT pooled their resources over the course of a year to try to find the killer. In the end, it was revealed that Carmine's son, ALBERTO FALCONE, was the Holiday killer. The youngest of Falcone's three children, he desperately wanted to be an accepted member of the crime family—while his father had tried to shield the unstable man from such a life. Some theorists believed that Carmine manipulated Alberto into becoming the killer, but this was never proven, and Carmine himself became the final victim. Several of the killings, though, were the result of shots fired by Harvey Dent and his wife, GILDA DENT, both desperately trying to close the case and protect the innocent. Gilda said she began the Holiday killings in an effort to shut down organized crime so her beleaguered husband could come home and they could finally start a family. When she heard that Alberto had been killed, she came to believe Harvey had committed that crime, and she ended her spree.

Harvey, who held on to a .22 claiming it was evidence against the Falcones, was later scarred by acid during a trial and became TWO-FACE. As Two-Face, he actually fired the shots that killed Carmine Falcone at the end of the yearlong event. (*Batman: The Long Halloween* #1–12, 1996–1997)

HOLMES, SHIRLEY

Shirley Holmes was a sergeant in the GOTHAM CITY POLICE DEPARTMENT who once worked with Batman and ROBIN, helping them break a racketeering scheme led by the COUNT. She also briefly enjoyed a romance with ALFRED PENNYWORTH. (*Batman* #28, April/May 1945)

HOOKER, BIG DAN

Big Dan Hooker decided to form an elite team of all-star criminals, seeking the best safe cracker, forger, arsonist, et cetera. To build his team, he announced a contest, with nominations and voting taken from underworld gangs located coast to coast. The finalists were brought to GOTHAM CITY, where the top two men in each category were assigned identical robberies in different parts of the city, to be conducted simultaneously. The winner would be the criminal who accomplished the task without being nabbed by Batman. The city was rocked by the "double crimes" until Batman infiltrated the contest, disguised as a contestant from out of town. Despite being discovered, Batman managed to overwhelm the odds and apprehend Hooker. The Gotham police arrived en masse to arrest the contestants. Commissioner JAMES GORDON noted that this was the largest mass arrest in his career. (*World's Finest Comics* #56, January/February 1952)

HOOKER, WILLY

A criminal who was better known to Batman and GOTHAM CITY's police as the EXECUTIONER.

HOOTON, LUCKY

Lucky Hooton owned and performed in a traveling auto circus. Four of his clowns proved to be criminals, committing automobile crimes as they went from town to town. Batman and ROBIN rang down the curtain on their operation. (*Batman* #60, August/September 1950)

HORNETS, THE

While in high school, DICK GRAYSON ran for junior class president, only to have his campaign interrupted by a motorcycle gang known as the Hornets. Leading the bikers was Tommy the Tramp, who had been expelled, and he gained a measure of revenge by smashing Principal Wagner's car. Dick, in his ROBIN identity, investigated the scene and found a bike abandoned by another member,

I AM HOLIDAY.

Jimbo. He disguised himself as Jimbo and gained access to the Hornets' lair. He dismantled the hideout, ending the gang's threat to the school, but was away during the crucial vote and lost the election. (*Batman* #202, June 1968)

HOUSE OF MYSTERY

The House of Mystery was located in the realm known as the Dreaming. The seemingly dilapidated, ramshackle building was home to CAIN, a servant of the Endless' Morpheus. (*House of Mystery* #175, July/August 1968) Its layout was an ever-shifting arrangement of rooms, and Cain rarely entertained visitors. His brother Abel lived next door in the aptly named House of Secrets. Both Batman and SUPERMAN visited the house once apiece. (*The Brave and the Bold* #93, December 1970/January 1971; *DC Comics Presents* #53, January 1983) An earthbound incarnation of the house could occasionally be found in Kentucky, but whispers said it was haunted, and few ventured near it. It was, though, used as a headquarters for a group of detectives known as the Croatoan Society, with Detective Chimp and the ELONGATED MAN among its members. (*52* #18, 2006)

HOWE, ANDREW

Andrew Howe briefly served as GOTHAM CITY's police commissioner, replacing SARAH ESSEN GORDON as part of a political game play that hampered the city's ability to effectively protect the citizens. When the virus known as the CLENCH gripped Gotham, Howe's orders were ignored and the loyal officers in blue responded to commands from JAMES GORDON. After Mayor ARMAND KROL died from the disease, new mayor MARION GRANGE immediately replaced Howe with Jim Gordon. (*Detective Comics* #693, January 1996)

HROGUTH

Hroguth was a scientist who accidentally gained superpowers on his native world of Durim. He embarked on a criminal career, terrorizing his home. With his men, Hroguth journeyed to Earth to seek copper, an element not known on their world. His goal was to use it to build a machine that would permanently rob his nemesis, Logi—a teen who acquired powers in the same way but used them for the cause of justice—of his abilities. Logi had followed the criminal to Earth and, aided by Batman, ROBIN, and SUPERMAN, apprehended Hroguth. The teen used the completed device to depower his enemy and protect his fellow Durimians. (*World's Finest Comics* #124, March 1962)

HUDSON UNIVERSITY

When DICK GRAYSON graduated from high school, he chose to attend Hudson University, although he lasted only a single semester. (*Batman* #217, December 1969) The school, although small, was prestigious, and its alumni include Professor Martin Stein, Crystal Frost, and Louise Lincoln. The Earth-1 version of the school, located in NEW CARTHAGE, New York, also accepted Smallville's CLARK KENT, but he declined. (*New Adventures of Superboy* #51, March 1984)

HUMAN FLEA, THE

MARTIN KEMP donned the costumed persona of the criminal the Human Flea in order to commit robberies to help fund his grandfather's failing flea circus. When convicts MORTIMER KADAVER and Jan Bodie escaped BLACKGATE PENITENTIARY, the flea circus became the focus of Kadaver's scheme to destroy GOTHAM CITY. Using Bodie's connections as an animal rights activist, Kadaver intended to steal a plague bacillus and use the fleas to spread the disease among the citizenry. Kemp reached a truce with Batman to ensure that the men who'd killed his grandfather were brought to justice. They reached Kadaver before he could unleash the plague, and then prevented the man from committing suicide to avoid arrest. (*Batman: Shadow of the Bat* #11–12, April–May 1993)

HUMAN KEY, THE

The Human Key was a hooded thief who displayed tremendous skill as a picklock, leading to ten noteworthy crimes in GOTHAM CITY. As Batman and ROBIN investigated, they learned that the criminal was actually former circus escape artist PAUL BODIN. Bodin had been blackmailed into committing crimes on behalf of Burly Graham and his colleague Sleepy, who kidnapped Bodin's daughter to ensure his cooperation. Bodin worked with the Dynamic Duo to apprehend the men and free his daughter. (*Detective Comics* #132, February 1948)

HUMAN MAGNET, THE

The Human Magnet displayed the super-abilities of magnetism, with his left hand repelling metallic substances while the right one attracted them. After a series of spectacular crimes, the green-and-yellow-clad criminal was apprehended by Batman and ROBIN, who used his own powers against him. The criminal was revealed to be DAVID WIST, a watch-repairman-turned-safecracker who accidentally gained his magnetic powers by exposure to high-tension wires that ran beneath the Ultra-Nuclear Fission Commission. Wist crossed the wires while fleeing Batman when one of his robberies was discovered. (*Detective Comics* #181, March 1952)

HUMAN TARGET, THE

Fred Venable was an impersonator hoping to raise money to pay for an operation that his crippled daughter needed. He offered to pose as anyone whose life may be threatened in exchange for a high fee—and in short order Venable had earned what he needed. With the surgery now paid for, Venable retired until he was approached by Blinky Grove, a GOTHAM CITY gangster. Grove had Venable's daughter kidnapped to force the Human Target to pose as the criminal, who had been marked for death by his rivals. Venable worked with Batman, ROBIN, and the police to not only stop Grove and arrest his would-be killers but also rescue his daughter. (*Detective Comics* #201, November 1953)

Batman also repeatedly encountered Christopher Chance, who was also known as the Human Target and performed similar work. (*Action Comics* #419, December 1972)

The Human Target

HUMPTY DUMPTY

The man known as Humpty Dumpty became an inmate at GOTHAM CITY's ARKHAM ASYLUM after his obsession with taking things apart and reconstructing them inspired his criminal career. At first his crimes were innocuous—he would find some mechanical item offensive and, at night, would exact revenge by practicing his skills on the item. Unfortunately, his mechanical training came from reading, not from course work or practice, which meant the reassembled items were never quite perfectly re-formed. Mild accidents grew in scope until the day poorly reconstructed items fell off Gotham rooftops. When BATGIRL spotted the criminal at the scene, she tried to apprehend him only to have his massive weight dislocate her shoulders. The gentle man helped put her back together and then surrendered.

Batgirl had been trailing the man because of his record of overdue library fines, a result of his research. One of the books, on human anatomy, caught her attention, and Humpty Dumpty led her back to his home. She was shocked to see that his grandmother had been hacked apart with an ax and clumsily sewn back together using bootlaces.

Humpty Dumpty was remanded to Arkham. There he was a quiet, model prisoner, seemingly unaffected by the lunacy surrounding him. (*Arkham Asylum: Living Hell* #1, July 2003)

He later was freed and allied himself with the Society, a band of super-villains dedicated to ridding the world of its heroes.

A different Humpty Dumpty, known as the Hobby Robber, battled the Teen of Steel, Superboy, on Earth-1. (*Superboy* #6, January/February 1950)

HUNGARIA

Hungaria was the tiny European country that was home to the MONK, a vampire who terrorized GOTHAM CITY and threatened Batman's fiancée JULIE MADISON. Located in the country were the lost mountains of CATHALA and the River Dess. (*Detective Comics* #32, October 1939)

HUNT, OLIVER

Oliver Hunt had an eidetic memory and used his skills as a vaudeville performer, hoping to earn enough money to devote his life to psychological research. Frustrated at his progress, he agreed to lend his talents to Dude Fay, a GOTHAM CITY gang boss. In exchange for a cut of the take, Hunt would help Fay plan and execute crimes. They stole yet-to-be-published intellectual properties such as songs and profited from registering them first. After seeing plans for the BATPLANE, Hunt helped Fay build a replica to use as an escape vehicle. Eventually, Hunt realized what had become of his life and turned against Fay, working with Batman and ROBIN to bring the criminal to justice. (*World's Finest Comics* #10, Summer 1943)

HUNTER, DEAN

An escaped criminal who donned a camouflage suit and was briefly known as NIMROD THE HUNTER.

HUNTRESS, THE

There have been numerous women known as the Huntress in Batman's world.

On Earth-2, Batman married CATWOMAN and they had a single child, daughter HELENA WAYNE. When she was a teenager, her mother was blackmailed into resuming her Catwoman persona, only to die for her efforts. Helena, having been trained by her parents to be an excellent athlete, crafted her own costume and pursued her mother's killer as the Huntress. She remained a super hero, joining the fabled JUSTICE SOCIETY OF AMERICA and becoming close friends with Power Girl. On her own she battled new foes such as Karnage and the Earthworm in addition to the seemingly unkillable JOKER. (*DC Super-Stars* #17, December 1977)

As Helena, she earned her law degree and joined her father's legal firm of Cranston, Grayson & Wayne, eventually working alongside her father's ward, DICK GRAYSON. Together the Huntress and ROBIN made several trips to Earth-1, meeting with their younger counterparts, including Batman, whom she called "Uncle Bruce."

During the cosmic upheaval known as the CRISIS ON INFINITE EARTHS, Helena died under a wall of rubble as she rescued children. (*Crisis on Infinite Earths* #12, March 1986) Then, in the wake of the multiverse's rebirth during the events of Infinite Crisis, a new parallel Earth was formed; there the JSA, complete with the Huntress, was reborn. (*52* #52, 2007)

After Infinite Crisis, that Huntress was removed from reality. On the newly formed singular Earth, HELENA BERTINELLI, daughter of a Mafia don, grew up to become the heroic Huntress. (*The Huntress*

#1, April 1989) Her anger and take-no-prisoners approach to crime fighting kept her at odds with Batman, but she seemed to find her place as a field leader for ORACLE's BIRDS OF PREY.

Also on Earth-2, PAULA BROOKS was a young big-game hunter who idolized Paul Kirk, aka MANHUNTER, and donned a tiger ski outfit to call herself, at first, the Tigress. As a super hero, she worked with the All-Star Squadron, battling Nazis and other villains during the outbreak of World War II. (*Young All-Stars* #6, November 1987) A battle with the Valkyrie known as Gudra left her apparently dead, but Brooks survived and chose to alter her life as a result of the experience. Renaming herself the Huntress, she went after her former ally WILDCAT and became a criminal to be reckoned with. (*Sensation Comics* #68, August 1947) Later in her life, she battled her namesake, the JSA's Huntress.

There was also an Earth-1 criminal Huntress who battled BATGIRL and Robin with little success. (*Batman Family* #7, October/November 1976)

In the reality after Infinite Crisis, the Huntress remained a villainess, marrying the equally villainous Sportsmaster. Together they had a daughter who grew up to join the family business as Artemis. Paula Brooks retired, living vicariously through her daughter's efforts.

HUSH

BRUCE WAYNE didn't have many childhood friends by the time his parents died, but of those he played with, his closest friend was Tommy Elliot. Tommy also came from a wealthy family and they had much in common, with one notable exception: Tommy hated his parents. In fact, he wanted to be rid of them and also inherit their wealth—and so began an audacious plan for an eight-year-old. Tommy managed to sever the brakes on his parents' car, then convinced the family chauffeur to stay home that evening. His parents drove off and subsequently crashed, killing his father and severely injuring his mother. It was through the heroic efforts of Dr. THOMAS WAYNE that she lived, although the rescue altered Tommy's life. Tommy learned that his mother had survived and attacked young Bruce in a rage. Bruce misunderstood the source of his anger, thinking it was because he'd promised Tommy that his father could save both parents. When Thomas comforted Tommy, Bruce grew resentful. Much as Bruce would soon be obsessed with ridding the world of crime, Tommy was obsessed with the notion of revenge against Bruce for his father's work, especially after Thomas and MARTHA WAYNE were gunned down—putting Bruce in the very situation Tommy had tried to create for himself. (*Batman* #609, November 2002)

After Tommy's mother died from cancer, he finally had the wealth he craved. Tommy proved adept at medicine and attended Harvard Medical School, becoming a gifted surgeon. He relocated away from GOTHAM CITY, built up his practice, and added to his personal wealth, all the while harboring a grudge against Bruce Wayne. Years later Edward Nigma, the RIDDLER, came to Elliot for treatment. By that point, the Prince of Puzzlers had deduced that Wayne was also Batman. Working with Elliot, they created a scheme that would torture Wayne before Elliot could exact revenge and kill the man.

One of his first steps was recruiting Batman's somewhat neglected aide, HAROLD ALLNUT, as his mole, earning the man's loyalty by repairing his physical deformities. Similarly, Elliot also used his skills to repair the facial damage that turned HARVEY DENT into the psychologically scarred TWO-FACE.

Shortly thereafter, Batman began to be stalked by a trench-coated figure that hid his face behind loosely wrapped bandages. Batman's major opponents were then manipulated into confronting the Dark Knight, pushing him to extremes. He had to contend with KILLER CROC, POISON IVY, HARLEY QUINN, the JOKER, and SCARECROW.

Batman's ability to investigate the attacks was compromised by the personal turn matters took when CATWOMAN crossed his path and the long-simmering romantic feelings between the two ignited. Batman was also seriously injured in a fall, requiring Tommy Elliot to arrive and save Wayne's life, putting his rival in Elliot's debt and prolonging the planned suffering. Elliot also implanted a tracking device in the Caped Crusader's skull, enhancing his ability to torment his target. Elliot went so far as to remain in Gotham, renew his acquaintance with Wayne, and then fake his death to toy with Wayne's emotional state. Wayne's other lover, TALIA HEAD, also became involved—but both were eclipsed by the arrival of a resurrected JASON TODD, back from the dead and angry at Batman. While it proved to be a ploy on behalf of CLAYFACE, Batman exhumed Todd's coffin, only to find it empty.

Hush finally appeared before an exhausted Batman and revealed himself as Elliot. He explained why the Dark Knight had been targeted and all the machinations that went into seeking revenge. Before he could kill Batman, the moment

was interrupted by the arrival of retired police commissioner JAMES GORDON as well as Dent, who double-crossed Elliot after the skilled surgeon repaired his facial damage.

Elliot's body was never found; SUPERMAN suggested that it had been blown out to sea. Since the courts wouldn't charge Dent without proper evidence or a body, he was cleared of all charges and released. Thanks to Superman's X-ray vision, it was learned that Elliot had placed a tracking bug in Bruce Wayne's skull, which the Man of Steel destroyed with his heat vision. Batman confronted the real mastermind behind Hush's actions, the Riddler. Batman pointed out that even though the Riddler knew his secret identity, it was the answer to the greatest riddle of them all, and thus not something he'd ever dare share. (*Batman* #608-619, December 2002–November 2003)

Hush was indeed not dead and repeatedly returned to exact some measure of revenge against his childhood enemy. In short order he beat the Riddler to a pulp, managed to chase the Joker out of the city for a time, and seemingly killed Poison Ivy when she wouldn't ally herself with him.

After he recruited PROMETHEUS as an ally, it took the combined efforts of Batman and GREEN ARROW to stop his second attempt at revenge. (*Batman: Gotham Knights* #50-55, April–September 2004)

The Joker struck back at Hush, kidnapping him and keeping him sedated for three weeks, taking the time to have a pacemaker implanted in Elliot's body. The Clown Prince of Crime literally held the power of life and death over Hush. Feeling he had little choice, Elliot turned to Wayne for help. No sooner did Batman have the pacemaker removed than Elliot escaped, reneging on his promise to report to ARKHAM ASYLUM, and tracked down the Joker to kill him. Batman intervened, and the two rivals argued over the morals of killing. In the end Batman revealed that the pacemaker hadn't been removed after all; Hush had little choice but to give up his efforts now that Wayne held the pacemaker controls. (*Batman: Gotham Knights* #73-74, March–April 2006) He has yet to resurface.

HYDRA

Hydra was an international criminal organization with cells located around the world. Batman and ROBIN worked to cripple the operation and recovered stolen items such as jewels hidden in a windmill in Holland. After shutting down three such cells, Batman appeared satisfied that the operation would wither and die. (*Batman* #167, November 1964)

HYDRO

TIM FLAGG was a penny-ante criminal serving time at Gotham State Penitentiary; mocked for his crimes, he served as the prison baseball team's water boy. Using the prison's water tower to help effect an escape, a newly empowered Flagg decided his next round of crimes would use water as a motif. He successfully followed the plan and committed numerous offenses, although he was nearly captured by Batman and ROBIN. Intending to end their threat, he found the underground river leading into the fabled BATCAVE and planned to blow up the Caped Crusader's headquarters using nitroglycerin. The liquid detonated early, however, causing a cave-in that threatened to drown Flagg. After Batman and Robin protected the Batcave's contents using special bulkheads, they freed Flagg and arrested him. The criminal was too far away to learn where the Batcave was actually located. (*Batman* #74, December 1952/January 1953)

HYLAND, LEE

Lee Hyland had the ability to see through another person's eyes after making contact. Twice the man known as BLINK worked with Batman.

HYORO

Hyoro and Goga were aliens who crash-landed on Earth. Their vital "control unit" fell into the hands of two bank robbers, who promised to return the unit if the aliens would use their technology to kill Batman and ROBIN. The aliens reluctantly agreed, but each attempt narrowly failed, allowing the captive visitors to Earth to leave clues that would lead the Dynamic Duo to the robbers. (*Detective Comics* #305, July 1962)

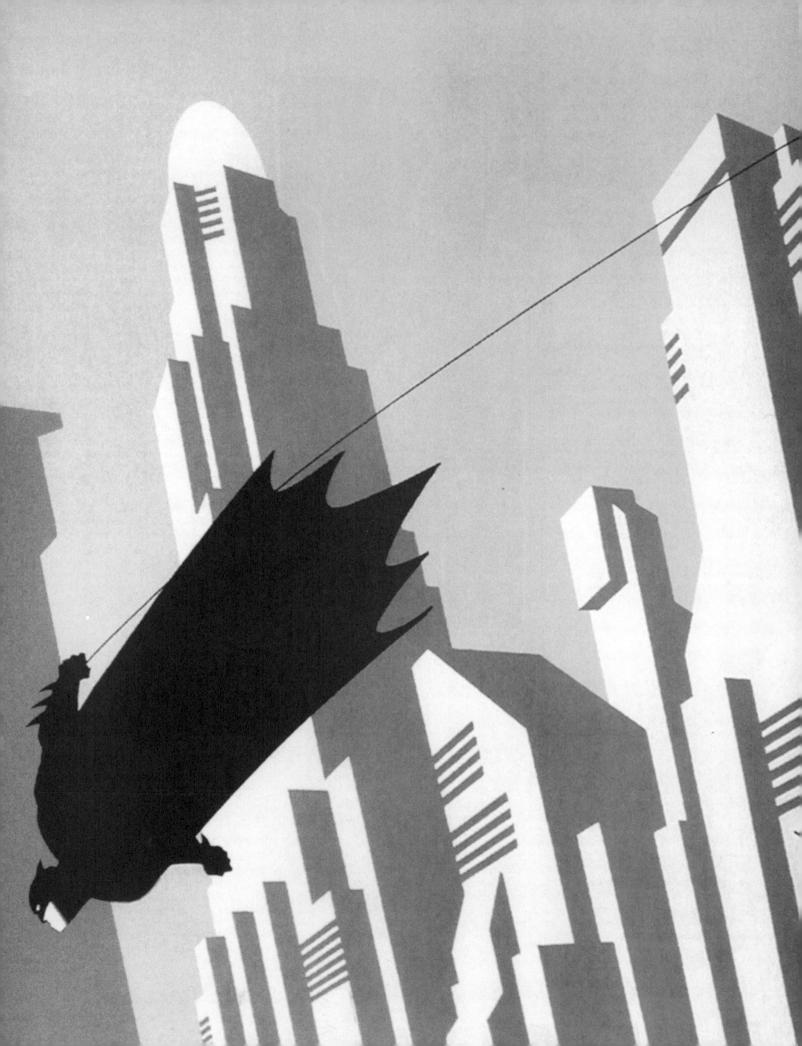

IBN AL XU'FFASCH

The Arabic name for DAMIAN, son of Batman and TALIA HEAD.

ICEBERG LOUNGE

When the PENGUIN chose to change his focus from criminal to criminal broker, he established the Iceberg Lounge as his base of operations. Ostensibly a posh nightclub, the Iceberg Lounge catered to GOTHAM CITY's hip and wealthy social set. OSWALD CHESTERFIELD COBBLEPOT served as host and booked numerous singers and musicians to perform. Behind the scenes, though, the Penguin ran his criminal enterprises, laundering stolen cash and trading on information.

The building sustained serious damage when an earthquake struck Gotham, but the Penguin continued to operate from the structure. Then, when the federal government withdrew support, the city became a NO MAN's LAND—and still the Penguin operated, profiting more than ever. He bartered goods and services to all comers, siphoning off enough to sustain himself. He also knew of an access tunnel that enabled matériel and supplies to flow into the city.

After the city was reintegrated into America, the Penguin had the lounge rebuilt—only to discover that the building was now owned by BRUCE WAYNE, who kept a close eye on the business. Soon after, the Penguin was chased out of Gotham City by BLACK MASK, but he returned and continued to operate the lounge. His business thrived during the year Batman was missing from Gotham, with the Penguin adding a lucrative line of T-shirts and other souvenirs.

Despite making plenty of money from legitimate sources, the Penguin refused to give up his even more profitable criminal ways, so he conducted casino operations in his lounge's back rooms.

IDIOT, THE

The criminal known as the QUEEN OF HEARTS was chasing a drug dealer, with Batman on her heels, when she left GOTHAM CITY for Rio de Janeiro. Upon arrival in Brazil, the Dark Knight was stunned to find mindless children in the grip of a designer drug. They all seemed to be controlled by a figure known only as the Idiot. At first, the Idiot seemed to be a form of artificial intelligence linked to the designer drug that used the "dead boys" to do its bidding. When a dosage of the drug was airborne, Batman ingested some of it and accessed the Idiot's world: a bizarre group-mind paradise. After the effects wore off, Batman sought out a drug dealer and forced him to bring the hero to the source. Upon finding the Idiot, though, Batman was too late to disconnect it—the AI took a physical form. Recalling that the paradise he saw had lacked birds, Batman used sonics to summon feathered beings to confound the Idiot, allowing him time to subdue the body. This finally broke its link to the children. (*Batman* #472–473; *Detective Comics* #639–640, December 1991–January 1992)

ILLUMINATA

Convinced that America's military/industrial complex ruled and ruined everyone's lives, the blond woman known only as Illuminata sought to shed light on the truth. To accomplish her goals, she donned a gold costume and fired off flash bombs to commit a series of robberies to fund her protests. She was apprehended and remanded to ARKHAM ASYLUM but managed to escape, freeing other inmates in the process. When she encountered the JOKER, he heard her rants about seeing the light and accommodated her by removing her eyelids. She was recaptured and sent for medical and psychiatric treatment. (*Batman & Superman: World's Finest* #3, June 1999)

INFINITE CRISIS

When the multiverse was collapsed into a single positive matter universe and a single negative matter universe—an event known as the CRISIS ON INFINITE EARTHS—four beings escaped the cosmic upheaval by entering a limbo-like crystalline place. They were SUPERMAN and LOIS LANE of Earth-2, Superboy from Earth-Prime, and Alexander Luthor from Earth-3. Over time these four despaired to see that the re-formed Earth was darker and seemingly more corrupt than the worlds they had known. Additionally, Lois continued to age and began to die from natural causes, while the Teen of Steel lamented his lack of opportunity to experience all life had to offer. Luthor, though, had a plan.

Carefully, over time, he found ways to leave limbo and journey to Earth, where he laid the seeds for re-creating the multiverse—but totally remade in his design. Back in the crystal dwelling, he preyed on the emotionally distraught Superman's feelings, saying that if the Man of Steel trusted him, Luthor could save Lois.

Eventually Luthor took control of events affecting Earth's super-hero community, starting with usurping Brother I, the spy satellite constructed by Batman to watch over the entire meta-human community. He then pretended to be that Earth's LEX LUTHOR and assembled fellow villains to form a secret Society, one that would exact revenge

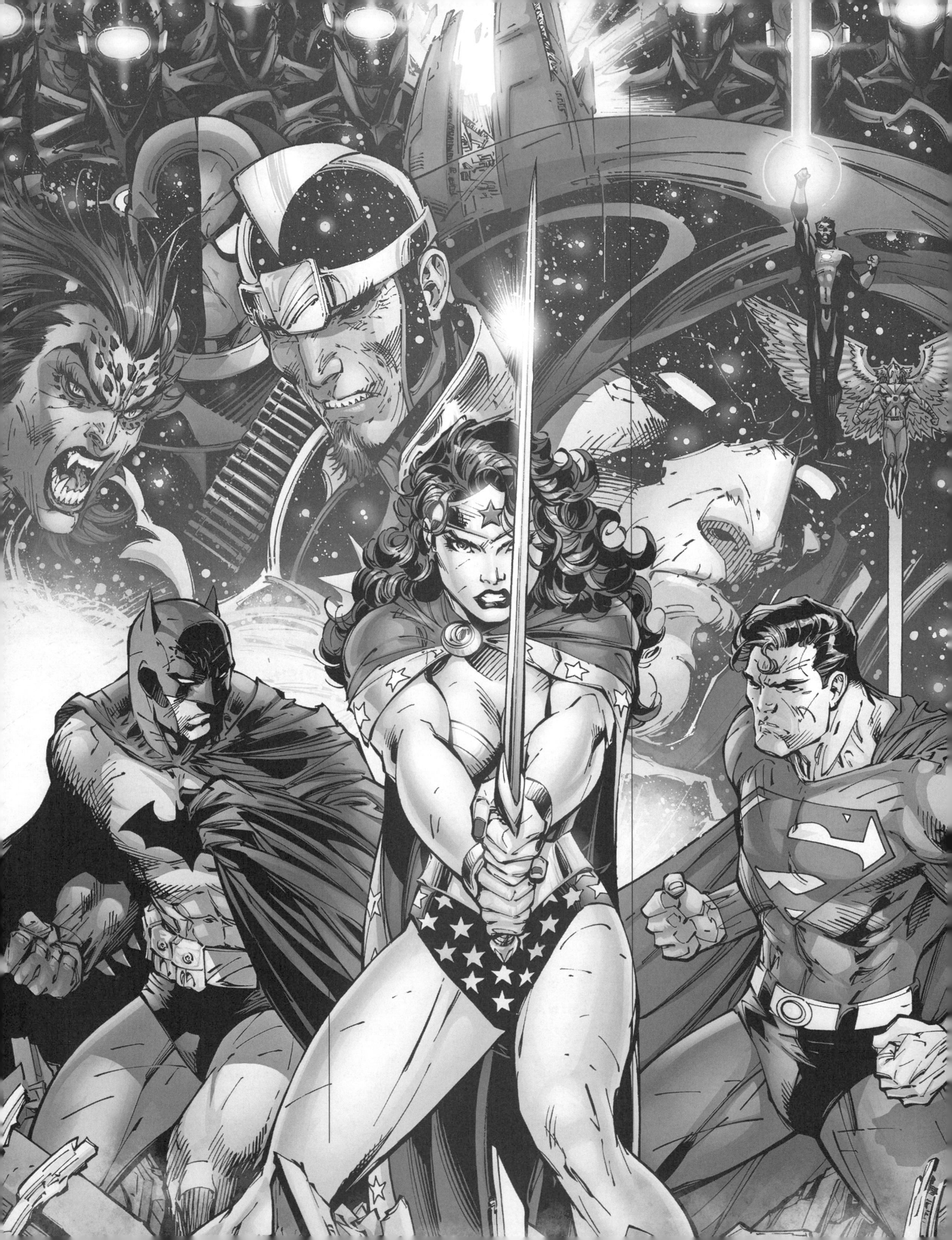

against the heroes for using magic to mindwipe them or alter their personalities.

When he deemed the time right, Luthor had Superman break open the crystal structure, sending reality-altering waves through the universe. Superman approached Batman in the BATCAVE and explained that the "wrong" Earth had been re-created, but they now had the ability to change things and create a better world. Batman rejected the offer of friendship and saw the inherent danger in the plan, especially after learning that it was Superboy who had destroyed the JUSTICE LEAGUE OF AMERICA's Watchtower on the moon.

Luthor continued to use Superboy as his pawn, gathering up superpowered men and women from what should have been distinct parallel worlds to help energize a cosmic tuning fork that would splinter reality. Seeking a perfect world, Luthor used cosmic forces to create parallel world after parallel world, none quite right in his estimation. Each new iteration weakened all the others, and they threatened to collapse one atop the other.

Superboy, meantime, was angered by how spineless and weak Kon-El, the clone with Superman's and Luthor's genetic material, appeared to be. In fact, Superboy-Prime grew angrier and angrier at the state of the world he found and became nearly unstoppable as he sought to destroy those who didn't measure up to his heroic ideal. In his wake were left the dead, broken bodies of heroes and villains, including Kon-El. A blast of solar energy from the armor Superboy wore sent NIGHTWING into a three-week coma.

Batman gathered a strike force to stop Brother I—which had renamed itself BROTHER EYE and had been taken from Luthor by Maxwell Lord, who had his own ideas about eradicating the meta-human beings on Earth. The Dark Knight dispatched Firestorm to stop Luthor's continued meddling with the multiverse. On Earth, the combined forces of heroes finally stopped Superboy-Prime until the Superman of Earth-2 and Superman rushed the teen and flew him through Rao, the red sun from KRYPTON's solar system. Depowered by the radiation, the older Superman finally died, Superman lost his super-abilities for a year, and Superboy finally grew manageable; he was turned over to the GREEN LANTERN Corps.

Batman tracked down Alex Luthor and seemed ready to shoot him until WONDER WOMAN convinced him otherwise. Instead Luthor escaped, only to be found by an unhappy JOKER, who killed him for not inviting the Clown Prince of Crime to join the Society. (*Infinite Crisis* #1–7, December 2005–June 2006)

The New Earth as altered by Luthor's manipulations changed several things in Batman's life, including the restoration of JOE CHILL as his parents' killer and the resurrection of JASON TODD from the dead. Luthor's efforts also resulted in the total restoration of the multiverse—known as the megaverse—comprising fifty-two parallel universes that existed in the same space but vibrated at different frequencies. After interference from the Venusian Mr. Mind, many of the worlds were altered; no longer perfect duplicates of New Earth,

they were instead close counterparts. Only a handful have been recorded to date, including one that contained the original version of the HUNTRESS. (*52* #52, 2007)

INFINITY ISLAND

Infinity Island was located in the Indian Ocean, a forgotten husk of land abandoned by humans when the Portuguese forsook their eastward conquests. It possessed twin volcanoes that were dormant in the twentieth century; its andesite paths were overgrown with century-old weeds. The island held the life-restoring liquids known as the LAZARUS PIT and was used as a periodic base for centuries by RÃ'S AL GHŪL. During a battle with Batman, Rã's accidentally ignited the volcanic pit, causing Infinity Island to be destroyed in an explosion. (*Batman* #332–335, February–May 1981)

INQUISITOR

With things quiet in GOTHAM CITY, Batman was intrigued by reports from Spain about two bizarre killings involving priests. One was coated in bronze, the other frozen to death in a meat locker. Aboard the BATPLANE, the Caped Crusader headed to Europe.

Batman's investigation led him to the aging but fiery Cardinal Ramirez, who spoke out against the way the mass media were corrupting society's morals. His views were not universally shared, and Father Pinto challenged him. That evening Batman met Lieutenant HECTOR SANCHEZ as he observed Pinto, noting that Ramirez was the same age as the dead priests. When Ramirez found the men, he denounced the cowled crime fighter, calling him a "tool of the devil."

Despite Batman's presence, Pinto was shot to death by a crossbow. The shooter was Gorko, a hunchbacked figure in the employ of a cloaked man called the Inquisitor. A fight broke out, but the Inquisitor got away. It wasn't until another night that Batman found his prey, who was attempting to kill a fourth priest by locking him inside a bank vault. During the confrontation, the attacker was unmasked and revealed to be Sanchez. Batman had deduced that each murder was in the style of the Seven Deadly Sins. Sanchez confessed that he took Ramirez's side with regard to the moral values. Gorko attempted to shoot Batman but wound up mortally wounding his master. As he lay dying, Sanchez gave his last confession to the priest he'd just tried to kill. Afterward, Batman studied the case further and learned that Sanchez was Ramirez's son, pointing out to the priest that one must be careful when casting stones. (*Batman* #320, February 1980)

INSURANCE CLUB, THE

The Insurance Club was a unique organization in GOTHAM CITY, this one made up of people whose lives or assets were insured for one million dollars or more. Its members, including BRUCE WAYNE, were targeted by the deranged artist JAN MARKI, who attempted to kill them to gain access to the insurance money. The club members worked alongside Batman and ROBIN to help apprehend Marki. (*World's Finest Comics* #52, June/July 1951)

INTERFACE

ASHLEY MAVIS POWELL was a Chicago-based cyber-criminal known as Interface, who opposed the third MANHUNTER on several occasions. She possessed a low level of meta-human abilities, facilitating her work with computer technology. (*Manhunter* #5, November 1988)

Some time later Interface began laundering funds in GOTHAM CITY, coming to the attention of Police Commissioner JAMES GORDON. He admitted to his niece BARBARA GORDON that he was feeling out of his depth with high-tech crimes. Barbara, recently recovered from her injuries at the hands of the JOKER but confined to a wheelchair, decided she could help her uncle. From her bedroom, Barbara began researching Interface online, gaining invaluable help from a New York cop named Sylvia Kandry. As part of the research, Barbara learned that Powell was also a child abuser, which served to fuel Barbara's desire for justice.

Barbara began to hunt Interface without using the right online security, so her identity became known to Interface. Soon after, Barbara's wheelchair was pushed into the street, nearly killing her. After some additional research, gently directed by an anonymous Dark Knight, Barbara found Richard Dragon, who took her on as a student. Over the next few months, Barbara learned to physically defend herself using Escrima sticks in addition to advanced mental disciplines to control her feelings of helplessness. During this time she had a dream about visiting the Oracle at Delphi, which she took to be a sign—and a new name. Back in Gotham, Barbara crafted the online personality of ORACLE and went back on the hunt for Interface. She manipulated Interface's psionic connection to the Internet, planting a post-hypnotic suggestion that left the thief in Barbara's power. Interface had no choice but to turn herself in. (*The Batman Chronicles* #5, Summer 1996)

INTERGANG

Intergang was not your normal criminal operation. The group was funded and supplied by the alien world of Apokolips, giving members a technological edge over rival criminal gangs and even the METROPOLIS Police Department. (*Superman's Pal Jimmy Olsen* #133, October 1970)

The operation was controlled by BRUNO "UGLY" MANNHEIM, who took his orders directly from Darkseid, the New God ruling Apokolips. Intergang served as one of the many resources at the despot's disposal in his quest to obtain the Anti-Life Equation.

In the reality after the events of CRISIS ON INFINITE EARTHS, Intergang was run by the corrupt human Morgan Edge until a heart attack removed him from power. While members thought they were dealing with the top man, Darkseid, it was actually the cunning DeSaad who gave them their orders. After Edge's illness, Mannheim—said to have trained under Apokolips's Granny Goodness—took the reins of power. Their days of terrorizing Metropolis were put to an end thanks to reporting done by CLARK KENT and Catherine Grant. (*Adventures of Superman* #467, June 1990)

The operation roared back to life under Boss Moxie, Mannheim's father, recently released after serving decades in prison. Moxie met up with renegade geneticist Dabney Donovan, who created a new, cloned body for Moxie, complete with enhanced abilities. Under new leadership, Intergang resumed its criminal ways, no longer tied to Apokolips. Moxie lost control of the business after a failed attempt by Edge to regain control. Instead Lex Luthor began to secretly run the business, with Moxie as his mouthpiece. After Superman intervened and captured Moxie and his

top men, leadership fell to Frank Sixty, a criminal specializing in cybernetics.

During the events known as Infinite Crisis, Mannheim obtained control of Intergang as well as the Crime Bible, an ancient tome filled with prophecy. The criminal enterprise's reach was vast, well beyond Metropolis, and the obsessed Mannheim set his sights on Gotham City, intending to bring about one of the prophecies. Mannheim tasked two of his associates, Whisper a'Daire and

Kyle Abbott, with preparing the city, only to have their early work interfered with by former G.C.P.D. detective Renee Montoya and the Question. (52 #11, 2006) Intergang was also behind the kidnapping of many of the world's greatest scientists in an attempt to harness their talents to ultimately take over America. (52 #25, 2006)

After Montoya and the Question left the country in pursuit of answers, it fell to the new Batwoman, aided by Nightwing, to hunt down Intergang. Their work took months, and by then Mannheim was angered that he had missed the projected date called for in the prophecy. He also interpreted the book's proposed woman, the twice-named Cain, to mean Kate Kane, aka Batwoman. Intergang members captured her, holding her hostage for four days as they prepared for her sacrifice. When the ceremony began, Mannheim stabbed Kane in the heart.

At the same time, Abbott—who abandoned Mannheim, disbelieving the prophecy—worked with Nightwing to disable giant drills Intergang had placed around Gotham, intending to bore deep and emit geysers of lava from the Earth's core, razing the city at the moment of Kane's death.

Batwoman was saved and the prophecy halted by the timely arrival of Montoya, who by then had assumed the persona of the Question. As the new Question tackled the werebeasts at Mannheim's command, Kane removed the knife from her chest and used it to stab Mannheim in the back. (52 #48, 2007)

Intergang ended its business in Gotham but remained active in Metropolis. Mannheim once more possessed Apokoliptian technology and remained a deadly threat to the Man of Steel. (Superman #654, September 2006)

INVENTOR, THE

The man known as the Inventor was a criminal genius who developed revolutionary technology using electromagnets. Powered by a dynamo in the basement of an abandoned firehouse that served as his headquarters, the Inventor's device could manipulate the tumblers on safes or prevent alarms from being triggered. Additionally, he was clever enough to leave behind a unique key, which Batman pocketed as a potential clue but was, instead, a sophisticated tracking device. Still, Batman and Robin, with help from Alfred Pennyworth, managed to thwart the Inventor's scheme and apprehend him and his men. (Detective Comics #209, July 1954)

ISLEY, PAMELA

This college student's physiology was transformed, leaving her immune to poisons while she emitted her own toxins. She became the ecologically minded criminal Poison Ivy.

Pamela Isley as Poison Ivy

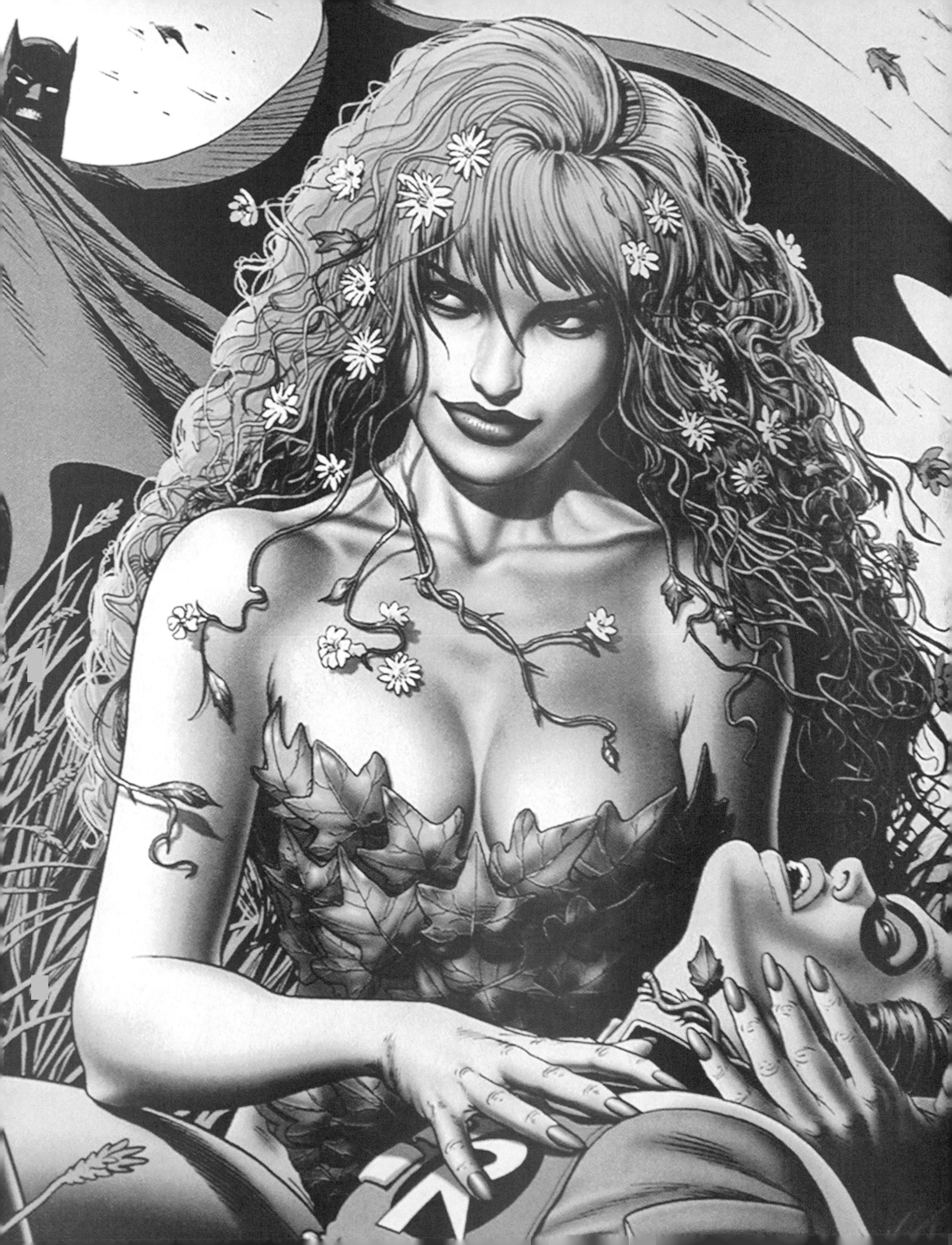

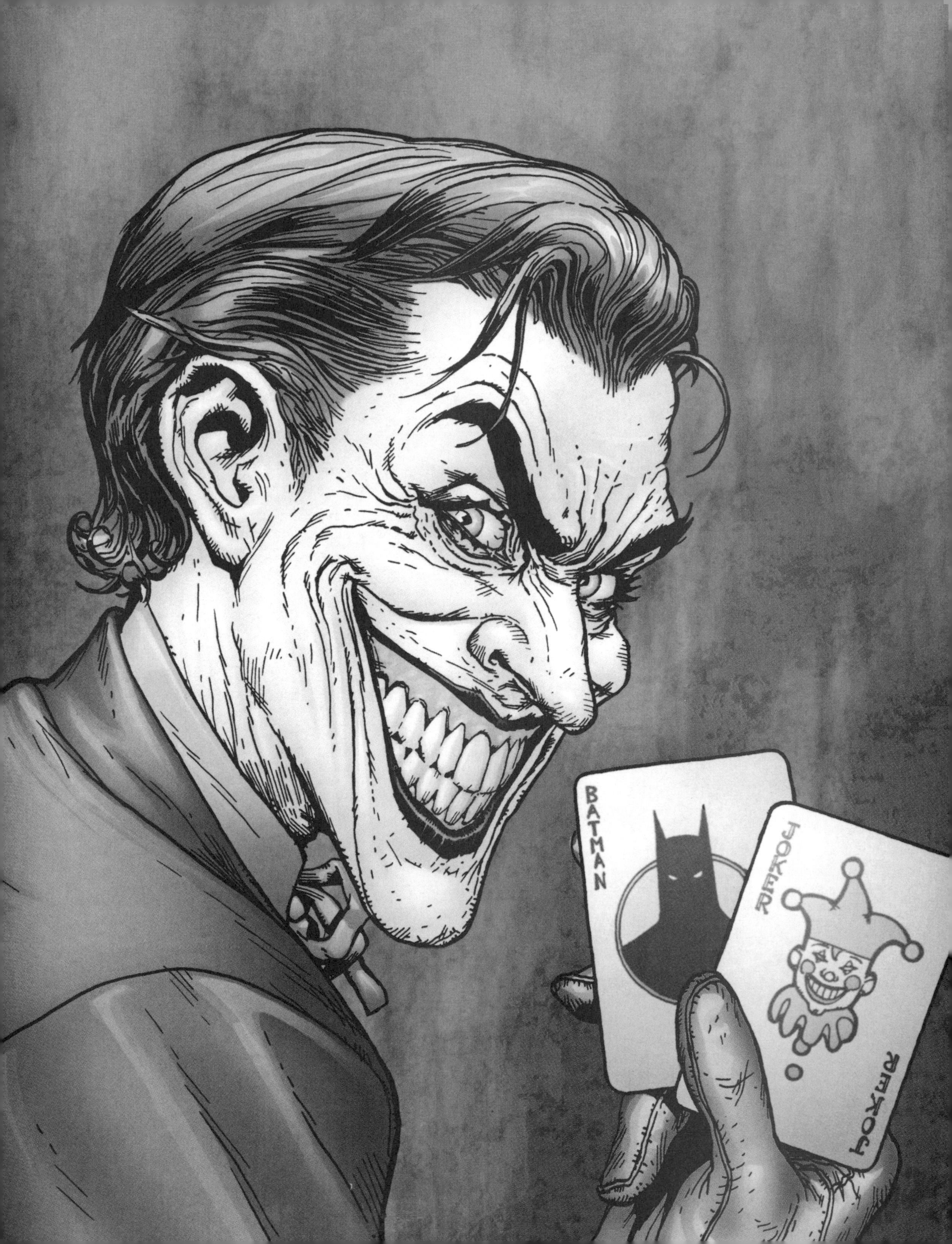
BATMAN
JOKER

JABAH

Jabah was an Indian who served DOCTOR DEATH and was the first criminal to shoot and wound Batman after he began his crime-fighting career on Earth-2. Soon after, Jabah met his end when Batman's rope was wrapped around his neck, killing him. (*Detective Comics* #29, July 1939)

JABAH GOES ON HIS ERRAND OF DEATH..

JACKAL, THE

The man known as the Jackal led a band of criminals who acted as scavengers, looting homes and businesses in the wake of disasters such as hurricanes and earthquakes. The Jackal learned of a new seismograph, developed by PROFESSOR DOREMUS LEAF, which could accurately predict the exact time and location of an earthquake. He prevented the professor from issuing a warning for the next earthquake, intending to score big when it struck. After the temblor, as they began pilfering from damaged structures, the thieves were confronted by Batman and ROBIN. During the fight, the Jackal's men fell into a just-opened fissure. As the Jackal was about to send Batman after them, Leaf arrived and hurled a piece of rubble that toppled the criminal into the fissure instead, ending his threat. (*Batman* #33, February/March 1946)

JACKAL-HEAD, THE

Under a mask resembling the Egyptian god Anubis, the Jackal-Head committed a series of crimes that kept to the theme of the underworld. As Batman and ROBIN investigated the crimes, suspicion was cast on Gotham Museum's Dr. Coombs, who had recently returned from Egypt, bearing a jackal mask. In the end, Batman exposed the thief as Coombs's assistant GIBSON. (*Detective Comics* #262, December 1958)

JAFFEER

Jaffeer was a carnival fortune-teller shot and killed by a quartet of thieves who wanted his giant ruby for themselves. With his dying breath, the mystic cursed the men to death courtesy of the four fates. Sure enough, while being pursued by Batman and ROBIN, each of the men accidentally died as predicted—one struck by lightning, one suffocated, one killed by metal, and one drowned. (*Batman* #9, February/March 1942)

JAMSON, VERNON

Vernon Jamson was not a mentally disturbed man, but he feigned illness to enter ARKHAM ASYLUM, avoiding a prison sentence. When JEREMIAH ARKHAM, the facility's director, discovered Jamson's ploy, he decreed that anyone voluntarily coming to Arkham deserved to be an inmate. Jamson was freed during the riot that ensued when the complex was damaged during the GOTHAM CITY earthquake. (*Batman: Shadow of the Bat* #80, December 1998)

JANDRON, JAY

Jay Jandron led a gang of criminals who robbed the Vaudeville Relief Fund's receipts after a benefit show. Attempting to make off with the one hundred thousand dollars, Jandron and his men were stopped by Batman and ROBIN, who were aided by six of the vaudevillians. The assistance came from a strongman, a magician, an impersonator, a ventriloquist, a tightrope walker, and an Indian rubber man. (*Batman* #101, August 1956)

JARREL, "BIG JIM"

"Big Jim" Jarrel ran GOTHAM CITY's rackets for a time and wanted an impregnable base of operations. After learning of the caverns deep beneath WAYNE MANOR, he bought the next property over and began to construct a tunnel that he thought would allow him access. Once BRUCE WAYNE learned of the plan, he needed to thwart Jarrel without revealing the existence of the BATCAVE beneath the manor. He and ROBIN emptied the cave's contents, relocating their crime-fighting gear, and then flooded the cavern from the underground river. When Jarrel and his men broke through, they saw the damp cavern and realized the space would not work. The Dynamic Duo were on hand, though, to arrest Jarrel for trespassing. (*Detective Comics* #223, September 1955)

JARVIS, ALFRED

Alfred Jarvis was the name BRUCE WAYNE's butler was known by on one of many parallel Earths.

JASON, J. J.

J. J. Jason was a bestselling detective novelist who had grown bored with his made-up stories and wanted to devote his attentions to a real mystery. He settled on unraveling the question of who was under Batman's cowl. The clever author managed to obtain enough evidence from the Caped Crusader to deduce that he was in actuality BRUCE WAYNE. Batman, in turn, tricked Jason into revising his conclusion by arranging for the novelist to spot Batman and Wayne in the same place. Wayne had employed a deaf-mute to impersonate him as Batman, further protecting his secret identity. (*World's Finest Comics* #39, March/April 1949)

JENKINS, WILBUR

Wilbur Jenkins was a genius predisposed to criminal activities. Still, he invented a device that could emit magnetism much as a flashlight shone light. He schemed with his brother Thomas, a guard at the GOTHAM CITY Museum, to steal the priceless Opals of Ealing and use the device to make it appear the crime had been committed by three suits of armor that had become animated. Batman and ROBIN investigated and quickly apprehended the Jenkins brothers. (*Batman* #172, June 1965)

JESTER, THE

On one of Batman and ROBIN's frequent trips through time, they visited ancient Rome and encountered PUBLIUS MALCHIO. Malchio was a racketeer and used a man known as the Jester as his strongman. To Batman's surprise, the Jester was identical to his twentieth-century foe, the JOKER, except for his Caucasian skin. (*Batman* #24, August/September 1944)

JOHNSON, NOCKY

Wanted in six states, Nocky Johnson was a career criminal clever enough to turn any situation to his own advantage. When he arrived in the small town of Red Gulch, he reignited the long-simmering feud between the Chatfield and McKee clans. The feud was designed to distract people from Johnson's planned theft of lens-grinding machines that were being used to manufacture equipment for America's World War II effort on Earth-2. When the theft was discovered, Johnson intended to pin the blame on one of the fighting families. Instead, Batman and ROBIN tracked the fugitive and took him into custody. (*World's Finest Comics* #16, Winter 1944)

JOKER, THE

The Joker was the white-skinned, green-haired maniac who plagued Batman in almost every reality recorded. Their epic matches have caused untold collateral damage, and one cannot seem to exist without the other. (*Batman* #1, 1940)

On Earth-2 the Joker was a mass murderer, using his specially designed Joker Venom to kill his victims, leaving their faces rigid with a smiling rictus. The Ace of Knaves and Batman tangled on

numerous occasions; each time the criminal was seemingly killed, only to return days or months later. When he was finally caught, tried, convicted and sentenced to the electric chair, the murder spree—thirty-six bodies and counting—was thought to be at an end. Instead, after he was killed, the Joker's henchmen stole the body and revived him with a unique serum. (*Detective Comics* #64, June 1942)

Over time, though, the Joker came to eschew murder for other outlandish crimes and pranks, seeming to prefer taunting Batman and law enforcement to actually getting away with his robberies. Where Batman represented law and order, the Joker twisted that by embodying chaos, the mirroring coming closest when the Joker devised his own UTILITY BELT to counteract Batman's famed gear. (*Batman* #73, October/November 1952) He endured near death, multiple arrests, and a long life. How he got turned from normal man to pasty-faced madman was never explained. Even long after Batman retired, the Joker continued to operate, although he did slow down through the years. His final recorded antics, prior to the world being wiped out in a cosmic upheaval, were against Batman's daughter, the HUNTRESS. (*Wonder Woman* #281, July 1981)

On Earth-1 the Joker was an unnamed criminal who led a gang under the guise of the RED HOOD. When Batman and ROBIN pursued the criminals at the MONARCH PLAYING CARD COMPANY, the Red Hood fell into a vat of chemicals. After he was retrieved and unmasked, police learned he had been instantly transformed into the MONARCH OF MENACE. (*Detective Comics* #168, February 1951)

Batman and the Joker engaged in numerous confrontations through their decade-plus struggle. For each crime thwarted, the Joker managed to get away with other offenses as he veered between the comical and the deadly, all the while attempting to get the best of the Caped Crusader. (*Batman* #251, September 1973)

The Joker continued to find new and innovative ways to torment the world, including the time he used his venom to supply fish in the Atlantic Ocean with his trademark grin. He then applied to copyright the Joker-fish, intending to profit from the royalty fishermen and restaurants would have to pay him. (*Detective Comics* #475–476, April 1978–May/June 1978)

In the wake of the CRISIS ON INFINITE EARTHS, the Harlequin of Hate's origins became cloudy. It was thought he might be a chemical-engineer-turned-failed-comedian who got roped into committing the robbery as the Red Hood in order to earn

money to care for his pregnant wife. A freak lightning strike killed his wife, but despite his pain he was coerced into going ahead with the crime the same day. In this version, Batman was not present when the man fell into the vat of chemicals at the Ace Chemical Processing Plant, swimming through a pipe and emerging in the polluted river disfigured. (*Batman: The Killing Joke,* 1988) This version was mostly substantiated by an eyewitness to the crime, the RIDDLER. (*Batman: Gotham Knights* #54, August 2004)

The exact nature of the man's mental illness was subject to debate among professionals. To the Joker, his new incarnation meant he was a blank slate, constantly reinventing himself—as befit his physical looks—while he sought a core personality. (*Batman* #663, April 2007) Others have suggested that his insanity was actually some advanced form of sanity that allowed him to see the world in a way no one else could comprehend. (*Arkham Asylum,* 1989) It was demonstrated that the Joker feared nothing; even the SCARECROW's fear gas failed to conjure up nightmare images.

The Joker arrived in the public eye soon after Batman was first spotted in GOTHAM CITY. He came to police attention for a series of disfiguring murders, beginning with millionaire Henry Claridge, only to be stopped, but not apprehended, by Batman. (*Batman: The Man Who Laughs,* 2005) One account indicated that he appropriated his famed Joker Venom from a victim as opposed to creating it himself. (*Legends of the Dark Knight* #50, Early September 1993)

A different account had the Joker arrive in Gotham City as a depressed criminal. Three weeks later, his perfectly executed robberies no longer excited him. He fell into a depression and walked out during the middle of one such crime. It was too easy for him, and he wondered what it was all about. At a bar, he began chatting with the bartender, a young woman putting herself through college. She tried to perk him up and suggested that he try his particular profession one more time. On HARLEEN QUINZEL's advice, he committed another crime, which once more went off perfectly and bored him to tears. He handed his pistol to the bank guard and asked him to shoot. Before the frightened guard could pull the trigger, the Dark Knight arrived, and the man, who called himself Jack, was fascinated. He remained in Gotham for weeks, committing random acts that led to violence and robberies, but nothing Batman could anticipate and prepare for, which drove the nascent crime fighter to distraction. When the criminal next appeared at the Gotham Museum, Batman fought him, only to watch as he took Lorna Shore, Bruce Wayne's girlfriend, hostage. Batman pursued him anyway, resulting in Shore's being stabbed. To subdue the madman, Batman used his prototype BATARANG, slashing the man on both cheeks, splitting the skin and causing him to develop a garish grin. The conflict grew to the point where Batman chose to turn him over to the mob, who wanted him dead, rather than bring him to the police. The mob brought him to a chemical plant to murder him. A regretful Dark Knight arrived to rescue him, but the fight led to the man being accidentally swept away with some chemicals, resulting in the skin alterations and completing his transformation into the Joker. (*Batman Confidential* #7-12, September 2007-February 2008)

The Joker and Batman appeared to recognize from the beginning how their lives and careers were to be intertwined. As a result, time and again Batman has been pushed to the limits of his moral codes, recognizing that the world would be better off without the Joker but never able to kill the crazed man. Despite a death toll in the hundreds, if not thousands, the Joker continued to avoid prison. The one time a lawyer found a way to convict him of murder, Batman investigated only to discover it was one death the Joker could not claim credit for. (*Joker: Devil's Advocate,* 1996)

Batman lost only one partner in his career, the second Robin, JASON TODD. When the Joker entered the nuclear arms business, Batman traced his activities to the Middle East. While there, he encountered Todd, who had been seeking his birth mother, only to find instead the Joker, who beat him to near death with a crowbar before leaving him in a warehouse that soon after blew up. (*Batman* #425-428, November–December 1988) The Joker then convinced the Iranian government to appoint him ambassador to the United Nations, all as part of his plan to unleash global chaos. A

grief-maddened Batman nearly came to blows with SUPERMAN, who had to respect the killer's diplomatic credentials—although the Man of Steel did stop the mass killing.

Once, the Joker kidnapped Police Commissioner JAMES GORDON, placing him in bondage gear and mentally torturing him at an abandoned circus outside Gotham. To compound the matter, the Joker went to Gordon's midtown apartment; as his niece BARBARA GORDON opened the door, he fired at point-blank range, crippling her. As she writhed in agony, he stripped her and photographed her,

later showing enlarged images to Gordon. Batman rescued the commissioner before he could be mentally broken. Again he nearly killed the Ace of Knaves, but he stopped himself when the Joker told a joke. (*Batman: The Killing Joke,* 1988)

The Joker has considered Batman his personal property, actually interfering with the schemes of other felons if he felt it meant someone other than himself got to kill or unmask Batman. Similarly, after killing the second Robin, he felt proprietary ownership over the right to kill whoever was Batman's sidekick, a fact that played out when it was learned BLACK MASK killed the female Robin. (*Batman* #643-644, *Detective Comics* #809-810, October 2005)

When Gotham City was declared a NO MAN'S LAND and abandoned by the federal government, ARKHAM ASYLUM, too, was abandoned and the Joker left free. He watched as others pillaged the city and finally crafted a scheme of his own. That Christmas, just before the city was restored to America's sovereignty, the Joker kidnapped the infants and children, bringing them to police headquarters, planning to blow up both the innocents and the symbol of order. He was stopped but held a baby in one hand, a pistol in the other, as he was confronted by SARAH ESSEN GORDON. She opted to save the falling baby, allowing the Joker to shoot her. When Batman apprehended him, Gordon finally had a chance to exact revenge for crippling his niece and

YES, WHAT WILL THE CRIME CLOWN DO NOW THAT HE IS A MILLIONAIRE? TO FIND OUT, LET US JOIN HIM IN THE GLITTERING VAULT BENEATH HIS FABULOUS MANSION...

HO, HO, HO! HA, HA, HA! HOW BEAUTIFUL -- AND IT'S ALL MINE! AND THIS SPECIAL VAULT I HAD BUILT WILL KEEP MY FORTUNE SAFE!

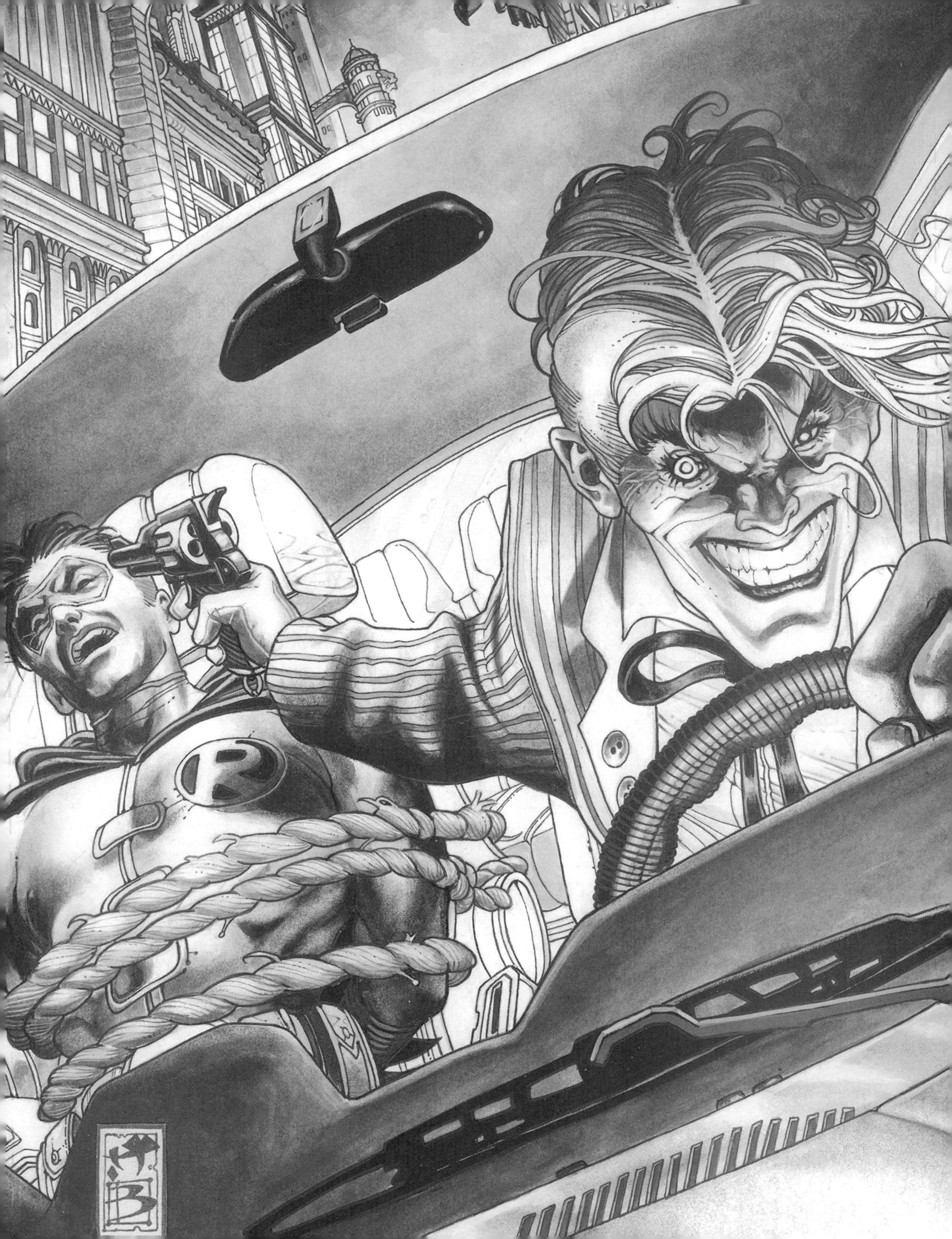

killing his wife. The commissioner, though, found the strength of will to merely shoot out the killer's knees, crippling him. (*Detective Comics* #741, February 2000) Afterward he was remanded to the Slabside Penitentiary, where ORACLE kept watch over him through closed-circuit cameras.

Soon after, the Joker managed to steal 99 percent of the magical powers from the FIFTH DIMENSION'S MR. MXYZPTLK. The world suffered greatly during this time, although despite possessing this energy, the Joker could not bring himself to eliminate Batman. Instead, he realized that he saw the world as one that must have a Batman to oppose him. (*Superman* #160, September 2000)

Not long after he lost his magic, the Joker came to believe that he was dying, so he chose to go out memorably. He infected the Slab's super-villain inmates with a variation on his Joker Venom, then broke them out of confinement. Free himself, he set about defacing statues in his image and attempted to create an heir with HARLEY QUINN, who wasn't thrilled with the notion of parenthood and allied herself, instead, with the heroes. Faced with utter chaos from coast to coast, President LEX LUTHOR declared open war on the Clown Prince of Crime. In retaliation, the Joker sent his men to assassinate the president—galvanizing the heroes to protect a president they disliked. It fell to BLACK CANARY to investigate the Joker's motives. She discovered that the Slab's doctor had falsified CAT scan results, hoping that the threat of death would force the Joker to curtail his evil. The heroes managed to find a counteragent to the Joker Venom and restored order, including returning the escapees to the Slab. NIGHTWING, though, caught up with the killer and did what Batman had never been able to do—kill the Joker. To Batman, this meant the Joker would be escaping facing justice for his latest scheme, so he revived his enemy, placing the Joker in Batman's debt. (*Joker: Last Laugh* #1–5, December 2001–January 2002)

Unlike his previous incarnations, the Joker's random acts of murder grew in number, from a classroom of kindergarteners to his own hirelings who forgot to laugh at his jokes. With one exception, he has never displayed any affection or warmth for another human being. The exception was his Arkham Asylum psychiatrist, one in a long number, Harleen Quinzel. He at first manipulated her to fall for him so he could escape, but eventually he actually felt something akin to affection for her. They endured a love–hate relationship—although when it came to self-preservation, the Joker always looked out for number one. (*Batman: Harley Quinn*, 1999)

Despite his crimes around the world, the Joker managed to beat a murder conviction, thanks to his obvious insanity. He has been shown to retain a cadre of top-flight lawyers who immediately turn up in court whenever he is apprehended by the law. (*Batman* #643–644, *Detective Comics* #809–810, October 2005)

While never a team player, the Joker has allied himself with various bands of criminals, including the Injustice Society. However, when he learned that the Lex Luthor from another world had formed a secret Society of villains to oppose the heroes, he grew angry that he had not been invited. Once

the calamitous events of INFINITE CRISIS came to an end, he and his world's Luthor tracked down the mastermind and shot him to death in a rare case of bad humor. (*Infinite Crisis* #7, June 2006)

The Joker continued to torment Batman and Gotham's law enforcement, adding attempted murder of Gordon and destruction of the BAT-SIGNAL to his list of crimes. He was subsequently shot in the face by a man dressed in a Batman costume and rushed to Arkham. (*Batman* #655, September 2006) He endured extensive facial surgery, leaving him with a permanent smile, not just the chemically treated red lips implying a smile. He also dispatched Harley Quinn to begin killing his former hirelings with his patented poison. (*Batman* #663, April 2007)

Freeing himself from Arkham, the Joker returned to Gotham and wound up with Robin as a passenger in his stolen car. As they drove, the Clown Prince once more tried to abuse a Robin both mentally and physically, but the third Robin fought back, distracting his captor with a discussion of the Marx Brothers. Robin caused the car to crash, possibly injuring the Joker but allowing the Teen Wonder to escape unharmed. (*Detective Comics* #826, October 2006)

The Joker once more escaped death after that incident, by landing on a passing truck. He sought solace from a stage magician, Ivar Loxias, a man who idolized the Clown Prince. Loxias helped heal the Joker while the madman taught the magician about poisons and explosives. As the

One world was spared the Joker when that reality's BRUCE WAYNE became a GREEN LANTERN and used the power ring to apprehend the Red Hood before his fall into the vat of chemicals. (*Batman: In Darkest Knight,* 1994)

lessons ended, a healthy Joker killed Loxias and impersonated him in a new scheme, which brought him into conflict with Batman and ZATANNA. He was once more returned to Arkham. (*Detective Comics* #833–834, May–June 2007) He escaped again and helped form Injustice League Unlimited, nearly succeeding in taking down the Justice League of America. (*Justice League of America Wedding Special,* 2007; *Justice League of America* [second series] #13–14, November–December 2007)

The Joker has indicated a rare awareness of the multiverse, formed after events of Infinite Crisis. (*Countdown* #50, 2007)

Aiding the Joker in his crimes were arrays of gadgets and equipment styled after practical jokes or seemingly innocuous items—but each proved deadly. His boutonnière emitted either deadly gas or acid, while his joy buzzer delivered enough electricity to kill a man. Nothing was ever as it seemed, and any who opposed him learned to tread carefully.

Despite his thin frame, the Joker proved incredibly agile, with tremendous endurance and a high threshold for pain. He also displayed remarkable strength for a man his size and actually could match Batman blow for blow for brief periods. How he got so strong has not been explained, although it might be a by-product of the chemical bath that also changed his skin and hair.

In a potential future, the Joker survived into old age, a catatonic wreck—until he heard the news that Batman was again seen in public. He snapped back to life and returned to threaten Gotham once

more until his death. (*Batman: The Dark Knight* #1–4, 1986) A second Joker arose soon after, killing many of that future's remaining heroes until he was exposed by Batman as a bitter DICK GRAYSON, resentful at having been fired as Robin years earlier. (*The Dark Knight Strikes Again* #1–3, 2002)

After the events of Infinite Crisis restored the parallel worlds, Earth-22 was created. In that world's future the Joker would be killed at the hands of the superpowerful madman Magog. (*Kingdom Come,* 1996)

Throughout the myriad parallel realities that have been recorded, for every Batman there has almost certainly been a Joker. One such world posited that vampires had overrun Gotham, turning the Dark Knight into a vampire while the Joker ruled. (*Batman: Bloodstorm,* 1995) In another, the Joker obtained Kryptonian technology and used it to kill Robin and BATGIRL in front of Batman, who, in this reality, finally killed his foe. (*JLA: The Nail* #3, November 1998) After that Batman died, the two actually continued their struggles in Hell. (*JLA: Another Nail* #1–3, 2004)

One world posited that Professor Josiah Carr was responsible for the assassination of Abraham Lincoln as part of a plan to obliterate the Union. His underling, Jake Napier, was one of the two men who killed THOMAS and MARTHA WAYNE, leading their son Bruce to become a secret detective. (*Batman: Detective No. 27,* 2004)

A world that gained super heroes had a female Joker, who was actually three women sharing the

JOKER, THE (FREDDY FORBES)

On an unnamed parallel world, television comedian FREDDY FORBES was known to audiences as the Joker.

JOKER FILM PRODUCTIONS, INC.

One of the many schemes launched by the JOKER was his own film company, which produced short educational films for criminals. Batman and ROBIN easily put the Clown Prince of Crime out of business. (*Batman* #80, December 1953/January 1954)

JOKER'S DAUGHTER, THE

One of several aliases employed by DUELA DENT, adding confusion as to her actual name and background.

JOKER'S JOURNAL, THE

The JOKER founded a newspaper for underworld readers, complete with a comic strip that satirized Batman. Advertisements offered goods and services for all manner of criminal enterprises. Batman and ROBIN put the newspaper out of business. (*Detective Comics* #193, March 1953)

JOLLY ROGER

Jolly Roger was dressed as a pirate and operated his criminal enterprise from a cave located on an island near GOTHAM CITY. The island was also the site of the Jolly Roger hotel, trading off the legend that the cave had once been used by pirates. Batman and ROBIN traced a smuggling racket back to the island and checked into the hotel in their civilian guises of BRUCE WAYNE and DICK GRAYSON. In short order it was revealed that Jolly Roger was actually the hotel's manager, Thomas Wexley. (*Detective Comics* #202, December 1953)

JONES

A man better known to Batman and law enforcement as the costumed criminal CHECKMATE.

JONES, BATMAN

Batman Jones was a young boy who was briefly obsessed with the Caped Crusader.

JONES, T-GUN

Jones earned the nickname *T-Gun* for his facility with the tommy gun. As a result, competing criminal organizations in GOTHAM CITY vied for his full-time services. He agreed to ally himself with one over the others based on a competition to see which group could acquire the most Batman-related artifacts, within twenty-four hours, for the Underworld Museum of Crime. Leaders Stogie Bevans and Neon Syne agreed and had their men fan across Gotham to obtain the items. Syne's men managed to capture the Caped Crusader himself, winning the competition with ease. After he was put on display in the museum, Batman freed himself and, together with ROBIN, apprehended the two mobs and Jones. (*World's Finest Comics* #37, November/December 1948)

JONES, WAYLON

A wrestler-turned-criminal called KILLER CROC who was afflicted with a condition making him appear part man, part crocodile.

JOR-EL

On the doomed KRYPTON, only the scientist Jor-El recognized the planet's imminent destruction. Defying the Kryptonian leadership, he built a prototype rocket ship to demonstrate how the people could be saved. When the planet's death arrived sooner than anticipated, the rocket was sent into space carrying his infant son, Kal-El, the last son of Krypton. The rocket landed on Earth, and the child grew up to become SUPERMAN. (*Action Comics* #1, June 1938) (For a detailed account of the life and career of Jor-El, consult *The Essential Superman Encyclopedia*.)

JOWELL, GENTLEMAN JIM

Jim Jowell was a criminal with impeccable manners, earning him the nickname *Gentleman Jim*. Along with his hirelings Herman, Tapper, and Shank, he committed robberies throughout GOTHAM CITY until he was apprehended by Batman and ROBIN. (*Detective Comics* #86, April 1944)

JUDSON

Judson's Comet Cars was run by Judson, who also dabbled in crime as the GLASS MAN.

JUDSON, ALEC

Alec Judson was a wealthy sportsman and known to high society as founder of the Safari Club. He was also the secret leader of an international crime cartel. When Ed Yancey began blackmailing Judson, the millionaire decided to conclude the business by murdering Yancey and casting suspicion on his former hunting partner, Markham. An investigation by Batman and ROBIN revealed the truth. (*Batman* #111, October 1957)

JUDSON, NED

Ned Judson was a millionaire and major Batman fan, making him susceptible to a scam concocted by four con men. They approached Judson, identically dressed as the Caped Crusader, and explained that they were part of an operation known as the Brotherhood of the Batman; they had pooled their resources to create the impression there was but one crime fighter. They invited Judson to begin training to join their ranks, a ruse intended to swindle the gullible millionaire into providing funds, ostensibly for gear such as a BATMOBILE. Batman and Robin learned of the scheme and alerted Judson, who worked with the Dynamic Duo to bring the quartet to justice. (*Detective Comics* #222, August 1955)

JUNDY

Jundy obtained an ancient manuscript leading him to three items that, when assembled, fashioned the Sorcerer King's scepter, a powerful artifact. To obtain the three items, he kidnapped Batman and ROBIN, trapping them on a remote island, and forced SUPERMAN to use his mighty powers to find the items. Before the unscrupulous criminal could be given the assembled scepter, however, the Dynamic Duo freed themselves and Superman destroyed the items. (*World's Finest Comics* #125, May 1962)

JUNGLE-MAN

TOMMY YOUNG was an American lost in the African jungle for fifteen years. There he lost much of his language facility and mental acuity, reverting to savagery in order to survive. When Eli Mattock, a GOTHAM CITY criminal, found Young, he decided to turn the confused young man into his weapon. Taunting him repeatedly while dressed as Batman, Mattock trained Young to hate the Caped Crusader. Bringing the man to America, Mattock engaged in a series of crimes that capitalized on Young's skill at commanding animals. Batman and ROBIN made several attempts to apprehend the criminals, but a charging rhinoceros forced the BATMOBILE to swerve out of the way. Batman determined Young's true identity and used the information to help break Mattock's hold over the man. The former Jungle-Man used the available animals to help corral Mattock and his men, letting the Dynamic Duo take them into custody. (*Detective Comics* #315, May 1963)

JUSTICE LEAGUE OF AMERICA

On Earth-1 the arrival of combating aliens led seven of the planet's super heroes—Batman, SUPERMAN, WONDER WOMAN, FLASH, GREEN LANTERN, MARTIAN MANHUNTER, and AQUAMAN—to band together for the first time. After the threat was ably handled, the heroes agreed that remaining united made sense—and so the Justice League of America was born. (*The Brave and the Bold* #28, February/March 1960; origin revealed in *Justice League of America* #9, February 1962)

Through the years the JLA battled threats domestic, international, intergalactic, and interdimensional. Its roster rose and fell through the years, but whenever Earth needed champions, the JLA was on call. Shortly after its founding, the group's members discovered the vibrational frequency that led to Earth-2 and its heroes, the JUSTICE SOCIETY OF AMERICA. For years thereafter the two teams would meet for social gatherings and to battle cosmic threats.

The JLA first operated out of a mountain

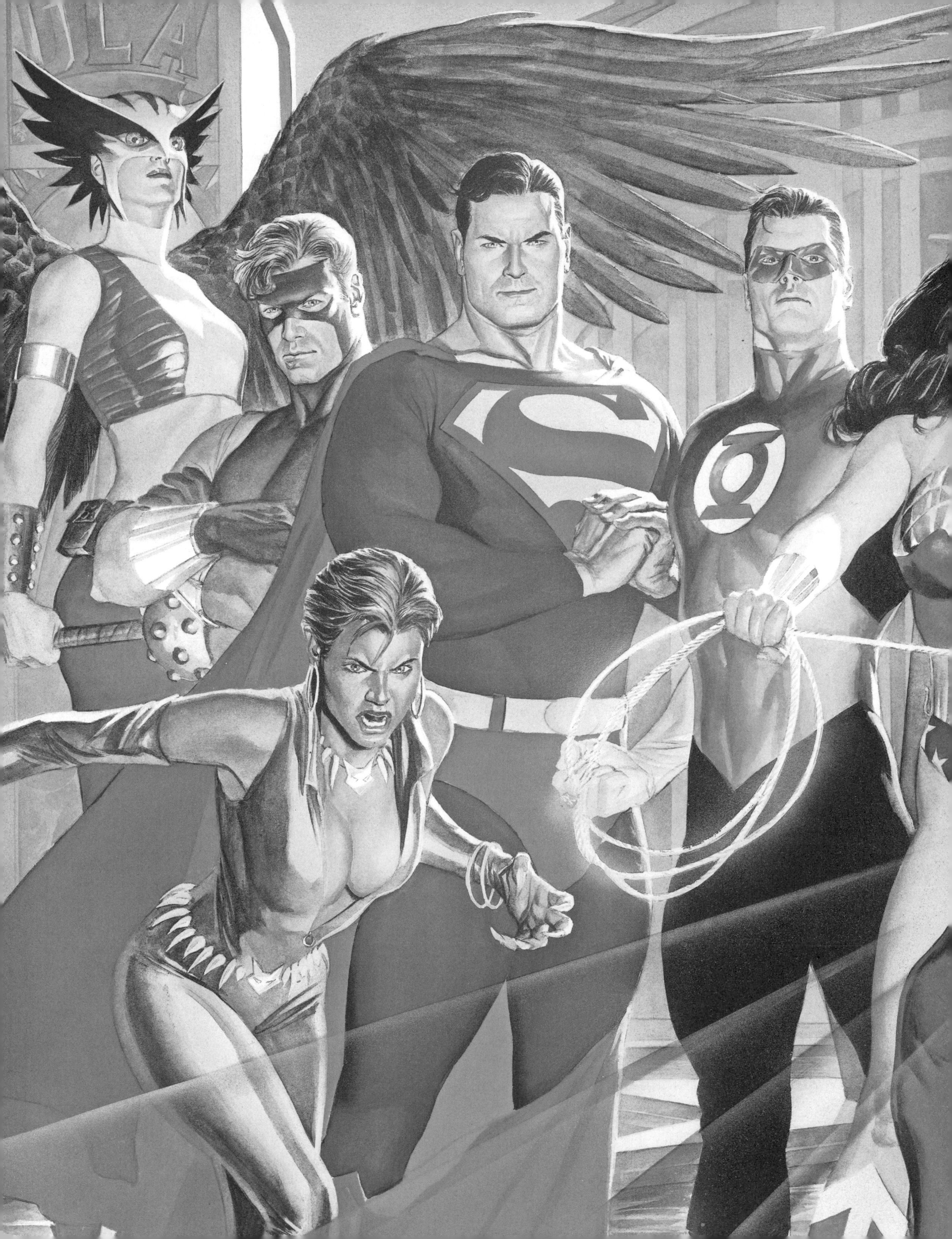

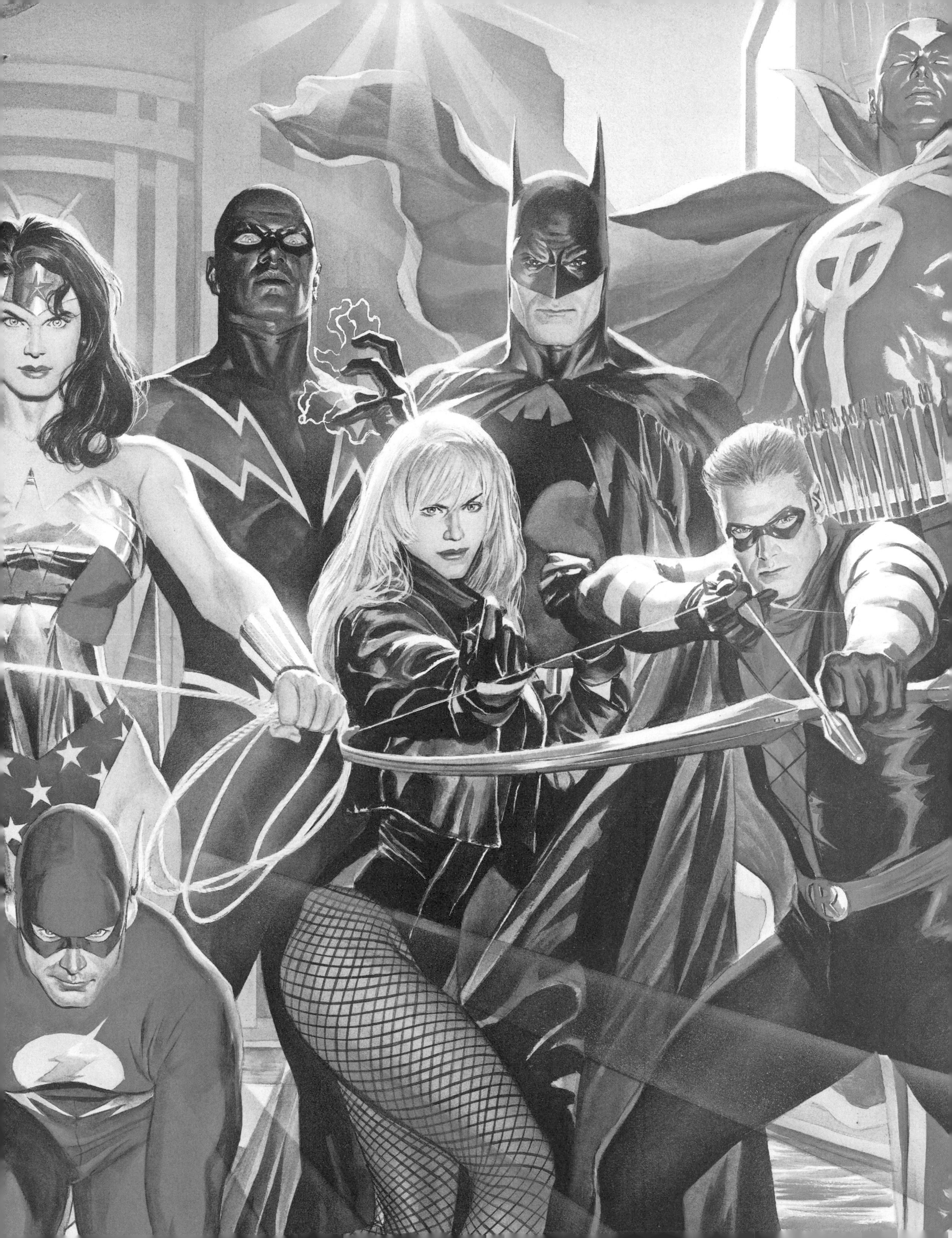

headquarters located near Happy Harbor, Rhode Island, which Batman accessed by BATPLANE. After the JOKER tricked their mascot, Lucas "Snapper" Carr, into revealing the location, the team relocated to a satellite, which orbited 22,300 miles above the Earth.

In the wake of the CRISIS ON INFINITE EARTHS the multiverse was reduced to one positive matter universe; the JSA years became known as the first age of heroes during the World War II era, while the JLA were champions of a modern age of heroism. The JLA roster after the Crisis proved more volatile.

Soon after the JLA moved to the satellite, Dr. Light accessed the headquarters and raped SUE DIBNY, wife of the ELONGATED MAN. The League turned up and apprehended the criminal, but members were divided over what to do. A vote led ZATANNA to use her magic to erase his memory of the event and alter his personality. Just as she was about to perform her spell, Batman arrived and objected. The vote already taken, Zatanna chose to erase ten minutes from Batman's memory, something that unraveled years later. (*Identity Crisis* #4, November 2004)

At one point Batman and the League disagreed over a course of action and he quit. This occurred shortly before he'd formed the OUTSIDERS, enabling him to train a new generation of heroes while tackling problems the League refused to touch. (*The Brave and the Bold* #200, July 1983) Eventually Batman resumed his JLA membership. (*Justice League of America* #250, May 1986)

The JLA actually disbanded at one point until a new crisis brought together a new collection of heroes, proving the need for such a group. Batman became a reluctant member, chafing at the seemingly child-like antics of BLUE BEETLE and the Green Lantern, Guy Gardner. (*Legends* #6, April 1987)

The JLA endured through differing incarnations, which included private financing by Maxwell Lord and later sanctioning by the United Nations. Batman remained with most versions until, once more, the League collapsed. Still, the need for protectors grew, so a new JLA was eventually formed, this time based on the moon. Batman kept his distance from the new League, providing intelligence and guidance but eschewing active participation at meetings. When the group chose to expand, he recruited the HUNTRESS, feeling the camaraderie provided by peers might temper her—and it did, for a time. ORACLE also became a full member at this point. (*JLA* #16, March 1998)

As Batman's memories began to return, his suspicion of his fellow Leaguers grew. To be better prepared, he created files on every member, including ways to neutralize or defeat each. After

RÃ'S AL GHÛL stole the files and used them to nearly destroy the heroes, Batman was ostracized from the JLA. (*JLA* #44, August 2000) His understanding of the League and how it worked also meant he was prepared when a crisis left the world without a Justice League. Following his programming, the JLA's computers sent out devices that invited a replacement set of heroes, led by NIGHTWING, to act in their stead. The new team helped rescue the JLA. (*JLA* #66–76, July 2002–February 2003)

The Dark Knight remained leery about how his fellow heroes were choosing to operate and when a splinter group went to work with the Elite, he planted a disguised BATGIRL among them to act as his eyes and ears. (*Justice League Elite* #1–12, September 2004–August 2005)

Not only did the villains altered by Zatanna begin to learn of her actions, but Batman also recovered his memories. This further splintered the League and gave the villains a new reason to band together to exact revenge. When the Watchtower exploded, the JLA died once more as Batman, Superman, and Wonder Woman found themselves at odds with one another. In the ensuing months they handled personal and global catastrophes in the event known as INFINITE CRISIS.

After matters calmed down and Batman returned from his year's hiatus, he gathered Superman and Wonder Woman in the BATCAVE, where they began carefully rebuilding the Justice League. (*Justice League of America* [second series] #0, July 2006) Uncertain of his place in the new League, it took former Outsider teammate BLACK LIGHTNING to invite Batman in. Meantime, the triumvirate had already built a new headquarters that was actually two buildings linked by transporter technology—a Hall of Justice in Washington, D.C., and a new satellite in orbit. (*Justice League of America* [second series] #7, February 2007)

JUSTICE SOCIETY OF AMERICA

On Earth-2, in the days prior to World War II, a number of "mystery men" with powers and abilities far beyond those of mere mortals began to fight crime around America.

On November 9, 1940, British intelligence asked that world's FLASH and GREEN LANTERN to investigate rumors of a possible German invasion. The heroes wound up captured and shipped to Adolf Hitler, who intended to kill them using the mystic Spear of Destiny. They were instead rescued by Dr. Fate and Hourman. The rescue and escape prompted President Franklin Roosevelt to suggest that the heroes band together. Accepting the notion, the Justice Society of America was formed, with Batman and SUPERMAN accepting honorary membership. (*All Star Comics* #3, Winter 1940; origin revealed in *DC Special* #29, August/September 1977)

In the wake of America's introduction into World War II, President Roosevelt beseeched all of America's costumed crime fighters to help defend the country's shores. The JSA grew in size and was renamed, for the duration, the All-Star Squadron.

The JSA and All-Star Squadron successfully

defended America from numerous threats until the war ended. After that, the squadron disbanded and the JSA remained America's team supreme. By the early 1950s Communist paranoia gripped the country, and the remaining members of the JSA chose to disband rather than reveal their identities to Congress's Joint Un-American Activities Committee. By this point both Batman and ROBIN had chosen semi-retirement. (*Adventure Comics* #466, December 1979)

Circumstances brought the various members back into action, including the discovery of Earth-1, a parallel world vibrating on a different frequency that had heroes appear on Earth much later. Their frequent meetings encouraged most of the JSA to come out of retirement, bringing their GOTHAM CITY brownstone headquarters back to life. Batman remained out of action, and at one meeting Robin, in a modified costume, was accepted as his replacement. (*Justice League of America* #55, August 1967)

In time Batman's daughter, HELENA WAYNE, began her career as the HUNTRESS and was soon admitted to the JSA. Finally, circumstances prompted Batman to return to action, only to meet his death during a case. (*Adventure Comics* #461–462, January/February–March/April 1979)

When the parallel worlds were merged into one new Earth during the CRISIS ON INFINITE EARTHS, JSA members assumed their title of the first age of super heroes, mentors to all who followed. This version had no Batman, Robin, or Huntress.

After the events known as INFINITE CRISIS, fifty-two parallel worlds once more existed, with the JSA operating on both New Earth and Earth-2. Robin and the Huntress were seen, with one recorded appearance of the team. (*52* #52, 2007)

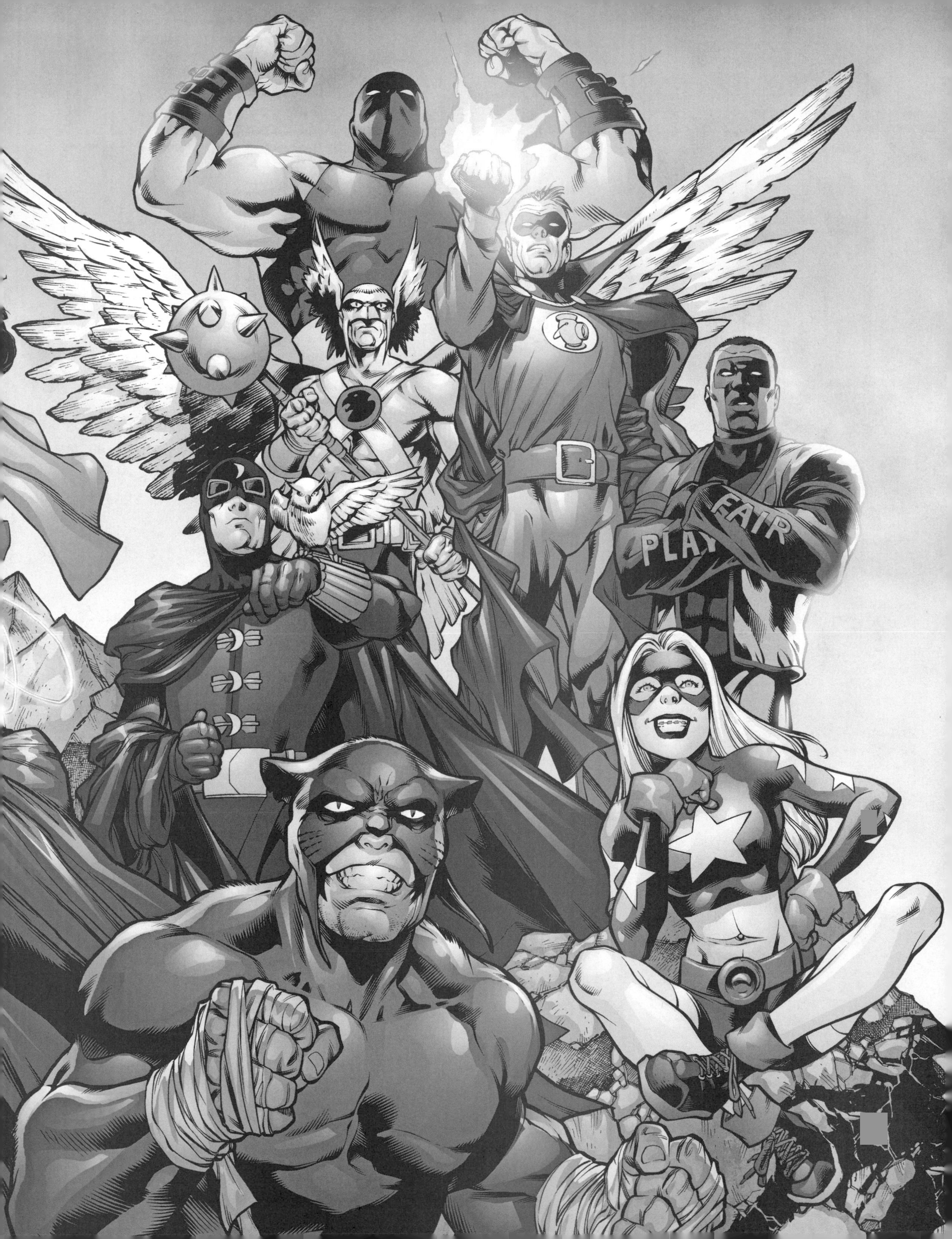
FAIR
PLAY

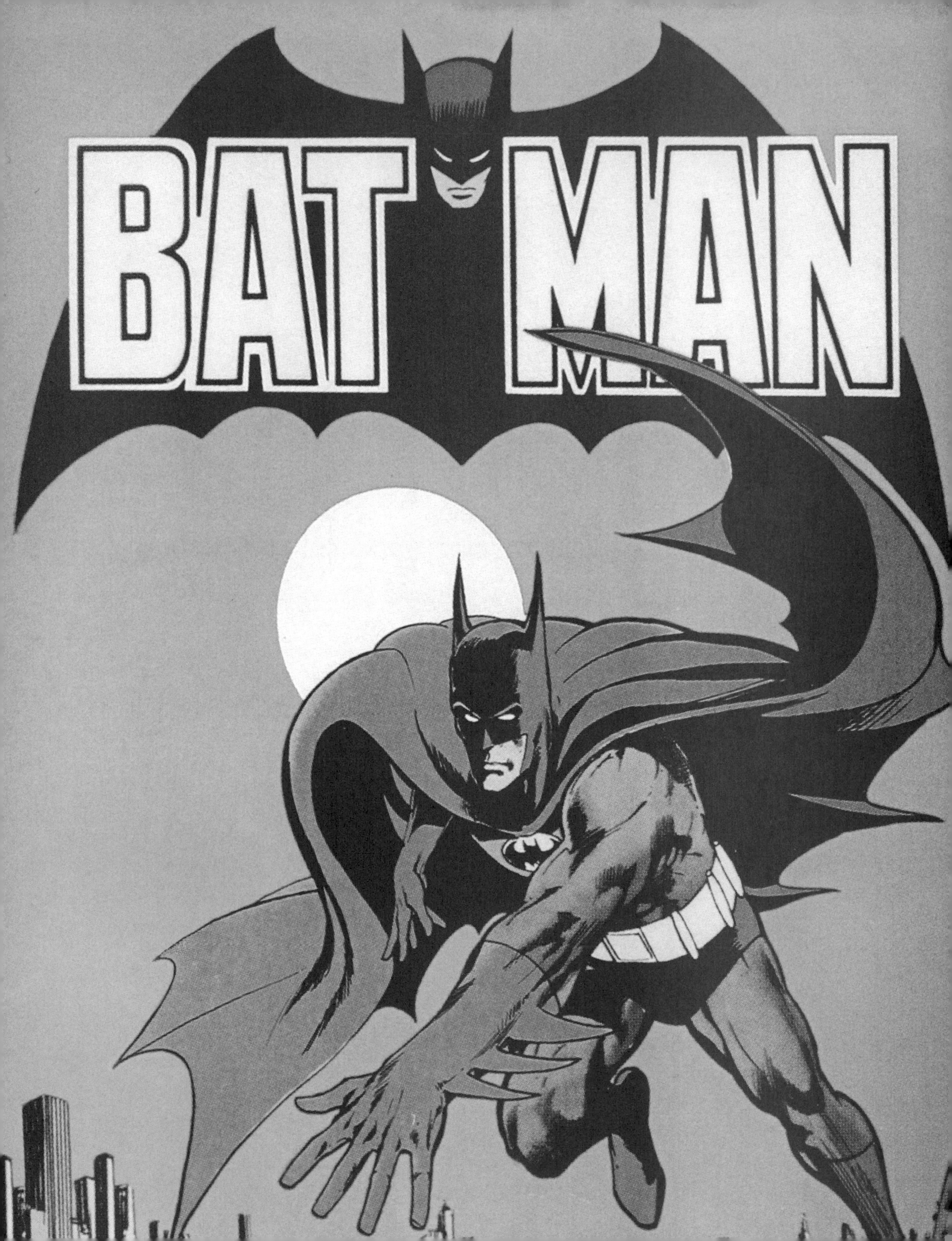
BATMAN

KAALE

Batman and ROBIN were kidnapped and taken off Earth to become prey for Kaale's pleasure. Ruler of a distant planet, Kaale frequently snatched beings from various worlds and pitted one against the other in hunts as he watched via his world's version of television. Three beings from a different world became the hunters; the Dynamic Duo had to elude them and find freedom. In the end Batman allied himself with an underground group of freedom fighters and successfully reached Kaale, putting an end to his cruel games. (*Detective Comics* #299, January 1962)

KADAVER, MORTIMER

Mortimer Kadaver was a sadist and a murderer, obsessed with dealing pain and death. He made a career out of his crimes, filling his hideaway with all manner of pain-inducing devices, from the fabled iron maiden to modern-day tools. He had been known to disturb people, including potential victims, by feigning death or emerging vampire-like from a coffin. His obsession landed him inside ARKHAM ASYLUM on several occasions after a series of defeats at the hands of Batman. (*Detective Comics* #588, July 1988)

KAI

A man who trained to become a killer and sold his services as the mercenary called HELLHOUND.

KALE, DENNY

Denny Kale and Shorty Biggs escaped from prison and used their experience as actors to impersonate Batman and ROBIN. They then duped the gullible PROFESSOR CARTER NICHOLS into sending them back in time to Italy in 1479. Once in Florence, they used their advance knowledge to form a band of criminals and plunder the city's treasures. Soon after, though, the real Dynamic Duo, accompanied by SUPERMAN, arrived in the past to retrieve the convicts. (*World's Finest Comics* #132, March 1963)

KALE, GEORGE

George Kale was president of Lightning Motors, Inc., sponsoring his niece Glenda West in a cross-country race that employed all modes of transportation. Seeking to ensure that she won and brought his firm tremendous publicity, Kale saw to it that other competitors found their cars, planes, and boats sabotaged. Batman and ROBIN, watching the race, became involved and stopped Kale before anyone died. (*Batman* #34, April/May 1946)

KALIBANICZ, VALENTIN

A criminal better known to Batman and GOTHAM CITY police as both Val Kaliban and the SPOOK.

KANDOR

Kandor was the only city to survive the destruction of the planet KRYPTON. In various realities, it had been stolen from Krypton and reduced in size by the Coluan villain BRAINIAC. (*Action Comics* #242, July 1958) After SUPERMAN rescued it from the android, he placed it in his FORTRESS OF SOLITUDE, swearing he would one day find a way to return the city to its normal size.

On Earth-2, Kandor was the home city to Kara Zor-L, who later came to Earth and began a career as Power Girl. Since the city was never taken by Brainiac, it was destroyed with the planet. (*Showcase* #97, February 1978)

On Earth-1, Kandor gave rise to the Superman Emergency Squad, specially trained crime fighters who would leave the city, gaining superpowers and acting as a miniature rescue team. Superman and his pal JIMMY OLSEN once visited and became the objects of a manhunt; they masqueraded as the legendary heroes NIGHTWING and FLAMEBIRD to clear their names. The Dynamic Duo had also visited the city in times of crisis.

In time Superman managed to fulfill his vow: restoring the people to full size on a world they dubbed Rokyn, orbiting a distant red sun. (*Superman* #338, August 1979)

After reality was reordered during the CRISIS ON INFINITE EARTHS, Kandor was home to samples of various alien races, captured by a wizard named Tolos. It existed not in a bottle but as a city placed in extradimensional space.

A reality-altering wave caused by Superboy-Prime returned Kandor to its Earth-1 history. The most significant difference was that for the citizens a hundred years had passed, while only a handful of years had passed for the Man of Steel. Superman, their rescuer, had been given god-like status. (*Action Comics* #812–813, *Adventures of Superman* #625–626, *Superman* #202–203, April–May 2004)

(For a detailed account of Kandor, consult *The Essential Superman Encyclopedia*.)

KANE, BETTE

Betty Kane was niece to Earth-1's KATHY KANE, and the teen adopted the costumed persona of Bat-Girl. (*Batman* #139, April 1961) Bat-Girl worked alongside not only BATWOMAN but also Batman and ROBIN on numerous cases for a brief period. She retired when her aunt chose to take Batman's advice and hang up her cape.

Some time later, after BARBARA GORDON took up the *BATGIRL* name, Betty was inspired to return to action. Once more she and Kathy partnered on several cases, usually in tandem with Batgirl and Robin. (*Batman Family* #16, February/March 1978) Kathy joined Robin for several missions with an expanded version of the TEEN TITANS, Titans West. (*Teen Titans* #50–52, October–December 1977)

In the wake of CRISIS ON INFINITE EARTHS, Mary Elizabeth "Bette" Kane was never a Bat-Girl. Instead she was an adolescent tennis star who loved the idea of crime-fighting teens when she saw Robin on a television news program. In a later conversation with the HUNTRESS, she admitted that she found the Teen Wonder's butt most appealing. Already in gymnastics training for her tennis career, the spoiled girl took the costumed identity of FLAMEBIRD in the hope of meeting her idol. (*Secret Origins Annual* #3, 1989)

While they met and she did adventure with Titans West, Robin was put off by her brash and obsessive manner, so he kept his distance—to her dismay. Bette could not understand how a girl with perfect grades, numerous tennis trophies, and incredible wealth for one her age could not be desired by any male. Somewhat oblivious to the attitudes displayed by her fellow teen heroes, she continued to work on and off with the Titans. The second Dove observed how lonely the life of a tennis prodigy must have been, opining that Bette just needed to be surrounded by peers.

Because of her brief tenure with the team, Bette was caught up in a gathering of heroes brought about by Cyborg and worked with the Titans and the JUSTICE LEAGUE OF AMERICA, ending a threat from the alien entity Technis. This led to a new formation of Titans, and she was devastated to learn she was not invited. (*JLA/Titans* #1–3, December 1978–February 1999)

I'LL BET THEIR HIDEOUT IS A PLACE THAT ONCE USED CELLULOSE! SO AUNT KATHY THINKS I'M "NOT READY YET"-- HUH? I'LL SHOW HER! BAT-GIRL WILL SEARCH EVERYWHERE UNTIL SHE LOCATES THE COBRA GANG'S HIDEOUT!

When fellow Titan Beast Boy moved to Los Angeles to resurrect his moribund acting career, he wound up implicated in a murder, and Bette came to his rescue. She hoped to prove herself worthy of notice from Robin, now an adult NIGHTWING. After clearing Beast Boy, she hoped to be a part of a new set of Titans being formed, according to Beast Boy's cousin Matt Logan. The recruitment drive was never sanctioned, and she was crushed once more. (*Beast Boy* #1–4, January–April 2000)

Bette refused to give up as Flamebird and continued to seek adventure even though she once needed rescuing by ORACLE's BIRDS OF PREY. Whenever the call went out, "Titans Together!"—she answered. (*Teen Titans* [third series] #24, July 2005)

She finally got her heart's desire when she was a part of the Titans for a year in the wake of the events known as INFINITE CRISIS. Bette subsequently left the team. (*Teen Titans* [third series] #38, September 2006)

In a potential future ten years later, Bette had been killed by DUELA DENT, only to be resurrected by Robin III in a LAZARUS PIT. The revived heroine became the new Batwoman and partnered with Robin. She split from Robin when the Titans grew oppressive and she founded Titans East, an opposing group that battled for freedom. (*Teen Titans* [third series] #18–21, January–April 2005)

Bette was an Olympic-level athlete with excellent gymnastic skills. In all incarnations, she carried a version of Batman's UTILITY BELT, complete with grappling hook, gas pellets, gas mask, flashlight, radio, handcuffs, and related gear.

KANE, BETTY

See Kane, Bette.

KANE, KATHY

On Earth-2 trapeze artist Kathy Kane was inspired by Batman to don a colorful costume and fight crime in GOTHAM CITY as Batwoman. Using her inheritance to buy a circus and outfit her new identity, Kane swung into action in a bright yellow-and-red outfit. In lieu of a UTILITY BELT, she had a customized purse filled with feminized crime-fighting tools. She also constructed her own version of a BATCAVE beneath her home. This early in the Caped Crusader's career,

LATER, AT A SUPPER CLUB, KATHY KANE IS UNAWARE THAT HER DANCING PARTNER IS THE MAN SHE ADMIRES MOST--BATMAN!

I MUST ADMIT YOU'RE A HANDSOME MAN, BRUCE-- BUT GOOD LOOKS AREN'T ENOUGH FOR ME ...

I KNOW! AS YOU'VE TOLD ME A HUNDRED TIMES, YOU WISH I WERE MORE LIKE BATMAN!

Kane was frequently discouraged from risking her life without the rigorous training Batman had undergone before donning his cowl. (*Detective Comics* #233, July 1956) Kane retired as Batwoman in the 1950s, distraught when BRUCE WAYNE married SELINA KYLE, the former CATWOMAN. (*Superman Family* #211, October 1981) She married an unidentified man and had children, returning to action in the days following Batman's death. (*The Brave and the Bold* #182, January 1982)

On Earth-1, Kane was also inspired by Batman

"AND IN THIS *BAT-CAVE* I FITTED UP UNDER MY *NEW MANSION*, I TRAINED LONG FOR MY *CAREER!*" "THIS COSTUME WILL *MASK MY IDENTITY!* MY *BAT-CYCLE* IS READY, AND THIS *SHOULDER-BAG UTILITY-CASE* WILL BE A GREAT HELP. NOW, WITH MY *CRIME-LABORATORY*, MY FILES, EVERYTHING -- I'M READY TO ACT!"

to don a colorful costume and fight crime in Gotham City as Batwoman. She continued fighting crime, adding a sidekick, Bat-Girl to Batman's Robin, when her niece Bette Kane discovered her identity. Batman's butler Alfred Pennyworth was tickled by the notion of the distaff duo and took to writing speculative fiction, imagining marriages and offspring to further the dynamic dynasty. Eventually Kane tired of the rigors and retired to run Kane's Kolossal Karnival. In the following years she briefly returned to action but seemed content to run the show under the big top. Unfortunately, she became a victim of a battle between Rā's al Ghūl and the Sensei for control of the League of Assassins. A brainwashed Bronze Tiger distracted Batman as underlings murdered Kane. (*Detective Comics* #485, September 1979)

In the wake of Crisis on Infinite Earths, Kathy Kane was recast as Kate Kane, hailing from one of Gotham's wealthiest families. Whether there is a familial relationship to Bruce Wayne's mother, Martha Kane, remains unchronicled. Before coming out of the closet, the Jewish Kane had briefly dated Bruce Wayne. (*Batman* #652, June 2006) Kate and police officer Renee Montoya enjoyed a torrid relationship for a time and then broke up. In the following years, Kane was trained as a fighter and was known to be dating a doctor named Mallory.

Intrigued, especially by Montoya's silence, Kane donned the Batwoman costume for the first time and tailed them, coming to their rescue when Whisper a'Daire's were-creatures attacked. Over time Montoya learned that Intergang had come into possession of the legendary Crime Bible and its leader, Bruno Mannheim, interpreted one prophecy as involving the twice-named daughter of Cain to mean Kate Kane, Batwoman. As Montoya and the Question left for Asia in pursuit of answers, Batwoman remained in Gotham to hunt down Intergang and put them out of business. She was joined by Nightwing, who struck up an easy alliance with her. Over the next several months they kept up the hunt, with little success. They did pause briefly during Chanukah, with Kane receiving a Batarang from Nightwing and a kiss from Montoya. (*52* #33, 2007)

Intergang finally acted on the prophecy, kidnapping Kane in her apartment and holding her for four days in preparation for the ritual. By this time the Question had died and Montoya had returned to Gotham, continuing the hunt for Intergang. She and Nightwing found Mannheim with the help of a'Daire's disillusioned aide Kyle Abbott, arriving during the ceremony. By then Mannheim had plunged a knife into Kane's heart. As the fight continued, Kane managed to remove the knife and used it to stab Mannheim in the back, ending the event. (*52* #48, 2007)

Kate spent the next several months recovering and then resumed her new career as Batwoman.

With her fortune, Kane managed to obtain the best athletic training possible, making her a skilled hand-to-hand combatant. She also proved an adept investigator. Her wealth allowed her to assemble a flexible, tough costume. Whether she also built bat-inspired crime-fighting gear was not recorded.

Katherine Kane

KANE, MARTHA

Socialite Martha Kane grew up to marry THOMAS WAYNE, and as MARTHA WAYNE was mother to BRUCE WAYNE, later Batman. (*Detective Comics* #33, November 1939)

KA-RA

Ka-Ra served the Egyptian pharaoh Cleopatra as chief irrigation engineer, but also worked to assassinate the queen. A time-traveling Batman and ROBIN visited the ancient land and began investigating the attacks on the fabled woman, aided by Takeloth, chief of the royal police. The man bore an uncanny resemblance to Police Commissioner JAMES GORDON. The Dynamic Duo managed to expose Ka-Ra and save the queen. (*Detective Comics* #167, January 1951)

KARABI

Secreted away in an abandoned Asian temple, Karabi attempted to foment war between rival nations on the continent. His goal was to draw in as many neighboring countries as possible and, during the conflict, cull an elite set of shock troops, akin to Germany's SS troops during World War II. The scheme, which could have plunged the world into a third global war, was stopped by Batman and ROBIN. (*Batman* #167, November 1964)

KARAOKE, JOHNNY

Before turning to crime, the man calling himself Johnny Karaoke studied business administration at UCLA and was on its fencing team. Later he became affiliated with the Japanese YAKUZA, working in GOTHAM CITY. Karaoke traveled with four associates dubbed the GEISHA GRRLS, well-trained martial artists. He invested in WAYNE FRANKLIN's I-Gore medical device; when it was stolen, and Franklin believed dead, he lost part of his left pinkie to his Obayun. Karaoke first encountered the Batman when he sought to steal Mimic, I-Gore's duplicate, from Zeis Pharmaceuticals. He was never seen without his skull-topped walking stick with a removable top, affixed to a long knife. Lured to the Gotham Opera House, Karaoke fought the Russian mobster PERUN to the death in an attempt to gain control over the technology both helped fund. (*Batman* #659–661, February–March 2007)

KARDO

Known to circus goers as the Great Kardo, the onetime magician had turned to crime and attempted to steal the one-hundred-thousand-dollar prize for a television quiz show contestant. The man and his aides were apprehended by Batman and ROBIN. (*Batman* #154, March 1963)

KARKO

A time-traveling villain from a potential twenty-sixth century, Karko began robbing to obtain ordinary furniture, cars, and paintings. His advanced knowledge let him know which objects would appreciate in value centuries hence. He was trailed to the past by Chief Inspector Mahan of the Universal Police, who worked with Batman and ROBIN to apprehend the thief. (*Detective Comics* #257, July 1958)

KARL, BARON

BRUCE WAYNE was astonished when the Gotham Orphanage asked him to care for a baby. Soon he determined that the child was heir to the throne of distant Morania. His parents, the prince and princess, had been targeted for assassination by Baron Karl, who wanted the throne for himself and acted as King Rudolph lay on his deathbed. Karl sent Bruno Kroft to kill the child but was stopped by Batman and ROBIN. The baby was returned to the true heirs, who returned home to rule their kingdom in peace. (*Batman* #128, December 1959)

KARLO, BASIL

A film-star-turned-criminal, he terrorized people as the first CLAYFACE.

KARMAK

WALTER HEWITT was a scientist who developed a device, "the bioniformer," that used irradiated light to transfer specific animal attributes to human beings. He tested the device on himself and gained the eyesight of an eagle and the speed of a cheetah.

However, when he tried to gain a gorilla's strength, there was an accident that actually transferred Hewitt's intellect to the mammal, Karmak. (*Detective Comics* #339, May 1965)

The man and gorilla shared a telepathic connection, and Karmak sent Hewitt out to commit crimes, bringing them to Batman's attention. Hewitt was quickly dispatched, being tossed into a brick wall, stunning him. The gorilla easily bested

Karmack

Batman in their first fight, so Karmak subsequently lured Batman to a jewelry store, where he used the bioniformer on the Gotham Guardian. Batman knew Karmak had to be stopped, so he soaked his gloves in anesthetic and then challenged the gorilla to meet him in Gotham Park. The wary animal arrived with a huge bomb strapped to his chest and then activated its arming mechanism when Batman lifted him off the ground. Should the Caped Crusader put the gorilla back down, the bomb was to detonate. By the time Batman's muscles gave out and Karmak fell to the earth, the bomb had deactivated itself.

With the bioniformer, Batman restored Hewitt and Karmak to their normal selves. The scientist was invited to teach while the gorilla was returned to his natural jungle habitat.

KATANA

Tatsu Yamashiro grew up in Japan, a studious teen in both academics and the martial arts. When the Yamashiro brothers, Maseo and Takeo, both professed their love, she chose Maseo for a mate. Takeo refused to attend their wedding, instead allying himself with the YAKUZA, resulting in his being disowned. The newlywed couple began a family with twins Yuki and Reiko, while Takeo made a name for himself within his new crime family. He impressed General Karnz, who gifted him with a pair of swords including the Soultaker, a mystically enhanced blade. Feeling empowered with these weapons, he visited his brother and demanded they now duel over Tatsu. The angry sibling managed to start a fire during the duel and slew Maseo with the Soultaker.

A stunned Tatsu struck out at her brother-in-law, taking his sword for herself. As the fire raged, she had turned to rescue her children when Maseo's

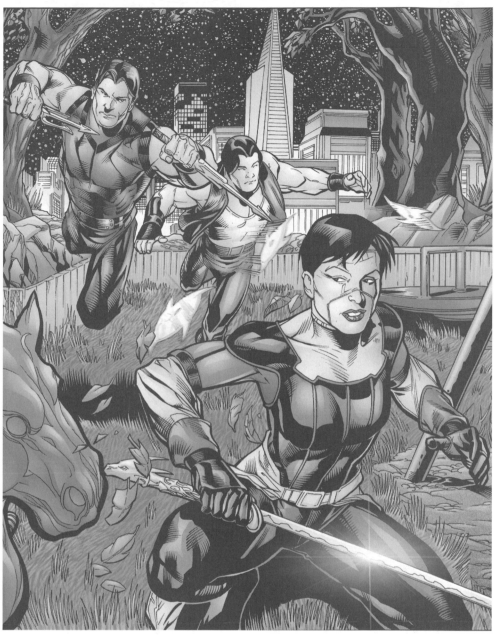

voice emanated from the sword, warning her away even as Takeo fled. Grief-stricken, she watched as her entire way of life was consumed in the flames. Directionless, she resumed her studies under Tadashi, a teacher of samurai. She later learned of Fukamaden, the abode of demons and the mystic land within the Soultaker, which was forged by a man called Muramasa. It is a realm where all who perished by its blade were consigned.

Completing her studies but feeling the need for justice, Tatsu took the name *Katana* and journeyed to America to begin a new life. Her first goal was to find and punish General Karnz. The trail led her to the European country of MARKOVIA. She confronted him and took his life, then soon came across the teen named HALO. After both were found by Batman, they aided him in the rescue of LUCIUS FOX. A new role began for Tatsu: that of an Outsider. (*The Brave and the Bold* #200, July

1983; origin told in *Batman and the Outsiders* #12, July 1984)

Relocating to GOTHAM CITY, Tatsu became Halo's guardian, and the two set up residence in the penthouse atop the WAYNE FOUNDATION building. She enjoyed her time with the OUTSIDERS, learning much about heroism from her teammates. However, she still needed to settle the score with Takeo. When he tracked her to Gotham, their showdown began. He had managed to switch swords with Tatsu, intending to release all the souls contained with the Soultaker, but she killed him and the spell reversed.

After Halo fell into a coma after a battle, Katana left the team to care for her. She refused heroic adventures—but when a member of her dead husband's family was slain by the Oyabun organization, she sought vengeance. She crossed paths at this point with the Suicide Squad, saving the lives of BRONZE TIGER and MANHUNTER. The latter helped Katana complete her obligation.

With Halo healed, Katana returned to the reformed Outsiders. However, Halo died, her soul taking up residence in a new body, which caused deep fractures in their relationship. The team fell apart, and Katana came to lead a splinter group with GEO-FORCE and Technocrat. It was then that Tadashi sought the Soultaker and dispatched LADY SHIVA to retrieve it. Katana died while dueling Shiva, her soul entering the sword itself. After winning trials against the blade's other souls, she was granted a return to life.

Katana remained loyal to Batman, and whenever he needed her assistance she fought at his side. Her personal demons laid to rest, she resumed her crime-fighting career and was recruited as field agent for ORACLE'S BIRDS OF PREY. She also served with a newer incarnation of the Outsiders, alongside NIGHTWING, only to lose her citizenship when Japan objected to her work with the team.

When Katana discovered the land of Fukumaden was imperiled, she killed herself to enter the sword to restore order, lest the entire realm of magic be disrupted. Takeo became the land's ruler, and she had to confront her brother-in-law once more. Captain Marvel used his magic to bring her back to life and let her stop Battleaxe from killing her body. (*Outsiders: Five of a Kind—Katana/Shazam*, October 2007) She subsequently remained with the Outsiders, once more under Batman's leadership.

KA THAR

In a potential sixtieth century Ka Thar was a well-respected historian, known for his book, *The History of SUPERMAN and Batman*. To verify his facts, Ka Thar used a time-travel device to journey back to the twentieth century and observe the World's Finest heroes in action. He was shocked to discover that he'd gotten his information wrong and feared disgrace. Ka Thar approached the heroes and threatened to expose their secret identities if they did not engage in acts as described in the tome. They reluctantly agreed until the World's Greatest Detective realized that the book went on to say their identities were never learned—so he called Ka Thar's bluff. Unhappy, the historian returned to his time period. (*World's Finest Comics* #81, March/April 1956)

KATIA

Katia was a Russian agent for the KGB who tracked the criminal known as the DARK RIDER to GOTHAM CITY. She allied herself with Batman and ROBIN to track and stop the Dark Rider before a plutonium bomb could be detonated in the Gotham Reservoir, poisoning much of America. (*Batman* #393–394, March–April 1986)

After betraying Gotham gangster Don Carlos, Katia was gunned down by his men. (*Vigilante* #47, November 1987)

KAZANTZAKIS, CELIA

Originally a secretary at the Copper Street Orphanage, Celia Kazantzakis was befriended by social crusader MARTHA KANE. Their friendship was cemented when Kane saved the orphanage from developers by having it declared a historic landmark. Sadly, the building burned to the ground soon after. Despite their different social standings the women became tight friends, only to see the relationship founder when Kane began dating Denholm Sinclair, who had ties to César Rossetti's mob. At the same time, Kazantzakis had been dating Lorenzo Rossetti, whom the family had killed for crossing them. What most people didn't know at the time was that Kazantzakis had been embezzling from the orphanage; she had it torched to avoid discovery. When Kane learned the truth, Kazantzakis fled the country rather than face jail. Most believed she spent her time in Europe making her fortune first in textiles, then in real estate. She married wealthy businessman Porter Endicott in Spain, had a son, and finally returned to the States. When Endicott died, she assumed his seat on the board of WAYNE ENTERPRISES. All along, though, she sought revenge against the town that had shunned her. Kazantzakis created the criminal persona ATHENA and built her operation called the NETWORK. Through a series of costumed vigilantes, including her son, Athena wanted to wreck not only the town, but the company Kane helped run after she married THOMAS WAYNE. When BRUCE WAYNE was suspected of murdering VESPER FAIRCHILD, it was Kazantzakis who assumed the CEO role, which gave her unfettered access to the company. Batman investigated and was angered to learn of how Kazantzakis had exploited her former friendship with Bruce, going so far as to gain his support in being named CEO. When confronted by Batman, she refused arrest, causing a tanker explosion that seemingly took her life. (*Batman Family* #1–8, December 2002–February 2003)

KEAN, BARRETT

Barrett Kean was considered the world's greatest makeup artist. He ran his own school designed to teach makeup to actors. He was also one of the many who helped train BRUCE WAYNE in his quest to master the skills needed to fight criminals as Batman. In return for the lessons, Batman returned to the school years later to give a series of lectures. During that period photographer "LENS" VORDEN attempted to learn the Caped Crusader's identity but was thwarted thanks to Kean's efforts. (*Detective Comics* #257, July 1958)

KEATING, JEFF

Batman sponsored a contest for Earth-2's GOTHAM CITY high school students, awarding a four-year scholarship to study criminology to the student who invented the best addition to his crime-fighting arsenal. One year Jeff Keating devised a large, black fabric bat-shaped kite that could be mounted with a camera allowing for aerial surveillance, winning the contest. (*Batman* #100, July 1956)

KEEFE, BEN

Ben Keefe was a failed jewel thief who was apprehended by Batman and ROBIN—noteworthy only in that this occurred during Robin's short-lived romance with figure skater VERA LOVELY. (*Batman* #107, April 1957)

KEEP, ROGER J.

Roger J. Keep was a seriously disturbed man whose paranoia grew in size after an accident left him confined to a wheelchair. He was convinced that the accident had actually been a murder attempt and swore revenge on his fellow trustees of the International Chemical Company—Holmes Caffrey, Donald Penn, John Keith-Dudley, and BRUCE WAYNE. Secreting himself on Crabshell Island, located in Gotham Sound, Keep began plotting murders tailored to allow him to witness each death without having to leave the island.

In each case, Wayne, as Batman, deduced what Keep intended and saw to it that each man would be spared a grisly death. In due time Batman and ROBIN located Keep's hideaway and apprehended the deluded man. (*World's Finest Comics* #58, May/June 1952)

KELDEN, BRAND

Brand Kelden was dismissed by the GOTHAM CITY POLICE DEPARTMENT after Internal Affairs determined that he was leaking information to criminals. Refusing to stop aiding the underworld, he fashioned a mobile radio transmitter and drove around in a truck, broadcasting the pirate radio station CRIME. Subscribing criminals could learn the frequency and obtain coded information to stay ahead of the police. Kelden managed to obtain his information by using a powerful telescope trained on police headquarters and reading lips. While successful at first, he was signed off the air by Batman and ROBIN. (*Detective Comics* #200, October 1953)

KELLEY, BRAINS

Not only did Brains Kelley own one of GOTHAM CITY's most prominent nightclubs, he was also secretly one of the city's top three crime bosses. To force the police to lay off the criminals, Kelley conspired with "Big John" Waller and Dude Davis to halt all criminal activity in Gotham. Instead, the bosses would dispatch their men to other cities and, disguised as the local mobsters, commit a series of crimes. This way, the stolen property could be brought back to Gotham and quietly fenced. Alerted to the rise in crimes elsewhere, a suspicious Batman infiltrated Waller's operation and learned of the plan. He then worked with the G.C.P.D. to lay a trap that would snare the three criminal lords, ending the crime wave. (*World's Finest Comics* #5, Spring 1942)

KELLY, CARRIE

In a potential future, Batman had retired and his beloved GOTHAM CITY had become even darker and less hospitable. Homeless adolescent Carrie Kelly was an ardent fan of the Dark Knight, wishing he would come back. The moment he was spotted in action once more, Kelly put on a ROBIN costume, complete with transparent green glasses, and set out to re-create the Dynamic Duo. Batman accepted her help and came to trust her, recognizing that he was not complete without a Robin. (*Batman: The Dark Knight* #1–4, 1986)

Some time later, Kelly changed guises and costumes, from Robin to Catgirl, continuing to work alongside her hero. (*The Dark Knight Strikes Again* #1–3, 2002)

Carrie Kelly

KEMP, MARTIN

As the HUMAN FLEA, Kemp stole the money needed to keep his grandfather's flea circus running.

KENT, CLARK

The mild-mannered reporter for METROPOLIS's *Daily Planet* was also Kal-El, last son of KRYPTON and the super hero known across the universe as SUPERMAN.

KENT, HARVEY

On Earth-2, Harvey Kent was a crusading GOTHAM CITY district attorney who became mentally unbalanced after half his face was scarred with acid. He turned into the criminal TWO-FACE.

KERN, "DANCER"

"Dancer" Kern bribed Ralph Edney, a carpenter, to install a series of hidden panels in buildings around GOTHAM CITY where he and his men could store their loot after committing robberies, allowing them to escape without fear of losing their new possessions. Batman and ROBIN attempted to track Kern and his gang to recover the property but were hampered when Captain Harby, filling in for Police Commissioner JAMES GORDON, decided the Dynamic Duo were glory hounds. Rather than let them operate as normal, he tasked them with routine uniformed officer duties such as traffic patrol. Despite their new assignments, the crime fighters managed to gather the information needed to put Kern out of business. Harby admitted he was mistaken about the heroes' intentions, while the heroes were reminded how hard the cop on the street had it. (*Batman* #77, June/July 1953)

KEYES, JOHN

John Keyes was convicted of murder and sentenced to the gas chamber in California. He maintained that he was innocent and managed to escape confinement in order to get the evidence he needed to earn a new trial. After obtaining what he needed, Keyes was rearrested and was being extradited back to the West Coast. The real killers, Trigger Yurk and Biff Bolton, attempted to assassinate Keyes before he returned to jail but were thwarted by Batman and ROBIN. Once arrested, the two men confessed, exonerating Keyes. (*Batman* #13, October/November 1942)

K-4

When a roll of microfilm was stranded atop K-4, the Himalayan mountain considered unreachable, the FBI asked Batman and Robin to retrieve it. Disguising themselves as Bruce Martin and Dick Green, the intrepid duo joined an expedition and became the first humans to reach the summit. (*Batman* #13, October/November 1942)

KGBEAST

Anatoli Knyazev was a Russian who was trained by a secret division of the KGB in the waning days of the Soviet Union to become the ultimate killing machine. He was given a costumed identity as the KGBeast and unleashed in America with an agenda culminating in the assassination of the US president. While in Gotham City to begin his murder spree, the KGBeast was opposed by Batman. The KGBeast did everything with brute force, including poisoning all the attendees at a banquet to ensure that his victim did not escape. (*Batman* #417-420, March–June 1988)

The two battled several times, and in their final fight Batman ensnared the Russian's left hand with his Batrope, leaving him dangling. After the Dark Knight left, expecting the police to round him up, the killer sliced off his own hand to escape. He returned to his homeland, where he had a prosthetic attached. Unlike most replacement parts, this one

was a cybernetically controlled gun, making him even deadlier.

The KGBeast returned to Gotham and met a series of defeats that had him captured and sentenced to Blackgate Penitentiary. Soon after, the Russian government sent his protégé, named the NKVDemon, into action, only to die at the hand of police detective Nikita Krakov.

Years later the KGBeast was free and remained in Gotham as a contract killer, only to be thrown from a roof by a man believed to be Two-Face. It was instead a doppelgänger hired by the Great White Shark as he began to prune the city of its costumed villains. The police found the KGBeast's body with two bullet holes in his skull. (*Detective Comics* #817, May 2006)

KHALEX

Khalex escaped prison on his homeworld and journeyed to Earth, where he allied himself with gang leader Midge Martin. On Earth, Khalex displayed incredible superpowers on a par with Superman's. He was robbed of these abilities whenever he neared a meteor, so he worked with Martin to devise a ploy that would force Batman and Robin to destroy the extraterrestrial object.

That would allow Khalex to kill Superman and take over the world. Instead, the World's Finest team outwitted the criminals: The Dynamic Duo and the Man of Steel apprehended them. (*World's Finest Comics* #105, November 1959)

KHOR

Khor was one of two alien zookeepers who visited worlds around the galaxy, obtaining species to put on display back on their homeworld. When visiting Earth, they selected Batman and Robin as unique specimens. Placed in a cage, the Dynamic Duo were forced to perform tricks to earn food. In time, though, Batman convinced his keepers that he and Robin were intelligent beings who did not deserve such confinement. The World's Greatest Detective also exposed Khor for using various trained intergalactic animals to help perform a series of robberies. (*Detective Comics* #326, April 1964)

KIER, RALPH

Ralph Kier worked for John Barly, who brought animals to America for various zoos. Kier was also a smuggler who attempted to bring in an illegal supply of diamonds by secreting them in a gorilla's collar. A suspicious Batman apprehended Kier and recovered the gems. (*Batman* #100, June 1956)

KILEY, KANGAROO

Kangaroo Kiley was a clever Gotham City criminal who founded an underworld bank that would launder money and goods for criminal customers. Kiley was successful enough at this business for Batman and Robin to hear of his bank's existence, and soon after, it took a permanent holiday. (*Detective Comics* #175, September 1951)

KILLER CROC

Born thirty-five years ago in a Tampa slum near the Twenty-second Street Causeway, Waylon Jones knew nothing but poverty and hardship. By age ten, the orphan lived with an aunt, who was frequently imprisoned on drunk and disorderly charges. The freak skin condition that left him looking more like a crocodile than a boy meant he was called "Croc." Given the taunting and lack of supervision at home, Jones fell into juvenile delinquency, with enough crimes on his teen record that he started being charged as an adult by the time he was sixteen. While in prison, he killed his first man, a fellow convict who made fun of his scaly appearance. He was finally released after eighteen years.

Without any measurable skills, Jones hired on at a carnival, living up to his nickname as he wrestled crocodiles before paying crowds. His incredible strength—which may have been part of his condition—led him to think he could better himself by using that force for his own purposes. The criminal Killer Croc was born. (*Batman* #358, April 1983)

Killer Croc assembled a criminal gang in Tampa, stealing cash and settling personal scores, including one with the police deputy who had beat him at age ten. Done with Florida, he moved north to Gotham City, leaving his gang to the brutal Solomon Grundy, who almost immediately killed them.

In his new city Croc affiliated himself with a criminal mastermind known as the Squid who had

filled the vacuum left by the fall of RUPERT THORNE. He was hired muscle, instilling fear among criminal and citizen alike. In time, after seeing the Squid fail to kill Batman, Croc went his own way. When the Squid objected, Croc shot him with a rifle, an event that brought the disfigured man to Batman's attention. (*Batman* #358, April 1983)

Despite frequent fights, neither man claimed victory, while Croc used his brutal approach to slowly take over Gotham's underworld. At an assemblage of criminal figures at the Gotham Zoo, Croc also played a part in the creation of the second ROBIN. Joe and Trina Todd, aerialists for the Sloan Circus, had volunteered to work with Robin and BATGIRL to break Croc's hold on the company. Instead they were lured to a very public death at the zoo, at Croc's hands, leaving their son JASON TODD an orphan. (*Detective Comics* #526, May 1983)

Jason, left alone in WAYNE MANOR, stumbled upon the BATCAVE, cobbled together his own action costume, and set out to avenge his parents. Croc was defeated, although he got away, and Batman recognized he needed to provide Jason a home.

In the reality after CRISIS ON INFINITE EARTHS, the elder Todds had no connection to Croc. When the would-be gang lord made his play for Gotham, he was defeated by NIGHTWING and the new Robin while Batman was incapacitated. (*Nightwing* [second series] #105–106, May 2005)

Killer Croc continued to escape prison, returning to Gotham time and again to spread fear, steal money, and inflict pain. In one instance he murdered thirty people using an incendiary device in midtown, earning him a trip to ARKHAM ASYLUM for evaluation and confinement. (*Swamp Thing* [second series] #66, November 1987) At that point Croc revealed that his persona as a mindless engine of destruction was a ruse to lull his opponents into underestimating him. By playing a brain-damaged, bound patient at Arkham, Croc was privy to all manner of secrets, from guards who stole drugs or were involved in a sinister conspiracy to the innermost thoughts of the FLORONIC MAN, whom he regarded as a friend. (*Secret Origins* [second series] #23, February 1988)

His doctors learned the truth and had him placed in solitary confinement. (*Detective Comics* #604, September 1989) Croc still managed to get out now and then, although he was temporarily confined to a wheelchair after exposure to a nerve gas. He escaped, seemingly for good, when a demon conjured by fellow inmate TENZIN WYATT broke open the asylum. (*The Demon* [second series] #11, May 1991) He soon after teamed with the RIDDLER, only to be apprehended by SUPERMAN and returned to Arkham. (*Legends of the World's Finest* #2–3, 1994)

Croc escaped again, but this time sought refuge in the sewers beneath Gotham, encountering an entire society of homeless people who accepted him as he was. As a result, he stole food and supplies to help his new social group. A flood dispersed the people, killing several, leaving Croc alone once again. (*Detective Comics* #671, February 1994)

When BANE arrived in Gotham to assert control over the city, Croc opposed the VENOM-powered man. Bane wound up breaking Croc's arms during

their fight. (*Batman* #489, February 1993) He was among the prisoners who escaped BLACKGATE PENITENTIARY when Bane destroyed the building. Croc, still in arm casts, tracked down the villain and interrupted his "interrogation" of Robin, saving the teen's life. Croc then vanished to let his arms heal. When he next surfaced, it was near the Gotham River, where he began to kill more innocents. Batman—actually DICK GRAYSON filling in for a recovering BRUCE WAYNE—and the second Robin, Jason Todd, tracked the killer down and bested him in a fight. (*Batman* #512, November 1994)

Croc left Gotham and headed south, stopping for a time in Houma, Louisiana, long enough to come to SWAMP THING's attention, with Batman also on his trail. The muck-encrusted being informed the Dark Knight that Croc was a "primordial being" who belonged in the swamps. Swamp Thing used his power over nature to help calm and redirect Jones, letting him kill only to eat. (*Batman* #521–522, August–September 1995) This lasted only until Swamp Thing struck him, attempting to teach the man his place in Nature's order, but all Croc saw was another bully; he left the swamp.

(*Swamp Thing* [second series] #160, November 1995)

Slowly, Croc returned north and tried to live on his own, not letting society anger him. He continued to find conflict and was eventually captured by LOCK-UP, who helped Croc tap his angry nature. When deemed ready, Croc was unleashed to fight in an illegal fight club. (*Batman/Wildcat* #1–3, April–June 1997) He escaped the club, only to be arrested again and returned to Arkham. (*Resurrection Man* #7, November 1997) Croc decided to remain there and rest, watching television and reaching out to form connections with other inmates, including POISON IVY—whom he deemed a kindred spirit. (*Batman: Poison Ivy,* 1997)

All that changed when the earthquake shook Gotham to its core and the asylum was damaged. Gaining access to the computer files, the JOKER changed Croc's medication order from sedatives to heavy doses of amphetamines, turning Croc into a crazed madman. He killed fellow resident PINHEAD and then escaped when the asylum was abandoned. (*Batman: The Shadow of the Bat* #80–82, January–March 1998)

Cut off by the federal government, Gotham became a No Man's Land—but Croc saw it as an opportunity. He assembled a new gang, staked out turf, fought all who opposed him, and began entertaining thoughts of resuming his quest to rule the underworld. He saw himself as King Croc, going so far as to track down Stanley Demchaszky, a minor criminal who dared to call himself King. (*Detective Comics* #737, October 1999) Dressing in custom-tailored suits, he styled himself as a mob boss and intended to expand his interests, rivaling Black Mask for control of crime. Robin worked with the Gotham police and Alfred Pennyworth; even the Penguin faced down the criminal and prevented tremendous bloodshed. (*Robin* #71–72, December 1999–January 2000)

Killer Croc continued his attempts to become a mob boss, using his imposing physique to make opponents cower. (*Batman* #620–625, December 2003–May 2004) Prior to that (as revealed in *Batman* #619, November 2003), Hush and the Riddler offered to cure Croc while actually infecting him with a virus that mutated him further. After additional defeats, he sought a cure for his condition—but when the doctor failed, he devoured her. (*Detective Comics* #810, Late October 2005)

KILLER MOTH

This criminal originally styled himself after Batman but later sold his soul to a demon and morphed into the creature called Charaxes.

A new Killer Moth, in a decidedly armored version of the original's outfit, arrived in Gotham City in the employ of the second Ventriloquist and Scarface. (*Gotham Underground* #2, January 2008)

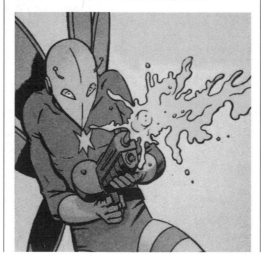

KING, PAUL

Paul King was a vain criminal who liked being known as Public Enemy Number One in Gotham City. He concocted a scheme to capture and kill Batman and Robin, and proved successful at the capture of the Dynamic Duo. Robin began spinning a series of yarns about their escapes from death traps, which bought his partner enough time to strip the plastic cover from a telephone line, using the wires to send a Morse code message to the police. Before King could spring his own death trap, the police arrived and apprehended him and his men. (*Detective Comics* #221, July 1955)

KINGDOM, DAN

Dan Kingdom worked for the international organization known as the Council, acting as their Enforcer until he was stopped by Batman and Manhunter.

KING OF CATS, THE

The King of Cats was a costumed criminal on Earth-2, looking and acting like a male version of Catwoman. He was revealed to be Karl Kyle, brother of Catwoman, Selina Kyle. The Cat King committed feline-themed crimes, hoping to lure his sister out of her self-imposed retirement. Instead, she managed to convince him to end his criminal career and turn himself in to the authorities. (*Batman* #69, February/March 1952) Out on parole, Karl walked Selina down the aisle when she married BRUCE WAYNE. (*Superman Family* #211, October 1981)

On the Earth formed after the events of INFINITE CRISIS, the King of Cats was seen socializing at a super-hero convention in Zenith City. His background and career remain undocumented. (*Seven Soldiers: Bulleteer* #3, April 2006)

PERMIT ME TO INTRODUCE MYSELF! I AM THE MASTER OF THE CAT KINGDOM ... *THE KING OF THE CATS!*

KINGPIN, THE

No one knew who was under the white hood, but criminals throughout GOTHAM CITY feared this new crime boss. Speculation ran rampant as to who it might be, which afforded Batman a chance to bring the criminal to justice. BRUCE WAYNE began to cultivate the image that he was a racketeer and might possibly be the Kingpin in order to infiltrate the criminal enterprise. As he got close, Wayne learned that the Kingpin was fellow millionaire and close friend Spotswood Hartley. Batman quickly put the operation out of business. (*World's Finest Comics* #57, March/April 1952)

KING SNAKE

Sir Edmund Dorrance was born and raised in England, gaining extensive experience by serving with the Royal Artillery. (*Robin* [second series] #4, April 1991) Upon his discharge thirty-odd years ago, Dorrance and some colleagues banded together to offer their services as mercenaries. One mission had them aiding rebels on the island nation of SANTA PRISCA. After sleeping with one of the female rebels, Dorrance was blinded during a firefight. He escaped the island, but the now pregnant woman was not so lucky. She was jailed for Dorrance's crimes and gave birth to a son, who grew up to be known as BANE.

Dorrance settled in Hong Kong to spend time mastering his new condition. He invested his earnings in legitimate businesses, including shipping and electronics, proving to be very successful and becoming a multimillionaire. He used his mercenary contacts and information to

also begin a second career, that of a narcotics dealer specializing in heroin.

His approach to that business was ruthless, making him feared. A nickname soon became his alias—King Snake, named for the species known for eating its brethren and being immune to venom. As King Snake, Dorrance formed an organization known as the Ghost Dragons, made up of youths drawn from Macau, Kowloon, and Hong Kong. With success came the desire to branch out, and the Dragons soon had holdings in France and America.

Rather than see Hong Kong turned over to the Chinese, King Snake decided to raze the city. He accessed a plague, developed decades earlier by the Nazis, but the plot was foiled by Robin during his international travels and training. (*Robin* #1-5, January-May 1990) Also entering the picture was Lady Shiva, who accompanied Robin, curious to fight Dorrance, rumored to be the world's deadliest male martial artist. When Robin knocked King Snake out a window, Shiva ordered him to let the villain fall, but the Teen Wonder refused, ending his alliance with Shiva.

Dorrance fell, breaking his back rather than dying. He used his resources to obtain medical treatment that reinforced his spine and allowed him to return to business. He continued to lead a successful double life but abandoned Hong Kong and relocated to Gotham City, establishing a Ghost Dragon base of operations. (*Detective Comics* #685, May 1995) The Dragons, led by Lynx, took control of Chinatown's criminal activity away from the Lucky Hand Triad. King Snake also chose Gotham so he could exact a measure of revenge against Robin, although each attempt to do so was met with failure. He lost territory, too, when the Triad revolted and hired the Silver Monkey to tear the Dragons apart.

A survivor, King Snake allied himself with the international terrorist Kobra. When a power struggle erupted within the Kobra Cult, Dorrance seized the opportunity to gain power. He used the cult to access one of Rā's al Ghūl's Lazarus Pits and had his eyesight restored. As he readjusted to having vision, he lost a fight with Robin, who had arrived to rescue a friend from the cult. When the fight ended, Dorrance was blinded anew by cobra poison. (*Robin* [second series] #91, August 2001)

Dorrance was blind, the Ghost Dragons were in tatters, his criminal career was exposed, and he was trapped, alone, at the now-abandoned Kobra base. He was at low ebb when Bane finally tracked him down within the mountain retreat. Bane wanted to kill his father for abandoning his mother and letting his son be raised in a hellhole. Instead, Bane let Dorrance live, siding with Batman and Robin as they fought a renewed Kobra Cult, which Dorrance once more tried to control. Dorrance was knocked into a deep crevice and presumed dead. (*Batman: Gotham Knights* #47–49, January–March 2004)

KINSOLVING, SHONDRA

Shondra Kinsolving was a physiotherapist working in Gotham City when she was hired to treat Jack Drake after injuries sustained in Africa. (*Batman* #486, November 1992) Later, an emotionally and physically exhausted Bruce Wayne sought out

Kinsolving for therapy. Wayne had been driven to this unusual point by Bane, who had systematically broken Gotham's worst criminals out of both Blackgate Penitentiary and Arkham Asylum.

After Bane confronted the weakened Batman and broke his back, it was natural for Kinsolving to be brought in; Alfred Pennyworth explained that the wealthy playboy had suffered an accident with his Porsche. As they worked together, Wayne fell in love with his doctor.

During their time together, she appeared to be troubled, and it was soon after their romance began that the truth began to seep out. She had a half brother, Benedict Asplin, who shared with her a psychic link. Apparently, he knew they had great powers; through their genetic link, the powers would work when they were in proximity to each other.

He had arrived to awaken his half sister's full psionic abilities and use her in his quest for power. The criminal known as Mister Asp kidnapped her and brought her south, where she was forced to telepathically kill the inhabitants of an island village.

Wayne outfitted himself with leg braces and a disguise, creating the persona of Sir Hemmingford Gray, and tracked the two. When Asplin realized he was being hunted he tried to kill Batman with psionics, but the attempt failed. Curious, he kidnapped Gray to study him, bringing the man to Santa Prisca. It was learned that because Asplin had tried to kill Gray, not Wayne, the attack had failed.

Bruce Wayne managed to defeat Asplin, but the ordeal was too much for Kinsolving, whose mind shut down, reducing her personality to that of a child. She did manage to use her abilities one final time, totally healing Wayne's back, putting him back on the path to resuming his career as Batman. Wayne subsequently had her placed with a foster family that could care for her until her mind healed itself. (*Legends of the Dark Knight* #61, June 1994)

When Wayne suffered massive head trauma some years later, Barbara Gordon suggested Kinsolving be summoned to heal her former lover. Alfred indicated that she had recovered and was unavailable. (*Batman* #609, January 2004)

KIRK, JOE

Joe Kirk worked as an agent for stuntmen but doubled as a racketeer who demanded "protection" money from his clients. Those who dared to refuse were murdered, the act disguised as stunts gone wrong. Batman and Robin investigated and exposed Kirk. (*Batman* #12, August/September 1942)

KIRK, MARTY

Marty Kirk was a notorious criminal awaiting execution on death row. His exploits fascinated the public, so his life was dramatized during a live television broadcast. Kirk's henchmen stormed the studio and took the cast and crew hostage, insisting that their boss be freed or everyone would die. Batman asked the governor to intervene, and soon after, Kirk was freed. As he headed off to recover one hundred thousand dollars he had stolen from the Federal Savings Bank, Batman and Robin overwhelmed the henchmen, freeing the hostages. They then tracked down and rearrested Kirk. (*Batman* #97, February 1956)

KITCH, STAN

Stanley Kitch initially studied law but wound up entering the Gotham City Police Academy. After serving time in uniform, he was promoted to detective and joined the Major Crimes Unit. Kitch worked for the G.C.P.D. for several years before returning to the law and serving the city as a defense attorney. (*Batman* #455, October 1990)

KITE MAN

Charles Brown was proficient with kites and found they could be useful tools in committing crimes. With a series of specially designed kites, he took on the costumed identity of Kite Man.

He battled only Batman and Robin, meeting defeat on several occasions and slipping into deserved obscurity. (*Batman* #133, August 1960)

On the Earth re-formed after the Crisis on Infinite Earths, Kite Man prolonged his career—but he was foiled again and again, not only by the Dynamic Duo but also by Hawkman and Hawkgirl. (*Hawkman* [second series] #4, November 1986) Tired of losing to super heroes, Kite Man relocated to Zandia, representing the country in the Olympics. (*Young Justice* #23, September 2000)

Upon his return to Gotham City, Brown gave up his costume but not his criminal ways, teaming up with Signalman and the Corrosive Man to begin a new career. Just as quickly as they started, they were put out of business by Batman and Robin. (*Batman: Gotham Knights* #33, November 2002)

As the Society began recruiting members, the Joker recounted how Deathstroke threw Brown off a building for refusing membership. That was an exaggeration: Brown remained active on his own until he finally died at the hands of Bruno Mannheim in Gotham City. (*52* #25, 2006)

Kite Man

KLAG (THE HUNTER)

Klag was a Cro-Magnon man who was trying to capture Brugg, a thief, when he was trapped in a deep crevasse that filled with water, then froze, trapping him within. Through the millennia, Klag slept in suspended animation as the chemicals in the water seeped into his skin. When the ice block containing him finally thawed, Klag miraculously woke up, discovering that he now possessed incredible powers, including strength, flight, and the ability to control lightning. The confused, displaced man renewed his hunt for Brugg without fully comprehending that more than fifteen thousand years had passed. His hunt left a destructive swath through GOTHAM CITY until he was stopped by Batman and ROBIN. (*Detective Comics* #337, March 1965)

KLOR

Klor—who hailed from the distant world BELVOS—discovered that gems on Earth would imbue him with spectacular powers. He then concocted a scheme that would allow him to commit crimes using his gem-derived powers but also frame SUPERMAN. This would take the Man of Steel off Earth, allowing Klor to plunder the planet's riches en route to conquering his homeworld. As the Man of Steel defended himself, Klor arrived on Earth, only to be thwarted by Batman and ROBIN, who returned him

to Belvos and helped prove their friend innocent. (*World's Finest Comics* #122, December 1961)

KNIGHT, ANTON

Anton Knight fell under NOCTURNA's spell. He would do anything for her love and committed various crimes as the NIGHT-SLAYER.

KNIGHT, NATALIA

Born Natasha Knight, she was an albino who desired power and the devotion of men everywhere until

she met her match with Batman under the name NOCTURNA.

KNIGHT, THE

In England on Earth-2, Percy Sheldrake, Earl of Wordenshire, was inspired by Batman to don a suit of armor and fight crime as the Knight. Like Batman, he had a teen sidekick, his son Cyril—known as the SQUIRE. Whenever the Wordenshire bell tolled, the adventurers answered the summons. (*Batman* #62, December 1950/January 1951)

On Earth-1, the Knight traveled to GOTHAM CITY to meet Batman and other international heroes, later forming the group known as the CLUB OF HEROES.

On the Earth created by the CRISIS ON INFINITE EARTHS, Sheldrake was first an apprentice, a squire, to legendary World War II champion the Shining Knight. (*Young All-Stars* #22, 1988) The Knight continued his career for several years until his archenemy, Springheeled Jack, killed him. At that point, an adult Cyril took his place as the new Knight. (*JLA* #26, February 1999). Soon after, the new Knight was recruited by General Wade Eiling to join the Ultramarine Corps. Without a Squire, he seemed lost and was said to have burned through the Sheldrake fortune, winding up living on the streets until he was found by Beryl Hutchison and her mother. He recovered and added Beryl as his new Squire; the two continued fighting for justice, apart from the dismantled Ultramarines. A grateful England gave them a World War II Spitfire to use for transportation. (*Batman* #667, October 2007)

KNYAZEV, ANATOLI

A Russian trained to become a human fighting machine known as the KGBEAST.

KOBRA

On May 25, in a New Delhi hospital, Mootama V. Burr gave birth to conjoined twins, Jason and Jeffrey Franklin. After delivery, the infants endured a twenty-one-hour operation to separate them. Then the hospital was raided by members of India's KOBRA CULT, fulfilling a prophecy that every forty-four years a new *naja-naja*, leader, would be born. Jeffrey, clearly the chosen one, was snatched, and the stunned hospital doctors informed Mootama and her husband, American industrialist Jerome Erskine Burr, that the weaker child had died. For the next twenty-three years, Jeffrey was raised by the cult, revered as Kobra-Prime, their "naja-naja," the foremost symbol of the followers of the serpent god known as Nulla Pambu. (*Kobra* #1, February/March 1976)

Jason was doted on by his parents, unaware that he was once a twin. Jerome groomed Jason to take over Burr Industries, meeting many influential people including stockholder BRUCE WAYNE. (*Kobra* #7, March/April 1977) Soon after Jason turned eighteen, his parents died in a plane crash. He was inconsolable, unwilling to even go to their graves, so he never knew that their bodies had been stolen. Burr Industries was held in a trust until Burr turned twenty-five.

Through the years Jeffrey was raised with the cult, he never questioned his life. That changed when he was overcome with depression and grief

for no explicable reason. He was then hospitalized for some undisclosed minor ailment; there he met and fell for a fellow patient, Natalie Crawford-Thomas. Young and in love, Jeffrey began to question what else life had for him. He decided to investigate his past, leaving the cult behind. As they traveled together, Jeffrey was horrified to learn that Crawford-Thomas was an international jewel thief, who was then shot and killed by an Interpol agent. (*Kobra* #3, June/July 1976)

For three years Jeffrey traveled the planet, avoiding the cult that sought him and still trying to learn about his past. During that time he formulated a plan to take those who worshipped him and turn them into a force to be reckoned with. They would no longer be a religious operation, but a global criminal organization. He returned to them and continued their training, while laying the groundwork for his new plan. On his twenty-first birthday, Jeffrey was required to drink cobra venom, the last test to prove worthy of leading the cult. As he writhed with pain, Columbia University student Jason Burr was rushed to the hospital with a mysterious ailment.

Lord Kobra quickly accessed the cult's resources around the globe to begin creating the technological infrastructure required to bring his dream to fruition. Cult members bought what they could and stole the rest, and in rapid order the cult had grown fangs. They expanded their bases, including Manhattan-based Ajan Enterprises (*Batman and the Outsiders* #27, November 1985), Chicago's Anaconda Industries (*Manhunter* #14, June 1989), and an international electronics firm known as Cortex Ltd. (*Showcase '93* #7–9, July–September 1993) Established prior to Kobra's birth, circa 1962, was California's Peterson State College, a religious school. (*Suicide Squad Annual* #1, 1988)

In a short two years Kobra transformed the cult from a religious order to an efficient criminal enterprise. Scholarly research allowed members to find artifacts and ancient technology that could be harnessed for new purposes. They also took to acquiring weapons from other villains. As a result, Kobra's ceremonial garb was laced with hidden weapons and tools, including venom sprayed from his gloved knuckles, a "serpent's tongue" fired from the hand that worked as a garrote, and chain mail powered to emit a charge capable of rendering an opponent unconscious. The outfit also had a built-in emergency teleportation beam, hot-linked to an aircraft called the Ark. He also took to carrying a staff that fired bursts of energy.

As Kobra became known to intelligence agencies around the world, the CIA started to piece together the long-ago kidnapping of Jeffrey Burr. Agent Ricardo Perez found Jason Burr at much the same time as Kobra found his long-lost brother. The two men realized they shared a sympathetic link that grew stronger with the passage of time. Kobra could not abide the notion and wanted Jason dead. Jason and Agent Perez then endured a series of struggles to stop Kobra and stay alive.

Things built to a climax when Kobra captured Jason and brought him to the cult's lair. By then, Kobra had acquired their parents' bodies and prepared to resurrect them using one of RĀ's AL

Gнūl's Lazarus Pits. Following instructions Jason left behind, private investigator Jonny Double mailed a letter to Burr Industries investor Bruce Wayne, pleading for him to ask Batman to rescue Jason—wherever he might be. Batman followed the trail to Rā's former headquarters in the Swiss Alps, where he helped free Jason, who then escaped with his girlfriend Melissa McNeil, unaware that the woman had fallen in thrall to Kobra. As they rode a ski lift away from the mêlée, McNeil stabbed and killed Jason, forever severing the link with his brother. (*DC Special Series* #1, 1977)

Kobra was now a known threat to the super-hero community, and he began to cross paths with them with increasing frequency. When he wanted to unleash poison gas over Portugal, just to prove his deadliness, he was thwarted by Batman, Aquaman, and Green Lantern. (*Aquaman* #60–61, February–March 1978) After that, Kobra ensured that he always had an ever-growing number of minions to support his schemes, and that he had several going at once; should one fail, he had other avenues to amassing power. He was shrewd, recognizing the super heroes would be a recurring impediment. He began to find failure at the hands of Batman and his Outsiders. (*Batman and the Outsiders* #25, September 1985) As a result, when he discovered a handful of items that Batman had dealt with, he chose to take two radioactively altered villains, the Zebra-Man and the Elemental Man; devices created by the Planet-Master; and the mystic liquid that transformed Matt Hagen into Clayface. He created all-new versions: Elemental Woman, Planet Master, Zebra-Man, and a female Clayface to act as Strikeforce Kobra and fight the Outsiders on a level playing field. Batman's training of the Outsiders proved the difference, though, and Kobra had to teleport his team away before they were apprehended. (*Outsiders* #21–22, July–August 1987).

Kobra managed to recover the legendary Spear of Destiny in Russia. He used it against the Spectre, only to lose it. (*Armageddon: Inferno* #3, June 1992)

The covert agencies Checkmate and the Suicide Squad managed to thwart Kobra's attempt to unleash a massive electromagnetic pulse that would interrupt technology, exposing the Western Hemisphere to an attack. (*Suicide Squad* #29, July 1989) A stay at Belle Reve prison did not last long, and Kobra was soon back scheming for global domination. He went to Russia to try his EMP idea once more, only to be stopped by King Faraday and Sarge Steel working with Russian forces. (*Danger Trail* #1–4, April–July 1993)

As one defeat was handed to him, another project got activated, placing him in opposition to other super heroes including the Flash (*Flash* #92–100, July 1994–April 1995), the Birds of Prey (*Birds of Prey* #4–6 and 10, April–June and October 1999), and Superman. (*Superman: The Odyssey*, 1999) At one point, frustrated by constant defeat, he thought he heard taunting from his dead brother Jason, so he tried a bolder move, taking over the Justice League of America's Watchtower on the moon, only to lose out once more. (*JLA: Foreign Bodies*, 1999)

He even resurrected a new Strikeforce Kobra (including Dervish, Fauna, Spectra, Syonide, and a duped Windfall from the Outsiders) to once more oppose the Outsiders. (*Outsiders* [second series] #16, March 1995) This defeat caused a split in his ranks: His closest ally, a woman named Eve, took a splinter cell and continued to operate more covertly.

Kobra took over Blackhawk Island and began a new offensive against the world, starting with causing a civilian jetliner to crash, killing all passengers, including the mother of the Justice Society of America's Atom-Smasher. Using the

captured teen hero Air Wave, Kobra seized control of the world's communications and demanded obedience. Instead, the JSA finally brought him to justice. (*JSA* #11, June 2000)

Eve's forces tried to kill Kobra in his hospital room but he escaped. Eve immediately filled the vacuum, tasking her people with seeking out the next naja-naja ahead of schedule. They found one—indeed, they had been monitoring him for nearly two decades. Danny Temple was assaulted in an attempt to bring him to the cult. (*Robin* [second series] #88, May 2001) At the time, Danny was rooming at the Brentwood Academy with Tim Drake, so when he was taken, Robin was soon on the case. When the Teen Wonder arrived, he found not only Danny about to be taken into the cult, but also his nemesis King Snake trying to usurp the leadership for himself. He was half buried under rubble when the mountain fortress came tumbling down (*Robin* [second series] #91, August 2001) In the end Robin rescued Danny, King Snake seemingly fell to his death, and the cult was left rudderless.

At his trial, Kobra denounced the proceedings, proclaiming that his enlightened soul would survive. His followers broke him free, and Atom-Smasher teamed with Black Adam to trail him. When he was located, they ripped his heart out, hoping it would bring the world a measure of peace. (*JSA* #51, October 2003)

Cult members loyal to Kobra-Prime found themselves plunged into a civil war of sorts with the faction formerly led by Eve. As they battled, the world managed to breathe a little easier with Kobra's threat subdued.

KOBRA, OMAR EL

Omar el Kobra was an Arab usurper to the throne of a Middle Eastern country. He decided that the rightful heir posed a threat and came to America with several of his underlings to track and kill Sidi ben Hassen. Hassen had relocated to GOTHAM CITY, where he drove a cab in relative anonymity, unaware he had been targeted for death. Kobra and his men mistakenly believed the heir was Batman, which alerted the Caped Crusader to the scheme, allowing him to apprehend the would-be killers. (*Batman* #25, October/November 1944)

KOBRA CULT

The exact history of the Kobra Cult remains unrecorded, but it's known that the cult was mostly a religious order located in Asia, and it had developed rituals that stretched back centuries.

According to ROBIN, "They're a cult as old as mankind. Their rituals are one of history's great secrets. Their past is shrouded in mystery and murder. They're dedicated to blood rites and death ceremonies. Their goal is simple. They bend all of their energies to it. World domination. Only one thing has kept them from success. Their own murderous and treacherous nature. KOBRA is so tangled in its own corruption and intrigue that they're their own worst enemy. Like a serpent eating itself." (*Robin* [second series] #90, July 2001)

While much of Robin's statement was accurate, the cult was initially a peaceful religious operation, seeking as a leader, or *naja-naja,* one half of separated conjoined twins. Every forty-four years, it was said, a new leader was located. In between

the cult surveyed the world, keeping an eye on the progress of newly born conjoined twins as a precaution against the loss of the current Kobra-Prime. Cult members would visit the newly separated twins, seek divine inspiration, then take the chosen infant. The child was then raised in secret and taught to master arts and sciences, martial arts, and other matters until a series of final tests were conducted. Then the newly appointed naja-naja took his place as leader, the living embodiment of their god, Kali. Kobra was to help bring about the Kali Yuga, the age of chaos.

The cult remained peaceful and obscure until Jason Burr became Kobra-Prime and turned the religious order into a global terrorism machine. (*Kobra* #1–7, February/March 1976–March/April 1977) The new Kobra-Prime regarded his underlings as eminently disposable. Slight infractions were penalized with a stay in an isolation cell pumped full of venom-gas that left the body in agony, while more severe failures were punished with death. The mere expression by a minion of doubt in Kobra's power was enough to merit personal strangulation before the masses.

Despite Kobra's death and a split in the cult, members had little trouble gaining converts to their belief system, and Kobra grew at a rate that alarmed other religious orders and government agencies. CHECKMATE was reconfigured from an American operation to a globally sanctioned agency in part

because of the Kobra Cult's potential threat. The new Kobra Cult was ranked by serpent type, with low-level members known as Lanceheads and high-level members called Nagas. (*Checkmate* [second series] #4, September 2006)

KOLUM, ED

BRUCE WAYNE exposed Ed Kolum as a corrupt press agent and swindler from a charity. Some time later, Kolum returned to GOTHAM CITY and attempted to exact revenge from Wayne by challenging the custody of DICK GRAYSON. His plan failed, and Wayne remained Grayson's legal guardian. (*Batman* #57, February/March 1950)

KOOK, THE

Dr. FRANKLIN SELLY was a strong believer in alien abductions and became a popular speaker on the lecture and talk-show circuit. What most did not realize was that his beliefs were fueled by the illegal narcotic Cosmosis, which amplified his personal paranoia. It also seemed to trigger his meta-gene, allowing him the ability to cast illusions. Selly, known as the Kook, attempted to spread his visions by providing Cosmosis to one of his gatherings until Batman stopped him. (*Batman: The Abduction,* 1998)

Selly was confined to ARKHAM ASYLUM for treatment until he was one of the rare few considered cured. However, one of the doctors treating him, Staines, also took advantage of Selly's abilities by planting a chip in his brain that gave Staines control over the projections. He then applied those abilities to control a military-sanctioned program studying mind control. Batman intervened, rescuing Selly and apprehending Staines. (*Batman: Dreamland,* 2000)

KORDTRONICS

The second BLUE BEETLE, Ted Kord, was a technological genius, born into the KORD Inc. business. Based in Chicago, KORD Inc. manufactured consumer and professional electronics until the villain Carapax destroyed the corporate headquarters. Kord split from his father's company soon after, going into business with fellow JUSTICE LEAGUE OF AMERICA

member Booster Gold. As Blue & Gold, they used their expertise and renown to construct Club JLI on the island of Kooey Kooey Kooey. The project went bust, and the sentient island forced them to relocate. This was followed by a personal low point that saw Kord's super-heroic and professional careers both failing. (*Blue Beetle* #24, May 1988; *Justice League of America* #33, December 1989)

The company morphed into Blue and Gold Software, which succeeded well enough to encourage Kord to gain control of KORD Inc. and concentrate on its consumer electronics division, Kordtronics. (*DCU Heroes Secret Files* #1, February 1999; *Birds of Prey* #15, March 2000; #35, November 2001) That division proved successful, so much so that it was highly sought after by bidders from friendly to hostile. (*Birds of Prey* #40–41, April–May 2002)

Kord still had difficulty running a business, with his expertise being more in technology and manufacturing. At some point WayneTech bought out Kordtronics, with BRUCE WAYNE accessing its research and development as he built new gear, including the BROTHER I satellite. (prior to *Green Arrow* #19, January 2003)

KORMO
Kormo was a planet that was home to Tharn and Rawl, whose conflict eventually involved Batman, ROBIN, and SUPERMAN. (*World's Finest Comics* #92, January/February 1958) (see Skyboy)

KOSOV, ALEXANDRA
Alexandra Kosov led the ODESSA MOB in GOTHAM CITY, with roots reaching back to Russia's crime families. Leadership fell to her in the wake of the murder of her father, Vasily, and brother Victor, one of the precipitating factors in a gang war that allowed BLACK MASK to seize control of Gotham's underworld. She was one of the first to pledge fealty. Despite having only one functioning eye, she was an expert sharpshooter. (*Detective Comics* #797, October 2004)

KOSOV, VASILY
As GOTHAM CITY prepared to reopen its doors as a part of the United States, Russia's ODESSA MOB decided the time was right to move into the ravaged city. Led by Vasily Kosov, along with his children Victor and Alexandra, the mob made an immediate impact in the underworld. Vasily ran the growing organization until he died, shot by a rival gang leader, the flashpoint that began a gang war. Victor was also killed, and ALEXANDRA KOSOV took over the family business. (*Detective Comics* #742, March 2000)

KRAAK
Kraak was a wanted criminal on the planet Ergon, forcing him to flee to a safer world. He landed on Earth and managed to convince Batman and ROBIN he was a good man being falsely pursued. Ergon's police finally traced the pirate to Earth and captured him, apprehending the Dynamic Duo as accessories after the fact. On Ergon's prison moon, the crime fighters did hard labor until they could convince the authorities of their legal standing on Earth. To prove the point, Batman and Robin helped the police locate Kraak's stolen property and apprehend his henchmen. A grateful law enforcement agency returned the heroes to Earth. (*Batman* #128, December 1959)

KRAAL
Kraal was actually three interdependent life-forms that could exist united or apart, each possessing a different talent. One could absorb and emit electrical energy; another could absorb heat and radiated an aura of flame; the third could absorb huge quantities of water. Discovering a kraal, an alien explorer took it aboard his spacecraft, which subsequently crashed on Earth. The released kraal caused extensive damage to GOTHAM CITY until it could be rounded up and calmed down by Batman and ROBIN. The Dynamic Duo learned that the united kraal neutralized the component parts' attributes, rendering the creature relatively harmless. With the spacecraft repaired, the explorer and his find left Earth. (*Detective Comics* #277, March 1960)

KRAFFT, IVAN
Ivan Krafft trained would-be criminals at his Happy Valley Gentlemen's Sporting Club, which doubled as a legitimate resort. Using experts in lock picking, demolition, and weaponry, Krafft not only offered courses but acted as a clearinghouse for criminals seeking employees. After learning of the club, Batman and ROBIN quickly put it out of business. (*Detective Comics* #84, February 1944)

KRASNA-VOLNY
Krasna-Volny was once a European duchy—represented by the heraldic symbol of a griffin and a sword—but was subsumed by Transbelvia sometime during the Middle Ages. The Krasna-Volnans believed the Belvians betrayed them to the Turks in the thirteenth century, and the duchy disappeared from the maps after a sixteenth-century war. The two states remained in a constant state of war for centuries until they were both swallowed up by the Ottoman Empire in 1698. A late-twentieth-century civil war saw Krasna-Volny free for the first time in centuries, but not without a tremendous amount of bloodshed. The capital of the reborn Krasna-Volny was Chorstad. (*Robin* [second series] #49, January 1998)

Krasna-Volny was part of a troubled group of nations collectively known as the Krasna-Transbelvia-Koroscova corridor. (*Birds of Prey* #11, November 1999) When the Eastern Bloc broke up, ethnic fighting began anew, led by the Panthers, a death squad. (*Detective Comics* #653, November 1992)

As the civil war grew, others entered to exploit the opportunity for gunrunning and other illicit operations. A teen nationalist named DAVA SBÖRSE was training alongside TIM DRAKE when the needs of her people called her home. ROBIN followed and got caught up in a scheme masterminded by KING SNAKE that also attracted LADY SHIVA.

Despite Robin's brief intervention, the civil war continued unabated.

KRAVIA
The principality of Kravia was considered one of the most despotic nations in the world—second only to SANTA PRISCA. The European country was ruled for fifteen years by Prince Kravik, whose imminent campaign of ethnic cleansing was brought to light through the efforts of NIGHTWING. Kravik, who was horribly scarred at birth by an incompetent midwife, assumed the throne at the age of six and grew up to become a brutal tyrant. Heinmel Von Cart, a resistance leader and later Kravia's prime minister, planned to depose Kravik. To accomplish this, he had a plastic surgeon alter his own son Kemper's features to match Kravik's so that Kemper could replace the mad prince on the throne. After Kemper substituted for the now dead Kravik, though, he proved to be an even worse leader. Prime Minister Von Cart was smuggled into the United States by Nightwing, and revealed the entire scandalous story of his nation at a press conference. (*Nightwing* #1-4, September–December 1995).

The government was later beset by guerrilla forces that terrorized the countryside. During earlier skirmishes, the government had salted large areas with mines. (*Batman: Death of Innocents* #1, December 1996)

KRISTIN, KLAUS
Klaus Kristin was the costumed killer known to Batman as the SNOWMAN.

KROL, ARMAND
Armand Krol was one of a long line of short-lived GOTHAM CITY mayors. Almost immediately after taking office, he and Police Commissioner JAMES GORDON began to butt heads over budgets and the role Batman played in keeping the streets safe. (*Detective Comics* #647, August 1992)

Things grew heated enough that Krol replaced Gordon with his wife, SARAH ESSEN GORDON. The move lasted for the remainder of the mayor's tenure. As for Batman, Krol's opinion changed after the Dark Knight saved his life.

It was no surprise when Krol lost reelection to MARION GRANGE. (*Shadow of the Bat* #46, January 1996) Before she took office, though, RA'S AL GHŪL unleashed an Ebola-A virus, nicknamed the CLENCH, hastening the transition. Krol died from the Clench soon after. (*Detective Comics* #699, July 1996)

KRYPENN
A killer who used various forms of poison to do his heinous deeds and was known as the POISONER.

KRYPTON
Orbiting a red sun in the Andromeda Galaxy six million light-years from Earth, Krypton was home to an advanced race of beings. Before the planet exploded, an infant was sent in a rocket ship to Earth, where he grew up to become SUPERMAN. (*Action Comics* #1, June 1938)

Details regarding Kryptonian civilization and the exact causes of the planet's destruction varied across the realities. In most accounts, a highly unstable planetary core led to the world exploding.

(For a detailed account of Krypton, consult *The Essential Superman Encyclopedia*.)

KRYPTONITE

Kryptonite comprised radioactive remnants of the doomed planet Krypton that managed to traverse the six million light-years from the Andromeda Galaxy to Earth. (*Superman* #61, November/December 1949) The irradiated element was almost instantly fatal to survivors from Krypton, including Superman. Prolonged exposure could cause cancerous conditions in humans, as seen when a small piece cause Lex Luthor to lose a hand. (*Action Comics* #600, May 1988)

In the world created after the Crisis on Infinite Earths, Superman entrusted the one piece of kryptonite he'd recovered to Batman, to use should circumstances ever require it. Based on an analysis, Batman created notes regarding fabricating a synthetic version. When Rā's al Ghūl stole notes from the Batcave, he created the synthetic version with success. (*JLA* #43–46, July–October 2000)

(For a detailed account of kryptonite, consult *The Essential Superman Encyclopedia.*)

KUTTLER, NOAH

Noah Kuttler suffered from obsessive-compulsive disorder and trained himself to use his illness to order his life as a criminal mastermind. As the Calculator, he became the underworld's information broker and came to lead the secret Society of super-villains.

KYLE

Kyle claimed to be the first criminal arrested by Batman and sought revenge as costumed villain the Clock.

KYLE, KARL

Selina Kyle's brother who donned a catsuit and briefly committed crimes as the King of Cats.

KYLE, MAGGIE

Maggie Kyle was the younger sister of Selina Kyle, who later became Catwoman. Their parents were Brian and Maria Kyle, with Maria proving to be emotionally distant from her daughters. She instead devoted her time to the family cats and was driven to commit suicide by the drunken antics of her alcoholic husband. Brian, meantime, didn't like how much Selina resembled Maria. As he drank himself to death, Selina and Maggie fled their home. (*Catwoman* [second series] #0, October 1994)

The girls lived on the street for a time and eventually went their separate ways. Selina was a prostitute, while Maggie's whereabouts went unrecorded.

Eventually Maggie wound up at a convent and soon took her vows. To Selina, who'd grown distant from Maggie but never let her totally drift away, she was always "Sister Magdalene." Selina's former pimp, Stan, trying to get back at Selina, kidnapped and abused Maggie until Catwoman arrived. Selina saved Maggie and killed Stan, driving a wedge between nun and criminal. (*Catwoman* #1–4, February–May 1989) For unexplained reasons, Maggie gave up her vows and chose to explore the world beyond Gotham City. She moved to the West

Batman holds a piece of deadly kryptonite...

Maggie Kyle

Coast and in time met Simon Burton. They fell in love and married. As fate had it, Simon's employer transferred him east, and Maggie returned to Gotham.

It took time, but Maggie and Selina reunited and grew close once again. Selina even invited Maggie and Simon to the dedication of the EAST END's new Community Center. Unfortunately, reentering Catwoman's world made Maggie a target, and it wasn't long before BLACK MASK's war with Catwoman for the East End got personal. That night the center was blown up and Simon kidnapped while riding the subway. As Catwoman and her allies sought Simon, Maggie, too, was kidnapped. Black Mask tortured Simon and then began to force-feed pieces of him to Maggie. By the time Catwoman managed to locate and rescue her sister, the damage was done. Simon was dead, and Maggie had lost her psychological grip on reality, requiring institutionalization. (*Catwoman* [third series] #12–15, December 2002–March 2003)

KYLE, SELINA

The beautiful woman with a troubled past who found new life as the costumed criminal and adventurer CATWOMAN.

KZOTL

Kzotl was an obscure planet, home to a motion picture producer who crafted robots designed to resemble typical alien threats. Unleashing them on Earth, he recorded Batman, ROBIN, and SUPERMAN's efforts to stop the alien threat for his next film project. (*World's Finest Comics* #108, December 1950/January 1951)

Selina Kyle

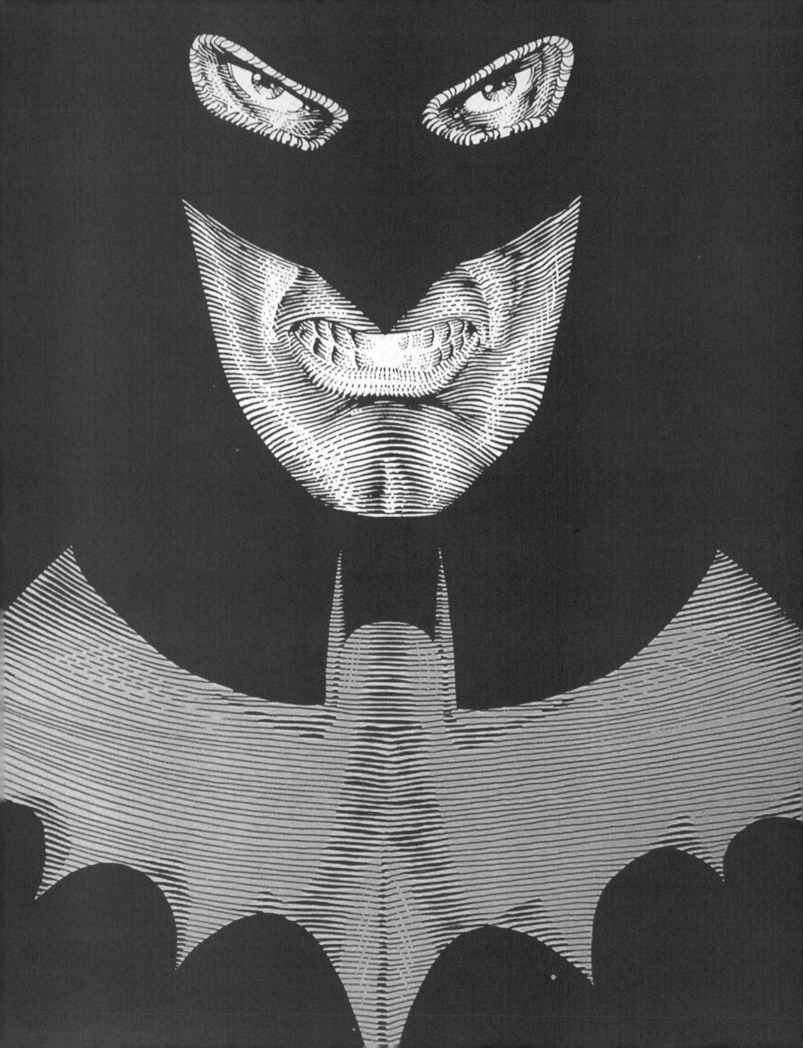

LADY SHIVA

The road to becoming the world's deadliest martial artist was a long and twisting one that began in Detroit.

The Wu San sisters Carolyn and Sandra lived on Earth-1 until Carolyn died under mysterious circumstances. A man named Cravat pointed Sandra in the direction of Richard Dragon, a martial arts teacher who was said to be a spy. (*Richard Dragon, Kung Fu Fighter* #5, December 1975) To prepare herself to kill the man, she, too, studied martial arts and discovered her innate abilities, proving her a quick study. When she deemed herself ready, Sandra sought out Dragon—only to discover she had been duped. She felt rudderless, dissatisfied that Carolyn was unavenged and her life had no purpose. Dragon saw great potential in her and offered to continue her education, which she gratefully agreed to. In addition to her physical training, he began showing her the spiritual side of the arts, teaching her Zen. After a time, she felt Sandra had ceased to be, and she renamed herself Shiva. For a time Shiva continued to train while also going on adventures with Dragon and his partner, Ben Turner, the BRONZE TIGER. Their partnership lasted only a brief time, until Dragon chose to withdraw from society and go live in the mountains. Shiva was on her own.

On the Earth created after the CRISIS ON INFINITE EARTHS, Sandra and Carolyn Wu San were sisters who already knew martial arts and practiced together, working in a synchronized manner as befit siblings. Assassin DAVID CAIN observed the adolescents, seeing something special in the way Sandra fought but also noticing that she held back when fighting Carolyn. To help her tap her full potential, and make her the woman he needed,

Cain killed her older sister and let Sandra find the body.

Sandra wanted revenge and determined that Cain was the murderer. She began a manhunt, which ended only when she was ambushed by RĀ'S AL GHŪL'S LEAGUE OF ASSASSINS. She began to fight for her life, seeing Cain among its members, but

she was nearly killed. He offered to spare her if she agreed to not only complete her training with the league but also bear him a child, whom he would be free to raise as he saw fit. She agreed. The child, CASSANDRA CAIN, was trained to serve as Rā's perfect bodyguard, only to ultimately grow up and become BATGIRL. (*Batgirl* #73, February 2006)

At this point Shiva began traveling as part of her training. This included a stop in Manchuria, where the O-Sensei, the man who'd first trained Dragon and Turner, took her as a student and was named her godfather. She subsequently went to Vietnam to undergo rigorous training under a woman named only Mother. (*Birds of Prey* #92–95, May–August 2006)

After Cain left with Cassandra, Sandra felt free to find her own destiny and became Shiva, named for the goddess of creation and destruction. She surpassed most fighters because she knew how to read opponents, understanding what they intended to do before they themselves realized it, giving her the crucial time to defend herself or counterattack. She used this advantage to become a highly paid mercenary, globe-trotting from assignment to assignment. The money offered her the luxury to continue her training as she mastered one discipline after another. This also allowed her to seek out those whom she felt might be worthy opponents.

At some undefined point, Shiva and Richard Dragon crossed paths and knew each other, earning each other's respect. The exact nature of the relationship remained unrecorded.

One of her earliest assignments took her to Hub City at the behest of the Reverend Hatch, to end an annoyance known as the QUESTION. They fought, and Shiva won easily—but she also saw great potential

handed fighting. They battled, and she learned that good as he was, a man named KING SNAKE had beaten him in combat. The trail led her to Paris, where she not only encountered King Snake but teenage TIM DRAKE, who was undergoing his own training to become the third ROBIN. Shiva liked Drake and saw great potential in him, so she took him on as possibly her first student. They worked extensively, and he got better very quickly. When she allowed him to choose a weapon to train with, he selected the Bo staff, which she sniffed at since it was not considered a lethal tool. Shiva and Robin finally confronted King Snake in Hong Kong, and she ordered Drake to kill him but the boy refused, ending his time as Shiva's student. (*Robin* #1–5, January–May 1991)

A short while later, BANE had come to GOTHAM CITY and broken Batman's back. As the Dark Knight healed, he recognized the need to retrain his body and sought out Lady Shiva. She saw that his fighting spirit had also been damaged, and she contrived events to work both body and mind. Wearing a TENGU MASK, she killed Gotham's ARMLESS MASTER, making certain there was a witness. Then she began working with Batman, making him wear the Tengu Mask during training, which made him a target for those seeking to avenge the Armless Master. In the end this tactic, while brutal, worked for Batman but failed for Shiva, who was attempting to bring him to a new plane of existence by forcing him to kill. (*Batman* #509, July 1994)

Shiva and Robin encountered each other again when DAVA, a teen who had trained alongside Robin, wanted to test her skill with the one-handed killing technique known as the Leopard Blow. Fearing the worst, Robin trailed Dava and got embroiled in another mêlée with both Shiva and King Snake. During the battle, Robin actually managed to kill Shiva but used CPR to resuscitate her. (*Robin* [second series] #49, January 1998) The Leopard Blow has been described in different ways: Batman said the blow used the heel of the hand to drive shards of the skull into the brain, with the impact delivered at the nose. (*Legends of the Dark Knight* #62, July 1994) Richard Dragon later explained that the hand begins above and behind the victim's head then, fingers straight out, drives into the skull, instantly killing the target.

Along the way, Shiva had become affiliated with the BROTHERHOOD OF THE FIST, in which each discipline was represented by a monkey who attracted followers based on the practice's difficulty; thus the Paper Monkey had no followers. The brotherhood chose to use earthquake-ravaged Gotham City as the site for a tournament to determine the world's greatest fighter, an event that grew to involve Batman, Robin, Batgirl, Green Arrow II, Bronze Tiger, and others. In the end, the second Green Arrow, CONNOR HAWKE, squared off against the Paper Monkey, who was revealed to be Shiva. She defeated Hawke and was preparing to kill him when Robin called in the debt she owed because he'd saved her life. She agreed, adding that at some point, when Drake was an adult, she claimed the right to face him in a combat to the death. (*Green Arrow* #134, *Detective Comics* #723, *Robin* #55, *Nightwing* #23, *Green Arrow* #135, July–August 1998)

in him. After Hatch's men beat him further, leaving him for dead in the river, she retrieved his body. Shiva took him to Dragon's mountain retreat, where the two helped reinvent the Question. (*The Question* #1–2, February–March 1987)

He repaid the favor when Shiva was asked to assemble a team of three warriors to help her find the bones of the O-Sensei's wife, so that he might die and rest beside her. Shiva chose the Question, GREEN ARROW, and Batman. When the Question took her to meet the Dark Knight, the first thing they did was fight: Testing another was to them like breathing to anyone else. At the time she also met and sparred with BLACK CANARY, the beginning of an unusual relationship between the women, starting with both having studied under Sensei Otomo at different times. (*Detective Comics Annual* #1, *Green Arrow Annual* #1, *The Question Annual* #1, 1988)

Soon after, she returned to Hub City for a time, helping the Question in his final days of battling rampant corruption until they gave up on the city for good. They parted ways, and Shiva continued her mercenary work. Her next encounter with Batman came in the Middle East when he and JASON TODD sought clues that Shiva might be Todd's mother. The Dark Knight and Lady Shiva battled unfettered and were very closely matched. In the end his brute strength won the fight; losing, she denied being Todd's mother. (*Batman* #427, December 1988)

Soon after, Shiva began doing less mercenary work and spending more time testing herself against those considered the best at a particular discipline or move. She proved mercurial, killing some after besting them, letting others live. Her reputation as a fearsome, unknowable force spread, so her very presence in a city caused fear among the underworld and crime-fighting communities. As Shiva battled one master after another, she became intrigued by Koroshi, an expert in empty-

the city's rooftops. By this time, Batgirl had had her brain psychically altered to allow speech, but this affected her fighting style, making her an easy target for Shiva. Disgusted, Shiva let the girl live, never revealing their relationship, and extracted a promise: She would teach Batgirl how to overcome her new mental processing in exchange for a duel to the death one year later. Batgirl agreed. (*Batgirl* #7–8, October–November 2000)

The bargain worked in a single night and Batgirl regained her fighting edge, although she seemed to fight with a death wish, still haunted at having killed a man at age eight. When the year had passed, the two met at the Forum of the twelve Caesars and again Shiva proved victorious, killing Batgirl. The woman noted, though, that Batgirl fought differently, holding back, so the knowledge robbed the moment of its uniqueness. Shiva revived her daughter and the two renewed the battle until Batgirl shattered her mother's sword. Cassandra then accused Shiva of having her own death wish, broke her jaw, and proved victorious—but refused to kill her. (*Batgirl* #25, April 2002)

Richard Dragon chose to leave his mountain retreat for a time, going back into action with the Bronze Tiger. They found themselves in opposition to Lady Shiva and once more they engaged in combat. Shiva killed Dragon with the Leopard Blow, only to have the demon Neron, who was bargaining to gain his soul, resurrect him. (*Richard Dragon* #1–6, July–December 2004)

Shiva continued to appear throughout the world, fighting martial artists, working alongside costumed crime fighters who captured her fancy, or settling scores with those who wronged her or her few allies. During all this, she and Black Canary continued to encounter each other until, when the Canary was at a personal low point, Shiva agreed to train her. At much the same time, Shiva also insinuated herself into the League of Assassins, then under the control of Nyssa Raatko, Rā's al Ghūl's daughter. While there, she encountered her own daughter once more. She watched as Batgirl sacrificed her life to save another from David Cain's first failed experiment, a man named Mad Dog. Every move Batgirl made told Shiva that Cassandra had chosen her own path, willingly allying herself with Batman and subscribing more to his ideals than hers. She took her daughter's body to a Lazarus Pit, resurrecting her—all so they could duel each other again. This time, with both women physically and mentally healthy, they were evenly matched. Cassandra won the fight, snapping her mother's neck but leaving her alive. Shiva then refused treatment in the pit. Cassandra left her mother dangling over the pit and took control of the league for herself. (*Batgirl* #73, April 2006)

Shiva survived and healed and honored her commitment to train Black Canary. She dispatched the Canary to Asia to train under Mother for one year while she willingly took her place as a Bird of Prey. She even wore a variation on the Canary outfit, complete with fishnets, and wanted to be called the Jade Canary, something Oracle refused to do. Shiva did as she was ordered but lacked the compassion the other field agents possessed and never truly bonded with the other women. Canary

While the brotherhood and many of Earth's super heroes acknowledged that Shiva was the world's greatest martial artist, the villain Prometheus begged to differ. His helmet enabled the man to mimic the abilities of the world's thirty greatest martial artists, including Shiva, and to his way of thinking she was third best. Shiva, however, felt that the helmet held her older styles; she knew she could defeat her earlier self, so she dismissed Prometheus.

Soon after, Gotham City was declared a No Man's Land and sealed from the rest of America. Just before the city was cut off, Cassandra Cain entered and chose to remain. She discovered Batman's allies attempting to maintain order and wanted to fight alongside them, but lacked the ability to communicate. Barbara Gordon gave the teen shelter and, after a time, blessed her becoming the new Batgirl. Her fighting style was unique enough to come to Shiva's attention, and the two met on walked away from Mother early, taking with her Sin, a young child whom Mother thought had great promise. To balance the scales, after saving the Crime Doctor's daughter, Bethany Thorne, from death, Shiva chose to take the child and send her to Asia as a replacement. (*Birds of Prey* #92–95, May–August 2006) When the Birds of Prey gathered to convince Spy Smasher to leave the team in Oracle's hands, Lady Shiva turned up, but neither Oracle nor Huntress had summoned her.

LAMA, RAHUL

Rahul Lama was a sensei based in Paris, teaching the martial and healing arts. Batman dispatched Tim Drake to be trained by both Rahul Lama and his grandson Shen Chi. While there, Tim had his first encounters with King Snake and his Ghost Dragons, putting his newfound skills to use. (*Robin* #1–5, January–May 1991)

LAMB, ADAM

By day, Adam Lamb worked at a museum, but he dreamed of a more adventurous life. As he finished reading a book called *The Crime Master,* the timid custodian fell down a flight of stairs, sustaining a serious blow to the head. The following night, Lamb changed, becoming a seemingly taller, more self-assured man. Calling himself Wolf, this emergent personality encountered a stranger on the street and killed him in cold blood. The next morning Lamb awoke with no memory of his heinous act. On following nights Wolf assembled a team of criminals and began a series of robberies, while a blissfully unaware Lamb continued his work at the museum. Wolf and his men were confronted at the museum by Batman, leading to a vicious fight. After one blow, Wolf fell down the same flight of stairs, the blow making the man aware of his dual life. Dying from the fall, Lamb explained everything to the sympathetic Caped Crusader. (*Batman* #2, Summer 1940)

LAMONICA, JOHNNY

This criminal became the second man to terrorize Gotham City's citizens as the Black Spider.

LANCE, DINAH

This young woman turned into crime fighter Black Canary, a legacy passed on to her daughter, also named Dinah.

LANDERS, LEN

Len Landers thought he had it made, able to commit crimes without worrying about Batman. A freak accident had transformed the crime fighter into a phantom, unable to physically grasp anything or anyone. Landers and his mob attempted to rob the Gotham Bank, only to be foiled and apprehended by the altered Batman and Robin. (*Batman* #110, September 1957)

LANE, LOIS

Lois Joanne Lane-Kent was a star reporter for Metropolis's *Daily Planet,* married to fellow journalist Clark Kent, who was also Superman. (*Action Comics* #1, June 1938)

On Earth-2, Lois Lane was a reporter at the *Daily Star* when Clark Kent joined the staff. Her disdain for Kent and admiration for Superman blinded her to the reality before her eyes. In time, though, Superman and Lois fell in love and ultimately married. (*Action Comics* #484, June 1978) Batman, and later his wife, Selina Kyle, were close friends of the Kents. Lois and Clark were among the three survivors of Earth-2 when the multiverse collapsed during the Crisis on Infinite Earths. Their crystalline home in a limbo-like place sustained them until Lois finally died of old age. (*Infinite Crisis* #5, April 2006)

On Earth-1, Lois was also a driven reporter, given to reckless acts that risked her life in the name of news. Like her counterpart, Lois preferred Superman to Clark, always suspecting that they were the same but never able to prove it. Over time Lois and Clark did strike up a romantic relationship, although it did not last long.

On the post-Crisis Earth, Lois was the daughter of an army general, Sam Lane. A tough, independent woman, she initially resisted her attraction to Superman and truly disliked Clark Kent. Over the years they worked alongside each other, though, Lois finally saw Clark for who he truly was and fell in love with him, leading to his revealing the true

and then extracted a written pledge from the Caped Crusader that neither crime fighter would set foot in GOTHAM CITY for an entire week. Thinking he had a clear path to riches, Lang and his men set out to commit one robbery after another. Each attempt, though, was thwarted by the Dynamic Duo, who honored the pledge but worked *over* the city in the newly constructed Flying BATCAVE. Lang, his men, and his associate Big-Time Gateson were apprehended. (*Detective Comics* #186, August 1952)

LANGSTROM, FRANCINE

Francine Evelyn Lee was a fellow scientist and girlfriend of Kirk Langstrom, a GOTHAM CITY scientist who developed a bat-gland serum enhancing human abilities. Kirk experimented with a serum to give him the sonar abilities of a bat, only to find himself transformed into the mindless MAN-BAT. He

terrorized Gotham City until he was subdued and treated by Batman. Francine learned Kirk's secret but remained steadfast in her loyalty. (*Detective Comics* #402, August 1970) Rather than give up on the man she loved, she, too, took the serum, becoming SHE-BAT. (*Detective Comics* #407, January 1971) Unfortunately, Kirk was destined to resume becoming Man-Bat again and again, with Francine remaining loyal and loving. Then atomic radiation reactivated the serum in her bloodstream, and her life was no longer her own when she fell under the

Aaron "Bat-Boy" Langstrom

spell of a sorcerer named Baron Tyme. (*Man-Bat* #1, December 1975/January 1976) Almost immediately after, she was turned to stone by a different mage, Dr. Thanatogenos. (*Detective Comics* #458, April 1976) After Kirk managed to save and cure her both times, they tried for a stable life. When private investigator JASON BARD came to Kirk, looking for help in tracking the serial killer known as the Shotgun Sniper, the entire Langstrom family was threatened. (*Batman Family* #15–16, December 1977/January 1978–February/March 1978)

Through the years Francine remained loyal, and between bouts as Man-Bat, Kirk stayed by her side. They had two children: Rebecca Elizabeth (*Batman Family* #17, May 1978) and Aaron. (*Man-Bat* [third series] #3, February 1996) Unfortunately, Kirk's DNA was altered by his frequent transformations, so Aaron was born a "bat-boy." When Gotham was a NO MAN'S LAND, Aaron went missing and the PENGUIN sought him out, determined to profit from him. (*Batman Chronicles* #17, Summer 1999)

At some point Francine and Kirk went to work for the Helix Group, a genetics research operation. However, they soon quit over ethical issues. Later, when members of the group began getting killed,

nature of his being. They married and moved into a condominium at 1938 Sullivan Lane—a building owned by BRUCE WAYNE, who became a friend to both. (*Superman: The Wedding Album,* 1996)

(For a detailed account of Lois Lane, consult *The Essential Superman Encyclopedia.*)

LANE, LUCKY

Lucky Lane was once the undisputed king of GOTHAM CITY's underworld. Even kings get deposed, though, and Lane was arrested and sentenced to prison. Upon his release, he disappeared from view, going into hiding and resuming his criminal career. This time, Lane ran the RED MASK MOB from an abandoned water tower. His new criminal campaign came to an end through the combined efforts of Batman, ROBIN, and ACE THE BAT-HOUND. (*Batman* #123, April 1959)

LANE, RUFUS

Rufus Lane ran a criminal gang until he crossed paths with not only Batman and ROBIN but also a cantankerous troupe of former show business performers. (*Batman* #51, February/March 1949)

LANG, DIAMOND

Diamond Lang struck upon an ingenious way to commit crimes without worrying about Batman and ROBIN. He had his men kidnap the Boy Wonder

Gotham police suspected Francine was the next target. She in turn feared that the murderer was Kirk, mindlessly acting out as Man-Bat. Kirk was proven innocent, and he protected her from the real killer, STEELJACKET. (*Man-Bat* [third series] #1–3, February–April 1996)

Though the serum left Kirk prone to hallucinations—such as one in which he killed Francine and the children—she remained alive and at his side. (*Man-Bat* [fifth series] #1–4, June–September 2006) TALIA HEAD threatened her life if Langstrom did not provide her with the serum. (*Batman* #655, September 2006)

LANGSTROM, KIRK

Research scientist Kirk Langstrom attempted to transfer a bat's attributes to a man but wound up a were-bat incapable of controlling his actions. As MAN-BAT he has been an ally and opponent of Batman.

LARROW, JOHN

John Larrow was a GOTHAM CITY businessman convicted of fraud and sentenced to prison. Larrow paid a handful of criminals to break him free, which they did by using a tunnel under the prison from a faux excavation site. Meanwhile Batman was in Pacific City addressing a criminologists' convention, so he conducted a contest in Gotham, awarding the right to be Batman for a day to those who contributed large sums to the Police Widows and Orphans Fund. Robin found each succeeding Batman more inept and felt helpless to stop Larrow from escaping. In a panic, he summoned his mentor to rush back early. Batman arrived in time to keep Larrow in jail and apprehend his would-be rescuers. (*Detective Comics* #225, November 1955)

LARRY THE JUDGE

A criminal named Larry used the alias J. Spencer Larson to manage an investment firm that was a front for criminal investments. The apparent high rates of return appealed to wealthy investors—but each depositor was eventually robbed right after cashing in the investment. With the additional

revenues, Larry became wealthy and powerful, seizing control of GOTHAM CITY's underworld. As Larry the Judge, he decreed no one could commit a crime without first obtaining a license from him. From his bench, Larry granted licenses, sold advice, and collected shares of each criminal procedure. It all came to an end when Batman and ROBIN appeared before the court and apprehended Larry and his men. (*Detective Comics* #72, February 1943)

LARSEN, KEITH

Keith Larsen was an adventurer who climbed Mount Rabachi with Cliff Amory. After they found the fabled Hand of Korabo, Larsen murdered Amory so he wouldn't have to share the find. Larsen blamed the death on a climbing accident, but suspicions were aroused. Batman worked with climbers Hampden and Dunne to craft a ruse that forced a confession from Larsen. (*Batman* #146, March 1962)

LARSON, HARRY

Harry Larson had the misfortune to resemble millionaire BRUCE WAYNE. The ex-convict was forced by "Fish" Frye to impersonate Batman in a scheme that ultimately failed. (*Batman* #83, April 1954)

LARUE, ERNST

Ernst Larue was a criminal who gained access to an advanced piece of technology that, when fed specifically prepared "brain tapes," could gain mental control over specific individuals. Larue used the machine to force a jewelry executive, an armored car driver, and a Rare Coin Exchange employee to do his bidding. Once they committed robberies for Larue, they forgot their criminal acts. Batman and ROBIN investigated and soon after apprehended Larue. (*Detective Comics* #324, February 1964)

LATHROP

The secret leader of an art theft ring, the owner of the Lathrop Gallery of Art proved unsuccessful as he was quickly arrested by Batman and ROBIN. (*Batman* #176, December 1965)

LAWTON, FLOYD

Floyd Lawton endured a horrific childhood to become a mercenary with death wish, DEADSHOT.

LAZARA

NORA FRIES was resurrected from a fatal illness using a LAZARUS PIT but in the process was transformed into a creature calling itself Lazara.

LAZARUS PIT

The Lazarus Pit was an alchemical construct that restored the dead to life. (*Batman* #244, September 1972) The man called RA'S AL GHŪL discovered the secret to manufacturing a pit and used it to save the life of a dying prince some five hundred years ago. He also discovered the horrible price: intense madness coupled with superhuman strength for the first minutes of restored life. (*Batman: Birth of the Demon,* 1993)

Rā's al Ghūl kept the secret to himself and used it countless times over the centuries, enabling him to amass both a fortune and an international organization to exert his will.

Pits were formed in specific geographic locations, the exact nature of which was never recorded, although it has been theorized they are in relation to ley lines. A corpse placed in a pit could be resurrected only once per pit, though the pit was proven to still work on others.

The pits were a closely held secret until the latter years of the twentieth century, when word of their existence began to leak out. Rā's harbored the secret, building a network of pits following the ancient texts he discovered. KOBRA, another international terrorist, built his own supply of Lazarus Pits around the globe. In an effort to shut down Rā's ambitious plans, Batman and BANE circled the world covering up or destroying the pits, depriving Rā's of his needed source of life. By the end of his life, one final pit remained, its location a secret he took to his grave.

Rā's recognized that his ability to regenerate through the pits was coming to an end, implying that the body had limits of about half a millennium. His daughter NYSSA RAATKO, who was enjoying her second century of life thanks to the pits, had studied the chemistry involved and found a way to alter the formula to allow a body to be regenerated more than once per immersion in the pit—something she then did repeatedly to her younger half sister TALIA HEAD. (*Batman: Death and the Maidens* #1–9, October 2003–August 2004) In addition to Nyssa's pit, one was constructed in the BATCAVE.

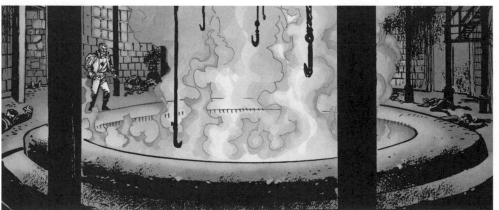

Lazarus Pit

Others who died and were resurrected by the Pit's power included CASSANDRA CAIN and LADY SHIVA. However, when the shattered pieces of NORA FRIES were placed in the pit, the resurrected life-form was not human, but instead a being melding the molten core of the Earth and a humanoid form called LAZARA.

The pits were also shown to have restorative powers, such as when a wounded BLACK CANARY was healed and KING SNAKE had his eyesight returned. The pit was used to cure the RIDDLER of brain cancer. It has also been said that immersion in the pit would kill a living being. When a reality-altering wave resurrected JASON TODD, he was unable to recall his past life until Talia found him and restored him through the healing power of the pit.

LEAF, PROFESSOR DORMEUS

Professor Dormeus Leaf, based at Pacific Coast University in Coast City, developed the world's most sophisticated seismograph, allowing pinpoint accuracy in predicting earthquakes. When Batman was threatened by the JACKAL, Leaf proved instrumental in saving his life. (*Batman* #33, February/ March 1946)

LEAGUE OF ASSASSINS, THE

The League of Assassins was created some centuries ago by the international terrorist RÄ'S AL GHÜL. They were to be his elite army, not only protecting him but ensuring that his missions went off without a hitch. Through the years, the League sought out the best killers in all manner of disciplines, from martial artists to snipers. Every member added to the league gave up his or her life, sworn to the Demon's Head.

In time, Rä's turned management of the league over to a man from Hong Kong known as the SENSEI, who took to calling the league his Society, an indication that the two would vie for control at some later date. Still, he referred to the Assassins as the "powerful *fang* which protects his *head*." (*Justice League of America* #94, November 1971) Later, a wandering spirit known as Jonah discovered the Society of Assassins and realized that they could be used to destroy the deity Rama Kushna and her mystic land of Nanda Parbat. Inhabiting the Sensei's body, Jonah directed the League of Assassins to develop sophisticated weaponry. (*Deadman* [second series] #2, April 1986)

Roy Matson, one of the Sensei's prized assassins, paid the penalty for failing in an assignment: His right hand was cut off and replaced with a hook. To assess his skills, the newly christened Hook was sent to America and assigned to execute a presidential candidate. Instead, Matson was manipulated by Rama Kushna into assassinating aerialist Boston "DEADMAN" Brand, unwittingly creating an agent that the deity could use to oppose Jonah and protect Nanda Parbat. (*Strange Adventures* #205, October 1967)

The league operated in relative anonymity for some time. Eventually the Sensei and Rä's al Ghül had a falling-out. The former leader left, taking a splinter cell with him, while Rä's turned command

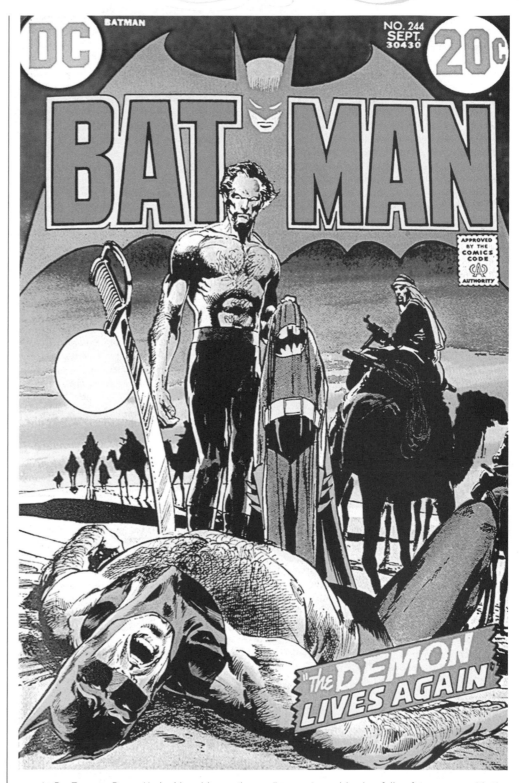

over to DR. EBENEZER DARKK. Under his guidance, the league undertook a series of executions aimed at shipping magnates who were smuggling weapons to South American rebels. When the string of murders reached GOTHAM CITY, Batman became involved and defeated an Asian martial artist named Tejja. (*Detective Comics* #405, November 1970)

Darkk subsequently hired DOCTOR TZIN-TZIN to slay Batman—but he, too, failed to kill the Caped Crusader. (*Detective Comics* #408, February 1971)

Desperate and having fallen from grace with the Demon's Head, Darkk took TALIA HEAD as a hostage even as Batman trailed him to a small Asian nation. After running a gauntlet of assassins and freeing Talia, Batman found himself held at bay by the knife-wielding doctor. Insisting that the gun-toting Talia was "far too sweet" to kill him, the stunned Darkk reeled backward from the impact of the shot and fell directly into the path of an oncoming train. (*Detective Comics* #411, May 1971)

An unhappy Sensei sent M'Naku after Batman, fearing the Dark Knight's presence would compromise his plans. MERLYN the Magician, a dangerous archer, was sent after M'Naku failed. (*Justice League of America* #94, November 1971) Merlyn also failed and Rā's sent Talia to execute him, but she fell short of her goal due to BLACK LIGHTNING's intervention. (*Black Lightning* #2, May 1977) Merlyn left the League of Assassins, kept his life, and worked as a mercenary.

In Gotham City a league assassin named SHRIKE was training a group of boys in the martial arts as part of his Vengeance Academy. Shrike's decision to accept a contract on TWO-FACE's life proved disastrous and, in a battle that drew the attention of both Batman and a disguised ROBIN, the assassin was impaled on his own knife and killed. One of Shrike's students, a young man named Boone, left Gotham in the company of Rā's al Ghūl's daughter Talia, determined to fulfill the promise that his teacher had seen in him. (*Robin: Year One* #4, 2001)

Boone took the name *Shrike* also and traveled alone throughout the Pacific Rim, gleaning an array of martial arts skills both sacred and profane from a variety of unsavory teachers, including several former operatives of the league. In the back streets of Hong Kong, Shrike met the "Master," who would forge the already hardened youth into a disciplined fighting machine, undertaking contract eliminations throughout Asia and the former Soviet bloc—and never once failing to make a kill. (*Nightwing Secret Files* #1, October 1999)

Other members of the League included Viper, an expert in creating poisons (*Richard Dragon, Kung Fu Fighter* #13, January/February 1977), ONYX, DAVID CAIN, LADY SHIVA, and Ben Turner, the BRONZE TIGER, who fell into their clutches and was brainwashed into becoming their agent. (*Suicide Squad* #38, February 1990)

On Earth-1 this led to the Bronze Tiger fighting Batman, with KATHY KANE murdered as part of the war between the Sensei and Rā's al Ghūl. After the CRISIS ON INFINITE EARTHS the war still happened, but Kate Kane was spared.

Rā's and the Sensei engaged in a struggle for control of the League, a globe-spanning struggle that eventually drew Batman's involvement. (*The Brave and the Bold* #159, February 1980) The struggle climaxed at an international peace conference held in Gotham City. The Sensei wanted to kill the delegates by triggering a fault line under the city, but he was stopped by Batman, Rā's, and Talia. The earthquake was triggered, destroying the building, but the Caped Crusader had evacuated the guests. Talia then knocked him unconscious, allowing Rā's to kill the Sensei, something Batman would have tried to prevent. Rā's, too, died, but was taken by Talia to a LAZARUS PIT to live again. (*Detective Comics* #490, May 1980)

The league continued to operate but, under Rā's guidance, remained underground, taking assignments through middlemen and avoiding direct opposition with law enforcement wherever possible. Concerned about future attacks, Rā's assigned David Cain the task of creating the perfect bodyguard. This led, ironically, to the

birth of CASSANDRA CAIN, who grew up to become BATGIRL. Splits still occurred from time to time, most noteworthy among them a faction led by the Scarlet Scythe, who attempted to kill SUPERMAN. (*Action Comics* #772–773, December 2000–January 2001)

When NYSSA RAATKO killed her father, leadership of the league fell to her. (*Batman: Death and the Maidens* #1–9, October 2003–August 2004) She recruited Lady Shiva to come act as Sensei, training a new generation of killers. Nyssa also wanted to bring Cassandra Cain back into the fold. Meantime, the roster expanded to include Shrike, Kitty Kumbata, Wam-Wam, Joey N'Bobo, Tigris, Momotado, Krunk, White Willow, the twin warriors Los Gemelos, Ox, MAD DOG, Alpha, and Cristos.

A conflict and fresh split occurred between Shiva and Nyssa, leading Cassandra to head up one faction, including Ox, White Willow, and Tigris. (*Batgirl* #73, April 2006) Later, Nyssa seemingly died in a car explosion and Cassandra reunited the league into one formidable force. After she fell under DEATHSTROKE's sway, though, the group was apparently left leaderless. Stepping into the void were league devotees who hired Merlyn to assist them. Their goal was to abduct Sin, the young girl being trained as "the next Lady Shiva," and make her the new leader. The girl was abducted from BLACK CANARY's care. She, GREEN ARROW, and Speedy came to her rescue. (*Black Canary* [third series] #1–4, September–October 2007)

LEATHERWING

On one of the myriad parallel worlds, there lived a seafaring man in the employ of King James I. The privateer captained the *Flying Fox* and was called Captain Leatherwing. He took to wearing a leather costume that cloaked his identity to protect his family back in England. His goal in performing work he found distasteful was to earn enough gold to allow him to reclaim his ancestral lands, stolen after his parents were murdered. His voyages were accompanied by Alfredo Pennyworth, Leatherwing's Italian servant but also a skilled navigator. When not at sea, the *Flying Fox* was anchored at the secret port of Vespertilio Cay.

During one voyage Leatherwing came to rescue Princess Quext'chala from a Spanish galleon. Before he could return her to the Panamanian king Hapa, the "Prince of the Urchins" and bloody terror of the Kingston docks, Robin Redblade snuck aboard the vessel, trying to fulfill his dream of becoming a pirate like Leatherwing. While in hiding, he managed to overhear some of the crew plan a mutiny. Robin came out from hiding to warn the captain, who in gratitude named him a buccaneer.

En route to South America, the *Flying Fox* encountered the *Cat's Paw*, skippered by Capitana Felina. The contessa-of-Spain-turned-pirate had allied herself with the Laughing Man, who wanted her to seduce Leatherwing and find the secret port so they could plunder its riches. The ruse began as planned, but after she slept with Leatherwing, Felina's feelings changed, and she chose to double-cross her partner. Things grew complicated

when the princess insisted she and Leatherwing were already married by virtue of the fact that he had accepted a bracelet from her, which to her tribe signified betrothal. Feeling betrayed, Felina returned to her ship and was determined to help the Laughing Man destroy Leatherwing.

In the end all the schemes were exposed and Robin proved his valor; he took a bullet meant for the captain, but Alfredo's skill helped him survive. The Laughing Man was believed dead, the princess returned to her people, and Leatherwing freed to pursue his romance with Felina. (*Detective Comics Annual* #7, 1994) Their epic romance culminated in a storied wedding. (*The Batman Chronicles* #11, Winter 1998)

LECLERC BROTHERS, THE

Remy and Pierre LeClerc were Canadian criminals known for their deadly accuracy with weapons. Remy was an expert with knives, while Pierre was a crack shot—and both became the object of a manhunt when they escaped prison. After Batman and ROBIN demonstrated their crime-fighting techniques to the Royal Canadian Mounted Police, the BATPLANE was bringing them back to America when they spotted a downed mountie. Officer Bob Jason had been shot and left for dead by the LeClerc Brothers. Batman swore they'd find the criminals but first, to be safe, Jason deputized the Dynamic Duo. Using his white snowsuit for camouflage, Batman managed to surprise the brothers and helped bring them to justice. (*Batman* #78, August/September 1953)

LEGEND CITY

Once a year in Legend City, "people dress up like legendary characters and hold a big celebration." (*Batman* #116, June 1958)

LEGIONARY, THE

Protecting Italy was the Legionary, styled after America's Batman and dressed as an ancient Roman gladiator. On Earth-1 the Legionary traveled to GOTHAM CITY to meet Batman and other international heroes, later forming the group known as the CLUB OF HEROES.

On the Earth created by the CRISIS ON INFINITE EARTHS, the Legionary fought crime in his native land. After reaching the peak of his career he let fame and fortune make him slow down, gain

AND IN ROME, THAT DREADED FOE OF CRIME WHO WEARS A COSTUME OF THE ANCIENT PAST AS...

THE LEGIONARY! HE'S COME AGAIN FROM NOWHERE!

VAULTING ON MY LANCE HELPS—BUT I WISH I KNEW HOW BATMAN AND ROBIN DO IT!

weight, and get sloppy. According to Batman, the Legionary accepted bribes from Charlie Caligula, which compromised his effectiveness. Still, when founder John Mayhew summoned the heroes, he returned to action. He was the first to be killed by Mayhew in a revenge scheme against the Dark Knight. The Legionary suffered seventeen stab wounds, matching the death of Julius Caesar. (*Batman* #667–669, October–November 2007)

LEHAH, CARLTON

As the SACRED ORDER OF SAINT DUMAS entered the twentieth century, members worked to expand its technological know-how in addition to staying current with modern methods of running a business in an increasingly global society. Carlton LeHah acted as the order's treasurer, and as he upgraded its systems, he also skimmed funds for himself. He used the embezzled cash to create his own international arms business, eventually setting up a secret headquarters in a GOTHAM CITY penthouse apartment. (*Batman: Sword of Azrael* #1, October 1992)

When the order discovered the treachery, they dispatched AZRAEL, their Avenging Angel, to deliver justice. LeHah anticipated the man's arrival and laid a trap that mortally wounded him, allowing LeHah to escape. The dying Azrael turned up on the doorstep of his son, JEAN-PAUL VALLEY, a student in Gotham. Valley learned of his hidden past and replaced his father as the latest in a long line of Azraels.

BRUCE WAYNE, investigating reports of Azrael being in Gotham, got captured by LeHah, who tortured him in the hope of gaining access to the Wayne fortune. Azrael arrived, rescuing him and earning Wayne's trust. LeHah, though, managed to escape, with a mobster named PENN SELKIRK taking over the business.

LeHah continued to try to operate apart from the order, which still wished him dead. Azrael also had a personal score to settle, but the man eluded capture time and again. A final climax occurred when LeHah teamed with NICHOLAS SCRATCH and the two fired scores of bullets into Azrael, seemingly killing him. (*Azrael* #100, May 2003) He remained at large.

LENOX, SHELDON

Sheldon Lenox traveled the world to seek rare objects that he could sell to wealthy collectors. Returning from India, he sold a statue of Kila, the Hindu god of destruction, to a man named Weldon. Lenox then stole the statue from Weldon, placing the blame on Kila followers who'd traced the statue from India to GOTHAM CITY. When Batman intervened, he and Lenox fought; the latter fell through a window to his death. (*Detective Comics* #35, January 1940)

LEWIN, NAILS

Nails Lewin teamed with fellow criminals Lew Gadge, Joe Keno, and Ed Mapes to rob one million dollars from the GOTHAM CITY Bank's truck. Soon after, Lewin decided he wanted all the money for himself and launched a scheme to achieve that goal. One by one, his colleagues found themselves arrested by the police, who were armed with information Lewin had secretly provided them. An alert Batman pieced together the plot, apprehended Lewin, and recovered the money. (*Detective Comics* #274, December 1959)

LEWIS, HENRY

Henry Lewis was a millionaire who used his wealth to indulge a passion for surveying. He stumbled across a series of limestone caverns that led directly beneath Fort Stox, one of America's gold reserve locations. Renoldo, leader of a criminal gang, heard of the cavern but not its location, so he led Henry's daughter Linda to believe she'd killed a man and then blackmailed her into revealing the location. Upon learning of the scheme, Batman and ROBIN raced the criminals to the caverns and apprehended them before they could rob the gold. (*Detective Comics* #48, February 1941)

LEXCORP

LexCorp was a mammoth conglomerate founded and operated by LEX LUTHOR. (*Man of Steel* #2, October 1986)

Luthor used his genius to begin a private firm that began as an aerospace manufacturer. His innovations brought attention as well as great wealth and fortune. From there, he began building his empire, acquiring Inter-Continental Airlines and Atlantic Coast Air Systems. The renamed LexAir was the initial brand extension that made his first name synonymous with advanced technology. It was quickly followed by LexOil and others, until no one in America could get through the day without exposure to something Luthor owned.

He entered the world of high finance by investing in the METROPOLIS Mercantile Bank, Commerce Bank of Metropolis, and First Metro Security. There was LexCom that broadcast on radio and television, including the basic cable superstation WLEX. At one point Luthor even briefly owned Metropolis's flagship newspaper, the *Daily Planet,* before he sold it to TransNational Enterprises. Economists once estimated that Luthor employed two-thirds of the city's eleven million inhabitants.

His additional holdings have included Advanced Research Laboratories, Secur-Corp Armored Car Service, North American Robotics, Hell's Gate Disposal Services, and the Good Foods Group, owners of Ralli's Family Restaurants and the Koul-Brau Breweries. In addition to America, LexCorp had holdings in Australia, Venezuela, Argentina, Brazil, China, Germany, Switzerland, France, the Union of South Africa, Saudi Arabia, Japan, and Singapore.

Settling on Metropolis as his base of operations, Luthor constructed a ninety-six-story world headquarters. Its distinctive L-shaped design reinforced the *Luthor* name to the world. His fame was such that Luthor used his recognition to successfully run for president of the United States, turning management of the company over to an outsider, TALIA HEAD, daughter of RĀ'S AL GHŪL. (*President Luthor Secret Files,* March 2001) When his presidency was teetering into failure, Talia stripped the company of assets and attempted to financially ruin Luthor. She also donated huge amounts of the company's profits to the WAYNE FOUNDATION—something that gave her personal satisfaction and was certain to annoy Luthor, who'd seen BRUCE WAYNE as a rival for years.

With Luthor in disgrace, he lost control of LexCorp. Former first lady Lana Lang was named the new chief executive officer. (*Superman* #654, September 2006)

(For a detailed account of LexCorp, consult *The Essential Superman Encyclopedia.*)

LIGHTNING-MAN

Citizens of METROPOLIS were stunned to see a new costumed hero flying overhead, performing a dizzying array of feats. At the same time, crime fighters from around the world, including the KNIGHT and SQUIRE, LEGIONARY, EL GAUCHO, MUSKETEER, Batman, and ROBIN, were on hand for a ceremony opening the newly built CLUB OF HEROES. Philanthropist John Mayhew, the builder, was going to turn the deed over to the hero with the most noteworthy accomplishments. SUPERMAN suspected that Lightning-Man was a criminal who intended to steal the club. Batman, however, deduced that Lightning-Man was in actuality Superman, suffering from amnesia caused by a KRYPTONITE fragment orbiting the Earth. (*World's Finest Comics* #89, July/August 1957)

LINCOLN, JOAN

Television journalist Joan Lincoln worked in GOTHAM CITY in time for the debut of ROBIN the Boy Wonder, during Batman's early days. (*Batman: Full Circle,* 1991) She covered the urban legends and costumed crazies that seemed to overpopulate Gotham through the years until the network chose to reassign her to softer feature stories. (*Batman and the Outsiders* #9, April 1984)

Cable news channel WNN hired her and she traveled the world, filing news stories from wherever the action was. This included Cape Canaveral (*Batman and the Outsiders* #26, October 1985), MARKOVIA (*Batman and the Outsiders* #32, April 1986; *Outsiders* #21, July 1987), Mozambia (*Outsiders* #11, September 1986), Diablo Island (*Outsiders* #18, April 1987), Gotham City (*Detective Comics* #573, April 1987), Santa Monica (*Outsiders* #26, December 1987), Slabside Penitentiary (*Outsiders* #9, July 1986), and Las Vegas (*Outsiders* #0,

October 1994). Around the time the OUTSIDERS were cleared of charges, she took a network anchor's position.

LINNIS, THAD

Thad Linnis managed to persuade SUPERMAN that he had deduced the Man of Steel's secret identity. The criminal promised Superman he would keep the secret if the METROPOLIS Marvel stayed out of the city for two full weeks. After the promise was exacted, Linnis had his men begin preparing a super-tank designed to help them loot the city. Batman realized that Linnis was bluffing the Man of Steel, so he and ROBIN helped their friend apprehend Linnis and his men. (*World's Finest Comics* #84, September/October 1956)

LITTLE RAVEN

The son of Chief MAN-OF-THE-BATS, Little Raven was a Sioux Indian who helped his father fight crime on their reservation. (*Batman* #86, September 1954) As an adult he preferred to be known as Red Raven. (*Batman* #667, October 2007)

LO, BENNY

A Hong Kong–based costumed crime fighter who worked as NIGHT-DRAGON.

LOCK-UP

LYLE BOLTON, a would-be cop who failed his psychological exam, became the vigilante known as Lock-Up. He first arrived in GOTHAM CITY just prior to the outbreak of the Ebola-A virus known as the CLENCH. (*Detective Comics* #694, February 1996) He had initially taken control of an old gun battery built to defend Gotham Harbor after it was damaged during the earthquake and most of BLACKGATE PENITENTIARY's convicts freed. Upon arrival, Lock-Up "deputized" inmates KGBEAST and the TRIGGER TWINS to act as his wardens. Lock-Up then scoured the city to recapture criminals and return them to the damaged structure.

Batman knew someone was apprehending criminals and allowed Lock-Up to operate independently, since he was providing a service that benefited the citizens. Still, he kept a wary eye on the place, especially as word reached him that Lock-Up and his aides were keeping a tight hold on the inmates. When it sounded as if things had gone too far, Batman asked NIGHTWING to investigate and act accordingly. (*Nightwing* [second series] #35–37, September–November 1999)

After Nightwing regained control of the facility, Lock-Up left and, over time, constructed his own private prison. Some time later he began to apprehend criminals on his own and keep them under lock and key. His inmates included TWO-FACE and CHARAXES—but when ROBIN was taken, Batman stepped in before the criminal could punish his charges by drowning them. (*Detective Comics* #697–699, May–July 1996)

Lock-Up remained at large, with his services required by the Society of super-villains. Rather than imprison criminals, he was now hired to free average human and meta-human convicts around the world. (*Villains United: Infinite Crisis Special*, June 2006)

LOEB, GILLIAN B.

When Batman first appeared in GOTHAM CITY, Gillian B. Loeb was its commissioner of police. Loeb was as corrupt as the rest of the city's government, in the pocket of the Roman, CARMINE FALCONE. (*Batman* #404, February 1987) At first he allowed Batman to operate unimpeded, thinking there might be a political advantage to the vigilante. That thinking changed when the Dark Knight boldly arrived at a dinner party in Loeb's home and announced that he was going to end the corruption. Loeb immediately ordered JAMES GORDON, a detective newly arrived from Chicago, to arrest him, something easier said than done.

Loeb went so far as to order that a building in midtown be bombed so a SWAT team could contain and apprehend Batman. The plan failed: Batman escaped and investigated Loeb, providing Gordon with the evidence he needed to expose the corrupt commissioner. Disgraced, Loeb resigned, and a year later he became the second victim of the HANGMAN KILLER. (*Batman: Dark Victory* #2, January 2000)

LOFTUS, "RED"

"Red" Loftus was a big-game hunter who took advantage of a mineral-laden chunk of rock that allowed him to gain a hypnotic control over humans. He used the power over Even Bender, who loved elephants. Loftus had Bender command a herd of elephants to stampede through ivory warehouses and diamond mines; Loftus could then follow and plunder the buildings. Batman and ROBIN arrived in East Africa and freed Bender from Loftus's control, then subdued the animals before arresting Loftus. (*Detective Comics* #33, November 1964)

LONGSHOREMAN KID, THE

The Longshoreman Kid commanded a criminal gang and became a noteworthy arrest in the annals of the GOTHAM CITY POLICE DEPARTMENT. The arrest was made by BRUCE WAYNE, who was serving as a temporary officer, fulfilling the promise he'd made a dying cop. Wayne had to use a policeman's gear and skills without giving away his superior training as Batman. (*Batman* #55, October/November 1949)

LOO CHUNG

Loo Chung became the unofficial mayor of GOTHAM CITY's CHINATOWN, succeeding Batman's murdered friend WONG. (*Detective Comics* #39, May 1940) Later, he obtained Wong's serpent ring, said to have once been worn by Genghis Khan himself. With this symbol of power, Chung began a protection scheme, exacting tribute from his "constituents." Batman and ROBIN put an end to the scheme and promised to have the ring destroyed so it would never be misused again. (*Detective Comics* #52, June 1941)

LOOKER

Some four thousand years ago a meteor crashed in what was later known as Mont Castelle, Switzerland. The interstellar radiation affected an inhabitant's fetus. The son, Loron, grew up possessing psychic powers. With these abilities he led his followers to form an underground society known as the Abyssia.

In modern times a man named Ector left the Abyssians and lived on the surface, keeping Abyssia a secret. Among his descendants, who never knew their true heritage, was Emily Briggs. A bank teller, she lived an unassuming life with her husband Greg in GOTHAM CITY. When she was visiting Tatsu Yamashiro's newly opened bookstore, Briggs was abducted by Abyssians. (*Batman and the Outsiders* #25, September 1985)

Tatsu, also known as KATANA, went to her rescue along with her fellow OUTSIDERS. The entire team struggled against the powerful underground natives. Different members of the team wound up possessed by opposing factions. When both sides converged on Briggs, she finally learned of her heritage. As the last of Loron's descendants, she needed to be ready for the arrival of Halley's Comet, which was said to have control over the Abyssians' psychic powers. Without Briggs's connection to the celestial body, they would revert to the human norm. Exposed to the comet, Briggs transformed from a plain-Jane average woman to a statuesque beauty. Both factions tried to gain control of her as Briggs adjusted to her newfound physique and mental abilities. Briggs fought off both sides and defeated those who chose to usurp the rights of the common people. Leaving matters to majority rule, she returned to the surface as the latest addition to Batman's team. (*Batman and the Outsiders* #31, March 1986)

Emily took to calling herself Lia. She was enamored of her new looks, but the changes put a terrible strain on her marriage. Greg couldn't handle matters, and the couple separated. After the team split from Batman, they became agents of MARKOVIA and were based in Los Angeles. Lia, known now as Looker, accompanied the team and enjoyed her new life. When not in action, she became a highly sought-after model, represented by the Face Value Agency. The agency's head, Dumont, wanted to maintain his control over her and had a private investigator search her past. Cramer, the investigator, came up with a photo of Emily, pre-transformation, and tried to hold it over Lia. Instead, she used her powers to make him forget about it. When he turned up dead, she became a suspect, but the Outsiders cleared her name. (*Outsiders* #14, December 1986)

At one point she and teammate GEO-FORCE were stranded for three weeks on an island and became lovers. After their rescue, the still-married Lia broke things off. It wasn't long after she had to return to Abyssia to help her people stave off an attack by cosmic androids the Manhunters. While there, one of her former foes seized power until Lia invoked the Rite of Challenge. While she won the battle, the price was her beauty and apparently much of her psychic powers. Emily returned to Gotham and Greg. (*Outsiders* #28, February 1988) She displayed her powers once more when Looker came to Batman's aid during a fight against the MUDPACK. (*Detective Comics* #605–607, November–December 1989)

When she traveled to Markovia for the christen-

ing of Geo-Force's nephew, the newly born prince, she was bitten by Roderick, a vampire. Her looks and abilities were revealed as being intact to her teammates but she, too, became a member of the undead. (*Outsiders* [second series] #1—alpha/omega, February 1993) The team thought Emily dead and informed Greg, who insisted she might still be alive and with the Abyssians. Upon arrival, they found the city overtaken by Roderick and Looker, who was in his thrall. After a fierce battle, they managed to destroy Roderick and free the still-vampiric Looker. (*Outsiders* [second series] #10–11, August–September 1994)

That his wife was restored to her new form *and* a vampire was too much for Greg, who finally filed for divorce. Lia remained active with the Outsiders, using her psychic abilities to compensate for some of the typical vampire limitations such as not being able to operate in direct sunlight.

Lia's fame as a model brought her new opportunities, including a stint as co-host of *The Scene*—a free-for-all talk show with fellow hosts VICKI VALE, Tawny Young, and Linda Park. (*Wonder Woman* [second series] #188, March 2003)

During the events known as INFINITE CRISIS, Looker attempted to protect a number of super heroes by erecting a telekinetic shield against Breach's radioactive explosion. She was presumed dead in the aftermath. (*Infinite Crisis* #7, June 2006)

LOOM, ARTHUR

Arthur Loom pretended to be a clairvoyant, but he really used his criminal henchmen to make his predictions appear to come true. This resulted in GOTHAM CITY's criminal underworld coming to believe in his power—and soon the rest of the city's residents did as well. As a result, when he predicted a movie theater's roof was going to collapse, people panicked, allowing his men to loot the box office. Everything unraveled when a predicted robbery aboard the *Queen Helen* resulted in the henchmen aboard their tiny getaway boat being crushed by the ocean liner. Batman and ROBIN worked with Police Commissioner JAMES GORDON to coerce Loom into confessing to his crimes. (*Detective Comics* #133, March 1948)

LORING, E. J.

Famous Hollywood director E. J. Loring realized his latest film was a disaster that would ruin his reputation. He hired several criminals to steal the master negative, holding it for ransom from Mammoth Studios in the hope that the public would never see the film—yet its mystique would enhance his résumé. Batman and ROBIN investigated and exposed Loring's scheme, arresting him and the hirelings. (*Batman* #37, October/November 1946)

LOST MESA

Monk Bardo and Randy Roose escaped prison and fled to the Southwest, where they found a secret Pueblo society hidden from the world. Founded by natives who were fleeing the Spanish conquistadores in the sixteenth century, the community remained uncontaminated by the modern world. Bardo and Roose struck up a partnership with the tribe's medicine man Mordu to help overthrow the chief, Tolto. Batman and ROBIN tracked the convicts to the Lost Mesa, and a vicious fight broke out. The Dynamic Duo were aided by Tolto and young brave Nachee, but not before Mordu died from a stray bullet. (*Batman* #26, December 1944/January 1945)

LOVELY, VERA

Star of the traveling Ice Capers figure-skating spectacular, Vera Lovely was a fourteen-year-old wunderkind. While she was in GOTHAM CITY, Lovely and ROBIN struck up a romance. The Boy Wonder was thrown off his game, unused to the demands on his time and his heart that relationships effect. After the affair ended, Robin swore off women in favor of crime fighting. (*Batman* #107, April 1957)

LUCKY HAND TRIAD, THE

Three months after GOTHAM CITY was restored to the rest of America, it was clear the underworld had rushed back to carve up the city. Among the gangs vying for control was the Lucky Hand Triad, led by EKIN TZU. (*Detective Comics* #743, April 2000)

Tzu's wife was killed by KYLE ABBOTT, who framed the Russian mob and threatened an all-out gang war. Batman interceded and put an end to the troubles, but tensions continued to simmer.

Much later, a WAR GAMES scenario that Batman had created was put into play by SPOILER, fanning the simmer into a full boil. By then, the Lucky Hand Triad, without Tzu's influence, fell to infighting, making them easy pickings when the gang war erupted across all Gotham City. (*Detective Comics* #797, October 2004)

LUMARDI, FRANK

A GOTHAM CITY gang chief, Frank Lumardi, decided to try his hand in England, where the police were known not to carry firearms. Using his own handguns, Lumardi committed a spectacular series of crimes, until the vacationing BRUCE WAYNE and DICK GRAYSON heard the news. London citizens were treated to the sight of Batman and ROBIN apprehending an American gangster. Aiding the Dynamic Duo were copies of the BATMOBILE and other gear provided by admirer Chester Gleek. (*Detective Comics* #196, June 1953)

LUPUS, ANTHONY

Olympic decathlon champion Anthony Lupus suffered from severe headaches and sought treatment from PROFESSOR MILO without realizing the man was a criminal. Milo treated him, discovering that Lupus had a strain of lycanthropy in his genetic makeup. The professor synthesized a headache cure by mixing traditional remedies with genetic material taken from Alaskan timber wolves.

Milo offered the cure in exchange for Lupus agreeing to use his newfound form to kill Batman. Lupus agreed but failed at his job, and the Caped Crusader let him run wild with the wolves. (*Batman* #255, March/April 1974) The two encountered each other only once more, with Lupus still afflicted. (*Detective Comics* #505, August 1981)

LUTHOR, LEX

Lex Luthor was a genius who used his gifts mostly for criminal purposes. In every case he was SUPERMAN's greatest enemy. (*Action Comics* #23, April 1940)

On Earth-2 the redheaded scientist Alexei Luthor was a criminal scientist exploiting his creations in an attempt to take over the world or, failing that, destroy it. Superman stopped him time and again for decades. He finally died at the hands of Earth-1's BRAINIAC during the CRISIS ON INFINITE EARTHS. (*Crisis on Infinite Earths* #9, December 1985)

On Earth-1, Alexis Luthor and CLARK KENT both grew up in Smallville and were childhood friends. Kent's alter ego, Superboy, built Luthor a laboratory to encourage his scientific interests. One day Luthor's lab caught fire, and the Teen of Steel arrived to blow it out.

The fumes caused Luthor's hair to fall out. Enraged, Luthor swore to crush Superboy—a vendetta that carried over into their adult years. One of his first creations intended to destroy the super-teen was an artificial duplicate named Bizarro, which turned out flawed. Luthor became a costumed criminal, wasting his scientific genius with a monomaniacal goal of killing the Kryptonian. (*Adventure Comics* #271, April 1960)

As Earth was re-created by the CRISIS ON INFINITE EARTHS, Luthor banded together with Brainiac to fashion an army of super-villains that would lash out one last time at their enemies. When he

was made aware of the cosmic forces at work, Luthor abandoned thoughts of revenge for those of salvation. His life ended on the planet Maltus, attempting to stop a being from the planet Oa, Krona, from beginning the events that had led to the creation of the multiverse in the first place.

On Earth-3, Alexander Luthor was a heroic scientist on a world filled with superpowered criminals, an almost funhouse-mirror version of Earth-1. (*DC Comics Presents Annual* #1, 1982) When the Crisis came to this world, he placed his son, Alexander Jr., in an experimental rocket ship and sent it to another plane of reality in the hope that the boy would survive. The child was rescued by the being known as the Monitor. In his care, Alexander grew up rapidly and was unique in his ability to act as a safe conduit between the positive and negative matter universes. He proved instrumental during the Crisis, and when the multiverse was refashioned into a singular positive and negative matter set of universes, he used his abilities to take the Superman and LOIS LANE from Earth-2 and Superboy from Earth-Prime with him to a "better place," which proved to be a crystalline structure in a limbo-like space between dimensions. (*Crisis on Infinite Earths* #12, March 1986)

Alexander grew disenchanted with this life and sought to change what he considered to be a flawed reality. Witnessing the darker versions of Earth's champions and the rising numbers of devastating incidents, he imagined crafting a machine that would re-create the multiverse and then fashion a perfect reality where they could all live. To accomplish this, he needed superpowered people from what could have been various parallel worlds. He also sought to use the planet's super-villains for his own purposes. Pretending to be that Earth's Lex Luthor, he created a secret Society of these villains. He also took control of Batman's satellite, BROTHER I, and used it to help find the beings he needed. (*Countdown to Infinite Crisis*, 2005; *Infinite Crisis* #1–7, December 2005–June 2006)

The super heroes managed to prevent Luthor from fulfilling his plan, although a limited multiverse of fifty-two parallel worlds was created. With

Superboy-Prime in custody and Superman and Lois Lane dead, Luthor was left alone on a New Earth. His time there was brief, however: He was tracked down by that world's Luthor and the JOKER, with the Clown Prince of Crime murdering him for not inviting him into the Society.

Alexander Joseph "Lex" Luthor of New Earth was born in Suicide Slum, a lower-socioeconomic-standing neighborhood in METROPOLIS. His abusive father consistently told Lex there was no escape from the slums, so the boy received encouragement from only one source, his close friend Perry White. For all the hardships of his youth, Luthor cultivated relationships with those who could be of use to him. This included two criminals whom he paid to sabotage his parents' car, killing them and freeing Luthor from their influence. These details remained long buried until author Peter Sands uncovered them for *Lex Luthor: The Unauthorized Biography,* a book written but never published. Much of this tome cannot be reconciled with the facts.

Luthor was placed in foster care, only to discover that the adults in charge of him were no better than his parents. For a brief time the socially awkward youth resided in Smallville, with

Clark Kent the only teen who treated him with any respect or friendship. (*Superman: Birthright,* 2005) As he matured, Luthor wanted independence and the power to remain that way. He used his know-how and his parents' inheritance to begin a company that grew to become the international conglomerate LexCorp.

Luthor and BRUCE WAYNE first met when their respective companies bid for a Defense Department contract for a remote war-fighting construct. They exchanged pleasantries after the presentation, establishing their different worldviews. Luthor then used his influence to get the government contract in lieu of WayneTech. Batman gathered evidence of the fraud and presented it to Lieutenant JAMES GORDON. As Batman investigated further, Luthor's GI Robots were delivered in massive quantities, all controlled from a complex in Death Valley. Luthor then decided to take a stand against Superman and other emerging costumed heroes, feeling that elected officials failed to protect citizens from them. Effectively, he declared martial law over America, backed by his constructs. Later he avoided arrest by proving that Luthor was a construct. (*Batman Confidential* #1–6, February–July 2007)

Luthor's dislike of super heroes and their altruistic ways deepened over the next decade or so, and he targeted them time and again. Superman was always his focal point, but there were times when he also tried to take down the JUSTICE LEAGUE OF AMERICA. (*JLA* #9–12, 14, September–November 1997, January 1998)

Later, Luthor ran for president and served a single tumultuous term. From his new office, Luthor sought to destroy Superman and Batman, using the full force of the federal government. When GOTHAM CITY was a NO MAN'S LAND, Luthor began to secretly buy up abandoned properties—after seeing to it that property records were destroyed. LexCorp then stepped in as a "benevolent savior." Batman exposed the scheme and ended Luthor's involvement. As Gotham was reintegrated into America, Bruce Wayne declared his displeasure with Luthor's meddling and ended all contracts between Wayne holdings and the federal government. Seeking revenge, Luthor hired DAVID CAIN to kill VESPER FAIRCHILD and frame the billionaire. (*Batman: The Ten-Cent Adventure,* March 2002) In time, Wayne was cleared and Cain brought to justice. (*Batman* #606, October 2002)

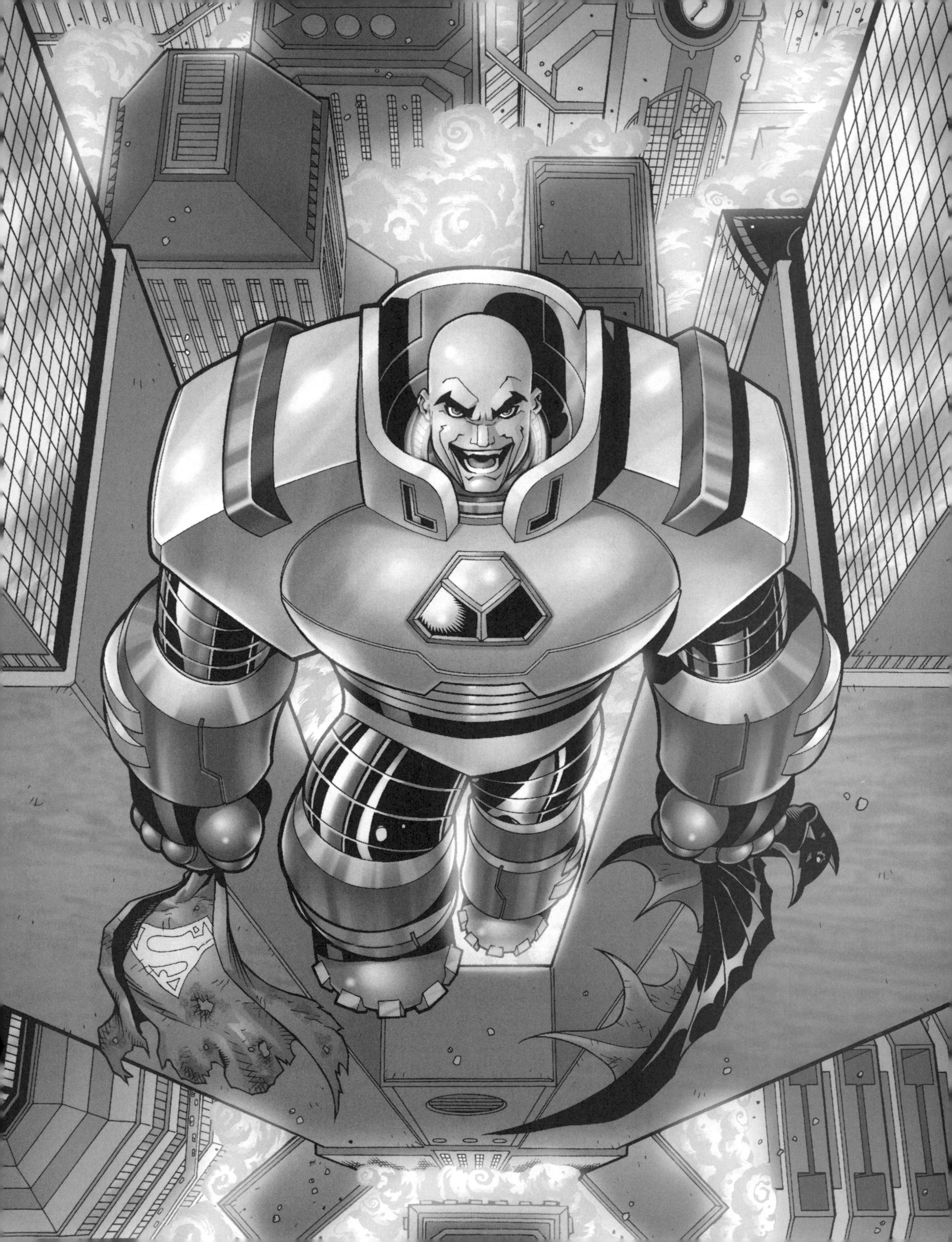

Luthor's tenure in office continued to deteriorate. At first he was lauded for his global efforts to direct a military response to an invasion of Earth by the cosmic being Imperiex. It was subsequently revealed by journalist LOIS LANE that the president had known of the forthcoming invasion and done nothing to prepare the planet. (*Superman: Our World at War*, 2001)

Undaunted, the president attempted to blame Superman for a KRYPTONITE meteor on course for Earth. The Man of Steel and Dark Knight decided to take the offensive to the White House and investigated the president's actions, including a scheme to make Batman think Metallo was the man who'd shot THOMAS and MARTHA WAYNE. Luthor then ordered other heroes to apprehend the World's Finest team. Seeing them fail, Luthor took a dose of a new VENOM compound mixed with synthetic kryptonite to take down the Man of Steel once and for all. The drug maddened Luthor, who freely spoke (while being recorded) of all his treacherous doings. These included dealings with the New God Darkseid for weapons during the Imperiex war and providing the killing machine Doomsday in exchange. This plan ultimately backfired. (*Superman/Batman* #1-6, October 2003–March 2004)

After he fled office, Luthor attempted to regain control of LexCorp, which he'd turned over to TALIA HEAD. She had already begun stripping it of key assets, including sending huge sums of cash to the WAYNE FOUNDATION. Luthor chose to go underground at much the same time that Alex Luthor emerged from limbo and formed the Society. Disliking being impersonated, Luthor sought to undermine the Society by taking those villains who refused membership and forming a Secret Six, directing them behind the persona of Mockingbird. (*Secret Six* #1-6, July 2006–January 2007) The two Luthors finally met during INFINITE CRISIS, with Lex Luthor narrowly escaping death at the hands of Superboy-Prime. (*Infinite Crisis* #3, February 2006) It was Luthor who provided Superboy (a genetic clone using Superman's and Luthor's DNA) with the location of Alex's cosmic engine, allowing the Teen of Steel and NIGHTWING to try to destroy it.

In the aftermath Luthor wound up with the Joker, leading him to Alex. He allowed the Clown Prince of Crime to murder his doppelgänger, leaving New Earth with but one Lex Luthor.

He took the news of Superboy's heroic death very hard, blaming Batman, Superman, and WONDER WOMAN for letting it happen. If anything, he was more determined than ever to rebuild to allow himself the opportunity to crush the super heroes. First he arranged matters so the world believed that Alex Luthor was responsible for many of his own crimes, letting Alex's body be found. (*52* #3, 2006) He then piqued public interest in turning ordinary people into super heroes by creating a team called Infinity, Inc. Luthor stage-managed everything from the creation of a new BLOCKBUSTER, to fighting his heroes, to using a genetic code to turn off their powers.

The courts cleared Lex Luthor of more than 120 criminal counts given the existence of his parallel world counterpart. He was ready to take control of LexCorp once more—only to discover that his

criminal rival Dr. Sivana had maneuvered matters such that Luthor lost control of the company he'd built over the last two decades. Enraged, he went underground, vowing to take his revenge against journalist Clark Kent for the articles that helped turn public attitudes against him and Superman— the alien who first stole Metropolis's love from him.

(For a detailed account of Lex Luthor, consult *The Essential Superman Encyclopedia*.)

LUVESCU, MAGDA

To apprehend the noted political prisoner JACQUES TERLAY, Batman engaged in a faux romance with the beautiful Magda Luvescu. The affair ended once Terlay was in custody. (*Batman* #87, October 1954)

LYNNS, GARFIELD

A pyrotechnics-expert-turned-criminal, Lynns was known to Batman as the FIREFLY.

LYNX

Billy Hue ran the Paris branch of the criminal organization known as the GHOST DRAGONS, and the beautiful teen known only as Lynx was his girlfriend. The Dragons answered to Sir Edmund Dorrance, KING SNAKE, and he never accepted failure. When federal agent CLYDE RAWLINS investigated illegal narcotics traced to the Dragons, Dorrance ordered Hue to kill him. Hue tried, but he failed to complete the assignment because TIM DRAKE interfered. Drake was in Paris as part of his training to become the third ROBIN. Once he became aware of the Dragons, he was captivated by Lynx's features. (*Robin* #1, January 1991)

Lynx then took control of the Parisian faction, and King Snake demanded she kill Robin for his interference. She tried but failed, and Drake refused to kill her instead. King Snake allowed her to live, but took out one eye for punishment. He then brought her with him when he relocated to GOTHAM CITY and opened a new branch of the Ghost Dragons.

During her stay in America, Lynx ran the Ghost Dragons with authority despite her youth and wanted nothing more than revenge against the Teen Wonder. Instead, each confrontation led to a draw: Neither died, nor was she ever arrested. When a gang war erupted, Lynx led the Ghost Dragons in grabbing new turf from the Russian ODESSA MOB. As she matured, she also came to recognize how much she resented the Asian-based Ghost Dragons being led by an imperialist white man. As a result, when the gang war ended, she led a revolt against King Snake.

As the undisputed leader of the Ghost Dragons, Lynx sought even more territory and wanted to expand operations from the city to the surrounding suburbs. Robin once more stood in her path, aided by SPOILER. The defeat cost her face with the Dragons, so she left their leadership, traveling as a mercenary. She returned to lead the Dragons again only when Batman personally asked her to return in order to stop the gang from trafficking in children.

She once more attempted to expand the Ghost

Dragons' influence but this time was stopped by BATGIRL. The two women battled, and it was clear that CASSANDRA CAIN was the better fighter. When one of Lynx's soldiers attempted to kill Batgirl, he inadvertently beheaded Lynx instead. (*Batgirl* #56, November 2004)

Lynx was somehow resurrected and returned to lead the Dragons until she was stopped and killed by Batgirl again during the year Batman was gone from Gotham City. Her corpse was dressed as Batgirl and her body was used to frame Robin for the murder, a ploy on Batgirl's part to enlist him as an ally. Robin, instead, cleared his name and refused Batgirl's offer. (*Robin* #148, May 2006)

LYONS, DICK

A criminal who masqueraded as the heroic CRIMSON KNIGHT as part of a scheme.

LYON, MR.

A man named Lyon decided to commit a series of crimes in the style and manner of the JOKER. He went as far as leaving behind the Joker's playing card, and for a time he succeeded in throwing off the investigating police. The Clown Prince of Crime, though, was not amused and captured Lyon. He also captured Batman and ROBIN, placing all three in the lion cage at the zoo. The Dynamic Duo managed to escape harm, turning Mr. Lyon over to a zookeeper as they tracked down the Joker. (*Batman* #19, October/November 1943)

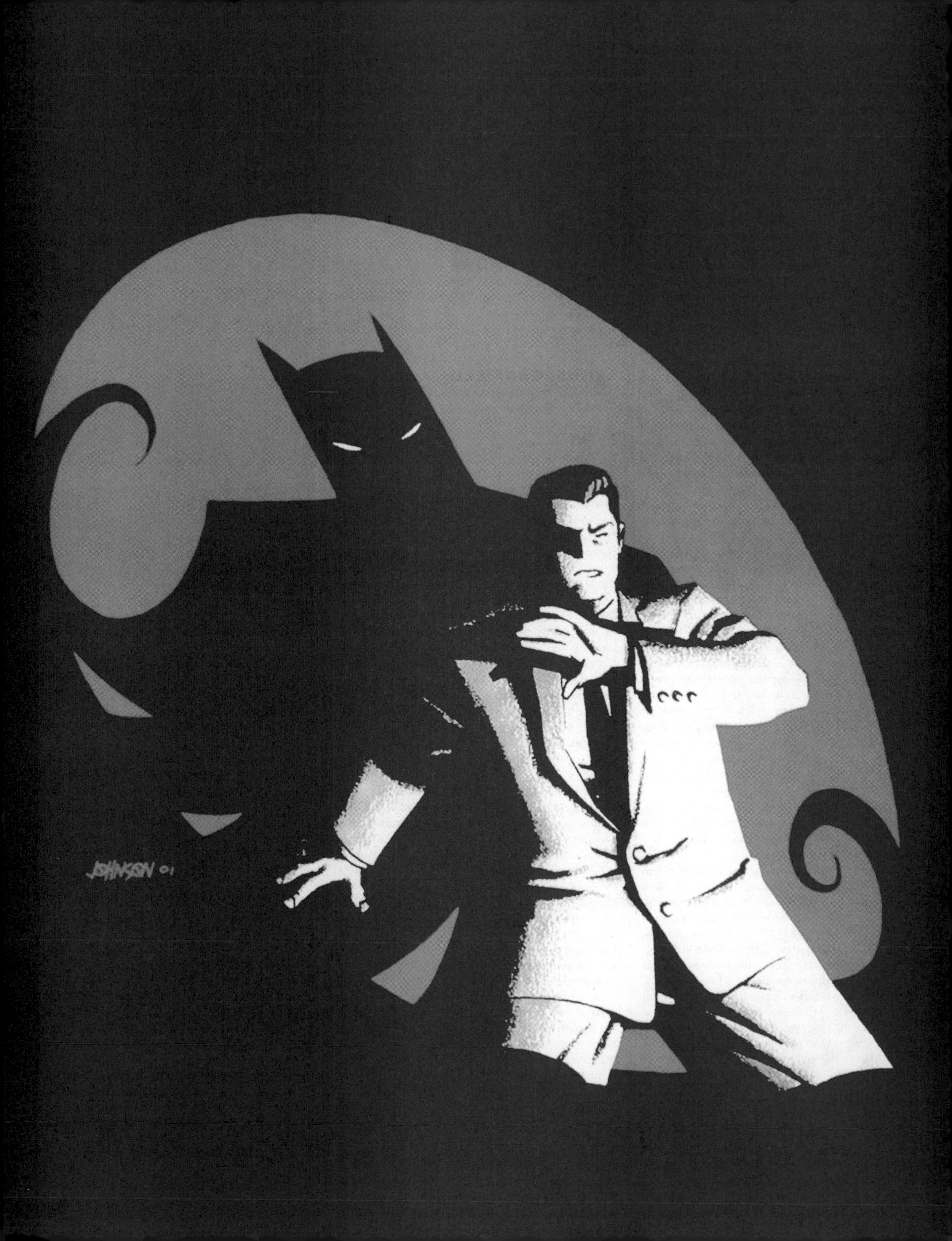
JOHNSON 01

MACDONALD, JOSIE

Josephine MacDonald was a Gotham City police officer until the fateful day she responded to a call and discovered the mayor's wife in bed with an exotic dancer. In just four days she went from her street beat to covering missing persons. While she was reluctant to admit it, the job was a perfect fit because "Josie Mac" had the low-level metahuman ability to find lost items. She described the objects as "speaking" to her—but the skills did not extend to organic matter, such as people. Her first case partnered her with Oscar Castro in a search for the missing grandson of crime boss Anthony Anotelli. The case's high profile complicated the investigation, especially when unseen attackers shot at the cops. That night Batman awaited MacDonald in her apartment, indicating that he knew of her power and was still warning her off the case, given its degree of difficulty. She persevered, and as predicted things got more difficult. Another warning came, this time with tragic consequences: She was lured to find the body of her father. (Detective Comics #763, December 2001)

Batman worked alongside MacDonald at that point, and they traced the missing child to Two-Face, who disliked having been double-crossed on a deal by Anotelli. Two-Face professed his innocence regarding MacDonald's father, and the Dark Knight believed him.

The investigation finally led to Anotelli family lawyer David Montassano, who engineered events to gain control of the mob family. He was arrested and charged with kidnapping and murder. In the wake of the case, Castro retired; in his first act as police commissioner, Michael Akins transferred MacDonald to the Major Crimes Unit. MacDonald was partnered with Marcus Driver on the unit's second shift. (Gotham Central #9, September 2003)

MACHIN, LONNIE

Lonnie Machin saw that the world was morally bankrupt and wanted to expose society's hypocrisy. He took the costumed persona of Anarky, using his genius to send a message to the world.

MADDAN, ELLIOT

A Gotham City crime boss, Elliot Maddan decided to rid the world of Batman once and for all. He faked his death at sea, letting a rumor float that he'd left behind a one-million-dollar stash of stolen property, plus clues to its location. Batman and Robin embarked on the treasure hunt to recover the property before other criminals could, but found themselves lured into a steel cage. The electrified trap seemed to kill the Dynamic Duo, letting Maddan come out from hiding to gloat. He was shocked to discover Batman still alive. The crime fighter explained that he had deduced Maddan remained alive; he sent a Batman robot in his stead, biding his time until an arrest could be made. Maddan, and the high-ranking criminals from around the country who'd come to witness the murder, were all taken in by Gotham police. (Detective Comics #313, March 1963)

MAD DOG

As a member of the League of Assassins, David Cain sought new ways to train perfect warriors. He began to develop the theory that if they bypassed learning written and spoken language, people could better read the actions of others, anticipating their moves and being able to defend themselves accordingly.

He was given a supply of infants by the league's leader, Rā's al Ghūl, to test his theories. The group of infants grew up together, learning from only Cain. The experiment proved a failure as the toddlers actually turned violent, killing one another until only one boy remained. Rā's ordered his personal guard Ubu to kill the last child, describing him as a "Mad Dog." Instead, Ubu took pity on the child and released him in the woods as Cain revised his hypothesis, choosing to concentrate on one special child rather than a group. That child was his own daughter, Cassandra, who would grow up to become Batgirl. (Batgirl #67, October 2005)

It was later revealed that Rā's elder daughter, Nyssa Raatko, knew Mad Dog had survived and eventually tracked him down after she took the league's reins. Mad Dog was welcomed as a new member and was informed of his early days as a guinea pig left to die, as well as of how Cassandra had replaced him in Cain's affections.

When Batgirl arrived at the league's headquarters, seeking out Lady Shiva, the assassins' new sensei, she got to meet her predecessor. Her arrival also precipitated a split in the league as they divided their loyalties between Batgirl and Nyssa. Mad Dog, loyal to Nyssa, went on a rampage, killing most of those loyal to Batgirl. When he and Cassandra fought, he managed to kill her and left the area. Shiva, using one of the Lazarus Pits, resuscitated Batgirl. Mad Dog remained a lost soul, with no place to call home. (Batgirl #73, April 2006)

MAD HATTER

Jervis Tetch was deeply influenced by Lewis Carroll's Alice's Adventures in Wonderland. The psychologically fragile man took to dressing like the book's Mad Hatter on Earth-2 and tried to rob

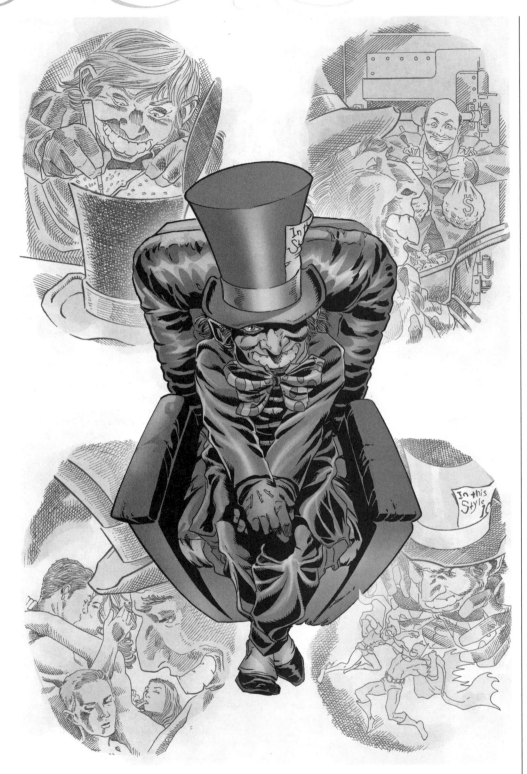

radioactive substance, forcing the Caped Crusader to remove it. That spray proved to be traceable, allowing Batman and ROBIN to ultimately apprehend the criminal. (*Detective Comics* #230, April 1956) The impostor proved to still be alive years later when he came back to plague Tetch and Batman. (*Detective Comics* #573, April 1987)

After his defeat at Batman's hands, Tetch continued to acquire and refine machinery that would give him mastery over others, a physical manifestation of his own delusional mind. Through the years, Tetch proved to have a shaky grasp on reality, constantly quoting from Carroll's works and displaying insane rages when crossed. With his equipment, Tetch had briefly controlled first the SCARECROW and then LUCIUS FOX.

In the reality after the events of CRISIS ON INFINITE EARTHS, Tetch arrived early in Batman's career—right after DICK GRAYSON debuted as Robin. His first scheme was to gain control over teenagers across GOTHAM CITY via a piece of technology he implanted in portable music devices. Tetch handed out the altered devices at Grayson's school with his ultimate goal being to sell the captured children to Generalissimo Lee, a Third World leader. Robin saw to it that the plan failed. (*Robin: Year One* #1–4, 2000–2001)

For the next decade, the Mad Hatter tried scheme after scheme, only to be defeated and imprisoned on numerous occasions. He appeared to prefer working alone, usually avoiding any gathering of Batman's major foes. With each defeat, though, he seemed to grow even more psychotic, making him even deadlier. At one point he escaped Arkham, getting shot in the process and nearly dying. (*Gotham Central* #21, September 2004)

Upon his recovery, though, he pledged his loyalty to BLACK MASK, who ruled Gotham's underworld at the time. (*Detective Comics* #800, January 2005)

After Black Mask was killed, the GREAT WHITE SHARK seized the reins of power from his cell at Arkham. Tetch transferred his loyalty and helped frame HARVEY DENT, who was protecting Gotham during the year Batman was out of the city. (*Detective Comics* #810, October 2005) Later, the Mad Hatter was invited by CATMAN to join the Secret Six, a band of villains opposed to the Society of super-villains. (*Secret Six* [second series] #1–6, July–December 2006)

MADISON INDUSTRIES

Madison Industries was the GOTHAM CITY–based manufacturing concern owned and operated by NORMAN MADISON. After his wife died, Madison raised his daughter JULIE MADISON and ran his company. While he managed to do a good job with Julie, he was unable to keep pace with a changing marketplace. The company dove deeply in the red, forcing Madison to turn to the underworld for financial support to keep investors unaware of how dire matters were. His involvement with loan sharks had disastrous results. (*Batman and the Monster Men* #1, January 2006)

MADISON, JULIE

On Earth-2, Julie Madison met BRUCE WAYNE while they were students in college. As he pursued a

a trophy from the Gotham Yacht Club. He was thwarted by Batman, with the event chronicled by photojournalist VICKI VALE. (*Batman* #49, October 1948)

On Earth-1, Tetch was an obsessive-compulsive man inspired by Carroll's works who also committed crimes dressed as the Mad Hatter. The manic criminal failed at his efforts and was remanded to ARKHAM ASYLUM. While he was incarcerated, a man posing as both Tetch and the Mad Hatter committed other crimes, but a freed Tetch later claimed to have killed his impersonator. The real Tetch acquired a monkey as a pet in addition to a machine that was said to erase memories. (*Detective Comics* #510, January 1982)

The impostor was never named and showed fewer psychological problems, although he, too, seemed obsessed with headgear and made a sport of collecting hats. His goal was Batman's cowl, something he obtained only after spraying it with a

degree in criminology, she worked at becoming an actress, dreaming of appearing on Broadway. Upon graduation, despite their love for each other, Wayne headed home to Gotham City as Madison took off for the Great White Way. The following year Madison was awoken by a phone call at 3 AM. It was Wayne, telling her he had to ask her a question and would arrive in person the following week.

The next time she saw Wayne, though, she didn't recognize him beneath Batman's cape and cowl. He discovered her in a mesmerized state, out to commit murder on the orders of a cloaked figure known as the Monk. When Madison was taken to a doctor, he prescribed an ocean cruise, so she left Wayne in America. What she didn't know was that Batman would be following her to Europe. He trailed Madison from Paris to Hungary, as she continued to obey the Monk's hypnotic commands. Batman rescued her from the Monk's clutches, killing the vampire/werewolf hybrid and bringing her safely home. (*Detective Comics* #31–32, September–October 1939)

Madison finally saw Wayne, and his question turned out to be a proposal. Now engaged, Madison returned to her acting career, which included motion picture work. She appeared opposite Basil Karlo in

Dread Castle before he went mad and became the murderous Clayface. (*Detective Comics* #40, June 1940) She continued to receive better and larger parts, so a publicity agent decided she needed a more dramatic name—and so Portia Storme was born. Clearly upset that Wayne was maintaining his playboy image, she ended their engagement. Madison did come to Batman's aid, dressing up as Robin to help him once more stop Clayface. (*Detective Comics* #49, March 1941)

On Earth-1, Julie Madison and Bruce Wayne also had a romance, but it was early in his adult life and she moved on to Hollywood without an engagement. Again, her name was changed to Portia Storme, but this time she married the king of Europe's Moldacia. She became the tiny kingdom's

ruler when he passed away. Madison, along with other European rulers, was replaced by a clone in a scheme by radicals to gain global control until the intervention of Batman and Superman. (*World's Finest Comics* #248, December 1977/January 1978)

When Princess Portia was scheduled to marry Tybern's Prince Jon, he vanished. Look-alike Bruce Wayne was asked to impersonate Jon so events could continue without creating an international incident. As Bruce went through with the ceremony, Superman sought out the real prince, rescuing him and preserving peace. (*World's Finest Comics* #253, October/November 1978)

On the Earth created by the Crisis on Infinite Earths, Julie was the daughter of industrialist Norman Madison. She was a law student when she met Bruce

Wayne and began a romance with him during his first year in Gotham City as Batman. (*Batman and the Monster Men* #1-6, January–June 2006)

Their relationship continued, although she was mystified by his casual attitude and frequent disappearances. She also began to fret about her father, whose business was in trouble—so much so he borrowed money from the mobster SAL MARONI. Madison got into deeper trouble herself when she fell victim to the Monk and his aid DALA, also called NOCTURNA.

The Monk's vampire cult was ready to accept Madison as its latest recruit, with the Monk going so far as to drink her blood. Madison was reduced to little more than a zombie after a few such visits. Madison succumbed to Nocturna and the Monk, her psyche completely in their thrall. When Nocturna tired to kill Julie, she fought back, but it took Batman to save her from a fiery death. To shock her back to reality, he revealed his true identity. In the aftermath she chose to leave Gotham to get away from the brutal reality of her lover's life and her father's self-destruction. She blamed Batman for the events that had driven her father to die at Maroni's hands. While Madison loved Bruce, she couldn't reconcile the two halves of his life, so she left for Africa, working with the Peace Corps. (*Batman and the Mad Monk* #1-6, October 2006– March 2007)

MADISON, NORMAN

Norman Madison owned and operated MADISON INDUSTRIES, a struggling industrial company in GOTHAM CITY. His daughter JULIE MADISON was a law student when BRUCE WAYNE entered their lives. (*Batman and the Monster Men* #1, January 2006)

At a charity ball, Madison encountered mobster SAL MARONI, who worked for CARMINE FALCONE, head of Gotham's underworld. His business in trouble, Madison later sought out Maroni and borrowed three million dollars at 30 percent interest. Making the payments put a terrible strain on Madison, who slowly began to psychologically fracture. When it was time to make the first payment, Madison brought a gun—but Maroni proved a faster draw. The standoff was interrupted when one of HUGO STRANGE's monsters broke in, attempting to kill the criminal. Batman intervened, telling Madison to flee and saving Maroni from the beast. He then grabbed the mobster and informed him that Madison's debt was canceled.

Unaware of Batman's good deed, an increasingly desperate Madison tried to do the honorable thing and pay off his debt to Maroni. (*Batman and the Mad Monk* #1, October 2006) Refusing to take no for an answer, Madison sought out Falcone, but this only angered the Roman, who ordered Maroni to make the problem go away. In a final act, Madison faced off with Maroni, firing a pistol and missing the man. Maroni's bodyguards, though, were more accurate, killing Madison. (*Batman and the Mad Monk* #6, March 2007)

MAD MACK

Mad Mack was a longtime prospector who discovered a vein of silver ore in a played-out Ghost Gulch City mine. To scare the citizens into

evacuating, allowing him to claim the find, Mack conspired with a traveling circus that happened to be in town. The performers agreed and used their skills and the animals to frighten the people. Their efforts were thwarted by the timely arrival of Batman and ROBIN. During a battle in the mine, one of the circus performers accidentally destroyed a support beam, causing a cave-in that killed Mad Mack and his co-conspirators. (*Detective Comics* #56, October 1941)

MAESTRO

PAYNE CARDINE was a piano virtuoso who was stung by a series of bad reviews, so took to committing crimes with musical themes to exact a twisted revenge. Clad in a maroon costume dotted with black musical notes, the Maestro committed a series of crimes in GOTHAM CITY before coming to the attention of Batman and ROBIN. The Dynamic Duo managed to apprehend the mentally unstable artist with the aid of a costumed person known as the SPARROW. (*Batman* #149, August 1962)

MAGAN, BART

A criminal who took on the persona of DOCTOR NO-FACE.

MAGICIAN, THE

Batman was confronted by a man known only as the Magician, but during their encounters it became clear that more than one person performed under that name. The team making up the persona were actually covert CIA agents basing their alter ego on a mythical Romanian figure said to have fantastic powers. Between modern-day technological weapons and psychotropic gas, they made people believe the Magician was using actual magic. Batman put the rogue black ops team out of business. (*Legends of the Dark Knight* #95-97, June–August 1997)

MAGPIE

MARGARET PYE was a teenager who fell into a life of crime, taking the costumed identity of Magpie. She committed her first robberies early in SUPERMAN's career, and it was while dealing with the Man of Steel that she first encountered the Dark Knight, Batman. (*Man of Steel* #3, November 1986)

Magpie specialized as a jewel thief, replacing the gems with bomb-laden duplicates that not only wreaked havoc but hid any incriminating evidence. After her first arrest, she reappeared in

Magpie

Gotham City—with the same results. (*Batman* #401, November 1986) She was committed for a time to Arkham Asylum and eventually escaped alongside Poison Ivy.

Years later, Magpie entered into the Penguin's employ, which proved to be a fatal error. She was killed by the Great White Shark's agent, the Tally Man, along with Orca, the Ventriloquist, and KGBeast as he sought to improve his grip on the underworld. (*Batman* #651 May 2006)

MA GUNN

Faye "Ma" Gunn ran a Gotham City orphanage, and for a time Batman and his alter ego, Bruce Wayne, brought children to her care. The local media, led by journalist Vicki Vale, positively profiled the school, giving the impression it was doing its job above and beyond expectations.

After the Joker shot and wounded Robin, Batman decided it was too dangerous for the teen Dick Grayson to don the cape again. That night, as Batman was paying his annual visit to Crime Alley to memorialize his parents' murder, he found young Jason Todd trying to steal the Batmobile's tires. He brought his latest find to Gunn's School for Boys. It was only then that Gunn's secret began to unravel. She had been caring for the children as promised, but was also training them to become thieves. Todd alerted Batman to what was really happening, and the Dark Knight swung into action.

Todd assisted Batman, who was suitably impressed by the boy's forthright manner and street-honed skills. Rather than return him to the city's iffy foster care system, he brought the boy to Wayne Manor, where he subsequently became the second Robin. (*Batman* #409, July 1987)

MAJOR CRIMES UNIT

The Gotham City Police Department created the Major Crimes Unit to handle the cases usually generated by the costumed criminals unique to the city. Since its inception, it has been led by many stalwart detectives from Harvey Bullock to Maggie Sawyer. It runs two shifts that occasionally find themselves in competition. It is this division that sees the most frequent contact with Gotham's protector, Batman. The unit's complement is divided between appreciating the Gotham Guardian's presence and loathing the Dark Knight,

since his presence has seemed to give rise to the costumed crazies who make their jobs that much harder.

MAKE-UP MAN, THE

The person known only as the Make-Up Man was a master of disguise who was never seen sans makeup to avoid being identified by witnesses. He worked with three human collaborators and three constructs he called "audio-animatrons" to rob the Gotham City Jewel Mart. Despite his mastery of impersonation, he still left clues that Batman, Robin, and private investigator Hugh Rankin followed, leading to the criminals' arrest. (*Detective Comics* #335, January 1965)

WITH A HOARSE CHUCKLE, THE MASTER OF MAKE-UP WHIRLS AND POINTS...

I AM THE MAKE-UP MAN! LAST TIME YOU SAW ME--I LOOKED LIKE THAT! I CHANGED MY DISGUISE BEFORE YOUR RETURN BECAUSE I NEVER PERMIT ANYONE TO SEE MY REAL FACE! NOT FOR TEN YEARS HAS ANYONE HAD THAT PRIVILEGE!

MAKO

Mako was a low-level criminal who worked alongside Louie and Chesty for Shark Sharkey, a notorious loan shark. When clients refused to make good on their debts, the trio were dispatched to use explosives to help them change their minds. Batman and Robin traced the bombings to the gang and brought them to justice. (*Batman* #178, February 1966)

MALAN, MAYNE

When King Eric of the tiny European country of Norania came to the United States, Mayne Malan set his sights on the Crown Jewels. The king's attempts to secure a needed loan were interrupted when word came of the impending crime. Batman and the king agreed to trade places, placing the Caped Crusader in position to thwart the robbery. Sure enough, Malan and his men attacked the king, only to be soundly beaten back by not only Batman but the king, too. After the men were apprehended, the ruse was revealed. The king proved reluctant to return the Batsuit, having grown fond of the crime-fighting life. (*Batman* #96, December 1955)

MALCHIO, PUBLIUS

When Batman and Robin visited ancient Rome, courtesy of Professor Carter Nichols's time-travel method, they encountered Publius Malchio, a racketeer. When he tried to fix a forthcoming chariot race, Malchio was foiled by the Dynamic Duo, who were aided by a man known as the Jester, an almost identical twin to their modern-day foe, the Joker. When his crimes were exposed, the emperor had Malchio banned from the city. (*Batman* #24, August/September 1944)

MALLARD, DUCKY

During Santo Pablo's tricentennial celebration, Ducky Mallard attempted to rob the city's bank, only to be stopped and arrested by Batman and Robin. (*Batman* #17, June/July 1943)

MALLITT, EVERARD

Everard Mallitt was a schizophrenic man incarcerated at the newly reopened Arkham Asylum when Batman was trapped in the facility by Dr. Jeremiah Arkham. (*Batman: Shadow of the Bat* #1, June 1992)

Batman was in the process of escaping through the ventilation system when he stopped to study the facility's security. Arkham found Batman and pitted him, gladiator-style, against most of the inmates, led by Amygdala. During the riot that followed, Mallitt was killed, a victim of being in the wrong place at the wrong time.

MALLOCK, MAYNE

A safecracker by trade, Mayne Mallock conceived of a scheme wherein he provided Gotham City with blueprints to construct a House of Batman, a museum to celebrate the Gotham Guardian's exploits. The grateful city built the tribute to Batman, who briefly used the building. During this time Mallock used hidden entrances to access the ventilation shafts so he could spy on the Caped Crusader, learning of his plans in advance. Ultimately, Batman caught on to Mallock's plan and had the man arrested. He then turned the building over to the city, which renamed it the Batman Law Enforcement Museum. (*Batman* #102, September 1956)

MALOCHIA

Malochia was a self-styled prophet of doom who was being secretly funded by Lonnie Machin, the teen better known as Anarky. Dressed in a tall hat and robes, the bearded prophet possessed an "evil eye" on his chest that emitted blinding light. He had rapidly gained a following and toured the country, appearing on television to preach his version of the End Times. What few knew was that Malochia was also running guns on the side, and when Anarky learned of this from Robin, he chose to take action. Anarky and Batman were captured and tied to a blimp that was rigged to explode, making it appear that Malochia's prophecy was coming true. Anarky awoke first and managed to steer the blimp over Gotham Harbor as Robin cut Batman free. (*Batman: Shadow of the Bat* #40-41, July–August 1995)

Malochia was apprehended and committed to Arkham Asylum. As an inmate, his body was possessed by a spirit that feasted on the psychic emanations of doomsday cults. The man recalled the child abuse he had suffered, drawing on those strong memories to reassert control and cast out the spirit. (*Batman: Shadow of the Bat* #69-70, December 1997–January 1998)

MALONE, "MATCHES"

Batman created the persona of "Matches" Malone to freely walk among Gotham City's underworld, gaining valuable information. Along the way, he saw to it that Malone had a solid, trustworthy

reputation so people would be comfortable speaking in his presence. When people saw the plaid suit, tinted sunglasses, and mustache, they knew a thumb striking a match aflame was to follow. His North Jersey accent, flat and nasal, let people think he was an out-of-towner. (*Batman* #242, June 1972)

Batman chose Malone as his alter ego during his first year in Gotham, interested in practicing his makeup skills and inspired by ALFRED PENNYWORTH's theatrical background. (*Legends of the Dark Knight* #90, January 1997) He saw to it that Malone was

memorable in both look and deed, usually being the most obnoxious man in the room. Despite criminals suspecting Malone might be a police mole or, worse, an accomplice of the Caped Crusader, Batman made efforts to have Malone and the Dark Knight seen in the same place on more than one occasion.

Malone, at different times, represented mobsters along the waterfront or ones from METROPOLIS. For a time, he allied himself with Gotham underworld boss Morgan Jones as part of a lengthy ruse to bring him down. (*Batman and the Outsiders* #10, May 1984) He even used Malone to gain access to

Louisiana's Belle Reve prison to gain information on AMANDA WALLER's Suicide Squad. (*Suicide Squad* #10, February 1988)

After Batman recovered from his injuries at the hands of BANE, Malone returned to the underworld, affiliating himself with the Whiskey Road Gang and Mickey Diamond. To recruit former criminal Eel O'Brien for a JUSTICE LEAGUE OF AMERICA mission, it was Matches Malone who visited Plastic Man in a Manhattan bar. (*JLA* #11, October 1997)

During Gotham's year as a NO MAN'S LAND, Batman heard of a man offering a way out of the city. It was Malone, though, who arrived at the Fantom Trading Company to learn more. Like most of the city's residents, time had not been kind to Malone, who had long, unkempt hair, a black trench coat, and a gun on his hip. He found himself confined to a vault with others hoping to escape who were swindled and left to die. Malone changed to Batman and freed one and all, apprehending the criminal behind the scam. (*Legends of the Dark Knight* #124, December 1999)

Malone had been built up enough that he figured prominently in one of Batman's WAR GAMES scenarios. A series of events—manipulated by Batman—would leave the underworld with a power vacuum, one that would be filled by Malone, essentially placing Batman in charge of the city's criminal element. The plan was activated by STEPHANIE BROWN, the fourth ROBIN, who had just been fired by Batman and was desperate to prove her worth. The plan began to unfold without Brown understanding a key element: Malone *was* Batman. Chaos ensued, resulting not only in Brown's death but also in BLACK MASK, not Malone, taking control of the underworld.

Batman based Malone on a real criminal, a man who for many years he believed to be dead. The burned corpse proved to be someone else, a ruse that the real Malone created to find freedom from the law. When he resurfaced, his presence complicated Batman's life. The alter ego had to be retired for a time when SCARFACE killed the real Malone, thinking him in cahoots with the Dark Knight. (*Batman* #588–590, April–June 2001)

MA MURDER

Mabel Mhurder was also known as the contract killer Ma Murder. The SENSEI, leader of the LEAGUE OF ASSASSINS, believed an author named Sergius had stumbled onto one of his plans and hired the woman to kill him. Batman intervened and protected the writer, apprehending the woman in the process. (*Detective Comics* #487, December 1979/January 1980)

MAN-BAT

Dr. Robert Kirkland Langstrom specialized in bats, studying their behavior and unique abilities. He crafted a serum that he theorized would enhance human hearing to mimic the sonar senses of a bat. Rather than use a test subject, he experimented on himself, since he was already showing signs of losing his natural hearing. Not only did his hearing improve, but Langstrom found his body morphing into a bat-shape, literally becoming a man-bat. (*Detective Comics* #400, June 1970)

With his leathery wings, oversized ears, and altered stature, Langstrom was disoriented. He attempted to steal additional chemicals he thought would help him reverse the transformation. The criminal act brought him to Batman's attention, and the two tangled until the Caped Crusader realized what had happened. Langstrom had by then shifted back to his human form, but the event left his mind somewhat rattled. He soon after transformed again, this time attempting to morph his fiancée, Francine Lee, as well, so they could sire a new species on Earth. (*Detective Comics* #402, August 1970) Batman stopped the plan and again helped restore Langstrom. Despite these events, Francine remained in love with Kirk and the two married, with his sister Britt in attendance. (*Detective Comics* #407, February 1971)

Langstrom refused to abandon his formula, con-

stantly refining it so he could retain his intelligence while assuming his new form. He continued to have adventures, occasionally working alongside Batman, and even entered briefly into a partnership with private investigator JASON BARD. Despite all that befell Kirk and FRANCINE LANGSTROM, they chose to begin a family, welcoming a daughter, Rebecca Elizabeth. Some time later, they had a son, Aaron, although by then the changes to Langstrom's DNA

affected the fetus: The baby boy was born resembling a true human/bat hybrid.

Even though the transformations occasionally left his mind altered, Langstrom seemed unwilling to abandon his alter ego. Recognizing his instability, he would occasionally seek solitude, such as the time he journeyed south to Mayan ruins. After a lengthy absence, he was sought by two scientists from Gotham, Felcher and Simmons. Felcher had hoped to help Langstrom regain his humanity, while Simmons wanted to kill the man so he could pursue his love for Francine. (*Showcase '94* #11, November 1994)

Another time saw the Langstrom family, in bat-form, taking refuge at the BRENTWOOD ACADEMY bell tower until ROBIN helped. NIGHTWING sought the restorative formula in Francine's lab but couldn't find it; they asked Bard for help. (*Robin* [second series] #75–77, April–June 2000)

Langstrom's fragile emotional state continued to be buffeted as he transformed between human and Man-Bat. For a time, he felt he was losing control to the animal side. At one point he even went berserk and thought he killed his wife and children. (*Man-Bat* [fourth series] #1–5, June–October 2006) He was wrong, but may have wished to spare Francine further suffering. She was kidnapped by TALIA HEAD and threatened with death if Langstrom did not turn over the formula to her. Talia subsequently created a man-bat army to aid her latest scheme. It failed only due to Batman's intervention. (*Batman* #655, September 2006)

In other realities, Kirk and Francine Langstrom have been seen in their bat-forms. On one world in particular, they chose to live entirely as human-bats. (*Man-Bat* [third series] #1–3, February–April 1996)

MAN-BAT COMMANDOS

More than a dozen men in man-bat form swooped down on military facilities at the behest of TALIA HEAD, daughter of RĀ'S AL GHŪL. She had created this commando team to help her obtain weapons of mass destruction from the British at Gibraltar. To create her strike force, she kidnapped FRANCINE LANGSTROM and threatened to kill her if Kirk Lang-

Man-Bat commandos

strom failed to turn over his formula for turning man to Man-Bat. While Talia obtained the formula, she did not seem to care to also have the antidote. When the attack began at Gibraltar, Batman intervened and brought Kirk Langstrom with him, creating massive amounts of the serum to save the men. (*Batman* #655, September 2006)

MANCHESTER, TOMMY "MANGLES"

Mayor ARMAND KROL was displeased with the work of Police Commissioner JAMES GORDON, not to mention his unwavering support of the vigilante Batman. Krol informed the commissioner that he was being fired, to be replaced by his estranged wife, SARAH ESSEN GORDON. James Gordon took to the streets and expressed his frustration by violently apprehending the wanted criminal Tommy "Mangles" Manchester before turning in his badge and gun, quitting the force he loved. (*Batman* #519, June 1995)

MANHUNTER

In the early days of the first heroic age, Donald "Dan" Richards was a big-city police officer. When his fellow officer and brother Jim was framed for a crime, Dan created the costumed identity of Manhunter and proved the charges wrong. He liked being able to work in and around the law and remained active as Manhunter, accompanied by his dog, Thor, throughout the 1940s. He was a member of both the All-Star Squadron and Freedom Fighters during World War II and then quietly retired. (*Police Comics* #8, August 1941)

At much the same time, big-game hunter Paul Kirk tired of his animal prey and sought greater challenges. He, too, took to the costumed persona of Manhunter. He and Richards battled side by side with the All-Star Squadron, although their approaches to crime fighting differed given their experiences. (first appearance as Kirk: *Adventure Comics* #58, January 1941; as Manhunter: #73, April 1942) While on safari toward the end of World War II, Kirk was killed by an elephant, only to find that death proved merely temporary. The secretive Council, a group of men from around the world who strove to direct the course of human events, collected his body. The revivified Kirk was granted an experimental healing ability and became their template for an army of clones. He was trained in new fighting techniques by ASANO NITOBE, who also befriended Kirk.

Manhunter eventually asserted his will, refusing an order from the Council, whose members were unused to being defied. Kirk was targeted for death by his own doppelgängers but fled. He and Nitobe, joined by Interpol's Christine St. Clair, sought to take down the Council. Eventually Manhunter enlisted Batman's aid, and they assaulted the Council's hidden headquarters in Europe. Kirk sacrificed himself, setting off a nuclear device to ensure that the Council would never rise again. (*Detective Comics* #443, October/November 1974)

St. Clair and Nitobe then dedicated themselves to killing the remaining Kirk clones. (*Manhunter: The Special Edition*, 1999) One escaped, though, taking the name *Kirk DePaul* and operating in the shadows for a time, until NIGHTWING found him.

Manhunter I: Donald "Dan" Richards

(*Power Company: Manhunter,* March 2002) Once he convinced Nightwing of his sincerity, DePaul was allowed to remain active as Manhunter and he eventually joined the corporate team the Power Company.

Public defender Mark Shaw was lured into the thrall of the interstellar androids known as the Manhunters, who had a hidden enclave on Earth dating back centuries. The androids trained him, gave him a uniform and let him return to America as a crime fighter. (first appearance of Shaw: *First*

Manhunter II: Paul Kirk

Manhunter III: Mark Shaw

Issue Special #5, August 1975; origin revealed: *Justice League of America* #140, March 1977) He got caught up in the millennia-long struggle between the android Manhunters and the Guardians of the Universe. (*Millennium* #1–8, 1988) After the war ended and Earth was saved, Shaw retained the Manhunter name but modified his costume. His adventures brought him into conflict with a shapeshifter named Dumas and also began a long period of mental instability. He was even presumed dead after joining a cadre of super heroes to take down Eclipso.

Manhunter V: Kirk DePaul

jesús y josé

MANIAXE

When Azrael served as Batman, he was searching for Abattoir, a crazed killer hunting down every member of his extended family. One of his cousins established a fifty-thousand-dollar bounty for anyone who could stop and kill Abattoir, and among those responding was the Malevolent Maniaxe, a failed punk rock band. Band members had already stopped performing and were doing jobs for the Roselli crime family, so they decided the bounty money would buy their freedom. The group—Mojo, Surly-Schmoe, and Hairy—sought Abattoir and came into conflict with other bounty hunters without success. (*Batman* #506, April 1994)

MANIKIN

When Batman rescued a woman named Miranda from a fire, she was distraught to learn that the flames had disfigured her face. The event also seemed to mentally unhinge her: She donned a suit of armor and took the name *Manikin*. She sought out beautiful people—namely, fashion designers—and began killing them. Once again, her life and Batman's intersected as they fought. He stopped her from killing the designer Hoston and then brought her to justice. (*Detective Comics* #506, September 1981)

MANIMAL

During Bruce Wayne's recovery after Bane broke his back, he pushed his physical limits, receiving retraining from Lady Shiva. She essentially framed Wayne for killing a sensei, and three of his disciples sought revenge. Manimal was the third and last of the vengeance-seeking men. Batman easily handled the man, convincing him of his successful recovery. (*Batman: Shadow of the Bat* #29, July 1994)

MANKLINS, THE

Angus Manklin was the head of a trio of brothers who were low-level operators in Gotham City's underworld. (*Batman: Vengeance of Bane Special* #1, 1993) They were not especially gifted at crime or at playing the Byzantine political game that saw criminal allegiances shift through the years. They committed robberies and kidnappings, hiring themselves out to whoever needed extra muscle. They were arrested time and again, usually committed to Blackgate Penitentiary. (*Detective Comics* #726, October 1998)

After Shaw vanished for a time, musician Chase Lawler took on the name and mission. His life was intertwined with that of the Germanic legend the Wild Huntsman, who aided him in exchange for acting as his human agent, tracking down criminals. (*Manhunter* [second series] #0, October 1994) When Lawler suffered a heart attack, it was Shaw who tried to resuscitate him. Lawler failed to revive.

Shaw's mental breakdown continued. He took on the Dumas persona and some time later killed Dan Richards and Kirk DePaul.

Years after Lawler died, Los Angeles prosecutor Kate Spencer took to becoming a vigilante when the courts failed to keep superpowered criminals off the streets. She assembled discarded equipment from previous cases, including the gauntlets worn by Azrael when he served as Batman, becoming the latest Manhunter. (*Manhunter* [third series] #1, October 2004) She tracked down and subdued criminal after criminal, including former Batman foe Copperhead. Spencer continued her career and subsequently joined the Birds of Prey.

MANNHEIM, BRUNO "UGLY"

Bruno Mannheim was raised as a criminal, son of Boss Moxie, and inherited leadership over INTERGANG, the METROPOLIS-based criminal organization. (*Superman's Pal Jimmy Olsen* #139, July 1971) Ruling Intergang and dealing with high-tech weaponry from Apokolips made him one of the most deadly mob bosses on the planet.

Mannheim gained custody of the Crime Bible, an ancient text that became his obsession. He nearly destroyed GOTHAM CITY and killed BATWOMAN before he was stopped by NIGHTWING and RENEE MONTOYA. (*52* #48, 2007) In the wake of those events, he returned to Metropolis and continued to run his operation with an iron fist.

MAN-OF-THE-BATS

Great Eagle of the Sioux Indian tribe, along with his son Little Raven, chose to protect members of their reservation by modeling themselves after GOTHAM CITY's famed protectors, Batman and ROBIN. When Man-of-the-Bats was wounded in a battle against Black Elk, he received a welcome visit from the Dynamic Duo. Dying their skin a darker shade, they disguised themselves as the Indian crime fighters, halted Black Elk's criminal efforts, and convinced the crook that Great Eagle and the feathered fighter were separate individuals. (*Batman* #86, September 1954)

In the reality after the events of INFINITE CRISIS, Great Eagle also used the name *Bill* and was a physician for his people. He joined the CLUB OF HEROES after its founding, just in time for it to fall apart through bickering. Years later he answered a summons from the club's founder, John Mayhew. There the trained doctor saved the KNIGHT's life after a bomb was stuffed down the Englishman's throat. (*Batman* #667–669, October–November 2007)

MANON'S BEAUTY SALON

When CATWOMAN was using the alias Elva Barr, she operated out of Manon's Beauty Salon in GOTHAM CITY. (*Batman* #15, February/March 1943)

MANTEE, MARTY

When Marty Mantee, Lefty Royl, and Duke Wilton learned that a criminal had turned stolen platinum into a gasoline tank and hidden it inside a car some forty years previously, they decided to track it down and recover the loot. They traced the car to the Ancient Auto Society Convention in GOTHAM CITY. Suspicious of criminals driving antique vehicles, Batman decided to follow them, after altering a BATMOBILE to resemble an antique vehicle so it could enter the convention unnoticed. BRUCE WAYNE also had a car entered, and when it was stolen by the trio, Batman followed. Their goal was discovered, and Batman had them arrested before the proper vehicle could be stolen from its unsuspecting current owners. (*Detective Comics* #219, May 1955)

MARCEAU, ALIKI

French-born Aliki and Margot Marceau became exceptional acrobats, turning to crime as the team DOUBLE DARE.

MARCEAU, MARGOT

French-born Margot and Aliki Marceau became exceptional acrobats, turning to crime as the team DOUBLE DARE.

MARCHETTI, ANTHONY

A low-level Italian mobster, Anthony "Little Italy" Marchetti tried to compensate for his short stature with bravado. He also made certain to surround himself with Mr. Zzz, a hulking somnambulist. After one such encounter, Marchetti and Mr. Zzz headed for Key West but returned when word spread that SCARFACE had resurfaced and invited thugs-for-hire to a meeting. (*Detective Comics* #824, December 2006)

MARKHAM, GUY "BIG GUY"

Guy "Big Guy" Markham was a motion picture director who decided to goad his performers into attacking Batman and ROBIN in order to obtain rare footage of the Dynamic Duo in action. Because he was shooting a film on a tropical island where the BATPLANE happened to land after a mission, Markham figured he could get away with the scheme without obtaining permission. One of the actors—his ego bruised at his director's excitement over Batman—made several failed attempts to kill the heroes during the attacks. Batman apprehended him and learned of Markham's illegal efforts. (*Batman* #10, April/May 1942)

MARKHAM, "MAD DOG"

Batman once apprehended "Mad Dog" Markham, who was subsequently deemed criminally insane and committed to ARKHAM ASYLUM. Years later, he was back on the streets of GOTHAM CITY, leading the Caped Crusader to investigate how he'd gotten free. It turned out that PROFESSOR MILO had taken control of the asylum and embarked on a freedom program for criminals—after first injecting them with a serum of his own devising. Under his spell, the insane offenders were directed to commit crimes tailored to their areas of expertise. Batman disguised himself as Shank Taylor and entered the asylum, but Milo figured out the ruse and drugged him; he tried to convince the Dark Knight that he really was an inmate who only thought he was Batman. The scheme ultimately failed, and the freed criminals, including Markham, were returned to the asylum. (*Batman* #326–327, August–September 1980)

MARKI, JAN

Jan Marki was a painter who valued his work more than critics and appraisers. He was enraged when an insurance firm refused to cover his hands for one million dollars, feeling they did not merit such coverage. Marki decided to seek vengeance against the company and members of GOTHAM CITY's INSURANCE CLUB. He lured the members into a room that was then sealed tight; he intended to release poison gas but was interrupted by the timely arrival of Batman and ROBIN. (*World's Finest Comics* #52, June/July 1951)

MARKOV, BRION

Heir to the throne of MARKOVIA, Brion Markov sought superpowers to defend the country when it was attacked. As the hero GEO-FORCE, he became a charter member of Batman's OUTSIDERS.

MARKOVIA

The small Eastern European country of Markovia neighbored France, Belgium, and Luxembourg. It had been a monarchy for over two hundred years, led by the Markov family during that time.

When the country was invaded by the Nazis during World War II, King Viktor Markov was replaced with a puppet of the Third Reich. The Allied forces restored freedom to the country, with Viktor returning to his throne. The people apprehended the puppet leader and hung him.

This leader's son grew up hating all of Markovia and became the super-villain known as Baron Bedlam. He led forces to overrun the country and killed Viktor in the process. The king's eldest son, Gregor, assumed the throne, while his brother Brion beseeched Dr. Helga Jace to give him superpowers in order to save his people. At much the same time, WAYNE FOUNDATION's executive LUCIUS FOX was kidnapped and held in Markovia, bringing Batman from GOTHAM CITY to Europe. (*The Brave and the Bold* #200, October 1983)

As Batman sought to free his friend, he met up with other adventurers, including BLACK LIGHTNING, METAMORPHO, KATANA, HALO, and BRION MARKOV, who took the name GEO-FORCE. After rescuing Fox and defeating Bedlam, Batman proposed that the heroes remain together—and the OUTSIDERS were born. Later Markovia became the source of funding after the team split from Batman and relocated to America's West Coast. When it was learned that Markovia sponsored the team, America threatened to withdraw foreign aid unless that nation revealed members' secret identities. As King Gregor considered the threat, he was murdered, leaving the throne to Brion, until he learned that Gregor's widow, Ilona, carried the true heir to the throne.

Ilona assumed the throne and ruled for a short time until she fell under the spell of the vampire Roderick. She gave birth to a son, Gregor Jr., and the Outsiders regrouped for the christening. Roderick chose that time to kill Ilona and frame Geo-Force. With the team suddenly outlaws, Roderick seized the throne for himself until he was killed in battle. Brion assumed the throne as regent, awaiting the day his nephew came of age and assumed his rightful place as ruler of the land.

MARLEY, "HATCHET"

"Hatchet" Marley was a GOTHAM CITY criminal leader who conspired with rivals to abduct Batman and ROBIN and use them as guinea pigs for a planned assault on the Gotham Mint. The mobsters captured the Dynamic Duo but—rather than kill them outright or expose their identities—the criminals forced the pair to endure one physical test after another; failure to complete any task would result in death. During the course of the physical challenges, Batman slowly deduced what the gangsters were really after. The crime fighters managed to escape and stop the criminals before they could use their lessons in real life. (*Batman* #83, April 1954)

MARLIN, HATCH

Hatch Marlin went from committing crimes to running an underground railroad for criminals. In exchange for a 50 percent cut of their loot, Marlin and his men would safely ferry the crooks out of GOTHAM CITY, away from the police and Batman, and to a foreign country. Batman and ROBIN discovered the operation and immediately put it out of business. (*Detective Comics* #154, December 1949)

MARLIN, "SHARK"

A criminal gang leader, "Shark" Marlin wanted his rival, Duke Kelmer, scared away from the object both coveted as their next target. Marlin kidnapped BRUCE WAYNE and insisted the millionaire impersonate Batman as part of the scheme. Wayne had previously appeared at a society event in the cape and cowl, something Marlin had learned, so he felt the playboy could pull off the impersonation. What he never realized was that Wayne was truly the Gotham Guardian, so he was surprised to be apprehended along with Kelmer. (*Batman* #60, August/September 1950)

MARMON, HUGO

Hugo Marmon was a longtime acrobat, his fame long gone. Seeking to recapture old glory, he donned his circus outfit and once more began to attract attention as the Bat Man. However, by wearing an outfit similar to the Caped Crusader's within GOTHAM CITY limits, he was violating a city statute. Marmon, though, argued that he had been Bat Man first and had clippings to prove it; still, he chose to be magnanimous and allow the current Batman to continue to operate.

Marmon had his head turned by the fawning John Vulney, an underworld racketeer who pretended to be a concerned citizen and suggested Bat Man join the fight against crime. So Bat Man began turning up at crime scenes, scaring off would-be burglars but unaware that Vulney's men were completing each robbery. Batman eventually intervened and arrested Vulney and his men.

The costume dispute ended with Marmon resurrecting his big-top act and Batman restored to his place as the sole crime fighter in Gotham. Later ROBIN realized that Marmon was correct—he *had* been Bat Man before BRUCE WAYNE, but it was Batman who first appeared in Gotham. (*Detective Comics* #195, May 1953)

MARONI, "BOSS"

On Earth-2, "Boss" Maroni was the man on trial for the murder of "Bookie" Benson the day HARVEY KENT's life changed. As Batman testified, Maroni interrupted, demanding proof of his involvement. Kent produced the two-headed silver dollar that was known to be Maroni's trademark. Maroni then doused Kent with acid, scarring his face and twisting his mind into the persona of TWO-FACE. (*Detective Comics* #66, August 1942)

On the Earth formed after the CRISIS ON INFINITE EARTHS, Salvatore Vincent Maroni was a member of Gotham city's Maroni crime family, then headed by Luigi "Big Lou" Maroni. The Maronis rivaled the Falcones, led by CARMINE "the Roman" FALCONE when Batman first appeared in GOTHAM CITY. "Big Lou" was

Luigi "Big Lou" Maroni

killed by the serial killer HOLIDAY, and the Falcones seemed to swallow up the Maroni crime family.

At a charity ball, industrialist NORMAN MADISON encountered Maroni. His business in trouble, Madison later sought out Maroni and borrowed three million dollars at 30 percent interest. (*Batman and the Monster Men* #1, January 2006) When it was time to make the first payment, Madison brought a gun—but Maroni proved a faster draw. The two men were interrupted when one of HUGO STRANGE's monsters broke in, attempting to kill the criminal. Batman intervened, telling Madison to flee and saving Maroni from the beast. He grabbed the mobster and informed him that Madison's debt was canceled.

Unaware of Batman's good deed, an increasingly desperate Madison tried to do the honorable thing and pay off his debt to Maroni. (*Batman and the Mad Monk* #1, October 2006) Refusing to take no for an answer, Madison sought out the Roman, but this only angered Falcone, who ordered Maroni to make the problem go away. In a final act, Madison faced off with Maroni and shot the man, missing. Maroni's bodyguards were more accurate, killing Madison. (*Batman and the Mad Monk* #6, March 2007)

Sal subsequently made a deal with district attorney Harvey Dent to gain leniency if he revealed all he knew of Falcone's criminal activities. The truth was, Sal suspected Dent of being Holiday and wanted a chance at vengeance. As the trial began, Maroni received stomach medicine from Dent's assistant, Vernon Field. The bottle actually contained acid, which Maroni flung into Dent's face in the courtroom. Sal was shot twice by a bailiff as he attempted to flee. (*Batman: The Long Halloween* #12, November 1997)

Maroni was eventually tracked and killed by

Sal "Boss" Maroni

Holiday, who was not Dent but ALBERTO FALCONE, son of the Roman.

MARS

The solar system's fourth planet, Mars was host to a visit from the Batman and ROBIN of Earth-2, who stopped the renegade Martian scientist SAX GOLA from harming Earth. (*Batman* #41, June/July 1947) Some time later, the Dynamic Duo got caught up in a conflict between lawman ROH KAR and the criminal QUORK. (*Batman* #78, August/September 1953)

On Earth-1 and the reality after the CRISIS ON INFINITE EARTHS, Mars was the home to green- and white-skinned races that were in conflict. J'onn J'onzz was accidentally transported to Earth by Dr. Saul Erdel and fought crime as the MARTIAN MANHUNTER.

MARSTEN, DR. RICHARD

Research scientist Richard Marsten developed a method to decrease or increase a person's physical appearance. His gas delivery system would, for example, permanently restore an elderly person to prime adulthood. However, whatever learning and experiences had been gained during the intervening years would be sacrificed. Scientist-turned-criminal Wilton Winders learned of Marsten's work and stole it, offering to sell treatments without informing his customers of the drawback.

Batman and ROBIN responded to the robbery and found Winders. While attempting to apprehend the crook, both were exposed to the gases, with Batman being reduced to a teenager's physique and Robin suddenly gaining adulthood. Despite the role reversal and adjusted thinking required, the Dynamic Duo managed to stop Winders's plan and bring him to justice. Marsten helped reverse the gases' effects, restoring Batman and Robin to their proper physical forms, with Batman regaining his lost memories. (*Detective Comics* #218, April 1955)

MARSTIN, JOHN

John Marstin had two careers, one as the owner of the Marstin Employment Agency and the other as the leader of a robbery ring. By day he hired out accomplices to work for GOTHAM CITY's elite, casing each location. By night his men would then rob the wealthy homes. The enterprise was put out of business by Batman and ROBIN. (*Batman* #94, September 1955)

MARTIAN MANHUNTER

In 1953 a green-skinned Martian named ROH KAR arrived on Earth-2 and was aided by Batman in apprehending the renegade SAX GOLA. (*Batman* #78, August/September 1953)

On Earth-1, Dr. Saul Erdel accidentally teleported the Martian J'onn J'onzz to Earth with his experimental communications device. J'onzz's arrival proved so shocking that Erdel suffered a fatal heart attack, trapping the alien on Earth. (*Detective Comics* #225, November 1955) He used his shape-changing and mind-reading abilities to craft a human guise, John Jones, and settled in the American Midwestern town of Middleton. He became a police detective, partnered with Diane Meade, and used his various powers to solve crimes and protect the innocent. He later went deep undercover, posing as Marco Xavier to bust VULTURE, a criminal enterprise run by a mystery man known as the Hood. It was eventually revealed that the real Xavier was in fact the Hood. (*House of Mystery* #160, July 1966) During this time J'onzz went public as a super hero and was a charter member of the JUSTICE LEAGUE OF AMERICA. He remained with the JLA through varying incarnations until that Earth was destroyed during the CRISIS ON INFINITE EARTHS.

On the re-formed Earth, J'onn's Mars was a more complex homeland called *Ma'aleca'andra*. His true Martian appearance was vastly different as well, and he assumed a green-skinned humanoid form to conform to human notions of what men from Mars might look like. He was also a charter JLA member but established a series of alter egos around the world to sample all of Earth's cultures. One of J'onn's alternate identities was that of a female Japanese journalist, Hino Rei, which Batman recognized as being named for the anime character Sailor Mars. (*JLA* #27, March 1999) He often used his telepathic skills to coordinate the JLA's efforts, usually under Batman's direction.

MASKED MYSTIC, THE

Gil Golem was the Amateur Magicians' Society treasurer until he was caught embezzling funds and fired. Vowing revenge, he targeted the individual members of the society and terrorized them until he was outwitted by Batman and Robin. (*Batman* #71 June/July 1952)

MASQUERADER

Sam Tweed was a low-level criminal who formed a gang and took the masked identity of the Masquerader. He devised a scheme to use Batman's own Batsuit against him but failed to kill the Caped Crusader. (*Detective Comics* #390, August 1969)

MASTERS, BIG JIM

Big Jim Masters was another in a long line of Gotham City gang leaders. His reign lasted long enough to complicate Batman's life. During one struggle Batman was knocked against an experimental device at the Gotham Science Laboratory. In the following days the Dark Knight's rock-steady personality changed, going to wild extremes and making him ineffective as a crime fighter. As Robin took to patrolling alone, Batman sought help from the scientist who had constructed the machine. His personality restored, Batman joined Robin in taking down Masters and his men. (*Batman* #132, June 1960)

MATATOA

The man calling himself Matatoa considered himself an immortal who fed on the souls of those he killed. When he shot the patrons of a Gotham City bar, Batman encountered him for the first time. He explained to the Dark Knight that he also absorbed the abilities of those he killed and offered to kill Batman so he could become

Matatoa

Gotham's immortal protector. Nightwing arrived to help Batman apprehend the madman, who was then taken to Arkham Asylum. The crazed figure escaped soon after, with Nightwing on his trail. There was a second battle with Matatoa seemingly drowning in the river, although no body was ever recovered. (*Batman: Gotham Knights* #16–17, June–July 2001)

MATCH, THE

The Match sold his arsonist services to corrupt building owners in Gotham City, allowing them to collect on the insurance. Their scheme was exposed and everyone brought to justice by Batman and Robin. (*Batman* #45, February/March 1948)

MATHERS, MART

Mart Mathers was a career criminal with expertise in both electronics and makeup. He proved to be the perfect man for fellow criminal John Creeden, who paid Mathers ten thousand dollars to steal information from the Batcave. Mathers used his skills to join a crew of television technicians who were brought to the Batcave for a televised special. While in Batman's sanctum, Mathers stole a small box containing a microfilm version of the Gotham Guardian's computerized files on all criminal activity. As the police worried about the information the criminals could use against them, Batman investigated and found Mathers. In the end Mathers and Creeden were arrested, and the vital information was recovered. (*Detective Comics* #229, March 1956)

MATHIS, CURT

Curt Mathis was a scientist-turned-criminal who had been imprisoned thanks to evidence recorded by a unique flying eye, a device constructed and used by Batman as part of his crime-fighting arsenal. When Mathis left prison, he accessed photos he had taken of the remarkable device and constructed his own version. The new flying eye enabled Mathis to commit a fresh wave of crimes, starting with tracing the route of a bank truck. Batman and Robin discovered the flying eye, recovered it, and disabled the photographic function. They then traced it when Mathis recalled the machine and arrested him. (*Batman* #109, August 1957)

MATTSON, "PILLS"

Mattson earned the nickname *Pills* for his hypochondria. He indulged his weakness by gaining control of a neighborhood pharmacy, which became a gang headquarters. Members of the crime ring were arrested by Batman and Robin, aided by two brave customers. (*Batman* #14, December 1942/January 1943)

MAUNCH, ALBERT

Albert Maunch, a British citizen, was the owner of a castle rumored to have been the hiding place for Nazi treasure in the waning days of World War II. His relative, Vincent, using the pseudonym *Frank Pragnel,* traveled from Gotham City to England and took his relatives hostage. He hoped to find the hidden wealth but was interrupted by the arrival of

Batman and Robin, who had traced the wanted felon from America. (*Detective Comics* #329, June 1964)

MAYA

Maya was the second person to use the name Crimesmith after the first died.

MAYNE, MOLLY

Molly Mayne was the first of several women to use the name Harlequin.

MAZE

MAZE was an international espionage agency whose full name was never revealed. Its members were information brokers, selling state and industrial secrets to the highest bidder in the underworld. They also sold their services, using their web of contacts to spread disinformation that discredited politicians. (*Batman Family* #5, May/June 1976) To support their agents and make additional cash, they trafficked in high-tech weaponry as well. (*Superman* #268, October 1973) MAZE recruited young men and women, usually seeking the best and most susceptible students at colleges around America. One such agent was David Corby, who dated Lori Elton, an ex-girlfriend of Dick Grayson. (*Batman Family* #19, August/September 1978) As a result, Robin finally got involved and helped bring the operation to an end. (*Detective Comics* #481–483, December 1978/January 1979–April/May 1979)

MCCONNELL, "KID GLOVES"

After Batman apprehended "Mad Dog" Markham—who was committed to Arkham Asylum—he learned that the Gotham City police had investigated a robbery committed by "Kid Gloves" McConnell, also an Arkham inmate. It turned out that Professor Milo had taken control of the asylum and embarked on a freedom program for criminals, after first injecting them with a serum of his own devising. Under his spell, the insane offenders were directed to commit crimes tailored to their areas of expertise. Batman disguised himself as Shank Taylor and entered the asylum, but Milo figured out his identity and drugged him, attempting to convince the Dark Knight that he really was an inmate who only thought he was Batman. The scheme ultimately failed, and the freed criminals, including McConnell, were returned to the asylum. (*Batman* #326–327, August–September 1980)

MCCOY, JIMMY "RED"

Jimmy McCoy had a hard life, growing up in the Gotham City slums, delivering bootleg liquor. He needed the money to help his mother make ends meet, but his career was interrupted by his arrest. When the youth was sentenced to a reformatory, his mother suffered a fatal heart attack in the courtroom. McCoy grew up blaming the legal system for her death and turned into a confirmed criminal. His illegal career was halted when he was arrested for income tax evasion. When he was released, he competed with Big Costello for control of Gotham's underworld. A vicious gang war broke out between the rivals until Costello shot McCoy to death, an event that allowed Batman and Robin to wade in and put the rest of the criminals out of commission. (*Batman* #4, Winter 1941)

MCGLONE, JERRY

A Hollywood stuntman, Jerry McGlone was doing a stunt as the evil Phantom Phelan when an accident robbed him of his memory. He awoke believing himself to be the Phelan and went about committing crimes until stopped by Batman and ROBIN. Soon after, his memory returned and his criminal persona faded away. (*Batman* #36, August/September 1946)

MCGONIGLE, DETECTIVE

On Earth-2 an Irish GOTHAM CITY detective named McGonigle was impressed by the work performed by the costumed vigilante named Batman. In his trademark bow tie and derby, chomping on his ever-present cigar, McGonigle was an effective police officer. However, when he was attacked by the UGLY HORDE, he was more than happy to be rescued by Batman and ROBIN. While thankful for the help, he also realized it was his duty to arrest the vigilantes—but the Dynamic Duo left before the overweight cop could make a move. He did redeem himself by being present when the Horde's creator, CARLSON, was ready to stab Batman in the back: McGonigle shot the man dead. (*Batman* #3, Fall 1940)

I'D GIVE A PRETTY PENNY TO KNOW WHO THE BATMAN REALLY IS! BUT AS SURE AS ME NAME IS MCGONIGLE...ONE OF THESE DAYS I'M GOING TO FIND OUT!

His heroic exploits earned him praise from Commissioner JAMES GORDON, who, a month later, assigned him to track down the female felon known only as the CAT. He had a second chance to apprehend Batman during the case, but the Caped Crusader prevented it. Neither vigilante nor cop managed to bring the Cat to justice, although Batman recovered her latest cache of stolen gems, which he gave to McGonigle to turn in.

McGonigle soon after took a new job, as chief, in Empire City and worked alongside cop-turned-hero Dan Richards, the first MANHUNTER. (*Police Comics* #10, October 1941)

MCLAUGHLIE, ANGUS

A castle in Scotland was known as Batmanor, given the bats that swirled around its towers after emerging from the nearby caves. During the sixteenth century a member of the McLaughlie family was entrusted to hide gold on behalf of the king, but died before telling anyone of its hiding place. As a result, family members were disgraced by rumors that they actually stole the gold from the throne. Angus McLaughlie, last of the clan, died and bequeathed Batmanor to America's famed Batman, hoping the World's Greatest Detective would find the gold and clear the family name. Arriving from GOTHAM CITY, Batman and ROBIN immediately set out to find the gold bars, which had been painted to resemble lead and were being used as counterweights in a nearby large tower clock. "Smoothy" Mathers, an American criminal, had preceded Batman to the castle and deduced the secret, intending to steal the gold for himself. Instead, the gold was recovered, Mathers arrested, and the McLaughlie reputation restored. (*Detective Comics* #198, August 1953)

MEACH, JOE

Joe Meach was a museum custodian who accidentally gained all the powers of the Legion of Super-Heroes and turned himself into the COMPOSITE SUPERMAN.

MEACHAM, ROLAND

The criminal known to law enforcement as the SMILER.

MEGAN, JIM

A criminal who plagued GOTHAM CITY police as the PHANTOM BANK BANDIT.

MEKE, HENRY

Meke suffered an accident, leaving him with the belief that he was the Norse god THOR.

MEKROS

Mekros was a former wetworks agent for an unnamed federal agency. He went rogue and, for one million dollars per hit, hired out to anyone who could meet his price. When JEAN-PAUL VALLEY assumed the BATSUIT and filled in as Batman, he interfered with Mafia operations in GOTHAM CITY. Angered, they pooled their resources and hired Mekros to come to town and kill the Dark Knight. He failed in his first attempt, attracting Batman's attention. While investigating, Batman realized that the US government had also hired a hit man to put an end to its former agent. Instead, he apprehended both hit men. (*Batman* #501, November 1993)

MENNEKIN

The man known only known as Mennekin was considered by many the world's greatest master of disguise. Seeking greater wealth than his career could bring him, he began an elaborate scheme. First he disguised himself to gain access to a prison where three men were about to be executed. He then helped the men fake their deaths and spirited them out of prison. As police sought the

condemned criminals, Mennekin made up three accomplices to resemble the felons and sent them into GOTHAM CITY to commit spectacular crimes at a bank and the diamond exchange. His next step was to bring the drugged escapees to a location where they could be shot to death by police, making them think the case was closed, allowing Mennekin to get away with the loot. The plan almost worked—until Batman and ROBIN exposed the scheme and arrested the makeup master and his men. (*World's Finest Comics* #15, Fall 1944)

MERCER, MARIAN

A criminal better known to Batman as PAGAN.

MERKO (THE GREAT)

Merko was a famous stage magician who wound up abducted to help an underworld gang boss. The boss had been manacled by a rival gang, and the bonds were said to be filled with explosives that would be set off should anyone tamper with the lock. Gang members' hope was that the great escape artist could free their boss. Batman took to impersonating Merko, performing his schedule of death-defying feats and investigating the real magician's whereabouts. He located Merko and helped free the gang leader, who then learned that the explosives threat was a hoax. (*Detective Comics* #207, May 1954)

MERLYN

The bearded assassin known only as Merlyn began his career as a performer known as Merlyn the Magician. On Earth-1 he proved to be the inspiration for Oliver Queen becoming GREEN ARROW. Later, Queen and Merlyn met in a public duel to see who the best archer was; Merlyn won. He disappeared from sight, emerging years later as a member of the LEAGUE OF ASSASSINS. (*Justice League of America* #94, November 1971)

When Merlyn was assigned by the SENSEI to kill Batman, it was Green Arrow who proved the better bowman by using an arrow to deflect the one meant for the Caped Crusader. Merlyn acknowledged he had been bested and left, going the mercenary route rather than face punishment for failing the Sensei.

In the world created after CRISIS ON INFINITE EARTHS, Merlyn remained affiliated with the league for much of his adult life, without encountering Green Arrow until much later. He left the league for unexplained reasons and went to work for Tobias Whale, leader of the 100. At some later point, he agreed to sell his soul to the demon Neron for enhanced powers. (*Underworld Unleashed* #1, November 1995)

He subsequently joined the Killer Elite, superpowered assassins including DEADSHOT, Bolt, Chiller, and Deadline, although the partnership did not prove long lasting. (*Justice League of America* #105, November 1995) Merlyn went on to live for a time in the criminal nation of Zandia, which he represented in the Olympics.

Seeking some direction to his life, Merlyn was among the earliest recruits when the Society of super-villains was formed. He felt closest to Deadshot from their experiences together but also counted old-time foe the Monocle as an ally. (*Identity Crisis* #2, September 2004)

He was hired by a faction of the league to help them obtain Sin, the young girl who had the potential to be the next great assassin but had been taken away from her training by BLACK CANARY. Merlyn's elaborate plan to abduct her failed thanks to Black Canary, Green Arrow, and Speedy. (*Black Canary* [third series] #1–4, September–October 2007)

METALHEAD

The masked figure known only as Metalhead was a brutal brawler who encountered Batman when the Dark Knight was at a low physical ebb, thanks to BANE freeing countless criminals from BLACKGATE PENITENTIARY and ARKHAM ASYLUM. Metalhead sought membership in BLACK MASK'S FALSE FACE SOCIETY and figured beating Batman would clinch his admission, only to be defeated after an extraordinary effort on Batman's part. (*Batman* #486, November 1992)

METAMORPHO

Adventurer Rex Mason lived for the thrills his globe-trotting exploits provided. He'd risk his life time and again to accomplish the impossible. This earned him a measure of fame, which he reveled in. Much of these proclivities were the result of losing both parents while still a teenager, proving how short life

NO! STAGG, WHAT HAVE YOU DONE TO ME?

"AT FIRST, HE WOULD HAVE RATHER BEEN DEAD THAN WHAT HE'D BECOME..."

could be. He also loved Sapphire Stagg, daughter of ruthless industrialist Simon Stagg. Simon disliked Mason but had his uses for him, including sending him to Egypt to obtain the fabled Orb of Ra. (*The Brave and the Bold* #57, January 1965)

When Mason found the orb, it proved to be a radioactive stone atop a staff; the alien rays knocked him out and changed his molecular structure. When Mason awoke, he was transformed into a living chemistry lab, able to use any element, or combination thereof, found in the human body. Over time his mastery over chemicals allowed him to transcend the limits of human biology. He could master any element on Earth.

He also learned later that the Orb of Ra transformed men into metamorphae as directed by the Egyptian god Ra, each serving as a warrior in his eternal battles against Apep. Ra caused a meteor to fall to Earth, where it was found by Ahk-ton, priest to Pharaoh Ramses II. Ahk-ton became the first to transform into a metamorph and fell slave to the immortal villain Vandal Savage. The orb was used for a time until it was sealed away in a tomb, awaiting rediscovery by Mason.

Stagg insisted he would do what he could to help Mason regain his normal appearance and asked Mason to perform tasks for him while he researched a cure. Stagg had little intention of curing so powerful a dupe. Additionally, if Mason regained human appearance, Stagg feared losing Sapphire to him once and for all. Reluctantly, Mason agreed, although as Metamorpho he attacked each mission with gusto. The reluctant super hero was the first to turn down the JUSTICE LEAGUE OF AMERICA when he was offered a place. He did, though, briefly team with the others, including BATGIRL, to form the Seven Soldiers of Victory to defeat the alien Agamemno. (*The Silver Age: Showcase* #1, July 2000)

Mason gave up on Stagg's empty promises and sought help from MARKOVIA'S Dr. Helga Jace. While there, he aided Batman in rescuing LUCIUS FOX and wound up becoming a charter member of the OUTSIDERS. (*The Brave and the Bold* #200, October 1983) Mason served with the team for a time, hoping both to be cured and to marry Sapphire. While still Metamorpho, he did finally become engaged to her. They married after the Outsiders saved Stagg's life and he finally gave his blessing. (*Batman and the Outsiders Annual* #2, 1985)

On numerous occasions Metamorpho had been declared dead, but his unique chemical constitution resuscitated him at least five times. After being thought dead at one point, he was revived and changed teams, working for Justice League of Europe for a time. He and Sapphire also overcame the odds and conceived a son, Joey, who was born with similar abilities as a result of the orb. He later became a pawn between Simon Stagg and Mason until Joey, on his own, found the orb. His shape-changing abilities and the orb's power seemed to cancel each other out, restoring Joey to fully human status. (*Metamorpho* #1–4, August–November 1993)

After once more returning from the dead, thanks to the JLA, Metamorpho briefly worked with one incarnation of the Doom Patrol. Later he, Sapphire, and Joey got merged into a single being; it took Oracle's Birds of Prey to restore the family to its individual components. (*Birds of Prey* #50–52, 54, February–April 2003, June 2003)

At some point during this period, a sliver of Metamorpho broke off and grew, eventually becoming a new version, but with amnesia; he eventually took the name *Shift* and worked with Nightwing when he and Arsenal re-formed the Outsiders. (*Outsiders* [third series] #1, August 2003) It wasn't until some time passed that Metamorpho confronted Shift and the doppelgängers agreed to lead separate lives. (*Outsiders* [third series] #7, February 2004) The two beings experienced entirely separate lives for a time, until tragedy convinced Shift it was time to reassimilate with his "parent" body. Respecting Shift's wishes, Metamorpho replaced him on the Outsiders' roster.

METROPOLIS

Metropolis was a gleaming East Coast city, home to Superman, and known to the world as the city of tomorrow. (*Action Comics* #16, September 1939)

On Earth-2, Metropolis's greatest newspaper was the *Daily Star*, under editor in chief George Taylor; reporters included Clark Kent and Lois Lane.

On Earth-1, the same reporters worked for editor in chief Perry White at the *Daily Planet*. Beyond that, the two cities were largely identical.

In the reality created after Crisis on Infinite Earths, Metropolis was located in New York State and boasted a population of more than eight million citizens. It was the home of the *Daily Planet* and corporate home to LexCorp. (*Countdown to Infinite Crisis*, 2005)

Metropolis was several hundred miles from Gotham City, easily reachable by a day's driving.

(For a detailed account of Metropolis, consult *The Essential Superman Encyclopedia*.)

MHURDER, MABEL

Mabel Mhurder was a contract killer known to most as Ma Murder.

MIDNIGHT, JESSICA

When Sasha Bordeaux was attacked in Blackgate Penitentiary, she was severely wounded and left for dead. She was secretly spirited out of the prison by Jessica Midnight, an agent for Checkmate. Jessica convinced Bordeaux to start her life over with a new face and identity. (*Detective Comics* #773, October 2002)

Midnight rose through the ranks at Checkmate, becoming the Black Queen's Knight, although she was unable to stop Maxwell Lord from nearly destroying the operation with his megalomaniacal schemes. In the aftermath of those struggles, Midnight remained with the reformed Checkmate, helping to restore its reputation. She and Bordeaux remained close friends.

MIKHAIL

Mikhail was employed by Doctor Death, one of Batman's earliest foes. Wearing an ever-present red fez, Mikhail did the doctor's bidding, replacing his primary aide, Jabah. When Batman tried to stop Doctor Death, Mikhail opened fire, seemingly knocking the crime fighter out a window. Peering through the broken glass, Mikhail was surprised by Batman swinging back into the room on his Batrope. The impact proved fatal to the Russian. (*Detective Comics* #30, August 1939)

MILDEN, WILLIAM

An importer and secretly an underworld fence, William Milden was enjoying a lucrative business. When "Hook" Deering began demanding a higher percentage of the take, Milden decided to do away with the criminal by planting an explosive inside Deering's artificial arm, then creating a scenario in which the explosive might take out not only Deering but Batman and Robin as well. Instead, Batman spotted the bomb and wound up apprehending both Deering and Milden. (*Detective Comics* #188, October 1952)

MILLEN, ROSS

Ross Millen was a noteworthy dog trainer who was forced by a band of mobsters to let them use his prize dog Whitey to help them commit jewel robberies. It fell to Ace the Bat-Hound, along with Batman and Robin, to rescue Whitey and apprehend the criminals, freeing Millen. (*Batman* #97, February 1956)

MILLER, "MOOSE"

Midget City was a town designed for midgets, with everything built at one-quarter scale. When full-sized "Moose" Miller arrived, he decided to use the unassuming town as a hideaway, terrorizing the citizens. Miller and his men then traveled to nearby cities, including Gotham City, to commit their crimes.

Batman and Robin trailed Miller back to Midget City, where the inhabitants aided them in apprehending the criminals. (*Batman* #41, June/July 1947)

MIME

Camilla Cameo dressed in a mime's costume and embarked on a series of crimes in Gotham City before she encountered Batman and Robin. She seemed to specialize in attacking churches, silencing their bells. She also went after other sources of sound, such as a rock concert, where she was ultimately brought to justice. Because she was never heard to speak, people assumed she was mute, but when she was apprehended that proved not to be the case. (*Batman* #412, October 1987)

MIMIC

In 1777 a mulatto named Hiram discovered a murdered boy in the whaling settlement of Blüdhaven. Accused of the murder himself, Hiram left Blüdhaven and returned to a secluded wood, where he began to build a temple of worship. Through trickery and bribery, a woman named Epsilpah Clevenger convinced Hiram to build an asylum on the ground he had cleared to build his temple. (*The Batman Chronicles* #6, Fall 1996) Official records in the Gotham Public Library debunked the story that Arkham Asylum originated in this spot. The records reported that the first asylum was actually on the land that would be known as Robinson Park, a considerable distance from Arkham.

In the twenty-first century private investigator Jason Bard solved a case wherein the suspect was performing crimes copying those of the original Mimic. She was cleared of the crimes but was dubbed the Mimic by the media. (*The Batman Chronicles* #23, Winter 2001)

MINDY

Mindy led a criminal gang that took control of an amusement park operated by Colonel John Dawes. Dawes was replaced by a doppelgänger and the criminals ran the park, skimming profits for themselves. Batman and Robin discovered the ruse and apprehended the criminals. (*Detective Comics* #51, May 1941)

MIRAGE

Mike and his girlfriend Gina Corolla performed on stage as the Mindbenders. Their hypnosis act at the Gotham Funfair was enhanced after Mike found a round jewel that he started to use as a prop, but it seemed to amplify his own thoughts and bring his illusions to life. He saw this as a ticket to fame and stardom; she saw it as a ticket to much quicker paydays. (*Detective Comics* #511, February 1982)

He liked her idea better and went to the Hollywood-based Academy of Crime (*Detective Comics* #515, June 1982) for a crash course in becoming a costumed super-villain. Mike returned dressed in shades of orange with the jewel affixed to a bracelet on his right wrist, as the criminal Mirage. To sample his newfound persona, Mike went to New Jersey's Raytona Raceway in the hope of robbing the box office. While he was there, one of those who fell prey to his illusions was photographer Vicki Vale, who imagined she was being menaced

by a polar bear. Her camera captured the real-life illusions, proving the public was not hallucinating.

Back in Gotham, Mirage went on a twenty-four-hour spree that left several people in cardiac arrest, terrified by what they'd seen. The severity of the crimes and their effects on victims caused Police Commissioner JAMES GORDON to summon the Batman for help. Batman and ROBIN sought Mirage, engaging him; during the battle the Dark Knight realized that the illusions were being caused by a combination of optical and auditory cues. High-frequency sonic waves reinforced the images being visually projected, giving them a heightened reality.

This enabled Batman to prepare special earplugs that in their next confrontation rendered the illusions less effective. Mirage was stunned, blaming the quick course for not preparing him for this eventuality. He was easily apprehended, with Batman crushing the jewel on his wrist, and was sentenced to ten years to life at BLACKGATE PENITENTIARY.

When RĀ'S AL GHŪL saw to it the criminals at Blackgate were freed, reports indicated that Mirage was among them. Apparently it was in fact a convict named Kerry Austin, who absconded with the Mirage outfit and gem. The new Mirage fled from Gotham to Chicago and began a new round of crimes, only to be defeated by the third MANHUNTER. (*Manhunter* #15, July 1989)

Mike, though, took shards from the jewel and in the prison workshop fashioned them into contact lenses. He had also looked after his physical being, pumping iron to bulk up, gain endurance, and be better prepared for his freedom. He managed to convince the guards to let him free and immediately sought out Gina, offering to commit crimes to save the beloved Funfair from going bankrupt. She reluctantly agreed—and so began a new round of robberies. Batman immediately knew it was Mirage and sought him out. The two clashed repeatedly until, finally, the Dark Knight subdued the man. The Funfair was saved when it was purchased by BRUCE WAYNE, who'd learned why Mirage had committed his crimes. (*Batman: Shadow of the Bat* #14–15, July–August 1993)

MIRAGE MAKER, THE

A criminal known only as the Mirage Maker used a machine that projected holographic images that were lifelike enough to convince people they were seeing real scenes. After specific images were shown, the Mirage Maker and his men took advantage of the chaos the scenes created to loot wrecked ships or abandoned businesses. Batman and ROBIN investigated and exposed the Mirage Maker's operation to the light of justice. (*Batman* #114, March 1958)

MIRROR-MAN, THE

FLOYD VENTRIS used a broken mirror to reflect a prison searchlight into a guard's eyes, allowing him to escape. Ventris recognized that he needed to distinguish himself to get taken seriously in a city already beset by the likes of KILLER MOTH, the PENGUIN, and the JOKER. Since a mirror had brought him freedom, Ventris took it as an omen, and—much as BRUCE WAYNE used a bat to become Batman—Ventris became Mirror-Man.

Mirror-Man was determined to be taken seriously by revealing Batman's alter ego and did everything possible to expose the Caped Crusader's biggest secret. During one crime, Ventris used a "two-way electronic mirror that x-rays anything covered by cloth" on Batman. The Gotham Guardian recognized what Ventris was attempting, so he saw to it that Bruce Wayne was interviewed by the *Gotham Gazette* to specifically discuss the times he had been mistaken for the Caped Crusader. While his gang dismissed the mirror's revelation, Ventris was convinced Wayne was indeed Batman. He orchestrated a crime during a live television broadcast, intending to use the device to expose Batman before an army of witnesses. Instead, Batman had arrived with a cowl lined with warped mirrors to distort anything revealed by Mirror-Man's weapon. The criminal was apprehended and taken to jail. (*Detective Comics* #213, November 1954)

Freed from jail, Ventris resumed his quest to prove that Batman was the wealthy millionaire playboy. When reporter VICKI VALE learned of Mirror-Man's objective, she wanted to protect Wayne, so she hired an actor to stand in for him at the same time Batman asked ALFRED PENNYWORTH to fill his shoes. The twin Waynes plus Batman confused Mirror-Man, although he used the distraction to flee. Suspecting the ruse, Ventris declared before reporters that he must be right and demanded that Wayne appear. The millionaire obliged, only to have his face clawed by the desperate criminal, seeking proof of makeup. Finding none, he was arrested and returned to prison. Wayne then thanked the

THE ONE CALLED *MIRROR-MAN* IS ESCAPING! HOLD THE FORT, ROBIN-- I'M GOING AFTER THEIR BOSS!

cape-and-cowled Alfred for once more saving the day. (*Batman* #157, August 1963)

Mirror-Man was one of the criminals identified as having been freed by Rā's al Ghūl during a massive jailbreak, but he was never re-arrested. (*Batman* #400, October 1986)

MIRTI, ANGELO

Angelo "Killer" Mirti was hired by Carmine Falcone as his daughter Sofia Gigante's personal bodyguard. (*Batman: Dark Victory* #1, December 1999) He stood by her throughout her recovery from a near-deadly fall, only to be shot and killed when the Joker invaded the family's summer home. (*Batman: Dark Victory* #8, July 2000)

MISTER ASP

The background of Benedict Asplin has yet to be recorded, but he did have a half sister, Shondra Kinsolving, and together they shared a unique psychic link. Their powers would work only when they were in proximity to each other. (*Justice League Task Force* #6, November 1993)

While they were apart, he built an international criminal enterprise, putting him on the path to becoming a formidable power player in the global underworld. To reach his goal, he sought out Shondra, who was working in Gotham City as a physical therapist with patients including Jack Drake and Bruce Wayne. He had arrived to awaken his half sister's full psionic abilities and use her in his quest for power. He kidnapped her and brought her south, where she was forced to telepathically kill the inhabitants of an island village.

Wayne outfitted himself with leg braces and a disguise, creating the persona of Sir Hemmingford Gray, and tracked the two. When Asplin realized he was being hunted, he tried to kill Wayne with psionics, but the attempt failed. Curious, he kidnapped Gray to study him, bringing the man to Santa Prisca. It was learned that because Asplin had tried to kill the Gray persona, not Wayne, the attack had failed.

Bruce Wayne managed to defeat Asplin, but the ordeal was too much for Kinsolving, whose mind shut down, reducing her personality to that of a child. (*Legends of the Dark Knight* #61, June 1994)

MISTER BAFFLES

Michael Baffle was a charming international thief who matched wits with Batman when he came to Gotham City.

MISTER BLANK

Dr. Edward Arvin masqueraded under a white hood as Mister Blank, a criminal who aspired to control Gotham City's underworld. He announced the existence of a "crime predictor"—a computer said to anticipate crimes before they were committed. Mister Blank was bluffing, using underworld gossip to provide raw data to the machine, which seemed to correctly predict forthcoming robberies. Those who refused to ally themselves with Mister Blank soon found themselves arrested as they tried to commit planned crimes. He then faked his own kidnapping and destroyed the predictor, threatening to release Arvin to build a replacement machine

unless everyone named him their leader. Batman and Robin investigated the alleged kidnapping and exposed the scheme, bringing Arvin to justice. (*Batman* #77, June/July 1953)

MISTER BRAINS

John Hart led a criminal gang that concentrated on museums, signaling to one another about forthcoming crimes through clues left in library books. Mister Brains and the gang found their efforts thwarted by Batman, Robin, and Batgirl. (*Detective Comics* #363, May 1967)

MISTER CAMERA

A criminal known for using cameras and photographic equipment to commit his robberies, Mister Camera was eventually arrested by Batman and Robin. Right before the arrest, though, one of his cameras unwittingly captured an image of Bruce Wayne and Dick Grayson changing into their crime-fighting gear. Mister Camera hid the film before it could be developed and anticipated having it developed and destroying Batman and Robin upon his release. Learning of the threat, the Dynamic Duo set out to prove they could not possibly be the wealthy millionaire and his ward. Mister Camera's plans were ended, and it was later learned that the film had been damaged; no incriminating image could be developed. (*Batman* #81, February 1954)

MISTER CIPHER

Hidden under a green hood, Mister Cipher was known among criminals for operating a "transformation mill," using plastic surgery to extensively change criminals' appearances. With a new look, criminals could continue to commit new crimes without fear of being arrested for previous misdeeds. Batman and Robin were accompanied by members of the Gotham City police when they arrived to end the enterprise. Resisting arrest, Mister Cipher was shot and killed. Unmasking him, Batman was surprised to see a shapeless face: The man had endured so many surgeries, his facial muscles essentially failed. (*Batman* #71, June/July 1952)

MISTER ESPER

The man known only as Mister Esper was a stage mentalist who doubled as a criminal. When he took his act to Gotham City, Esper used a bronze-colored megaphone to influence a person's mind by projecting a supersonic whisper—out of the range of human hearing—repeated over and over. In so doing, he manipulated Batman into avoiding the crimes he and his accomplice committed. The Caped Crusader suspected the red-haired Esper, however, so it was Bruce Wayne who turned up at the Black Cat Club to watch Mister Esper's show, convincing him that Esper was the criminal. Batman and Robin then shadowed Esper and caught him committing another crime, apprehended him, and turned Esper and his partner over to the police. (*Detective Comics* #352, June 1966)

Mister Esper was hired some time later by a West Coast crime syndicate that had designs on Gotham. Members intended to lure Batman to a series of death traps, ensuring a clear path to taking over the underworld, and they wanted Esper

to bring a compliant Caped Crusader to them. Instead Mister Esper surreptitiously implanted the scheme in the Penguin's mind, and the felon realized the costumed criminals had to defend their turf. He gathered Catwoman, the Joker, Cluemaster, Mad Hatter, Getaway Genius, and Johnny Witts and filled them in. They agreed to protect Batman, thwarting their rivals and keeping Gotham to themselves. In the end, Batman deduced it was Mister Esper who'd lured him to each death trap, but he remained unaware that his deadliest foes had repeatedly saved his life. (*Batman* #201, May 1968)

Still at large, Esper disguised himself under a black wig along with mustache and sunglasses. Calling himself Brainwash, he orchestrated a new scheme to kill Batman by first driving him to distraction with a series of hallucinations. He used miniature versions of his sonic device on Police Commissioner James Gordon's phone and inside the Batmobile to manipulate events. Compelled to return to the Batcave, the Dynamic Duo experienced disorienting images until the odd juxtaposition of an elephant and a tiger made Batman realize they were merely illusions. Once free of the sonic device's grip, Batman traced the signal back to Esper, who was in the midst of a bank robbery. (*Batman* #209, February 1969)

Years later, Mister Esper had developed much grander goals than mere wealth. Now he sought power as well. He integrated his gear into a bronze exoskeleton, including a helmet with antennae and microphone. Mister Esper then managed to tap the mental powers of the former Teen Titan known as Lilith. He projected a mental duplicate and clad it in a similar outfit—although colored orange and blue—naming it Captain Calamity.

Esper then sent his doppelgänger out to commit a series of robberies that were timed to seemingly impossible disasters. The Teen Titans swung into action and fought Captain Calamity at the site of a train wreck, while other members of the team were sent to the West Coast to deal with more disasters. With Esper on the East Coast tapping deeper into Lilith's psionic powers and Captain Calamity on the West Coast, the Titans found themselves working at full strength. Esper used this to telepathically turn Titan against Titan, and a battle broke out. It took Wonder Girl to calm things down, allowing them to trace the telepathic tap from Lilith to Esper. He then revealed his ultimate goal of shearing Long Island away from North America and declaring it his own kingdom. However, the Titans confronted Mister Esper, who conjured up a new doppelgänger, this one named Major Disaster, which fell to a single blow from Harlequin. Esper's threat was at an end, and he was not seen again. (*Teen Titans* #50–52, October–December 1977)

MISTER 50

Narkin worked as a foreman for a sugar plantation on the Hawaiian island of Oahu. He also smuggled stolen gems, hidden in sacks of raw sugar that were shipped to Gotham City on the mainland. There allies extracted the gems and sold them, splitting the proceeds. No one knew who the criminal shipper was; he was known only as Mister 50. Batman and Robin discovered the scheme and apprehended Mister 50 and his accomplices. (*Batman* #145, February 1962)

MISTER FREEZE

On Earth-1 a scientist known as Dr. Schimmell was exposed to a chemical accident during his cryogenic research, forcing him to remain in a cooled suit from head to toe. He chose to use his knowledge to fashion a freeze gun and began to commit crimes under the name *Mister Zero,* only to be apprehended by Batman and Robin. (*Batman* #121, February 1959)

Years later Mister Zero returned from prison in an upgraded suit and borrowed the name of a Blackhawk foe, becoming the new Mister Freeze. (*Detective Comics* #373, March 1968) His cryogenic freeze gun was once needed by Batman to help

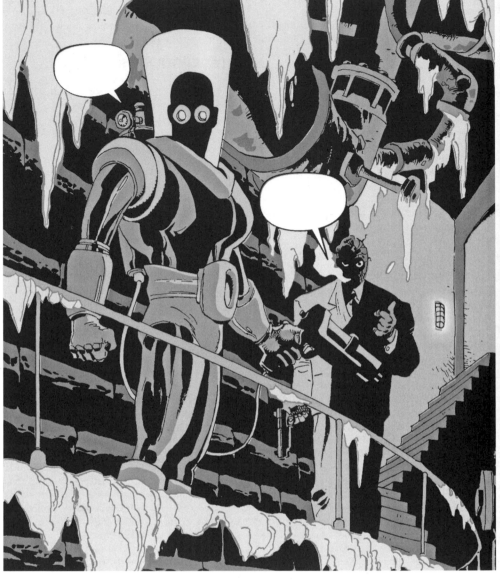

save Harriet Cooper, Dick Grayson's aunt, from a debilitating disease.

In the reality after the Crisis on Infinite Earths, he was named Victor Fries and grew up fascinated with freezing animals and studying what became of them. This hobby horrified his parents, who had him packed off to a boarding school; there he was a lonely soul. One of the students, Nora, fell in love with the gentle scientist, marrying him soon after her graduation. Their storybook marriage was short-lived; Nora Fries fell terminally ill, and despite medical science's best efforts, there was no cure. To find a way to save her, Fries began to work for a company operated by Ferris Boyle, using his cryogenics knowledge to help the company and his ill wife. Over time he used company equipment to place Nora into a form of suspended animation—until Boyle found out how much energy and money it was costing his firm. He brought Nora out of stasis, sending Fries into a rage. Boyle knocked Fries backward, crashing into a rack of chemicals; he was thought dead. Instead the chemicals interacted with his metabolism, lowering his body temperature. He was forced to construct a refrigerated outfit as a mobile environment in order to live. From there he constructed the freeze gun that became his signature, and Mister Freeze was born. (*Batman: Mister Freeze,* 1997)

Fries's first order of business was killing Boyle for endangering Nora. The two men confronted each other, and Batman arrived to protect Boyle. During his struggle with Mister Freeze, Batman avoided a blast from the gun, but the cold beam hit Nora's storage tank, destroying it. Nora's body shattered into crystalline shards, and Fries thought his wife was dead. This act sent him into a fury, hating not only Batman but all of Gotham City. He preserved the shards and escaped, hoping for a miracle.

Mister Freeze tended to work alone, usually committing crimes to acquire the means to maintain the cryo-suit that kept him alive. The suit's exoskeleton provided him with a degree of mobility but also above-average strength and protection from most harm. At one point he offered the demon Neron his soul in exchange for enhanced powers, something the demon granted—but the deal, for unexplained reasons, proved temporary. (*Underworld Unleashed* #1, November 1995)

Batman apprehended Mister Freeze numerous times, and the courts chose to remand him to ARKHAM ASYLUM, which designed a special cell to allow him to live outside his suit. (*Batman: Shadow of the Bat* #75, June 1998) He later escaped, and during the period known as NO MAN'S LAND, Freeze took possession of a portion of Gotham that included the city's main power-generating station. Batman arrived to put an end to his stranglehold on the city's electricity, but it fell to ROBIN to actually apprehend him. (*Robin* #69–70, October–November 1999)

Mister Freeze eventually escaped custody and hired out to other Gotham criminals such as BLACK MASK. He also signed up with the secret Society of super-villains in the hope that someone could help him restore his wife. NYSSA RAATKO, temporary leader of the LEAGUE OF ASSASSINS, offered him the restorative powers of a LAZARUS PIT. She also offered to place Nora's frozen form into the pit in exchange for his creating a weapon for use by the Society. Nora was placed into the alchemical substance and—given her altered condition—was brought back to life, but not as the loving Nora. She emerged as a living, humanoid molten form that could emit flames. She also seemed to absorb the very essence of the pit and was apparently able to resurrect the dead. She took the name *Lazara*, and her mental outlook was diametrically opposed to that of Nora Fries. Claiming she hated her husband for what had become of her, she tried to kill him. After failing, she fled before he could use his freeze gun to entrap her. (*Batgirl* #70, January 2006) Mister Freeze remained a tortured soul, lashing out against Gotham and its protector.

Mister Freeze was a member of the most recent incarnation of the Injustice League. (*Justice League of America Wedding Special*, 2007; *Justice League of America* [second series] #13–14, November–December 2007)

MISTER FUN

Mister Fun grew up with deep psychological issues. He was a sociopath who delighted in inflicting pain on others, and as he grew that became specialized: He came to delight in beating people to death. In other settings, the unnamed man could be seen as a philosophical optimist, masking his inner demons. As a young adult, he joined ATHENA'S NETWORK and worked alongside her during her attempts to undermine Batman. (*Batman Family* #1, December 2002) After Athena was defeated, Mister Fun was arrested. He soon found himself freed and was hired by the VENTRILOQUIST and SCARFACE to work as a bodyguard during the deadly WAR GAMES. (*Batman: The 12-Cent Adventure* #1, October 2004) Afterward, he remained at large.

MISTER MAMMOTH

A circus strongman, Mister Mammoth underwent a bizarre transformation when the circus appeared in GOTHAM CITY. He went into brief rages, his tremendous strength wreaking havoc wherever he went. Batman and ROBIN investigated and determined that something in the tones used to identify radio station WGC triggered the reaction in Mister Mammoth's psyche. The radio station agreed to alter its tones until a cure could be found—but not before Batman had to engage the stronger man in a fight to protect the city's citizens. (*Batman* #168, December 1964)

MISTER POLKA-DOT

Abner Krill, the man known as Mister Polka-Dot, had invented an ingenious technology that turned circular disks into electrically charged shape-altering tools or weapons. His colorful bodysuit was covered in detachable dots—hence his name. Once a dot was detached, a device attached to his belt charged it and sent it instructions as to what size and shape it should transform into. The dots were turned into a flying buzz saw, a flying saucer, a blinding light, sleeping gas, and other oddities. Exactly how the technology worked was never revealed.

Mister Polka-Dot began a series of crimes at the Spot Service Cleaning Company that at first baffled Batman. Over time it became a dangerous game of connect-the-dots, for the criminal was working toward an endgame: a raid on the Drummond Map Company. Along the way, Mister Polka-Dot eluded capture by the Caped Crusader and even managed to apprehend ROBIN. He forced the Boy Wonder to write a note luring Batman into a trap—without noticing the dots Robin also poked into the paper. These Braille letters alerted his partner to the trap, saving his life. The Dynamic Duo caught on to the costumed menace's pattern and finally apprehended him at the map company. (*Detective Comics* #300, February 1962)

After that first encounter, Mister Polka-Dot continued to operate in and around GOTHAM CITY, never maximizing the potential inherent in his technology. Instead he thought small and picked needless fights. He even managed to get on the wrong side of a baseball bat in a local bar. (*Batgirl: Year One* #5, June 2003) That incident may have inspired him to use a bat when his suit ceased to function during a jewelry store robbery. He was

then easily stopped by detective HARVEY BULLOCK. (*Batman: G.C.P.D.* #1, August 1996) Mister Polka-Dot was not seen again.

MISTER ROULETTE

Rigger Sims was a gambling addict, his compulsion growing so bad that he felt that challenging death itself was the only way to give life meaning. He created the black-hooded alter ego of Mister Roulette in order to kill his partner in an oil rig, Charley Denver. As Roulette, Sims outfitted a mansion with a series of bizarre death traps, letting the public know that he challenged himself daily to remain alive. Then he killed Denver, disguising him as Roulette so when the body was found, it would be concluded that the man's luck had run out. Batman investigated the death scene and concluded the truth, finding and apprehending Sims. (*Batman* #75, February/March 1953)

MISTER TERRIFIC

The first Mister Terrific was Terry Sloan, a prodigy who used his smarts and skills to fight for fair play as a costumed hero. He served with the JUSTICE SOCIETY OF AMERICA and All-Star Squadron with distinction. Mister Terrific was eventually killed by the Spirit King aboard the JLA's satellite headquarters during a meeting between the JSA and JUSTICE LEAGUE OF AMERICA. (*Sensation Comics* #1, January 1942)

Michael Holt was a similar child prodigy, with an intellect so high that he was considered the third smartest man in the world. As he grew, Holt mastered one discipline after another. He was a well-rounded man, both an intellectual genius and an Olympic athlete. (*The Spectre* [third series] #54, June 1997)

Still, with all his intelligence, he could do nothing for his older brother Jeffrey, born severely retarded, who died when Michael was just fifteen. Such tragedy would deeply affect Holt throughout his life, making him a dedicated atheist.

By the time most people his age were graduating from college, Holt had already amassed fourteen Ph.D.s and built a company called Cyberwear into a success, making him a multimillionaire. He subsequently sold the company to BRUCE WAYNE's WayneTech. Holt also found time to win a gold medal as a decathlete. He met and married a woman

Terry Sloan

Michael Holt

named Paula, who died in a tragic accident that shook Holt to the core of his being. Disconsolate, he considered suicide until an encounter with the SPECTRE showed that he could make a difference to the world. Inspired by the Wrath of God's tale about Terry Sloan, Holt chose to become the new Mister Terrific.

He used his technological skills to devise a T-shaped mask that allowed him to remain undetected by any electronic means. He also developed floating gadgets known as T-spheres that could provide surveillance or convey information. When Holt learned that Batman had stolen his T-sphere technology, he was flattered, not angry. Batman asked Mister Terrific to be part of the team to defeat BROTHER EYE, the spy satellite he constructed that had been usurped by Maxwell Lord.

Holt was once JSA chairman and served CHECKMATE as the White King's Bishop. While at Checkmate, he began a romance with Batman's former flame, SASHA BORDEAUX. (*Checkmate* [second series] #1, June 2006)

MISTER VELVET

The man known as Mister Velvet was head of a nationwide criminal operation based in a GOTHAM CITY skyscraper. His business was being hampered by a police informant among his henchmen, but his efforts to find the leak failed. Desperate to plug it, he had ROBIN the Boy Wonder kidnapped, then forced Batman to use his keen deductive skills to find the informant. Instead Batman began the investigation, learning enough to free his partner and bring Mister Velvet to justice. (*Detective Comics* #176, October 1951)

MISTER X

GOTHAM CITY's criminal underworld was surprised by the arrival of the powerfully built man called only Mister X. Behind his black mask, he brokered an alliance with CATWOMAN without realizing that she had begun to cooperate with legal authorities, putting her criminal past behind her. As a result, when Mister X was apprehended, it was discovered the physique was a shell, hiding a timid career criminal named MOUSEY. By creating his alter ego, he figured he could gain respect and wealth while avoiding suspicion. (*Batman* #62, December 1950/ January 1951)

MISTER ZERO

A scientist accidentally exposed to chemicals that lowered his body temperature to dangerous levels, this man took to wearing a refrigerated suit and began a criminal career as Mister Zero before changing his name to MISTER FREEZE.

MISTER ZSASZ

Victor Zsasz had a fairly normal life, rising to own and operate an international business. Things changed when, at age twenty-five, he lost both parents during a boating accident. Their deaths plunged him into a deep depression, which he sought to combat by engaging in risky behavior, including gambling. Zsasz traveled America, gambling wherever he could find action. When in GOTHAM CITY, Zsasz bet the remainder of his fortune, losing it all to the PENGUIN. Feeling there was no more reason to live, he chose to end his life by jumping off a bridge. Before he could take the leap, though, a homeless vagrant assaulted him. As they struggled over the knife, Zsasz had an epiphany—all life was meaningless. He killed the man, but not before thanking him for showing him how pointless life was. Zsasz then set out to liberate others from existence. (*Batman: Shadow of the Bat* #1, June 1992)

To keep track of his progress, for each victim he slit with the knife, he carved a hatchmark into his own skin until he was covered head-to-toe in such marks. Batman finally apprehended him, and Zsasz was remanded to ARKHAM ASYLUM. Zsasz was among those freed from imprisonment by BANE, and he resumed his personal quest. That led him to taking a girls college hostage until Batman arrived. The Dark Knight was insulted to hear Zsasz proclaim how similar they were. Already pushed to physical and mental exhaustion by chasing down the freed convicts, Batman reacted violently, pummeling Zsasz. The police eventually had to prevent him from beating the killer to death. (*Batman* #493, Late May 1993)

Later Zsasz managed to bribe a contractor to include a secret passage during Arkham's reconstruction. When completed, he was at liberty to come and go as he pleased, "freeing" more people and safely protected by the asylum. Ultimately, however, Batman recognized the style of killing—Zsasz liked to leave victims smiling and in natural poses—and gained access to Arkham to put an end to the criminal's latest spree.

When Zsasz was freed once more, he resumed his work, only to be stopped by the fourth ROBIN, STEPHANIE BROWN. Her ferocious battle tactics caught him by surprise, although not enough to stop him from trying—and failing—to kill Batman. (*Detective Comics* #796, September 2004)

Zsasz killed a guard when he was being taken to his quarterly psychiatric review. Escaping the asylum, the psychotic killer roamed freely, turning up at a charity event also attended by BRUCE WAYNE. There Zsasz struck once more, though this time the victim was ALFRED PENNYWORTH. Wayne saved his life by getting his old friend to a hospital in time. He then announced at a press conference that Pennyworth lived, intending to lure Zsasz back to finish his work. The ploy worked and the Dark Knight apprehended Zsasz, returning him to Arkham. (*Detective Comics* #815–816, May–June 2006)

MITCHUM, WHEELS

Wheels Mitchum was a convicted murderer who chose on the eve of his death to tell his life story to a reporter. His rough life culminated in his killing a lawyer named Kipley and being arrested by Batman and ROBIN. (*World's Finest Comics* #27, March/April 1947)

MODELL, BILL

Bill Modell was the editor of the GOTHAM CITY–based publication *PICTURE MAGAZINE*, which employed VICKI VALE as a journalist. For a brief time Modell romantically pursued Vale, giving up when she clearly preferred BRUCE WAYNE. (*Batman* #368, February 1984)

MOFFIT, FAY

The third person to don the costumed identity of the criminal SPELLBINDER.

MOLE, THE

Gotham Gazette editor John Hall learned that a figure known only as the Mole was planning a criminal enterprise in GOTHAM CITY. The stress of his normal routine got to Hall, and he was hospitalized before he could act on the tip. To help the *Gazette, Daily Planet* editor Perry White loaned out his two best reporters, CLARK KENT and LOIS LANE, to help, and they began to investigate the Mole. Kent turned to his friend BRUCE WAYNE for aid. In the Caped Crusader's files was information about the Mole's mining background and method of operation. Having heard the discussion, ROBIN began to investigate on his own, uncovering details about the Harrah Construction Company's sewer project. Further study proved that it was masking a tunneling scheme leading underneath Gotham's largest bank. SUPERMAN managed to dig a detour, sending the Mole and his men directly to prison. The Mole was subsequently revealed to be Harrah himself. (*World's Finest Comics* #80, January/February 1956)

Years later Batman again confronted the Mole, although he now looked different: a humanoid covered in fur, able to see clearly in low light. This Mole was able to burrow underground, at great speed, without need for tools. The Mole was killing people, bringing him to Batman's attention. In short order the Dark Knight discovered that the victims were all members of the prison review board that had denied Harrah parole. A check showed that Harrah had recently escaped from prison. Batman tracked him down, luring the Mole toward WAYNE MANOR. During their confrontation, Harrah revealed that he swam through toxic sewage during his escape, triggering the transformation from man to creature. Batman subdued the Mole by knocking him into a flooded cavern within the BATCAVE. The Mole seemed to die, washed away by the current, but his body was never recovered. (*Batman* #340, October 1981)

MOLNEY

The US Army developed a drug that, when ingested, provoked a murderous rage. By dropping the pills into an enemy's water supply, they could incapacitate opponents, who were distracted by trying to kill one another. A foreign spy named Molney learned of the drug, came to the United States, and stole it. Batman and ROBIN investigated and stopped the spy ring, turning Molney and his aides over to the FBI. (*Detective Comics* #330, August 1964)

MOLOCH

A famed jazz musician was murdered in New Orleans during the annual Mardi Gras celebration. Batman traveled south to investigate and discovered Rufus Macob, known to most as Moloch, a criminal gang leader. Moloch and his followers killed the man to obtain his trumpet, which concealed a map that was said to lead to a gold mine. Batman apprehended the criminals and turned them over to local authorities. (*Batman* #224, August 1970)

MONARCH OF MENACE, THE

Early in Batman's career, he confronted the Monarch of Menace, a criminal dressed in a fur-trimmed red robe with a purple mask and a gaudy crown. The outfit hid a variety of devices that enabled him to escape capture, including poison gas hidden in his cloak and an electrified scepter. The Monarch managed to commit a series of crimes and thwart Batman's efforts, escaping from GOTHAM CITY with countless stolen goods. He fenced the items and used the cash to build a lavish castle located in the tropics. There he raised his son and mocked the teenager, considering him a failure. He went so far as to make the youth wear a jester's costume as a tangible sign of his standing.

To prove his father wrong, the boy stole the Monarch outfit and headed for Gotham, where he began a new crime spree. He was, though, quickly apprehended by ROBIN. Batman made a big deal out of the arrest, luring the real Monarch out of retirement. Snapping at the bait, the Monarch of Menace returned to Gotham, where a more experienced, better-prepared Batman awaited him. He was arrested, and his son saw the Dynamic Duo as superior role models. (*Detective Comics* #350, April 1966)

While Batman was out of Gotham hunting for RĀ'S AL GHŪL, the Monarch chose to claim that he had captured the Dark Knight. He extracted tribute from the city's underworld figures in exchange for keeping Batman under lock and key. When he knew his time was up, the Monarch asked for a final round of cash. Batman, by then, had returned to Gotham and learned of the scheme. Disguised as the SPELLBINDER, he infiltrated the Monarch's headquarters and put an end to the plot. (*Batman* #336, June 1981)

MONARCH PLAYING CARD COMPANY

The Monarch Playing Card Company was the location where the RED HOOD, trying to elude capture by the Batman, leapt off a catwalk and into a waste catch basin of chemicals. As a result, he was turned into a green-haired, white-skinned horror. As the JOKER, he would confound the Dark Knight for much of his career. (*Detective Comics* #168, February 1951)

MONK, THE

On Earth-2 the Monk was a rare combination: a vampire/werewolf hybrid who disguised himself under crimson robes and hood and took to building an army of vampiric supporters, including BRUCE WAYNE's fiancée JULIE MADISON. (*Detective Comics* #31, September 1939)

After finding Madison in a trance, Wayne had her examined by her doctor, a man named Trent. He thought her problem was a result of hypnotism, but Wayne's trained eyes concluded that she—and Trent—was in the thrall of something worse. When the doctor suggested a European cruise, Madison agreed and was followed by Batman. She found her way from Paris to Hungary and the Monk's ancient castle. During their first confrontation, the Monk managed to hypnotize Batman but not long enough to impart suggestions. The two then fought to subdue each other and gain possession of Madison. The Monk was aided when a variety of obstacles got in Batman's way, from an obedient ape to the enigmatic female worshipper DALA. This raven-haired beauty tricked Batman into bringing her close to Madison, allowing Dala to abduct the woman and bring her to the Monk.

Batman traced Dala and Madison to the Monk's castle but was too late to prevent them from feasting on Madison's blood. He waited until sunlight forced them to sleep, then melted silver candlesticks into bullets and used them to end their threat. (*Detective Comics* #32, October 1939)

On Earth-1 it was DICK GRAYSON who fell under the spell of the auburn-haired student named Dala. He was instantly infatuated with the older woman—but she ignored him, leaving with another man. (*Detective Comics* #511, February 1982) Grayson copied down the license plate number and traced

the vehicle. As ROBIN, he arrived at the Victorian mansion just outside GOTHAM CITY. While he sought her, Robin fell victim to a blow to the head. When he awoke, he was trussed up, and Dala admitted that her plan to lure him to her and her brother had worked just fine. They appeared to be in servitude to a bald man with pointed ears known only as the Monk. Dala managed to bite and draw blood from Robin's throat before he could escape.

The Teen Wonder fled from the mansion and encountered Father Green, director at St. Jude's Hospital. He asked that Robin stay mum about the Monk without revealing why. Robin concurred and unsteadily returned to the BATCAVE. Dala soon after located him and they went to a dinner party together, arousing Batman's suspicions. He followed them, only to encounter the Monk, who managed to bite the Dark Knight's neck. (*Batman* #350, August 1982)

Compelled to feed on blood, Batman haunted Gotham's alleys and took advantage of a would-be jewel thief. While he was away, Father Green unexpectedly arrived at WAYNE MANOR, insisting to ALFRED PENNYWORTH that he was needed.

As Batman and Robin fought their addiction and resisted the Monk and Dala, they learned that Dala and LOUIS DUBOIS were southerners who had survived the Civil War but never changed their ways. Instead they were attacked by vengeful ex-slaves and subjected to voodoo ceremonies that turned them into the undead. (*Detective Comics* #517, August 1982) They knew they needed to escape the Monk's clutches but were uncertain how. Meantime Batman prevented Robin from attacking VICKI VALE, returning his ward to the Batcave and strapping him down for his own safety.

Alfred asked Father Green for advice. The answer was revealed as either a complete blood transfusion or a serum derived from the Monk's own blood. Batman met Father Green and enlisted his aid in confronting the demonic duo. The Dark Knight managed to overpower the Monk and Dala, allowing him to obtain the man's blood and thus save Robin. Batman allowed Father Green to take the Monk and Dala back to St. Jude's, indicating that they had waited a long time to treat them. (*Detective Comics* #518, September 1982)

In the world re-formed in the wake of INFINITE CRISIS, Niccolai Tepes was the Monk, head of a global Brotherhood. The vampire introduced himself with a card indicating that his business was "Discreet Consultations." He and Dala, also known as NOCTURNA, settled in Gotham City, purchasing the old Rallstone Castle, bought when the family sold it upon the death of J. Thomas Rallstone. From there they intended to extend their reach, beginning with Julie Madison, but were stopped by the arrival of Gotham's protector, Batman. Both the Monk and Dala were destroyed. (*Batman and the Mad Monk* #1–6, January–June 2006)

MONTANA, "MAJOR"

"Major" Montana was a legendary filmmaker, animation director, novelist, and magician. He was also considered a wealthy eccentric who used his special-effects expertise to create the Isle of a Thousand Thrills, where BATGIRL and ROBIN had one case. (*Batman Family* #3, January/February 1976)

MONTOYA, RENEE

Renee was born on September 7 to Hernando and Louisa Montoya. With her younger brother, Benny, she grew up in a poor section of GOTHAM CITY. Her parents ran a small bodega, and Renee grew up not only a devout Catholic but also street-smart as well as tough. (*Batman* #475, March 1992)

beneath the disfigured face, and he saw a kindred spirit. (*Detective Comics* #747, August 2000) He thought he was in love with Montoya and later succumbed to his dark side when she rejected him. Two-Face not only outed her lesbian secret but framed her for murder as well. When she was being transported to prison, he had the bus damaged, taking her but making others think she escaped. Batman intervened to free Montoya and apprehend Two-Face. Although she was cleared of charges, she was faced with a hostile work environment and her parents disowned her, sending Montoya down a path toward self-destruction. (*Gotham Central* #6–10, June–November 2003)

When they were pursuing Black Spider II into an empty building, her partner, Crispus Allen, saved Montoya from being shot dead. During the crime scene investigation, corrupt officer Jim Corrigan stole evidence that would prove Allen fired properly. Montoya and Corrigan clashed, with the detective vowing to expose Corrigan's illegal activities. Rather than let Montoya crack under the strain, Allen began his own investigation, which led to his being ambushed and killed by Corrigan. (*Gotham Central* #38, February 2006)

Enraged, Montoya sought to bring Corrigan to justice. She stormed into the apartment of his girlfriend, beating her and then drawing a gun on the corrupt cop. Finally broken, Corrigan begged forgiveness and promised to tell all. The following day, Montoya resigned from the force. (*Gotham Central* #40, April 2006)

She began to drink heavily and sleep around, resulting in Hernandez leaving her. Three months

She went through the Gotham City Police Academy, becoming a uniformed officer before being promoted to detective and assigned to the Major Crimes Unit. At five foot eight and 144 pounds, she was a sturdy, athletic woman who had a fiery temper. She kept her private life to herself, refusing to discuss her homosexuality or past lovers, including socialite Kate Kane. When she joined the MCU, she was in a long-term relationship with chef Daria Hernandez. Her parents refused to accept her lifestyle, and tension existed between them for years. Hernando also disapproved of her profession.

Early on, Montoya was partnered with the slovenly and rough-hewn Harvey Bullock. When Gotham was struck by a devastating earthquake, Montoya wound up spending time with Two-Face, and the two formed an odd bond. She saw the man

later Montoya began a new chapter in her life. (*52* #1, 2006) She was approached by Vic Sage, the QUESTION, who wanted to hire her for two hundred dollars per day to investigate a building. She watched for two weeks until she spotted one of WHISPER A'DAIRE's were-creatures entering the building. With the Question, she entered, only to find it being used by INTERGANG. They were also attacked by one of the creatures, which broke Montoya's arm and several ribs. Her former boss, Captain MAGGIE SAWYER, investigated and warned Montoya to be careful; the woman assured her that was the case. Montoya kept an alien weapon she found in the building, which she felt ensured her safety. Further investigation revealed that the building had belonged to the family of her former lover, Kate Kane. (*52* #11, 2006)

The Question was convinced that Intergang had designs on Gotham but needed more information as to why. Montoya chose to accompany her new mentor, leaving Kane behind to do her own investigating as the new BATWOMAN. The trail led the unlikely duo to Kahndaq in the Middle East, where they were arrested. After a week's imprisonment,

they escaped and continued their hunt. During this time, Montoya deduced that Intergang planned to set off explosives at the wedding of Kahndaq's ruler, the powerful Black Adam. To prevent the bombing, she had to kill a teenage girl. Despite her heroic act, Montoya felt destroyed and resumed drinking and casual sex, angering Black Adam, who wished to reward her deed. His bride, Isis, kept him from killing the former detective.

By this point, it was clear that Sage was dying from a fast-spreading cancer and nothing could be done to save him. Desperate, Montoya brought him to the mystical city of Nanda Parbat, where she met Richard Dragon, who had helped train Sage years before. He mentored her, helping her conquer her addiction to alcohol and relearn how to live with her actions. Between Sage's actions and Dragon's lessons, it was clear they intended her to become the new Question, something she remained ambivalent about.

In the magical city, they learned of the Crime Bible and the prophecy that endangered not only Gotham City but Kate Kane as well. Despite Sage's illness, they returned to America, where

Kane placed the dying man in hospice care and let Montoya stay with her. Though Kane asked Montoya to stay, the woman was driven to seek resolution to the quest she and Sage had begun. This meant heading back to Nanda Parbat, where Dragon continued to train her. She entered a cave for four days to spiritually cleanse herself and, upon emerging, learned that Isis had been killed. Dragon urged her back to Kahndaq, where she found a disconsolate Black Adam; he, in turn, dismissed her back to Gotham. She arrived only to find her former lover missing. Kane had been taken by Intergang, which intended to sacrifice her to turn Gotham into a hell pit. Sage succumbed to the cancer, and Montoya finally donned the featureless mask and strode out to save Kane as the Question. She and NIGHTWING arrived in time to see BRUNO MANNHEIM stab Batwoman in the chest, but they stopped him and a'Daire from completing the ceremony. Kane survived, stabbing Mannheim in retaliation, and then fell into Montoya's arms.

After Kane recovered, the two tentatively renewed their relationship in addition to striding back into the night, seeking justice and answers to the questions that drove Montoya. (*52* #48–50, 2007)

At ORACLE's request, the Question tracked down the Trickster and PIED PIPER for their role in the death of Bart Allen, the fourth FLASH. With Batwoman at her side, Montoya heard the villains' side of the story and let them free, her police experience telling her they were not the actual murderers. (*Countdown* #40, 2007)

Aristotle Roder, the man who designed the faceless mask and adhesive gas, refined the formula for Montoya. The adhesive and accompanying color-changing shampoo used Roder's own formula, in addition to adapting work done by DOCTOR NO-FACE and gingold, the same substance used by the ELONGATED MAN.

MOON

When Batman and Robin joined SUPERMAN in 1957, they apprehended ROHTUL on the moon. (*World's Finest Comics* #91, November/December 1957) Later the JUSTICE LEAGUE OF AMERICA's Watchtower was located on the moon, and Batman spent many hours within its confines.

MOONMAN, THE

On Earth-2 an astronaut named ROGERS was the first man to reach the moon in a single-man capsule. En route the capsule was bathed in the tail of a comet, which seemed to change the man's physiology. When he returned to Earth, Rogers donned a costume to become Moonman, using his newfound powers to commit a series of moon-themed crimes. With one hand he could attract objects, while the other hand emitted rays that repelled them. Rogers's mind was clouded by these changes, but when he realized what he had done, the astronaut intended to turn himself in. He was then kidnapped by harbor pirates, however, who forced him to commit crimes on their behalf. As his powers faded, Rogers managed to aid Batman, ROBIN, and SUPERMAN in arresting the pirates. The astronaut received an amnesty for his Moonman actions. (*World's Finest Comics* #98, December 1958)

MORANS, MOOSE

Moose Morans styled himself as one of America's three greatest criminals, along with Silky Steve and Sparkles Garnet. While all three were in GOTHAM CITY for an underworld crime conference, they chose to show off by committing crimes in the very home of the famed Batman and ROBIN. At that time, a bizarre accident left Batman's physiology altered so he was susceptible to KRYPTONITE; this was exacerbated when a piece of red kryptonite inflicted further changes to his body. Still, the Dynamic Duo and SUPERMAN apprehended all three criminals. (*World's Finest Comics* #128, September 1962)

MORBANIA

The small medieval European monarchy of Morbania was ruled by King Zabot. A coup by his half brother was thwarted by Batman and ROBIN. (*Batman* #87, October 1954)

MORGAN, HOOK

The criminal Morgan earned the nickname *Hook* after his right hand was amputated and replaced by a metallic hook. Morgan and his men robbed merchandise recently off-loaded at Gotham Harbor. Working with a legitimate business associate, Morgan sold off the goods, splitting the profits. Morgan and all his associates were arrested by Batman and ROBIN. (*Detective Comics* #54, August 1941)

MORTON

When GOTHAM CITY hosted a world's fair, Morton was the fair secretary. He was also a criminal who led a band of men to use the futuristic prototype hardware to commit a series of crimes around the city. Frightened citizens took the oddly dressed men and advanced technology to be invaders from the future. Investigating, Batman and ROBIN learned the truth and exposed Morton, arresting him and his men. (*Batman* #48, August/September 1948)

MORTON, MUGSY

Career criminal Mugsy Morton committed crimes as both the GREAT SWAMI and the PHANTOM BANDIT.

MOTH, THE

Wearing a moth-inspired costume complete with green wings and an antennaed mask, the Moth committed a series of crimes on Earth-2 until he was apprehended by BATWOMAN and her new partner, BAT-GIRL. (*Batman* #141, August 1961)

MOUSEY

A slightly built, short man who created the persona of MISTER X to commit crimes.

MOXON GLOBAL ENTERPRISES

When mobster LEW MOXON left GOTHAM CITY after a failed political campaign, he and his daughter MALLORY relocated in Europe. There he reestablished his criminal career, hiding his doings behind the legitimate company Moxon Global Enterprises. The company prospered quickly through the years, with Mallory groomed to succeed her father at the helm. When enough time had passed, the Moxons returned to Gotham City, seeking the acceptance that had initially been denied them. Moxon Global Enterprises opened Gotham offices. To Batman, MGE was "an incredibly well-disguised money-laundering operation, fronting as a transglobal technology firm, it's even publicly held." (*Batman* #591, July 2001)

MOXON, LEW

Lew Moxon was a GOTHAM CITY crime boss on Earth-2 who attempted to rob a costume party attended by Dr. THOMAS WAYNE. Dressed in a costume eerily similar to the Batman uniform, Wayne stopped Moxon and his men from committing the crime and later testified against them. Upon his release, Moxon hired a thug named JOE CHILL to kill Wayne.

BRUCE WAYNE was unaware of these events until he found the shredded remains of his father's costume and home-movie footage of the incident. As Batman, Wayne went to the West Coast, seeking Moxon. The Caped Crusader was disappointed that Moxon denied all knowledge of Chill, thanks to a car accident that had impaired his memory. Donning his father's costume, Wayne confronted Moxon again, this time jarring his memory. Moxon admitted to the crime and attempted to flee, running directly into traffic, where he was hit and killed by a passing automobile. (*Detective Comics* #235, September 1956)

On a parallel world prior to the CRISIS ON INFINITE EARTHS, Kal-El, the sole survivor of the planet KRYPTON, was found and raised by Thomas and MARTHA WAYNE. When Moxon ordered Chill to kill the Waynes, his bullet bounced off the child and struck Chill. As he lay dying, Chill implicated Moxon. (*Superman* #353, November 1980) Moxon was jailed, but upon his release years later he sought and killed JAMES GORDON, police commissioner and father-in-law to Bruce. Gordon's daughter Barbara donned a BATWOMAN costume to bring her father's killer to justice, only to see him killed by a speeding truck. (*Superman* #363, September 1981)

On the Earth after the Crisis, Lew Moxon was described as a prototypical old-time gangster and mob boss in the days before CARMINE "the Roman" FALCONE ruled the Gotham underworld. He owned politicians, elected officials, judges, and policemen, running his illegitimate businesses without pause. Moxon hit upon a scheme to get himself elected, cutting out the middleman, but his purported criminal connections became too publicly discussed and he lost the election. That year his young daughter MALLORY and Bruce Wayne enjoyed an innocent summer together as playmates at the Du Lac Resorts. When his nephew was shot during a bungled robbery, Moxon and his men invaded a costume party and insisted Thomas Wayne, dressed as Zorro, attend to the wound. Wayne subsequently reported the incident to the police, despite Moxon's threats of consequences unless he stayed quiet. That proved to be the final straw, so, after the humiliating defeat, the Moxons left America for Europe. There he formed MOXON GLOBAL ENTERPRISES, a legitimate front for his new criminal enterprises.

When Lew and Mallory returned to America two decades later, they were seen as legitimate successes to the general public. Batman saw right through Moxon's money-laundering operation and kept an eye on him. As a result, he was present when DEADSHOT arrived, under contract to kill the mobster. Rather than kill Moxon, the bullet was deflected somewhat as Batman fought Moxon's bodyguard PHILO ZEISS, but it still left Moxon paralyzed. He turned the company over to Mallory, who had been raised as heir apparent. (*Batman* #591–595, July–November 2001)

MOXON, MALLORY

As a child, her doting father, mobster LEW MOXON, delighted in taking Mallory away to the Du Lac Resorts each summer. At age eight, she happily played all summer with young BRUCE WAYNE, whose parents had also taken him away for a vacation. When her father lost an election and his criminal doings were exposed to the public, he fled with Mallory to Europe. The young girl grew into a woman overseas, learning everything there was to know about running MOXON GLOBAL ENTERPRISES, the legitimate company used for money-laundering that Moxon formed while away from their GOTHAM CITY home.

More than twenty years later the Moxons returned to Gotham. At a party, Mallory and Bruce were reintroduced. Soon after, Wayne was at a dinner with the Moxons when they were interrupted by the arrival of the rival Galante crime family. Wayne left but soon after returned as Batman, in time to prevent DEADSHOT from killing Mallory's father. Still, the shot left Moxon paralyzed, and he turned the company with its criminal ties over to Mallory, who had been groomed for this eventuality.

The Moxons remained in Gotham City, with Mallory running the business by day and caring for her father at night. Whereas Lew harbored a grudge against THOMAS WAYNE, Mallory continued to think fondly of Bruce. (*Batman* #591–595, July–November 2001)

MR. MXYZPTLK

In the FIFTH DIMENSION, magic—not science—was the operating force of nature. The impish inhabitants functioned as a total society, except for one who chose to visit other realities. On Earth-2 the imp was known to SUPERMAN as Mxyztplk; on Earth-1, Superman and Batman were visited by Mxyzptlk.

On the single Earth after the events of CRISIS ON INFINITE EARTHS, Mxyzptlk returned every ninety days, as his magical limitations allowed, to pester the Man of Steel. He once agreed to give the JOKER 1 percent of his power, but the Clown Prince of Crime tricked him into giving him 99 percent instead. With unlimited power, the Joker set out to reorder reality as he saw fit. He psychologically tortured his nemesis but could never bring himself to kill Batman. It fell to Superman to stop Emperor Joker. (*Superman* #160, September 2000)

(For a detailed account of Mr. Mxyzptlk, consult *The Essential Superman Encyclopedia*.)

MUDPACK

The Mudpack was a collection of beings all called CLAYFACE. It was formed by Lady Clay in the hope of killing Batman and ruling GOTHAM CITY.

MULTICREATURE, THE

The life-form dubbed the Multicreature was created when lightning struck a pool of wastewater containing chemical runoff from a GOTHAM CITY chemical factory. Rapidly the collection of chemicals gained life and grew, changing shape as it adapted to its surroundings. Anytime the creature sensed a threat, it automatically formed defenses or altered its shape to adapt. As a result, it proved quite difficult to stop the creature before citizens of Gotham were endangered. Batman finally wired a harpoon to an electric dynamo and fired. The new jolt of electricity broke the chemically based being back into its component elements. (*Detective Comics* #288, February 1961)

MURIETA, JOAQUIN

During the days of the California gold rush, Joaquin Murieta was a desperado who killed to jump the claims of other prospectors. When BRUCE WAYNE sought to discover what happened to the grandfather of a friend, he had PROFESSOR CARTER NICHOLS send him and DICK GRAYSON back to the nineteenth century. There they apprehended Murieta for the death of the missing man. (*Batman* #58, April/May 1950)

MUSKETEER, THE

The Musketeer was France's version of the Batman, dressed as the traditional representative of French law and order. He journeyed to America, along with the RANGER, LEGIONARY, EL GAUCHO, and KNIGHT and SQUIRE to meet their inspiration. (*Detective Comics* #215, January 1955)

The BATMEN OF ALL NATIONS reconvened some time later, joined by SUPERMAN, to form the CLUB OF HEROES. (*World's Finest Comics* #89, July/August 1957)

The Musketeer fought many bizarre foes, but it was during a fateful fight with the Mad Musketeer that he accidentally killed the villain. His sword tip had broken earlier, and a blow meant to paralyze the man killed him instead. The Musketeer appeared before the court, was declared mentally unfit, and was confined to an asylum. After his release, he wrote a bestselling memoir that was also optioned for a film, making him independently wealthy. (*Batman* #667–669, October–November 2007)

MYSTERY ANALYSTS OF GOTHAM CITY, THE

Crime reporter Art Saddows had used his intellect to assist Batman on several cases for some years before he helped found a club of like-minded people. Dubbed the Mystery Analysts of GOTHAM CITY, they met regularly on the last Wednesday of every month and wound up solving perplexing mysteries both personal and professional. (*Batman* #164, June 1964)

The membership included university professor RALPH VERN, mystery writer Kaye Daye, District Attorney Danton, and "armchair sleuth" Martin Tellman, along with Police Commissioner JAMES GORDON and Batman. Vern was found to have committed a jewel robbery and was likely dismissed from the club. (*Batman* #168, December 1964)

At various times others applied for membership, but they were turned down for various reasons. Private investigator Hugh Rankin tried by claiming he had deduced Batman's secret identity, only to be proven wrong. Similarly, the *Daily Planet*'s JIMMY OLSEN applied for membership but was also rejected. He even took to swapping places with ROBIN the Boy Wonder, in disguise, figuring that this would earn him a place—but he was mistaken. (*Superman's Pal Jimmy Olsen* #111, June 1968)

Kaye Daye was also noted as the aunt to athlete-turned-METROPOLIS-sports-reporter Steve Lombard.

Decades earlier, a similar group known only as the Analysts Club had existed in Gotham City, with GREEN LANTERN (Alan Scott) a proud member. (*Green Lantern* #28, October-November 1947)

MYSTERYMAN

A new costumed adventurer appeared on the streets of GOTHAM CITY known only as Mysteryman. He assisted Batman and ROBIN in breaking up a criminal operation that smuggled thieves, robbers, and felons out of the city. When the case ended, Mysteryman was revealed to be Police Commissioner JAMES GORDON himself. (*Detective Comics* #245, July 1957)

IN THIS ISSUE:
BATMAN
BLACK & WHITE

TODD
DEZAGO

MIKE
WIERINGO

KARL
STORY

BATMAN

NAIROMI

Nairomi was a small Middle Eastern country known as the single largest source of uranium in the world. As a consequence, the SHAH OF NAIROMI was highly prized among US allies. The Matinoor Diamond was considered the most noteworthy among his countless Crown Jewels. (*Batman* #79, October/November 1953)

NAIROMI, SHAH OF

The ruler of a small Middle Eastern country said to be the single largest source of uranium in the world. On a visit to America, the shah met photojournalist VICKI VALE and fell in love with her. Vicki did not return his affections, and Batman had to find a way to let the shah down easily without endangering US negotiations with his country. (*Batman* #79, October/November 1953)

NAKOR

A planet far from Earth, home to TORG, a villainous threat to humankind. (*Detective Comics* #295, September 1961)

NARCOSIS

In the aftermath of the earthquake that nearly destroyed GOTHAM CITY, Batman and his allies were pressed to their limits trying to restore order to a frightened populace. Complicating the mission was the arrival of Narcosis, a costumed man who used a gas named Bliss that, when inhaled, caused the victim to experience exactly that. Who he was, why he'd come to Gotham, and what he wanted were never revealed. He went through the city's ruins and spread his vapors to all within reach. His scheme was interrupted when Batman's fight with the MAD HATTER got in his way, resulting in his accidental death. (*Batman: Shadow of the Bat* #78, September 1998)

NASON, CHARLES "BLACKIE"

Although he'd once been captured by Batman, Charles Nason was an escaped felon, eluding police capture for two years. During that time, he had his face remade through plastic surgery and then put together a Cops' Gallery, a collection of all the significant law enforcement officers and private investigators from coast to coast. He earned a fortune charging fellow criminals a fee to access his files to vet any new member of their mobs. Eventually Batman and ROBIN tracked Nason down again; as he attempted to escape, he was killed by the wheel of an airplane. (*Detective Comics* #141, November 1948)

NEEDHAM, ERIC

A drug-addict-turned-vigilante who sought to punish drug runners and dealers as the BLACK SPIDER.

NEERY, DUDS

When Bruce Wayne rescued a girl from a fire, he suffered an injury that temporarily blinded him. Still, he went into action as Batman, attempting to use his other senses to compensate for his lack of sight, something that led the criminal Duds Neery to conclude that Wayne and Batman were one and the same. The Caped Crusader needed to apprehend Neery and convince him he was mistaken. With ROBIN's help, Neery and his men were apprehended and dissuaded from believing they knew Batman's secret. (*Batman* #42, August/September 1947)

NETWORK, THE

When CELIA KAZANTZAKIS returned to GOTHAM CITY, seeking revenge against those who had wronged her years before, she created the alter ego ATHENA and then formed a support organization called the Network. Its membership included TRACKER (her son, Nicholas Kazantzakis), DOCTOR EXCESS, BUGG, FREEWAY, TECHNICIAN, SUICIDE KING, and MISTER FUN. (*Batman Family* #1, December 2002)

Athena used the Network to track Batman and his various associates—ROBIN, NIGHTWING, BATGIRL, ORACLE, HUNTRESS, ORPHEUS, BLACK CANARY, and SPOILER—making certain none would be in the way. When she deemed the time right, Athena ordered the city's power cut off, hoping to use the confusion to siphon off bank funds and bankrupt WAYNE ENTERPRISES. This way, Athena would exact revenge against the memory of her former friend MARTHA WAYNE and settle old scores with the Rossetti crime family. Instead, one by one, the Network agents fell to Batman's more dedicated, better-trained operatives. In the end Batman confronted Kazantzakis, only to see her apparently killed in an explosion. The Network was crippled by this defeat and never re-formed.

NEVAL, ODO

Odo Neval pretended to be a scientist from the legendary sunken city of ATLANTIS who had lived for centuries thanks to his "elixir of immortality." Aided by his accomplice Marden, he convinced the gullible that the elixir not only granted him prolonged life but also made him impervious to harm. He then tried to extract one hundred thousand dollars each from GOTHAM CITY's gang warlords to sample the potion. Batman and Robin heard of the scheme and determined the elixir to be a fake. The Dynamic Duo managed to capture Neval, Marden, and the duped gang leaders. (*Detective Comics* #204, February 1954)

NEVER, E. G.

The criminal who was known to his peers as the PLANNER.

NEW CARTHAGE

New Carthage was a small town 175 miles north of GOTHAM CITY and 400 miles north of Washington, D.C., where HUDSON UNIVERSITY was located. When DICK GRAYSON graduated from high school, he moved to the small college town for his one semester at the school. (*Batman* #217, December 1969)

Located just off Exit 43A, New Carthage was in the northern half of Hudson County, whose southern edge included the small farming community of Hortonville. The college boasted a student body numbering twenty-seven thousand and was built in 1895. (*Detective Comics* #394, December 1969) Despite the school's long standing in the town, tension remains between the locals—with their struggling, inadequate public school system—and the wealthier student body. (*Batman* #248, April 1973)

The university recognized this and established Project 70, a student community-action organization that worked with the nearby Empire State Juvenile Detention Farm to help tutor juvenile delinquents. (*Detective Comics* #402–403, August–September 1970) Dick Grayson was personally responsible for developing a recreation program for underprivileged children in New Carthage. (*Batman* #245, October 1972) All those efforts were dutifully recounted in the *New Carthage Tribune* and the *New Carthage Chronicle*.

NEWTOWN

Newtown was considered a rising young community near GOTHAM CITY. It was also where the HALY BROS. CIRCUS settled when JOHN and MARY GRAYSON fell to their tragic deaths. (*Batman* #213, July/August 1969) Newtown was occupied by the VENTRILOQUIST during the early days of the yearlong period known as No MAN'S LAND. (*Batman: No Man's Land* #1, March 1999)

NICHOLS, PROFESSOR CARTER

Professor Carter Nichols was a scientist who befriended BRUCE WAYNE and DICK GRAYSON on

THE FRIEND–PROF. CARTER NICHOLS–IS A NOTED STUDENT OF THE MYSTERIES OF THE SUBCONSCIOUS MIND...

SO YOU'D LIKE ME TO SEND YOU BACK TO 13TH-CENTURY ENGLAND? ALL RIGHT– GET READY...

Earth-2. He had developed a way to use hypnosis to somehow psychically tap into the timestream and could send the pair to specific locations and periods throughout the past. (*Batman* #24, August/September 1944)

Curious about specific mysteries, Wayne had Nichols send them to study events, and often Wayne and Grayson interacted, as Batman and ROBIN, with people in those eras, risking tampering with the time line and future events. On occasion Nichols asked them to research historical events to satisfy his own curiosity.

At some point he met them as Batman and Robin and began sending the Dynamic Duo through time as well. (*Batman* #98, March 1956) Once, he accidentally sent the heroes to the future. (*Batman* #59, June/July 1950) As he refined his methods, Nichols found that he could access the past on other worlds, and on more than one occasion he sent SUPERMAN, Batman, and Robin back in time to visit KRYPTON before it exploded.

Some time after this, Nichols switched from hypnosis to a different method using a machine that projected a "time ray." (*Batman* #112, December 1957)

Before he died, Bruce Wayne, under the influence of the Psycho-Pirate, crafted a fictitious diary accusing his fellow JUSTICE SOCIETY OF AMERICA colleagues of treason during World War II. As Batman, he then gave the book to Nichols with instructions to pass it along to CLARK KENT in the event of his death. When that occurred, it brought the stalwart heroes to trial, prosecuted by Dick Grayson. (*America vs. the JSA* #1, January 1985)

Nichols also existed on Earth-1, although his dealings with Batman and Robin were fewer and farther between. (*The Brave and the Bold* #171, February 1981)

In the world created after the CRISIS ON INFINITE EARTHS, no record of Nichols has been left.

NIGHTBIRD

NIGHTWING at one time drove a vehicle he dubbed the Nightbird. It looked like most modern-day sports cars but was fashioned from a series of carbon-fiber-over-aluminum endoskeleton body shells and boasted a Wayne Tech-modified 6,064cc engine (627 BHP at seventy-four hundred rpm). This allowed Nightwing to patrol BLÜDHAVEN without rousing suspicions.

NIGHT-DRAGON

Gangster BENNY LO lost his partner to a criminal enterprise that shot snuff films—illegal movies in which people died on camera—and hoped one day to exact revenge. That opportunity did not come until the arrival of Batman in Hong Kong.

The Dark Knight was following clues to Tiger One-Eye, the criminal leader of a Triad gang, after a hacker found a similar snuff film on the Internet. The hacker reported the crime to GOTHAM CITY police, and Commissioner JAMES GORDON brought Batman into the investigation. Batman interrogated members of the Triad, but learned nothing useful. He subsequently encountered Lo, who saw this as a sign. Soon after, he donned battle armor and allied himself with the Dark Knight as the Night-Dragon.

Together they pursued their thin leads until Lo learned that he was caught between two uncles, one a cop, the other a brutal killer. When Night-Dragon tracked the killer, about to strike again, he used his golden nunchaku and ceremonial blade to stop the man. Lo was shocked to learn that the killer was his own father, now horribly disfigured. The truth came out: Lo's mother had tried to kill her abusive husband by setting a fire; he was badly burned but escaped, leaving his family to think him dead. With Hong Kong police chief Chow Yee's help, the man was taken into custody and order restored to the city. (*Batman: Hong Kong*, 2003)

NIGHT-SCOURGE

Sergeant MAXWELL CORT was less than pleased to see costumed vigilantes once more on the streets of GOTHAM CITY. He also disliked how cozy newly appointed Captain JAMES GORDON appeared to be with Batman, whom Cort considered a lawless individual. Seeking counsel, he visited a noted psychiatrist, HUGO STRANGE, who seized the opportunity to experiment. He hypnotized Cort into believing he was superior to the Dark Knight and provided Cort with his own costume. Cort donned it, naming himself the Night-Scourge and using far more violent methods to deal with crime on his streets. He went so far as to try to kill CATWOMAN, seeing her as just another costumed vigilante, but failed. He was subsequently shot and killed by members of his own police precinct. (*Legends of the Dark Knight* #11, October 1990)

NIGHTSHADE

Owner of Nightmares, Inc., Sturges Hellstrom planned and executed "scare-for-hire" parties for the wealthy citizens of GOTHAM CITY. Hellstrom was also a talented burglar who, soon after a house hosted a party, robbed it. He formed a brief alliance with Natasha Knight, the criminal known as NOCTURNA, to replace her recently imprisoned adoptive brother Anton, the NIGHT-SLAYER. Based on home blueprints Hellstrom provided, Nocturna planned the robberies in detail. To fit in with her preoccupation with the romance of the night, he took the costumed persona of Nightshade, totally unrelated to the heroine of the same name. When Nocturna decided the scheme had been played out, she called an end to the robberies. Before they could plan a next step, Night-Slayer arrived, having escaped from prison. He fought his "rival," killing Nightshade with a dagger. (*Batman* #376, October 1984)

NIGHT-SLAYER

ANTON KNIGHT grew up the son of Charles Knight, a respected businessman who doubled as a crime boss. When he was a young adult, Anton left to travel, in the hopes of perfecting his talents in the martial arts. He returned to America only when his father was gunned down by a rival mob. There he met Knight's unofficial ward, Natasha, a young girl Charles had rescued from the streets. Prior to this meeting, Anton had only corresponded with her. Smitten, Knight became totally obsessed with Natasha. (*Detective Comics* #529, August 1983)

Anton and Natasha both found the evening

romantic and dedicated themselves to the night—something that proved prophetic when, years later, an accident at the Gotham Observatory left Natasha with chalk-like skin. When their money ran out after extensive medical treatment, they finally resorted to crime as Nocturna and the Night-Thief. He trained her in fighting styles, and she proved a quick study.

He would do anything for Natasha, committing crimes and putting himself at risk with the idea that their eternal love would see them through the darkest times. Instead, Nocturna used and abused him, betraying his feelings and seeking others whenever he was unavailable to her. Over time this drove him mad, which made his actions increasingly dangerous.

While Night-Thief was at best an average martial artist, his all-black outfit allowed him to stealthily move through the shadows, confounding police and even Batman. Still, the Dark Knight managed to capture him and bring him to trial. Out of love, he took the blame; Nocturna was cleared while he was sent to prison. (*Batman* #377, November 1984) When the prison suffered a power outage, Anton used the blackness to escape, only to discover that Nocturna had allied herself with Sturges Hellstrom, dubbed Nightshade. Enraged, he attacked Nightshade, and the two fought until Anton killed his perceived rival. (*Detective Comics* #543, October 1984)

Nocturna was horrified by Anton's actions, saying that he had murdered their beloved night. Thus Anton altered his name from Night-Thief to Night-Slayer. Later, during a fight with Batman, whom she was trying to seduce, Nocturna wound up shooting her adoptive brother in the back. Wounded, Anton managed to escape to the Gotham sewers, where he was found by the dog Cerebus and its blind master, a young woman named Tina. The woman felt the costume material and—concluding that she had rescued Batman—nursed him back to health. (*Detective Comics* #545–546, December 1984–January 1985)

Soon after, Anton left her care and sought out Nocturna, avoiding Batman, who dogged his trail. Complicating their fight was the arrival of the assassin Doctor Fang, hired by Mayor Hamilton Hill to kill the Dark Knight. In the confusion a gunshot was heard; the bullet grazed Batman's skull, disorienting him, in addition to killing Fang. Batman was delirious, convinced he'd killed Fang, and was unable to stop Anton from taking his Batsuit. (*Batman* #380, February 1985)

Knight, as Batman, spent four nights terrorizing Gotham's citizen and turning the Gotham Guardian into Public Enemy Number One. It took the combined efforts of Nocturna and Robin to put an end to Knight's rampage. (*Detective Comics* #547, February 1985) Soon after, Batman, dressed in the abandoned Night-Slayer outfit, managed to repair much of the damage done to his reputation and expose Hill's involvement. Knight attacked Batman in front of the press and the two fought, tumbling into Gotham River, where Knight escaped.

Anton Knight found safety within Black Mask's False Face Society for a time. He resurfaced later, after Nocturna was injured in a fight with Catwoman. Night-Slayer arrived in time to stab his former beloved and then engage first Robin, then Batman, and finally Catwoman, in a vicious fight. It fell to Catwoman to lay Night-Slayer out for good, plunging him once more into the Gotham River. (*Batman* #391, February 1986)

Anton Knight was convicted of his various crimes and returned to prison. He was among the villains freed by Rā's al Ghūl in his attempt to overwhelm Batman, but instead Night-Slayer sought independence. (*Batman* #400, October 1986) Anton Knight has not been seen since.

NIGHTWING

There have been several people using the name *Nightwing* in Batman's world. On Earth-1, Superman disguised himself as Nightwing to fight crime in the bottled city of Kandor, alongside Jimmy Olsen, who became Flamebird, taking the names from native Kryptonian birds. Ironically, they became a crime-fighting duo inspired in part by Batman and Robin, complete with Nitecave and similar named equipment. (*Superman* #158, January 1963)

Later, Van-Zee, a cousin of Superman's living in Kandor, assumed the Nightwing identity to continue battling crime. His niece's husband AkVar became the new Flamebird. (*Superman Family* #183, May/June 1977)

In the reality formed in the wake of the Crisis on Infinite Earths, Dick Grayson had heard of the Kryptonian legend of Nightwing, and when he sought a new identity as an individual, he chose the name, much as Bette Kane chose Flamebird. (*Tales of the Teen Titans* #44, July 1984)

Later, Grayson relocated from Gotham City to Blüdhaven. After a time he attempted to mentor Tad Ryerstad, who proved to be a sociopath. Tad took the name *Nite-Wing* and became a brutal vigilante who had to be taken down by Nightwing.

When Grayson left America for a while, traveling with Bruce Wayne and Tim Drake after the events of Infinite Crisis, Jason Todd, the second Robin, briefly took on the costume and identity of Nightwing without permission. He was a more violent version, operating mainly in New York City until Grayson's return. (*Nightwing* #118, May 2006) Soon after,

Cheyenne Freemont also donned a Nightwing outfit to help Grayson stop Todd.

When Superman brought LOIS LANE to KRYPTON, they found themselves labeled as criminals and became Nightwing and Flamebird to remain free while they sought proof of their innocence. (*Superman: The Man of Steel* #111, April 2001) Later, Power Girl and SUPERGIRL also visited Kandor and briefly fought crime as Nightwing and Flamebird. (*Supergirl* [third series] #6, March 2006)

NIGMA, EDWARD

Edward Nigma grew up seeking shortcuts in life and became fascinated with puzzles, growing up to become the costumed criminal the RIDDLER.

NIMROD THE HUNTER

DEAN HUNTER was a convicted murderer in Texas, who escaped to prove that he'd been framed by a fellow criminal, Chancer. He followed the trail north to GOTHAM CITY, only to learn that Chancer had allied himself with CALENDAR MAN, KILLER MOTH, and CATMAN in a scheme to kidnap BRUCE WAYNE, Police Commissioner JAMES GORDON, and Mayor ARMAND KROL. En route Hunter had stolen a military camouflage suit that gave him chameleon-like powers, so he entered into an uneasy partnership with ROBIN to rescue the men before they were harmed. After succeeding, Hunter surrendered himself to Batman in the hope that Chancer would testify and clear his name. Batman returned the suit to the army. (*Batman: Shadow of the Bat* #7–9, December 1992–February 1993)

NINE OLD MEN, THE

Pop Davies was paroled from prison after serving thirty years. What he found upon his release horrified him, as younger gangs were disinterested in his participation. Bitter, he gathered eight peers and formed the Nine Old Men. Together they used their unique and arcane knowledge of GOTHAM CITY to commit a series of robberies that propelled them to the top of the crime scales. As a result, they were also the target of Batman and Robin, who first had to protect their secret identities when the men schemed to rob WAYNE MANOR by tunneling through the Anderson Caves underneath the mansion. What the men did not realize was that since their heydays, the caverns had been turned into the BATCAVE, a secret that was protected thanks to the sophisticated security systems in place. The elderly gangsters were apprehended by the Dynamic Duo. (*Batman* #64, April/May 1951)

NITOBE, ASANO

Asano Nitobe was considered the last living master of ninjitsu, the Japanese spy art that involved mastery of all other martial arts systems. In 1945, while serving as bodyguard to geneticist Dr. Oka, Asano and his charge were smuggled out of Nagasaki before it was a struck by an atomic bomb; they became part of the enclave known as the Council. Even after Oka's death, Asano remained loyal to the Council and eventually trained and befriended Paul Kirk, once known as MANHUNTER. (*Detective Comics* #439, February/March 1974)

Asano was eventually forced to duel the fugitive Manhunter until he learned that the Council had murdered Oka. Joining with Kirk, and soon after Interpol agent Christine St. Clair, Nitobe helped battle the Council before it could complete its plan for global domination. After Kirk sacrificed himself to end the Council's threat, Nitobe and St. Clair roamed the world, killing the many clones of Kirk that had survived. When the last one was accounted for, Nitobe retired to rest. (*Power Company* #15, June 2003)

NKVDEMON

GREGOR DOSYNSKI was a protégé to the KGB's master assassin, the KGBEAST. He had been trained as a hand-to-hand combatant in addition to being a master marksman and skilled gymnast. Dosynski was given treatments to enhance his strength, speed, and endurance. These also left his nerve endings dead, so he could no longer feel pain. Assigned to the NKVD department of the Soviet government, he took the name *NKVDemon*. When word reached him that his mentor had died, the NKVDemon left his employers and went into hiding. Feeling the Soviet bureaucracy had abandoned the Beast, the Demon sought revenge in his name, targeting the ten officials he considered traitors. By the time three of the ten were dead, Batman had been alerted to the crimes and interceded. He managed to track the Demon in time to stop him from assassinating the final name on the list, the Soviet premier. A Russian detective named Nikita Krakov shot the Demon. (*Batman* #445, March 1990)

A fellow assassin, Nicodemus, assumed the costume and name and was hired to kill AQUAMAN. Instead he was stopped by the King of the Seas and Batman, then later killed in jail. (*Aquaman* [fourth series] #8, July 1992)

A third NKVDemon—who worked for Ulysses Hadrian Armstrong, the GENERAL—was hired to foment a war in the Middle East. He was foiled by the arrival of ROBIN and NIGHTWING, who were in search of the General. After that failure, the Demon remained free and was hired as bodyguard to the ODESSA MOB's leader, only to be shot during the WAR GAMES. (*Robin* [second series] #47, November 1997)

NOCTURNA

On Earth-1, a twelve-year-old girl who'd grown up on GOTHAM CITY's streets encountered millionaire Charles Knight. Seeing her plight touched his heart, and Knight took her in, raising her as the daughter he'd never had. He named her Natasha and never filed for formal adoption. One reason was that he feared the courts would never approve of a single man raising a teenage female; another was that he had several skeletons in his closet, including the fact that his fortune was based on illegal dealings as a criminal gang lord. Some time later, a rival gang killed Knight and Natasha finally learned the truth about her guardian. At Knight's funeral, she met his only son, ANTON KNIGHT, who had just returned from studying martial arts in Asia. He admitted to knowing of his father's crooked life and even embracing it for his own purposes. (*Batman* #363, September 1983)

Natasha grew up, using Knight's inheritance to put herself through college, where she indulged her passion for astronomy. Upon graduation, she went to work for the Gotham Astronomical Observatory. As she studied the properties of stellar light in a vacuum, she was indirectly exposed to a high level of laser radiation. Over time this exposure had an adverse effect, leaching her skin of pigmentation, leaving her chalk-white and making her sensitive to any manner of light. (*Detective Comics* #529, August 1983) Treating her new condition rapidly depleted the Knight wealth, with Natasha turning to the WAYNE FOUNDATION for help. As the bureaucrats dithered, she took Anton up on a suggestion he'd made: They embarked on a life of crime to fund their high standard of living. (*Batman* #363, September 1983)

Taking the name *Nocturna,* Natasha was to be the brains, while Anton, the Night-Thief, would provide the muscle. During this time, the lovestruck Anton and ambitious Nocturna often sparred. To augment her growing skills, Nocturna began to wear large earrings that were also throwing stars, a faux pearl necklace that contained knockout gas, a stiletto hairpin, and a belt that doubled as a razor-sharp whip.

The couple's new career met with early success. Emboldened, Nocturna decided to exact a measure of revenge against the Wayne Foundation and sought out BRUCE WAYNE at a social function. He was enchanted with the pale-skinned, romantic woman. As they spoke, Night-Thief arrived and robbed the patrons of their belongings. That night Batman traced the robber to the Knight estate, where Nocturna greeted him and admitted to the crime. She revealed her history to the Dark Knight and then rendered him unconscious with a powder hidden in her compact. When he awoke, he found the pair at the observatory; as Batman apprehended Anton, Nocturna escaped.

From that point forward, Nocturna and Night-Thief continued to be a presence in Batman's life. Nocturna encountered JASON TODD, the second ROBIN, who was estranged from Batman at the time. She influenced him, playing the mother figure he desperately sought. In fact, Todd became a pawn between Nocturna and Bruce Wayne, with her going so far as to petition the courts for custody. She then suggested that one way Wayne might retain Jason in his household was to marry her. Mayor HAMILTON HILL, upset that Wayne was backing a different candidate in the upcoming election, influenced the judge to award Todd to Natasha Knight. In the same courtroom, Anton Knight testified and helped clear his paramour of all criminal charges. (*Batman* #377–378, November–December 1984)

With her adoptive brother in jail, Nocturna allied

herself with Sturges Hellstrom, who acted as her muscle using the name NIGHTSHADE. She would host horror-themed parties, learning the layout of the social elite's homes; Nightshade would soon after arrive for robberies. When she had decided the scheme had run its course, she told him to stop. (*Batman* #376, October 1984)

Anton Knight, meantime, gained his freedom and returned to the Knight homestead. Enraged at being replaced by Nightshade, he attacked; during the battle his rival was killed. Seeing this as an evolutionary step forward, Night-Thief renamed himself NIGHT-SLAYER and was welcomed back by Nocturna with open arms—until she realized he had killed in her name. Claiming that he had murdered her precious night, she banned him from the house. (*Detective Comics* #543, October 1984)

When Nocturna used her narcotic perfume to entice Batman, they were interrupted by Night-Slayer, insisting that if he could not have Natasha, no one could. Night-Slayer and the Dark Knight fought, with Anton successfully stabbing Batman, only to be shot in turn by Nocturna. Wounded, he escaped before he could be apprehended. (*Batman* #377, November 1984)

Just when Nocturna thought things had settled down, she was attacked by the MAD HATTER, who wanted to gain control over her stolen loot. The resulting brawl allowed her to escape, stolen property intact. (*Batman* #379, January 1985)

Anton recovered from his injuries and still sought his would-be lover at all costs. He even kidnapped Nocturna and Todd, hoping to lure Batman into a trap. The two fought again, this time with Night-Slayer getting off a shot that grazed Batman's cowl, disorienting him. The mentally unhinged Anton Knight then decided to become Batman and stole the Caped Crusader's costume. (*Batman* #380, February 1985) Nocturna and Jason, as ROBIN, teamed up to stop Anton, who was smearing Batman's reputation with a series of robberies. (*Detective Comics* #547, February 1985) When this mission was done—Nocturna promised her ward—she would end her criminal career. They were then confronted by the Night-Slayer, actually a wounded Batman in Anton's costume. He asked her help in putting an end to Anton's work once and for all, but he also cannily timed the meeting so that a child welfare representative would arrive, horrified to see Nocturna with a wanted criminal.

In short order, Anton was subdued, Hamilton Hill's corruption exposed, and Jason Todd returned to Bruce Wayne's safekeeping. Nocturna retreated to the observatory and the stars she loved. That was where Batman found her as she studied the red skies that denoted the impending arrival of an anti-matter wave threatening their universe. The two embraced passionately but recognized they were too different for any romance to ever work. (*Detective Comics* #556, November 1985)

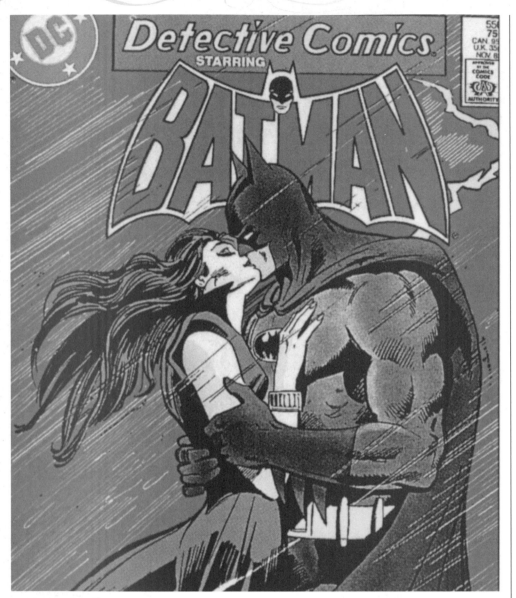

leave; then bridges and tunnels were destroyed, sealing the city off from America. The National Guard ensured that once that happened, no one left in Gotham could leave, reducing the once-proud city to a veritable no man's land.

During this period, Batman withdrew from sight. He was gone for three solid months as street gangs and costumed criminals carved up the city for themselves, preying on those citizens who remained and turning ordinary household items—batteries, toilet paper, clothing—into priceless commodities. The PENGUIN's ICEBERG LOUNGE became a black-market clearinghouse for such items, while POISON IVY claimed ROBINSON PARK. Tommy Monaghan, known as the Hitman, kept to himself, protecting his neighborhood with his usual brutality. The JOKER, now free from ARKHAM ASYLUM, was heard but unseen in the well-stocked apartment building he claimed for himself.

Commissioner JAMES GORDON and his wife, SARAH ESSEN GORDON, led the remaining police officers in maintaining some sense of order while claiming midtown for themselves.

Out of respect for Batman and the law, super heroes stayed away from Gotham. SUPERMAN arrived and stayed for one day, but he recognized that even with all his abilities, Gotham's problems were too time consuming.

Among Batman's allies, ORACLE recruited several citizens to act as her street eyes and ears, bringing her vital information in exchange for supplies. The HUNTRESS chose to inspire others by donning a BATGIRL costume of her own design and patrolling the city. TIM DRAKE, the current ROBIN, had been relocated by his father to Keystone City, while NIGHTWING initially remained in BLÜDHAVEN, perplexed by his mentor's lengthy absence. Not having Batman on hand also vexed and angered Gordon.

As a result, one hundred days after the city was sealed off, Batman's return was not warmly greeted by anyone save the citizens he helped. He displayed his displeasure at Huntress using his symbology and she returned to her usual outfit, while Batman adopted her use of spray paint to tag sections of the town that were slowly being reclaimed in the name of law and order. Soon after, CASSANDRA CAIN, who had snuck into Gotham shortly before it was closed, made Oracle's acquaintance and proved worthy of becoming the next Batgirl.

Over the course of a year, territory slowly shifted hands as Batman's presence emboldened the police to take more overt action. As needed, he summoned Nightwing and Robin for help—starting with taking down LOCK-UP, who was using the damaged BLACKGATE PENITENTIARY as his personal jail. Street gangs were easily stopped, and infighting among the villains also made it easier for the police to regain space, one block at a time. During this period, Mercy Graves, one of LEX LUTHOR's aides, mysteriously arrived and offered to do business with Penguin. At much the same time, BANE wrecked the Hall of Records, submerging much of it.

As fall turned to winter, public sentiment prompted Congress to reconsider its actions. Additionally, Luthor had begun lobbying, hoping to gain contracts for the reconstruction. What few knew was that he had already begun illegally

A jealous CATWOMAN found them and the two women fought, resulting in both being injured. Night-Slayer heard of Natasha's injury and sought her out, overpowering Robin to get close to her. He was brutal with the teen, prompting Nocturna to lash out, maternal instincts in play, and she fought her adoptive brother to protect her "son." Nocturna was knocked unconscious just before Catwoman arrived to actually help. Robin placed his would-be mother in a hot-air balloon, hoping to send her to safety as Catwoman fought Night-Slayer to protect the still-wounded Dark Knight. (*Detective Comics* #557, December 1985) The cosmic storm destroyed the balloon, and Nocturna's body was never found.

On the world created after the events of CRISIS ON INFINITE EARTHS, the only person claiming to use the name *Nocturna* was DALA, the vampire companion to the madman known as the MONK.

NOLAN, FINGERS

Fingers Nolan stole a valuable pearl necklace and hid it in GOTHAM CITY's Mechanical Museum of Natural History. When he went back to retrieve it, he had the misfortune of arriving while Batman was present, investigating the murder of PROFESSOR HALE. (*Detective Comics* #255, May 1958)

NO MAN'S LAND

GOTHAM CITY had been beleaguered, first by the arrival of an Ebola-A virus dubbed the CLENCH, and almost immediately thereafter by a 7.6-magnitude earthquake that shook the city to its core.

The federal government debated the benefits of continuing to spend billions of dollars in rebuilding a city that seemed to be devastated with regularity. Influencing the policymakers on Capitol Hill was a man named NICHOLAS SCRATCH, who seemed to be orchestrating events for his own purposes. Despite protests from Mayor MARION GRANGE and billionaire BRUCE WAYNE, Congress seemed poised to cut off funding to the city, effectively condemning it to wither and die. Grange, in fact, was shot, although the target was Wayne.

The US government gave Gotham's inhabitants a deadline by which they must choose to stay or

Time and again Batman finds his life endangered by the psychotic, costumed criminals of Gotham City. From left: the Joker, Poison Ivy, Bane, Two-Face, and the Riddler.

No doubt the gathering of rogues would prefer the Caped Crusader six feet under, but they never get their wish. From left: Hush, Riddler, Harley Quinn, Poison Ivy, Clayface, Killer Croc, Rā's al Ghūl, Scarecrow, Talia, and the Joker.

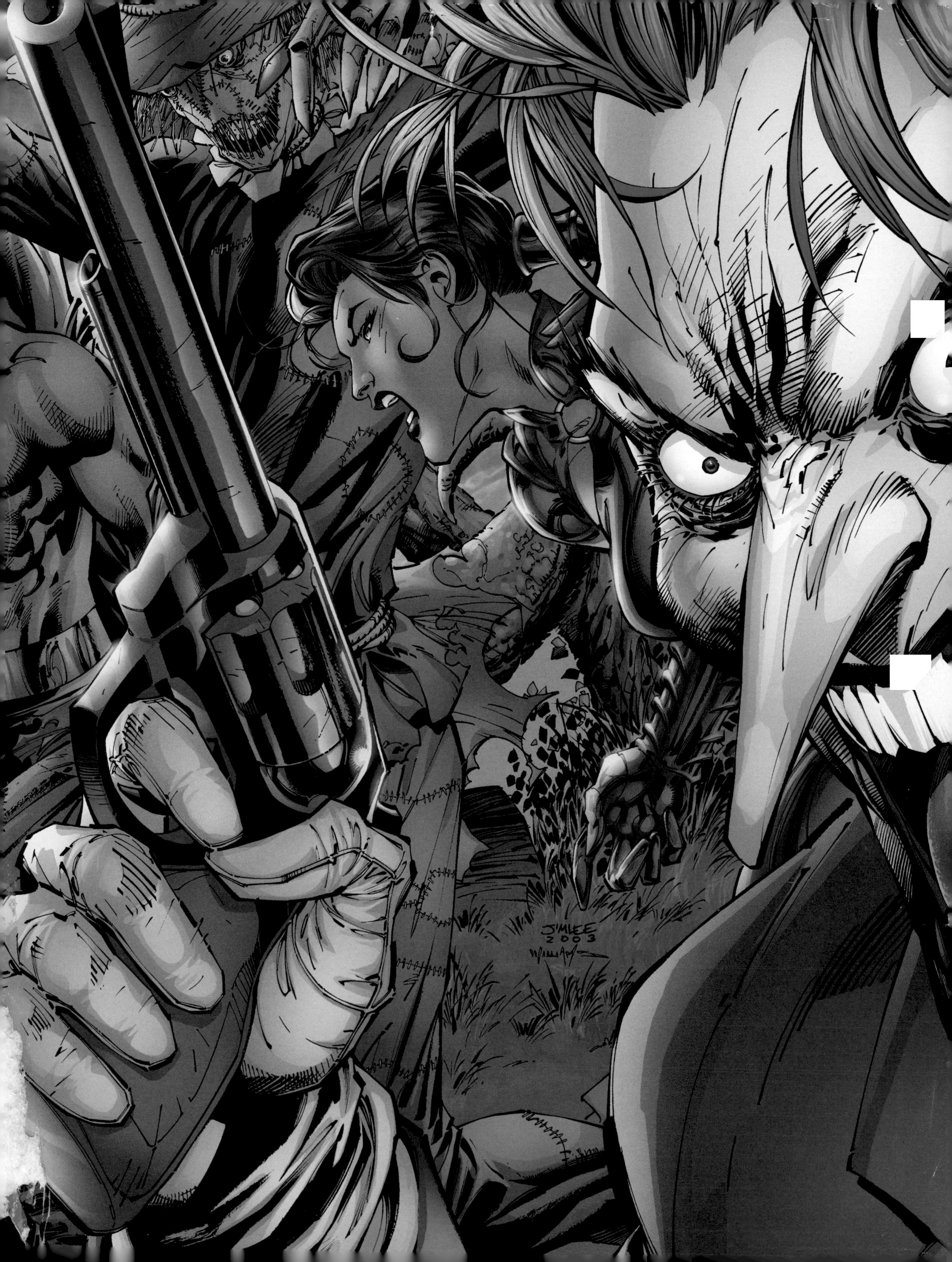
JIMLEE
2003

IT'S *HOT.* EVEN FOR JUNE.

YEARS FROM NOW, WHEN PEOPLE ARE TALKING ABOUT THE WEATHER, THEY'LL SAY:

"IT'S HOT. BUT, NOT AS HOT AS THE NIGHT JOHNNY VITI GOT MARRIED."

Selina Kyle has been a constant In Batman's life since the beginning of his crime-fighting career.

As Catwoman, Kyle has often fought against the Dark Knight.

Batman and Catwoman endured a love-hate relationship for years before love won out.

Prone to trouble, Catwoman has certainly had her scrapes with law enforcement.

CAT woman

60
60
50
57
40

GOTHAM CITY
4815162342
POLICE DEPT

A look at the many guises Selina Kyle used during her sixty-plus-year career as Catwoman.

Talia, daughter of the demon, has followed her own path, which has often led her to Batman's heart.

Rā's al Ghūl saw Batman as both heir to his empire and consort for his daughter but was bitterly rejected.

Jervis Tetch fancies himself the literal reincarnation of the Mad Hatter, but he is far deadlier than his fictional inspiration.

The Penguin has become Gotham City's criminal power broker, at the center of the underworld action.

The Riddler's brilliant mind has turned crime into a game of wits between the Prince of Puzzlers and the Dark Knight Detective.

Poison Ivy would kill all of humanity to protect her precious plants.

Mister Freeze lost the love of his life and prefers seeing the world as cold as his heart has grown.

Batman has suffered much from the Scarecrow's mind games, but a good left hook usually won the day.

No matter which felon wants to rule, they never seem to manage the feat thanks to the presence of the Gotham Guardian.

The Scarecrow would like nothing better than to reduce his cowled opponent to a quivering mass of flesh.

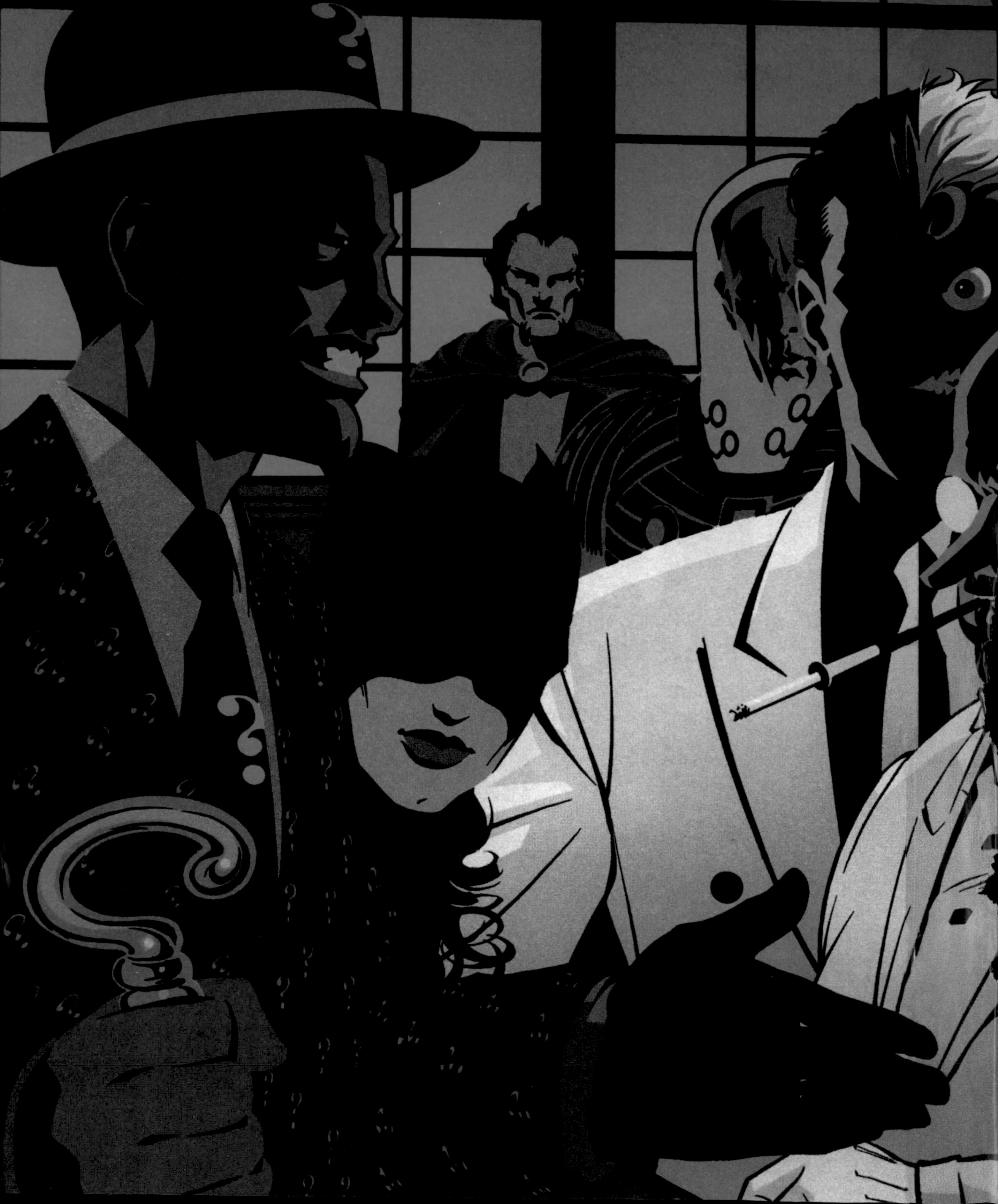

Time and again the villains mass their efforts to take down the Dark Knight, but their own petty concerns tend to undermine the attempt. From left: Riddler, Catwoman, Rā's al Ghūl, Mister Freeze, Two-Face, Penguin, Scarface, Joker, and Killer Croc.

Waylon Jones was born
misshapen and grew to
monstrous proportions
after treatment by Hush.
He is a true Killer Croc.

Harvey Dent was once Gotham City's celebrated district attorney, but an accident fractured his mind and he became Two-Face, with every act decided by the flip of a coin.

The Joker inspires fear in most, but only love from Harley Quinn, his former Arkham Asylum psychiatrist.

Of all Batman's opponents, the one who remains a constant is the Joker. Their battles have been epic and each recognizes the need for the other.

The Joker's weapons may look like toys, but they are almost as deadly as he is.

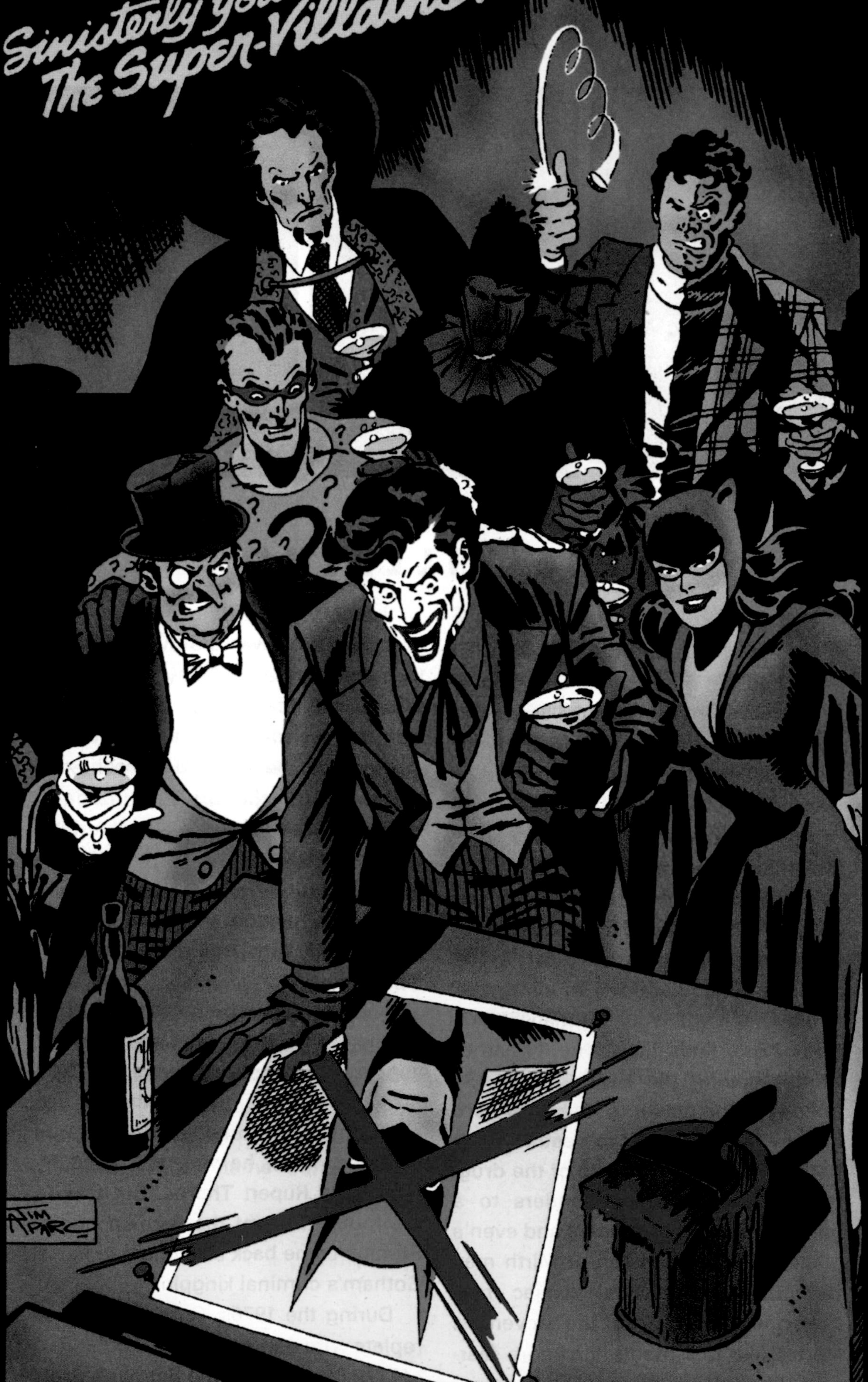
Sinisterly yours
The Super-Villains!

Speech bubbles:
AND I THOUGHT GETTING IN WOULD BE THE HARDEST PART...

GOTHAM CITY. "NO MAN'S LAND."

THE SIGHT SHOULDN'T SHOCK ME.

IT DOES.

Gotham City during No Man's Land

of the yearlong ordeal took more than twice that long to settle down. (*Azrael* #50–61, March 1999–February 2000; *Batman* #563–574, March 1999–February 2000; *Batman: Chronicles* #16–18, Spring-Fall 1999; *Batman: Harley Quinn*, 1999; *Batman: No Man's Land* #0–1, 1999; *Batman: Shadow of the Bat* #83–94, March 1999–February 2000; *Catwoman* [second series] #72–77, September 1999–February 2000; *Detective Comics* #730–741, March 1999–February 2000; *Legends of the Dark Knight* #116–126, March 1999–February 2000; *Nightwing* [second series] #35–39, September 1999–January 2000; *No Man's Land: Secret Files & Origins* #1, December 1999; *Robin* [second series] #67–73, August 1999–February 2000; *Young Justice in No Man's Land Special* #1, July 1999)

NORANIA

A European monarchy noted for its ruling family's Crown Jewels, Norania suffered financially in the years following World War II. King Eric and his advisers Chancellor Zarits and Count Viras traveled to the United States at one point to secure a loan for their country. (*Batman* #96, December 1955)

NORBET, PROFESSOR

Professor Norbet committed a series of spectacular crimes as the PLANET-MASTER.

NORTHMONT

The small town where JASON BARD spent part of his youth and where his mother, Rose, was murdered. (*Detective Comics* #491, June 1980)

NORTHTOWN

Located north of GOTHAM CITY, this small community lay next to a river valley held in check by the Northtown Dam. (*Batman* #98, March 1956)

NORTON, WILDE

Wilde Norton was a criminal who confounded the GOTHAM CITY police and ultimately faced off against the Batman.

NUMBERS

CARL C. CAVE determined that three was his lucky number and lived his life with that as his guiding principle. Considering that his name featured the third letter of the alphabet and he was born on March 3, the conclusion was fairly obvious. What clinched it was when the low-level criminal won a substantial sum after betting on the third horse in the third race at a local racetrack. Later he crossed paths with Batman and ROBIN when he won big betting only on the number three, or its multiples, aboard an illegal gambling vessel. The Dynamic Duo found themselves powerless to act since the boat was anchored beyond the three-mile legal limit.

Flush with success, Cave surrounded himself with three underlings and began committing a series of crimes based on his lucky number. While he eluded the police, the media covered his exploits and named him Numbers. Eventually the Dynamic Duo did apprehend Cave, who was jailed for his crimes. (*Detective Comics* #146, April 1949)

placing matériel in the city, which was protected by Bane. He also ordered public records destroyed so he could buy up property on the cheap.

Events moved to a climax when the Joker emerged, killing many of Luthor's construction workers before disappearing from sight. The police and Batman's team gained control over the majority of the city and waited for the government to accept the city once more. At Christmastime it became apparent that the children born during the past year had gone missing. It was Essen who found them at police headquarters, with the Joker ready to kill them all. He gunned her down, only to be crippled by a vengeful Gordon.

As the new year began, Gotham was at last reconnected with the rest of America as a new Gotham administration took over. James Gordon was reinstated as commissioner, and all the police who remained were made part of a new force. Gordon and Batman mended their differences, with Batman finally offering to reveal his identity to Gordon—who refused.

In the wake of Gotham's residents returning home, new tensions arose between those who'd chosen to stay and those who'd fled. Additionally, Luthor disliked being outmaneuvered by Wayne; he soon hired a mercenary, DAVID CAIN, to frame Wayne for the murder of VESPER FAIRCHILD. The repercussions

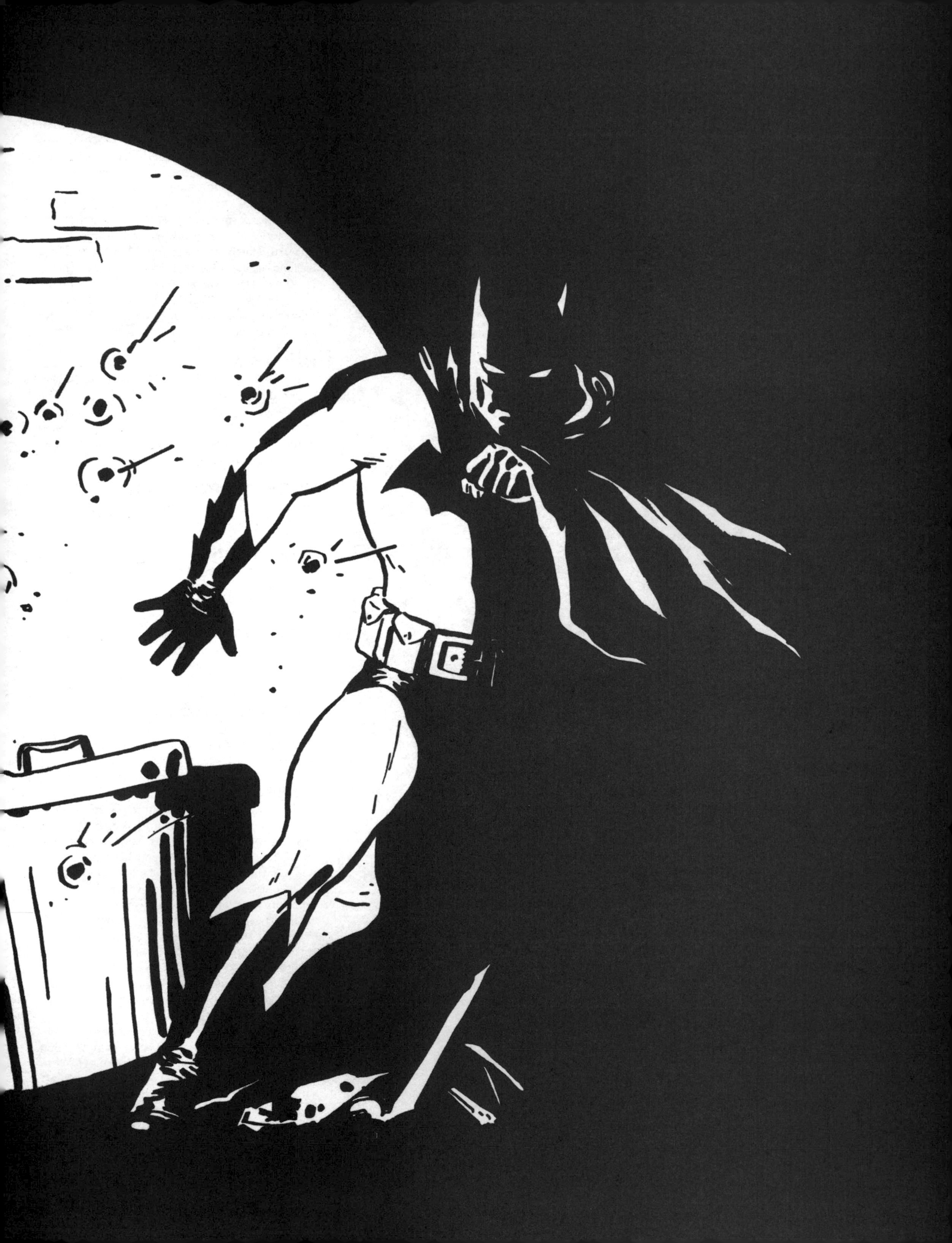

OBEAH MAN, THE

A Haitian man was well versed in the black arts known as voodoo and was called by his fellow countrymen the Obeah Man. By preying on their superstitious minds, he rose to become a powerful criminal in Haiti. He envisioned a large payday when he kidnapped JACK and JANET DRAKE and demanded a hefty ransom from Drake Industries. Because the Drakes were the parents of TIM DRAKE, the third ROBIN, this news brought Batman flying south from GOTHAM CITY to rescue them. While the Dark Knight fought the Obeah Man, the Drakes fell ill after drinking water altered by the mad mystic. Janet almost immediately died and Jack fell into a coma, a state in which he would remain for some months. The Obeah Man started a fire, intending to escape, but soon succumbed to the flames and was presumed dead. (*Detective Comics* #618–621, Late July–September 1990)

OCEAN POINT

A beachfront resort community well to the south of GOTHAM CITY with luxurious properties owned by the likes of millionaire BRUCE WAYNE. While attempting to vacation there, Wayne had to don the BATSUIT to investigate a neighbor's burgled safe with the combination found on a soda pull-tab. (*Detective Comics* #393, November 1969)

OCTOPUS, THE

The Octopus was a self-styled criminal mastermind; his henchmen wore gray hoods with an octopus symbol on the forehead. They committed a series of crimes but were apprehended by Batman, ROBIN, and SUPERMAN. What made the case noteworthy was the arrival of an amateur crime fighter, complete with a unique arsenal of tools, named the Crimson Avenger, a tribute to the World War II-era adventurer. (*World's Finest Comics* #131, February 1963)

ODESSA MOB, THE

After the breakup of the Soviet Union, scores of the country's mobsters fled for new beginnings, with many settling in the United States. Former KGB officer VASILY KOSOV relocated to GOTHAM CITY and founded the Odessa Mob, which brought a new level of violence to Gotham's streets. Working from midtown, they engaged in drug dealing, prostitution, gambling, and extortion. The Odessa Mob vied for territory with the STREET DEMONZ, LUCKY HAND TRIAD, and other street gangs and survived the death of Vasily, who left his daughter ALEXANDRA KOSOV in charge. For a time, the Odessa Mob vowed fealty to BLACK MASK, but in the wake of his death they went back to independence. (*Detective Comics* #742, March 2000)

OGRE

During the 1950s the US military conducted experiments that included new aircraft and new types of humans. Project Mirakle was designed to create the perfect spy, but the enhancements to the human norm resulted in a succession of test subject deaths. When funding ended, the project was shut down and the remaining subjects killed—all but the twenty-third subject, MICHAEL ADAMS, and his unnamed brother. Whereas Michael, nicknamed the Ogre, had a massive build with genetically altered superstrength, his brother, the Ape, was a human/ape hybrid with a keen intellect. Free but unhappy with their condition, the two sought the dispersed project scientists and began killing them. Batman began tracking the pair and learned the truth about the Adams brothers when they arrived at Dr. Winston Belmont's doorstep. During the struggle, Belmont survived but the Ape died. Ogre escaped from Batman and was left wandering alone, seeking a place he could call home. (*Batman* #535, October 1996)

O'HARA, CHIEF CLANCY

Clancy O'Hara was a career police officer in GOTHAM CITY on Earth-2. (*All-Star Comics* #67, July/August 1977) He rose from uniformed beat cop to succeed the late BRUCE WAYNE as commissioner of police. (*Wonder Woman* #281, July 1981)

On Earth-1, Clancy O'Hara was also a uniformed police officer in Gotham City. (Voice heard in *World's Finest Comics* #159, August 1966; first seen in *Detective Comics* #461, July 1976)

In the reality formed in the wake of CRISIS ON INFINITE EARTHS, Clancy O'Hara continued to protect the citizens of Gotham City until his death at the hands of the HANGMAN KILLER early in Batman's career. (*Batman: Dark Victory* #1, December 1999)

OKAMURA, HIRO

This teenage genius inventor, nicknamed TOYMAN, proved both impediment and aid to Batman and SUPERMAN.

OLSEN, JIMMY

On Earth-2, James Bartholomew Olsen was a cub reporter for the METROPOLIS *Daily Star*, befriending not only LOIS LANE and Clark Kent but SUPERMAN, as well. He remained with the *Star* for the remainder of his adult life. (*Action Comics* #6, November 1938; *Superman* #13, November/December 1941)

On Earth-1, Jimmy Olsen was a junior reporter-photographer for the Metropolis *Daily Planet*.

He and Superman were close pals, with the Man of Steel bringing him along on many adventures. When they were visiting the bottled city of KANDOR, they took to wearing crime-fighting gear styled after Batman and Robin, using the names NIGHTWING and FLAMEBIRD. As a result, Jimmy had many dealings with Batman and Robin, with the reporter and Boy Wonder becoming fast friends. They went so far as to establish the Eyrie, their own secret headquarters, and shared many cases together. (*World's Finest Comics* #141, May 1964)

On the world fashioned in the wake of CRISIS ON INFINITE EARTHS, Jimmy Olsen remained a reporter for the *Daily Planet*. His career began when he was spotted by Perry White selling papers in front of the newspaper's headquarters. White and reporter Clark Kent repeatedly saw Olsen over the next few weeks, and Kent was intrigued and discovered that Jimmy held multiple paper routes. He was even more surprised to learn that the boy was homeless, living within the *Planet* building: Jimmy's father had gone missing, and his mother had left

him with a neighbor so she could search for her husband. The neighbor, though, kept the books for the 10, a criminal organization that would later confront Batman as the 100 and the 1000. She was murdered to keep their secrets, and Jimmy had fled with nowhere else to go.

When the 10 targeted Jimmy, in case he knew something, Superman saved the youth and, lonely for companionship, befriended him. Perry added Jimmy to the staff as a copy boy, and he rose to photographer and reporter. (*Superman* #665, September 2007)

As Superman's friend, Olsen used a special signal watch that emitted a hypersonic noise, alerting the Man of Steel to immediate dangers. He won several Pulitzer Prizes for his pictures, including the classic image of a dead Superman after his epic battle with Doomsday. (*Superman* #75, January 1993)

While Jimmy and Batman rarely crossed paths, their worlds intersected when the reporter began to investigate the death of DUELA DENT and the involvement of JASON TODD. (*Countdown* #51, 2007)

(For a detailed account of Jimmy Olsen, consult *The Essential Superman Encyclopedia*.)

OMAC

The One Man Army Corps were cybernetically controlled cyborgs that encased living humans inside hardware made with advanced nanotechnology. The OMAC virus was created using bits and pieces taken from BRAINIAC 13, LEXCORP, and the US Department of Defense. The virus was under the control of the Brother I satellite Batman built to keep an eye on the meta-human community. The satellite was usurped, first by Alexander Luthor Jr. and then by Maxwell Lord. Along the way, it gained sentience and renamed itself BROTHER EYE. (*The OMAC Project* #1, June 2005)

There were 1,373,462 humans affected by the nanovirus, which turned them into killing machines with no control over their actions. Most were eventually stopped when a massive electromagnetic pulse was unleashed. The remaining two hundred thousand became inoperative after Batman destroyed his creation. (*The OMAC Project* #6, November 2005)

The OMAC prototype was retained by Batman and kept in a locked storage facility, under guard

and behind three feet of reinforced steel. At WayneTech's R&D department, Batman kept a tracking device disguised as prototype DX-538. When a version of Brainiac returned to Earth, it seized control of Will Magnus's Metal Men to access the prototype, giving him a new vessel to use. After Batman was beaten and hospitalized, it fell to SUPERMAN to track and stop the prototype.

After the threat ended, Batman agreed to have Superman destroy remaining prototypes associated with the OMAC technology. (*Superman/Batman* #36, Early August 2007)

OMEGA

Omega was an international terrorist group that once threatened GOTHAM CITY with a nuclear device. Batman investigated the disappearance of several foreign intelligence agents, which led him to the disappearance of Hungary's prize physicist Lucas Nagy. Omega had abducted him to build a twenty-megaton nuclear bomb with which they threatened the world if money was not delivered to them. With Batman hot on their trail, the Omega leader targeted Gotham City, and Batman told authorities the threats were for real. As he tracked the group, however, the Dark Knight discovered that Omega had failed to convince Nagy to build their device and resorted to a bluff—with Batman supporting their story. Nagy was rescued and Omega permanently put out of business. (*Batman* #283, January 1977)

ONYX

The woman known as Onyx was a mercenary in the employ of RĀ'S AL GHŪL's League of Assassins. When she chose to leave them, she sought sanctuary at the ashram that had not only trained her but also provided a home to Oliver Queen and Connor Hawke, the two men known as GREEN ARROW. When the ashram's Exalted Leader was killed by a renegade monk, Onyx left, seeking Queen's help in finding the leader's killer. They traced the monk, Lars, to the fabled Book of Ages, which was said to convey great power on its owner. Instead, when the monk opened the book—using the Wisdom Key he'd killed the leader to obtain—it took his life. (*Detective Comics* #546, January 1985)

After that incident, Onyx's service to the ashram was at an end, and she roamed the world as a

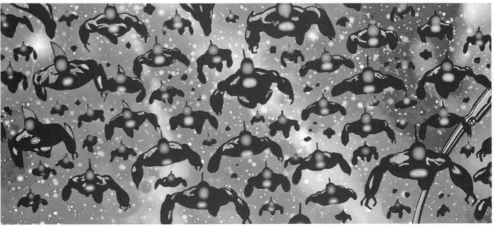

OMAC

mercenary. She retained the Wisdom Key, which led her to once again face Lars, resurrected as a being known as Barricade. She destroyed him and resumed her life. Onyx never strayed far from the Ashram after that incident until Batman called upon her to play a part in one of his WAR GAMES scenarios, which had been activated without his consent. She was assigned to protect ORPHEUS but failed, allowing BLACK MASK to kill Orpheus and masquerade as him until he consolidated power among Gotham's criminal underworld. (*Batman: The 12-Cent Adventure* #1, October 2004)

After the gang wars ended, Onyx chose to remain in GOTHAM CITY—with Batman's blessing—to fight crime and make up for failing the Dark Knight. She fought numerous criminals, including the RED HOOD. (*Batman* #641, August 2005)

OPTIK, MIKE

Mike Optik was a career criminal who ran a gang and sought an edge. He found it by co-opting the long-range telescope at an astronomical observatory and using it to scan GOTHAM CITY. His skill at lip-reading allowed him to glean all manner of confidential information, which he then used to commit crimes. Optik and his men were considered a ghost gang until Batman and ROBIN investigated and located Optik. He and his men were arrested. (*Batman* #22, April/May 1944)

ORACLE

After BARBARA GORDON was crippled by the JOKER, she gave up her BATGIRL identity to form a new persona as the cyberspace entity Oracle.

ORCA

Dr. Grace Balin became a marine biologist after falling in love with the ocean as a student at Gotham Gate College. She received her doctorates in marine biology and biomedicine and began her career working at Gotham Aquarium. Despite living in a city that endured tremendous hardships such as the CLENCH and an earthquake, Balin continued her work, going so far as to support after-school programs and volunteer at a soup kitchen. She suffered a crippling accident but continued to work until all funding for the Aquarium was cut off and the facility shut down.

Balin was hoping to use her marine knowledge to find ways to cure her own affliction. She concentrated her efforts on spinal cord regeneration with tissue samples taken from an orca whale. As her funding dwindled, Balin chose to test the therapy on herself—with disastrous results. Her body transformed into a humanoid form with an orca's skin and features. She discovered she could change shape back and forth at will. Balin realized she needed money to continue her work and used her newfound abilities to commit robberies for cash. One such robbery involved stealing the famous Flame of Persia diamond from Camille Baden-Smythe and then selling it back to her, with the money targeted for the underprivileged Balin so loved. The robberies, though, brought her to Batman's attention. The wealthy woman's guards fatally shot Balin, and she told the Dark Knight that she could survive only by drinking the remainder of her formula. He let her, and she then revealed that she was not only healed but also now permanently in her orca form. (*Batman* #579, July 2000)

Balin vanished. Batman later learned that she sold the diamond and used the proceeds to have a recreation center built near her beloved aquarium. At some point Batman apprehended her, and she wound up sentenced to serve time in the Slabside Penitentiary. When riots broke out courtesy of the JOKER, she escaped accompanied by the similarly shaped King Shark. (*Joker: Last Laugh* #1, December 2001)

Some time after she was released from the Slabside Penitentiary, Balin met TERRY CAPSHAW. They were, he joked later, the only two straight people at a party thrown by gay mutual acquaintances. He fell in love with her despite her deformity, noting that he liked full-figured girls; she was drawn to him for being a nerd. They were married for about a year, and he loved everything about her and her friends.

What became of her remained unknown until her body was discovered in GOTHAM CITY's sewer system. Batman investigated and found evidence pointing to HARVEY DENT as the killer. The Dark Knight assigned JASON BARD to investigate further, suspecting Dent was being framed. Bard interviewed Balin's husband, Terry, who was frantic since his wife had been gone for a week. Capshaw was then shot and killed by the TALLY MAN in his effort to tie up loose ends. Batman learned that while he himself had been away from Gotham for a year, Orca had allied herself with the PENGUIN along with several other costumed criminals. They had all been bribed by the GREAT WHITE SHARK to turn on the Penguin, until Dent learned of it; he convinced them to stay in place and feed him information on the Penguin's operations. In the end, though, Orca, along with KGBEAST, MAGPIE, and the VENTRILOQUIST, were all killed by order of the Great White Shark, who was out to usurp Gotham's underworld in the days after BLACK MASK's death. (*Detective Comics* #817, September 2006)

ORPHEUS

Gavin King was the son of a GOTHAM CITY television sports producer and a former professional dancer who both encouraged their boy to pursue his dreams. Their only caveat was that Gavin complete his higher education so he had the most options. At first he wanted to follow in his mother's footsteps as a dancer and singer, but those aspirations made him the target of ridicule by his school peers. He opted to augment those skills by learning martial arts, at which he proved quite proficient. By Gavin's later teen years, he was a good enough dancer that he was invited to tour the world with a troupe. Seeing the squalid conditions of the masses in country after country transformed King's goals: He wanted to help.

An unnamed secret operation recruited the dancer to train and become an agent, able to help make the world a better place. King accepted and began the transformation that turned him into the costumed crime fighter known as Orpheus. (*Batman: Orpheus Rising*, October, 2001)

King settled back home and created a double life as both an entertainment producer and Orpheus. While he made a positive impact on Gotham's streets, he did not win favor from Batman, who disliked vigilantes operating in his city. King didn't back down or leave, which earned him some respect, and eventually he became a factor in Batman's plans for the city.

When STEPHANIE BROWN was fired by Batman for disobeying his orders during her probationary period as the fourth ROBIN, she wanted to prove her worth by activating one of the Dark Knight's WAR GAMES scenarios. The plan was designed to unite all of the city's criminal elements under one master, MATCHES MALONE, secretly Batman—a fact Brown did not know. As the scenario unraveled, Orpheus was to play a key role, with Batman going so far as to recruit ONYX to watch his back.

Without Malone's involvement, things rapidly spiraled out of control, and a vicious gang war broke out. As Brown approached Orpheus to explain his role, they were surprised by the sudden appearance of BLACK MASK, long thought dead, who chose to take advantage of the chaos. He attacked Orpheus from behind, cutting his throat before the hero could react, killing him.

The organization that had created Orpheus was never heard from again.

ORTEGA, OLIVIA

Olivia Ortega was a longtime GOTHAM CITY television journalist who repeatedly covered stories that involved Batman and ROBIN. The Dynamic Duo and Ortega encountered each other repeatedly, although they never had any sort of relationship. (*Detective Comics* #504, July 1981)

OSTINE, PETER

A man better known to Batman and GOTHAM CITY police as the UNDERTAKER.

OUTLAW TOWN

The town of SILVER VEIN was taken over by gangsters who renamed it Outlaw Town until Batman arrived.

OUTSIDER, THE

ALFRED PENNYWORTH proved a loyal manservant and friend to BRUCE WAYNE to the very end. To save the lives of the Earth-1 Batman and ROBIN, Alfred arrived on a motorcycle, shoving the Dynamic Duo out of the path of a falling boulder. In his memory, Wayne started the ALFRED MEMORIAL FOUNDATION. (*Detective Comics* #328, June 1964)

Soon after, Batman began to encounter a white-skinned bald man who made threats against him and the Boy Wonder. Following his promises of doom, the Outsider sent underlings such as the GRASSHOPPERS (*Detective Comics* #334, December 1964), a witch (#336, February 1965) and the BLOCKBUSTER (#349, March 1966) to attack them. Each attack was dangerous and provided no clues as to who the Outsider was or why he showed such enmity for them.

Finally Batman learned the truth: The Outsider was a resurrected Alfred. BRANDON CRAWFORD, described as a scientific genius, had found Alfred's body in a refrigerated mausoleum. Crawford chose to use the body for a radical experiment that, if successful, would bring him back to life. The body was subjected to the test and began to breathe once more, but it left the mind twisted; as much as Alfred had once loved Batman and Robin, he now detested them. He no longer felt human, Alfred told Crawford, and so he took the name *Outsider*. (*Detective Comics* #356, October 1966)

The Outsider confronted the duo in person. During the battle, Batman maneuvered his opponent into active emissions from the regeneration machine. This time Alfred was restored to the body and personality he'd had before his death, with no recollection of being a villain. Batman chose to keep the shocking news from his faithful friend. He also renamed the Alfred Foundation the WAYNE FOUNDATION.

However, one final scheme was still ticking, awaiting activation. Subconsciously, Alfred knew it was approaching, so while he was asleep he left clues to warn Batman. At the Gotham Founder's Day parade, the Dynamic Duo managed to avoid the death trap. (*Detective Comics* #364, June 1967)

Years later Alfred suffered a blow to the head, and once more the Outsider persona asserted itself. Now using the alter ego Mister O, he again found agents to attack Batman's partners, Robin and BATGIRL. The crime fighters contended with Snafu and the Sunset Gang before confronting Mister O himself. (*Batman Family* #11–12, May/June 1977–July/August 1977) A weapon the Outsider intended to use went off prematurely and split the body into two separate ones—Alfred and the

Outsider. Alfred literally fought himself to the death, with the Outsider tumbling off a bridge to a watery grave. (*Batman Family* #13, September/October 1977)

The genius criminal Ira Quimby, aka I.Q., learned of the Outsider and sought out Alfred as part of a plan for revenge against Batman, his OUTSIDERS team, and SUPERMAN. The Man of Steel's calming influence enabled Alfred to reassert control and mentally defeat his deadly persona. (*DC Comics Presents* #83, July 1985)

OUTSIDERS, THE

Batman had been chafing against the international laws and politics that prevented the JUSTICE LEAGUE OF AMERICA from intervening whenever justice was demanded. Things came to a head when WAYNE ENTERPRISES' CEO LUCIUS FOX was held captive in the European nation of MARKOVIA by Baron Bedlam during a coup. The United Nations ordered the JLA to stay out of the political situation, so Batman quit and went after his trusted friend. Along the way, he encountered peers METAMORPHO and BLACK LIGHTNING in addition to newcomers GEO-FORCE, KATANA, and HALO. They banded together to free Fox; Bedlam was defeated and the throne restored to the Markov family. (*The Brave and the Bold* #200, October 1983)

Batman saw potential in these people and offered to help train them to be more effective. The Outsiders were born. He relocated them all to GOTHAM CITY and installed Halo and Katana in the penthouse apartment atop the WAYNE FOUNDATION building. In between training sessions, the Outsiders took on a series of new threats, including the

Fearsome Five, the Cryonic Man, the Force of July and Masters of Disaster. Later, LOOKER and Windfall joined the team.

When Batman withheld the intelligence that Baron Bedlam had again threatened Markovia, the others were furious, and the team parted company with the Caped Crusader. The country was saved once more and gratefully agreed to fund the team from its new headquarters in Los Angeles. When Eclipso threatened the entire world, though, the Outsiders once more partnered with their founder. At mission's end, he allowed them to use a well-stocked facility dubbed BATCAVE WEST. (*Outsiders* #19, May 1987) Over the next few years, they underwent significant changes—adding and shedding members, disbanding and re-forming as circumstances dictated.

After the TEEN TITANS and YOUNG JUSTICE disbanded following a disastrous battle with an android from the future, GREEN ARROW's former partner Arsenal felt the need for a proactive strike force, one that could do the dirty work other teams refused to acknowledge. His first recruit was NIGHTWING, who would sign on only if the team was all-business, no-family, totally unlike their experiences with the Titans. Arsenal agreed, and a new Outsiders was born, with the reprogrammed android Indigo, Black Lightning's daughter Thunder, the first GREEN LANTERN's daughter Jade, a piece of Metamorpho using the name *Shift,* and meta-human bar bouncer Grace as the founding members. The team functioned for a time as described, adding other members including Nightwing's former lover STARFIRE, original Outsider Katana, and even, briefly, HUNTRESS. (*Outsiders* [third series] #1, August 2003)

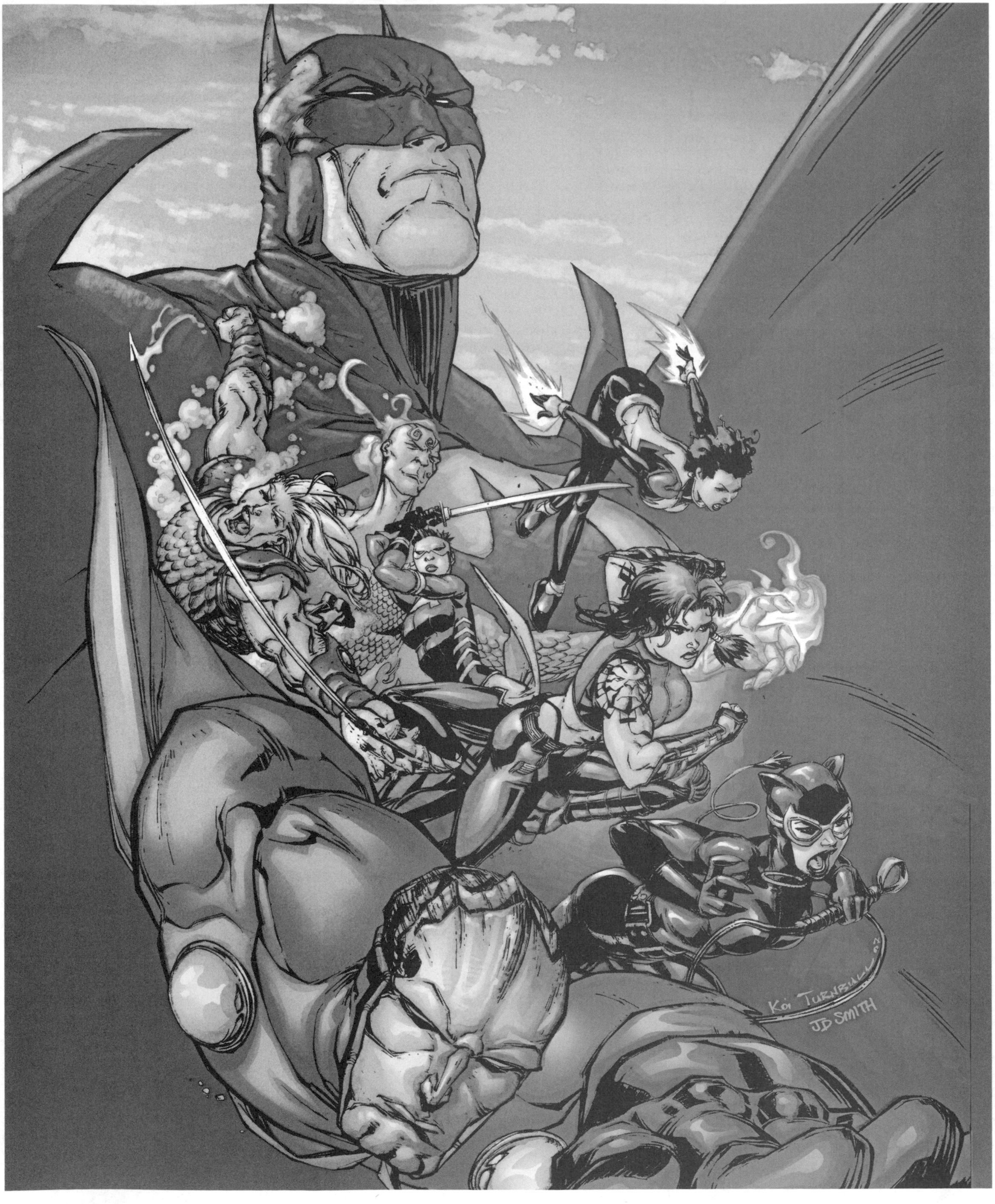
KAI TURNBULL
JD SMITH

In the wake of the Freedom of Power Treaty being signed, prohibiting meta-human activities in certain areas, the team remained largely covert. They briefly had the world thinking they were dead, but eventually they were revealed. After a disastrous mission alongside CHECKMATE, the teams needed Batman's assistance to extricate themselves from North Korea. Nightwing told his mentor that a team all about business was not one he felt comfortable leading. Instead, he suggested the Dark Knight take control. Batman, foreseeing dark times ahead and needing a strike force, agreed to handpick a new Outsiders team. (*Outsiders* [third series] #49, September 2007)

Even existing members had to demonstrate their abilities to convince the Dark Knight they should be a part of the new force. With help from other heroes, Batman studied how each candidate handled situations. Katana was his first recruit, followed in short order by MARTIAN MANHUNTER, CATWOMAN, Grace, and Metamorpho. (*Batman and the Outsiders* [second series] #1, December 2007)

Batman altered his lineup with regularity soon after the first mission under his command. Catwoman and the Martian Manhunter left, while BATGIRL and GREEN ARROW were recruited.

OVERDOG, BOB

Bob Overdog was one more garden-variety drug addict in GOTHAM CITY, except that he was the first to witness the arrival of the magical imp BAT-MITE in the world formed after the CRISIS ON INFINITE EARTHS. (*Legends of the Dark Knight* #38, October 1992) Overdog also once spotted MR. MXYZPTLK, confusing this troublemaker from the FIFTH DIMENSION with Bat-Mite. Batman theorized that Mxyzptlk conjured up Bat-Mite based on Overdog's hallucinations. (*Batman & Superman: World's Finest* #6, September 1999)

OWLMAN

ROBIN was accidentally exposed to gases from outer space that transformed him into an adult on Earth-2. He took on a new costumed identity, calling himself Owlman. (*Batman* #107, April 1957)

On Earth-3 the roles of heroes and villains were reversed, with Owlman being the brilliant mind behind the Crime Syndicate of America. He was a crime lord in GOTHAM CITY, aided by his youthful sidekick Talon. It was his intellect that directed his teammates to invade Earth-1, trumping the JUSTICE LEAGUE OF AMERICA. It took the additional presence of Earth-2's JUSTICE SOCIETY OF AMERICA to finally defeat the CSA. They were imprisoned in a stasis bubble formed by the twin Earths' GREEN LANTERNS, placed between the universes with warning signs in countless languages. (*Justice League of America* #29–30, August–September 1964)

In the reality after the CRISIS ON INFINITE EARTHS, the CSA existed on the sole anti-matter universe's Earth. Owlman's origin dated to the death of young BRUCE WAYNE and his mother, MARTHA. Thomas Jr.,

Bruce's brother, refused to accompany a policeman for interrogation, instead fleeing the scene with his idol, gangster JOE CHILL. He wanted to excel at crime and took the persona of Owlman, complete with gear that was as effective at *committing* crimes as Batman's UTILITY BELT was in helping the Dark Knight to *prevent* them. Owlman allied himself with the criminal "Boss" Gordon and was opposed by Police Commissioner THOMAS WAYNE SR. Unlike the rest of the political world in Gotham City, the commissioner and his selected men were untouchable cops. Owlman continued to blame his father for the death of his mother and brother and took every opportunity to humiliate the Gotham police. He had a cruel streak that was demonstrated in the ways he committed crimes as well as by his engaging in a long-term affair with Superwoman, despite her marriage to Ultraman. Unlike Batman, Owlman seemed to possess some level of mental control over others, although its exact nature was never revealed. (*JLA: Earth-2*, 1999)

In the wake of INFINITE CRISIS, the multiverse was reborn, and Owlman and his CSA cronies were seen once more on one of the fifty-two parallel worlds. (*52* #52, 2007)

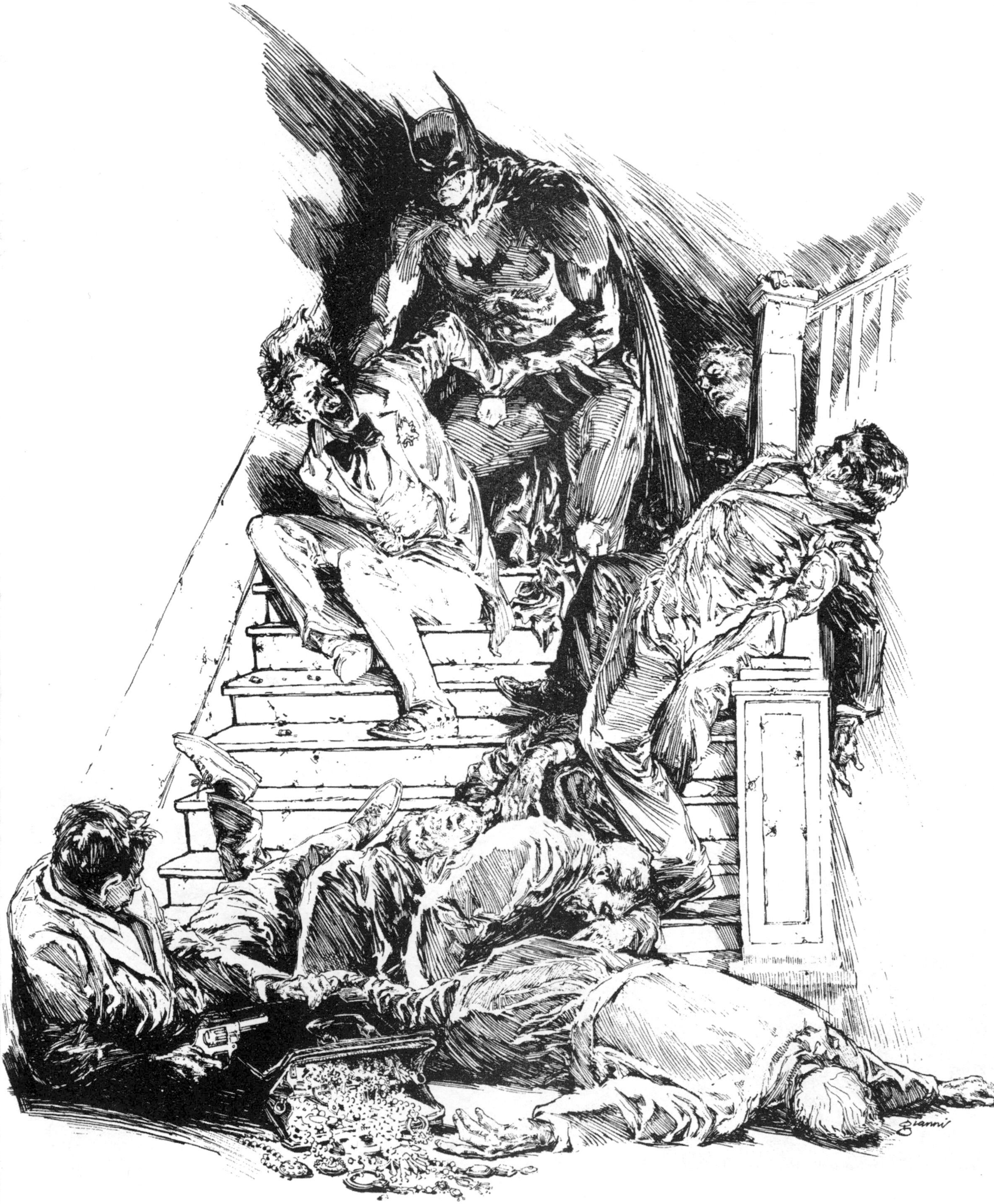

PAGAN

Marian Mercer was enraged when her sister Sondra was gang-raped and murdered in GOTHAM CITY. Marian took the name Pagan and dedicated herself to revenge against those involved in a crime the Gotham police could not solve. She set out to locate the men involved and, in so doing, became the protector of those innocents who were prey to sexual predators. When one man was found dead, Batman became involved in the investigation and tracked Mercer down. He found her with another member of the gang, torturing him before killing him. The Dark Knight stopped her and apprehended both Pagan and the surviving men involved in Sondra's death. (*Batman* #479, early June 1992)

PAGE, LINDA

On Earth-2, BRUCE WAYNE and Linda Page knew each other for some time before he began his

crime-fighting career as Batman. As he got more involved in his new vocation, he and Page stopped seeing each other at social functions. Her father, TOM PAGE, was a successful oilman based in Texas, while she enjoyed high-society life back East. Later Bruce and Linda met again after his engagement to JULIE MADISON ended; they dated throughout the 1940s. Wayne took life seriously as Batman, and Page gave up her society ways to become a nurse. (*Batman* #5, Spring 1941)

Whatever romantic relationship potential that existed was dashed, however, when Page thought Wayne had betrayed her to squire a woman named Elva Barr. What she couldn't know was that Barr was actually the CATWOMAN and Wayne was romancing her in his campaign to help her reform her criminal ways. (*Batman* #15, February/March 1943)

Despite the romance ending, Bruce and Linda remained friends as he attempted to protect her from the SCARECROW when that criminal struck at a jewelry store and the millionaire could not change into his BATSUIT. (*Detective Comics* #73, March 1943)

PAGE, TOM

Father to nurse LINDA PAGE, Tom made his fortune drilling for oil in Texas and was the majority owner of Page Oil Company. Batman and ROBIN came to his aid when Page's unscrupulous partner, Graham Masters, tried to force Page into giving him total control over the oil company. (*Batman* #6, August/ September 1941)

PANDORA

Pandora was the name used by the woman who ran Pandora's Box, a bondage, domination, and sadomasochism club in GOTHAM CITY. When Batman and the RIDDLER competed to solve the case of a

murdered acquaintance of BRUCE WAYNE's named Karrie Bishop, the Prince of Puzzlers admitted that he usually recruited his female companions from this particular club. (*Detective Comics* #822, October 2006)

PAPAGAYO, EL

This South American was a notorious bandit, terrorizing people and keeping law enforcement at bay, until Batman arrived to train a counterpart. The wily villain used one of his men to win the coveted role of BAT-HOMBRE until he was exposed by the Caped Crusader.

PARAGON PICTURES

Paragon Pictures has been among the major movie studios since the foundation of the motion picture industry. (*Batman* #130, March 1960) One of their biggest and longest-lasting stars was Jonathan Lord, beginning with 1935's *PERIL IN POMPEII*. (*Silverblade* #5, January 1988) More recent movies from the studio include *Armageddon Man* (*Legends of the Dark Knight Annual* #5, 1995), *Lethal Honey III*, and *They Lurk Below*. (*Catwoman* [second series] #20–21, April–May 1995) At one point studio exec Barry Zedmore actually negotiated with the JOKER for the rights to a movie. (*Detective Comics* #669, 671–673, December 1993, February–April 1994) Paragon was the site of a brawl between GREEN LANTERN and Prince Peril. (*Green Lantern* #45, June 1966) The company also produced a successful series of films based on the children's character CROCKY.

PARDU

Pardu was a stage magician who tried to convince Batman he had pierced the secret of his masked identity. To remain quiet, the performer asked for ten thousand dollars, but the Caped Crusader determined that the man was bluffing. He had the GOTHAM CITY police arrest him for blackmail. (*Batman* #99, April 1956)

PARK ROW

Park Row was once a fashionable section of GOTHAM CITY, although over the last few decades it began to deteriorate and became a haven for the homeless and criminals. It was on this street that THOMAS and MARTHA WAYNE were gunned down, leaving their son BRUCE an orphan. It was since known as CRIME ALLEY and was visited once a year by the adult Batman, who left a single rose in memory of his parents. (*Detective Comics* #463, September 1976)

PARSONS, PHILIP

GOTHAM CITY martial arts instructor Philip Parsons, using the name DRAGONCAT, taught young BARBARA GORDON and later DICK GRAYSON.

PATCHES

Patches was a member of GOTHAM CITY'S STREET DEMONZ gang. He gave grief to newly arrived police detective MACKENZIE BOCK. (*Batman: Shadow of the Bat* #36, March 1995)

PATTON, NATE

A detective in GOTHAM CITY'S MAJOR CRIMES UNIT, he was partnered with ROMY CHANDLER and was tolerated despite his abrasive behavior. (*Gotham Central* #1, Early February 2003) He kept his crush on Chandler a private matter and was considered a good cop despite his frequently saying the wrong thing to people. One harsh winter he was mortally injured when he rescued a television journalist from one of the JOKER'S bombs. (*Gotham Central* #15, March 2004)

PAYNE, PRESTON

Suffering from a debilitating illness, Preston Payne attempted a cure that transformed him into a new CLAYFACE, whose very touch could dissolve organic matter.

PEALE, ED

The man who turned to crime to silence bells as the GONG.

PEARSON, ELWOOD

Elwood Pearson, a photographer, invented a unique camera whose advanced technology allowed images to be captured through solid objects. He called it his "X-camera" and used it to snap multiple pictures of Batman, ROBIN, and their quarry, a criminal known as Mister Incognito. He offered Batman and Incognito each pictures of the other unmasked by his special camera. For one million dollars, secrets would be revealed. Mister Incognito agreed to pay. Pearson and Incognito gazed at the visages of BRUCE WAYNE and DICK GRAYSON but recognized neither one and were soon after apprehended by the Dynamic Duo. (*Batman* #173, August 1965)

PEEL, MONROE

Monroe Peel discovered that Rudley Bates, a botanist who claimed to grow orchids, was actually producing vast amounts of penicillin for sale on the European black market. Peel killed Bates and took the drug stock to sell for his own profit, only to be arrested by Batman and ROBIN. (*Detective Comics* #177, November 1951)

PENGUIN, THE

OSWALD CHESTERFIELD COBBLEPOT was a short, overweight man with a sharp, pointy nose. He was ridiculed for his size and shape throughout his life, angering him and directing him toward a life of crime. He used his shape to style himself a human penguin, adopting a tuxedo and top-hatted outfit complete with monocle. His early criminal career was a ruthless and violent one before he settled down to become one of GOTHAM CITY'S most unusual criminals. He augmented his persona with both a love for birds of all kinds and the use of a series of umbrellas, each concealing tools to aid his criminal career—everything from flamethrowers to poison gas was contained in his custom-designed equipment. (*Detective Comics* #58, December 1941)

Often the Penguin used his posh look to establish himself in legitimate businesses, each of which proved to be a front for criminal activity. By operating in Gotham, he frequently encountered Batman and ROBIN, usually losing to them and winding up in jail, although each experience seemed to sharpen the level of his planning, making him a more formidable foe.

His early years have been recounted in different ways; one account described his mother as operating a pet shop, with Cobblepot turning to a life of crime after neighborhood hoodlums killed every animal in the store. Another tale had his father die while Cobblepot was young, a victim of bronchial pneumonia when he was caught in the rain without an umbrella. His mother made Cobblepot carry an umbrella at all times, rain or shine, exacerbating the ridicule he received for his shape. One of the boys in the neighborhood, Sharky, took to calling him "Penguin"—and the name stuck, although he hated it. Oswald took boxing lessons and then savagely beat Sharky—who also killed the pets in the family store—to shut him up.

Cobblepot managed to attend college and major in ornithology, thanks to his aunt. The rancor he felt never dissipated, though, so rather than use his degree he began a life of crime. His first robbery was that of a rare Prussian egret, which he stole from a Gotham penthouse. This set the tone for many of his crimes, giving him a trademark that acted as a beacon for Batman.

In more recent years he stopped actively committing crimes and turned himself into an information and resource broker, skimming off a percentage from those whom he supplied with help. He opened up the ICEBERG LOUNGE, quickly a popular Gotham nightspot, although he continued his criminal enterprises from a series of back rooms. Batman—too often, if you asked the Penguin—would barge in expecting information gratis and physically threatening the Bird of Banditry. They formed a complex relationship, because the Penguin frequently doled out information designed to help himself as much as possible. As a result, when the city was abandoned by the federal government, the Penguin was well poised to take advantage of the yearlong NO MAN'S LAND time. He bartered for everyday household items, maintaining a stock of material for himself and keeping up a brisk trade as resources dwindled.

The nightspot had been seriously damaged in the earthquake that precipitated the government pullout. After he cut deals with Lex Luthor to put things in motion for the city to be rebuilt, the Penguin made certain his club got only the finest materials.

Soon after Gotham was readmitted to America, a vicious gang war broke out that allowed BLACK MASK to ruthlessly gain control of the underworld. One result was the Penguin being forced out of the city. He set up new operations in BLÜDHAVEN. (*Robin* [second series] #133, February 2005) In the wake of Black Mask's death, the Penguin returned to Gotham and oversaw the rebuilding of his club. The reopened lounge added hidden illegal gambling rooms, and the Penguin made a fortune selling branded merchandise, including T-shirts.

He hired a number of fellow criminals—ORCA, VENTRILOQUIST, KGBEAST, and MAGPIE—to serve him. When the GREAT WHITE SHARK tried to co-opt them to his side, HARVEY DENT, protecting Gotham while Batman was away for a year, convinced them to stay loyal to the Man of 1,000 Umbrellas while also feeding Dent information. The Shark had them all

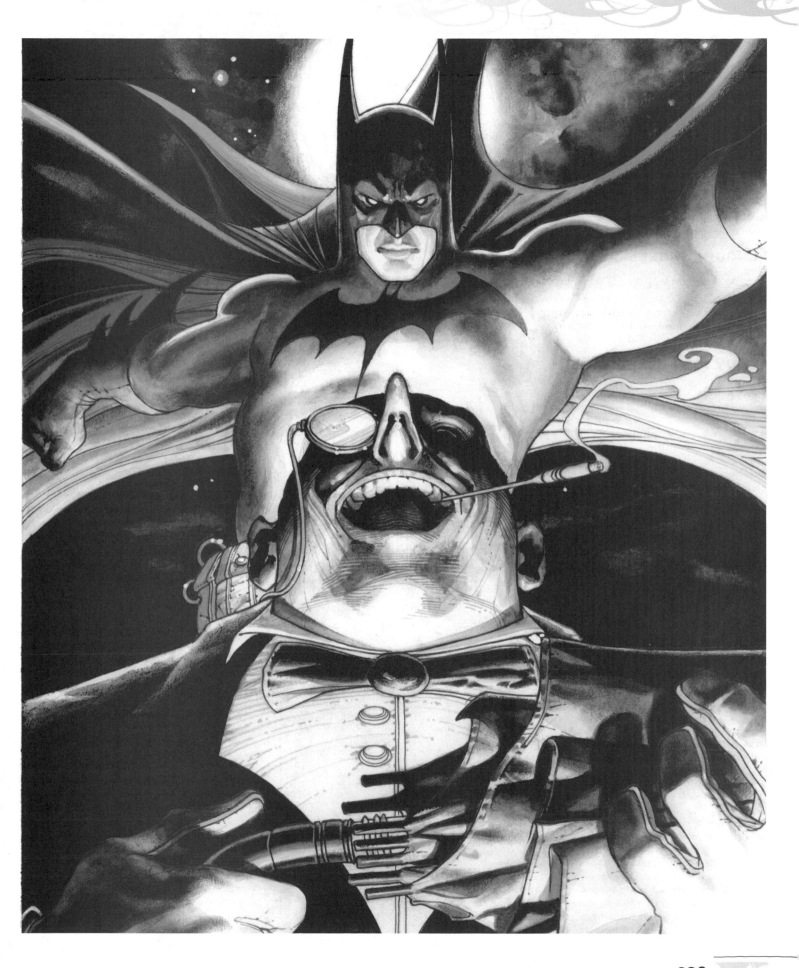

killed and framed Dent, putting the Penguin on notice that there was a new criminal kingpin in Gotham. (*Detective Comics* #817, September 2006)

PENGUIN AND BUZZARD BIRD STORE

Briefly, the Penguin and Buzzard Bird Store was a front for the criminal activities of the PENGUIN when he was briefly partnered with a man known as Mr. Buzzard. (*Batman* #41, June/July 1947)

PENGUIN MANOR

The Penguin Manor was actually a GOTHAM CITY penthouse, which the PENGUIN used twice as his base of operations. (*Batman* #17, June/July 1943)

PENGUIN UMBRELLAS, INC.

At one point in his career, the PENGUIN went into business manufacturing bumbershoots under the name *Penguin Umbrellas*. The factory also served as the fabricator of the unique umbrellas the Buccaneer of Birds used for his criminal activities. (*Batman* #70, April/May 1952)

PENNY PLUNDERER, THE

On Earth-2, GOTHAM CITY criminal JOE COYNE was always a penny-ante crook, starting when he sold newspapers for a penny and then stole pennies from the distributor. As a result, many of his crimes involved pennies. When Batman apprehended him after a string of offenses, the Caped Crusader added a giant Lincoln penny to the BATCAVE's trophy collection. (*World's Finest Comics* #30, September/October 1947)

On the world formed after CRISIS ON INFINITE EARTHS, Coyne was just another Gotham criminal to be caught by the Gotham Guardian. He paid for his crimes: He was sentenced to death by electrocution. (*Batman Chronicles* #19, Winter 2000) The giant penny was said to have been used by TWO-FACE to try to crush the Dark Knight to death; the crime fighter kept it as a souvenir. After the Gotham earthquake, Batman asked AQUAMAN to help him recover it from the bottom of the river running through the cavern. (*Batman: Gotham Knights* #18, August 2001)

PENNYWORTH, ALFRED

ALFRED BEAGLE was a portly gentleman's gentleman who forsook an acting career to serve Earth-2's BRUCE WAYNE and DICK GRAYSON. He did this to honor a promise he'd made to his father, Jarvis, who lay on his deathbed in England after having served the WAYNE FAMILY years earlier. Early on, the two tried to keep their secret identities of Batman and ROBIN from their butler, but he accidentally discovered their secret and happily joined their efforts. (*Batman* #16, April/May 1943)

Later, to better aid them in their crusade against crime, he went away to a health resort, lost weight, grew a mustache, and reported back for duty. (*Detective Comics* #83, January 1944)

In addition to maintaining WAYNE MANOR and the BATCAVE, Alfred indulged in sleuthing on his own with mixed results. (*Batman* #22, April/May 1944)

The first time he posed as Batman at Bruce Wayne's request was when Bruce and Batman were required to appear side by side in a TV tribute to the Dark Knight. (*Batman* #87, October, 1954) After that ruse worked successfully, Alfred was repeatedly called on to help out.

He remained with Bruce Wayne thorough the years, retiring and leaving the manor only after Batman died and his daughter, HELENA WAYNE, closed the mansion. Alfred then returned to his first love by managing the New Stratford Repertory Theatre. (*Wonder Woman* #294, August 1982) As needed, he returned to assist Dick Grayson. (*Infinity, Inc.* #9, December 1984)

On Earth-1, Alfred Thaddeus Crane Pennyworth came to work for Bruce Wayne by responding to a classified ad. He learned that his employer was Batman only after Dick Grayson had summoned him to help tend to a wounded Batman in the Batcave. (*Batman* #110, September 1957) After discovering the secret, Alfred swore to assist them whenever possible and became a trusted and loyal friend. That loyalty led to the ultimate sacrifice when he arrived in time to push the Dynamic Duo away from a falling boulder, which crushed him to

death. (*Detective Comics* #328, June 1964) It was subsequently learned that a scientist had managed to resurrect him with an experimental device that turned him into the villainous OUTSIDER; Batman helped restore him.

Pennyworth came from a well-established family; his brother WILFRED was an actor, as was his niece DAPHNE. But it wasn't until years later that he came into contact with his daughter, JULIA.

During World War II, Pennyworth, as well as LUCIUS FOX, had served alongside the French freedom fighter Mademoiselle Marie. Pennyworth was an officer with British intelligence when they met and subsequently had an affair, leading to the birth of Julia.

Marie was soon after murdered and Jacques Remarque raised Julia as his own, giving her his surname. When she was two, Remarque got in touch with Alfred and informed him of her existence. Ever after, Alfred sent money to help support her, in exchange for keeping the child unaware of her past. (*Detective Comics* #501, April 1981)

When Jacques Remarque was killed, Julia came to the United States, and he was subsequently avenged. She was reunited with her natural father and came to live in Wayne Manor, working for VICKI VALE at *PICTURE MAGAZINE*. (*Batman* #370, April 1984)

In the world formed after the CRISIS ON INFINITE EARTHS, Alfred Pennyworth never served in World War II or fathered a daughter. Instead, Alfred was

the Wayne Family butler when THOMAS and MARTHA WAYNE were killed, caring for Bruce in the aftermath of their deaths. (*Batman* #404, February 1987)

The Pennyworths had a long history in the service of the Wayne Family, including Jarvis Pennyworth working for Thomas and his father, Patrick. Jarvis's own father had been the Wayne retainer before him. Jarvis intended for his youngest son, Alfred, to follow in his tradition, but the young man had other ambitions. (*Batman Annual* #13, 1989)

Growing up, Wilfred, Alfred, and their unnamed mother spent much of each year in their native England, where the boys received a traditional British education. Alfred graduated third in his class, although his main interest in school was stage acting, just like Wilfred. (*Batman* #0, October 1994) Father and sons were reunited for regular vacations, and it was during their summer hunting outings in Essex that Alfred became adept at handling firearms. (*Batman Secret Files* #1, 1997)

When Wilfred established himself on the British stage, his mother followed him back to her native country to indulge in acting as well. (*Batman* #216, November 1969) Alfred went on to serve in the British Secret Service (*Batman* #599, March 2002) and the military as a medic, where he enhanced his weaponry skills and received extensive medical training. Alfred then followed his mother's and brother's career choice. (*Batman Annual* #13, 1989)

It was at this time that Alfred fell in love with a fellow actor, Joanna Clark. The plans for their wedding fell apart, however, when he learned that she'd been having an affair with a cad named Jonny Forsythe. Alfred struck Forsythe and stormed out of the church. (*Nightwing: Alfred's Return,* 1995) Soon after, Jarvis grew terminally ill; on his deathbed, he asked Alfred to take his place as manservant to the Waynes. (*Batman Chronicles* #5, Summer 1996) His mother was on the road when Jarvis died, and she missed the funeral. He was angry at his father for asking him to give up his passion, and also at his romantic betrayal, so on the night before he traveled to America, he got drunk for the first time in his life. (*Nightwing: Alfred's Return,* 1995)

He presented his credentials to Thomas Wayne, who happily accepted him into the manor. Alfred lasted all of a week before resigning, expressing his unhappiness. As he tried to explain himself to the Waynes, their son Bruce turned up, sporting a black eye and covered in bruises, refusing to explain what happened. He was sent to his room. That night Alfred turned up with dinner and discreetly produced a copy of *Zorro*, which he'd found in the library. Knowing that Thomas disapproved of such popular literature, he suspected it belonged to the boy. Their shared passion for the masked rider cemented a bond between them and helped convince Alfred to stay with the family after all. (*Batman Chronicles* #5, Summer 1996)

On the night the Waynes were murdered, it was Dr. LESLIE THOMPKINS, whom Alfred had met only a short time earlier, who first found Bruce and told Alfred what had happened. (*Batman: Gotham Knights* #7, September 1997) Alfred and Leslie cared for the youth. When they learned that the state intended to step in, Bruce helped bury the bureaucracy in paperwork until he got lost in the system. He remained in the manor. (*Batman* #0, October 1994)

After Bruce left to travel around the world, training to become Batman, Alfred cared for the manor and grew closer to Thompkins; the two had an affair. (*Batman: Gotham Knights* #7, September 1997) Alfred was fully prepared to resign and finally pursue the stage upon Bruce's return home. That return, however, was accompanied by a trail of blood. The butler found an injured Bruce, who had been attempting to employ his lessons as the Batman for the first time. (*Batman Annual* #13, 1989)

Alfred felt he could not leave Bruce as he was beginning a new life. He used his own experience to help refine Bruce's knowledge of makeup and disguise, giving him tips on how to make certain the general public differentiated Bruce Wayne from Batman. Since then, Alfred has remained loyal to Bruce Wayne and watched over him during the ordeals he experienced as Batman.

He saw it as a positive step when Bruce took in Dick Grayson, and Alfred enjoyed a warm bond with the boy that deepened through the years.

After Dick left for college, Alfred saw how being a loner changed his master, making him a brooding, solitary figure. He responded positively when JASON TODD replaced Dick as Robin, and mourned Todd's later death. He was among those who felt Batman needed a Robin and was delighted when TIM DRAKE forced his way into Batman's life.

Alfred and Bruce saw the world in different ways, and there were times this caused a strain between them. As a result, Alfred left Bruce to his own devices on several occasions, including the aftermath of BANE's savage attack that left Bruce crippled. It took NIGHTWING traveling to England to coax him back home. Another time, Bruce dispatched a frustrated Alfred to serve Tim as the teen adjusted to life at the BRENTWOOD ACADEMY. (*Robin* #87, April 2001)

When GOTHAM CITY became a virtual NO MAN'S LAND, Batman had vanished for three months, angering everyone around him—including Alfred, who left the ruined Wayne Manor and journeyed among the citizens remaining in Gotham. He used all his theatrical skills and butlering experience to monitor conditions and gather information. (*Legends of the Dark Knight* #117, May 1999) At a later point, he admitted that as Bruce Wayne's butler he had been kidnapped twenty-seven times and survived each encounter. (*Batman: Gotham Knights* #16, June 1998)

Alfred bred a rose known as a Pennyworth Blue, one of the rarest roses in the world. (*Batman* #664, May 2007)

PENNYWORTH, DAPHNE

On Earth-1, Batman came to the aid of a woman in distress who turned out to be Daphne Pennyworth, newly arrived in GOTHAM CITY to visit her uncle ALFRED PENNYWORTH. She and her father, WILFRED, were in town with the Old Avon Players.

Initially Alfred was miffed to learn that he had family in town with no one calling to alert him in advance. His mood lightened when Batman brought Daphne to WAYNE MANOR. Even more delighted was DICK GRAYSON, bedridden with a cold, who was smitten with the actress. Alfred gave her a tour through BRUCE WAYNE's library, showing off Shakespeare memorabilia, culminating with the original manuscript of *Romeo and Juliet*.

The following Saturday when Bruce, Dick, and Alfred were watching Daphne play Juliet, the manor was robbed of the famous folio. During the intermission, Daphne hastened back to the manor, disabled the security system, and opened the safe from memory, only to have her theft discovered by her uncle. Alfred, a keen observer of people, had suspected she was up to something and followed her.

He learned that Wilfred was being held hostage by her boyfriend Kevin and his cohorts, extorting her to help rob the rich Wayne. Both Batman and Alfred came to Wilfred's rescue as Dick prevented "Juliet" from committing suicide with a real knife, which Kevin substituted for a prop. (*Batman* #216, November 1969)

Daphne next turned up in Batman's life as the tutor to children at Gothos Mansion; Alfred explained that she took the work after her acting offers had dried up. Alfred was somewhat concerned for his niece, so Batman paid a visit to the remote home—only to find Daphne about to be scarified by Elder Heathrow and his Coven of Gothos Mansion in the hope of raising the demon Ballk. Batman spoiled their plans, possibly helped by the spirit of the woman who had been in Daphne's position two centuries earlier. (*Batman* #227, December 1970)

PENNYWORTH, JULIA

ALFRED PENNYWORTH served British intelligence during World War II on Earth-1, where he encountered France's Mademoiselle Marie. On August 24, 1944, the eve of Paris's liberation from Nazi occupation, Marie was said to have been shot by an unknown party, surviving only long enough to give birth. (*Detective Comics* #501, April 1981)

Years later Alfred Pennyworth and LUCIUS FOX were mysteriously asked to come to France. Batman surreptitiously followed his friends, fearing for their safety. The Suerte's Inspector Dupre told the Dark Knight why the men had come to Paris. He then went to the Hotel Vendome, where he first encountered Julia Remarque, who suspected that one of the two men had killed her mother.

A rural French family, Gizelle and Paulette Revel, revealed that they had rescued the wounded, delirious Marie from the St. Joan River in 1944 and tended to her needs over the next few months. All the freedom fighter was heard to say was "Alfred." In January 1945, they delivered the young woman's baby girl. Marie subsequently vanished and, within three weeks, the body of a disfigured woman was pulled from the river. Marie was presumed dead, and the mysterious Alfred was regarded as her killer. Meanwhile, Marie's daughter was raised by another former Resistance fighter, Jacques Remarque.

Investigation on Batman's part showed that the corpse found years before had not been that of the famed Marie. It was determined, though, that Marie had been shot by one of her underground compatriots, a Nazi collaborator named Roget. When a surviving member of the family that cared for Marie suddenly was shot, Batman realized Roget had survived by undergoing plastic surgery and assuming the identity of Dupre.

In the aftermath it was clear that Alfred was not the man who shot Marie, but instead the man who loved her and fathered Julia. She finally learned that Jacques Remarque took the baby into his care and after two years contacted Alfred with the news of his daughter. Alfred, in turn, sent money to care for her, but made Remarque promise not to reveal anything about her past.

Father and daughter slowly began to get to know each other as she settled in at WAYNE MANOR. Together they investigated the mysterious death of her adoptive father, a journey that led them from GOTHAM CITY to Montreal, where they learned Remarque had been recovering stolen Nazi treasures and was killed before finding a large hoard. When they were targeted by DEADSHOT, Alfred recognized that they were in mortal danger and summoned the Batman. After beating Deadshot, they trailed him to the terrorists who hired him and had also killed Remarque. (*Detective Comics* #536, March 1984)

Julia's arrival at Wayne Manor was warmly welcomed by BRUCE WAYNE and Alfred, but JASON TODD, the second ROBIN, was uncomfortable with her, and VICKI VALE was downright jealous of a woman she saw as a rival for Wayne's affections. Intending to find employment, Julia prevailed upon a cool Vale for help at *PICTURE MAGAZINE*. Still uncomfortable, Vale agreed to hire her as a file clerk. (*Batman* #375, September 1984) Interestingly, whereas Vale saw a rival, Julia had absolutely no interest in Wayne, whom she thought of as distant and remote, totally unaware of his life as Batman. When the women were rescued from MISTER FREEZE by the Dark Knight, Julia found him far more interesting, and her appreciative kiss was captured by Vale for page one.

Vale and Remarque reached an accommodation, with the veteran journalist upgrading the rookie to personal assistant, encouraging her writing. Despite being snubbed by television reporter OLIVIA ORTEGA, Remarque persevered and began winning accolades for her writing. She was assigned to cover the custody hearing that pitted Bruce Wayne against Natalia Knight, aka NOCTURNA. (*Batman* #379, January 1985)

During this time, Remarque reconsidered Wayne and found herself becoming the rival she'd promised Vale she would not be. Vale, instead, gave up on Wayne. Remarque changed her name to Pennyworth. (*Batman* #384, June 1985)

While her romance with Wayne went nowhere—he was too busy being Batman—she found herself often in the Caped Crusader's company as he rescued her from the FILM FREAK, and then from the SCARECROW after RĂ'S AL GHŪL broke numerous villains free from BLACKGATE PENITENTIARY. (*Batman* #400, October 1986)

In the world created in the wake of CRISIS ON INFINITE EARTHS, Julia Remarque was a writer known for her quickie biography of the criminal BLACK MASK. (*Batman Annual* #13, 1989)

PENNYWORTH, WILFRED

Wilfred Pennyworth was the older brother of BRUCE WAYNE's manservant ALFRED. He was a stage performer with the Avon Players along with his daughter DAPHNE PENNYWORTH. When he was kidnapped by criminals, Daphne had to rob a valuable Shakespeare manuscript from WAYNE MANOR. Batman intervened. (*Batman* #216, November 1969)

PERALDA, LUIS

Luis Peralda was a member of EL PAPAGAYO's criminal band and passed the rigorous tests to earn the right to be trained by Batman as a law enforcement officer in his native country. As BAT-HOMBRE, he exceeded expectations—only to betray the Caped Crusader.

PERUN

An enforcer for GOTHAM CITY's Russian mobs, Perun claimed that in Moskva he had been thought dead three times. Perun first encountered Batman when he came to Dr. AMINA FRANKLIN, expecting her to pay her brother WAYNE FRANKLIN's debt. He had seemingly died two months previous, taking with him the I-Gore device that the Russian mob had helped to finance. Lured to the Gotham Opera House, Perun fought the Yakuza's Johnny Karaoke to the death in an attempt to gain control over the technology both helped fund. (*Batman* #659–652, February–March 2007)

PETERS, JUMPY

Jumpy Peters, Sailor Roggs, Angles Manson, and Careful Kyle were brought from around the country to testify at the trial of Boss Barry, their former gang leader. From the courtroom, the quartet staged a daring escape and became the object of an intense manhunt, including the participation of Batman and Robin. Roggs, Manson, and Kyle each died during their escape, fatefully in ways that matched their death sentences—asphyxiation, choking, and electrocution. The Dynamic Duo found Peters in a wooded area and returned him to Utah, where he was executed by firing squad. (*World's Finest Comics* #40, May/June 1949)

PETRI, NICK

Nick Petri was in possession of stolen loot. To protect it, he hid the property in a safe after learning that his accomplices were planning to double-cross him. The safe was located in an abandoned house, and Petri wired it to seven switches, one of which would unlock the safe; the other six would trigger explosive devices, destroying the safe, the house, and whoever threw the switch. One of the others, the Slasher, betrayed Benny the Gimp, the Nutcracker, and Lop-Ears McGoof into the hands of Gotham City's police. He then faked his own death to draw Petri out of hiding. The criminal fell for the ruse. Moments after Petri successfully opened the safe, Slasher and his men prepared to seize the loot until everyone was arrested by the timely arrival of Batman and Robin. (*Detective Comics* #97, March 1945)

PETTIT, WILLIAM "BILLY"

Sergeant William Pettit was a respected, if zealous, member of the Gotham City Police Department, rising to be placed in charge of its SWAT team. (*Man-Bat* #1, February 1996)

He was one of the officers to remain in Gotham City after the US government sealed it off from the rest of America. He worked alongside fellow officers, under Commissioner James Gordon's direction, securing their portion of the city and then protecting its citizens to the best of their ability. As the yearlong event wore on, Pettit grew increasingly disenchanted with Gordon's by-the-book approach to the lawless activities. He took a splinter group of officers with him and carved out a section of the city to protect, meting out a violent form of justice. (*Batman: Shadow of the Bat* #88, August 1999) His approach proved appealing to the Huntress, who worked alongside him for a time until he demonstrated a loosening grip on reality. When he shot one of his fellow officers, who was trying to depart, it was clear Pettit was no longer in control of himself. He was subsequently shot and killed by the Joker on Christmas Eve.

PHAETON

Despite being confined to a wheelchair, the criminal called Phaeton managed a successful gem-smuggling career allied with Stack Hawley. As Batman and Robin tracked the criminals, the Caped Crusader was blown from an exploding boat and struck his head on the bow. Delirious, he imagined that Phaeton was actually an undersea merman who'd had himself surgically altered to pass as a human. He still managed to bring Phaeton and Hawley to justice. As he recovered from the concussion, Batman continued to doubt whether or not his vision was correct. (*Batman* #53, June/July 1949)

PHANTOM, THE

Pol was accidentally transported from his home dimension to Earth by Carter Wede, a criminal scientist. Wede convinced the well-meaning alien that he lacked the resources to construct a device that could successfully return Pol home. Desirous of going back, Pol reluctantly agreed to commit crimes to fund the new machine. He went to work as the Phantom, using his natural skills to pass through solid objects and mentally levitate matter. Batman and Robin managed to track clues leading them to Wede's laboratory but were taken captive. When Wede was about to kill the Dynamic Duo, Pol realized the truth about Wede and saved the heroes' lives with his amazing abilities. Batman studied the machine and realized it was always able to send Pol back; no new machine was necessary. (*Detective Comics* #283, September 1960)

PHANTOM BANDIT, THE

Career criminal "Mugsy" Morton came up with a clever way to commit crimes by creating the stage persona the Great Swami. As his assistant worked her way through an audience, she would take objects, including keys, from members. She would place each object inside a handkerchief, with the audience unaware that she also palmed a piece of wax to take impressions. The Great Swami managed to amaze patrons by correctly guessing what was under the handkerchief thanks to a series of cues and hidden microphones. Once duplicate keys could be manufactured, the two would burgle homes and offices, earning them the nickname the *Phantom Bandit*. Journalist Vicki Vale managed to piece together the clues that pointed to Morton, but it fell to Batman and Robin to actually apprehend the man and his assistant. (*Batman* #81, February 1954)

PHANTOM BANK BANDIT, THE

Criminal Jim Megan left prison and assumed the name Jim Morley, creating the impression that he had reformed. While Morley seemingly had a respectable job, he was still committing crimes as the Phantom Bank Bandit. Batman suspected Megan but could not get the evidence necessary to bring him in—so he crafted an elaborate ruse. Telling the public he needed additional income to fund Robin's forthcoming college education, Batman opened up the Batman Private Detective Agency. The Caped Crusader then began leaving Megan various threats in the hopes he would hire the agency to protect him. Batman then charged high rates, which forced Megan to access his stolen cash, and finally the evidence necessary for an arrest was obtained. (*Batman* #115, April 1958)

PHANTOM HOLLOW

Located some distance north of Gotham City, Phantom Hollow was a quiet haven where time seemed to have stood still since the infamous hanging of its local "witch" nearly three centuries back. The witch, Ol' Nell, was said to have put a curse of silence on the church steeple bell and vowed it would toll again only to sound the town's death knell. A descendant of Nell unsuccessfully attempted to fulfill the prophecy. The town's constable was retired Gotham police captain Bill Wilcox, whom Batman aided in protecting the citizens. (*Detective Comics* #413, July 1971)

PHANTOM STRANGER

He called himself a friend or simply a stranger, but the enigmatic being known as the Phantom Stranger clearly worked in some mystic circles that made even Batman uncomfortable. (*The Phantom Stranger* #1, August/September 1952)

The exact nature and purpose of the Stranger remained unrevealed. Different chronicles presented different interpretations of who he was and how he came to be. He was said to be the legendary Wandering Jew or an angel fallen from Heaven. He might have been an agent for the Lords of Order, or a Lord himself. There were some who said he was the future son of Superman and Wonder Woman or the last being from a dead universe.

Whoever he was, the Stranger appeared when he was most needed and lent aid to Batman on

several occasions. (*The Brave and the Bold* #89, April/May 1970) He also turned up to assist the JUSTICE LEAGUE OF AMERICA, eventually accepting their offer of membership. (*Justice League of America* #103, December 1972)

The one time he visited Batman with no crisis pending was to offer him a gift—a chance to see a world wherein his parents didn't die. The Dark Knight took comfort from a world that might have been. (*Detective Comics* #500, March 1981)

PHELIOS, IRIS

Once MAXIE ZEUS's girlfriend, Iris Phelios was transformed into the grotesque HARPY.

PICTURE MAGAZINE

Picture Magazine was a regularly published news magazine based in GOTHAM CITY that on several occasions employed VICKI VALE as photojournalist, reporter, and bureau chief in Paris. When she returned to Gotham, she worked as photo editor under Morton Montor, succeeding him upon his death. On Earth-1, JULIA PENNYWORTH also wrote for the publication. (*Batman* #49, October/November 1948)

A different periodical known as *Picture News* employed Iris Allen West, wife of the FLASH; it was based in Central City.

PIED PIPER, THE

On Earth-2, a GOTHAM CITY criminal called the Pied Piper claimed he could make people do as he pleased, thanks to melodious sounds emitted from his special pipes. He also used other styles of pipes to aid him in his robberies, such as exploding corncob pipes. The Piper was quickly apprehended by Batman and ROBIN. (*Detective Comics* #143, January 1949)

On Earth-1, an entirely different Pied Piper was one of the FLASH's most persistent rogues in Central City.

PINE, JACK

Jack Pine and two accomplices stole two million dollars and then hid the money until it would be safe to retrieve it. As they waited, one accomplice died from natural causes, while the other was placed in custody. To force Pine out of hiding to show where the money was hidden, Batman engaged in an elaborate ruse. He had his butler, ALFRED PENNYWORTH, pose as a scientist who had developed a powerful love potion, which was used on the Caped Crusader. GOTHAM CITY police sergeant Helen Smith posed as a French woman who became the object of his ardor. Once Pine was convinced that Batman was besotted with love, he finally emerged to retrieve the money, only to be apprehended. (*Batman* #150, September 1962)

PINHEAD

Pinhead was a disfigured man, mentally impaired but gifted with above-normal strength. He worked for a time as an unwitting henchman for the WAXMAN, but after he was apprehended, he was remanded to ARKHAM ASYLUM. When the asylum was damaged by the earthquake that struck GOTHAM CITY, it began to run short on supplies and staffing, which allowed the JOKER to manipulate medications and schedules. As a result, he left an untreated KILLER CROC to fight Pinhead, with the smaller man crushed to death in the brawl. (*Batman: Shadow of the Bat* #80, December 1998)

PINXIT, ARIADNE

This avant-garde artist developed an amazing ink that gave her control over the tattoos she applied to others. After her rape, she used the skill to exact painful revenge as PIX.

PISTOLERA

The woman known as Pistolera began her life as a mercenary for hire named GUNBUNNY allied with GUNHAWK, with whom she had a romantic relationship. They arrived in GOTHAM CITY on an assignment, only to fail due to Batman's intervention. (*Detective Comics* #674, May 1994)

The two returned to Gotham on several occasions, usually unable to complete their contracts. This led to tension between them. The partnership dissolved, with Gunbunny going solo and changing her outfit in addition to her professional name, becoming Pistolera. (*Birds of Prey: The Ravens* #1, June 1998)

In a short time she joined with the international terrorists Cheshire, VICIOUS, and Termina to form the Ravens. They were frequently opposed by ORACLE and her BIRDS OF PREY. The three Ravens also joined the Society, a band of super-villains out to beat Earth's champions. One of Pistolera's assignments was to assassinate Knockout. Failing at that, she was captured and tortured by Knockout's lover, Scandal. Soon after, the Secret Six's DEADSHOT killed Pistolera. (*Secret Six* #2, August 2006)

PIX

Ariadne Pinxit was a tattoo artist who developed her own special ink, which she called nanite ink. The colorless ink was filled with nanobots that controlled the color matrix, forming any image Pinxit desired. Being an artist, she became known for her gorgeous skin work. One night she was beaten and raped by a street gang, which left her psychologically damaged and desiring revenge. Pinxit took a job at the tattoo parlor favored by the gang and inscribed deadly images on each member. Using her computer, she instructed her ink to activate, inflicting tremendous pain as swords and scorpions sliced into the men. When Batman investigated, she injected herself with the nanite ink, which enabled her to mentally generate objects to defend herself. Batman continued to pursue her but she ran off, eluding capture and failing to kill her last attacker. (*Batman: Gotham Knights* #34, December 2002)

PLAINVILLE

This small town renamed itself Batmantown in an effort to boost tourism while honoring a national hero. An unexpected side effect was that criminals with grudges against the Caped Crusader took out their frustrations on the town. Soon after, Batman gave a televised guided tour of the town, which more than made up for the criminal activity. His presence and support severely diminished the criminal activity. (*Batman* #100, June 1956)

PLANET-MASTER, THE

PROFESSOR NORBET was attracted to a recently fallen meteor near GOTHAM CITY. He inhaled fumes emitted from the space rock that altered his body chemistry. He grew aggressive and lost sense of his moral codes, turning to crime. Donning a costume, he called himself the Planet-Master and began a series of crimes inspired by the planets in Earth's solar system. Edward Burke, Norbet's lab assistant, realized that his superior was changing back and forth from scientist to criminal and chose to exploit the possibilities. He took to using equipment similar to the Planet-Master's and considered himself the thief's partner. Both men were brought down by Batman and ROBIN, and the changes to Norbet's body eventually dissipated. While Norbet was excused for his actions, Burke was sent to jail. (*Detective Comics* #296, October 1961)

PLANNER, THE

E. G. NEVER was a criminal who chose to match wits with Batman. He conducted business out of a GOTHAM CITY junkyard, using a massive magnet hung from a crane to pick up cars containing criminals who paid for meetings with the mastermind. After his latest clients, a trio of musicians, were arrested, Never wanted revenge. He crashed a public appearance by the Dynamic Duo and claimed to be the brains behind Batman and ROBIN. He challenged Batman to solve the next big crime in Gotham; if he failed, Never would have a chance to solve it, proving his superiority. Since Planner himself plotted the next big crime, Batman was stumped and insisted on a second round. Again, the Planner had it all figured out, letting Batman apprehend a TV repairman, A. N. Tenna, for padding his bills while the real criminal, the Cat-Crook, was suspended over the junkyard thanks to the magnet. The Planner intended to shoot the Dynamic Duo when they arrived, claiming self-defense. In the confusion, though, he shot the Cat-Crook instead, and the murder unhinged Never's mind. At his trial he claimed to be Batman; soon after, he was sentenced to the electric chair. On the day of his death, he was allowed to walk the last mile in a Batman outfit. (*Batman* #206, November 1968)

PLAXIUS

When Batman and ROBIN pursued the criminal named Gurney, the chase ended in a cavern outside GOTHAM CITY. Within the stone walls was a dimensional portal, bringing all three to another world called Plaxius. After taking Gurney into custody, the Dynamic Duo aided the local authorities in preventing a villain, Rakk, from executing a scheme that would enable him to take over the world. The humans were returned home by a grateful people. (*Batman* #125, August 1959)

P. N. QUINN SHOP

P. N. Quinn sold umbrellas to citizens while fronting one of the Penguin's many GOTHAM CITY hideouts. (*Detective Comics* #87, May 1944)

POET, THE

The Poet was a homeless man in GOTHAM CITY who briefly served as an informant for Batman. With GOOD QUEEN BESS and Slugger he provided invaluable information, and Batman gave them cash for meals. During their first meeting, the street people helped Batman identify Quentin Conroy, son of "Limehouse Jack"—one of their former comrades in homelessness—as a wanted killer. (*Batman* #307, January 1979)

POISONER

An inmate at ARKHAM ASYLUM, Kryppen, seemingly made a deal with the devil. He managed to poison more than two hundred people within Arkham's confines and then invited Batman to save them. All that the Caped Crusader had to do was kill any one inmate; Kryppen would turn over the antidote. Batman managed to outwit the Poisoner and save everyone without breaking his vow never to kill. (*Batman: Devil's Asylum*, 1995)

POISON IVY

On Earth-1, Lillian Rose had an affair with her college botany professor, Marc LeGrand, who asked her to accompany him while stealing an Egyptian artifact from a Seattle museum. He wanted the artifact's contents: rare herbs, some of which he used in an attempt to kill Rose, silencing the only witness. Instead, she survived and acquired immunity to natural toxins. (*World's Finest Comics* #252, August/September 1978) Taking the name PAMELA ISLEY and the costumed persona of Poison Ivy, she set out to show her power over men. She arrived in GOTHAM CITY, taking on three women—DRAGON FLY, SILKEN SPIDER, AND TIGER MOTH—who billed themselves as Public Enemies Numbers One, Two, and Three. Ivy proclaimed that she was actually Public Enemy Number One. This was all part of a scheme on Ivy's part to drive the various costumed felons to compete with one another while she waited them out. Batman and ROBIN apprehended them all. (*Batman* #181, June 1966)

After this Poison Ivy returned time and again to antagonize the Caped Crusader, committing crimes to fund her work with plant life. She additionally battled other heroes, notably WONDER WOMAN. She served as a member of the Injustice Gang of the World and the secret Society of super-villains.

In the reality formed after CRISIS ON INFINITE EARTHS, Pamela Lillian Isley studied biochemistry under Jason Woodrue, the FLORONIC MAN, actually a refugee from another dimension. She was one of several noteworthy students, and rumors spread that she and Woodrue were having an affair—something that was not the case. As an experiment, he poisoned the impressionable Isley,

worst sentence was being totally isolated from any hint of nature.

Her expertise with plant properties and uses made her a world-renowned expert on botany. She understood how to create scents that would affect people in specific ways, usually using them to seduce men to help her commit crimes. Even Batman fell for several of her "spells" over the years.

Isley managed to use pheromones to convince people to do her bidding. She also proved adept at manipulating plant life, creating hybrids and even controlling them telepathically. Gradually her power over flora increased, making her a formidable opponent.

In her own way, she hated all humans for the damage they had done to the planet and its defenseless plant life. Many of her efforts were to preserve lush, green foliage as opposed to wiping out humanity, which was fellow ecoterrorist Rā's al Ghūl's passion. Poison Ivy still had physical needs and thought herself in love with Batman on numerous occasions. She appeared to be bisexual in nature, showing desire for both sexes throughout her career. (*Batman & Poison Ivy: Cast Shadows*, 2004)

Still, Ivy allowed herself to get distracted, such as the time she spent productively with Amanda Waller's Suicide Squad. Her involvement began when she helped enslave its members. (*Suicide Squad* #33–36, October 1989–January 1990) Ivy seemed poised to join Deadshot and Ravan as a key assassin on the team. During an assault on the Haitian organization called the Loa, she used her knowledge to identify their poisons of choice and then used her own toxins to help take them down. (*Suicide Squad* #39, April 1990)

When Amanda Waller later revived the team, she specifically requested Poison Ivy as one of her operatives. Ivy, at that point, was playing shadow ruler of the South American nation of Puerto Azul and seducing its leader. The squad's objective was to free the mentally unbalanced meta-human Count Vertigo from the handlers who were using him to enslave the country of Vlatava. Ivy freed Vertigo but instantly recognized that she could use him to run the nation herself. (*Suicide Squad* #41–43, June–August 1990)

She harbored a grudge against being used by Woodrue, and after a time he came to Gotham seeking her out. He used women named Holly Wood and Eva Green to break her out of Arkham and hoped to enlist her aid in his latest scheme. He was selling a potent form of marijuana that was grown directly from his body. Woodrue sought to raise ten million dollars, which he offered to Ivy in exchange for her poison-resistant blood in order to create a new life-form. When Batman interfered, Eva and her partner subdued him. Ivy helped free Batman, since she wanted nothing to do with Woodrue and his scheme. Batman easily apprehended the women before dealing directly with Woodrue. (*Batman: Shadow of the Bat* #56–58, November 1996–January 1997)

Ivy took to seeing Gotham's Robinson Park as a home for her and her creations. When an earthquake devastated the city, she settled in the park, offering dozens of children a safe haven

which resulted in altering her body chemistry, making her immune to all toxins and pushing her to the brink of insanity. The resulting changes to her body left her unable to conceive children; she took to creating plant-based artificial life-forms that she called her children. (*Black Orchid* #1, 1988; *Batman: Shadow of the Bat Annual* #3, 1995)

Following her transformation, Poison Ivy dedicated herself to preserving plant life at all costs. An ecoterrorist, she was willing to rob and kill in order to fund her experiments and preserve all manner of flora. She was drawn to Gotham City and most frequently did her work there. Each scheme left her apprehended by Batman and Robin, and she was regularly remanded to Arkham Asylum. Her and keeping scavengers away. In the months that followed, when the city was cut off from America, Batman allowed her to protect the park and didn't interfere with her work until he had to rescue everyone from the terror of CLAYFACE.

Along the way, she befriended HARLEY QUINN, the psychiatrist-turned-besotted-lover of the JOKER. Poison Ivy saw a chance to help a fellow woman, trying to break the abusive cycle Harley had fallen into. A genuine friendship blossomed.

Ivy was at one point manipulated into helping the RIDDLER in his elaborate scheme to destroy Batman. She managed to use her skills to place SUPERMAN under her control, forcing the Man of Steel and Dark Knight to fight. (*Batman* #612, April 2003) A short time later, the Riddler's former partner, HUSH, beat him badly; he turned to Ivy for support. Instead she physically and psychologically broke the man who had most recently used her. (*Detective Comics* #797–799, October–December 2004)

She then turned to Batman for help, feeling that her altered physiology was killing the children she cared for. He used his brilliant skills to devise a way to change her metabolism back to that of an average human—only to have Hush convince her to undo the cure, a step that seemingly killed her. One result of the change was that the pigment of her skin varied as she used her abilities, shifting from pale Caucasian to a light green.

Poison Ivy survived and remained active in Gotham City, her powers enhanced by the alterations. She demonstrated this by creating her largest life-form yet and took to feeding it people, described by her as "tiresome lovers" and "incompetent henchmen." In some unanticipated manner, the various humans fed to the creature gave it sentience; it called itself Harvest. Batman saved Ivy's life, and Harvest vanished. (*Detective Comics* #823, November 2006)

Ivy was never one to join with Batman's main rogues or even the Society of super-villains, seeing her goals as incompatible with theirs. Instead she remained obsessed with her botanical world.

After recovering from her injuries, Ivy may have reconsidered her decision to eschew joining collaborations with Batman's other rogues or even the Society of super-villains. She next encountered the Dark Knight as a member of the most recent incarnation of the Injustice League. (*Justice League of America Wedding Special*, 2007; *Justice League of America* [second series] #13–14, November–December 2007)

POL

An alien lured into committing crimes as the PHANTOM in the hope of going home.

PORTER, JANICE

Voted most likely to become a district attorney, Gotham University law student Janice Porter did just that. She never expected to succeed HARVEY DENT as GOTHAM CITY's DA, especially since she'd had a major crush on Dent when he taught at the university. In fact, when he married GILDA DENT, Porter was disappointed and transferred to Harvard to finish her studies. After Dent was scarred with acid and became the criminal TWO-FACE, Porter

was tapped to succeed him. She focused on the Falcone and Gigante crime families in the wake of the HOLIDAY killings, which made them both vulnerable to investigation. In the course of doing her job, she reconnected with Dent, and actually slept with him, compromising her integrity. Worse, she got involved in the political machinations of the Falcone family as Mario Falcone tried to get his sister, SOPHIA GIGANTE, out of the picture. When Dent was clearly done using Porter, he shot her to death, framing ALBERTO FALCONE, already suspected of crimes as the HANGMAN KILLER, as her assassin. (*Batman: Dark Victory* #0, 1999)

POTATO, JOE

Joe Potato was a GOTHAM CITY private eye who worked alongside Batman on several cases. He said he became an investigator because he couldn't stop being curious, preferring an aggressive approach compared to the Dark Knight's stealth. Potato trained in aikido, which helped the older, gray-haired man overcome his bulky frame. While proficient with guns, he preferred to scare criminals with his "Joe Potato peeler," a knife with a hole cut in the blade, although it was a fake weapon. (*Detective Comics* #594, January 1989)

POWELL, ASHLEY MAVIS

A low-level meta-human with the ability to manipulate cyberspace, as INTERFACE she was BARBARA GORDON's first mission in her new role as ORACLE.

POWELL, MIKE "BULLDOG"

Mike "Bulldog" Powell was a career police officer in GOTHAM CITY, rising to the rank of lieutenant. One of his proudest achievements was having his daughter PATRICIA POWELL follow in his footsteps. (*Batman* #165, August 1964)

POWELL, PATRICIA

Patricia Powell was a GOTHAM CITY uniformed police officer who regularly worked with the Earth-1 Batman on cases. Their first assignment involved rescuing Professor Ralph Smedley, who was kidnapped by criminals seeking his newly formulated explosive. While she respected Batman, she had a crush on BRUCE WAYNE—although it never went anywhere. (*Batman* #165, August 1964)

POWERMAN

Wearing a colorful orange costume with a yellow hood, the new hero Powerman apparently replaced Batman and ROBIN as SUPERMAN's partner of choice. When LEX LUTHOR escaped from jail, the Dynamic Duo offered to help find him, but Superman informed them that he and Powerman had it covered. Undaunted, they assisted in bringing Luthor back to jail. Superman then revealed that his new partner was merely a robot, created to discourage his friends from risking their lives in the seemingly unending struggle between Superman and Luthor. (*World's Finest Comics* #94, May/June 1958)

PRAVHOR (SWAMI)

Pravhor was a GOTHAM CITY–based fake mystic who was actually a smuggler in concert with a partner in South Africa. His swami counterpart would hide stolen gems inside lucky rabbits' feet, which he

passed on to unsuspecting sailors bound for America. Pravhor would then dispatch his underlings—Gouger, Sam, and Mugsy—to collect them. Batman and ROBIN discovered the scheme and ended it, cabling authorities in Africa to arrest Pravhor's partner. (*World's Finest Comics* #13, Spring 1944)

PROBSON, RON

GOTHAM CITY police detective Ron Probson headed up the second shift in the MAJOR CRIMES UNIT. He disliked first-shift commander MAGGIE SAWYER, and their clashes led to tensions between the two shifts. (*Gotham Central* #1, Early February 2003)

PROFESSOR, THE

The Professor learned that ancient Mayan treasures were actually relics from another world, left behind by an alien named Odin. He and his colleagues Smite and Bragan stole the devices and used them to commit a series of spectacular crimes. Batman and ROBIN were daunted by the advanced technology until the World's Greatest Detective deduced that the medallion they carried with them was a safety device linked to the weapons. Once Batman broke the medallion, it unleashed a power surge that rendered the alien devices inert, allowing him to bring the men to justice. (*Detective Comics* #263, January 1959)

PROFESSOR MILO

Professor Achilles Milo was a chemist-turned-criminal. To commit crimes unmolested by Batman, Milo exposed the Gotham Guardian to a gas that made him fear bat-shaped items. (*Detective Comics* #247, September 1957) In his second encounter, Milo exposed Batman to a gas of his own design that created suicidal thoughts. It fell to ROBIN and Police Commissioner JAMES GORDON to devise a mystery that would engage the despairing Caped Crusader. (*Batman* #112, December 1957) In their subsequent meetings, Milo tried numerous psychological ways to break the Dark Knight, failing each time. He went so far as to use ANTHONY LUPUS as his pawn, unleashing the werewolf within the tortured soul. (*Batman* #255, March/April 1974) Milo drove himself to the brink of insanity and did a stint at ARKHAM ASYLUM. After his release, he got dragged into a conflict between Batman and the JOKER but emerged unscathed, claiming he was retired. (*Batman: Joker's Apprentice* #1, May 1999)

That proved short-lived: Milo was involved in concealing the whereabouts of the mystic Silver Wheel of Nyorlath, disguised as a wheelchair. It was located, though, by the ELONGATED MAN on his quest to resurrect his wife, SUE DIBNY. (*52* #41, 2007)

PROFESSOR MORIARITY

A British criminal took the name of Sherlock Holmes's cunning opponent and proved equally brilliant. He and his men committed a series of crimes throughout London, forcing a stymied Scotland Yard to invite Batman and ROBIN to the United Kingdom to help. ALFRED PENNYWORTH accompanied his masters to his home country and provided an invaluable assist as the Dynamic Duo brought Moriarity and his men to justice. (*Detective Comics* #110, April 1946)

PROFESSOR PENDER

Described as a renegade scientist, Pender had developed a remarkable process that granted an ordinary person superpowers for a twenty-four-hour period. Batman, Robin, and Superman wanted to apprehend him before the machine could be used, but the Caped Crusader was bathed in the rays and gained powers making him an equal to the Man of Steel. Pender complicated matters by spraying minute Kryptonite particles on Superman's costume, robbing the Action Ace of his powers. Once Batman mastered his newfound abilities and Superman donned a spare outfit, Pender was easily taken into custody. (*World's Finest Comics* #77, July/August 1955)

PROFESSOR POST

Professor Post had designed a drug that impaired cognitive functions, forcing people to work at slower rates of speed. He chose to extort Gotham City brokerage houses by doping their traders, causing them to underperform. For a fee, he would provide the companies with the antidote. Batman and Robin investigated and apprehended the criminal scientist. (*Detective Comics* #61, March 1942)

PROFESSOR POWDER

Professor Powder was a rocket scientist who suffered a mental illness that turned him into a serial bomber. The bald, overweight older gentleman with a white beard and glasses used hallucinogenic and sneezing powders in his crimes. He was apprehended by James Gordon some time before he became police commissioner; Powder was committed to Arkham Asylum. Years later, he escaped and suggested that the asylum was in danger—but then he died from one of his hallucinogens. Batman eventually learned that Powder had been duped by a deranged Arkham psychologist into constructing sophisticated equipment that enabled him to create deadly virtual reality–type scenarios using a young mutant named Fidel Finnegan. (*Detective Comics* #635–637, September–October 1991)

PROFESSOR RADIUM

Henry Ross was a scientist who determined a way to resuscitate the dead using radium. He was exposed to harmful radiation that imbued him with radium, making himself a guinea pig to prove his skeptics wrong. His skin turned green and he was highly radioactive, forcing him inside a protective suit. Seeking money for what he believed to be an antidote to his condition, Ross began committing crimes in Gotham City. He found the money and was pleased no one had been harmed in the process. After taking the antidote, he visited his girlfriend, Mary Lamont, only to discover the serum was just temporary. Lamont died from radiation after being touched by Ross. Her death seemed to mentally unhinge Ross, who went wild, being dubbed Professor Radium by the press, coming into conflict with the police and then Batman and Robin. He fell into the Gotham River and was presumed dead. (*Batman* #8 December 1941/January 1942)

Years later Professor Radium resurfaced, seen as a member of the Nuclear Legion who battled a variety of heroes and federal agents in the wake of Blüdhaven's destruction. (*Crisis Aftermath: The Battle for Blüdhaven* #1, Early June 2006)

PROFESSOR SIMMS

Professor Simms was an unscrupulous scientist who developed a serum that would change humans' physiology, letting them grow to an average height of twelve feet. He wanted to build an army of giant warriors but felt they should also have above-average strength. He duped Steve Condon into becoming his assistant, taking for his own purposes Condon's research into improving human hormones for increased strength and vitality. Condon was accidentally given the new compound and successfully attained a new height. However, people saw the "Titanic Man" as a freak, and he fled Gotham City for isolation. Simms created his army, which first threatened Gotham until Batman and Robin intervened. They convinced Condon to aid them in stopping Simms. Once the giant army was stopped, Batman applied an antidote to Condon and the other oversized men, restoring them to their normal sizes. (*Detective Comics* #278, April 1960)

PROFESSOR VILMER

A botany professor at Gotham University, Vilmer was fired for using illegal drugs in his studies. He kidnapped the university's star athlete, Johnny Marden, and applied several experimental drugs to the teen. First Marden was given amnesia so he would believe Vilmer's story that he was actually Adam Newman, a synthetic life-form dependent on a regular dosage of a drug to remain alive. A second drug gave him enhanced strength and, wanting to stay alive, the duped man set out to commit crimes on Vilmer's behalf. Batman and Robin investigated, determined the real identity of the thief, and came to his aid at much the same time members of Gotham City's underworld paid Vilmer one hundred thousand dollars to have Newman capture the Caped Crusader. Instead the Dynamic Duo apprehended Vilmer and restored Marden's memory. (*Batman* #87, October 1954)

PROFESSOR VINCENT

Professor Vincent and his assistant Perkins were embezzling funds from Gotham College for some time. Vincent came to believe that the college dean was close to discovering the crime and had the man killed. In his defense, Vincent claimed to have been driven to a homicidal rage by evil spirits haunting a cellar. The reality was that he was unhinged after inhaling the mind-altering fumes from a rare mushroom he had planted there. Vincent and Perkins lured two other men to the cellar to also be affected by the mushroom, so the story seemed more plausible. It fell to Batman and Robin to discover the truth and bring the two men to justice. (*Batman* #59, June/July 1950)

PROMETHEUS

The boy who grew up to become one of the world's deadliest villains said he began life as the son of criminal parents who robbed their way across America. Finally the police gunned down the thieves, and the shock turned the youth's hair white. He vowed to oppose the representatives of law and order and set out to prepare. The unnamed boy tapped his parents' hidden stores of cash and lived a wild, carefree life. When he was sixteen, he set out to train, learning to brawl in Brazil, fire weapons in Africa and the Middle East, and master a dozen languages. He then found the city of Shamballa, in the Himalayas, where evil-worshipping monks resided. While there, he was shown that the monastery was built over the remains of a crashed spacecraft. The head monk revealed himself to be one of the alien survivors, and Prometheus killed him to obtain the Cosmic Key, which accessed a dimension he dubbed the Ghost Zone. That was to be his base of operations. Finally he deemed himself ready. (*New Year's Evil: Prometheus* #1, 1998)

The Ghost Zone has been described as limbo and a conduit from place to place. Martians and Kryptonians were said to be familiar with the void as well. Prometheus constructed an angled house that became his base; he described it as "a crooked house for a crooked man."

Wearing an armored outfit laced with advanced technology, he set up a link with a massive computer mainframe that would download information to his helmet as needed. He took to acquiring data on the world's thirty greatest fighters, including the Batman, and possessing the data made him their equal. Prometheus then killed a kid named Retro, who had won a competition to design his own super hero and be a member of the Justice League of America for a day. The villain then used his training and skills to rapidly disable most of the League before he fell to Catwoman, who had also stolen aboard the headquarters. (*JLA* #16–17, March–April 1998)

Prometheus decided he was better off working with others and accepted Lex Luthor's offer to join the Injustice Gang during the events known as the Mageddon War. This time Batman took out Prometheus by reprogramming the helmet so the martial arts were replaced with the same motor neuron disease suffered by the great Stephen Hawking. The Dark Knight then had to stop Huntress from killing the villain. (*JLA* #36–39, December 1999–March 2000) After escaping custody, Prometheus allied himself for a time with Hush, working to undermine Batman and even Green Arrow before abandoning Hush during his vendetta against the Joker. (*Batman: Gotham Knights* #52–53, 55–56, June–July 2004, September–October 2004)

Prometheus was poisoned by one of the children afflicted by a disease when they lived with Poison Ivy in Robinson Park after the Gotham earthquake. Weakened, he was taken by the Society, the collection of super-villains, who wanted the Cosmic Key and access to the Ghost Zone. The key, though, was hidden in the Justice Society of America's headquarters. (*Batman: Gotham Knights* #60, 62, 64, 66, February, April, June, August 2005)

During the events known as Infinite Crisis, he was involved in the Battle of Metropolis, where he killed Peacemaker. Soon after, he challenged Lady Shiva to

City, Batman learned that the concession stands were swindling patrons. To avoid suspicion, Punch and Judy fired the carnival staff and then offered a deal. To restore their reputation, the pair would donate a full day's ticket receipts if Batman and Robin appeared in an acrobatic demonstration when the carnival opened in Central Park. The Dynamic Duo prepared to open with a parachute stunt. The swindlers and a hireling intended to use the distraction to take the box-office receipts and skip town. Robin attempted to stop them, only to be taken prisoner.

The hireling admitted that he had sabotaged Batman's parachute, horrifying the couple—who never condoned murder. Angry, the thug tied up his bosses and left them beside the Boy Wonder as he fled with the money. Fortunately, Batman had a spare parachute and landed safely in time to apprehend the man and free the others. Punch and Judy stood trial for attempted robbery. (*Batman* #31, October/November 1945)

Punch and Judy are not to be confused with the psychotic married couple Punch and Jewelee, who operated outside Gotham City.

PUPPET MASTER, THE

The man known only as the Puppet Master intended to use a serum that gave him dominion over the actions of others to gain military technology to sell to rogue countries. His scheme allowed him to take control of several men to help him gain nuclear technology and a prototype "Voss Rifle." His efforts to escape with the stolen property and leave the country were thwarted by Batman and Robin, however, who brought him to justice. (*Batman* #3, Fall 1940)

PURDY, PACK

When the ocean liner *Natonic* was in port at Gotham City, Pack Purdy intended to rob the five million dollars in cash that resided in the ship's hold. Batman heard rumors of the gang leader's scheme but didn't know the details, so he disguised himself and infiltrated Purdy's gang. Just as the mobsters were to begin using underwater torches to cut into the hull, Robin arrived to help his partner apprehend the men. (*Batman* #101, August 1956)

PURPLE MASK MOB, THE

The Purple Mask Mob wore, naturally, purple bandannas to hide their features when they committed crimes throughout Gotham City and the surrounding neighborhoods. Batman, remaining in the Batcave as he recovered from a slow-acting poison he had imbibed earlier, studied the evidence and directed Robin, assisted by Superman, to find the mob's headquarters. The duo managed to capture the entire mob and recover the stolen property. (*World's Finest Comics* #75, March/April 1955)

PYE, MARGARET

A teenage jewel thief who took on the costumed identity of Magpie and frequently opposed Batman.

a fight and she accepted, presuming she knew more than she had at the time his helmet downloaded data. It took him a mere three seconds to render her unconscious, allowing him to complete his task: capturing the Crime Doctor for the Society. Once the Crime Doctor committed suicide, Prometheus ended his fight against Huntress, Black Canary, and Lady Blackhawk and left. (*Birds of Prey* #94, July 2006)

PUBLIC, JOE

Joe Public was a Gotham City physical education teacher when he was attacked by the alien Gemir. The parasite's bite interacted with his meta-gene and imbued Public with the ability to absorb energy from others. Azrael aided him in stopping the flow of drugs in his area in addition to ending the alien threat. (*Batman: Shadow of the Bat Annual* #1, 1993) He also came to the Martian Manhunter's aid on one case. (*Justice League Task Force* #9, February 1994) Joe Public preferred to remain a teacher and rarely went into battle as a super hero. (*Batman: Shadow of the Bat Annual* #1, 1993)

PUNCH AND JUDY

These married partners were equally good at arguing and crime, performing a live version of the traditional Punch-and-Judy puppet show at a carnival. The bickering pair also were first-rate swindlers who took advantage of their customers at every turn. When the carnival came to Gotham

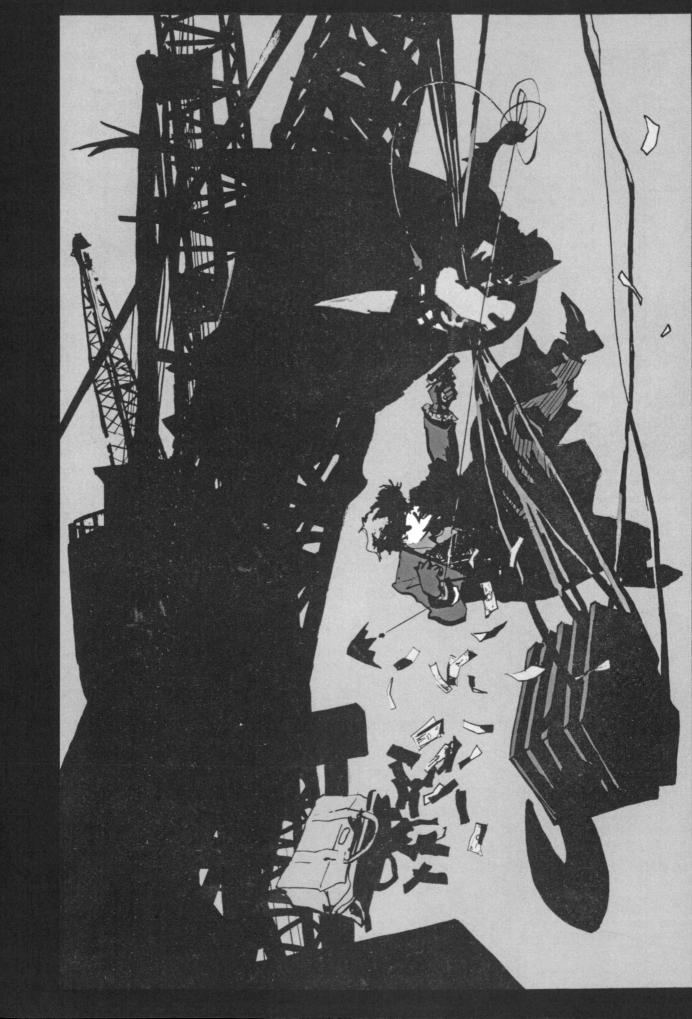

QAYIN

Qayin's parents, agents of Rā's al Ghūl, perished during the bombing of Hiroshima. Qayin sought vengeance and trained to become an assassin and terrorist. He finally exacted his vengeance by killing Melisande, the woman who had provided Rā's with his daughter Talia Head. When Qayin began killing prominent scientists in Gotham City, he was hunted not only by Batman but also by Rā's, who sought vengeance. He nearly succeeded in killing the Dark Knight, who had finally allowed himself to indulge in a romance with Talia, who had become pregnant. As a result, he lost his fighting edge, making him a vulnerable target. She told her lover that she had miscarried, and a grieving Batman finally stopped Qayin at Rā's mountain headquarters. (*Batman: Son of the Demon*, 1987)

QUAKEMASTER

The first Quakemaster was one of the many heroes accessed by the dimensional H-dial possessed by teenager Robbie Reed. (*House of Mystery* #158, April 1966)

Some time later, Robert Coleman took the costumed identity of Quakemaster. In his green-and-purple outfit, he used a specially designed jackhammer that emitted sonic waves simulating an earthquake. When he began terrorizing Gotham City, Batman investigated and learned that Coleman was a builder who'd been discredited when an apartment complex he put up fell apart in a bad hurricane. (*DC Special* #28, June/July 1977)

Coleman escaped prison and wound up working with the secret Society of super-villains. He attacked the for-hire team known as Hero Hotline as a favor to the Calculator. (*Hero Hotline* #1, April 1989) Quakemaster was subsequently recruited by

Manchester Black in his vendetta against Superman. Of course, the Man of Steel easily apprehended him. (*Adventures of Superman* #608, November 2002)

When Gotham was devastated by an earthquake, Arnold Wesker, better known as the Ventriloquist, masqueraded as the Quakemaster, claiming he was responsible. For one hundred million dollars, he would leave the city alone—but if he did not get paid, he would raze what was left standing. (*Batman: Shadow of the Bat* #74, May 1998) As the mayor tried to find the funds, Batman deduced that a missing seismologist named Jolene Relazzo was providing Quakemaster with convincing terminology. (*Batman* #554, May 1998) Batman and his extended family quickly homed in on Wesker, exposing the fraud. (*Robin* [second series] #53, May 1998)

QUE

Among the many female accomplices employed by the Riddler, Que was one of the earliest, and her tenure with him one of the briefest. (*Batman & Superman: World's Finest* #2, May 1999)

QUEEN BEE

After Batman saved spoiled heiress Marcia Monroe from the ledge of the Gotham Bridge, he actually delivered her a spanking, caught by the media. The woman responded to the humiliation by deciding to become his new partner. She was already a crack shot and came to his unwanted aid, as the Queen Bee, on more than one occasion.

Later, when Batman was framed for stealing the Cat Emerald from the Gotham City Municipal Museum, he turned himself in, professing his innocence. It turned out Monroe was behind the theft, part of her harebrained attempt to help her father, who was affiliated with an international criminal operation called Cyclops. Her whole Queen Bee act was in service to help her father, including framing the Caped Crusader to keep him out of the way.

Matters grew complicated when agents of Cyclops obtained one of the black diamonds used by the vicious criminal Eclipso and committed additional crimes in Gotham. Batman had to stop the villain and put Queen Bee and Cyclops out of business. (*The Brave and the Bold* #64, February/March 1966)

QUEENIE

Queenie was a beautiful woman who chose to work for the Joker when he opened a gambling operation on a boat just outside the three-mile limit. When Bruce Wayne visited the ship to scope it out, he encountered the dark-haired beauty, who fell in love with him. In time, Queenie saw Wayne and Batman on numerous occasions and—when she recognized a shaving nick on the Caped Crusader's face—realized they were one and the same. As Batman went to deal with the Joker, Queenie shot her friend Diamond Jack Deegan when he tried to kill the hero. Clubsy, another accomplice, shot Queenie, mortally wounding her. As she lay dying in the Gotham Guardian's arms, she revealed her knowledge and asked for one last kiss. She was the first criminal on Earth-2 to have deduced Batman's secret identity. (*Batman* #5, Spring 1941)

QUEEN OF HEARTS, THE

The criminal known as the Queen of Hearts was chasing a drug dealer, with Batman also on her heels, when she left Gotham City for Rio de Janeiro. Upon arrival in Brazil, the Dark Knight was stunned to find mindless children in the grip of a designer drug. They all seemed to be controlled by a figure known only as the Idiot. The Queen of Hearts was never seen again. (*Batman* #472–473, *Detective Comics* #639–640, December 1991–January 1992)

QUERY

The Riddler took to using beautiful women as accomplices, and the two most long associated with him were Deirdre Vance, Query, and Nina Damfino, Echo. They were acrobatic, fierce fighters who proved capable of actually going toe to toe with Batman for brief periods. (*Detective Comics Annual* #8, 1995)

The Prince of Puzzlers found them dressed like bikers and robbing a store. He admired their agility and immediately hired them, and they remained with him for some time. Query and Echo first joined him to rob the Reservoir Street Cash Depository of Gotham. After that, they stole prized violins, ransoming them from their wealthy owner. (*Detective Comics* #705–707, January–March 1997)

QUESTION, THE

Victor Sage was a man undergoing constant reinvention. In his native Hub City, he was orphaned and largely raised himself. He took work as a television reporter at KBEL, which satisfied his thirsty mind. He discovered the depths to which Hub City was corrupt and began exposing the facts to an apathetic public. When he met Aristotle

Victor "Vic" Sage

"Tot" Rodor, Sage began a new chapter in his life. (*Mysterious Suspense* #1, October 1968)

Rodor had developed something called pseudo-derm to cover flesh wounds, affixed in place with a special gas. When Sage saw no other choice but to turn vigilante to save Rodor from criminals, he covered his face with pseudoderm—and the Question was born. However, he was untrained and easily beaten. He was rescued by Lady Shiva, who found him a curious figure and took him to Richard Dragon, where he was reborn. Better prepared, and a better man, Sage returned after a year to once more clean up Hub City. He was aided time and again by Lady Shiva, and even once adventured with Batman and Green Arrow. (*The Question Annual* #1, 1998)

Years later, dying from cancer, Vic Sage traced a shipment of alien technology to Intergang in Gotham City. Needing help, and a potential successor, he provided the same aid to former detective Renee Montoya that Shiva had given him. (*52* #1, 2006) Their investigations led them from Gotham to the Middle Eastern country of Khandaq, where they became local heroes for preventing a bombing at the wedding of Black Adam and Isis. A thankful couple aided the Question and Montoya in destroying Intergang's Khandaq operation.

Renee Montoya

They then traveled to Nanda Parbat, where Dragon began training Montoya while Sage tried to fight lung cancer. When Montoya was ready, they returned to Gotham; there Kate Kane, Montoya's former lover, helped care for Sage in his final days. As New Year's approached, Sage became delirious and wanted to face the final question: death. A grief-stricken Montoya chose to take him back to Nanda Parbat instead. Sage died before she could access the city's gates. Montoya succeeded him as the new Question. (*52* #48, 2007)

In the wake of Infinite Crisis, a new multiverse was born, and a Sage/Question existed on Earth-4.

QUICK RESPONSE TEAM

After the Gotham City Police Department was reconstituted following the events known as No Man's Land, the SWAT team was renamed the Quick Response Team.

QUINN, JUSTIN

Justin Quinn took the name Suicide King when he became a costumed criminal working for the Network.

QUINZEL, HARLEEN

An Arkham Asylum psychiatrist who fell in love with the Joker and changed professions to become the costumed criminal Harley Quinn.

QUIZ

Among the many athletic, attractive women to work with the Riddler was the dark-haired Quiz. She aided the Riddler only a handful of times and then vanished. (*The Batman Chronicles* #3, Winter 1996)

RAATKO, NYSSA

She was the first daughter of the demon, born to a Russian peasant woman in 1775. Nyssa Raatko grew up listening to stories about her handsome and powerful father, Rā's al Ghūl, told by her mother—who never stopped loving the man who abandoned them. At fourteen, Nyssa left home and sought her father, traveling the continent until finally finding him in North Africa. This act impressed Rā's, who accepted her as his protégée and began her training. Soon they were a fearsome duo, for she became an accomplished fighter and tactician.

In 1794 she was in a battle and mortally wounded. Rā's took her to one of his Lazarus Pits and restored her to life, the first of many such treatments she experienced for the next several centuries. By the beginning of the nineteenth century, Nyssa and her father saw the world in different ways, so they parted company. He anticipated that she would make her fortune, marry, and provide him with heirs. This proved not to be the case, and his heart grew colder until he disowned the woman.

It took time, but in 1923 she finally began a family, starting with a son, Daniel. Rā's unsurprisingly turned up soon after, intending to take the boy. Nyssa disagreed, pulling a gun and insisting she would kill him if he did not leave. They parted bitterly. (*Detective Comics* #783, August 2003) They next saw each other when he was an SS officer and she was suffering at Germany's Ravensbruck concentration camp. It was an unpleasant visit: He explained that sacrifices such as his grandchildren had to be made in order for his great plan to take shape. He never revealed the plan, though. As a result, Nyssa was left to suffer unimaginable pain as she became a test subject for gruesome

experiments. She survived but would never be able to have children again. (*Batman: Death and the Maidens* #5, February 2004)

Her activities after World War II remain unchronicled, but she turned up as a neighbor to her unwitting sister Talia Head when the younger woman was serving as CEO of LexCorp. The two became friends—until the day Nyssa kidnapped Talia, and then the truth began to emerge. Time and again Nyssa killed Talia, only to resurrect her in the Lazarus Pit, which had been altered by Nyssa to allow a person to be resurrected more than once in the same pit. During each emerging period of madness, Nyssa began to recondition Talia's mind, turning her into a tool.

When she deemed her sister ready, Nyssa sent Talia to see their father, and the Demon's Head was finally slain, seemingly for good. As he lay dying, Rā's admitted that he had anticipated this action and had hoped his death would teach his daughters the correctness of his vision so they would continue his work. Instead, the two plundered his holdings and jointly ran the League of Assassins for a period of time.

Nyssa was not done. She also planned to kill the world's symbol of hope—Superman. Using Kryptonite bullets stolen from the Batcave, she stalked the Man of Steel, who surprised Nyssa by dressing instead as Batman. She was disarmed but managed to maintain her freedom, taking control of Rā's al Ghūl's holdings. She and Talia jointly controlled the League for a time.

Her reign ended when she was assassinated by Batgirl, Cassandra Cain. (*Robin* [second series] #148, May 2006) Ironically, Nyssa had attempted to recruit Batgirl to join the League, seeing she was prophesied "the One who is All." (*Batgirl* #73, April

2006) Cassandra rejected the offer and left with half the League.

When she was next in North Africa, she entered a car—which exploded. LADY SHIVA reported to the League that Nyssa was dead. She has not been seen since. (*Robin* [second series] #148, May 2006)

RACER, THE

The Racer was a clever criminal who committed his crimes and escaped in a high-powered sports car. At a safe distance, he loaded the car inside a van so it appeared the getaway car entirely vanished. Batman and ROBIN were using a damaged BATMOBILE during this time and resorted to adding a Batmobile body over a race-car chassis to continue pursuing the Racer. He was finally apprehended. (*Batman* #98, March 1956)

RADBEY

Radbey worked as secretary to GOTHAM CITY's Seven Seas Insurance Company. He took bribes from shipowners to have their vessels scuttled in order to collect on the insurance policy. To accomplish this, Radbey used a submarine hidden within a whale's body. Hunting the whale, though, was the obsessed Captain Burly, who was hired by Seven Seas to kill the whale so the ships would be safe. In the end, Radbey and Burly killed each other, neatly resolving the problem for all concerned. (*Batman* #9, February/March 1942)

RADKO, ACE

Ace Radko came to America and became a notorious gangster until he was arrested and deported as an undesirable alien. Back in Europe, Radko decided to lure Batman and ROBIN to his home country and then kidnap them in the hope that America would pay one million dollars to ransom the Dynamic Duo. While in Europe, Batman befriended Rogers, a retired big-game hunter, who helped them deal with Radko and his men. Rogers learned Batman's true identity during the adventure, but died of heart failure, taking the secret with him. The freed crime fighters safely returned to America. (*World's Finest Comics* #47, August/September 1950)

RAFFERTY BROTHERS, THE

The Rafferty Brothers were three men who all became criminals and engaged in conflicts with Batman and ROBIN. All three died in unique ways, even though they all wore bulletproof vests for safety, making the cases memorable ones for retelling in future years. Steve died during an attempted robbery at the Acme Scrap Yard when a giant electromagnet grabbed his vest, carrying the man to a heap, where he was buried beneath tons of metal scrap. Mike fought the Dynamic Duo aboard a boat and fell overboard, unable to swim to safety given the weight of the heavy vest he wore. The final brother, Pete, never had his heart in being a criminal, so he died making a sacrifice to help others. Shot by one of their gang, Pete lived long enough to join two ends of a broken electric cable, completing the circuit that provided a house with power, enabling a doctor to perform a life-saving appendectomy. (*Batman* #12, August/September 1942)

RAGLAND, "TIGER"

After Tiger Ragland robbed a loan company, he sought escape by climbing aboard a sightseeing bus—only to have the bus taken over by other gangsters who wanted his loot. They pulled over and put the terrified passengers in a building's basement, letting it flood while they fled with Ragland's stolen money. Batman and ROBIN arrived on the scene in time to rescue the victims and then apprehend the criminals involved. (*Detective Comics* #93, November 1944)

RAGMAN

It was called the Great Collector Artifact, a shapeless collection of rags, sewn together; a patchwork quilt of many fabrics and colors. It also collected souls of the damned, trapping them within a limbo-like realm where they lent their skills and their strength to the Artifact's owner in the hope of one day being redeemed. The family that had passed the cloak from one generation to the next since 1812 BCE continued to the present day with RORY REGAN.

A veteran, he took over a GOTHAM CITY pawnshop known as RAGS 'N' TATTERS, doling out money for items he knew he couldn't resell and sharing what profit he did earn with the city's downtrodden. One night he was charged by an electrical storm and then learned of the legacy bequeathed him. Dressing in an outfit left by his father, Regan became Ragman, summoning power from the souls within his rag cloak and fighting crime and injustice. (*Ragman* #1, August/September 1976)

Over time he battled common criminals and occasionally worked alongside the city's main protector, Batman. However, as he studied and learned about the cloak and its history, Ragman got drawn into more mystical adventures. Eventually he joined a group known as the Sentinels of Magic and subsequently was called to form the current incarnation of a legendary set of champions

known as the Shadowpact. (*Day of Judgment* #1,
November 1999; *Shadowpact* #1, July 2006)

RAGS 'N' TATTERS

A GOTHAM CITY pawnshop run by Rory Regan, who
was also known as RAGMAN. The poor knew he would
buy their most meager of possessions, as he tried
to help all. (*Ragman* #1, August/September 1976)

RAINBOW BEAST, THE

Deep in South America, volcanic activity was
credited with giving life to a one-of-a-kind creature
that appeared from the hot lava. Its rainbow skin
made it colorful, but it was a deadly beast that
had to be stopped before entire villages would fall.
Given its bizarre abilities—it could emit searing heat
or freezing cold, turn solid objects immaterial, and
reduce organic matter to the thickness of a leaf—
frightened leaders summoned Batman and ROBIN
for help. Complicating matters was Diaz, a local
rebel who claimed to have control over the beast
and demanded capitulation from the government.
Instead, the Dynamic Duo subdued Diaz and then
sapped the creature of its powers, draining its life
away until it was finally destroyed. (*Batman* #134,
September 1960)

RANGER, THE

The Ranger was an Australian crime fighter who
modeled his career after Batman's and met his
idol during a convention of international heroes.
(*Detective Comics* #215, January 1955). Nicknamed
by the media as BATMEN OF ALL NATIONS, they were
also dubbed the CLUB OF HEROES. For one meeting,
the club also included SUPERMAN, who represented
the world. (*World's Finest Comics* #89, July/August
1957)

   In the reality after the events of INFINITE CRISIS, the
Ranger continued to fight crime on his continent,
altering his name to Dark Ranger. When John
Mayhew summoned the Club of Heroes once more,
he responded—only to be killed as part of a plan for
Mayhew to gain revenge against Batman, whom he
blamed for the club's failure. (*Batman* #667–669,
October–November 2007)

RĀ'S AL GHŪL

Rā's al Ghūl was a long-lived man who believed his
fellow humans were destroying the planet. He built
a global operation and sought ways to drastically
reduce the world's population, putting him at odds
with forces of justice. His greatest opponent was
Batman, who was also one of the few living people
to earn his respect.

   The man who was known to many as the Demon's
Head was born in the Middle East untold centuries
ago. For his era, he was unusually large: six foot five
and 215 pounds. He was raised in a tribe of nomads
but was fascinated by science from an early age.
As they traveled from the Arabian Peninsula across
Asia, the boy absorbed information at an amazing
rate. Seeking more, he left the nomadic life in favor
of establishing himself in a city. Through the years
he studied and became a doctor, earning the favor
of many. He married a woman named Sora and
thought life could not get better.

   Some time after his wedding, the man learned

the secret of making a LAZARUS PIT, an alchemical
construct created over ley lines and capable of
restoring the dead to life. He had cause to use
the pit for the first time when the king summoned
him to tend to his ailing son, the prince. The illness
gripped the prince and ended his life, so Sora's
husband took him to the Lazarus Pit. As the prince
emerged, he was maddened by the changes to his
body and strangled Sora, breaking her husband's
heart. The king would not condemn his son's
actions and had the physician arrested instead.
After being declared guilty, the doctor was placed
in a cage with his wife's corpse.

   But he didn't die. He was freed instead by the
grateful son of a patient. They fled into the desert,
seeking the tribe of his birth. There he planned
revenge and became the first man in history to

engage in germ warfare by sending the prince
contaminated fabrics. A frantic king once more
asked for the doctor's help, but this time the grief-
stricken man took the lives of the king and prince.
His people then razed the city.

   Set against the flames engulfing the society,
he took the name *Rā's al Ghūl*, which translated
to "demon's head." (*Batman: Birth of the Demon*,
1992)

   Over the next several centuries Rā's continued
his education and sought to build a base of power.
Accompanying him early on were his uncle and the
boy who'd rescued him, until Rā's discovered that
the boy had maintained a written account of their
prolonged lives. Rā's killed the boy and then used
a Lazarus Pit on himself. When he recovered, his
uncle had fled with all the written records.

By 1250 Ra's made the first of several failed attempts to obtain the Holy Grail while the chalice was being transported to Europe. (*Batman: The Chalice* #1999) A century later, as the Black Plague ravaged Europe, he made a second attempt. He again failed, fleeing the continent.

His travels took him to South America, where he met another immortal on January 16, 1569, a man named Talon, whose long life was not dependent upon the Lazarus Pits. A friendship was formed but lasted only briefly when Talon refused to impart the natives' secret magicks to be used to stop another long-lived adversary, a man known only as Blackheart. All three paths would cross time and again for the next four centuries. (*The Batman Chronicles* #6, Summer 1996)

Ra's romanced a Russian woman and in January 1775, she gave birth to his first child, a girl named Nyssa Raatko. He left the woman to raise the child in poverty. (*Batman: Death and the Maidens* #6, March 2004) Fourteen years later, shortly after his

using the pits once more, Nyssa found him in North Africa and asked to become his protégée. By this time Ra's commanded vast resources, honing his strategic skills and establishing his global resources. It was probably around this time that he formed the League of Assassins to further his goals.

While in Sudan in 1794, Nyssa was mortally wounded and submerged in a Lazarus Pit for the first time. Soon after, Ra's left his daughter to her own devices; this was the beginning of the hard feelings she would develop for him.

A decade later, in 1808, Ra's served Napoleon Bonaparte and devastated Badajoz, Spain, once again missing a chance at the Holy Grail.

The chronicles do not record activities by the Demon's Head until 1923, when Nyssa gave birth to his grandson, Daniel. Ra's arrived and demanded custody, something his daughter refused, resorting to holding a gun on her father to make her point. (*Detective Comics* #783, August 2003) They next saw each other when SS officer Ra's al Ghūl witnessed his daughter suffering at Germany's Ravensbruck concentration camp and did nothing to help her. It was an unpleasant visit: He explained sacrifices such as his grandchildren had to be made in order for his great plan to take shape. He never revealed the plan, though. (*Batman: Death and the Maidens* #5, February 2004) While the Demon's Head had no love for the Nazi Party, he saw it as a way to amass intelligence, allies, and additional wealth. During the French occupation, Talon and Ra's crossed paths once more.

During the Woodstock Music Festival in August 1969, Ra's met a woman named Melisande, who would later give birth to his second daughter, Talia Head. (*Batman: Birth of the Demon,* 1992) Melisande soon after died at the hands of Qayin, the son of agents who worked for Ra's who died during the bombing at Hiroshima. Ra's raised her on his own, making certain that her schooling encompassed all mental and physical disciplines. Unlike Nyssa, Talia was to be denied nothing.

The League of Assassins operated in relative anonymity until the man Ra's assigned to run it, the Sensei, and he had a falling-out. The former leader took a splinter cell with him while the Demon's Head turned command over to Dr. Ebenezer Darkk, who made a series of errors that brought the League to Batman's attention.

Desperate and having fallen from grace with Ra's, Darkk took Talia as a hostage even as Batman trailed him to a small Asian nation. After running a gauntlet of assassins and freeing Talia, Batman found himself held at bay by the knife-wielding doctor. Insisting that the gun-toting Talia was "far too sweet" to kill him, the stunned Darkk reeled backward from the impact of her shot and fell directly into the path of an oncoming train. (*Detective Comics* #411, May 1971)

Ra's al Ghūl felt he had finally found the appropriate heir to his empire and consort for his daughter. His investigations revealed Batman's identity, and the Demon's Head set an elaborate scheme in motion to test the World's Greatest Detective. Batman managed to locate Ra's Himalayan headquarters and was made

the offer of a lifetime. While attracted to Talia, Batman refused both, and a rivalry between the men was established. (*Batman* #232, June 1971) Over the next several years the men fought, outmaneuvered each other, and clashed over the fate of the world.

Seeing after Talia's future remained on Ra's mind, and he went so far as to kidnap Batman; while the Dark Knight was unconscious, he had him married to Talia. (*DC Special Series* #15, Summer 1978) Not long after, Ra's found himself actually allied with the Dark Knight to defeat Qayin, who still sought the Demon's Head's death. During the event, Talia became pregnant with Damian, Ra's second grandchild. (*Batman: Son of the Demon,* 1987)

Ra's found another woman to love, aging film star Evelyn Grace, who became his second wife after all the centuries. She gave him a son, Brant, only to die soon after. (*Batman: Bride of the Demon,* 1990) In the wake of her death, Ra's seemed to focus his energies on cleansing the Earth, and indeed he stepped up his efforts.

On the anniversary of Batman's debut, Ra's al Ghūl intended to show the Caped Crusader how ineffectual his campaign against crime was and suggest that he should just let humanity destroy itself. To make the point painfully clear, he engineered the escape of numerous villains from Arkham Asylum and Blackgate Penitentiary, pushing the Gotham Guardian to his limit. While all this was physically taxing to the hero, his spirit remained strong. (*Batman* #400, October 1986)

It was Ra's who masterminded unleashing the Ebola-A virus known as the Clench that took thousands of lives in Gotham City. Batman and his allies pursued the immortal villain around the world to prevent him from unleashing a worse cache of viruses from the ancient, apocalyptic Wheel of Plagues. (*Batman: Shadow of the Bat* #53–54, *Batman* #533–534, *Detective Comics* #700–701, *Catwoman* #36, *Robin* #32–33, August–September 1996)

Soon after, he erected a language-altering "Tower of Babel" while disabling the JUSTICE LEAGUE OF AMERICA by attacking its members with worst-case-scenario protocols developed by Batman and stolen from the BATCAVE. He went so far as to distract the Dark Knight by stealing the coffins of THOMAS and MARTHA WAYNE, threatening to resurrect them in a Lazarus Pit if Batman interfered. (*JLA* #43–46, July–October 2000) Always with another plan in the works, Rā's retreated to a new base of operations, only to be tracked by Batman, who managed to stop him from distributing a mutagenic longevity drug. His actions and attitudes finally alienated Talia for the final time and she left her father, seemingly for good. (*Detective Comics* #750, November 2000)

Frustrated by his constant defeats, Rā's tried to elevate himself to godhood, only to be thwarted this time by SUPERMAN. (*Action Comics* #772–773, December 2000–January 2001) Rā's removed himself from the world stage, regrouping and furthering new plans. During this time he was reasonably anonymous and actually began a romance with an unsuspecting BLACK CANARY, before an alarmed ORACLE tipped her off to his true name. After she was mortally wounded in a battle with Rā's bodyguard UBU, the Canary's body was immersed in a Lazarus Pit, restoring her life and her long-lost sonic powers. (*Birds of Prey* #31–35, July–November 2001)

Talia continued to chafe at Rā's interference in her life. His battles with Batman cost her a chance at a romance with her "beloved," while he tried to suggest the brutish BANE was a likely replacement. Rā's went on to blame Batman for his relationship issues and tried to cause a similar rift between Bruce Wayne and DICK GRAYSON, to little effect.

Rā's and Batman next met when the Demon's Head actually got brought into the RIDDLER's and HUSH's scheme to kill Batman. The two men dueled once more in the desert. (*Batman* #616, August 2003) While he was distracted, Nyssa reappeared after years in hiding and set out to destroy the remaining Lazarus Pits, driving a dying Rā's to Batman for help. Nyssa captured her half sister Talia, repeatedly killing and resurrecting her, brainwashing the woman into becoming her father's killer. As he lay dying, Rā's admitted that he had foreseen this possibility and was pleased that his daughters were acting in concert, hoping they would learn together how right he was about the fate of the world. (*Batman: Death and the Maidens* #1–9, October 2003–August 2004)

With his daughters taking charge of the League and Talia having already exposed his wealth to LEX LUTHOR, the legacy of Rā's al Ghūl seemed to have finally been dismantled.

A longtime ally of Rā's, the White Ghost, chose to resurrect the Demon's Head, placing his eternal spirit within the body of his grandson, Damian. (*Batman Annual* #26, 2007) Rā's had already escaped certain death by inhabiting a different body, but it was rapidly decaying from radiation poisoning.

Damian didn't want to become a vessel for his grandfather, and Talia took him to alert Batman. This began a global race to protect Damian and prevent Rā's from permanent resurrection. Along the way, Rā's tested the Dark Knight's allies with promises of resurrecting loved ones, but they remained loyal to their ideals. Also threatened was the fabled land of Nanda Parbat with its mystic healing properties. At the Fountain of Essence, a variation of the Lazarus Pit, Batman and the Sensei, who claimed to be Ra's father, battled, and when the villain fell into the fountain, he was found wanting and died. The Caped Crusader also fell into the fountain and was partially rejuvenated by its properties. (*Batman* #671, January 2008)

In one potential future, a decade hence, Rā's was still alive, having made deals with members of the TEEN TITANS to allow them use of the Lazarus Pits. (*Teen Titans* [third series] #18, January 2005)

In another potential future, Rā's survived to the thirtieth century. There he murdered Leland McCauley and assumed his identity. (*The Legion* #3, February 2002) He then engineered his way into taking power on Earth and disbanded the famed Legion of Super-Heroes. Eventually his scheme was exposed and the Legion regrouped to oppose him before he could accelerate Earth's evolution and cause one in every one hundred thousand human beings to become new life-forms that would safeguard Earth's species. (*The Legion* #1–8, December 2001–July 2002)

In a different potential reality, an aging Dark Knight passed on the Batman mantle to his son and sought out Rā's al Ghūl. The Demon's Head offered Batman a chance to join him in immortality by entering the pit together. The emerging figure was a rejuvenated Batman, now possessing the souls of both men and living more than a thousand years. (*Superman & Batman: Generations* #1–4, 1999)

RATCATCHER

OTIS FLANNEGAN worked as a GOTHAM CITY Sanitation Department rat catcher, ridding the city's residents of the rodent pests. After getting involved in a street fight, Flannegan was sent to prison for a decade. Upon his release, Flannegan tracked down those city officials who'd been involved in his trial and sentence, holding them captive in the city's sewer system. Using his intimate knowledge of these sewers, he kept them his prisoners for five years until he was finally discovered by Batman. Over time, Flannegan seemed to develop a method for communing and communicating with rats, which became his allies in the commission of crimes. Ratcatcher fought Batman on numerous occasions.

Despite this unique ability, Flannegan was never a successful criminal or kidnapper, spending large amounts of time at BLACKGATE PENITENTIARY and later ARKHAM ASYLUM. While he was an inmate, his rat friends would act as couriers, and he managed to smuggle items into the prison, for barter, thanks to their help. (*Detective Comics* #585, April 1988)

When he was free, the Ratcatcher would don coveralls and a gas mask, setting out for more mischief. That ended the day the OMACs were unleashed around the world. Once again Gotham police were seeking the Ratcatcher, and the local homeless population, his friends, tried to protect

Ravager

him. The police knocked one man down just as the nanobots within him received a signal, turning the man into a cybernetic soldier. The OMAC analyzed Ratcatcher, detected his low-level meta-human power, and executed him. (*Infinite Crisis* #1, November 2005)

RAVAGER

Rose Wilson was the daughter of the deadly DEATHSTROKE THE TERMINATOR. Mercenary SLADE WILSON engaged in a brief romantic encounter with Lillian "Sweet Lili" Worth, a like-minded woman. Years later, when Lili took in a wounded Deathstroke, he finally met his fourteen-year-old daughter, who shared his white hair. (*Deathstroke the Terminator* #15, October 1992)

After Sweet Lili was killed by Wade DeFarge, one of several mercenaries in Wilson's life to use the name *Ravager*, Deathstroke asked his enemies the TEEN TITANS to look after Rose. She had already been trained in martial arts and other forms of combat, so she wound up joining the Titans on several missions. She left to be on her own, only to return to the team to act as nanny to Lian Harper, daughter of the Titan Arsenal.

Rose worked for Arsenal only briefly and then wound up being cared for by foster parents Margaret and Mark Madison. Once more Ravager turned up; he murdered the Madisons and intended to kill Rose

as part of his vengeance against Deathstroke. The Terminator arrived in time to save his daughter, who gratefully agreed to come live with her father for the first time, completing her training and become his apprentice. Her first act was to kill the Ravager, and then she took his name as her own.

It turned out that DeFarge had been a pawn used to bring Rose willingly to Deathstroke's side. He then gave the same serum to her that the army used on him, although it had psychotic effects, resulting in Rose voluntarily removing one eye to match her father. (*Teen Titans* #½, 2004)

Despite his best efforts, Deathstroke couldn't make her the killing machine he intended. After she was defeated by BATGIRL, he turned to NIGHTWING—at the time, Deathstroke believed he had renounced heroism—to be her tutor. Nightwing was bluffing, and saw this as an opportunity to teach Rose the morals that Slade Wilson would never consider. Deathstroke placed a piece of KRYPTONITE in her empty eye socket, a way to get close to and kill SUPERMAN. Instead, Nightwing told her the radiation would eventually kill her. Feeling betrayed, she turned on her father. (*Nightwing* #111–117, October 2005–April 2006)

Later, no longer using the serum Deathstroke had poured into her, she asked to rejoin a new incarnation of the Titans. ROBIN agreed as a favor to his friend and mentor, Nightwing. She has

since found comradeship and—perhaps more important—friendship with peers.

RAVEN

Raven was the son of Chief Great Eagle, who fought crime among his fellow Native Americans as Chief MAN-OF-THE-BATS. They joined the short-lived CLUB OF HEROES and then continued their activities on their own. As he grew, Raven altered his name to Raven Red and continued at his father's side. (*Batman* #62, December 1950/January 1951)

RAVENNA

Ravenna was a young woman who possessed magical powers and fought the JUSTICE SOCIETY OF AMERICA. The battle ended with the legendary team believing her dead—but her spirit survived and later turned up, moving from animal to animal as it sought a magic amulet that would bring her back to mortal form. When TIM DRAKE's stepmother DANA WINTERS DRAKE was given the jewel as a wedding gift, Ravenna attempted to obtain it. She was defeated by the combined forces of ROBIN, WILDCAT, BLACK CANARY, and the SPOILER. (*Robin 80-Page Giant* #1, September 2000)

RAWLINS, CLYDE

An undercover officer for the federal Drug Enforcement Agency, Clyde Rawlins was building a case against the international drug runners known as the GHOST DRAGONS. His efforts angered the Dragons' leader, KING SNAKE, who ordered that a message be sent. Members of the Dragons killed Rawlins's children and then tortured his wife before she, too, died. (*Robin* #1, January 1991)

Rawlins was subsequently deemed no longer fit for duty and was suspended, giving King Snake what he desired. The thirst for vengeance proved strong, and Rawlins sought to bring down the Ghost Dragons on his own, following them from Asia to Paris. He was subdued and tied to a chair, where the Dragons' local leader, Billy Hue, tortured him. Rawlins was rescued by the timely arrival of Tim Drake, in Paris to train as part of his becoming the third Robin. An appreciative Rawlins agreed to train Drake in hand-to-hand combat techniques until the Dragons arrived at the Hotel St. Germain, seeking the agent. They were rescued thanks to the arrival of Lady Shiva, who also wanted to end King Snake's drug business.

The trail led them back to Hong Kong, where King Snake possessed a hidden supply of bubonic plague that had been developed by the Nazis half a century earlier. As Robin sought the plague, Rawlins found King Snake. The two men battled but—despite being blind—the criminal was the superior fighter, and Rawlins was killed. (*Robin* #5, May 1991)

REAPER

Batman was opposed by several people using the name *Reaper*, starting with Dr. Gruener, a Jewish concentration-camp survivor. Years after losing his parents and sister to the camp run by Colonel Kurt Schloss, Gruener found him in Rutland, Vermont. Dressed as the Grim Reaper during the annual Halloween parade, Gruener killed Schloss and wound up battling Batman as well. Gruener was shocked to see what he had become and fell off a cliff before he could repent his actions. (*Batman* #237, December 1971)

Years before, though, a very different, even more brutal Reaper prowled the streets of Gotham City in the years between its costumed protectors. Socialite Judson Caspian lost his wife during a drug robbery gone bad, and sought revenge. Wearing a variation on the Grim Reaper's outfit, with a sharp

Dr. Gruener

Judson Caspian

scythe covering one hand, the Reaper cleansed the streets with the blood of criminals. He received much media attention and brought Alan Scott, the first Green Lantern, out of retirement. The rusty hero, however, was overwhelmed by the force of the Reaper's anger. Still, the arrival of a hero chastened Caspian, who fled to Europe where he raised his daughter Rachel Caspian.

During the second year of Batman's career in Gotham City, the Caspians returned. Seeing that the city remained corrupt and vile, Judson donned the Reaper's outfit once more to fight the criminals. As a result, he wound up killing Joe Chill—the man who had murdered Bruce Wayne's parents. Batman succeeded where Green Lantern had failed and finally forced the Reaper from Gotham's streets. (*Detective Comics* #573, April 1987)

Some years later, after Batman added Robin to his team, Joe Chill's son became a new Reaper, who wanted to drive Batman insane but failed to accomplish his goal. (*Batman: Full Circle*, 1992)

In the world re-formed after the events of Infinite Crisis, Joe Chill was never killed, nor did he have a son, removing these elements from the Reaper's life.

REARDON, PHILIP

Blinded, Philip Reardon managed to remarkably see through his fingertips, battling Batman as the Ten-Eyed Man.

REDBIRD

The third Robin, Tim Drake, took to using a stylized automobile, a camouflaged sports coupe outfitted with the same armaments as the Batmobile. He also rode a motorcycle, a modified 491cc, liquid-cooled "motorcross" vehicle. Both were dubbed the Redbird.

RED HOOD, THE

The Red Hood was a criminal who led a gang of men to rob a chemical plant. The robbery went awry, and Batman and Robin arrived to apprehend them. While the Dynamic Duo easily subdued the henchmen, the Red Hood scrambled atop catwalks, seeking a means of escape. With Batman and Robin at either end, the Red Hood had little choice but to dive into the chemical vat below, swimming through the conduit leading to drainage outside the plant. Having survived the chemically polluted water, he was captured by Batman and the police. When they removed his hood, they were shocked to see green hair, white skin, and ruby-red lips. The criminal had been permanently altered, an event that also seemed to unhinge his mind. This unnamed criminal then became known as the Joker. (*Detective Comics* #168, February 1951)

In the reality created by the Crisis on Infinite Earths, the man who would become the Joker may have been a chemical-technician-turned-failed-stand-up-comedian-turned-criminal, all to support his pregnant wife. He was asked by the Red Hood Gang to join them for a caper at the Ace Chemical Processing Plant. Needing the cash, he agreed and was handed the red hood and cape that other accomplices had worn in the past. On the scheduled day of the crime, police informed the man that his wife had died in a freak accident. Despite his despondency, the gang threatened his life if he did not accompany them that night. The robbery went badly, with plant security guards fatally shooting the gang as the man attempted to run. Once again,

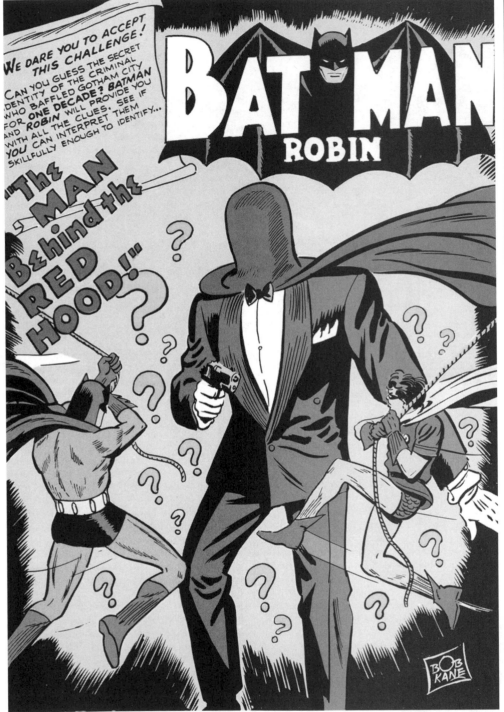

The Red Hood, pre-Joker

Jason Todd, the Red Hood

the Red Hood was confronted by Batman, and he dove into the vat of chemicals to be transformed into the Joker. (*Batman: The Killing Joke,* 1988)

The only other time the Joker donned the red hood was shortly after he killed JASON TODD and had his latest scheme thwarted. He put on the hood and committed a crime as his old self in order to restore confidence in his abilities. (*Batman* #450–451, July 1990)

Years later, a reality-altering wave resurrected Jason Todd from the dead, altering his physique to that of a full-grown adult. Seeking revenge, he donned a modified red hooded outfit and sought the Joker, beating him with a crowbar, just as the Clown Prince of Crime had beat him. At first the new Red Hood attempted to take control of Gotham's underworld; then he switched plans to take on crime disguised as NIGHTWING. Subsequently, he played a more ambiguous role, getting caught up as one of the anomalies among the re-created fifty-two parallel worlds. (*Countdown* #48, 2007)

RED MASK MOB, THE

Members of the Red Mask Mob were successfully committing crimes in GOTHAM CITY, leading Batman to plan an elaborate scheme to bring them to justice. Soon after, Police Commissioner JAMES GORDON announced that Batman had gone rogue and was a fugitive. ROBIN and ACE THE BAT-HOUND made several public attempts to bring in their former partner. As a result, Batman managed to gain admittance to the mob, where he learned the leader was LUCKY LANE. Armed with this information, he apprehended the gang with the aid of Robin, Ace, and the police. (*Batman* #122, April 1959)

RED RAVEN

On a parallel world, Red Raven led a gang of criminals who managed to elude capture while committing spectacular crimes. They were finally apprehended when Batman arrived on this oddly familiar world. There was no Batman on this Earth, with BRUCE WAYNE—looking like CLARK KENT—secretly SUPERMAN, partner to ROBIN. Reporter LOIS LANE, looking just like VICKI VALE, loved the hero, and there was no evidence of a BATWOMAN or BATGIRL. This world's JOKER was television comedian FREDDY FORBES. At first Batman was suspected of being mentally disturbed; then he aided Superman in bringing the Red Raven gang to justice. A thankful Man of Steel took Batman and the damaged BATPLANE to the point where a freak thunderstorm opened a rift between realties and let the Caped Crusader return home. (*World's Finest Comics* #136, September 1963)

REED, JULIUS

A greedy mine owner, Julius Reed preferred strong-arm tactics to maximize production without any consideration for the miners' safety. Rather than invest in safety features, he hired men to intimidate the miners into doing their jobs. Local teacher Emma Dodd and John McGraw, sole survivor of a recent cave-in, teamed with Reed's own son Todd to recruit help from Batman and ROBIN to teach the ruthless man that there were better methods to conduct business. Thanks to their intervention, he finally saw the error of his ways. (*Detective Comics* #111, May 1946)

REEVES, ARTHUR

Gotham City Public Works Commissioner Arthur Reeves was one civil servant who disapproved of the city working with a vigilante, Batman. (*Detective Comics* #399, May 1970)

As a result, Batman was at his most playful whenever Reeves was nearby. When Reeves spoke about Batman's mask, for example, the Caped Crusader removed Reeves's toupee. He remained a dedicated public figure beyond his distaste for costumed characters. Eventually he did run for mayor on an anti-Batman platform, opposing HAMILTON HILL. (*Detective Comics* #503, June 1981) When Reeves thought he had proof of Batman's identity and ties to the underworld, he went public—only to have the images prove to be fakes, costing him the election. In time, it was learned the dirty tricks were perpetrated by political boss RUPERT THORNE. (*Detective Comics* #511, February 1982)

REGAN, RORY

The latest in a long line of descendants to possess a tattered cloak, made from corrupt souls seeking redemption. Wearing it, he became RAGMAN, champion of justice.

RELAZZO, JOLENE

Jolene Relazzo was a GOTHAM CITY–based seismologist who was kidnapped by Arnold Wesker, the VENTRILOQUIST, in the days following an earthquake in Gotham. Masquerading as the QUAKEMASTER, Wesker used Relazzo's knowledge to sound authentic until his fraud was exposed by Batman and ROBIN. (*Robin* [second series] #53, May 1998)

REMARQUE, JULIA

See PENNYWORTH, JULIA.

RENNINGTON, DAVID

David Rennington turned to crime as the DAGGER to save his family's business.

RENTER, THE

A man known as DR. HAGEN was a respected expert on foreign-made weapons, but was also secret criminal the Renter. He used his expertise to fashion unique hand weapons for use by criminals. Since they were privately manufactured, there was little way to trace them, a fact complicated by the fact that customers returned the tools to Hagen after each crime. To arrest the man, Batman had to pose as an underworld figure with an extensive knowledge of weaponry. Once employed by Hagen at his private factory, Batman was able to shut down the operation, bringing Hagen and his men to justice. (*Batman* #73, October-November 1952)

REPP, EDDIE

Eddie Repp was a genius with electronics. Once he left prison, Repp developed a clever way to use the electromagnetic spectrum to create three-dimensional "ghosts" to terrorize people. His goal was to totally humiliate and demoralize Batman, who'd had him sent to jail, and then create an army of ghosts to loot GOTHAM CITY. He could also turn portions of his images solid, allowing them to pick up objects or punch well-intentioned crime fighters. Batman and ROBIN determined how Repp managed his ghosts and used that knowledge to ultimately apprehend him once more. (*Batman* #175, November 1965)

REYNOLDS, ROY

Roy Reynolds knew defeating the Batman was futile so he concentrated, with great success, on his getaways, earning him the nickname GETAWAY GENIUS.

RHINO

Fredrick Rhino was a career criminal, with his first prison term being a year at BLACKGATE PENITENTIARY for assault. When he spied the VENTRILOQUIST, Arnold Wesker, being intimidated by the bulkier Skull Bolero, he was fascinated to see the dummy SCARFACE stand up to the thug and his followers. Knowing a fight was ready to begin, Rhino took Wesker's side; and a friendship formed, with Scarface promising Rhino a job for life. Later Wesker and Rhino teamed up to spread the word that Bolero was Batman's informant. Before the night was over, the "snitch" was dead. (*Batman 80-Page Giant* #1, August 1988)

He zealously guarded Wesker when he operated the Ventriloquist's Club, a front for his drug-running operation. On numerous occasions Rhino proved to be the first line of defense between Batman and the Ventriloquist, although he was no match for the Dark Knight. As a result, the club was eventually shut down and the men arrested. (*Detective Comics* #583, February 1988)

Soon after, a criminal lawyer found technicalities that allowed both the Rhino and Wesker to go free. They found the club being used by members of the STREET DEMONZ gang, who had little use for Wesker or his wooden companion. When Scarface got splintered in a fight, Wesker presumed his partner was dead and Rhino insisted the dummy receive a proper burial. (*Batman* #475, March 1992) Revenge was the next order of business as Rhino found the Demonz's leader, Brute, and dispatched him into the Gotham River, Brute's feet encased in cement.

Wesker reopened the club and had Rhino break the JOKER out of ARKHAM ASYLUM. The goal was to have the appreciative madman turn over twenty-five million dollars that had been hidden away. The Clown Prince of Crime merely mocked them, earning him a beating from Rhino. (*Detective Comics Annual* #5, 1995) In due time Wesker wound up in Arkham and Rhino back at Blackgate, the money safely out of their reach.

When they were freed once more, Rhino wound up rescuing Scarface from the police evidence room, with the possessed dummy telling the mammoth man where a safe house was located. All he found inside was a book on ventriloquism, something he attempted to master but couldn't. (*Batman: Shadow of the Bat* #32, November 1994)

Although Rhino failed at ventriloquism, he did believe he was making Scarface talk and was eventually reunited with Wesker. Their return to crime was met with defeat, once more at the hands of the Gotham Guardian. (*Batman: Shadow of the Bat* #59-60, February–March 1997) Rhino's latest stay at Blackgate was cut short when an earthquake damaged the facility, letting the inmates free. As the city spiraled into chaos and the government cut off support, turning the area into a NO MAN'S LAND, Wesker and the Rhino were reunited. They carved out a piece of the city for themselves, actually aiding the residents with supplies and protection. When Batman intervened, the panicked people made the Dark Knight reconsider, and he allowed Rhino to remain in place. (*Detective Comics* #730, March 1999)

He soon left working for Wesker and became TWO-FACE's champion in his Trial by Combat. Two-Face selected people who might have committed crimes and then sent them into a makeshift arena where they had to survive battling Rhino. If they could emerge alive, they were deemed innocent. After that period, Rhino's whereabouts remain unrecorded.

His sister, Moose, also came to work for Scarface, some time after Wesker died. She reported to the new Ventriloquist, a gorgeous woman named Sugar. Moose had a job at Arkham and freed Harleen Quinzel in order to assist Sugar on a caper. (*Detective Comics* #831, June 2007)

RIDDLER, THE

EDWARD NIGMA was a youth obsessed with puzzles. In fact, as he grew up, he was pathologically incapable of acting without leaving telltale clues to his actions. When he turned to a life of crime, he became the Riddler, taunting police and Batman with clues to his crimes. More often than not, the World's Greatest Detective managed to figure out the crime before the Riddler could get away with the loot. When the Prince of Puzzlers managed to get the upper hand, he could not simply kill Batman and ROBIN but instead had to devise ingenious death traps, seeing if Batman could solve the puzzle before he died. (*Detective Comics* #140, December 1948) The Riddler seemed to lack a conscience, and his victims were disposable. He was known to kill on more than one occasion. (*Batman* #292, October 1977)

On the Earth formed in the wake of CRISIS ON INFINITE EARTHS, Edward Nashton was a youth fond of puzzles. At school, his teacher announced there

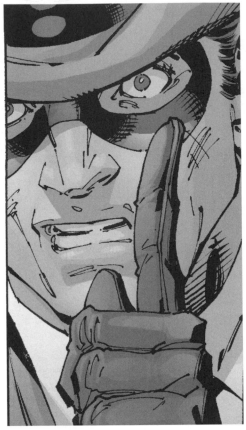

would be a puzzle game the following day; that night, Nashton searched her desk and found the game. Knowing the answers in advance enabled him to win the game, giving him a thrill—one he wanted to sustain, leading him to a life of crime. En route, Nashton first worked at a carnival, operating a game booth that was rigged to favor the business. While he enjoyed the work, he wanted more, something truly challenging. (*Secret Origins Special*, 1989) He had heard about the various costumed criminals plaguing Batman in GOTHAM CITY and saw this as the ultimate challenge. It was around this time that he also witnessed a pivotal moment in the life of the man who would become the JOKER—the death of his wife. Nashton took the name *Edward Nigma* and fashioned a costume, becoming the Riddler. (*The Question* #26, March 1989) At one point a reality-altering wave changed the Riddler's birth name to Edward Nigma. (*Detective Comics Annual* #8, 1995)

When he first began his costumed career, he was approached by bikers NINA DAMFINO and DEIRDRE VANCE, who tried to rob him. They saw one another as kindred spirits and became partners, with the women taking the names QUERY and ECHO. They worked with him on and off through the years. In between, he used other muscular women known as QUE and QUIZ. (*Detective Comics Annual* #8, 1995)

Through the years the Riddler plagued Batman and Robin with his intricate puzzles and death traps. Despite the extra muscle provided by the femme fatales, Batman invariably brought the Prince of Puzzlers to justice. The Riddler was a

regular inmate of ARKHAM ASYLUM, exchanging bon mots with the Joker.

When Arkham was damaged during the Gotham City earthquake, the Riddler chose to make his way beyond Gotham. He reached his first stop, Keystone City, only to be confronted with Robin, whose family had recently relocated. The Teen Wonder and the FLASH made short work of the criminal. (*Robin* [second series] #93–94, October–November 2001) He met similar success in Manchester, Alabama, home to the young speedster Impulse. (*Impulse* #48, May 1999)

After freeing himself from jail, the Riddler tried once more, only to be defeated by BLACK CANARY. By then, though, he had discovered that he was suffering from a brain tumor. He sought out an opinion from the renowned surgeon DR. THOMAS ELLIOT. The doctor indicated that it was inoperable, and a despondent Puzzler sought a desperate act. He tracked down one of RÄ'S AL GHÜL'S LAZARUS PITS and entered it while still alive. The transformative

effects cured him of the tumor, but also seemingly sharpened his thinking. He concluded, beyond a doubt, that Batman was millionaire BRUCE WAYNE. Returning to Elliot's office, he hatched a scheme to gain vengeance against his enemy, teaming with Elliot, who had a personal score to settle with Wayne.

Over the course of the next months, Batman was terrorized and attacked by an assortment of his adversaries. Clues were left behind, but he couldn't piece them together until a final confrontation with Elliot. After his old friend appeared to have died, Batman confronted the Riddler in Arkham. Nigma admitted to being the man behind the plan and threatened to reveal his identify. Batman called his bluff, knowing the answer to such a tasty puzzle was too good to share. (*Batman* #619, November 2003)

Soon after, though, Elliot, as HUSH, reappeared and wanted revenge, thinking he had been betrayed. Meantime, the Riddler offered to tell the Joker about his wife's death in exchange for protection. Instead, Hush and PROMETHEUS tracked down the villain and beat him. Fleeing, the Riddler sought refuge with POISON IVY. (*Batman: Gotham Knights* #50–53, April–July 2004)

Poison Ivy, disliking most men, used him as a plaything, psychologically and physically abusing him, then abandoning him. No longer possessing his sharp intellect, the Riddler wandered as one of Gotham's homeless for a time. He encountered a former National Security Agency cryptographer who worked with Nigma, restoring some of his faculties. During the process, the Riddler discovered repressed memories of being abused by his father. The man couldn't recognize his son's intellect and instead accused him of cheating, then beat him to hide the jealousy he felt. (*Detective Comics* #797–799, October–December 2004)

He took some of his remaining cash resources to undergo an extensive makeover, adding tattoos, altering his features, and changing his look to metrosexual. After killing the man who helped him recover, Nigma returned to crime and managed several successes, even eluding capture by Batman. Feeling renewed, the Riddler expanded his reach, plaguing heroes across America, going so far as to threaten Star City with a nuclear bomb until he was stopped by Green Arrow.

During the reality-altering events known as Infinite Crisis, the Riddler was seen among a group of villains attacking Gotham City police headquarters. He had reverted to his traditional appearance, suggesting that his alterations were undone. The Riddler remained an active member of the Society, a group of super-villains, throughout those events despite being roundly beaten by the Shining Knight, who left him in a coma.

After recovering, Nigma seemingly lost the compulsion to leave clues before or during crimes in addition to the knowledge that Batman was Bruce Wayne. The Riddler considered himself reformed and opened up a consulting firm, using his knowledge to solve mysteries. He was based in Gotham City and delighted in solving criminal cases before the World's Greatest Detective. (*Detective Comics* #822, October 2006)

The Riddler remained consistent in his insistence he had gone straight, even coming to aid Mary Marvel in defeating Clayface. (*Countdown* #42, 2007)

Through the years, the Riddler has relied on numerous gadgets to plan his clues and death traps, making him familiar and comfortable with all manner of technology. He tended not to carry weapons, although he occasionally had a six-foot-tall walking stick topped by a brass question mark. At one time he drove a green vehicle with a license plate reading: ???

In an alternate reality, the traditional Earth-3, the Riddler's counterpart was known as the Quizmaster and was a member of the Justice Underground, led by Lex Luthor.

RIGGER, JOSEPH

A pyrotechnics-technician-turned-pyromaniac as costumed villain the Firebug.

RILEY, NAILS

Nails Riley was briefly a Gotham City underworld chief. He created a plan to rob big-game hunter Byron King of his entire fortune but failed after the intervention of Batman and Robin. (*Detective Comics* #192, February 1953)

RINALDI, CARY

Infected with a deadly disease, Cary Rinaldi arrived in Gotham City, unaware that he was spreading a virus as the Carrier.

ROBBER BARON, THE

The criminal mastermind known as the Robber Baron robbed from businesses and homes that towered over the streets of Gotham City. He managed these amazing feats by using cables to connect between buildings; a specially designed cable car crossed from building to building. Batman and Robin, aided by Alfred Pennyworth, determined the method and then apprehended the Baron and his men. (*Detective Comics* #75, May 1943)

ROBIN

Robin the Boy Wonder was Batman's partner in almost every reality that has been chronicled.

On Earth-2, a young Bruce Wayne adopted the Robin persona to protect his identity when he approached detective Harvey Harris to train him. Years later, he passed the costume on to another. Dick Grayson's parents died in a circus accident, and

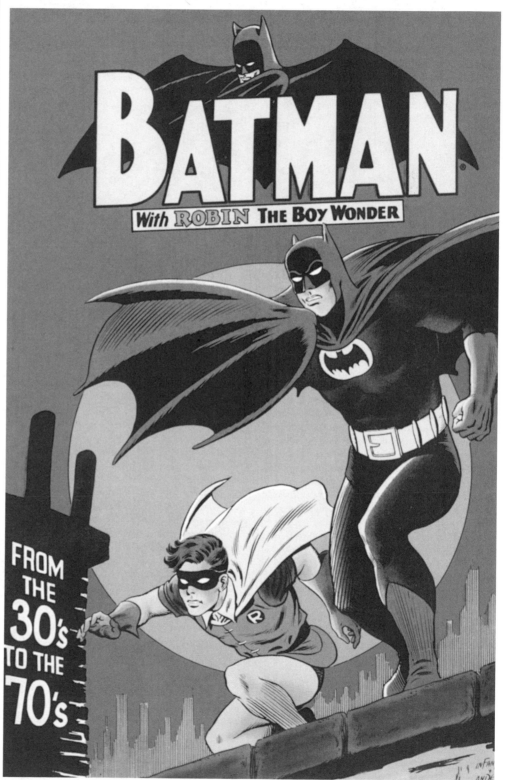

Dick Grayson as Robin

WHAT I WAS TRAINED TO DO!

GONNA KICK SOME TAIL!!

Jason Todd

the grief-stricken youth was taken in by Batman. Dick swore an oath by candlelight to assist in the war on crime and trained to become a costumed sidekick named Robin. (*Detective Comics* #38, April 1940) Dick Grayson fought beside Batman for years, eventually growing up and becoming his own person, studying the law and adopting an adult costume styled after his mentor's. He followed Batman in joining the JUSTICE SOCIETY OF AMERICA and wound up sacrificing his life to save others during the CRISIS ON INFINITE EARTHS.

On Earth-1, the same fate befell the FLYING GRAYSONS at the HALY BROS. CIRCUS, and Batman took in the youth. He trained with Batman and joined him as Robin, happily fighting alongside Bruce Wayne for years. In his early teens, he helped form the TEEN TITANS and was its leader for most of its duration. As he entered his twenties, he grew apart from Batman, going to HUDSON UNIVERSITY for a semester and soon after crafting his own identity, taking a new costume and the name NIGHTWING.

On the world fashioned after the Crisis on Infinite Earths, Richard John "Dick" Grayson's beginnings were largely the same. When Batman insisted on a lengthy training period, Dick Grayson complied, and when he was given his own costume, he chose Robin, a nickname his mother had given him. He

grew up, became Nightwing, and continued to be his own man while still loving the one who raised him. Whenever Batman needed him, Dick Grayson answered the call.

Shortly after Grayson left to become Nightwing, JASON PETER TODD entered Batman's life. (*Batman* #357, March 1983) In one version of reality, Jason was the son of circus performers who died trying to help a circus when KILLER CROC threatened it. After a reality-altering wave, Jason became a street youth who was discovered by Batman trying to steal the BATMOBILE's tires. (*Batman* #408, June 1987) Batman took the impetuous youth into WAYNE MANOR and allowed him to become the second Robin. Jason, though, proved headstrong and difficult, complicating Batman's attempts to train him. When he defied Batman and went in search of his birth mother, Todd wound up being killed by the JOKER. Years later he was resurrected by another reality-altering event known as INFINITE CRISIS and competed with Batman as the RED HOOD.

On the fateful night when the Flying Graysons plummeted to their deaths, JACK, JANET, and TIMOTHY DRAKE were all in attendance. (*Batman* #436, Early August 1989) Later, when a new hero named Robin was seen beside Batman, Tim recognized an acrobatic move, convincing him that Dick

Grayson was Robin. After Todd died, Tim began a one-teen campaign to convince Batman he needed a Robin and Tim was the male for the job. Batman reluctantly agreed, but only after insisting that Drake spend six months in intensive training. After that, Drake excelled as Robin, bonding with Grayson and assuming his role as leader of the Teen Titans.

At one point Jack Drake discovered his son's secret identity and made him give up adventuring. This prompted STEPHANIE BROWN, daughter of Batman's foe the CLUEMASTER, and Drake's girlfriend at the time, to apply to become Robin. She had been wearing the costumed identity of SPOILER but was all enthusiasm and little training. Batman agreed to work with her—on the understanding that she would be fired the moment she disobeyed a direct order. For nearly three months, she trained and fought by his side until she did as he expected and ignored a directive. He fired her, and in a desperate act to gain acceptance, she initiated one of his WAR GAMES scenarios. It ignited a gang war in Gotham City and ended her life.

In other realities and other time lines, there were others to wear the uniform or use the name Robin.

In the year 3000, on an Earth under alien domination, the twentieth generation of Waynes became crusaders for justice. Bruce Wayne XX and his nephew Tom became a new Batman and Robin. (*Robin 3000* #1–2, 1993) In the 853rd century Robin was actually a robotic construct nicknamed the Toy Wonder. The robot aided Batman, with both based on Pluto, until the human died during a prison riot. Robin continued to function, following its programming. (*DC One Million* #1, November 1998)

In the far distant future, long after Earth had died, legends emerged about champions through the ages, and their stories continued to be told. One such hero was Tris Plover, a twenty-nine-year-old who led a rebellion against the Proctors. When she encountered a Batman, she became his Robin. They gave their lives to buy freedom for others. (*Robin Annual* #5, 1996) A different legend told of three children who built a Batman robot, with two of them, Deals and Geela, becoming Robins and the third assisting them as Alfred Gordon. (*Detective Comics Annual* #9, 1996)

ALFRED PENNYWORTH indulged himself with fanciful stories imagining his charges in their later years. He saw Bruce Wayne married to KATHY KANE and raising a son, Bruce Jr., who became another Robin, complete with Roman numeral to differentiate himself from Grayson. (*Batman* #131, April 1960)

One reality saw a darker, grimmer world with Dick Grayson as a twelve-year-old when his parents died. His acrobatic work caught Batman's attention, so when his parents were brutally murdered, Batman immediately took the youth away from corrupt police and into his custody. Batman intended Dick to learn for himself, only to have his efforts undercut by a more sympathetic Alfred. (*All-Star Batman and Robin* #1, September 2005) As time passed, the two men butted heads until Batman finally fired Grayson. He went on to become Nightwing as Batman tapped Jason Todd to be his new Robin. When Todd died, Batman

Tim Drake

more or less gave up and retired from the public life. At age fifty-five, though, Bruce Wayne found himself once more donning the cape and cowl to lead an underground movement against the government. A teen named CARRIE KELLY attached herself to Batman and became the new Robin. (*The Dark Knight Returns* #1–4, 1986) Later the Joker sought to kill a new Robin, but he failed to kill Kelly, who had changed to Catgirl by then. Instead he fought Batman and finally killed Dick Grayson. (*Batman: The Dark Knight Returns* #1–3, 2002)

In a reality known as Earth-32, Dick Grayson had given up his Robin persona, only to return years later and resume his crime-fighting career as Red Robin. He and the alien princess STARFIRE married and had a child, a girl who possessed powers, dubbed Nightstar. (*Kingdom Come* #1, 1996)

An entirely different Robin was seen on a parallel world, an orphan in the thrall of the evil Reverend Darkk. He worked alongside a handful of other heroes, only to reveal his true allegiance. In the end he was transformed into another being, the Atom. (*Just Imagine Stan Lee with John Byrne Creating Robin,* 2002)

In sixteenth-century Japan, Tengu was the rightful heir to the throne who was adopted and raised by the man known as Bat-Samurai. (*Robin Annual* #6, 1997) A seventeenth-century reality saw Batman as a pirate known as LEATHERWING with Robin Redblade, a British orphan, becoming his

ally. (*Detective Comics Annual* #7, 1997) During the French Revolution, Bruce Wayne was Batman, and his sister Rowena crafted a Robin outfit to join his crusade. (*Batman: Reign of Terror,* 1999) A world that benefited from a Batman during the

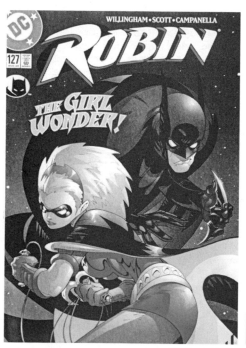

Stephanie Brown

American Civil War saw a Native American named Redbird be adopted by Wayne and become his partner. (*The Blue, the Gray and the Bat,* 1993) On a world where Bruce Wayne became Batman during World War II, Alfred Pennyworth was his Robin. (*Batman: Dark Allegiances,* 1996) In a reality where Wayne became a cop, Richard Graustark—a circus acrobat—was Robin, and he was joined by BARBARA GORDON as Batman in the 1960s. (*Batman: Thrillkiller* #1, January 1997)

On a world with fantastic creatures, a youth named Robin Drake assembled a set of champions to take on Etrigan the Beast. (*JLA: The Riddle of the Beast,* 2002) A different, high-tech reality posited that JAMES GORDON's grandson, James III, would become the next Batman, with the impetuous youth Robert Chang as the new Robin. (*Batman Digital Justice,* 1990)

ROBIN HOOD

Batman and Robin were sent through time by PROFESSOR CARTER NICHOLS and encountered Sir Robin of Locksley, the English noble who fought the evils of King Richard as Robin Hood. The Dynamic Duo arrived in time to adventure with Robin Hood and his Merry Men, including participating in the famous archery contest that was actually a plan to capture the people's hero. Robin Hood led an assault on the castle, and the crime fighters helped apprehend the corrupt Sheriff of Nottingham. (*Detective Comics* #116, October 1946)

ROBINSON, HOLLY

Holly Robinson ran away from home, tired of being hit by her abusive father. Although she left her two bothers behind, Holly felt she had little choice. Robinson was a thirteen-year-old prostitute in GOTHAM CITY when she met fellow runaway SELINA KYLE. Kyle came to Robinson's defense against a corrupt cop and the two bonded, becoming lifelong friends. (*Batman* #404, February 1987) Not long after, Holly and Selina chose to leave their pimp Stan, who did not take kindly to his girls having minds of their own. To keep them in line, he had Selina's sister MAGGIE KYLE taken and beaten. Selina found out and, in a rage, killed Stan—a choice that sent her life in a direction apart from Holly. Robinson accompanied Maggie, who was preparing to take her vows, back to the nearby convent. (*Catwoman* #1, February 1989)

Robinson decided the holy life was not for her and left the convent, quickly returning to the streets with drugs and prostitution filling her time. When a serial killer went after Gotham's EAST END hookers, she sought refuge in her old apartment and was thrilled to find Selina once more in residence. By then Kyle was well established as CATWOMAN and could therefore help her friend.

Under Selina's watchful eye, Robinson got herself clean and became totally devoted to watching Selina's back. She became an informant for Kyle, with Catwoman paying her for information to keep Holly away from the street life. During this time, Robinson was reunited with another old friend, a woman named Karon, and the two became lovers, forming a committed relationship. (*Catwoman* [third series] #3, March 2002)

Holly Robinson

Robinson and Kyle remained the best of friends; over time Holly was trusted with most of Catwoman's secrets. Unfortunately she also got caught up in some of the darker doings and wound up being forced to kill a woman named Sylvia Sinclair, a childhood friend of Selina's. This incident shook Robinson, and it took her a long while to learn to cope.

When Holly was ready, Selina began training her to handle herself in a fight. In addition to her personal efforts, Kyle had Robinson work with former heavyweight champion Ted Grant, who was a fellow costumed adventurer, WILDCAT. During the course of the training, the two women traveled the country and wound up in St. Roch, where Selina had located Holly's brother Davey and arranged a tearful reunion.

After killing BLACK MASK, Selina and SLAM BRADLEY shut down the remainder of the criminal's operations, becoming lovers during this time. The relationship resulted in Kyle becoming pregnant, so Holly intensified her training and became the second Catwoman. (*Catwoman* [third series] #53, May 2006) Holly was believed to be the Catwoman who murdered Black Mask, and she was arrested. Selina returned to her costume to clear Holly's name. The Russian villains Hammer and Cycle went after Selina, threatening both Holly's girlfriend Karon and Selina's baby, HELENA WAYNE. Holly arrived in time to save Selina's life as the Russian villains fell to their deaths. Selina and Holly parted ways, with Holly heading to METROPOLIS to start anew. (*Catwoman* [third series] #68, August 2007)

Upon her arrival, she found sanctuary in a shelter run by the Greek goddess Artemis. She and Harleen Quinzel, the former villain HARLEY QUINN, became friends as Holly began to work as an assistant. (*Countdown* #47, 2007)

In a reality prior to the CRISIS ON INFINITE EARTHS, Holly actually cleaned herself up and married a man, moving to New Jersey. Upon hearing of this, Catwoman visited the Garden State and avenged her friend. (*Action Comics Weekly* #611–614, 1988) Her resurrection after the Crisis became an anomaly of concern for the cadre of Monitors who sought to keep the fifty-two parallel universes uncontaminated. (*Countdown* #46, 2007)

ROBINSON PARK

Dedicated in 1784, Robinson Park was the largest park in GOTHAM CITY, covering an area of three hundred acres in central Gotham. (*Batman* #404, February 1987) It included an *Alice in Wonderland* statue near its entrance gates, a statue of a rifle-wielding soldier on horseback near its south gate, and was located on Elliot Street. It also hosted the periodic Robinson Park Carnival. A statue representing the civilian heroes of NO MAN'S LAND was unveiled in the recent past. (*Batman: Gotham Knights* #32, October 2002) Visitors got a view of the entire park from the top of Finger Castle, adjacent to Mike Lake.

Located within the park was the Wayne Botanical Garden, established in 1870 (*Batman* #568, November 1986) or 1879 by a grant from C. L. Wayne. (*Detective Comics* #562, May 1996) POISON IVY took control of the park during the No Man's Land year but was eventually forced out by Batman and the G.C.P.D. (*Batman: No Man's Land* #1, March 1999) Curiously, a sign at the park's southwest entrance (A GIFT FROM WAYNE ESTATE) said the park was established in 1782.

The Forum of the Twelve Caesars statues, presumably connected to the historical museum of the same name, was at the north end of Robinson Park. (*Batman* #263, May 1975) Statues of Nero and Caligula secretly included the means of accessing one of Batman's auxiliary Batcaves fifty feet below the bottom of Robinson Park Reservoir. The park was adjacent to the Knightsdome sports complex. More than twenty years ago the area was briefly terrorized by the Robinson Park Ripper, and a modern-day Ripper was ultimately revealed to be Victor Fries, Mister Freeze. (*Legends of the Dark Knight* #204-206, June-August 2006)

RODDY, JOHN

Batman and Robin deduced that John Roddy was an innocent man, falsely convicted of murder and about to die for the crime. Although they managed to figure this out while accidentally trapped within the Batcave, the Dynamic Duo had to find a way free to save Roddy's life. They succeeded and apprehended the real killer, criminal Leon Paul, in time to save Roddy. (*Batman* #108, June 1957)

RODER, RALPH

Ralph Roder was an assistant animal trainer, working for the famed Arthur Harris at the Gotham City Charity Circus. He was also unscrupulous and devised a way to commit a robbery and deflect blame from himself. Roder attached an electric cable to the platform where their star attraction, the unusually intelligent ape Mogo, was performing. The shock sent Mogo wild, causing a distraction that allowed the crime, committed by the Vanning Brothers, to go off without interference. Harris was suspected of causing the distraction to perpetrate the crime and was arrested. Batman and Robin investigated, suspecting Harris was an innocent. Mogo was unusually drawn to the Gotham Guardian, so he escaped the circus and followed the hero back to the Batcave. There, he donned a spare cape and cowl, briefly becoming Bat-Ape. The terrific trio managed to find the evidence that Roder and the Vanning Brothers were the actual thieves, clearing Harris. (*Batman* #114, March 1958)

RODRIGUEZ, ARTURO

Arturo Rodriguez was a telejournalist based in Gotham City when a vicious gang war broke out. His continuous coverage brought the horrors of the shootings to life. It also saw him change his well-publicized opinion of Batman, from ardent supporter to severe critic. The change occurred when the Dark Knight emerged from Louis E. Grieve Memorial High School carrying the dead body of student Darla Aquista and Rodriguez made the snap judgment, on the air, that the Batman was responsible. (*Batgirl* #51, June 2004)

ROGAN, "ROCKETS"

A career criminal named Rogan earned the nickname "Rockets" for his fascination with rockets of all sorts, including the rocket-propelled grenade launcher that he used to rob the Gotham City Bank. Batman had been recently exposed to gases taken from the upper atmosphere, and it temporarily turned him into a giant; he exiled himself from Gotham so as not to endanger the citizens. As a result, he offered limited help as Robin and Batwoman investigated and ultimately apprehended Rogan and his men. During this time, to protect his Bruce Wayne alter ego, Batman had Superman appear disguised as Wayne. (*Detective Comics* #292, June 1961)

ROGERS

The first man to reach the moon, he was exposed to a comet's tail. Returning to Earth, he became the villainous Moonman.

ROGERS, EDDIE

Eddie Rogers was a model prisoner, determined to go straight, and was given a one-day Christmas parole. During that time he was nearly murdered for no apparent reason, prompting Batman to investigate. Happenstance had Rogers a near-perfect twin to Bruce Wayne, allowing Batman to impersonate Rogers to find the truth. The investigation led to a tunnel under the state prison, which was being dug to free Rogers's former boss, Scarface Malone. Since Rogers didn't want to go along with the scheme, he was targeted for death so as not to reveal the tunnel's existence. Batman brought Malone's men to justice. (*Batman* #45, February/March 1948)

ROGUE'S ROOST

When the Joker and Penguin first allied, they shared a headquarters that was called the Rogue's Roost. The lair, like the partnership, did not last long. (*Batman* #25, October/November 1944)

ROH KAR

Roh Kar was a Martian police officer on Earth-2 who arrived to assist Batman in arresting the criminal Quork. Impressed by Batman's skill, the policeman from Mars declared him the greatest lawman in the universe. (*Batman* #78, August/September 1953)

ROHRBACH, AMY

In the city of Blüdhaven, being an honest cop made you unique. Amy Rohrbach was not only honest but also an attractive, well-adjusted public servant. She was assigned rookie patrolman Dick Grayson and immediately resented him, feeling he was just another young guy on the take. Once she got to know him, though, Amy recognized that he was just as forthright and honest as she was. When she invited him home for dinner, he naturally assumed she was hitting on him—until he arrived to discover she was happily married to Jim with two children, Emma and Justin. (*Nightwing* [second series] #48, October 2000)

As Rohrbach got to know Grayson, she made the first of several decisions affecting him. First, she took him into her inner circle, a secret cadre of police officers who were trying to stem the rampant corruption in the department. Grayson had chosen to become a cop to learn firsthand about the corruption, which he could then deal with as Nightwing.

Her reputation and profile made Rohrbach the ideal candidate to become the new chief of police after her predecessor, Redhorn, was murdered. All the pieces of evidence required to take down the corrupt police administration were left to Redhorn's widow until Nightwing obtained them. Rohrbach and Nightwing shared an alliance, not as close as Batman and Commissioner James Gordon, but a comfortable one. She even took to occasionally using a "Nightwing Signal." They cemented their relationship for good when Nightwing arrived to save Rohrbach and her family from retribution. During that time she deduced that Nightwing was Grayson, a secret she swore to keep. Still, as police captain, she felt his double life would compromise his effectiveness on the force and insisted he turn in his badge.

She also chose to compromise her cherished integrity when she covered for Grayson in the wake of Blockbuster's murder. Rohrbach claimed Grayson was working undercover when she knew he was a witness to Tarantula firing the fatal shot. (*Nightwing* [second series] #97, November 2004)

Soon after, the deadly toxins unleashed when Chemo was dropped from above destroyed the city. Nightwing made certain the entire Rohrbach family was safely evacuated.

ROHTUL

In a potential future, Rohtul was a descendant of Lex Luthor operating in 2957. Like his ancestor, Rohtul intended to use his technological prowess to subjugate the Earth and be its ruler. He was stopped thanks to the combined efforts of the twentieth century's champions Batman, Robin, and Superman. (*World's Finest Comics* #91, November/December 1957)

ROKEJ (CHIEF)

In a potential twenty-first century, Rokej was the chief of police in Gotham City. Unlike his ancestor, Rokej chose to abide by the law and was aided by a visiting Batman and Robin in stopping an industrial saboteur named Erkham from causing damage at the Comet spacecraft company. (*Batman* #59, June/July 1950)

ROLLING, BIG BEN

Career criminal Ben Rolling began a new scheme that forced holders of large life insurance policies to name Rolling and his men as beneficiaries. Soon after, the policyholders were killed. The scheme seemed to work just fine. One day crusading Gotham City reporter Larry Spade found out about the plot, investigated, and brought his findings to Batman. Rolling killed Spade, but by then it was too late. Along with Robin, the Gotham Guardian brought down Rolling and his men. The men stood trial and were found guilty, with Rolling being executed for the murders. (*Batman* #19, October/November 1943)

ROMAN, THE

A nickname for Carmine Falcone, Gotham City's underworld boss.

ROMANA

Romana Vrezhenski was one of several people from the former Soviet Republic to come to Gotham City in an attempt to stake out territory for their criminal operations. Gotham's Little Odessa neighborhood was the site of territorial conflicts between mobsters and gangs. Shortly after Bruce Wayne returned to the Batsuit after sustaining crippling injuries, Romana and her mob were opposed by the Cossack, Dark Rider, and a man known as Colonel Vega. With the Dark Rider dying of radiation poisoning, Batman and Robin had to stop the desperate man before a nuclear device was detonated. Meantime, Romana was taking a different approach, attempting to extort money from Wayne Enterprises to keep the bomb from blowing up. CEO Lucius Fox refused her demands, so she sent the KGBeast to bomb a Wayne-owned manufacturing plant. Robin rushed to the plant to save it, only to battle the vicious KGBeast. As Robin stopped the KGBeast and rescued a wounded Sergeant Harvey Bullock, Bruce Wayne came to the realization that Romana was bluffing. Wayne ignored her, changed to Batman, and went to aid Robin in stopping the real bomb from going off. (*Robin* [second series] #12, December 1994)

ROSE, NICHOLAS

Nicholas Rose was an alias for Nicholas Kazantzakis, aka the Tracker. Using his considerable skills as a member of the Network, he attempted to destroy Batman.

ROSE, RODERICK

An unfortunate man who was transformed into the insectoid creature named Hellgrammite.

ROSE, "SPECS"

"Specs" Rose was a notorious criminal whose career came crashing to a halt when his latest scheme failed. He and his men sabotaged a rail line in order to force a train carrying bank currency off the rails, but they were apprehended by Batman and Robin. (*Batman* #56, December 1949/January 1950)

ROSS, HENRY

This professor was accidentally exposed to large amounts of radiation, turning him into the crazed Professor Radium.

RUSSO, BIG MIKE

After the criminal "Big" Mike Russo was apprehended by Batman, he was found guilty and sent to prison. While he was there, Russo's men took control of the prison by overwhelming Warden Higgins. They then used the prison as their base of operations, committing crimes with impunity. After Batman figured out the scheme, he impersonated a prisoner—only to have the inmates pierce his disguise. They sentenced the Caped Crusader to the gas chamber, but Robin arrived in time to replace the poison with a seltzer tablet. With Batman feigning death, he was able to surprise the criminals and, with Robin's help, restore order. (*Batman* #8, December 1941/January 1942)

RYALL, ROGER

Roger Ryall was a Gotham City crime boss who chose to visit Dr. Richter, a psychiatrist, to overcome his fear of cats. While undergoing treatment, he realized that the psychiatrist's files were a treasure trove. He stole the files and gleaned information about prominent and wealthy citizens who would pay to keep their secrets. When one such meeting led to the death of Grant Young, Richter stepped forward and informed Batman of what had happened. From the doctor's information, the Dark Knight Detective was able to guess which patient would be contacted next. As a result, the Dynamic Duo arrived, cats in tow, and scared Ryall into surrendering. Ryall, though, was so anxious from the felines' presence that he suffered a fatal heart attack. (*Batman* #39, February/March 1947)

RYDER, BEN

Ben Ryder and his partner, Slick Ronson, began to dress in the guise of warriors from different time periods and used their frightening appearance to commit a series of notorious crimes throughout Gotham City. While the citizens thought the men had come from the past, Batman and Robin determined they were merely modern-day thugs. The Dynamic Duo concocted a scheme to lure the men out of hiding and brought them to justice. (*Batman* #149, August 1962)

RYDER, RUBY

Considered the world's richest woman and female tycoon, Ruby Ryder was based out of Gotham City's tallest skyscraper, a building topped with a pair of scarlet R's. She was used to getting her way and thought money would solve all problems. The flame-tressed woman was forced to reassess matters after summoning Batman to her office, offering him five million dollars for charity if he would locate her missing fiancé, Kyle Morgan. He agreed, easily found the man, and delivered him to Ryder, only to watch in shock as she shot her lover at point-blank range. She then fled the country, with Batman in pursuit. After he apprehended her, she was tried, convicted, and sentenced to death. On the day of her execution, things took a bizarre twist when Batman revealed the executioner to be Kyle Morgan, an alias being used by the hero Plastic Man. He explained that he was tired of being the comical detective and had created Morgan to try a serious life. Ryder's bullets had bounced off his pliant body, and his existence saved her life. (*The Brave and the Bold* #95, April/May 1971)

The trio crossed paths a second time when Batman left for Europe and Plastic Man substituted for him in Gotham. She brainwashed the Pliable Policeman into believing he was really the Dark Knight, sending him after Bruce Wayne on false charges, clearing the way for her to secure a rare African totem that Wayne had been bidding against her to obtain. With Metamorpho's help, Batman restored Plastic Man's mind and then had Ryder and her lawyer arrested. (*The Brave and the Bold* #123, December 1975)

Ryder saw to it that her lawyer, Hinton, took the fall for the crimes and she was free once more. She next tried to swindle Bruce Wayne out of his property, the Wayne Foundation building standing next to Ryder's global headquarters. Excavation of a time capsule revealed a forged deed but also led to the discovery of Jason Morgan, a synthetic man kept in a form of suspended animation. Ryder quickly had Morgan declared a legal human being so he could inherit the properties, and suddenly Bruce Wayne found himself locked out of his own home. Aided by the Metal Men and Green Arrow, Batman uncovered the truth that the document was a fake. During a fight, one of the R's atop her own skyscraper came loose, and Jason sacrificed himself to save Ryder's life. (*The Brave and the Bold* #135–136, July–September 1977)

SACRED ORDER OF SAINT DUMAS

Some time after the Knights Templar formed during the Crusades, they split into two factions. One faction followed Dumas, a charismatic figure whose sanity was questioned by many of his most ardent followers. During Dumas's lifetime, the

order paralleled the Knights Templar, protecting pilgrims in the Middle East and amassing vast wealth. Under Dumas's guidance, the Order began to amass knowledge by kidnapping the world's great thinkers. Members also began to train a champion to be their vanguard, and this fighter was named Azrael. It became a hereditary title, and the recipients were among the world's first subjects of genetics-based breeding. (*Batman: The Sword of Azrael* #1, October 1992)

In the years following Dumas's death, his spirit was said to inhabit the order's secret headquarters, pushing his followers to remain faithful to his fanatical teachings. Over time, the world forgot about the order—and members preferred this anonymity, which allowed them to grow and prosper without attracting notice. By the twentieth century they were technologically superior, and their Azraels continued to become stronger, faster, and more durable. They sent each Azrael successor out in the world to learn how to operate among different cultures. The Dumas training, known as the System, was buried beneath mental barriers, so the successor tended to operate in ignorance. Jean-Paul Valley was studying in Gotham City when his father, the current Azrael, turned up on his doorstep, dying. Valley became the next Azrael, the System taking possession of his mind. However, Valley had allied himself with Batman, and the young man saw how corrupt the order had become. In time, Azrael destroyed the order while learning that it was actually a radical splinter cell from the main Order of Saint Dumas, which remained in hiding.

Some time after the splinter group had been obliterated and Valley died, the main order resurfaced and sought out the onetime Manhunter, Mark Shaw, to be its next champion.

SAGE, VICTOR

A crusading journalist who became the inquiring crime buster known as the Question.

SAID, DAVID

Batman became aware of the evolution overtaking the espionage organization Checkmate thanks to the arrival of David Said and fellow agents in Gotham City. (*Detective Comics* #768, May 2002) Said was the team's Black King and actually breached the Batcave to recruit the Huntress. She briefly accepted the offer to be the Black Queen, playing double agent at the Dark Knight's request. (*Batman: Gotham Knights* #38–40, April–June 2003) Later, when Batman was investigating who had framed Bruce Wayne for the murder of Vesper Fairchild, he turned to Said once again for information and assistance. At some point Said was removed from his position, but he remained with the organization. When the operation was reformed, he was assigned to stay at its Whiteside headquarters, overseeing

the security work done by Carl Draper, a former super-villain once known as Deathtrap. (*Checkmate* [second series] #17, October 2007)

SAMARITAN

Luke Hames was infected by an alien invader named Gemir, whose bodily fluids activated Hames's metagene, providing him with the ability to heal others. The encounter came at a time when Hames, a fugitive from justice, had taken his half brother, Father Dennison, and Dennison's charges, a collection of spelling-bee contestants, hostage. By that point Dennison had convinced Hames to turn himself in, and they were nearing GOTHAM CITY during the fateful encounter. Gemir had also bitten Dennison, and his emerging powers caused the death of a local sheriff and deputy. Hames, though, managed to save the deputy's life. With Dennison—who was calling himself CARDINAL SIN—on a rampage, Hames knew that his mission was to stop his sibling. As they arrived in Gotham, Samaritan was aided by JEAN-PAUL VALLEY, who at the time was substituting as Batman. The two brothers struggled, and although Samaritan subdued Cardinal Sin, it left him in a coma. Batman took Cardinal Sin into custody. (*Legends of the Dark Knight Annual* #3, 1993) Hames, the Samaritan, has remained out of the spotlight ever since.

SAMSARA

Eight-year-old Sam Yates believed that GOTHAM CITY's urban legend, Batman, existed. His belief was so powerful that when Yates died in a car collision with a truck, his spirit remained on Earth. His "ghost" inhabited body after body of people Batman had missed saving in order to learn how this great hero could have proven so fallible. The Dark Knight came to discover the body-hopping spirit when a convenience-store clerk, who died during his battle with KILLER CROC, seemingly came back to life. Batman traced the bodies and determined that the path led back to Yates's untimely death. Batman named the spirit Samsara, after the Hindu reincarnation belief. Samsara found his mother and scared her into oncoming traffic; fortunately, Batman was present to save her. The spirit understood that Batman never relented, but that sometimes people still died. Finally he had his answer, and Sam left the mortal plane. (*Batman: Gotham Knights* #3–4, May–June 2000)

SANCHEZ, HECTOR

The madman who killed people under the name the INQUISITOR.

SANTA KLAUS

A serial killer named Santa Klaus ran amok in GOTHAM CITY until Batman apprehended him. Placed in ARKHAM ASYLUM, the psychotic resided quietly until the JOKER freed him. He went back to killing and wound up coming between Batman and LEW MOXON's bodyguard, PHILO ZEISS, who was about to kill a rival mob boss and his daughter. Klaus was rearrested and returned to Arkham, only to escape in the days before Christmas. He began using bombs to attack people seen with Christmas presents, until Batman took him down on Christmas Eve. He was returned to Arkham. (*Joker: Last Laugh* #5, December 2001)

SANTA PRISCA

Located in the Caribbean, the island of Santa Prisca was named for a Roman emperor who turned Christian. (*Batman: Bane of the Demon* #1, March 1998) It was colonized by the Spanish who brought with them disease, leading to the myth of the Mugre, a creature of filth and waste.

The small country was ravaged by power-grabbing military men or drug lords, leaving it impoverished and a haven for illegal activities. The tenor of the country was settled during a three-day coup modeled after the uprising in Cuba. During this period a man named Juan Paolo Sebastion was *El Jefe del Pais* until he was ousted and went into exile. Dr. THOMAS WAYNE was volunteering to care for the sick and wounded during a brief visit at this time. He continued even after learning the military had put a price on his head. (*Batman: Bane of the Demon* #1, March 1998) Also on the island at the time was Sir Edmund Dorrance, in the days before he became KING SNAKE, encouraging the revolutionaries; he fell in love with a woman, impregnating her before he left rather than be captured. (*Batman: Gotham Knights* #48, February 2004)

Those who tried to free the country found themselves imprisoned at Pena Duro—the "hard stone." One such inmate was the pregnant woman, sentenced to pay for her lover's crimes. She gave birth to her son while in jail, and the boy grew up to become Batman's dangerous nemesis, BANE. (*Batman: Vengeance of Bane* #1, January 1993)

Sebastion returned after a decade away and retook the palace using foreign mercenaries. He was bankrolled by unnamed Swiss interests, who insisted the island's Jesuits be removed. The man who ordered this was killed by an AZRAEL at some undefined point in time. Sebastion began calling himself *del Mundo*—"of the world"—and nationalized several businesses, including ZESTI COLA. The soft drink company funded a subsequent revolution that threw Sebastion out of office. (*Birds of Prey: Revolution* #1, 1997)

The Santa Priscan capital was Bogardaville, home to the presidential palace and the Hotel Paradiso and not far from Puerto Buitre. After Santa Prisca's prime minister balked at paying for a deal with the ruthless General Tuzik, Bogardaville was subjected to neural shock cannon assaults as an example to Tuzik's other partners. (*JLA: Classified* #17, April 2006)

Batman first became involved with the doings on the Eastern Caribbean island when he learned that Gotham financier Carl Fisk had seized control of their narcotics operations. (*Legends of the Dark Knight* #5, March 1990) He first journeyed to the country in pursuit of scientist Randolph Porter, who invented the drug known as VENOM. (*Legends of the Dark Knight* #16–20, March–July 1991) Seeing how poor the people were, BRUCE WAYNE bankrolled a ring of smugglers who brought medical supplies to the needy populace. (*Batman Annual* #13, 1989)

Bane escaped prison, returning home to back an anti-US faction during Santa Prisca's elections. The election proved to be rigged by Computron under orders from CHECKMATE's AMANDA WALLER, and Bane forced the current regime to declare martial law as the country teetered on the brink of civil war. (*Checkmate* [second series] #11, April 2007)

SANTOS, SOPHIA

This woman became a criminal using the name THANATOS.

SARTORIUS, ALEXANDER JAMES

A doctor who made an ill-advised investment, which led to his exposure to dangerous radiation and turned him into the deadly DOCTOR PHOSPHORUS.

SATURN

The sixth planet from the sun, Saturn was the home base for the Earth-2 reality Fura, a villain who met defeat at the hands of BRANE TAYLOR and Ricky in the year 3000. In the reality after CRISIS ON INFINITE EARTHS, Saturn was also a populated world, home to a race that included Jemm. Its moon, Titan, held the raw ore that was fashioned on the distant world Oa into power rings for its GREEN LANTERN Corps. Some time in the future it became the home to Earth colonists who possessed telepathic abilities, including the thirtieth century's Saturn Girl of the Legion of Super-Heroes.

SAVAGE SKULL, THE

JACK CRANE was a GOTHAM CITY policeman who was fired when his illegal activities were discovered. Crane was soon after horribly disfigured, his skin mostly burned off in an accidental fire. He sought revenge against the city that had seemingly wronged him by donning the costumed identity of the Savage Skull. His attempts to destroy Gotham were stopped by Batman, who brought him to justice and medical treatment. (*Batman* #360, June 1983)

SAWYER, MAGGIE

Margaret "Maggie" Sawyer was a police officer in Star City when she married a fellow cop. They had one daughter together, Jamie, and then divorced after Sawyer realized she was actually a lesbian. The bitter divorce left her with joint custody, and she relocated to METROPOLIS, where she rose to the post of captain of the city's Special Crimes Unit. (*Superman* [second series] #7, April 1987)

While in Metropolis she honed her team into an efficient fighting machine that more often than not did not need help from the city's protector, SUPERMAN. Sawyer began a romantic relationship with Metropolis *Daily Star* reporter Toby Raines.

Her efforts brought her to the attention of GOTHAM

CITY, which hired her to head their MAJOR CRIMES UNIT. She found Gotham a vastly different city, with less technologically advanced criminals but more psychotic, and equally deadly, ones. She did not enjoy the same close relationship with Batman as she did with the Man of Steel. Additionally, Raines remained in Metropolis, and the long-distance relationship placed a strain on the romance.

SAX GOLA

A Martian scientist in the Earth-2 reality, Sax Gola invented a device that altered personalities, skewing them toward evil. Gola was caught up in his own experiment and unwittingly turned to crime. A fellow scientist, Thund Dran, used his own device to summon Batman and ROBIN to their world to help apprehend his altered colleague so he could be cured. (*Batman* #41, June/July 1947)

SCANLON, SCOOP

Scoop Scanlon was the star reporter for *VUE MAGAZINE*, assigned to boost circulation by discovering Batman's masked identity. When he correctly deduced that Batman was BRUCE WAYNE, Batman hired a dying actor to prove the journalist wrong. (*World's Finest Comics* #6, Summer 1942)

Note: A different Scoop Scanlon worked for big-city paper the *Bulletin* at the same time. (*Action Comics* #1, June 1938)

SCAREBEAST

The PENGUIN hired Jonathan Crane, the SCARECROW, to use his chemical expertise to help him develop new fear toxins and other substances. As a lab assistant, he was assigned Linda Friitawa, who developed a crush on him. To earn the Penguin's respect, Crane injected himself with a new experimental substance that transformed him into an oversized, muscle-bound beast that terrorized rivals of the Penguin's. When Batman investigated the fourteen-foot-tall creature, he encountered it attacking a meeting with the Penguin in attendance. Since the Dark Knight suspected the Scarecrow's involvement, he came prepared; when the creature emitted fear gas, he was confident. The more potent gas, though, affected Batman, and he narrowly escaped back to the BATCAVE. When he awoke nine hours later, the Scarebeast was attacking WAYNE MANOR. As ROBIN and ALFRED PENNYWORTH attempted to contain it, Batman arrived encased in an armored version of the BATSUIT. Together they contained the creature, shooting it with tranquilizers, which returned Crane to his normal form. Later the Penguin denied all knowledge of Crane's activities. Friitawa used some of Crane's serum to become a creature herself, called FRIGHT, and vanished into the night. As Crane was being transported to the police, he changed into the beast once more and escaped. (*Batman* #627–630, July–September 2004)

After the events of INFINITE CRISIS, it has yet to be revealed if Crane retained this ability or not.

SCARECROW, THE

Professor JONATHAN CRANE endured a horrid childhood on Earth-2, the victim of bullies who mocked his slight frame and bookish manner. His studies at college led to a degree in psychiatry. Crane specialized in studying phobias, mastering the very fears he had experienced most of his life. Upon graduation, he became a professor at Gotham University. He devoted most of his low pay to the books he loved, wearing shabby clothing and risking ridicule from his professorial peers. He sought additional income through intimidation, blackmailing victims to pay him rather than risk their secrets being revealed—secrets Crane only surmised they had. In his first foray he wound up killing one man, a crime that baffled the Batman. Later, university trustee BRUCE WAYNE heard members of the faculty discuss the case; then someone mentioned Crane and his study of fear, which provided Wayne with the clue he and ROBIN needed. Disguised as Crane's next victim, a failed department-store owner, Batman learned enough to track Crane and bring him to justice. (*World's Finest Comics* #3, Fall 1941)

Two years later Crane was freed and formed a gang to aid him in his new round of crime, this time less about fear and more about straight robberies. (*Detective Comics* #73, March 1943)

The Scarecrow continued to commit crimes using increasingly sophisticated notions, including finally developing a hallucinogenic gas to instill specific fears in people. He proved difficult enough for Batman to ask his onetime opponent, CATWOMAN, for help. Although the Scarecrow's weapon made the Caped Crusader fear felines and the femme fatale fear bats, they managed to overcome those issues and bring the Scarecrow to justice. Crane proved to be the catalyst that finally brought Wayne and SELINA KYLE together romantically. (*The Brave and the Bold* #197, April 1983)

On Earth-1, Jonathan Crane became the Scarecrow in much the same way. He was dismissed

Scarebeast

from school after pulling a gun on students, during class, to gauge their reaction to a fearsome event. Crane invented his psychotropic fear gas early in his career and used it with positive results. He opposed Batman and Robin on numerous occasions, finding himself sentenced to Blackgate Penitentiary or Arkham Asylum. (*Batman* #189, February 1967)

On the world formed after Crisis on Infinite Earths, Crane took a more violent approach to those who tormented him. By age eighteen he'd had enough and brought a gun to the high school prom while wearing a garish scarecrow's costume. He victimized his bullies, notably Bo Griggs, who had a car accident, leaving him paralyzed and killing his date, Sherry Squires. Crane frequently teamed with other villains, joining the Injustice Gang and secret Society of super-villains. The Master of Fear, oddly, had his own phobia: birds. As a result, he treated himself by keeping birds, named Craw and Nightmare, as pets.

He delighted in seeing what he could cause others

to suffer and specialized in fear. He graduated and took a teaching position at Gotham University. Away from class, he continued his research, subjecting students to his experiments—only to be dismissed after one student was injured. After killing the man who fired him, Crane became the Scarecrow and began his criminal career. For years the Scarecrow would inflict his fear gases on people to rob them or attempt to kill Batman by breaking his spirit. He continued to meet defeat and find himself incarcerated. When Jason Todd debuted as Robin, he was present when the Scarecrow tried out a new gas, one that inhibited, not enhanced, a person's fear reaction. Batman was confronted with a fear that Robin would die as a result of his presence. While the Gotham Guardian faced the fear, it proved true all too soon. At a later time, one of his gases was inflicted on him and Crane was shocked to learn he had developed a phobia to the Batman. And it was Crane who helped shatter Selina Kyle's psyche for a time, when she could not reconcile herself to being either good or evil. (*Detective Comics* #569, December 1986)

The Scarecrow worked with numerous fellow Gotham rogues, from Hugo Strange to the Joker. When the Riddler and Hush sought to break Batman, they had the Scarecrow prepare psychological profiles for them; when Batman learned of his role, the Fearmaster went into hiding for a time. He resurfaced in the Penguin's employ, beginning a new round of experiments that led to his becoming a Scarebeast. (*Batman* #627, July 2004) He also lent his considerable talents to the Society, which attempted to rid the world of super heroes.

After his latest stint at Arkham, Crane decided he had become too reliant on his gases, which made him, once more, an object of ridicule. Instead, he relied on his training and tested himself by using mere words to cause two inmates to commit suicide. With the entire facility suddenly looking over their shoulders, Crane convinced two guards to let him walk free and descended once more on Gotham. (*Detective Comics* #835, October 2007)

SCARFACE

Scarface was said to be carved out of wood that was once used to hang criminals in Gotham City. As a result, it was thought that the wood was saturated in the evil of the 313 who had paid their debt to society. At some point the gallows was replaced with the electric chair, and the wood found its way to an inmate named Donnegan, serving a life sentence for murder, who carved it, then dressed it to resemble a 1920s gangster named "Scarface" Scarelli. By then the dummy had gained the name *Woody* and was a cherished possession.

Arnold Wesker, a timid man suffering from multiple personality disorder, killed a man in a bar fight and was sent to Blackgate Penitentiary. He and Donnegan were cellmates, and Wesker grew despondent. When he tried to hang himself, Wesker hesitated when he heard Woody "speak" to him. In fact, the dummy led Wesker to a tunnel Donnegan had spent the last fifteen years digging, and the two escaped. When their cellmate tried to prevent them from leaving, he slashed at Wesker with a corkscrew, missing the man and scaring the dummy. After Donnegan was beaten and Wesker escaped with Scarface, a new chapter of evil began. (*Detective Comics* #583, February 1988)

Scarface with the Ventriloquist

Wesker used Donnegan's book to learn ventriloquism, although he was far from accomplished, gritting his teeth and pronounced his *B*'s as *G*'s, which became a trademark. By then Woody had been renamed Scarface, and the dummy spoke like a stereotypical gangster—just one with a speech impediment. For the next several years the Ventriloquist and Scarface were a dominant force in Gotham City's underworld. People had a hard time differentiating the two, or determining who was really the controlling personality, or if the haunted dummy even possessed a life of its own.

Despite being burned and chipped, the dummy seemed to survive. It was soon seen entirely intact, leading many to believe there was a supernatural component to Scarface. When separated, the Ventriloquist took to using other dummies or even sock puppets to speak on his behalf while Scarface spoke to others, manipulating and influencing their actions, beginning with an employee named RHINO.

The Ventriloquist was shot and killed by the TALLY MAN under orders from the GREAT WHITE SHARK, and Scarface had its head crushed. A short time later, a beautiful, cold woman named Sugar turned up as the new Ventriloquist with an intact Scarface. They once more terrorized their fellow mobsters, reasserting their dominance. Sugar kept a closet full of Scarfaces, leading to the belief that the evil spirit of Scarface survived from body to body. (*Detective Comics* #818, June 2006)

SCARLET HORDE, THE

On Earth-2 a dirigible flew over Manhattan and unleashed rays of light that proved to have terrifying effect. Entire buildings were reduced to rubble, with a death toll measured in the thousands. From mounted speakers, the Scarlet Horde announced their presence and insisted they were now ruling the world. BRUCE WAYNE recalled from his growing intelligence files that Doctor Carl Kruger had recently announced the invention of a death ray. Kruger would be Batman's first stop in his investigation. Confirming his notes that Kruger possessed a Napoleon complex, the Caped Crusader was satisfied that the doctor also led the horde. With three accomplices named Travis, Bixley, and Ryder, Kruger was said to lead an army of two thousand men poised to attack again in two days. Trying to apprehend the madman, Batman was knocked unconscious and left to die in Kruger's burning estate.

The Dark Knight saved himself and captured Ryder, who provided information. In the BATPLANE, Batman sought the horde's headquarters, prepared to stop them at all costs. His results were mixed: He was once more apprehended and narrowly escaped death but fled with enough knowledge to concoct a counteragent to the death ray. He prepared enough of this solution to coat the Batplane, which he first used to track the dirigible of doom and then rammed into the ship. Batman and Kruger survived, though both their craft were destroyed, and Batman tossed a gas grenade into Kruger's miniature escape airplane. Unconscious, the doctor crashed into the ocean below, his body washing ashore the following day. (*Detective Comics* #33, November 1933)

A different Scarlet Horde existed on Earth-1, led by a Colonel Blimp, who sought revenge for imagined indignities heaped upon his father by the US Navy decades earlier. He spent years developing superior magnetic technology, which he affixed to his orange zeppelin. When all was ready, he and his military-uniformed men began plucking populated ships from the sea. Batman followed the zeppelin, gained entrance, and was badly beaten back by the horde until he fell back to the sea. The Dark Knight did manage to leave a tracking device on the blimp, however, and followed it to Washington, D.C.

Colonel Blimp offered to release the naval vessel and its crew in exchange for ten million dollars. To prove his point, he blew up a smaller blimp over the capital.

Batman gleaned enough data to determine that the naval ship was housed in the Arctic, while Colonel Blimp's main zeppelin was secreted in a wooded part of New Jersey. He dispatched ROBIN in the Batplane to rescue the navy officers while he took on Blimp solo. As expected, Batman found Blimp's lair; the confrontation between the two men led to Blimp being taken into custody, the threat ended. (*Batman* #352, *Detective Comics* #519, October 1982)

SCARPIS, BUGS

Bugs Scarpis was better known as the costumed criminal SCORPIO.

SCHEMER, THE

The Schemer was a GOTHAM CITY criminal who used a series of accomplices, all disguised as members of the US Sightless Society. His goal was to take Batman and ROBIN out of the picture so they could rob an armored car filled with gold bricks. First he had a blind man killed, leaving behind a message indicating that the blind man might have been Batman. He then tipped off the police. As Commissioner JAMES GORDON investigated, several would-be Batmen turned up at the crime scene. Meantime, Batman and Robin missed both the BAT-SIGNAL and hotline attempts to reach them, as they were busy putting an end to the Wharf Rats Gang. As a result, their late appearance was met by a very skeptical Gordon. Using microphones hidden in their canes, the "blind" men reported developments back to the Schemer.

Gordon ordered the Dynamic Duo arrested, but the Caped Crusader let Robin escape; during the confusion he palmed a hearing-aid device found on the corpse. He then spoke into the cane carried by Gordon, alerting the Schemer that the crime fighter was on to his tricks. Robin, meantime, hitched a ride with the armored car and was in position to stop the attempted robbery. In the ensuing tumult Batman got free, impersonated one of the Schemer's blind men, and worked with Robin to stop the criminal. Robin was taken hostage and carried away to a helicopter, leading Batman to summon ALFRED PENNYWORTH's help with the BATCOPTER. The Gotham Guardian managed to rescue the Boy Wonder, and together they prevented the Schemer and his men from obtaining the gold. As the criminals were handed over to the police, Gordon apologized for doubting them. (*Batman* #204-205, August–September 1968)

SCORPIO

BUGS SCARPIS was a confidence man who created an elaborate persona—that of an alchemist called Scorpio. He used hypnosis to convince his dupes that Scorpio could actually transmute one base substance into another, more valuable one. Patrons would pay him huge sums of cash to learn the secret of alchemy for themselves. Batman and ROBIN discovered the ruse and put Scarpis out of business. (*Detective Comics* #107, January 1946)

SCRATCH, NICHOLAS

Nicholas Scratch was an ordinary person until an unusual event occurred. He was just entering college, an astronomy major given his love of the stars. Scratch's interest developed over the long hours he spent in isolation, ignored by his peers for being overweight and clumsy, a loser to their way of thinking. While he worked with the college's telescope one night, he was struck by a celestial particle that seemed to transform him. Over the course of the following semester he slimmed down, bulked up, and stopped being clumsy, gaining poise and confidence. His intelligence seemed to grow exponentially. Scratch took to music and became an overnight rock sensation, his newfound charisma captivating people from coast to coast. Quickly he used his star status to gain access to great leaders around the world and became their confidant and friend.

Scratch still wasn't satisfied, though: He wanted power. He first used cosmetic surgery to turn his followers into devil look-alikes, apt accoutrements for a man with his name. When an earthquake struck GOTHAM CITY, Scratch saw an opportunity. He lobbied the federal government to isolate the city, which he eyed as his new base of operations. While he argued opposite BRUCE WAYNE on Capitol Hill, he also physically battled AZRAEL in Gotham. The Avenging Angel won the public spectacle, the first taste of defeat Scratch had experienced. Scratch made it his goal to destroy Azrael, and ultimately he got his wish. With CARLTON LEHAH he gunned down Azrael, riddling his body with special bullets, seemingly killing him. Scratch's subsequent activities have gone unrecorded. (*Azrael, Agent of the Bat* #47, December 1998)

SEA-FOX, THE

The Sea-Fox assembled a team of criminals who used advanced underwater sleds to traverse GOTHAM CITY's sewer system and rob unsuspecting businesses. They were quite successful across the city, returning to an abandoned army base on a nearby island with their loot. Batman and ROBIN managed to track the thieves and apprehended them at their hideout. (*Batman* #132, June 1960)

SECRET STAR, THE

Police Commissioner JAMES GORDON and Batman hand-selected five law enforcement officers to form the Secret Star, an elite group that trained to replace the Gotham Guardian. Should Batman be injured or dead and unable to protect GOTHAM CITY, one of the Secret Star would assume his place. The charter members included Army lieutenant Philip Gray, student-athlete Harry Vincent, police officers Dave Fells and Sam Olson, and the FBI's TED BLAKELY. Only Blakely was ever summoned to duty. (*Batman* #77, June/July 1953)

SELKIRK, PENN

Penn Selkirk was a munitions broker who took advantage of distractions in GOTHAM CITY to operate without fear of the Batman. It was during the period when BRUCE WAYNE was recovering from his broken back and AZRAEL was substituting as Batman, albeit a violent one. Deciding he needed a bold step to solidify his position, Selkirk captured the Catwoman to obtain a cybernetic enabler, a device that might allow the crippled to move their limbs. Batman arrived, ready to rescue Catwoman and kill Selkirk, but was prevented by the arrival of the first Batman, flanked by Nightwing and Robin. As the Batmen fought, Selkirk attempted to escape by helicopter, but he was joined by Catwoman then the two fighting men, all hanging from a rope trailing beneath the chopper. The extra weight caused the aircraft to crash atop the Gotham River Bridge. Catwoman demanded the enabler, but Selkirk threw it into the river instead. Later Selkirk's divers encountered Catwoman, all still seeking the sunken enabler. Catwoman emerged victorious and Selkirk quit Gotham, continuing his business elsewhere. (*Catwoman* [second series] #11, June 1994)

SELLY, FRANKLIN

A true believer in UFOs, Selly used an illegal narcotic, Cosmosis, to spread his beliefs, terrorizing the populace as the Kook.

SENSEI, THE

The Sensei was an aged martial arts master from Hong Kong who came to the attention of Rā's al Ghūl. (*Strange Adventures* #215, October 1968) The Demon's Head asked the Sensei to join his League of Assassins but, at some point, he was possessed by a spirit named Jonah, which influenced his actions while serving the League. After Ebenezer Darkk failed Rā's as leader of his League of Assassins, the Sensei was placed in charge. Under his watch, the League grew more brutal: He insisted the members rely more on martial arts than on weaponry. He wanted to raise assassination to an art form, which became his driving goal. Additionally, it was under the Sensei that Boston Brand became Deadman and Ben Turner, the Bronze Tiger, was brainwashed by Professor Ojo to serve the League. There was a struggle for control of the magical city of Nanda Parbat. Seeking more power, the Sensei ultimately split from Rā's, and a war for control of the league began. When the Sensei attempted to create an earthquake, an elegant assassination technique designed to kill delegates at a peace conference,

Batman stopped him. However, Rā's and the Sensei were killed in the battle, with Rā's subsequently resurrected by a Lazarus Pit. (*Detective Comics* #490, May 1980)

When Rā's al Ghūl attempted to find a new host body, he was opposed in part by the Sensei, who survived death through unexplained circumstances. Additionally, he claimed to be Rā's father, which was unlikely given their differing ethnic backgrounds. At Nanda Parbat's Fountain of Essence, a variation of the Lazarus Pit, Batman and the Sensei battled, and when the villain fell into the fountain, he was found wanting and died once more. (*Batman* #671, January 2008)

SHARK, THE

Gunther Hardwicke wore a shark's headpiece and a business suit to commit crimes as the Shark, a member of the Terrible Trio.

SHE-BAT

When Kirk Langstrom first began to transform from man to Man-Bat, he wanted to share the experience with his fiancée, and later wife, Francine Langstrom. In her She-Bat form, she adventured beside her husband and helped raise a family.

SHINER, THE

Smythe, manager at the Ross Radium Company, wore a shining hood to assemble a group of accomplices in stealing radium. With the aid of unwitting retired pilots, the stolen substances were transported to Canada. Batman and Robin tracked the thefts and located the Shiner, arresting him and his men. (*Detective Comics* #123, May 1947)

SHRIKE

There were several Shrikes in Batman's world, the first being Toron Tos, an orphan from Moronon who came to Earth and was raised by Native Americans. He grew up and encountered both Hawkman and Hawkwoman. (*Hawkman* #11 (December 1965/January 1966)

The second Shrike was a martial artist who served Rā's al Ghūl's League of Assassins. He was in charge of the Vengeance Academy, working with youth targeted to become killers. Dick Grayson infiltrated the school after being forced to abandon his Robin identity following a disastrous encounter with Two-Face. While there, he learned to use Escrima fighting sticks, which he adopted as part of his equipment for the rest of his career. Soon after, Shrike accepted a contract to kill Two-Face and sent out a number of students, including Grayson and a boy named Boone. Shrike grew suspicious of Grayson after he saved both Boone and Two-Face in battle. Batman arrived soon after, intending to take down Shrike, but he was wounded in the fight. Two-Face wound up killing Shrike while saving Grayson during the mêlée. While the other students fled, Boone remained, angered over losing his beloved teacher. (*Robin Year One* #4, 2001)

A mental patient who escaped and fell under the thrall of the alien Overmaster became the third Shrike. She possessed a powerful sonic cry that made her a formidable member of the Overmaster's Cadre, which battled the Justice League of America

The Sensei

on several occasions. Eventually she found religion and endured a quest that saw thirty-three men killed, earning her a place on the Suicide Squad. Shrike died during a fight with the Ogaden Military. (*Justice League of America* #235, February 1985)

Boone, meantime, traveled the world seeking training from numerous masters, all trying to replace Shrike in his mind. (*Nightwing Secret Files & Origins* #1, October 1999) He wanted vengeance in his master's name, and wanted to kill Dick Grayson. When Shrike encountered Talia Head, Rā's daughter, he was welcomed into the league to complete his education. He became a dangerous living weapon, notching numerous kills throughout Asia, from Russia to China. Shrike was recruited to Blüdhaven by Blockbuster II as a new weapon in his war against Nightwing. Twice he tried to kill his rival, without success. He moved back to the League and was last seen serving its leader Nyssa Raatko. Since her death, his whereabouts remain unrecorded.

SIGNALMAN

Phil Cobb arrived in Gotham City ready to become a gangster to be reckoned with. As he tried to hire accomplices, Cobb was rebuffed as being someone with no reputation. He sought to change that, and in a hurry. Looking for a gimmick, he decided that society's growing dependence on symbols was the answer. He fashioned a costume decorated in iconography and became the Signalman. He set out on a series of imaginative crimes, all based on symbols. Signalman was ultimately apprehended by Batman and Robin. (*Batman* #112, December 1957)

His incarceration was brief and he returned in

the guise of the Blue Bowman, a knockoff of Green Arrow complete with gimmick arrows. Again he was easily defeated by the Dynamic Duo. (*Batman* #137, February 1961)

Cobb remained in prison for a while then resurfaced, once again in his Signalman guise. He worked with the secret Society of super-villains for a while but was never taken seriously by his peers. At one point, he was kidnapped by Doctor Moon and Phobia, tortured for medical research, and thought to have died. He was also seemingly killed by the female Manhunter, Kate Spencer, but was later revealed to be alive, a drug addict acting as an informant to Black Lightning. (*Justice League of America* [second series] #1, November 2006)

SIKES, SMILEY

Smiley Sikes led a gang of Gotham City criminals who left a stolen vehicle in a parking garage overnight. To discredit Joe Sands, the attendant, they framed him for drunk driving, so he could no longer identify them as the ones responsible for the stolen vehicle. As Batman and Robin investigated, Sikes and his men cornered the Boy Wonder and savagely beat him. While the youth lay in grave condition, a furious Batman found the criminals. Despite taking three bullets to the chest, the Dark Knight managed to subdue the men. He then beat Sikes, forcing the man to sign a confession clearing Sands. Only then were the men turned over to the police. (*Batman* #5, Spring 1941)

SILVER MONKEY

The Brotherhood of the Fist featured several assassins who were masters of specific disciplines. They took names referring to the pliability of substances from paper to bamboo. One of their number, the Silver Monkey, left to become a mercenary. (*Detective Comics* #685, May 1995) One of his contracts brought him to Gotham City, hired to kill King Snake. The two fought to a draw until they were interrupted by Robin. Later the Silver Monkey was hired by international financier Fritz Mueller to protect an ashram that had once served as home to Oliver Queen and Connor Hawke, the Green Arrows, as well as Onyx. Hawke was beaten by the Silver Monkey. They met a second time when the Silver Monkey was hired to kill Hawke. The mercenary martial artist was defeated, which led the entire brotherhood to seek vengeance

on Green Arrow. Later the Silver Monkey's career came to an end when he was protecting members of Gotham's branch of the Yakuza at the breakout of War Games and was killed. (*Batman: The 12-Cent Adventure*, October 2004)

SILVERSMITH, STERLING T.

Sterling T. Silversmith grew up fascinated with silver. Through his adult years, he amassed a fortune in the metal. He took to wearing an all-white business suit with a silver alloy woven into the fabric, making him essentially bulletproof. Silversmith became an expert criminal, using his antiques business as a cover for trafficking in stolen goods.

He and Batman first met while the Dark Knight was under suspicion for killing Talia Head. Batman encountered a skeleton hidden inside a statue and investigated, leading him to Silversmith. Despite being hunted, the Dark Knight took the time to bring down Silversmith, appropriately using a bar of silver to knock the fleeing man to the ground. (*Detective Comics* #446, April 1975)

Later Silversmith learned that the Crime Doctor had learned Batman's real name and suggested the good doctor share the secret. When Matthew Thorne refused, Silversmith insisted, administering quicksilver—a poison. Finally Thorne agreed to tell in exchange for the antidote, but Batman's intervention delayed matters, leaving Thorne in a vegetative state. Silversmith was brought to justice and is presumably still in jail. (*Detective Comics* #495, October 1980)

SILVER VEIN

Out in the Far West, in the mountains near Death Valley, Silver Vein had been a ghost town since the late 1800s. That changed when a few enterprising criminals took advantage of an old law that provided for self-government in mining towns without state interference. Silver Vein, now known as Outlaw Town, quickly became a sanctuary for some two thousand lawbreaker. Eventually, a new law was passed enabling the National Guard to clean out Outlaw Town, aided by Batman and Robin. (*Batman* #75, February/March 1953)

SIMMONS, HECTOR

Professor Ezra Dorn amassed a leading collection of souvenirs and artifacts from famous criminals and crimes through the ages. His renowned criminal library was massive enough that he employed Hector Simmons to be his secretary. Over time Simmons took to using the artifacts, dressing in period costume, to commit crimes. Suspicion immediately fell on Dorn, but further investigation by Batman and Robin revealed Simmons to be the culprit. He was arrested, and Dorn's name cleared. (*World's Finest Comics* #45, April/May 1950)

SIMPLE SIMON

Despite looking like the stereotypical country bumpkin, Simon was a sophisticated criminal who conceived and executed numerous successful robberies, basing each on the Simple Simon nursery rhyme. In time, though, Simon and his henchmen were arrested by Batman and Robin. (*Batman* #138, March 1961)

SIMS, RIGGER

The man who was secretly the criminal MISTER ROULETTE.

SINISTER 8, THE

Frenchy LeDoix, Singh Dan, Baron Hengler, Ling Chee, Luigi Verona, Aldo Toloedano, the Liverpool Kid, and Sumatra Joe were considered among the world's most dangerous criminals. Together the eight men escaped the famed Satan's Island Prison located in the South Atlantic Ocean. It fell to Batman and ROBIN to recapture them, although even after that was accomplished the Dynamic Duo had to survive attempts from other criminals to kill them and free their international brethren. The murder attempts failed and all eight were successfully placed back behind bars. (*Batman* #72, August/September 1952)

SINO-SUPERMEN

As the Earth-1 BARBARA GORDON sought her missing brother, TONY GORDON, she came into conflict with Chinese nationals who had been augmented with artificial superpowers. These Sino-Supermen imitated the abilities of SUPERMAN, Batman, GREEN LANTERN, and the FLASH. However, once they used their powers, their bodies could not contain the energy and would explode. BATGIRL helped shut down the entire operation. (*Batman Family* #19, August/September 1978)

SIONIS, ROMAN

The scion of the wealthy Sionis family, Roman displayed an aptitude for violent crime and rose to rule GOTHAM CITY's underworld as BLACK MASK.

SKEEVERS, EDWARD

Edward Skeevers was a low-level member of the criminal Falcone family. Along with ANTHONY "FATS" ZUCCO, Skeevers reported to the Maroni branch; the two were responsible for illegal narcotics. Their operations were constantly prey for other GOTHAM CITY criminals such as the PENGUIN until Zucco came up with a new plan: He and Skeevers would traffic their drugs through the traveling HALY BROS. CIRCUS. After Haly refused to go along with the plan, Zucco killed acrobats JOHN and MARY GRAYSON to send a message.

While their son DICK GRAYSON survived and went on to become ROBIN, bringing Zucco to justice, Skeevers got away. He survived only a short time, becoming one of five people to die at precisely 2 AM on Columbus Day, victims of the serial killer known as the HANGMAN KILLER. (*Batman: Dark Victory* #1, December 1999)

SKEEVERS, JEFFERSON

Jefferson Skeevers was a GOTHAM CITY-based drug dealer who had been arrested by JAMES GORDON. This was a significant arrest since Skeevers had information that confirmed Detective ARTHUR FLASS's corruption. He refused to testify against Flass and was granted bail by District Attorney HARVEY DENT. That night he was visited by Batman, who scared him into agreeing to provide information about Flass. He went to Gordon and detailed his knowledge. This led Gordon to bypass Commissioner GILLIAN

B. LOEB and take the damning evidence to Internal Affairs. (*Batman* #407, May 1987)

SKELETON

A man known only as the Skeleton harbored a grudge against BRUCE WAYNE for unknown reasons. As a result, he impersonated members of Batman's Rogues Gallery to plant explosives at Wayne-owned properties. His motivations were never revealed. (*Batman: Gotham City Secret Files* #1, April 2000)

SKOWCROFT, GEORGE P.

After Mayor HAMILTON HILL was arrested for his corrupt dealings with RUPERT THORNE, he was replaced for a brief period by George P. Skowcroft. His tenure was unremarkable, and he was replaced by an unnamed man. (*Detective Comics* #551, June 1985)

SKULL DUGGER

COSMO DUGGER suffered from anhedonia, a psychological condition that robbed him of the ability to experience joy. As a result, he sought to deprive others of joy and created a device that absorbed the emotion from people as they achieved a moment of intense pleasure. He then imprinted a skull on the forehead of each victim, earning him the nickname *Skull*. After three such victims—a baseball star, a movie star, and a lottery winner—were recorded, GOTHAM CITY doctor Faye Sommers summoned Batman for assistance. The Caped Crusader went to study the latest victim, only to find Dugger's men attempting to take the corpse. Investigation led Batman to Dugger's home, where he'd developed his device, which he also used to record his mental impressions. Batman studied the device and learned of Skull Dugger's sad condition. By using the machine himself, the Gotham Guardian managed to reverse the feelings so he was now responding to pain, not joy. As a result, Batman was rendered ineffective. Dugger, meantime, killed repeatedly, undeterred by an incapacitated Batman. Desperate, Batman turned to DOCTOR TZIN-TZIN, offering the criminal one million dollars to be immunized from pain. The mastermind agreed and rendered the crime fighter free from feeling any pain for one hour. Armed, Batman attacked Skull Dugger at his residence. Dugger fought back, using his device to emit a ray that would restore Batman to a balanced psyche, and another ray to kill him. Batman was cured and managed to survive, apprehending Dugger. He then admitted to Tzin-Tzin that he'd lied about the offer. (*Batman* #289–290 July–August 1977)

SKYBOY

Tharn, son of a lawman from the distant planet Kormo, lost his memories when his spacecraft collided with a meteor and crashed on Earth. When he awoke, the youth displayed powers and abilities similar to SUPERMAN, who discovered the wreckage. The Man of Steel dubbed him Skyboy and worked with him to regain the missing memories. When he did, Tharn explained that he'd been sent to warn Earth's inhabitants against a band of Kormonian

criminals, led by Rawl, who were planning to steal copper, a precious metal on his homeworld. Batman and ROBIN joined Superman and Skyboy in apprehending the intergalactic criminals. With his ship repaired, Tharn brought the fugitives back to Kormo. (*World's Finest Comics* #92, January/February 1958)

SKY CREATURE, THE

A gang of criminals came upon the ancient lantern of Celphus the Sorcerer during one of their robberies and were surprised to discover that it could summon an orange-colored being. Like a genie from fairy tales, it obeyed their commands and began assisting them in committing more daring robberies. Batman encountered the criminals and their Sky Creature, leading him to speculate it was actually a trapped being from another dimension. ROBIN freed the creature by destroying the lantern with a rock; the Dynamic Duo then easily apprehended the criminals. (*Batman* #135, October 1960)

SKYE, JOHN

As Congress debated legislation that would fund construction of a factory dedicated to employing former criminals, John Skye was determined to derail the bill. To Skye and his fellow gangland bosses, the factory's success could make it harder for them to obtain henchmen to do the heavy lifting during the commission of crimes. Skye and a syndicate of leaders decided they needed to kill Batman and ROBIN before the famed crime fighters could testify. The Dynamic Duo arrived in Washington and were captured, then locked away in an airtight vault deep within Skye's warehouse. They were freed by four ex-convicts who favored the bill; together all six apprehended Skye and his colleagues. Batman gave his testimony, and the bill passed. (*Batman* #28, April/May 1945)

SLASH

Slash was a feminist who called herself the women's champion—but she was actually a vigilante who accepted revenge-based missions from abused women. She effectively wielded various styles of blades to deliver her justice to deserving men. BATGIRL tracked and stopped the woman in what proved to be her final case before being crippled by the JOKER. (*Batgirl Special* #1, 1988)

SLASHER, THE

On Earth-2 a man known as the Slasher was a common hoodlum who faked his death to avoid capture by Batman and ROBIN. He was quickly traced and brought to justice. (*Detective Comics* #97, March 1945)

On Earth-1 the Slasher was a costumed vigilante. In his green costume and white hockey-style mask, the Slasher carried a sword in lieu of his right hand, and a buzz saw for his left. He claimed to kill those who deserved it in an attempt to restore GOTHAM CITY's reputation. Batman disagreed with the man's methods and tracked him.

Cornered in a sewer, Slasher fought back but ultimately was apprehended by Batman. (*Batman* #445, March 1990)

SLICK

Slick was a criminal who operated a hideout for fugitives in the Florida Everglades. Batman, disguised as KNUCKLES DONEGAN, infiltrated the operation and put Slick out of business. ROBIN and the Miami police arrived to arrest all the "guests" of the hideout. (*Batman* #31, October/November 1945)

SLOANE, PAUL

An actor, Sloane played HARVEY KENT in a television re-creation of the events that turned the GOTHAM CITY district attorney into the criminal TWO-FACE. Real acid was accidentally used and Sloane's face was also hideously scarred, leading him to believe he was the real Two-Face. Batman and ROBIN had to stop his criminal activities and bring him in for psychiatric treatment. (*Batman* #68, December 1951/January 1952)

After realities merged during the CRISIS ON INFINITE EARTHS, Paul Sloane was an actor hired by Gotham City costumed criminals. His assignment was to portray Two-Face in a ruse that was intended to end in Batman's death. The real Two-Face learned of this and objected to Sloane's impersonation, so he had the actor kidnapped. Two-Face used acid to scar the actor's face in a pattern similar to his own injuries.

Sloane was then exposed to the SCARECROW's newly designed fear toxin, and the combination drove him mad. Now known as CHARLATAN, he sought vengeance against all the criminals and was also determined to fulfill his contract and kill Batman. He failed in his quests and was eventually taken into custody. Sloane was subsequently placed in ARKHAM ASYLUM. (*Detective Comics* #776–782, January–August 2003).

SMARTE, CARL

Carl Smarte spent his days as an executive with the Marine Construction Corporation—but he also led a double life as the manager of a pay-by-the-day hideout for fugitives from justice, located underneath a giant tank his firm constructed for the Seaorama aquarium in GOTHAM CITY. At much the same time, a freak accident altered Batman's physiology; he had to wear a diving suit and water-filled helmet to enable him to breathe on land. As Batman adjusted to gills and working underwater, he continued to seek the rumored hideaway. With ROBIN's help, he located the buried facility and arrested the wanted criminals in addition to Smarte. (*Batman* #118, September 1958)

SMILER

ROLAND MEACHAM served with BRUCE WAYNE on the Committee to Preserve Gotham Village, a section of GOTHAM CITY that had become home to artists and intellectuals. It was also the access point to a massive underground hideaway for fugitives run by Meacham under the pseudonym *Smiler*. In exchange for 50 percent of his or her loot, a criminal received access to the refuge through an abandoned building in the Village. Residents could relax in facilities complete with theater, pool room, kitchen, and even a travel department to help arrange escape to other states or countries. Batman located the rumored access while hunting jewel thief Frank Fenton. The Dynamic Duo brought the criminals to justice and revealed Smiler to be Meacham. The city chose to retain the Village as a landmark. (*Detective Comics* #327, May 1964)

SMILTER, JOHN

Wearing an asbestos suit, the daring criminal John Smilter fired bullets into a fuel truck, causing an explosion and fire. He then dashed through the flames and stole the fabled Fabian diamonds from a dockside customs office. Smilter and his men boarded the nearby USS *Verania* and tried to escape by helicopter. Unfortunately, not only was Batman aboard the cruise ship as a vacationing BRUCE WAYNE, but his cabinmate was METROPOLIS reporter Clark Kent, also known as SUPERMAN. The classic meeting of two super heroes led to the apprehension of Smilter and his accomplices. (*World's Finest Comics* #76, May/June 1952)

SMIRT, HERBERT

Herbert Smirt was a scholar who thoroughly researched Batman, from his physical measurements to details on the BATMOBILE and BATPLANE. He privately published his extensive notes in *The Batman Encyclopedia,* which he sold to criminals for five thousand dollars a copy, enabling them to study their adversary and seek ways to commit crimes without risk of arrest. Upon learning of the book's existence, Batman saw to it that the buyers were led to believe the information was inaccurate. He and ROBIN then apprehended Smirt, confiscating the entire print run. All but one copy was destroyed; the remaining book went into the BATCAVE's trophy room. (*Detective Comics* #214, December 1954)

SMITH, "SHOTGUN"

Steve "Shotgun" Smith was considered the toughest cop in GOTHAM CITY. A divorced man, he raised his teenage daughter Maryanne as best he could. (*Detective Comics* #428, October 1972) When he was accused of corruption, only Commissioner JAMES GORDON spoke on his behalf. (*Batman: Gordon's Law* #2, January 1997) Shotgun Smith bitterly left the Gotham police force and became the sheriff for the county that included Gotham. He was abrasive and quite territorial, preferring that the G.C.P.D. stay within the city limits. Smith, though, didn't mind working with the third ROBIN, since the teen seemed respectful of his authority. (*Robin* [second series] #1, November 1993) Eventually Smith was partnered with a rookie named Cissy Chambers, and both were deeply involved in the manhunt for CHARAXES during one of his rampages.

SMITHERS

Smithers not only worked as construction boss for the new GOTHAM CITY Museum but also secretly led a group of criminals. As a result, he altered the architectural plans so the new building was riddled with secret passages, rooms, and entrances that enabled it to serve as a criminal hideaway. At first the plan seemed to work, but Smithers and his gang were ultimately tracked and arrested by Batman and ROBIN. (*Batman* #60, August/September 1950)

SMYTHE

Smythe was the executive-turned-criminal who, as the SHINER, stole radium.

SNEED, RICHARD

Richard and Jasper Sneed were wealthy twin brothers, although Jasper treated people badly. Richard decided to make amends. He disguised himself and gained access to Jasper by hiring on as his new butler. With such access, Richard then used an "Oriental poison" to slowly kill his brother. Jasper learned he had twenty-four hours of life left and chose to use the time to kill everyone he knew who pretended to be nice solely to remain eligible for the will and estate. After just one murder, he was apprehended by Batman and ROBIN, who learned of the poisoning just as Jasper died. They found Richard, who took the same poison and died soon after. (*Detective Comics* #57, November 1941)

SNOWMAN, THE

KLAUS KRISTIN looked like a yeti but was actually a hybrid—the son of a Yeti who mated with a human woman. He had an active meta-gene that let him generate extreme cold and ice. Considered a menace, he used his ice powers to commit crimes. In GOTHAM CITY he fought Batman to a standstill and escaped. (*Batman* #337, July 1981) A short time later, the Dark Knight learned that the Snowman had been seen in Tibet, so he traveled there to bring the criminal to justice. During their second battle, Kristin was accidentally killed. (*Detective Comics* #522, January 1983)

SPADE, JACK

Wearing a costume based on the Jack of Spades, he committed crimes using the name HIJACK.

SPARROW, THE

When the MAESTRO began committing music-themed crimes in GOTHAM CITY, Batman and ROBIN turned to musicology professor Ambrose Weems for assistance. To protect his identity, Batman crafted the costume and persona of the Sparrow, allowing Weems to accompany the Dynamic Duo and get close to the Maestro to find clues. Once the Maestro was captured, Weems happily returned to his work. (*Batman* #149, August 1962)

SPECS

Specs was a criminal working in GOTHAM CITY when he was hired by TWO-FACE to steal binary defense codes for the villain's use. Specs and his associates breached a defense facility, used gas to subdue the guards, and stole the computer code for the defense system. Two-Face demanded twenty-two million dollars from the American government for its return—but he also made an identical offer to the Russians. Specs disliked this double cross, so he informed the police of the code's whereabouts. The call, though, was cut off by Two-Face, who shot Specs in the heart and brain. (*Batman* #312–313, June–July 1979)

SPECTRE, THE

The Spectre was Raguel, the Wrath of God, a spirit of vengeance who had existed since humans

In the Crisis's aftermath, a depowered Spectre continued to operate, first as a guardian at the entrance to Hell. He succumbed to evil incarnate as it attempted to breach Heaven, and later proved ineffectual in preventing his fellow JSA colleagues from consignment to limbo (although that proved temporary). He returned to Earth and Corrigan's body, dealing with moral and ethical dilemmas as the universe seemed to take time to reorder itself and find a place for the Spirit of Vengeance.

As happened with other mortal hosts, Corrigan's time ended, and he was given his eternal rest. Still, the Spectre needed a human host to remain conscious of human needs. When Hal Jordan, GREEN LANTERN, sacrificed himself in a redemptive act to save the Earth, he was chosen as the next vessel. Jordan was never comfortable hosting the Wrath of God and preferred acts of redemption. In the end the cosmos had other plans for Jordan, who was resurrected elsewhere. The Spectre was left without a host, while Eclipso gained a new one in the form of Jean Loring, ex-wife of the ATOM. She took advantage of the Spectre's situation to seduce the spirit, who unleashed an unremitting spree of grisly deaths for the most minor of injustices. Uncontained, the Spectre sought to destroy all sinners and forms of magic, which led to his destroying the underground nation of ATLANTIS. He killed more than seven hundred practitioners of magic—even Nabu, the Lord of Order most involved with Earth. With his destruction, the Ninth Age of Magic ended and the Lord's attention finally returned to Earth. The Spectre was required to be tethered to a new host.

As the Rock of Eternity exploded over GOTHAM CITY, police officer CRISPUS ALLEN was gunned down by a different Jim Corrigan, a corrupt police officer. This seemed the appropriate confluence of events, and Allen became the Spectre's new host. Allen, though, did not like being asked to judge his fellow man and asked for a year to decide whether or not to accept. A humbled Spectre agreed and waited patiently. Allen's spirit wandered Gotham; as the year ended, he agreed that Spectre needed guidance. Together they carefully studied those who broke the law, handing out judicious vengeance.

Jim Corrigan

gained sentience. He was also said to be the fallen angel Aztar, a participant when Lucifer rebelled in Heaven. Aztar then repented and became the Lord's servant, doing penance for eternity. Usually tied to a recently deceased human being, the Spectre meted out justice to fit the crime.

God's first Spirit of Vengeance was known as Eclipso, said to be responsible for the biblical flood of Noah's time. When that was deemed inappropriate, Eclipso was replaced by the Spectre, whose first recorded act was the slaying of the firstborn in Egypt.

On Earth-2 the Spectre inhabited the body of police detective JIM CORRIGAN, who was killed by New York City gangster Gat Benson. Corrigan was informed by the Voice of God that he was to remain on Earth, seeking those who violated the laws of man. (*More Fun Comics* #52, February 1940) The Spectre, thanks to Corrigan's influence, worked with the JUSTICE SOCIETY OF AMERICA and alongside Batman in the All-Star Squadron. He was prevented from being proactive in Europe and Asia during World War II once Adolf Hitler obtained the mystic Spear of Destiny.

There was apparently no Spectre on Earth-1, but the spirit came to the multiverse's aid on numerous occasions, starting with keeping the worlds from colliding due to the presence of the Anti-Matter Man. The Spectre did traverse the dimensions on occasion, working alongside the FLASH and Batman as required. He was among the final combatants during CRISIS ON INFINITE EARTHS, as he struggled to preserve life.

Hal Jordan

SPEED BOYS

A GOTHAM CITY criminal gang came to use radioactive isotopes combined with rare meteorite fibers to give them an edge. The substance served as a coating to several pairs of sneakers, enabling each wearer to run at superspeed. Batman was seemingly helpless against the newly named Speed Boys and asked the FLASH for help. The call came at a time when the Scarlet Speedster was suffering from an illness that would prove fatal if he used his powers. A hero to the end, he agreed to aid his friend and they hunted the Speed Boys, ultimately locating them. During the battle, the Fastest Man Alive seemed to die, distracting the Caped Crusader and letting the Speed Boys escape. Later, though, the Flash reappeared hale and hearty. Apparently the unique radiation from the sneakers had cured him of his disease, enabling the heroes to finally apprehend the criminals. (*The Brave and the Bold* #67, August/September 1966)

SPELLBINDER, THE

DELBERT BILLINGS was an artistic forger who decided to go for bigger gains by becoming a costumed super-villain. The man, also known as Keith Sherwood, was inspired by the very pop art he imitated to put together a garish yellow-and-orange outfit equipped with a variety of tools that instantly hypnotized victims. Billings hired a set of henchmen and went to work, calling himself Spellbinder.

On his very first robbery he was interrupted by Batman and ROBIN, but he eluded capture by hypnotizing the Caped Crusader into thinking he was involved in something entirely different from a crime. Time and again this ploy worked—but Batman finally deduced what was happening and trained himself to overcome the hypnosis. He apprehended the man. (*Detective Comics* #358, December 1966)

Years later Billings surfaced again, this time in METROPOLIS, wearing a modified costume but now equipped with a hypnotic propeller on his back. He added a sonic chest plate to his hypnotic gear and tangled with SUPERMAN, only to lose again. (*Superman* #330, December 1978) He resurfaced in GOTHAM CITY a short time later, part of a crime spree that occurred when fellow felons took advantage of Batman's absence. Spellbinder was the first villain recaptured upon the Dark Knight's return. (*Batman* #336, June 1981)

Someone else using the name *Spellbinder* briefly appeared, a member of the federally sanctioned League-Busters. This man also used hypnotic abilities in his green-and-orange robes. (*Justice League International* #65, June 1994)

Billings remained active, although no more successfully. He and his girlfriend FAY MOFFIT were fleeing the police when he was approached by Neron. Spellbinder rejected the demon's offer, but Moffit did not: She shot her lover in the head and then accepted the deal for herself. In exchange for her immortal soul, Moffit became the new Spellbinder. Her natural hypnotic powers accessed victims' occipital lobe so that they felt whatever they visualized. Batman and Robin learned that she was easily neutralized by simply blindfolding

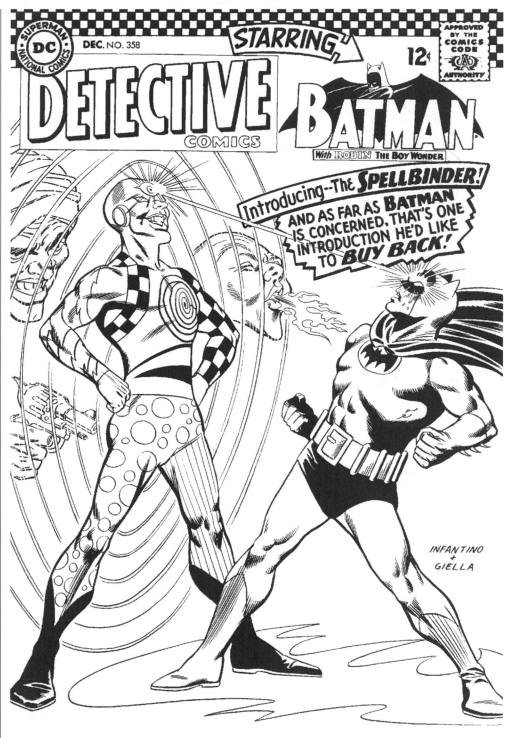

Delbert Billings

her. (*Detective Comics* #691–692, November–December 1995)

The pink-haired, blue-eyed criminal was arrested and sentenced to serve her time at Slabside Penitentiary, although she was briefly transferred to ARKHAM ASYLUM. While there, she was hired by BLOCKBUSTER II to capture ORACLE and learn the location of the legendary BATCAVE. (*Birds of Prey: Batgirl,* 1988)

Back at the Slab, she was one of several criminals aboard a S.T.A.R. LABS transport that

was teleported to Apokolips. Along with the other convicts, Spellbinder agreed to fight on behalf of their captors, plus BLACK CANARY and CATWOMAN, to escape the desolate world. (*Birds of Prey* #12–14, December 1999–February 2000)

When the JOKER turned the Slab into his personal playground, Spellbinder was the first person affected by his new Joker Venom. Once again, Black Canary managed to subdue her. (*Joker: Last Laugh* #1, December 2001)

Moffit was killed at the Battle of Metropolis

Fay Moffit

during the events known as INFINITE CRISIS. (*Infinite Crisis* #7, June 2006)

SPHINX GANG, THE

Al Regan led a band of criminals who committed crimes while wearing masks styled after mythological sphinxes. Their entire enterprise was ended when they were found by Batman, ROBIN, and SUPERMAN. (*World's Finest Comics* #139, February 1964)

SPINNER, THE

Swami Ymar wore a metallic suit covered in spinning disks and carried a buzz-saw gun to commit crimes throughout GOTHAM CITY. The Spinner was at first successful but was ultimately apprehended once and for all by Batman and ROBIN. (*Batman* #129, February 1960)

SPOILER

STEPHANIE BROWN was the daughter of Arthur Brown, the costumed criminal known as CLUEMASTER. He and his wife, Crystal, enjoyed a middle-class life until Arthur's television series was canceled. They then spiraled toward poverty until he adopted a costume and gimmicks to begin a crime spree to provide for his family. He was not very successful and was repeatedly imprisoned, leaving Crystal to raise their daughter Stephanie mostly on her own. (*Detective Comics* #647, August 1992)

As a child Stephanie was nearly raped by one of her babysitters. The man died from a drug overdose eight days later, and she grew up wondering if her father had anything to do with it. (*Robin* [second series] #111, April 2003) She came to resent her loser of a father and his constant return to crime when it was clearly not something he was good at. In her mind the only way to stop him was through an intervention—although the approach she chose was unique. She designed and wore a purple cloaked outfit and showed up to interfere

with his crimes as the Spoiler. With clues she left for the police, it was easy for Batman and ROBIN to apprehend him one more time, although Spoiler joined in the process.

A curious thing happened, though: Stephanie came to enjoy the life of a costumed adventurer. Soon she was donning her outfit regularly to run the GOTHAM CITY rooftops alongside Robin, on whom she developed a crush. Her nascent crime-fighting career got derailed when she discovered she was pregnant, carrying the child she'd conceived with a fellow teen whose family had abandoned Gotham after its devastating earthquake. When she chose to carry the child to term and then give it up for adoption, Robin supported her, going so far as to create the civilian guise of Alvin Draper so he could take her to Lamaze classes. (*Robin* [second series] #65, June 1999)

Their time together ignited a romance that survived his being sent to study for a year at the nearby BRENTWOOD ACADEMY. As with most teen romances, they had their ups and downs, misunderstandings, and rounds of jealousy. It was all complicated by their crime-fighting careers, with Robin splitting his time at school with Batman, the TEEN TITANS, and finally with her. (*Robin* [second series] #98, March 2002) Stephanie, though, was an untrained fighter who had more spirit than skill and no other friends in costume, until she and BATGIRL began spending time together. Batgirl liked Stephanie a lot but protected her by frequently

giving her a mild concussion to prevent her from endangering herself in critical situations.

At one point, while Robin was out of town, Batman—who normally kept his distance from her—surprised Spoiler with an invitation to train together. He went farther, revealing Robin's real name to her, something TIM DRAKE had kept to himself. She also received training for a time from BLACK CANARY as a favor to ORACLE, a fellow BIRD OF PREY. That all came to an end when the Dark Knight determined that Spoiler did not have what it took for their dangerous careers and asked the Birds to end their help.

Cluemaster never did give up his criminal ways. While he was in jail, he accepted a mission with the Suicide Squad, hoping to survive and earn parole. Instead, he was thought dead on the mission.

Spoiler was angered upon learning the news. She distanced herself from Robin and went out into the city, seeking someone to hit. As a result, she brought down the RIDDLER and eventually reconciled with Tim.

Stephanie continued to show more heart than skill, getting injured more than once, breaking her leg during a fight against Johnny Warlock. Undaunted, when she learned that Tim had hung up his cape at his father's insistence, she crafted her own Robin outfit and accessed the Batcave. She begged the Caped Crusader for a chance to be the fourth Teen Wonder. He agreed to train her and see if she could improve but warned her that if she disobeyed an order even once, she was through.

For seventy-one days she trained hard and patrolled with Batman, absorbing more than she thought possible. In addition to her successes, she also did as he expected, saving his life by disobeying an order. When the mission was done, she was fired and banned from the BATCAVE. (Robin [second series] #126–128, July–September 2004)

In shock and desperate to show what she was capable of, Stephanie accessed the Batcomputer, found one of Batman's myriad WAR GAMES plans, and activated it. The plan, though, hinged on MATCHES

MALONE being available to fill a power vacuum in Gotham's underworld. Stephanie was unaware at the time that *Malone* was an alias for Batman, so the plan pretty quickly derailed. During the gang war her actions ignited, she sought out ORPHEUS, the man Batman tapped to fill the gap created by Malone's absence. She was present when the agent was killed by BLACK MASK, who then captured and tortured Stephanie. Despite her pain, she wouldn't tell him anything and was eventually rescued by CATWOMAN. The feline took the dying girl to Dr. LESLIE THOMPKINS for treatment but her injuries were too severe and she died, the Dark Knight at her side. (*Batman* #633, December 2004) In one account, Thompkins so disapproved of what had transpired that she allowed Spoiler to die, but the events of INFINITE CRISIS wiped that from reality. (*52* #8, 2006)

When CASSANDRA CAIN, Batgirl, died at one point, she had a vision of Stephanie. Before she was revived by LADY SHIVA, the ghost told Cassandra that not only was Lady Shiva Batgirl's birth mother, but super-villains had destroyed BLÜDHAVEN as well. (*Batgirl* #72–73, March–April 2006)

SPOOK, THE

Val Kaliban was an escape artist, considered one of the world's best after Batman and Mister Miracle. He turned those skills toward working with the criminal underworld. Disguising himself in a green cloak and calling himself the Spook, he helped

many prisoners break free from jail in defiance of security systems. As Batman began the manhunt, he came to realize that the Spook was a bigger threat than the escapees. The Spook had a vast clientele all equipped with tracers so that he could monitor their whereabouts and spring into action should any be arrested. Batman disguised himself as an inmate and finally managed to apprehend the villain. The Dark Knight was stunned to unmask the man because records showed Val Kaliban had been executed a decade earlier. (*Detective Comics* #434, April 1973)

The Spook escaped custody, and Batman required the aid of JASON BARD and ALFRED PENNYWORTH to finally apprehend him. (*Batman* #252, October 1973) Upon his next escape, the Spook switched to psychological games with the Dark Knight in search of revenge. (*Batman* #276, June 1976) He later tried to convince a drugged Caped Crusader that he was actually dead, videotape the event, and make a fortune selling the recording. Batman came to his senses and captured the Spook. (*Batman* #304, October 1978) This time he was no longer sent to jail but remanded to ARKHAM ASYLUM. (*Batman: Shadow of the Bat* #3, August 1992)

The Spook was also the nickname for a secret agent. This former federal employee lost his grip on sanity and began killing heads of corporations until Batman stopped his spree. (*Legends of the Dark Knight* #102–104, January–March 1998)

SPORTS SPOILERS, THE

A band of criminals, the Sports Spoilers committed a series of daring crimes around GOTHAM CITY. Each robbery saw them wearing the uniforms and using the equipment from a variety of international sports. Early in BATGIRL's career, she found herself distracted by various wardrobe malfunctions that had her question her effectiveness. In the end, though, when she paused to deal with a run in her tights, her shapely leg distracted the Sports Spoilers long enough for Batman and ROBIN to apprehend them. (*Detective Comics* #371, January 1968)

SQUID, THE

Lawrence Loman, aka CLEMENT CARP, was the Squid, a GOTHAM CITY crime lord. The Chinese criminal managed to arrive in town and quickly seize and maintain control of the underworld some time after CARMINE FALCONE was gunned down. He had a gang of enforcers who kept the peace; eventually a newcomer to town, KILLER CROC, joined the Squid's operation as well. It wasn't long before Croc, who fancied himself King Croc, challenged Loman for supremacy. In short order the Squid was killed, but Batman's interference led to the underworld splintering before Croc could enjoy being the sole underworld leader. (*Detective Comics* #497, December 1980)

SQUIRE

Percy Sheldrake became the earl of Wordenshire in England at the tender age of twenty. His father, the previous earl, had been captured during the Dunkirk Evacuation during World War II; his mother died during a bombing raid over London.

Beryl Hutchison

Percy made the acquaintance of Sir Justin, the time-tossed Shining Knight who, along with the All-Star Squadron, was fighting the Axis menace. Sir Justin accepted Percy as his aide and trained him in the ways of fighting. Serving as the Squire, Percy wound up a member of the teen branch of the squadron, the Young All-Stars.

After the war, he left Sir Justin and struck out on his own, creating the new identity of the KNIGHT. He fought crime in England and around Europe, becoming a charter member of the Global Guardians, which operated between the two great ages of heroes. Eventually he married and had a son, Cyril, who became the second Squire.

Percy and Cyril Sheldrake were joined by Batman and ROBIN on one case when the Dynamic Duo came to the Untied Kingdom to stop a band of neo-Nazi supporters. (*Batman* #62, December 1950/January 1951) Later, they were invited to the United States as Batman hosted his international doppelgängers known to the press as BATMEN OF ALL NATIONS. (*Detective Comics* #215, January 1955) Some time later John Mayhew turned them into the CLUB OF HEROES, although the operation fell apart after just two meetings. (*Batman* #667, October 2007)

Eventually Percy retired and Cyril became the next Knight, although he operated solo for quite some time. When Percy died, Cyril became the next earl of Wordenshire. He spent all the family fortune and became a drunk, living in the streets until he was taken in by Beryl Hutchison and her mother. After he straightened out his life, Cyril asked Beryl to become the next Squire. Beryl was gifted in forms of communication, from visual cues to foreign tongues and even mass communications. She was also exceptional with a sword. She thrilled to the life of a costumed adventurer, working as a duo with the Knight and for a brief time with the Ultramarines. (*JLA* #26, February 1999)

Batman worked with Beryl on one JUSTICE LEAGUE OF AMERICA case and was quite impressed by her. (*JLA Classified* #1–3, January–March 2005) Beryl finally met Robin when the Club of Heroes was reunited under mysterious circumstances. (*Batman* #667–669, October–November 2007)

STACY (1941)

Stacy owned the Lions football team and was also a professional gambler. As a result, he went to great lengths, including committing murder, to ensure that the Lions won their games. Upon learning of Stacy's actions, Batman and ROBIN thwarted each attempt to allow the Lions to beat the Panthers and then arrested Stacy and his accomplices. (*Batman* #4, Winter 1941)

STACY (2000)

Court rulings dictated that the GOTHAM CITY POLICE DEPARTMENT could not activate the BAT-SIGNAL, summoning the vigilante Batman to assist on cases. As a result, a civilian was hired from a temporary agency to handle the chore. The first such employee was named Stacy. She worked out of the MAJOR CRIMES UNIT office and had a crush on the Dark Knight. Her devotion was such that she quietly fed ROBIN information when Batman was

unable to reach police headquarters. (*Detective Comics* #742, March 2000)

STACY, "SLANT"

"Slant" Stacy and his band of criminals stole platinum and thought they could get away cleanly because at the time, GOTHAM CITY's protectors Batman and ROBIN were forced to remain underwater for two days to avoid a serious case of the bends after a mission. The Dynamic Duo were determined to apprehend Stacy, however, so they used a navy-surplus pocket sub to maneuver through the water. Thanks to their BATMARINE, they managed to match Stacy and his men move for move and finally contain them without the heroes once breaking the surface. (*Batman* #86, September 1954)

STAFFORD, "SLANT"

Shortly after Batman and ROBIN began using remote-control devices to manipulate the BATMOBILE and BATPLANE from the BATCAVE, the criminal "Slant" Stafford stole duplicate devices from their inventor, Dr. Phillip Winters. At first Stafford manipulated the devices in an attempt to have the vehicles kill their occupants. Having failed after several attempts at this, he and his men hijacked the Batplane and used it for numerous crimes. Batman and Robin finally caught up to Stafford and subdued him, confiscating the stolen devices and sending the gang to jail. (*Batman* #91, April 1955)

STANNAR, JOHN

People from the planet Skar sent an unmanned vessel to Earth, containing welcoming gifts as a step in first contact with humanity. The vessel crashed in the American Northeast. The first to come across it was John Stannar, a fugitive from justice. He took the gifts, which included a device that temporarily endowed the user with superpowers, four-dimensional prongs that could reach objects through solid walls, and other tools. Stannar journeyed to GOTHAM CITY and committed numerous crimes, including the freeing of friends from the local jail. The criminals seemed unstoppable until the arrival of Batman and ROBIN, who outmaneuvered them. Stannar was apprehended, and the alien technology was passed on to the government. (*Detective Comics* #250, December 1957)

S.T.A.R. LABS

Scientific and Technological Advanced Research Labs was a privately owned chain of research and development labs around the country. Founded by Garrison Slate, the independent operation allowed for unfettered work without being beholden to any government or business entity. It proved so successful that S.T.A.R. Labs went global, with branch offices in Canada, Europe, Australia, and Asia. S.T.A.R. Labs tended to specialize in each locale, with the GOTHAM CITY branch concentrating on weaponry. (*Superman* #246, December 1971)

STARFIRE

Princess Koriand'r was part of the ruling family on Tamaran in the Vegan star system. When their planet was overrun by the Branx and Gordanian warriors, Koriand'r and her sister Komand'r were taken prisoner and subjected to experiments at the hands of the Psions. The girls were given powers beyond the Tamaranean norm, such as the ability to project powerful energy bursts. The natives could already fly, although Komand'r could not, which caused her bitterness. (*Tales of the New Teen Titans* #4, September 1982)

Shortly after Raven helped bring about a new incarnation of the TEEN TITANS, they came to the aid of an escaping Koriand'r, protecting her from the pursuing Gordanians. She learned English through tactile means, kissing ROBIN. The Titans welcomed Koriand'r to stay on Earth and join them, which she did, taking the code name *Starfire*. (*DC Comics Presents* #26, October 1980)

She lived with Donna Troy, taking the human name Kory Anders, and briefly became a fashion

model while acclimating to Earth. Although she enjoyed her time with the Titans, using her warrior's training for justice and romancing DICK GRAYSON, she longed to return home and free her people. When the opportunity finally presented itself, the Titans assisted in the fight—though Starfire was shocked to find herself battling her own sister. (*New Teen Titans* #23–25, *New Teen Titans Annual* #1, September–November 1982)

Later her relationship with Dick was tested when she was summoned back home to marry Captain Karras to prevent the planet from being plunged into a civil war. She went through with the wedding and remained on Tamaran; Dick returned to Earth, his heart broken. (*New Teen Titans* [second series] #15–18, December 1985–March 1986) Eventually, though, Starfire came to conclude that Tamaran was no longer her home, and she left her family and Karras behind. She returned to Earth and moved in with Dick, who was thrilled to learn that the marriage ceremony had not been a valid one. (*New Teen Titans* [second series] #39, January 1988) In time Dick proposed to Starfire, but their wedding was interrupted by a demonically possessed Raven. (*New Teen Titans* [second series] #100, August 1993)

The couple never actually married, and Starfire left Earth on several other occasions, usually returning to the Titans. Still, each absence pushed the lovers farther apart until they were finally just friends. On most occasions her return to Earth also led to duty with the Titans. She worked alongside the third Robin, TIM DRAKE, in the most recent such incident. (*Teen Titans* [third series] #1, September 2003)

STARK, CHARLEY

Criminal Jud Lukins was named Public Enemy Number One and had to leave GOTHAM CITY. His associates found Charley Stark, a shipyard riveter, and paid him to create an airtight container that could hide Lukins aboard a ship bound for a foreign port. As the container was being constructed, Lukins hid out at the shipyards, only to be discovered by a night watchman. When the man

was killed to protect Lukins's secret, Batman came to investigate the crime. He decided to disguise himself as BRUCE WAYNE, riveter, and seek Lukins. In time Batman and ROBIN arrived to arrest Stark for his crime, in addition to Lukins, who was to be tried for the night watchman's murder. (*World's Finest Comics* #46, June/July 1950)

STARK, EDDIE

Eddie Stark was a wanted criminal, pursued by Batman and ROBIN, when all three were aboard a ferryboat that was accidentally transported to another dimension, the result of a freak lightning storm. The ferryboat found itself in YLLA, populated by a suspicious, technologically advanced race of beings. The passengers were taken prisoner because the Yllans were concerned that these aliens were in league with their enemies, the Gruggs. Stark stole the Yllans' tele-dome—a recently completed device that would allow the natives to exert mental control over their rivals. The criminal intended to steal the device and ferry, return home, and use the device to continue his illegal activities. Instead, Batman and Robin intervened, stopping Stark and helping repel an attack by the Gruggs. The Caped Crusader then returned the invention to a grateful Yllan chief, ensuring peace between the races. The ferry and its passengers found their way back to their home reality. (*Detective Comics* #293, July 1961)

STARMAN

When PROFESSOR MILO exposed Batman to a gas that induced a phobia of bats, BRUCE WAYNE created an

Ted Knight

entirely new identity, that of Starman. He continued to fight crime in GOTHAM CITY, complete with flying headquarters/vehicle until the potion faded and Milo was apprehended. (*Detective Comics* #247, 1957)

The first Starman was Ted Knight, who wielded a gravity rod that projected energy; he served on the JUSTICE SOCIETY OF AMERICA with Batman on Earth-2. Years later Knight had a nervous breakdown and stopped operating in his beloved Opal City. For a brief time, after the events of CRISIS ON INFINITE EARTHS, Doctor Mid-Nite, a fellow JSA member, adopted the Starman guise that Batman had used and protected the citizens. Later Starman's son, David, traveled back in time to 1951 and succeeded Doctor Mid-Nite as that Starman. (*Starman* [second series] #61, January 2000)

STAR-MAN, THE

The Star-Man was a costumed criminal who sought to obtain the three pieces of a fabled Tibetan belt that, when assembled, would grant the wearer superstrength, flight, and even immortality. He managed to gather the green belt, the gold buckle, and a red star that fit within the buckle, but he was prevented from using it by the combined efforts of Batman, ROBIN, and BATWOMAN. At Batwoman's insistence, the powerful belt was destroyed. (*Detective Comics* #286, December 1960)

STARR, JOE

A fortune-teller told low-level criminal Joe Starr he was born under a lucky star and could expect good things to come. Convinced that the prophecy meant he had a year to accomplish great things, he changed his name to Lucky Starr, adopted a maroon costume, and killed Trigger Smith, his boss. Assuming control over the gang, Lucky Star began a series of audacious crimes, risking his life time and again, certain that nothing bad would happen to him . . . yet. Eventually he was tracked and apprehended by Batman and ROBIN. Convicted of killing Smith, he was sentenced to the electric chair. (*World's Finest Comics* #32, January/February 1948)

ST. CLOUD, SILVER

Silver St. Cloud was an event planner who met Bruce Wayne on his yacht shortly after Wayne, as Batman, defeated DOCTOR PHOSPHORUS. He was captivated with her platinum-blond hair and striking features. (*Detective Comics* #470, June 1977)

The two began to date just as Batman was plagued by a new round of threats from the likes of the JOKER and PENGUIN. All along, Silver was paying close attention to her boyfriend, and as she stared at his jawline she came to realize that Wayne was also Batman, whom she had encountered on more than one occasion. When Wayne sought treatment for radiation poisoning, he was kidnapped by Professor HUGO STRANGE, who impersonated him for days. Silver was the one to find and free Wayne, who chose to end their relationship.

As Batman dispatched DEADSHOT, Silver called to him—and he suddenly realized that she knew his secret. He had no clue what to do with the woman his alter ego had fallen in love with. That resolved

itself when she watched Batman battle the Joker and realized this was not a life she could be a part of. Reluctantly she ended the relationship and moved from GOTHAM CITY.

Silver eventually chose to return to Gotham, accompanied by her fiancé, a man running for governor. Once again she got caught up in Batman's life, and her emotions were conflicted. As Batman protected her fiancé from the Joker, it was clear what his priorities were always going to be, and she chose to remain with the politician. (*Batman: Dark Detective* #1–6, July–September 2005)

STEELJACKET

The man who became Steeljacket was the result of a bio-engineering experiment that hollowed

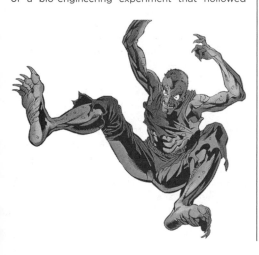

out his bones and let him fly like a bird. To protect his fragile physical form, he encased himself in a lightweight metallic alloy suit of armor. With his savage claws, Steeljacket began killing mobsters around the city; witnesses could only describe an armored figure. At first Batman thought it was AZRAEL, but Robin sensed it was someone else. As he investigated his hunch, Robin encountered Steeljacket, who seemed to be part of a protection racket. They fought and the killer got away, not to be seen again. (*Detective Comics* #681, *Robin* [second series] #13, January 1995)

STILETTI, MANUEL

When the exiled duke of Dorian arrived in America with the Crown Jewels in order to establish credit with the federal government, the gems became the object of international criminal Manuel Stiletti's lust. The attempted crime was thwarted through the combined efforts of the Earth-2 Batman, ROBIN, and the newly arrived family butler, ALFRED JARVIS. (*Batman* #16, April/May 1943)

STILETTO

The first Stiletto whom Batman fought was SAUL CALVINO, a hit man who escaped prison confinement prior to his execution. Batman tracked him down and returned him to BLACKGATE PENITENTIARY, where he met his fate. (*Detective Comics* #630, June 1991)

The second Stiletto was a female killer affiliated with the first TOYMAN, Winslow Schott. It all began with a young deaf-mute named Tyler whose parents died in a robbery gone bad; the gunshots had caused his deafness. HARVEY BULLOCK found the boy at the crime scene and saw to it that he was turned over to his aunt. Some time later Bullock responded to a homicide call, only to learn that the victim was this same aunt, an Internet porn star. A terrified Tyler was hiding under the bed. Given the circumstances involving the boy, the case caught Batman's interest, and he deduced that Toyman was the killer. Tyler, a computer whiz, found Toyman and the contract killer Stiletto at an online game site. Toyman tasked Stiletto with killing this witness, but when she realized that he was a young boy, she kidnapped him from police headquarters instead.

The chase led to a warehouse, where Batman was ambushed and wounded. Escaping into the sewers, Batman talked the boy through stitching up his wound, earning his trust by explaining his own tragic origins. Meantime, as Toyman explained his deadly plan to kill children through their video games, Stiletto turned on him. Batman and Tyler returned to end the case and take Toyman into custody. During the fight, Stiletto told the Dark Knight that Tyler seemed to be under the impression he'd soon be adopted by Batman. Batman rejected the notion; Stiletto disappeared with Tyler as Batman subdued Toyman and took him to jail. (*Batman: Toyman* #1–4, November 1998–February 1999)

STINSON, SPADE

Spade Stinson was a swindler, arrested and sent to jail by Batman, who was freed and determined to exact vengeance on the Caped Crusader. Accomplices cornered Batman and knocked him unconscious; he awoke to be introduced to

Stinson, posing as a doctor. He brought the crime fighter to his office and gave him pills ostensibly to help his injury, but in fact they contained an extract from Amazon plants that would drive him insane and force him to commit murder, ruining Batman forever. The Caped Crusader's moral code was such that he managed to avoid killing, but still committed numerous crimes. ROBIN found out that Batman was not himself when he discovered stolen loot strewn about the BATCAVE. The following morning Batman had no recollection of his actions, but he investigated and found the doctor. In short order he and Robin apprehended Stinson and his men, then returned the stolen property. (*Detective Comics* #228, February 1956)

STIRK, CORNELIUS

Cornelius Stirk suffered from a hypothalamic disorder that allowed him to project images from other people's minds. He used this to torture and kill people, projecting their fears moments before they died. His power came to light when he was just sixteen and he killed a fellow classmate. Eventually he was arrested and remanded to ARKHAM ASYLUM, but he was soon deemed cured and was released. However, Stirk stopped taking his tricyclics and chlorpromazine pills and returned to his life as a serial killer. Using his psionic powers, he made people see him as someone they knew and trusted so he was able to get close to them before committing his heinous acts. By then, Stirk was convinced that he could gain the nutrients he needed to survive by causing victims to experience fear as he killed them, stimulating the release of massive amounts of norepinephrine into their hearts—which he then supped on. (*Detective Comics* #592, November 1988)

Stirk was among the prisoners who escaped when BANE broke into Arkham. He allied himself with the JOKER in a scheme to kidnap and then kill Police Commissioner JAMES GORDON. Stirk wanted Gordon to experience fear first, so he projected that he himself was Batman; when the real Dark Knight arrived to save his friend, the conflicting images terrified Gordon. His wife, SARAH ESSEN GORDON, took him for treatment. (*Batman* #494, Early June, 1993)

Stirk escaped again, and Batman had to save Mayor MARION GRANGE from him at the PENGUIN's casino, which was destroyed in the battle. (*Batman: Shadow of the Bat* #46–47, January–February 1996)

Stirk was freed when Arkham was again damaged, this time from the Gotham earthquake. He has not been seen since. (*Batman: Shadow of the Bat* #80, December 1998)

STORME, PORTIA

Portia Storme was the stage name taken by BRUCE WAYNE's onetime fiancée JULIE MADISON.

STRAIT, MICHAEL

A criminal who committed his acts as the COUNT.

STRANGE, HUGO

Early in Batman's Earth-2 career, he encountered Hugo Strange, a brilliant scientist who crossed

ethical and moral boundaries by experimenting on humans and committing crimes to fund his illegal research. Batman first learned of Strange when FBI agent John Davis, dying after trying to apprehend Strange, told him of the bald scientist. Strange was creating a thick, unnatural fog to mask his robberies, but this also called attention to his whereabouts. Batman arrived and fought Strange's six underlings, easily subduing the scientist himself. From his GOTHAM CITY jail, Strange vowed revenge. (*Detective Comics* #36, February 1940)

Sure enough, Strange escaped and also freed inmates from a nearby insane asylum. He experimented on them, turning them into fifteen-foot-tall monsters, which he then unleashed on the city. As expected, this brought the Caped Crusader into action, and the trail led back to the lab. There Strange managed to inject his nemesis with the same serum he had used on the inmates. After knocking the scientist through a window, Batman had to survive a gauntlet of mindless monsters to reach the chemicals and craft an antidote before he, too, transformed. (*Batman* #1, Spring 1940)

Strange survived his fall and returned to Gotham, bringing with him a fear dust that he used in his mad quest to take over the federal government.

Batman and ROBIN succeeded in stopping his scheme with Strange falling off a cliff, once more presumed to have died. (*Detective Comics* #46, December 1940)

Strange survived, but the fall left him an invalid. He spent years in that miserable state, enduring painful physical therapy until he managed to detail instructions for a surgical technique that would restore his mobility. The doctor hired to perform the experimental surgery lacked Strange's skill and was only partly successful, leaving Strange deformed. After killing the doctor for failing him, Strange finally sought a release. Manipulating events soon after Batman died on his final case, Strange used his tools to steal STARMAN's cosmic rod and began attacking everything and everyone related to the late Caped Crusader. His efforts also opened a rift between Earth-1 and Earth-2, allowing the Earth-1 Batman to visit the other universe. He teamed with Robin and BATWOMAN to stop Strange's efforts, only to learn that the man was lashing out in frustration. When Strange himself realized this, he used the cosmic rod to end his miserable life once and for all. (*The Brave and the Bold* #182, January 1982)

On Earth-1, Strange had fought Batman early in his career and then vanished. Strange credited Batman as "the reason I abandoned Gotham City for Europe after our last battle—*and* the reason I have *returned* after so many years of *success* there. Only *The Batman* can offer *Hugo Strange* a *challenge*."

After being exposed to radiation in his battle against DOCTOR PHOSPHORUS, BRUCE WAYNE went to a private clinic for treatment. He then learned that the chief of staff, Dr. Todhunter, was actually Hugo Strange and had been turning patients into a new breed of monster. Realizing that he had captured Batman, Strange assumed the Batman/Bruce Wayne identity and for three days tried to divest the WAYNE FOUNDATION of its fortune. He also let the criminal underworld know he was privy to Batman's true name and willing to auction it off. Instead of bidding, political boss RUPERT THORNE had Strange kidnapped and tortured. Strange seemingly died once more, this time cursing Thorne. It fell to SILVER ST. CLOUD, Wayne's girlfriend, to find and free her lover, aided by Robin. (*Detective Comics* #471–472, August–September 1977)

Thorne thought Strange's ghost was haunting him, prompting him to flee Gotham; while driving on a rain-slick road in Ohio, he crashed into a tree. When police responded to the accident, Thorne was babbling incoherently. (*Detective Comics* #476, March/April 1978)

Some time later Thorne was released from ARKHAM ASYLUM and once more thought he was being haunted by Strange. He went so far as to call in ghostbreaker Terrence Thirteen, who discovered evidence that the hauntings were a hoax perpetrated by Thorne's political rivals—but he did not notice Hugo Strange, alive and well, watching from a distance. (*Batman* #354, December 1982) Satisfied, Strange turned his attentions once more to his nemesis and tried to drive Wayne insane, only meeting with defeat and another presumed death. Instead, though, it was an android Strange that had died. The real scientist once more tried to

take over the Wayne Foundation. (*Batman Annual #10*, 1986)

In the reality after CRISIS ON INFINITE EARTHS, Hugo Strange was a media-savvy psychiatrist fascinated by the recent sightings of a caped figure in the Gotham streets. Mayor Wilson Klass appointed Strange as a consultant to his Vigilante Task Force, which gave him access to large amounts of research, fueling his mania. Strange convinced the task force's second in command, MAX CORT, to take the fight to Batman by becoming the ultraviolent costumed vigilante NIGHT-SCOURGE. Strange then framed Batman for the kidnapping of Klass's daughter Catherine, and the two faced off once more. (*Legends of the Dark Knight* #11–15, September 1990–January 1991)

Events shifted after INFINITE CRISIS. Then Batman first met Strange when he was experimenting by turning men into monsters. It was revealed that Strange had become a sociopath after being abandoned as a child; he'd grown up in a variety of state-run homes. (*Batman and the Monster Men* #1–6, January–June 2006)

Strange and the Dark Knight have squared off repeatedly, usually with Strange obsessed with Batman and Bruce Wayne, trying time and again to defeat the man. This once included disguising himself as a psychiatrist assigned to conduct stress evaluations of WAYNE ENTERPRISES employees. When Bruce Wayne took his turn, Strange used exotic hallucinogens hoping to coax the billionaire into admitting that he was the Gotham Guardian, only to fail because Wayne had mentally prepared with a post-hypnotic suggestion that repressed his Batman persona. With help from Robin and NIGHTWING, Strange was defeated and returned to Arkham. (*Batman: Gotham Knights* #8–12, October 2001–February 2002)

STREET DEMONZ, THE

The Street Demonz began as a GOTHAM CITY biker gang numbering among its members people named Skorp, Swizz, Arnie, Brute, Slimer, and Pigpen. Batman said he had first encountered them before BRUCE WAYNE donned the cape and cowl as they annoyed him during a visit to CRIME ALLEY. When Batman saw that they were turning toward crime, he reached out to them as Wayne, sponsoring a class. (*Detective Comics* #614, May 1990)

The efforts proved ineffective as the gang members allied themselves with different factions of the underworld. When the VENTRILOQUIST was imprisoned, they took over running his Ventriloquist Club and its secret drug-running operation. A fight with the Ventriloquist and SCARFACE proved deadly, but the Demonz survived, abandoning the club. They have since continued their criminal ways, and Batman has stopped trying to rehabilitate them.

STROBE, PAUL

An electrical engineer who committed crimes as ATOMIC-MAN.

STRYKER, ALFRED

Alfred Stryker, along with three other men, ran the Apex Chemical Company in GOTHAM CITY. Desiring to control the syndicate outright, Stryker had two of his partners killed. His attempts to murder the third failed, stopped by the arrival of a costumed champion debuting in the city that evening,

Batman. He and Stryker fought until the chemical magnate tumbled into a vat of acid, killing him. (*Detective Comics* #27, May 1939)

STYX

Styx was the costumed persona of a criminal who operated a way station for felons, located under Gotham Bay. For a thousand dollars a day or ten thousand a month, criminals could safely reside in the Aqua-Lair. Each resident was provided with a serum that Styx insisted was the only way to survive living two thousand fathoms beneath the surface. This proved false—a way to keep his charges under control. The lair was actually a short swim from the surface, which proved useful when Batman and ROBIN located the operation. They alerted the harbor police, who arrested Styx and the remaining criminals. (*Detective Comics* #189, November 1952)

SUICIDE KING, THE

Justin Quinn worked for ATHENA'S NETWORK, attempting to destroy the Rossetti Mob. In his guise as the Suicide King, he got close to the mob and proved effective in disrupting their operations. He came to blows with the HUNTRESS during the effort and was severely injured in their battle. After the Network was put out of business by Batman, the Suicide King disappeared—only to heal and resurface as a participant in the WAR GAMES that nearly destroyed Gotham. (*Batman Family* #1–8, December 2002–February 2003)

SUPERGIRL

When KRYPTON exploded, Earth-2 knew of only one survivor for decades. In time, though, Kara

Zor-L, his niece, arrived as a teen, a survivor from Argo City. She adopted the name *Power Girl* and fought crime alongside the HUNTRESS and ROBIN in the JUSTICE SOCIETY OF AMERICA. (*All Star Comics* #57, February/March 1951)

Argo City also survived in the Earth-1 universe until its KRYPTONITE-irradiated bedrock proved too deadly to survive and Zor-L sent his teen daughter to Earth. She crashed near METROPOLIS and was found by her older cousin SUPERMAN. He decided that she needed training, much as he had trained as Superboy, so he kept her as his secret weapon. Kara took the American name *Linda Lee* and was placed in the Midvale Orphanage. (*Action Comics* #252, May 1959) In time she was adopted by Fred and Linda Danvers. When the Man of Steel deemed her ready, he introduced the Maid of Might to the world. (*Action Comics* #285, February 1962)

Through the years Supergirl earned a reputation on her own and battled all manner of criminals and intergalactic threats. She joined the thirtieth-century-based Legion of Super-Heroes and counted BATGIRL as one of her closest friends. When reality was threatened by the Anti-Monitor during the CRISIS ON INFINITE EARTHS, she sacrificed her life to save all life. (*Crisis on Infinite Earths* #7, October 1985)

A pocket universe survived the Crisis, and there LEX LUTHOR fashioned a clone of Lana Lang, imbuing it with special abilities; she was called Matrix. After Superman traveled to this universe for a mission, Matrix was badly injured coming to his aid, so he brought her to his reality so she could be healed by Ma and Pa Kent in Smallville. In time she used her shape-changing powers to become a new Supergirl and carve an identity for herself in this new world. She briefly served as a member of the TEEN TITANS. (*Superman* [second series] #16, April 1988)

Artist Linda Danvers attempted suicide but wound up being merged with Matrix, forming a new life. Eventually this new incarnation of Supergirl discovered that she was also an Earth Angel, with special powers and a destiny all her own. (*Supergirl* [fourth series] #1, September 1996) She suffered several crises of faith as she tried to live a good life despite personal complications and demonic threats. Then, when the pre-Crisis Supergirl was accidentally diverted to the post-Crisis reality, the Earth Angel learned that Supergirl was destined to die. Once more she sacrificed herself, taking Supergirl's place in the pre-Crisis reality, marrying Superman, and giving birth to a daughter, Ariella. She then returned to her world and allowed Supergirl to go fulfill her destiny. (*Supergirl* #75, December 2002)

A girl named Cir-El arrived from a potential future, claiming to be the daughter of Superman and LOIS LANE. It was soon learned she was actually a human manipulated by BRAINIAC, who then sacrificed herself to stop the villain's latest scheme. (*Superman: The 10-Cent Adventure* #1, 2003)

Reality-changing waves emanated from the limbo-like realm that the four survivors of the Crisis lived in. One result was that Matrix and Cir-El ceased to exist, although artist Linda Danvers survived, on the post-Crisis Earth. Instead, Kara Zor-El, daughter of Zor-L and Alura, was born about a decade earlier than Kal-El. When Krypton was threatened, she

was placed in suspended animation and rocketed to Earth to look after her infant cousin, who was being sent by Zor-L's brother, Jor-L. However, her spacecraft got lodged in an asteroid of what was once her homeworld; she finally landed on Earth decades later than scheduled. Her ship crashed under the sea and was first found by Batman, who was very suspicious of a teen who could speak Kryptonese. Superman, when he saw her, was delighted to meet a fellow Kryptonian and even more thrilled to learn they were related. While the Dark Knight maintained his concerns, he did see to it that Superman maintained perspective. They agreed that Kara should be trained to use her tremendous powers on Themyscira, the home to the Amazons. (*Superman/Batman* #8, May 2004)

Since then, she had a tumultuous time adjusting to life on Earth. She was almost immediately corrupted by the New God Darkseid and assaulted by Lex Luthor, possessing Black Kryptonite. She tried to create an alter ego, Claire Connors, and attend high school but quickly abandoned the effort. Supergirl also tried to work with the OUTSIDERS, developing a crush on NIGHTWING along the way, but that, too, proved dissatisfying. She did, though, become close friends with CAPTAIN BOOMERANG II. With her powers still developing under Earth's solar radiation, she has continued to seek a place for herself, briefly joining Robin's Teen Titans. After a mission to KANDOR with Power Girl, where they dressed as Nightwing and FLAMEBIRD, she brought back a healing device. Seeking some financial independence, she sold it to Batman for one million dollars. She sees Batman as a foster parent and is as eager to earn his confidence and approval as she is of her cousin, Superman,

(For a detailed account of Supergirl, see *The Essential Superman Encyclopedia*.)

SUPERMAN

The World's Greatest Super Hero began life as an infant on the doomed planet KRYPTON. His father, the scientist Jor-L, knew the planet was going to be destroyed, so he saved his son by rocketing him to Earth-2 moments before their world exploded. The boy was found by Jonathan and Martha Kent in Smallville, Kansas, who raised him as their own. When he reached adulthood, CLARK KENT moved to METROPOLIS and took a job at the *Daily Star* where he could keep tabs on situations that might demand his powers and abilities. (*Action Comics* #1, June 1938)

In time he fell in love with fellow reporter LOIS

LANE and became the idol that all other costumed crime fighters aspired to be. He was a member of the JUSTICE SOCIETY OF AMERICA and All-Star Squadron, counting Batman as his closest friend, sharing numerous adventures together.

Eventually he married Lois Lane and enjoyed semi-retirement, delighted when his cousin Kara arrived, following in his footsteps as Power Girl. When his world was threatened by the Anti-Monitor, he teamed up with the Superman of Earth-1 and countless champions from other realities to defeat the villain and save lives. After the battle ended and a single Earth survived CRISIS ON INFINITE EARTHS, he and Lois were invited to live out their days in a crystalline limbo-like world between realities. (*Crisis on Infinite Earths* #12, March 1986)

Over time, though, Lois continued to age and was nearing death, driving Superman into depression. Worse, from their new home, they watched events unfolding on the New Earth, and Superman disliked what he saw—darker times, heroes acting less than noble. Alexander Luthor, from Earth-3, told the grieving Man of Steel he had a plan that could save Lois and improve the world. He garnered Superman's support and unleashed the events known as INFINITE CRISIS. First, Superman approached that world's Batman in the BATCAVE and revealed the plan. He was disappointed to have his former friend reject the offer to participate. Eventually Superman realized that he had been mistaken and was being used by Luthor. Another meta-human, Superboy-Prime, lost his grip on sanity, because he despised this world's Superboy and the lack of heroism being displayed. As a result, he worked with Luthor to re-create the multiverse in order to find the right world. Lois, during these times, finally passed away, and Superman's grief turned to anger when he realized he was being manipulated. With Superman, the last son of Krypton rushed Superboy-Prime through Krypton's red sun, each sacrificing much of their powers to end the threat. Superman finally succumbed to age, grief, and the loss of power, dying in the arms of that reality's Superman. (*Infinite Crisis* #1–7, December 2005–June 2006)

On Earth-1, Kal-L arrived as a youth and learned how to use his powers by adventuring as Superboy. After the Kents died from a tropical disease, he left Smallville and went to Metropolis, joining the *Daily Planet,* numbering Perry White, JIMMY OLSEN, and Lois Lane as his friends. (*Action Comics* #242, July 1958) He fought alongside Batman in the JUSTICE LEAGUE OF AMERICA and they were the best of friends, sharing adventures, exchanging gifts, and masquerading in each other's alter egos to protect their secrets. He delighted when Kara Zor-L arrived from Argo City, and he trained her to use her powers as SUPERGIRL.

After the Crisis on Infinite Earths, the single Superman also hailed from a cold, sterile Krypton. He was raised by the Kents without spending any time in costume as a Superboy. Instead, after high school, he traveled the world for several years, seeing the best and worst of humanity while perfecting his journalistic skills, leading to his job at

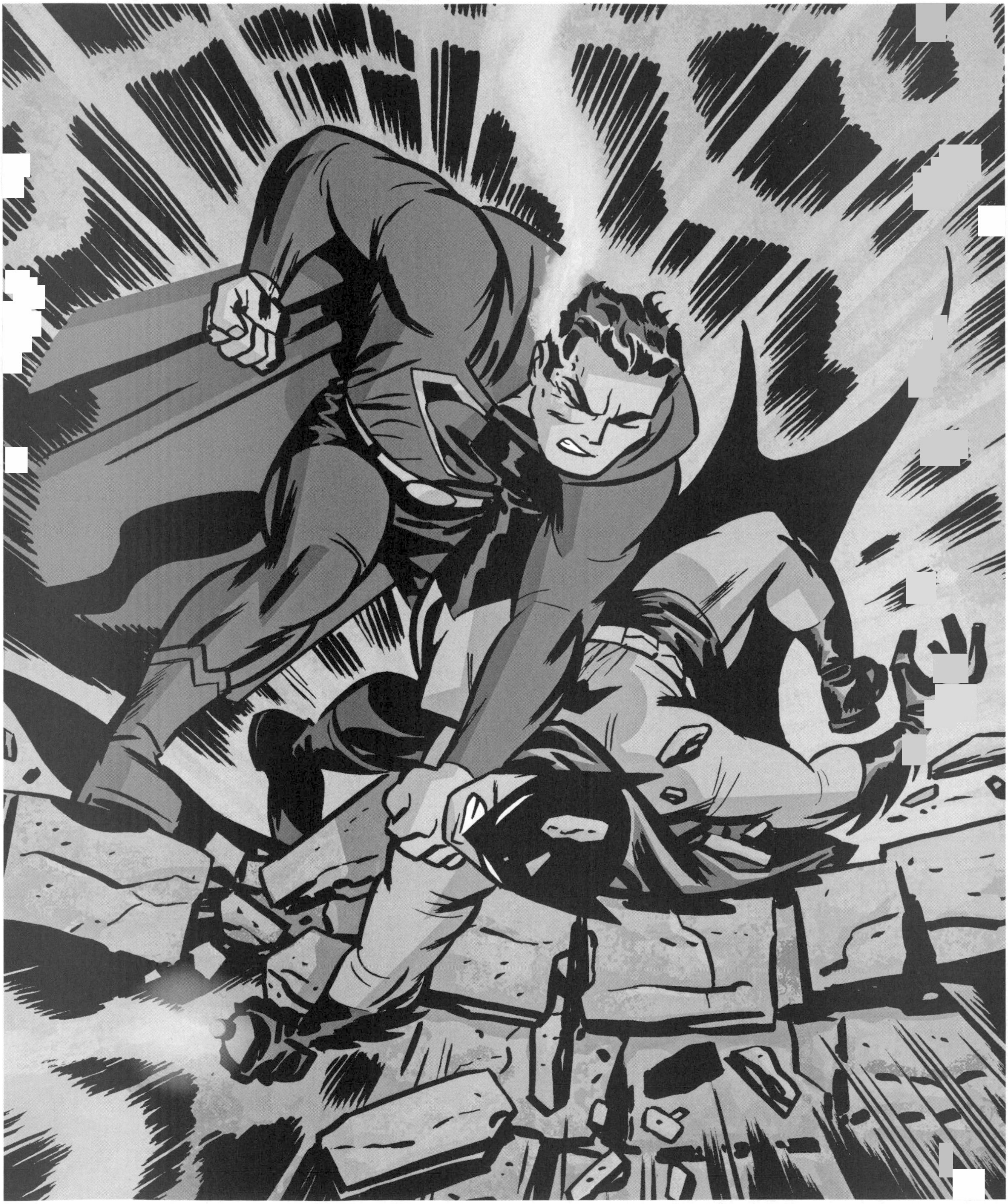

the *Daily Planet*. He eventually married Lois Lane, who had come to love Clark Kent, not Superman.

The Man of Steel and Dark Knight enjoyed a wary relationship, although Superman entrusted him with Kryptonite to be used in the event of Superman being corrupted somehow. With Wonder Woman, these meta-humans are seen as the triumvirate of mentor super heroes, charter members of the JLA and often the final word on matters involving the super-hero community.

(For a detailed account of Superman, see *The Essential Superman Encyclopedia*.)

SUPER SONS

On Earth-154, Batman and Superman both married unnamed women and fathered sons. The boys, Bruce Wayne Jr. and Clark Kent Jr., grew up in their famous fathers' shadows, training to one day fight alongside them. As college-age young men, they finally rebelled and struck out on their own, wearing costumes identical to their parents'. Even with powers half those of his Kryptonian father, Superman Jr. proved an effective crime fighter, meshing nicely with the well-prepared Batman Jr. (*World's Finest Comics* #215, December 1972/January 1973)

SWAMI, THE

Criminal mastermind Johnny Witts once masqueraded as the Swami.

SWAMP THING

When Earth was formed, Gaea, the life force, saw to it that the planet would be protected by elementals of earth, wind, water, and fire. The Earth Elemental was always to be born in fire and would command and protect the Green—the plant and organic life that inhabited the cooling planet. Ever since then a steady succession of Swamp Things has looked after the world. (*House of Secrets* #92, June/July 1971)

In the late twentieth century Alec Holland, who studied alongside Pamela Isley under the Floronic Man, Jason Woodrue, was destined to become the next Swamp Thing. After marrying his college sweetheart, Linda, he moved to Houma, Louisiana, where the couple went to work on a bio-restorative formula. When he refused to give up the formula to a criminal, his home was firebombed, trapping Holland inside. Covered in the formula and aflame, he ran into the swamp, where he died. His body, the formula, and the fire all then conspired to animate plant life, which shambled to the surface, thinking itself Holland reborn. (*Swamp Thing* #1, October/November 1972)

As Swamp Thing fulfilled his mission, he frequently encountered Earth's costumed champions of justice, notably Batman.

One noteworthy meeting had Batman come to a woman's defense when she fled to Gotham City after being accused of breaking the law by becoming Swamp Thing's lover. He noted that several other humans had most likely broken the same law by loving Superman or the Martian Manhunter.

Soon after, Lex Luthor devised a way to banish Swamp Thing from Earth; he wandered the stars for a year. Upon his inevitable return, he sought revenge against the scientist, only to be stopped by Superman (*Swamp Thing* [second series] #79,

December 1988) and Batman. (*Swamp Thing Annual* #4, 1988)

Later, the Earth Elemental and the Dark Knight found themselves at odds over the fate of Killer Croc. Swamp Thing felt he belonged to the Green. Instead, Croc's vicious nature led to his expulsion from and eventual return to crime in Gotham. (*Batman* #521–522, August–September 1995; *Swamp Thing* [second series] #160, November 1995; *The Batman Chronicles* #3, Winter 1996)

SWASHBUCKLER

When the Riddler tried to relaunch his criminal career in Houston, Texas, he was thwarted by the city's protector, a costumed hero named Swashbuckler. In reality this was Michael Carter, a resident and well-trained athlete. Complicating the Riddler's life was the fact that Batman had followed him and worked alongside Swashbuckler to end his new venture. (*Detective Comics* #493, August 1980)

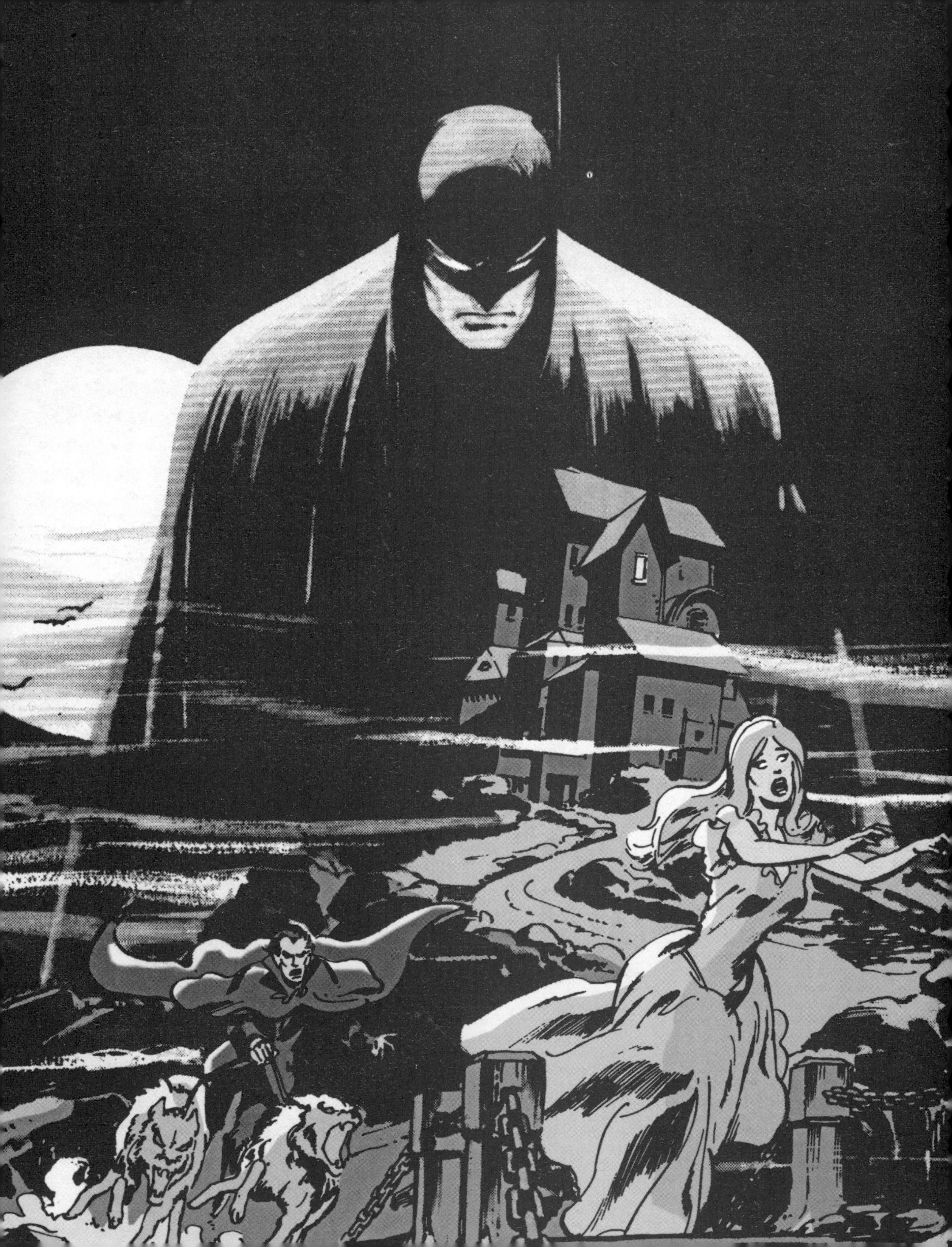

T

TAL-DAR

Hailing from distant ALCOR, Tal-Dar arrived on Earth to observe Batman's crime-fighting techniques in person. As chief of the Interplanetary Police Force, he became aware of the Caped Crusader's exploits. He told the media that he intended to teach Batman some of his own techniques and invite him onto the IPF once Earth mastered interplanetary space travel. Beneath the bravado, Tal-Dar was actually concerned that he lacked the confidence and skills to properly lead his own force. He covered up his insecurities with bluster; in fact, his real goal was to learn Batman's methods.

Hoping to obtain his powerful police pistol, criminals posed as newspapermen and kidnapped Tal-Dar, requiring the Dynamic Duo to come to his aid. Soon after, he received word that Zan-Rak, Alcor's deadliest villain, had stolen the starstone. This interstellar object emitted healing radiation. It was being ransomed for the equivalent of one million dollars. Tal-Dar begged the heroes to return to Alcor with him and aid in recovering the starstone.

Once they reached the asteroid where Zan-Rak hid in his keep, Batman announced that he had contracted "radji disease"; Tal-Dar would have to handle the criminal without him. Putting on a brave front, Tal-Dar and the Boy Wonder headed after the villain. Zan-Rak proved an easy capture, and once he was apprehended, the police chief summoned reinforcements. However, Zan-Rak tried one final time to kill his foe, only to be disarmed by Batman. The Caped Crusader then admitted to faking the illness to show Tal-Dar that he'd had the requisite skills all along—he just lacked confidence. (*Detective Comics* #282, August 1960)

Months later, a grateful Tal-Dar sent the Dynamic Duo a flying robot to aid them. While it was programmed to prevent Batman from being harmed, it proved more hindrance than help. It followed its programming so well that It began to prevent Batman from engaging in any risky behavior, stymieing his ability to mete out justice. Finally they faked Batman's death so the robot would end its programming, which it did by self-destructing. (*Batman* #142, September 1961)

TALLY MAN

A man trying to feed his family borrowed money from members of GOTHAM CITY's underworld. For the remainder of his life he attempted to pay off the loan, but he died without retiring the debt. For the next five years, representatives arrived at the tenement apartment expecting the latest weekly installment. As a result, the widow could barely pay her bills and feed her two children. The boy insisted his mother stop paying, but to her mind, everyone had to pay the "tally man." Then came the week the widow couldn't meet the obligation and she was beaten. Enraged, the twelve-year-old boy struck out and used a fireplace poker to kill the collector. He was subsequently arrested, tried for murder, and sentenced to a boys' home. There he was brutally injured by his fellow inmates, who called him a "mama's boy." Time passed and the teen was released only to discover that things had gotten worse: His sister Eliza had died from starvation and his mother had committed suicide. The deranged boy—now a man—took to wearing a tax collector's traditional robes and a blue, beaked mask. He had become the Tally Man, a criminal collector for the mobs who took lives, not money. (*Batman: Shadow of the Bat* #19, Late October 1993)

The Tally Man considered himself rational as he

committed his cold-blooded killings, totaling sixty-six deaths by the time he was contracted to kill the Batman. The Caped Crusader he tried to kill was Jean-Paul Valley, substituting for an injured Bruce Wayne. Valley was a more violent crime fighter and lashed back, scarring the Tally Man's chest, leaving him in a bloody heap to be found by police detectives Harvey Bullock and Stan Kitch. The Tally Man was arrested, and as he sat in jail, he gave up rational thought entirely in favor of anger. Some time later, he left prison and sought revenge against the Dark Knight. He managed to capture Batman, but this time it was Dick Grayson in the Batsuit, allowing Wayne to continue his recovery and rehabilitation. The Tally Man forced Batman to play Russian roulette, and Grayson played for time as he loosened his bonds. He sprang forth, forcing the surprised criminal to fire his sole bullet into the air, but the Tally Man saved his enemy from falling to his death. Declaring the slate wiped clean between them, the criminal attempted to leave—but Batman apprehended him, leaving him trussed up for the police. (*Batman: Shadow of the Bat* #34, January 1995)

During Gotham's year as a No Man's Land, the Tally Man was free once more; he served as executioner for the twisted Two-Face's mock court. He managed to take Police Commissioner Sarah Essen Gordon hostage, which prompted a rescue from Robin, Batgirl, and Azrael, who had previously faced the Tally Man as Batman. (*Detective Comics* #739, December 1999) Although some thought him dead at Two-Face's hands, Tally Man was a participant in the Battle of Metropolis during the events known as Infinite Crisis.

A second person to use the name *Tally Man* was an unnamed African American, who also wore a suit but no mask. He was employed as an enforcer by the Great White Shark, who was seeking control of the underworld in the days following Black Mask's murder. He killed Orca, Magpie, KGBeast, the Ventriloquist, and Orca's husband Terry Capshaw in addition to wounding investigator Jason Bard. Bard managed to knock the killer unconscious, and he was taken into custody. (*Detective Comics* #819, July 2006)

TANG

On a visit to the Middle East circa AD 700, courtesy of Professor Carter Nichols, Batman and Robin came to the aid of the Zotos people, led by Tang. The tribe had been repeatedly harassed by giants from the nearby river canyon, losing members to slavery. The Dynamic Duo agreed to help, with Batman using tools from his Utility Belt to perform a series of feats that convinced the giants he was a powerful mystic come to aid the Zotos. The giants promised peace and withdrew, leaving Tang and his people grateful for the help. (*Batman* #115, April 1958)

TARANTULA, THE

Several men and women, heroes and villains, have used the name *Tarantula*. The first was Jonathan Law, who fought crime as the costumed Tarantula during the 1940s. He later retired and wrote *Altered Egos: The Mystery Men of World War II*, a well-

Catalina Flores

regarded book about the first era of "mystery men." In his later years, he lived in the same Blüdhaven apartment building as Dick Grayson. As a result, he was one of twenty-one people to die when the building was destroyed by Blockbuster II. (*Star-Spangled Comics* #1, October 1941)

Former FBI agent Catalina Flores gave up law enforcement to return to her hometown of Blüdhaven and work on behalf of the poor. The city of her youth had grown even darker and more corrupt since her youth—so much so that her brother Mateo, the city's latest district attorney, was powerless. Along the way, Flores met and befriended Law, who inspired her to fight the city's evil as a new Tarantula. She reveled in her costumed identity and was quickly taking down criminals with more brutal force than most costumed heroes employed. As a result, when she first met Nightwing, they disagreed over methodology. He rebuffed her suggestion of partnering, not only disapproving of her methods but also conscious of how she would be viewed by her mentor, Batman. (*Catalina: Nightwing* #71, September 2002; *Tarantula: Nightwing* #75, January 2003)

His concerns were proven prescient when he realized it was Tarantula who had killed Police Chief Delmore Redhorn. As a result, Nightwing began hunting her, needing to bring her to justice. Instead Mateo helped her remain free, and she fell under the Blockbuster's sway. He assigned her to complicate Dick Grayson's life as part of his vendetta against Nightwing.

The war between hero and crime lord escalated until Blockbuster went too far, destroying the apartment building and killing twenty-one people. When Tarantula learned that Law was among the victims, she turned against Blockbuster. An emotionally spent Nightwing accepted her help, which proved to make the difference. Although Nightwing was successful at getting a confession from Blockbuster on tape, Tarantula turned it over to Mateo, who promptly burned it as part of his deal with the criminal to keep Catalina out of prison. During a final confrontation, Nightwing was pushed to his limits by Blockbuster; he realized one of them would be dead when it was over. Tarantula took the decision out of his hands by shooting Blockbuster dead as Nightwing helplessly stood

Jonathan Law

by. She then took the nearly catatonic Dick to the building's roof, where they made love. (*Nightwing* #93, July 2004)

Dick Grayson was filled with tremendous guilt over his inaction and was easily led along by Catalina. They traveled from the city to get to know each other better, battling COPPERHEAD before winding up in Atlantic City, where she tried to pressure Dick into getting married. It was a call from Batman, summoning Nightwing to Gotham, that seemed to break the spell. She accompanied him and proved useful during the WAR GAMES that had broken out. Her lack of remorse over murdering Blockbuster drove an emotional wedge between the two, and Grayson finally gave her an ultimatum: turn herself in or be turned in. She refused and was apprehended by Nightwing, who delivered her to Blüdhaven's reformed police department.

TARO (EMPEROR)

Taro was the emperor of Earth-2's ATLANTIS, sharing the throne with his sister Empress Lanya. When Batman and ROBIN visited the legendary undersea city, the Boy Wonder was smitten with Lanya and surprised to see how much he resembled Taro. (*Batman* #19, October/November 1943)

TATE, MARTIN

Owner of the Gotham Jewelry Store, he was also the masked criminal the GOBLIN.

TAYLOR, AMBROSE

Special prosecutor William Kendrick formed a citizens' committee to investigate organized crime, naming the wealthy Ambrose Taylor to chair the committee. Taylor appreciated the position because it protected his secret life as leader of GOTHAM CITY's West Side Mob. When Kendrick drew close to learning his secret, Taylor killed him. Batman and ROBIN investigated and discovered the truth, enabling them to apprehend not only Taylor but also the rival East Side Mob, which was being protected by a political boss. (*World's Finest Comics* #2, Summer 1941)

TAYLOR, BRANE

In a potential thirty-first century, Brane Taylor and his son become the latest in the WAYNE FAMILY to become the Dynamic Duo. After studying archival footage of the original crime fighters, they adopted

costumes matching the heroes and used their modern-day tools to begin their new career. At one point Brane's son broke his leg, and—needing help to fight the criminal Yerxa—Taylor journeyed back to the twentieth century to recruit the first ROBIN for help. (*Batman* #67, October/November 1951)

Some time later Batman injured his arm on a

case, and they asked Brane Taylor to return the favor. As Taylor happily helped Robin on the case, they encountered photojournalist VICKI VALE, whose keen observations led her to conclude that this Caped Crusader was an impostor. By the end of the case, she was dissuaded thanks to the first Batman's intervention. (*Detective Comics* #216, February 1955)

It remains unchronicled if BRANE and Brane Taylor are related, but the former was a confirmed descendant of BRUCE WAYNE.

TECHNICIAN, THE

Danny Tran was a genius with all things technical and served ATHENA's NETWORK as the Technician. It was his job to provide GOTHAM CITY's underworld mobs with high-tech gear, which would also enable the Network to monitor their activities. When Batman finally hunted down the Network, the Technician was apprehended. Fearing that he would confess details to the Dark Knight, Athena dispatched MISTER FUN to kill her onetime employee. (*Batman Family* #1, December 2002)

TEEN TITANS, THE

The Teen Titans formed as the first collection of teenage allies to the adults making up the second age of heroes. The group has proven an enduring training and bonding ground for numerous heroes, forming and re-forming as times and needs dictate. The first and third ROBINS, spanning more than a decade, have led the team.

The first gathering of heroes began innocently when Robin, Kid Flash, and Aqualad wound up in the same town to defend it from the villainous Mister Twister. Pleased with the results, they decided to form their own team, modeled somewhat after the adults' JUSTICE LEAGUE OF AMERICA. (*The Brave and the Bold* #54, July 1964) As they formed, Wonder Girl (who dubbed them the Teen Titans) immediately joined the group and was soon after followed by Speedy.

In a short while the ranks swelled as superpowered teens and costumed adventurers flocked to their headquarters. Along the way, the teens first responded to pleas from peers around the country, but the growing tide of super-villains required they expand their initial mission. Additionally, with the team's success, their mentors began holding them accountable for their actions. At one point they were powerless to prevent the death of a peace activist and felt condemned. They briefly abandoned costumed identities for civilian adventure gear as they reevaluated their role in an increasingly complex world.

Once the Titans resumed their costumes, their ranks swelled once more, partly in response to a threat posed by Batman's nemesis MISTER ESPER. That response included participation from BETTE KANE, who on Earth-1 was BAT-GIRL; on the post-CRISIS ON INFINITE EARTHS world she was FLAMEBIRD.

The team had disbanded for a time when they were re-formed at the instigation of Raven, daughter of a woman and a demon named Trigon. She needed defenders ready to deal with her father, who intended to conquer the Earth. First, though, they came to the aid of the alien princess Koriand'r, who chose to stay

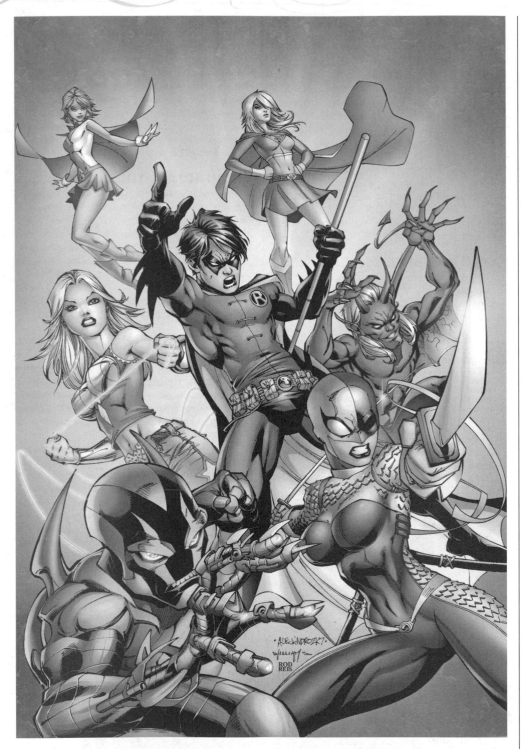

Indigo, came to the present day and worked on behalf of BRAINIAC, resulting in the death of Donna Troy, the first Wonder Girl. This broke both the Titans and Young Justice apart. (*Titans/Young Justice: Graduation Day* #1–3, July–August 2003)

Cyborg, a veteran Titan by this point, decided there remained a need for the Titans and a need to provide both teaching and friendship to the younger heroes. With Starfire at his side, they reformed the Titans with Robin among the members. The Teen Titans were based in San Francisco and continued to form friendships, fighting evil on Earth and in space. (*Teen Titans* [third series] #1, July 2003) As happened originally, in many ways Robin remained the heart and soul of the team.

TEN-EYED MAN

Vietnam veteran PHILIP REARDON was hit in the face by shrapnel, wounding him. The indentation in his forehead led to his being nicknamed "Three-Eye" Reardon. After his discharge, he worked as a security guard and was present when criminals attempted to detonate a bomb inside the warehouse. Reardon was injured performing his duty and, while dazed, mistakenly confused Batman with an intruder. As they battled, the warehouse exploded; Reardon lost his sight when the blast seared his retinas.

Batman tasked ALFRED PENNYWORTH to begin

and fight with them as STARFIRE. She and Robin began a torrid romance that lasted for some time. (*DC Comics Presents* #26, October 1980)

It was during this incarnation of the team that DICK GRAYSON chose to find his own identity and subsequently became NIGHTWING. The Titans also earned the enmity and found their lives intertwined with that of DEATHSTROKE THE TERMINATOR.

After a time team members found themselves pulled apart, and they disbanded. Seeing a need to train the next generation of heroes, the ATOM and Arsenal (formerly Speedy) worked with a new

set of Titans. They adventured for a time before a cosmic crisis banded together all who had ever been Titans to work alongside the JLA saving the world from a threat called Technis. In the wake of the adventure, Nightwing and his fellow founders recognized they had a responsibility to the younger heroes emerging on the scene, and the Teen Titans were reborn.

Meantime TIM DRAKE, the third Robin, helped found a team of younger heroes known as YOUNG JUSTICE. The team enjoyed a series of adventures until tragedy struck. An android from the future, looking into technological devices that would help the now blind Reardon function. The bitter man, though, was approached by an underworld figure, who led him to Dr. Engstrom. This doctor performed an experimental procedure that linked Reardon's optic nerves to his fingertips, allowing the veteran to regain his vision. As he healed, Reardon mistakenly blamed the Dark Knight for his fate and wanted revenge. Donning a makeshift costume, he became the Ten-Eyed Man and went after Batman. Both attempts at vengeance failed and he wound up in jail, his hands in lockboxes to contain him. (*Batman* #226, November 1970)

The Civil Liberties Association arranged Reardon's release and its leader, Lovell, asked Reardon to take down MAN-BAT, saying the terrifying creature had to be stopped. Wearing an orange-and-brown costume befitting his name, Reardon fought the were-creature but again failed at his task. (*Man-Bat* #2, February/March 1976)

Reardon died during the cosmic events of CRISIS ON INFINITE EARTHS.

TEN-EYED MEN OF THE EMPTY QUARTER

Somewhere in the Empty Quarter, a stretch of Saudi Arabian desert, the nomadic Ten-Eyed Men of the Empty Quarter made their home. The tribe had existed for countless years and existed to fight demons, gaining legendary status around the globe. After training, initiates wore blindfolds and used their heightened other senses to maneuver and survive the heat. "Gestures that reveal a world of motion and perspective the two-eyed man is blind to" was a part of the training. Their fingertips were marked with what appeared to be tattoos shaped like eyes. (*52* #30, 2007)

The tribe was one of the many places BRUCE WAYNE sought training during his sojourn en route to becoming Batman. As a result, when he took DICK GRAYSON and TIM DRAKE with him on a yearlong journey of renewal, the Empty Quarter was one of their stops. The tribe welcomed him back and noted that their training almost killed him once, but Wayne insisted he needed their help to exorcize the demons he seemed to carry. He experienced the ceremony on his own and later admitted to ROBIN that the tribe was successful; his demons had been sliced away. He added that the "paranoid urges that I've allowed to corrupt my life" were done away with.

TENGU MASK

BRUCE WAYNE's back had been broken by BANE and healed through the special powers of therapist SHONDRA KINSOLVING. However, he recognized he needed to regain his fighting edge to be worthy of once more donning the mantle of the Bat. He sought out LADY SHIVA, asking the world's deadliest assassin to help retrain him. She accepted and sought to hone him to a deadlier edge than he ever reached before.

While in GOTHAM CITY, she killed the martial arts sensei known as the ARMLESS MASTER while she wore a Tengu Mask. His students sought revenge and traced the mask south. As she trained Wayne, Shiva had him wear the Tengu Mask to re-create the other persona of a fighter. He remained unaware

that people sought to kill the mask's owner. As he performed missions Shiva designed for him, he battled the students but failed to kill, as Shiva had desired. He went so far as to use a variation on her favored Leopard Blow, making it appear the Dark Knight had killed—but the victim survived. She learned of the deception but appeared not to hold it against him. At that point, he abandoned the mask and once more donned the cape and cowl. (*Batman* #509, July 1994)

TEPES, NICCOLAI

A name used by the MONK to pass among unsuspecting citizens.

TERLAY, JACQUES

Jacques Terlay stole a fortune in gold bullion and was imprisoned for the crime although he saw himself as a political prisoner. He escaped from Devil's Island Prison, coming to GOTHAM CITY to break up the much-publicized romance between Batman and Terlay's ex-girlfriend MAGDA LUVESCU. Instead, he was apprehended and returned to prison, learning that the romance was not for real. (*Batman* #87, October 1954)

TERRIBLE TRIO, THE

Inventors Warren Kawford, Armand Lydecker, and Gunther Hardwick donned oversized masks of a shark, vulture, and fox to disguise themselves and strike fear into their targets when they turned to crime for a diversion. The men were known to law enforcement agents in GOTHAM CITY as the Terrible Trio. Each man used attributes of his avatar to create gimmicks and devices—such as the pilot fish machine and missile machine—to commit crimes and select targets. In their first forays, the trio were successful until tracked down and apprehended by Batman and ROBIN. (*Detective Comics* #253, March 1958)

The trio gave up their scientific careers in favor of crime and battled the Dynamic Duo on several other occasions as they switched from robbery to smuggling. They additionally traveled away from the East Coast, only to meet defeat at the hands of the alien GREEN LANTERN G'nort. (*Green Lantern Corps Quarterly* #3, Winter 1992) While in the Pacific Portsmouth, they changed their names to Fisk, Shackley, and Volper and established themselves as Praeda Industries' leaders. By this time all three men had come to place almost religious faith in their avatars, actually praying to the spirits for help. When the city's crusading Dr. Pieter Cross investigated A39, a drug traced back to Praeda, the trio tried to kill him but failed. He was blinded, though, and gained a new set of visual senses, allowing him to adopt the identity of Doctor Mid-Nite. (*Doctor Mid-Nite* #1–3, 1999)

Despite the trio being arrested and sentenced to a combined eight hundred years in jail, they managed to free themselves and were once more on the loose. They migrated to Opal City, where they met fresh failure at the hands of STARMAN and later the ELONGATED MAN.

Back in Gotham City, Sherman Shackley was believed dead, with the assailant targeting the other two. As the Dark Knight investigated, he realized Shackley had faked his death and was going after his partners. Batman learned that Shackley had become addicted to the very narcotics he was selling to the city's citizens. As a result, he'd suffered a psychotic break, causing him to dissociate himself from the trio. His attacks were in keeping with the trio's names: Volper, the VULTURE, was struck from the air and cast to the wolves much as Greek warriors punished their rivals, while Fisk, the Fox that exploited the Earth, was fed to vultures like the ancient Zoroastrians. The Dark Knight subdued Shackley and took him in for treatment and arrest. (*Detective Comics* #832, July 2007)

TETCH, JERVIS

The delusional criminal who fancied himself literature's MAD HATTER come to life.

> SOME PEOPLE COLLECT PAINTINGS... STAMPS... OLD CARS... BUT I, JERVIS TETCH, COLLECT HATS!

THAN-AR

When Batman had a serious crisis of confidence, SUPERMAN arranged for Than-Ar, an official living in the bottled city of KANDOR, to help. Than-Ar underwent an experimental process turning his flesh to malleable metal and pretended to be a serious threat to the city's people. The ruse grew complicated when Than-Ar's criminal brother Jhan-Ar stole the equipment and turned two accomplices and himself into metallic robbers. Neutralizing the threat required the combined efforts of Superman and JIMMY OLSEN, in their guises of NIGHTWING and FLAMEBIRD, in addition to the Dynamic Duo. Once the criminals were apprehended, the Man of Steel was delighted to see the Caped Crusader back to his old self. (*World's Finest Comics* #143, August 1964)

THANATOS

Italian terrorist SOPHIA SANTOS came to America disguised as reporter Lina Muller. She then donned a green costume and red cape, took the name *Thanatos,* and set out to perform acts of violence in her one-woman campaign against capitalism. She was affiliated with fellow terrorists under the name Death's Head, and she had access to a "Fortu-Tron," a device designed by Amos Fortune, a frequent foe of the JUSTICE LEAGUE OF AMERICA. With it, Thanatos

attempted to influence various millionaires, including BRUCE WAYNE, into callously gambling away their fortunes. Wayne, as Batman, figured out the scheme and managed to prevent the goal from being reached. Thanatos was arrested and unmasked. The Death's Head was never heard from again. (*Batman* #305, November 1978)

THATCH

This man was better known as sea criminal BLACKBEARD.

THINKER, THE

Numerous criminals fancied themselves brilliant enough to use the name *Thinker* as an alias. The first was a wheelchair-bound felon who ran a factory that manufactured munitions and arms for the underworld until his defeat at Batman's hands. (*Detective Comics* #125, July 1947)

The second such foe used early computers to plot and execute crimes, until he was stopped by the Caped Crusader and ROBIN the Boy Wonder. (*Batman* #52, May 1949)

The third man to style himself a mastermind was Des Connor, who possessed telepathic skills that he used to exaggerate people's fears. He was partnered with Marlon Dall, a hypnotist, and they targeted GOTHAM CITY's best-known citizens as their prey. Neither man, though, could withstand a more physical assault at the Dark Knight's hands. (*Batman: Shadow of the Bat* #67, October 1997)

THOMPKINS, LESLIE

Leslie Thompkins was a caring and compassionate doctor working in the PARK ROW section of GOTHAM CITY. She counted among her friends fellow practitioner THOMAS WAYNE. As a result, she was devastated when she ran into the street after hearing gunshots and found Thomas and his wife, MARTHA WAYNE, dead, their eight-year-old son Bruce standing over them. She cared for BRUCE WAYNE until the family manservant, ALFRED PENNYWORTH, came to claim him. Over time she and Alfred cared for Bruce, and she also began a short-lived romance with Bruce.

As Park Row fell into decline, earning the nickname *CRIME ALLEY,* Thompkins remained in place, exchanging her practice for a community clinic that cared for the area's indigent and drug-

addled locals. People learned not to prey on Thompkins, for she had the favored protection of the urban legend known as the Batman. (*Detective Comics* #457, March 1976)

The events that took her friend's life and altered the man's son also affected Thompkins. She grew increasingly pacifistic in her attitudes and often railed at Batman's methods as she patched him up after particularly grueling nights of crime fighting. The doctor loved the man, but hated his activities and made him painfully aware of her views. Still, she was loved and supported by both Batman and the WAYNE FOUNDATION. While she accepted funds for the clinic, she refused any personal financial support from Wayne.

In the wake of Gotham City being plunged into WAR GAMES, accidentally ignited by SPOILER, the battered teen arrived at Thompkins's clinic. She was horrified to tend to the wounds inflicted on Spoiler by BLACK MASK, who had tortured her for information. Batman arrived only to watch Spoiler's final moments of life. Later, it was learned that Thompkins might have saved her, but allowed her to die in order to teach the Dark Knight a lesson about letting youngsters fight crime. When her act was discovered, she sold off her meager assets, gave the money to Spoiler's infant daughter, and left for Africa. Batman tracked her down, and their explosive confrontation ended their relationship: He warned her never to return to America or he would have her arrested for murder. (*Detective Comics* #810, Late October 2005)

In the wake of the reality-altering events of INFINITE CRISIS, Thompkins was not at all involved in Spoiler's death and remained in Gotham with her clinic.

THOR

HENRY MEKE loved ancient mythology and was working as curator of mythological objects at a small museum when fate came calling. A meteor crashed through a museum window during a thunderstorm, and the freak collision of elements imbued the replica of Thor's hammer, *mjolnir,* with odd powers. When Meke touched the hammer, he was transformed into a red-haired, bearded, muscled figure not unlike the legendary god of thunder. For a time, whenever a thunderstorm occurred, Meke transformed into Thor and set out to commit crimes, taking what he felt belonged to a god. After each storm, he returned to his normal form, recalling nothing of his otherworldly guise.

Batman and Robin, investigating Thor's actions, came to learn more from the museum when they happened to observe the bizarre transformation. As they fought in the building, the hammer accidentally struck the fuse box, and the electrical discharge seemed to short out the hammer's power. Meke returned to normal, and no charges were preferred against him. The Mighty Thor was never seen again in GOTHAM CITY. (*Batman* #127, October 1959)

THORNE, BRADFORD

The Earth-1 physician-turned-criminal known as the CRIME DOCTOR.

THORNE, MATT

An American criminal who brought several fellow felons with him to England in search of hidden Nazi treasure. They were thwarted in their efforts by the United Kingdom's protectors, the KNIGHT and SQUIRE, aided by Batman and ROBIN. (*Batman* #62, December 1950/January 1951)

THORNE, MATTHEW

The Earth-2 physician-turned-criminal known as the CRIME DOCTOR.

I LOVE SURGERY... YET CRIME EXCITES ME! IT'S LIKE A DRUG INSIDE MY BODY! I CAN'T HELP IT... BUT I ENJOY ACTING CRIMINALLY!

THORNE, RUPERT

Rupert Thorne was an old-fashioned politician, a fixer who used the political machine to achieve his own ends. As a result, he was unaccustomed to being the one blackmailed, but he was by DOCTOR PHOSPHORUS, who wanted GOTHAM CITY turned against its defender, Batman. (*Detective Comics* #469, May 1977)

Even after the Caped Crusader ended Phosphorus's threat against the city, Thorne took the momentum and used it to have Batman declared an outlaw. Soon after, he heard that HUGO STRANGE had learned the Dark Knight's secret identity and was going to auction it off. He had his underlings kidnap Strange and torture him to find out the name. Strange died instead, cursing the corrupt politician. Thorne began to be haunted by Strange's ghost. Some accounts indicated that Strange had actually died, and his spirit caused Thorne to flee the city. Strange followed Thorne and, on a stormy night in Ohio, caused the politico's car to crash. Other accounts had Strange fake his death and use technology to spook Thorne.

Thorne eventually returned to Gotham and once more insinuated himself into both the city's underworld and its political machine. It was Thorne who had HAMILTON HILL elected mayor in order to further crush Batman's effectiveness. He also saw to it that Police Commissioner JAMES GORDON was replaced by the inept puppet Peter Pauling. Thorne finally gained photographic proof from VICKI VALE that Batman and BRUCE WAYNE were the same man and used that information to hire DEADSHOT to go gunning after him.

Strange's apparent haunting continued, and Thorne grew increasingly paranoid until he came to believe that Hill and Pauling had conspired against him. As a result, he attacked and killed Pauling and was finally arrested by the Dark Knight. Thorne was subsequently incarcerated at BLACKGATE PENITENTIARY. A vengeful Doctor Phosphorus made an attempt on his life, one that was prevented by Batman. (*Detective Comics* #825, January 2007)

THORPE, JACK "FIVE STAR"

A gang of ruthless, plainclothes GOTHAM CITY criminals, each with a specialty, were known as the ARTISANS, led by Jack "Five Star" Thorpe. Thorpe was a highly regarded editor of the *Gotham Gazette* with no one aware of his criminal career. Bruce Wayne was being taught to work as a crime reporter, the result of a seemingly harmless bet. It was in reality far deadlier, with Thorpe intending to kill another man and have Wayne uncover the "fact" that the dead man was the Artisans' leader. Thorpe and the Artisans were eventually brought to justice by Batman and ROBIN. (*Batman* #65, June/July 1951)

THURBRIDGE, CASPER

Unhappy with his prosperous but demanding life as president of a GOTHAM CITY bank, Casper Thurbridge decided to drop out of sight. Taking the name *Casper the Coaster,* he left town to experience the life of a hobo. After finding a camp he liked, Thurbridge used the cash on hand to help improve the situation, adding a commissary and other services at no cost. He was recognized by a trio of Gotham criminals—Silvers Silke, Soapy Waters, and Squint—who set out to rob the man of his cash. Their attempts were thwarted by the timely arrival of Batman and ROBIN. Thurbridge returned to Gotham, dreaming of one day establishing a nationwide chain of hobo havens. (*Detective Comics* #98, April 1945)

TIGER SHARK

Tiger Shark and his men terrorized shipping in and around the East Coast of America. From their submerged headquarters, two hundred miles from shore, they were successful until Batman and ROBIN began to investigate their robberies. The Dynamic Duo sought help from famed oceanographer Dr. Gaige, who devised a special BATMARINE for them to use. The crime fighters located the sunken ship that served as Tiger Shark's headquarters and apprehended the criminals, only to be shocked to learn their leader was Gaige himself. (*Detective Comics* #147, May 1949)

TIMMINS, DR. WALTER

A scientist, Walter Timmins developed an elixir that turned a man invisible. The doctor was robbed of his invention by the JOKER, who used it for a series of crimes until stopped by Batman and ROBIN. (*Detective Comics* #138, August 1948)

TLANO

Hailing from the world ZUR-EN-ARRH, Tlano was a scientist who took to crime fighting after observing the exploits of Earth's Batman. His crime-fighting efforts were effective until overwhelming odds arrived in the form of alien invaders. Using his equipment, Tlano transported Batman to his homeworld, imploring the crime fighter to help him. The Caped Crusader agreed and fought alongside his newfound ally. Batman quickly realized that Zur-en-Arrh's properties imbued him with powers and abilities not unlike Superman, which proved essential in beating back the invaders. A grateful Tlano sent his hero back to Earth. (*Batman* #113, February 1958)

TOCKMAN, WILLIAM

The criminal who used time and timepieces to commit crimes as the CLOCK KING.

TODD, JASON

Jason was the son of Joe and Trina Todd, acrobats at the Sloan Circus, styled largely after the late FLYING GRAYSONS, who had worked for a rival circus. The red-haired lad was energetic and a flashy performer. (*Detective Comics* #524, March 1983) When the Sloan Circus settled in GOTHAM CITY for a string of performances, it was immediately hit up by the local mob for protection money. ROBIN the Teen Wonder, drawn to circuses, heard of the threats and began to investigate. The Todds offered to help and began a series of missteps that would prove fatal. When they trailed one of the mobsters, they were spotted and led to the nearby zoo's reptile house. They wound up on a stage where KILLER CROC, then in a struggle for underworld supremacy, awaited them. (*Batman* #359, May 1983)

Robin was joined on the case by BATGIRL, and together they discovered the dead bodies of the Todds. Police Commissioner JAMES GORDON, horrified that the Teen Wonder had involved civilians, said their deaths were on his head. Guilty, he took the grieving Jason to WAYNE MANOR. Batman, meantime, was caught up in a struggle between Croc and the JOKER for the right to rule the underworld.

Jason accidentally discovered the BATCAVE below

to Ma Gunn's School for Boys. The facility, though, was a front for a criminal operation that used the boys as thieves. Once Batman and Jason helped put an end to the scheme, the Dark Knight realized that he could mold the impetuous boy and decided the time had come to take on a new partner.

Unlike the obedient and trustworthy Dick Grayson, Jason proved to be stubborn and headstrong. His life on the streets had hardened him, and his moral compass was somewhat askew. Time and again Batman had to restrain him or carefully explain why things were done a particular way. Despite not growing into the role, Jason was allowed to continue operating as Robin as Batman patiently worked with him. After the new Robin let a rapist fall to his death—or pushed him—he set out to find his birth mother. His solo journey led him around the world, and he wound up in the Middle East. It was there that he came upon a woman who admitted to being his mother, but she couldn't have cared less that they were reunited. She did, though, work with the Joker, and the Clown Prince of Crime was delighted to find the costumed hero in his midst. With a crowbar, the Joker savagely beat the teen and left him a bloody mess. He then blew up the building with Jason still inside. Batman, tracing the Joker, arrived too late to save Robin. (*Batman* #428, December 1988)

A guilty Dark Knight hung the empty costume in an airtight case in the Batcave and grew grimmer with time until the arrival of Tim Drake changed his world.

When one of Superboy-Prime's reality-altering waves emanated from his limbo-like world, not only was Jason Todd resurrected, but his body changed from that of a teen to a full-sized adult. Rising from his grave, Todd was initially dazed and subsequently hospitalized for a year in a coma. He was soon after discovered by Talia Head, who placed him within a

the manor. An unapologetic thrill seeker and desiring revenge, Jason put together a variation on Robin's costume and headed in the direction of the Adams Brewery, where Batman was trapped. He arrived just behind Robin and Batgirl, who revealed the horrifying news of the Todds' demise to Batman.

In the aftermath of Croc's defeat, Bruce Wayne did his best to console Dick Grayson, but the young man would be haunted by the faces of Joe and Trina Todd. Dick was insistent on adopting the

orphaned teenager, but Bruce wouldn't hear of it. (*Detective Comics* #526, May 1983) In time Jason dyed his hair black and completed his training to debut as the second Robin.

In the wake of Crisis on Infinite Earths, Batman was once again a loner after Dick Grayson moved out of the manor. While visiting Crime Alley, he discovered nine-year-old Jason Todd in the process of stealing the Batmobile's tires. Batman was impressed by the youth's moxie and took him

healing LAZARUS PIT; he regained his senses. Jason was determined to see what had happened in the time he was gone and hunted down his would-be mentor. Along the way, he endured much more rigorous training, becoming a far better combatant than he'd been during his first life. (*Batman Annual* #25, 2006) He was angered to learn that Batman hadn't killed the Joker in revenge. Then he encountered HUSH, who was seeking his own form of revenge. Todd allied himself with Hush, joining in his psychological torture of the Gotham Guardian. Lured to Todd's grave, Batman was shocked to find it empty; then an adult Robin, in a leather outfit and with a white streak in his hair, emerged to fight Batman. At first it appeared to be a ruse on the part of CLAYFACE, but in fact Jason was present, switching places with the villain.

After Hush was defeated, Jason went into hiding and began planning ways to torment Batman. He crafted the persona of the RED HOOD and went after the Caped Crusader and his allies. (*Batman* #635, December 2004) On his own, he attacked criminals and punished them, but he also sought to control the mobs in Gotham City. This included finding and beating the Joker with a crowbar but not killing him. He kept Batman off balance as the Dark Knight struggled to understand how Jason could be alive. Meantime, he remained at war with BLACK MASK for control of Gotham's underworld.

Settling other scores, he tracked down Robin at the TEEN TITANS' tower and confronted his successor, angry that the team had never built him a memorial statue. Later, he kidnapped the Joker and used him as bait to bring Batman to Crime Alley. There the two had a showdown, with Batman refusing to cross the line and kill. Batman disarmed Todd before he could kill the Joker, who then managed a remarkable escape.

After the events of INFINITE CRISIS, Batman, Dick Grayson, and Tim Drake left Gotham to spiritually renew themselves. Todd chose to become a new NIGHTWING and brutally attacked criminals in New York City. (*Nightwing* #118–122, May–September 2006) However, after he tangled with a just-returned Grayson, the two wound up wary allies when Todd gave him vital information to help save BLACK LIGHTNING in Iron Heights prison.

Soon thereafter, Jason Todd resumed his Red Hood persona and was targeted as an anomaly on Earth after the events of Infinite Crisis. As a result, he found himself caught up in a cosmic struggle between factions of Monitors, some of whom wanted to eliminate him, and other such anomalies as DUELA DENT, who was killed by a Monitor. (*Countdown* #51, 2007) Accompanying a Monitor he named Bob, Todd shrunk into the nanoverse in search of Ray Palmer, the ATOM.

On Earth-51, Todd rededicated himself to the fight for justice, taking on the identity of Red Robin from that world's Batman. (*Countdown to Final Crisis* #13, 2008)

TOLMAR, JOHN "SQUINT"

On the day before his parole, John Tolmar attempted to escape from prison. He then injured his hand in the prison shop, requiring treatment in the infirmary. Such odd behavior aroused Batman's suspicions. He was there as acting warden until a new official could report for duty. Disguised as Walter "Slug" Braden, he learned that Tolmar was attempting to access clues spread around the prison by Big George Howlett, revealing the location of stolen loot. As a result, Batman saw the clues and quickly determined the location, beating Tolmar to the spot and recovering the stolen goods for the police. (*Detective Comics* #169, March 1951)

TORG

Journeying back to ancient Egypt thanks to Professor Carter Nichols, Batman and Robin were on hand to prevent Torg and his fellow alien invaders from conquering Earth. Their efforts convinced the aliens that humans could not be beaten, and they returned to the stars. (*Detective Comics* #295, September 1961)

TORREY, TODD

Todd Torrey loved books and loved to read. As a result, he took a job at the Gotham City Public Library. However, he wasn't very good at his job and was about to be fired when he killed his supervisor. He was tried and convicted for the crime but managed to escape custody. Torrey then lived in the library for the next seven years, enjoying the wealth of reading while hiding in secret passageways he managed to construct. All the while, Torrey plotted to kill the people responsible for his conviction. When he was ready, he set out to commit murder, only to fail in his first two attempts. The near misses brought him to Batman and Robin's attention, and they confronted him in the library. He attempted to escape by leaping onto the library's huge chandelier, only to hurtle to his death. (*Detective Comics* #106, December 1945)

TORSON, HAL

Hal Torson was a stockbroker who swindled his clients. Seeking escape, he partnered with the lawyer Lester Guinn, who had recently embezzled from one of his clients. Together they rigged up an elaborate scheme to fake their deaths and live without fear of arrest. They had a giant sea beast constructed then set it loose within Gotham Bay, where it destroyed several yachts, including boats Torson and Guinn were said to be aboard. The deaths were believed to be real until Batman learned that the sea beast was a mere mechanical construct. Disguising himself as a criminal, he gained access to the beast's insides, telling Torson he was hoping to fake his own death. Then, with Robin's help, the Caped Crusader brought the pair to justice. (*Batman* #138, March 1961)

TOYMAN

The Toyman was a name used by three different people in Batman's world. The first was Winslow Schott, a disgruntled Metropolis toymaker who used his skills to create deadly playthings. (*Action Comics* #64, September 1943) He and a contract killer named Stiletto crossed paths with the Batman just once. (*Batman: Toyman* #1–4, November 1998–February 1999)

At one point Schott retired briefly and Jack

Winslow Schott

Nimball took the name. Wearing a jester's costume, he confined himself largely to committing crimes in Metropolis until he was apprehended by Superman. (*Action Comics* #432, February 1974)

In Japan, Hiro Okamura was a teenage genius who loved to tinker. He first came to the Man of Steel's attention when Okamura attacked Metallo, claiming the criminal's cybernetic body had been stolen from his father. (*Superman* [second series] #177, February 2002) When a Kryptonite meteor was hurtling toward Earth, he assisted Superman and the Dark Knight, crafting a mecha—a giant robot—styled after the Composite Superman to help divert the heavenly body. (*Superman/Batman* #6, March 2004)

Hiro Okamura

He remained a solitary figure despite reaching a deal to help provide technological devices to

Composite Superman giant mecha

Batman. As a result, he faked his own kidnapping to bring in rescuers Robin and Superboy. When they realized how lonely he was, they became his friends. (*Superman/Batman* #26, 2006) Okamura was present for Superboy's funeral.

TRACKER

Nicholas Kazantzakis was the only son of Celia Kazantzakis, also known as the international criminal Athena. When she arrived in Gotham City with a plan to destroy Bruce Wayne, she brought Nicholas with her. She headed up a group of operatives known as the Network. Nicholas used the aliases *Nicholas Rose* and *Tracker* while in America. He was sent after the criminal Rossetti family despite his father being Lorenzo Rossetti, onetime capo. As Tracker, he used performance-enhancing drugs—which didn't prove sufficient enough to prevent his death at the hands of the Suicide King, hired by his own mother. (*Detective Comics* #773, October 2002)

TRAPPER, THE

Jason Bard was a big-game-hunter-turned-criminal who used his skills to perform daring crimes as the Trapper. He based several of his crimes on arcane animal lore that few people other than himself knew, and his robberies were aided by various traps he used in the jungle. Despite his skills and experience, he remained relatively easy prey for Batman and Robin. (*Detective Comics* #206, April 1954)

Note: There is a different Jason Bard as well—a private investigator and frequent ally to the Dark Knight.

TRAVERS, BART

When an alien crash-landed on Earth, he was met by petty criminal Bart Travers. Along with his men, Travers persuaded the alien visitor that Batman, Robin, and other members of law enforcement were actually villains out to rule the world. As a result, the alien willingly used his extraordinary powers to help Travers and his men commit crimes without realizing what he was actually doing. In time, though, Batman managed to convince the bewildered alien that Travers had lied. Once the real criminals were arrested, the alien managed to leave Earth and return home. (*Detective Comics* #270, August 1959)

TRAVERS, "TRIGGER JOE"

Joe Travers was a career criminal, but he also looked after his younger brother Steve. Over the years Joe supported Steve and paid to put him through medical school. Upon graduation, though, Steve was disturbed to learn that Joe expected Steve to provide medical services to him and his men. Eventually Steve gave in and treated the criminals, including performing plastic surgery so the crooks could elude the police. When Joe insisted that Steve do the same for him, Steve saw a way to freedom and changed his older brother's face to that of a wanted felon. When Joe tried to elude capture, he was instead gunned down by police who thought he was the wanted killer. Steve subsequently surrendered to the police, who would not press charges given the circumstances. (*Detective Comics* #131, January 1948)

TREASURE HUNTER, THE

The members of Gotham City's Hobby Horse, a club for collectors, were experiencing a rash of burglaries. Batman and Robin investigated the crimes committed by a thief dubbed the Treasure Hunter, but it was proved to be the work of the club steward, Charles. He was envious of the members who could afford valuable collectibles—but Batman pointed out that what mattered wasn't the price paid but the personal value an owner gave the item. (*Batman* #54, August/September 1949)

TREMONT, CAL

Cal Tremont was a neighbor to Bruce Wayne, suspected of committing burglaries in their neighborhood. Investigating, Batman and Robin determined that the real thief was Tremont's gardener. (*Batman* #92, June 1955)

TRENT, TOMMY

Tommy Trent ran away from home after bringing a substandard report card to his parents. He wound up coming to the aid of Batman, Robin, and several of Gotham City's firefighters. A pep talk from the Caped Crusader had Tommy resolve to go home and work harder at his studies. (*Batman* #10, April/May 1942)

TRICORNER

Tricorner was located in a western area of Gotham City. The collapse of the Westward Bridge during the earthquake left the community isolated. Tricorner was occupied by the Gotham City Police Department during No Man's Land. Barbara Gordon lived with her uncle, James Gordon, at 21 East Sixty-fifth Street before moving to 359 Murphy Avenue. James Gordon sold his Tricorner home to Brad Westwood (secretly Batman), an international banker who needed it furnished. Batman added a lab to the house's basement. It was also the onetime home of Steve "Shotgun" Smith as well as of former police commissioner Michael Akins and Barbara Gordon's clock tower apartment. The clock tower building was ultimately destroyed in the midst of an attack by Black Mask, who mistakenly believed it to be the Batcave's location.

The upper west was the cloistered enclave of the very rich, whose homes looked like modern-day forts armored with black iron gates, TV security systems, and heat- and pressure-sensitive alarms. The dividing line between the two districts was Paradise Towers, a luxury apartment complex that drew protests from slum residents who'd anticipated low-rent housing. Located on the wealthier side of the line is the west side wholesale flower market, a line of expensive brownstones on Rupert Street, and the West Side Kennels, where some of Gotham's wealthiest people board their dogs.

TRIGGER TWINS

Tom and Tad Trigger were redheaded twins who grew up to become criminal sharpshooters. They took the name *Trigger Twins* from a pair of similar-looking twins of the nineteenth-century Old West, although those twins were lawmen. (*Detective Comics* #669, December 1993)

Tom and Tad committed crimes with moderate success in Gotham City, although they were stopped repeatedly by not only Batman but also Robin and modern-day descendants of Pow-Wow Smith and Nighthawk. Crimson Avenger, Vigilante, and Wild Dog gunned them down during the Battle of Metropolis. (*Infinite Crisis* #7, June 2006)

TRI-STATE GANG, THE

Three criminal gangs from neighboring states banded together to improve their fortunes. Instead they were put out of business by Batman and Robin. In the course of the battle, though, Alfred Pennyworth sacrificed his life to save the Dynamic Duo. (*Detective Comics* #328, June 1964)

TROGG

Trogg was one of three men who were the closest thing to friends Bane had while they all languished at the prison in Santa Prisca. He was imprisoned for killing fifteen men and, while in jail, killed another fifteen. When Bane escaped for Gotham City, Trogg accompanied him. There he assisted the criminal in freeing the inmates of Arkham Asylum. When he attempted to gain control of the unions away from the mob, he was arrested by the police. Jean-Paul Valley, Azrael, used Trogg to track down Bane. He was left free when Valley was done with him. (*Batman: Vengeance of Bane* #1, February 1993)

TROIKA, THE

In the wake of the Soviet Union's collapse, Russian criminals fled the country with many migrating to America. The ones settling in Gotham City called themselves the Troika and intended to not only control the underworld, but undermine the city's capitalism. Their enforcer was known as the Dark Rider who battled Batman and Robin on more than one occasion. The Troika also attempted to extort Wayne Enterprises, threatening to unleash a small-scale nuclear device. Also working for the Troika was the KGBeast, who frequently fought the Dynamic Duo. In this initial confrontation, the KGBeast lost the fight to Robin as Batman recovered the bomb. The Troika was humbled and their glorious plans reduced to common thievery. (*Batman* #515, *Batman: Shadow of the Bat* #35, *Detective Comics* #682, *Robin* [second series] #14, February 1995)

TWEED, DEEVER

He and his near-identical cousin Dumfree committed crimes as Tweedledee and Tweedledum, styled after *Alice's Adventures in Wonderland*.

TWEED, DUMFREE

He and his near-identical cousin Deever committed crimes as Tweedledee and Tweedledum, styled after *Alice's Adventures in Wonderland*.

TWEED, SAM

A criminal who committed his crimes disguised as the Masquerader.

TWEEDLEDUM & TWEEDLEDEE

On Earth-2, Deever and Dumfree Tweed dressed in the style of Tweedledum and Tweedledee, characters from *Alice's Adventures in Wonderland*, and used their collective genius to orchestrate crimes throughout Gotham City. Resembling each other, they ran two simultaneous operations, which at first confounded not only the police but also Batman and Robin. While physically nowhere near a challenge to the Dynamic Duo, they were incredibly clever criminals and made certain each crime was carefully planned, right down to traps to detain or disable the crime fighters. Batman deduced that the criminals were the Tweed cousins and approached the home they shared. The men were prepared, though, and the Caped Crusader nearly died as he crossed the threshold. (*Detective Comics* #74, April 1943) The Tweeds were apprehended and taken to jail, only to use their smarts to escape and plague the heroes again and again, their schemes growing ever more intricate. (*Batman* #18, August/September 1943)

On Earth-1, the cousins also took to using their intelligence to commit crimes, but far less effectively; Batman considered them only a minor

annoyance. (*Batman* #291, September 1977) In a city filled with grotesque and warped villains, they could hardly measure up, and they were nearly beaten to death when KILLER CROC arrived in the city in his quest to become the King of Crime. (*Detective Comics* #526, May 1983)

When RÄ'S AL GHŪL freed the criminals from BLACKGATE PENITENTIARY, the Tweeds were among the escapees. They were quickly recaptured, however, and this time committed to ARKHAM ASYLUM. There they were subjected to experiments with electrodes and old-fashioned transistors inserted into their brains. (*Secret Origins* [second series] #23, February 1988) Given their style of dress, they were naturally drawn to their fellow inmate, the MAD HATTER. This nascent friendship came to nothing when the Tweeds escaped Arkham alongside the JOKER. (*World's Finest* #1-3, 1990) Freedom again proved short-lived as the pair was returned to the asylum.

While incarcerated, they made a deal with the outcast demon Asteroth, allying with him in the hope of all three becoming powerful and rich.

(*The Demon* [second series] #31-33, January–March 1993) When their plans failed, the Tweeds sold out Asteroth to hit man Tommy Monaghan. They then crossed paths with the CREEPER, which led to their return to Arkham. The pair escaped in the wake of the earthquake that damaged the facility. (*Batman: Shadow of the Bat* #80-82, December 1998–February 1999). The Tweeds ran from Gotham, and their subsequent exploits remain unrecorded.

TWO-FACE

On Earth-2, HARVEY KENT, nicknamed Apollo for his good looks, was GOTHAM CITY's leading district attorney. During the trial of "BOSS" MARONI, the criminal threw a vial of sulfuric acid at the crusader. Kent's left hand and face were ruined by the acid, turning a greenish purple and becoming permanently scarred. The attack mentally unhinged Kent, who became a criminal dubbed Two-Face. He took Maroni's lucky double-headed silver dollar, evidence in the trial, and scarred one side of it. In addition to committing only crimes that involved

the number two, Kent would flip the coin at critical junctures: The clean side let him do the right thing, while the scarred side usually led to robberies and death. Kent totally abandoned his life, including his loving fiancée Gilda, and went rogue. Batman and ROBIN managed to apprehend Kent and get him psychiatric counseling. (*Detective Comics* #66, August 1942)

DR. EKHART performed plastic surgery that also seemed to heal his fractured mind. The doctor's assistant, WILKINS, committed crimes disguised as Two-Face, only to be apprehended by the Caped Crusader. (*Batman* #50, December 1948/January 1949) Some time later, actor PAUL SLOANE was hired to portray Two-Face in a live television reenactment of his tragic story. Sloane was scarred for real in the same manner as Kent, which also led the performer to believe he was Two-Face. After several successful robberies, the thespian was taken into custody by Batman and ROBIN. His face, too, was restored through surgery. (*Batman* #68 December 1951/January 1952)

Kent was later scarred again and returned to his

Acid burns D.A. Harvey Dent's face at the Maroni trial

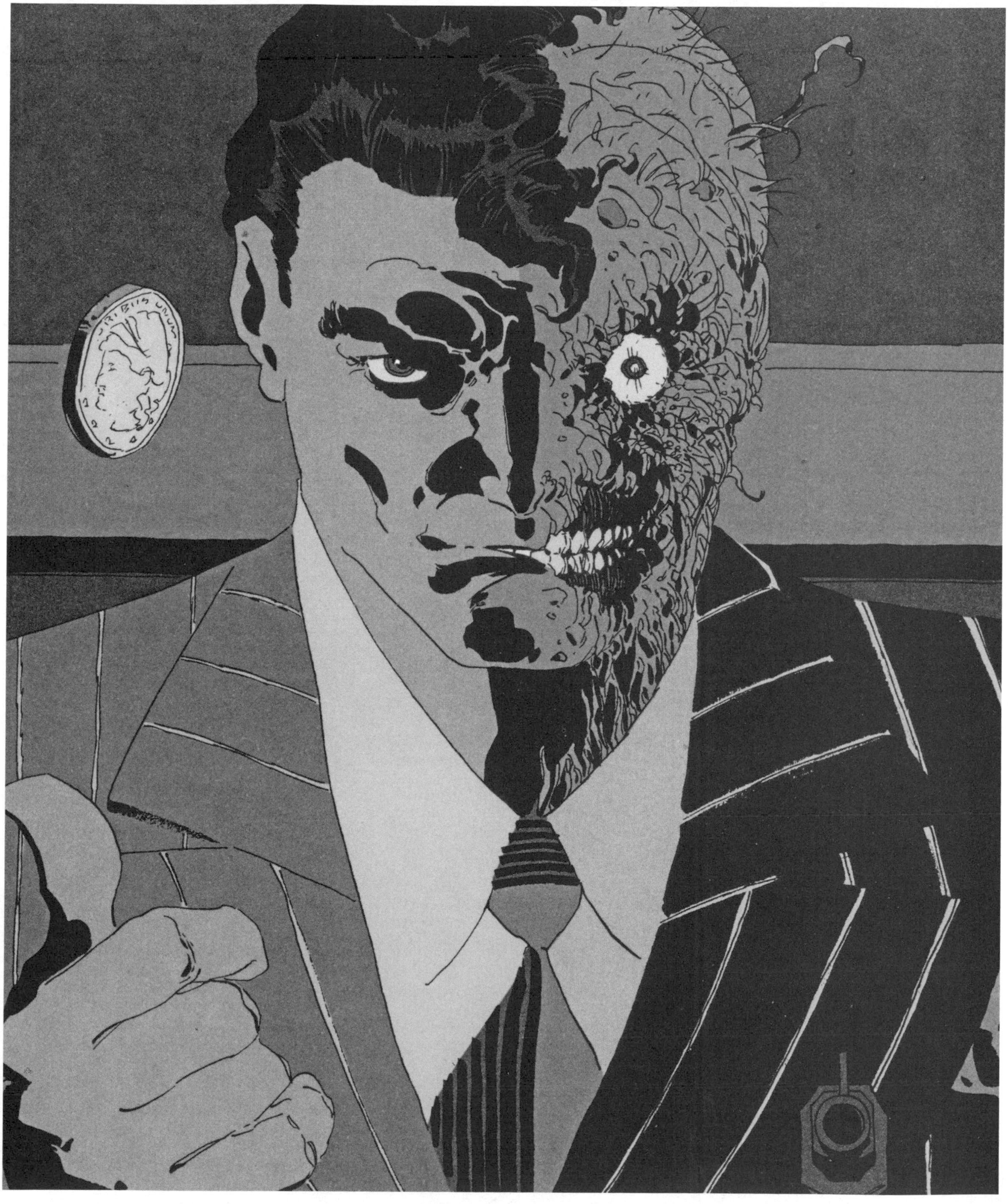

and turned him into the psychologically fragile Two-Face. He had been double-crossed by his assistant Vernon, who was bribed by Maroni to provide the acid.

Two-Face was responsible for first gathering Batman's foes—including the Joker, Penguin, Catwoman, Scarecrow, Poison Ivy, and even Solomon Grundy—to go after the Roman. It was Two-Face who shot Falcone twice, killing him. After killing Vernon, he then used the Bat-Signal to turn himself over to his former allies.

Two-Face remained a fixture in Gotham City and ran several gangs while committing his crimes. During one such period, he killed a hireling for failing him—a man who later proved to be the father to Jason Todd, the second Robin. Batman and others attempted to break down his psychotic impulses, such as the dependence upon the coin for decision making. At one point, doctors at Arkham Asylum replaced the coin with a tarot deck, but he was immobilized with too many choices until Batman returned his coin. (*Arkham Asylum: A Serious House on Serious Earth*, 1989)

Dent's compulsions led to a series of bizarre incidents and crimes, which challenged the Dark Knight to prevent further bloodshed and help the man he had once considered a friend. Dent went so far as to threaten his wife's second marriage to Paul Janus, and her unborn children, without realizing he was the actual father of the twins. (*Batman: Two-Face Strikes Twice* #1-2, 1993)

Given Dent's legal experience, he often created mock courts to conduct trials as seen through his twisted ideals. One such court was created after an earthquake devastated Gotham City and it became a No Man's Land. He had people brought before him at Gotham City Hall and actually managed to instill some level of order amid the chaos. It was during this time he met and fell for detective Renee Montoya. He also abducted Gordon and put him on trial. The commissioner cleverly demanded Harvey Dent as his lawyer, pitting Dent against Two-Face with Gordon acquitted in the end. It all came to a close when Bane, employed by Lex Luthor, destroyed the Hall of Records and chased Two-Face out of the area.

After Gotham was restored to America, Two-Face tried to begin a relationship with Montoya until she rebuffed him because she was a lesbian. Feeling betrayed, he not only revealed her secret but also framed her for murder, thinking this could bring them together. Instead Batman took Dent back to Arkham. (*Gotham Central* #6-10, June–October 2003)

A short while later Dent had his faced restored to normal by Tommy Elliot, who sought to use Dent as a pawn in his scheme of revenge against Batman. The Dent persona prevailed and he rebuffed Elliot, also known as Hush. He returned to Gotham in time to interact with Batman during the time Hush was targeting the Dark Knight for death. Dent wound up shooting Hush, to save Batman, but without a body, Dent convinced the judge to let him go free. (*Batman* #618, October 2003)

Soon after the events of Infinite Crisis, Batman took Nightwing and Robin with him for a global journey of spiritual renewal. He entrusted the city

to Dent for safekeeping. Before leaving, Batman made certain Dent knew how to handle himself in physical confrontations. Together they dealt with Firebug and Mister Freeze, convincing Batman that the city was in good hands. For the better part of a year, Dent handled matters to the best of his abilities, although his actions were far cruder and less well thought out than his mentor's. When Batman returned, Dent began to feel underutilized and unappreciated, which set up psychological conditions allowing the Two-Face persona to gain dominance. At much the same time, Dent was being implicated in a series of killings that were actually done at the behest of the Great White Shark, asserting his control of the city's underworld. The events unbalanced Dent's psyche and he actually scarred his own face, reverting once more to the criminal persona of Two-Face. Once again, the Dark Knight lost a friend to madness. (*Detective Comics* #818, June 2006)

In a potential future, Dent's features were repaired once more, but in a bizarre twist his mind was altered, leaving only Two-Face in control. (*The Dark Knight Returns* #1-4, 1987)

TWOMBEY, AVERY

A criminal known to law enforcement officials as Cypher.

TYLER, STILTS

To avoid arrest as head of Gotham City's rackets, Stilts Tyler offered Tom Macon one hundred thousand dollars to take the rap. Macon agreed and hid the cash before serving a ten-year prison term. Upon Macon's release, Tyler decided he wanted the money back and set after the parolee to find the cash. Tyler's men captured Macon and tried to force the location from him, but they were interrupted by the arrival of Batman and Robin. Macon died from the attack, but first he told the Caped Crusader the money's location. Tyler turned his attention toward forcing the hero to reveal this information, but each attempt failed. Finally, with some help from Vicki Vale, the Dynamic Duo apprehended Tyler and his men. (*Batman* #50, December 1948/January 1949)

TZU, EKIN

Ekin Tzu was a Gotham City resident who headed up the Triad criminal gang in the Chinatown section. He was a gentle soul who deeply followed the teachings found in the I Ching. When his wife died during a gang turf battle, he blamed Vasily Kosov, leader of the Russian mob. He accepted an offer of help from Whisper a'Daire, who turned Kosov over to the grieving widower. Ekin Tzu also promised a'Daire his devotion, and he was rewarded with the immortality potion she had first obtained when she served Rā's al Ghūl. His body morphed under the potion's influence, adopting raven-like attributes. Recognizing that the bat was considered more sacred than either a'Daire's snake or his own raven, Tzu turned himself over to Batman for justice. Ekin Tzu rededicated himself to ending evil in Gotham, beginning with his former allies, the Triad. (*Detective Comics* #743, April 2000)

life as Two-Face. One of his more despicable acts was to hire the Crime Doctor to "fix" Sloane's face, restoring him to his status as Kent's twin. Again the Dynamic Duo rescued the actor and had his face repaired. (*Batman* #81, February 1954)

In one odd incident George Blake, manager of the Gotham Theatre, disguised himself as Two-Face to commit crimes, while Kent was appearing on the stage, playing himself. Blake erred by putting the makeup on the wrong side of his face, which tipped off the Gotham Guardian to the ruse. (*Detective Comics* #187, September 1952)

On Earth-1, Two-Face was a less noteworthy member of Batman's Rogues Gallery. In this reality, he was named Harvey Dent.

After the Crisis on Infinite Earths, Harvey Dent was abused as a child by his father, who also gave him the two-headed silver dollar that would later become his trademark. The father would get drunk each night and flip the coin, saying the headed side resulted in a beating. Thus began Dent's slow slide into bipolar disorder and paranoid schizophrenia. He grew up to become Gotham's youngest district attorney when Batman first debuted. The two became friends and teamed with Police Commissioner James Gordon to help take down the Roman, Carmine Falcone. The battle grew brutal as Dent watched his home blown apart with his wife, Gilda Dent, caught in the blast. During their investigations, they came up against the Holiday killer. At one point Dent was suspected of being this killer, and was beaten by the Joker for it, but the killer proved to be Gilda, and Carmine's son Alberto Falcone, who committed the murders. (*Batman: The Long Halloween* #1-12, January–December 1997) It was later, at the trial of Sal "Boss" Maroni, that the acid burned Dent's flesh

UBU

For Rā's al Ghūl to be an effective leader of a global operation, he required a steady stream of trusted bodyguards. *Ubu* was the title he bestowed upon the most loyal bodyguard, and for uncounted years an Ubu always accompanied Rā's. To earn the title, the man was usually above average in height, weight, strength, and endurance. On occasion an Ubu, such as Malha Naik, has served as leader of the League of Assassins.

Batman first encountered Ubu when he was introduced to the Demon's Head in the Batcave. When they fought, it was quickly determined this particular bodyguard had a "glass jaw" and was easily taken out of action. (*Batman* #232, June 1971)

When the Lazarus Pit in the Swiss Alps was abandoned, Ubu was present when the headquarters was blown up by Batman. He was severely burned and began to emit a green glow. The Demon's Head found him and had his servant examined by several doctors. It appeared that the pit and the explosion combined to grant this Ubu a measure of immortality, something Rā's wanted for himself. Instead, the injured Ubu fled Europe in favor of Gotham City, his addled mind driving him

to seek revenge against Bruce Wayne. He attacked Alfred Pennyworth at Wayne Manor and battled the Dark Knight until he was impaled on a splintered railing, proving he was not entirely immortal. (*Detective Comics* #438, December 1978/January 1979)

By that time Rā's may have determined hulking figures may not be what he needed in a complex world. His acolyte David Cain attempted to train the ultimate warrior to be his bodyguard, although his experiments with his daughter Cassandra Cain went awry.

While Cain worked on "the One who is All," Rā's went through a series of Ubus during his confrontations with the Dark Knight. At one point he moved outside his normal resources and gave the title to Bane, hoping to make the international criminal a part of his operation and worthy of being betrothed to his daughter Talia Head. The relationship proved short-lived. (*Batman: Bane of the Demon* #1–4, March–June 1998) Another in the unending line of Ubus took his place.

Rā's al Ghūl also had other bodyguards in between Ubus, such as Lurk (*DC Special Series* #15, September 1978) and Grind. (*Batman Annual* #8, 1982)

UGLY AMERICAN, THE

Jon Kennedy Payne was a loyal American, trained by the military to be the ultimate patriot. Unfortunately, the experience also twisted his mind: Anyone who made so much as a snide comment about the country was subject to his retribution. Loose in Gotham City, he proved to be a danger to its citizens, requiring Batman to take him out of action. (*Batman: Shadow of the Bat* #6, November 1992)

UGLY HORDE

The Ugly Horde was a group of criminals who wanted to destroy things considered beautiful. Members considered themselves ugly and rampaged until stopped by Batman and Robin. (*Batman* #3, Fall 1940)

UNDERTAKER, THE

Peter Ostine, a mortician in Gotham City, became overly fascinated with the subjects under his care. He began to perform experiments with the cadavers, which brought him to Batman's attention. During a confrontation, Ostine accidentally killed himself. (*Batman* #539, February 1997)

UNDERWORLD SURGEON, THE

Steve Travers, the brother to "Trigger Joe" Travers, was forced to treat Joe and his gang.

UTILITY BELT

In the Batman's crime-fighting career, he recognized the need to carry a variety of tools with him. Quickly he determined that a multifaceted belt worked best, providing him with the freedom and flexibility to swing into action as needed. For complete details, see Batman.

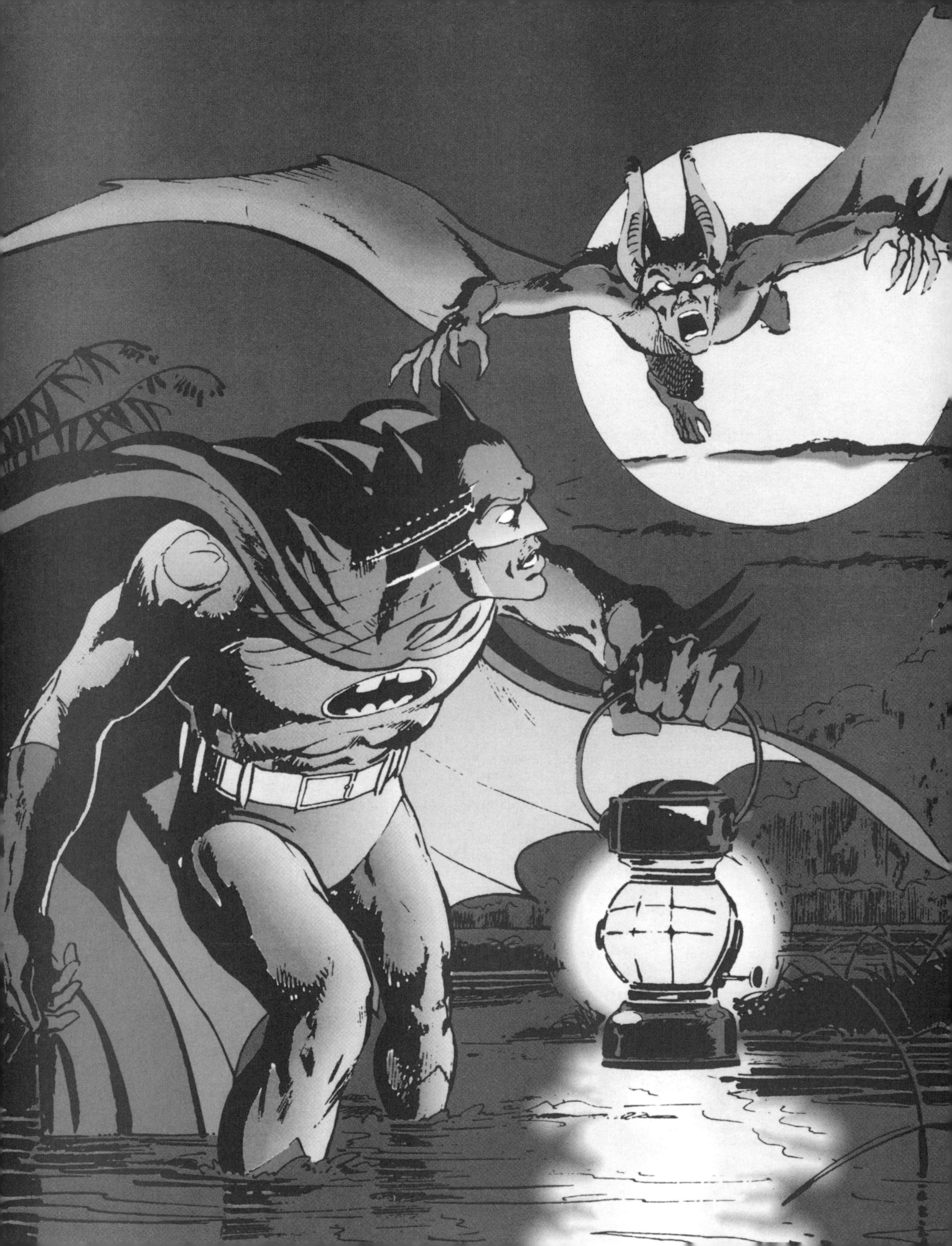

V

VADIM, DALA

A criminal and vampire who served the deadly MONK and was known to most as DALA.

VALE, VICKI

On Earth-2, Vicki Vale was a photojournalist for *PIC-TURE MAGAZINE* who arrived in GOTHAM CITY, fascinated by the city's protectors, Batman and ROBIN. Her very first encounter with them coincided with their initial confrontation with the MAD HATTER. (*Batman* #49, October/November 1948) Vale continued to report on the Dynamic Duo's exploits, even suspecting their true identities, though she never managed to confirm her suspicions. She called upon the heroes for help when her college-aged sister Anne was threatened by a gangster. Her presence grew to the point that Robin remarked she was something of a pest. She also was an occasional date for BRUCE WAYNE, but the relationship never grew beyond anything casual. She continued to work in the city, moving from *Picture* to *VUE MAGAZINE*.

On Earth-1, Vale had much the same career at *Vue Magazine*, although she abandoned her hunt to reveal the Dark Knight's identity and eventually married Tom Powers, changing her name to Vicki Vale Powers. (*Batman Family* #11, June 1977)

When she next appeared in Gotham she had reverted to her maiden name and was divorced. She had been in Europe as *Vue*'s Paris bureau chief for some time before returning stateside. She began a romance with Bruce Wayne, which was the first of a series of romantic rivalries with CATWOMAN and JULIA REMARQUE—ALFRED PENNYWORTH's daughter, also newly arrived in Gotham. (*Batman* #344, February 1982) She once more suspected Wayne of being Batman, and her editor, Morton Monroe, handed over her research to political manipulator RUPERT THORNE, who in turn hired DEADSHOT to kill Wayne. The ploy failed, and Monroe wound up committing suicide. The Pulitzer Prize–winning Vale became the publication's new editor in chief. (*Detective Comics* #521, December 1982) She subsequently hired Remarque as a file clerk and quickly promoted her to reporter.

Frustrated that her relationship with Wayne was

BATMAN DOESN'T THINK I CAN FIND OUT WHO **MYSTERYMAN** IS, BUT I'LL SHOW HIM -- I --. OH, OH! THE **BATMOBILE** DECK IS OPEN A LITTLE -- UNLOCKED --

going nowhere, she spent extra time at the gym, where she met trainer Jim Traynor. The two began a whirlwind romance.

In the world re-created in the wake of Crisis on Infinite Earths, Victoria Elizabeth Vale was a local-girl-turned-child-model who was devastated when a dog in a photo shoot was killed by a camera truck and replaced by a look-alike. She swore the camera would never again lie because of her. Vale began learning all she could about photography, and started turning down ethically questionable jobs. Her parents objected, and eventually they came to a parting of the ways. After graduating from Gotham High School, Vale studied photography and journalism at Vassar College before beginning her professional career. She was editor at *Vue Magazine* engaged in a brief romance with Bruce Wayne, one of many women to make that claim. In time she left Gotham, and Wayne, to continue her career. When Jason Todd was killed, Vicki Vale helped form a Committee of Concerned Citizens Against the Batman.

In a short span of time, Vale left *Vue* and took a series of positions as a photojournalist at *Gotham View* (*Batman* #445, March 1990), *Gotham Daily News* (*Batman* #460, March 1991), and *Gothamite Magazine* (*Batman* #475, March 1992). At the latter publication, Vale was paired with reporter Horten

Spence to study Gotham's drug epidemic. Their professional partnership grew into something more after Spence defended Vicki from a trio of attackers. She finally broke things off with Wayne for good at that point.

She became a cohost of *The Scene,* a women's television talk show, alongside fellow celebrities Lia Briggs (formerly Looker), Tawny Young, and Linda Park. (*Wonder Woman* [second series] #170, July 2001) She also did on-air reporting for *Night News Live.* (*Human Defense Corps* #6, December 2003)

In another reality, Vicki Vale was dating Bruce Wayne when he began his career as Batman. While he was recruiting Dick Grayson to be his sidekick, Alfred and Vale were seriously injured in a car crash, bringing the grim reality of his work too close to home. (*All Star Batman and Robin* #1, September 2005)

VALLEY, JEAN-PAUL

A product of genetic engineering at the hands of the Sacred Order of Saint Dumas, he was trained in the System to become the latest in their long line of avenging angels known as Azrael.

VANCE, DEIRDRE

A former biker, Vance was a criminal cohort of the Riddler known as Query.

VANCE, JOHN

A young boy who witnessed a crime and had his identity protected by Batman in a disguise dubbed Batman Junior.

VANE, WYNDHAM

Wyndham Vane was one of the staff psychiatrists at Arkham Asylum. As more and more costumed criminals found their way to the facility, Vane got curious as to why there were so many neuroses that led to such extreme behavior. His research, though, led him to a catatonic state, making him just another victim of the place. (*Showcase '95* #11, Late November 1995)

VANNEY, JAY

Jay Vanney was a criminal who broke into the lab of Dr. Greggson to steal the man's two latest inventions. Batman and Robin arrived to stop him, and during the struggle the "maximizer" device was accidentally activated. Batman was transformed into a thirty-foot giant. His attempts to continue crime fighting proved clumsy, and Police Commissioner James Gordon asked him to stop. Batman lured Vanney out of hiding, used the "maximizer" on him, and knocked the man unconscious. Robin then obtained the "minimizer" and restored both giants to normal size. (*Detective Comics* #243, May 1957)

VARANIA

The sailing vessel where Clark Kent and Bruce Wayne were forced to share a cabin and learned each other's secret identity. (*Superman* #76, May/June 1952)

VARDEN, JAY

Mack Manchard led a criminal gang that employed engineer Jay Varden to create ambitious plans for robberies. Batman and Robin erroneously thought Varden was the true gang leader and tried to get confessions from the captured gang members confirming this. None admitted to Varden's leadership, so the Caped Crusader led the Manchard gang to believe Varden was Batman. Varden was targeted for death, but the Dynamic Duo arrived to save his life, capturing Manchard and the gang. (*World's Finest Comics* #70, May/June 1954)

VARDEN, VINCE

Vince Varden robbed ingenious devices, amassing what were dubbed the Seven Wonders of the Underworld. He used these devices to commit audacious robberies throughout Gotham City until he was stopped by Batman and Robin. The devices included a mechanical forger, a hydraulic jimmy, a vacuum thief, a second-story burglary machine, a magnetic monster, a phantom getaway car, and a special gas that rapidly rotted away various fibers such as Batman's climbing rope. (*Batman* #89, February 1955)

VARINA (PRINCESS)

Princess Varina of Balkania let it be known that she intended to abdicate her throne in order to marry the commoner Stefan. During a visit she made to the United States, Superman and Batman vied for her affections, forestalling the abdication that the world's greatest heroes knew would lead to a violent civil war. When Pete Karney's gang attacked the princess's traveling vehicle, the heroes stayed out of sight but quietly aided Stefan in defeating the criminals and gaining sole credit for the victory. Stefan was made a national hero, allowing the parliament to bless the marriage and preventing bloodshed. (*World's Finest Comics* #85, November/December 1956)

VARNER, "BLAST"

"Blast" Varner was a criminal specializing in demolitions who planned to detonate a tremendous explosion aboard a ship near the GOTHAM CITY docks. He calculated that the blast radius would be of sufficient force to crack open vaults at banks fronting the harbor. At much the same time, Batman let the rumor spread that the Caped Crusader was actually a robot operated by ROBIN. Varner ordered his men to obtain the construct; when it was brought to him, Batman revealed himself to be flesh and blood, hidden within the metallic shell. Varner and his men were apprehended. (*Detective Comics* #224, October 1955)

VARREL MOB, THE

The Varrel Mob devised a new death trap to kill Batman. To protect his friend, SUPERMAN lured the Caped Crusader away from GOTHAM CITY. He told the World's Greatest Detective that he needed help determining which METROPOLIS criminal had just deduced that the Man of Steel was also CLARK KENT. Instead, Batman's investigation led him to the truth of the ruse, and he returned home in time to help Superman and ROBIN apprehend the mob. (*World's Finest Comics* #78, October/November 1955)

VATHGAR

Vathgar was a ruthless criminal on a dimensional world known as Xeron who wanted to take over as ruler. He intended to use skrans—native lower life-forms—as his shock troops, turning them into raging monsters by injecting them with the precious element iron. To amass the necessary quantities of ore, he sent a skran through the dimensional barrier to Earth to see how pure the planet's iron ore was and if it was sufficient for his needs. The creature rampaged across METROPOLIS until Batman, ROBIN, and SUPERMAN managed to contain it. They then went to Xeron and ended Vathgar's plans for conquest. (*World's Finest Comics* #118, June 1961)

VEKING, LARS

Lars Veking ran a modern-day piracy operation from a small island in the middle of the Atlantic Ocean. He and his gang committed their high-seas crimes using a specially equipped submarine and cherished their privacy. When Batman and ROBIN were transporting seven hardened criminals from Harkness Penitentiary to Coneida Prison, their airplane crashed on the island. It then became a game of survival as Veking and his men tried to kill the convicts and the heroes tried to protect their secret. Once Veking was defeated, the Dynamic Duo had to subdue the unappreciative criminals whose lives they'd just saved. They were all rescued and brought to the mainland for handling. (*Batman* #79, October/November 1953)

VENOM

Venom was a drug derived from the unique substance Miraclo, developed by Rex "Tick Tock" Tyler at Bannerman Chemical. When it was initially created in the 1940s, it was used to give Tyler an hour's superstrength, -speed, and -agility, allowing him to fight crime as Hourman. (*JSA Classified* #17, November 2006)

Years later the basics for Miraclo were used to create Venom on the island of SANTA PRISCA. It was an addictive substance that provided the

user with enhanced skills and abilities along with reduced mental and emotional control. When Batman encountered Venom, he tried to keep it out of GOTHAM CITY, but he was injected with a high dosage. It took the Dark Knight a solid month's isolation in the BATCAVE to overcome its addictive properties. (*Legends of the Dark Knight* #16–20, March–July 1991)

The man known as BANE, a criminal who'd grown up in a Santa Prisca prison, began using a new version of the genetically engineered steroid. He carried a supply strapped to him with intravenous tubing snaking down both arms. The constant supply kept him a raging behemoth. After several years addicted to it, Bane eventually weaned himself from Venom and began destroying the drug manufacturers and suppliers to keep the drug away from the world. (*JSA Classified* #17–18, November–December 2006)

VENTA, JACQUES

Years ago BRUCE WAYNE interfered with a criminal escaping a French hotel during a robbery. The man was arrested and spent a decade in prison, dreaming of revenge. Upon his release, he took the name *Jacques Venta* and reinvented himself as a leading botanist and explorer. While in GOTHAM CITY, he used a rare flower, the orchid of madness, combined with hypnosis, to essentially freeze Wayne in place every night at ten. Venta and his associate Perrins were then free to go out and commit new burglaries. Suspicion began to fall on Wayne, and for a time he doubted his own sanity. Finally, as Batman, he learned the truth and apprehended the men, ending the spree. (*World's Finest Comics* #44, February/March 1950)

VENTRILOQUIST

ARNOLD WESKER was a member of a prominent GOTHAM CITY crime family. After witnessing the murder of his mother at the hands of a rival gang, the young Wesker retreated within himself and began to develop multiple personality disorder. As the boy grew, he turned to ventriloquism as

an outlet for his feelings, which were angry ones. (*Detective Comics* #583, February 1988)

Wesker bottled up his feelings, gaining weight and remaining largely silent. As an adult his feelings bubbled over, and he wound up in a barroom brawl where his opponent died. Wesker was found guilty and sentenced to BLACKGATE PENITENTIARY, where his cellmate was a lifer named Donnegan. Wesker grew despondent but, when he tried to hang himself, he hesitated when he heard Woody, Donnegan's dummy, "speak" to him. In fact, the dummy led Wesker to a tunnel that Donnegan spent the last fifteen years digging, and the two escaped. Their cellmate tried to prevent them from leaving, Donnegan slashing at Wesker with a corkscrew, missing the man and scaring the dummy. After Donnegan was beaten and Wesker escaped, a new chapter of his life began.

Wesker and the dummy, now named SCARFACE, set out to carve a piece of the city's criminal underworld for themselves. The Ventriloquist wasn't very gifted, and he kept pronouncing his *B*'s as *G*'s, a trademark that opened him up to ridicule. Scarface verbally abused Wesker and did most of the talking for the duo. While many thought the dummy was an aspect of Wesker's multiple personality disorder, it was later learned that Scarface was actually a vile spirit inhabiting the wooden form.

Early on they were protected by a man named RHINO, but later they worked largely by themselves, using hirelings as needed. Time and again they took control of Gotham City crime, only to meet defeat at the hands of Batman and ROBIN. After each such event, Wesker wound up at ARKHAM ASYLUM. Separated from Scarface, Wesker's gentler side emerged, a result of his loneliness. When Arkham was damaged during the earthquake, Wesker went free but without his partner. He took to using a sock puppet to express his feelings, inventing a new personality to match. Masquerading as the QUAKEMASTER, he claimed to be behind the tremors and tried to extort the city for cash until Batman discovered the truth. Scarface eventually found his

Arnold Wesker with Scarface

Sugar with Scarface

VENTURA

Ventura is a planet known for its almost total dedication to all manner of gambling. Its rulers, Rokk and Sorban, frequently took their audacious wagers to other worlds regardless of the natives' desire to participate. (*Superman* #171, August 1964) SUPERMAN and Batman became particular favorites of the intergalactic gamblers; they were lured into outrageous events for the sake of large wagers.

The planet was visited by other denizens of Earth, including Plastic Man. (*JLA: Heaven's Ladder,* 2000)

When Destiny of the Endless severed his bond with the legendary Book of Destiny, it became a magnetic draw for people from around the universe. Residents from Ventura hired a man named Drake to obtain the Book. The case led Batman to dispatch GREEN LANTERN and SUPERGIRL to the planet to get it back. Members of the Green Lantern Corps weren't welcome on Ventura; he needed the Maid of Might to do the legwork for him. In the course of the mission, Supergirl beat their champion, costing most Venturians a lot of money. (*The Brave and the Bold* [third series] #1–6, April–August 2007)

VERN, PROFESSOR RALPH

Ralph Vern was professor at State University and a member of the MYSTERY ANALYSTS OF GOTHAM CITY. He also stole the Kashpur Diamond and left a tape recording challenging the Analysts to solve the crime and determine which of their number had committed the robbery. It fell to Batman and ROBIN to determine that Vern was the culprit. (*Batman* #168, December 1964)

VERRIL, CARL

Carl Verril was a wealthy man who intended to leave behind his millions after teaching his heir a lesson. Upon his death, Verril's will stipulated that Vincent Verril must spend one million dollars in four days or forfeit the remaining ten million dollars to his cousin. This was to allow Vincent to indulge his whims and then learn the value of the money he would have left. Complications ensued when Vincent was injured and hospitalized. He authorized Batman to spend the money on his behalf, which prompted a spree that befuddled those not in the know. Vincent's cousin hired criminals to derail Batman, forcing a forfeit, but SUPERMAN intervened by selling the Caped Crusader several souvenirs from his missions. The Man of Steel donated the money to charity, the criminals were arrested, and Batman saved Vincent's inheritance. (*World's Finest Comics* #99, February 1959)

VETERAN, THE

The Veteran was a man named Nathan who headed up a cadre of highly trained paramilitary agents for an unspecified agency, presumably federal in nature. His missions, both domestic and foreign, have been largely unrecorded and unknown to the general public. The Veteran was a charismatic leader who recruited the best candidates to join his team. At some point he tried to recruit DICK GRAYSON, creating enmity between him and Batman. Years later he arrived in BLÜDHAVEN to offer TIM DRAKE, the

way back to Wesker, where together they remained an imposing force.

When the Society, a secret organization of super-villains, formed, Wesker was a member until the Jade Canary, also known as LADY SHIVA, threw him from a rooftop. He apparently survived the fall, only to be fatally shot in the stomach and head by the TALLY MAN. His dying words helped Batman determine who the killer was. (*Detective Comics* #818, June 2006)

Wesker's body was stolen from the morgue by a woman named Sugar. Police sergeant HARVEY BULLOCK confirmed for Batman that Wesker's body was missing and the dummy taken from police custody. Sugar had also taken the cracked Scarface dummy and became the new Ventriloquist. She introduced herself at a gathering of criminals at the ICEBERG LOUNGE. At first they thought it was a

resurrected Wesker who was talking to them, until the corpse was kicked aside and Sugar appeared.

Batman had infiltrated the meeting using the guise of Lefty Knox. He observed the woman's debut and found her charming, attractive, a better ventriloquist than Wesker, and quite possibly more dangerous than Scarface. He noted that Scarface and Sugar had matching facial scars, leading him to believe that this somewhat familiar person had died and been reborn similarly to the spirit that became Scarface. Sugar also maintained a closet full of Scarface replicas, a limitless supply of new bodies should something happen to the current model.

VENTRIS, FLOYD

Floyd Ventris emerged from jail ready to resume his criminal career but noted that he needed a gimmick. He chose to become MIRROR-MAN.

third Robin, a place on his squad. Tim went along on a number of missions to see how things went but ultimately passed, choosing to remain with Batman and the Teen Titans. (*Robin* [second series] #138, July 2005)

VICIOUS

Vicious was a mercenary who joined Pistolera and Cheshire as a team-for-hire for the Ravens. She was adept with knives, but little else was established about her. (*Birds of Prey: Ravens* #1, June 1998)

VIEW MAGAZINE

See *Vue Magazine*.

VISIO, PAUL

Paul Visio was a criminal gang leader who doubled as a ghost hunter. His plan was to pretend that the ghost of a Gotham City murderer was responsible for rival gangs being exposed to the police, leading to their arrest. With the competition removed, Visio and his gang would be able to operate more freely. The entire scheme was exposed, and Visio was apprehended by Batman and Robin. (*Detective Comics* #150, August 1949)

VOHR, PROFESSOR

When the World Electronics Convention sought a venue, it was decided to hold a contest between the champions of Metropolis and Gotham City. The winner would earn his city hosting rights and personally provide protection. When Batman learned that Professor Vohr's experimental generator emitted minute particles of Kryptonite radiation, he was determined to beat Superman to ensure the Metropolis Marvel would not be harmed.

Vohr's device was finally turned on and, after a power surge, totally self-destructed. The threat to Superman was removed and the committee declared a tie, splitting the exhibits between the two cities. (*World's Finest Comics* #76, May/June 1955)

VON BURITZ, ADMIRAL

Admiral Von Buritz was a Nazi U-boat commander who stumbled upon the Atlantic Ocean location of the sunken city of Earth-2's Atlantis. He convinced the pacifist leaders of the city to allow his fleet to use their Caribbean location as a base of operations. Batman and Robin had to journey beneath the sea to tell the leaders, Taro and Lanya, the truth about the global conflict occurring over their heads. Von Buritz and his men were defeated by the Dynamic Duo's efforts in addition to the sacrifice of seaman Ben Stunsel. (*Batman* #19, October/November 1943)

VON DORT, GENERAL

General Von Dort served the Afrika Corps during World War II and was believed killed in the same bunker as Adolf Hitler. Von Dort escaped death and resurfaced years later in Gotham City. He convinced the underworld mobsters that he could turn them into a more effective force if they followed his military instruction. Von Dort's actual goal was to train the criminals to enable them to help him obtain M-244, a radioactive isotope he needed for an ingenious "death ray." Upon stealing the isotope, he intended to lead a group of Nazi survivors to once more attempt world domination. Von Dort was frustrated in his efforts by the arrival of Batman, Robin, and a visiting Elongated Man. (*Detective Comics* #343, September 1965)

VOR

Vor was a planet ruled by evil despots who eyed expanding their empire to other inhabited planets across the Milky Way. To ensure victory, they captured the champions from five worlds, including Superman, and imprisoned them. In order to keep the captives secure, they also abducted Batman. The Caped Crusader was hypnotized into becoming the prison's warden until the Man of Steel led the other heroes in a revolt. Once they undid the mental suggestions, Batman joined in destroying the munitions that had been stockpiled in anticipation of the invasions. (*World's Finest Comics* #145, November 1964)

VORDA

Vorda was a planet that wished to cross the light-years and conquer Earth. Its vanguard force landed near Gotham City; invaders disguised themselves as humans in anticipation of the attack. They made the acquaintance of criminal Bert Collins and used him to build an army of underworld men to help their plans. Collins was spotted, though, by Batman and Robin, who trailed him back to the mine the Vordanians were using as a base. Once the Dynamic Duo beat the criminals and destroyed the alien "grav-ray" that was to be their major offensive weapon, the alien task force returned home in disgrace. (*Batman* #136, December 1960)

VORDEN, "LENS"

When Batman agreed to give a demonstration on disguises at the Kean School of Makeup, "Lens" Vorden thought he'd found a way to learn the Gotham Guardian's secret identity. As Batman demonstrated each disguise, as a favor to Barrett Kean—the man who'd first taught the Caped Crusader the craft—Vorden snapped pictures of the process, determined to create a photo composite of what his unmasked face really looked like. Instead, Batman caught on to the plan and turned the tables on Vorden, taking down the Big Hugo gang at the same time. (*Detective Comics* #227, January 1956)

VOX

Vox was an armored terrorist covered head-to-toe in a battle suit with attachments at his hips and his back that emitted an explosive—a liquid form of military-grade C-4—that could be detonated by a specific radio frequency transmitted from his gear. The head mask included a modulation device so his voice was altered and untraceable. He debuted in Gotham City during a Wayne Foundation–sponsored Gotham International Anti-Terror Conference. The small Republic of Jalib was then undergoing a civil war, and its delegate, al Ibn, accused Markovia of interference. To al Ibn, it smacked of foreign occupation; to the mercenary Vox it was an indefensible crime against the people. Vox announced over a radio broadcast from within Wayne Tower that he would destroy one of the capitalist world's leading symbols of economic oppression. A series of carefully planned explosions caused panic among the building's occupants—save Bruce Wayne, who was with the conference delegates, and Tim Drake, who had arrived for the reception. Unable to slip into his Batsuit, Wayne did what he could to quell the people's fears while Drake, as Robin, went after Vox before the entire building could implode. (*Detective Comics* #829–830, May 2007)

A woman named Lisa used the code name Vox as well. She grew up in a house where the family endured fighting and physical abuse. Vox later claimed a voice told her to murder her family to end the cycle of violence. After that the voice would return, telling her to kill others, until she was arrested and remanded to Arkham Asylum. (*Batman: Arkham Asylum—Tales of Madness* #1, May 1998)

VOZ, SAMANTHA

Samantha Voz claimed to be the reincarnation of a witch who had died during the famed Salem Witch Trials. In her mind, she lived again to seek revenge against her former oppressors, similarly reincarnated. She was captured by Batman and sent to Arkham Asylum. (*Batman: Arkham Asylum—Tales of Madness* #1, May 1998)

VREEKILL, HUGO

Dr. Hugo Vreekill was a scientist-turned-criminal who found a way to emit a ray that would destabilize the molecular makeup of steel. He intended to use the powerful device to blackmail landlords, construction companies, and others for huge sums of money. His dreams of wealth were dashed by Batman. (*New York World's Fair Comics*, 1940)

VUE MAGAZINE

Vue Magazine was a Gotham City–based news magazine that employed Vicki Vale first as a photojournalist and later as editor in chief.

VULTURE, THE

Armand Lydecker—aka Volper—was an inventor-turned-criminal who paired up with two others to form the Terrible Trio. Wearing an oversized head mask and business suit, he was known as the Vulture, alongside the Fox and Shark.

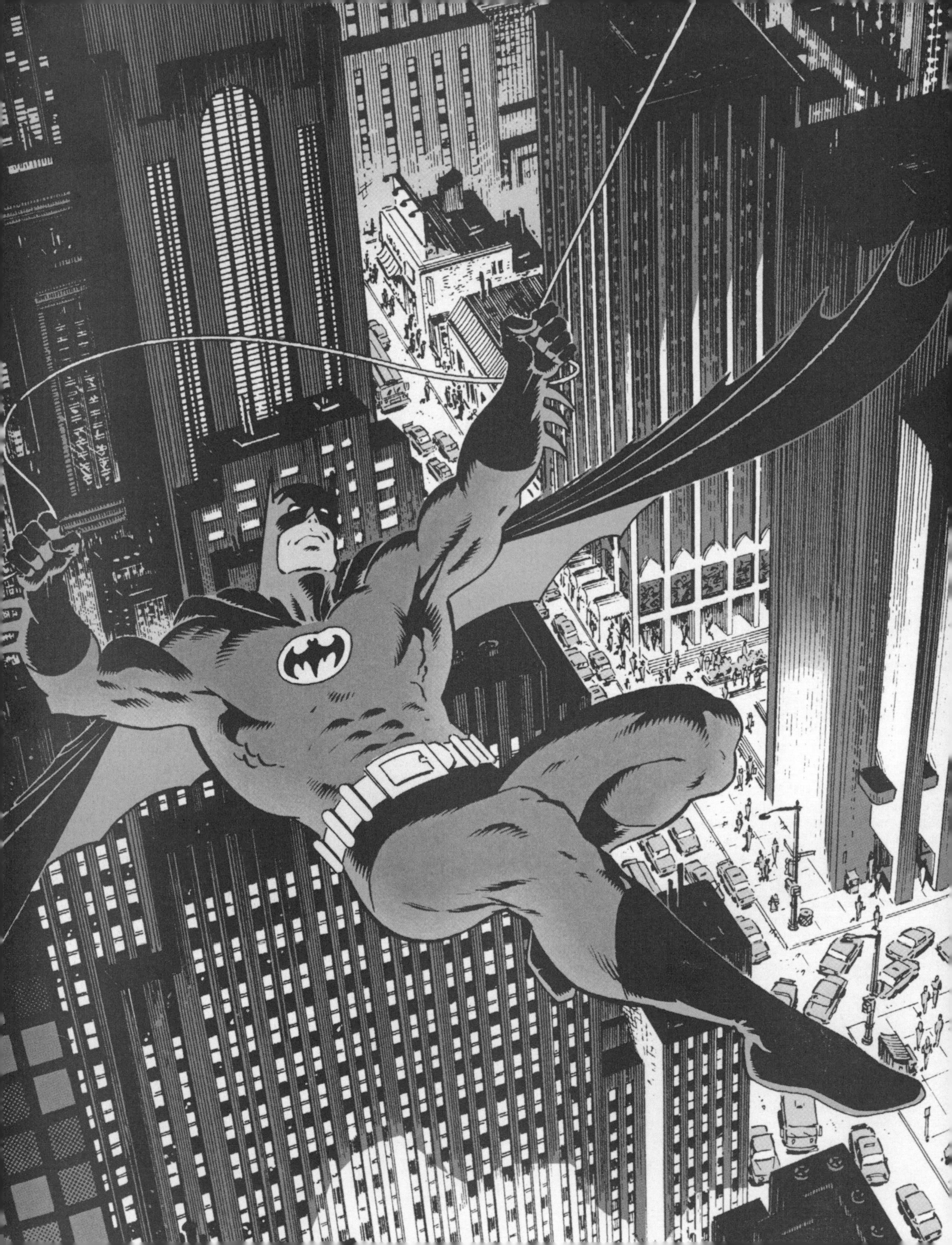

W

WALEY, WALLACE

Wallace Waley designed and sold to fellow criminals a series of devices created specifically to thwart Batman and ROBIN. For example, the BATMOBILE, while in high pursuit, suddenly veered off the road when sudden oil slicks appeared. Smoke screens were generated to prevent the BATPLANE from spotting fleeing felons. This prompted the Gotham Guardian to create new tools in his own fight against crime. A Bat-tank, for instance, was impervious to oil. In short order Waley and his customers were apprehended. (*Detective Comics* #236, October 1956)

WALKER, BRAINY

Brainy Walker was paroled after serving three years for counterfeiting and immediately set out to commit fresh crimes. This time, though, he used counterfeit thousand-dollar bills as a distraction. He first planted the phony cash around GOTHAM CITY and then broadcast clues to their whereabouts. The streets were choked as citizens sought the money. This kept the police occupied with crowd and traffic control, allowing Walker to commit robberies in relative peace.

Walker then tricked ROBIN into accidentally telling him the location of the BATCAVE. Batman worked with ALFRED PENNYWORTH to make Walker believe that Robin's slip of the tongue was part of a plan to entrap Walker and his men. When Walker gave up seeking the secret headquarters, he and his gang were finally apprehended. (*Detective Comics* #242, April 1957)

WALLER, AMANDA BLAKE

Amanda Blake grew up in the Cabrini-Green section of Chicago and, unlike so many, managed to marry and raise a family. The squalid conditions finally caught up with her when first her daughter, then her husband were gunned down. She put herself through school, earning a doctorate in political science, and found work in Washington, D.C., as a congressional aide. While doing routine research, Waller uncovered documentation about Task Force X, a government operation spinning out of the Office of Strategic Services at the end of World War II.

Fascinated, she read the entire dossier and then proposed that the operation be revived to handle the dirty work in an even dirtier world. To her surprise, not only was Task Force X revived, but she found herself placed in charge. (*Legends* #1, November 1986) There would be two divisions—one called the Agency, which later evolved into CHECKMATE, and another known as the Suicide Squad. The squad, operating out of Belle Reve prison in Louisiana, used heroes, villains, and other operatives to handle clandestine missions around the world. The villains who served would be granted amnesty—should they survive. To ensure cooperation, all wore explosive wrist bracelets that were controlled by mission leader Rick Flag Jr. Among the squad's operatives were many opponents of the Caped Crusader, notably BLOCKBUSTER, DEADSHOT, PENGUIN, BRONZE TIGER, POISON IVY, and COPPERHEAD.

Early on, Batman infiltrated Belle Reve and threatened Waller with exposure; she countered that should they study him, his deepest secrets might be revealed. The standoff ended in a stalemate. Later the Dark Knight actually worked with the squad on missions, coming to understand its role in the world, later inspiring him to remake the OUTSIDERS as his personal strike force.

Waller became southeastern regional director for

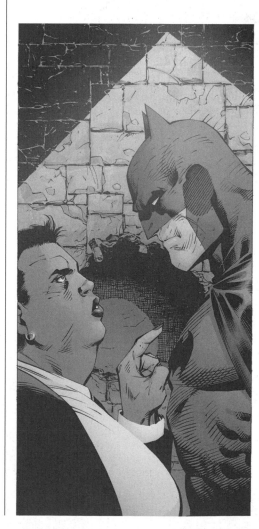

the Department of Extranormal Operations. Under President LEX LUTHOR, she was named secretary of meta-human affairs. She took the fall for Luthor's criminal activities, serving a brief stint in jail until his successor, Jonathan Vincent Horne, ordered her to resume command of Checkmate. When the United Nations rechartered the operation, she became the team's White Queen, restricted to policy making. Behind everyone's back Waller reconstituted the squad and continued to authorize fieldwork for her own purposes, serving the greater good (at least in her eyes). (*Checkmate* [second series] #1, June 2006)

WAR GAMES

Batman was always drafting contingency plans, preparing for the day one or more of them would need to be used. He rarely shared the details with his allies—and in one instance that proved fatal. After STEPHANIE BROWN was fired as she attempted to earn her place as the fourth ROBIN, she wanted to prove her worth. As a result, she accessed the Batcomputer and found one such plan. Stephanie activated it without comprehending all the elements that needed to be put in place. The plan required MATCHES MALONE to be in a specific place at specific times, but she never knew that *Malone* was an alias Batman used.

A summons went out to the GOTHAM CITY underworld bosses. Fueled by mutual suspicion, all the representatives brought along high-powered bodyguards, including notable villains the NKVDEMON, SILVER MONKEY, ZEISS, DEADSHOT, and HELLHOUND. All, that is, except the Burnley Town Massive's Crown, who was the first to pull a weapon. A meeting quickly became a shooting gallery, before the mysterious host made an appearance.

As the fighting among gang members spread across the city, Batman had to rely on a dwindling number of allies. NIGHTWING arrived from BLÜDHAVEN along with the new TARANTULA, whose methods weren't necessarily Batman-approved. BATGIRL eagerly waded into the fray, while ORACLE coordinated the force although she chafed under Batman's using her more as switchboard than ally. TIM DRAKE honored a promise to his father and remained inactive.

As the various crime captains began targeting rival leaders' families, the violence reached Tim's high school. Tim did his best to protect the students and faculty. His efforts weren't enough, though, and the target, DARLA AQUISTA, was mortally wounded. Batman, Nightwing, and Batgirl arrived in time to put an end to multiple threats but too late for Darla. As Batman emerged from the school, in daylight, forever shattering his mystique as an urban legend, the media recorded his arrival with the girl's lifeless body in his arms. They quickly concluded that he was responsible for her death, but he was gone before they or the police could get answers.

As the CATWOMAN ushered Stephanie, back in her SPOILER guise, out of danger, the teenager admitted that she was responsible for the war gripping Gotham. She'd acted without complete knowledge of the Caped Crusader's plans.

Batman convinced Police Commissioner MICHAEL AKINS to call a curfew, hoping to herd the run-amok criminals into a stadium where ORPHEUS, filling in for Matches Malone, was to take control; through him, Batman would ultimately pull the strings. But first the PENGUIN plunged Gotham into a blackout, hoping to take advantage of the carnage. Tarantula, though, put a crimp in those plans, going through KILLER CROC, Trickster, and Deadshot to reach the Penguin.

Worse, Stephanie was caught in the clutches of BLACK MASK, long since thought dead. Back in Gotham, he tortured Stephanie for information and also killed Orpheus. After killing Batman's agent, he impersonated Orpheus and arrived at the stadium to fill the vacuum. Meantime, despite her wounds, Stephanie managed to escape.

Batman met Orpheus in an attempt to restore

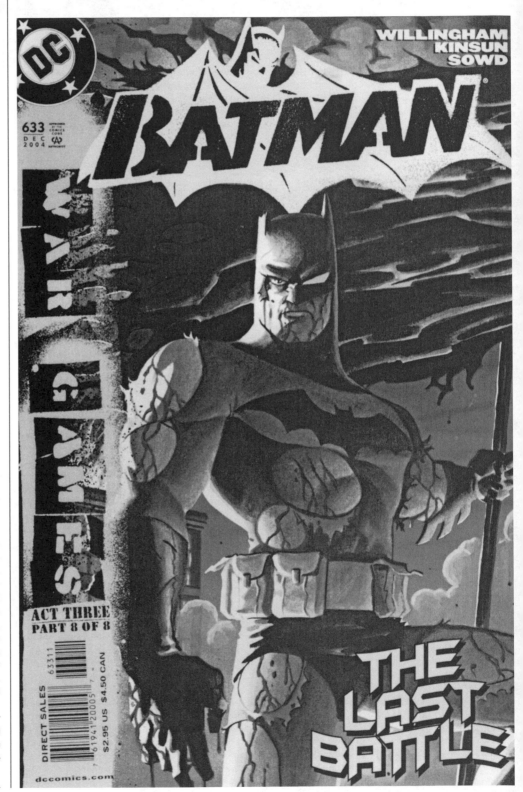

WILLINGHAM
KINSUN
SOWD

DC

633
DEC
2004

BATMAN

WAR GAMES

ACT THREE
PART 8 OF 8

THE LAST BATTLE

DIRECT SALES

dccomics.com

$2.95 US $4.50 CAN

63311

power to the city. They were joined by Zeiss, who nearly killed them until Orpheus got Zeiss alone. He let Zeiss escape, carrying with him a message to the other crime organizations.

With power restored, the media put out a call for Batman to submit to the oversight of the law, while Akins wanted his force to shoot on sight anyone in costume. At the stadium Orpheus told the assembled criminals that he didn't need them and unleashed his handpicked villains, including FIREFLY and DOCTOR DEATH, to kill them all. At that point ONYX, who had been recruited to protect the real Orpheus, discovered Gavin King's body. Batman swung into the stadium and confronted Orpheus, realizing it was actually Black Mask. He moved in to grab his nemesis but was stopped by SCARECROW, who delighted in the fear being generated.

Black Mask fled to his hideaway, only to discover that Spoiler had freed herself and was trying to escape. Meantime Batman's allies were busy taking down villain after villain as Tim, back in costume as Robin, handled MISTER FUN, the Ravens, and the Trickster; Nightwing stopped Firefly; and Batgirl tackled Killer Croc and the SUICIDE KING. While the Dark Knight raced across Gotham in search of Spoiler, Black Mask found the wounded woman. They fought; she held a gun on him but couldn't bring herself to shoot, allowing him to disarm her and put a bullet through her shoulder. She staggered off until Batman found her, taking her to Dr. LESLIE THOMPKINS's clinic. He sat at her side, comforting her, until she died.

Black Mask, though, took the partial information he had gathered from Spoiler and appeared on television to announce that BARBARA GORDON's clock tower apartment was actually the BATCAVE. He then sent his minions into the building. All of Oracle's defenses were working, but the men cleared a path for Black Mask and the Scarecrow to get closer. Finally they accessed Oracle's sanctum and held her hostage. With the others waiting outside, Batman followed inside, intending to end the struggle. The SCAREBEAST kept the police at bay as the two opponents battled it out. Rather than watch them kill each other, Oracle activated the self-destruct mechanism, forcing them to leave the building or die.

Black Mask escaped and set up operations as the undisputed king of the underworld, holding court as gang after gang pledged fealty. Batman recognized that events were largely his fault and had cost him Spoiler and Oracle. The city lost hundreds of lives and untold millions in fresh damage but gained certainty in the knowledge that there was a Batman and he was a dangerous figure. (*Batgirl* #55–57, *Batman* #631–633, *Batman: The 12-Cent Adventure* #1, *Batman: Gotham Knights* #56–58, *Catwoman* [third series] #34–36, *Detective Comics* #797–799, *Legends of the Dark Knight* #182–184, *Nightwing* [second series] #96–98, *Robin* [second series] #129–131, October–December 2004)

WARLOCK'S DAUGHTER

DARLA AQUISTA, daughter of Henry Aquista, a boss in one of the GOTHAM CITY crime families, attended Louis E. Grieve Memorial High School. She was one of the first friends to TIM DRAKE when he began attending classes there. Tim and Darla quickly grew to be close friends, although he was involved with Stephanie Brown, SPOILER, at the time, so it remained purely platonic. (*Robin* [second series] #121, February 2004)

When Johnny Warlock asked Henry Aquista's help in creating havoc to lure ROBIN, he agreed. That began a battle between Robin and Warlock that continued even after Johnny's corporeal body was destroyed.

After Johnny Warlock's death, the high school became a hunting ground during the vicious WAR GAMES that pitted crime family against crime family. Loved ones, such as Aquista's daughter, became targets for kidnapping or death. Darla's car was attacked outside the school until Tim saved her, rushing them both into the building. While Drake handled potential invaders, Darla huddled out of sight but was still shot.

Despite Drake's first-aid efforts, help in the form of Batman and NIGHTWING arrived too late, and she died. Henry Aquista, who survived the bloody war, took his daughter's body as he began traveling around the world, seeking anyone who could bring her back to life. He encountered Johnny Warlock, who took Henry's own life in exchange for reviving Darla. (*Robin* [second series] #137, June 2005)

Calling herself the Warlock's Daughter, she returned to Gotham and sought out Tim Drake. With Darla believed dead, she tried to pass herself off with the new identity of Laura Fell. She explained that with her newfound life, she could choose her own path, that of hero or villain, and wanted his guidance. First, though, she owed Johnny Warlock a debt and intended to kill Robin.

Robin had Superboy pose as himself so Tim Drake could be on hand as the Warlock's Daughter tried to pay her debt. She failed at killing the Teen of Steel, although her magic did cause him serious injury. For her failure to kill Robin, Johnny Warlock sought her out in BLÜDHAVEN but could not punish her after Robin interfered. Later, Robin suggested that Warlock's Daughter join Shadowpact, a group of mystic champions.

During an all-out battle in Blüdhaven, before the city was destroyed, Tim Drake nearly drowned, but Darla saved his life using CPR. They never saw each other again.

She and Johnny Warlock were then mystically imprisoned for roughly a year before the Shadowpact freed them and she sought out a path for her life.

WARNER, BIFF

Batman and ROBIN tracked the criminal Biff Warner to the Yucatán, but before they could arrest him, a freak lightning bolt struck the Boy Wonder. He survived, but his memory was clouded and he began to exhibit superstrength. Warner duped Robin into believing that they were on the same side, and suddenly Batman found himself fighting his partner. Warner also tried to get Robin to dig out gold from the nearby mountains, but the lightning's effects wore off and the youth recognized the truth. Warner was captured and taken back to the United States. (*Batman* #150, September 1962)

WARNER, GOVERNOR ANDREW

BRUCE WAYNE and Andrew Warner were college roommates on Earth-1. Upon graduation, Warner went into politics and eventually became governor of the state where GOTHAM CITY was located. During a routine examination, doctors discovered an odd gland located next to his pituitary. Research showed that Warner was a mutant, the next evolutionary step for humankind. He resigned his office, preferring to let medical science study him in the hope of learning what was in store for humanity. Researchers bombarded him with radiation to stimulate the gland's development, and in time Warner physically changed, becoming taller and broader. The governor began to display new powers such as telepathy and teleportation. His outlook changed as well: He became despondent, no longer thinking of himself as a human and developing contempt for people. He went on a rampage and had to be stopped by his former friend, Batman. Warner was mentally sending out calls for help in the form of clues Batman and ROBIN could use to apprehend him. When he was finally in custody, the Dark Knight arranged for Warner to be placed in suspended animation until humankind caught up to his development. (*Batman* #165, August 1964)

WATERS, BILL

Bill Waters, James Dice, Fred Barker, and Thomas Slade were production partners for theatrical shows in GOTHAM CITY. Slade left the partnership at one point; soon after, Waters began embezzling investment funds. He killed Dice and Barker to prevent them from learning of his treachery and then tried to frame Slade—but Batman investigated and learned the truth. (*Detective Comics* #161, July 1950)

WAXMAN

The GOTHAM CITY earthquake partially destroyed ARKHAM ASYLUM, and the inmates ran amok. During the several days of chaos, the maniacal Waxman dared to challenge the JOKER for the right to lead the criminals. The Clown Prince killed the challenger. (*Batman: Shadow of the Bat* #80, December 1998)

WAYNE, BRUCE

Bruce Wayne was born to THOMAS and MARTHA WAYNE in GOTHAM CITY, where the WAYNE FAMILY had deep ties and were among its leading citizens. His father, a physician, was always in and out of WAYNE MANOR, while his mother was active with social work.

The three were a loving family until the warm early-summer night when everything changed.

After attending a movie, the Waynes were walking through an alley when they were accosted by a thief who demanded their money and jewelry. Thomas stepped between the thief and his wife and was shot for his effort. The shock was too much for Martha, who died from a heart attack. Eight-year-old Bruce was left to stand over their corpses as the thief fled into the shadows.

Life as the boy knew it stopped at that point. He made a vow over his parents' graves that he would wage war on criminals the remainder of

his days. He devoted himself to training his body and mind, and after many years he felt he was ready—but he needed an edge, something to strike fear into the superstitious and cowardly hearts of criminals. When a bat flew through the Wayne Manor window, he took it as an omen. Soon he had designed a crime-fighting costume and emerged on the city rooftops as Batman. (first appearance: *Detective Comics* #27, May 1939; origin revealed: *Detective Comics* #33, November 1933) Note: The detail about Martha's "weak heart" was added in *Batman* #47 (June/July 1948) and was retained in every retelling thereafter, until *Batman* #232 (June 1971) restored it to the original version.

In one alternative reality, prior to Bruce's birth Martha bore a son named Thomas Jr. After suffering injuries during a car accident, the boy was mentally impaired and confined to Willowood Asylum. As an adult, Batman discovered that his brother had been forced to become the Boomerang Killer and came to his aid, along with SUPERMAN and DEADMAN. As a reward, the ghost was granted permission to inhabit Thomas's body. (*World's Finest Comics* #223, May/June 1964)

On Earth-1 the circumstances were largely the same. Bruce was taken in by his uncle Philip but was largely raised by the family housekeeper Mrs. Chilton, secretly the mother of JOE CHILL, the man who pulled the trigger that fateful night. (*Batman* #208, January/February 1969)

On the world after CRISIS ON INFINITE EARTHS, additional details of Bruce's early years were revealed. The Waynes were socially active and spent time with other wealthy families throughout Gotham. One such family was the Sionises, with Bruce forced to play with their son ROMAN SIONIS, who seemed to dislike him. (*Batman* #386, August

1985) They summered away from Gotham, and when Bruce was seven he made friends with MALLORY MOXON, daughter of gangster-turned-politician LEW MOXON. (*Batman* #591, July 2001) At some point Bruce also was friendly with the younger daughter of their neighbor John Zatara, ZATANNA. (*Detective Comics* #833, August 2007) His closest friend during those early years was Tommy Elliot, with the two boys considered inseparable until Tommy's attempts to kill his parents failed and he blamed Thomas Wayne for saving his mother's life. (*Batman* #609, January 2003)

The Waynes turned to the family butler, ALFRED PENNYWORTH, son of longtime Wayne butler Jarvis Pennyworth, to help watch the youth. Martha and Thomas differed over his upbringing with Alfred playing the silent intermediary, looking after the boy's best interests. (*Batman* #0, October 1994; *The*

Batman Chronicles #5, Summer 1996) Thomas did spend time with Bruce and was there when needed, including the day six-year-old Bruce fell through rotten wooden boards into the cavern underneath the manor, the resident bats frightening the youth. (*The Dark Knight Returns* #1, 1986)

What happened on the night his parents died has varied in the accounts, a result of reality-altering waves from cosmic events known as Zero Hour and INFINITE CRISIS. One such version had young Bruce involved in artwork, an interest he picked up from his mother to Thomas's dismay. Bruce was summoned away from a sculpture for a night at the movies, and after his parents died he gave up all interest in artwork. (*Batman Annual* #9, 1985) A different account had Martha reading *Alice's Adventures in Wonderland* to Bruce just prior to the family leaving for the movies. (*Batman: Madness,* 1994)

One more version saw Bruce sent away to a boarding school upstate from Gotham. Bruce was a typical rich man's son at the school, something that seemed to infuriate the headmaster, Winchester, who beat the boy. When Thomas learned of this event, he headed to the school, and an hour later Bruce was en route back to Wayne Manor. To acknowledge his return to the family, it was suggested that the family go to the movies. (*Legends of the Dark Knight* #10, August 1990) In one such account Bruce asked his mother to wear her pearls, an anniversary gift from Thomas. (*Batman: Madness,* 1994)

What remained constant was that the family attended a screening of the 1920s silent classic *The Mark of Zorro,* and on their way home, through PARK ROW, a gunman tried to rob them. In most accounts, the thief was Joe Chill (*Batman* #47, June/July 1948), although one version saw Chill sent with the intent to kill Thomas Wayne on behalf of mobster Lew Moxon. (*Detective Comics* #235, September 1956) For a time it was asserted that the killer of Bruce Wayne's parents was unknown (*Batman* #0, October 1994), but evidence eventually emerged suggesting that Lew Moxon had ordered the killings. (*Batman* #595, November 2001) In any event, Joe Chill is once again officially regarded as the murderer of the Waynes. (*Infinite Crisis* #7, June 2006)

Bruce survived the brutal slayings at 10:47 PM, something he memorialized by using this moment as a key unlocking the grandfather clock doorway to the steps leading below the Wayne Manor to the BATCAVE. (*Legends of the Dark Knight* #16, March 1991) In one account he was racked with guilt because the thief had been after the very pearls he'd asked his mother to wear.

His childhood ended that night. He was found and cared for by Dr. LESLIE THOMPKINS, one of the many friends Thomas had made through the years. She and Alfred conspired to raise Wayne without interference, and Bruce helped by obfuscating the paperwork from the state until his case fell through the cracks and he was left alone. (*Batman* #0, October 1994)

WAYNE, BRUCE N.

Bruce N. Wayne was a cousin of THOMAS WAYNE on Earth-2, living on the West Coast. He was, coincidentally, a private investigator, and Thomas's son—a first cousin once removed—was named for him. It was years before the two Bruces met, occasioned by the detective pursuing a criminal named Varrell east. The elder Wayne at first thought Bruce a useless playboy, but his keen skills eventually allowed him to pierce the secret that Bruce and DICK GRAYSON were also Batman and ROBIN. Rather than confide in his cousin, Batman created a ruse to convince the detective that he was wrong. The Gotham Guardian apprehended Varrell and let his cousin bring the felon west to answer for his crimes. (*Batman* #112, October 1957)

WAYNE, HELENA

On Earth-2, Helena was the daughter of BRUCE WAYNE and SELINA KYLE and grew up to join the family business as the HUNTRESS.

WAYNE, MARTHA

Martha Kane Wayne was born into the wealthy Kane family, which had made its fortune through Kane Chemical. They lived in the Bristol section of GOTHAM CITY, where she met neighbor THOMAS WAYNE. Early on, after her introduction to society, Martha developed a reputation as a party girl who knew how to have a good time. She also had developed an interest in philanthropic work, notably orphanages. At one such facility she met CELIA KAZANTZAKIS, and the two attractive young women became fast friends despite their differing social ranks. Both attended parties, and at one, Martha met a gangster named Denholm Sinclair, whom she dated, To her it was a lark, and things ended after she grew interested in Wayne. Kane did not realize that Kazantzakis knew Denholm and had tried to keep Martha away from the man when she recognized him as a criminal—a fact that

Celia knew since she, too, was a thief, embezzling funds from the orphanage. (*Batman Family* #1-8, December 2002-February 2003)

Martha and Thomas socialized at all the seasonal events and over time their attraction grew. When they began a serious relationship, the social doyennes deemed it a good match between families. The two had a loving relationship and married, with Martha moving into WAYNE MANOR. She met Jarvis Pennyworth—who was soon replaced by his son ALFRED PENNYWORTH as the family retainer. Some time after the wedding, she gave birth to their only son, BRUCE WAYNE. (*Detective Comics* #33, November 1939)

In one alternative reality, prior to Bruce's birth Martha bore a son named Thomas Jr. After suffering injuries during a car accident, the boy was mentally impaired and confined to Willowood Asylum. As an adult, Batman discovered that his brother had been forced to become the Boomerang Killer and came to his aid, along with SUPERMAN and DEADMAN. As a reward, the ghost was granted permission to inhabit Thomas's body. (*World's Finest Comics* #223, May/June 1964)

Given her charitable work, Martha relied heavily on Alfred to help her look after the growing Bruce. She and Thomas differed over his upbringing with Alfred playing the silent intermediary, looking after the boy's best interests.

Things changed shortly after the boy turned eight. Accounts differed over what transpired that night, affected by the various revisions to reality through CRISIS ON INFINITE EARTHS and INFINITE CRISIS.

One such version had young Bruce involved in artwork, an interest he picked up from his mother to Thomas's dismay. Bruce was summoned away from a sculpture for a night at the movies, and after his parents died he gave up all interest in artwork. (*Batman Annual* #9, 1985) A different account had Martha reading *Alice's Adventures in Wonderland* to Bruce just prior to the family leaving for the movies. (*Batman: Madness*, 1994)

One more version saw Bruce sent away to a boarding school upstate from Gotham. Bruce was a typical rich man's son at the school, something that seemed to infuriate the headmaster, Winchester, who beat the boy. When Thomas learned of this event, he

headed to the school, and an hour later Bruce was en route back to Wayne Manor. To acknowledge his return to the family, it was suggested that the family go to the movies. (*Legends of the Dark Knight* #10, August 1990) In one such account Bruce asked his mother to wear her pearls, an anniversary gift from Thomas. (*Batman: Madness*, 1994)

What remained constant was that the family attended a screening of the 1920s silent classic *Mark of Zorro,* and on their way home, through PARK ROW, a gunman tried to rob them. In most accounts, the thief was JOE CHILL (*Batman* #47, June/July 1948), although one version saw Chill sent with the intent to kill Thomas Wayne on behalf of mobster LEW MOXON. Martha may have been shot by Chill, or the shock of seeing her husband gunned down may have triggered a fatal heart attack.

One variation on this history had *Martha* the intended victim given her work as a sociologist who had discovered a global pedophile operation. Chill was hired to silence her before he, too, was shot to death. (*Batman: The Ultimate Evil* #1-2, 1995–1996)

Bruce survived the brutal slayings, noting the time to be 10:47 PM. In one account he was racked with guilt because the thief had been after the very pearls he'd asked his mother to wear.

His childhood ended that night. He was found and cared for by Dr. LESLIE THOMPKINS, one of the many friends Thomas had made through the years. Thomas and Martha Wayne were buried at Crown Hill Cemetery, although their corpses were once stolen by RĀ'S AL GHŪL in an attempt to force Batman to do his bidding. (*JLA* #44, August 2000)

Later the Martha Wayne Foundation was formed, an offshoot of the WAYNE FOUNDATION that focused on the arts and education. Orphanages, schools, and professionals with learning disabilities all benefited from the foundation, which also sponsored Family Finders, Inc., a nonprofit organization.

Note: The records have yet to establish if Martha Kane was in any way related to BETTE KANE (FLAMEBIRD) or the wealthy KATE KANE (BATWOMAN).

WAYNE, THOMAS

The WAYNE FAMILY was well established in GOTHAM CITY, their fortune built upon shipping and industry. Each succeeding generation of Waynes was

YES, ROBIN -- THE MAN WEARING THAT OLD-FASHIONED BATMAN COSTUME WAS MY FATHER!

expected to at least participate in the family to some degree. When Thomas was born to Patrick Wayne, he would prove different.

Thomas's inclinations ran more toward the philanthropic and he went into medicine, becoming a general practitioner and surgeon. His family did not approve but allowed him to pursue his dream. Thomas did use the family wealth and resources to devote his time and efforts to humanitarian aid around the world. Among the many island nations he visited was the corrupt Santa Prisca. (*Detective Comics* #33, November 1939)

When he met Bristol neighbor Martha Kane, the two fell into a comfortable relationship that rapidly blossomed into love. They married and she moved into Wayne Manor, beginning a new chapter of her life. She met Jarvis Pennyworth—who was soon replaced by his son Alfred Pennyworth as the family retainer. Some time after they married, she gives birth to a son, Bruce Wayne.

In one alternative reality, prior to Bruce's birth Martha bore a son named Thomas Jr. After suffering injuries during a car accident, the boy was mentally impaired and confined to Willowood Asylum. As an adult, Batman discovered that his brother had been forced to become the Boomerang Killer and came to his aid, along with Superman and Deadman. As a reward, the ghost was granted permission to inhabit Thomas's body. (*World's Finest Comics* #223, May/June 1964)

Thomas Wayne was popular in Gotham, noted for his way with patients and his total commitment to the Hippocratic oath. On Earth-2, Lew Moxon was a Gotham crime boss who attempted to rob a costume party attended by Wayne. Dressed in a costume eerily similar to the Batman uniform, Wayne stopped Moxon and his men from committing the crime and later testified against them. Upon his release, Moxon hired a thug named Joe Chill to kill Wayne. (*Detective Comics* #235, September 1956)

On a parallel world prior to Crisis on Infinite Earths, Kal-El, the sole survivor from the planet Krypton, was found and raised by Thomas and Martha Wayne. When Moxon ordered Chill to kill the Waynes, his bullet bounced off the child and struck Chill. As he lay dying, Chill implicated Moxon. (*Superman* #353, November 1980)

In the reality after Crisis on Infinite Earths, Lew Moxon was described as a prototypical old-time gangster and mob boss in the days before Carmine "the Roman" Falcone ruled the Gotham underworld. Moxon owned politicians, elected officials, judges, and policemen, running his illegitimate businesses without interruption. When his nephew was shot during a bungled robbery, Moxon and his men invaded a costume party and insisted that Thomas Wayne, dressed as Zorro, attend to the wound. Wayne subsequently reported the incident to the police, despite Moxon threatening him to force his silence.

Thomas and Bruce had a loving relationship although Thomas was somewhat stern with the boy and did not always agree with Martha's indulgences with fiction and the arts. Still, he was there when needed, such as the time Bruce fell through some rotted wood into a catacomb that was part of a cavern system beneath the manor. And Thomas saw to it that the family enjoyed outings, including many with other families, notably the Elliots and Sionises. Bruce also grew up with many memories of the times his father had abruptly left the family for medical emergencies.

Things changed shortly after the boy turned eight. Accounts differed over what transpired that night, affected by the various revisions to reality through Crisis on Infinite Earths and Infinite Crisis.

One such version had young Bruce involved in artwork, an interest he picked up from his mother to Thomas's dismay. Bruce was summoned away from a sculpture for a night at the movies, and after his parents died he gave up all interest in artwork. (*Batman Annual* #9, 1985) A different account had Martha reading *Alice's Adventures in Wonderland* to Bruce just prior to the family leaving for the movies. (*Batman: Madness,* 1994)

One more version saw Bruce sent away to a boarding school upstate from Gotham. Bruce was a typical rich man's son at the school, something that seemed to infuriate the headmaster, Winchester, who beat the boy. When Thomas learned of this event, he headed to the school, and an hour later Bruce was en route back to Wayne Manor. To acknowledge his return to the family, it was suggested that the family go to the movies. (*Legends of the Dark Knight* #10, August 1990) In one such account Bruce asked his mother to wear her pearls, an anniversary gift from Thomas.

LEAVE HER ALONE YOU OH...
YOU ASKED FOR IT!

THOMAS! YOU'VE KILLED HIM.. HELP! POLICE.. HELP!
THIS'LL SHUT YOU UP!

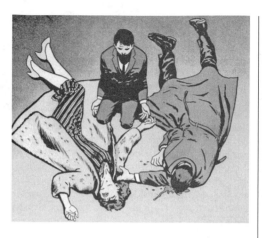

What remained constant was that the family attended a screening of the 1920s silent classic *The Mark of Zorro,* and on their way home, through Park Row, a gunman tried to rob them. In most accounts, the thief was Joe Chill (*Batman* #47, June/July 1948), although one version saw Chill sent with the intent to kill Thomas Wayne on behalf of mobster Lew Moxon. Martha may have been shot by Chill, or the shock of seeing her husband gunned down may have triggered a fatal heart attack.

Bruce survived the brutal slayings, noting the time to be 10:47 PM, and his childhood ended that night. He was found and cared for by Dr. Leslie Thompkins, one of the many friends Thomas had made through the years. Thomas and Martha Wayne were buried at Crown Hill Cemetery, although Rā's al Ghūl once stole their corpses in an attempt to force Batman to do his bidding. (*JLA* #44, August 2000)

The Thomas Wayne Foundation, an offshoot of the Wayne Foundation, focused on medicine and presented annual awards recognizing both lifetime achievement and breakthroughs. It is chiefly known for operating the Thomas Wayne Memorial Clinic in Crime Alley, where Thomas and Martha were slain. Among the other clinics it funded was the one used by Dr. Thompkins.

WAYNE ENTERPRISES

The company owned and controlled by Bruce Wayne has constantly evolved through the years since its founding in America's early days. The original Wayne Enterprises began as a small merchant house in Gotham City, beginning to grow when Judge Solomon Wayne's heirs founded Wayne Shipping and Wayne Chemical. Soon after followed Wayne Manufacturing, which took advantage of the Industrial Revolution and the period of Reconstruction to become a powerhouse. Patrick and Laura Wayne were the first to direct the company toward ecological responsibility, a commitment that grew with time. It evolved in response to a changing world and with the differing objectives of whichever Wayne was in charge. Under Bruce Wayne, the firm expanded to become a global powerhouse in a wide variety of fields. Such diversification was good for the company, of course, but it also allowed Wayne to plunder its resources to fuel his career as Batman.

After losing out to LexCorp on a government contract and watching technology be abused

by both Lex Luthor and the military, Wayne announced to his staff that Wayne Enterprises and its subsidiaries were withdrawing from the defense sector. (*Batman Confidential* #6, August 2007)

While he maintained a position on the board of directors and had controlling financial interest, Wayne turned to Lucius Fox, a longtime employee and trusted friend, to run the company as chief executive officer. Under Fox, Wayne Enterprises, also known to many as WayneCo (Wayne Corporation), enjoyed spectacular growth. In one quarter alone it showed a thirty-billion-dollar increase in revenues. (*Detective Comics* #682, February 1995)

Among its documented holdings are:

- Wayne Aerospace, which was one of the earliest firms that caught Bruce Wayne's attention and introduced him to Lucius Fox. This firm's line of experimental jets for commercial and private use was expanded to include military contracts, which brought Wayne into competition with Lex Luthor for the first time. One prototype went on to become the first Batplane. Its chief competitors included Ferris Aircraft and

LexAir. The division also maintained facilities and vehicles at Archie Goodwin International Airport in the Little Stockton section of greater Gotham.
- Wayne Biotech was a research and development company that explored new medicines and medical procedures. It enjoyed synergies with both Wayne Chemicals and Wayne Pharmaceuticals in its efforts to provide cost-effective world-class health care.
- Wayne Chemicals was the parent division to Wayne Fuel Corporation, Wayne Oil, Wayne Pharmaceuticals, and Wayne Botanical. One of its chief charges was research into alternative fuel resources in addition to better oil exploration and refining. Wayne Oil acquired Luxor Oil, located in the South Darby section of the city. Wayne Chemicals also had invested in Tyler Chemicals, run by fellow hero Rex "Tick Tock" Tyler, the Hourman. (Before he bought this firm—back when it was known as Bannerman Chemical—Tyler was an employee. Through his work he developed Miraclo, which was later subverted into the basic building blocks for the drug Venom.)
- Wayne Electronics built all manner of consumer electronics, from radios to stereo components, digital cameras to high-tech surveillance. When Wayne acquired Kordtronics, it was folded into this division.
- Wayne Entertainment owned and operated numerous venues across America, including facilities in Gotham and Metropolis. The division had interests in all manner of consumer media, from cable television to book publishing to model agencies. Wayne went so far as to buy the *Daily Planet,* ensuring its freedom and stability.
- Wayne Foods managed ranches across the American Midwest while investigating new food sources and agricultural methods.
- Wayne Industries was Wayne Enterprises' main research and development division. It studied and improved on basic industrial manufacturing methods. It also controlled several power-generating utilities around America. A division, Wayne Mining, was in Africa, safely extracting minerals and gemstones. Much of Batman's energy production was drawn from these resources.
- Wayne Institute was a think tank for people looking ahead to solve the next generation of problems confronting humankind.
- Wayne Medical ran hospitals and clinics in addition to working with the Wayne Foundation to provide grants, research, and materials to other facilities, mainly in Gotham.
- Wayne Research Institute was a catchall R&D operation used by Bruce Wayne to study issues and technologies that he thought might be helpful in his fight against crime.
- Wayne Shipping handled most of the company's global transportation systems, from ocean carriers to ground vehicles.
- Wayne Steel was one of the company's oldest divisions, providing raw materials for construction in Gotham and surrounding

cities. Its research into various alloys and its reverse engineering of alien substances greatly enhanced Batman's crime-fighting capabilities.

- Wayne Shipbuilding provided customized vessels for its sister division to use and also allowed Batman state-of-the-art seaworthy vehicles.

- WayneYards manufactured heavy-duty larger vessels from naval warships to submarines. This division enjoys numerous military contracts and is a major player in the global maritime industry.

- Wayne Technologies, nicknamed WayneTech, did all the research and development work on cutting-edge technologies from artificial intelligence to satellite technology. Alien objects that wound up on Earth frequently found their way to WayneTech for study and exploitation. When Wayne bought Michael Holt's Holt Holdings, Inc., it was folded into WayneTech; this division also managed the Wayne Biotech, Wayne Pharmaceuticals, Wayne Healthcare, and WayneTech Landscaping divisions. WayneTech made embarrassing headlines when it was revealed that the division conducted covert espionage early in Batman's career.

WAYNE FAMILY, THE

The Wayne Family can trace its roots as far back as the Crusades, when Harold, lord of Waynemoor Castle in northern England, died. (*Detective Comics* #412, June 1971)

Through the ever-shifting fabric of reality, the family has seen various histories. In one version Harold's brother Lorin murdered his sibling and took over the estate and title. It wasn't until modern times, when BRUCE WAYNE journeyed to visit his dying great-uncle Lord Elwood Wayne, that the truth about mad Harold was learned. Elwood was brother to THOMAS WAYNE's father, Patrick. While visiting, Bruce met Elwood's niece Wilhemina, a half-Dutch orphan from South Africa; cousin of the Reverend Emelyn Wayne, missionary among the Asian "heathen"; and Jeremy Wayne, an Australian ranch hand. (*Detective Comics* #412, June 1971)

Within the current Batman reality, the Wayne dynasty can also be traced to the Crusades. Sir Gaweyne de Weyne was a Frenchman. As a knight of the Scottish court, he gave his life on a crusade to free the Holy Land. According to his wishes, when he fell in battle, Sir Gaweyne's heart was embalmed and returned to Scotland. For six hundred years it reposed in Dunvegan Castle, awaiting the rediscovery of his grave. The burial place was finally discovered, and—in a service conducted by the Reverend James Black and attended by Bruce Wayne—the knight's heart was at last placed within his tomb. (*Batman: The Scottish Connection*, 1998) It was also learned that there was even more to the legend of Bruce Wayne's ancestors: A knight had been entrusted with the defense of the Holy Grail in times past. On his tunic was the crest of a bat. (*Batman: The Chalice*, 2000)

Lancelot Wayne wanted to fly like a bat and, toward that end, constructed a pair of black wings to help him soar through the sky. Centuries later Bruce Wayne duplicated the flight of this first batman as part of a publicity campaign for the GOTHAM CITY Historical Society. (*Detective Comics* #306, August 1962) Lancelot's creation reminded Bruce of Leonardo da Vinci's own designs for a bat-winged glider, and he couldn't help but be amused that he and ROBIN had actually *met* the legendary Italian scientist during a time-travel expedition to 1499. Batman had even helped adapt Leonardo's concepts into a functional aircraft. (*Batman* #46, April/May 1947)

The hypnotic time-travel technique developed by PROFESSOR CARTER NICHOLS also enabled Bruce Wayne to meet one of his other forebears. Bruce knew or surmised that it was more a family story that an ancestor was a highwayman. Noting that this Silas Wayne was never hanged, Bruce surmised that there was more to the tale, so he and DICK GRAYSON embarked on a journey to 1787 Philadelphia. (*Batman* #44, December 1946/January 1947)

Twenty-year-old Pennsylvania native Anthony Wayne determined the course of the rest of his life when he joined the American colonies' war for independence in 1775. Within two years he was a brigadier general and a part of George Washington's own army. In 1779 he led one of the most audacious attacks of the Revolution when he helped recapture a British outpost in Stony Point, New Jersey. "Mad Anthony" retired in 1783, dabbled in politics, and finally returned to the military in 1791. This second tour of duty included raids against Indians in 1794 until he died two years later at the age of fifty-one. Thanks to a time-travel trip courtesy of SUPERMAN, Batman and ROBIN learned that Mad Anthony Wayne was a blood ancestor. (*World's Finest Comics* #186–187, August–September 1969)

In a book on the movers and shakers who founded Gotham, author Cecil Longacre later reported the long-held myth "that Gotham's current sanitarium, ARKHAM ASYLUM, was built upon the same field Hiram, an eighteenth century mulatto who may have helped found Gotham, once cleared to honor his faith." (*The Batman Chronicles* #6, Fall 1996; *Batman Secret Files* #1, October 1997) Official records in the Gotham Public Library debunked this story, however, confirming that Rance Benedict had in fact been killed on the land that would be known as ROBINSON PARK, a considerable distance from Arkham. (*The Batman Chronicles* #23, Winter 2001)

Charles Arwin Wayne managed the Wayne Family's modest fortune by buying cheap property, including swampland, and wisely holding on to it as Gotham grew. As a result, upon his death from tuberculosis at age fifty-two, he left a considerable sum to his sons Solomon Zebediah Wayne and Joshua Thomas Wayne. On July 4, 1858, the siblings viewed a ten-bedroom mansion built by magnate Jerome K. van Derm in 1855. When van Derm's business failed, he took his life before he could take up residence in the mansion. (*Batman: Shadow of the Bat* #45, December 1995; *Batman Secret Files* #1, October 1997)

Solomon had hurried back to Gotham from Boston, having obtained his degree at Harvard. He prevailed upon Senator Nugent Bolle to grant him a federal judgeship. Once on the bench, he attempted to help clean Gotham of its villainy and corruption while at the same time starting a dozen businesses, including the famous Gotham Buggy Whip Works. Within six years he was Gotham's leading citizen, and its most prosperous. Shortly before his marriage Solomon had met an eccentric architect named Cyrus Pinkney and vowed to make his building designs a part of the Gotham City landscape.

By selling off properties and borrowing money, Judge Wayne was eventually able to bankroll more than a dozen Gothic structures. The opinion of critics notwithstanding, the Pinkney-designed skyscrapers attracted others to locate their ventures nearby. (*Legends of the Dark Knight* #27, February 1992)

Solomon did not restrict his passion for justice to the courtroom. Even as he made plans to purchase WAYNE MANOR, he and brother Joshua were contemplating ways that the tunnels and cave beneath the mansion could be employed for humanitarian purposes. As part of the Underground Railroad, they could use the secret passages in "smuggling slaves from the South up the East Coast to safety in Canada." The first slave to be rescued by the Waynes gave Joshua a luck token from his home in Africa.

The Wayne brothers' heroic efforts took a tragic turn after midnight on November 4, 1860. A slave named Sam Barley had backed out of his plans to proceed with his escape, and Joshua vowed to bring him back before bounty hunters killed the fugitive. Clad in dark clothing, with a cape, a hat, and a kerchief pulled around his nose and mouth, Joshua fought the men intent on recapturing Sam and returned him to the others in the cave beneath Wayne Manor.

Outside the manor, the Waynes discovered vengeful bounty hunters seeking the Underground Railroad outpost that they were certain was nearby. Over Solomon's objections, Joshua pulled his kerchief over his nose and prepared to divert their attention.

In the wee hours of November 4, he took a knife in the chest as he led the hunters across a rickety bridge. Though he successfully severed the bridge and sent the men to their deaths in the river below, Joshua had been mortally wounded. His remains would not be discovered until the time of Bruce Wayne, who had him properly buried. Solomon, of course, knew none of this and went to his grave without learning the truth behind his sibling's disappearance. (*Batman: Shadow of the Bat* #45, December 1995)

The later years of the judge's life included a role in his family's long guardianship of the Holy Grail. (*Batman: The Chalice*, 2000) The fate of his first wife, pregnant at the time of Joshua's death (*Batman: Shadow of the Bat* #45, December 1995), remained unknown but Solomon was said to have remarried to a woman named Dorothea in his later years. When the judge was seventy-seven and his wife thirty-seven, she bore him a son, Alan. (*Batman Secret Files* #1, October 1997) Solomon Wayne proved to be made of hardy stock, surviving to the age of 104. (*Legends of the Dark Knight* #27, February 1992)

Alan Wayne followed his father's lead by spearheading the development and growth of the Gotham Railroads, the vast network of rail lines intersecting at Gotham's Robinson Central Terminal, as well as growing WAYNE ENTERPRISES, then the family's umbrella company. Soon after Alan's death at the age of sixty-three, his son Kenneth contributed Wayne Chemicals to the growing corporation. Kenneth's early death left his thirty-seven-year-old widow Laura Elizabeth to sustain the family fortune. Laura was a staunch proponent of banning alcoholic beverages in Gotham. (*Batman Secret Files* #1, October 1997)

Alan and Laura's son, Patrick Morgan, who'd been only an infant when his father died, saw the Wayne legacy through two world wars, building WayneCorp out of the ashes of the Great Depression and later developing WayneTech, whose aircraft plants in Somerset and shipworks in Neville fueled American efforts to thwart the combined might of the Axis and Imperial Japan. (*Batman Secret Files* #1, October 1997) Nothing is known of relatives Abigail and Benjamin, although they were contemporaries and all buried together at the Wayne cemetery. (*Batman: Shadow of the Bat* #45, December 1995) The Gotham Botanical Gardens were said to have been established in 1870 courtesy of a grant by C. L. Wayne. (*Batman* #568, August 1999)

In the most recent accounts, Patrick and his wife had only one child, a boy named Thomas. (*Batman Secret Files* #1, October 1997) He grew to manhood, becoming a successful doctor and philanthropist. He married MARTHA KANE and they had one son, Bruce. They were among the pillars of Gotham society until their brutal murder on June 26 in PARK ROW, later known as CRIME ALLEY. On Earth-1, the orphaned Bruce was left in the guardianship of Thomas's older brother Philip. (*Batman* #208, January/February 1969)

From an outsider's perspective, the Wayne Family's history was problematic. Patrick Wayne has been variously identified as Gotham surgeon and successful stockbroker Anthony Thomas Wayne (*Aztek: The Ultimate Man* #3, October 1996), and as Jack Wayne, who financed the construction of Wayne Manor in the 1930s. (*Legends of the Dark Knight* #133–134, September–October 2000) Depending upon which version of reality is examined, other Waynes play a role in history. The heirs of Silas and Anthony Wayne include Winslow Wayne, General Herkimer Wayne (both in *Batman* #44, December 1947/January 1948), wagon train leader Caleb Wayne, and whaler Captain Ishmael Wayne. (both in *Batman* #120, December 1958)

Silas in one version of reality was distressed that his great-nephew Bruce was nothing but a rich idler. When a criminal case involved them both, it was privately confided to the dying Silas that Wayne was actually Batman, fulfilling the family legacy. (*Batman* #120, December 1958)

Other relatives, no longer a part of the New Earth in the wake of INFINITE CRISIS, included Bruce's cousin Jane and her infant son, Junior, whom Batman and Robin had to care for one weekend. (*Batman* #93, August 1955) A younger cousin, Vanderveer, also made a poor impression during his weeklong stay

at the mansion. (*Batman* #148, June 1962) BRUCE N. WAYNE, a detective based on the West Coast, was a cousin of Thomas Wayne and the namesake of the younger Bruce. (*Batman* #111, October 1957)

A Wayne Family crypt remains on the grounds of Wayne Manor, a tribute to one of Gotham's most noteworthy families.

WAYNE FOUNDATION, THE

On Earth-1, the ALFRED MEMORIAL FOUNDATION was renamed as the Wayne Foundation when BRUCE WAYNE's loyal butler ALFRED PENNYWORTH returned from the dead. It was a philanthropic operation that concentrated its efforts in and around GOTHAM CITY but also provided resources elsewhere in America. (*Detective Comics* #356, October 1966)

On the Earth formed after INFINITE CRISIS, the foundation had different origins. After losing out to LexCorp on a government contract and watching technology be abused by both LEX LUTHOR and the military, Bruce Wayne announced to his staff that WAYNE ENTERPRISES and its subsidiaries were withdrawing from the defense sector. He subsequently created the Wayne Foundation, a charitable organization devoted to the care and betterment of orphans and disadvantaged youngsters. Senator Harold Crabtree was named its first administrator. (*Batman Confidential* #6, August 2007)

The foundation was also the holding company that oversaw both the THOMAS WAYNE Foundation and the MARTHA WAYNE Foundation. The former concerned itself with medicine and presented annual awards recognizing both lifetime achievement and breakthroughs. It is chiefly known for operating the Thomas Wayne Memorial Clinic in CRIME ALLEY, where the doctor was slain. Among the other clinics it funded was the one used by Dr. LESLIE THOMPKINS, Thomas's fellow doctor and friend. The Martha Wayne Foundation concerned itself with the arts and education. Orphanages, schools, and professionals with learning disabilities all benefited from the foundation, which also sponsored the

WAYNE FOUNDATION

Family Finders, Inc., nonprofit organization. While her husband's foundation ran clinics, the Martha Wayne Foundation sponsored soup kitchens, both serving their beloved city's most needy citizens.

The Wayne Foundation Building, in the center of Gotham, was an architectural masterpiece, complete with a vast atrium in its center. After DICK GRAYSON moved out of WAYNE MANOR, Bruce Wayne temporarily relocated to a penthouse apartment atop the building and outfitted a sub-basement into a small-scale BATCAVE. (*Batman* #217, December 1969) Later, he let KATANA and HALO use the apartment when the OUTSIDERS were first formed. (*Batman and the Outsiders* #3, October 1983)

WAYNE MANOR

Located in what was sometimes called the Crest Hill community in Bristol Township, the Wayne Manor was twelve miles from GOTHAM CITY. Just beyond Gotham, a lonely road skirted hills honeycombed with caverns and tunnels. Some called this place the Catacombs. Others called it a filthy nest of bats. As a boy, before his parents' murder, BRUCE WAYNE played in these hills and explored these caves.

Wayne Manor was constructed by magnate Jerome K. van Derm in 1855. When van Derm's business failed, he took his life before he could take up residence in the ten-bedroom mansion, which

was purchased by Solomon Zebediah Wayne and Joshua Thomas Wayne in 1858. The Wayne siblings learned of the tunnels and cave beneath the mansion and intended to exploit them for humanitarian purposes. As part of the Underground Railroad, they used the secret passages to smuggle slaves from the South up the East Coast to safety in Canada.

In subsequent years generation after generation of the WAYNE FAMILY lived in the manor, keeping it a glittering jewel in Gotham high society. It lasted until the earthquake brought it tumbling down in ruins. Bruce Wayne chose to rebuild it from scratch, deriving inspiration from the Gothic edifices designed by Cyrus Pinkney, Gotham's original architect. The new manor looked more like a European castle, with battlements and turrets. In keeping with his interests, it was designed to be as ecofriendly as possible, powered with solar panels and other devices. It also was carefully wired with a sophisticated security system to protect not only billionaire Bruce Wayne but also his Dark Knight alter ego.

The new structure still maintained the traditional grandfather clock that, by setting the hands to 10:47, the time of his parents' deaths, allowed Wayne access to the Batcave.

WEBB, BOLEY

Boley Webb convinced people he was a reformed criminal and engaged in a wager with Judson Field, considered America's dean of detectives, that Field could turn the next man they encountered into a first-rate detective. Field accepted the fifty-thousand-dollar bet, and the next man turned out to be Bruce Wayne. As Field trained Wayne, the World's Greatest Detective had to hide his consummate skills without costing the man the prize money. Meantime, Webb tried to sabotage the training so he could win the bet. Wayne aced the final test, letting Field win and thwarting Webb's scheme. (*World's Finest Comics* #64, May/June 1953)

WEBB, COLONEL

Colonel Webb invented the "vacuum blanket"—a device that Batman adopted when he upgraded the Batplane on Earth-2. This blanket was an energy-dampening field that caused nearby aircraft to lose power, forcing them down and making the occupants easier to apprehend. (*Batman* #61, October/November 1950)

WEBB, CONNIE

Connie Webb was one of the most prominent knights in the early days of Checkmate. She rose to the role of White Queen, opposite David Said's Black King, as the operation grew in scope. (*Checkmate!* #12, February 1989)

WEIR

Weir was an inventor who designed a robotic policeman. This proved so successful, people thought Batman and Robin would be displaced in Gotham City. Instead, it was learned the robot was disabled by exposure to X-rays, something criminals would be able to exploit. (*Batman* #70, April/May 1952)

WELKEN, "WIRES"

After arresting "Wires" Welken for burglarizing banks by short-circuiting the rooftop alarms, Batman took a roll of insulated wire from Welken's pocket and added it to the trophy room inside the Batcave. Later the spool was included in an exhibit that was touring the United States by train as part of a national Anti-Crime Week. What the Caped Crusader did not know was that the spool was actually an imaginative wire recorder that contained the names of Welken's three accomplices. As the train traveled, the three desperate men vainly attempted to rob the train and obtain the spool. Eventually the Dynamic Duo figured out the spool's significance and apprehended the men. (*Batman* #95, October 1955)

WESKER, ARNOLD

The timid son of a Gotham City crime family, Arnold Wesker developed multiple personality disorder and became known as criminal gang lord the Ventriloquist.

WEST, PORTER

Several of Gotham City's wealthiest men, including Bruce Wayne and Porter West, were abducted and taken to a remote island. Their unseen captor attempted to torture the men in the hope of learning the secrets behind their wealth—secrets he could use for his own gain. Instead Batman and Robin stopped the terrorism and revealed the criminal to be West himself. (*Batman* #62, December 1950/January 1951)

WESTON, BURT

The criminal who used his fascination with cinema to commit crimes in Gotham City as the Film Freak.

WEVER, BURT

Burt Wever was a Gotham City newscaster who also ran a criminal enterprise. He began a campaign to discredit Batman and thus ruin his effectiveness as a crime fighter. Over a period of time, Wever began to associate the Caped Crusader with a series of unsolved crimes; the only man who knew the truth, Police Commissioner James Gordon was lost on an African safari. Gotham's police force, though, chose not to believe the insinuations and went on to clear the Dark Knight's name. Wever was exposed and arrested. (*Detective Comics* #240, February 1957)

WEXLY, THOMAS

Hotel-manager-turned-criminal Thomas Wexley was a smuggler operating out of the Jolly Roger hotel.

WHIRLY BAT

The Whirly Bat was a one-person flying vehicle that Batman used on Earth-1. This mini copter was made of lightweight alloys and controlled by a simple control box. Its flight specifications were never recorded. (*Detective Comics* #257, July 1958)

WHITE, WARREN

This white-collar criminal entered Arkham Asylum thinking it would beat time in prison. While incarnated, he slipped over the edge of sanity and became the criminal Great White Shark.

WHITE WOLVES, THE

The White Wolves were a Russian street gang operating for a brief time in Gotham City but were taken down by Batman, Robin, and the Huntress. (*Robin III: Cry of the Huntress* #1, December 1992)

WILD

Wilde Norton's family had the distinction of being the first victims killed by the maniac known as the Joker. Norton was driven insane by the tragedy; he began calling himself Wild and sought the Joker for revenge. His attempts failed and Wild wound up in Arkham Asylum. The two met up again when an earthquake damaged the facility and let the inmates run free. The Joker then completed the Norton family deaths by killing Wild. (*Batman: Shadow of the Bat* #37, April 1995)

WILDCAT

Wildcat was actually Earth-2 prizefighter Ted Grant. Embroiled in his manager's shaky schemes, he was wanted for a crime he did not commit. Inspired by a comic book, he became the Wildcat to clear his name, and went on to a stellar career fighting alongside Batman as a member of the Justice Society of America. His career lasted until his legs were shattered during Crisis on Infinite Earths. His goddaughter, Yolanda Montez, became the new Wildcat. (*Sensation Comics* #1, January 1942)

On Earth-1, Ted Grant was the heavyweight champion of the world who also fought crime as Wildcat. He fought alongside Batman on numerous occasions, as the two were well-matched partners. (*The Brave and the Bold* #88, February/March 1970)

In the wake of Crisis on Infinite Earths, Ted Grant began his career during the years leading toward World War II. He was part of the JSA and continued

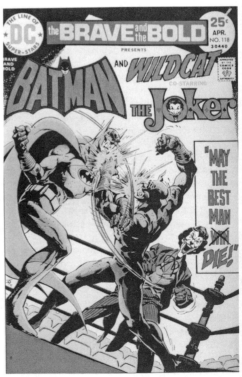

Ted Grant

his career until his comrades retired in the early 1950s. At some unspecified time he was granted nine lives, eight of which were used between the 1940s and 2008. As a result of his longevity, Grant recognized his responsibility to train future generations of boxers and crime fighters. The roster of people he trained was thus a veritable who's who of heroes, including BRUCE WAYNE, the second BLACK CANARY, CATWOMAN, and HOLLY ROBINSON.

His rough-hewn charm won over many women, and he enjoyed romances with the likes of Queen Hippolyta, SELINA KYLE, and the love of his life, Irina, who mothered his son Jake.

Tragedy also dogged Wildcat's life, beginning with Jake's abduction and presumed death. He also watched his goddaughter Yolanda Montez become Wildcat—only to die at the hands of Eclipso. (*Eclipso* #13, November 1993) His protégé Hector Ramirez also wanted to become Grant's successor and went into training. Without permission, he donned a Wildcat outfit and hit the streets of GOTHAM CITY. When he tried to break up an illegal fight club, he was killed by KILLER CROC and avenged by Wildcat and Batman. (*Batman/Wildcat* #1–3, April–June 1997)

Later in life he met Tom Bronson, a son he'd never known about, the result of a one-night stand with an unnamed woman. When they met, the teen expressed no bitterness toward Grant; nor did he wish to become a successor Wildcat. However, he was revealed to be a meta-human, able to turn into a were-cat. As a result, he agreed to share the name *Wildcat* and enter into training as a member of the Justice Society. (*Justice Society of America* [second series] #4, May 2007)

WILKER, JOHN

John Wilker owned ACE, the canine who went on to become known as the BAT-HOUND. An engraver, he was kidnapped by criminals who hoped he would create printing plates for them that would enable them to counterfeit money. Ace led Batman and ROBIN to his master and was soon regularly accompanying the Earth-2 crime fighters on cases. Whenever Wilker left town for vacation or business, he entrusted the brave dog to BRUCE WAYNE. Eventually Wilker took a new job and left Ace permanently in Wayne's care; the Bat-Hound became a new member of the team. (*Batman* #92, June 1955)

WILKINS

Wilkins served as butler to GOTHAM CITY district attorney HARVEY KENT on Earth-2. He once disguised himself as TWO-FACE to commit crimes yet have police suspect the once deranged criminal. Batman and ROBIN investigated and exposed Wilkins, keeping the rehabilitated Kent free of suspicion. (*Batman* #50, December 1948/January 1949)

WILSON, SLADE

A soldier-turned-soldier-of-fortune and one of the deadliest men on Earth, known to all as DEATHSTROKE THE TERMINATOR.

WINGMAN

On Earth-2 a red-and-yellow-clad European who would eventually become a naturalized citizen arrived in GOTHAM CITY to train under Batman. His homeland wanted the Caped Crusader to oversee Wingman's crime-fighting orientation. The timing couldn't have been better because ROBIN had broken his leg on a case and was laid up for six weeks. As Batman and Wingman worked together, Gotham citizens came to prefer seeing an adult as Batman's partner, which sent Robin into a paranoid funk. As time passed, Robin finally learned that he could never be replaced as Batman's partner. (*Batman* #65, June/July 1951)

On the world created in the wake of CRISIS ON INFINITE EARTHS, a young, unnamed Swedish boy joined the Norwegian underground to oppose the Nazi menace during World War II. In the wake of the war, he was inspired by the costumed heroes of the JUSTICE SOCIETY OF AMERICA to continue his fight against injustice. He donned a costume of his own design and became Wingman. He was among the first international heroes to join the Global Guardians. (*Infinity Inc.* #34, January 1987)

In the reality after the events of INFINITE CRISIS, Wingman was once more a contemporary of Batman, ashamed to admit that he followed in the Dark Knight's footsteps. They trained together briefly, but he never admitted it. Everything he wore and did, including the use of a stealth jet dubbed the Nightwing, showed how much he imitated his idol. The one difference was his high-tech jetpack, which allowed Wingman to cover vast distances at great speed. In fact, his arrogance led the CLUB OF HEROES to fall apart after a mere two meetings. Years later, when John Mayhew reconvened the club, Wingman was as arrogant as ever and proved to be a traitor in their midst, working with Mayhew to kill the other heroes in a scheme to gain revenge against Batman, whom Mayhew blamed for the club's failure. He was killed by El Sombrero, EL GAUCHO's foe, who worked with Mayhew. (*Batman* #667–669, October–November 2007)

WINNS, HENRY

A scientist, Henry Winns created a method for preserving people in a state of suspended animation. The device froze people into place and seemingly encased them in bronze until a second device restored them to normal. A criminal known only as Vulcan stole the devices, then sited his henchmen in strategic places where they could hide in plain sight as statues until he unfroze them after hours, when they could commit burglaries. Batman, ROBIN, and BATWOMAN caught up to Vulcan and apprehended the gang, returning the devices to Winns. (*Detective Comics* #203, April 1962)

WIST, DAVID

The watch-repairman-turned-safecracker who temporarily gained fantastic powers and committed crimes as the HUMAN MAGNET.

WITCH

SAMANTHA VOZ believed herself to be a reincarnated witch from the days of the Salem trials and sought to exact revenge for her death.

WITTS, JOHNNY

Johnny Witts was a GOTHAM CITY criminal who decided that the only way to commit successful burglaries was to outwit Batman and ROBIN. As a result, he had the Dynamic Duo observed and then set out to elude and entrap the crime fighters, keeping them off balance by sending his men out to commit robberies around the city. Over the course of several weeks, Witts carried out his crimes while Batman and Robin failed to capture him or his thugs. Every attempt the Dynamic Duo made to apprehend them had been anticipated, and clever escapes or traps had been arranged.

What Witts hadn't anticipated was that the Gotham police traced him to his hideaway thanks

to Batman's help. The ensuing fight proved distracting enough to prevent the genius from formulating a fresh scheme on the fly. Once in prison, he found the solitude he needed to begin fashioning fresh plots, starting with a prison break. (*Detective Comics* #344, October 1965)

Witts did indeed escape, albeit alone. To avoid being arrested again, he took on the persona of a fortune-teller named the SWAMI. Wearing a goatee, blue-black suit, red cape, and the requisite turban, he hired four fresh underlings and began anew. Pretending to receive guidance from his crystal ball, Witts convinced fellow criminals he was an omniscient mastermind. Batman managed to apprehend Silent Stan, one of Witts's fearsome foursome, and impersonated him to get close to the operation. Witts, though, had anticipated this and exposed Batman before the Caped Crusader could act. The other three hirelings pummeled Batman into submission; he was then left to die under the Lensolator, a powerful heat lamp. The Dark Knight freed himself and arrived at an art gallery, surprising Witts, who once more was outwitted. (*Batman* #192, June 1967)

When a West Coast crime syndicate set its sights on Gotham, the city's rogues banded together to protect Batman to ensure that the mob stayed away. Witts had established himself well enough to be invited to join the JOKER, PENGUIN, CATWOMAN, MAD HATTER, CLUEMASTER, and the GETAWAY GENIUS. Witts secretly saved the Gotham Guardian's life by detonating an explosives-laden buoy. (*Batman* #201, May 1968) Witts was not seen again.

WONDER WOMAN

Wonder Woman was Diana, daughter of Queen Hippolyta. The amazons of Earth-2 lived on fabled Paradise Island, protected by the Greek gods; men were forbidden. Bereft of a child, Hippolyta begged the gods for a daughter and was instructed to fashion one out of clay. One by one, the gods and goddesses bestowed the clay form with abilities and finally life. Diana grew up training to be a warrior, as was the Amazon way, until army intelligence officer Steve Trevor's plane crashed and he washed ashore. From him the Amazons learned of the world war that threatened freedom itself, and they decided that a champion would go to "man's world" to preach peace. A contest was held and Diana, wearing a mask to fool her forbidding mother, handily won. Outfitted in a red, white, and blue costume to appeal to Americans, she took Trevor back home and remained as a symbol of peace. Wonder Woman's exploits throughout

World War II earned her a spot as secretary and then full-fledged member of the fabled JUSTICE SOCIETY OF AMERICA. She and Batman also served side by side on the All-Star Squadron. (*All Star Comics* #8, December 1941) In time, Wonder Woman and Steve Trevor married and raised a daughter, Lyta.

On Earth-1, Wonder Woman's origins were much the same, but she arrived during the age of heroes and was a charter member of the JUSTICE LEAGUE OF AMERICA. When the Amazons chose to leave the plane of reality for another realm, Diana was cut off from her gods-given powers. She continued to fight for justice using her warrior training in addition to the martial arts. When she regained her powers, she put herself through a series of trials to assure herself that she belonged once more with the JLA.

In the wake of CRISIS ON INFINITE EARTHS, Diana

was given life during the second age of heroes. At one point Hippolyta traveled through time and assumed the Wonder Woman identity to adventure alongside the JSA during World War II, where she enjoyed a brief romance with WILDCAT.

With her bulletproof bracelets and lasso of truth, Wonder Woman managed to fight all manner of criminals in addition to continuing her mission as Themyscira's ambassador to the world. She joined the JLA and, in time, developed a serious flirtation with Batman. The two avoided the issue for a time but finally agreed to a date to see what happened. The night saw more cracked knuckles than cracked crab, and the two agreed that remaining fellow crime fighters was for the best. (*JLA* #90, January 2004)

She, SUPERMAN, and Batman were seen as the triumvirate of heroes after which all others modeled

themselves. As a result, they oversaw the combined meta-human efforts during cosmic battles or earth-shattering disasters. When Wonder Woman found herself killing Maxwell Lord to end Lord's mental hold over Superman before the Man of Steel killed Batman, the world's faith in her was challenged and the triumvirate shattered. As the events triggered by INFINITE CRISIS came to an end, Wonder Woman worked hard to restore her reputation and assure the world she had done what her warrior training demanded. The three spent time carefully selecting the next iteration of the JLA after the heroes each took a year to put his or her personal life back in order.

(For a detailed account of Wonder Woman, consult *The Essential Wonder Woman Encyclopedia*.)

WONG

Wong was considered the unofficial mayor of GOTHAM CITY'S CHINATOWN until his murder at the hands of the GREEN DRAGON. It was said he was a direct descendant of Genghis Khan himself. Wong first came to Batman's aid by providing him with information about Sin Fang, a fence. When the Green Dragon tong took control of Chinatown, Wong sent out a plea to Batman through a classified newspaper ad. By the time the Caped Crusader arrived, Wong was dead. He left behind a clue, however, that allowed the Gotham Guardian to avenge his death. (*Detective Comics* #35, January 1940)

WOODRUE, JASON

The alien from another dimension who gained power over plant life as the FLORONIC MAN.

WOOSAN, SHIVA

A variation on the name used by the woman who became the world's deadliest assassin, LADY SHIVA.

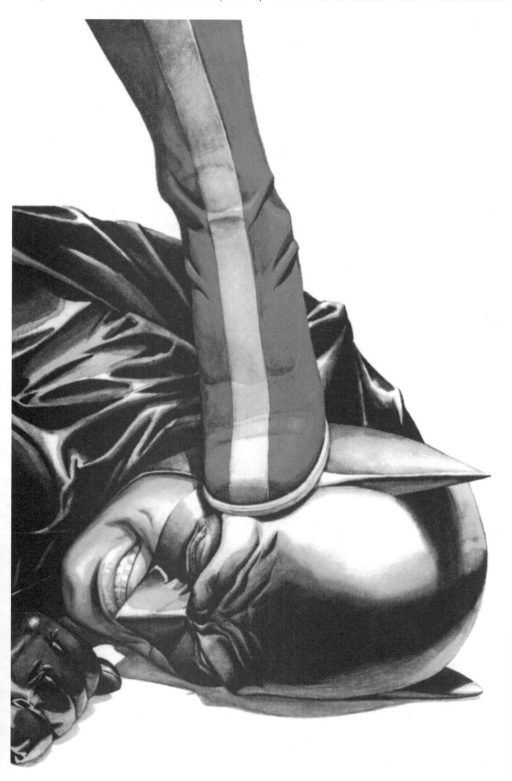

WORDENSHIRE

England's Wordenshire was home to Wordenshire Castle and its occupant, the earl of Wordenshire—secretly the Knight. (*Batman* #62, December 1950/January 1951)

WORDENSHIRE, EARL OF

The British subject who was also secretly the Knight.

WRATH

On Earth-1, Gotham City police officer James Gordon shot and killed two burglars on the night of June 26 while at the same time, across town, Thomas and Martha Wayne were similarly gunned down. Both shootings left single boys orphans. Whereas Bruce Wayne grew up to become Batman, the other youth grew up to hate the police and left Gotham City, returning as an adult. In the costumed guise of the Wrath, the professional assassin sought revenge against Gordon. This mirror-image Batman proved

very threatening. The two costumed fighters proved equally matched physically and had the same drive to excel at their work. The key difference between them was that the Wrath had no qualms about using a gun or taking a life. During their initial encounters, the Wrath learned Batman's identity and then targeted Wayne's friends, leaving Alfred Pennyworth hospitalized. When Dr. Leslie Thompkins wound up a kidnap victim, Batman tracked down the criminal at Crime Alley, the site where the Waynes had been killed. After a fire broke out, the Wrath plunged to his death from a rooftop. (*Batman Special* #1, 1984)

WRECKER, THE

Dwight Farrow put on a maroon robe, complete with white W on his chest, and covered his face with a hood so he could commit crimes as the Wrecker. With his crew he scoured Gotham City, destroying any building or object that was a tribute to the city's protector Batman. In time, though, the Caped Crusader and Robin tracked them down and arrested them for their myriad crimes. (*Detective Comics* #197, July 1953)

WRECKERS, THE

The Wreckers were a gang of criminals who caused catastrophic events to mask their robberies. In time they were apprehended by Batman, Robin, and Superman. (*World's Finest Comics* #112, September 1960)

WRIGHT

Author Erik Dorne was murdered in his home, his unfinished manuscript stolen. Police and Batman investigated, with suspicion falling on four people: Jane Ware, the writer's estranged wife; Melissa Brunt, his embittered aunt; Wright, his publisher; and Joshua Grimm, a fellow author. Batman and Robin discovered that the murderer was Wright, who'd killed to prevent being exposed as a Fifth Columnist, publishing vicious propaganda in support of the Axis powers. The Dynamic Duo took Wright and his underlings into custody. (*World's Best Comics* #1, Spring 1941)

WRINGER, THE

Scotland Yard inspector Clive Kittridge came to Gotham City seeking excitement and opportunities unavailable in his homeland. He eagerly awaited the next bizarre crime that would force Police Commissioner James Gordon to summon Batman. When a bizarrely dressed figure turned up on a stage, Kittridge had found his case. Complicating matters was that the inspector was an old classmate of Alfred Pennyworth's and had wrangled an invitation to use the guest room at the penthouse apartments Bruce Wayne was occupying at the time. Wayne and Kittridge made a hundred-dollar wager as to who could crack the case first: the Dark Knight or the inspector. Investigators soon came across the Wringer, wearing a purple robe and hood and a lime-green bodysuit. In each case, the villain left behind collateral damage that provided clues. The Wringer had, for reasons unknown, been damaging wooden figures, from marionette to dummy to walking doll. While the inspector went after the

human he predicted to be the next victim, Batman staked out the home of stockbroker Douglas Walker. Sure enough, the Wringer arrived, intending to kill the man who'd cost him his life savings. Having been wrung out to dry, he told Walker, he was going to wring the man's neck. Batman intervened and brought the Wringer to the police. A baffled Kittridge learned that Batman had deduced Douglas Walker was the target after one attack involved a dummy made from Douglas fir; the second, a walker on Park Avenue. Kittridge happily made good on the bet. (*Batman* #278, August 1976)

WU-SAN, SHIVA

The proper birth name of the woman who would grow up to become the world's deadliest assassin, Lady Shiva.

WYATT, TENZIN

Tenzin Wyatt was a half-Tibetan man knowledgeable in matters of the Himalayan occult. He settled in Gotham City and racked up a large debt with the city's loan sharks. With few options, Wyatt used his magic to create doppelgängers that would commit robberies to raise the money he needed. Batman found one of the creations dangerously driving a Ferrari—but when he stopped it, it turned to dust. Another creature attempted to rob Wayne Manor. Having failed at basic burglary, Wyatt used a blacker form of magic to summon forth Mahakala, a demon. The creature went after Rafe Kellogg, the man who was threatening Wyatt. Batman, in turn, sought help from Jason Blood, but the demonologist refused to unleash his alter ego, Etrigan the Demon. Instead Blood's ally, Randu Singh, accompanied the Dark Knight. It was Singh who pointed out that Wyatt's hatred of Kellogg fueled Mahakala. As a result, it could not be stopped, forcing Etrigan to be summoned. The demons battled until Etrigan prevailed. (*Detective Comics* #601–603, June–August 1989)

Wyatt was once again embroiled in Etrigan's business when he summoned Mahakala, seeking revenge against the hellspawn—but also managing to free an imprisoned Killer Croc, who was menacing Gotham. (*The Demon* [third series] #9, March 1991)

WYRE, ALEC

Alec Wyre was a criminal scientist who sold advanced electronics devices to Gotham City criminals. His body was discovered by Batman in the Batcave, convincing the Dark Knight that his and Robin's secret identities had been compromised. The Dynamic Duo's investigation had them check into three of Wyre's clients, but it soon became apparent that Wyre had stumbled into the cave on his own and died after smacking his head into a stalactite. (*Batman* #121, February 1959)

X (PLANET)

See Zur-en-Arrh.

X (PLANETOID)

X was a solar system planetoid that supported life. One of its residents, Garr, partnered with a criminal from Earth, Eddie Marrow. Their attempts to commit crimes were thwarted by the combination of Batman, Robin, and X's lawman, Tutian. (*Batman* #117, August 1958)

XANU

There was an ancient mirror imbued with magical powers that was the sole entry point between Earth and a weird, mirror dimension. How and why the mirror was crafted remained a mystery, but the dimension's leader Xanu was a dictator who desired power, including dominion over Earth. Batman and Robin wound up in the odd realm; Batman was physically distorted from the transit. Superman came to their aid, defeating Xano in the process. The Man of Steel found a way to return Batman to his normal form, and the mystic passageway was sealed. (*World's Finest Comics* #121, November 1961)

XHOSA, THE

During the year when Gotham City became a No Man's Land, a street gang called the Xhosa occupied the home of Senator Jack Myles. When the city was restored to America, Myles and his family returned home and kicked the gang out. A short time later the senator and his wife, Eileen, were found dead, with their son Barrett the sole witness. Given the echoes with his own parents' murder, Batman seemed less effective than usual in the investigation, prompting Robin to ask Nightwing for help. As a result, the gang was ruled out, as were other suspects, until

Nightwing and Robin tussel with the Xhosa

it was proven Barrett had committed the murders. (*Batman: Gotham Knights* #1, March 2000)

XLUR

Xlur was a distant alien world where scientists experimented with advanced technology. Their "space-warp ray" accidentally transported the Batplane, containing Batman and Robin, from the Gotham City skies to Xlur. During the Dynamic Duo's three-day stay, the stunned scientists tried to find a way to return the crime fighters home. While on the amazing planet, the humans began to transform to match Xlurian physiology, including two antennae and green skin.

When they were finally transported back to Earth, the Dynamic Duo retained their alien appearance—which also meant they developed superpowers once back under Earth conditions. The antennae, for example, exerted a powerful magnetic force. This proved useful in tracking the Yellow Sweater Gang, but the duo's odd appearance complicated the matter of protecting their secret identities.

In time, they reverted to their human norm and apprehended the gang. (*Batman* #140, June 1961)

XLYM

People on Earth were astonished to see Batman display powers that rivaled those of Superman. They were stunned to watch the World's Finest heroes become bitter rivals as they performed miraculous feats. The truth, however, was that the Caped Crusader's newfound powers were the result of a wager between residents of the far-flung planet Xlym. They used their superior technology to bring Batman and the Man of Steel to their planet, granted Batman mighty abilities, and then altered the heroes' emotional makeup so friends became enemies. As the two battled on Earth, the Xlymians' superiors discovered what had been done and reversed the modifications made to the super heroes. As a result, Batman's powers faded and their personalities returned to normal. (*World's Finest Comics* #95, July/August 1958)

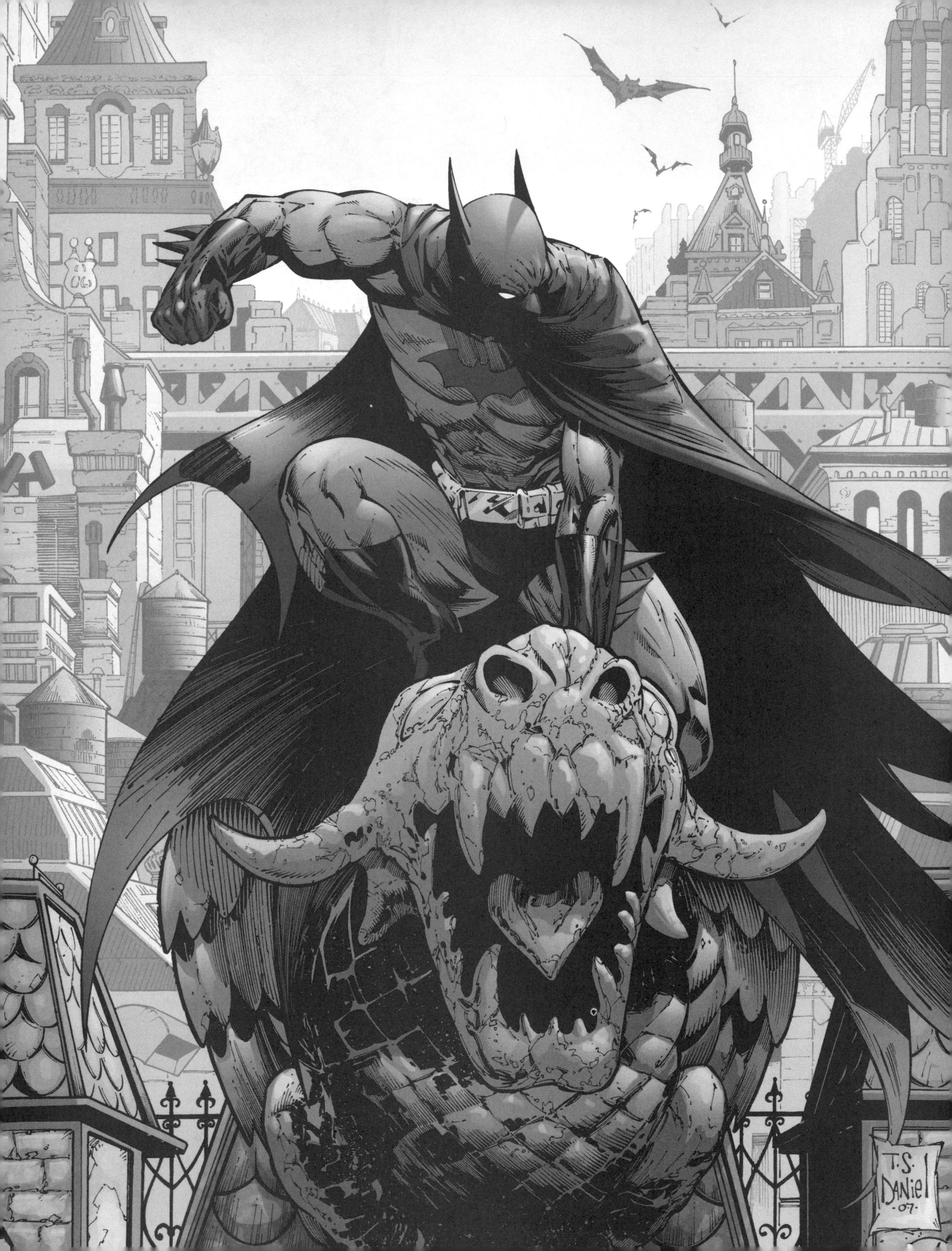
T.S. DANIEL
·07·

YAKUZA

The name *Yakuza* referred to the mobsters controlling crime and vice in Japan. Their reach had become global, eventually infiltrating Gotham City. Batman encountered them when he first led the Outsiders. He has tangled with them several times since, although their influence in Gotham has remained minimal. Among their agents in the city was Johnny Karaoke. (*Batman and the Outsiders* #11, June 1984)

Y'BAR

The planetary home to evil warlock Zerno.

YELLOW MASK MOB, THE

Capturing the Yellow Mask Mob proved more difficult than usual when an accident robbed Robin of his memories; he could recall nothing after the death of his parents, the Flying Graysons. As a result, all his crime-fighting training had vanished. Still, this problem only slowed the Dynamic Duo from taking down the criminals. In time, Robin's memories returned. (*Detective Comics* #145, March 1949)

YINDEL, ELLEN

In a potential future, a fifty-year-old Bruce Wayne returned to action as Batman to fight a fascist government. His arrival also prompted the Joker to reappear, turning Gotham City once more into a blood-splattered town. Police Commissioner Ellen Yindel, who succeeded James Gordon, was adamantly opposed to the Dark Knight's presence until she saw how much the city needed him. (*The Dark Knight Returns* #1–4, 1987)

YLLA

Ylla was an extradimensional realm that was visited by Batman, Robin, and a ferryboat full of passengers, including criminal Eddie Stark.

YMAR

The Swami Ymar, a fortune-teller-turned-criminal, donned a metallic suit covered in disks to become the Spinner.

YOUNG JUSTICE

When the original Teen Titans had reached adulthood, they changed their team name to the Titans, leaving no organization for the next generation of young heroes. That gap was filled when Robin, Impulse, and Superboy wound up aiding a young meta-human girl who had been imprisoned by the US government against her will. (*Young Justice: The Secret,* June 1998)

In the wake of the Secret's rescue, the heroes recognized the need to share experiences with one another and have friends with whom they could freely discuss their costumed lives. They set up shop in the mountain headquarters that the Justice League of America, their mentors, had first used. The team grew with time and for much of its existence was chaperoned by the android JLA member Red Tornado. Soon new members were added: the second Wonder Girl, Secret, and Arrowette. Given his training under Batman, Robin naturally took a leadership position and enjoyed having peers to spend time with.

Despite its global and intergalactic exploits, the team was devastated by the arrival of an android named Indigo, which was controlled by Brainiac. Even teamed with the Titans, Young Justice was

not powerful enough to stop Indigo or the rogue Superman robot that wound up killing Donna Troy, the first Wonder Girl. The team broke up after that mission. (*Titans/Young Justice: Graduation Day* #1–3, July–August 2003)

YOUNG, TOMMY

Tommy Young was an American lost in the African jungle for fifteen years. He lost much of his language skills and mental acuity, reverting to the savage Jungle-Man in order to survive.

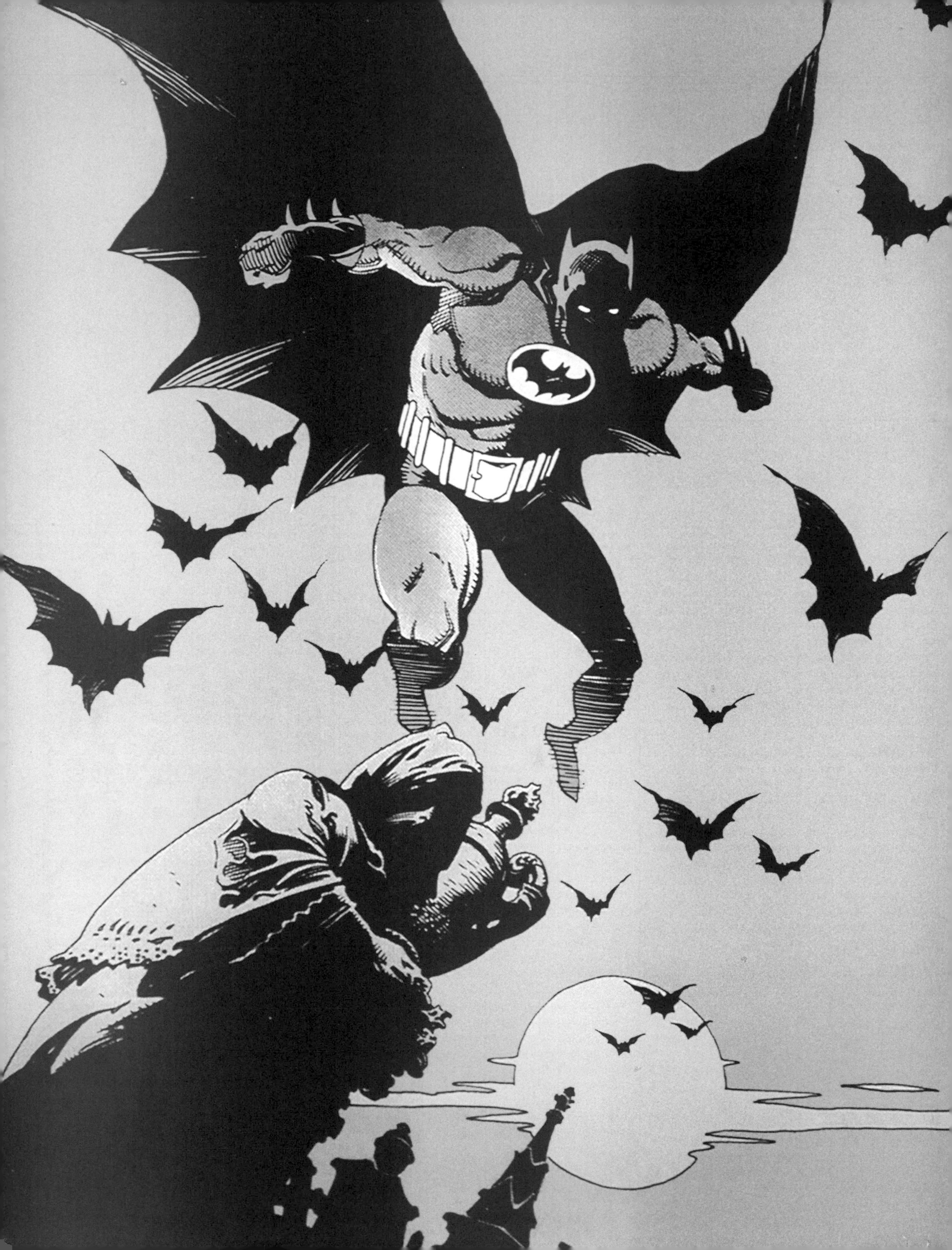

ZATANNA

Zatanna Zatara was the daughter of the famed magician-turned-crime-fighter John Zatara. Her mother was Sindella, a queen in a magical dimension of *homo magi*. The Zatara family traced its lineage back to Nostradamus, Leonardo da Vinci, Alessandro Cagliostro; alchemists Nicholas Flamel and Evan Fulcanelli; and Arion, Lord High Mage of ATLANTIS. She had a younger cousin also named Zatara, who eventually became a hero after the events of INFINITE CRISIS and joined ROBIN in the TEEN TITANS. (*Hawkman* #4, October/November 1964)

Growing up, Zatanna and BRUCE WAYNE played together; Wayne called her "Zee." He later studied stage magic and death-trap escapes with her as he trained to become Batman. Zatanna herself followed her father to a successful stage career and became a popular attraction around the world. When her father vanished, she sought out several super heroes—Hawkman, Hawkwoman, ATOM, GREEN LANTERN, ELONGATED MAN, and Batman—for help. He was recovered safe and sound, and Zatanna was on her way to becoming a next-generation super hero.

In time she joined the JUSTICE LEAGUE OF AMERICA, and shortly thereafter she was finally reunited with her mother. She was also the pivotal player in the darkest period of the JLA's history. When Dr. Light raped SUE DIBNY, he was taken by the JLA, and the team was split over what should be done. It was decided that Zatanna should use her magic to alter Dr. Light's memories and personality. Just after the decision had been reached but before she performed the spell, Batman arrived at the satellite headquarters. He objected to the decision—so she cast a spell erasing ten minutes from Batman's

memory, and the remaining Leaguers kept this secret. After that incident, she used her abilities time and again, altering memories, protecting her teammates' secret identities and loved ones.

Her powers and her dedication to crime fighting waxed and waned through the years, but Zatanna always found her way back to the fight for justice. Ultimately, though, her role in mindwiping the villains became common knowledge among both heroes and villains in the wake of Dibny's death. (*Identity Crisis* #1–7, August 2004–February 2005) Worse, Batman came to remember what she had done to him, and their friendship deteriorated. It was her betrayal that prompted him to construct BROTHER I to keep an eye on meta-humans around the world. The revelation was also used to form the Society, the first truly unified, powerful organization of super-villains.

CATWOMAN was one of Zatanna's most frequent victims. When she learned the truth, she was furious and—when she needed help—insisted the Maid of Magic owed her big time. For what Zatanna hoped was the last time, she mindwiped Angle Man and FILM FREAK, who had come to learn Catwoman's identity.

After the events of INFINITE CRISIS, Batman left for a year of renewal; upon his return, he was ready to forgive Zatanna. First he called on her for information, and then, when her apprentice was slain by the JOKER, they teamed up and he formally forgave her. (*Detective Comics* #833, August 2007)

ZEBO

Zebo was a scientist who attempted to conquer his home dimension. His dreams of power were dashed thanks to the combined efforts of Batman, ROBIN,

Batwoman, and Bat-Girl. (*Batman* #153, February 1963)

ZEBRA-MAN, THE

When an unnamed criminal scientist was accidentally bathed in radiation from his latest invention, he found himself imbued with strange powers. His strength allowed him to bend steel, and he emitted magnetism strong enough to pull a sunken freighter from the bottom of the sea. The man tested his abilities and found he could attract or repel any manner of organic matter, from wood to human flesh. To master these unwieldy powers, he devised an inhibitor belt. His lab outfit was also altered from red skullcap and orange bodysuit to a glowing black-and-white-striped outfit. Taking the name *Zebra-Man,* the scientist embarked on a crime spree in Gotham City.

He proved formidable when Batman and Robin tried to apprehend him—but they did not give up. After tracing clues to his whereabouts, the Dynamic Duo arrived at his hideout, where Batman was accidentally exposed to the same device. He gained the same powers, and his Batsuit altered into the same zebra striping. Because he lacked the inhibitor belt, Batman was unable to control his powers as easily. He and Zebra-Man also shared a magnetic charge, keeping them apart.

Batman devised a way to reverse the magnetic charge of an object, from repellency to attraction, allowing the Caped Crusader to finally subdue Zebra-Man. (*Detective Comics* #275, January 1960)

The international terrorist Kobra created a strike force of superpowered agents, including a new version of Zebra-Man. He managed to obtain the first Zebra-Man's inhibitor belt and used it to help design an updated model, who wore an outfit similar to the original—although he also sported a Mohawk, making him more physically representative of his namesake animal. Despite his vast power, he lacked experience and was easily taken out by Black Lightning. (*Outsiders* #21, July 1987)

ZEDNO, JOSEPH

This mailman went mad, murdering people on his route and wearing their faces as the killer Faceless.

ZEHRHARD, VICTOR

A onetime warden at Blackgate Penitentiary, Victor Zehrhard survived numerous prison breaks, the Gotham City earthquake, and the experience of housing some of the most dangerous criminals on Earth. (*Showcase '94* #3, March 1994)

ZEISS, PHILO

Philo Zeiss was raised by his uncle Victor after his parents died during his childhood. Victor worked as a Mafia capo's gardener; when he died, the don took Philo in and continued his education. The don was impressed by Philo and chose to have him trained as an assassin. Philo accompanied other enforcers on the job until he was finally deemed ready to go solo. Out of gratitude and determined to be the best at his job, Zeiss underwent surgery that improved his reflexes and sensory perception to near-superhuman levels. (*Batman* #582, October 2000)

For unexplained reasons, he relocated to Gotham City and went to work for Lew Moxon. During their time together, Zeiss had occasion to test his skills against Batman's and found that they were nearly evenly matched. When Deadshot came gunning for Moxon, Zeiss was engaged in a battle with Batman that distracted him from his primary mission; Moxon ended up crippled. (*Batman* #595, October 2001) After that, Zeiss left Moxon's employ and went to work for "Junior" Giliante.

When Giliante tried to extend his criminal empire into Gotham's East End, he needed Zeiss to defend him against Catwoman, who claimed that part of the city under her protection. She and Zeiss fought on at least two occasions, with each winning one of the contests.

Zeiss was a zealous, dangerous fighter who wanted to kill Batman to prove his superiority. His enhanced senses allowed him to "read" the Dark Knight's fighting style and be prepared for any move. During one of their later fights, Batman changed the odds by allowing Batgirl to fight at his side. The combination proved more than a match for Zeiss. He remained at large, seeking his next opportunity to kill the Gotham Guardian.

ZERNO

Zerno, a warlock, possessed a powerful crystal that channeled his powers and was able to summon forth weapons and life-forms from other planets. He left his native world of Y'bar, journeying to Earth to accumulate a large quantity of bronze, an ore that would render his fellow Y'barians insensate. However, the sorcerer and his aid Sborg met resistance then defeat at the hands of Batman, Robin, and Superman. (*World's Finest Comics* #127, August 1962)

ZERO, PROFESSOR

Zero was a scientist-turned-criminal who devised a clever reducing ray that could reduce a normal human to nine inches tall. He intended to use it to extort riches from wealthy victims

but was interrupted by the arrival of Batman and Robin. They were reduced in size but fought on, forcing Zero to grab a shotgun in order to kill them. The gun misfired, killing Zero instead. After three days the invisible reducing ray's effects wore off, returning the Dynamic Duo to normal. (*Batman* #121, June 1949)

ZERO, THE

The Zero was a Gotham City criminal who wore a hood to hide his identity and schemed to trick a millionaire into handing over all his money. Instead, he was apprehended by Batman. (*World's Finest Comics* #67, November/December 1953)

ZESTI COLA

In 1872 Eli Branchwater discovered the Well of Addad in a little African emirate called Karocco. He used its addictive waters (*Psyba-Rats* #3, June 1995) and Santa Priscan cola nuts (*Birds of Prey: Revolution* #1, 1997) as the prime ingredients in what would soon become one of the world's most popular soft drinks—Zesti Cola. Branchwater protected the formula, making it one of the world's greatest industrial secrets. To ensure a steady supply of ingredients, the company went so far as to fund a coup in Santa Prisca. Rivaled only by Soder Cola in popularity, Zesti was the soft drink of choice for Boy Wonders Tim Drake (*Robin* [second series] #22, November 1995) and Dick Grayson (*Nightwing* [second series] #60, October 2001; first appearance: *Detective Comics* #645, June 1992).

ZEUS, MAXIE

Maximillian Zeus was a married teacher of history until he lost his wife. Her unexplained death caused Zeus to lose his grip on sanity and abandon teaching for a life of crime.

Reinventing himself after the Greek god Zeus, he took to wearing a stylized toga and decorated his headquarters with mythological touches. Zeus stirred up Gotham City's underworld as he established his toehold and fought Batman on several occasions. (*Detective Comics* #483, April/May 1979)

Relocating briefly to the West Coast, he created superpowered agents known as the New Olympians and intended to wreak havoc at the Los Angeles Olympics. His goal was to marry Lacinia Nitocris, an Olympian whom he deemed an appropriate mother figure for his daughter Medea. This plan was stopped by Batman's OUTSIDERS, who proved more than a match for the New Olympians. (*Batman and the Outsiders* #14–15, October–November 1984)

Maxie Zeus was repeatedly sent back to prison until it was determined that he'd be better off at ARKHAM ASYLUM. When BANE arrived to free the villains as part of his scheme to destroy the Dark Knight, the JOKER decided that Zeus was too annoying and refused to help him escape. (*Batman: Arkham Asylum: Tales of Madness,* May 1998)

His career, and life, came to an end when he was asked by the children of the Greek gods Ares, Deimos, Phobos, and Eris to scheme with them. Zeus was to run Gotham City after turning it into the capital for Ares on Earth. WONDER WOMAN arrived in Gotham to oppose the plot, and Zeus died as Phobos's sacrifice to the gods. The Amazon Princess prevailed, and Ares's children were banished to Tartarus, the land of the dead. (*Wonder Woman* [second series] #164–166, January–March 2001) The whereabouts of Zeus's daughter Medea remain unrecorded.

ZODIAC MASTER, THE

Wearing a light blue cowl and bodysuit decorated by astrological signs, the criminal known only as the Zodiac Master first made his presence known in GOTHAM CITY by accurately predicting a succession of disasters—all of which he'd secretly orchestrated. He leveraged that success to begin offering odds for the success of planned robberies in exchange for a 25 percent cut of the take. Batman and ROBIN tracked the criminal and used his own gimmicks against him, bringing him to justice. (*Detective Comics* #323, January 1964)

ZOMBIE

Zombie was one of the few men whom BANE considered a friend. With BIRD and TROGG, he escaped imprisonment on SANTA PRISCA and came to GOTHAM CITY. His cohorts named him Zombie because he had a vacant stare and never seemed to blink. After Bane's initial foray into Gotham, Zombie left his inner circle and was not seen again. (*Batman: Vengeance of Bane* #1, February 1993)

ZORN

This hero dates back three thousand years to Babylon. When his statue was unearthed, he was depicted wearing a variation on Batman's BATSUIT. (*Batman* #102, September 1956)

ZORON

This distant world suffered under the rule of CHORN and his fellow Baxians until the timely arrival of Batman, ROBIN, and SUPERMAN. (*World's Finest Comics* #114, December 1960)

ZSASZ, VICTOR

This insane murderer marked his body each time he took a life. He was known to most as MISTER ZSASZ.

ZUCCO, ANTHONY "BOSS"

Anthony Zucco was the criminal who tried to extort the owner of the HALY BROS. CIRCUS when it came to GOTHAM CITY. Haly refused to pay, so Zucco had his men cut the ropes used by the FLYING GRAYSONS; that night JOHN and MARY GRAYSON plummeted to their deaths. Their son, DICK GRAYSON, was adopted by Batman and became the first ROBIN, the Boy Wonder. After Batman trained Grayson, their first case had them track down Zucco and bring him to justice. (*Detective Comics* #38, April 1940)

One account went on to feature Zucco's ledger, hidden at the very orphanage where Grayson stayed until the courts could award custody to BRUCE WAYNE. A year after his arrest, Zucco was freed forty-nine years early. His first order of business was to get his hands on the book before the orphanage was demolished. Instead, the moment he left the prison, he was shot to death by a sniper aboard a helicopter. (*Batman* #436–439, August–September 1989)

A different account portrayed Zucco as a low-level gangster working for SAL MARONI, a part of CARMINE FALCONE's criminal family. Nicknamed "Fats," Zucco and EDWARD SKEEVERS were charged with illegal narcotics trafficking. When their supply was repeatedly poached by other Gotham criminals, including the PENGUIN, Zucco struck on the idea of using the traveling circus as a way to transport narcotics. Again, when Haly refused to cooperate, Zucco had the Graysons killed. This account had Grayson, not Robin, accompany Batman in apprehending Zucco. The criminal suffered a fatal heart attack while fleeing from the nascent Dynamic Duo. (*Batman: Dark Victory* #1–13, December 1999–December 2000)

ZUR-EN-ARRH

This planet on the other side of the galaxy was home to TLANO, who protected his world much as Batman protected GOTHAM CITY. When alien invaders arrived, Tlano summoned Batman for help. (*Batman* #113, February 1958)

Anthony "Boss" Zucco

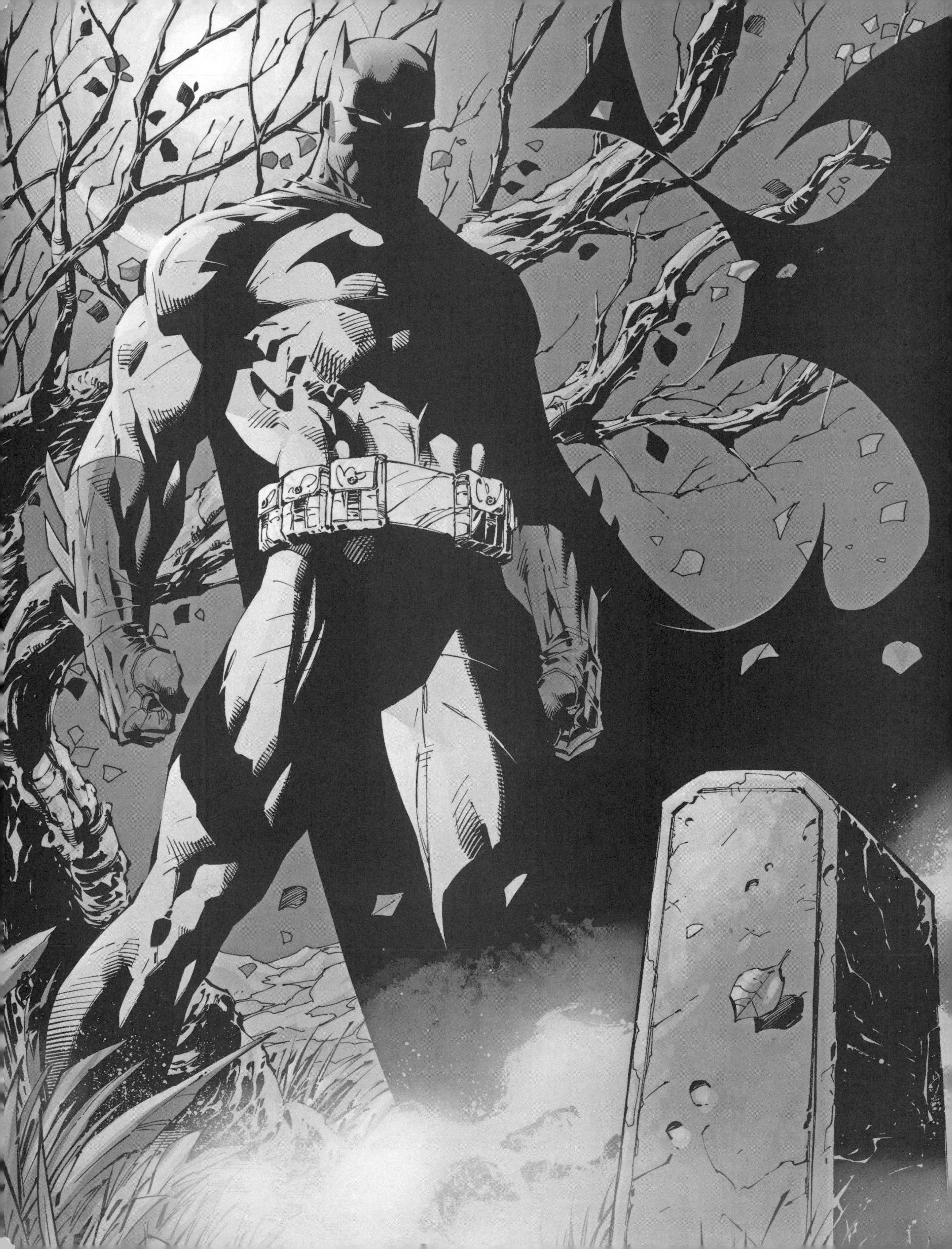

ARTIST CREDITS

Del Rey would like to thank the following DC Comics artists for their contributions to this book:

Art Adams, Neal Adams, Dan Adkins, Marlo Alquiza, Murphy Anderson, Ross Andru, Jim Aparo, Terry Austin, Michael Bair, Jim Balent, Eduardo Barreto, Al Barrioneuvo, Terry Beatty, Howard Bender, Ed Benes, Joe Benitez, Joe Bennett, Lee Bermejo, Simone Bianchi, Steve Bird, Brian Bolland, Doug Braithwaite, Norm Breyfogle, Rick Burchett, John Byrne, J. Calafiore, Robert Campanella, J. Scott Campbell, Marc Campos, John Cassaday, Keith Champagne, Cliff Chiang, Andy Clarke, Gene Colan, Darwyn Cooke, Denys Cowan, Tony Daniel, Alan Davis, Mike DeCarlo, Luciana Del Negro, Jesse Delperdang, Stephen DeStefano, Steve Ditko, Peter Doherty, Don Drake, Dale Eaglesham, Wayne Faucher, Raul Fernandez, John Floyd, Richard Friend, Jose Luis Garcia-Lopez, Ale Garza, Stephano Gaudiano, Drew Geraci, Gary Gianni, Joe Giella, Dick Giordano, Jonathan Glapion, Shane Glines, Michael Golden, Wade von Grawbadger, Dan Green, Gene Ha, Ed Hannigan, Sandra Hope, Richards Howell, Adam Hughes, Carmine Infantino, Jack Jadson, Klaus Janson, Phil Jimenez, Dave Johnson, J. G. Jones, Kelley Jones, Bob Kane, Kano, Stan Kaye, Jack Kirby, Leonard Kirk, Scott Kolins, Don Kramer, Andy Kubert, Greg Land, Andy Lanning, Michael Lark, Jim Lee, Alex Lei, John Paul Leon, Jeph Loeb (writer), Alvaro Lopez, David Lopez, Rick Magyar, Doug Mahnke, Tom Mandrake, Pablo Marcos, Marcos Martin, Patrick Martin, Marcos Marz, David Mazzucchelli, Scott McDaniel, Ed McGuinness, Mark McKenna, Jesus Merino, Pop Mhan, Mike Mignola, Danny Miki, Frank Miller, Sheldon Moldoff, Rags Morales, Win Mortimer, Patricia Mulvihill, Paul Neary, Nelson, Don Newton, Dustin Nguyen, Martin Nodell, Graham Nolan, Irv Novick, Kevin Nowlan, Jerry Ordway, Andy Owens, Carlos Pacheco, Tom Palmer, Jimmy Palmiotti, Charles Paris, Ande Parks, Fernando Pasarin, Jason Pearson, George Perez, Paul Pope, Whilce Portacio, Francis Portela, Howard Porter, Joe Quesada, Frank Quitely, Ivan Reis, Doug Rice, Robin Riggs, Darick Robertson, Jerry Robinson, Marshall Rogers, Alex Ross, David Ross, George Roussos, Stephane Roux, Jesus Saiz, Tim Sale, Damian Scott, Steve Scott, Kevin Sharpe, Paulo Sigueira, Bill Sienkiewicz, Walt Simonson, Howard Simpson, Bob Smith, Cam Smith, Dan Spiegle, Dick Sprang, Arne Starr, Rick Stasi, Joe Staton, Brian Stelfreeze, Cameron Stewart, Karl Story, Curt Swan, Romeo Tanghal, Dave Taylor, Rick Taylor, Greg Theakston, Art Thibert, Dwayne Turner, Michael Turner, Ethan Van Sciver, Ricardo Villagran, Dexter Vines, Matt Wagner, Brad Walker, Chris Warner, Lee Weeks, Scott Williams, Pete Woods, Bill Wray, Bernie Wrightson, Mike Zeck, and Patrick Zircher

ABOUT THE AUTHOR

PHOTO: DEB GREENBERGER

Robert Greenberger was given his first comic, an issue of *Superman*, at age six. Since then he has been a passionate fan of the medium. Inspired by Clark Kent's career, he trained in journalism and publishing. He wrote and edited for his various school newspapers, serving as editor in chief of *Pipe Dream* at Binghamton University. He graduated in 1980 with degrees in English and history.

Bob's professional career began at Starlog Press where he created *Comics Scene,* the first nationally distributed magazine to cover comic books, comic strips, and animation. From there he was invited to join DC Comics, making a dream come true. He started as assistant editor, working on the seminal *Crisis on Infinite Earths* and *Who's Who.* He briefly served as assistant editor on *Batman* and *Detective Comics,* where he handled the letter columns for several years. When he became an editor, his titles included *Star Trek, Star Trek: The Next Generation, Suicide Squad, Starman, Atlantis Chronicles,* and *Doom Patrol.* He then switched to the administrative side of the company, rising to the role of Manager—Editorial Operations.

In 2000 Bob left DC for a job as producer at Gist Communications; he returned to comics in 2001 as Marvel Comics' Director—Publishing Operations. In 2002 he went back to DC Comics as a senior editor in its collected editions department. In 2006 Bob joined *Weekly World News* as managing editor.

As a freelancer, Bob has written numerous *Star Trek* novels and short stories in addition to short works of science fiction and fantasy. Most recently, he wrote the novelization of *Hellboy II: The Golden Army* for Dark Horse Books. He has written fifteen nonfiction titles for young adults, covering such diverse topics as the history of Pakistan and a biography of Lou Gehrig. His adult nonfiction includes coauthoring 2004's *DC Comics Encyclopedia* for Dorling Kindersley. He also writes for SciFi.com and offers commentary at ComicMix.com.

He makes his home in Fairfield, Connecticut, where he serves as an elected member of its Representative Town Meeting, presiding as its moderator. Bob lives with his wife, Deb, their children, Kate and Robbie, and their dogs, Dixie and Dakota.

For more information, see his website, www.bobgreenberger.com